6th November 2023

234x153mm • 1184 pages

HB • 9781786697288 • £2...
XTPB • 9781786697295 • £16.99
E • 9781786697271

Publicity • Polly Grice
polly@headofzeus.com
020 3089 0379

Sales
sales@headofzeus.com

An odyssey through a frozen realm, through political, criminal, scientific, philosophical and amorous intrigues to stand face-to-face with something utterly alien.

14th July 1924. It should be high summer but Warsaw is buried under feet of snow and Benedykt, a dissolute young Polish mathematician, is about to be roused from his bed by two officials from Russia's Ministry of Winter.

Russia and Europe are being devoured by the ever-westward march of a supernatural winter. Agriculture has collapsed and people have flocked to cities seeking protection from the deadly cold. But out there, on the ice, there is an incredible new wealth to be had. In winter's wake, 'black physics' transmutes matter into strange and valuable forms, allowing new technologies, industries and economies to prosper.

At the heart of it all lies Siberia – the 'Wild East' – a magnet for all the political, religious and scientific fevers shaking the world. And that is where Benedykt, once he has been woken, will be sent.

And he will have to decide whether to embrace the ice, or to destroy it.

JACEK DUKAJ read his first Stanislaw Lem novel at the age of six, published his first short story at the age of fourteen and has gone on to publish six novels, five novellas and three short story collections. He is a six-time winner of the Janusz A. Zajdel Award, a four-time winner of the Jerzy Zulawski Award and a winner of a European Literary Award and a Koscielski Award. A short animated movie by Tomasz Baginski based on this short story Katedra (The Cathedral) was nominated for an Academy Award in 2003. Dukaj lives in Cracow.

First published as Lód in Poland in 2007 by Wydawnictwo Literackie

This edition first published in the UK in 2025 by Head of Zeus Ltd,
part of Bloomsbury Publishing Plc.

9 7 5 3 1 2 4 6 8

A catalogue record for this book is available from the British Library.

ISBN (HB): 9781786697288
ISBN (XTPB): 9781786697295
ISBN (E): 9781786697271

Author photogragh: Albert Zawada

Printed and bound in Great Britain by CPI Group (UK) Ltd, Croydon CR0 4YY

Head of Zeus
5–8 Hardwick Street
London EC1R 4RG

WWW.HEADOFZEUS.COM

ICE

Jacek Dukaj

Translated by Ursula Phillips

An Ad Astra Book

Contents

Dramatis personae vi

Part I
WARSAW

CHAPTER THE FIRST 3
On the thousand-rouble son 3
On what cannot be put into words 17
On the laws of logic and laws of politics 20
On Mr Tadeusz Korzyński's finger 30
On the blinding darkness and other obscurities 37
On the delusions of frost 43

Part II
TRANS-SIBERIA

CHAPTER THE SECOND 57
On the miasmas of luxury 57
On the Hungarian count, Russian power, English
 cigarettes and American shadow 63
On the power of shame 83
On pens and revolvers 91

CHAPTER THE THIRD 101
On two-valued, three-valued and valueless logic, as well
 as on the logic of women 101
On what cannot be thought 109
On the heroes of hazard and the speed of the Ice 111
On the machine that devours logic and other inventions
 of Doctor Tesla 120

On several key differences between the European sky
   and Asian sky   131
On the Yekaterinburg frost   139

CHAPTER THE FOURTH   **151**
On forty-seven half-murderers and two would-be
   investigators   151
On the arsenal of Summer   170
On some of the means by which God communicates
   with man   184
On the hidden talents of Miss Muklanowicz and other
   obscure matters   214
On truth, and what is truer than truth   220

CHAPTER THE FIFTH   **268**
On the light and dark sides of a light and dark katzenjammer   268
On the dreams of Princess Blutskaya   281
On death in the past tense   292
On the necessity of controlling History by hand   313

CHAPTER THE SIXTH   **326**
On the dreams of Benedykt Gierosławski   326
On the angels of shame and shamelessness   335
On the Siberian madnesses   347
On the great significance of a brief difference of opinion
   between Doctor Konyeshin and Herr Blutfeld   360
On Winter   376

CHAPTER THE SEVENTH   **398**
On the sculpting of smoke   398
On foreseeing the future   418
On the temperature at which truth freezes   428
On the power of contempt   437
On the unrealised   448

Part III
THE WAYS OF THE MAMMOTHS

CHAPTER THE EIGHTH   **459**
On the City of Ice   459
On a night in the cemetery and rising from
   the grave in the morning   471
On the charms of family life   481

Dramatis personae

Sergey Andreyevitch Aktchukhoff, political exile and religious thinker
Salomon August Andrée, Swedish engineer and polar explorer
Herr Bittan von Asenhoff, wealthy Prussian nobleman and former industrialist
Grigory Grigoryevitch Avksenteyeff, senior editor at *The Irkutsk News*
Mariolka Belcik, Jelena Muklanowicz's companion
Nikolay Aleksandrovitch Berdyaeff, Russian philosopher and theologian
Herr Blutfeld, German traveller on the Trans-Siberian Express
Frau Gertrud Blutfeld, his wife
Prince Blutsky-Osey, high-ranking tsarist official and diplomat
Princess Blutskaya, his wife
Karol Bohdanowicz, Polish exile, geologist, explorer and mining engineer
Stanisław Brzozowski, Polish philosopher
Grisha Buntz, Warsaw pimp
Izydor Chruściński, Polish vodka merchant
Ciecierkiewicz, Pilsudtchik and Yapontchik
Aleister Crowley, British occultist and mountaineer
Jan Czerski, Polish exile, palaeontologist, geologist and explorer
Aleksander Czerski, son of Jan
Roman Dmowski, Polish politician, founder of National Democracy movement (Endecja), opponent of Józef Piłsudski
Zahary Feofilovitch Dushin, tsarist privy councillor close to the Blutskys
Benedykt Dybowski, Polish exile, naturalist and zoologist
Tigry Etmatoff, Tungus tracker and guide
Ünal Tayyib Fessar, Turkish businessman
Mitschka Fidelberg, Polish revolutionary
Christine Filipov, American travelling with Nikola Tesla
Abraham Fishenstein, Jewish banker
Pavel Vladimirovitch Fogel, functionary of the Russian state security police
Captain Frett, hussar in the Imperial Russian Army

On ministerial mammoths and the cartography of
   the Underground World   501
On old and new friends known and unknown   526
On the peculiar glory of the Atra Aurora   549
On the last kopeck   583
On what cannot be felt   607
On gleissen blood   616
On death in the present tense   644
On black physics, on the Un-State, on the fine art of
   saying farewell and the reason for authority figures   681
On the Brotherhood of War against the Apocalypse   724
On the Daughter of Winter and beautiful devotchkas,
   on the war between spirit and matter and the difficult
   love for the body   764
On the Kingdom of Darkness   813
On the delight of temptations repulsed   842
On the great designs, that is, on the power of man over
   future and past   869

CHAPTER THE NINTH   **917**
On a Lyednyak soul   917
On the jama-u-mu-kon bone   935
On the measure of mirkdom   958
On the corpse-eaters   975

PART IV
UN-ILU

CHAPTER THE TENTH   **989**
On the coldest of fathers   989
On the Ice   995
On what cannot be known   996
On the non-necessary   1003
On the founding of the first History Industry Company Ltd   1040
On the collective soul and dictatorship of mercy   1106
On us   1148

Ex Libris   1159

Glossary   1161
About the author and translator   1165
Translator's postscript   1166

Nikolay Fyodorovitch Fydoroff, Russian religious thinker and scientific resurrectionist

Benedykt (Benek) Gierosławski (aka Venyedikt Filipovitch Yeroslavsky), Polish mathematician and logician

Filip Gierosławski (aka Filip Filipovitch Yeroslavsky), Benedykt's father, exiled to Siberia for anti-tsarist conspiracy

Kazimierz Grochowski, Polish mining engineer, explorer, geographer and ethnographer

Saturnin Grzywaczewski, deputy director of Krupp in Irkutsk

Leokadia Gwóźdź, Filip Gierosławski's partner in Irkutsk

Henrik Iertheim, Dutch engineer employed by Krupp

Edmund Gerontyevitch Khavroff, Fyodorovian, editor-in-chief of *Resurrection*

Doctor Konyeshin, Russian physician

Tadeusz Korzyński, Polish gentleman in Warsaw, former comrade of Józef Piłsudski

Tadeusz Kotarbiński, Polish philosopher and logician

Professor Kryspin, physician and director of a Siberian ice sanatorium

Krzysztof (aka Adin), Pilsudtchik and Yapontchik

Modest Pavlovitch Kuzmentsoff, Russian lawyer

Vladimir Ilyich Lenin, Russian revolutionary, leader of the Bolsheviks

Tadeusz Lewera, aspiring Polish author

Prince Georgy Yevgenyevitch Lvoff, Russian aristocrat and statesman

Nikolay Panteleymonovitch Lushtchy, black-market trader, former railway employee

Pavel Nikolayevitch Milyukoff, leader of the Constitutional Democratic Party (Kadets)

Jelena (Jelenka) Muklanowicz, Polish traveller from Warsaw

Nikolay Nikolayevitch Muravyoff-Amursky, Russian statesman and explorer who expanded the Empire in Siberia

Myerzoff, Russian general fighting on the Japanese front

Zenon Myśliwski, secretary of the Last Kopeck Club

Dietmar Klausovitch Nasboldt, captain in the Imperial Russian Navy

Zygfryd Ingmarovitch Ormuta, director general of the Ministry of Winter in Irkutsk

Sasha Pavlitch, Nikola Tesla's Russian assistant in Irkutsk

Ivan Petrukhoff, guest at the governor general's ball

Józef Piłsudski (nickname Ziuk), Polish politician and freedom fighter exiled to Siberia

Aleksandr Aleksandrovitch Pobebedonostseff, founder and chief executive of the Siberian

Coldiron Industrial Company (Sibirkhozheto)

Porfiry Pocięgło, Polish businessman from Irkutsk, advocate of Siberian independence

Nikolay Petrovitch Privyezhensky, captain in the Imperial Russian Army

Mefody Karpovitch Pyelka, Martsynian

Piotr Rappacki, Polish high official in the tsarist Ministry of Winter

Grigory Yefimovitch Rasputin, leader of a Martsynian sect, former friend of the Imperial family

Pyotr Leontinovitch Razbyesoff, senior civil servant and provincial prosecutor

Zinovy Petrovitch Rozhestvensky, admiral in the Imperial Russian Navy, commander of the fleet at the Battle of Tsushima

Boris Viktorovitch Savinkoff, leader of the Fighting Wing of the Social Revolutionary Party (SRs)

Ivan Dragutinovitch Schembuch, high functionary in the Irkutsk Ministry of Winter

Timofey Makarovitch Schultz-Zimovy, governor general of the Irkutsk governorate

Tchingis Shtchekelnikoff, Benedykt's Siberian bodyguard

Wacław Sieroszewski, Polish exile, ethnographer and novelist

Juliusz Słowacki, Polish romantic poet, author of narrative poem *Anhelli*

Ignacy Sobieszczański, Polish industrialist in Irkutsk

Pyotr Arkadyevitch Stolypin, Russian statesman and former prime minister

Pyotr Berngardovitch Struve, Russian philosopher, economist and politician

Bolesław Szostakiewicz, Polish mayor of Irkutsk

Aleksey Fyodorovitch Tchushin, Russian industrialist

Alfred Teitelbaum, Polish Jewish philosopher, mathematician and logician

Nikola Tesla, Serbian American electrical engineer and inventor

Trotsky (Leff Davidovitch Bronstein), Russian revolutionary

Frantishek Markovitch Uriah, functionary in the Irkutsk governor general's chancellery

Yury Danilovitch Vazoff, undercover agent on the Trans-Siberian Express

Jules Verousse, Flemish journalist

Fryderyk (Fredek) Weltz, fellow student of Benedykt Gierosławski

Maria Weltz, Fredek's mother

White-Gessling, British engineer travelling on the Trans-Siberian Express

Wojsław Wielicki, Polish businessman in Irkutsk

Halina Wielicka, his wife
Marta Wielicka, his sister
Mieczysław Wolfke, Polish physicist employed by Krupp
Jeż Wólka-Wólkiewicz, journalist and editor of *The Free Pole*
Sergey Aleksandrovitch Yesyenin, Russian poet
Kliment Rufinovitch Yurkat, professor of cold-temperature physics
Filimon Romanovitch Zeytsoff, former Marxist and political prisoner, disciple of Aktchukhoff
Arkady Hipolitovitch Ziel, Pobedonostseff's secretary and messenger (his Angel)
Zygmunt, biology student, Benedykt's friend and flatmate in Warsaw

'We shall not freeze'

PART I

Warsaw

'If a soldier fires from a rifle, then in that moment a wound begins to exist, inflicted after a while by the bullet on the enemy; if someone consumes a dose of untreatable poison, then in that moment the ultimate trial of mortality begins to exist, even though its moment may come only after a few days. The Ancients spoke correctly: we died already in the moment of our birth. We have no power over the further progress of the bullet or poison (and, in part, over the further progress of our lives).'

CHAPTER THE FIRST

On the thousand-rouble son

On the fourteenth day of July 1924, when the tchinovniks of the Ministry of Winter came for me, on the evening of that day, on the eve of my Siberian Odyssey, only then did I begin to suspect that I did not exist.

Beneath feather quilt, beneath three blankets and an old gabardine overcoat, in fustian long johns and wool-knit sweater, in socks pulled over socks – feet only protruding from under quilt and blankets – thawed out at last after ten or more hours of sleep, curled almost into a ball, head wedged under pillow in its thick pillowcase, so that sounds reached me already mellowed, warmed, wax-coated, like ants trapped in resin: slowly and with great effort they forced their way in, through sleep and through pillow, little by little, word by word:

'Gospodin Venyedikt Yeroslavsky.'

'The same.'

'Asleep?'

'Yes, Ivan Ivanovitch. Asleep.'

One voice then another, the first low and husky, the second low and sing-song; before I lifted blanket and eyelid, I already saw them bending over me, the husky one by my head, the sing-song one at my feet, my tsarist angels.

'We have woken young Master Venyedikt,' declared Ivan when I raised a second eyelid. He nodded to Biernatowa; the landlady obediently forsook the chamber.

Ivan drew up a low stool and sat down; he kept his knees together and on his knees a black bowler with narrow brim. His high starched vatermörder collar, white as snow in the afternoon sun, dazzled my eyes, white vatermörder and white clerical cuffs blinding against the solid black background of their uniforms. I kept blinking.

'If you'll allow us, Venyedikt Filipovitch.'

They allowed themselves. The other sat at the foot of my bed, dragging down the quilt with his weight, so I had to let go. Clutching in turn at the blankets, I rose on my pallet, thereupon exposing my back; the cold air stole under my sweater and long johns, I shuddered, wide awake.

3

I flung my overcoat over my shoulders and drew up my knees under my chin.

They watched me in amusement.

'How's your health?'

I cleared my throat. A night-time phlegm had accumulated in my gorge, a corrosive acid resulting from the combined contents of my stomach, garlic sausage, gherkins, whatever else we had ingested the previous day, warm dogwood vodka and cigarettes, a great many cigarettes. I leaned towards the wall and coughed violently into the spitting-box. Till I was bent double. Bent double, I went on hacking for a while.

I wiped my mouth on the torn sleeve of the overcoat.

'Oxlike.'

'That's good, good, we were afraid you wouldn't get out of bed.'

I got up. My pocketbook lay on the windowsill, stuffed behind a dead geranium in a pot. I took out my bumaga and thrust it under Ivan's nose.

He spared it not a glance.

'But my dear Gospodin Yeroslavsky! Think you we're some type of lowly beat constables?' He straightened his back still further on the stool; I had thought it impossible, but he straightened it further until the walls appeared crooked, the wardrobe hunchedbacked, the door-frame scoliotic; offended, the tchinovnik lifted his chin and puffed out his chest. 'We invite you most cordially to accompany us to Miodowa Street, for tea and sweetmeats, the Commissioner always has his sorbets, petit fours, cream horns delivered straight from Semadeni, real overindulgence of the palate, if I may so put it – what say you, Kirill?'

'You may, Ivan Ivanovitch, by all means,' Kirill replied in his sing-song lilt.

Ivan Ivanovitch had a bushy, heavily pomaded moustache with up-ward-curling tips; Kirill, on the other hand, was entirely clean-shaven. Ivan took a watch on a tangled chain out of his waistcoat pocket and announced it was five minutes to five, Commissioner Preiss was a stick-ler for punctuality, and what time was he going for dinner? He had arranged to meet the major general at the Hotel Francuski.

Kirill offered Ivan some snuff, Ivan offered Kirill a cigarette; they watched me as I dressed. I plunged my face into the basin of icy water. The stove tiles were cold. I turned up the lamp-wick. The room's only window looked out onto a poky yard, the glass panes so encrusted with grime and hoarfrost that even at midday very little sunlight filtered through. As I shaved – was still shaving – I had to stand the lamp in front of the mirror and turn the flame up full. Zygmunt had parted

company with his razor immediately on arrival in Warsaw and cultivated a beard worthy of an Orthodox priest. I glanced at his bedding
on the far side of the stove. On Mondays he had lectures and had
doubtless risen at dawn. On Zygmunt's bed lay the black fur shubas of
the tchinovniks, their gloves, a cane and a scarf. The table meanwhile
was piled high with dirty crocks, bottles (empty), books, magazines
and jotters; Zygmunt liked to dry his socks and undergarments by
hanging them over the edge of the table, secured by anatomical atlases
and Latin dictionaries. And in the middle of the table, on top of a
well-thumbed, grease-stained copy of Riemann's *Über die Hypothesen
welche der Geometrie zu Grunde liegen* and a heap of yellowing back
issues of the *Warsaw Courier* – kept as kindling or for plugging cracks
expanded by the frost or for dehumidifying shoes, but also as wrapping for butterschnitten – soared a two-tiered colonnade of wax
candles and candle stubs, the ruins of some stearin Parthenon. Against
the wall opposite the stove, meanwhile, towered level stacks of hard-
bound volumes arranged according to format and size or frequency
of reading. A gorget with an image of Our Lady of the Gate of Dawn,
hanging on the sooty wall above the books – the only relic of the previous tenants, whom Biernatowa had evicted onto the street because of
their 'unbecoming conduct' – had turned thoroughly black and now
resembled more a mediaeval breastplate for Lilliputians. Ivan scrutinised it for a long time, with great concentration, seated stiffly on the
stool, left hand and cigarette thrust backwards at an angle of forty-five
degrees to his body, right hand resting on his thigh beside the bowler,
frowning and wrinkling his nose, ruffling his moustache – then I understood that he was practically blind, that he was an office myope;
on his nose and below the eye sockets were pince-nez marks, without
his pince-nez he had no choice but to rely on Kirill. They had come in
directly from the frost and Ivan must have removed his spectacles. In
here, my own eyes sometimes water. The air inside the lodging house is
dense and heavy, scarred by every bodily odour, human or animal; no
one opens the windows, doors are instantly slammed shut and cracks
above the doorsteps stuffed with rags, so that no warmth escapes from
the building – firewood has to be paid for, after all, anyone able to
afford coal wouldn't normally be cooped up in such dark holes, where
the air is dense and heavy, and you breathe it in as if you'd drunk the
water spat out by your neighbour as well as by his dog, as if your every
breath had previously passed a million times through the consumptive
lungs of peasants, Jews, coachmen, butchers and whores; hawked up
from black larynxes, it returns to you again and again, filtered through
their saliva and sputum, processed through their mould-infested,
louse-infected, pus-incrusted bodies, coughed up by them, blown out

5

through their noses, spewed up straight into your mouth, but you have to swallow it, you have to breathe it in, so breathe, breathe!

'E-excuse me.'

The privy at the end of the corridor was luckily unoccupied at that moment. I vomited into the hole, from which an icy stench blew up into my face. Cockroaches crawled from under the shit-stained boards. When they reached as far as my chin, I squashed them with my thumb.

Coming out again into the corridor, I saw Kirill standing in the doorway of our room – he had his eye on me, was standing guard, making sure I didn't escape into the frost in my long johns and sweater. I smiled knowingly. He handed me a handkerchief and pointed to my left cheek. I wiped it. When I tried to return it, he took a step back. I smiled a second time. My mouth is wide, it smiles very easily.

I donned my only presentable outfit, that is, the black suit in which I'd sat my final examinations; were it not for the layer of underlinen, it would have hung on me now as on a skeleton. The officials watched as I tied my shoelaces, buttoned my waistcoat, fought with the stiff celluloid collar attached to my last cotton shirt. I took my documents and re-maining loose change, three roubles and forty-two kopecks – any bribe offered out of this would be purely symbolic, but in an office a man with empty pockets feels naked. There was nothing I could do instead about my old sheepskin coat, the patches, stains, crooked stitches, I had no other. They scrutinised me in silence as I squeezed my arms into the asymmetrical sleeves, the left one longer. I smiled apologetically. Kirill licked a pencil and scrupulously noted something on his cuff.

We left. Biernatowa was clearly watching through her half-open door – and immediately appeared alongside the tchinovniks, flushed and rattling away, in order to conduct them back down the stairs from the second floor and across both well-yards to the main gate, where the watchman Walenty, adjusting his cap with its bronze spangle and tucking his pipe into his pocket, swept the snow hurriedly from the pavement and helped the tchinovniks into their sleigh, clasping the gentlemen by the elbows so they didn't slip on the icy curb; Biernatowa, meanwhile, as the seated officials wrapped their legs in their plaids, regaled them with torrents of complaints about malign tenants, bands of Vistula-bank thieves, who break into houses even in broad daylight, as well as the merciless frosts, due to which damp window frames warp from the inside, pipes burst within walls and no plumbing and no sewage system lasts long in the ground; finally she assured them fer-vently that she'd long suspected me of all sorts of crimes and iniquities, and would definitely have informed the appropriate authorities were it not for the thousand and one other cares piling up on her head – until the driver, seated on his box behind Kirill's back, cracked his whip and the horses jerked the sleigh to the left, forcing the woman to step aside, and so we moved off in the direction of the Warsaw delegation of the Ministry of Winter, to the former Palace of the Bishops of Cracow, Miodowa Street number 5, on the corner with Senatorska.

Before we turned from Koszykowa Street onto Marzałkowska, a fine snow had begun to fall; I pulled my shapka over my ears. The officials in their voluminous furs and walnut-shell bowlers, seated on the low benches of the sleigh, Ivan opposite me and Kirill with his back to the izvoztchik, resembled the beetles I had seen in one of Zygmunt's textbooks: fat oval torsos, short paws, small heads, all glossy-black, enclosed within the geometrical symmetry of ellipses and circles. A shape so close to the ideal sphere, its very nature debars it from this world. They stared ahead of them with passionless gaze, mouths tightly shut and chins held high owing to their stiff collars, passively yielding to the movement of the sleigh. I thought I would glean something from them on the way. I thought they would start demanding donations in return for their goodwill, for their lack of haste and urgency. They said nothing. I shall ask them – but how? About what? They will pretend they haven't heard. Flakes of sticky snow swirled between us. I tucked my cold palms into the sleeves of my sheepskin.

Lights were burning in the Pâtisserie Française; the electric blaze beat through the great windows and spun woolly haloes around the silhouettes of passers-by. The summer sun ought still to have been standing high in the sky, but as usual heavy clouds hung over the city, the streetlamps had even been lit – very tall, with spiralled pinnacles. We turned northwards. From Ostrowski's cakeshop, at the junction with Piękna Street, some girls in red coats and white hooded capes came running out, their laughter penetrating for a moment above the hubbub of the street. I was reminded of my unfinished letter to Julia and her final questioning scream. Next door to Ostrowski's, at Wedel's, I used to arrange to meet Fredek and Kiwajs for an evening round of cards. Right here, behind the Sokół Cinema, at Kalka's, the Kind Prince used to hire a room for our night-time sessions. Were I to raise my head and look to the left, above Ivan's bowler, I would see the window on the second floor of the residential building at number 71, from which Fredek had fallen.

At the intersection with Nowogrodzka a fat cow hung frozen to a lamppost, connected by a tendon of dark ice to the top of the façade of a four-storey building. The cow must have come from the last roundup of cattle to the Ochota slaughterhouse; the hiberniks had not yet chopped it down. Further down the street, above the roof of the 'Sphinx' apartment house, there loomed a blue-black nest of ice, a vast coagulated mass of frozen matter as hard as diamond, joined by a network of icy threads, icicles, spans and columns to the residential buildings on either side of Marszałkowska and Złota Streets – to residential buildings, lampposts, stumps of frozen trees, balustrades of balconies, bay windows, spires of cupolas and ornamental turrets, attics and chimneys. The 'Sphinx' cinema had long been closed, of course; on the topmost floors no lights were burning.

The sleigh slowed down as we passed Nowogrodzka. The driver pointed to something with his whip. The carriage in front veered onto the pavement. Kirill looked behind him. I leaned out to the right. Two policemen stood at the intersection with Jerusalem Avenue, herding the traffic away from the centre of the thoroughfare aided by whistles and shouts – for there, a gleiss was freezing its way across the road.

For a few minutes we were stuck in the congestion it had caused. Usually, gleissen translocate above the roofs, rarely coming down to earth in cities. Even at that distance I seemed to feel the waves of cold flowing off it. I shuddered and instinctively buried my chin in the collar of my sheepskin. The tchinovniks from the Ministry of Winter exchanged glances. Ivan looked at his watch. On the other side of the street, behind an advertising column covered in bills announcing a wrestling match at the Okólnik circus, a man dressed in the English style was setting up an antiquated camera in order to photograph the gleiss; his pictures would surely never appear in any newspaper, confiscated by the people from Miodowa Street. Ivan and Kirill paid him no attention.

The gleiss was exceptionally fast-moving, before dusk it should have succeeded in crossing to the other side of Marszałkowska, in the course of the night have climbed onto the rooftops, by Friday have reached the nest above the cinema. Last year, when a similar icer crossed the river from Praga to the Royal Castle via the Aleksandr Bridge, the bridge was closed for nearly two months. Meanwhile this glacius here – were I to wait a mere quarter of an hour, I would surely be able to perceive its movement; how it freezes from place to place, shifts position in the ice, as ice, from ice to ice, how one and then another crystal thread bursts and slowly scatters a bluish-white crumble, one minute, kshtr, two minutes, kshtr; the wind snatched up the lightest particles along with the snow, but the majority froze back into the black ice sheet that was causing street mud to congeal in the gleiss's wake, the ice of ice; meanwhile, the path of this rugged frozen mass was stretching like a huge track of snail slime fifty metres or so to the east of Jerusalem Avenue, both over the pavement and up the front elevation of an hotel. The rest had already been hacked off by the hiberniks or had thawed of its own accord; yesterday afternoon the thermometer at Schnitzer's showed five degrees above zero.

The gleiss was not moving in a straight line, nor did it maintain a constant height above the cobbles (gleissen also freeze into the ground beneath the earth's surface). Three or four hours earlier, judging by the brittle architecture of the ice, the gleiss had begun to alter its trajectory; before, it had shifted barely a metre above the middle of the street, but then, three hours ago, it had moved upwards along a sharp parabolic curve, above the pinnacles of lampposts and crowns of frozen trees. I saw the row it had left of slender stalagspikes; they glowed in the reflected light of streetlamps, in the gleam of neon colours, in the radiance streaming from windows and shop displays. The row of stalagspikes broke off above the tramlines – the gleiss hung with its whole weight upon a star-shaped network of frost-strings, spreadeagled horizontally and stretching towards the façades of the corner buildings. It was possible to walk underneath, were anyone foolhardy enough to try.

Ivan nodded to Kirill and the latter clambered out of the sleigh with a reluctant grimace on a countenance made red by the smarting cold. With a bit of luck, I thought, we'll perhaps be late, Commissioner Preiss will leave for his supper booked with the major general and they'll dismiss me from Miodowa empty-handed. Thanks to you, dear God, for that monster icicle. I shifted position on the bench and leaned my shoulder against the back of the sleigh. A newspaper vendor came running up – 'Hirohito Defeated!', 'Express Special, Myerzoff Triumphal!' I turned my head. Crowds were gathering alongside the blockages in the city centre, street hawkers appeared, sellers of cigarettes and holy water, or holy fire. Policemen were chasing pedestrians away from the gleiss, unable to protect everyone. A gang of street urchins stole up from the direction of Briesemeister's restaurant. The pluckiest, wearing a muffler wrapped around his face and thick shapeless mittens, ran within a few feet of the gleiss and flung a cat at it. The mouser flew through the air in a high arc, spreading wide its paws, howling at the top of its lungs... a terrifying shriek broke loose. It was most likely dead already when it hit the gleiss, only to slide off slowly into the snow, frozen to the marrow: an ice sculpture of a cat with splayed limbs and tail straightened like a wire. The boys ran off almost writhing with joy. A Jew with side curls shook his fist at them from the doorway of Epstein the Jeweller, swearing bitterly in Yiddish.

Kirill meanwhile had laid hands on the older policeman and, having seized him by the elbow so he didn't dash off in pursuit of the urchins, began to reason with him about something in subdued tones, but with the conspicuous assistance of sweeping gestures from his other hand. The constable averted his face, shrugged his shoulders, scratched the crown of his head. The younger of the two was shouting to his companion, get a move on, help! On Jerusalem Avenue the runners of two sleighs had become hooked together, causing even greater hullabaloo; carriages were driving onto the pavements; pedestrians, cursing in Polish, Russian, German and Yiddish, were fleeing from under wheels and hooves; outside a wine store, a matron the size of a Danzig cupboard had tumbled on the frozen mud, three gentlemen were trying to help her up, a portly officer hastened to their aid, and so all four of them heaved together, at the count of one – she fell again – two – she fell again – three – and the whole street was splitting its sides with laughter, whilst the poor woman, red as a cherry, squealed in terror, swinging her fat little legs in their tiny boots… No wonder it took the crack of lacerated metal and splitting wood for us to look back towards the junction. An automobile had hit a coalman's cart; one horse had fallen, a wheel had come off. The policeman brushed Kirill aside and ran towards the crash. The motorist trapped inside the covered vehicle began to honk his horn; in addition, something went off beneath the bolide's bonnet as if fired from a double-barrelled shotgun. This was too much for the grey nag harnessed to the sleigh alongside us. Startled, it lurched forward straight towards the gleiss. The driver grabbed at the reins but the horse itself must have sensed into what wall of frost it fell – it reared to one side even more energetically, overturning the sleigh on the spot. Did the runner catch the curb? Did the grey nag slip on the black surface of the ice? I was already standing up in the ministerial sleigh observing the accident together with Ivan above the line of sleighs in front, but everything occurred too swiftly, too unexpectedly; there was too much movement, shouting, too many lights and darks. The grey nag had fallen, the sleigh drawn by it had overturned and shed its load – a dozen or so bulbous cylinders packed in sawdust-filled baskets; the baskets and cylinders rolled towards the middle of the junction, some must have smashed, since a shiny celadon liquid was spreading over the ice – naphtha, I thought – when fire flared up, ignited by an electric spark from the automobile, by a discarded cigarette, by an iron-shod hoof striking the cobbles – I have no idea by what. The blue flame leapt across the entire width of the puddle, tall, taller and taller still, a metre, a metre and a half high – almost reaching the gleiss frozen into the network suspended overhead.

The photographer, bent over his camera, gradually, methodically, took snap after snap. And what he'll see later will be what is captured on glass and printed on paper: snow – snow – pale haloes around streetlights – dark mud, dark cobbles, dark sky – grey elevations of residential buildings against a wide ravine of city – in the foreground, the chaos of angular vehicles held in a traffic jam – and between these and between people's silhouettes the brilliance of pure fire erupting, so intensely bright that the photographic paper in this spot appears totally unexposed – and above this, above the white flame whiter than white, at the heart of the hanging arabesque of ice, sprawls the gleiss, the gleiss, a massive thunderbolt of cold, a star of hoarfrost, a living bonfire of chill, the gleiss, the gleiss, the gleiss above ladies' fur toques, the gleiss above men's caps and bowlers, the gleiss above horses' heads and carriage hoods, the gleiss above the neon lights of coffee houses and salons, boutiques and hotels, pâtisseries and fruit shops, the gleiss above Marszałkowska Street and Jerusalem Avenue, the gleiss above Warsaw, the gleiss above the Russian Empire.

As we drove later towards the Saxon Garden and along Królewska Street, past the Garden itself, lifeless beneath longstanding permafrost, and the colonnade strung with icicles, past towers covered in snowy overhangs and the Russian Orthodox cathedral on Saxon Square, towards the thoroughfare of Krakowskie Przedmieście, that picture – the afterimage of that picture and what it represented – came back to me again and again, an insistent memory of obscure significance, a sight seen but not understood.

The officials exchanged gruff remarks under their breath, the driver shouted at inattentive passers-by; the snowstorm had abated, but the day was growing colder and colder; my breath, suspended in a white cloudlet before my face, froze on my lips; the sweat-covered horses moved forward in clouds of sticky damp – the Royal Castle drew closer and closer. Before the turning onto Miodowa Street, I caught a glimpse of it above the Zygmunt Column: the Castle encased in a block of shadowy ice – and a great nest of gleissen positioned above it. A purplish-black, clotted mass stretched over half the rooftops of the Old Town. On sunny days, around the Great Tower, it was possible to see waves of cold stood upright in the air. No thermometer has a scale capable of measuring such cold. On the boundary of Castle Square, gendarmes keep watch by their bonfires. Whenever a gleiss freezes its way out of the nest, they close off the streets. A cordon of dragoons from the Fourteenth Malorossiysky Regiment had been stationed there by the governor general, but the regiment had been expedited in the meantime to the Japanese front.

The rooftop of the Palace of the Bishops of Cracow, however, remained free of icy accretions. Stylish shops still occupied the annexes entered by way of Senatorska Street – electric floodlights illuminated the displays for Nikolay Shelekhoff's Exclusive Delicatessen and teas from Sergey Vasilyevitch Perloff's Moscow Trading House – but the main wing, entered from the Miodowa side, with its rococo finials, pilasters and Corinthian capitals, was the property of the Ministry of Winter. Above both entrance gates hung the two-headed black eagles under their Romanoff crowns, incrusted with onyx tungetitum.

We drove into the inner courtyard, the runners of the sleigh scraping the cobblestones. The officials alighted first, Ivan immediately vanished through a door, planting the tsviker on his nose; Kirill stood on the steps before the threshold and turned in my direction. I opened my mouth. He raised his eyebrows. I looked down. We entered.

The janitor relieved me of my sheepskin and cap whilst the warden pushed towards me a great ledger in which I had to sign in two places; the pen slipped from my fingers, stiff from the cold: should I sign for you, sir, no, no, I can do it myself. Illiterate plebs also darken the corridors of the Directorate of Winter.

Everything here sparkled with cleanliness: marble, parquet, glass, crystal and the rainbow sheen of coldiron. Kirill led me up the main staircase and through two secretariats. On the walls, beneath portraits of Nikolay the Second Aleksandrovitch and Piotr Rappacki, hung sunlit landscapes of steppe and forest, Saint Petersburg in spring and Moscow in summer, from the days when spring and summer still had access to them. The secretaries did not raise their heads from their desks, but I saw how councillors, administrators, clerks and scribes followed me with their eyes and then exchanged oblique glances. At what hour does the clerking end? The Ministry of Winter never sleeps.

Commissioner Extraordinary Preiss V.V. occupied a spacious office with antique masonry stove and disused fireplace, the high windows of which looked out onto Miodowa Street and Castle Square. When I entered, crossing paths in the doorway with Ivan, who had clearly just announced me, the Commissioner was busying himself with the samovar, his back turned. He too had the figure of a samovar, bulging pear-shaped torso and small bald head. He moved with phrenetic energy, hands flapping above the table, whilst his feet never stopped dancing, step to the left, step to the right – I was sure he was humming to himself under his breath, smiling under his breath, merry eyes looking out upon the world from a ruddy countenance; the smooth forehead of the Commissioner of Winter unfrowning. In the meantime, since he failed to turn around, I stood by the door, arms folded behind back, letting the warm air fill my lungs, wash over my skin, thaw the blood congealed in my veins. In the office it was almost hot, the great painted majolica stove never cooling for one moment; the windowpanes eventually misted over so much that through them I saw mainly the blurred rainbows of streetlamps, strangely flooding and pouring down the glass. It is a matter of great political importance that within the Ministry of Winter, cold never prevails.

'Well, why don't you sit down, Venyedikt Filipovitch? Have a seat. Have a seat.'

Ruddy face, merry eyes.

I took a seat.

Sighing audibly, he slumped into a chair on the far side of the desk, cradling in his palms the porcelain cup of steaming tchay. (He did not offer me any.) He had not been overlong in charge, the desk was not his; behind it he looked like a child playing at a being a minister, definitely minded to change the furniture. They must have sent him only recently, the tsarist commissioner extraordinaire, sent – from where? From Saint Petersburg, from Moscow, from Yekaterinburg, from Siberia?

I took a deeper breath.

'If Your Esteemed Nobleness will permit... Am I under arrest?'

'Arrest? Arrest? Whence such an idea?'

'Your officials –'

'My officials!'

'Had I received a summons, I would myself –'

'Did they not invite you courteously, Mr Gierosławski?' He, at last, pronounced my name correctly.

'I thought –'

'Bozhe moy! Under arrest!'

He was panting.

I clasped my knee in my hands. It's worse than I'd imagined. They're not going to throw me into gaol. A high-ranking tsarist official wishes to have a *conversation* with me.

He began taking papers out of the desk. A fat wad of roubles. Official stamps. Perspiration streamed over my body neath my undergarments.

'Ye-es.' Preiss slurped his tchay loudly. 'Kindly accept our condolences.'

'I beg your pardon?'

'Last year your mother died, no?'

'Yes, in April.'

'You were left alone. I am sorry. A man without a family is like... well, he's alone. That's bad, oy, bad.' He turned over a leaf of paper, slurped, turned over the next leaf.

'I have a brother,' I muttered.

'Yes, yes, brother by birth, at the ends of the earth. Where did he go, Brazil?'

'Peru.'

'Peru! And what might he do in Peru?'

'Build churches.'

'Churches! Writes often, no doubt.'

'More often than I.'

'Nice. He must miss you.'

'Must.'

'And you don't miss...?'

'Him?'

'Your family. When did you last hear from your father?' Leaf of paper, leaf of paper, slurp.

Father. I knew it. What else could it be?

'We don't correspond, if that's what you mean.'

'Dreadful, oy, dreadful. Don't you care if he's alive?'

'Is he?'

'Ah! Is Filip Filipovitch Gierosławski alive! Is he alive!' Preiss sprang up from behind his theatrical desk. By the wall stood a large globe on a lightweight pedestal made of wet coldiron, on the wall hung a map of Asia and Europe; he rotated the globe and slapped the back of his hand against the map.

When he turned back to look at me, not the slightest trace remained on his chubby cheeks of his recent jollity; his dark eyes stared with clinical concentration.

'Is he alive,' he whispered.

He picked up the yellowed papers from his desk.

'Filip Gierosławski, son of Filip, born in the year eighteen hundred and seventy-eight at Wilkówka in the Kingdom of Prussia, in East Prussia, Heilsberg District; since nineteen hundred and five a Russian subject, husband of Eulagia, father of Bolesław, Benedykt and Emilia, sentenced to death in nineteen hundred and seven for his part in a plot against the life of His Imperial Exaltedness, as well as armed rebellion; well, by way of reprieve, the sentence was commuted to fifteen years' hard labour with deprivation of nobility rights and sequestration of property. In nineteen seventeen he was granted amnesty with a prikaz to reside for the remainder of his life within the General Governorate of Amur and Irkutsk. He didn't write? Never?'

'To my mother. Perhaps. At the beginning.'

'But now? Recently? Since seventeen. Not at all?'

I shrugged my shoulders.

'I am sure you know better than I when he writes and to whom.'

'No insolence, young man!'

I smiled weakly.

'Apologies.'

He scrutinised me for a long time. On a finger of his left hand he wore a ring with a dark stone set in precious tungetitum, engraved with the emblem of Winter; he rapped the ring on the desktop, trook, trookk, even raps stronger than odd.

'You graduated from the Imperial University. What are you doing now?'

'Preparing for the rigorosum –'

'Supporting yourself on what?'

14

'Private lessons in mathematics.'

'And you make much on such lessons?'

Since I had already been smiling, all I could do now was lower my eyes onto my clenched hands.

'Much, not much.'

'You're a regular guest of the moneylenders; all the shylocks on Nalewki Street know you. To Abiezer Blumstein alone you owe upward of three hundred roubles. Three hundred roubles! Is it true?'

'Were Your Esteemed Nobleness to state on what matter I'm being interrogated, it might be easier to confess.'

Trook, trookk, trook, trookk.

'Or maybe you really have committed some crime, for you to sweat out your fear so profusely, eh?'

'Perhaps Your Esteemed Nobleness would deign to open a window.'

He stood over me; had no need even to expressly stoop to talk straight into my ear, first a whisper, then a soldier's bark, eventually little less than a scream.

'You are a gambler, my Benedykt, an inveterate card player. Whatever you win, you lose – whatever you earn, you lose – whatever you borrow, you lose – whatever you beg from friends, you lose – you no longer have any friends – no longer have anything, yet you lose even that, you lose everything. Pontoon, baccarat, blizzarder, poker, anything will do. Once you won half a sawmill and lost it the very same night. You have to lose; you can't rise from the table without losing so utterly that no one wants to play with you. No one wants to play with you anymore, Venyedikt Filipovitch. No one wants to lend to you anymore. Your entire life is indebted for two years ahead. Bolesław doesn't write to you; it is you who write to him, begging for money, but he won't send more. You don't write to your father because your father has no money. You wanted to get married, but your father-in-law-not-to-be set his dogs on you when you pledged your betrothed's dowry and lost it. Had you at least blown your brains out as befits a noble-born, but you won't do it, tphoo, that's the kind of scum noble you are!'

I continued to smile apologetically.

Commissioner Preiss heaved a sigh, after which he clapped me amicably on the shoulder.

'There now, never fear! We also fraternise with scum. It's of no consequence to us that you're as little interested in your father's fate as in the Emperor of Japan's gout – on the other hand, you are interested in a thousand roubles! Am I right? A thousand roubles interest you like… well, they interest you very much. We will give you a thousand, and maybe a second thousand later, if you perform well. You are going to visit your father.'

Here he fell silent, obviously anticipating a reply. As he received none, he returned to his desk and steaming tchay (it had cooled slightly, so now he slurped longer and louder), to his papers and stamps. Wielding a massive pen, he entered his signature on a document, struck it with a stamp, corrected it with a second; satisfied with what he had done, he rubbed his diminutive hands together and sat back in the leather armchair.

'Here are your passport and orders to our delegation in Irkutsk, they'll look after you on the ground. They purchased the ticket at once, you leave tomorrow for Moscow, otherwise you won't catch the Siberian Express – today is the first of July, your ticket is for the fifth, departure is at ten in the evening from the Yaroslavsky Station, you'll be in Irkutsk on the eleventh, there they'll put you on the Winter Line to Kezhma. Here you have a thousand, sign the receipt. Buy yourself some decent clothes so you look human! And should it occur to you to take the money and lose it all at cards – on second thoughts, lose it if you must, so long as you reach Baikal. Come on, sign!'

A thousand roubles. What are they expecting me to do there? Drag out of my father names not betrayed at his trial? So why is the Ministry of Winter turning to me with this and not the Ministry of Internal Affairs?

'I will go,' I said. 'Visit my father. What else? Is that it?'

'Talk to him.'

'I'll talk to him.'

'And when you talk to him, well, then it will be all right.'

'I don't understand, what Your Esteemed Nobleness…'

'He sent no letters, but you're not surprised, why should you be, ha?' Commissioner Preiss opened a baize- and tortoiseshell-embossed briefcase. 'Irkutsk informs us… He was a geologist, is that right?'

'I beg your pardon?'

'Filip Filipovitch studied geology. He continued to pursue it in Siberia. Here I am informed… From the beginning he was very close; then his convict work gang was attached to the second or third expedition that went there in the spring of nineteen ten. The majority perished from frostbite. Or froze to death on the spot. He survived. Then he returned. To them. I don't believe it myself, but that's what they write to me here. They have given the order, given the money, so now I am sending the man. Your father converses with gleissen.'

On what cannot be put into words

My life is governed by the principle of shame.

One gets to know the world, gets to know a language for describing the world, but does not get to know oneself. The majority of people – almost all, I would say – never learn as long as they live a language in which they could describe themselves.

When I say of someone that he is a coward, it means I consider that he behaves in a cowardly fashion – it means nothing more, because, obviously, I will not look into his soul and will not find out whether he is a coward. I cannot use this language, however, to describe myself: within the scope of my experience, I remain the only person for whom his words, actions, failings, are but a pale and fundamentally random reflection of what lies hidden beneath them, of what comprises their cause and source. The existence of this source I experience directly, whilst I am not conscious at all of certain aspects of my behaviour, and receive everything in an incomplete, distorted manner. We are always the last to learn what a fool we have made of ourselves in company. Better do we know the intentions behind our actions than those actions. Better do we know what we wanted to say than what we actually said. We know who we want to be – we do not know who we are.

A language for describing our actions exists, because many people experience this reality and are able to discuss amongst themselves someone else's ostentatious affability or someone else's faux pas. A language for describing myself does not exist, because no one except myself experiences this reality.

It would be a language for one-person usage, an unutterable, unwritable language. Everyone must create it themselves. The majority of people – almost all, I am convinced – never acquire it as long as they live. At most they repeat in their minds other people's descriptions of their own person, as expressed in that derivative language – in the language of the second kind – or they imagine what they would say in it about themselves, were they able to see themselves from the outside.

In order to say anything about themselves, they have to make themselves strangers to themselves.

My life is governed by the principle of shame. I have no better words with which to tell this truth.

A beggar extends his hand in an imploring gesture, I have money, I could give him at least five kopecks, at least two, at least one kopeck; no one else is watching, there are only the two of us, me and the beggar – I give nothing, I turn and walk quickly away, hiding my head in my shoulders.

Who smashed the jar of jam? Mother raises her voice. Who smashed it? Not me, I haven't a clue, it was Bolek, or Emilka, but Mother asks again, and again, and then I point emphatically at Bolek. Him.

Laughter in company, we are making fun of a shared acquaintance, obviously not with us here and now; one after another we evoke memories of his disgrace and weakness. I stand up, laughing no longer, frowning, lips pursed, stand up and – Aren't you ashamed of yourselves!

The drunken girl clings to me, spills over my arms, slides onto my chest, my lap, as the droshky slows down and stops outside the gate to the old town house where I rent a room with Kiwajs. Kiwajs is with his distant family in the provinces, the room is empty, the krasavitsa giggles, gnawing at a button on my frock coat – the cabby turns around, winks at me, your lordship needs help? I glance about, terrified. Press a crumpled rouble into his fist. Drive the bitch away, wherever you want! I throw off the drunken girl, leap from the droshky and flee into the dark hollow of the gate.

In the forest behind grandfather's village, in the pit of an uprooted tree above a stream, lies the corpse of a roe deer. Devoured by predators and scavengers, under a black canopy of flies. I tell no one that I come every morning and every evening, poke at it with a stick, turn it over, watch how the insects crawl over it anew, how the flesh changes colour and dark fluids flow out of the body, seeping slowly into the soil. Where are you spending so much time, my grandfather asks. I lie. He sees that I lie. Where am I going, he asks. I say nothing. He chastises me with his belt. I weep. I do not tell the truth, do not tell anything. Throughout the entire summer I walk in the forest seeking dead animals. Carrying a fat stick, like a cudgel. With that stick I beat the carcass in mindless frenzy, until the putrid matter falls away from the bone. So take that! And that! And that!

Eighteen and seventy-four! Eighteen and seventy-four! Announcing the winning numbers, the fairground crier screams himself hoarse. We'd all bought lottery tickets on entering the fair. All smiles and laughter, red from frost and slivovitz, we now search our pockets for the bits of card. I find mine, extract it. Eighteen and seventy-four. Enacting their great disappointment and fury, the others cast their tickets into the mud, cursing their bad luck and mocking the nincompoop who does not come forward to claim his prize. I tear up the winning ticket and do the same as they.

At night, when no one is watching, I practise pulling gruesome faces, bulging my eyes and baring my teeth, rather too wildly for them to signify anything in the language of human physiognomy; gruesome faces, but also absolute deadness of mien, motionlessness of the most infinitesimal muscles of the skull, which in the light of day and amongst people I never manage to achieve; I have no control then over the grimaces of my face. At night, when asleep, I see under my eyelids a diagram, like one of Zygmunt's yellowed drawings, an anatomical diagram of that betrayal: dozens of threads of hard twine strung beneath the skin of my cheeks, eyebrows, chin, lips, whilst the other ends of these threads are held by the people surrounding me, in their hands, between their teeth, roped around watch chains and cufflinks, tied to wedding rings, cane heads and pipe stems; some of these people themselves have them sewn into facial muscles, and also into their hearts, straight through the chest and breastbone. Then that drawing comes to life – it is day – there is movement – people – me –

I am smiling – smiling – smiling.
...

I am recalling behaviours, availing myself of the second language...

I have to make myself a stranger to myself.

Benedykt Gierosławski was a good child. Who would not have wanted such a child? He was well-behaved – always obeyed his parents, obeyed his elders, never spoke out of turn, stirred up no trouble, didn't fight with other children, said his prayers before bed, and had the best marks at school. Other boys gallivanted around town, spent time on the streets – he read books. Other boys spied on girls and teased their sisters – he taught his sister the alphabet. Washed behind his ears. Said hello to neighbours and acquaintances. Did not pick his nose or stick out his tongue. Was never ill. Caused his parents no problems. Who would not have wanted such a child?

When he'd completed seventeen years and entered the Imperial University, he met other men who had been good children.

They recognised one another from their smiles.

Was it already too late? Could I have gone back? – gone back to what, to whom, to what kind of me? There is no moment in the past which, miraculously transformed, would have turned around the course of my life, no catastrophe that *befell* me, as a result of which I am different from what I ought to be; I cannot point to any such thing.

It is precisely the other way around: whatever time I might reach back to in memory, I always discover beneath the fine epidermis of my words and deeds this same principle, the muscle of disquiet, hope and disgust strained in this same direction, when I was three years old, thirteen or twenty-three. It's not a feeling, but something else, not a thought – it flees, ducks away, slips out, immaterial, indescribable – Halt! Look me straight in the eye! – you, you – I am naming you Shame, though you are not it, I am naming you Shame, because no better words exist in the speech of men.

On the laws of logic and laws of politics

Alfred Teitelbaum was waiting for me in Herszfeld's restaurant. He sat by the big window that opens onto Simons Passage reading a newspaper which was folded askew. He had ordered peisachovka and goose scratchings and was probably already on his second helping; from Miodowa to Długa Street is only three paces, but as I was telephoning him from the Palace lobby, I was accosted again by Ivan and Kirill: forms had to be completed, a certificate of trustworthiness obtained, more minor travel documents written out... When I entered the restaurant, the clocks were indicating seven.

'Here, take it.'

Alfred stared at the banknotes thrown onto the tabletop. Had he any recollection still of the debt? Or had he given up all hope I'd ever settle it? I hung up my sheepskin and cap. He was counting the roubles, slowly shuffling them between fingers.

I sat down.

'I'm leaving.'

He raised his head.

'For how long?'

'No idea.'

'Where to?'

'Siberia.'

He cleared his throat.

'What's happened?'

I told him about my father, showed him the documents.

'You were afraid I'd not believe you,' he muttered.

'You've been threatening me for a month with your move to Lwów.'

He lit a cigarette. To warm myself, I ordered vodka. Outside the window, on the opposite side of the street by a shop door neath a milliner's sign, two young women were conversing, dressed in elegant chic stoles. Half-turned towards the window, we talked above blue smoke and the voices of other guests, Herszfeld's was full at this time of day; we talked loudly and distinctly as if declaiming from a stage, or testifying before a high tribunal. The women under the milliner's sign were laughing, covering their red mouths with black-gloved hands. The frost made their beauty still more pronounced, lit a sparkle in their eyes, dabbed rouge on their cheeks, chiselled their nostrils.

'Leśniewski and Sierpiński are inviting me officially, in the name of Lwów University.'

'They've just broken ranks with Kotarbiński.'

'I shall do my doctorate there in a year, two years.'

'Starting all over again?'

'Bah! I was wondering whether to change my name.'

'You jest.'

Alfred shrugged his shoulders.

'Byezhkoff heard I was applying for a permanent post, a teaching position. And you know how he runs down Jews.'

'Łukasiewicz is to lecture at the Imperial from the autumn. Perhaps _'

'Lecturing in the Polish language isn't all. This boycott has gone on for too long. The Imperial University goes back more than half a century, we have to reckon with tradition.'

'So, it's abroad to Lwów? You've decided?'

'You say yourself you don't know when you'll return. Besides, admit it, we've struck an impasse with this work.' He reached into a briefcase shoved under his chair, extracted a thick file of papers, a good half-ream. 'Please, take the lot, including my latest valiant attempts.'

I leafed through absentmindedly. Indeed, there was even Kotarbiński's article from *The Philosophical Review* from eleven years before as well as the final, rejected version of our *Theories and Applications of More-than-Two-Valued Systems of Logic*.

'And so? Now we're left only with set theory and Boole?' I snarled peevishly.

'I can no longer bring myself to look at the *Principle of Contradiction*. I shall have to mull over again from scratch the elementary propositions for the logics in *Principia Mathematica*. If you take the quantifiers of the propositional and functorial variables... Besides, I already told you.' He sighed.

The conversation ran dry.

I rumpled Alfred's newspaper in my hands.

The war is nearly won. Russia cracks down on enemies closer to the Empire's heart. In Saint Petersburg, a high-profile political trial. *Vilinkovitch A.D. is charged with membership of a faction aiming to introduce a democratic republic in Russia. Cross-examined by the prosecution, the accused confessed at the end of the third day of his trial.* In the financial columns, questions of customs tariffs and speeches against free trade in the British Parliament, as well as bankruptcies in heavy industry. *American billionaire Morgan negotiates with German and French banks over establishing a grand anti-coldiron trust and has already offered, together with these banks, an exclusive trade deal at guaranteed prices to governments of countries so far unaffected by the Ice, demanding however an anti-Russian customs embargo. We say: Let Mr Morgan fund his own country!* Ppff, hard to find a topic I cared about less. I drained the glass of vodka. A column further on, below an advertisement for J. Joujou's School of Good Manners – a caricature of women rampaging in automobiles. *New excesses by the suffragettes. English suffragettes employ ever more violent methods in their campaign. The day before yesterday a suffragette burst into the office of Election Minister Carr; a moment after the minister's departure, she threw hot liquid over the documents and manifestos lying on the table. A drop of the liquid splashed into the eye of the minister's secretary, scalding it painfully. Despite the acute pain, the secretary gave chase to the assailant; she, however, having fled the place, climbed into an automobile and tore up the narrow street against the flow of traffic. The plucky secretary continued the chase on a borrowed bicycle, but the demented lady accelerated without respect for people or animals, thereby escaping the arm of the law. Thank God such vulgar customs are foreign to us in the Kingdom and in imperial Russia.*

I rumpled the paper, my own mind empty of thought.

The last customers were leaving the milliner's shop; the women stepped away from the entrance, vanishing from our field of vision. The haberdashery next door was also closing; lights went out inside.

I squeezed tight my eyelids, as if a snowflake had suddenly flown into a pupil.

'I can't forget that sight, when I drove onto Miodowa Street… You know, there's a gleiss stood over the junction of Marszałkowska and Jerusalem Avenue.'

'Aha.'

'There was an accident, a spill of naphtha, flames sprang a good metre high, or higher, two metres. Except that, you see, the gleiss was hanging above the fire, already frozen to buildings, streetlamps, advertising columns. Earlier it had been dragging itself along the ground – but above the junction, it had risen in the air. It must have begun to rise a good half-day beforehand. But, Alfred, that accident was entirely unforeseen! One coincidence after another!'

He stared at me half-amused, half-terrified.

'What's this supposed to be? Field tests in logic?'

'Bu-ut, is logic a science founded on empeiria? On the surface, what could be more removed from empeiria? And yet in such reflections, we all depend on our experience, on observation of events taking place in the world – in our world and in our observation. Truth and falsehood do not exist outside of our heads. Without the language in which we express them, and without the sensory impressions on whose basis we have learned everything – there would be neither truth nor falsehood.'

He stubbed out his cigarette in the ashtray.

'Without the language… Precisely in this language! In this language, in which we speak, there is no truth or falsehood.'

'In the language in which we speak…' I began and broke off, experiencing for the thousandth time this one unassailable truth: that in the language in which we speak, all these tragic deformations and limitations of the language in which we speak cannot be expressed. It is not even possible to relate why certain things cannot be related.

'You're still haunted by the antimony of the liar,' I tutted in disgust.

A man stands before you and says that he is lying. He told the truth? Therefore, he was not lying. He lied? Then he was telling the truth.

What value are we to ascribe to such statements? Since they are neither true nor false.

'Help me!' Alfred Teitelbaum rapped the ashtray on the tabletop. 'Where does the error reside?'

'We assume that human language is generally bound by the laws of logic. Whilst it is the other way around: it is language that impedes logic.'

'To tailor language to logic – but then it would no longer be our language.'

'So what? If logic is the reflection of objective reality, and not merely a prejudice living inside our heads sanctified by tradition – then we should proceed in the same way as the physicists, gradually tailoring the language of the mathematical description of the world to this world.'

'To find such a language, in which it would be possible to express the truth... That means: in which everything that can be expressed will either be true or false. Mm-hmm.' – Again, he stared out of the window at the snowy passage. 'First, you would not be able to speak in that logical language about yourself. In order to circumvent the antimony of the liar, you would have to banish beyond language all true or false assertions about propositions made in that language.'

I snorted.

'Therefore, once again it would be a language unfit for expressing the truth.'

'No! You would be able to say that snow is falling,' he waved towards the windowpane, 'but you would not be able to say that you spoke the truth when saying that snow is falling. Not in that same language. Do you see?'

'But that still does not match up to our world. Do we really have in it only truth or falsehood?'

'Bu-ut that's another kettle of fish! Kotarbiński is right: certain statements can be neither true nor false, until the events occur to which they refer. Leśniewski is an orthodox follower of Laplace, and that's why he takes his entire future as already realised. But the statement "Tsar Nikolay the Second did not live to see his sixtieth birthday" will not be true or false for another four years. But when such events occur, and when those statements become true or false, they cannot then cease to be so with time.'

'Because you look at the process as if it were some kind of logical meat mincer, into which you stuff from one side – that of the future – misshapen chunks of the meat of events; we grind them through the Present and, hey presto, there emerges from the other side of the mincer – into the past – a logical mince divided into two equally sized ribbons: truth and falsehood.'

'Well, that more or less agrees...'

'So freeze it now.'

He bridled.

'What?'

'Freeze it, hold on to it, stop it in its tracks. You can be certain only of your Now. Everything else – everything that clings to your Now but is not contained within its confines – is doubtful, exists only as speculation built upon Now, and only insofar as you are able to deduce it.'

Teitelbaum was already staring at me pityingly.

'You really believe that we render judgements about the past either true or false – when we uncover it? And that we rob them of falsehood or truthfulness – when we forget, and thus lose this knowledge? Benek!'

'That's what happens with judgements about the future after all, on which we are agreed, no? God makes no use of three-valued logic, because He knows everything; His is the language of "Yea, yea, Nay nay." So says the Bible and Doctor Einstein. And since people can only know those events that affect their Now... What in that case am I to say about gleissen? The one I saw at the junction today... Tell me: were we to perceive reality differently, were we to live in a different reality, a different time stream – would we make use of the same logic? You know we would not.'

Alfred ordered coffee. Unbuttoned his collar and even leant back in his chair.

'Which means that without someone to articulate this truth in words, it is not possible to assert that the world exists, correct? The statement "the world exists" will not be true – or false – until someone expresses it.'

'Earlier, there would have been no possibility of such a statement, so –'

'How does it happen then that in all cultures, at all times, all languages create the same categories of truth and falseness, bah! that they all invoke the principle of non-contradiction?'

'Because they continue to be human cultures, built upon experience entering through two eyes, two ears, mulled over inside a monkey brain... You studied biology after all. Think: how many earthly species there are endowed with a different sensory apparatus, set in different environments.'

'So how is it then: you have one objective logic, rooted in reality itself – or hundreds of different logics dependent on the thought and sensory apparatus of a particular species?'

'But each to a different degree and from a different angle approximates the logical principles of the universe.'

'Ah! And according to you, gleissen –'

'They perceive not the world as we perceive it. They live in another world.'

'You have in mind a world that's completely deterministic? Animals without will knowing their whole future?'

'No, no, had it known the future, it would not have crawled there!'

'So what then –'

'A riddle: a world best described by the logic of Kotarbiński – and a world described according to my logic, in which only judgements about the present are frozen: true or false. By what criteria would you differentiate these worlds?'

'Mm-hmm. By the fluidity of their truth about the past?'

'What does that mean? Talk to anyone about nineteen twelve or the January Uprising.'

'Facts are one thing; the memory of them, the opinion of them, is something else.'

'Memory!' I snorted angrily. 'Such memory is not a gift but a curse: because we remember only the past, and we remember one single past, each his own, we succumb to the delusion – Doctor Kotarbiński too succumbed to it – that past events remain established for all eternity, frozen in truth. And we construct all logic based on this delusion.'

Alfred wound and unwound his white handkerchief pensively.

'By what criteria would I differentiate these worlds? ... Am I to conclude you consider them undifferentiable? But in your world, many pasts, equally true and untrue, would exist simultaneously, just as at this moment there exist many possible futures to our rendezvous here: in some of them you depart first, in some I do, in some we meet –'

'My dear Mr Teitelbaum! My dear Mr Gierosławski! Whom do my fair eyes behold!'

Thus appeared before us Mitschka Fidelberg of the Mutual Aid Association of Shop Assistants of the Mosaic Faith of Warsaw, secretary of the Warsaw Socialist Circle and distant cousin of Abiezer Blumstein. Already tipsy and sweating profusely under his freshly starched shirt, his face alight with alcoholic glow, so much so the wall lamps were reflected in his smooth cheeks as in the cupolas of the Aleksandr Nevsky Sobor; when he bent over me, with a fiery blast aimed straight at my nose, it was as if a hot searchlight had ignited before my eyes, a roaring furnace opened its jaws. Mitschka weighed nearly two hundred kilos, and was also the right height for them. When he leaned on the tabletop, we heard the crack and snap of wood, the rattle of glass; when he stood upright again, the neon streetlights were eclipsed behind his back.

'My respects, my respects, let me kiss my geniuses, Benedykt, damn you, well, well –'

'Mitschka, how goes it?'

He belched over me garlic and condensed euphoria.

'Come now! Have you not heard?' He grabbed the crumpled newspaper and brandished it over his head like a standard. 'Myerzoff has defeated the Japs at Yule!'

'Possibly so, the newspapers vendors were hollering about it – but why should it prompt such delight in you?'

'There'll be a winter ceasefire! A great amnesty! New ukases on the zemstvos! Taxes down, support for Ottepyelniks up!' He pulled out a roll of flimsy agitational brochures and thrust a few at each of us. 'Have some! Have some!'

'And a good communist is pleased at the emperor's triumph, why so?'

'What do I care about triumph – triumph or disaster, so long as we don't have a thirteenth year of war with no end in sight, aim or sense. But things are moving now!' He kissed me with a bold flourish on both cheeks, right, left and right again. 'Things are moving! Thaw! Spring!'

Alfred pushed aside the propaganda, wiped his mouth and forehead with the handkerchief, took out another cigarette.

'Revolution is most easily ignited by the flames of war, is it not? Ordinary people won't come out on the streets to die for words and ideas, but for bread, work and a few extra kopecks a day – certainly. Therefore, the better the state of the economy, the less the chance of an all-Russian uprising. A long, drawn-out war between two world powers always brings hope of economic collapse. But who'll rise up against His Victorious Imperial Exaltedness in peacetime?'

Mitschka drew up a chair, then sat on it with an extended sigh, as if releasing steam from a samovar, pfffch! – and he's already rolling up his sleeves, loosening his collar, setting wide apart his elephantine legs; the chair creaks as Mitschka Fidelberg leans over towards his interlocutor and puffs out his chest, prepared with his own chest to defend the Revolution.

'Nineteen-oh-five!' he roared. 'Nineteen twelve! How many more times, gentlemen! How many more times the same mistakes! The Bolsheviks and SR-men never learn; the Bund at least has come to its senses. Had we a working class like England or Germany – but who's going to make a revolution here, I keep asking myself the same question: uneducated peasants? How the Narodniks have come out of this, we know; it's easier for them to recruit Okhrana agents to their idea than the peasantry; a people tied to the land is itself a reactionary class. What of it that they shoot the tsar's ministers, blow up his generals? The tsar's got plenty of generals!'

'Which means what? Are you joining the Struvists and court socialists?'

'I spit on them!' he spat. 'It's not about this or that camarilla, but History! Because the whole point is that in the present state of the country, revolution has no chance of success. We have seen it for ourselves from our own bitter experience, paying twice over with worker's blood, in nineteen-oh-five and twelve, yet it seemed in those days too that the autocrat was weakened by Japanese wars and everything pointed to our advantage. But for the same reason, gentlemen, you'd never have made a social revolution in Ancient Rome! Marx was well aware of it: History progresses according to the iron rules of logic and you can't simply skip one stage or other – just as a butterfly can't be born at once, first you have to have the caterpillar and then the chrysalis.'

'Lenin –'

'Lenin does nothing these days except bite the legs of Swiss nurses.'

'Mitschka,' I leaned towards the breathless Fidelberg, 'am I understanding you correctly? You are going to support the bourgeoisie and the capitalists, because only after them can there be a real proletarian revolution?'

'You have to have a proletariat to make a proletarian revolution! Perhaps you believe in god-building or the pipe-dreams of Berdyaeff *et consortes* or those socialist Narodniks who've suddenly taken a shine to Herzen and Tchernyshevsky and still harp on today about Russia's historical mission, and that we don't have to chase after the West and repeat its mistakes; instead, without townsmen and bourgeoisie, thereby bypassing the intricacies of capitalism, they cultivate an autochthonic Russian socialism out of the unblemished, collective popular spirit, ugh. Rusky mysticism! What, on the other hand, says Trotsky? Even if by some miracle – a conspiracy of the Four Hundred, insanity of the ruler, a natural or unnatural disaster – even if one nation-state were to fall under the control of the working people, all states of the old order near and far would immediately throw themselves upon it and smash it to smithereens, not giving socialism a chance to develop to strong maturity. Revolution would have to embrace all nation-states, at least the majority, where majority is measured according to economic and military power. It's not enough to add up the history of one country; only History can be calculated effectively, by which I mean the all-embracing, all-regulating historical system. Do you see that, my gentlemen mathematicians? You must see it!'

'What then is to be done? Open the can! Drag Russia into the twentieth century, even against her will! Yes, yes: defrost History by force! Defrost History, I say! First Ottepyel, then Revolution! But not a Thaw of divine conferring, transported from metaphysical cycles,' here he clenched his club-shaped fists, 'but made with our own human hands! Out of our work, intelligence, science, money! So that,' he panted, catching breath at the very end, 'is the sort of new Ottepyelnik I am...'

'I have long ceased following the perturbations in the Duma – aren't the Trotskyites now in some tactical league with the Struvists and Stolypinist trudoviks? Besides, does any of it really change anything? What difference does it make to a Pole? One form of Russian power, another form of Russian power.'

'A reborn Poland must be a socialist Poland! And it will be!'

'Well, that doesn't add up either.' Teitelbaum inhaled a drag of tobacco smoke. 'If you enter alliances that result in the softening of reactionary politics, then you will only hamper the revolutionary work: isn't that the whole point – that tsardom and the bourgeoisie should oppress the proletariat, no?'

I raised my finger.

'Dialectics, Alfred, dia-lec-tics!'

'Why can't we expect revolution then also in Germany, England, America?'

'Those Western capitalists have no idea how to oppress. Only a Russian knows how to oppress the weak and poor, so that they even cease caring whether they're alive or dead.'

'What drivel!' Mitschka banged his fist on the tabletop. 'There the bourgeoisie keeps an even firmer grip, because it's had more time to take root and become intrenched. Whereas in Russia – in Russia, well, here in the Kingdom, we've been ready since the beginning! Let History get off the ground, let us achieve the necessary conditions – and revolution is inevitable!'

'How should I know... With Pyotr Struve at the helm and socialists sitting for twenty years in the Duma...'

'Perhaps it would be better to bank on some massacre at the front or riots on the streets... And hunger in the countryside. Though until now they've been starving to death humbly enough without butchering nobles or tchinovniks, Pugatchoff long forgotten.' Alfred winced sceptically. 'And then there's the military, the military first and foremost – not some mutinous battleship or other, but regiments, armies.'

'Starting to return home right now.'

'The economy should pick up, definitely,' I admitted. 'Though I am not sure it's such good news for the moneylenders.'

Fidelberg slapped his sweating forehead, which resounded like a succulent smack.

'Agh, Benedykt, grandfather is already –'

'Oh, that's right, Mitschka!' I beamed. 'Be so good as to ask the old fellow whether he mightn't lend me, in circumstances of sudden dire need, a mere ten roubles? A long journey awaits me, expenses.'

'Archangels defend me!' Fidelberg leapt to his feet and retreated through the restaurant, waving his great hands in front of his red face and making signs to ward off evil. 'As if such mediations hadn't already cost me more than enough! Begone!'

Alfred followed him with his eyes.

'Really, Benek, no need to return it now, if –'

'Worry not! Before they get around to demanding back a loan, you have to ask for the next – they're happy to escape for the time being with their wallets intact.'

'I suppose so,' he stubbed out the cigarette, buttoned his jacket, picked up the briefcase. 'So, when are you leaving?'

I turned over in my hands Mitschka's legally illegal pamphlet, filled with obscure miniscule print, a dozen articles in dubious spelling speckled with exclamation marks, a single daubed political cartoon and one poem by Yesyenin at the foot of the final page.

'Tomorrow.'

'To Siberia, you say. Via Tyumen and Irkutsk, yes?'

'What now?'

'Nothing, nothing,' he hesitated, pondering for a moment. 'When I received that award from the Mianowski Fund... Financed mainly by Eastern fortunes, Poles from Asia, from the Caucasus and Far East. Were you at the banquet...? No, probably not. I met one of those magnates who sells furs, gold, coal and coldiron, he was funding several scholarships for young mathematicians from the Kingdom, Bielecki or Bielawski...'

'And so?'

'He opened his heart over a bottle of vodka, so much so I thought he was going to recite his whole family tree; I barely managed to get rid of him, such is his nature, offers you the world, then thrusts it down your throat. Every Christmas and Easter he sends me unspeakably hideous cards with his felicitations and promises that when he is next in Warsaw... Ye-es, I'll find his address, write you a letter of introduction. Maybe it'll be of use. The train departs from Terespol Station?'

'Mm-hmm.'

'Chin up! Don't give in to gleissen, Benek! Don't give in to the Ice!'

Biting my tongue, I folded the brochure into geometrical squares, Yesyenin on top.

A snowbound plain, the moon's orb white,
Beneath the Ice, land locked in plight.
Inhuman icers grip the birchwood stream.
To slumber here? To freeze? Of Revolution dream.

On Mr Tadeusz Korzyński's finger

Not every creditor can be approached with the same tactics as Abiezer Blumstein; it doesn't pay to behave in that way towards everyone. From Herszfeld's I walked straight to Bielańska Street, to the house of the Korzyński family. The master was at home, I was invited into the drawing room. It took me a long while to clean the snow and mud off my boots under the watchful eye of the valet before he admitted me onto the parquet floors and carpets. We stepped from the brightly lit hall up the wide wooden staircase to the first floor. There was a scent of cinnamon and vanilla. From the depths of the corridor I could hear women's voices, perhaps too that of Staszek. Here the gas lamps were burning, but in the drawing room the drill roller-blinds had not yet been drawn over the windows, nor the heavy curtains of English chintz. Beneath the dark sky woven with snow-laden clouds, it is easy to forget that we are actually in summer, that the Sun rises and sets according to summer hours. Less warmth and light as ought in July penetrate the winter aura and reach the earth; it is still nevertheless a July sun – you need only glance at the angle at which it slices through the clouds, how it bounces off the snow, in what colours it paints the windowpanes. The drawing room windows faced west; the eerie twilight of a wintry summer evening reigned within, a grey luminosity.

Tadeusz Korzyński was looking out onto the street. I trod softly over the thick carpet, but he must have heard me; he turned around, pointed to a red re-upholstered chair.

'What's happened, my Benek?'

Usually I come to see Staszek on Tuesdays, Thursdays and Saturdays.

'I have not come about lessons, sir.' I extracted a roll of roubles; I had earlier counted out the exact sum. 'I should return the advance.' He neither moved nor extended his hand, so I laid the roubles on the table. 'I am very sorry, I will recommend another tutor.'

'Has Staszek –'

'No, not at all, nothing to do with Staszek.'

He waited, arms folded behind back, erect, in his narrow-cut *tout jour* frock coat. He stood between two high windows against the backdrop of a gilt-framed mirror – a silhouette of a man, or dark reflection of a silhouette in the mirror, there was no telling them apart. The July winter light described a dark line around him from both left and right, as if he were a saintly figure depicted on a stained-glass pane. He waited in silence, capable of waiting like that for long minutes. I felt my lips part in a sickly ingratiating smile: caoutchouc, junket, lard melting on a piping hotplate.

I told him about my father, the Pilsudtchiks, the sentence and Siberia. He continued to say nothing. I told him about the visit to Miodowa Street and ticket to Irkutsk. He said nothing. I told him about my father and the gleissen. Without uttering a word, he left the drawing room by a side door. I sat with hands clasped around my knees; in front of me on the table lay the red-hued diengi, above me on the wall hung a hussar and young woman decked in flowers, and all around me – a cornucopia of fragile trinkets and family memorabilia belonging to Mr and Mrs Korzyński. A large grandfather clock struck eight.

Mr Korzyński returned with a large tome under his arm and a small casket in his hand. He summoned the maid to light the lamp. Having sat down at the table, he scrutinised me for a moment from under thick eyebrows. With his left, healthy hand, adorned with a massive signet ring bearing the all-seeing eye inside its triangle and glory, he mechanically stroked the casket lid, covered in intricate plant symbols.

When the maid had closed the door behind her, he opened the large tome. It was a photograph album.

'I was not acquainted with your father, young man, but know that it was no coincidence that you were recommended to me as a teacher for Staszek. We try to assist the families of old comrades. A friend of a friend had written about you; I had written to friends.'

He paused.

I lowered my eyes.

'I had guessed as much –'

'In nineteen twelve,' he began, interrupting me, 'I took part in a raid to recapture fellow combatants belonging to Piłsudski's Union of Active Struggle transported to Yekaterinoslav and Sebastopol for the Black Sea Trials. As I am sure you are aware, the raid was successful, but afterwards we were pursued with even greater tenacity. We split into groups; cities were unsafe; the majority tried to make it into Galicia, many of us were caught. My unit chose the route towards Rumania. Eventually, we were chased across the Borderlands and cut off by the Dniester; we had been fleeing for three weeks, it was already October, and we knew that Piłsudski had been captured, the Revolution had collapsed in Russia and the Japanese were withdrawing along the whole front. All we had to do now was lose the Cossacks; in the end, we nearly lost ourselves. We rode across the steppe, far from human habitation. Hamlets could be discerned from afar by smoke rising into the sky. That particular one, we stumbled upon after dusk and quite by surprise. We imagined they must have seen us too, and since we needed provisions… A wretched Ukrainian khutir, a few hovels, more like dugouts, mud huts. Nowhere fire, smoke, lights, only silence, that silence of the steppe which sends shivers up your spine; no dog barks, no cattle low, no cart scrapes its wheels. Nothing. We ride in, our guns cocked. Immediately it's obvious that something is untoward. Not one of the hovels stands upright: walls are lopsided, doors pushed out of frames, roofs have subsided. The same with furniture and tools, as if someone had twisted them in a vice, floorboards skewed, wheels buckled, poles split open. We ride up to a well – the well has collapsed. We peer into farmyards. The cattle are dead, only flies swarm over corpses. Plague, someone whispers. Our commander orders us to check on the people. We look inside the hovels. It's the same with the people, just corpses. We chase off the flies. The faces are swollen, flabby, as if all had drowned. But at the same time, red and black as if burned. We ride around the village examining the ground. A track leads from north to south, the width of four peasant carts; the earth is churned up, overturned, torn asunder, not from ploughing but as if it had scattered itself about, crumbled of its own accord, you understand, there is no trace of any tool. Even the stones along this tract are split open, ground to a gravel. We glance at one another. To the south, says our commander. We ride south – but it's night-time, we have to stop. In the morning, the track peters out. It's there and then no longer there – in the middle of the steppe, a place like any other place, but here the earth is churned up, yet a few paces farther on the grass grows green. Back north, says our commander. We ride. We pass a village, the track is very distinct, it's safe to trot. In the afternoon, some thirty miles ahead, we see it on the horizon. At once the temperature drops. A little nearer, and the breath freezes on our lips. A gleiss, we suspect. You will remember that in nineteen twelve, to the west of the Bug, people knew about gleissen only from hearsay. A gleiss, we say to ourselves, as we lace up our tunics, wrap our greatcoats around us, spur on the horses. Only later, when I returned to the Kingdom and read newspapers from Galicia, did I understand what it was. An expedition from Königsberg had found something similar in the Nyland guberniya, in the Grand Duchy of Finland. The first icecradle.'

He turned the photograph album to face me. Now, as the lamp burned on the table, whatever lay beyond its reach was doubly hidden in shadow; as soon as you glanced into the patch of light, anything outside of it surrendered to the reign of night. Instead, here in the light, objects drew closer, grew warmer, friendlier towards human beings, willingly presenting themselves to the touch, lifting themselves to the eyes. I stretched out my hand towards the album. Tadeusz Korzyński's hand, the right, deformed one, was pointing to photographs on the first page.

Eight men pose for the camera, stand in a field holding their guns or leaning on the barrels, in a row. Their tunics recall the old military uniforms of the Rifles, but the rest of their clothes resemble rags. They are unshaven, but their faces are clean. They do not smile. It is day, above them the bright sky. Behind them – a vast massif of dazzling white.

The black stump points to further photographs. Here we see the same icecradle. It extends about fifty metres, maybe more. The photograph is not of the best quality; whoever of them had brought the camera had definitely not brought the best equipment. He'd also been unable to take a panorama of the icecradle from above; it showed a plain with no elevations. There are only eye-level shots, taken perhaps from the saddle, and only of the outer layers.

It is neither building nor sculpture nor living organism. Gleissen go in and out of it, but it could equally be said that an icecradle swallows gleissen and spits them out. Likewise, no one can say whether the nests of gleissen hanging over cities of Asia and Europe are merely places where a few or several gleissen have frozen together – or whether they are also something more, something altogether different.

An icecradle is in relation to a nest what a nest is in relation to an individual gleiss. But in the case of the icecradle, we now know with certainty that it consists of something more than a simple congregation of gleissen. Immortalised in the photographs are fragments of agricultural tools imprisoned in the ice, household utensils, half a table, an old cauldron, an icon, a fragment of anvil, as well as more perishable things like a wholegrain pancake, string of onions, ring of sausage, and also body parts, animal and human, and internal organs, and other objects impossible to identify in the black-and-white images. The ice formations seem to correspond to the shapes of the paraphernalia trapped within them. A large icespike growing at an oblique angle out of the ground, in which half a corpulent woman hangs suspended above the plain, is crowned by a weird caricature of a human foot.

White glints of steppe sunshine, reflected in the ice, erase however any precise details of the icecradle.

'Without a magnifying glass you can't see it, but this fragment here,' – the talon, which had once been the bone of his index finger, touches a photograph – 'has the look of a face about it, even has a plait attached to the other side, except that it's completely stretched out vertically, look, the nose, the mouth. Here, here. Seven metres at least.'

He shows me more pictures. I bend over, almost touching the album with my nose. The lamplight warms my face and neck.

'We have no more photographs; the camera did not withstand the cold. It was meant to be a chronicle of freedom, not a panopticon of ice.'

He closes the book.

I return to my upright position; my hands remain in the circle of trembling brightness – I withdraw them when Korzyński lowers his eyes towards them.

'Farther on, beyond this fragment,' he begins again, clearing his throat, 'there was a bay, that is – a break in the external formation of the ice and a breach leading to its interior, like a corridor between two white walls. I wanted to try riding in there, to see at least what lurks inside an icecradle, whether anything more lurks there beyond what we had seen. Our commander forbade it.

'Then, just beyond the entrance to the corridor, in the second wall, the eastern wall, we espied this young man imprisoned in the ice. There is no photograph, you have to trust my memory. He was submerged in ice up to his ribs. But he was not trapped in a standing position, rather lying – some three metres above the ground. Above him, a lump of permafrost was also suspended with half a potter's wheel locked inside; the whole mass was roughly semicircular. We immediately turned our attention to the youth trapped in the ice, but only when someone shouted: "Breath!" did we see the cloudlets of steam before the livid face, beneath the head covered in frosty hair suspended over the chest. He was alive. He was breathing.

'Hack down the icecradle! We could barely get close enough to touch the poor wretch. Cold rolled over us in sharp waves; inhale it deeper, and a man's soul freezes within him. Someone fired a shot into the wall, a metre below the imprisoned youth. The bullet stuck in the ice; not even a scratch-mark appeared. What to do? Our commander ordered us to light a bonfire underneath the boy. We gathered branches and brushwood. Thanks to the fire, it was possible to stand there longer and lead a horse to the wall. I still had a drop of homemade vodka and attempted from the saddle to give the poor fellow a drink. Still unconscious, he hung there limply. I was unable to part his lips so there was no way of pouring the beverage down his throat; his head slumped forward as far as anatomy allowed; he lay in that ice with his back to the sky, face down, as if he'd been trapped by the transparent slabs from above and below before he'd had time to crawl out from between them. Then I realised the best we could do was gift him a few more hours of life – or shorten his agony, would that be any worse outcome? Were he actually to regain consciousness before dying… Usually people who perish from cold simply fall asleep, so I am told, allegedly unaware of approaching death. So why wake him? Half his internal organs, guts, liver, pancreas, kidneys, must surely have already changed into hard clods of ice. What breathes – is no longer a man – though nails and hair still continue to grow also on a corpse.

'I moved my hand over his chest (he was wearing a coarse hemp shirt) in order to ascertain where life still reached. My hand,' here Tadeusz Korzyński raised his right hand towards the lampshade and splayed the black stumps under the light, 'slid towards the ice, maybe my horse shifted under me, maybe I lost my bearings in the stultifying cold... I touched the ice. I froze to it. I must have cried out dreadfully; they told me I screamed as though I'd been flayed. True, the skin came away from my flesh like torn-off paper. My horse took fright, reared away from the ice and the fire. I fell off. My fingers,' here he moved what was left of them under the lamp as if playing with the shadows cast, 'remained in the ice. I had fallen onto a large icespike, knocked out several teeth, gashed my skin. Behold the wound.'

He leaned towards me, grinning. The scar twisted on his visage in harmony with the joyless grin, a thick welt like the mark of a single bullet.

'They dragged me away. Bound my hand. The cold cauterized the wounds. They made me drink the vodka I'd tried to give the icelocked boy. I slept. In the morning, the youth was no longer breathing, a dark hoarfrost had spread over his eyelids, nose, mouth. I went there with a high torch to burn my fingers out of the ice, after a few minutes they fell off. The whole thumb, bits of three others. During the night they had managed to freeze deeply into the icecradle. Had they also left imprints of their shapes? I examined the thumb. A piece had been bitten off, traces were clearly visible, the savaged muscle at the base and a tooth stuck in it, wedged between the bone and the cartilage, my own molar tooth which I had lost when falling.'

Tadeusz Korzyński opened the Japanese lacquered casket. Inside was a small bundle wrapped in chamois, the shape and size of a cigar. He took it out and then gently unwound the material.

The thumb looked mummified, petrified – uniformly black, straight, with the nail blending into the skin, which was firmly and smoothly pulled over it. Mr Korzyński rolled the thumb over on the chamois cloth, turning towards the oil lamp's waxy light the other side of its base, where – as I leaned over the table – the yellow root of a tooth protruded from black bone.

The grandfather clock struck half-past eight.

Mr Korzyński laughed quietly. I glanced at him inquiringly – was he going to explain the joke? He was not joking, he himself was staring at the thumb, lost in sombre thoughts.

'I looked for those missing teeth in the grass and in the mud and in the snow, but I did not find them. On my return I gave an account of everything to my Master, handed over the photographs. Brothers from France were already taking great interest in the gleissen, I was invited to collect further information. Initially, the Russians did not impose such censorship on research in guberniyas in the vanguard of the Ice. I was unable to devote much time to it, but since the gleissen reached Warsaw...' He raised his eyes to me. 'What precisely did they tell you about your father?'

I repeated what I had said.

He shook his head.

'He talks to... Hiberniks – people who have survived the proximity of a gleiss – are no more than ordinary paupers, for whom falling asleep drunk in the snow has proved a blessing in disguise. The Ministry of Winter exploits them and pays them to keep order in the city after gleissen, since that initial touch immunises them against the cold.'

'It may also be different, the other way around.'

'I beg your pardon?' He leaned stiffly towards me, submerging his puckered countenance again in the cloud of yellow brightness above the dark tabletop.

'What I am saying,' I stammered, 'What I am saying is that it's a false diagnosis. We know only that those who survive are exceptionally resistant to frost – yes, but they would not have survived, would they, had they not been resistant in the first place?'

'I am not sure to what –'

'Does katorga make our Sybiraks exceptionally resistant and resilient? Or do the less robust simply not return, and so we never take them into account? Perhaps there is no miraculous change – merely selection.'

He straightened his back, vanishing again in shadow.

'Yes, I see, you are right.'

'Cause and effect are illusions of a weak mind,' I muttered under my breath.

He reclined slowly in the twilight.

'Benek, dear fellow' he began again gently after a while, 'even if your father were a hibernik... Truly, I know not which is worse. Listen to me. Why I tell you this. In the spring of twenty-one, intelligence reached me that someone was seeking volunteers to throw bombs at a nest of gleissen. Locked up by the Okhrana, this SR-man, who was meant to manufacture the bombs, then turned out to be an Okhrana agent. But, apparently, volunteers had already come forward claiming to be capable of approaching the nest, bah, and placing a bomb at its very heart, and that they would do it for a fitting sum: renegade Martsynians. It was then that I heard about the sect of Saint Martsyn. Folk who deliberately walk into the clutches of a gleiss. They die, of course, frozen to death. There are degrees, thresholds of initiation, or rather thresholds of recklessness. How close can a believer get? Two metres. A metre. For a second; or can he withstand longer? You can hold your breath – that helps, if air off the gleiss doesn't enter the lungs. Get too close and breathe in deeply – and you drop dead, the heart stops. They practise it. Bathe in ice-holes. Sleep in snow. Slow down the blood in their veins, lower their pulse. Move slowly, speak not, eat not, consume only liquids, regularly let blood, regularly swallow ice. Allegedly, Rasputin is also one of them – he martyrs himself by swimming in the Neva under ice floes. Allegedly, the most highly initiated Martsynians really do touch – not the warmer icecradles, empty of gleissen – but gleissen themselves. No one has met these adepts of Winter. Perhaps they live there, in Siberia.

'You say Filip Gierosławski converses with gleissen. That is what they told you.' He rewrapped the dead thumb in the soft material, tucked it away in the casket. 'If you do not have to, if you have any choice... perhaps it would be wiser to spare yourself this meeting.'

He stood up.

'And take the money.'

'Thank you.'

Different tactics have the desired effect with different creditors. And there are also those with whom it pays to be honest.

On the blinding darkness and other obscurities

The gleiss still hung over Marszałkowska Street. I dropped into the 'dairy-house' on the corner but found no Zygmunt. Quickly swallowed a plate of boiled potatoes with dill, washing it down with kefir. The hot steamy air filling the eatery – a greasy haze – penetrated my lungs and impregnated my clothes with aromas of cheap cuisine. Scratching myself under the sheepskin, I thought perhaps I had already achieved that level of abnegation when, smelling the odours of others, I had ceased to smell my own. Those looks and smirks from the tchinovniks of Winter... Had not Tadeusz Korzyński also discreetly moved away from me, leaned back from the table? I am capable of not noticing what I wish not to notice; capable of smiling through the stench.

I walked to the Messalka bathhouse. The façade of the tall townhouse opposite the Holy Cross Church had recently been renovated; stained frostoglaze panels, their pieces held together by frozen coldiron, had been mounted into the office windows fronting the street, matching designs in the baths. Silhouettes of passers-by were reflected in the coloured glass, drifting past in shoals like exotic images of undersea life, wondrous flora and fauna beneath the brightly coloured surface of the water – overcoats, shubas, sheepskins, stoles, muffs, capes, hats, bowlers, caps, fair-skinned faces, faces with black growth, wrapped in scarves, wearing pince-nez... I stopped in my tracks. There: bowler hat, azure-blue eyes beneath the black rim, smooth cheeks – I spun around – he had vanished amongst the people. An hallucination, or was it really Kirill from Miodowa Street? But even if – but why assume at once that Kirill was following me? Why should he be? And why he, and not some anonymous spy of the Okhrana? I chose not to believe it.

Soaking in the hot water, I went over in my mind the words of Korzyński's tale. The photographs had left less of an impression than his words – I had seen in Austrian and Prussian newspapers a fair number of shots of gleissen, their nests and even an icecradle; besides, already in Stolypin's day, Gebethner & Wolff had published a monograph by natural scientists from Saint Petersburg; the Ministry of Winter had not confiscated the entire print-run and the photographs were of considerably better quality. But Korzyński's black frozen thumb with the tooth embedded in it – the thumb, which he had not bitten – yet had bitten –

On the other hand, maybe it was a common affliction of older people: swallowed by their own memory, they live less and less on what they experience every day and more and more on what they remember. The scale-pan of the past outweighs the scale-pan of present and future, and it happens that in answer to a question about a weather event outside their window, they will describe a storm remembered from childhood – for the fifth, tenth time – not even realizing that they repeat themselves; since the very fact that they already said it has slipped their memory.

How many times had Tadeusz Korzyński repeated his story? Always no doubt in a dark room, after dusk, beside a single burning lamp, in the silence. How many times had he taken out the casket and lovingly unwound the honey-coloured chamois? *There is no photograph, you have to trust my memory.* The common affliction of older people. He must be at least fifty. I was reminded of Fredek Weltz's mother, not much his senior. Since Fredek's death, her memory has stopped still like a frame in a photoplasticon, moves not forward, accumulates no fresh images – accepts not a world in which Fredek is no longer amongst the living. It is a form of benign derangement often affecting cheerful, trusting, gentle-hearted people in the twilight of their lives.

She never goes to bed before midnight, then dozes instead for most of the next day; I knew she would receive me. As a rule, I look in on her on my way home from the Korzyńskis – how was your day, how are you feeling, Mrs Weltz, has the landlord forgotten again to bring the coal, and this handful of roubles, they are from Fredek, he couldn't come himself, unfortunately, he'll come tomorrow for certain, he came yesterday, did he not?

She opened the door; I had barely knocked, it was as though she were lurking in wait behind the door or watching out for me through the window. The maid had returned to the Germans who rented the six-room flat on the fourth floor; she would drop in on the widow for only two or three hours. The rest of the day Mrs Weltz spent alone. She never left the building. Sometimes neighbours, or friends of neighbours, came to see her – she would tell their fortunes from cards, or read their palms, or interpret their dreams. What else remained in old age to a woman from a nice respectable home? Gossiping, embroidering on her tambour frame, matchmaking for the young, reminiscing about her own youth. Once she prophesied I would marry five or six women, beget four sons, amass a worldwide fortune, and on top of all that, die very young.

'Come in, Benek dear, I'll pour the tea, another cruel frost, did you see those clouds in the west, there'll be so much snow tonight that –'

'I've only come for a moment, tomorrow I won't be able, so –'

'This morning Fryderyk came for breakfast, left something for you, please, there, on the sideboard.'

'Ah, Fryderyk… yes.'

Mrs Weltz pulled me almost by force from the hallway into the parlour, a petite, slightly stooping woman in black dress, black bonnet, covered from top to toe in black lace – for nine years she had worn mourning for Engineer Weltz, who had died of pneumonia during the first winter of the gleissen. I kissed the desiccated, puckered skin of her hand (smelling of camomile and naphthalene). Immediately, she tore it away, smiling, and scampered off to the kitchen.

The little parcel on the sideboard was the size of a cigarette case. I undid the paper wrapping. *Wiener Spielkarten – Ferd. Piatnik & Söhne.* A deck of playing cards. Fredek mainly played with Piatniks, used to buy half a dozen packs at a time, the cheaper sort.

'Where did you get these?' I asked, when she returned with tea and biscuits on a tray.

'What, those cards?' She gave me a fleeting glance. 'I have been telling him to stop gambling, no good will come of it, honestly, Benek dear, couldn't you bring him to his senses somehow, you are such a sensible young man, but Fryderyk, my God, if only he took after his pater of blessed memory and not what he likely inherited from his grandma Horacja, a good heart, but a butterfly and a scatterbrain – as soon as he knows no one is keeping an eye, he immediately listens to what the evil spirit prompts…'

Where did she get that deck of cards? Surely, she must have found it amongst her son's belongings – but only today? Was she waiting with it – but for what purpose?

I hid the cards in the pocket of my sheepskin. Reached for my pocketbook, counted out twenty roubles, then, on second thoughts, another five.

'Mrs Weltz, I must return these to Fredek, would you be so kind as to convey them to him when he calls? I am departing for a few weeks, please don't alarm yourself that I won't –'

'Escaping to the sun, to the country, are we, Benek dear?' She measured a spoonful of honey from the jar. 'I am not in the least bit surprised; the doctor tells me it's too dangerous here for my health and I should move out of Warsaw, but where would I move to, and is it worth it – not much life remains to me, but you young people, undoubtedly… has the university term already ended?'

'The Imperial has its break in winter. Mrs Weltz –'

'So where are you going?'

I gritted my teeth.

'To visit my father.'

She blinked, confused.

'But did you not say your father's dead…?'

'What are you saying, no, nothing of the kind. He's alive. Still alive. Probably.'

'Ah!'

She observed me carefully, inclining towards me her bony head in its black bonnet, the honey spoon half-raised to lips pursed in contemplation. At this point I should have turned away and walked out – fled – ignoring her pleas and entreaties. Except that she was silent – watching me with wide-open eyes, as if waiting for some sort of sign; the hand raised in the air shook more and more conspicuously.

Eventually, she put down the spoon and smacked her lips loudly.

'But what are you so afraid of, my child?'

I smiled, unsure of myself.

'Come,' she nodded encouragingly. 'Come, I won't eat you.'

She grabbed my hand.

'Show me.'

She succeeded only in straightening my fingers and shaking her head over nails so badly bitten they were bleeding; before she could turn over my hand so that the palm faced upwards, I had torn it away.

'I won't let you go like this,' she grumbled, rising to her feet. 'Do you want me to worry myself to death? Fryderyk also tells me nothing, none of you ever tell me anything. If Wincenty, God rest his soul, had listened to me and not gone that day to Praga –'

'I've no time for your patience games!'

'Sshhh, my child, we shall explain everything in just a moment, explain, illuminate, undarken – just a moment and we shall see, *lux in tenebris*, everything shall be revealed, wait, wait.'

Humming briskly under her breath, Mrs Weltz took from the sideboard a small jar containing a black candle-end; cleared from the table the tray with its cups and saucers, the little basket of dried flowers, her needlework and yarns, and also the bundle of roubles; adjusted the lace tablecloth, and transferred the lamp to a heavy cabinet that concealed a broken-down orchestrion behind its ornamental doors. She took out the candle-end and placed it in the middle of the table on the upturned jar lid. Then she took my arm, the sleeve of my sheepskin, and pulled me energetically towards a spot opposite the window. 'Here,' she indicated, having placed me a metre or so from a wall covered in faded wallpaper with reeds-and-cranes motif. 'And please don't move, please, I implore you.' I muttered something as a sign of agreement. I stood facing her with my hands in the pockets of the unfastened sheepskin, one leg already retreating towards the door. She returned to the table. Licking her fingertips, she twisted between them the pitch-dark braid of the blackwicke, twisted, smoothed and began to purr with satisfaction. She was amusing herself perfectly; I doubted not that she lived for such moments. She moved a burning match towards the braid. I could see Maria Weltz sideways on, how she bent over the mahogany table and gingerly reached from above towards the blackwicke, the flame almost touching her fingers. A hushed pop was audible like the snapping of a delicate bone or thwack of a leather thong against wood, and the fire leapt onto the blackwicke, reversing colour within a split second. The room filled with a vibrant darkness. Trembling unlicht flowed into the world, absorbing into its thick shadow the circular table, Maria Weltz stooping over it, the empire chairs, the orchestrion, the gilt-framed portrait of Madonna and Child, the old sideboard, the photographs of the deceased engineer, the Berlin porcelain dinner service, the dozen clay juglets standing on the low jardinière, the gramophone with its cracked horn, the roller blinds, the curtains and the decorative fern neath the window. The unlicht surely leaked out farther, beyond the window – it must have gone darker on Chłodna Street, and should any passer-by have raised his head, he would have seen on the second floor of the rented townhouse, amongst the brightly lit yellow rectangles, one window that was pitch black. Whereas here, indoors, the boundaries of darkness were defined by objects lying in the path of the unlicht – the glintzen cast by these objects appearing as geometrical patches of luminosity: under the table, in the corner behind the wardrobe, behind Mrs Weltz. Whenever she moved, her refulgent glintz also moved. The unlicht did not consist, however, in a simple reversal of light: it did not circumnavigate obstacles lying in its direct path, whilst the very boundaries between darkness and glintz did not remain unchanged. The wardrobe did not move, the blackwicke did not change position, and yet the rectangle of brilliance on the paper behind the wardrobe's side now shrank, now expanded, the borderline between light and darkness constantly bending ellipsoidally, now outwards, now inwards; from an upper corner of the glintz, every now and then, there grew a funnel-shaped extension to the glare, broadening across the ceiling, only to immediately wind back into itself and stab the glintz with a crooked fang of dark. The feverish fluttering of light and unlicht did not falter for a second. 'Stand still.' I stood still. Maria Weltz, hurriedly mumbling the Litany of the Blessed Virgin Mary, walked around the table and then hid in the radiance in the corner behind the wardrobe. From there, she could clearly see the glintz dancing on the wallpaper behind my back. Instinctively, I wanted to look over my shoulder, interpret the shape of the light cast onto the wall. 'Stand still!' I froze. Forced now to look straight ahead of me, I glanced inadvertently at the black flame of the blackwicke and for a long time was dark-blinded; a greasy tar poured into my eyes. I squeezed the lids together. Mrs Weltz continued to mumble under her breath, the words merging into a melodic purr. What images was I projecting onto the faded wallpaper with its reeds and cranes? On Saint Andrew's Day, people pour hot wax through key-heads into cold water; those images are likewise meaningless, childish fortune-telling, amusement, superstition. 'And now think of him.' 'What?' 'Your father. Think! Conjure him before your eyes! And again!' Irritation got the better of me. I swung around on my heels, turning to face my own glintz, and opened my eyes. A silhouette of cold fire spread its arms before me, its head a bushy crown of spark-thorns, standing upon the tangled roots of thunderbolts, as if in a robe woven of electrical threads, a long needle pointing obliquely towards the earth. I staggered forward, terrified. 'Put it out!' Maria rushed to the table and covered the blackwicke with the palm of her hand, smothering the coal-black flame. The lamplight and grey luminosity of the wintry July evening outside the window returned to the room.

I rubbed my eyes, twice blinded – by the darkness and by the light – convinced that under my eyelids, the pupils still pulsated like two will-o'-the-wisps of unlicht.

Widow Weltz gave me hot tea, pushed the biscuits in my direction.

'No one can tell their own fortune from a blackwicke, Benek dear, you should not have looked. What did you see?'

'I was dark-blinded.'

'Not good, not good. Are you sure your father lives?'

'Why do you ask?'

'Nothing, nothing, I hope he is alive and well, please forgive me, I meant not to frighten you –'

'Frighten me?' I laughed dryly. 'With what?'

For the first time, her eyes avoided mine. She stowed the blackwicke in the jar, screwed on the lid, placed the jar on a shelf in the sideboard and locked the door. She moved with the exaggerated caution typical of the elderly, as if she had to first think through every movement, plan it, and only then carry it out.

Rare were the moments – like this, like now – when expressions of joy deserted her face; when they did, the flabby skin revealed all its wrinkles, the birdlike folds distended neath chin and throat, the eyelids sagged.

'When Fryderyk visits me, I tell him his fortune too, insofar as I can. I try to forget, but since I cannot forget, I try to ward off fate – warn him to avoid his fate. I know the light of death, the glintz which he casts, it is his destiny – I tell him so, but he heeds me not, please watch over him, Benek dear, please, I implore you – were he to perish as well, like the blackwicke shows, suddenly, young, tragically, in anger, were he to perish too, I know not what I would do.'

She sat down cautiously on a chair, almost hunched in half; with quivering hand, she raised a batiste handkerchief to her face.

'And now you too are leaving – and it's the same – the same – I know that light! – who will watch over you?'

With every word she shrank farther into her chair, more and more fragile, powerless, unhappy, more and more like a lost little girl – beneath her million wrinkles, in her black mourning.

'I shall pray for you every day. Benek dear. Please go now.'

On the delusions of frost

On Żelazna Street, manure had poured from a shattered cart, liquid horse-muck was freezing on the cobbles, on the pavement. I trod carefully, staying close to the wall. From around the corner, from Ceglana Street, rushed a group of drunken workers, I almost fell over. They hurled coarse abuse at me and went noisily on their way, accompanied by raucous singing, oafish shouts echoing from the hostelries, taverns, seedy dens and dives, whilst the strains of mandolin and accordion emanated from annexes and basements. Farther down Żelazna, where fires blazed in charcoal braziers above the snow, beaten metal resounded like a fractured bell. Trams were meant to follow their normal routes, at least in summer; solid ice, however, had frozen over the tracks, whilst the passage of a single gleiss was enough to pulverise the best steel to something akin to chalk. City mayor Miller had taken the decision therefore to switch all tramways to coldiron; a contract worth millions of roubles had been signed with Sibirkhozheto, so now, day and night, the Warsaw streets reverberated with the pounding of hammers. I passed small gangs of workmen, stripped to their shirts despite the cold. They would also have to change the traction. Horse-drawn trams were back in favour. Since the time gleissen had crossed to the west bank of the Vistula and through the Powiśle district in order to build their nest on Leszczyńska Street close to the electrical power station, La Compagnie d'Électricité de Varsovie had experienced constant problems, coming close at one time to bankruptcy; meanwhile, the Electrical Society of Schuckert and Co. was paying the city regular fines, since the street lighting repeatedly refused obedience, and whole quarters were steeped in darkness. The western precincts of the city were still poorly electrified. A beat constable leaning against a gas lamppost puffed on his pipe, killing the reek of industrial burning. Unstifled by the low temperature, sharp aromas drifted likewise from kitchens and laundries, deep drains and dark courtyards. This district I aimed to traverse as quickly as possible. Somewhere behind me, another passer-by had encountered the merry band of proletarians; cries rang out in Russian, full of indignation at first, then – terror. I didn't even glance back. Snow had stopped sprinkling; all plane surfaces, horizontal and sloping, were coated in pure white, sparkling like crystal in the gas or electric lights of the metropolis – in such moments, Warsaw is indeed beautiful: since it resembles not so much Warsaw as a picture postcard of Warsaw.

I lived in this city, but the city lived outside of me. Our bloodstreams did not merge, nor did our thoughts intersect. In this way, victims and parasites live alongside one another, on top of one another. But who is living off whom? One pointer may be the behaviour of the gleissen: they nest amongst the greatest densities of population.

Outside the Kalisz Railway Station, I bought bread, sausage, a jar of sour rye soup and dried plums. Yesterday's café-terrace beggar – today's almost richling; yesterday, one of Warsaw's eternal students with the prospect of a thousand more evenings spent over vodka, cigarettes and cards, on the road to premature senility, crowned by a more or less Romantic descent into consumption and syphilis – today... who? And yet for more than a year, since my mother's death, I'd been waiting for just such an occasion, waiting for money – in order to escape. Away from this city, away from these people, away from myself in this city. What a godsend are the people we know not: I shall tell them I am an innocent young teacher of mathematics oppressed by the Russifiers of the Congress Kingdom. Such shall I be unto them, and at once be it also unto myself; Benedykt Gierosławski shall fall from me, be shed like the skin of a snake – for how else can we be born again in this life, reborn in this world? – what a godsend – strangers, others.

And so, Cape Province, the Antipodes, the West Indies, perhaps Constantinople. A thousand roubles will suffice.

A stray dog had caught a whiff of the smoked sausage; it barked at me all the way from the waterworks to the Artillery Barracks. But outside my own gate, a consumptive little runt in a railwayman's cap caught up with me; I wrested myself from him, concealing my purchases under my armpit. The consumptive was brandishing a piece of paper, coughing wheezily. I was about to shout for Walenty when the stranger calmed down. Pressing hand to chest, he breathed shallowly, nodding his head rhythmically, as if he were indeed swallowing air; steam issued from his mouth in short gusts. Then I noticed that his left ear was missing and all that remained under his cap were a red scar and bloated shred of flesh. Most certainly frostbitten.

'M-mister Benedykt Gie-rossławski,' he whistled.

'Honoured,' I muttered, moving along the wall towards the gate.

'S-s-son of Filip. We have a reques-st for you.'

'I've just drunk my last kopeck. Let me pass, for Christ's sake, or I shall summon the watch!'

He stuffed the paper into the pocket of my sheepskin – a sealed envelope.

'G-give it-t to him, he will know.'

'What?' I wrenched the envelope from my pocket and threw it in the snow. 'Be off with you!'

The consumptive looked at me accusingly. Picked it up, brushed off the snow, wiped it with his sleeve.

'D-do you think we don't know what-t they're up to on Miodowa? Tchinovniks talk.' He coughed again. 'Take it!'

Should I shout? Run away? Split his head open with the jar?

I cautiously accepted the envelope into my gloved hand.

'If this be some damned Piłsudtchik –'

'Be not afeard, my s-son. A few words from his friends in the Rifles.'

'Haven't you got your own people in Siberia?'

'It will be five years s-since our people s-saw him.'

I shrugged my shoulders.

'Well. If it's so fiendishly important, why not spirit it there by special messenger.'

The one-eared fellow replied not – I stared at him, he turned away – and then I understood that the Polish Socialist Party-men and Piłsudtchiks depended on my father for precisely the same reasons as the tsarist officials.

I glanced around at the street; the night was young, pedestrians still flitted past along the pavements, hauling their sleds and carts over the icebound cobbles. I retreated into the shadowy gateway.

'Winter is stalking me.'

'No longer.'

I retreated until I had entered the first courtyard of the lodging house. The little consumptive remained by the gate, a slight figure within the semicircular frame of the dark entrance. He watched me from under the crooked peak of his cap, hands in the pockets of his long greatcoat.

'Give it him. He will know.'

'But what if you're a pawn of the Okhrana!'

'Be not afeard.'

He pulled the cap over his earlessness and walked away.

Zygmunt had not yet returned. I bit into the sausage and bread, sipping the cold rye soup. The envelope I flung onto the pile of books; the rectangle of pure white continued to catch my eye. I went downstairs to Biernatowa, purchased a bucket of coal and lit the stove. Having cleared part of the clutter from the table, I opened Alfred's file – but was at once reminded of my unfinished letter to Julia. I found it inserted in the latest issue of *Mathesis* magazine. Now I was going to have to persuade her of entirely the opposite… I blew on my fountain pen, dipped the nib in warm saliva. *Forget what I said above. Events have occurred in the meantime which make carrying out our plans to the end, as we envisaged them, impossible. I am leaving and shall not be in the Kingdom for a month, probably longer. My father, whom you know not, although, as comes back to me now in memory, you did meet him once or twice, when we were still children* – At Wilkówka, nineteen-oh-five or six, early spring, fresh green grass and icy morning dew on the apple trees in the orchard, white puffy clouds in the sky and smooth furrows of earth in the fields, earth so black it's almost purple, spring, and the joyous chirping of birds outside the windows at dawn, young spiders in chinks in the wooden walls, scent of fresh butter in the air, and fresh cattle dung when the cows emerge from the byre, and what else: the scent of childhood, when I wake with hot sun on my lips, under clean linen, on goose down, and the manor house is already creaking and scraping and groaning, the old floorboards squeaking under the footsteps of Greta, our nanny, as she mounts the stairs to us in the loft, to wake the children and oversee their morning prayers, and beyond the window – clank-clunk, the well chain, quack-quack-honk-honk-cluck-cluck, ducks, geese and chickens, and sometimes the clipped barking of a dog, the shouts of the farmhands, the clatter of hooves and jangle of a carriage, as the guests descend.

… Our cousins the Trzcińskis had arrived, and Uncle Bogasz, and our mother's relatives from West Prussia, and a multitude of people whom I had never seen before, until the manor was transformed into an alien house filled with alien individuals, alien voices, where all were equally hosts and guests. Whole families passed through it and through the forester's cottage, with their children, servants, dogs and servants' children. At first, it was all very exciting: usually, we had to drive to fairs to glimpse something new, travel to a city, but here the new came to us, people we knew not, clothes we had not seen, speech we had not heard, neither Polish nor German, French nor Latin; also, an automobile might arrive at the manor amidst much roaring and smelly exhaust, for us it was a red-letter day, we would stroke the shining *carrosserie* with reverence, until Andrucha shooed us away, yelling from the porch... But after a few days, childish boredom would prevail, exhaustion at the constant pressure of new attractions; I distinguished not between one relative and the next, counted not the guests, whether they'd just arrived or merely returned from their drive to the lake – I would lie in the hayloft in the stable, observing the farmyard through a knot hole in the wood, fall asleep like that in the cool hay; until mother, who always knew where we were, appeared at the bottom of the ladder, and then it was the time to wash our hands and sit down to supper.

... For a week or maybe two, Julia also appeared with her parents; we even played together. I don't remember what she looked like – she says she was an awkward child; but I do remember that Alicja, the governess, always indulged her slightest whim. I remember asking my mother if Julia could stay longer – how much easier our lessons would be, were the governess to look favourably on at least some of our caprices. My mother clearly kept that in memory as proof of my liking for Julia.

... Emilka was still alive then, she followed us everywhere, whilst she was followed by Michałek's limping dachshund – they would stand at a distance and watch our games with great dewy eyes. The orchard in particular lent itself to games of hide-and-seek, cowboys and Indians, hare and hounds. We were chased away only by Utchay the Tatar who, bent low towards the earth, made his round of the coppices every day, embracing the trunks and stroking the slender branches and newly sprouting leaves. The older children, the children of the visiting guests, would mimic him cruelly. He'd threaten them with a birch cane. For Emilka, he kept mallow caramels in his pocket; Julia saw this and, lo and behold! began to fawn and ingratiate herself, rolling her bright-blue eyes and chewing her plait – until the old fellow fought her off too. Then she would sulk the whole day long.

... Father appeared only when the family councils were drawing to a close, when some of the visitors had returned to their own homes. One evening, leaning over my bed, a shadow in the pale gleam of moonlight,

Bolek whispered: 'He's come!' And I remember how I could not then sleep the whole night through, lay with eyes wide open, listening intently to the protracted breathing of the house and rustle of night-time insects. Father had come! In the morning, I saw him shouting angrily at the relatives assembled in the drawing room; we watched through the window until our mother shooed us away. I don't remember what I remembered from beforehand – whether father was different from my image of father, or whether they merged into one in my memory so that no accidental features could change him, in shirt or frock coat, with beard or without beard, shouting or smiling, in sound health or emaciated, like this or otherwise – Father. Because we saw him so infrequently, once every few months, I had to remember my image of him all the more vividly. Had he never appeared at all, deprived of body, face, voice and characteristic features, would he have been any less real? Existence is not a necessary attribute of a good father.

... Before dinner they all went out into the garden, there they split into small groups, intrafamilial factions, which gradually parted company amongst the trees. We, the children, had obviously no idea what the adults were discussing so acrimoniously. It did not pass off without threatening with fists, raising of shoulders towards the sky, invoking the name of God in vain, and even hand-to-hand fights, when one or other of them aimed a blow at his opponent, and yet slowly enough for other moustachioed and bearded uncles to catch the clenched fist in mid-air. They dispersed and came together again. Greta and Michałek's wife brought out cold milk and lemonade from the manor, beer cooling in the well and water taken straight from it. Then the relatives wandered amongst the trees with beer-mugs and tumblers in their hands; metal beakers and porcelain teacups when other vessels ran out.

... I hid amongst the apple trees, peeping out from behind trunks and neath branches – that was how I watched them now, eavesdropped, an Indian in white shoes and straw hat, the cowboy with sleekly cut parting. This too was a game; I giggled soundlessly, charging from tree to tree. Having eyes only for my father's gesticulating pipe, I almost collided with Utchay. He tried to grab me by the collar, I escaped, forfeiting my hat – escaped in the wrong direction. 'Whose pups are these!' my father erupted. 'A man gets no peace even here! Do they have to muck about right under our feet!' 'Don't you recognise your own son?' 'Bolek?' 'Benedykt,' old Utchay corrected in his croaky voice. 'Ah yes, yes,' my father muttered, smiled and ruffled my hair. I raised my head, smiling broadly in response. Already he was looking above and beyond me at Uncle Bogasz, who was pontificating about the price of land and rents in Warsaw, and that such and such would be better for the whole family, and they can't all suffer because of one *aufbrausender*

Dummkopf. 'Don't disturb papa,' my mother pulled me aside. I stood obediently beside Emilka. 'Bolek!' giggled little Emilka, pointing her finger at me. 'Bolek!' The dachshund, similarly amused, thrust out its long tongue. Kick that dog! Pull out Emilka's golden locks! Push her into a cow pat! Throttle her! And if that's not possible, run away from here, before I grow red all over, before I dissolve into tears. And if that's not possible – 'Bolek!' I laughed along with her. 'Bolek!' we laughed – at what? I was unable to restrain myself, the principle of shame was stronger even than anger, even than –

'But you didn't have to throw bread on the floor!'

I heaved myself up from the table, drowsy from sleep. The last page of the letter had stuck to my cheek; I blew – and it glided onto the floor, where Zygmunt, on bended knee, was brushing dirt off half a bread roll.

I yawned noisily.

'I go out – there's no you; I come back – there's no you; yesterday you got legless with us, yet today you're once again the early bird, oo-oo, nauseating.'

Zygmunt lay the bread on fresh newspaper, sniffed the second stick of sausage, raised an eyebrow.

'They let you go, hah.'

'You've already been swallowing tales.'

'And what tales! That half the Citadel came for you, dragged you off in shackles to the Tenth Pavilion.'

I found a clean sheet of paper, sharpened a pencil with a pocket-knife.

'I shall write down for you all the names and amounts. Give it only to them, no one else, even should they swear on the cross; and only this much, not a kopeck more. Have them write a receipt, without fail. Aha, and you don't know when I'll be back.'

'When will you be back?'

I took out my pocketbook, counted the notes.

Zygmunt had thrown off his top sheepskin, tightened his fox-lined bekesha, and was about to go to Biernatowa's kitchen to boil water – but at this sight he sat down, lit a cigarette, twirled his moustache.

'I didn't know you had such generous friends.'

'Not going to ask about the interest?'

'Such tender-hearted shylocks. Well, all right, spit it out.'

I told him about my father's sentence and the Ministry of Winter's proposal.

He tugged at his beard till tears sprang to his eyes.

'And you're going there?'

I shrugged my shoulders.

'A thousand roubles and, well, to fall at the feet of my darling papa...'

'If I didn't know you, I might believe you.' He flicked cigarette ash amongst the old candles. 'This diengi is for the Jews – but are you leaving me something for the rent? Am I to start looking at the university for a new lodger? Do you ever mean to return from your Sybir?'

'Why?'

'Oy, there's something you're not telling me.'

'Don't get any ideas.' I counted another sixteen roubles. 'Here, take it, pay in advance. In case of need, I'll telegram.'

He moved closer to me.

'Are they blackmailing you with something?' he whispered. 'What, Benek?'

I smiled.

'Let's say I have a premonition.'

He nodded.

'A premonition! You won't admit to yourself the obvious, so what's left? A foreboding. You know very well what this is about. They intend to use you against him, evidently having no other means. People tried in nineteen fourteen and fifteen are completing their sentences, but it would be more convenient to keep them where they are, in exile. Some kind of police provocation, a planted letter with an assassination plan, or bomb in a suitcase… You remember the affair with those cabbage-headed SR-men. What are you getting into, Benek, by Christ's wounds!'

'Miodowa tells me it's about gleissen.'

'And you believe it!'

'Want a dried plum?'

He tugged at his beard for a final time and went to boil water.

I pulled out my old sac de voyage from under the bed. The delegation of Winter in Irkutsk had purchased me a place in a first-class carriage, such a ticket costs almost three hundred roubles, I wondered whether to exchange it for a cheaper and profit from the difference. I would have to inquire in Moscow. Either way, Commissioner Preiss was right: I must procure some decent clothes; at this precise moment I had very little to pack. From under the bed, I also pulled out my leather ankle boots. When did I last wear those? The brown leather was damp and encrusted with a kind of mildew or moss… Well, I also needed to buy something suited to real winter. It was hardly summer, but on the other hand – Siberia, and on the third hand – the Ice. What exactly did it look like? The world of the gleissen. I should have inquired at Miodowa Street.

The door slammed shut.

'Zygmunt, you've surely heard something in the department…'

'Eh?'

'Gleissen. What do the professors say?'

'On what topic?'

'Well, on how it lives.'

'It doesn't live.'

'What?'

'Cannot live, it's so extremely cold there that nothing can live, it prevents all movement in living organisms.'

'But they move –'

'Well, so what? Movement, change – what should that make us presuppose?' He poured the boiling water over the dregs, clasped the hot mug in his hands, hissed. 'Look how the hoarfrost spreads over the window.'

'Mm-hmm?'

'Look at the frost.' He indicated with his head. 'Even in shape it resembles a living plant.'

'Is that what naturalists are saying about gleissen?'

He shrugged his shoulders.

'I don't know. Bondarczuk from Saint Petersburg was meant to deliver guest lectures, but they were cancelled. There are various theories. Sometimes I hear one thing, sometimes another. Siberian companies as well as the tsar are pouring money into research; the Siberian Coldiron Industrial Company has funded a Chair of Ice at the Saint Petersburg Technological Institute; people from the Imperial and from Lwów University are going there, sooner or later it will be explained.'

'If it can be explained by research.'

'What?'

I tore my eyes from the windowpane.

'The question of existence.'

Zygmunt merely snorted.

'I'm just a simple practitioner. If a broken leg needs setting, I will set it, but whether or not that leg exists – that problem requires other doctors.'

I knew he would don that mask. *I'm just a simple practitioner.* Now he'll start wailing like an illiterate peasant and scratching his backside. Shame governs us in different ways; now I see it wherever I look. I turned my back on Zygmunt, ostentatiously ignoring him, and leaned over my sac de voyage. Look not, listen not, remember not. It's the only way.

Zygmunt's father was born in a coal merchant's cottage; Zygmunt's grandfather used to kowtow to my grandfather, kiss the master's hands and defer to the manor. Were I to inquire of Zygmunt, would he call that shame? I daresay not as well – in the language of the second kind, we have to describe the symptoms differently: this is anger, envy, hatred, contempt, this is compassion, this is friendship.

No one would call that shame. But I know, I see. His concern for me; how perturbed he was and how he began asking whether they were not blackmailing me, whether it was not some provocation; that brusque cordiality, as if we'd lived since childhood in great intimacy, yet we've been residing barely a year under this roof, seeing each another not at all often; how he always worries over my troubles and immediately wants to help... Is he not sincere? But he is as sincere as he possibly can be! And to whom could I entrust so much money, knowing for certain he wouldn't keep a kopeck for himself? Only to him, only to Zygmunt – I had never had and never could have a better friend.

That friendship, from his point of view, is undeniably genuine – erected on the foundation stones of the principle of shame.

He went to bed. I transferred the lamp to the table, swept the crumbs off the floor and pulled from under the heap of broadsheets and grease-stained papers two thick files bound with twine. Availing myself of a bent-pronged fork, I unravelled the knots. I had not opened these files since Easter. Maybe it would be better to consign them to the flames forthwith? I raised the first page to my eyes. *In the present work we attempt to demonstrate not only that the logical conceptions of truth and falsehood deriving from Classical thought are incorrect, but also that new formulations of them are equally incorrect.* We had demonstrated that our own were also worthless. I opened the stove door with the poker and forced the bundle into the embers. The second one – I recognised it from the inkblot on the cover – was the rough draft of my unfinished polemic with Kotarbiński; in my thoughts I had called it the 'Book of the Dead'. *Is the 'position of a dead man' really 'so strong that people are unable to oust him from the past, even though they have all deliberately forgotten about him'? In what sense then does something still 'exist', which no longer exists? Are all assertions about the past necessarily either true or false?* Somewhere here, there ought also to be Alfred's notes to his version. Maybe some of it is still fit for publication. I undid the file. At least I would have something to keep me occupied on the journey.

Alfred is right however: we had lost the heart for it, I had lost heart. I sense that something is still deficient here – all these logics are flawed, but we, but I, see it all the more clearly now that I have liberated myself from the old patterns of thought. I am unable, however, to point to a better solution that could be defended with mathematical rigour. So, what is left to me: premonitions, fleeting associations, vivid impressions – like the returning memory of the gleiss suspended over the fire in the city centre. As well as intuitions, which even like this – in images, words – I am unable to describe: knowledge constructed in the language of the first kind, locked forever in my heart.

Zygmunt was muttering to himself in his sleep (sometimes he held long conversations with his nightmare demons), it was impossible to make out individual words, but the intonation was clear: bewilderment, fear, irritation. I shut the stove door. The sweep had only just unclogged the damper, yet even so the air bit into my eyes, clawed at my throat; by morning the wall and ceiling above the vent would again be black-ish-grey from the smoke. Our neighbour below returned from his shift at the city pumping station, I recognised the raspy lilt with which he swore at his mother-in-law and her family; in a moment his wife would join in the workaday opera. From behind the stove I pulled out some rags, scorned by the Jewish old-clothes man, and stuffed them in the gap between the door and the threshold – at least the night-time frost would not sneak in through there. Outside the window a ferocious bliz-zard had blown up, it was surely ten degrees below zero. I shuddered involuntarily, remembering the cat which had frozen solid. In the be-ginning, people had tried to measure the temperature of gleissen with mercury thermometers – but the scale did not go low enough. After all, hiberniks do not really touch gleissen. The Martsynians can claim what they like – if what Korzyński said is true – but a man is a man, he has to breathe, blood has to circulate in his veins, muscles must func-tion. I turned up the tubular wick of the naphtha lamp, lit a cigarette from the blue flame. How, in God's name, do you *converse* with gleis-sen? He might just as well conduct dialogues with a geological feature. Just as well hold a conversation with a mathematical equation. I took a drag, cleared my throat. *Movement, change – what should that make us presuppose?*

To gaze at the hoarfrost on the windowpane, at those would-be flowers overgrowing it from shutter-frame to centre… It's only frost, the pressure of outside conditions; under such pressure, moisture man-ifests itself in this or a different guise. What if the frost were to assume still more complex forms, what if it reacted faster to changes in external conditions, what if deeper meanings were to appear in its intricacies – would we then recognise it as a sovereign conscious being?

Why then do we speak of gleissen as if they had an 'I'?

Why do I speak of myself as if I had an 'I'?

Do I exist more, exist more really, than the frost-ferns etched on the windowpane? Because I am able to capture myself in thought? What of it? The capacity for self-deception is but one more flourish in the form of ice, a baroque ornament frozen for show.

In such a way arises the illusion of existence: a pattern imposed by unknown laws organises random elements; then successive, ever-lon-ger branches of hoarfrost freeze to it, spreading in both directions, into the future and into the past, reproducing the same illusory regularity:

that it was, that it is, that it lived, that it lives, that it will live – the frost flower – the gleiss – I.

One has to try at last to liberate oneself from the language of the second kind, express truth in a way in which it can be expressed. *I do not exist.* One does not exist. Exist not. It's not I who thinks it. Not I stood here, staring through the frosted window at a snowstorm above the Warsaw roofs, at eddies of white dust sucked into the trapdoor of the courtyard well, at dirty lights flickering through the blizzard from windows opposite: not I who throws a cigarette butt into the stove, pulls a wool-knit sweater over my back, dons a second pair of socks, fustian long johns, frayed overcoat; not I who gathers up from the table the yellowing scribbles, unfinished letter, Teitelbaum's papers, not I leafing through the notes and typescripts. Each action occurs; what happens, happens – but it's not the ice blossom advancing across the pane, merely the frost hardening. It's growing colder.

Grow colder, need to stoke the stove. Stoke the stove. Throw in some logs. Adjust the lamp-wick. The wind howls outside the window, rooftiles rattle. Pee in the chamber pot. Snuggle under the quilt, three blankets. Blow into the numbed palms. Zygmunt snores loudly. Hear how he tosses from side to side and smacks his lips in slumber.

Close the eyes. And then the images return, words and thoughts. The ruddy complexions of the tchinovniks of Winter above their stiff high collars. The gleiss over the naphtha flame at the junction of Marszałkowska Street and Jerusalem Avenue. Commissioner Preiss with his hand on the old globe, his florid face, merry eyes. Mitschka Fidelberg thundering the truths of relentless revolution. Mr Korzyński emerging from the gloom in a cloud of yellow light, black stump resting on the ice album. The furious glintz on the wallpaper in Maria Weltz's parlour. The silhouette of the earless Pilsudtchik – and his envelope white as the Siberian snow. *Be not afeard.* Father with revolver in hand, a double bloodstain on his white shirtfront, like red quotation-marks enclosing scream, shot and carnage.

The wind roars and whistles. Vermin scuttle around the dark room.

To go? or not to go?

Even if not all roads lead to absurdity, perhaps there is none so well-trodden that would not lead there, were someone outlandish to lead along it. Someone who is there where he does not have to be – extending a hand in our moments of exhaustion – when we seek him, he hides inside us and directs our inquiring gaze – goes before us unnoticed and lightens our way with dark light – our unlikely guide, enemy, friend?

PART II

Trans-Siberia

'There truly is beyond existence and non-existence a third eventuality, just as beyond the assertion that the lamp is an animate animal and the assertion that the lamp is an inanimate animal, there lies the eventuality that the lamp is not an animal at all. Of course, if the lamp is an animal, then it must be either animate or inanimate in the sense of its mortality. Both when we say of something that it is alive or is not alive, we suppose that it is an organism. Similarly, when we say of something that it exists, thereby confirming the something, and when we say that it "does not exist", when we negate it, thereby pronouncing a judgement of denial, we suppose a certain common condition of existence and of so-called non-existence. But it is possible to negate also this condition: to say that the lamp is neither an animate animal nor an inanimate animal, only that it is not an animal at all; to say that a given object neither is nor "is not", only that it "is not" in another, broader sense – that not even that exists, which is the condition for being able to state correctly that a given object "is not" in the first sense. Language does not distinguish between such things.'

CHAPTER THE SECOND

On the miasmas of luxury

On the seventeenth day of March 1891, according to the Julian reckoning, Tsar Aleksandr the Third published a rescript ordering the construction of a railway running from the Miassa Station via Tchelyabinsk, Petropavlovsk, Omsk, Tomsk, Krasnoyarsk, Irkutsk, Tchita, Blagoveshtchensk and Khabarovsk to Vladivostock. On the nineteenth of May, in Vladivostock, the heir to the throne, future Emperor of All the Russias, Nikolay the Second, laid the foundation stone under the iron track subsequently known as the Great Siberian Way, the Transsibirskaya Zhelyeznodorozhnaya Magistral, the Transsib.

It was brought into service in stages – just as construction advanced in stages simultaneously from different stations – ultimately linking the line with Moscow and Saint Petersburg; in October 1904 it stretched from the Pacific Ocean to the Baltic Sea. The Transsib is nearly ten thousand kilometres long. The laying of the line depleted the Imperial Treasury of upward of one and a half milliard roubles.

A dozen pages or so of the brochure are devoted to the history of the Trans-Siberian Railway and details of its construction, yet the Manchurian question and the Russo-Japanese wars are barely mentioned. The shortest route to Vladivostock leads not through Blagovyeshtchensk and Khabarovsk, but through Manchuria, through Zabaykalsk, Harbin and Ussuriysk. In August 1905, according to the terms of the peace treaty concluding the first Russo-Japanese War, Manchuria was ceded to the 'exclusive dominion of China' following the loss of Port Arthur to the Japanese and defeat of the Russian fleet at the Battle of Tsushima Strait. At the start of the second war, however, Russia regained it, subsequently concentrating efforts on controlling the warm-water Amur ports and Sakhalin as well as securing Kamtchatka and the northern Siberian routes; the question of Korea, the Liaodong Peninsula and Port Arthur receded into the background. According to the Sino-Russian treaty of 1911, Manchuria came officially under the Tsar's dominion, costing Russian diplomacy two million roubles in bribes to ministers of the Middle Kingdom. What, however, were those millions in comparison with the budget for building the

Transsib? Whilst the whole route of the Magistral was at last located on Russian territory.

The final pages of the brochure, which every passenger in Deluxe class found in their compartment, contained a description of the Around-the-World Railroad project, into which the Transsib would transmute once connection was assured with the line running from the Tchukotka Peninsula across the Bering Strait to Alaska; the Transsib would then become the Paris-to-New York Tricontinental Railroad. A licence to build this line had been received by the Edward Harriman consortium, financed in the main by investors on Wall Street, and in 1917 construction of the tunnel had begun under the Strait, digging from east to west. The construction, in itself an ex-traordinarily difficult engineering feat, was constantly being delayed and suspended due to various external factors: first it was the war with Japan; then the court intrigues of several Grand Dukes, who – as shareholders in the Lena Gold Mining Company Lenzoto – had a direct interest in keeping the Americans well away from the Siberian riches; then petitions from the Duma, where resentments were voiced every moment over the sale of Alaska to the United States; and even-tually, more or less open acts of sabotage against Harriman by various competing *Sociétés Anonymes, Aktiengesellschaften* and Limited Companies, which had proliferated unrestrictedly in Tsarist Russia under the governments of Stolypin and Struve – yet grown ever more firmly and deeply embedded in the economic organism of Russia; whereas it was they whom Russia most had to thank for improving the economic situation, despite crashes on the global markets. The only goods that do not lose value in times of crisis are precious stones and metals, and extracting the earth's natural resources is the surest way to make money. During the building of the Transsib alone, scores of seams of metal ore and coal were discovered. Foreign geologists were speculating besides about oil deposits hidden in western Siberia. Exports of coldiron were rising by over twenty per cent per year; the Sibirkhozheto Tower in Irkutsk was allegedly the tallest building in Asia. In December 1923, on the New York Stock Exchange, one ounce of tungetitum sold for 446 dollars and thirty cents, more than twenty times the price of an ounce of gold.

There was doubtless a large dose of tsarist propaganda in all this – but that great riches were flowing out of Siberia was attested if only by the décor in the first-class carriages of the Trans-Siberian Express, 'the most luxurious train in the world'. Learn from the brochure that the current rolling stock – third generation following the impressive sump-tuousness of the train exhibited at the World's Fair in Paris in 1900 – was the work of the L. Zieleniewski Railway Carriages Factory in Sanok and the Lwów Engine, Boiler and Pump Manufacturing Company. So, the undercarriage and steel skeleton at least were the handiwork of Polish engineers; the interiors were designed by Russians, modelled in part on the empire-style mirror-filled salon-carriage of Nikolay the First, also built in fact by Poles. The ceiling and walls above the boiserie of the compartment were upholstered in dark-green silk twill adorned with gold-and-grey plant motifs. The brass trimmings – knobs, doorhandles, locks, latches, frames, fittings, bars, brackets and hooks – were so highly polished that when they shone in the electric light they resembled droplets or blobs of liquid metal suspended in mid-air. All features were endowed with sophisticated albeit impractical shapes, often so complex they completely masked their actual functions. Study for a good minute the symmetrical grips on the window, cast in the form of roaring lions with raised tails. Thus, in order to open the compartment window, it was necessary to pull the lions' tails; in order to shut it, press on the metal tongues protruding from the beasts' maws. Electric light bulbs concealed behind coloured globes were switched on by twisting a decorative knob on the wall: a golden Sun with thick spiral rays. Realise that the knob is most certainly real gold. The bedlinen sewn exclusively of the airiest cotton and silk. A thick rust-coloured carpet covers the floor. Untie the shoelaces and stand on it only in socks, then without socks – how it caresses the bare feet. Feel the touch, fragrance and colours of luxury as they seep through the skin, penetrate air and light, wave after wave, settling in the muscles, in the blood, in the bones – tiny molecules of bliss.

The Trans-Siberian Express departed from Yaroslavsky Station in Moscow on the eighteenth day of July, a Friday, at ten o'clock in the evening, in accordance with the timetable printed in the *Putevoditel*. On the compartment wall, alongside a miniature escritoire and wardrobe, opposite the washbasin concealed behind a mirror, was a small drinks cabinet. Pour a glass of shampanskoye from the complimentary bottle nicely cooled in welcome, as the train begins to gather speed. Cheers! Down the hatch! To Benedykt Gierosławski as he shall be amongst those who know not Benedykt Gierosławski! Shades of suburban buildings flashed by beyond the window, then villages and trees – the train rode out of the Moscow winter; suddenly the glass pane became steeped in the vivid cherry-crimson of the summer sun, a twilight afterglow, since the Sun itself had already sunk below the horizon, but even so, all the highly polished fixtures shone like living flame; the boiserie and fabric wall-coverings were alight. Jerk the lion tails, open the window, and summer pours into the compartment, warm wind swelling the embroidered net and velvet curtains. Stand with head immersed in the stream of that wind, beneath the cataract of sunny rose-pink, with half-closed eyes and half-open lips. A minute, two, or more, until the sense of time is lost – and there remains only one measure: took-took-took-TOOK, took-took-took-TOOK.

The luggage lies unpacked. Three valises and a handheld bag – the worn-out sac de voyage having been sold in a Moscow pawnshop, like the sheepskin coat and remainder of old clothes, that is to say, the few they wished to take. Acquire in this same pawnshop a stylish cane with dolphin-shaped ivory head, a Waterman pen (Eyedropper with gold-filled overlay) and also a watch on a silver chain bearing the inscription Uhrenfabrik von J. Rauschenbach – as well as a bloodstone-set signet ring engraved with the Korab coat of arms. How did a signet ring with a Polish coat of arms end up at an Arbat pawnbroker's? To leave it there unbought, discovered so serendipitously, would be like turning one's back on love at first sight. Traditionally, Gierosławskis use the Lubicz seal, but what difference does it make to those who know not the Gierosławskis? A nobleman is a nobleman, one breed of dog, as long as the signet lies well on his pinkie.

Stow the valises in the cubbies, retrieving only pyjamas, dressing gown and toilet accoutrements. (In Deluxe class there are spacious, fully equipped bathrooms.) Before it grew totally dark, the carriage provodnik knocked on the door, a fatty with a peasant face, dressed in a Cossack-style uniform with gold braiding and shiny galloons. He was welcoming all the new passengers and inquiring if they required anything, if they found the compartments comfortable, and should any need arise – at your service, at your service, your lordships! Thrust a three-rouble note into his podgy fingers. Night and day, Your Esteemed Nobleness! Then he brought a jug of hot tchay; one of the main tasks of a provodnik is to tend the fire in the carriage samovar. The tea comes in useful: the earless Pilsudschik's envelope had surfaced amongst some papers. Open it – open it under the steam, whistling and beating time with the heel. Benedykt Gierosławski would have burned the envelope without opening it – but that Benedykt Gierosławski was receding with each rotation of the Express's wheels, took-took-took-TOOK, time to forget about Benek, poor sod.

Inside the envelope was a single sheet of paper, folded three times over, on which twelve meaningless rows of letters had been banged out in thick greasy type:

XROZOJLBEXWABTXVEFIS
AMOKOREWSDXWFCEYTKUY
HVOZLFARJSODLAYTOREE
KsJPVORAABTXWBATFBAOG
LJZBKNCGBBKVNYEUTJCF
JCARSXSFBYOKMXDLNGWZ
AHSALREZSXDRJCARYDWH
HJMSPMZPJXCPFYILMWIR
JYRGFLIDARMPFGBYPWLB
UNXUJNWPFAZZUJRLNDXR
VAYLSYRGZKEKAREEAHJL
TI

Hah, they knew they couldn't trust the messenger! Anyone would have opened the envelope – it was a miracle to have held out for so long.

And yet, embarrassment immediately raises its head and something akin to anger – at whom? They had expected dishonesty and, voilà, they were right!

Transcribe the encoded letter, chew the cap of the pen. How to break this code? Is it breakable at all? Mathematicians do not go in for codes, it's the domain of linguists, specialists on the structure of language; classicists in particular like to play at it, Latinists, Hellenists. Upon what is such a code based? Upon the substitution of certain letters for others, on changing their order, on inserting letters that obscure the content? Perhaps the arrangement of the signs on the page is significant, these eleven lines each with – count them – twelve letters, and the twelfth line with only two. Try to read every third, fourth, fifth letter as if it were the next in an alphabetical sequence. Try to trace words concealed horizontally, vertically, diagonally and even according to the chess knight's moves. To no avail, meaninglessness translates into meaninglessness, xvzafy robllr ozkrig zlnedz…

Pschaw! Wake up only when the train jerks suddenly, the Express brakes violently, blocked wheels squeal on the rails. Letter, pen and writing-pad filled with phrases of unutterable gibberish slip off the narrow surface of the escritoire. Glance at the watch. Ten minutes to two, Moscow time. According to the brochure, the train should already have passed Vladimir on the Klyazma River and left the Golden Ring; no stops were envisaged here.

Open the window, look out into the night. The train stands in open country, the only lights coming from the carriage windows. Out of the window next door, on the right-hand side, leaned the round head of an elderly gentleman, in wire-rimmed spectacles, with a not yet fully developed bald patch and impressive moustache. Exchange smiles and courtesies. Why this emergency stop, he asked in broken Russian, had there been an accident? He introduced himself as Engineer White-Gessling, an Englishman employed by one of the partners of Sibirkhozheto. Switch to German.

'I can see what looks like a main road in the distance, some sort of buildings. The driver's probably hopped out for vodka.'

'You jest, Mr Gerosasky.'

'Yes, of course.'

The Express moved, slowly gathering speed. Left behind were the lights of an automobile turning around on that road.

'It seems someone has joined us, Engineer.'

'Someone so important they stop the Express for him? Who is it, the tsarevitch?'

'Or Rasputin's favourite ballerina.'

Have to retreat inside the compartment, pull down the window; night wind was lashing the eyes.

Someone knocked – the engineer had come for a word. Lift the hasp and open the door. The provodnik was walking down the corridor; behind him lingered three men in dark suits, the eldest – silver-haired with a dignified mien – was in the process of adjusting the pince-nez on his nose and unravelling the papers taken from under his arm. The engineer had not come for a word – only now had he stepped out of his compartment, likewise summoned by the knock. From over his shoulder his bleary-eyed spouse watched him, half asleep.

'They are inspecting documents.'

'What, the police?' he asked.

'If not worse.'

All the passengers of the third Deluxe carriage had already emerged into the corridor. The compartments had been designed as alternate single and double cabins: on the other side, from under number four, loomed two ladies, a big-boned matron and a skinny, morbidly pale young girl under her wing; farther on, beyond them, a grizzled gentleman with a glass eye was proving his identity.

'If you will allow me, my dear,' Engineer White-Gessling, paying no heed to the nocturnal hour, pyjamas, state of dishabille and exceptional circumstances, set about the formal introductions, 'Count Benedykt Gero-Sasky.'

Wrapped in a white dressing-gown, she extended a hand from behind the back of her corpulent husband.

'Nice to meet you, Count.'

Whence, devil take it, had sprung that count?! The word had not been uttered at all in the conversation through the window. Whatever had got into the daft Englishman's nut?

Raise the head. There was no opportunity to deny the falsity, for as soon as the head rose from the clawed hand of the engineer's wife, the policemen were there, courteously proclaiming themselves to be especially assigned functionaries of the Department for the Protection of Public Security and Order; the silver-haired officer even introduced himself: Pavel Vladimirovitch Fogel – and they requested the travel documents. Fogel spoke in German. In reply to the Englishman's question about the reason for the night-time inspection, he evasively mentioned terrorists – but there's no cause for alarm, please sleep peacefully, we are very sorry for the trouble. Return with the documents, whilst that other man behind Fogel, as soon as he had cast an eye over the inscriptions and stamps and sweeping signatures of the Ministry of Winter, was all but standing to attention; handing them back with an ingratiating smile and bow, he effusively wished everyone goodnight. The engineer, unable to fully understand the stream of words in Russian, observed their behaviour all the more closely. Well, now also, it was too late to persuade him in two sentences out of that count; he'd have to be put straight in the morning.

Lock the door to the compartment. In the glass windowpane lined with velvet darkness flickered the portrait of a young man. Claret-coloured smoking jacket with green piped edgings, white braided cord with tassels, pale complexion above the broad lapels, narrow nose, black hair clipped halfway up the nape of the neck and combed back from the high forehead, stuck to the skull by the shining brilliantine applied by a Moscow parikmakher, black moustache drooping down towards the chin around the wide mouth – and when he raised his hand to the smoothly shaven cheek, a massive signet ring with coat of arms still flashing in the reflection. Stare in amazement.

What a curse – strangers, others.

On the Hungarian count, Russian power, English cigarettes and American shadow

'Count Gyero-Saski, if you'll allow me, Count: Herr Blutfield and his wife, Doctor Konyeshin, Monsieur Verousse, Captain Privyezhensky.'

Bow to them.

'*Je suis enchanté.*'

'Ah, what company. You come under Franz Ferdinand, yes, Count?'

The waiter offers a chair. Sit down.

'Dear lady –'

'Except that the accent sounds not quite right, I have a good ear, do I not, Mr Blutfeld?'

Frau Blutfeld's consort muttered in assent, his mouth full.

'Let me guess,' Frau Blutfeld continued in the same breath, 'Hungarian blood on the father's side and kinship with Polish nobility through marriage to Prussian ancestors, true? Oh, Count, please don't pull such a surprised face, I am never mistaken in such matters: last year in Marienbad I recognised Countess von Meran from the shape of her mouth; and how she implored me not to compromise her incognito, I tell you –'

'I am not a count.'

'But did I not say so! A woman's intuition!' She looked about her with pride, as if the entire Deluxe dining car were admiring in dumb fascination her genealogical expertise.

'Have no fear,' she whispered theatrically, leaning over the table, lace cockade hovering over the sour cream, her formidable bosom adorned with heavy brooch threatening to flatten the porcelain. 'We will not betray your secret, Count. Will we?' She spread her gaze around the table. 'Will we?'

Could there be any doubt that by midday, even the engine driver's youngest helper would have heard of the Hungarian count, Graf Gyero-Saski?

Tuck the serviette under the chin.

'Let us suppose,' speak with deliberation, 'but only suppose, that I am really not a count, and my name is as it appears on my documents, Gierosławski, Gie-ro-sław-ski, there you have it, impoverished minor nobility – what might I say or do to convince you that you persist in error?'

'Nothing!' she cried triumphantly. 'Nothing!'

Apart from this, breakfast passed in more or less animated conversation on current political affairs, or inconsequential society gossip. (At which the dependable Frau Blutfeld excelled.) Beyond the windows of the speeding Express, the birch groves flashed by, glowing green above the white-and-black stripes of their slender trunks, everything blurred by the momentum, like on the canvasses of French Impressionists, colours, lights, shadows, shapes: birch forest in July sun – the mere notion of a forest. Daniloff and Buy had long been left behind, the train resting for barely fifteen minutes at each; when it left Buy, the provodniks came down the Deluxe corridors knocking on doors and reminding passengers that breakfast was served. Wonder whether not to press a few more roubles into the hands of the attendants and ask them to bring meals to the compartment, even if cold. In this way, contact with other passengers might be avoided; at most, it would be in the corridor on the way to the bathroom and back. The spiral of shame was already making itself felt: each day spent in seclusion would make stepping out all the harder; the fears and morbid revulsions would only accumulate – Count Gyero-Saski curled in a quivering ball behind the door, a cornered beast, biting his fingers and pressing his ear to the wall, in order to hear above the clickety-clack of the wheels the sound of approaching footsteps – after a week of journeying, it would indeed be possible to reach such a state, it was not unimaginable. Therefore, it was essential to face the world on the very first morning with a smile on the lips, dressed in white English suit with carnation twisted rakishly in the buttonhole, and head with easy stride towards the restaurant car, which was directly attached to the third Deluxe passenger carriage, and unblinkingly accept the invitation of Engineer White-Gessling to join him at table, bowing gallantly, and how... 'Ladies, gentlemen, *énchanté*.'

Conversation was conducted in German, with shorter or longer interpolations in French when Jules Verousse stumbled over the German syntax. In addition, Monsieur Verousse stammered and generally spoke very obscurely: he would begin sentences, mumbling inaudibly under this breath, or, if he finished them at all, sometimes the middle part only of the utterance was audible above the table, sometimes his clauses lacked a predicate. Learn that Verousse is a famous and well-heeled journalist, bought from *Le Petit Parisien* for some horrendous sum by Maurice Bunau-Varilla. Travelling to Siberia to write a series of reportages for *Le Matin* from the Land of the Ice. He was Flemish by descent and harboured a profound disrespect for all reigning dynasties and governing cabinets, including Bunau-Varilla himself with his ostentatious fortune and notorious anti-Communist passion. Verousse's speeches of few words customarily consisted of political mockery or French aphorisms. Thin as a rake and very tall, he served every person at table within reach of his spindly arms, offering this or that platter, the salad bowl, the swan-shaped salt-and-pepper shakers. The table sat eight people, four with four facing, and Monsieur Verousse occupied the seat second from the aisle – he sits directly opposite: horsey jowls, hooked nose and wire-rimmed spectacles resting on that nose.

Since Captain Privyezhensky spoke not at all, and Herr Blutfeld never stopped eating – he ate, ate and ate, as if eating had totally replaced breathing, and were he to cease stuffing his oral orifice, he'd immediately drop dead, his tumid face purple from foodlessness – since they spoke not, and the engineer's wife confined herself to nodding at her husband's words, the discussion circulated between White-Gessling, Gertrud Blutfeld, Count Gyero-Saski and Doctor Konyeshin.

Doctor Konyeshin – a bourgeois city man with a stern face framed by fiery red sideburns – was travelling to Vladivostock to research the White Plague ravaging the colonial communities of eastern Siberia and the Pacific ports. 'They're afraid the rest of the Pacific Fleet will die of it,' Frau Blutfeld hastened to explain in whispers, scarcely exchanging a glance with the thickset doctor. 'The Ministry of War certainly had no intention of issuing them with a propusk to return home, but now, after Myerzoff's victory, medicine has to come to the Ministry's aid. So that our lovely little sailors don't mutiny again. They'll tear our poor doctor limb from limb.' – As Gertrud Blutfeld's whisper was more piercing than the loudest *zwischenruf* from Monsieur Verousse, Konyeshin must have heard it. But he merely wiped his pince-nez and returned to methodically cutting a hard-boiled egg into four, eight and sixteen pieces (he then placed the slices of white and yolk onto a slice of white bread in symmetrical patterns).

Frau Blutfeld whispered information gleaned from her *Who's Who* of gossip, whether or not anyone wished to listen; the Hungarian count was likewise an opportune victim – well, let's be honest, a slightly more attractive one. The Blutfelds were travelling from Saint Petersburg and were already acquainted with several of the passengers; the histories of others Frau Blutfeld had learned by her own secret methods (phrenology, genealogy, a glass of wine, a dream at dawn, or such was the assumption). Listen therefore to her accounts first of the table companions, then of other passengers in Deluxe class, and then of absent others.

A banker and his nephew – a mother and child, wife of a fur-trade magnate – the prosecutor of the Amur Oblast returning from a ministerial briefing – a young lady consumptive and her aunt on their way to an Ice sanatorium (the next-door neighbours glimpsed in the night), but no cause for concern, the young lady is no longer infectious – a tsarist naval officer assigned to a warship at Nikolayevsk – profligate brothers from a Moravian beer-producing dynasty on their journey around the world – a retired cavalry captain from the Kaiser's hussars – an elderly American chemical or electrical engineer, along with his wife, also under contract to Sibirkhozheto – a young widow travelling alone, who was too provocatively beautiful for her to be, in Frau Blutfeld's eyes, a respectable woman – an old man on his way to visit the graves of his exiled sons on Sakhalin – a pastor from Lorraine with his family, disembarking before the Urals –

And two tables away – 'Only don't look now!' – Prince Blutsky-Osey was sipping his morning coffee, allegedly travelling to Vladivostock on a personal errand for Nikolay the Second.

'May the apoplexy strike me down, if it's not because of him we have to suffer night-time emergencies!'

'Secret police, Special Corps of Gendarmes, the Third Department, perhaps even the Okhrana – no doubt they've assigned someone to him,' muttered the doctor. 'After all they knew when and where he's travelling, they didn't have to hound the whole train at night. No doubt he also has his own people.'

'Perhaps they received intelligence of terrorist designs only at the last moment,' suggested the engineer.

'… last-moment leaks very convenient always…'

'Yesterday evening the matter was explained to us in detail. Officially, the prince is travelling to America to visit his younger daughter, Agafya, who married the vice-chairman of the Russo-American Company, but he's in fact going to negotiate a peace treaty with the Japanese. Imagine, ladies and gentlemen, how many people in Russia and in Europe would be gratified, were the negotiations to prove ineffectual.'

'How many?' Ask in naïve amazement. 'Who really depends on this war? Who amongst those who chuck bombs and shoot at dignitaries?'

'All of them,' said the doctor. 'Anarchists and socialists of all shapes and sizes prey on misfortunate and chaos. What chance would they have, were it not for the war? Remember oh-five and twelve.'

'It was then they suffered bloody defeats, was it not?'

'Bah, it was then they came closest to making their revolution succeed. A great war, discontent amongst the people, bloody massacres – this is exactly what they need. Ditto those various Narodnik rebels, damned Poles, *excusez-moi, mon comte,* Circassians and Georgians, all just waiting for the emperor's moment of weakness, and immediately they're leaping at Russia's throat.'

'The doctor was on Kreshtchatik in Kieff on Red Saturday,' Gertrud Blutfeld informed everyone in her theatrical whisper.

'Indeed, I was, I ran from my home as soon as it went off. We were bringing in the wounded, gathering up the killed until evening. Torsos separately, limbs separately, guts, gallons of blood.'

'… by accident chemicals – when students half-educated take for bombs…'

'Were it not for the Ice, we'd have had an epidemic in the city in the middle of summer; all it takes is for a single mass grave not to be drenched quickly enough in liquid lime, I have seen such things at the front.'

The Englishman and his wife exchanged glances of distaste and embarrassment.

'Doctor, really, my dear sir…'

'Forgive me,' muttered Konyeshin, and returned to methodically spreading marmalade on his toast.

Frau Blutfeld chuckled, covering her mouth with her handkerchief.

'The doctor has already provoked a few ructions here. The personage sat there by the window – not anymore, he's gone – that unshaven fellow in black, very unfashionable, you saw him, Count; well, yesterday he and the doctor locked horns, and so, it's at once evident what man he is: Filimon Romanovitch Zeytsoff, have you not heard, Count? – Well, neither had I, but he's apparently an important figure amongst the Reds, agh, I know nothing about politics – am I right, Doctor, sir?'

'Zeytsoff, newspaper rabble-rouser, gaoled after nineteen twelve, clearly not for long enough.'

'And blood immediately rushed to the good doctor's head!' Frau Blutfeld savoured the memory of a delectable minor scandal.

'... communists in first class revolutionising out of excess comfort...'

Wince sceptically, 'You're not suggesting, are you, that this Zeytsoff was targeting the prince? Those quick to shed ink usually faint at the sight of blood.'

Frau Blutfeld, the theatrical conspirator, glanced behind her with ostentatious discretion.

'Oh! That one in the corner! Hunched over his salad. The one with the broken nose.'

Take a quick look. The fellow had the posture of a retired wrestler: broad shoulders splitting the sleeves of his poorly cut jacket; livid blue scar across shaven head, a long ridge of hideously conjoined tissue. Absolutely, he was as suited to the first class of the Transsib like a knuckleduster to a china shop.

Engineer White-Gessling scrutinised the broken-nosed wrestler with avid interest, now through his eyeglasses, now from above them.

'What? Our next revolutionary?'

'Hardly! He was talking to the natchalnik of the Express, we saw him, they signed some sort of printed papers, true? Husband, dear?'

Herr Blutfeld gurgled in assent.

'And then, just as we were going to supper,' she continued, leaning again over the table towards her interlocutor, the sign of an imminent sensation, 'through the half-open compartment door – what should we see? He was loading a revolver! Just like that!'

'A policeman, if I understand correctly.'

'They must have assigned him to the prince,' replied Doctor Konyeshin. 'After all, I told you so.'

'Only one?'

Wipe the mouth with the serviette and move away from the table: 'Were his death so important to me, I would simply unbolt the rails.'

'... no danger as still more policemen here at night,' Verousse inter-rupted again. 'Informed of terrorists on train but who on train to derail himself?'

'Those who usually perish from bombs cast by themselves. Mm-hmm. Yes. Ladies. Gentlemen.'

The men crossed into the smoking car to drink coffee, smoke a pipe, cigar, cigarette; only Herr Blutfeld declined, following doctor's orders to take half an hour's nap after meals. A wide sliding door beneath coldiron archivolts (from which the sightless eyes of a Queen of Winter with snow-white breasts peered down, supported by icicle-winged putti) divided the smoking area from the main space of the saloon car. In it were a billiard table – the most absurd extravagance – and a small library, restocked at station stops with the current edi-tions of local newspapers. A tall radio receiver with illuminated dial also stood there. Every so often the signal slipped off the frequen-cy, doubtless due to vibrations and jolts of the speeding train; soon, however, it would find itself beyond the reach of European radio stations – the farther it travels east towards Winter, the fewer they are and weaker they become. Beyond the next door was the saloon proper, where the ladies had repaired. The original plans for the com-position of the first-class carriages of the Trans-Siberian Express had included a chapel car (with a small bell tower projected above the roof), a gymnastics car... Now other extravagances were in vogue. The parlour car, located just ahead of the saloon, might feasibly have served as a ballroom; it was fitted with fireplace, and equipped with upright piano. It opened onto a glass-panelled gallery, from which the passengers could admire the landscapes as the Trans-Siberian Magistral sliced them into two continents. Beyond the gallery there was also an observation platform surrounded by a fanciful iron-work balustrade, under smoke-protective shield.

The smoking-room area, decorated according to the Russian version of Art Nouveau, that is, with exaggerated oriental splendour (more gilt trimmings and heavy ornamentation), nevertheless gave the im-pression of being bright and roomy. Blinds had been rolled up and the cover of the oval skylight removed, the ventilation vents left slightly ajar – into an interior drowning in browns and blacks, sunlight streamed in sheaves of living azure and green fired from sky and forest depths. Shafts of dazzling brightness pierced the Armenian carpet with mo-mentum, raising cloudlets of shimmering dust.

Sit down in the corner armchair under a mirror. The Englishman handed around Wild Woodbines. The steward proffered a light. Smoke. The man from Flanders and the doctor also reached into the engi-neer's silver cigarette case; Captain Privyezhensky, instead, took from his pocket a pipe made of light-coloured wood and a leather tobacco pouch.

The cigarette smoke formed itself into phantasmagorical shapes in the sunlight, glimmered and flickered. The movement of the train, its jolts and bounds, affected not at all the slow hypnotic pantomime of these silvery billows.

'There stands the next,' Konyeshin pointed with a movement of his head to a powerfully built man with Asiatic facial features and neck like a joint of gammon. Leaning against the window, the man seemed engrossed in his newspaper.

'And those three during the night? Are they in second class?'

'Or in the service van. They're not going to throw out passengers to make room for themselves in Deluxe.'

Sit with one leg folded over the other, with loosened foulard cravat, unbuttoned jacket; smoke a cigarette, observe the kaleidoscopic interplay of light and smoke. In the opposite corner, under an ornamental palm, sits the American engineer, whom Frau Blutfeld had pointed out in the dining car. He was reading a book, making hurried notes every now and then on a piece of paper slipped under the jacket; not once did he lift his head. Have him in direct line of vision, at the far extent of the gaze, which penetrates the smoke and encounters no resistance, in order to focus solely on the other side of the carriage. The sun did not reach all nooks and crannies of the smoking car; behind the American was only shadow. The Yankee was tall, had sharp features and dark skin and hair (black with a single silver streak on the right) combed towards the sides from a central parting. His profile resembled that of Gypsy patriarchs. The bony chin, thrust forward, rested on his stiff collar. The bushy eyebrows were knitted, as he mused over the book. In order to turn a page, he raised a white-gloved hand – whilst the shadow, of course, also raised its hand. Observe that shadow. Movement, no movement, movement, no movement, the light trembling – how is it possible, it's not possible – because if he moves not in his armchair under the palm tree, and the streams of light move not, if the windows change not their position in the carriage, nor the Sun its position in the firmament, and the train swerves not on its tracks, then how is it that the shadow behind the American dances on the wall like the cigarette smoke in the air, like fluid dissolving into fluid, swims from figure to figure, warps and contracts, warps and swells, dallies with itself, and sparkles like reflections on flowing water.

Shadow, not light – shadow as glintz, the living negative of the negative – an impossible image seen on the oak boiserie of the smoking car of the Trans-Siberian Express.

In the parlour car, someone was playing Chopin on the piano, mutilating him cruelly.

Flick the cigarette over the cup of a glass tulip before speaking, 'I believe, however, that from the political point of view, ending this war is in everyone's interests. As a rule, wars lead to crises, carry nations from one era into the next – but this war is leading nowhere and will change nothing. Even Lyednyaks are not especially clamouring for it in the Duma; whilst Ottepyelniks depend absolutely on withdrawal from the Asian impasse. We can expect irrational acts of desperation on the part of some terrorists or other, we can always expect them – I cannot see, however, any concrete plan whereby anyone in Russia would gain from the death of Prince Blutsky before he signs the peace with Japan.'

'... the hope win war and lose not to Japan again now rematch of rematch...'

'Bah, but the whole thing hinges on the fact that Russia is incapable of conducting or winning wars!' Laugh. 'She never was! She cannot, and that's that. It is a queer phenomenon of History.' Raise the cigarette above the head. 'Look at the last two centuries, gentlemen, when Russia became a European power. She suffered far more war wounds than she inflicted. Where are her thundering successes in battle, where her leaders of genius, glorious campaigns from which cadets at L'École militaire de Saint-Cyr and West Point learn their strategies and tactics? There are none. And how many times was she miraculously rescued from truly devastating defeats? Remember Pyotr the First besieged by the Turkish army on the Prut River, where he had no choice but to capitulate. Remember Aleksandr the First after Austerlitz and Friedland, von Diebitsch after Wawer and Iganie. Or even the last Turkish war: the Muscovites would have fled in ignominy from Osman Nuri Pasha's Plevna were it not for the Rumanians. From whom afterwards, of course, in order to demonstrate their gratitude, they seized Southern Bessarabia.

'Instead, Russia has brilliant diplomacy, adept at the art of division and setting at loggerheads, which thwarts in time any anti-Russian alliance; possesses cunning and eloquent agitators ready to proclaim Russia's triumphs with infinite effrontery in all the capital cities of Europe, as well as the superiority of her reasons of state in moments of her greatest humiliation and defeat. And thanks to this policy pursued for generations, Russia has managed to inculcate an incomprehensible Russophilia not only in the salons of Paris, Berlin, Vienna, but also amongst the nations slung in the mud by her own hand and demeaned under her boot: Czechs, Lithuanians, Poles. Such is the victory of victories: it's not enough to conquer, you must also force the conquered – no, not force them – ensure that they come of their own freewill to kiss the knout of the oppressor.'

'... after Kishineff and massacres Anglo-Saxon press won't give to Russia, Jews and Western socialists won't give, n'est-ce pas?'

What exactly is happening to that man's shadow? Scrutinise the Yankee from under squinting eyes, through the smoke and sunlight. Maybe it's not about the man but the place, that twilight corner where the rays of summer reach not. But no: Yankee stands up, nods to the steward, crosses for a moment into the saloon to fetch a glass of water. Turn the head to follow him, gaze after him from behind the tulle curtain of smoke – whilst the shimmering tremulous shadow, shadow-not-shadow, arabesque of dazzling light and slightly weaker light, this vibrant optical phenomenon tracks the American, surrounding him like a wandering pillar of heat, distorting images, bleary perspectives. But it all happens very subtly, delicately, lightly, on the borders of his silhouette, along the sutures of gloom. Glance at the people sitting in the smoking car. They are paying no attention to the lean figure of the Yankee hidden in the corner beneath the palm.

'Perhaps we are gazing at the wrong stars,' said White-Gessling. 'You've forgotten, gentlemen, why this war broke out in the first place. The first conflict with Japan was over Manchuria; Japanese and Russian ambitions clashed in China, it was about Korea and spheres of influence – but the second time, everything started with the economy, with the Tunguska deposits. And, I tell you, this is how it will end. One hundred per cent of the world's deposits of tungetitum and coldiron are located on Russian territory; Russia controls all the trading routes leading to them. Should we be surprised then that the Japanese risked war for the sake of moving the treaty borders a few hundred miles? Especially since, Ice or no Ice, this was already hanging in the air: in nineteen eleven, they were already rebuilding militarily after the first war, deadlines of their various international contracts were about to expire, and well, above all, they had to achieve their goal before the United States of America opened the Panama Canal, so as not to be caught in fire from both sides. But both in Russia and in Japan, businessmen influence decisions. Do you know, gentlemen, how much profit Sibirkhozheto made last year?' The Englishman snorted and blew smoke towards the ceiling. 'So, who stands to gain from the murder of Prince Blutsky? I will tell you who: the competitors of Sibirkhozheto's subsidiaries. Those who lost out in the battle for concessions. They. These are profits reckoned in tens of millions, hundreds of millions of roubles. Or: the foreign firms, for whom the market may collapse when Asia is connected to America via the Alaskan Line. Whilst the war continues with Japan, construction is delayed, hence for the time being they are relatively safe. Or –'

'So, you say: not anarchists and socialists, but greedy bourgeois?' Konyeshin smiled.

'One does not rule out the other.' Comment in undertones, 'What could be simpler than slipping hot-headed SR-men precise information about time and place? And who would search afterwards for the secret informers? Terrorists themselves confess, deny not their idea. If murder you must, then let it be by someone else's hand, gentlemen, someone else's hand.'

The doctor winced in distaste, wiped his nose, adjusted his pince-nez.

'Were we to reason in this way, behind every bomb thrown at high-ranking tchinovniks by a naïve anarchist, we should assume a palace power struggle between Ottepyelniks and Lyednyaks, a conspiracy by one syndicate of coldindustrialists against another, the private ambitions of some minister or Grand Duke...'

'Not to mention the quarrels in the Duma: the upcoming elections, and Struve may lose his majority, were he to flunk the peace negotiations.'

'The Minister of War –'

Captain Privyezhensky burst into loud laughter. All conversation stopped, several people even glanced in from the billiard room. The captain covered his mouth with his hand. Doctor Konyeshin peered at him inquiringly with raised eyebrows, Engineer White-Gessling – was nonplussed.

Privyezhensky put aside his pipe and crossed his arms over his uniform.

'What are you talking about, gentlemen?' he asked quietly, still with a trace of laughter in his husky voice. 'Please forgive me, but I can no longer contain myself. Engineer,' he addressed White-Gessling, 'these economic calculations of yours, sir, analyses of the struggle of business interests...'

'What?' the Britisher's hackles were up. 'What are you –'

'No, no,' the captain made a great effort to suppress his hilarity, which was not altogether sincere. 'You are quite right, of course. That is – you would be right, were this Great Britain. You see, sir, things have worked out in such a way that in my still-short career, I have managed to rub shoulders with people from the inner circles of power, to peep, so to speak, under the palace carpets... What are you talking about, gentlemen, on the Saviour's wounds!' He shook his head in mocking incredulity. 'This is Russia!'

'... for noting this fact we fail not express gratitude...'

'Please don't be angry, Engineer, but you have no clue, sir, of the principles by which our country is governed.'

'Really?' White-Gessling snorted, twirling a second cigarette between his fingers.

'It is not even a question of power and how the country is governed, in the way you reason. A few decades ago, Russia still *belonged* to His Sovereign Majesty the Emperor; the emperor owned it – the lands, the riches concealed in them, and everything which grew upon the land, as well as mountains, rivers, lakes, a quarter of a continent.' Captain Privyezhensky encompassed with a sweeping gesture the sunlit expanses flashing by outside the windows of the Express. 'He *owned* it, just as you gentlemen own your watches or shoes. Only recently did he agree to graciously introduce a division into what belonged to His Imperial Exaltedness and His Family, and what belonged to Russia. For himself, he kept half. Thus I am not talking about any United States of America, not talking about France or Great Britain with her Magna Carta or their parliaments – but about a completely different type of dominion from the one you know, even from the most reactionary of European monarchies. Please understand, sir: the Habsburgs *rule*, Emperors of All the Russias *possess*.

'You assume, gentlemen, great political disputes and conflicts of high finance behind the decisions of the autocrat. My God. If only that were so! If only these hypotheses about conspiracies and many-layered intrigues could be true! Even this train in which we are travelling, the Trans-Siberian Railway. How do you think the Manchurian Line arose and the first war broke out with Japan? Politics? Economic calculations, what, Engineer? Reckoning the benefits of investment? And perhaps behind it all lies Russia's whole strategy for colonising Far-East Asia…? Hah!

'The truth stems from the fact that our emperor, Nikolay the Second Aleksandrovitch, in his childhood and youth, abandoned himself intemperately to the sin of Onan. When the general apathy, fatigue and day-time weakness of the heir to the throne became rather more than apparent, professors from abroad were summoned. Their diagnosis eventually reached the ears of His Imperial Exaltedness, who ordered that the shameful educational problem be resolved as soon as possible. Thus, the elderly generals, privy councillors and ministers of the court, following lengthy consultations, chose the time-honoured method: a natural outlet had to be found for the young man's virile energy. On sundry occasions, therefore, they began to parade the glossiest krasavitsas before the eyes of Tsarevitch Nikolay Aleksandrovitch, usually the daughters of families closely connected to the court. In the beginning, the imperial advisers were congratulating themselves on the success of their plan, for indeed the tsarevitch quickly realised which sin tasted better, and completely gave up the first for the second. It soon transpired, however, that in this too he knew no moderation, turning it into a craving visible to all. But it's a matter of great political import that nothing should stand in the way of a future alliance with another major power through the wise marriage of the emperor. A new headache therefore arose for the privy councillors and retired generals: to break up all Nikolay Aleksandrovitch's love affairs before he became too attached to any favourite and his affections burgeoned. Whilst the tsarevitch confined himself to late-night excursions to the Saint Petersburg drinking dens and homes of reputable prostitutes in the company of Grand Duke Sergey Aleksandrovitch, there was no great danger. But soon the costs began to mount: thus, in exchange for breaking off the relationship between the heir to the throne and Mademoiselle Myatleff, the empress paid the Myatleff family three hundred thousand roubles by purchasing their property on the main Peterhof road at many times the going rate. And it went from bad to worse. The tsarevitch completely lost his head over the ballerina Kshesinskaya. His Sovereign Majesty the Emperor, when he learned of it, and the fact that she was from the Polish Krzesiński family and ready to lead the future emperor through the boudoir from Orthodoxy to Roman Catholicism, plunged into ultimate despair. An order was prepared at the highest level to banish the stunning ballerina from Saint Petersburg by the administrative route, and the chief inspector of Saint Petersburg police, General Gresser, was sent to deliver it. Kshesinskaya received Gresser politely and invited him into her boudoir – and who should be in her boudoir but Tsarevitch Nikolay Aleksandrovitch? Nikolay, without giving it a second thought, tore up the paper and showed Gresser the door. Now all the court councillors saw clearly that the Empire's future was threatened. It was not possible to remove temptations of the heart from Nikolay Aleksandrovitch – so it was necessary to remove Nikolay Aleksandrovitch from them. How to do it? Well, he was put on a naval cruiser and sent on a journey around the world. But a warship is not a monastery, and the tsarevitch not a monk. The iniquities and debaucheries that took place aboard the *Memory of Azoff* during the tsarevitch's voyage were recorded by the world's press, whereas only those facts reached His Imperial Exaltedness that had to reach him. In India, the tsarevitch's younger brother, Grand Duke Georgy, who had been travelling with him, left the ship; he returned home a broken man, chest smashed and barely alive. Then it emerged: during one of their bouts aboard ship, the highborns had drunk so much that the wildest ideas occurred to them, and Grand Duke Georgy had had a bet with a Greece prince on who could climb higher up the mast. The Greek won; as for

His Highness Grand Duke Georgy Aleksandrovitch, he fell from a great height, and thanks only to drinker's luck or divine intervention did not break his neck. The next port of call for the young heir to the throne, before Vladivostock, where he was to take part in the opening ceremony of the Trans-Siberian Railway, was Japan. It goes without saying, of course, that every time the heir to the Empire stepped ashore, he was accompanied by huge manoeuvres on the part of the forces of order; you may imagine, gentlemen, in what immense fear the reigning family lives of assassination. It was no different then, whilst a cordon was meant to circumscribe the tsarevitch's independent movements. All such precautions, however, as well as armies of Japanese constables lining the streets, were of no avail. On the tsarevitch's return journey to Kyoto from Lake Biwa, a fanatic raised on nationalist ideas – not some random passerby, for there were certainly none of those anywhere in sight, but one of the agents placed in the police cordon to protect the illustrious guest – threw himself upon him. He would have attacked earlier, at the first opportunity, but he'd been unable to distinguish the tsarevitch from the other foreigners. He was helped only by the dragon tattoo, which His Imperial Highness Nikolay Aleksandrovitch had acquired in Nagasaki, when he was amusing himself with the Greek prince in the local bawdy-houses. The Japanese press described the image on the skin of the tsarevitch's right arm in detail: a dragon with yellow horns and red belly. That was how the crazed samurai recognised the heir to the Russian throne. Before he was overpowered, he managed to hack Nikolay Aleksandrovitch twice with his sword; the tsarevitch attempted to flee, but were it not for the Greek prince's bamboo cane, he would not have lived, that's for sure. Both slashes struck the head. In the beginning, however, the wounds appeared superficial: after a few days the future emperor was again on his feet, left with a scar, not an especially ugly one. But from that moment on, His Imperial Highness Nikolay Aleksandrovitch has suffered from various psychological indispositions. Which with time have intensified. For instance, our emperor sees cobwebs everywhere and lashes out to tear them down, orders the servants to sweep the rooms and corridors. The Japanese sword has marked His Most Serene Majesty for the rest of his life – excruciating migraines, hallucinations, bouts of depression, apathy and mental weakness, all of which make him prey to charlatans, spiritualists, mesmerists, mystics and holy fools. From *père* Philippe, who was to ensure that the empress would bear an heir to the throne and who summoned on demand the spirits of Nikolay Aleksandrovitch's ancestors so they could dictate to him state policies, and who proved eventually to be a barber from Marseilles – to the Galata Virgin, who prophesied to the emperor the outcomes of wars – to the immortal

Rasputin. In his day too, a certain Bezobrazoff possessed a similar mesmeric power over the autocrat's will, once a government adviser and member of the Black Hundreds. Bezobrazoff regarded himself as an expert on Far-Eastern policy and on these affairs in particular he imposed his opinion. When Witte opposed him – 'Who does your Highness trust more: a private individual or your shtats-sekretar and minister?' – the emperor appointed Bezobrazoff shtats-sekretar. Bezobrazoff entered into numerous partnerships with officials in His Sovereign Majesty's Chancellery, with the Russian consul in Korea, with the Grand Dukes, investing millions of roubles of even the emperor's own estate. They created a joint-stock company, which received concessions from the Korean government to exploit forests and minerals in Korea. In order to realise these and other financial phantasmagoria, Bezobrazoff hypnotised the Emperor of All the Russias into decisions affecting the establishment of Alekseyeff's viceregency, the Manchurian Line of the Transsib, the management of Port Arthur and the Far East, and as a result the war itself with Japan. The exploitative licence awarded to Bezobrazoff was in fact the main cause of the first war: Russia's territorial demands corresponded to the lands conceded to his joint-stock company. You were speaking, Engineer, of calculating businessmen's interests? The emperor's profits from shares in Bezobrazoff's enterprise can have amounted at most to tens of millions of roubles – whereas the viceregency itself has been devouring a hundred and twenty million a year. To say nothing of the costs of the war. You were speaking, sir, of causes and effects, of the consequences of rational political choices and plans. So, there you have the causes and the kind of rationality behind the policies of the Russian state: a samurai sword, suffocating delusions and the voice of a charlatan whispering in the imperial ear.

'The same principle operates just as much at the autocrat's court as in the most destitute village, the empty steppe, the cold taiga – there is no line, no boundary, beyond which you, sir, could safely apply your intellectual tools. There is only one Russia. You have found yourself, Engineer, in a land where people – no, not people, but human-objects – are subject to an infinitely superior being, whilst that being shapes their reality at will according to his whimsical caprices and fleeting desires, in no way explaining anything, because these things too are not for explaining. As to understanding – it is possible to understand the laws of nature. But would man still understand the laws of nature, were God to keep changing them for no apparent reason, from one second to the next?'

Say nothing. Who tells in public of the practices of the boudoir, who speaks in seemly company of such shameful matters as habits engendered by the body's animal urges? And matters affecting not any person

– but the reigning monarch? An army officer! This cannot be! Shame, shame, shame! Ought he not to self-combust right here on the spot? What inner daemon had set Privyezhensky ablaze? Stare out of the window – at fields and forests, at river floodwaters, at a white boulder, took-took-took-TOOK, already left behind.

Konyeshin, White-Gessling and Verousse exchanged idle remarks, digesting the young captain's words with uncertain mien.

'… well honestly Yoshihito none too normal either…'

'There must be something in this spiritualism, very fashionable again in Saint Petersburg salons, Princess Blutskaya has promised us a real seance here today, consider yourselves warned, gentlemen…'

'If the captain tells such tales to random travelling companions – it can't be so bad with civil liberty in Russia.'

Privyezhensky smiled bitterly.

'And have you any idea, Engineer, why I've been banished from Saint Petersburg to the other end of the world?'

Light another cigarette. Smoke stings the eyes; blurred images loom out of the bright sunlight and dissolve in the sun.

The Yankee closed his book, stood up, pulled at his shirt-cuffs, glanced around the smoking car and then went out into the neighbouring carriage. The Asian bruiser, walking past the palm tree a moment later, cast on the boiserie crowned by ivy-leaf carvings a shadow which was as normal as possibly could be, with sharp stable edges. Whatever that phenomenon depended on was therefore directly associated with the person of the American.

'… Count, as you possess Polish roots, I should have taken this into account.'

'I beg your pardon?'

Turn to face the Captain. Privyezhensky remained focused on cleaning the stem of his pipe, raised not his eyes.

'At the Britisher, I am not surprised, but that you, Count –'

'There is no affinity between our nations.' Speak dryly.

'I heard what you said, Count, about Russian soldiers and diplomats. All conquered nations are afterwards –'

'Conquered? You conquered us? In which battle, pray? In what war?'

'… now now calm down gentlemen no grounds in train excuse for une querelle d'Allemand…'

Light a cigarette. Privyezhensky tapped his pipe on the arm of his chair. Cross the legs comfortably, tug at the trouser crease.

'Russia does not conquer.' Adopt a gentler, softer tone, just audible above the rhythmic rattle of steel. 'Russia seizes. Germany conquers. France conquers. Turkey conquers.

'You bear a grudge against your commanding officers, Captain, so it's easy now to pour out your bitterness against them – is there some lesser Bezobrazoff behind your transfer? – but you won't disown your motherland. Would you wish Russia to be otherwise? Then it would not be Russia. And that, after all, is the greatest apostasy of all revolutionaries: they deny Russia. Permit me, Captain to ask…'

Privyezhensky frowned. Wait. He makes an encouraging gesture with his pipe.

'Were it to lie within your power, were you to possess such divine might, would you order the liquidation in Russia of autocracy?'

'What does that mean: liquidate? And leave the government to whom? The Duma?'

'For instance. At any rate, in the hands of representatives of a system radically different from autocracy. Would you order it? Tell me honestly. You regard yourself as an Ottepyelnik, true?'

Privyezhensky chewed the mouthpiece of his cold pipe. Head resting on the back of his chair, he let his eyes wander across the ceiling and blue above the skylight. A few seconds longer and his very silence gave a clear enough answer.

Laugh quietly.

'I am curious how much these Narodniks and revolutionaries believe in their utopias. When they overthrow autocracy – what will they build in its place? Whatever they decide on, even on handing power to the working masses, in the end they'll give rise to some form of autarchy.

'There is no kinship between our nations, Captain. We believe in the same God, but that belief sits differently in our hearts. For your people, the most important is redemption after death; happiness beyond the grave overshadows all virtues of this life – after all, salvation is possible only after forsaking the world. This world will always be evil to you, unjust, full of pain and injury, which cannot be repaired in life. Upon what nobility of spirit, therefore, do you set your eyes? – not upon that which glorifies action, resistance and deeds which change the face of the Earth, but the silent bearing of inevitable sufferings in passive asceticism, in humility, in worship of God despite the sufferings; life spent dreaming about happiness after death. Blackest pessimism and fatalism enshroud this belief like a pall a living corpse. Hardly surprising then that your peasants, the lowest of the low, give the impression of being touched by a hereditary form of apathy, animal-like resignation and lack of will carried in the blood. Even as they perish in their thousands from starvation, they perish without rebelling, their empty eyes fixed on heaven. The same image is portrayed by your art, your literature – nihilism or apocalypse – every time I read Dostoyevsky – I want to drink myself to death.

'And where to seek kinship, when our traditions of government and law are so different? Poland, the one never to open its doors to absolutism, is forced now to tolerate the institutions and practices of autocracy. With us, the law made man secure and equal before even the king – with you, the place of law is occupied by the principle of power. The freedom of the boyars can never be compared to the freedom of even our farmhands. Ah, just like water flowing over stones, it filters down from the very heights to the very pits: every executor and under-executor of the autocrat's will feels himself omnipotent and above the law. Therefore, you have no genuine nobles, at best fake foreign aristocrats, doglike dvoryanins; your tchinovniks, on the other hand, are the most formidable in the world. When, with us, any upstart peasant or townsman, as soon as he starts climbing and exceeding his station his life, wants to turn into a nobleman, although, obviously, he cannot, yet he's fixated on such an ideal – what are the ideals of your parvenus? Neath the boot of the autocrat, this pale substitute for chivalric tradition never had an opportunity to flourish; there's no place for honour, since blind obedience to the autocrat stands above all other qualities. Instead of honour, pride, integrity, independence of mind – a pliable neck and flexible knees ready to bend, courtly cleverness, ingratiation, cruelty and duplicity.

'There is no kinship between us, never was and never shall be...'

Captain Privyezhensky got up and walked away without a word.

Stub out the cigarette in the flower-shaped ashtray. Catch the eye of Doctor Konyeshin. The doctor narrowed his eyes behind the pince-nez angled on the bridge of his nose, but his look was sharp, searching.

'Where are you disembarking, Count?'

'In Irkutsk.'

'Just as well. Ever fired a gun?'

'You joke, sir.' Bristle at this. 'Tsarist officers face trial and demotion.'

'True. Yet I would swear, Count, that you were deliberately provoking him.'

'I have never seen him before, know him not – why should I...?'

'Agh, *pour passer le temps.*'

'But you are not offended by my words.'

Konyeshin laughed. Hear his laughter for the first time: a sound resembling something between a hiccup and a cough.

The doctor stuffed his handkerchief into his mouth, bowed his head – only then calmed down.

'I know Poles, my dear Count,' he said after a while. 'I lived in Vilna. I believe I even know that book.'

'What book?'

'The one you were citing, Count. *Know Your Enemy*, or something along those lines.' The doctor folded the handkerchief and wiped the pince-nez with it. 'Like in the anecdote about the Jew who reads the antisemitic press: "You see, sir, in our papers they write only about misfortunes, poverty and persecution – but here I read that we rule the world; it instantly warms the heart!" Konyeshin bared his wide straight teeth. 'I adore these Polish squibs. I'm almost ready to believe that we Russians really have straddled and broken in the daemon of History.'

Answer him with a smile.

'Happy to provide some entertainment. A long journey awaits us, we should fill the boredom, as you rightly observed.'

'... about what gentlemen for God's sake so I understand somebody explain joke or is he serious duel and you Poland Russia friends enemies Doctor Count somebody me or nothing of it and then write down so please explain me...'

Lean towards Verousse.

'Please don't take it to heart, no one understands it.'

'Peculiar habits of the locals,' nodded the doctor. 'Always add piquancy to reportages.'

The lanky Fleming flailed about offended, no doubt in the belief he was being mocked. He rose from his chair, straightened his back, hesitating for a moment over what to say or whether to say goodbye – gave up and marched off with his stork-like stride deeper into the saloon car.

Nod to Konyeshin to come closer.

'Did you hear, Doctor, what Frau Blutfeld was saying about that American engineer? I am ashamed to confess most of her monologue escaped my attention.'

'American...?'

'He was sitting over there.'

'Ah! I believe he is called Dragan. A shady figure, if you ask my opinion, Count.'

'Oh?'

'That woman he's travelling with... He could be her grandfather.'

'They're not married?'

'On dit.'

Exchange knowing glances with the doctor.

'On a journey, when we commingle for a short time with people we'll never meet again, we let ourselves reveal considerably more truth about ourselves than is wise or decent,' said the doctor, also extinguishing his cigarette. 'There is something magical in it, it's a magical time.'

Smile ironically.

'More truth?'

'Truth – the truth we know and the truth we know not.'

Konyeshin stood up, brushed ash off his jacket. At exactly that moment the train swung into a bend and the doctor, teetering slightly, rested a shoulder against the rolled-back door of the billiard room.

Raise the eyes towards him. He tilted his head confidentially.

'Whilst Frau Blutfeld, trust me, has already managed to describe all of us in precise detail from the worst possible angle.'

He hiccup-coughed once more and walked away.

Remain in the smoking car till the birch forest beyond the window changes to mixed taiga and the sun sails away from the asymmetrical skylight in the carriage roof. Now flight into the compartment and spending the day in isolation no longer came into play: every minute spent amongst people, every exchange of opinions with other passengers, every cigarette smoked in the Deluxe smoking car – made the departure from Count Gyero-Saski all the harder; yet it was just the same cage and just the same beast yelping behind bars – when he breakfasted on silver and porcelain, when he declaimed his national sermons.

The little book in question was entitled *The Situation of Russia in History, or What Every Pole Should Know concerning His Enemy*, and was written by Filip Gierosławski shortly before his deportation; until the assassination of Dmowski, it even enjoyed a certain popularity. Reading it was unavoidable, of course – but that it should remain so well lodged in the memory... Who could have foreseen that Count Gyero-Saski would turn out to be such a hardened patriot-cum-Russophobe? (At least he's not devoid of a sense of humour.) Whose words, however, was he to use: whence, from whom, from what shadow were his words wrung – words which when uttered aloud in the presence of other people proved to be his truest truth – whence came that Count Gyero-Saski, who answers a tsarist officer's anger with lazy irony, with an effortless gesture of hand and cigarette? Existence is not a necessary attribute of a father, and when travelling – well, travelling is a magical time.

Decipher the letter! Bump into the thin consumptive girl in the corridor. 'Excuse me.' 'Excuse me.' And the light of sudden recognition in her eyes, spontaneous sincerity. 'I thought no one else from Poland was travelling with us...!' 'You and your auntie as I understand it.' 'Yes, it would be very nice, if...' 'Benedykt Gierosławski.' Kiss her hand. She curtsied awkwardly in the narrow corridor. 'Jelena Muklanowicz.' 'Thank God, I nearly fell foul of some palace army man, I'd go crazy within a week in such company.' She giggled. 'Frau Blutfeld has invited us...' 'Oh, God!' Break free. 'Then I'm taking cover!' 'But should you care to join us at our table –'

She had painted around her dark eyes with powerful henna, as a result of which her complexion seemed all the paler, bordering on the deadly anaemic. Stop for a moment with the key already in the compartment door, hand on the golden heather-sprig that formed the handle, as a thunderbolt of bad associations struck: Frau Blutfeld – Count Gyero-Saski – ostensibly unintentional tête-à-tête – unmarried young lady, bachelor, sly old aunt – five days to Irkutsk on the same train. Shake the head and burst out laughing. To describe this whole story to Julia, she'll be in very heaven.

Open the window, take out the writing pad bound in canvas and rubber. The Pilsudchiks' letter lay inserted in a page farther on from where it had been left. Bite the lip. Someone had broken into the compartment and rifled through everything. And what could be more interesting to a spy than a piece of encoded secret information which is so obviously a piece of encoded secret information? On the door, on the lock – not the slightest trace. A pro.

Sit down, undo completely the already-loose cravat, steady the breath. From behind the dividing wall of the compartment came the suppressed voices of Mr and Mrs White-Gessling. Those people who broke in... If they know not the key to the code – what are the chances they'll break it whilst still on the Trans-Siberian Express? Had they brought a specialist with them for the purpose? Doubtful. Smack the lips under the moustache. And hence: who will be first? Mind against mind. Take the cap off the Eyedropper, shake the nib. Maybe Zygmunt was right and this is Okhrana provocation, and the only reason for the code is so that the bearer should not know that he carries in person his own death sentence – but perhaps, behind this dysalphabetic babble, the secret of his father really is hidden. Who then had broken in, if not Mr Scarface or Mr Gammon Neck? An adherent of Saint Martsyn concealed amongst the first-class passengers?

The pen leaps up and down above the paper and plants inkblots in time to the rhythm of the galloping train, tap-tap-tap-TAP. In the head – puzzles and plots, in the heart – cold fear, and outside the window – Russia basking in the sun. Hospodi pomiluy.

On the power of shame

'Count! Over here!' cried Frau Blutfeld. Prince Blutsky-Osey nodded assent.

Hesitate mid-stride. Miss Muklanowicz pulled a disappointed face. Shrug the shoulders resignedly and turn towards the prince's table.

Bows followed and exchanges of ritual civilities. Who knows what forms are binding in the presence of Russian princes and dukes? Adopt therefore the principle of strict taciturnity, always a safe option. The steward offered a chair. Soup sloshed about in tureens, bowls and plates whenever the Express leapt over a set of points.

In addition to the Blutfelds, whose presence in any company ought not to provoke surprise, a not-so-young tchinovnik with hawkish stare in slightly slanting eyes took a seat at the prince's table. Frau Blutfeld introduced him as Councillor Dushin (privy and extraordinary, naturally). He stared at everything and everyone with inquisitive suspicion – at the amber wall-clock chiming the dinner hour, at the *consommé* served with diablotins and croutons, at the Astrakhan caviar, at the insufficiently white gloves of the waiter attending him and at the Hungarian count.

The conversation revolved around fashion; the old princess, ugly as sin, was discussing Western decadence, always a topical subject, with Frau Blutfeld.

'Yet in Paris, have you not seen? It beggars belief! The models they're introducing to young women, having rejected corsets altogether? No sense of style, elegance or even a healthy figure, nothing – there's no sticking to a strict cut or pattern, skirts hang off them like they were scarecrows, waistline completely lost somewhere, and how they all slouch, how it looks!'

'At first, they wanted to wear the same in Berlin and Stuttgart; thank God, they got over it. But two years ago, Your Highness, when we were in Italy – that very same fashion was in vogue, if one can call it fashion, honestly!'

'Were it only in some way presentable… But the worst is, you venture onto the street and don't know where to cast your eyes, or what to say to the children – it's the height of impropriety, ankle and half the calf, sometimes as far as the knee; raise your eyes, and again a pretty face under a totally unladylike haircut, cropped almost to the skin, I've seen it myself – and how they ride on those velocipedes in slit skirts – well, and when we were at Des Terreaux in Lyon, you wouldn't believe what outfits the girls play tennis in!'

The prince bore this in silence. Certainly, neither Herr Blutfeld, swallowing the viscid borscht with the efficiency of a fireman's pump, nor Councillor Dushin, who inspected every piece of broccoli from four separate angles before tentatively raising it to his lips, offered little opportunity for interesting conversation.

'And so,' the prince sighed melancholically, dipping his moustache into fish soup, 'it was you who tried to pick a fight with our captain over political principles?'

Glance in terror at Frau Blutfeld.

'A misunderstanding, Your Illustriousness, a mountain out of a molehill.'

Frau Blutfeld had caught that glance and rushed to the rescue.

'The count is travelling incognito,' she announced in her alarmist whisper. 'He asked me not to mention the name Gyero-Saski.'

The prince assumed a pouting expression, curious to know more.

'You see, my dear,' he said to his wife without raising his eyes from his plate. 'Here we have womanly discretion: he could not have chosen a better confidante.'

Gertrud Blutfeld knew not whether to be insulted or pretend to be insulted, or pretend not to have understood the prince's irony, though she may well have not understood it – pressing her lips together, she said no more.

'Gyero-Saski from Prussia, well yes,' the prince muttered in the meantime. Think: He must be nearly seventy years old, but for such an old man, bearing up well. The sole indications of his high birth were two enormous rings set with precious stones and the glittering decoration lying over his heart. His left hand trembled slightly as he manipulated the heavy cutlery. Could the tsar really not send a more capable negotiator to talks with the Japanese? Captain Privyezhensky would no doubt laugh mockingly: yet what have palace decisions to do with intellectual competence?

'Those Prussian Junkers who married into aristocratic Danubian families are now sitting on fine estates; your family keeps villages near Kaunas, yes? Who was it, ah – Pyotr Davidovitch Korobyel sold you a piece of land beyond our forests in the Illukst uyezd; were you ever there, young man? I recall never tasting better meads, Poles know how to make excellent mead, one has to admit.'

'A wealthy family,' remarked Dushin, narrowing his eyes.

'Really, you exaggerate, Your Illustriousness.'

'Ah, but we visited Tódor Gyero in Vienna in the spring of last year, you remember, my dear, immediately after the scandal at the Prünzels, when that southern violinist threw himself out of a window and broke both arms and legs; God's finger, I tell you, is present in such tragedies, nothing happens without a moral: the man used to entice and seduce virtuous women with his sensuous art, now he won't take up violin or bow again. Tódor was renovating his manor near Gödöllő, we stayed with the Vyershins – he renovated it in the end, did he not? It must look beautiful in summer.'

'Indeed.' Mutter, eyes lowered towards plate. 'In summer especially.'

'And Graf Gyero's daughter is marrying von Kuschel, who is a cousin three or four times removed of my wife's half-sister on the Battenberg side, so in a sense also related to His Sovereign Majesty the Emperor – when was the engagement announced, April, May? In May, we were in the Crimea, the rain was relentless, young von Kuschel seems an agreeable fellow and wise beyond his years, which runs with them in the family, fast-maturing blood, *non*?'

'Mm-hmm… I am not so well acquainted.'

'Decent people on the whole, funded a hospital after the epidemic in nineteen eleven, I saw the thanksgiving plaque in the entrance hall. You show up there too, eh?'

'Certainly.'

'Nothing happens without a moral,' the incandescent Prince Blutsky went on, crumbling rusks into his wine; insofar as teeth remained to him at all, he moved his lower jaw as if the bones had already putrefied to the consistency of rubber, eating in an identical manner to old Utchay, who invariably chopped apples, pancakes and meats into tiny slices with a pocket-knife, since only in that way could he swallow them without biting. 'And I am telling you, young man, that every evil you do and say shall return to you sooner or later and slap you in the face like a woman betrayed; and why so? why, because birds of a feather flock together, similar things seek each other out; have you ever wondered why it always works out like this – why in cities: with districts and streets, such and such people, robbers' alley, cutthroats' passage, loose women's boulevard, as well as merchants' quarter, and high-born quarter, and when the bells ring out in temples of worship, why you stop and listen, moving by ear from tserkoff to tserkoff; the same it is in any company – remember at school, if your father sent you to school, or in the army, wherever you gather people together of different provenance and different life experiences, at once they start mixing and seeking each other out, joining and pulling together, like to like, other to other, and look: here you have troublemakers and brawlers, here dodgers and toadies, there noble souls, there dreamers. And it's the same in life, nothing happens without a moral, a man of simple upright heart won't suddenly find himself amongst criminals and you won't witness hardened murderers dwelling happily amongst honest men, thus everything returns to you and creates its moral symmetry, evil to evil, good to good, truth to truth, lie to lie; you should know this, young man, whoever you are, because Pyotr Davidovitch sold no property in Illukst ujezd, I know not and have never heard of the Magyar house of Gyero; neither did we visit them in Vienna, von Kuschel is the name of one of my greyhounds, and may I be struck dumb if you, you good-for-nothing, ever in your life donated a kopeck to any charitable work, let alone funded a hospital, so begone from my sight before I have you cudgelled and thrown off the train, you brazen rogue, ahem, ahem – and might I request for dessert, a cup of hot milk with a smidgeon of butter and honeydew honey, thank you.'

Burn now, from the head downwards, from the red face and lips stretched in an ingratiating doggy smile, to the fingers palpitating as if in an onrush of fever, knocking against the table and serving dishes, tugging at the tablecloth. Crumble to black ash on the spot, so as not to have to look them in the face, listen to their whispers; for a great silence suddenly befell the dining car and all eyes were focused on the prince's table. The prince had not raised his voice, yet were any present who had not heard his words? they had all heard. Burn! Yet no fire struck. The fever burns without flame. They're speaking louder and louder – indistinguishable words; the heart beats too powerfully, blood roars in the ears. What they say – is clear enough.

Now came the time for truly heroic action; what had to be done was beyond a man's strength. Drop the hands, retract the feet, stand up, shift the trunk and push back the chair, all with eyes cast directly down, towards the chasm of hell; turn around, step to the side and then towards the aisle and –

Almost burst into tears: the lips had begun to tremble whilst some muscle vibrated neath the skin between chin and cheek; tears welled in the eyes. It's beyond human might! Shame crushed the larynx and windpipe, the throat dried up in seconds; impossible to swallow saliva, impossible to catch breath, something was strangling inside the chest, pressing on the lungs – how to move, whence draw energy, arms like stones, legs leaden. Impossible. The hands shook more and more vigorously; nudged by a thumb, a fork fell to the floor. The struggling breath resembled the squeal of a wounded horse, saliva oozed from a corner of the mouth; but in this state there was no controlling even the mouth – above all, the mouth.

Yank the left leg. The chair scraped on the carpet. Frau Blutfeld stood up to make room. What humiliation could be greater! Sobs mounted in the chest. Burn! Yank the right leg. The thighs do not obey; have to lean on the elbow-rests. The first time, the hands slip, the second likewise; stand only at the third attempt. Now a step to the left. If the knees don't give way. Feel the calves aquiver: a terrible impression when your own body slides out of control and collapses under you like a house of cards; the quivering reached into the shins and shook even the muscles of the belly.

Take that one step and cry out almost in relief.

Raise the head.

All were watching.

Smile.

Take a second, third, fourth step with that smile still burning on the countenance – the stewards stepped aside, the sitting passengers moved away with their chairs, the provodnik opened the door – a fifth, sixth, seventh – amidst the hush; close now, flight from their eyes is at hand, escape from their stares. For the time being, a reflection stays in the windowpane, a final image of the dining car from over the shoulder: all are watching.

Smile.

Even when the first and second doors have slammed behind, when the passage into the corridor of the next carriage has been traversed, and the corridor of that one to the very end, carriage after carriage, running, banging the shoulder against doorframes and pushing aside people who cannot be looked directly in the face, on and on, into the saloon, through smoking car and billiard room, across the parlour carriage – in panic-stricken flight – through the empty open gallery, it's still not enough; the accursed smile won't quit and will have to be clawed off with nails, knives, broken glass, so run on farther still. The iron door onto the observation platform is jammed – so break it down.

Fall out into the fresh air, into a blaze of afternoon sunshine and the clamour of great machines speeding along tracks, directly onto –

The muscleman with the scar was throttling Engineer Dragan, pinioning him with his knee to a metal seat and mangling his neck in his great square paws. Beside them on the carriage terrace lay the second okhrannik, the one with the Asiatic physiognomy – with shattered skull.

Stand and stare, catching breath in the wide-open mouth. They were frozen in mortal embrace – hands on neck, hands on hands clutching the neck – their swollen faces directed towards the door, motionless in half-murder as in an ancient sculpture, the very image of mythic struggle: cruel strongman and victim, brute strength and helpless old age.

Retreat a step to the threshold of the gallery.

Upon which Scarface turned his head and resumed the throttling, crushing the Yankee's chest with his knee.

Dragan, however, refused to look away; he will die with eyes fixed on the face of the accidental witness – cannot cry for help, cannot make a gesture, can only stare unflinchingly. He had dark, deep-set eyes.

Take another step back.

Dragan watched. Had that accursed smile finally crawled off the mouth? Was the American staring precisely at that smile? The intensity of his stare was too great, forbade an averting of the gaze.

The butt of a revolver fastened in a leather holster peeked from under a flap of Scarface's dishevelled jacket. The strangler was a whole head taller, whilst the jacket was almost splitting on his Herculean shoulders. His dark teeth were bared; sweat dripped from the tip of his crooked nose onto the forehead of the engineer, who was losing consciousness.

Flee whilst still possible!

But shame already ruled supreme. Extract the gold-filled Eyedropper from the suit pocket, undo the cap and, with a smile hovering on those wide lips, jump over to Scarface and plunge the pen into the back of his neck.

Crooked Nose roared and fell on his knees, releasing the old Yankee from his grasp. With one hand he reached for the Waterman protruding above his collar, with the other – for the revolver. Kick him on that hand – and the weapon flew in a high arc over the balustrade, landing on the embankment and immediately disappearing from sight.

Dragan, coughing and brushing his back against the wall, rose to his feet. He indicated with his eyes the body of the second policeman. Was he also armed? Pounce upon the corpse. A hard shape under the fabric – tug at the lapel, buttons shoot off – here the leather braces, the holster, the black butt. Take out the cold revolver. Dragan rattled something incomprehensible. Look around. Scarface was running away.

His route into the gallery was barred, whilst the door into the next carriage beyond the long platform and shock-absorbing coupling lacked even a handle, being locked from the inside – this was already the service van, and beyond it were only the tender and engine – so what was left to the killer? He climbed onto the balustrade, sculpted here in the form of a vine, seized the edge of the roof and crawled onto it with a single thrust of his legs, with monkey-like dexterity, despite the blood pouring down the back of his neck and collar of his shirt; one, two seconds passed when the re-soled underside of his shoe was still visible against the azure backdrop of sky – and Scarface was gone.

Shove the long-barrel revolver into the belt, under the waistcoat and jacket. Leap onto the balustrade in Scarface's tracks. When shoulder and face emerged above the tunnel chiselled out of the air by the locomotive, they were hit by a cold wind, as the loose-fitting suit billowed in the blast. Feel the swift tugs of tiny hands, soft fingers ruffling the hair and pulling on the ears – wind, the force of speed with which the massive Express strikes the air. Trees and fields flashed by in blurred streaks, no longer even impressionistic clouds of colour, but the impression itself of the image and movement within the image, the brightly coloured light of a summer idyll. Only the sky above the roof, now successfully ascended, only the sky was peaceful, motionless, photographically sharp.

He could have been standing there, lying in wait just above the brink, to kick the temples of the first fool to poke up his head – a thought that had not occurred. But he was not standing there, not lying in wait. Climb onto the roof, creeping like a lizard, chest pressed onto the filthy surface, arms splayed wide. Scarface was moving on all fours a few metres ahead. The wind had whipped his jacket over his head; the fellow fumbled with it till he had to stop and remove his arms – it flew off into the taiga, flapping above the left-behind carriages and green crowns of trees, a black flag, vestige of a raven's wing, a feather, a dark dot, until it vanished. Scarface gave a shout but it was impossible to make out his words in the boom of rushing air and roar of the speeding train, in the drawn-out wheeze of the steam engine. Shouting, he looked over his shoulder, as if he'd received a warning from somewhere in answer to that whimper. See then that Scarface had torn a piece of material from his shirt and bandaged his whole neck with it; but the nib must have gone deep, the temporary bandage was already soaked in blood, a red patch spreading down Scarface's back.

He shouted for a second time and flung himself back the way he had come, rotating on his knees – he saw not the revolver aimed at him, so this was his chance. But his left knee slipped on the greasy gunge covering the carriage roof and Crooked Nose slid onto his side, the impetus of his own movement spinning him around with his back to the edge; he tried to grab hold of the rivets, could not reach, and his shoes went over the margin of the roof, he flew faster and faster, legs lashing, mouth opening in comic inhaling-exhaling, like a butchered fish, a hungry fledgling – his knees gave way under him, and he fell.

Move cautiously towards the edge. Scarface was hanging on with both hands dug into the coldiron ferrules of a tall sash window. Did the passengers see him? The bandage unwound itself from his neck, wind bore away droplets of blood, his ripped shirt fluttered. See how the muscles of his arms tremble from effort, his fingers white, his face contorted in grimaces of pain.

He glanced up. Look him straight in the eye. Turn away? Watch him fall off and perish? Do something, do nothing – these are deeds and renunciations, but what lies before them, at their source? Still the beacon of shame is unextinguished. Reach out and offer the man a hand.

Lie afterwards on the back, gasping for air, head towards Asia, legs towards Europe, and watch how single clouds sail across the blue; in the blue, nothing changes but they. Well, from time to time, coils of grey smoke from the locomotive flit by on high. Once a bird flew past.

Scarface was gasping more heavily still.

'A cursed man. Punish him, O, God! Oy, I shall give up the ghost here.'

'So it seems.'

'Egh, and such a life, tphoo.'

'You shouldn't have raised a hand against the divine commandments, sin has finally rebounded.'

'You speak true, sir. But what can I do. A man serves, Tsar Batyushka commands.'

'The tsar ordered you to strangle the American? You don't say.'

'A-ah, the will of higher authority, whoever's there to profess it, first Lyednyaks, then Ottepyelniks, each his own threat and cry.'

'And that other – wasn't he from the Okhrana? From the prince perhaps?'

'Princes dine with swine. If that wagon hadn't left Saint Petersburg sealed – but now, it's all shit under the bridge.'

'Meaning – the American?'

'What American? Lightningbolt devil. Father in heaven, All ye Saints, it grips me already, khh.'

'Don't move.'

'Say me a blessing.'

'What, am I a priest to bless people?'

'Priest or no priest.'

'It was I after all who –'

'Always easier with a kind word. Well.'

'What's your name?'

'Vazoff, Yury Danilovitch, khh, mother Vasilisa, née Martchik, from Borisoff.'

'Yury, I believe you could have been a good man.'

'Yes, yes.' His shallow breathing quickened rapidly as he approached the finish. 'True.'

'No grace in me from God to bless you in His name according to what you are, no grace from people to bless you in their name according to what you did to them; my sole grace comes from your begging for this blessing, so I give it from a sincere heart: may you stand in such humility before the Lord. And I beg your forgiveness.'

'Khhr. Bozhe moy. They didn't let me. Yes.'

Turn the head to the left. His open eyes – already empty – lay a warm breath away. Wind had wiped the saliva from his parted lips. Yury died with hands clasped around his neck, in the same cross-choke with which he'd have strangled the elderly engineer.

White clouds scudded across the sky like blots of milk dropped in ink. The golden Eyedropper must have pierced an artery – not an artery, because the fellow would have bled to death instantly – but with every movement, with his every effort, the embedded nib, a fragment of nib – opened farther the wound, and so his heart gradually pumped the life out of Yury.

Skeins of ducks startled by the passage of the Express flew up from the forest; braids of smoke from the locomotive's high chimney wove from left and right, twisting in time to swerves in the track. A rare occurrence, but the train was moving directly east; whenever it swung into a bend, however, and leant at an angle, it was essential to grab the rivets, press down on the sun-baked metal sheet with arms outspread.

The corpse, instead, travelled on the roof unconstrained. Soon or later, it would slip off.

Imagine the crew appearing at once: Dragan will bring help, the okhranniks from second class come running, there'll be a great scandal and sensation, maybe the natchalnik will even stop the train. Wait for that jolt, wait for their shouts and exhortations. In vain. Reach inside the waistcoat pocket – the watch, crushed to bits, indicated an absurd hour. So, what next? Go back down and – and – glance at the suit, once white, now brownish-grey with streaks of black slime, a ripped sleeve, soaked to boot in Yury's blood. And in such a suit, how can a snot-nosed tatterdemalion brave those people? Count! It's a kind of scourge. *Nothing happens without a moral.* A plague on all your heads!

Remove from the finger, swearing and biting the lips, the signet ring with the Korab coat of arms set in bloodstone – it slides smoothly over the layer of slippery filth – and fling it away. Bouncing up and down, it rolled along the roof of the carriage.

But this removal was but an empty gesture; breaking free was not so easy. For why not deny it at the very beginning? Why were White-Gessling and Frau Blutfeld not put right? Why was the confabulation allowed to escalate till it became impossible to straighten? There is no escaping from shame, except into other shame. Cower even here, on the roof of the Trans-Siberian Express speeding through the taiga, in the sole company of a corpse, under the great blue firmament and high Sun – cower even here, with knees pulled up under the chin, forehead lowered, arms tightly intertwined, festering in dry sobs; shake to the rhythm of the train and despite it, in unstoppable shudders – of shame.

Till the train began to slow, and lights and columns of smoke appeared in the distance ahead of the engine, against the backdrop of a low line of hills looming on the horizon – the next station on the Transsib, Svetcha or Kotelnitch; there's nothing to wait for, now or later, it's all the same, time to go back down, to return to the compartment.

Descend carefully to the balustrade and jump onto the observation platform. No trace of the remains of the second okhrannik. Well, there was a trace: a few drops of blood. Had he perhaps survived? Take off the jacket, turn it inside-out and place it folded over the forearm below the breastbone – it should conceal the dirtiest fragments of shirt, waistcoat and trousers. Smooth the hair dishevelled by the wind (greasy filth on the fingers instead of brilliantine). The hands are still shaking whilst the head, treacherously light, sways like a kite on the breeze. Calm down, calm down, calm down. One more deep breath... The doorhandle.

There was no one in the gallery. Approach the door to the carriage with the fireplace; place an ear against it. A voice, voices, a woman's voice, men's voices. Maybe wait here? They will leave eventually.

Either that or they'll enter the gallery. And discover the man lurking in the corner. There's no escape.

Yank open the double doors and step inside.

Black gloom fell on the eyes, coal tar streamed neath the eyelids. In the uniform blackness, distorted glintzen of several persons and several pieces of furniture, a round table, chairs, were pulsating on the carriage walls and ceiling. The silhouette nearest the table cast in unlicht – the figure of a woman – was pointing at the opposite wall with straightened arm. On the wall danced the glintz of a tall man. Unlicht suffused everyone and everything, blurring sharp edges, drowning forms in murk and flattening solid bodies. The only certainty came from the glintzen themselves: volatile, vibrating, deformed by being cast upon uneven surfaces – yet quantifiable, visible to the human eye. The man by the wall raised his hand, most likely adjusting his spectacles. The woman moved her hand over the table, projecting onto the ceiling a dazzling radiance that blinded them all for a moment, until they instinctively jerked back and averted their heads, which in turn emboldened their glintzen all the more, and for a moment the refulgent silhouettes leapt over the walls, flapping their limbs like crippled angels. A wave of whispers surged around the room in Russian, German and French.

'He!' cried Princess Blutskaya. 'He will tell us what it was!'

'*Une créature de la vérité*,' said Jules Verousse, moving away from the wall and expanding to enormous size in his glintz like a white blemish on an instantly developed photograph. 'Monster enthrones *die Dunkelheitmat* over over over machines.'

Retreat towards the gallery. Try to leave unobserved, but the back collides with the double doors, arm holding the jacket drops, and from under the unbuttoned waistcoat a beam of cold fire bursts into the room, as if a dragon hidden in the guts were belching forth a sulphurous flame through the belly button. Stare in terror at the filthy waistcoat. Stretch out the hand – it enters the fire as into a soft stream of water; brilliant light irradiates the fingers, illuminates the nails, skin, tendons and muscles, blood vessels – the hand hangs in it like in orange jelly, casting pink afterglows across half the room. Recalling those devotional pictures where Christ opens his breast and golden rays blaze in solid shafts out of his pierced heart. All participants of the séance froze, women and men, sitting, standing, around the table, by the walls, truly blinded now, pressing together their eyelids, shielding their faces: long-sleeved dresses with ruches, guipure lace and high necklines neath lockets and cameos; stiff shirt collars, dress collars turned down onto steep yokes, tightly wound cravats, pleated and smooth, velvet and foulard; silk neck-ties, batiste jabots and rabats, cockades and tulles, gold, silver and amber cufflinks, coral cigarette holders and ivory pipes, white shirt-cuffs, white plastrons framed by the dark lapels of frock coats and jackets of woollen deux-pièces and three-piece tailcoat suits with the triangles of folded handkerchiefs in the breast pocket; the gleam of watch chains, gleam of tortoiseshell lorgnons, monocles and pince-nez fastened to those stiff collars by long chains – a collective portrait of Europeans *Anno Domini* 1924 scorched beneath the eyelids as in the flash of a magnesium bulb. Someone shouted, someone fell over, a young lady fainted, slumping limply on her chair. Stretch the irradiated hand deep into the fire, covering again the waistcoat with the jacket. The fingers tightened their grip on the butt of the revolver.

Darkness was not restored for long – the princess immediately snuffed out the blackwicke and evening sunlight poured into the carriage.

Raise the head.

All were watching.

Smile.

On pens and revolvers

It was cold to the touch, covered in pearly dew and in stronger light shimmered along its curvatures and edges in every colour of the rainbow – the simplest way to recognise coldiron metals. Rotate it in the hands with exaggerated caution: no firearm had ever landed in these hands before. It was light, which was the first surprise. Wash hastily in the compartment basin (the time for bathroom expeditions will come in a few hours when others have fallen asleep) but even so, fingerprints remain on the smooth steel. Despite the rainbow-coloured glints and afterimages, the coldiron itself was uniformly black – but polished to such mirror-like purity, it was possible to count the papillary lines of the thumb when it rested for a moment on the cock. The cock was shaped like a scorpion with long curved tail raised to sting; precisely this tail had to be pulled back and released, and the scorpion would hit the primer with locked pincers. However, the whole revolver looked as if designed by a French devotee of Art Nouveau, an expensive bauble made to individual order; this was the second surprise. The asymmetrical hilt proved to be the spiral coil of a snake, which at the end, at the bottom, opened its maw, revealing a few fangs and a curled-up tongue – between these fangs and the tongue, it was possible to thread a leather strap or suspend a steel ring. The trigger guard consisted of flower stalks whose calyces led directly into the chambers of the cylinder. There were five chambers. The cylinder did not shift sideways – in order to load it, the revolver had to be broken in two. Look inside the chambers, extract and reinsert the cartridges: matte-black finish with blunt, almost flat tips. Switch on a lamp and examine them under the light bulb. Around the base of every bullet ran a delicate engraving consisting of three Russian letters: П. Р. М., as well as a three-digit number: 156, 157, 159, 160, 163. Examine more closely the revolver itself. The long barrel had been cast in the shape of a bony reptile, some kind of lizard-like creature with spikey comb that piled up along the length of its spine, only to explode above the back of its neck into a protuberance akin to a slanting horn – this was the bead. The lizard had no eyes, but its wide-open gob – the muzzle of the long barrel – displayed a complete set of sharp teeth – painstakingly honed on the edge of the barrel, fang after fang. On its belly was engraved a series of letters composing a single word:

Гроссмейстеръ

Fold away the Grossmeister, wrap it in a dirty towel and hide it at the bottom of a valise.

But what if they should break in again and search the compartment? Hesitate. There's no alternative; it must always be kept on the person.

And then it will burst again into cold fire at the least expected moment…

Three times they knocked on the door of the compartment; the provodnik knocked a fourth, announcing the supper hour. Admit no one. Leave the key turned in the lock, so that the provodnik can't open it with his own from the other side. Draw the curtains over the window, so that none can peer in at a station stop.

The knocking passengers protested effusively, urging the opening of the door – first, naturally, was Frau Blutfeld, then Miss Muklanowicz, then Councillor Dushin. The latter, on leaving, thrust a visiting card under the door with a compartment number inscribed on the back. Gertrud Blutfeld was interested above all in material for gossip, Jelena came in an awkward attempt to console, but Councillor Dushin – Dushin did not appear in his own name but in the name of Princess Blutskaya, who clearly demanded an explanation from the intruder who had sabotaged her séance. No one inquired, on the other hand, about the dead or vanished functionaries of the Okhrana.

Calculate the time of day according to the timetable of the Transsib as recorded in the *Putevoditel*, since the watch no longer worked. The train had stopped at Vyatka, so it must be gone ten in the evening.

At roughly half past ten, Engineer Dragan knocked on the door.

'You are there, sir,' he said in German devoid of any trace of accent. 'You can hear me. You saved my life. I looked out for you at supper. Please open up. I'm not going to stand out here.'

Open the door a crack. He gave it a shove and stepped inside the compartment. Move aside – he was taller by at least ten centimetres, forcing a craning of the neck. The distance at which a man positions himself in relation to another depends not on bulk or height, but on the angle at which they size each other up. Children and women show greater tolerance; whereas men constantly seek a better position, like those gunslingers in cinema Westerns. The science of the soul, should it arise, will arise on the basis of stereometry.

He shut the door behind him, then extracted from an inner pocket of his jacket the broken Waterman pen.

'Please.'

He was deadly serious, no muscle twitched on his face; his gesture nevertheless bore a kind of ceremonial formality. To accept or not accept, either way, it will have a significance greater than that which can be expressed in language of the second kind. Dragan waited with proffered arm.

'Thank you.'

Sit down on the made-up bed, rotating the crippled Eyedropper in dirty fingers. The absurdity of the situation was in some way reassuring. It was true, the man's life had been saved. He is grateful, has to be grateful, has a debt of gratitude.

How… embarrassing it is.

Raise the eyes to look at the American, only to lower them immediately – he was standing and peering down, swaying gently to the rhythm of the train, in his impeccable double-breasted suit of ashen hue with wide white scarf wrapped around his neck, upright, morbidly thin, eyes glowing like hot coals under the brow ridges. He'll incline his head and they'll burn brighter, suddenly almost grey-blue.

Mutter under the breath: 'It's taken in blood.'

He heard.

'Pen beats sword,' he laughed huskily. 'Where is it?'

'What?'

'You took it from Mikhail. Everyone in the train is talking about *the angel in unlicht*.'

'I own no angelic blade. What's become of Mikhail's body?'

'My dear sir, you saved my life, I'm not asking what happened later on the roof.'

The shadow of this man was once again performing strange antics, swelling and subsiding, as if someone were alternately inflating it and then sucking it out from behind Dragan; the line between shadow and light kept arching and vibrating.

Bite into the thumbnail.

'You work for the Russo-American Company. Maybe it's about the Alaskan Line. The Russian competitors hired a saboteur; it was for your protection that those three policemen caught up with us last night. They're not sitting in second class, not all of them – at least one is travelling in the service van behind the tender. That's where they carried Mikhail's body; they did not drag it after all through the gallery and fireplace room, nor did they throw it off the train. Why were you walking on that observation platform, sir, knowing you were in danger? It was an ambush; Mikhail had laid a trap for Yury. Were they both from the Okhrana? Lyednyaks and Ottepyelniks support different Siberian companies, and the Ottepyelniks generally oppose Sibirkhozheto; you were caught between hammer and anvil. But Yury had been travelling in Deluxe from Saint Petersburg; warning must have come about someone completely different. Now you are afraid, sir, because you are left without Mikhail, without protection in first class. You don't know who it is.'

He moved the tabouret from the escritoire and sat down. Took out his cigarettes and lit up. His gaze ran almost parallel to the floor. Lift the eyes, look him directly in the eye. The compartment despite everything was narrow and confined – were Dragan to lean a little farther forward, were he to rest his hands on his knees, it would have been possible to swallow the smoke straight from his lungs. That corner, that distance… confessor and confessant, lawyer and accused, a young lady's father and the bachelor seeking her hand, master and pupil.

He muttered something to himself in his husky tongue, glanced around the compartment. Show him the ashtray. He was old; from his silhouette and movements, he appeared not so, yet he could have been the peer of Prince Blutsky.

'That revolver,' he said after a while, 'is worth more than its weight in gold. I understand. You are a poor man. Forgive me, I have no wish to offend you, sir. You are a poor man taking advantage of the chance to rub shoulders with high society, to enter a better world, and then what – the unfortunate incident with His Highness. Allow me to suggest a ransom for the trophy. You shall name the price, sir. I beg you, no offence. You have no idea what you have taken into your hands, Mr… Gerosłaski.'

'Gierosławski.'

'Gierosławski. Yes?'

'Yes. Benedykt Gierosławski.'

He smiled.

'What, in the end, are the real circumstances of your birth?'

'*Moi, je suis mon ancêtre.*'

'Ah! If only someone could say that of himself honestly! Even Frankenstein's monster... You have read Mary Shelley? Don't you find it fascinating how in literature electrical force always –'

'It's coldiron, some sort of coldiron coolbond. Bullets made of tungetitum. I had no idea they manufactured such weapons.'

'They do not manufacture them.'

'And what for? Whatever could you kill with tungetitum bullets that you couldn't kill any other way? Since it is so expensive.'

Dragan gestured encouragingly with his white-gloved hand.

Bite the nail off a second finger.

'It is not a weapon against people. It is a weapon against gleissen.'

'Aha?'

'I'm wondering... Drat, what a shame I read no more about it. What properties does tungetitum possess at high temperatures, under high pressure? That coldiron coolbond... If only I hadn't covered up that fulminating glare –'

'With what? Your hand, your clothes? It cannot be covered up. I have a dozen patents for tungetitum lighting systems – at these prices, however, exceptionally impractical – I know what I'm saying.'

'What do you mean: cannot be covered up? After all –'

'Dammit, think, young man!' barked Dragan, whereupon he crossed one leg over the other and pulled on his cigarette.

Remember examinations at the university and that typical irritation of professors restraining themselves with a last vestige of willpower from exploding before the student's obtuseness, crying out to heaven for vengeance – so the student finds it all the harder to collect his thoughts – so they become all the more irritated – so the student burns alive and dreams only of vanishing from their sight – so they send him packing with a resigned wave of the hand. He walks away from the firing squad, and returns to life and reason.

Now he can demonstrate his genius and knowledge! He cannot, for no one asks.

In the same way, the good sapper is not the one who manages to dismantle a model of a landmine, but the one who disarms real mines that threaten to blow him in the air – so, too, the good student is not the one who parades his knowledge and skills, but the one who parades them before the harshest examiners.

It seemed initially, and for a long time, that this was a generalisation merely serving to justify college loafers; then it became clear that such division runs between people in general, in any sphere. How many people are there who cope perfectly with any fake in life, yet when it comes to attempts on their real life – their hands tremble? Top students in meaningless fields of learning, excelling in answers to questions that were not asked, become omniscient a moment later. Were they only allowed to take the exam one more time, given one more mine to disarm, one more life…!

'It's a reaction induced by unlicht, yes? I covered over the source of the unlicht and the reaction stopped.'

'Coldiron nickel with a peculiar bond symmetry. It reacts to unlicht like pure tungetitum. In the braids of blackwickes, carbon compounds of tungetitum are burned, but in cheaper blackwickes, even frozen-through carbon itself. In turn, certain oxidation reactions of cryocarbon isotopes –'

'For what purpose had Mikhail that weapon? Has some gleiss in disguise sneaked aboard the Express?' Chortle.

Lost in thought, Dragan examined the stub of his cigarette.

'I do not work for the Russo-American Company. It is not about the Alaska Line. I am not involved in overland engineering.'

'You're not an engineer?'

He smiled faintly.

'I studied it, you know, but somehow never obtained a degree in engineering. Doctorates – why, of course.'

'It's not about industrial sabotage? So why do they want to kill you?'

'I shan't be surprised should it transpire that Pobedonostseff is paying a million roubles for my head. Have you heard, sir, that the son-in-law of the third shareholder of Sibirkhozheto is travelling with us? They see in it some kind of safeguard… Pyotr keeps an eye on Pavel, who keeps an eye on Jan, who hold a razor to Pyotr's throat. Those two okhranniks – poor bastards – to how many masters must they remain loyal at one and the same time? Well, it's torn them to shreds like a horse pulling in four directions. And now too – whom have they sent in their panic? Not obvious gendarmes, but retired tchinovniks of the Third Department of His Imperial Exaltedness's Own Chancery, portly pen pushers, who – just imagine – are today agents of the Okhrana, bah, they even have papers to prove it!' He put out his cigarette. 'I ought not to burden you with all this, Mr Gieroszewski, or whatever you wish to call yourself, young man. Since you won't return the revolver – though what use is it to you, if not to sell? – too bad, you won't. I implore you, however, to be on your guard. You are quite right to suppose that there's something to fear. With that entry before the princess, you declared yourself to the whole train, they'll take you for God knows whom; what could be simpler than pushing a few roubles into the provodnik's hand, as I did, and discover on what ministerial papers you're travelling?'

He rose to his feet.

'If I could somehow in future... The provodnik also told me that you're going as far as Irkutsk, is that true? Second carriage, compartment number eight, that is letter H. Please don't hesitate, I shan't forget what you did.'

'My name is Benedykt Gierosławski, Dragan, sir.'

'A curious coincidence, for I too have been forced to hide temporarily behind a false identity. Mm-hmm, no longer important, since we are already en route. Remember the words of the great Goethe. "Travelling is like gambling, always accompanied by winning or losing, and usually when least expected." He adjusted his gloves. 'My name is not Dragan; I come from a zadruga named Draganic, hence the pseudonym. I am an American citizen, but was born a Serb, in Smiljan, Croatia. My name may have reached your ears: I am Nikola Tesla.'

He bowed stiffly and went.

At midnight the Trans-Siberian Express completed the nine-hundred-and-seventieth kilometre of the Magistral. The first day of the journey was ended.

CHAPTER THE THIRD

On two-valued, three-valued and valueless logic, as well as on the logic of women

'For pity's sake, Benedykt, sir, you cannot not eat anything at all!'

'*Qui dort dîne*. And besides, I can pay them to bring what's left of breakfast.'

'Please be reasonable! Open the door.'

'I'm not yet up.'

'Sleeping so much is unhealthy; melancholy gets the better of you, apathy chokes and migraines torment.'

'Do you intend, miss, to shout through the door for long?'

'The wall's not much thicker.'

'You can't let it rest, can you! Has your esteemed aunt not taught you it's improper to accost strange men?'

'Am I to summon my aunt? Auntie!'

'One moment!'

Miss Jelena Muklanowicz: dressed in white silk blouse, lace cuffs spilling over her hands, raven-black velvet choker, high corset constricting her body; in narrow beige skirt under which only the tips of her leather slippers were visible, black hair gathered tightly in a bun and pierced by two silver-headed pins. Dark eyes, pale skin, made whiter still by powder – were it not for the gloss on her lips, the devushka would have seemed drained of all blood and colour. She sat down at the escritoire, rotating her legs to the left so that the soft material flowed from her hips in a single continuous wave. Hands clasped on lap.

Rise not to greet her. Sit on the bed covered by its counterpane, next to the window, in smoking jacket thrown over the shirt.

Miss Muklanowicz looked like a governess reprimanding an unruly six-year-old.

Turn the eyes towards the rain-drenched landscape beyond the window.

'The door has closed behind you, whatever will people think?'

'My God!' Jelena whispered in a voice *à la* Frau Blutfeld. 'A scandal!' She clapped her hands in jubilation. 'Yes!'

Rest the temple against the cool pane.

'I surrender.'

She smacked her lips disapprovingly.

'For a start, the young gentleman could remove his hands from his pockets.'

Remove them.

'But how come… Agh.' At last, she was disconcerted – but only momentarily, since she at once assumed a new air. 'Not very nice. Papa never dipped the little boy's fingers in vinegar? If the young gentleman is that hungry, then all the more reason to eat breakfast – and not his own fingers.'

This tone of hers… Either she had raised younger brothers or really had worked as a governess. But governesses are not in the habit of travelling first-class in the Transsib.

'It's not funny.' Knock the head against the pane, once, twice, harder. 'You have found some diversion, miss, to pass the journey-time, but as for me –'

'How can you! Here I am agonising and making no mean laughing stock of myself in order to entice you back to the world, prompted by Christian compassion…' But now she was smiling again and the imp bouncing in her pupils and in the quivering corner of her lip – '…and you dare to say such things, sir!'

Clearly, she expected a rejoinder proffered in a flippant tone – then she would laugh out loud, and it was already felt in her voice just how infectious that laughter might be, how irresistible; so, she would laugh out loud and then everything would drift down a plainly demarcated track – towards greater naturalness, sincerity, openness. This is how people get to know one another, how strangers become friends; from such material, it's easy to build bridges linking shores of alien worlds. And Miss Muklanowicz is an engineer exceptionally adept at erecting interpersonal bridges; it was obvious from the first meeting, the few phrases hurriedly exchanged in the narrow passageway – and at once there were jokes, barbed cordialities. That she's a compatriot – is of no great consequence. In fact, what she says is also of no great consequence, nor in what language she says it. She'll burst out laughing – it's enough. Had she been encountered at home on a Warsaw street, naturally, it could not happen so quickly and simply, but – this is the Trans-Siberian Express, travelling is a magic time, hours stretch into days, days into months. She will burst out laughing.

No. Avert the face towards the windowpane. Maybe she'll go away. The silence grew protracted, silence, meaning the hypnotic clatter of the train, took-took-took-TOOK. Stare at Jelena's transparent visage in the window, suspended against a backdrop of wooded hills and rain-laden clouds; it drifted across the landscape like a reflection over a watery surface, the pale ghost of a pale girl. A black lock, escaped from her coiffure, she tucked behind her ear, lifting to her face the hand in its cloud of white lace; even this gesture invited conversation. Whenever Jelena turned her head, a dark-red star flashed on the velvet choker – a ruby? Black pearls sparkled in the silver settings of tiny earrings. Her features were superimposed onto a distant memory of – a cousin? neighbours' daughter from Wilkówka? Too-large eyes, too-sharp a nose, beauty born of imperfection, underlined further by her black-and-white maquillage; hard to tear away the eyes, hard to forget.

She glanced around the compartment, seeking an outlet for her impatient energy, an excuse to defuse the situation. Her eyes alighted upon the papers scattered on the tabletop.

'What's this? a code?'

Spring to the feet, leap towards the escritoire.

'A-ah, no.' Burst into laughter, bundle the typescripts and manuscripts into the folder. 'Not a code; just a game of mathematical logic.'

'Oh?'

Glance at her suspiciously.

'Mathematics interests you, miss?'

She assumed an offended air.

'May I not take interest in something I know not? Isn't any healthy mind most intrigued by the very things it has not yet had a chance to confront, things as yet inconceivable, mysterious and exotic – as opposed to what is known and already tedious? Why so surprised, Benedykt, sir?' She reached for one of the sheets. 'Tell me, this for example, what's it all about?'

'Oh. That's something that cannot be… Well, all right, but please don't look like that.'

My God, is there any more banal conversational ploy? A man should be allowed to wax lyrical about his work, his hobbies, allowed to impress the salons; let him believe the woman really is interested and listening attentively; let the peacock spread his tail. The principle, after all, was well attested.

And yet:

'Logic, mm-hmm, logic deals with the rules of reasoning, with the correctness of methods for drawing conclusions, you really want to hear about this, miss?'

'When people ask what you do, what say you?'

'That I somehow make ends meet.'

She raised her eyebrows.

'So all right.' Sit down opposite Miss Muklanowicz, lay the folder on the knees, smooth out the papers. 'I am working on the logic of propositions. Every statement has some logical value. Value – in relation to truth. But not everything we say is a proposition in the logical sense. Questions, for example, are not propositions; nor are commands, nor utterances lacking a subject, nor predicates otherwise semantically distorted. The bambarara bimbers the bomberick. Is that true or false? Do you understand?'

'Yes, yes.'

'Since Antiquity, since Aristotle, Classical two-valued logic has been accepted as valid. Called two-valued because it operates with two values: truth and falsehood. Every statement is either true or false. Also from Aristotle come several fundamental principles of logic, of which you may have heard. The principle of non-contradiction, which claims that the same statement cannot at one and the same time be true and false. We are talking and we are not talking. I am alive and I am not alive. I am a man and I am not a man. Obvious absurdities. Also, there is the principle of excluded middle – that for any statement there are only two possibilities: either the statement is true or it is its negation. It is raining or it is not raining. It is day or it is not day. We are travelling by train or we are not travelling by train.

'Already in Antiquity, people polemicised with Aristotle's principles of logic.' Gather momentum. 'From Cicero, we know of the dispute between Chrysippus and Diodorus over the validity of the divinations of the augurs or of the Chaldean soothsayers. Amongst the Stoics, there were hardened determinists and believers in two-valency, *omnem enuntiationem aut veram, aut falsam esse.* Though Aristotle himself, in *De interpretatione*, had his moments of doubt, when he considered, for example, the sea battle which may but does not have to take place tomorrow. Later it flashed through mediaeval scholasticism; Paul of Venice, in his *Logica Magna*, thrust all those future sea battles into the category of "undecidable" propositions, *insolubilia.* But a few years ago, Doctor Kotarbiński raised the problem afresh, proposing, instead of two-valued logic, a three-valued logic.

'And so, not all meaningful statements are true or false in their moment of utterance. "Every truth is eternal, but not every truth is immemorial." This means, Jelena,' gather momentum almost to the point of logorrhoea, 'that when some event occurs, the truth about it becomes fixed and whatever we assert about it will from then on be true or false; however, until the course of that event becomes a foregone conclusion, any assertions about it are neither true nor false. Such statements possess a different logical value, they are precisely "undecided". Will we reach Irkutsk on time? Whatever I say about it now can have nothing whatsoever to do with truth or falsehood.'

'Have I understood it right: the old logic is to affect only the past, yes?'

'More or less. On this point I differ from Kotarbiński. I lack that certainty. There are three questions we have to answer:

'Are the laws of logic sewn into reality itself – like the warp in fabric, the rhythm in a melody, the colour in light – or do we also create them for ourselves as a special kind of language for telling about the world? Would they therefore be different if we spoke differently, thought differently, came from a different culture, a different History, participated in the world through different bodies, received the world through different senses? Would they be different for us, were we not people? Are they therefore different for gleissen?

'Is there one general truth to which every logic relates, truth as such, that is, an objective, absolute measure of the correctness of all judgements – or do we have only incomplete approximations, based on what we know, what we can recognise, being as we are, the way we're born? If, however, there is no objective and absolute truth, then we have no right to talk about any approximations to it: we can be closer to or farther away from a concrete point, at a distance calculated according to a concrete scale – but we cannot be nearer or farther away from a place which does not exist or which remains undefined in space. Therefore, either we have been given objective truth, irrespective of who recognises it, or there is no truth or falsehood at all in the sense in which everyone makes use of these words.

'And finally: what argument lies behind giving special status to events of the past, so that two-valued logic is applied to them, but not to future events? The latter remain undefined; the less predetermined they are, and the farther from our direct experience, all the more so. Why do we not apply an analogous principle of three-valuedness to things of the past? Isn't this merely a prejudice arising from human nature – because a human being remembers the past, but only imagines, only foresees, the future? Should not two-valued logic be valid therefore only in relation to our most directly given present?'

Miss Muklanowicz listened with great attention, chest out, forehead up, eyes wide open; she played very well, it has to be admitted, the role of interestedness.

'I don't think I fully understand, however, help me please, Benedykt. How would that differ from acknowledging that we simply know not what happened in the past? Just as we know not what will happen in future?'

'You are mistaken. "I know not what was happening in these forests a hundred thousand years ago" – either I know or I know not. If I say instead: "A hundred thousand years ago, fires were raging" – then irrespective of whether I know, or am guessing, or had a dream, or deduced the thing from geological strata, or – on the contrary – am convinced I am lying, the statement according to the logic of Aristotle and Kotarbiński is either true or false, full-stop.'

'But according to your logic… Half-truth, half-falsehood, one of the possibilities, yes? Where then is that region,' Miss Muklanowicz described a circle in the air, 'that region of certainty, in which logic – '

'Freezes? The present. Here and now. What we receive with our senses.'

'So not even yesterday? Have you no faith in your own memory?'

'Well, different people remember different versions of the same events… Naturally, regarding what happened yesterday, I can draw more definite conclusions. Kotarbiński wrote about a determined future: I swallow now some poison which will kill me without fail after one hour, and already in this moment I can genuinely state that tomorrow I shall no longer be alive. Similarly, I can state this or that about a past determined by the present. That if I am alive today, then I was also alive yesterday. Though perhaps we should use a different word for determinism directed against the current of time. But that is precisely how we deduce the existence of things lying outside our direct experience.' Encompass with a swift gesture the interior of the compartment, the train, the rainswept plain. 'Of what existed several years ago… we can be considerably less sure.'

Miss Jelena Muklanowicz pressed her nail to her red lips.

'So perhaps, in spite of everything, you are that count, eh?'

'O God!'

'That you are one-tenth him, mm-hmm?'

And she burst out laughing.

Stow away the folder of papers in the drawer of the escritoire.

Jelena extended her marble-white hand; the devushka's light touch rested on the sleeve of the smoking jacket, slid down the sleek material to the wrist; she had cool, dry skin.

'Come now, don't be angry, I beg you. Everything you said is truly fascinating. Word of honour! Only you take yourself so dreadfully seriously… Could you but see your face… And how you took to heart that whole affair with Prince Blutsky…! Do you ever smile? Please give me a smile. Come on! I am asking so nicely, Benedykt, sir!'

Bare the teeth.

'I'm as merry as the day is long.'

'Oh! Better already! I shall convert you yet, you'll see. And in case you were thinking –'

A knock on the compartment wall.

'Jelenka, time for your medicine!'

The devushka averted her eyes.

'Coming, Auntie!'

Bite the thumb.

'Eavesdropping, eh?' Inquire in a whisper.

Jelena shrugged her shoulders. She stood up; the train jumped on its tracks and she grasped hold of the golden snakes on the wardrobe doorknob. Instinctively stand up too.

She placed the index finger of her left hand on the shawl collar of the smoking jacket, at heart level.

'But now,' she began in a sterner tone, 'promise me you'll come to the dining car, eat breakfast like a normal human being, calmly smoke a cigarette afterwards in the smoking car to aid your digestion and –'

'Jelena, miss!' Bristle up.

'What? Well, what? I'm not leaving till you promise! You think I'm joking?'

And for greater effect she stamped her foot, noiselessly, admittedly, as the carpet dampened the blow of her slipper.

'And what are you laughing at now, huh? Now you laugh!'

Take her hand off the chest, raise it to the lips and skim it lightly against them.

'I promise, Jelena, I promise.'

At that the blushes washed over her – bright red against the pallor of her complexion like frostnip blemishes.

She wrested away the hand, withdrew. Sudden shyness now prevented her from lifting her eyes; her gaze wandered over the green walls, the swirling pattern of the carpet, the gilded ornaments and fittings.

With every step of her retreat, however, her self-assurance returned. Standing already in the corridor, she held open the door for a moment and leaned back inside the compartment.

'And, of course, we shall see one another at dinner!' she announced briskly. 'You still have to tell me exactly what happened at Princess Blutskaya's séance! Without fail!'

And she went.

Ye-es. My Aunt Laurencja, who had suffered from a chronic blood disease and spent most of her days in the hospitals and spas of Italy and Switzerland, whenever she suddenly improved and rose from her couch for a few weeks at a time, would explode with similar emotional energy, simply inflicting herself on relatives, acquaintances and non-acquaintances with the naïveté and frankness typical of children, with innocent curiosity about people and the world. Illness polarises character, the more critical the illness, the stronger it polarises; one emerges deflated, crushed, drained in body and soul, or, alternatively, with a great appetite for life, an eternally unsatisfied hunger for new impressions.

Don the grey suit, comb the hair, glance again in the mirror, check again the facial growth... but the longer this goes on, the greater the effort required to finally cross the threshold; the only salvation is in automatic reflexes and mindless impertinence – doorknob, key, lock, head up, onward march! So long as it's without smiling.

Find only two passengers still in the dining car; sit in the opposite corner. With impenetrable mien, the steward proffered the menu. Servants' faces always have a similar expression, masks of ambiguous indifference: whatever you seek in them, whatever you hope or fear to see in them – is what you will see. Glance not at the waiter when ordering. Those other two had left. Somewhere in the carriage a window was ajar and the dining car filled with the scent of rain, a cool damp hung in the air. Crocks and cutlery, porcelain and metal, glass and silver jingled in the silence (in the silence: that is, against the heavy ticking metronome of the train). The chief steward stood in the galley doorway, erect, napkin draped over his arm, eyes fixed on the far distance. He watched not, yet saw. Eat hurriedly, swallowing the unchewed mouthfuls. It was Sunday, the menu featured seven different English puddings described in four languages. Eating can be even faster.

Stop for a moment in the passageway to the saloon car. What madness to wittingly choose the path of torment. And for what, for nothing. The only thing that had to be done was to reach Irkutsk. As to promises made with smiling eyes – forget the promises. After all, it makes no sense. One step and they'll all gawp, as if at a two-headed calf. Enter the saloon.

The men looked up, the conversation died down. Approach the steward, request a light. Stare out of the window, taking the first drag; stare at the skylight, exhaling the first smoke. Gradually, they returned to their conversations. Wind bent the branches of spruce and pine, chased dark clouds across the sky; above the hills, white sunlight glinted between celestial rain-streaks, the electric fire of the gods, as the Express raced towards a rainbow. Was it safe now to turn from the window? Turn around.

The door to the billiard room was propped open. Chairs had been moved up to the large table, four men were playing cards. Banknotes lay strewn on the immaculate green; at the table edge stood teacups and shot glasses; ashtrays and spittoons had been shoved underneath. Doctor Konyeshin was shuffling the cards; beside him, with similar painstakingness, a bald southerner was trimming a fat cigar, sticking out his dark tongue from behind crooked teeth. Captain Privyezhensky was gathering to himself a pile of money and raised his eyes. Answer his glance without a smile.

Privyezhensky took his pipe from his mouth, squinted mockingly, scowled.

One of the chairs was empty. He tapped a ball-pocket with the stem of his pipe.

Draw out the bumazhnik and join the game.

On what cannot be thought

Most of our actions we are able to explain in the language of the second kind: we are able to articulate clearly and intelligibly why we behaved in such and such a fashion. Even when our interlocutor agrees not with the explanation, he still *understands* it.

There are acts, however – considerably fewer – which we are incapable of recounting to another person. We alone understand them, language of the first kind alone can embrace them; but language of the first kind consists not in words, is not bound by syntax corresponding to the grammar of the speech of men. When we embark then, despite everything, on an attempt at confession – in the confessional, in the arms of a lover, on our deathbed, before the high court – nothing emerges from our mouths but illogical gibberish, to which we hearken ourselves in helpless wonderment.

And finally, there are also those acts – the least frequent – which we cannot explain in the language of the first kind, even to ourselves.

We are able to imagine them (for we imagine the most absurd things, especially *post factum*), but we cannot account for them in the way that every action and every word of the characters in a play or book is accounted for by the logic of the sequence of events: in a given scene, the hero does this or that for this or that reason, because he is such and such a man.

But in this, life differs from accounts of life – in other words, from reflections of life distorted by the language of the second kind – because first of all there is truth, and only afterwards does it happen to be told.

Hence there are acts whose motives, causes, underlying emotions and thoughts we have no way of describing, even to ourselves.

If, however, a single rule exists which governs the behaviour of all people, then it's the Rule of Lesser Shame. We may work consciously towards personal suffering, even towards our own death – but no one works towards their own greater shame. Just as water flowing over an uneven surface always finds the lowest points, just as warmth escapes from the body, so too man is driven in any situation towards the lesser shame.

Sometimes, shame distanced in time, as a result of this distance, appears not to be so painful – this is how laziness is born – but who in his right mind will choose, from two shames threatening him directly, the greater? Know not the reasons for such a choice; the thoughts and feelings lying behind it cannot possibly be imagined. An impossibility just as fundamental as the Sun appearing in the night sky, or a married bachelor.

And yet –

Sitting in the attic at Zbyszek's place. On the table twenty-four roubles; for the first time, the play was for money, whose loss could have a real influence on life's course. The cards are bad, the rest of the savings are in the pocket; the right thing to do is abandon, give the excuse of the late hour, and leave, it's so obvious, so undoubtedly sensible and right – see it being done, hear what's said to them, hear them muttering in response their half-conscious farewells... Draw out the last diengi and stake all on the losing card.

Or:

Julia gesticulating hysterically and pulling angry faces from behind her father's back, who momentarily contained his fury and stood in the doorway with arms widespread: please, tell me why. So, open the mouth, in order to spit out the greatest shame – at whom, at Julia, at him, at everyone – it will gush forth like hot sputum, stick to their faces, clothes, glue together their hair, eyelids – listen to me carefully, sir – whilst Julia silently spells out with her lips: say it not, say it not, say it not – but the tongue had already torn itself from the palette; already the curse had been uttered. Her father turns pale, staggers, looks around at his daughter, but his dear little daughter had turned on her heels and fled deep into the house, slamming doors behind her, never to be seen again. The final image of Julia: her face covered in red blotches like burn scars, eyes dilated, eyes full of cold desperation. Shame struck like a poisoned arrow.

Or:

The Kind Prince sits down at his table, one hundred and twenty roubles in the pot, Kiwajs and Modrzykowski are writing out promissory notes; pairs in the hand again even, a round best missed unbid, as well as debts already so large, it'll mean taking credit from the prince for the umpteenth time and grovelling before the shylocks – so the intention is there, the thought and the will to throw down the cards and stand up from the game, but instead of that: 'Up the stakes.' And then, not the least surprise when the money for rent disappears, money for medicaments, money for life. Even the heart beats no faster. This time too there was no hope of victory. So why play?

They say: habit. Habit, or the persistent repetition of behaviours – yet how to ask in language of the second kind about what lies behind those behaviours? Here it breaks down completely; the questions remain and indicative sentences no longer make sense.

Nor is the language of the first kind equal to the task: *we know not why we do what we do.*

Deeds are not our deeds. Words not our words. The game is played, but there is no 'I' that plays.

The thought: 'I am' – means not that someone exists, who thinks he 'is'; it means only that a thought has been thought about existence.

Thoughts are thought, the body is seen, touched, the work of its dank mechanisms heard; the external world, objects belonging to this world, animate and inanimate – are seen, heard, touched, smelled, tasted, but what additional sense might register the existence of that supposed 'I'?

There is no such sense. Little children speak of themselves in the third person, only the conventions of the speech of men force them into the role of 'I'. And with time, grasping this most primal truth becomes more and more difficult – since these are things no longer thinkable.

On the heroes of hazard and the speed of the Ice

'Four.'
    'Four.'
        'Ditto.'
'Mine's eight.'
'Stick.'
'I'm good.'
'Anyone upping the stakes?'
'Eight.'
'Mr Fessar?'
'Nothing.'
'Captain.'
'Mm-hmm.'
'Benedykt?'
'Checking, checking.'
'Burned by the four.'
'Ice off the five.'
'Well, I beg to be excused! With two fiery queens in my hand, and twice in succession! How did you deal these cards, dear God!'
'Hee-hee, Gospodin Tchushyn shall fritter away his entire capital before setting eyes on his mines.'

'Don't fret over my mines, fret over your pocketbooks. We're upping the stakes to ten, agreed?'

Earlier, for a while, they had been playing whist and *vingt-et-un*, but for a few hours the gambling had been following the rules of blizzarder. Two others had joined the table for ten or so rounds; now only five remained again. People walked past, stopped, observed. The high sums in the kitty attracted attention. The stewards refreshed glasses, emptied ashtrays. Windows were opened and closed. Billiard balls rattled in the pockets as the train swung into a bend, braked or accelerated.

'What were they thinking of, putting a billiard table in a train?' wondered Ünal Tayyib Fessar. 'Whenever it seems I've grown used to this country and begun to understand it, I light upon something like this and am again racking my brains. King's laid down.'

'Ace down.'

'Nine down.'

'Gentlemen…!'

'I'm good.'

'Oho!'

'They must have built the whole carriage around the table.'

'Or lowered it through the roof. Second go.'

'Monumental idiocy encased in extravagant luxury.' Mutter under the breath.

'What's that you said?'

'The *grand seigneur* deigned to allude to our fatherland,' Captain Privyezhensky explained politely to the doctor. He could not refrain from sarcasm. Succeed for now in not answering him with gummy smile and beseeching glance – because not looking at him at all.

'Ace down.'

'But what hands you're dealing us, honestly… Seven down.'

'*Heureux au jeu, malheureux en amour,* as our journalist friend might say. Well, all right, but in truth – what's the point? Can there be anything more idiotic than a billiard table in a train?'

'Mm-hmm, we could create new rules.' Remark whilst selling a jack to the pot. 'There's chess and there's blizzarder.'

'What d'you have in mind?

'Billiards with, mm-hmm, an additional element of chance.'

'Man strikes, God carries the ball. Five down.'

'Ooh. All things in moderation, Doctor, including bluffs!'

'Tell that, Captain, to Aleksey Fyodorovitch.'

'Gospodin Tchushyn can afford a stupid bluff.'

Aleksey Tchushyn had inherited from an uncle (father-in-law, grandfather, some other relative or person affiliated by marriage) the majority shareholding in a company extracting coldiron, and was on his way to take possession of his unexpected fortune. Had he anything previously to do with mining? Any kind of business? Right now, during the journey, there was no way of verifying either way, nor did it much matter: Tchushyn was the man he presented himself to be to his fellow travellers. Dark-navy frock coat stretched over barrel-shaped torso like skin over a sausage; diamond-studded pin gleaming in black georgette necktie. The oldest of the players, he revealed great indecision with his cards and lack of coherent strategy; he would sell five, six cards in his hand, only to pass on the bidding. He wiped his high forehead with an enormous handkerchief and sighed deeply, shaking his head over the dealing. Wonder how much of this theatricality is natural to Tchushyn, and how much results from his belief that this is how an easy-going rich man ought to behave during a game of cards. He drank no coffee or tea, drank no vodka – asked instead for shampanskoye. Before dealing, he would wipe his chubby palms for a long time; the cards stuck to his fingers.

Our way of behaving during gambling games – and here, in fact, the size of stake is of no consequence if we genuinely engage in the play – betrays things about ourselves that we would otherwise never reveal. It's not a question solely of strong nerves; a man may have nerves of steel yet flounder in desperate bluffing. You won't tell a hero from a coward, so they say, until he's put to the test, that is, until someone holds a blade to his chest, until he stands under enemy fire. Because in workaday life, being neither cold nor hot, in domestic warmth, at body temperature – the soul rots like meat in the June sun. Gambling therefore offers one of the closest approximations to a genuine trial. War heroes, those who survive, in telling their battle tales, always remember the moments when – shrugging their shoulders, crossing themselves and spitting on the ground: 'One lives only once!' – they hurled themselves at mortal risk, surrendering to fate, often convinced they'd not emerge whole from the fray.

Captain Privyezhensky played very cautiously, refusing to sell hot hands and often passing immediately after dealing; three times, however, he consistently raised the stakes and bid to the very end. But because he did so with such military regularity, everyone quickly saw through him and withdrew as soon as he took up the challenge. So, although he maintains admirable calm and betrays himself neither in word nor gesture nor expression, our captain will never win large sums.

Doctor Konyeshin in turn was consistently unpredictable. Such players had been met before – when in luck, they sweep up fortunes, when luck runs out, fortunes are lost.

Ünal Tayyib Fessar was a special case. He was bored. Bored when he lost, and bored when he won. Everything at the table he did nonchalantly, involuntarily and mechanically. Were the play and the money really nothing to him and, thanks to this, no real test – or was this precisely the Turk's way of handling moments of trial? A bald barebones of Levantine charm, veins taut like the strings of a pianoforte neath the sun-tanned frost-burned tissue – in him no bones and muscles, only sinews and joints; when he smiles, crooked teeth crunch in his gums; when he swallows his thick viscous coffee, his Adam's apple stabs the skin of his neck like a silkworm chiselling out of his throat. He taps the card sleeves with long fingernails, clicks his fingers like they were castanets. Were someone to strike his egg-shaped skull, a dry knock would resound, as of oakwood.

Mr Fessar was returning from talks in Constantinople. In Irkutsk, he managed the business interests of a trading company selling the natural riches of Siberia in the Mediterranean basin, chiefly coldiron, tungetitum and tin. He claimed to have spent half his life in the Irkutsk guberniya.

Recounting to Aleksey Fyodorovitch picturesque tales from the Land of the Gleissen, he seemed a little less bored.

'Trust not, sir, the Western geologists, they'll flog you maps on which you can read the history of mountain ranges, position of prehistoric Yakut villages and deposits of the rarest minerals, but they have no nose for gleissen. Take the Russians, Poles, most recently men from the Balkans who've been through Austrian universities. Once we had a specialist from America, well, and whose turn is it now, Doctor, we had this slyboots from the Alaskan fields, why, *kurtlu baklanin kor alicisi olur*, twenty thousand went on blind bore-holes and warm outcrops.'

'I've heard a complete map exists of coldiron deposits…'

'Ah, the famous Grochowski Map! You may be sure, sir, that in the first week following your arrival you'll receive a dozen offers to purchase the Grohovshtchik. Dubious types, vagrants, former katorzhniks, Martsynians, fortune hunters, you have no idea, sir, what kind of place it is; not so long ago it was still Cape Province, before that California – but now adventurers and freebooters from the world over are flocking precisely there: beyond Baikal, into Winter. Benedykt, sir, are you selling or not? Come on, stop endlessly crumpling those cards – either put something down or fold. Eh, and my coffee's gone cold, slops fit for dogs.'

'Queen's going down in flames.'

'Eight down!' said Captain Privyezhensky. 'Wait, does Tchushyn's company not already possess the licences to exploit those deposits? They must know what they're digging up where?'

'Depends what they're dealing in. If we're talking in this instance about Tcheremkhovo frozen-through coal, then God bless them. But if the talk is of coldiron… What? Aleksey Fyodorovitch?'

Tchushyn mopped his brow.

'You like to frighten me, Mr Fessar, you're a bad man.'

'I frighten him! Well, watch out, gentlemen. I'm good and waiting, a ten and another ten. Doctor?'

'Stick.' Konyeshin put aside his completed hand and lit a new cigarette. 'One reads nevertheless the thick journals; Education or The Contemporary World recently published a substantial article. Siberian tungetitum… either way, there are no tungetitum mines, are there?'

'That's why there are magpies, local prospectors. Some are hunters, amongst them also Yakuts and Tunguses; why, tungetitum pays decidedly better than foxes, sables, otters and martens, and in truth it's easier now to come by. Some are Stolypin's peasants, some – former gold-diggers. Eventually, the usual Siberian riff-raff – once they've drunk their last kopeck, and since they feel such irresistible disgust towards honest labour in the ironworks and coldmills of Zimny Nikolayevsk, what do idlers and bezdyelniks choose to do? March north, become magpies.'

Ünal reached into an inner pocket of his jacket, extracted a fresh cigar, tore off the wrapper, then took out a heavy penknife, which looked more suited to skinning a tiger, whereupon he screwed up his left eye so as to cut evenly and precisely – probably the sole activity that sufficiently engaged his attention.

'Mm-hmm. Naturally, these prospectors also flog us tidings about deposits of coldiron – this too involves a whole gamut of imposters and fraudsters. But for information about a good deposit, we pay between ten and twenty thousand roubles. Then, of course, it's necessary to secure the mining rights, and quickly enough so that our competitors don't beat us to it. All the bigger companies employ spies to spy on each other. Ultimately anyone can be bribed, you have to keep an eye. The informant is then locked up so he can't sell the same location a second time.'

'But what if it transpires you are the second, or third?'

'That's why he's locked up, so as to then break his legs. They know. It's a business for sharp knives. Ye-es.'

He spun the penknife in his fingers, once, twice, putting it away only when he lit the cigar.

'But you're holding up the game again, Mr Saski; you sell a card, then you wait, reckon on a miracle, so what'll it be?'

'He can't decide whether to play coward or risk-taker,' muttered Captain Privyezhensky.

Glance at the cards for the umpteenth time. A hopeless deal, high flames only: queen of diamonds, ten of hearts, nine of hearts, seven of diamonds. The queen had already been sold and replaced by a cold king. Sell now the ten? They'll recognise a hot hand, equally good could be folding at once. Don't sell? Better then to skip this deal and get over losing the queen's dowry.

'I'm good.'

The Turk raised an eyebrow.

'Khorosho. Captain?'

'Cold nine down! In other words, sir, you are saying that all coldiron mines are opencast pits? Since, however, gleissen are already advancing towards the Oder...'

Smooth out a napkin at the edge of the table, nod to the steward.

'Might I request a pencil? Thank you.' Moisten automatically the tip with spittle. 'Mm-hmm, they reached Warsaw in nineteen fifteen, that is six years and some eight months; four thousand nine hundred kilometres in fifty-eight thousand three hundred and twenty hours, mm-hmm, eighty-four metres an hour, something doesn't fit: in the city, it's at most eight metres an hour, they advance no faster than that.'

'Evidently, they flow ten times faster through soil.'

'Soil better conducts the Ice, that's a fact.' Ünal nodded in agreement with his cigar. 'Show me that calculation.'

Hand him the napkin.

'Ye-es. An amusing question, we estimated it in our day in our company, made it close to one hundred metres an hour along the Ways of the Mammoths. If I remember correctly, ninety-six or ninety-seven.'

'It's slowing down.'

'Possibly.'

'At the very beginning it was considerably faster!'

'We ought not to make suppositions, however, based on my calculations. Perhaps the Ice is not spreading uniformly. Perhaps there exist privileged directions. Privileged places. Secondary epicentres. These also need to be taken into account. Why does Winter prevail in cities? The next stage would be to induce them on purpose to cluster and... Excuse me.'

The sinews on the Turk's face and neck were already tautening as he removed the cigar from his mouth – but he hesitated and froze just like that, for a second, two, three, wrestling with himself; in the end, he lost the battle and said nothing.

'Like a wave receding from the place of disturbance,' said Doctor Konyeshin. 'Aleksey Fyodorovitch, I understand, has folded?'

'Well... I suppose so, yes, yes.'

'Captain, sir.'

'Ten.'

'And I.'

'And I.'

'Please.'

'This is what I think.' Doctor Konyeshin slouched back in his chair, released the smoke from his mouth and tugged at his left sideburn, lost in thought. 'Throw a stone into a pond, and rings spread across the water. But there are different mediums, water, or not water, let some disturbance occur that has never occurred before in living memory. How shall we recognise it? We shan't recognise it. A phenomenon experienced a hundred times is a law of nature, a phenomenon experienced once – a miracle. And so, it spreads like rings on water...'

'Gleissen. The Ice.'

'Yes.'

'Except that, Doctor, it's incomparably more complex than the simple arithmetic of waves. We know not the laws that govern it, for how would we know?' Touch the palate with the tongue, seeking words that might conceivably approximate thought. 'But let us suppose a man stands for the first time on a beach, sees for the first time rollers breaking on the shore... Just as our ignorance of the laws governing the behaviour of liquids does not make, in our eyes, independent intelligent beings out of those waves, so too ignorance of the physics of the Ice should not make them out of gleissen. Mr Fessar, sir?'

'Yes. Ten and twenty and I go on. Captain?'

'Oh, I resign.'

'And what says our count?'

Nearly two hundred roubles lay on the table. Konyeshin and Fessar were still in the game, they had sold practically nothing – the doctor only one black seven; they were proceeding on cold cards. Or on hard bluffs. One way or another, they were out of reach: more than eighty roubles had been lost this day; not quite two hundred remained in the pocketbook, the change from the ministerial thousand. Obviously, no one would give credit to a compromised fraudster. Even were everything to be thrown at this round, the Turk could always outbid. And check. Yet the hand – the hand was on fire. Was it not the ideal way to flush out the final kopeck?

It was perfectly clear therefore what ought to be done: the intention is there, the thought and the will, to throw down the cards and stand up from the game.

Instead of that:

'Up the stakes.'

Lay all the banknotes in the bumazhnik on the table. Even the heart beats no faster.

They watched with interest. Tchushyn called for more shampanskoye. With a mocking smirk, Captain Privyezhensky tapped his pipe on the table. Mr Fessar chewed his cigar. People had stopped behind the players' backs as well as on the far side of the billiard table, lured by the sight of the laid-out cash. A woman even looked in from the saloon; recognise the rustle of her dress. Hold the gaze on a level with the cards.

'Ye-es,' sighed Ünal, counting out and throwing forty roubles onto the baize, and then a second forty. 'I must confess, I find the doctor's analogy incredibly fascinating. But why not take it further? Maybe life in general, maybe we – plants, animals, people – also consist purely of "more complex waves" spreading from the moment, from the place of First Impact? What? In what way do we differ? Doctor?'

Doctor Konyeshin reckoned with his eyes the laid-out stakes, adjusted the pince-nez on his nose, scowled.

'You'll forgive me, gentleman, I shall observe from the sidelines.'

'Gospodin Yeroslavsky?'

'You yourself believe not what you say.' Adjust the position on the chair, rest the wrists on the polished edge of the table. 'To you, sir, it seems too absurd to give it honest thought. You reason thus: "Certainly, I am not just some wave." You judge that we exist in a different, more independent way. You think that because you think, you are. You're mistaken.'

'Oh!' The Turk leaned across the table, finally aroused and intrigued. 'And so, you're dreaming us up now, yes? Am I right, young man?'

'Nothing of the kind. Neither do I exist. Forty and my forty.'

Ünal's eyes were blazing. With the fingertips of his left hand, he fondly stroked the tight-fitting skin on his rounded skull.

'You exist not. You are telling me that you exist not. Who then is telling me this?'

Wave a cigarette dismissively.

'Language, what kind of argument is that? I give these rays of the Sun an attractive name and then assert that there exists such and such an angel of light – for otherwise, who would be warming us here?'

'Agh, so it's not about you not existing at all, but –'

'It's exactly as the doctor said. We exist only insofar as gleissen exist, or the frost-flower on an icy pane. A momentary disturbance of matter, whose form happens to contain the ability to perceive a thought.' Outline with the hand in the air a sinusoidal curve.

'*Momentary?*'

'Momentary, which means relating only to the present, to this infinitely fine line, where the non-existent borders on the non-existent. I am unable to prove it, but convinced that when it comes to categories of truth and falsehood, we can speak only of that which freezes in the Now. Whereas there be many pasts and futures, equally true-and-untrue. That's the natural state. Whereas gleissen….'

'Yes?'

'They freeze anything they touch. Is that not what legends tell of the Kingdom of Ice? "And may thy speech be: Yea, yea, Nay, nay. For whatsoever is more than these cometh from evil." Are you playing, sir, or not, how long must I wait?'

Mr Fessar crossed his arms on his chest.

'Fold.'

'Fold?' Tchushyn jumped up. 'What are you doing, for heaven's sake…!'

'Fold.'

The amazement was too great, it froze the face and larynx; no emotion found its way out. Play on – play on – played on – and the game was won.

Scoop up the pile of roubles from the smooth green surface. The spectators gathered around the table exchanged loud remarks. Shuffle the cards held in the hand into the rest of the pack. In the doorway of the smoking car stood the chief steward announcing that dinner was served. The Express was slowing down, approaching a station; beyond the windows sprawled a wide network of railway tracks, timber yards. Tchushyn stood up and stretched his limbs, Doctor Konyeshin followed suit.

Cram the money into the pocketbook, stub out the cigarette-end, drink up the cold tea and spit into the spittoon.

He did not walk away, but continued to stand against the wall of the carriage, on the far side; see him without lifting the eyes, a restless dance of shadows around the tall silhouette. At what point had he begun to watch the play?

Try to make way for him in the passage; he raised a hand in its white glove and leaned slightly forward.

'Please drop by after dinner. Perhaps you will receive your proof.'

'I beg your pardon?'

'You know this young lady? Be so kind as to not keep her waiting.'

Jelena Muklanowicz cast a suspicious glance at the departing Doctor Tesla.

'Who was that?'

'I am not sure. Forgive me, ladies –'

'Oh, you shan't run away from me anywhere. Auntie – Benedykt Gierosławski.'

'Mm-hmm… *Enchanté.*'

On the machine that devours logic and other inventions of Doctor Tesla

'When I was studying at the Polytechnic Institute in Graz, bored by lectures from which I could no longer glean anything useful, I devoted more and more time to student games. In my third year, I recall, I used to play cards, chess, billiards, around the clock. We played for money, for greater or lesser sums. At that time, I survived on what my family sent. I won't say I suffered hardship, but you'd more likely encounter a bishop or general of our blood than a wealthy businessman. Was I out of luck or lacking in gumption? Neither, I think. If anything were to blame, it was too soft a heart. Seeing that an opponent could not withstand such serious losses, I would return my larger winnings. But no one felt obliged to reciprocate; I have to confess I was not popular with other students. So, I fell into serious debt. I wrote home. They sent more and more, more than they were able. In the end, my mother came. Appeared one day with a roll of banknotes. I believe it really was the last of their savings. "Have it, go and enjoy yourself," she said. "The quicker you squander everything we possess, the better. I know this fever will pass in the end." I took the money, went to a coffee house, won back with interest everything I'd lost and returned it to my parents. I tell you, sir, I was never tempted to gamble again; I was cured.'

'She shamed you.'

Doctor Tesla stared over his hands held in a pyramid.

'Yes, you could say that.'

Glass jingled in the drinks cabinet as the Express entered an exceptionally tight bend. The tracks here no longer ran so straight. More often too the train climbed steep inclines, causing mishaps at dinner in the restaurant car with soup, gravy and wine. After the halt in Perm, no extended station stops were envisaged until Yekaterinburg, already on the Asiatic side of the Urals. The Trans-Siberian Magistral ran mostly over mountain passes and slopes of low, disappointingly flat mountains, along the Bogdanovitch route. The window of Tesla's compartment looked out onto a south-facing valley, green, azure and yellow in the late afternoon sun, pitch black beyond the shadow-line. High above the Urals, overgrown by dense forest, hung clouds the colour of suds; it was one of few moments so far on the journey when the sky did not appear more beautiful than the earth.

Doctor Tesla half-opened the cabinet door. In the two-berth compartments, oval tables had been installed by the windows with delicate bentwood legs and tops set with mother-of-pearl. Little shot glasses embellished in gold knocked against the smooth white surface.

'Have you wondered, sir, why that Turkish businessman folded at the end? He shouldn't have.'

'Yes.'

'What do you mean: yes?'

'He shouldn't have. I have wondered.'

Tesla studied for a moment the label on the bottle.

'And?'

'He let me win, it's obvious.'

'But why?'

'It seems I convinced him.'

'Mm-hmm?'

'That I exist not.'

Having poured the liquid, Tesla held a glass up to the light, narrowed his eyes. An ironic half-smile, typical of him, strayed over his lips. Remember it from yesterday's conversation; but the irony was directed rather towards himself, not against his interlocutor.

'Not a very reliable method. You apply it often?'

'I kept him amused for a while.'

'But you, sir, are not amused, you believe in it. True?'

'Yes.'

'That you exist not. Mm-hmm.' Doctor Tesla sniffed the alcohol, tasted it. 'Gróf Keglevich, mm-hmm.' Sniffed again. 'Just as I thought, you are a very odd young man.'

Laugh.

'Have you looked in a mirror, Doctor? After dark, when the lights come on?'

'Ah!'

He leaned back, pressing his shoulders into the chair; his chin sank almost to his chest; hair slid over his temples as he gazed now from under raven-black brows, a single silver strand of hair pointing to a sharply delineated bone above the hollow cheek. Nikola Tesla's likeness to a Gypsy patriarch was thrown once again into stark relief. When he declared he hailed from a line of bishops and generals, he merely confirmed the original intuition.

'I might have expected you'd notice. Yes. There are certain side effects, of which… Mm-hmm. Have you spent much time of late, sir, in unlicht? Hours? In recent weeks?'

'No.'

'The human eye –'

'No.'

Sit at the table opposite him, back flat against the back of the chair, head inclined backwards, wrists on the tabletop. The symmetry of gazes was total – same height, same posture, as well as the same layout on either side of the space: made-up bed by one wall, made-up bed by the other wall, a streak of sunlight in between partially obscured by clouds – now the dialogue could proceed, in which every question and every answer would have equal weight.

Tesla moistened his lips in the cognac.

'In eighteen ninety-eight, Mark Twain embarked on a journey around Europe. All the salons on the continent were thrown open to him. Amongst others, he visited the court of His Imperial Exaltedness Nikolay the Second. Mr Twain wrote to me in advance, on his own initiative, acting as my agent *optima fide.* I had the honour to count myself amongst his friends, we'd met several years earlier through New York high society. In Great Britain, Germany and Austria, he also spoke in my name. In those days, it was mostly about selling the patents for polyphase alternating-current supply systems; ministries of war were interested too in my teleautomatons, I was working on remote-control torpedoes. Most of Mr Twain's efforts bore no fruit. For a long time, however, I had already been conducting my own personal negotiations with Tsar Nikolay Aleksandrovitch. Russia had expressed interest many times in purchasing my various patents with military applications; some she really did acquire. Only about ten years ago, however, when I experienced, mm-hmm, serious financial difficulties thanks to my partners' perfidy and dishonesty, and when the Ice began to spread with a vengeance across imperial Russia, the tsar offered me a long-term contract with resources to conduct research, leaving me the rights at the same time to the patents on any inventions created during the term of contract. The emperor seems to have, mm-hmm, a weak spot for me, perhaps because of my origins. You see, Benedykt, sir, in short, the terms were too good for me not to accept, especially given my situation then in America.'

Raise the glass to the lips. Concentric ripples ruffled the bright surface of the liquid in time to the rhythm of the vibrating train, took-took-took-TOOK. Doctor Tesla rotated mechanically the gilded glass between white-cottoned fingers. He was observing how cautiously his companion drank.

Cough.

'This contract with the tsar.'

'Yes?'

'What exactly, Doctor, did Nikolay Aleksandrovitch contract you to supply?'

Tesla smiled with genuine sympathy.

'Please do me the pleasure of stating that I'm not mistaken in you, that all this – is not blind chance.'

'But, my dear sir! I am not your assistant, for you to be constantly setting exams.'

'True. You are not. At present I have no assistant.'

The Hungarian cognac smarted unpleasantly on the tongue. Ram the glass on the tabletop; it sounded like the rattle of empty bones, the crack of a damp whip.

'The tsar has ordered weapons from you to fight the gleissen.'

'Yes?'

'The Grossmeister, the Grand Master, is only a pop-gun for shooting at sparrows. It's manual work – you can't have set up an assembly line – each specimen requires its own design and name. Genuine handicraft. How many pieces have been produced, a dozen?'

'Eight. Next question.'

Lick the lips.

'Those are just pop-guns, but you have fulfilled your contract, Doctor, you are travelling to test your inventions in the lands of the Ice; somewhere in the composition of this train is a sealed carriage, in which –'

'Yes.' He raised a white-gloved palm, stemming the stream of words. Tesla leaned over the table, suddenly breaking the symmetry. New contexts were imposed by the new symmetry of stares. 'You should understand, sir, that I am conversing with you now not because I owe you my life. We are both men of reason. Like minds attract; I have experienced it many times in life, people find one another unconsciously, know one another before they're acquainted, before they've heard of one another.'

'Evil to evil, good to good, truth to truth, falsehood to falsehood.'

'I will show you something. Please remain seated.'

He crossed to the other end of the compartment, to the corner by the door; on either side of the door were identical cubbies, he opened the left-hand one, reached down and pulled out onto the carpet a large sac de voyage. Judging by the effort with which Tesla swivelled it around and dragged it over to the table by the window, it must have been very heavy. Withdraw the feet. Doctor Tesla fished a small, elaborately worked key out of an inside pocket, bent over halfway and undid a lock on the black bag. Almost without parting its steel-riveted jaws, he reached steadily into an internal partition and brought out a red chamois case in the shape of a cylinder. Then, having straightened to his full height, he ejected from the case onto the palm of his hand a light metal telescope. Telescope, kaleidoscope, some sort of optical device with lenses at both ends, a slightly smaller and a slightly larger. He raised it to his eye and peered into the larger lens.

He muttered something in Serbian.

'Please.'

Clasp the apparatus with utmost caution. Bands of dark metal over-lapped, converging in white clamping rings made of ivory; on the central band was a little emblem depicting a symbolic eclipse of the Sun. The Sun was in yellow lacquer, the Moon in lustreless black.

Doctor Tesla watched expectantly. Shrug the shoulders.

'What it is?'

'An interferograph. Take a look.'

Look. Instinctively pointing the barrel at the window, towards the Sun and the Urals landscape – but this was no telescope; it brought the views no closer, showed nothing at all except a few beads of light flowing in a straight line across the diameter of the lens. The background remained uniformly black.

'And so?'

'You remember what you said about the Kingdom of Ice? "Yea, yea, Nay, nay."'

'That was more a feeling... The Ice... gleissen live in a world of two-valued logic. That is – if they do indeed live.'

'This is what you do?'

'Mathematics, logic. Well, I used to do them.'

'So, tell me yourself: can we regard it as a type of proof?'

'What?'

'Light.' He sat down, restoring the symmetry. 'I began taking an interest in it after my initial experiments with the combustion of tungetitum compounds. What exactly is unlicht? Darkness is the lack of light – how can darkness *force out* light? How can it cast shadows, which are light?'

'Fun and games for parlour spiritualists.'

'That as well. And yet...'

Lay the barrel on the table. It rolled between the shot glasses.

'You believe in such things, Doctor? Fortune-telling, clairvoyance, summoning spirits? Here in Europe, they still get a thrill from it, theosophists, Rosicrucians, Gnostics, anthroposophical occultists like Rudolf Steiner. Besides, you've seen how the princess amuses herself – have you seen?'

He wiped his bony nose, showing for the first time signs of confusion.

'Mistake me not for Edison, sir, it wasn't I who built a telephone to talk to the dead. They call me the Wizard because it's easy to dazzle ignoramuses, but I have been a man of science since childhood. A man of science, who appreciates how many phenomena science has still not grasped. In London, as a guest of the Royal Society, I had occasion to familiarise myself with proof of the transmission of thought. Lord Rayleigh showed me photographs of materialising ectoplasm. The wife of Sir William Crookes stunned me with her adeptness at the art of levitation. And I gleaned many helpful inspirations from my conversations with Swami Vivekananda on Vedic cosmology.'

'I know not all the properties of unlicht. One way or another, I take no interest in what I cannot see, measure, describe. That' – he pointed to the interferograph – 'is a simple gadget composed of glass, two compartments with slits, and a filter. The interference of light proves that light is a wave. That it's a wave has been obvious since Maxwell's time, since the experiments of Young. At the same time, it is obvious that light is composed of individual molecules, rushing ahead of themselves with a defined energy. In eighteen ninety-six, when Wilhelm Roentgen caused a furore with his shadowgraphs, I was conducting numerous experiments of my own, in which streams of light particles bombarded a fine gauze shield, thereby transmitting to it their impetus. A few years later Doctor Einstein captured the thing in his quantum theory. There is no doubt, therefore, that on this most fundamental level of reality, there is a contradiction: light is and is not waves, is and is not molecules. Were it to be only molecules, you would see in the interferograph two bright spots – points where the light rays pass through the two slits. But because light is also waves, it interferes with and overlaps with itself; there where the amplitudes augment each other, it is brighter, whereas where they cancel each other out – although there is no totally satisfactory explanation for this effect – you have a break in the line. In this very same place, the *Lichtquant*, the light particle or photon, is and is not; this same *Lichtteilchen* is both here, and there. Is that the logic of Aristotle? It's the negation of Aristotle! And yet we can see it with our own eyes.'

Raise the barrel again.

'Agreed.'

'Please keep it.' Hesitate, but he nodded. 'Please, it's easy to assemble according to Billet's scheme, all that's needed is a filter adapted for sunlight and precise measurement of the slits. Take a look in the interferograph when we reach our destination.'

Doctor Tesla handed over the chamois case. Rotate the apparatus again in the palm and put it in a pocket.

'And what shall I see then?'

He smiled. Reaching into his bag, he parted the steel jaws this time as wide as they would go. With a sharp energetic tug – so that his jacket strained across his back, emphasising the sharp shoulder blades neath the fabric, and his white neckerchief slipped, exposing above the stiff collar what looked like black bruises, negatives of Yury the Strangler's fat stubby fingers – he lifted onto the table a bulgy contraption made of wood and metal. Rescue the brandy glasses at the last moment from being crushed.

On one side of the bulk, Doctor Tesla tweaked a crank supplied with a rubber handle; on the other side, into a small orifice, he shoved a cable ending in a coldiron ring. The solid base of the contraption was fashioned out of dark wood; screwed into it were iron clamps and slats, against which the trunk rested, whilst locked inside it, as in a horizontally strung tight-mesh basket, were disks, cylinders, rods, wire coils and steel rings.

Set aside the glass. Espy, on closer inspection, a small, elegantly engraved brass plate in the centre of the wooden base:

Teslectric Generator
Tesla Tungetitum Co.
Prague – New York 1922

'What is this?'

'A teslectric dynamo-machine. The construction is similar to the construction of a direct-current generator, but instead of magnets I've installed pure tungetitum, whilst the winding is made of zinc-coated coldiron.'

'Pure tungetitum! You think such a thing might pay off?'

His eyes sparkled. Now he was happy as a child. The bony old man gave the impression he was about to rub his hands together and bounce up and down on his chair.

'It's not current that's produced here, my dear fellow, not current!'

'What then?'

'A different force. It flows freely into wood, into numerous coolbonds of coldiron, into plants and animals, into crystalline structures. High-carbon varieties of coldiron exist – like cryocarbon graphite itself – which, when connected to this obscure energy, emit unlicht. Upon this depends the patent for my dark bulb; one or two Siberian factories have already purchased it. Whereas uncontrolled release of teslectricity will produce an abrupt drop in temperature. The tsar supplied me with sufficient tungetitum; I could experiment to my heart's content. I already know that we can't apply directly here the rules of the old physics, and that this "teslectrical flow" does not behave like electrical current – but nor does it exactly resemble the flow of a liquid. It pours out, pours out, pours out; there are certain vessels, objects, materials that never seem to completely fill up, it goes on flowing endlessly.

'And in such a physical space, steeped in teslectrical energy – if you look then in such a space into the interferograph, you'll no longer see a drawn-out string of brighter and darker patches, but only the two solitary points of light.'

Fail for a moment to comprehend what he actually said. Then grab hold of the shot glass and knock back the remainder of the cognac. Reach for another. Did the hand tremble, or did the train shake as it turned onto a Urals pass?

Nikola Tesla was watching, a smile on his face.

All symmetry had gone to the devil.

'That...' Clear the throat. 'That is a powerful premise.'

He sighed.

'But it is not proof.'

'No. We cannot rule out that this tungetitum force acts like this only on the nature of light. How would I know? Does it straighten out the paths of the *Lichtquanten*? Logic... now that's something significantly more fundamental; logic cannot be reduced to one or another physical phenomenon. Even if your "teslectric force" indeed deprives light of its wave motion and traps the light quantum in a single place, to total existence or total non-existence.'

'That was exactly how I thought. Bah, after all, it hadn't crossed my mind until now that this unequivocal "freezing" of the nature of light could be anything more than a side effect of another change, so much more profound – despite all the Siberian legends, despite the accounts emanating from the Land of the Ice. Only today, before dinner, when I heard what you were saying about gleissen...'

'Yes.'

'A sudden illumination, as if I saw at once the contours of a ready-made solution, requiring merely interpretation. I am used to trusting such revelations, one once saved my life. Because look. If the teslectric force really does impose the two-valuedness of logic...' He sat hunched up as he was evidently wont to do in moments of enhanced cogitation, when his attention was distracted from control of his body. 'What you think, sir, what impact could it have on living organisms? On a human being?'

'I have no idea. All this is...' Make a chaotic movement with the hands. The right hand clasped the casing of the dynamo; the metal felt chilly, it wasn't coldiron, yet it was astoundingly chilly. Shudder and drop both arms. 'For such things, Doctor, there are no words; we are breaking the boundaries of language, breaking our own wits.'

'That's precisely what I'm asking. After all, you said that's what you do. Yes? Therefore, the mind: what kind of effect could it have on the mind?' He held two white fingers up to his temple like the barrel of a revolver. 'Should a man somehow... feel it?'

'You mean the inhabitants of Siberia? Maybe hiberniks, Martsynians?'

Tesla waved his hand dismissively, suddenly irritated, disappointed. 'You're incapable of telling me. Yes. Excuse me.'

Feel the hackles rise.

'But what are you getting at, Doctor! The effect on thoughts, or where thoughts come from? Thoughts! Hah! Such a man shouldn't breathe at all! For God's sake!' The higher the voice, the faster the speech, spoken with ever greater conviction. Lick the lips. Images from Zygmunt's anatomical atlases came rushing back, his words, the words of his medical colleagues, snatches of conversations. 'Were you to alter one chemical element, you would no longer have a human being. And this – this would be the greatest change of all! Flesh would drop off bones, blood decompose in veins, there would be no bones, there would be no flesh, no veins, no living tissue, nothing, nothing, nothing –'

He was already standing. In his left fist, he squeezed the coldiron ring that formed the end of the cable emerging from the teslectric dynamo-machine, and with his right palm grabbed hold of the crank. He began to turn it. Something clanged inside the machine and its steel bowels started to rotate inside the bulging belly; brighter and darker components began to whirl. Tesla wound faster and faster as the whirling exceeded the speed beyond which the human eye ceases to distinguish objects in motion, and perceives only motion itself, its direction and colour. The generator whistled and snarled. Doctor Tesla turned the crank steadily, his long arm working to a calm rhythm. He stood facing the window, once again upright, his cable hand raised in front of him to chest height, the cable dangling limply like a dead snake. Withdraw the knee so as not to get hooked in it accidently. Dryness caught the throat. Swallow the saliva, insipid from the cognac. A smell of burning began to emanate from the generator and prickle the nose. Miniscule droplets of moisture appeared on its metal trunk. Hairs on the skin stood on end; fingers, palate, tongue were all atingle. Rub the hands. They were cold; cold had taken hold of the compartment. Blow into their cupped hollows. Grey cloudlets of steam effloresced before the face of Nikola Tesla. He continued to turn the crank, the dynamo whirled, trrrrrrrrrr.

... Tesla's left arm, the stationary one, was the first to start going blurry. As if someone were wiping an image off an old photograph, or the photographic membrane itself were overexposed. White glove, shirt cuff, jacket sleeve, then the whole jacket, then the neckerchief and head, then his other hand, and his legs – Doctor Tesla was sinking into shadow, behind a perpendicular veil of grey twilight, like an ethereal shimmering afterimage, except that he was shimmering not from heat but from cold, and not in dazzling radiance but in darkness, that is, in unlight – you could see its black sparks, like negatives of electrical discharges, but out of focus, sluggish, sprouting in gentle arcs or tight clusters, dancing in fluffy tufts and tongues of black flame, along his shoulders and down his sleeves, on his hair and forehead, on the cheek-bones of Doctor Tesla – already he stood entirely shrouded in a haze of unlicht, in the glow of night. Trrrrrrrrrrrrrrrrrrr. Since he had the window before him, brightness glinted behind his back – the vibrant glintz of a tall silhouette, far sharper than any normal shadow cast in the light of day. Nikola Tesla was disintegrating into his own negative and negative of the negative, deposited as a bright-white patch on the carpet, door, wall of the compartment. Parabolic streaks of darkness began to leap between the doctor's body – his extended arm, upright torso, forehead – and the iron mass of the generator, glazing over now with hoarfrost. A covering of ice already glistened on the brass plate. Thrust the hands under the armpits, retreat along with the chair as far as possible from the accelerating dynamo. Trrrrrrrrrrrrrrrrrrrr.

... Tesla opened his mouth; tried to say something, but instead of words, a cloud of vapour, black as tar, issued from between the parched lips.

The Express began to brake and Tesla staggered despite his widely planted legs. He had to lean on the table; he let go the crank, let go the cable. The whirring gradually subsided. On the windowpanes, gilt fittings, fabric upholstery, metal and wood extravaganzas of the Deluxe carriage, on the brandy glasses, a snowy deposit sparkled like dew congealed by a spring ground frost.

Open the window to let warm air into the compartment.

Tesla straightened his back, mopping his mouth and forehead with his handkerchief. Removing his gloves, he painstakingly wiped his palms and each long, bony finger.

'The body, dear sir, the body is a mighty force, we don't deserve to have power over it.'

Struggle to conceal the embarrassment.

'Well, yes. A little gymnastics never harmed anyone.'

He was panting lightly. Seemed not in the least tired – then he was breathing more deeply, pink blotches appeared on his face, the pupils dilated.

'You've been doing it for long?'

'I noticed it helped me in my work. It purifies the mind, if one can put it that way.' He took out his cigarette case. 'There are also other effects, harder to describe.'

'What happens to your shadow –'

'I meant states of mind. The body is a mighty force, but the mind, *mon ami*, is the only thing a man is fully responsible for in this world.'

'And aren't you afraid of jeopardising it? What do you actually know in the end about this tungetitum force?'

Tesla laughed wholeheartedly.

'My dear fellow, once upon a time I used to pass electric current of one hundred and fifty thousand volts through my brain. Do you imagine, sir, we already know all there is to know about electricity? That's why we do experiments, to find out something new; we experiment not with what we know, because what's the point?' He lit a cigarette. For a split second, as Tesla blew out the match, it flared up like a blot of black ink. 'What is intriguing me now... Tell me, what experiments might I carry out in order to test your hypothesis?'

Kick with a shoe-tip the cable lying on the carpet.

'But what do we actually know about the relationship between teslectricity and gleissen? Where did you –'

The door to the compartment opened. His wife entered – not his wife, Nikola Tesla's companion, the young woman seen with him in the dining car. She entered and at once stood still, frozen on the threshold. Navy-blue skirt, part of an English suit, high waist, silver pendant on a jabot of Irish guipure lace, fair hair plaited in a crown braid. How old could she be, seventeen? Younger, without a doubt, than Miss Muklanowicz.

She glanced at Tesla, at the teslectric dynamo-machine, again at Tesla, screwed up her lips –

'Christine!' cried the doctor.

She spun on her heels and ran out, slamming the door.

Exchange knowing glances with Tesla. He threw his cigarette out of the window, pulled the white gloves back on, smoothed down his hair. Disassembled crank and cable from the generator, then removed the machine from the table and packed it in the bag. Fumbled to get the key into the tiny lock – for the train suddenly decelerated, everything shuddered more and more. Stand and stick the head out of the window as the doctor yanked the sac de voyage back to the cubby.

No station was there here, no buildings within sight, at least not on this side of the tracks; no sign at all of civilisation – nothing but mountains and mountain nature, the wild Urals. The sun emerged fully from behind dirty clouds and a succulent green burst forth from the woods stretching over the gentle mountainsides.

The brakes screeched, the carriage lurched forward one more time, and the train came to a halt. The wheezing of the locomotive and hiss of steam could be heard even here.

'What's happened?'

'Maybe an emergency. Maybe something with the tracks. We should ask the provodnik.'

Tesla glanced at his watch, grabbed his cane and opened the door.

'Sabotage!'

Follow him into the corridor. Passengers were pouring out of other compartments; a crowd had formed and a commotion arisen, everyone was asking the same questions. Meanwhile, no sign of the provodnik. Windows were opened. A draught wrapped the curtains around the heads of those looking out.

'Aren't you exaggerating, Doctor, after all –'

'Think, sir, *dammit*! Where do you get coldiron from? Without the slightest hesitation, they'd blow this whole Trans-Siberian Express into the air.'

'And themselves along with it? But what about the son-in-law of the Sibirkhozheto director?'

Tesla locked the compartment.

'That's precisely why in such moments I fear most for my prototypes.'

'At stations, at stops.' See now the gap in the reasoning elaborated yesterday at breakfast. Whilst the train is moving, a powerful bomb attack poses a threat to the whole train and all its passengers – but when the train is stationary, it is possible to safely blow up an individual carriage. And what follows from that: if the assassins are targeting a single Deluxe traveller – be it Prince Blutsky or Doctor Tesla – then indeed, they should place the murderer in the same class; if, on the other hand, they care solely about the carriage with Tesla's equipment, the bomber can travel equally well in second class.

The Serb defended himself with barely concealed revulsion against the pressing bodies, and pushed his way forward.

'Let me through, please,' he said in English. 'Forgive me, izvinite, please, *excusez-moi, entschuldigen Sie*, may I squeeze past, thank you.'

No one noticed the subtle washing-away of Doctor Tesla's silhouette as he forced his way through that throng, aided by his cane, half a head taller than almost all other passengers; they paid no attention to the flickering corona of shadow that Nikola Tesla cast upon himself – a tremulous noctaureole – afterimage of the unlicht.

On several key differences between the European sky and Asian sky

The wolf stood on a felled trunk, its wedge-shaped head protruding from behind branches.

'But when I approach –'

'You shan't approach, miss.'

'Aren't they afraid of people?'

'Not this one.'

'… gun or something to frighten it gentlemen of the train…'

'Animals grow used to things, *vous comprenez*, the wildest beast will become accustomed in the end, come sunrise or sunset, the passage of a steam engine, summer and winter, so long as there's regularity. Nature is the greatest of clocks.'

'Spare us your industrial poetics, Engineer.'

Ünal Fessar, rummaging until then with his cane in the ground, picked up a sizeable stone and slung it at the wolf. The other passengers shrieked loudly. The stone missed the animal and trunk by a good metre. The wolf shuddered nervously but budged not from its place. It bared its fangs and observed the people, inclining its head to the left.

Miss Muklanowicz tucked up her skirt and ran towards it. Monsieur Verousse and Engineer White-Gessling, standing nearest, tried to catch her, stop her, but she wriggled easily from their grasp. Ten or twelve metres separated her from the forest edge and the felled alder-trunk lying on that edge. Before anyone mustered courage to take decisive action, Miss Muklanowicz was approaching the wolf.

She stretched out her hand towards it.

'She's out of her mind, good God, wants to stroke it!'

'It'll bite off her fingers,' muttered Mr Fessar.

'Where's Doctor Konyeshin?'

'Probably still in the train.'

'But who is she anyway?'

'Miss Jelena Muklanowicz.' Say it.

She even knelt on the trunk, leaning her face over the animal's head, raised now towards her. Saliva glistened on the predator's yellow fangs; its curled-back lips were aquiver. The young woman reached from above towards its spine. The wolf wheeled around on the spot, jumped off the trunk and vanished into the forest.

Engineer White-Gessling clutched at his chest.

'What is she thinking of! It almost gave me a heart attack. Where's her guardian?'

Look about for Auntie Urszula. A tall woman with wide shoulders – there was no one on this side of the tracks with such a distinctive figure. No doubt she's reclining in the compartment under a hot-water bottle; at dinner she had complained of her circulation.

Walk up to Jelena. She was brushing her skirt with an innocent air.

'Suicide is a mortal sin.'

'You don't say! But had it been Captain Privyezhensky –'

'Then it would have been bravado worthy of admiration. Please.'

'Thank you.'

She accepted the proffered arm. Stroll back to the meadow. The passed-by Ünal Fessar doffed his hat. Miss Muklanowicz pretended not to have seen him. When she perceived, however, that Prince Blutsky, in the company of Privy Councillor Dushin and two men dressed in the prince's livery, was eyeing her from the engine – she stopped still and curtsied.

Draw the young lady in the opposite direction.

'The prince must have given them an earful. Do you think, sir, he really expected an attempt on his life? They were saying it's an accidental breakdown – well, what else could they say? We can't stop here for long, something else will drive into us. Another thing: those two okhranniks, who were roaming around the Deluxe carriages, are no longer with us, they must have got out yesterday evening. In other words, the matter has been clarified. Though the prince shows no great relief... Benedykt, sir! Really! What is it that you find so fascinating about the grass here? Are you listening at all?'

'I am listening.'

'You have an opportunity,' she whispered.

'Mm-hmm.'

'There's your wolf. He's waiting. Let's go.'

'What?'

'You think he'll bite? I wager he's not got many teeth left.'

Feel the hot flush on the cheeks.

'Enough.'

She raised her head.

'The first stars are coming out. Look. What constellation is that?'

'I know not.' Let go her arm. 'Forgive me, miss.'

Leap onto the metal footplate and hide inside the carriage. The idea of lying low behind the closed doors of the compartment until Irkutsk gains once more in attraction.

Frau Blutfeld appeared in the vista of the corridor. Jump out of the train on the other side.

Here, considerably fewer passengers were taking an airing. To the north, no green fields ascended to meet the mixed forest as they did to the south; almost immediately beyond the railway embankment, the naked scree began, broken on the western side by tiered terraces and dissected by a deep river of rocky rubble, and on the eastern stretching almost to the very summit that dominated the pass and valley like a watchtower. Scramble up a few metres, perch on a sun-baked sandstone boulder. The Express had stopped just before a bend, beyond which the tracks descended in an arc many miles long into a still lower valley. The passengers were dispersed across the terrain. Visible from here were the entire meadow on the far side of the train, the slopes of mountains lying opposite, strangely flattened and rounded; also, the ravine shrouded in evening shadow, out of which loomed the tracks. Even on their walks and in their choice of place to spread their blankets on the grass and improvise little picnics, the passengers upheld instinctively the division between first and second class: none of the Deluxe travellers wandered off to the west, beyond the line of the restaurant car, and likewise, few from the second-class sleepers crossed it either. Visible too were men's hats and bowlers and women's white parasols against the dark-green backdrop, as small groups of walkers approached the trees and thickets. There were children too – racing after one another, screeching between the carriages of the Express; the children, though few, made most noise. The Ural mountains meanwhile stood silent, tranquil – an image of sleepy wilderness from before the invasion of man. The low sun, with long strokes of the brush, added streaks of red, yellow and sepia. The colours were warm, yet a chill wind was stirring – button the jacket, draw up the knees. No one was watching. The prince and his entourage remained on the other side of the locomotive. The steel monster gave no sign of life; no breath rose from its chimney, nothing moved in the windows of the driver's cab.

Take out the cigarette case and lighter. Let's think it through calmly. Inhale the smoke. Could they really want to blow up the entire Express because of Nikola Tesla? And had that scene at the end of Princess Blutskaya's séance really attracted their attention? Tesla was clearly prone to megalomania and theatrical gestures, he could have exaggerated everything unintentionally. Was there really some personal danger? Someone had broken into the compartment earlier, rifled through the luggage. Prince Blutsky-Osey, the princess, Miss Muklanowicz, their little games – are not important after all. *Is there some personal danger of which to beware?*

True, were Tesla to succeed by some miracle in scorching the Ice out of Russia, he would liquidate at a stroke the whole coldiron industry. In any normal country, such a decision would be a question of working out profit and loss, balancing political and economic pressures. But in imperial Russia – Captain Privyzhensky had preached correctly – the emperor's dream prevailed, or Rasputin's holy vision. The samurai sword! And Nikolay had grabbed his pen and ordered from his Serbian namesake holy fire against the gleissen. What then remained to the Sibirkhozheto people and their henchmen, when rational arguments had no influence on the decision-making process?

By whatever means possible, Tesla's carrying out of the tsar's instructions had to be disabled.

Which carriage contains his priceless inventions? Glance towards the back of the train. Behind second class (third class and the cheapest carriages travel according to a different Transsib schedule) came several goods wagons, all boarded up. No one was standing beside them. Squint under the setting Sun. From precisely that direction, from the west – bright radiance hovering above her head, a dark skirt – the fair Christine, yes, for it was she, was clambering up the scree.

Stand up, offer a hand.

'*Merci*.' She was slightly breathless. 'I wanted a word with you, sir, without Nikola…' Spread a large handkerchief on the boulder; she sat down. 'He told me you had saved his life, so perhaps he will listen to you, sir, he has to listen.' An English accent weighed heavily on her German; some words required a moment's thought from Christine, when her forehead puckered and lips protruded. 'You saw what he does to himself.'

Cast away the fag end.

'Benedykt Gierosławski.'

'Ah, and I am – excuse me, Christine Filipov.'

'*Enchanté*.'

'I am very sorry it has to be like this… But I thought the opportunity might never arise. Could you, sir… Nikola seldom lets himself to be torn from his work, pays little attention to people. He talked to you, yes?'

'You mean about his tungetitum dynamo?'

'He attaches himself to it every day. I cannot bear to watch. Please, sir, he is sixty-eight years old! Sometimes it lasts for a quarter of an hour or longer; he cannot tear himself away. Then he talks to himself out loud, describes some sort of fantastical cities; demands to be led by the hand, because he can no longer distinguish those images from reality, loses himself in his imaginings as if in a fog. He even wanted me to wind up the machine. In Prague, he has electric-tungetitum generators, makes use of the city's electrical power plant. I had thought that now, since we have left… Could you appeal to his reason, sir!'

Who exactly is she to Tesla? Is she really the scandalously young paramour whom the Deluxe gossips would have her be? You can't ask directly after all. Indirect questions – 'What a likeness! Surely not his daughter? Granddaughter perhaps?' – would be no less offensive; she would see through them in a twinkling.

There is no likeness.

'You put me in an awkward position…'

'You saved his life!'

'Whatever arguments am I supposed to roll out? Is there anyone who knows better than he about this teslectricity?'

'Oh, he always thinks he knows best about everything!' She shuddered in the cold wind, despite her buttoned-up suit-top. Take off the jacket. Christine wrapped herself in it, crossing her hands over her chest. 'It's just so frustrating,' she said in English. 'I cannot bear the sight, he's really the sweetest man on Earth but…' She sniffed. 'You know, sir,' she continued in German, 'he's been doing it for years. Before, he used to connect himself directly to the electrical current. It's a craving! He says that when he was young, he once looked into a microscope and saw bacilli, how hideous they look when magnified, wanted to show me too; and because we inhale, drink these abominations, are constantly in contact with them – Nikola tries to protect himself from them at all costs. You understand, sir, he treated electric current as a bactericidal remedy. But since his laboratory on South Fifth Avenue burned down – so my mother told me – he began to feed on electricity; often ate no meals at all, just connected himself first thing in the morning to the apparatus. He says it keeps him healthy. Maybe. But now – it's no longer even electricity. I fear for him.'

'I don't know how much he's said about the purpose of this journey…' Pause. She gave an inquiring glance. 'You worry about his health, miss; you should worry rather about his life and yours. How come he brought you with him on this dangerous journey? From the very beginning, he has known what threatens him.'

'As if Nikola thought of himself as mortal man…!' she snorted. 'It was I who made him buy the ticket under a false name. I who chose this very train, on which Byelomishoff is travelling. I who wrote to the Tsar's Own Chancellery and telephoned the Ministry of Internal Affairs.'

'Ah. The Guardian Angel.'

She frowned.

'*Pardonnez-moi.*' Attempt to take her hand, but she conceals it beneath the jacket. 'Mademoiselle Christine, I feel honoured that you have placed so much confidence in me.'

'Don't make fun of me, sir, I know your reputation, maybe Nikola is actually mistaken in you –'

'My reputation!'

'The salon braggart!'

'Agh!'

Christine thought better of it, closed her lips, poised for the next invective. She pouted, now offended.

'Why do you force me, sir, to insult you? Does it afford you pleasure?'

Lean against the angular bed of warm boulder. Lift the face towards the pale constellations.

'Indeed, the stars are already out. The sky has cleared, swift winds blow here. A few hours ago, a few hundred kilometres to the west – on the horizon and along the horizon, a single slow storm still lingered. I awoke in the night, we were crossing a bridge over the Kama, it was already raining, some barges were passing below us, floating timber, long transports, the river was rough, most likely had burst its banks;

lights were burning on the shores, bonfires, lamps, as if signalling to each other through the rain, in the darkness of the night, and lights saluted on the river; the sky could not be seen, a wet blackness, only those flickering stars on land and on water. Were we moving? Sailing? Flying? Then I thought that I had dreamt it. They were signalling to each other.'

'Who exactly are you, Mr Yeroshaski?'

'Have I a reputation, or not?' Turn the head to the left, to the right, to the left. 'Look, miss, beyond the valley, between those summits. There it's already Asia. They say different stars shine above the Land of the Gleissen. Rare the days of clear sky; Winter has sorely mangled the weather. Look, please. Is it not suspended a little lower? You can see the curvature.' Describe an arc in the air. 'It presses, pushes down on the earth, stifling it. The European sky flees from the earth; they repel one another. But there, but here, in Asia – regarde! – a reversal of the poles is taking place – they are attracting. We have a good seat, a central loggia in the theatre of the continents, a view of everything as if it were laid on the palm of our hand. Under the European sky, you can stand upright, take a deep breath, leap without fear, build upwards, stare upwards. The Asian sky seems oppressive even from here, you have to stoop, lower your gaze, bend your spine towards the ground, move with a short careful step, build outward and downward. You see, Christine, how little space there is between the stars and the wilderness.'

'Maybe there are yet more highlands, and that's why.'

'Maybe.'

The devushka smiled hesitatingly. Her smile was ravishing – the cheeks grew round, swelled like two warm apples; a smile she had carried since the cradle.

'You are a poet, Mr Yeroshaski.'

'Au contraire, Mademoiselle, au contraire.'

She glanced around despairingly for a pretext to divert the conversation. She was too young, by a year, two perhaps – still too young.

'They are calling us!' she was relieved.

'Mm-hmm?'

'It seems to be repaired; we travel on.'

Descend to the tracks, help the young lady down the treacherous slope. The provodniks were running about counting passengers, parents were shouting at children, the locomotive was puffing softly. Christine returned the jacket. 'I know to you it seems childish...' She lowered her eyes. Strike the chest. 'I shall speak to Doctor Tesla, I promise.' She nodded her thanks and took cover in the carriage. Making promises to women comes too easily here. Worse still, such promises tend to be kept. Maybe she really is Tesla's Guardian Angel, removing the stumbling blocks from before his feet, since the doctor himself notices them not – or maybe merely playing at being Guardian Angel, and Tesla indulges her whims, old men have a weakness for naïve –

An unshaven stripling suddenly sprang over the coupling between carriages, catching his foot in the slack chain; the chain rattled loudly like a ship's bell. He stopped beside the staircase erected below the entrance to the Deluxe carriage.

A provodnik rightly identified him from afar as a lower-class passenger and took a determined stride towards him. The maltchik, however, paid no attention.

'Gospodin Gierosławski!'

Button up the jacket.

'What do you want?' Growl at him sharply, instinctively masking the sudden fear.

'Alight not in Yekaterinburg!'

'I'm travelling farther. What concern is it of yours, where –'

'Leave not the train! They've bin plotting against ya!'

'What? Who?'

'Cos you're in the pay of Ottepyelniks, they be sure of it.'

The maltchik sprang closer still, straining wide his bulging eyes; something sparkled in the left and began to pulsate, a black artery within a black pupil; he was terrified, awe-struck by his own fear. Try to thrust him off – but he grabs a wrist. His fingers were ice-cold, their touch almost scalding.

'We canna protect Your Esteemed Nobleness, no time were there, I couldna make 'em see. Get not outa the train.'

He crossed himself from right to left, instinctively pressing a cold-iron medallion to his livid lips.

'Preserve us in Thy care, we surrender to Thee, preserve us in Thy care.'

The provodnik seized him by the collar, but the youngling wriggled from his grip and ran off, immediately turning a corner behind the carriage. The provodnik threatened him with his fist.

'Tphoo, the pest, claws his way up to his betters and brings only shame – the youth of today – not a groschen of respect –'

'Wait, listen.' Stuff a banknote into his uniform pocket. 'Have a quiet word with the second-class attendants and find out who he is.'

'I already –'

'But secretly, my good man, secretly, on tiptoe, so the birdie won't take fright.' Mount the stairs. 'How much are we delayed?'

'Three hours, three and a quarter, Your Highly Esteemed Nobleness, but we'll be stopping for longer still in Yekaterinburg, have to switch engines and inspect the undercarriage.'

'Longer? How much longer?'

'For as long as it takes. Your lordship cares to visit the city? Yekaterinburg for sure is still in the grip of winter; last time, a bleeding icer was sat in the very heart of the Old Town. Well. All aboard! All aboard, please! We're about to depart!'

On the Yekaterinburg frost

Flakes of snow, silver needles, sugar crystals were falling from the sky, flickering playfully in the haloes of gas lamps. The station clocks showed two in the morning – in Yekaterinburg, it was already four, but all Imperial railways function according to Saint Petersburg and Moscow time. Before long the summer Sun will rise over the snowbound city – the night, however, belongs exclusively to Winter. A large crowd was milling nonetheless on one of the tall passenger platforms; locals mingled with travellers streaming from the carriages: touts for drivers and station porters, vendors of furs, vendors of amulets against gleissen and nuggets of tungetitum known as blacktungets (no doubt fake), babushkas proffering cabbage pirozhki in their loud sing-song cry, likewise lamb tcheburyeki; but the nimble maltchiks measuring oryeshki by the potful, very cheap and very flavoursome, created the greatest bustle. The provodniks invested little heart and effort in symbolic attempts to control the chaos – similar scenes were enacted at almost every station stop of the Trans-Siberian Express. On the other hand, the late hour had reduced the energy of the passengers; the majority travelling in Deluxe decided to sleep through Yekaterinburg. Monsieur Verousse, who took seriously his reporter's duties, alighted, as did the elderly man with the artificial eye and the prodigal Moravian brothers, as well as the French family with children from carriage number one; the latter immediately embarked on a jaunt around the city. A stop was announced of at least two hours. Some passengers were probably planning to call at the Orthodox cathedral for the late Sunday service; not all perhaps had given up, despite the delay. Snow, neither thick nor heavy, danced merrily in the yellow lights, settling softly on the wooden boards of the platform, on the recently erected station building made of Urals marble, on people's caps, shubas and greatcoats, on the warm carapace of the locomotive, silent now and holding its engine breath.

Fasten the warm sable-collared overcoat, pull on the gloves, step down onto the platform. A tout leaped up. Dismiss him impatiently.

'Time to stretch the legs?'

Look around. Ünar Tayyib Fessar.

'You want to take a look at Yekaterinburg? There's nothing interesting here, just one more paltry industrial townlet on a river; in decline now thanks to the Transsib and Zimny Nikolayevsk.' Thrusting his cane under his arm, he reached into his breast pocket and extracted two cigars from their case. 'Will you have a cigar, Benedykt, sir? Partagas, straight from Mexico.'

'Ah, thank you, thank you.'

He took out his penknife, snipped the coils of tobacco. Lit up. Light up too.

'Forgive me for asking, sir – but you don't seem to me like a fortune hunter, *un tricheur*, I don't believe these stories. I have a nephew not much younger… Was it a joke? A wager perhaps? Let me guess: tragically in love with a lady of high birth.'

Pull a wry face without uttering a word.

'What?' the trader raised his eyebrows, amused. 'A young gentleman who believes not in love?'

'It interferes with my other bad habits.'

Fessar laughed.

'Good one! I shall remember it. But seriously?'

'It was seriously.'

He cast a swift glance, no longer smiling.

'Aphorisms aren't meant to be lived, but to amuse company at table.'

Bow slightly.

'That one's even better.'

Sighing resignedly, he averted his eyes and pointed with his cane to the south, beyond the station.

'No doubt, sir, you wish to see a gleiss with your own eyes.'

'I am from Warsaw.'

'Ah, yes.' The Turk stroked the smooth mahogany dome of his skull. 'They've probably already reached Odessa. Mm-hmm.'

Set off at a leisurely pace out of the station towards the pale scattered lights of the city. Fessar attached himself without a word. A babushka holding a wide basket covered in white rag came tottering up, Ünar Tayyib purchased a stuffed roll. Wrapped it in a handkerchief and tucked it in the pocket of his voluminous fur coat.

Rotating on his hoof, he walked backwards for a while examining the footprints in the shallow snow; wherever frozen clay replaced boards and cobbles, he poked it several times with the heel of his Cossack boot, and even whacked it with his hefty cane.

'Mm-hmm, mm-hmm.' He emitted smoke along the tongue protruding over his lower lip, voluptuously licking up at the same time a few sparks of frost. 'I am curious as to whether anyone's been drilling bore-holes recently. And how is it with you? In Warsaw?'

'Pardon?'

'The soil, whether you've been checking the soil.' He jabbed with his cane at a hard furrow of mud. 'Our parley over cards has given me pause for thought. That calculation about the speed of the Ice. And other things.' He raised his eyes to the clouds. Yekaterinburg lay in a valley, the saddle of the Urals, at the Great Stone gates; on a clear night, shadow over the western constellations should indicate the boundary of the mountain chain. The Turk pointed to the left, towards the eastern horizon, dark, devoid of light. 'Maybe you'll take a ride over Shartash; in summer, it used to be a very pleasant lake. But for several years now, ice has never left it; there the frost is hardest. Ye-es, it travels via the soil, the perpetual permafrost. As Pobedonostseff's savages or the gentlemen geologists hired wholesale by Sibirkhozheto will tell you, it travels along black underground rivers, the Ways of the Mammoths. After all a single gleiss, even several stronger pockets of cold – won't alter the climate.

'Via the soil, very likely, yes, in Warsaw there was trouble with the waterpipes; roadworks also dragged on…'

Pass a solitary droshky waiting for the next passengers from the delayed Express; the driver was quaffing from a bottle concealed in a shapeless mitten. A gendarme standing guard beneath the station eaves cast envious glances at the peasant.

'Here the ice comes and goes, a warm month, a cold month – and yet it's closer to the Land of the Ice than your Warsaw. What is it that attracts it to some cities, whilst repelling it from others?'

'Bah!'

From the wide road running parallel to the railway tracks, two branches diverged at an angle, the left leading directly towards the few lights burning in second- and third-floor windows of buildings in the centre of Yekaterinburg. All houses visible from the street near the station were constructed of wood, designed as elongated rectangles. They more resembled outsized cottages than noble manors, not to mention the townhouses of Warsaw; low, slanting, they seemed half-buried in the shallow drifts. Wide shutters were slammed tight. Snow clung to chinks and crevices, settling on the sloping roofs in tiered layers, whilst a feeble wind dragged it into alleys and passages between dwellings.

Walk in silence.

'Benedykt, sir, why keep glancing around? Have you agreed to meet someone?' Fessar smiled with ambiguous irony. 'I am imposing on you – please just say it – I am imposing.'

A sudden thought: it's him, him, the deuced Turk, of course! he came out, waited, attached himself unasked; under that fur coat he could have two hunting rifles, a dozen bayonets, and how he smiles, it's him, him!

'You're looking quite poorly, sir.' Fessar stood still. 'It's not so very cold.' He looked closely. 'You're very pale. Your hand is shaking.'

Lower at once the cigar hand. Make off with the eyes – there: a small group of men with coarse ugly mugs, no doubt workers from some ironworks, are marching shoulder to shoulder, exchanging loud remarks, a crude genre scene – stare at them, not at the Turk, trying to give nothing away.

But he stood his ground:

'Here, by the Iset river, there's an entirely respectable restaurant in a hotel, and if you'll allow me to invite you, sir, to a very early breakfast, we would have a chance to talk privately, away from prying eyes and ears, which in truth is never possible aboard the train.'

'About what?' inquire sharply.

The Turk winced, facial sinews standing out under his skin as after some great exertion; he adjusted the cigar in his mouth, massaged the back of his head.

'They may prattle about ghosts and other figments of the imagination, but I have been in this business for years, I live in the City of Ice, I have seen the Tchyornoye Siyaniye and radiance of the Cathedral of Christ the Saviour; you may have tungetitum on you, pure or as a carbon coolbond, but who carries his own samovar to Tula, who?' Fessar gathered momentum, gesticulating with cigar and cane with ever greater zeal, no longer bored, oh no, speaking as a different man: 'And why these secrets, the false name, whilst Prince Blutsky-Osey is travelling allegedly to meet the Japanese – a well-known Ottepyelnik, and since he insults you so publicly, you must be thick with the Lyednyaks, so as not to vex Sibirokhozheto, because they'll be the first to take fright, well, but then it's an opportunity, a sin not to take advantage, ooph, so where are you rushing off to now, because –'

A sudden scream cut through the Yekaterinburg frost – the fitful rattle of a man in his death throes – the scream and rattle; a man was dying amidst the snowy night.

Glance between houses. There's movement in the shadows – a human form – low down – the black shape rises and falls. Take a step closer. For a moment, the visage of a dark-eyed youngling flows into the snowy brightness – *Preserve us in Thy care!* – wide-open mouth and smudge of dirt on his cheek, very pale. His arm rose and fell with a stone clasped in the fist, as he smashed the skull of a man splayed on the ground.

A penetrating whistle rang out. The whack of wood. Keel around. Ünar Tayyib Fessar, taut as a bow-string, teeth clenched on the cigar, his fur coat dishevelled, was taking a double-handed swipe from above his head with the heavy cane. Should he strike his target, bones would shatter. The frosty air was riven afresh, this time from rifle fire: the first of the workers collapsed in the middle of the street, face down on the ice. A second swerved to avoid the Turk's cane. They were carrying knives. Another shot fell. Spin around on the spot like a puppet on a stick, always one rotation behind. The cutthroats fled, tripping over their own feet, into the darkness of an alley; the last looked back in terror and rage – at the gateway of a house on the far side of the street.

Run towards that gate, feet tearing off the ground. A man in a yellow greatcoat rushed to escape.

The street was wide, deserted. Snow fell silently, snow upon snow. Run through the alien city shrouded in darkness: bolted doors, latched shutters, no living soul, a lone streetlamp at a junction, the junction also deserted; nothing but the rustle of wind, crunch of permafrost under the boots, and rasping breath. Chase after the man in the yellow greatcoat.

The street was as straight as the man flew, but stretched over hills, undulating up and down; he would disappear and reappear over the crest of a rise. Fear that he might turn off somewhere to the side, hide in the shadows – but no, he was racing directly ahead of him, seldom even glancing back; he had a definite goal, was not fleeing blindly.

Realise, as the temperature drops so low that the rasping breath turns to a stifling cough and frost screws its way like a threaded icicle into the throat – that the man in the yellow greatcoat was running farther, headlong into the embrace of the Ice.

Along the length of the embankment boulevard, a few streetlamps were burning, a yellow glimmer likewise drifting from the depth of an intersecting street; the sparkle of ice pierced the falling snow and twilight of the summer-winter dawn. A gleiss was freezing its way across the boulevard from building to building, astride three black spiderlegs of glazed matter, suspended at the height of the second floor. Snowy stalagspikes were springing up from the cobbles; the air was atremble, mangled by unearthly chills. Miraculously transparent icicles dangled below the glacius like a crystal beard, an upturned wheatfield of glass.

The man in the yellow greatcoat ran headlong into that ice. In a moment he'll exceed the bounds of human cold, death even to a hibernik – now it's perfectly clear – he must be a Martsynian who's fallen short of expectations – his one salvation – now, soon – is slipping away.

Wrench the Grossmeister from under the overcoat, unravel the rolls of varnished canvas and velvet, rag and oilskin, raise the weapon to eye level. Align the two-forked stinger of the scorpion with the lizard's horn. Press the icy coils of the snake; the palm flinched not – it was too cold – finger and all, it had frozen to the snake's tail.

Yellow coat – reptile horn – stinger – pupil. Hold the breath? Close the other eye? Won't the recoil shatter the wrist? Where to shoot – at leg, arm, so long as he's stopped? Pull on the viper's tail.

The Grossmeister erupted with cold. The entire right arm, from the gloved fingers to the shoulder, was benumbed. Cry out. Frost or fire, there's no difference – same pain, opposite trajectory. The right hand was plunged into a furnace of cold. A black afterimage still pulsated neath the eyelids, imprint of the unlicht's glare, as the report rang out and the tungetitum bullet hit the ground, struck the ice at the feet of the fleeing Martsynian. Missed, obviously. The cry was snuffed out in the frozen throat; bend over double, coughing. The Grossmeister fell not from the palm, since it had frozen to the glove, which had frozen to the skin. No feeling was there in the right hand; it drooped like a lump of dead wood, an unwieldy prosthesis.

Now the man in the yellow greatcoat was screaming. Raise the head. The tungetitum shell had exploded as Ice shrapnel, engulfing everything within a radius of a few metres in a wave of black cold. Long tongues of filthy permafrost jutted out of the hole shot in the ground, like the gigantic petals of a tulip-cup of razors. Fresh snow lifted off the street, shards of stone, mud, clay, gravel – had frozen in a split second into an intricate sculpture, an expressionist artwork suspended above the tulip on geometric strings of icicles, as if forced violently into the sky from the innards of that thrust-open bloom. Ice dust still glittered all around as loose clots of frozen detritus sank back to earth.

The man in the yellow greatcoat was stranded at the edge of the stricken area; the ice had not devoured him. It had shackled his legs as far as the knees, pierced his hip with a long icicle, pinned down his shoulders with a spiralling petal-blade of glazed matter, torn off a hand and coated his face in black hoar – but it had not devoured him. The man was screaming. Of the yellow greatcoat, only scraps remained.

Breathe into the sable collar so that no frost could flow directly into the lungs; slowly now, at a measured pace, a single breath for a single thought. He was screaming, capable therefore of speech. Approach the frozen man, pressing the limp arm into the side.

He was moving his head, the black hoar peeling in slivers off his neck; he jerked on his ice-stake cracking the frost on his eyelids – the Martsynian opened his eyes. He stared.

'Let me go!'

'Tell me, and I'll let you go.'

He shook his head.

'From cold to cold; for out of cold wast thou taken, and unto cold shalt thou return, frigid be the Lord God, from cold to cold –'

Step closer. The blast had struck him from behind and from the right. The Martsynian hung on that crooked icicle as on a tilted roasting-spit, a mediaeval pike; feet locked in ice but surely not touching the ground, a lump of earth twisting his spine at an impossible angle; he looked as if his neck were broken. The severed hand was nowhere to be seen. A small shred of yellow fabric had frozen below his shoulder.

Point with the left hand towards the eastern horizon, above the roofs of the city.

'Sunshine will soon appear. The gleiss is moving in the opposite direction. You'll melt, little brother.'

He tried to spit; saliva froze on his lips.

'Indeed?' Snarl at him. 'Is that how it'll be? Then rest in peace!' Turn away.

He burst into sobs.

'Forsake me not! I'll tell, tell! All I know – khrr – our most frigid father in Perm guberniya bade the brothers be vigilant, such and such a Polish gentleman, name of Venyedikt – khrr – Filipovitch Yeroslavsky will be travelling in the Siberian Express, and cannot get there, let me go!'

'And you obey these fathers of yours.'

'Sire!'

'And had I not left the train, what then?'

'But you left, you left, though we expected it not – O Most Immaculate Mother, if only you'd not left…!'

'Is it true your sole patriarch is Grigory Yefimovitch Rasputin?'

'Sire! Let me go!'

'So, tell me: are they waiting for me too in cities farther on? and in the train itself? is there someone? and why such hatred towards me, eh?'

'How should I know what's in other cities, let me go! What's in the train! For me it's the father's word, ice on heart, the most merciful, let me go!'

'But for what reason, there must be a reason!'

'You know which!' The Martsynian peered furtively from under the black hoar caking his eyelashes. Emaciated, his complexion savaged and discoloured by former frostbites, with several days' growth on sunken cheeks, he was like a caricature of a Sybirak convict; he lacked but the shackles. Now he was bound by fetters harder than iron. 'You yourself know best of all, khrr. Ottepyelnik plague: Trotskyite or Narodnik, anarchist or Petersburg Westerniser, or other revolutionary, but with only one thing in your heads: unfreeze, unfreeze, unfreeze our Russia.'

'What?'

'Let me go!'

'Are you hinting I want to…?'

'Wherefore then you going to the holy land? You're all the same! Fire in our eyes! But God's sent Russia the gleissen. So, kill the gleissen! Kill our Tsar-Batyushka! Destroy the country! You're all the same!'

'By Christ's holy passion, what are you blathering?!'

'G-gun in his hand fires ice, yet still he denies it, Russocide!' He jerked again. Were anger to truly burn with living fire, then the Martsynian would have melted clean through the glazed matter. 'They're waiting! The Devil be with you!'

Glance around at the street. This conversation will lead nowhere. The left hand carefully relieved the right of the Grossmeister. Return for the canvas and velvet...

'Let me go!' yelled the Martsynian. 'You said you'd let me go!'

Pick up the pieces of cloth, rewrap the revolver.

'Don't you know a lie when you hear one?'

More and more lights were burning in windows – wherever the Grossmeister's report and the Martsynian's screams had carried. Streets in Yekaterinburg intersect at right angles, the city having been built on an eighteenth-century grid; even the bridge spanning the City Pond on the Iset river was the direct extension of a street. In this direction – the bridge; in that – the station. Hide the Grossmeister, set off northwards at a brisk pace, massaging the benumbed arm. Thank God for this frost, otherwise some worthy townsman, roused from his sleep, would surely have bestirred himself to investigate the cause of the night-time racket. The Martsynian continued to scream.

Pause at the top of a hilly street, glance over the shoulder. Snow had not ceased falling; the first rays of the rising Sun were diffused by flakes swirling in the air, silver needles, sugar crystals. Blue shafts of light blossomed all around the gleiss and icy bowl of the crater, the crown of icicles surrounding it and the man hanging from it – throbbing in the radiance of the wintry summer dawn. Clouds were moving across the firmament; the window onto the sun closed momentarily and the shafts were extinguished; then they unfurled afresh – for a shorter time – for longer – for shorter... Tides of day broke upon the shallow shelf of night. The whole of Yekaterinburg was overlaid in white, covered in nothing but flat white surfaces, as if someone had set down a cardboard cut-out of pure white in the shape of a city, in lieu of a city; whilst under this sun, the card came to life, and white gave birth to colour. Even the gleiss radiated warmer hues; coldiron rainbows swam over branch-es of its asymmetrical permafrost. Except for the man in the yellow greatcoat: the more the warm light touched his face and waves of day broke over his black hoar, the greater the terror he bawled out. When, eventually, the ice slips from his shoulders and the Martsynian feels the wound of his severed limb – when the ice releases the Martsynian and the blocks of ice hanging above him tumble on the nape of his neck –

March at a brisk pace towards the station.

Ünal Tayyib Fessar stood over the cutthroat's corpse, leaning against a wheel of the empty droshky and smoking his cigar.

'Oh!' He spat out the smoke. 'Didn't they run after you?'

'Who?'

'The prince's men.'

Glimpse the droshky driver in the alleyway. He was shining a hand-held lantern for a gendarme, who was bent over the body with the smashed skull. Snow was falling on blood spilled in the snow.

'We should return to the train. The local police might try to detain us.'

'Mm-hmm?'

'As witnesses in the case.'

The Turk gazed with unhealthy curiosity.

'Councillor Dushin has it in hand. What happened to your arm, Benedykt? Are you wounded?'

'Councillor Dushin?'

'I tell you, sir, it was the prince's men.'

'Who?'

Fessar was alarmed.

'Come, come, it really would be better to return to the train. Please –'

'There's nothing wrong with me!' Spurn the businessman's hand. 'Why so Dushin?'

'But who shot them? I mean, the one lying here? Prince Blutsky's people.'

Glance again inside the alley. The gendarme was searching the corpse's pockets.

'No, not him,' said the Turk. 'And even if, they'll not admit it, an exceptionally ugly sight. Let's go.'

Shudder.

'Who –'

'But I see you can hardly stand. In fact, he could drive us, our superintendent genius can cope on his own, one moment –'

'No!'

'So, let's walk, let's walk.'

Retrace the earlier steps. Whom had the prince's servants been chasing? The boy with the black eyes? The remaining cutthroats? Probably.

'Sibirkhozheto will do anything to hold onto its monopoly,' Ünal Tayyib lowered his voice, staring in front of him and down at his feet. 'When Thyssen tried to set up a coldmill on a nest by the Danube, four fires burst into bloom, one after the other, till the gleissen dispersed and retreated. You need protectors. The prince is travelling to Vladivostock;

what arrangements did you make with him? Upon whom can you count there on the spot? Who's putting up the money? Who owns the shares? We could help you. Let us say exclusive rights to the new deposits and coldmills for India, Asia Minor and Africa for twenty-five years. What? Let it be fifteen years. Guarantees on the spot, and I open a letter of credit for a hundred thousand within an hour of arrival in Irkutsk, my word will suffice. What? *Je suis homme d'affaires*. Benedykt, sir.'

'I have no idea what you're talking about.'

'Just like you had no idea that they were waiting for you here, eh? I'm not blind after all, you well-nigh leapt out of your skin – and wherefore rush under the knife? Was that your agreement with Councillor Dushin? That you'd be the bait, and the prince's people would shoot them? Was that what the theatre was all about yesterday at dinner? Of no avail now. Just look at it, sir: Madame Blutfeld and our writer journalist are already gossiping, the station guard has blabbed everything, the street seemed empty, but a moment later the whole staff know. We'll say some gang tried to rob us, but it won't hold up for long – two corpses... or maybe three?'

'Two.'

'Two. You should not have left the compartment, sir, why go there?'

Sit for a moment on a station bench. The passengers remonstrating with the provodniks and a brawny droshky driver in the light of the platform lamps were fortunately not looking in this direction. A wave of snow stood in the air crosswise over the tracks, a crinkly curtain of cold. Had the shots been heard on the station? Were any of these people driving down that street? Had the gendarme come running of his own accord, or was he too summoned by Dushin? Fessar is right, it makes no difference, there's no way to stifle gossip.

'But you are wounded. I'll wake Doctor Konyeshin.'

'No!' Stand up. 'It's no wound. I'll be all right in a moment.'

'Why did you go there, why?'

The Turk shook his head.

'You won't understand... no one will understand... It cannot be told...' Try, obviously, despite this. 'I ought not to have gone. I was warned. I had no reason to go. All reasons were against.'

Fessar entered the carriage first and helped with climbing the stairs. Lean back against the corridor wall.

'I have been wondering why that name keeps hammering at my memory.' Ünal Tayyib reached mechanically for his watch, glanced absent-mindedly at the face. 'Another hour at least. And it's only now – when I was thinking about the maps circulating in the Land of the Gleissen – no, not Grochowski's – yet many Polish exiles work in these lands. Something must have landed in my hands – a map? A report?

perhaps a patent? Gierosławski, yes? Gierosławski. There was that geologist – with Krupp? Zhiltsoff? And of late, I believe, also on the wanted lists. Some notorious affair, and religious too. That is why, correct?'

Answer him not.

'That is why,' he whispered. 'Brother? Father? Some other relative? He discovered a method, at last.' The Turk put away the extinguished cigar, pulled on his gloves. 'No need to say anything, sir, now I understand, I understand.'

What had he understood? Clench the teeth. In such pain, it was impossible to think straight. Besides the Turk expected no answer.

'But that your ticket was paid for by the tsarist Ministry of Winter! That had me baffled. Politics, I thought to myself. And here Prince Blutsky-Osey bursts onto the scene. Well, yes indeed! The Ministry of Winter has been stuffed from the start with Ottepyelniks. Von Zielke. Rappacki. Whilst Pobedonostseff in turn has to pay the Lyednyaks, even if he'd rather not. And so, it goes round and round in circles –'

'Forgive me, sir, I have to –'

'*Hay hay, olur.*' He bowed and stepped aside, making way in the narrow corridor. He stood there a while longer leaning on his cane, in his heavy furs, like the silhouette of an old bear.

Struggle for a long time with the stiffened fingers of the left hand before finding the keyhole.

The door to the compartment, however, was open.

'Come in, please.'

He was sitting on the chair by the window. Had drawn the curtains – black suit and shadow in lieu of a face, bowler hat on knees, this much was visible. Memories came back of the tchinovniks of Winter, the first image of them blurring the pupils just after waking. Never a by-your-leave before they enter; theirs is the power.

'Shut the door.'

Switch on the light.

Pavel Vladimirovitch Fogel blinked and adjusted the pince-nez on his nose.

'Shut the door, Gospodin Yeroslavsky, my time is limited, please listen. I am told it would be better to leave you in ignorance, but that would not be honest. It is our –'

Slump onto the bedding. Head struck the boiserie. The silver-haired okhrannik frowned.

'Our task is to protect Doctor Tesla and his apparatuses. We received information that Lyednyaks had placed another man at the last minute amongst the Deluxe passengers. Somehow, they got wind of the fact we had nailed Vazoff. We dealt with Vazoff on day one; things went not to plan and we're immensely grateful, sir, for your intervention; in this manner, however, you've exposed yourself to danger.' Fogel leaned over the bed. 'Are you listening? We know not why you are so necessary to Winter, and know not what links you to His Highness. But we do know that the Lyednyaks see you now as a threat, no less a threat than Doctor Tesla. But our task is to protect Doctor Tesla and his apparatuses. You understand what I'm saying?'

'I am a marked man.'

'Maybe I shouldn't have. Act as you think fit. Now you know. It could be any of them.'

'Any and none and all at –'

'What?'

'Tsssss. Tell me, Fogel. Why the Lyednyaks? What do I… Khrr.'

'And your business with Winter? Why are you going there?'

'My father, Winter told me he talks to gleissen.'

'Ah! And you're surprised? At court too, they read Berdyaeff. I am a functionary of state order, sir, not appointed to rectify History. I pray not to the Ice. But there are those that do, on this side and on that.'

'That has no –'

'What's wrong, sir? Are you feeling all right?'

He stood up, leant over solicitously; the electric light turned his silver hair to gold. Someone's face – a familiar face – with aquiline nose and black moustache, contorted in great suffering, was reflected in the lenses of his pince-nez. He stretched out a hand. Curl up in the plaid.

'Gospodin Yeroslavsky?'

Shivering made plain speech impossible.

'Mel-mel-melt-ing.'

His exit went unnoticed, the departure from Yekaterinburg station unobserved. Lie unconscious in chill-induced fever when, shortly afterwards, the Express crossed the Siberian frontier; when, after two thousand and seventy-eight kilometres, the train passed the pillar marking the frontier – that totem of tsarist power over Europe and Asia, covered in farewell inscriptions, prayers and denunciations in many languages, as well as hundreds of Russian, Polish, Jewish, German and Arabic names: by this pillar the kibitkas once stopped, and families let go the exiles. Lie unconscious as in the organism Ottepyel triumphed over Lyod, and blood flowed again into the cold right hand. Dream of breaking ice floes, gushing streams of thaw and the Sun rising over the continents, dream – until the Sun really had risen, and it was summer.

CHAPTER THE FOURTH

On forty-seven half-murderers and two would-be investigators

Victory was hers, as she rotated a teaspoon on the tablecloth through ninety degrees. The combined forces of three porcelain mugs paralysed the butterdish. Tumblers and shot glasses fell before the bread basket; the brave charge of a vase with its bouquet of fresh flowers immobilised the ironclads built of metal plates. A knife sank in a quagmire of jam. Sunlight fell on the serviettes; the shadow of the salt cellar indicated the left corner of the table. Reserves of cold-meat dishes failed to materialise. The bread was white, fine-grained. It remained to surrender the salad.

Go to breakfast before the provodnik announced the meal, so as to pre-empt and avoid the remaining passengers. Turn shame to momentary advantage, whilst a different imperative demands the same behaviour: to lie low, keep the head down, bide the time. Because – *it could be any of them.* Choose the middle course, since it's impossible to tell which should be the most feared. The middle course, action along the path of least resistance, compromise choices – then we do not do all the more what we want to do; things happen of their own accord.

Sit at an empty table, nod to the steward. He pointed to the clock. Lean a shoulder against the window frame; early-morning sun flowed in warm waves from behind the back straight off the green plains, more far-reaching here than the blue firmament. Bogdanovitch had already been left behind, the Express should reach Tyumen before noon; the engine driver was trying to make up for the delay. The metal fittings of the dining-car door began to jangle. Look up. Miss Muklanowicz.

She smiled conspiratorially. From her own compartment, she must have heard the footsteps and rattle of the lock, there's no hiding from her. Yawning discreetly, she squinted in the sunshine flooding the empty dining car.

Naturally, she sat down at the same table. Kiss her hand.

'Where's your esteemed Auntie?'

'Auntie's feeling unwell.'

'Oh, I hope nothing serious.'

Miss Muklanowicz continued to smile. Remember that smile: mischievous imps in the eyes, mischievous imps at the corner of her mouth. She was scrupulously smoothing a serviette. An evil foreboding swelled within like a bubble of putrid gas.

She basketed her hands in front of her, fingertips touching.

'At dawn, I bumped into Frau Blutfeld.'

'I won't even ask.'

'You underestimate yourself, Benedykt. Alibaba needed forty thieves.'

'For pity's sake!'

'Whereas I was trying to help you, so you don't waste away in solitude, poor fellow. And lend courage before the prince. But you duped us all!'

'All right, I shall ask. So, what's that dreadful woman putting about now?'

'You, sir, have already been a count,' Jelena was adding up on her skinny fingers. 'A count, a drawing room knave, now you show yourself to be a nocturnal brawler, a bloodthirsty thug. Who are you really?'

Close the eyes.

'Just as you said.'

'Mm-hmm?'

'One tenth each. All at the same time.'

'You don't say.'

'But how can we know such things? You listen to other people, repeat what they say about you. Or listen to your own reveries and dreams. Count, brawler, philanderer, be my guest. Whatever you choose, miss. We are travellers, know nothing of each other, who'll defend us from trusting in gossip?'

'Gossip,' she began to hum. 'Gossip. Gossip.'

Raise the left eyelid.

'What?'

'Frau Blutfeld's gossip is no match for the truth.' She shook her index finger reproachfully. 'I know, I know, there's no denying it, Benedykt. You hatched the whole intrigue with Prince Blutsky; in Yekaterinburg blood was shed, it's all Saint Petersburg games, yes, yes.'

Make the sign of the cross with a vigorous sweep.

'As God is my witness, Jelena, the day before yesterday, on Saturday, was the first time I set eyes on Prince Blutsky; of Russian politics I know nothing at all, and I'm about as suited to street brawls as Frau Blutfeld is to the ballet! Oh, my hands are still trembling. Some drunken brigands attacked us, Mr Fessar can testify to it, local hoodlums, it was a miracle that the prince's men were nearby, otherwise I'd be riding in my coffin, well why are you making such eyes!'

'What lies you tell, sir!' Jelena Muklanowicz was enraptured and almost put her hands together in prayer. 'What lies you tell!'

Grind the teeth.

'Whereas you, miss, devil take it, have been reading too many crass romances and –'

'The train was not moving.'

'What?'

'The train was not moving.' She leant across the table, marble-white hand pressing the jabot into her chest. 'We were standing at the station. It was the middle of the night, so deathly quiet you could hear a pin drop.' She lowered her voice to a whisper. 'I was not asleep. I heard every word.'

'What are you –'

'"Our task is to protect Doctor Tesla and his apparatuses".'

'Oh God!'

'"It could be any of them".'

Cover the face with the hands.

Miss Muklanowicz began to giggle.

Groan quietly.

'Help.'

'Will you have club breakfast, or choose from the à la carte?'

'Please, please,' Jelena smiled at the steward.

Crockery appeared on the table, a highly polished samovar, juglets of milk, a bowl of fruit. Miss Muklanowicz, head slightly inclined, gazing out from under black eyelashes, began to toy with a dessert apple. Observe her through the fingers of the left hand, upon which the weight of the lifeless head now rested. The devushka was singing something under her breath, the sparky imp bouncing from her eyes to the ruby on her neck and back again. Sticking out the tip of her tongue with great deliberation, she set down the rosy apple between the samovar and the sugar basin, on a line dividing crosswise the eight-seater dining table. Glance at the apple, at the young woman, at the table, at the apple. She was waiting. Select a buttered roll from the basket and place it at the same distance on the opposite side of the samovar. Jelena pressed the back of her hand to her red lips. After reflecting a moment, she shifted the neighbouring place-setting, opening up a white plain of tablecloth on her left flank. Respond with a general rearrangement of the cutlery. Jelena, charmingly puffing out her cheek, positioned the water carafe in the centre of the stream of sunrays, casting blue-green rainbows onto her section of the table. Tug at the moustache, bite the nails. Salt cellar, all hope rested with the salt cellar.

No one knows the rules of the game, yet the game is played. Glance at Miss Muklanowicz with unconcealed suspicion. Was this merely the next overreaction of a nervy girl, or was she well aware of what she was up to? Perhaps it was not just this removed-from-life episode, the journey in the Transsib lasting a few days – but her whole life that she played like this. No one knows the rules of the game, yet the game is played. And so, wisdom is gained that cannot be gained in any other way. We are born – we know not why. We grow up – we know not to what end. We die – we know not wherefore. Chess has its rules, blizzarder has its rules, even court intrigues are governed by their own principles – but what are the precepts for life? Who wins at it, who loses, what are the criteria for victory or defeat? A knife is for cutting, a clock – for measuring time, a train – for transporting goods and passengers; but wherefore man? No one knows the rules of the game, yet the game is played. In relation to this game, all other games are childish simplifications verging on fraud, stupefying exercises in the mechanical dexterity of the mind. And yet the game is real. Its rules and aims remain obscure – conclusions may be reached solely in the course of the playing itself; only then do they manifest themselves, in our own moves. There is no umpire. You lose, you win – but whence and wherefore this certainty, you won't be able to express in any speech of men. The salt cellar checkmates the mustard pot. No one knows the rules of the game, yet the game is played.

Victory was hers, as she rotated a teaspoon on the tablecloth through ninety degrees. The combined forces of three porcelain mugs paralysed the butterdish. Tumblers and shot glasses fell before the bread basket; the brave charge of a vase with its bouquet of fresh flowers immobilised the ironclads built of metal plates. A knife sank in a quagmire of jam. Sunlight fell on the serviettes; the shadow of the salt cellar indicated the left corner of the table. Reserves of cold-meat dishes failed to materialise. The bread was white, fine-grained. It remained to surrender the salad.

Miss Muklanowciz accepted her triumph in silence. Said nothing as she ate. Calmly consumed her herbal tea, dabbed her lips with a serviette. Averted her gaze not once. Her smile fed on the sunshine illuming it, a true *perpetuum mobile*, joy in response to worry, joy in response to irritation, joy in response to indifference – it was impossible to remain indifferent. She raised and lowered her little finger in time to the music of the train, took-took-took-TOOK. Begin subconsciously to rap the tabletop with the knuckles, in counterpoint to her rhythm. She merely smiled more broadly, the continuation of the same game. Understand it now – from the first fleeting encounter, earlier even, from the brief glance that night, when the okhranniks were checking passengers' documents in the corridor – whether she even realised is doubtful. No one knows the rules of the game, and yet.

'Thank you.'

Get up from the table. The steward pulled back her chair. Open the door.

In the passageway, she suddenly stopped.

'So, we're commencing.'

'Commencing…?'

'The investigation.'

'Investigation.' Echo her dully.

'I've drawn up a list. Discounting the children and passengers who got in after Moscow, we have forty-five suspects.'

'You've drawn up a list.'

'It's obvious. We know that one of the Deluxe-class passengers is a murderer. The question is: who?'

'They've not murdered anyone yet.'

'Ah! Which makes the riddle all the harder! You must tell me everything exactly, sir. Doctor Tesla is that tall elderly man you were talking to yesterday evening after cards, true? But that little blonde woman, whom I saw you with during the evening stop?'

'You, miss, have been reading too many six-kopeck *Sherlock Holmeses* and *Adventures of Police Agents*.'

For greater effect, Miss Muklanowicz tried to stand with arms akimbo, but the corridor was too narrow; she contented herself by folding them over her bosom.

'And you, Benedykt, sir, what have you got against Sherlock Holmes?'

'Apart from his being an unreal detective solving unreal crimes? Nothing.'

'So, share your experience, sir, in solving real –'

'Quiet.'

The provodnik bowed and stepped closer. He glanced questioningly at the young woman. Motion with the hand. He bent over, pressing his lips to the ear, hot breath scorching the lobe.

'Your lordship wished to know about that boy in second class…' he broke off.

Reach with trembling hand for the pocketbook, fish out a banknote.

'He's called Mefody Karpovitch Pyelka,' the provodnik rattled off. 'Bunk seven top-left in the fourth car second class.'

'Where's he disembarking?'

'Bed paid to Irkutsk.'

'From Moscow?'

'From Buy, your lordship.'

Glance at Jelena. She was pretending not to eavesdrop, but it was a poor attempt at disguise; turning her head in a different direction, she leant towards the provodnik – the bang and clatter of the speeding train made eavesdropping difficult, especially here, near a passage between carriages.

'You want to find a murderer?' Whisper in Polish. 'Let's start with the molodyets who yesterday smashed a man to pulp.'

She opened her eyes wider. At once, however, the smile returned; she firmly embraced the proffered arm, holding her chin up high.

'Never fear, Benedykt; I shall defend you.'

The provodnik led the way.

The train's confined space hindered conventional gestures of emotion (conventional, that is, those in which a person draws close to another without drawing close at all). Hiss from pain, and in the corridor on the far side of the dining car, Jelena had to let go the arm.

'Something happened to you, sir? I should have asked, forgive me. That man yesterday, in the night, was also worried. Did they beat you?'

'No.'

'It's your hand.'

Beyond the dining car, the provodnik opened the door to the service areas. Allow Miss Muklanowicz to go ahead. She looked over her shoulder.

'I noticed at table that your hand was trembling.'

'And thought no doubt it was nerves.'

'It hurts, sir? What happened?'

'I got chilled to the marrow.'

'If you were frostbitten –'

'Have you never lost feeling in your extremities? Because blood has ceased to circulate in a hand, a leg; you touch your skin, yet touch makes no impression – it's foreign flesh over which you have no control, dead ballast; and then suddenly warmth returns, feeling returns and fresh blood. It tingles, itches, smarts, stings, aches. It hurts, true? Now multiply that a thousand times. As if someone were pouring hot acid into your veins. Ice is painless; it's the departure from ice that hurts.'

She stood still, looked attentively, eyes again greedy and head inclined towards her interlocutor, in the way only Mademoiselle Muklanowicz knows how.

'Are you speaking now of the body, sir?'

'Of what else?'

'What degree of frost must prevail in Yekaterinburg to cut down a man like that?'

'There was a gleiss. And Martsynians. Have you heard of Martsynians?'

'Professor Kryspin's sanatorium supposedly stands above the burned-down hermitage of the Holy Glaciator.'

'Well, yes. Then you've surely read about him and so will recognise him. Mefody Karpovitch wears a medallion depicting the saint in ice. Go ahead, please, the provodnik awaits.'

In the corridor of the second-class cars there was much more activity, almost all compartment doors stood open; from inside, sounds could be heard of conversations, sounds of hastily prepared meals; glass clinked against glass, someone was singing, someone snoring; life went on also in the corridor, a queue was huddling outside the bathroom, men were standing by the half-opened windows smoking cigarettes; a little girl was running the length of the carriage, peeping into every compartment in turn, giggling excitedly, probably playing hide-and-seek with someone. Enter a different world; it was a different train.

The difference in class – that is, in wealth – forejudged nothing in itself. Grasp this only in the moment of crossing into the next carriage. Here only Russians were travelling. The Deluxe passengers, even if subjects of the tsar by birth, shared not the customs of the Empire's common people, and had effectively detached themselves from ordinary folk. European etiquette, Saint Petersburg fashion, measured conversation in German, or in French… distance and restraint. Those are all artificial – natural instead is this spirit of unity, the everlasting memory of shared community; a few days suffice for people to instinctively create bonds with their travelling companions, so strong and heartfelt that they revert to the traditions of the land.

'Mefody? Ay, true, he must be already up. Fyodor Ilyitch, you seen the boy today?'

'Weren't he up before dawn?'

'Ah, before Bogdanovitch, ay, people joined the next-door compartment and made such a god-almighty din we was woken up. Someone looked in on the boy, they chattered for a while, went out. At the station stop, the water closet were under lock and key, if the fine lady will pardon me, they must have gone for a smoke.'

'And who was it? You know not, gentlemen?'

'We were asleep. Barely opened an eye to swear at this or that man, so he'd not disturb the sleep of others. Well, they went.'

'We would have met him in the corridor. Maybe he's sitting in one of the closed compartments.' Nod to the provodnik. 'Be so good as to go back and check.'

He sighed, turning on his heels.

'But what d'you want from the lad?' Fyodor Ilyitch was alarmed.

'Nothing, no more than to talk. This is where he sleeps?'

'Ay. But there's talk and talk, ever since Moscow them secret gendarmes have been coming –'

Laugh. 'No, not that kind of conversation. Where are his blankets?'

Fyodor shrugged his shoulders.

'Gave them to us. Said he had no use for them, he were too hot. Where you from, Litva? My sister Yevdokiya, may she rest in peace, lived in Vilna till nineteen twelve, maybe you were once in Lubicz's eating-house?'

'No.'

The provodnik returned.

'No sign.' Now he looked worried. 'Could have got off in Bodganovitch.'

'And left his things behind?'

Miss Muklanowicz assumed a clandestine look.

'The Mystery of the Disappearing Passenger,' she whispered.

The carriage provodnik appeared, since a crowd had begun to form and congestion to block the corridor – in such an enclosed community, any disturbance to the day's natural rhythm assumes sensational proportions.

'Better go to the duty room.'

The provodniks indicated the way. The second-class conductor immediately shut the door, bustled around the samovar, guests had to be entertained, no matter they'd just come from breakfast. The older official unbuttoned the braided tunic of his uniform; his belly spilled over the wide belt, and like this he made himself comfortable by the window. Tugging at his beard, he shook his head; what on earth must their lordships be thinking, in our train such things don't happen, we answer for every passenger, count every passenger, he must have secretly slipped away at the station stop and not returned in time; such a thing has never happened to Deluxe passengers and has no right to happen, I can assure you, your graces. He pressed hand to heart. His name was Sergey; the second-class conductor he addressed as 'Niko'. One was more embittered, the other more angry; both were embarrassed.

Glance at how Miss Muklanowicz was playing it. Now she only rotated the tea glass in her hands, only leant over the ebonite surface of the table, where detailed railway timetables and carriage distribution charts lay spread. In the blazing stream of sunlight, she moved not so much her head as narrowed her eyes against the blaze. What to do? Capitulate again? Bah, capitulation was already a fact – since she ought to have been dismissed at once following Sergey's first whisper about Mefody.

'So, you're saying, sir,' Jelena began, 'that this Pyelka took part in the brawl in Yekaterinburg. That he was a follower of Saint Martsyn. Then, not long afterwards, as we're leaving Yekaterinburg, someone comes to Pyelka's compartment, invites him outside – and that was as much as anyone saw of Pyelka. The provodniks can swear they never lose a passenger; one way or the other, our Mefody Pyelka is nowhere to be found in the second-class carriages.'

'He could have got out and been late for departure, as Sergey said. He must have got out.'

'Or jumped out.'

'Or jumped out.'

'Or was thrown off.'

'Also possible.'

'Or his corpse was thrown off.'

'Or.' Nod in assent.

The devushka moistened her lips in the steaming tea. Reach for the sugar. The train shook, grey crystals were scattered on the smooth black surface, like dry snow.

The compartment was no more spacious than the luxury compartments, four persons made a crowd, and because the window remained shut (with an open window, conversation would have been impossible whilst travelling) and the interior was warmed by the steppe sun pouring in through the glass pane as in a botanical hothouse, warmed too by the samovar and Sergey's sweaty bulk – the fug typical of second-class sleeping cars quickly set in, a greasy dampness forming droplets on the skin, trickling from palate to throat... Memories returned of Biernatowa's lodging house. Swallow the saliva, already thick, already viscous. The hot tea only raised the body temperature even higher. Imagine – those people in third, fourth class, in wagons barely fit for cattle, travel in a state of total stickiness, not man and woman, but collective and collective, great lumps of the muscular bulk of the Empire, many-gobbed, many-handed, many-tongued, but with one blood circulating within them, one saliva, one sweat.

'Yet you know this Pyelka, Benedykt – where from?'

Shrug the shoulders.

'I don't know him. Yesterday I saw him at his deadly handiwork. And ordered him to be found here, maybe he'd be able to explain something of it, but, obviously, he won't.'

'Interesting he left Yekaterinburg at all... Who was it there? Will you continue to maintain, sir, that they were random cutthroats?'

'Martsynians.'

'Aha!' Her eyes lit up. More and more she resembled a child taken unawares by successive presents: the greatest joy and excitement before she pulls the first ribbon, before she tears the wrapping paper. Whilst hermetically sealed and so attractively packed, the secret takes the breath away, contains within it the most marvellous possibilities. Criminal conundrums are not for untying; once untied, they cease to be useful.

'Those Martsynians there attacked you and Mr Fessar, and then the Martsynian Pyelka came to your defence, is that right? Mmm,' she took a long, drawn-out sip, 'to me, it looks like a religious matter, you must have trodden on their toes.'

'Bah! I'd only just heard of Martsyn. No doubt a schism within in the sect. Or some other squabble under the icons. That's when the brothers are at their harshest and cruellest, they show no mercy. But you, miss, don't believe me anyway, since I'm plotting after all with the prince and doubtless with the tsar himself. Devil take them! Who was he anyway – this Martsyn?'

The provodniks listened to the conversation conducted in Polish – hearing Martsyn's name, they exchanged glances, Sergey wheezed heavily, reached into a pocket of his uniform for his hip flask and laced his black tchay; having taken a slurp, he wheezed again... 'Martsyn, eeh, Martsyn.' He crossed himself. 'We know him, sir, they ride here that sort, we know them, oy.'

Who should know them better than the janitors of Siberia: the provodniks of the Trans-Siberian Express? Every pilgrimage of Martsyn's followers begins with the Transsib. Willingly or unwillingly, believers or not – these are the deacons of his Church.

Grunting at Niko to turn down the whistling samovar, Sergey began his tale, swiftly entering into the tone and melody of a courtly skazka: another's voice, another's words – out of the mouths of the lowliest heralds of the Ice.

Now the Avagensky Monastery in the Yakut land, since the days of the Schism and Patriarch Nikon's reforms, had taken the veil of ill fame as a den of renegades from the Church's bosom, of religious dissenters, a haven for old ritualists and all kinds of sectarians. It was there, so we hear tell, a hideaway was made ready for exiled Protopope Avvakum; but Avvakum was sentenced to be burned at the stake and slain after cruel tortures. Many at that time perished in fire, of their own freewill. They gathered their families, womenfolk, children, holy books, locked themselves in their tserkoffs, and set fire to the tserkoff. Whole communities of self-immolators burned. Years there were when upward of thirty thousand Old Believers ascended to heaven in smoke; Avvakum praised such self-immolation, this flight from a world totally in the thrall of the Antichrist along with Nikon's Tserkoff, this purification in flames.

'But why did that schism arise?'

'A-ah, your lordship, Nikon it was who admitted sermons into devotions, tserkoff processions away from the direction of the sun, three times *Allelujah*, the two-beamed cross, the sign of the cross with two fingers – he changed that too, so you can cross yourself with three fingers instead of two, oh.'

'Three fingers. And they burned themselves for that?'

'Your Esteemed Nobleness makes light of the truths of faith,' Sergey was offended.

'As if I should dare! Only to me it seems too slight a difference to forfeit your life because of it. And such an outward ritual gesture really belongs to the truths of faith? It's not these things that make up the substance of belief, you surely understand that.'

'In the Latin heresies, certainly it's of no consequence,' Niko mumbled, 'since they cross themselves any old how, so why not with the "three-fingered fig", that stamp of the Antichrist, neath which the mind darkens and ceases to tell good from evil, an existing thing from a bogus. But in true faith there cannot be two truths: if the two-fingered sign is in accord with Divine truth, then the three-fingered is not; and if the three-fingered is, then the two-fingered is not. But the dread deed was Nikon's permitting *both*. Allow disputes about God, and you deny God. Change one letter of the Divine Word, and you kill the Divine Word. Raise a hand to vote for or against God, and you renounce God. Only truth can be repeated faithfully; a lie can be recognised because a lie changes, because it's more than one.'

In addition, the year of the Antichrist was drawing nigh, 1666. Prophets appeared and other pretenders; when Shabbatai Tzvi proclaimed himself Messiah of the chosen people, nearly all Jews went over to him, the times were apocalyptic. And following the example of the Avagensky, believers began to make ready the monastery on the Solovetsky Islands as a refuge, where all the persecuted, opponents of Nikon and his reforms, were to find safety. Siberia gave sanctuary.

… Till authority caught up with them and an ukase came to crush those nests of heresy. Avagensky Monastery was the first in line. They destroyed it. Most of the monks escaped, hid in hermitages, khutors and mountain caves, in the wilderness. A century passes, another, and nothing changes; thus arose the Monastery of Siberia, scattered over thousands of versts. Fellow believers came to them, found them somehow, travelled from the ends of the earth, or were themselves Sybiraks, or Old Believers exiled by the tsar, Popovtsy and Bespopovsty, disciples, imitators, successors. Then they carried their writings out into the world, but more often they stayed – became rooted in the land. These or those died out, but later sectarians also fled to them, and so they replaced one another, generation upon generation, heresy upon heresy – there you will find immortals, and Dobrolyubovians, Evangelicals, Judaisers, Khlysts and Skoptsy, Shaloputs, Kapitonovians,

Vozdykhantsy, Skrytniki, Perfilovians, Nemolyaks, Strigolniki, Fedoseyevians, Melchizedeks and Babushkinians, Pastukhovians and Lyubushkinians, Akulinians and Stepanovians, wandering Beguny openly professed and secret and doubly secret, Molokans, Dukhobors, no doubt Shtundists and Tolstoyans as well, villages and communes, whole communities of sectarian dissenters, off the imperial maps and registers, outside the law and outside time, cut off from the world, you won't find them. Siberia gives sanctuary.

... Martsyn, the one from Martsyn's hermitage – no one knows what number counting from the master, but it's known the name is taken from Marcion of Sinope, one of the earliest heretics, a hundred years after Christ, and so impenitent he was excommunicated by his own father, bishop in Pontus. That former Marcion and his people, called Marcionites, proclaimed this heresy: the God of the Old Testament is not the God of Christ, but the real cause of man's sin and suffering – we inhabit a world of an evil creator – whilst knowledge and redemption must come from outside of this world – from a new God. And only the Gospel of the Apostle Luke is genuine, but even that not entirely, as well as a few of Apostle Paul's epistles. Those that travel here also claim that Marcion founded the New Testament and that there is no other Christian scripture, and it was only when people united against Marcionite scripture in order to deny the truth of Marcion of Sinope that our Bible arose; there you have it, that's what they tell.

... Now, when the Ice reached him, Martsyn saw in the icers this long-awaited other-worldly power and revelation of a God that would alter the face of the evil earth. The first Martsynians to enter the icy mists, icecradles and gleissen sought not self-glaciation, but the experience of enlightenment, illumination – and when some returned, so they say, and spoke of untold wonders and marvels, Martsyn wrote down his Prophecies of Winter. In nineteen twenty he vanished, at least that was the message spread throughout the Empire. His writings, his traditions and successors, remain. Whose numbers are growing as the Ice moves across Asia and into Europe and more and more new sects enter the Frost, until here, in Summer, such confusion arose because neither we nor they can agree who is a true son of Martsyn, who faithfully proclaims his word, and who warps their faith and twists the meaning of the Prophecies; whilst amongst them, there are those who eventually perceived in the gleissen the Antichrist, and amongst these, those who want to drive him out with fire and those who welcome him willingly, awaiting annihilation and the end of the world in the Ice; but there are also those for whom the treasures of Winter augur a Golden Age; and those who see in the Ice the prospect of eternal life, and travel there, to their holy land, for the ritual of self-glaciation, they buy one-way tickets on the Transsib for entire families – we have seen them, they remain in Siberia, in crystal blocks, in ice sarcophagi, yes.

'And have you any idea why Mefody Pyelka was travelling there?'

Sergey glanced at Niko; Niko raised his hands above his head.

'Even if he's a Martsynian, he told us not, your lordships.'

'We should search his belongings... But who could have called on him in the night? Didn't you see how he spoke to that someone?'

'He spoke with you, sir,' said Sergey. 'Didn't he say he meant to alight earlier? If you could certify, sir –'

'No.'

'Egh.'

Someone knocked at the door. Niko excused himself and went out into the corridor; at once noises were heard of a quarrel, two irascible passengers accusing each other of an unspecified insult.

Sergey sighed deeply for the umpteenth time. He buttoned his uniform, grunted: 'I too have work to do.' Still in the narrow doorway, he bowed awkwardly as he pushed past his fellow provodnik and the foul-mouths. The door slammed loudly. The Express was climbing a hill – the contents of cupboards and lockers in the duty room began to rattle, Sergey's unfinished tchay slid off the table. Catch it at the last moment.

Miss Muklanowicz rapped her tea glass on the tabletop.

'If I hadn't heard you myself,' she asserted, 'you, Benedykt, would be first on my list of suspects.'

'As if it were I who stole into second-class at night and threw Pyelka off the train?'

'It's extraordinary, sir, how you lie and lie.' She shook her head in amazement, silver pins glittering amid raven locks.

'And how you, miss, faultlessly detect it.'

'That I do, sir, and detect what you dare to repeat now: that you'd never seen Pyelka before and never spoken to him, nothing, nothing, eh?'

'I can repeat it again. You'll believe whom you wish to believe, me or Sergey. And by what means shall the truth be revealed to you out of this belief and disbelief?'

She frowned.

'So how was it? Spoke you with him or not?'

Shrug the shoulders, stir the tea, peer through the steamed-up window.

'Mademoiselle Holmes is beginning to perceive the difference between a bookish investigation and a real investigation. Does she recall what I told her about two-valued and three-valued logic? Crime stories, those written-down ones, paper ones, always play out according to the logic of Aristotle, always in a world of the principle of excluded middle and law of non-contradiction. At such and such an hour the murderer was here and here, whereas another suspect was – here, and a given witness – there, whilst here we have this particular alibi, and this particular truth, and whatever fails to conform is false, whereas memory is always true and the past is like a looking glass. In the end, the detective describes what he saw in it. It's a machine – a game of chess: because now we can see such and such an arrangement of elements, and knowing the rules governing them, we can recreate every one of their previous positions, just as we revoke a move on a chessboard, turn back the hands of a watch by winding backwards its precision works, or calculate the migration of heavenly bodies. And it's not enough that this mechanics of crime allows a picture of past events to be figured out – but everyone agrees with this picture! Even the murderer! There are no gaps, no hazy areas – places where perspectives are split in two and points of view made blurred: one person remembers this, another person – something else; there are no ill-fitting details, and above all, there's none of that great margin of uncertainty, no "perhaps", "approximately", "either – or", "insofar as". Whereas these, which proliferate so many times during the course of an investigation, should wash away all concrete detail from any image of things past, just as afternoon sun washes away the snowmen and ice castles put together by children. But in crime novels, witnesses invariably glance at a clockface moments before the crucial event, in order to accurately recall later the exact minute; the clocks are never slow or fast. Whilst a witness, should he lie, knows he is lying, and should he tell the truth, knows he is telling the truth. And the malefactor plans his crime like cannon billiards: if the angle be right and the strength of his strike be good, then the cue-balls will come to a halt in this or that place. And he succeeds! They stop! And thanks precisely to this, the sharp-witted detective, by examining the balls, can trace back their movements and demonstrate the beginning of the carom and the hand of the culprit. These are abstract logical games, which have nothing to do with the world we live in.'

Miss Muklanowicz stared in mounting horror.

'Great God, you killed him!'

Bridle at her words. 'What? Weren't you listening to what I said?'

'I was listening. Listening to how you went on. And on. And on. For Christ's sake, on and on!' She covered her mouth with a dainty hand. 'You killed him, sir.'

'A moment ago, you yourself gave me an alibi!'

'So, what. Alibi, lullaby. But now I see through it.'

Groan in despair, bang the head against the door of the duty room so hard something whacks inside and clatters ominously.

Jelena raised her chin.

'If not this Pyelka, then it's someone else. But you've got someone on your conscience. Maybe in Yekaterinburg? Admit it, I shan't betray you, sir, word of honour.'

'Congratulations. Indeed, who could resist your deductions? Tremble, all ye criminals! I wish you success.'

Stand up.

She grabbed a jacket-tail.

'I'm sorry. Don't be angry, Benedykt, sir.' She pushed aside her glass and likewise stood up, automatically smoothing down her skirt and straightening the sleeves burgeoning in guipure lace. 'I want only to help. Truly.'

Embarrassed, she sought appropriate words – sincere, yet not too sincere. Suddenly, memory returned of a confused Christine Filipov. Think: that's the difference, this hint of maturity, here runs the dividing-line between them.

'You are right, sir,' she said quietly. 'Nothing ever happens to me, throughout my whole life, only what I read in books, what I fantasise, what I see through the window. What I overhear. Please allow me. I couldn't sleep till morning.' She reached with trembling fingers deep into her sleeve, under the pearly lace, and fished out a crumpled roll of paper. 'I jotted them down, by name, according to the seats they occupy, because not all are known to Frau Blutfeld. Forty-five suspects in first class, one of them must be the man hired to remove Doctor Tesla, and you, sir, so please, all we have to do is tick them off until – until – please, I implore you.'

Seize her hand – the birdlike wrist, fragile twig of bone – and press it to the lips, a bit awkwardly, sideways; she resists. Hold the cold, dainty hand to the lips another moment, and another.

'The journey, Jelena, whilst the journey lasts, I may as well be a murderer too.'

And so in that cramped, stuffy space, fomented by the sun and human bodies, where behind dozens of little doors and hiding-places the provodniks' clutter rattles and rings to the rhythm of an iron drum, took-took-took-TOOK, and where the hubbub of voices and early morning bustle beyond the walls prevent the proximity of scores of strangers being forgotten for a second, there follows, here and now, that moment of mutual understanding – a moment of silence, when thought and meaning flow from person to person undistorted by the restrictions of the speech of men. Understanding reached in the course of an unknown game, and precisely for that reason, and only for that reason, possible – in a game without rules, stakes or aim.

As she shifts her gaze slightly to one side, raises the corners of her mouth, strains mechanically with her other hand towards the velvet choker, withdraws the hand, places it within the yellow stream of light, turns it over – gaze, naturally, at that radiantly illuminated palm and not at the devushka's face, at the palm, the early bird in the sunshine – seize this hand too, whether it be a good move or a victorious manoeuvre, now she can be pulled nearer or repulsed, but not very far, since the compartment is so confined – she raises her eyes, stares without smiling, yes, she understands what was not spoken, the squeezing of the wrist, the trembling of fingers, words that mean something else, mean nothing, whilst the journey lasts: I may as well be a murderer. See it in her dark eyes, in the throb of fine blue veins neath the delicate skin, she had understood. Namely what? That which cannot be expressed in words.

'Oy, oy, forgive me, your lordships, you can see for yourselves what I've on my mind, I'm not turning you out, nothing of the sort, but official business…'

'Well, since it's official…'

Step out into the corridor. The second-class passengers were watching a little askance, a little curious, herded together at the end of the carriage: the red-faced participants in the quarrel and the rest, amusing themselves at their expense. Pull Jelena farther away from that assembly. Everywhere here, someone is watching, someone is listening.

Miss Muklanowicz looked back over her shoulder.

'What was all that about?'

'Doubtless someone drank their vodka during the night, no one is guilty, Trans-Siberian goblins. Let's go. What have you done with your list?'

She spread the page against a windowpane. Sharp sunlight shone through paper and black ink; she had tiny regular handwriting, short, rounded letters, crammed together in serried ranks.

'You have removed – whom? The prince? The princess? Because you also included the fair sex, yes?'

'Yes.'

'You can cross off Miss Filipov, Doctor Tesla's young companion.'

'Ah yes. Forty-four.'

'But Auntie Urszula? And you?'

'I beg your pardon?'

'And what about me?'

'What?'

'Can you confirm that it's not me sent to harm Doctor Tesla?'

'But you also –'

'A very good way to wheedle one's way into Tesla's favour, don't you think?'

'You two were discussing it – the Ministry of Winter has sent you to find your gleissen father.'

'By Ministry, you mean which Saint Petersburg faction? Lyednyaks? Ottepyelniks?'

'You mock me, sir.'

'God forbid.'

She watched suspiciously; the moment of understanding had long passed, words were flowing again, words, words, words.

'You wish me to suspect everyone, sir, even yourself, even me. This way we'll never find the assassin.'

Pass into the next carriage. Hold the door open for the young woman. Somewhere she had dirtied her white blouse, now she was mechanically scraping the fabric with a spat-on thumb. Offer a handkerchief.

'Were he murdering the doctor before your very eyes, miss, you'd be able to claim: it's him. In the past, on the other hand, or in the future – there are as many murderers as there are possibilities.'

'But it's about catching him *before* he manages to kill!'

'In other words, we are to hunt down – what? a probability?'

'Thank you.' She returned the handkerchief. 'I have no idea how to talk to you, sir. It's your concern, after all, not mine. And yet you meddle and meddle. One of them,' she waved her piece of paper, 'is the Lyednyaks' man and knows very well why he is travelling to Irkutsk and what he has to do.'

Flick a nail at the paper: 'Quite the reverse. There are forty-seven half-murderers, of whom each is and is not a Lyednyak agent, is planning and is not planning a crime, knows and knows not what he does.'

Miss Muklanowicz pursed her lips.

'You shall describe to me all the details, sir, I shall question the crew, question the suspects, compare their statements and reach the truth; that's how it's done, you will see.'

Smile under the moustache.

'Quite the reverse. Criminals are not *discovered*; they are *created*. What do you mean to do? Gather inconsistencies till only one consistent possibility remains. That way you'll create a two-valued murderer in the world of three-valued logic.'

She was exasperated.

'And when he hurls a brick at that oh-so-clever head, what-valued bruise will sprout from it?'

'H-mm, ye-es, it depends how deep we travel into the Land of the Gleissen... Have they gone to sleep in there?'

Batter with the fist the closed door to the service carriage. Eventually the lock jangled and the ruddy face of a young steward appeared in the crack.

'Remember us? We're returning to Deluxe.'

He bowed and withdrew.

But Miss Muklanowicz at once put a foot inside the threshold, struck by a sudden thought.

'Listen, my good man, how is it: can anyone wander back and forth as they please between first and second class?'

'We-ell, no, missie, it's prohibited.'

'Prohibited to whom? To us or to them?'

Indicate with the fingers from behind the steward's back: diengi, diengi.

She made a wry face.

'But perhaps someone from Deluxe requested it last night? What?'

'Last night?'

'After Yekaterinburg.'

'I were asleep in the night, can't answer your lordships.'

Jelena tapped her heel on the wooden floor without taking her eyes off the steward. The chubby-cheeked Tatar knew not where to look; he folded his arms behind his back, stooped, shuffled his feet, burning from second to second with an ever-redder blush. Quizzed by anyone other than a young lady from Deluxe, he would surely have resisted with Asiatic insolence – the glances of Europeans slip off such smooth, well-rounded faces like water off a duck's back, Western shame touches not the people of the East.

Seize the young lady by the arm, draw her towards the dining car.

'Well what, well what!' she retorted. 'If that Lyednyak threw out Pyelka, then he must have crossed somehow from his part of the train to the second-class sleeping cars, he's not the Holy Ghost.'

'To be sure he crossed, but if he gave the senior attendant a back-hander, then the youngster won't confess, even were you to bring the gendarmes and threaten him with hard labour. Or you turn straight-away to the senior and pay even more. And if someone from Deluxe did indeed dispatch Pyelka to Abraham's bosom, then you can be sure a lot of ten-rouble notes landed in the pockets of the crew. Well, if Auntie Urszula can afford such extravagance… Why, what are you laughing at?'

Giggling, she carefully folded her list of suspects and slipped it back up her sleeve.

'Nothing, Mr Holmes, nothing, nothing.'

Enter the dining car. The passengers sitting opposite the entrance raised their heads and fastened their eyes for longer. They nodded discreetly to others; the whispering also began, likewise discreetly, stifled however at once, since everyone here was so well brought-up; an apologetic smile had already crawled out onto the lips. The silence proved even more embarrassing. Fessar was right: Frau Blutfeld or no Frau Blutfeld, gossip spreads like wildfire.

Luckily, Frau Blutfeld was not at table; Doctor Konieszyn was performing a solitary operation on the Viennese-style *Eier im Glas*. Walk quickly without glancing at Miss Muklanowicz.

At the last table, the balding Turk had sat down to his meal; now he made a movement as if to stand up.

'Allow me, Benedykt, sir –'

'But –'

'About your health, I wished –'

'Thank you, we've already eaten.'

'If –'

'Forgive me, sir, I can't, not now.'

'Ah! I understand, I understand.'

Jelena was out of breath; having run down the corridor, she leant against the partition wall.

'Well, whe-where to... what's driving you...'

'How did I get ensnared in this cabal!' Growl under the breath, staring at the door of the dining car. 'After all, I've not done anything! Never wanted to do anything! Just arrive there calmly. And now everyone. All imagining whatever they like. He too, that slippery Turk. God knows what. Lyednyaks, Sibirkhozheto, Martsynians, Okhrana or no Okhrana, Tesla and Pyelka and Prince Blutsky and Winter and no doubt also the damned Pilsudchiks as well.' Bite the thumb. 'Idiot, idiot, idiot!'

'You must... everything...'

'Ensnared. Well, so be it.'

'Tell me everything... ooph.'

'And you, miss, are a fine one! A harmless little scandal on a journey. They've already seen us together. Whatever might Fessar have thought?'

'You are so afraid of people.'

Is this fear? It is not fear.

Let out air, shrug the shoulders.

'If we stay in the saloon, in an open carriage – they'll give us no peace; if we shut ourselves in a compartment, mine, yours – worse still.'

'Stop moaning.' Jelena regained her composure. 'Come on.'

She led towards the front of the train, through the saloon and parlour carriage: the room with the fireplace, the observation gallery, the iron door – she gave it a shove. Step out onto the platform.

Glance instinctively underfoot. No blood. Overhead, across the azure sky, braids of dark-grey smoke and monumental stacks of white cloud were sailing past. On one side of the tracks stretched green forests, on the other – the open steppe; in the warm air, the scent of soil and damp wood penetrated through the reek of oil and iron. Shield the eyes from the sun.

Miss Muklanowicz leaned against the door.

'And now, sir, speak please.'

Feel in the pockets. Take out the chamois case, and from the case, the interferograph. Raise the barrel to the sky, hold the lens to the eye.

Along the diameter of the black ring ten or so beads of light were flickering.

Sigh in resignation and put away the apparatus.

Massage the aching right hand and begin: 'In an Arbat pawnshop, I bought myself a fountain pen, a gold-filled Waterman Eyedropper...'

On the arsenal of Summer

Nikola Tesla pressed the barrel to his temples and pulled the trigger.

There was a loud bang. His hair stood on end and his eyebrows bristled. Black lightning leapt across between the Serb's skull and the tungetitum mirror. The old Okhrana agent crossed himself three times. In the mirror glowed a bushy glintz, a portrait of Tesla in profile, head and neck and fragment of shoulder; the mirror was the shape and dimensions of a large oval wedding photo of bride and groom, thus allowing the natural size of his bust to be reflected.

The crucial thing was that the white negative burned on the coal-black surface – already fading, that is, growing darker – in no way resembled the physical form of the person portrayed. Could it be, as the doctor wishes, his symbolic 'karmagraph'? Have no high opinion of those esoteric oriental beliefs with which the inventor had been infected many years earlier by some shady guru. It's unbefitting, unbefitting.

'Better put aside that contraption, sir, I implore you.'

'But come closer, young man!'

'Please put it down.'

'Come closer, take a look and tell us what you see.'

His profile brought to mind the outline of a bird's head: slender neck, protruding beak, barbed comb on top. In lieu of a cheek, there gaped an empty hole. Other features radiated from his eye, possibly veins, possibly sparks, white-and-black shafts of lightning. There was no mouth, only the next claw-shaped lightning bolt, severing in two the blotch of his face or non-face.

'Of what were you thinking?'

'You tell me, of what I was thinking.'

Scratch the nape of the neck.

'Electrical machines and lightning storms?'

Tesla pressed a cable into a chest.

'I am nearly always thinking of electrical machines. Even when I'm not thinking.'

'In other words, it works?'

'I ought to have made arrangements in advance. Stepan! What d'you think?'

The okhrannik tugged at his watch chain, glanced nervously at the face.

'Oy, return to your compartment, Doctor, we're about to depart, Oleg Ivanovitch won't hold the train much longer, the telegram must surely have gone.'

Tesla waved a hand in resignation. Adjusting his white gloves, he took out a comb and began to tidy his upstanding hair with energetic strokes – first backwards, then symmetrically to the sides, outwards from the central parting. At the same time, he stared at himself in the polished casing of one of three vast metal cylinders: lying motionless on their sides in wooden surrounds, entwined in leather straps, hemp ropes and heavy chains, they occupied the greater part of the carriage. Old Stepan was keeping watch that the doors remained bolted; light entered only through small grated windows located at the very tops of the walls. Tesla stood hunched over, catching the reflections in the dark steel now in his left eye, now in his right.

'If there should be even a sliver of truth in it,' he muttered under his breath, 'it should be possible to reproduce the effect from any source of unlicht. They use blackwickes, because they're cheapest, powdered carbon tungetitum in the braid. But it's about the unlicht, man's effect on the unlicht: unlicht itself or whatever else always accompanies its release.' His squinting eyes ran the length of the cylinder. 'Agreed, Benedykt, sir?'

'Mm-hmm, that's how it seems to me too.'

'I was thinking about it during the night and then at breakfast. The princess pinned the English engineer to the wall. Speaking of which, where did you disappear to?'

'Only why do you have to immediately carry out all these experiments on yourself?'

Tesla pocketed the comb.

'Christine's been talking to you.'

Smooth down the moustache, survey the interior. The floor was sprinkled with sawdust; the boards were spliced together none too carefully, crooked lines of tar ran along their joins. The two Okhrana agents had made themselves at home in a corner behind piles of wooden and tin trunks; they had chairs, straw mattresses, blankets, a gasoline lamp. But how will they cope when the Express enters Winter?

'It makes no sense, Doctor. No one has to break in here in order to blow up the entire wagon. Or entire train. What kind of prediction were you seeking, sir? That you'd arrive in one piece in Irkutsk?'

'Light, these individual particles of light, not ether, but rays, *die Lichtquanten*, and perhaps the wave too whilst we are still in Summer – there must be something in the nature of light, in the nature of unlicht, on this nethermost level of prana permeating the entire akasha that interlocks directly with man's consciousness – are animals also irradiated by unlicht? – so that consciousness influences its course, its polarisation, so that man observes, or maybe only thinks, and – and – yes. Help me, sir.'

Grab the other end of the mirror.

'It's heavy.'

'Pure tungetitum on silver.'

'Must be worth a fortune.'

'Mm-hmm, you are right, sir, I had not thought of that.'

Tesla lowered the edge of the looking glass into a flat chest, wrapped it in tows and pressed down the lid. Hand him the padlock.

'Of what?'

'That they might also want to make money on it.'

'To plunder the whole wagon?'

Stepan nodded.

'Mademoiselle Filipov tried to insure it, but it's all still the property of His Imperial Exaltedness.'

'Have you estimated the value?'

'One hundred thousand roubles. More. How to estimate the value of the doctor's machines?'

Tesla snapped the padlock shut.

'Until I test them, no one knows if they're worth anything at all.'

'But that looking glass alone –'

'Looking glass! But it's not going to serve as a looking glass. What do you imagine it is?' With a dramatic gesture, he encompassed the whole interior of the goods wagon steeped in semi-darkness along with its contents. Doctor Tesla was undoubtedly prone to theatrical staging. 'This is the arsenal of Summer.'

He strode up to a pyramid of tin crates, each labelled with a serial number and the firm's emblem: *Tesla Tungetitum Co.*; the pyramid exceeded the height of even the tall Serb, stretching as high as the ceiling.

'These three flow-generators we shall connect to the electrical supply network in Irkutsk, we should get an onrush of the order of forty megamirks; here, I have almost a kilometre of cable insulated with silicon on a high-copper coolbond, but there – out of this, clamping rings will be assembled. And out of this – a cage of shadow. We shall see what pressure they will endure.'

Tesla will be passing through the gleissen a constant teslectric flow. Peep into the open chest. A cable with a firing pin attached and un-wieldy-looking trigger led from it into a bulgy case standing beside it, in which an invisible mechanism was snarling away; an identical cable ran out of it from another aperture, returning in over-long coils to the same chest, wherein squat jars filled with coal rested on wood shavings and rags. Coal?

'Isn't that precisely the gleissens' element?'

'You won't burn them, freeze them, smash them. Only that which gives them life can deprive them of life. In Prague there was no op-portunity to carry out tests... Besides, I have been advised against conceptual work in the Land of the Gleissen.'

Touch the rim of a jar. The glass was cold, lightly covered in hoar frost; moisture stuck to the fingers, prickled the skin.

'You want to – drain them? Suck them dry? Of what? Teslectricity?'

'When we set out into the desert, we take with us supplies of water, we seek the cool, build canopies to shield us from the broiling heat, spread out the shade. When we venture into the Arctic frosts, we go in furs, in warm clothes, we erect warm shelters. Now the gleissen have come – what do they bring with them? what saves them in a foreign land? That's what I have to take away from them!'

Raise the eyes. Tesla was checking the lead seals on the boxes, standing upright with his left hand behind his back, white shirt-front reflected like a triangular blotch on the grey tin. In the grubby semi-darkness, it was hard to state with certainty, but were not the shadows on the doctor's person, neath the creases of his attire, in the wrinkles on his face – spilling again out of their usual channels like rivers in full spate? were they not flowing in torrential streams despite the light and half-light?

Even more significant was the behaviour of the grey-haired agent of the Okhrana. Shrouded in silence, motionlessness and dark, he stood behind Tesla, moving only when Tesla moved from box to box; always beyond the Serb's field of vision, yet always close, like a mother observ-ing her son's first steps, like a male nurse standing guard over his patient – something of this there was in Stepan's silhouette, in the tension in his shoulders.

'Winter? Take away Winter?'

'Frost and snow and ice – well yes, these are the first things to occur to a layman. What are you looking out for there?'

'Miss Filipov keeps an eye on you in the compartment, yes, Doctor? You had to slip away here in order to take breakfast.'

'Breakfast?'

'You feed on that force, sir. What's in the jars?'

'Salt crystals impregnated with this black prana energy, with this murch. Mainly metallic salts from the iron group.'

'What?'

'I am trying various methods for accumulating teslectricity, seeking the most effective; right here I have ferric ammonium alum. What's she been telling you?'

'That it's stronger than you, sir.'

Tesla sat down on a container labelled with a paper skull-and-crossbones.

'Even if,' he said slowly, 'even if I had come to such a decision – namely, to surrender to it – whence the certainty that this was a bad decision?'

Bridle.

'For the love of God, you told me yourself of your struggles with the gaming habit! And don't I well know the grip of those invisible fetters? I know it! Have some regard for your own reason and mine!'

Tesla raised his index finger.

'*Bene*, Benedetto, consider also this: there are good habits. Things, actions, connections, to which we have willingly enslaved ourselves. If only physiological functions – pardon my rudeness – even if your life depended upon it, you would not, of your own free will, relieve your-self in your trousers. Consider the way in which you speak, the way you think. And also, this: that we differ from animals, from people brought up amongst animals, that there are certain things that we will not do; a hand withdraws of its own accord, legs refuse obedience, the mouth won't open. For by my every thought and deed, I demon-strate daily that I am no more than an automaton reacting to external stimuli which excite my senses; I think and act in response to them. I do not recall many instances in my life when I could not identify the earliest impression prompting a movement, thought or dream. So, every moment of genuine freedom of mind should be valued all the more, a sacred frenzy of reason! But civilisation – civilisation is a set of beneficial habits. For you rise from the table when a woman rises – before you think of rising. It's not you that govern the rising, but the rising that governs you.'

'The rising.'

'The rising. Yes. A child is in danger – the rushing to help that child. Speaking the truth when needing to, lying when needing to. The being polite. The washing. Respecting your elders. Not killing. You intend, sir, to fight such habits? It's possible, one can liberate oneself from them, I have known such people. Well?'

'But what habit so governs our discretion that we know which habits are good and which are bad?'

He smiled; he had a very sincere, attractive smile, a little shy. He approached the open chest, fastened again the cable ends into the apertures of the bulgy case, hitched a coldiron vice to the free end of the longer cable and then, having placed them in a jar, pressed the jaws of the device onto the grey crystal. In his other hand, he held the firing pin, fingers resting on the insulation and the trigger.

He watched serenely. Bite the nails.

'It will shoot.'

'No, I have switched it over, it's on free flow.'

'I should not –'

Grab the coldiron pin. Nikola Tesla pulled the trigger. The teslectrical tide began to flow, murch to boil in the body.

… And let go of the cold metal.

'… it's departing.'

'Yes, be quick.'

Stagger on faltering legs. Doctor Tesla swiftly unfastened the cables, rolled them up, put them away in the chest and lowered the lid. The door of the wagon had been pulled back, the younger okhrannik stood in the doorway. Squint in the afternoon sun beating off the Tyumen platform. The provodniks were summoning the passengers, the engine was chugging. Beneath the coldiron clocktower swung a wooden signboard with a row of crooked letters scrawled in red paint.

Льда нѣтъ

Tesla descended to the platform, waved his arm impatiently. Jump down – and trip over. The ground heaved underfoot like a wave; the bright-blue sky was blinding, Siberian air seared the lungs, all station sounds drilled into the ears. Into the ears, into the brain – a nest of buzzing bumblebees erupting under the skull.

Tesla assisted the return to the feet. Brush down the trousers.

'What happened? Doctor?'

'I can never remember either.'

'You made me –'

'Made?'

'Hypnotised –'

'You'll describe it to me later, sir, in detail, I insist.'

Tesla marched with long energetic strides towards the first-class carriages. Run after him – and run lightly, as kind spirits bore the body's burden above the earth. Yet still the horizon and blue sky and snow-white clouds in the sky and station building and serpent of the

Trans-Siberian Express and people swarming on the platform, still it all didn't quite compose itself into a harmonious whole, perhaps because the eyes were dazzled (blink, blink, blink!), or because of the shock of the fall. But run as if in a dream: softly, coming down to earth when feeling like coming down – and, were such a whim to occur, flying straight up to the clouds. And even though the image slowly cohered into a mosaic that made sense – consciousness remained that it was a mosaic, and that it could be composed in a different way. Clouds on the tracks, station in the sky, sky underfoot, houses blown out of the engine chimney, a coldiron horizon and sinewy rails – it could be like this; for now it is not, but it could be, remember that.

'But what was it actually about?'

Catch up with Tesla.

'Pardon?'

'You dropped by and at once tried to escape.'

'I couldn't in the presence of Stepan. In the night I had a visit from Mr Fogel. Have you any influence over them, Doctor?'

This distinctly annoyed him. He climbed the steps into the Deluxe car and stood with back turned, hesitating, resting an elbow on the open window looking out over the city. For the first time he took flight in his eyes, hid his face. Which does not necessarily herald a lie; it might equally herald an embarrassing truth.

'I mean to have nothing to do with it! They'd like to keep me the whole time in a golden cage!'

'But you must have heard, sir, about my adventure in Yekaterinburg. Mr Fogel said it was because of those wars at court between Ottepyelniks and Lyednyaks. And I had the impression it was not economic considerations that were the most important. Listen to me, Doctor! This is not science, pure and free – but matters of life and death. Have you ever had anything to do with Martsynians?'

This threw him completely off-balance. Tearing away from the window, with pursed lips and arms tightly pressed against the length of his torso, he bowed stiffly. 'Forgive me, sir.' And he walked off down the corridor, a tall, thin silhouette, white suit, rainbow of unlicht surrounding the white.

Here memory of an image was superimposed on the image and an arbitrary thought turned the head towards the windowpane – but sunlight was shining through the pane – and towards the polished fixtures of the carriage – but sunlight was bouncing off the steel. Hurry therefore to the compartment. Having drawn tight the curtains, peer into the mirror.

And in the mirror – pale shadow that had collected behind the shoulders and around the face flickered and danced like flame on a naphtha-lamp reflector; shadow and faint streaks of glintz, a shimmering afterglow at the limits of perception. Stand and stare. A minute, another minute, longer, motionless, whilst they romped and frolicked, moved about inside the looking glass and grew deformed in the backdrop – until the train jerked, the forehead hit the gilt frame and the spell was broken. This is hypnosis; this is coercion.

Jump up and down on the spot three times, bite into the base of the thumb, laugh emptily, lick the cold surface of the mirror, slurp, slurp, slurp, long strokes of the tongue across the glass. Sit then at the escritoire, resting the head in the hands so it doesn't tumble onto the desktop with a hollow thud. What to do? What to do? At once, the old temptation returned: to stay locked in the compartment, not to go out, have no contact with other passengers, no more conversations with Miss Muklanowicz, or, God forbid, with Tesla or Ünal Fessar. Maybe Fogel had been exaggerating, had meant to intimidate the ne'er-do-well so he no longer got in their way. (He had succeeded.) Pyelka was most likely snatched from the Transsib by Martsynians themselves, after all he had smashed their brother to a pulp. Therefore – don't go out. Tempt not fate. Settle matters with the Ministry of Winter in Irkutsk, pocket the second thousand, and back home. The sectarians and Lyednyaks will back off once they see that the son has as much in common with the father as a man with a monkey. So long as they are not provoked. Therefore, no more brawls. No public hints. Head in the sand. Yes. For as soon as a man steps out amongst people, he is caught between one shame and another, there is no rescue: deeds are more powerful than their subject, words more powerful than their narrator, the present more powerful than the past – there can be no control over every second's reaction, over every movement of a hand or facial grimace, or accursed smile. *Be afeared.* The lie of the moment triumphs.

The grabbing of the teslectrode, the burning in murch. Because hadn't the aim been to persuade the doctor to give up his abnormal addiction? Had not Mademoiselle Filipov been promised with chivalric intent? But the moment arrived and so it happened – happened like that; then there was the talk – that talk, and the action was taken – that action.

Had they been at least decisions of great moral weight! Fire and battle and storm and the blood of innocents or maybe even Lord Jim or some other precious human metal from Conrad's pages, which bends not, bends not, until it splits – with a great clap and echo resounding amongst fellow creatures. But no. But the reverse. A small shame, a shamelet, a baby shame, one, a second, a tenth, a hundredth, so miniscule it's invisible to the naked eye, the bacteria of the soul, against which there is no defence – unless the quarantine be strict.

If only this adventure with teslectricity brought no morbid consequences; fortune favours fools, but for the time being it's impossible to turn around on this train without falling into new traps. Calm the breath. The matter needs to be weighed up coldly and without prejudice. Firstly, one does not die of it. (Tesla has not died. Not yet.) Secondly, it passes, in any case it weakens and disappears with time. Thirdly – thirdly, what exactly happens…?

Raise the hand before the eyes. It trembled not. Blow into the hollow of the hand. No dark sediment appeared. Draw aside the curtains and peer into the interferograph. No change, light continues to interfere with light.

Feel, indeed, extraordinarily invigorated, but this again is nothing unusual, sometimes a shot of good vodka suffices. Tesla had been asking about the effect on the power of the mind. Memory – what is memory understood as a mental phenomenon: is it a repository of intellectual work or simply a direct reflection of states of the brain? Watch the last buildings of Tyumen flash by beyond the window. If the supposition is correct that there exists not one past, then neither can there exist one memory of the past: we remember many contradictory versions, whilst the intellect strives somehow to reconcile them, hence the washed-away recollections, false reminiscences, blank spaces, where memories have overlapped, erased and annihilated one another. But a man who has been enmurched, initiated into the logic of the gleissen, Yea, yea, Nay,nay, under the Aristotelian knife of truth – ought he not to remember the past clearly and distinctly, without any doubts?

But perhaps Tesla was simply justifying his habit in this way? Glance at the scraps of paper on the escritoire. Somewhere amongst them lies the Pilsudchiks' encoded missive. Find a pencil and, on the spur of the moment, in the margins of the Transsib brochure, recreate from memory the entire text, eleven lines with twelve letters and one more with two letters, rows of senseless combinations of signs, which even a mathematician cannot easily recall. Extract thereupon the actual missive.

Laugh in mockery. Indeed: on the spur of the moment, without any doubts, clearly and distinctly! Except it's totally different from the code itself. Toss aside the rotten fruit of memory.

But is there any sense at all in racking the brains over this epistle? They could have agreed in advance that a given letter or sequence of letters stands for a concrete word or phrase – there's no way of guessing.

Mm-hmm, but will the recipient of such a missive carry with him a book of codes, for years on end, in exile, in the wilds and frosts of Sybir, in taiga logging camps and deep mines, in his itinerant convict work gang, under the eye of guards and amongst ministerial spies – impossible, they made no agreement like that.

On the other hand, the code depends exclusively on what lies buried in the memory of the addressee. They cannot even be certain the recipient will find pencil and paper; maybe all that remains to him is to scratch in the snow with a stalk. So no books.

A method he has memorised for years, sufficiently secure and sufficiently simple. If there's a key, then it's a key easily retained in the head.

Can any such thing exist at all? Gnaw a fingernail in meditation. What method to choose in an identical situation? Shift the letters of the alphabet. A number of places agreed in advance. If it's one place, then B instead of A, C instead of B, D instead of C and so on. If it's more – mm-hmm, how many variants are there of such a code? As many as letters in the alphabet. In this missive, there are no Polish characters, so they are sticking to Latin notation. It suffices now to experiment with the first line: should the sense emerge at the very beginning of the text, there'll be no need to agonise over the rest.

Take a clean sheet of paper, jot down the Latin alphabet from A to Z, enumerating the letters from 0 to 25. All right, here we go, move forward one place. YSPAPKMCFYXBCUYWFGJT. Two places. ZTQBQLNDGZYCDVZXGHKU. Three…

Stare at the birch groves sailing past beyond the window against a backdrop of green fields, when all possible displacements had been tried in vain. A landscape like any landscape. Ride over these plains like a ship over an ocean, no wave distinguishable from the last; stars and clocks have to be trusted that the water clipped by its hull yesterday differs from today's. The hand crumples a last scribbled chit of paper and slings it into a corner. It really would be too simple a system, were a mere twenty-five attempts sufficient to break it.

How to complicate it without complicating an old political exile's very means of deciphering it? Glance at the alphabet jotted down on the previous paper, at the numbers above the letters. Something easy to remember – a key – a word, a phrase. JESZCZEPOLSKA. PRZECZZCAREM. FILIPGIEROSLAWSKI. EULAGYA. POLACYNIEGESIISWOJSZYFRMAJA. ABRAKADABRA. The idea is to not to always shift the letters the same distance in the alphabet, but – each letter according to the number of the corresponding letter of the key. Were the key to be JESZCZEPOLSKA, the first letter of the missive would be deciphered by moving it 9 places (J), the second – 4 places (E), the third 18 places (S) and so on, and then again from the beginning of the key.

How to break such a code? The number of combinations to check would be 26 times 26 times 26 times 26 times 26... a key that long. Abandon all hope, ye ignorant. Even were one to travel around the whole world, there'd be insufficient time.

Pinch the bridge of the nose. Fingers that had touched the jar containing immurched salt now left the same impression on the skin between the eyes: moisture, coldness, tiny needles prickling the flesh, a dull, smarting ache. Entirely pleasurable – like an ice compress on a feverish brow. Wipe the hand in a handkerchief. A delicate itching sensation arose.

Lower the window, light a cigarette. The papers on the desktop rustled and took wing. Gather them in a single sheaf and weigh them down with the inkstand. The Express was dashing along above some dried-up riverbed; perhaps an exceptionally long gorge, a shallow rift valley. A scar, a distinguishing mark on the otherwise smooth countenance of Asia. The wind, that is, air forced inside by the speed of the train – was surprisingly warm, dry. Drop the cigarette. Is this already the aroma of the steppes? Took-took-took-TOOK, took-took-took-TOOK. The valley ends; anonymous depths of grassy ocean return. Perhaps something in the sky, the contours of a mountain, a bird, a thunderstorm – no, nothing, only megalithic clouds like the limestone tombs of archangels.

Sunlight dazzled the eyes, the gaze drifted towards the shade, and in the shade shone a bright rectangle of paper. The Pilsudchik's missive remained uppermost. Flick ash out of the window. Took-took-took-TOOK, one day more, two, and even the heart will start to beat to the rhythm of the wheels. Such regularity can drive a person insane; for madness is precisely the addiction to excessive regularity, hunger for excessive regularity. Take another look. CAR. CAR. Tsar! OREE. REE. ORE. Bend over the escritoire. What does it mean? Does it mean anything at all? Certain sequences of letters are repeated. Pick up the pencil from the carpet. Draw circles around identical segments.

There were 5 repetitions. ABT and, 56 letters later, ABT. ORE, 32 later – OREE, 156 later – REE. JCAR, 32 – JCAR. YRG, 44 – YRG. All of them separated by an even number of characters. All separated by a number divisible by 4. But by 8 – no longer.

What does it mean? Anything at all? Inhale the smoke. Can this be coincidence? It can. But extraordinarily unlikely. Let's place a bet on the common and average. The key is a four-letter word. The missive has been encoded according to four shifts. Letters number 1, 5, 9, 13 and so on – are moved forward according to the numerical value of the first letter of the key; letters number 2, 6, 10, 14 – of the second letter of the key; numbers 3, 7, 11, 15 – of the third; numbers 4, 8, 12, 16 – of the fourth.

Except that the key itself remains a mystery. Sit down on the bed. At least the number of combinations to be checked is known: 456, 976. Were a quarter of an hour to be dedicated to each experiment... Chuckle under the breath. Madness.

The message consists of 222 letters. Up to 56 letters shifted according to the rule of the first and second, up to 55 – according to rule of the third and fourth. Stub out the cigarette end; 55 letters pulled out of the text, every fourth one. Like random chaff. No regularity will be found in this.

Glance at a page of Alfred's typescript. Yet it's not true: regularities do exist; you can see with the naked eye that in a text written in Polish, letters like A, E, I, appear considerably more often than J or G, not to mention X or Q. And when it comes to statistics, it is of no importance whether you take all one after another, or every fourth one.

Begin to calculate in this way the frequency with which letters occur. Calculate first how many times each is used in the first ten pages of Alfred Teitelbaum's article on Łukasiewicz's *Principle of Contradiction in Aristotle*, removing the accents to fit the Latin alphabet. The letters I, A, K, R came out on top, with G and H bringing up the rear. Then calculate the frequency of the appearance of letters in each of the four quarters of the missive. And commence by substituting them: the most frequent under the most frequent, the least frequent under the least frequent. Here, already no more than thirty combinations came into play. Some were excluded by the character of the language, a Pole would not utter RGRH or WCFZ; others in Polish were only too obvious. The first combinations to make sense emerged. NIE. CIE. PIE. WIE. NIA. TAK. TAK. Light the next cigarette. Too much sense for this to be pure chance. First letter of the key: B. Second letter of the key: J. Third letter of the key: A. Fourth letter of the key: H. Once again gibberish. But the missive deciphered according to it – contained explicit content:

```
WIOSNALUDOWTAKXODWIL
ZDODNIEPRUXPETERSBUR
GMOSKWAKIJOWKRYMNIEX
JAPONIATAKXPARTYAROZ
KAZUJECZASKOMPENSACY
ITAKROSYAPODLODEMXWS
ZYSTKIESRODKITAKXUWA
GAMLODZIIOCIEPIELNIK
IPRZECIWZIMIEXBRONLU
TEXNIEWIERZSTAREMUXK
URYERPRZYBEDZIEXZYJE
SZ
```

Transcribe the missive in calligraphic strokes onto a clean sheet of paper. The eyes ran over the text time and again, connoting words and phrases. Know it already by heart; the confusion mounted. PPS-men from the Kingdom had written to father after years of his Siberian exile – ALIVE – wrote the old revolutionaries to the familiar of icers – DEFEND THE GLEISSEN – they wrote in a tone of command – THE PARTY ORDERS – as if it were up to father to bring about all that – RUSSIA UNDER THE ICE – THAW TO THE DNIEPER – they wrote in cipher so that his son, God forbid, should not know their plans – ALL MEANS – but what, for the love of God, was that supposed to mean?!

The fingernail was completely chewed. Attack the cuticle of the thumb. What had that one-eared socialist said? That they were in touch with father? And yet this is meant to be their first message to him in five years? The consumptive was lying, that's clear. They had not learned about father from the people on Miodowa Street. Very likely they themselves had sent him to the gleissen. They want to exploit the Ice to stoke their revolution, for the triumph of socialism or the resurrection of the fatherland, whichever faction there at this moment –

The door slammed; the draught snatched up every paper in the compartment. Leap to shut the window.

'Benedykt!'

'What are you up to now!'

'I have him, sir!'

'You're trampling on my passport!'

Jelena was not listening. She grabbed a sleeve, tugging violently, almost unravelling the jacket seam.

Stand full height, resentful. 'What gall! Even gendarmes go about it with greater delicacy!'

She smiled joyfully, pale roses blooming on her habitually chalk-white cheeks; three, four black locks had escaped from her bun, ah, for Miss Muklanowicz – unheard-of untidiness.

'Yes?'

She lowered her voice to a whisper, moving closer still.

'Filimon Romanovitch Zeytsoff.'

'That communist?'

'Aha.'

Smooth down the moustache, regard her askance – she was very proud of herself.

'Why Zeytsoff?'

'Here's why. I took money from Auntie, went to buy over the provodniks and stewards. And –'

'What about Pyelka?'

'Nothing about Pyelka!' she snorted. 'Wake up, Benedykt, sir! Did

Fogel not say that the Lyednyaks had introduced their own man at the last minute? They couldn't know until Doctor Tesla decided – meaning – until Miss Filipov decided, under a false name besides. True? Have you any notion, sir, what the queues and registrations are like for the Transsib tickets? You have to wait months!' Again, she grabbed a jacket lapel. Step back against the wall, but this time Jelena was not letting go. 'You can still make it, sir, to a late dinner. Zeytsoff always comes at the very end, eats alone, you will sit with him – he's bound to betray himself!'

'But –'

'He will betray himself! The provodniks told me: he bought a ticket immediately prior to departure from Saint Petersburg, from some fur dealer, for one and a half thousand roubles. One and a half thousand! A bourgeois communist! Hah! It's him!'

She reached behind her, pressing down on the doorhandle. Glance helplessly around the compartment. Carpet, escritoire, bedding, everywhere papers, scores of pages filled with scribbled letter combinations tested during the course of the cryptoanalysis, at first glance – the notes of a madman, nothing more.

BJAH. And he was meant to remember it for all his years in Siberia? What a strange machine is the human brain: the stricter the order harnessing the world roundabout it, the greater the fury assailing the last hotbeds of disorder within it. BJAH! It cannot be, the key *must* mean something.

Jelena was saying her piece, persuading and imploring and tugging at the hand, like a tiresome younger sister unable to get her way; meanwhile the final mystery won't let itself be wrested from the mind, a nail in the skull, a wound in the head, it rankles, aches, gives no peace. Need to give it a scratch.

'Again, you're not listening to me, sir!'

BJAH. And if the letters really are meaningless? If it's even simpler still? Moving the letters one numerical place forward... 1-9-0-7. 1907.

They will forget everything, but not the year of their deportation.

'Seventeen years.'

'What?'

Peer above Jelena's shoulder. The man in the mirror had a very strange mien. Seventeen years. Father's face when he left for Siberia – remembered – not remembered – how much older had he been then? scarcely a few years; almost the same age! There are no photographs, no pictures, only the police description and the true-or-false memory. The mirror is the surest and in fact only means: only thus, only this far does father exist in the present, only in this form.

Jelena, frowning, looks over her shoulder. Does she see what's happening roundabout with the shadow? Perceive the shape of this ajouré penumbra?

Button the piqué waistcoat.

'Zeytsoff. His reasons could be totally different –'

'But! I questioned them thoroughly: everyone had tickets bought ages ago, except Zeytsoff, only he was added at the last minute, in someone else's place. So, it's either him – or no one. Unless Lyednyaks hearken to some kind of clairvoyants.'

Step over the threshold. Miss Muklanowicz curtsied before Mrs White-Gessling. Scandalised, the Englishwoman averted her head.

Jelena hissed in an urgent tone.

'I shan't drag you by the tie, sir, in case you're depending on that.'

'You were meant to lie down, you're about to faint.'

'Faint? What are you saying? How dare you, sir, ask such a thing of me?!'

Survey once more, key in hand, the messy compartment. On top of the papers thrown on the bed lay the Transsib brochure, open at the page scrawled with the erroneously remembered cipher.

Turn the key in the lock. Green shade drenched the windows as the Express plunged for a while between trees. The head begins to spin and a sudden thought occurs, just like that green, overshadowing the consciousness:

What if it were possible to decode also that missive?

On some of the means by which God communicates with man

Over the second vodka, Filimon Romanovitch took out a photograph of his mother.

'And you have to know, sir, that no photograph or painted image will convey her loveliness; so beautiful was my mother, as he, sober or drunk, was wont to tell – and I trust his word all the more when the firewater strips him bare – for as soon as his eyes rested upon her, my pater said to himself: my children she shall bring forth into the world, from out of this krasavitsa they shall take the good they shan't take from me. That's how he speaks, God in heaven, and he speaks aright, for this also you have to know, sir – what's your patronymic, ah, Filipovitch, pour me another, thank you – you have to know, Venyedikt Filipovitch, that my father, Roman Romanovitch, may be a kind-hearted man, yet he's one of evil passions. Envious tongues, of which there's no shortage in any uyezd, and especially in those zemstvos where all the high-born have known one another since time immemorial and every sin, every affliction, like every virtue, has tended to flow between them in the blood many times over, exchanged from generation to generation, all of us there being related, envious tongues, I tell you, vilified him as a voluptuary and shameless profligate. Unpalatable it is, when a son hears such things of his father; should he hear it from a stranger, he will deny it, defend his father's honour, but from relatives, familiars, friends – what happens to the son? With genuine tears in his eyes, he will begin to condemn his father's iniquity! The son! He the first accuser, he the guardian of righteousness! Cast off that grimace, sir. It was like that with me too.

'My father, as I was persuaded, had not one family and not one home, but at least three homes, and was entangled in such an intricate web of *liaisons du cœur* no clear account of his family ties can be given. We lived on the family estate; whilst in the town he kept two houses, wherein resided Sofiya and Yelizaveta, each with her own child, and with Sofiya also her younger half-sister, whom my father, as I see you've already guessed, sir, also counted amongst his lovers. And so, a libertine, and so, a loathsome sinner, paying no heed to human decency! Whereas I, growing up, had to listen for the hundred and thousandth time to tales of his fornications, since people take delight in discussing every tiny detail of the sins of others, for, unlike wounds to the flesh, wounds to the soul, clawed over, fingered and inflamed, afford greater pleasure when they're not your own; and the sensuality of it somehow suits the pleasures of the table – I speak still of sins – we relish them, sniff the bouquet, weigh up whether heavy enough, whether well tenderised, whether as thick as they should be, whilst those well-seasoned for years, for generations – are all the nobler, and those uncommon, exceptional ones – all the tastier; and feasts also take place not infrequently in the likeness of Ancient Rome: reclining in sloth, already sated, and yet not sated, with eyes closed and a smirk of sweet satisfaction, we listen avidly to the downfall of others; therefore imagine, sir, what I went through, forced to listen, to witness such banquets – as though those sins were being eaten out of my very side – Promethean torments. Endure it I could not; I did not endure.

'Maybe everything would have turned out differently, had my mother still been alive. She died in childbirth, entrusting us to the care of a nanny and a tutor, not so that our father shouldn't look after us, quite the reverse; she died giving birth to a second son, Fyodor; he was to remain at home. The old tutor, who had been her own preceptor, mother had brought with her from Yaroslavl; so in times of father's absence, when he was away on business, often for months at a time – when we could not help but worry where father spent his days and nights: was it not with another of his families, another wife, more beautiful, with other better sons whom he genuinely loved? – in such times the tutor managed the entire estate and then, in order to kill those thoughts, in order to occupy head and heart, I began to accompany him in the duties of a landowner and little by little even take them over. My eyes were opened to the lot of the Russian common folk. And if you're going to mock me now, sir... well, all right.

'Easy it is to arouse holy indignation in young heads and rage against injustice. Our common people are so accustomed to misfortunes and sufferings, they even fail to see, to understand the scale of the unnecessary injury they experience, family after family, hamlet and hamlet, guberniya and guberniya; even those wails, those laments of peasant women at the feet of the village priest and their tears before the icons, when you look upon them from the side – are likewise a ritual, likewise a custom sanctified by a thousand-year tradition. For what is needed is that someone should indeed look upon them from the side. He it is who sees the iniquity, who is able to name the wrong, the one who is unwronged – in him, I say, arises the remorse and the anger, the anger against injustice. You know, Venyedikt Filipovitch, the fate of Job. And that bargain of the Lord against Job, and Job's bargaining in the spirit of overbearing humility. "He destroys both the blameless and the wicked! The earth is given into the hand of the wicked, he covereth the faces of its judges – and if it is not he, who then is it?" But Job clung to the memory at least of his time of happiness, knew therefore the measure of his downfall and counted the days of wrong against the days of right – but the Russian peasant lies lower still than Job, and in this is more like a wild animal, more like a thoughtless beast than rational man, for no hope burns in him for a change to his fate, no lasting desire to alter his lot, just as you've never see a worn-out nag harnessing a driver to a shaft and sitting atop a box. And wonder not, sir, at my bitterness towards the people – how many days and evenings I sacrificed then, exploiting the forbearance of the old tutor, to efforts to improve their lives, going against the stewards and other landowners, yet who in the end brought all to naught, who ridiculed my endeavours? They themselves! The suffering folk! And I used to return from their miserable hovels, from their sickly children and haggard wives, from their cold, dark chambers, where if a candle burned at all, then only in the hanging lamp neath the holy icon, to a warm house, eiderdowns on my bed, to a lavish table, under the eyes of servants – and only then would the anger of injustice seize me, tug at me, cause me such a fit of trembling as you may have seen, sir, in people smitten by apoplexy, in them. Thus, the voice of Divine righteousness makes itself felt in man; and because in me, as I said, it had been aroused for better or worse due to my own father, I was all the more incapable of smothering it.

'That is the wrong! That is the torment only a Russian can comprehend! Not the suffering of Job, not the suffering of undeserving downfall – but the reverse, Anti-Job: the suffering of undeserving elevation! Gospodin Yeroslavsky! Can you not, can you not, can you – pour me another, brother! – not grasp it, I see you staring as if at a madman. And yet no pain is comparable: any Job is always noble and hallowed in his injury, for what is more deserving in heaven's eyes than the humble forbearance of blameless misfortune, what leads with greater certainty from this life on earth to the life eternal? – whilst Anti-Job is condemned in his torment, and for him you have no salvation: every luxury, every happiness, every triumph and satisfaction over and above his neighbour's is an ever greater pain for his conscience, a bloody wound lacerating deeper into the soul. Endure it I could not. No one imprisoned me there, after all, on the stage of my torment; I had a little money saved from my father's donations, the train to Saint Petersburg ran every Saturday... I did not endure. I knew not what might assuage this agony in Petersburg, yet I was not mistaken – pain cannot be shared with another person, but doesn't the very knowledge that we're not alone in it bring us some relief? In the city, I met those like myself, with similar experiences and convictions, became acquainted with the names of the enemies, read the prescriptions of Lavroff, De Laveleye, Pisaryeff and Marx himself, and the means for righting injustice... I joined the Marxist Narodniks and then the Socialist Revolutionary Party.

'The earth is given into the hand of the wicked! And his name is tsar, and his name is rich man and bourgeois and dark reaction! The faces of judges are hidden from simple men; nor shall you reach justice in your lifetime through violence, in this world, neath the sun of Evil. Nothing shall you gain against this or that human wrong, whilst the generals and tchinovniks stand behind it – first you have to destroy this world, which persists in evil, and create a different one that favours the well-being of all. Were there any certainty amongst us, it was precisely this. Those who began from below, from one man and one suffering, fell like Sisyphus; they gave up the struggle or came in the end to us. Minimalism proved impractical – maximalism alone realistic. There was clarity in it, a kind of sublimity typical of eschatological projects: a purpose bordering on miracle, transformation so total it can be likened only to the descent of the Kingdom of God – a necessary impossibility. If you could but imagine, sir, that state of soul... Sometimes, before a winter dawn, when sunlight streams over the city snow and ice and white mist rises above the silent streets, you'll fling your window wide-open after a sleepless night, gaze upon the sunrise in its immaculate purity, take into your chest the crisp, crackling air – your head will spin, but at the same time you'll feel such elation and wondrous lightness, as if you'd been irradiated by that bracing dazzle in body and soul, irradiated, cleansed and made as one with the angels, so that every thought shining in your head will be unavoidably real, sacredly correct – and you think YES.

'Our assassination attempts were therefore good, bombs thrown at dignitaries correct, the terror blessed. I attended the strikes of the First Revolution, described the history of the Council of Workers' Delegates. That failure was a terrible blow to us. The SR Combat Organisation was finally compromised in the Year of the Gleissen – but that was not the cause of my disillusionment. For a long time, our group had leant towards the Bolsheviks. I was close enough to take part in those debates, on paper and with people, saw how ideas shifted amongst them, how visions supplant visions, how somewhere between cigarette and cigarette, between a mass rally and a quarrel in a printing shop – a new necessity replaces the old. At first, the Bolsheviks spoke of revolution by the proletariat and peasantry to topple the autocracy, erase the practices of slavery and erect, on foundations of democracy, the Russian Republic. But then the revolution turns into a socialist one. Then such and such a government would arise, such and such a power – our – their – power do this and that, in this way, no, in that way, no, in still another way, and the more their hopes were dashed, the more the emperor felt secure, the better went Stolypin's reforms, whilst they, the fewer votes they had in subsequent Dumas, clashed all the more sharply over their own future government and methods for administering justice. You will say, sir, that I should have seen it at once after the affair with Lenin and the Mensheviks – that most horrifying dream of Anti-Job: for what was this struggle, if not a sure road to even greater elevation?

'I joined the anarchists, Bakuninist Brotherhood and Anti-Struvists. The second Japanese war broke out. Stolypin resigned, hunger entered the cities, Star Chamber invented Struve, Trotsky brought Lenin from Cracow, their last time together under one standard, we came to a halt on the barricades. I wasn't even scratched. The gendarmes took us sleeping, we'd fallen asleep in the frost, Winter had entered along with hunger. It transpired the Okhrana had had us all on record for a long time, they read me such things about myself, Gospodin Yeroslavsky, such things... An odd feeling to see yourself described by a satanic hand, hear your whole life out of the mouths of collectors of sin. They show you no faithful reflection, that's for sure, but their lying isn't random or irrational, bah, it's not even lying dreamt up by themselves:

they say what they see, but in every event and in every soul, they're capable of perceiving only what is dark, their eyes work only in shadow, in this they're like those blinded by unlicht, their ears hear only the sounds of night and the underworld, words of malice, anger and envy, such is the testimony they give and such the world they reflect. And only with time, years later, do you understand how much truth they told of you in that falsehood – for you would never see yourself in such harsh unlicht: *the worst man you could ever be.* As that kind of man, I stood before my judges. Whatever evil I could have done, but did not do – I did. Whatever foul deeds I could have committed, but did not commit – they will describe to me in detail. From temptations resisted – everything to which I succumbed. From the truth – lies. From the lies – truth. And from those noble deeds, which it is not in their power to deny – they will take away the nobility, revealing to me the blackest of perverse intentions propelling me towards them. It is a confession a thousand times crueller and more deeply wrenched from the soul than any admission made before God of your own free will. Of course, you can scream before the earthly judges and swear on holy images that it's all twisted and bears little resemblance to the truth; they will believe or not believe you, but this is not what it's about. Were you ever loved, sir, with a truly boundless love? And what saw you in the eyes of that besotted woman? What kind of you? The best you could possibly be, or not? And that also was a lie. But it is precisely by such lies that we learn the truth about ourselves.

'And who should hear it, who should be sitting from the very start on the first bench… He found me then, came for the trial – the father from whom I had fled in order to propagate good against his fornication. He paid off the lawyers, begrudged not the money spent on bribes; to no avail. Katorga awaited me, I was already enlisted before the prosecutor had uttered his first word. We were deported to Sybir.

'Truth and truth, the highest of truths, we need to keep repeating it: God knows what path to choose for us, what cross to lay upon our shoulders – in those days, there was no better life for me, no other deliverance, only katorga. Do you see these wounds, sir? And what you see not, what's covered by my beard growth, and these fingers, and what else I suffered on my body – all these are traces of my first year. Mainly we worked felling forests, not in the Land of the Gleissen itself, though later the Ice advanced there too – either way it was winter. The trunks of Siberian cedars froze to stone, as the earth froze to stone, snow to stone… You are travelling, sir, to Irkutsk, there you will see such frosts as there's no point in my describing. Men who had not procured clothing fit for Siberia at once lost fingers, ears, whole swathes of frostbitten skin, as if touched by leprosy. It was little better for our guards. And soldiers also turned up there as if exiled. When the Ice came, the tin buttons on their uniforms crumbled like dry clay. I shall never forget, oh, the first gleiss I saw in the taiga. The Buryats have this superstition that in the wilds, icers are attracted to open fire, a bonfire, smoke rising from an isolated cot, when such a fire has been kept going for several days; and that particular gleiss had settled on a stony clearing (for it had already sucked out all the grit and boulders from under the soil), in the midst of which three huntsmen were stuck huddled over a spit and its carcass: frozen to death – like stone. It sat on them like a spider on the corpses of flies. We had to register it with the natchalnik. There's a prikaz that every movement of gleissen is to be reported at once; apparently the Ministry of Winter uses them to plot its own Ways of the Mammoths, it possesses huge atlases, or, as our people say: geomantic horoscopes of the tides of the Ice. An order came from the higher natchalstvo: be vigilant and write with every post. Then two scholars arrived. Thus, I made the acquaintance of Sergey Andreyevitch Atchukhoff.

'Sergey Andreyevitch. He… But first – don't stint me, sir, come, fill it up, uh – but first…

'Ever been exhausted, sir? Really exhausted? Exhausted above all else? For how to measure exhaustion? This is how: by the things which lose importance for you when you're exhausted. So, in the beginning, you no longer care about food: you are so exhausted, all that matters is to crash onto your pallet and fall asleep in the warm. Then you cease to care about warmth – so long as you can escape from that reality into sleep and your exhausted body within it. The last thing to desert you is shame: when nothing arouses a shameful thought, when you no longer feel humiliated in relation to anyone in any situation and have grown indifferent to any debasement – that is the sign of ultimate exhaustion. For I have known men who did not raise a hand to shield themselves from a mortal blow, but dragged themselves onward in torment, so as not to give a hated guard the satisfaction of contempt. Contempt and shame: these are the Siberian thermometers of the spirit.

'Through exhaustion, therefore, began my return. Revelation came from the body. Exhaustion deprives us of all things, one after another, till naught remains but the body. You see it then with that same frosty, sublime obviousness – the mind is empty and pure – you see that man is no more than a simple mechanism of flesh. A movement of the hands, the lifting of an axe, the blow, the jolt, legs, shoulders, hands, the lifting of an axe, the blow, the jolt, legs, shoulders, hands, axe, hands, legs, shoulders, hands, legs, shoulders, hands, legs, shoulders, yes, yes, yes. And there is even no thought in it: "hands, legs, shoulders"; none. Only monotonous movement and the calm animal consciousness of movement, flowing in an unmuddied stream like water over ice, the mind is empty and pure. Wake up, defecate, swallow warm kasha, fasten clothing, boots, gloves, cap – we walk to the forest – left foot, right foot, we chop down trees, so hands, legs, shoulders, we eat, defecate, sleep, wake, hands, legs, shoulders, we eat, defecate, sleep, body, body, body, only so much remains, the mechanics of raw physiology. Day merges into day, time takes on the shape of a wheel, language ceases to convey complex thoughts – there are no other thoughts than simple reflexes of bodily processes – only verbal signals: "here", "there", "give me", "no", "yes", "foe", "non-foe", "warmth", "cold".

'Then I met Sergey Andreyevitch Atchukhoff. He spoke to me. That is, he spoke first to my body. I know not how I attracted his attention. People recognise one another on the basis of signals betrayed precisely by their bodies. When all thoughts depart and motivations melt away, the things most deeply implanted in the body remain: reflexes, mannerisms, rhythm, posture, but also something of the signs that physiognomists interpret, for it is not so that our face grows on our skull over years and years and remains untouched by our daily grind. Of course, we cannot describe them; were we able to control them, were they subject to our consciousness, such features would not belong to the order of the body, but the order of spirit. So, we say: chance. We say: the finger of God. We say: love at first sight. We say: kinship of souls.

'Sergey Andreyevitch is himself an exile, a high-born Tolstoyan, banished to Siberia at the instigation of an envious relative and courtier. Excommunicated besides by the Synod, whilst the Black Hundreds ensure he returns none too swiftly from Sybir. His friends have deserted him, his fortune he gave away. He was residing meanwhile in Tomsk and was a regular guest of Governor General Schultz-Zimovy in Irkutsk. Often, he travels in the wake of gleissen and writes letters to European newspapers from the lands of the Ice, conducts research. When I got to know him, he was still in his prime; you might take him for a peasant, sir, so modest is his dress, so rough his visage, and he has in him a kind of rigid humility, unruffled calm and great patience, characteristic of people bound by life to the slow rhythm of the soil, to the pulse of nature. I had to lead them to the gleiss's clearing, Sergey and his companion. That's how we met. And so? Chance, of course, chance.

'Sergey would relieve me of my labours. When we conversed... when it was no longer the body speaking... So, what then, apart from the body, over and above the body? He did not have to convince me; everything was in the questions. Beneath that Siberian sky, colder than the icebound earth, beneath those mountains – you might think, sir, that there is no man and never was any man amongst the animals of those wilds, that it's a genuinely pre-human land. It happened that we fell silent for hours. If not about the body, if not for the body, if not with the body – what then was there to talk about? think about? wherein the sense? wherefore the life? In that which is bodily, there is no answer. Look, sir! When a man has known the void hidden behind the mechanics of the flesh, lived in that treadmill of physiological inertia, he knows one thing beyond doubt: *the body cannot be the substance and purpose of the body.* The purpose of life is outside life. Man cannot be the meaning and justification of man – these lie outside of him, beyond matter, but what is matter? Only when you live for what is not matter do you truly live, that is, you are no longer simply a wave of repetitive movement: arm, leg, arm, leg, arm, leg, until thou art laid in earth, and then it's the maggots that move.

'I don't know myself when I told Sergey Andreyevitch my story. We tell it to strangers so they cease to be strangers – vodka helps, yes – but to non-strangers, what about non-strangers? A word contrary to their experience? They've already got to know the best truth about us they could know. It's then the lie is born: we try to explain, seek interpretations beyond ourselves, find reasons which come, obviously, from outside (from outside of our body). But Sergey knew nothing of me; everything I told him was the truth. I told him of the wrong done to Anti-Job, about the revolution, about the defeats of the Marxists. Yet what came out of my mouth, I myself already heard differently from before. Because what actually was to distinguish communism from capitalism? Both reduce man to matter. For both, man is but a body. And what he will eat, what he will excrete, and especially how much it's all worth, eschatology translated into figures and roubles, not the soul, but a balance of trade. So, no deliverance from there.

'The only genuine revolution, that is, transformation of the world, can take place through changing human nature – not through this or that transfer of matter, or system for disposing of material goods, but through changing what governs matter. Evangelisation, says Sergey Andreyevitch, the conversion of the Russian people. Do people believe in God? Even when they say they believe, they live as if they did not. You watch: this man lives like this, a second like that, that one there like this, yet another – like that. Who is a Christian, and who merely has a box of roubles jingling in his heart? You won't recognise him! Won't recognise him! How is it possible? What kind of faith is it, what kind of God, what kind of lost Christians are they, when by their own deeds and words they disavow their hopes every day, in every hour? Such a man will say: I have to do it, have to care for my family, secure them food and a roof over their heads, I have to obey my superiors, observe the law; nor can I deny myself violence, for how else should I defend myself against evil – am I not permitted to take up stick and stone, when an evildoer stands on my threshold and wishes to harm my little ones? Atchukhoff says: well no, you are not permitted; well no, if you be a true sparrow of God, if you have surrendered yourself to the sway of the invisible kingdom and placed your trust in timeless laws, if now you lie with your deeds and your neglect, behaving as if God existed not and as if only the law of the body, Caesar's law, could save you. Away with Caesar's law! – enact God's law! – create the reign of God on Earth! Only then will all people live according to this idea in every second of their consciousness – God is, God is, His power, His plan, His victory in the lowliest victory of the good, in Him the resurrection and bliss eternal – only then will the face of the Earth be changed and the Empire of Good arise.

'Such was the conversion of Filimon Romanovitch Zeytsoff neath the Siberian sky.

'When I returned from exile, I found my brother Fyodor married with children, still living in our father's house. Apart from this, everything was as before, but I was new and everything was different. What did those sideways glances of the neighbours, malicious whispers and vindictive gossip, mean to me now? I myself had brought with me my own shame, they slandered me, pointed the finger at me. Ah, the rebel! Ah, the criminal, the katorzhnik! Cursed anarchist! Then I looked upon them with the eyes of my father. For what remains to such a poor devil – will he give credence to strangers when portrayed by black tongues, or will he give credence to his own heart? Who sooner knows the truth about a man: the man himself or other people? But! You say, sir, a person knows not the truth. He knows it, knows it. Knows not that he knows it, yet knows. So, listen further: it happened that such snows fell on our town for a day and the next, so that those of us passing through as guests were trapped, unable to reach the provincial highway, and because the blizzard also found my father there, he forbade me to sleep overnight at the inn – for two days I put up in the house of my father's Sofiya. And there, oh, I saw such debauchery: a homely loving family, a man and a woman and their daughters, and that love between them which precisely a person unversed in such love sees all the more clearly – since it's neither gold, nor health, nor accolades, but precisely love that everyone envies first and foremost. And then, when Yelizaveta visited them, and then, when the little girls sang over the baby's cradle, and when I saw them all together in the one room with Sofiya's sister, Gospodin Yeroslavsky, the sole reason I didn't burst into tears was surely because my last tears had dried up long ago in Sybir. You speak of shame, sir! Only a man liberated from Caesar's laws of the flesh, only he can be ashamed before himself, or rather before the God within him. So here was this selfless fatherly love, born originally maybe out of passion, I know not, maybe so – unenvious, generous, measuring no boundaries and counting no interest – what beside such love were all our projects of justice for the people, our altruistic economic programmes? what our revolutions and uprisings?

'Verily, the honest voluptuary is closer to God than the greatest politician selling his soul to the good of humanity.

'You laugh, sir? You laugh? … Well, so be it.

'But what now – now too, thanks again only to my father's money, I am able to save Sergey Andreyevitch. How much it has cost me, I shan't say, a lot, a lot. Already his left lung, by all accounts, is completely shrivelled, another year in Winter and death will be certain, even though he's an old gleissenik. Three months I spent trudging around offices and palaces; I thought to rent lodgings in Saint Petersburg, in the old days you could bribe the right person and be sure the thing was fixed, today you have to buy off one authority, and then a second, in case one's not enough, and a third, in case that one changes its mind, but even then it's better to light a candle before an icon and say an occasional prayer; there's no certainty, so that I waited until the last moment for the papers with the reprieve, and if I don't oversee it myself, maybe they'll find Sergey no longer alive – and in the end I had to expend a fortune on the ticket, the only man with a seat to Irkutsk willing to come forward was that greedy Armenian; but from the second-class sleeping car, every man I tried to accost, imagine, sir, from the second-class car, no one on the platform wanted to resell their place, something incomprehensible, the world stood on its head, ungraspable by human reason; pour me another, sir.'

'Beautiful.'

'Oy, she was beautiful, beautiful.'

Hand him back the photograph.

'So, tell me, are you now a new Christian, therefore not for matter, not for the flesh, not to be confused therefore with the godless, yes?'

But he was already having to support his head with a hand, now the right, now the left, and thus he transferred the burden of his brain from fist to fist, until his bonce slipped from his grasp and his forehead hit the table, the glasses jangled and the ashtray leapt in the air – this sobered him up for a while longer. He straightened himself hastily in his chair, glanced around the saloon, blinking with a grim expression. The door to the billiard room was pushed back, a fierce game of blizzarder was again in progress with the participation of Captain Privyezhensky and Mr Fessar. Diagonally opposite the green table, by the travelling library, sat Miss Muklanowicz, pretending to be engrossed in a well-trawled ladies' magazine, *Le Chic Parisien* or *Wiener Chic*.

Earlier on, Privy Councillor Dushin had peered in. Observe that he has a great desire to approach and talk, and only the presence of

Zeytsoff – his matted mane of hair, crumpled frock coat, drunken sing-song and sweeping gesticulations – only the presence of the ex-convict constrained him. Reach automatically for the watch – but it's no longer there, smashed to bits. Glance at the face of the case clock. Already gone six, evening shadows will soon begin to spread beyond the windows. An entire afternoon wasted on a boozing bout with Zeytsoff.

'Not to be mistaken, not to be mistaken,' he muttered, 'but of course, for the flesh! Only for the body! Am I not a weak human being? One more slave! Yes, yes, you, sir, have seen through me – what of it that I know, what of it that I've recognised the way? We all know the path to happiness, and if we know it not, then we sense it, intuit it, and surely already discern the evil paths – but what of it, it's one thing to know the path and another to follow it, look at me, sir, a weak, weak man, and it was precisely then, on that day at Sofiya's, in front of my father and his women and my half-sisters, that I understood that I would disappoint Sergey Andreyevitch, must disappoint him, for were even a hair to fall from their heads, I would not hesitate to shed the blood of their injurer, nor would I rely on Divine Providence, and I disappoint him now precisely by buying him this reprieve, by kowtowing to Caesar. Do you suppose, sir, that I do not see it: I see it – if I rescue him from Winter, it will be against his will. Yes.'

Here he grabbed hold of the carafe and let the remaining alcohol slip into the decorative glass; raising the glass with a sure hand towards the dense wisps of his heavy moustache, into his black beard, he downed the vodka in a single gulp. Chest out, deeper breath, fists resting on the bone surface of the tabletop, eyes goggling, then a second breath, and *voilà*, Filimon Romanovitch Zeytsoff is as sober as a judge.

'Venyedikt Filipovitch,' he declaimed, upon which he raised a stubby finger to the height of his forehead as if aiming straight ahead from a pistol, screwing up even his eye and knitting his brow, 'I see you, see you plainly. You are from them. Do you think I don't know what you're up to? I see it very well.'

'You are drunk.'

'And what has that to do with it? I can recognise it. And Sergey also told me. That second doctor from Winter with Berdyaeff under his arm… they're all gleisseniks… you won't play cards or throw dice… or interpret dreams, dreams… under the Ice. Krrr, khrrrk!' He coughed violently. 'O holy Yefrem, all ye saints, what dryness – water, water! – save a suffering man!'

He rose – tried to rise to his feet; preparing to stand so sluggishly that disentangling himself from the chair demanded such gymnastics that it was possible to catch him in time, hold him down and summon the steward. A third carafe appeared.

Zeytsoff downed the next half-glass and his countenance smoothened.

'Don't be angry, Venyedikt Filipovitch, I meant no evil; when you say you've never been to the Land of the Gleissen, I believe you, why should I not believe you, but you can't surprise me either. You will see for yourself. Although, on the surface, it seems very much like your own, it's a different world, governed by different laws.' He looked round at the gamblers. 'We will ride into it, and at once they'll no longer feel like playing. You will recognise it, sir, after the first game of patience.'

'What you were saying about Lyednyaks – you and Lyednyaks –'

'Me and Lyednyaks! What – me and Lyednyaks?! Motherfuckers, Lyednyak dogs and their Lyednyak bitches!'

'Control yourself! Or they'll throw us out!'

Indeed, in the Deluxe saloon car, they had been watching Zeytsoff askance from the beginning. Now again they turned their heads. At the billiard table, a game was just finishing, the players were standing upright, stretching their limbs; Doctor Konyeshin, who stood nearest, almost sprang forward at the convict's vulgar outburst. Restrain him with an apologetic smile.

'Filimon Romanovitch, I ask you, have you ever had anything to do with Lyednyaks in high politics, do you hear me? – and what's all this business, the Ice and Berdyaeff, I mean, what's that all about – and also, what was it you discerned in me? But! Come, Filimon, dear man! Control yourself, for pity's sake, think of the shame before other people.'

'Shame before other people, shame before other people,' the bearded sloven kept repeating, scratching mechanically the scars on his frostbitten fingers, 'in other words, in other words, were it not for other people, sir, you wouldn't feel ashamed, correct? I tell you, we are all slaves.

'And as to what I discerned – as if you don't know already, half the engineers in Zimny Nikolayevsk are unlichted to the core. In the lobby of the Leaky Palace hangs a photograph, go there sometime and see for yourself; in nineteen thirteen, when the coldmills were set up, they all took commemorative snapshots – panoramas of the new town in the background, roofs, chimneys, fires, gleissen, whilst here, in the foreground, their whole brigade. Well, when they came out on those photographs, every other man looked like a ghost chased from the grave, his visage black as a Negro's, eyes, gob, hair, everything the wrong way around, whilst others still were bled of light and appeared only as men-shaped blotches, instead of men. And you ask me, sir! I see it clearly.

'And when in Petersburg I wiped the imperial antechambers with my knees, of what were the rumours, of what the whispers in the corners? As soon as I returned from Sybir, I went forthwith to the journals.

And there, old friends from conspiratorial days gave forewarning of the news. I had been in exile, whilst in Petersburg a new politics had taken shape against the backdrop of Winter, new parties and factions and secret coalitions, new alliances in the Duma and at court. There are those for whom it's fine as it is, who admit no change, only that everything should be frozen just as it is for as long as possible, but if changed, then changed in such a way so as not to change it; whilst there are those who dream of thaw and great transformation in Russia. Except that with a Lyednyak – everyone knows who he is and why; but an Ottepyelnik, a-ah! – one Ottepyelnik and the next Ottepyelnik are not the same, because he's a Struvist, and a whole-hearted socialist, and a silver-haired Narodnik, and an anarchist, and any old occidentalist, and even a Kadet, that is, a constitutional democrat, they all supposedly want change. But no alliance of any kind can arise between them. They merely wonder as one at why the old Russia is still as she was, as she is; barely touched by Stolypin and Struve, she freezes back immediately and becomes the laughing stock of Europe and the world, an autocratic empire opposed to the democratic monarchies of steam, iron and electricity – as it was in the eighteenth century, and in the nineteenth, so it is in the twentieth, and shall be forever and ever amen, Russia.

'Then Nikolay Berdyaeff writes his *History of the Ice* and explains after his own fashion, in the new *Questions of Life*, Russia's whole misfortune. Berdyaeff was also something of a Marxist, but now he's above all an ardent Christian and idealist of History. Thus, he writes: History should have proceeded otherwise. Do you observe, sir! He writes: it was not meant to be like this, truth has been concealed from us, we live in the age of the Antichrist, a false history of the world is being fulfilled. But in actual fact – you wonder, sir, and wonder rightly – how, according to what, can we recognise that our History is different? Different from what? Are we being given insight into separate courses of time, given a mirror onto different fates, so we might examine in it lives unlived, wars unwaged and emperors never even born? Only one History do we know: our own. Like when we glimpse only one animal of an unfamiliar species – there is no way you can tell whether it's the beast in its entirety and alike unto to its kin in everything or some kind of freak and wondrous oddity. But, as they say, Nikolay Berdyaeff is an idealist of History and does not believe at all that human reason cannot embrace it. History is governed by laws not so very different from the laws of nature, and whatever happens, happens not by chance. This means: not any sequence of events is possible. In fact, only that which is necessary is possible – and so epochs follow on after one another according to the method of logical emergence: the Renaissance out of the Middle Ages, the Enlightenment out of the Renaissance, and not, for example, the other way around. But! But! What Berdyaeff goes on to write: that before our very eyes, the impossible is in fact happening! that reality is contradicting the laws of History!

'Which, according to him, are such that with the end of the previous century, in the world of spirit, the dominion of the Renaissance idea came to an end, and an appropriate change ought to have followed in the world of flesh. For it is obvious that new thought and purpose and vision of the future do not arise spontaneously from the movement of matter, but are born in the spirit, and spirit then imposes them on sensory beings. Always, therefore, that which is not of the body precedes that of the body. Only slaves to the illusions spawned by capitalism and Marxism believe in the autonomy of the body. Why do you pull such faces, huh? It's the sacred truth after all! They are slaves! Were they honest men, they would not speak even for themselves. But somehow like this: my hand, my mouth, my head. That is, not "I was born", but "a body was born". Not "I speak", but "my mouth speaks", "my head speaks". Well what? Well what? We are all slaves, but not all of us have surrendered to the power of the flesh.

'The turning-point was to be accomplished therefore precisely in Russia – for Russia never fully emerged from the Middle Ages, there was no Russian Renaissance, here an epoch is born and closes, here the old converges with the new. We look at the world, at the West, and we see an end to the acceptance of any kind of spiritual order, everything hurtles now towards either extreme individualism or extreme collectivism. A revolutionary change had therefore to manifest itself, in matter out of spirit. Yet it has not manifested itself; there is no change. What has happened, so that nothing has happened? Well, Russia has frozen under the Ice, and our History has frozen.

'Because even when the reality of matter lies, the reality of spirit speaks truth; here, therefore, we need to be watching for the signs of History such as it ought to be. Berdyaeff travelled throughout Europe and every issue of *Questions of Life* published the results of his inquiry against matter. There was plenty of it there. A moment whilst I – er – rinse the abschmacks from my throat… Oh! Look at that fashionable young woman, sir, the lace, the baleen stays neath silk and satin, that singularly narrow skirt! Fashion! In what appears attractive to our eyes, tasteful and becoming, or not, we discover our likes and dislikes – and as in clothes so in furniture and home décor, so in architecture. You happen to see photographs of the metropolises of Europe and America. And what do you see? Differences plain to the naked eye. For the last ten, fifteen years – since the coming of the Ice; and plainest where the boundary runs – up to where the gleissen have reached. The whole of the Russian Empire, a bit to the south, the Balkans, Scandinavia and

China. But it is gradually spreading, like Winter, like the freezing temperatures: warmer here, cooler there. Berdyaeff says that in the final reckoning, but to a far-from-equal degree, the entire globe has been frozen. Which, obviously, there's no way of proving, or describing in detail. Well, but since it's so very striking in women's apparel – oh! – in all those flounces, frills and furbelows... Should you ever have occasion, sir, to peek in the Parisian journals –'

'I have.'

'I kiss your hand, Mademoiselle! You won't be angry, will you, at my pointing the finger, you see, Mademoiselle, I was about to –'

'I heard. You speak true, sir. Corsets there are an ancient memory. The cut of dresses is totally different, types of loose smock, flowing shawls, bayadère girdles, outer petticoats densely draped – whatever inspirations Monsieur Poiret takes from the Orient. Skirts barely reaching the knees, and sometimes not reaching; bah, so long as they're still skirts – but, jupe-culottes? I couldn't believe that ladies really wear such things.'

'Exactly so! And why didn't you believe it, miss? Why wouldn't you dress like that yourself?'

'Well, you know, sir... it's not proper.'

'Oh! And whence that little voice, miss, prompting in your pretty little head what is proper and what improper, eh? What is tasteful and what not? Why you like what you like, and like not what you don't like? Eh?

'And Berdyaeff also wrote about this: not only that things were freezing, but how they were freezing. Corsets, you say, miss. For, in the world of spirit, there is no great difference between restrictive, confining clothing and political confinement or imprisonment of the word. The same idea manifests itself wherever it can. We thought that vatermörders and high stand-up collars were *passé*, but here in the Europe of the Ice, *voilà*, they are once again popular!

'And why are inventions that have caught on over there not accepted here? Why does electrification of our cities proceed with such resistance? And automobiles? The closer we get to Winter, the fewer motorcars on the streets. And that invention called the cinematograph – have you ever seen a film, miss, moving images? In Warsaw perhaps. And the books we read? And the melodies played at balls and salons? Why is it that radio sets can't find buyers in Russia? And few are willing to send voice or music from house to house by wireless telegraph. Am I wrong? Benedykt, sir?

'So, here you have: the Ice and false History frozen in defiance of historical necessity. For were it not for the gleissen, says Berdyaeff, were it not for the gleissen, we'd already have had some revolution or other, or the collapse of our autonomous state: the end of Russia in her old guise; we'd have had a Russia torn apart between the extremes of the Postmediaeval Age. And yet, one way or another, Russia and the world have to go through this in order to fulfil the will of God and draw near to His Kingdom. Because, as I was telling you, sir – the young lady may not have heard – this is the most important thing of all: since, according to Berdyaeff, the whole movement of History and the laws turning its wheels are a manifestation of the divine plan and consequence of the one fact in History which is unique and completely divorced from the laws of matter, namely the birth and death of the Son of God, Jesus Christ – wherefrom begins the true History of Mankind.

'And by what means does Nikolay Aleksandrovitch Berdyaeff testify with such certainty to the will of God? Well may you ask, and you ask rightly. God reveals himself to us not in burning bushes, sends no prophets heralded by miracles, speaks not out of heaven. But we know our past, we know History, and we have been given the understanding to tell it to ourselves in clear words. *History is the sole direct means whereby God communicates with man.*

'And so you have Lyednyaks and Ottepyelniks, because, though not all who orientate politically along these lines in the Duma or in newspaper backbiting have read Berdyaeff, and not all who have read him believe in him, there are enough of them however in Saint Petersburg, in the Tauride Palace and in Tsarskoye Selo, in ministries, amongst courtiers and tchinovniks, and on both sides: Lyednyaks convinced that only the gleissen are defending Russia from downfall and bloody chaos, that only the Ice protects her from collapse; and Ottepyelniks persuaded that until they drive the Frost from the country, no reform will have any effect, that no coup, no revolution and no democratisation is possible, and that nothing will change for the good in this autocratic realm; there are enough of them to steer the politics of their parties and societies according to their own fears. But because no one expresses it openly, since we already have legions of holy duffers prophesying in the gleissen the Antichrist and annihilation of the world, apocalypses great and gloomy –'

'Martsynians.'

'Were it only they! You are a Pole, sir, not so? And the young lady is also from the Vistula Land – you have your own messianisms, to you such hunger is not foreign, hunger for what? With us, you see, mysticism doesn't end with religion. Or begin with it. Russian messianism spawned the Narodniks, and socialists, and anarchists; all politics and streams of ideas in Russia flow from mystical springs – why should it be different with Lyednyaks and Ottepyelniks? Imagine, sir, a non-human visitation befalling the land and turning summer into winter, here and there and there, towns and meadows into the Sybir of Sybirs, and a Russian not seeing in this the hand of God and a thousand spiritual symbols? Hah! It cannot be! Was I not telling you, Benedykt, sir – I told you, no? – of the fate of my fellow Marxists: this hunger in us is so great that we must take everything absolutely, totally and dogmatically – for many, even materialism has become a religion; I have known ascetics and mystics of materialism who had visions, rational epiphanies, whereby proofs were revealed to them of the non-existence of God and other sacred certainties of atheism, they experienced ecstasies of logic, of historiosophy.

'The young lady laughs, to her it seems, agh, *c'est tout à fait ridicule*, but it must be taken entirely practically. Our rulers know well this affliction of the common people: Russian obscurantism has its rationale. Midway through the past century, Minister of Education Prince Shirinsky-Shakhmatoff banned lectures in philosophy at the universities – they knew whence the real threat. But a few years go by, and another ukase comes from Saint Petersburg: philosophy is permitted and the natural sciences are prohibited. You see, miss, how in Russia things rumble on? At one time flesh is in the ascendant, at another – spirit. But the struggle is one and the same.

'So, what really lies behind the politics of Lyednyaks and Ottepyelniks? Were there no writings of Nikolay Berdyaeff, they'd be puffing themselves up with a different metaphysics of the Ice, as surely as two times two is four. It's just that –'

'Politics is a function of culture, and the heart of culture is, alas, religion.'

'Pardon?'

'Will you allow me to join you, lady and gentlemen?' Doctor Konyeshin crept from behind Zeytsoff's chair and stubbed out his cigarette in the ashtray right under his nose. Zeytsoff froze in semi-panicked reaction, knowing not whether to tuck his head into shoulders or leap to his feet and flee.

'As a matter of fact, Doctor, sir, we –'

'Thank you.'

Miss Muklanowicz had occupied the last of the three armchairs provided around the table. Doctor Konyeshin therefore grabbed a chair from beside the radio cabinet and sat down sideways-on, next to Jelena, whose hand he first smacked with a kiss, introducing himself in a half-bow. She fired a startled glance across the table. Gather the thoughts. What to do now? Drunk yet not drunk, whatever he had to confess, Zeytsoff had already confessed; more alcohol might still be poured into him, but what was the sense in that? Having serious doubts that Zeytsoff is that Lyednyak assassin. If such political thinking really does lie behind the Lyednyaks, then they would not have sent a sotted ex-katorzhnik – a man who is, after all, very far removed himself from Lyednyak thinking – in order to restrain Doctor Tesla and his machines. Would they really have shrunk from unbolting the tracks and derailing the whole Express? Even if half the management of Sibirkhozheto were on board along with their families?

Doctor Konyeshin crossed one leg over the other; the train jerked, the doctor lost balance and again placed his feet wide apart. At the same time, he lowered his hands onto his knees, leaning slightly towards the ex-convict – there was something false in this pose, a kind of exaggerated regularity of limbs, incompatible with man's nature, with the nature of the human body. Notice only now – perhaps because Zeytsoff's words about secret signs of the body and laws of physiognomy still rang in the ears – perceive only at this moment the geometrical symmetry which distinguishes the worthy Doctor Konyeshin: not only the arrangement of his whole figure, since this can be controlled by thought, but in the very appearance of his face, framed by ginger sideburns (so ginger they're almost red). Between those whiskers nothing spoilt the symmetry of the medic's physis. Every furrow, every hair and every sculpted feature of his counte-nance was reflected from right to left and from left to right. Blink. Perhaps the eyesight is deceptive, or perhaps the faltering light of the evening sun beyond the window casts insufficient brightness; they should already be switching on the lights... No, the truth is clear to the eye: Doctor Konyeshin has a body as symmetrical as an inkblot on a sheet of paper folded in two.

Why had this escaped the notice before? How many aberrations and miracles people remain unaware of, unable to perceive above all the nature of what is commonplace.

Blow into the cupped palm. Shadows flitted between the fingers. Better now not to smoke cigarettes. Spit not, sneeze not, cough not.

The symmetrical doctor pierced poor Zeytsoff with his stare.

'I am not sure I understood you properly, Mr...'

'Zeytsoff Filimon Romanovitch, at your service, sire, at your service.'

'Ye-es, I remember, I remember. Because you know: I've listened to enough mystical fairy tales, out of which someone's injury or misfor-tune always loomed in the end. On my own hands, I've felt blood shed by those mesmerised by such visions. And from what you were saying, sir, it appears that this Berdyaeff of yours is the next firebrand acting in God's name, wishing Europe and Russia a bloody revolution –'

'Not so, not so!' Zeytsoff waved his hands, almost knocking over the vodka carafe; startled, he pressed trembling palms under his armpits, crossing his arms over his chest. 'It's God's scourge, punishment for sins! Catharsis! Such is the necessity – there is no other path to the age of spiritual revival!'

'So, this is what God communicates to us? That we ourselves should take up pistols and knives and start killing our brothers and sisters?'

Miss Muklanowicz pouted sulkily.

'Well, it wouldn't be the first time, He's already given such orders. To kill.'

'How could you, Mademoiselle!'

'If only to Abraham.'

Zeytsoff went red in the face, saliva appeared on his lips, and something bad happened to his eyes: they began to tremble around the lids, shooting his vision now here, now there, like a garden hose dropped from the hand, showering water in random directions – at the doctor, at the ceiling, out of the window, at Miss Muklanowicz, at the billiard table, at the ceiling, at the doctor, at the bookcase, at the carpet, at the clock, at the glass, at the steward, at the ashtray, at Miss Muklanowicz, at the doctor, at Miss Muklanowicz.

'You know the Bible, miss? Imagine you have understood the Word of God? How many hours have you spent on it? How many days, nights, how many, how many? Do you know the Word or merely the dull echo of the Word issuing from your mouth? For thus it is written: God did tempt Abraham, and said unto him, Abraham, Abraham! And he said, Behold, here am I. And God said, Take now thy son, thine only son Isaac, whom thou lovest, and get thee into the land of Moriah; and offer him there for a burnt offering upon one of the mountains which I will show thee –'

Blow again into the palm, taking advantage of the interlocutors being distracted by the galloping Filimon Romanovitch and his drunken biblical sing-song. A mirror would come in handy... Here there is none; on the far side of the billiard room, there is.

See the penumbra – what of it, the penumbra of Nikola Tesla had been seen earlier when others saw it not. Nor do they see it now; or even if they see, they recognise it not, heed it not. Well, except Zeytsoff. Maybe because he dwelt for years in the lands of the Ice, maybe because he's had too much to drink; maybe for both reasons. Or maybe because he's Zeytsoff.

So, what rule to apply here? Need to sound out Doctor Tesla. Bah, but Tesla himself knows so little. Beset by doubt, he asks, seeks. He was experimenting on himself – or perhaps on someone else as well? How does he distinguish what's common to all from what's peculiar to him? More volunteers would be good.

True, he has found one. Touch the palate with the tip of the tongue. Still it tingles a little. Let's sum up: one, the light phenomena; two, the touch impressions: that smarting, itching, light-headedness and perhaps indeed surge of general energy; three, ah: even a few hours ago, the elderly Serb was laughable, but now, after deciphering the PPS-men's missive – the inventor's habit starts to become more comprehensible. Every time he bangs his head against the brick wall of a seemingly unsmashable problem, he faces temptation: the coldiron cable and jar of black salt or the teslectric dynamo – and maybe the wall will crack. How could he resist? You'll sooner cure an alcoholic.

And here, there is a new question: do they – the influence of alcohol and influence of telsectricity – mingle in the organism, and if so, with what impact? Reach for a glass. Murch freezes memory, murch straightens the paths of thought, and yet, the effects are not very different from the effects of a good allasch.

'And they went both of them together. And Isaac spoke unto Abraham his father, and said, My father: and he said, Here am I, my son. And he said, Behold the fire and the wood: but where is the lamb for a burnt offering? And Abraham said, My son, God will provide himself a lamb for a burnt offering –'

Swallow the remnants of the vodka, cough into the back of the hand. The empty glass put aside on the surface of yellowing bone swam in rainbows of pink, carmine and orange. The route of the Trans-Siberian Express ran here from north-west to south-east, and beyond the window, on the left-hand side but on the right side of the train, above the flat horizon, above the Asiatic plains and clouds daubed across the sky, hung the Sun, a red ovum, the Sun like a candied plum dripping liqueur juices onto the skyline, the setting Sun, whose white pupil could now be looked at directly without being blinded; stared at through long seconds without blinking, whilst no coloured blotches flooded the image after the eyes were averted. One, two, three – and so this is the fourth symptom. How much longer? An hour? a day? A single shock from the black current, or more – how many are needed? Before it truly enters the blood.

There were no coloured blotches on the eyes, but only after a while – perceive at what, at whom, the gaze is directed, with whom the gaze is exchanged. Captain Privyezhensky was watching over the top of his cards. Sitting at the far end of the billiard table, his back to the smoking room, separated by perhaps six or seven metres from Zeytsoff's table. He could not hear the conversation, of course – but the conversation of the cardplayers was equally inaudible. Were they talking about the notorious Benedykt non-Count Gyero-Saski, hero of the shootout in Yekaterinburg, who was now getting drunk in full view of the Deluxe passengers in the company of a communist ex-katorzhnik? The captain was smiling under his moustache as he threw banknotes onto the green baize. He said something without averting his eyes. The players chortled at length. Flee with the gaze. The setting Sun beat powerfully; doubtless for that reason the face felt so hot.

'And Abraham built an altar there, and laid the wood in order, and bound Isaac his son, and laid him on the altar upon the wood. And Abraham stretched forth his hand, and took the knife to slay his son –'

Why sit here any longer? turning into a laughingstock? As if the Lyednyak agent were to be caught! Let Jelena conduct her investigations, since she likes to dabble in them so much. But if this is to be taken seriously at all, then in truth, she ought to be dissuaded from the whole thing: assuming this secret agent really does exist, and Fogel described his intentions correctly – then when will the Lyedynak add a new target to his list: when left in peace, or when saddled with amateur detectives?

As though genuinely important problems did not weigh on the mind – problems from which it was impossible to escape, impossible to hide; they won't disappear like an empty memory on debarkation from the train. RUSSIA UNDER THE ICE, ALL MEANS YES. ATTENTION: YOUNG ONES AND OTTEPYELNIKS AGAINST WINTER! DEFEND THE GLEISSEN! But it wasn't just Petersburg factions, was it, but also Polish fighters, who gave credence to such daydreams? Bah, this letter sounded just like an order for father – an order for History – do this and this and that; wind up the gleissen, so that the Ice will congeal History as we have contemplated it. THAW TO THE DNIEPER! They had drawn lines for him on a map! As if it were in his power to choose this or that course of History, that is – flow of the Ice. Had they dreamed this up groundlessly, or had father given them word? Had he said he was going to the gleissen precisely for that? It was very like him.

Worse! Rest the feverish brow on the clenched hand. Worse, it's worse, for if the PPS knows, it's is still nothing – but if the Ministry of Winter knows? if the Russians know, their Ottepyelniks and Lyednyaks? those of Pyelka's ilk, the likes of Zeytsoff, genuine political fanatics? In which case they'd have killed father long ago! If they could. Maybe there is some obstacle? Is father still alive at all?

Memory of the interview with Commissioner Extraordinary Preiss V.V. rose before the eyes. *Is Filip Filipovitch Gierosławski alive! Is he alive!* And Preiss's behaviour. And how he inquired: *When did you last hear from your father?* He knew not whether to believe it or not. He had received instructions, he had to carry them out. How far had he been initiated? How much did he suspect? To what faction did he belong himself, whose man was he? Rappacki, the Minister of Winter, is said to be a diehard Ottepyelnik (they would not have placed another at the head of Winter), but this means nothing: he might be an Ottepyelnik in political matters, whilst a total disbeliever in the historical projections of Berdyaeff.

But if those Warsaw memories correspond to truth (if they don't come from a contradictory past), then it's also true that Preiss's people at once dispatched from Miodowa Street their own tchinovnik in the function of Guardian Angel. They were afraid it would leak out – they knew it would leak out. From a tsarist department – how could it not leak out? Since even the Pilsudchiks learned of it in that way, according to the consumptive postman.

So, here's the next puzzle: did the Pilsudchiks not know earlier? Had they forgotten about father, or what? The postman said also that they'd had no contact with father for years. Nothing of the kind! The very content of the missive belies it. Nonetheless, something must have happened for Winter to send urgent instructions to their Warsaw delegation along with a first-class ticket for the Transsib. Something must have – but what was it?

Nikola Tesla?

'Saith the Lord: for because thou hast done this thing, and hast not withheld thy son, thine only son: that in blessing I will bless thee, and in multiplying I will multiply thy seed as the stars of the heaven, and as the sand which is upon the sea shore; and thy seed shall possess the gates of his enemies; and in thy seed shall all the nations of the earth be blessed; because thou hast obeyed my voice.

'Such is the history of God's command unto Abraham. To bind and kill his son. You know the Jewish tradition – you know it not? – well then, there are other understandings of the binding of Isaac, *Aqedat Yitzhak*, and God saith many different things to Abraham and to people who read this story with unsullied thought. If they read it! If they think!

'There are Talmudists who do not see a command at all – but a favour. God requested a favour of Abraham; Abraham might not have granted the favour, but he did grant it, and because he granted God's non-command, that was why God rewarded him.

'And there are Talmudists who do not call it a favour either. For indeed, how could God not know the outcome? Not know what Abraham would do? God knows. Who then put whom to the test?

'And there are also those who regard it as God's favouritism towards Abraham. A sign for future generations and lesson for all eternity: here, you have the knife pressed to your throat, you lie bound to the stone and in this very second your own father shall cut you down – yet despair not, have faith in God, have faith to the end, and you shall be saved – He can rescue you from any plight.'

'Or course, yes indeed, if such a thing really did happen in the history of the Jewish people,' Doctor Konyeshin said calmly. 'It was about that one change in the custom of the Jews: that they should cease making sacrifices of people, and slaughter animals instead.'

'What are you saying, gentlemen!' Jelena bridled. Flustered, she took out a handkerchief and wiped her brow. Her pale skin seemed a little less pale. 'Talmudists this, Talmudists that, here we have a single monstrosity which can't be got around with lofty words, even were a thousand Jews to sit for thousands of years over their holy books. A test – definitely, a test: a test of Abraham's integrity. And Abraham was not up to it! Abraham disappointed! Is there any act more inconsistent with the morality of this world than a parent's murder of their own child? You won't find one; God knew what to command in this test. And what does Abraham do? Without batting an eyelid, he goes to murder his son! And that's meant to be a model? Of what, I ask! Why do we need such a parable?'

Smooth down the moustache before speaking. 'Notice, Jelena, how everyone here is splendidly obedient. Isaac to Abraham, Abraham to God. Who is also, after all, the father of Abraham. It's a tale about blind loyalty.'

Filimon Romanovitch, arms still crossed over his chest and with eye straying, keeled in his chair as though in a devotional trance.

'Inconsistent with morality, states Mademoiselle. But what was the morality of Abraham? The Word of God. Do you see, miss, this parting of the ways? Be so good as to listen to me now! I shall hand you control of this train; the switch for the points on our track rests in your dainty hand. So, we are travelling:

'On the left: God forbade killing, because killing is evil. On the right: killing is evil, because God forbade killing. And when you switch the points to left or right?

'On the left: it means, good and evil do not depend on God – God is subject to them, and we are subject to them. God, the omniscient, knows that killing is evil, therefore He gave the commandment: mind ye do no evil. Then, crucially, He himself could neither break nor change the commandments. Except that if not from God, then from whom, from what comes the Decalogue, whence precisely that division into good and evil? And why can it not be otherwise? Eh? Can you tell me that, miss? Without that knowledge, without a solid foundation, we will lose ourselves at once in this landscape, fall as into a swamp, condemned to our own powers, for who has ever pulled himself out of a swamp? That track leads into the abyss, should you choose to go there, miss, into the Land of the Destitute; and from thence, there is no return.

'On the right: as we enter these lands, we must be prepared that at any moment God may say: killing is good, evil is – oh! – travelling in trains and smoking cigarettes – and from that moment on, this is what shall be good or evil, because God is the sole and highest arbiter of morality and there is no sanction above God. It's the country of the autocrat of souls, the Land of the Tsar.'

'Therefore, therefore,' Jelena fumbled for words, 'therefore you are saying, sir, that just as He laid down the Ten Commandments, so too at any moment He may contradict them? Because whatever He commands, such and such will be good, because God commands it. Yes? Yes?'

Lean out of the chair, clasp the young woman gently by the elbow.

'There is no contradiction. Our Biblicist will correct me, should I should slip into error – will you not, Filimon Romanovitch? – but to the best of my knowledge, listen to me please, Jelena, there can be no contradiction here. God communicates with people by means of imperatives: "Thou shalt not kill". "Thou shalt kill". "Thou shalt not commit adultery". "Go forth and multiply". Imperatives never contradict themselves, just like questions. Contradictory at most can be reported statements about imperatives: "He said kill", "He did not say kill". But commands themselves can only be carried out, or not – they cannot contradict themselves. He commands that you do not kill. You are obedient, miss, or you are not. He commands that you kill. You are obedient, or not. The commands succeed one another, there is no contradiction. He, to whose commands you owe absolute obedience, is under no obligation to explain His intentions. The autocrat is always right, regardless of whether His command corresponds to previous commands. What do you think, Jelena, is this why Nikolay Aleksandrovitch so defends himself against writing down any kind of constitution for Russia?'

'Therefore, therefore – for you, sir, it's in order? You don't find this story cruel and corrupting? Don't see the abomination? Eh, you shan't escape me now!' Try to withdraw the hand, but she grasped it in time and held it in her grip. She had turned her back entirely on Zeytsoff, on Doctor Konyeshin, making it within a single heartbeat, single exchange of glances, a private conversation: she spoke to no one else, no one else heard, even if he heard. 'What would you have done, sir, in Abraham's place? Obeyed the command?'

Why does embarrassment not muddy the thoughts? Why does shame not entangle the tongue and mix up the words? Wherefore the calm voice and confident gaze, opposite her gaze? – why does the face not betray itself before her face?

Murch circulates in the veins, shimmers in the brain, flows under the skin.

'What would I have done? No offence, miss – but I don't care a toss about your question. In Abraham's place! *On ne peut être au four et au moulin*. Because my place is different, I see with the eyes of Isaac. For him, everything we've been so wisely and soullessly discussing is meaningless: whether He asked a favour or commanded, whether it was a test or whether God had the right, or whether He contradicted Himself... What do I care! I am lying on the altar. Know nothing. Know that my father has deceived me with lies and wants to kill me, shall kill me.

'And imagine, miss, imagine – I want to live! Not perish on that stone altar! I free myself from the bonds. Run away. Father chases me with his sword. Should he catch up with me, he'll slaughter me. He's old, I have a chance. So, tell me, miss, tell me, do I have a right to defend myself? Shall I do evil in standing up to my father, who wants to make a burned offering of me? Upon what would Isaac's guilt be founded?

'And would it make any difference to him, if he knew beyond all doubt that Abraham was doing it at God's command?'

'You are asking me, sir – if I hear aright – you are asking me, *if self-defence against God is morally permitted?*'

'God can do no evil!' Someone shouted from behind Zeytsoff's back. Raise the eyes. Leaning against the wall, in a cloud of cigar smoke, stood Ünal Tayyib Fessar. Dark-crimson sunlight rebounded off his bare cranium. He leaned a little closer towards the table, towards the interlocutors gathered around it, and showed his whole self in a flood of carmine reflections, as if drenched in blood from the very crown of his head. 'Stand against God, and you stand on the side of Satan!'

'The Tsar God,' muttered the symmetrical doctor. 'He, yes, He indeed "cannot" do anything evil. Whatever He does, He does good, because it is He that does it.'

Break free from Miss Muklanowicz. The eyes, however, did not free themselves but remained fixed on the Turk. On the thick lips of Mr Fessar, where flickered – that is, it was there and then not there – the before-image of a sneer, a hint of poisonous irony. A similar image of the dark-skinned countenance had been glimpsed once before, the undisguised self-satisfaction written on it already witnessed: night, whirling snowflakes, a heavy cane in his hand, a street in Yekaterinburg, blood on the ice. In the satisfaction of evil, there's something that makes us unable to keep it to ourselves, even when reason prompts otherwise, when it threatens us with highly unpleasant consequences – we have to give some sign, smuggle in an allusion or at least a twisted little smile: it was I! it was because of me! mine! I, I, I! even whereas for do-gooders, another person's joy is enough, awareness of the good deed itself, memory of the bright face of the beneficiary; good is sufficient unto itself.

But now the Turk did little even to hide his irony. When Doctor Konyeshin turned to look at him, the businessman winked.

Bristle. 'That's what you say, sir. Granted, you believe in it – but what would you really do?'

'God is God.'

'Would you not defend yourself, were He come to kill you?'

At that, Ünal Fessar straightened his back and broke away from the wall and, removing the cigar from his mouth, began to laugh. But how he laughed: chuckled not, chortled not, did not simply laugh – but roared with laughter, shook and uttered a kind of wolfish howl that drowned the voices of the gamblers and the strains of the upright piano in the neighbouring carriage and the rattle of the speeding train. Doctor Konyeshin rose to his feet and walked away from the table, scrutinising the Turk's attack of merriment with clinical interest. The game on the green baize must have ended, since the cardplayers too drew near in curiosity; suddenly there was a crush and confusion as they inquired the cause of the merriment. Take advantage of the moment to push towards the door. The doctor watched in silence.

'And thus it came to pass,' Filimon Romanovitch muttered in the meantime, as he rocked to and fro to the rhythm of the train, 'it came to pass that Jacob wrestled with God at the ford of Jabbok, and held Him in his grip throughout the night, until the breaking of the day, he held Him! – until God relented and surrendered and blessed Jacob, His conqueror; thus it came to pass.'

Someone pressed from behind, leant on the back; his whisper floated straight into the ear.

'… to see you later today. If, in spite of everything, you be a man of honour, sir.'

Glance over the shoulder. Dushin.

'What do you want now?'

'The princess –'

Miss Muklanowicz was hanging off the arm on the other side. Jerk in annoyance. With difficulty she caught her breath, searching for words.

'As far as I've heard, Benedykt, sir, and it doesn't have to be the whole truth after all, but he almost admitted himself that he gives credence to this Berdyaeff –'

'Just look at him now!'

Zeytsoff had taken out again the old photograph and, deeply engrossed in his alcoholic delusions, was swaying above it, hunched into an arch, his nose almost pressing into the cracked surface of the dark snapshot. 'Beautiful, beautiful she was.' Behold the reformed revolutionary, a true convert to the Russian idea – a son without a mother.

'And besides, Jelena, even if he does, for the love of God, then he's an Ottepyelnik through and through for as long as he lives, and would shield Tesla with his own breast. Let's go.'

'But! It's quite the reverse – because once they'd told him that your father talks to gleissen, then he had a thousand motives to scheme against your life.'

'You've fallen for this too! Fogel spoke of Lyednyaks – yes or no? Let's go!'

No chance; the privy councillor had dug his claw-like fingers into the other arm.

'Your father – what's she saying? – your father – to gleissen?'

'Let me go!'

'Your father talks to gleissen?!'

'Quiet!'

Unfortunately, Ünal Fessar had stopped laughing and so failed to drown out Privy Councillor Dushin. Not everyone heard, but Doctor Konyesin – certainly did. He leapt up as if stabbed by a spur, spinning on the heel of his shoe, already leaning over vigilantly with big (symmetrical) eyes and hands half-raised (symmetrically), a cry about to burst from his mouth.

But, also like lightning, he thought better of it; he retreated, his eyes dimmed, and he said nothing.

'What does it mean: talks to gleissen?' The younger of the profligate Moravian brothers frowned so deeply that his crop of fair hair flopped over his eyebrows. 'So gleissen *speak*?'

'Again, you try to fool people, you should be ashamed!' Aleksey Tchushin was incensed.

'I had been wondering what it would be today,' said Captain Privyezhensky, drawling on his words in a low tone. 'I was already wanting to place a bet, but our impostor has exceeded himself. Son of a confidant of gleissen! *Chapeau bas.*'

And again, they were all staring. But this time there was nowhere to flee to, no route open; they surrounded, locked in, pinned against a wall.

Jelena squeezed the arm.

'I'm sorry, I'm sorry, I'm sorry, I didn't mean to, I'm sorry.'

'Maybe the count will tell us this story?' the captain continued with an acidic sneer. 'For sure he'll tell it! Such an exemplar of Polish honour, pride and correctness – not like us Russians, as he said himself. "Ingratiating, duplicitous fakes, pliable necks".'

Smile at this? Possibly. Could anything be done? – something energetic, decisive, anything? – were it not for Jelena on one arm and Dushin on the other: jump over the armchair and table, fling the ashtray at Privyezhensky, seize the Grossmeister – could it be done? Possibly. And could anything be said? After all, they had not glued these lips together. Whatever could be said here and now – let it be said!'

And so, nothing was said.

'Will the count not grace us with an explanation?' Captain Privyezhensky buttoned up his uniform, slipped his officer's signet ring off his finger. 'No, the count will remain silent with his supercilious smile until the next poor unfortunate is duped by his innuendos and insinuations, and by that haughty look – you see, ladies and gentlemen, in this one thing he speaks the truth, you have no nation in the world prouder than the Poles.'

He took half a stride forward and his hand was swifter than the eye: from right side onto left cheek, from left side onto right cheek, from right side onto the jaw until the head recoiled.

Captain Privyezhensky wiped his hand on his handkerchief.

'Yes. Good. Remaining silent about flagrant lies – is the same as lying. But… Yes. Forgive me, miss, gentlemen.'

He turned around and walked away.

They stared greedily. As if disgusted, as if sympathising, as if confused, whilst each sinks his stealthy gaze into the victim's face, seeks its eyes, for any hint of a grimace of humiliation opening the mouth from emotion, ready to swallow the pain, the humiliation and the shame, the shame, the most delicious. It's a bodily reflex: sympathy – the shared feeling of pain, but also the shared feeling of pleasure at the hand that smites.

Ünal Fessar threw down his cigar between the vodka carafe and a glass, squeezed in front of Tchushin and pushed aside the privy councillor, who was still in shock.

'Why are you standing like that, you sad flunkeys? Make way!'

He elbowed his way through without ceremony, tugging at the coattail and collar. With his other hand he offered a handkerchief. 'Wipe yourself clean, sir, he smashed your nose, shirt, pity about the shirt.' Press the handkerchief to the nostrils. Feel not the loss of blood, feel not the pain of the blows or ripped skin. Only the knees trembled slightly as the train seemed to shake more than usual.

Pause beyond the passageway between carriages, resting a shoulder against the closed door of a compartment. Try now, only now, to swallow the saliva – heavy, viscous, cold – realise that it is not saliva streaming over the palate and gumming up the gullet.

Remove the handkerchief from the face, glance at the red stains. Thoughts rush ahead of themselves with lunatic calm. What about trying to burn this blood in the flame of a blackwicke…

Blink. Crimson sunlight was streaming through the windows into the corridor, everything was drowning in the warm rays of sunset, Mr Fessar, his bald mahogany scalp, the patterned carpet runners of Deluxe, the dark boiserie.

Cough.

'Thank you.'

'It's odd beyond words,' wheezed the Turk. 'Myself, I no longer know what to believe. Tell me, sir, no one can hear, we're alone – can you speak? do you feel all right? – tell me: do you have that technology, or not?'

Raise the head.

'It was you who threw Pyelka off the train.'

'What? Who? What? What?'

Extend towards him the hand with the blood-stained handkerchief; he thrust it angrily aside. The train jolted. The Turk leapt forward. Resist with a shoulder pressed into the wall, shove an elbow into Fessar's ribs. A clenched fist flashed before the eyes. Two bodies pummelled the compartment door and the side wall of the corridor, the sculpted fixtures, metal frames, glass and wood and coldiron. Fessar puffed and hissed through clenched teeth – were they words in Turkish, curses, threats, names of saints? The train sped ever onwards, took-took-took-TOOK. Free the tails of the jacket, punch the Turk in the chest. He flew backwards and tried to grab hold of a window knob, failed to catch it, banged against the casing and fell as if chopped down, in a position neither sitting nor kneeling, arms tucked behind him, head hanging limp, twisted in a bizarre pretzel-shape of limbs in the narrow corridor of the Transsib. Bright carmine spread over his smooth skull like sugar coating – a red liquid neath red light. Pick up the handkerchief.

'… wait, Benedykt, sir, it's my fault, I –'

Jelena Muklanowicz stood breathless in the passageway, her hand in a runaway gesture of distress – the gesture died, the devushka's hand dropped to her lips, muffling her cry.

Jelena took one look at the motionless body of Ünal Fessar – the expression on her morbidly pale countenance extremely serious, eyes unblinking, breath in, breath out, breath in – she raised her head, glanced around and pressed her ear to the door of the nearest compartment. From her black locks combed back in their bun, she drew a slender hairpin. Kicking aside the Turk's leg, which was blocking the corridor, with her dainty leather-booted foot, she knelt before the door and within five heartbeats had opened the Deluxe lock with the pin.

'Quick, move it! Grab him! They're inviting everyone to supper, they're coming! You take the arms. One, two! Inside!'

So saying, she seized the corpse beneath the knees.

On the hidden talents of Miss Muklanowicz and other obscure matters

Within five heartbeats she had opened the Deluxe lock with the pin.

'Quick, move it! Grab him! They're inviting everyone to supper, they're coming! You take the arms. One, two! Inside!'

So saying, she seized the corpse beneath the knees. Tuck the handkerchief in a pocket and grab him below the armpits. The young woman pulled, but he was heavy and unwieldy, and bent double – torso, limbs, head – like a broken doll, and kept catching some part of his anatomy against the window casing, carpet runner, furniture inside the compartment. Expect to hear a hollow thud as from a wooden mannequin. Shove it at last with all might onto the floor beside the bed; it folded in two. Miss Muklanowicz lifted her skirt, exposing calves clad in white stockings, so as to jump back over the body. She gave the door a violent push, shutting it at the last minute. Hear at once voices and footsteps, and even someone thumping on the compartment wall as he walked past. Jelena no longer looked so morbidly pale. Back pressed against the door, she was breathing rapidly, her bosom rising and falling to an asthmatic rhythm: every shallow breath made the next shallower still. She had to wait a minute in order to cough out a word.

'Stain.'

'What?'

'Blood!'

Touch the moustache, sticky from the already clotting blood.

'On the corridor carpet!' hissed Jelena.

'But it could be mine too, no? That's what they'll think.'

Take out the handkerchief, press it to the nose.

'All right,' Miss Muklanowicz breathed a sigh of relief. 'Whose compartment is it?'

Gaze squint-eyed from behind the handkerchief. On the escritoire stood a portable typewriter with a piece of paper wound in. Beside it lay a pile of thick books. On the bed – men's pyjamas with an oriental design. A clothes brush and wooden shoetree protruded from a small trunk standing under the window.

'But suppose he wants to pick up something on his way to supper?'

She clicked her tongue.

'Then we'll hang for it.'

She went to the window.

'Help me, sir.'

Jerk the window knob. Miss Muklanowicz pulled down the frame as far as it would go. The wind struck, roaring and whistling; the paper in the typewriter flapped like a flag, trfffrr, a blanket rolled back from the pillows, whilst the wardrobe door slammed against the wall.

Glance at the Turk and sit down on the bed with a sigh.

'We can't do it. He's too heavy. It's a metre and a half off the floor. Someone will see.'

'Like who, for instance? What will they see? Mr Gierosławski!'

'It's cost us so much effort to move him even this far! Imagine it, miss: legs first or head first, half a corpse juts out over Asia and swings its hands in the wind. And when we enter a bend, it'll be enough for someone to glance through a windowpane.'

'You're impossible! A walking ode to joy, honest to God.'

'Besides, he managed to mess up the carpet.'

'Sit there much longer, sir, dangling your arms, and the corpse will rot and flowers sprout from it.'

'Ha, ha, ha.'

'Suit yourself then!' She brushed her hands, offended. 'I am not imposing. Mr Benedykt Gierosławski can continue according to his own plan, pardon me for interfering.' She made for the door. 'Well yes, indeed, it's time for supper. Goodbye.'

Grab her by the waist without standing up. She loses balance as the carriage rocks. Clasp the devushka tighter still, dropping again the handkerchief.

'What do you think you're doing, sir?!'

'We, the murderers, are known for our loose morals. Any clean sheets of paper there?'

'A few.'

'We have to wipe away this blood. As much as possible. And so that it doesn't soak into the carpet. Imagine it, miss: the man returns to his *compartiment* and here, for no apparent reason, is a huge bloodstain.'

'And a corpse – in the cupboard? Everyone saw the Turk leave with you.'

'Please give them to me.'

She pulled out a pile of paper held down on the tabletop by a French dictionary. Take a look. Half the first page was taken up by a hydrographical description of the Tyumen region (many torrents and small rivers, long waterways) written in a dry French style with a great many errors, whole words crossed out and letters typed over letters; then there were lines and lines of one-letter sequences: aaaaaaaaaa, bbbbbbbbbb, cccccccccc et cetera.

'But clean ones. Leave those. Because he'll realise someone took them.'

Crumple a sheet in the hand, bend over Fessar's head.

'What, he'll be more moved by that than by the pool of gore beside his bed?'

Jelena looked down from on high, pointing with her finger.

'Here. And here. And here. Here, here, here. Over here! Here too.'

Groan. 'I'm beginning to understand poor Macbeth.'

'Make haste, Benedykt, he'll be back at some point from his supper!'

'Ugh. I'm all smeared like a butcher.'

'After all, the captain smashed your nose, you have an alibi.' She leaned forward. 'I can't see it, where's the wound? Roll him over.'

'One moment.'

Wipe the blood off the skin on the skull and carpet beneath it; still the stain remained, but at least the brightly coloured pattern partially masked it. Grasp the Turk's head by the chin and press the left temple into the floor. Blood flowed from a cut above the right eyebrow. Stretch out the hand for the next piece of paper.

'Since we're robbing him already,' Miss Muklanowicz digressed, 'perhaps he also has a towel to hand, we can throw it out as well, there'll be no trace.'

'Right, rip up the carpet at once.'

The corpse moaned and opened its mouth.

Spring to the feet.

Jelena was so taken aback that she sat on the escritoire, shedding the books and papers.

'You didn't examine him?!'

'I had no time. You immediately –'

'Had no time!'

'You saw for yourself, miss. A corpse like any other. That is, a dead one. That is… A very convincing cadaver, was what I meant to say.'

'The pulse! Or at least the breathing! Anything!'

'He didn't wake when we dragged him in here.'

'Better donate to a thanksgiving mass, sir, instead of complaining.'

'I am not complaining. I am only… Above all, it was an accident. It was you who made it into a murder!'

'Do I hear right…?'

'Yes! You are obsessed, miss! Murders, investigations, detective stories! So as soon as a body is covered in blood, it's definitely a corpse. And once there's a corpse, then it's definitely murder. A stupid accident, but Miss Muklanowicz appears on the scene and half a minute later we are disposing of the mortal remains, partners in crime. This was precisely what I was saying when you made fun of me! Thus, one becomes a murderer in Summer without having committed a murder. Besides – in this very same way I became that accursed count. And God knows what else.'

'Well, if we had thrown him out of the window of the speeding train, it would have been murder, no question.'

'You would have thrown him out, miss.'

'But I couldn't have lifted him on my own.'

'But you wanted to!'

'I wanted to help! Ungrateful man! Heart of ice! I'm forfeiting myself to crime, whereas he –'

'But did anyone ask you, miss? No! What is it you want from me?! You yourself came knocking at my door! Whoever saw the like! Where were you brought up! And now too – imposing yourself on me – with a corpse –'

'Otherwise, you'd be standing over it, wringing your hands: maybe dead and not dead, maybe they'll hang and not hang us, maybe a three-in-four chance I'll swing, tphoo, a man with zero-valued balls!'

'And language of the gutter to boot, yes, yes, but do indulge yourself, please!'

'Oo-oo, the swine…!'

Ünal Fessar sat up, ran his fingers over his head, blinked, and then raised his eyes towards the two people above him trading incomprehensible insults in Polish.

'*Excusez-moi, mademoiselle, mais je ne comprends pas…*'

Miss Muklanowicz fell upon him with great solicitude.

'And we were sick with worry!' Delicately she touched the torn skin. 'The bone is not broken, that's the most important.' She offered the businessman her hand. 'Will you stand?'

Seize the Turk by his other arm.

'Careful. You never can tell with head injuries.' Switch likewise to French. 'You must have heard our difference of opinion: as to whether you should be moved at all; doctors as a rule say no, but the train is shaking so much, we should send for Doctor Konyeshin – how are you feeling, sir, ought we to send for him?'

Mr Fessar rested on the bed; leaning against the headboard and pressing the batiste handkerchief offered by Jelena onto his wound, he glanced around slightly more consciously.

'Wait a minute. Mr Gierosaski. Miss –'

'Jelena Muklanowicz.'

'Ah yes, I remember. Wait a minute.'

He drew a finger over his forehead and stared at the red collected on his fingertip.

Pick up the dropped handkerchief for the third time. Mr Fessar squinted; he recognised his own property and raised his eyes. He made a wry face.

'That's it!' he snarled. 'That's what you are about!'

Jelena had meant to sit down beside the Turk; she stopped herself. Stood before the window. Wind tugged at her blouse, plucked at the lace.

'What are we about?'

'The honourable Mr Fessar' – speak slowly, checking whether the nosebleed had stopped once and for all – 'was very upset when I ventured the suggestion that he was the one responsible for, mm-hmm, the mysterious disappearance from the train of Mefody Karpovitch Pyelka.'

'Pyelka!' snorted the Turk. 'What Pyelka, damn it.'

'The honourable Mr Fessar' – speak, flinging at him the blood-soaked handkerchief, 'for reasons unbeknownst to me, has got it into his head that I possess, or am one of a partnership that possesses, the secret, mm-hmm, of cultivating coldiron outside the Land of the Gleissen.'

'Reasons unbeknownst!' the Turk yelled and clutched his head in visible pain; after a while, he continued in a whisper: 'You gave me to understand it very clearly, sir. Over cards. And later. And those people in Yekaterinburg. And the prince. You make a fool of me, sir.'

'The honourable Mr Fessar' – speak, reaching under the jacket and waistcoat, 'wished at all costs to acquire this technology. Or at least join the enterprise. He attempted to buy his way in, extort the details from me. Which, obviously, he did not succeed in doing, because there are no details; he had cooked it all up.'

'And Father Frost?' The Turk raised mechanically the second handkerchief and examined both for a moment in surprised consternation, one in his right hand, the other in his left, both white-and-red. He clenched his jaws. 'And you, miss, believe this scoundrel? You see how he lies. Through his teeth.'

'The honourable Mr Fessar' – speak, as the right hand felt beneath the unbuttoned waistcoat, 'therefore tried to gain the confidence in turn of my partner, that is, of the man he regarded as my partner. He must have seen Pyelka in Yekaterinburg. I have no idea what happened there; I ran away. Perhaps he had an opportunity to exchange a few words with him. Then, after the Express had departed, he went at once to Pyelka in second class. Summoned him out of the compartment. Where can you go there for a private chat at night? They went out onto the platform beyond the second-class sleeping cars. Mr Fessar tried to drag out of Pyelka the same as from me – but it wasn't enough that Pyelka, clearly, had no idea about anything, there was also the way Pyelka reacted unexpectedly to these proposals – he, a Martsynian. You didn't know, sir? You didn't know. Did you fight? Was there a scuffle? Did the train jerk? Yet you see how things can turn out unhappily.'

'Allah is great!'

'And so – he fell off, you pushed him, he fell off, perhaps earlier there was some fatal excess, but he fell off, there is no body. What a marvellous place for a murder: a train traversing two continents – who will find the mortal remains? Who recreate the circumstances of the crime? The place? The time? Who will gather the witnesses? Not the slightest chance. And you gave the crew so much baksheesh – only before the Last Judgement will they admit that they saw you at all; you can afford it.'

'*Abbas yolcuyum!*'

'Could it not have been like that? It could.'

'But it wasn't!'

'Let's be serious, Mr Fessar! How can you be sure of what did happen – in contrast to what could have happened? When we talk about the past, we always talk about what *could* have happened; only and exclusively about that. All statements in the past tense are hypothetical.'

'I don't know what's going on with you, young man, but I would recommend the Alpine sanatoria. Forgive me, miss.'

One more protracted stare – of scorn? of contempt? of disgust? of anger? – and hoisting himself up with great effort, Ünal Fessar advanced towards the door. Move out of his way, rotate into an awkward position so as not to have the back to him for one moment. Reeling, with one hand to his temple, he went out into the corridor. Here he stood for a while. Disorientated, he looked one way and then the other – where to go? where had he been going before he lost consciousness? – there. He stomped off with heavy steps.

Jelena was waiting with arms folded over her chest, rapping the edge of the furniture with her heel.

'But it was meant to be a joint investigation.'

'I'm sorry. I had a sudden illumination.'

'Illumination.'

'Enlightenment, endarkenment, a possibility… manifested itself.'

'Are you suffering, sir, from a stomach complaint? Auntie has mint drops that will save you.'

'What? No.' Wrest the hand from under the waistcoat, do up the buttons, 'Let's get out of here, no point in tempting fate.'

Shut the window. The devushka gathered up the crumpled, bloodied sheets of paper, put the books back beside the typewriter. From the doorway she cast her eyes once more around the compartment, reaching into her hair for the pin.

She stood stock-still.

'Oh, mother. Benedykt, how good is your eyesight?'

'Mm-hmm, today – hawk-like.'

'I must have lost it somewhere here.'

'Forget it, we'll never find it in this carpet for as long as we live.'

Jelena bit her lip. She removed another pin from the left side of her hair. Stepping out into the corridor, she glanced around quickly. Empty. She tucked up her skirt, knelt and – tshk, tshk, tshk – flicked back the spring in the lock. Help her up. She brushed down the dark material. A provodnik appeared in the passageway. Slipping the pin back into her hair, she looked over her shoulder. 'Benedykt, sir?' 'Fret not, miss, there's no trace.' 'My hem could have got wet…' 'No.' The provodnik withdrew. Open the door. Miss Muklanowicz examined herself in the narrow mirror in the passageway to the next carriage. Meticulously, she wound a black lock behind her ear. Moistening the tip with spittle, she ran her little finger over her eyebrows. 'Benedykt, sir?'

'Yes?'

'So, was it he who killed Pyelka in the end, or not?'

Heave a sigh. Take out the interferograph, pull off the red chamois. Turn to the window and look into the eyepiece of the barrel under the red sun: the same string of identical beads of light.

'Killed him, killed him not, it's still one and the same.'

On truth, and what is truer than truth

'Cognac?'

'Maybe we should go for a bite first.'

'Or maybe not. Cognac?'

'But you've already had a few too many with Zeytsoff.'

'I am as sober as five Laplacians. Cognac?'

'Yes, please.'

Pour both a glass, diluting it after the café fashion: half *fine à l'eau* and half ordinary water. Replace the bottle in the cabinet. Perched on the edge of the bed, Miss Mulkanowicz barely skimmed her lips with the glass. She was very tense: elbows tight against her body, bent slightly forward – but holding her head up high. She tasted the cognac and crinkled her nose.

Hang the jacket on the back of the chair. The pocket was stuffed with blood-smeared papers. Pull on the lion's tail of the window grip and cast the sheets to the wind. Against the backdrop of the setting sun, they scattered like a flock of startled birds. Close the window, and the rhythmic clatter of the train fell away. With her free hand, Miss Muklanowicz was pressing other sheets of paper into the counterpane: those filled with the Pilsudchiks' code. Gather them up as quickly as possible, tearing the last from the devushka's hands.

'And yet,' she murmured, 'and yet… you, sir, are somehow different.'

Hide the notes in a drawer.

'Am I swelling?'

'What?'

Step up to the mirror. No bruises discernible on the battered cheeks, at most a slight grazing of the skin neath one eye. Instead, the nose was indeed swollen, as was the upper lip, cut in two places; concealed to an extent by the moustache. Tomorrow it will be worse.

'I was observing you with Zeytsoff. To begin with, I thought it was arrogance –'

'Arrogance?' Glance furtively in the looking glass, flabbergasted.

'Has no one told you that you sometimes behave arrogantly?'

'I am not arrogant!'

'I know not.' She shrugged her shoulders. 'I am telling you, sir, what people see.'

Touch the lip. It was painful.

'I understand that such a man as Privyezhensky might nurse a grudge and detect a stuck-up nose in every native Pole...'

'But that's odd.' She moved to the centre of the bed in order to peek in the looking glass. 'Your reflection, sir –'

Turn around.

'Maybe you should sit on the chair, miss. It's improper for a young lady on a gentleman's bed...'

'You locked the door?'

'All the more reason.'

'*Bien*. No one sees, no one hears.'

'So long as your respected Auntie is not sitting there with her ear to the wall.'

'Auntie is not sitting there. Anyway, when we're moving, nothing can be heard.'

Smile crookedly (from now on, until the swelling subsides, this smile will always be crooked and sneering).

'You've tried?'

As should be expected, Jelena blushed and lowered her eyes. Again, with great caution, she raised the glass to her mouth. A pink tongue popped out and vanished between the lips. She drank not – she tried the alcohol as if it were poison, a drop to taste, a drop to test whether it mightn't kill.

'For a moment... it seemed to me I was saving your life, Benedykt, sir, there, in the saloon car.'

'What?'

'Have you forgotten that it's you they're after?'

'Fogel no doubt would prefer it that way.'

'Mm-hmm?'

'That I should believe it. But – in the saloon? my life?'

'When that kerfuffle arose. I was sitting almost opposite, saw him standing there, lurking by the door to the parlour car, a quarter of an hour, longer, smoking a cigarette; he withdrew, came back, and then immediately leapt at you from behind, from behind your back.'

'Dushin.'

'Well, yes, I speak of the councillor.' Pink tongue, cognac, lips. 'At once I thought: knife under the rib. Don't make such a face, sir! I admit to reading adventure romances, is there some law against it? That's how it looked – so I ran up, he saw me, and I thought...'

Smile: 'Romances.'

Miss Muklanowicz assumed an offended air.

'With you it's always the same.'

Sit down on the chair. The devushka lowered her glass, watched vigilantly.

'Romances.' Speak this time without smiling. 'I don't believe you, Jelena.'

She merely stared.

'Was it reading romances that made you a skilled picklock? Who are you?'

She lowered her eyes.

'One doesn't ask such questions.'

'But how else are we to spend the hours and days of our journey? A journey – it's just such a time – people exchange anecdotes, tell one another their life stories – what else is there?'

'I inquire not of you, sir,' she said quietly. 'Yet how many of these Benedykt Gierosławskis are there? I have just heard a new version, about some plans for cultivating coldiron – so coldiron is cultivated? – perhaps Mr Fessar was telling the truth and you, sir, were lying, I have no idea. Well then, who you are you really? Count? Mathematician? Fraudster? Adventurer of sorts? Agent of Winter? Son of a gleis-senik? Coldiron industrialist? Perhaps a renegade Martsynian? Only please don't say all at once! Or each one a tenth!' Nervously she rotated her glass. 'One doesn't ask such questions,' she repeated in a whisper.

Seize her left hand; she tried to withdraw the arm, muscles already taut – but stopped herself with conscious effort. She stared, confused. Cold fingers, the skin itself over dainty knuckles, blue veinlets under the skin – and when pressure is brought to bear, all those invisible components of the organism shift beneath it, between bones and between veins, and each is distinctly felt, each separately as well as the whole mechanical composition. Feel now what a human being is: lumps of matter.

For a kind of indecency may be perceived in the body's very existence

– not so much even in its exposure as in the revelation that we possess a body, in the acknowledgement of our corporeality. If it didn't hurt, if we weren't to die of it, if it were possible – would we open up to our closest friends also in this way: cutting open our skin, invitingly spreading our ribs, unpinning the muscles, unlacing arteries, displaying to the light of day and a lover's gaze the shaming wrinkles and curves of liver and guts, the irregularity of vertebrae, the vulgar curvature of the pelvis, in order, finally, to unveil the naked beating heart? That would be the highest and hardest form of bodily honesty.

'And even were I to tell you,' Jelena whispered, closing her palm into a fist, 'whatever I tell you –'

'You would not believe me either, miss.'

'Whatever you tell me –'

'Honesty in exchange for honesty.'

'But you said it yourself, sir: travelling is a magical time; as much as they know of us is what we are.'

'I said that?'

'Because no one will verify what is true and what is not.'

'No one will verify. But if it's untrue, if it's a lie – then the honesty is all the more profound.'

'What are you saying, sir!'

'My dear Jelena. Our lies betray more about us than the truest of truths. When you tell the truth about yourself – the truth is that which has really befallen you: your own snippet of world history. And yet you have no control and never had any control over it, chose not the place of your birth, chose not your parents, had no influence on how they raised you, chose not your own life; the situations in which you were placed were not of your creating, people with whom you had to mix were not creatures of your mind; nor did you consent to the fortunes and misfortunes that became your lot. Most of what befalls us is the work of chance. Lies, on the other hand, come entirely from you, over lies you possess total control, they are born of you, feed on you and answer only to you. In which then do you reveal yourself the more: in truth or in falsehood? Jelena.'

She raised her eyes.

'Am I to lie…?'

Let go her hand. She sat up straight; cupped both palms around the shot-glass, fingertips touching. She moved not away – but it was as though she were watching from the far end of a long corridor. Eyes half-closed in the red radiance. The sun, remaining to the rear of the hurtling Trans-Siberian Express, flooded her side of the compartment from the carpet to the ceiling reliefs, where the plump faces of nymphs peeped out from behind golden ivy and convolvulus; whilst in the warm light of the sunset, it all shone, flickered and glowed with deep-crimson flame – above the haughtily raised head of Miss Muklanowicz.

'Tell the truth.'

Took-took-took-TOOK, took-took-took-TOOK, took-took-took-TOOK.

Was it the solar reflection, or does that imp of childish perversity sparkle again in Jelena's eye?

'When I was twelve or thirteen years old,' she began, 'Auntie Urszula took me to the circus on Ordynacka Street. Before that, I rarely went to the city. I'd never been to the circus. I remember with what excitement I readied myself for this expedition, a real expedition; for a week, nothing else occupied my thoughts and dreams. For this dress, those boots, that kind of a cape, a different bonnet – and also what we would see, what animals, what clowns, what prodigies; the caretaker's niece brought me a placard, whereupon a slender female acrobat in chequered body stocking soared into the air through rings of fire, whilst from below, from beneath the fire, lions strained towards her with their gaping maws, huge teeth and claws.

'We drove to Okólnik in a covered droshky, I remember the dismal autumn sleet, it was still before the gleissen. First of all, we walked from Ordynacka to the pâtisserie, I was allowed cake; and I remember too its lemony tang, the sweet acid smarting my tongue; well I recall tastes and smells, seeming to remain forever in my body – on my tongue, in my head – some sort of carrier-particles of impressions, whereas sounds, whereas images, whereas touch leave no material imprint on a person; is that how it really is, what d'you think, Benedykt, sir?

'Then in the vestibule, Auntie bumped into some acquaintances, a colonel of dragoons with a lady; the colonel had a permanent seat in a box in the stalls' rotunda, near the arena, he invited us, shared his sweets with me, wanted to buy candyfloss; and of the colonel I remember his great moustache, oh, such candlewicks twisted in pomade. We sat in velvet. Other ladies, their gowns, feathers, hats, coiffures, the rustle of their fans, scent of their perfume – ah, Benedykt, sir, the scent of that perfume is within me still. I thought then it would take my breath away; you can skip a breath from too much excitement, as if someone laid a hand on your chest and pressed down on the bone with the flat of his splayed hand, here, just here –'

'On the breastbone.'

'Yes. A breath begins before the last has ended, air expels air, the lungs collapse, have you never felt it, sir? Poor Auntie must have been truly frightened because of me. The great gas candelabra under the cupola was lit. I saw that long frieze above the gallery, fantastical hunting scenes. Ladies' necklaces, earrings and rings shimmered like stars. Won't you wonder, sir, at a little girl? It was all too beautiful, too much like a fairy tale. Fairy tales don't lie. Here you may be right, Benedykt, fairy tales don't lie, especially when they don't tell the truth.

'Much later I discovered that in the boxes by the stalls – who has a seat there? Mainly ladies of easy virtue and officers' kept women.

'Before the first entr'acte we saw a fire eater, performing seals, a horseshoe crusher and a magician who drew rabbits and doves as well as snakes out of a top-hat, one snake escaped; the clowns were game, pulling it from each other's collars, ears, breeches. After the entr'acte a troupe of acrobats from Danzig was announced, I thought at once of that girl on the placard, and sure enough: a young woman in similar body stocking comes out with them and the ringmaster introduces her: The Incredible Felitka Caoutchouc! Clearly, an effective *nom de scène* – but there's instant applause when she bends her body like rubber, as if she had no bones, stretching her head back towards her heels, wrapping her legs around her neck, whilst the gymnasts pass her from one to another like a ball, and toss her onto a high scaffold, where she performs deadly acrobatics to a fast drumroll, and my heart leaps into my throat and I squeeze Auntie's hand, and then the girl really does jump through hoops of flame and bounce up from the trampoline somersaulting through fire; only there were no lions. At the end the whole troupe takes its bow around the ring, on our side as well, I lean out of the box. And Auntie says: I know her! She's the Boćwiałkiewiczes' daughter from Wrona Street! A coal merchant's horse trampled her and took all power from her legs, unhappy child, a helpless cripple for the rest of her life. But now we see that no, for she's – The Incredible Felitka Caoutchouc! The bell rang for the second entr'acte; the colonel offered to unravel the mystery (the lady whispered something in his ear). He sent a boy behind the scenes with a visiting card and banknote. Whatever did Felitka think? Did she always accept such invitations from officers? She appears, not yet out of her costume, in a cloak thrown over her shoulders. At once she recognises Auntie; kisses, hugs, laughter. She sat with us during the entr'acte. So, what had happened to her in all these years? She was not much younger than I when she'd fallen in the street under the hooves of a coal merchant's nag; trampled underfoot, she lost all strength in her legs, walked with crutches, if she walked at all, because, so she said, her parents preferred to keep her indoors – the courtyard from the window was as much as she saw, or the street from the courtyard when her father carried her outside. But not long afterwards, a tightrope walker gave a performance in their street – stretched his rope between rooftops and walked to and fro upon it three floors above the cobbles; a moment later the tightrope walker's daughter also stepped onto it, and marched back and forth in the air above the wide-eyed Felitka. Says Miss Caoutchouc: I watch and know that if I am to walk again, then it'll be in the air. Straightaway, there on the cobbled pavement, neath the wire stretched above her, she invented a future for herself and placed a wager on it. Shortly afterwards, feeling returned to her feet – do you understand, sir, she told us laughingly as if it were a joke, but it was no joke – feeling returned to her toes and so she became the Rubber Woman.

'Do you hear, Benedykt, what I'm saying? It's not about what I saw at the Okólnik circus, about how phantasies transform into life, life into phantasies. But the fact that Felitka, but some Boćwiałkiewicz girl from Wrona Street – wrote herself like a fairy tale, invented herself, told a lie and turned it into truth, and so there she stood before us, a living lie, a self-told fable, child of her own dreams. You are not what you are – you are what you make yourself to be! Do you understand, Benedykt, sir? The more exotic the circus, the more colourful the decorations and the greater the rapture in the child's eyes – the closer the borderline between impossibility and daydream, at hand's reach, at a touch. I tore a sequin from her body stocking, took it, stole it, keep it still in my jewellery box.

'And I admit to you, sir: I always read adventure novels where heroes survive fantastical affrays, travel through savage countries, fight cruel brutes devoid of honour and, by virtue of their own daring and wit, extricate themselves from the grimmest oppression. And such I have told myself to be, such a wager have I placed, such a lie I shall turn into truth.

'Think you, sir, this is the colour of my hair since birth? But the heroines of dramatic romances, not those timorous objects of the adventurers' affections – but *femmes d'esprit*, undaunted heroines, intrepid women spies, female robbers, they always have black hair and black brows. So henna, the magical henna. You sneer – because to you it's womanish coquetry, anything for the sake of beauty and pleasing men? Yet no, in fact! How, sir, do you think of yourself? What self-image does Benedykt Gierosławski carry in his head? Who art thou unto thyself? This is what it's all about! For only in this way can we begin to rewrite ourselves, lie about ourselves, that is make true the lie: a day, another day, a third, a month, and more, and still more, but regularly, consistently, without interruption, with every glance in a mirror, in every shop-window on the street, in every random reflection captured in the corner of an eye – until one day no other thought will arise in your head, because it will be the first image and the first association and the deepest truth about yourself, when you look there and see a brunette of Gypsy handsomeness and see yourself – for it will be you – the woman spy, the mysterious temptress, the acrobat of life. Who can open any lock with a hairpin and solve any mysterious crime.'

Took-took-took-TOOK, took-took-took-TOOK.

The sun shoots from beyond the horizon edge straight into Jelena's pupils; she pulled the curtain across her side, but it helped not; she raises a hand to her forehead, defends herself against the deluge of red. No means then of telling: is that a smile of mockery in the eyes of Miss Muklanowicz? are the pink shadows on her cheeks living blushes or the warm kisses of the sun? And everything she said – was it true or false? No sign does she give.

With her other hand she cautiously raised her glass. The ruby on her black velvet choker glinted blood-red; her modest finger-ring glowed. She tilted the glass. Tongue, cognac, lips.

'As to romances read in youth.' Clear the throat. 'You, Jelena, will appreciate this truth. As to romances. Stories of first loves, aye.' Clear the throat a second time. 'Her name was Anna, Anna Magdalena, I met her as if I'd not met her, that is, through numbness; it is hard to assume the spell of love at first sight, when this meeting is not connected to anything at all, washed away somewhere amid scores of others. With whom in that case, with what do we fall in love? – not with the concrete image of a concrete person, but with some rainbow-hued impression, a bouquet of mixed sensations, like the scent of a bouquet of a dozen different blooms is not the scent of any existing bloom – in whom do we fall in love? She, meanwhile, would flash by at the boundaries of perception, now seen, now unseen, now heard only behind a wall, when she did her piano practice – ah, I'm about to explain: I used to give her brother private lessons.

'The brother was unimaginably dense, I tell you, miss, those were roubles deservedly earned. After every lesson I felt I understood less and less of my own explanations, he would gawp at the simplest arithmetic, whilst a calf-like blessedness, unmoved by any rational thought, spread over his round countenance – in attempting to fathom his mental blocks, I lapsed myself into a kind of strange intellectual impotence, a swamp of stupidity; I had these flashes, or rather the opposite of flashes, eclipses, when I truly succeeded in looking upon the world through his eyes, and then the equations and graphs I'd just drawn with my own hand lost any sense, I can't imagine a more terrible feeling, and so there were moments when frustration got the better of me, I managed to shriek at him, fling rulers and copybooks, bang my fist on the table; he, naturally, only stared at me like a well-pastured cow, so I'd be almost tearing my hair out – and then Anna Magdalena would come into the room and ask if Jędruś was making progress. "Yes, miss, he's trying his best." Mother of God of Częstochowa, protect me from dense pupils!

'And so, a few months flitted by and I recall not how many times I exchanged formal courtesies with Anna and polite remarks about her younger brother; till one day I see that I am drawing him tangents of angles, yet thinking only thus: it's time to shout and raise a din, so that Anna Magdalena might deign to visit us. Because, if the truth be known, I would have spared myself that drudgery long ago, were it not for the hope of seeing her face, hope of a word, a fleeting touch, a glance. Take heed, miss: now I tell it so, but then I called not my feelings by name; we never name living feelings or we name them incorrectly, only their demise brings such ease, ease in the classification of dead objects, not to say: description of the entrails of a corpse. But in those days – thought was timid. A day, week, month. We converse whilst the imbecilic brother won't comprehend a word, as he carves in his copybook further algebraic abominations, his tongue lolling out. So boldness between us grows and grows, and with time also something akin to the excitement of a game, verbal gymnastics: saying a thing in such a way that no one but Anna will understand, and no one except me when she speaks; because although the blockhead brother was no great challenge, that's for sure, their parents, and grandfather by no means deaf, and housekeeper, and finally the snooping female cousin sheltering under their roof since the time gleissen settled on her townhouse, were also witnesses to our ever longer conversations. All too obviously – for again a month goes by and the day arrives: I am preparing to leave, and here on the threshold, the worthy begetter of Anna Magdalena and Jędruś detains me and invites me to drink tchay. Where the talk is deadly serious. Is he a respectable young man, and from what family, and what income, and where does he live, and what are his future prospects, and what says his heart? – what says his heart! – Bozhe moy, only now do I understood what was obvious to everyone except myself, and turned as red as boiled lobster. So, had I fallen in love? Was I thinking of marrying? You tell me, miss – what kind of scent is that – no bloom, and yet the bouquet is woven – woman, a thousand reflections of woman, a kaleidoscope of feelings.

'And so open affection and exchange of billets-doux and trifling keepsakes and longer tête-à-têtes behind closed doors, and the stupid brother laughing his face off. The fiancé! As to closed doors, I won't scandalise you more, because for this tale it's no longer important, but what is important – harken, miss. Anna Magdalena had a Danzig escritoire locked with a key and the key kept in a locket around her neck, and in the escritoire – her secrets, that is, all her letters, her diary, some girlish treasures and whatever else she desired to keep secreted from the world; I know, because I often came across her writing something, which she swiftly hid, or, if she wanted to hand me something in secret, she would take it out at once from under lock and key. And so the day arrives – or more accurately, evening, the gas lamps are already burning brightly – when I call on Anna, but she shouts to me from the servants' staircase that she won't be a moment, back in a jiffy, so I take off my overcoat, the housekeeper conducts me upstairs, I am left alone in the room; outside the window it's dark, my eyes turn to the light, a minute, alone, two minutes, alone, I saunter around, inspect the trinkets, and my eye alights on the escritoire, which is ajar. Ajar, whilst from under a pen case and lacquered box protrudes the corner of a folded paper; the pen case is likewise half-closed, on the paper a fresh inkblot. And what happens? My legs guide me to the furniture, a hand reaches out, fingers grasp the paper, extract it, unfold it, and it is read. I recognised Anna Magdalena's handwriting, and recognised her words: "My love!" – she always began like that. And so, a letter to me! She was in the process of writing, had not finished. I smiled inwardly. I shan't confess; I shall pretend not to have read it. Meanwhile, read on. "My love, a second day passes, and my body already aches for your body" – I remember, aye, but shall spare you, miss, you know what kind of letter it was. You know: *lettres d'amour* are not letters, their purpose is not to communicate information from sender to addressee; it is to conjure, in the absence of the object of love, those very same feelings prompted by their presence. As we write: that same elation, the letter-writer overcome by blushes, the heart pounding faster, both when we later recall what we wrote, and when we imagine the beloved who reads it – likewise when we receive it ourselves: that self-same euphoria and feeling of intimacy, and the thought of the one who wrote it, when they wrote it. With me it was no different: a few moments and blood throbs neath the skull, warm blissfulness envelopes the body, a kind of melting sensation spirits away all energy, not even in relation to Anna Magdalena, but to myself; these are Narcissus's pocket mirrors: love letters. *Verte*, the other side. And it was though I'd been hit on the crown with lead piping. A few more sentences and what should Anna write – she writes of his fair hair, of shared jaunts on horseback, refers to sinful pleasures that had never been our portion… I ought to have suspected earlier, but was blunted by the spell of self-admiration flowing from the love letter in which I had wanted to believe. I read the rest. Who, who is he, what's his name? She had not finished writing, there was a lack of detail. Maybe there's an envelope with his address? There isn't. What to do? I hear Anna Magdalena's footfalls, stand with her letter in my hand like a murderer caught red-handed with a blood-stained knife. What to do, attack her with accusations, hide the proof and run away, what to do? A split second to think – put the letter back in its place, withdraw to the window. Anna Magdalena bursts in, overjoyed, how nice you've come! – and I smile, smile, smile; I had tasted the sweet smack of betrayal.'

'Sweet?'

'But yes, yes, sweet, sickly sweet; warm putrefaction or a cadaver baked by sunlight gives off a similar odour, we don't want to but we breathe in the air, taste it, at once it makes us feel sick, but a little bit more, one more time – impossible to stop oneself. In its own nauseating way, it is pleasurable. In what might a betrayed man find consolation? In the very fact that he has been betrayed. Being betrayed very quickly proves to be a form of nobility of soul, a kind of exaltation; does Jelena understand me, or not, most likely not. It is also something that cannot be told to another person. Can we *imagine* how we would feel, were we to be betrayed – and by whom? Well, and can we point to someone on the street and *imagine* how we would feel, were we to love him?'

'It seems to me –'

'Follow me closely, Jelena. Thus it was I gave nothing away to Anna Magdalena. I say goodbye, take my leave. Kind of say something, do something, yet in my head there is but one thought: who is it, who, with whom, whom had she, who her, who? Get drunk? – that was never my method; besides, my stomach is too weak for alcohol. What then? I sit at my desk, jot down on a piece of paper: fair or auburn hair; rides horses; has a moustache; they met on this and that occasion; in this and that place; have known each other since – et cetera, whatever I could re-member from the letter. Yes, you assume rightly, miss: I began to spy on Anna Magdalena. Who visited them at home and whom did she go out to visit and whom did she meet on the street, in the shops, and whom did she regularly see in church? All men fitting the description were suspect. Were they the only ones! With time, suspicion began to spread like frost over water, gathering into itself ever further expanses. Because – you see the logic, miss – if she can cheat with one, why not with another? With a second, third, fourth, anyone? All were now suspect. If Anna Magdalena exchanged solely formal compliments with a neigh-bour in the gateway, then it was precisely not to give herself away before yet another devotee of her charms; if she responded not to a stranger's bow on Jerusalem Avenue, it was not because he was a stranger, but because she was remembering to keep up appearances; if someone of her circle greeted me cordially, then it was not out of cordiality but malice and being in league with the faithless woman. Follow me closely, Jelena! A week and a week and almost a month of miraculous betrayal. Her father! If her father had given his blessing, then why? – asks the betrayed man. And how was it possible he'd given away his only daugh-ter without a lot of haggling to such a shirker without a groschen to his soul and not the most spotless of names – by listening to the voice of his heart? – bah! All conspiracy and whorish theatre, *pardon pour le mot*. Papa must have been well aware of the real nature of the beautiful Anna. So, you see, miss – you cannot trust anyone. They conspired together, ensnared the penniless tutor. Did I not say that there is always something wherein consolation and satisfaction may be found?

'And God knows how long it would have gone on and how deeply I'd have sunk into the black pleasures of betrayal, were it not for Jędruś-the-cussed-idiot, Jędruś-to-the-rescue, who everywhere gawps except at what he ought, is interested in everything except in what he should be, and in the end espied me once or twice lurking in the shadows between the passers-by, and no doubt told his sister. In the beginning, Anna Magdalena likewise said nothing and sought to play games with me with a blameless face – but I already sensed something; then it transpired she'd noticed me herself, once by a window, once by a gate, since I'd not managed to disappear from view in time when she was visiting relatives in Powiśle. It could not have gone on endlessly. Because don't imagine, miss, that I was simply trailing after Anna and recording points of jealousy. It escalated. If only I'd caught her in flagrante, if only I'd seen with my own eyes…! But since I remained at the mercy of ever-more-monstrous assumptions, I had to reach for more radical means. I hired a pickpocket, so he'd clean out the pockets of men she saw – whether it was some billet-doux, scented handkerchief, the flimsiest trace. There was also an errand-boy, whom they often used, some street urchin, oh, a guttersnipe perhaps ten years old, who scampered off on errands for the whole household. One snowy evening I nabbed him on his own, wrapping a scarf around my head so he'd not recognise me, and began to question him, come now, when, to whom, with what, and what kind of letters, and what did the young lady say, and had he heard any gossip. Nothing doing. Then I shouted at him. Nothing doing, he runs away. So, then I grab him by the ear, hurl him against the wall and threaten him with my fist and, yes, I smashed the nipper in such frenzy that he dropped to the ground unconscious. And what's more –

'I couldn't last out endlessly. I enter, she's on the sofa, hands intertwined in a handkerchief, she raises her eyes, she's been crying; but her lips are tightly sealed. I see that it's about to snap inside her, mounting within her in silence, and precisely because of that Anna says nothing, so as not to burst all at once out of her masks and poses, for she can no longer withstand the charade, there had been some last straw, I know not what, Jędruś-cretin maybe, perhaps she herself has suspected that I suspected. But – these eyes of hers red from weeping! But her wrought little hands! Now she's the victim, now she's the injured one – oo-oo, never expected to see the day! Come on now:

admit it, admit it – I begin, my shouting, my pain – who is he, when did he oust me from your heart, if I ever dwelt in it, you have no heart, greedy whore! As if I'd bespattered her with spittle, she was convulsed by sobs. Her brother came running, I slammed the door, he pummelled it from the outside. Anna Magdalena is white as snow. "What is it you want from me? What harm have I done you? What madness! God!" And fresh tears. Here Fury touched me for a moment with her fiery hand, I remember not what I yelled; till it took my breath away and I trembled all over as if in a fever, grabbed hold of the furniture, would have collapsed. Anna is at my feet, clasping my knees. "It's not true," she wails, "it's all untrue, bad people were lying, don't believe them." Here strength fails me – bad people! telling lies! I grew hoarse, thus only in a whisper, very quietly: "I had the letter in my hand, inscribed by yourself." "What letter?" I point to the escritoire. She only stares and shakes her head. I whisper whole sentences engraved in my memory, her ardent confessions, the improprieties of which she reminded her lover. But, I see, she has understood – she shudders, lowers her eyes; so, I begin again, my whisper cold as a lancet blade, I know your sins, you harlot. No longer will she look me in the face, red blushes stream down as far as her neck, and again only a whisper remained – her whisper is so weak, I have to lean over. "No lover, no lover have I, no one apart from you, and I never have had." "The letter, your heartfelt letter!" "Yes, I have been writing letters, for years, all under lock and key, to him." "To whom?" "Since the time I began reading French romances, my lover, whom I never had, from romances, from books, for years, I've shared with him every thought, every sin, because I can write anything to him, he who exists not, exists not, exists not!" And so, Jelena, miss, what to say, what to do? All a result of reading romances! I probably tried to excuse myself, threw myself on my knees – she shoved me aside with not so much as a glance, her back turned, hiding her face, she drove me away, sobbing. In the doorway, her brother almost fell upon me with his fists: "Dummkopf, you dummkopf!" I fled. Afterwards, we would pass one another from time to time in the street, Anna Magdalena and I; she married the steward of Mrs Wodzińska's Tattersalls Club… but we never again looked each other in the eye.'

Took-took-took-TOOK, took-took-took-TOOK.

Tongue, cognac, lips.

'And did you not think, sir, that she might have left that letter intentionally, so that you'd find and read it?'

'To arouse my jealousy?'

'It never entered her head that you'd believe in her betrayal.'

'What for then?'

Jelena inclined her head forward, pursed her lips.

'There are things you won't say to someone's face, but will confess in a letter; and there are things that cannot be confessed in a letter either – but they can be given to be understood. In a different way. For a lady won't say directly: I want this and that. A lady must always be able to say no, and retreat without losing face. You say, sir, that with this imaginary lover of hers, she –'

'Let's let it rest.'

Miss Jelena Muklanowicz laughed discreetly, covering her lips with her palm. The Sun had already sunk so low and the tracks veered so far in relation to the Sun that little sunset light now poured into the compartment, and deep shadows, soft, undulating like thick velvet, had nestled down roundabout the young woman, wrapping her silhouette in the lavish material of night, until she sank so utterly into it that only by moving, only by reaching beyond the shadow – glass to mouth, to mouth an empty palm – did Jelena loom for a moment as a pale blotch, the outline of a remembered shape. What sort of laugh could be surmised therefore only from its muffled sound, smothered by the constant rattle of the train; the expression on the devushka's face cannot be read, nor the meaning of the laughter in her eyes. Derision? pity? mockery? sympathy? And does she now ask herself the inevitable question: true or false? But perhaps it seems to her she has already realised the answer – and for that reason, she laughs.

'You're amused, miss? A jolly little tale?'

'Please admit – no, you won't admit it. It sounds genuine enough, as if it really happened – but it's not a good fit, sir, not for you. You heard it somewhere? Someone told it you? And you repeat it now, cut to shape?'

'Not a good fit? Even if. Why do you think it false? Perhaps the falsehood is on the other side.'

'For it's as if I've got to know not Benedykt Gierosławski – but whom? a false Benedykt Gierosławski?'

'Got to know me!' Snort. Stand up, twist the electric light switch; the bulbs in the compartment flared in their coloured globes. Jelena blinked, covering her eyes with a by-now-familiar gesture. The night outside the window solidified into a black monolith, a smooth lump of carbonic ice. 'Got to know! – does that mean I have also got to know you?'

'Calm down, I beg you. I meant not –'

'What? Because, ordinarily you *get to know* people within two days?'

'Excuse me. That was foolish.' She removed her hands from her eyes. 'But looking at it from a third point of view: is betrayal with a non-existent lover less painful? less of a betrayal?'

'You're that certain, miss, that the story cannot be genuine!'

'You were very worked up, sir.' She stared, continuing to blink. 'And so – and so, it is genuine?'

Sit down again, cross one leg over the other, pull the crease of a trouser leg.

'That is not what I said. Your turn.'

Lost in thought, she touched with her nail the dimple below her lower lip.

'All men are monsters.'

'*Pardon…?*'

'All men are monsters. You will discover, Benedykt, sir, whether I am lying. Always I was sickly, especially from my eighth year of life, for the next five or six years – that was the hardest time, I no longer remember how many times the doctors foretold me a speedy expiry, obviously without telling me a thing, they just smiled, stroked my head and assured me that everything would be fine; but I always contrived either to eavesdrop or to drag it out of the servants or make it out from Auntie's faces and moods – that it was bad. The worst was that it was never a single mortal illness, but dozens of lesser infections and long-drawn-out indispositions, following on one after the other, overlapping and provoking one another: illness was a permanent condition, no specific illness, but a constant state of being ill, a kind of internal *diathesis*, because before I succeeded in emerging from one malignant fever, two different weaknesses had already built their nests in my organism, and so on endlessly. You could say that my main illness was precisely that extraordinary susceptibility to any infirmity, some inborn defect of the body, but how to judge, since I have been ill for as long as I can re-member – maybe everything was foredoomed by that first, innocent complaint, the pebble that launched the avalanche? Anyhow, I seldom left my bed.

'Now try, Benedykt, sir, to enter the world of a child bedridden for years. Here, out of necessity, the borderline between truth and fiction is kicked into the far distance. Signals from the outside world – slivers, echoes, traces left on people by the world, like the traces left by a mur-derer on the accessories to his crime – penetrate to the child, but she does not experience the world directly. So, what does she do? She con-structs the world in imagination. Not a city, but an imaginary notion of a city. Not a game in the snow but a notion of a game in the snow. Not a friend but a notion of a friend. Not life but a notion of life. The thought arises that reconstruction is possible, that all these traces must fit to-gether: a murderer exists; there was a crime. Experience is no longer necessary: it will always be random, fragmentary. Whereas imagination is *complete*. And it seems to me that you, Benedykt, as a mathematician

– I am not mistaken, sir? – know that feeling, that this primordial tendency of the mind is not foreign to you.

'Apparently, there are categories of insanity, rancour of the soul, which leave people totally severed from experience, cut off from sensory impressions. It is said: they live in their own world. In Professor Zylberg's clinic I saw catatonics. The tangible world is unnecessary to them, imagination has triumphed. Certainly, in the end, it has proved to be *truer*. Is this what you had in mind? If we lose the measure of truth – what decides? Anything whatsoever.

'It was a fever, very exhausting, the kind that makes the muscles ache and you fall asleep only in the chill morn after sweating all night, in a body now weightless and sodden; those are the rare pleasures of a long illness, which you, sir, no doubt have never had occasion to know, never had a taste of. But to me – they were ecstasy. Accompanied, however, by a strange lucidity of the senses; after such a night, you see things more distinctly, see, hear, feel with great keenness, because touch too, smells too, everything affects you with greater force – and all the more forcefully the weaker you are, the more you've been worn down by fever. Naturally, the mind is then at its weakest.'

'In the morning, after a sleepless night.'

'Yes.'

'Were you listening to Zeytsoff from the beginning?'

'But please don't interrupt me! So dawn arrives, the head is purged, the blinds are raised – and lo and behold, the eiderdown under my fingers is downier, the light in my eyes brighter, dazzling almost, the air is fresh even if it's not fresh, and the people new, even if they are the same. The doctor enters. The doctor is well over fifty years old, thick beard, balloon-like belly, fingers like stubby sausages, stinking of pipe-tobacco and ammonia; as he squeezes my wrist (and his skin is rough, like an elephant's), he mutters something under his breath, weird hoarse sounds. So I am already watching with eyes wide open, suspiciously, and – I see – wisps of grey hair growing out of his nose, little black clumps out of his ears, some strange organ like a pincushion moving under his beard, and when the doctor leers through the lenses of his eyeglasses, the watery stare of his enormous lights causes a shiver to run through me, and already the certainty, prompted by intuition, arises in my clear, lucid mind: this is not a being of my own species, it is something different – some sort of monster, an animal, not human. A low burble issues from its gob: "Ho-ow are we fee-ee-ling?" In terror, I barely whisper in response. That I'm all right.

'Do you think, sir, that I fell asleep in the end and the feeling passed off? But this is the whole point: it would have been better, had it not passed off! Because who, on a daily basis, brought me vestiges of extra-sickroom life, from whom could I read the reality lying outside my bedroom, who gave me the evidence for imagining the world? Auntie Urszula. Mama. Julka and old Guścowa. And sometimes Mrs Feschik, who came to read bedtime stories, because that was her greatest pleasure in life: reading bedtime stories to sick children. You see, sir? Women. Whereas the doctor called only when something changed in my condition, when it got worse, so precisely after a difficult night. And I saw what I saw; what I had to see. How long was it before imagination became fixed for good? The rule was irresistible. There am I, I and the other women; and there are they, like the doctor, these strange monsters, inhuman.

'In recollection, there is no difference between the world and the world imagined. Were you to imagine eating a locust – have you heard, sir, that there exist folk who live on locusts? – but imagine it precisely, until you get sensory impressions, so that after a while you cannot tell memory of the taste of locust from memory of the taste of bread: they taste different, but equally real. Well, I remember very well that I inhabited a world wherein men were the males of a different species of creature. What had happened to the other half of the human race? Men had surely killed them off in order to occupy their place. Mystification on an historic scale. They hid it from us, camouflaged their actions, dissembled, played roles – imperfectly, however, incompetently, sloppily, because they do everything clumsily and sloppily, such is their inhuman, menkindish nature. Not much is needed to see through them. For instance, how they behave amongst themselves, when they think we're nowhere near. At once their voices alter, coarsen, words lose in meaning, men switch to their own language, a kind of animal dialect of raucous grunts, growls, mumbles, croaks; of human language, they find use only for vulgarisms. Descended from scavengers, they eat like scavengers; I have seen rats biting into red meat, stuffing grub into their snouts till they go purple in the face from the strain and their lights pop out; oily sweat pours over their skin, yet their jaws work unflaggingly, all the faster, all the more, and the sounds that escape from them then, the wheezing, and the stench of their menkindish bodily excretions…! Or that rapacious fondness for blood and strife – despite their best efforts to hide it, it's enough to show them some butchery, or even a punch-up in the street, let one smash another's nose: and already their eyes are blazing, nostrils twitching – ah, they're onto the scent! – and off they go with muscles taut. In the evenings, after dusk and late into the night, in their caves, they hold their menkindish rituals, cultivate there the true mores of pain, sweat and violence; sometimes, they return to their homes, to us, without wiping away all the traces. In secret they pay homage to non-human gods with hideous likenesses. They've arranged everything anyway so we have no access to their meeting-places. Whole interiors, buildings, are out-of-bounds to us, where only men have access; entire districts, and maybe cities too, maybe there exist on earth cities not-for-women – wiped from the maps by male cartographers – underground metropolises, where men live in their natural state, free from the theatre of human culture, naked, covered in hog-bristles not only on cheeks and chin but all over their bodies, live in mud, in darkness and in a dark blaze of red fire, in scalding smoke, punching with their fists and biting indiscriminately in droves of a thousand, wallowing in the urine and blood of their victims, whilst he who suffers the most wounds and disfigures himself the most is made the idol of the horde and raised above other men, in order that they might admire the image of their god, in croaks, in vulgar cries, in spits and farts, free. And when they hunt down a woman unguarded by a man, a savage fight ensues at once over the right to be first to devour her. And when they have to return amongst women for longer, they pine and grieve at their exile and moan in their sleep and take revenge on us whenever they can, since it has befallen them to live in such bondage, concealment and oppression of their menkindish nature – and only then is there a small flash of joy and expression of satisfaction on their lumpen countenances, when they succeed in inflicting hurt, pain upon a woman. All men are monsters.

'How to free oneself from this world? Not possible, not entirely, the memory will always remain. Of course, it can sometimes be overshadowed by other memory. It came about like this, however, before I'd had time to grow accustomed to men... You were speaking, sir, of first love; it was not first love. I know not what it was – a hunting ritual perhaps. He used to steal up on me at the estate of my father's friends in Saxon Lusatia, their cousin, a young student spending his summer vacation there, whilst I felt well enough then to travel to the country, no serious illness, a real miracle, gleissen never reached those parts, so it was summer like the Lord God ordained, long evenings, warmth, crickets chirping, the scent of green grass and foliage – he used to steal up on me by the light of the moon. It wasn't true that I still lived in those imagined notions, after all I was no longer rotting for months under bedclothes; but it was also not true that I had completely forgotten, I am telling you, sir, I had not forgotten, I shall never forget. And so, he –'

'Won't you tell his name?'

'Artur. Artur. The landowning type, well-built, powerful legs from riding horses, burned by sun, hair the colour of overripe corn, he never combed it, a lion's mane – my God, Benedykt, do you hear how I describe him? From the very beginning, I saw more the animal in him. Are you able to judge, sir, the beauty of a steed of noble blood? How it moves, the walk, trot, gallop, canter, how the muscles flex beneath the skin, shining from warm sweat, and also the great harmony within, a rhythm like in music, great strength in the perfect body, perfectly tuned. Artur must have seen it in my eyes. My drawing teacher told me I had talent. Take a look some time at the way people gaze. How painters, sculptors, dancers and inhabitants of the South cast their eyes at once over a person's entire figure, even on greeting, on first meeting; not stopping at the face, they must survey the whole body. Artur recognised my gaze. I remember not what polite words he uttered when we were introduced. But I remember how he smiled: showed his teeth, bared his fangs. The hunt had begun: the man hunts down the human, that is, the woman.

'In the cool shades of the manor house and under the azure sky of harvest, in air atremble with noonwraiths and the heat of sun-scorched soil. With every passing day, everything resembled more and more my imagined notion, but perhaps it was I who was slipping back into it and dragging Artur after me by some mesmeric means – vain questions, I shall tell only what I remember. And so, with every passing day. In the beginning, we spoke little, but Artur very soon abandoned any illusion of human language, sticking to words in the menkindish dialect; so we conversed not at all, there being no common language between our species. The earth was baking – I wore no shoes, went barefoot, bare feet on bare soil for the first time in my life. He would entice me with a jug of cold lemonade, a juicy apple. Never came up to me, never gave it to me. He would stand with arm outstretched, and I had to draw near and take it. Then he would lean forward seeking my eyes with his eyes. What it was about was that with time, I should begin to eat out of his hand, literally, that is, without using my hands, straight from his hand into my mouth, with my tongue off his skin. He dogged me not, nor hastened after me like he'd hasten after ordinary game; and yet even on a solitary walk, I felt his presence always, his watchful gaze, and indeed, not once, not twice, he flashed by somewhere in the distance, a silhouette against the horizon or shadow amongst the trees, so that I acquired the habit of glancing over my shoulder, stopping and pricking up my ears – like a doe in the forest. At table, he never looked at me – he looked at those at whom I was looking, with whom I conversed. He went in and out of the room ahead of me. Then… We were returning one red evening from the riverbank, the master and mistress of the house, the steward's daughters, one of their neighbours, a slow walk along a dirt track; I was walking barefoot and cut myself on a sharp stone, it cut through the as-yet-unhardened skin between toes, I was hopping on one leg, and some drunken peasant, passing us on the road, made an indecent remark, I was left behind, limping, and then it transpired that Artur too had remained behind; Artur grabbed the peasant by the ear and began to twist it, pull and pinch it, until he dragged the drunkard down onto his knees and eventually landed his face in the dust of the road, almost ripping off that ear, the peasant was left there on the ground with blood on his snout. You understand, sir? I stood, watched, said nothing. Artur, of course, did not look back. I hobbled along behind him. Felt that the hunt was nearing its end, that it was a matter of days. There would be no warning. Nothing would he say, nothing ask, nothing beg, not him – long muscles under bronzed burned skin, menkindish melody of movement, mane of fair hair, white fangs. What to do? I was unable to sleep. He came not in the night. After dawn too, I fell not asleep. He came not during the day. I was unable to eat. At table, I followed Artur with my eyes; the others had already noticed, it had become all too obvious. Someone said something. Artur turned to me and, with a smile on his face, leant towards me, on his open palm a quarter of a juicy pear, the sweet syrup flowing over his fingers, over the bare skin of his hairy forearm. I licked my lips. Took the knife out of the apple-cake and plunged it into his chest.

'They sent me to Professor Zylberg's clinic. There I was treated for a "nervous breakdown" and there, when I fell ill, I fell ill with tuberculosis.'

Took-took-took-TOOK, took-took-took-TOOK.

Jelena Muklanowicz had grown increasingly apprehensive as her tale unfolded; now there could be no doubt: the unwholesome blushes, quickened breath, nervous movements of fingers on the shot-glass. Know not, however, of what these were the signs: truth or falsehood. Had confession to a man of honest truths provoked such emotional ferment – or had she become so upset whilst honestly lying? Under the electric lamp, every shade of violent emotion was clearly illuminated on her smooth face like a battlescape in a photoplasticon.

'Since you have allowed yourself, miss, such, mm-hmm, unrefined frankness, allow me to speak freely too, you won't be offended.' Drink up the cognac and energetically put aside the shot-glass; it almost shattered underhand. The duel continued, the stakes had been raised. 'Because I shall finally introduce myself in the appropriate manner: Benedykt Gierosławski, habitual gambler.'

'Agh!'

'Yes, yes, you have seen me playing, miss, and what were you thinking: strong, because he's mastered his shame? Hah! Weak, because he's not mastered his habit!'

'And you reckon only like that, sir?'

'What?'

She twirled her finger in the air.

'Strong, weak, strong.'

'Jelena, really, whether or not I reckon like that, of what importance is it; the stronger shall still conquer the weaker, even were I to name them in French with beautiful words and measure them in perfumery terms. But the gambler, but the habit in me – this *is* what is stronger.

'So, the story will be as follows. Seventeen years old, first year at the Imperial University, cards. There was this student of law, Fryderyk Weltz, because you should know, miss, that I remember the exact beginning perfectly, and the beginning was here, clear and concrete – insofar as anything at all exists in the past – a distinct dividing line between the gambling time and the time before gambling, since neither at home, nor in my family nor amongst my relatives and family friends, nor earlier at school, was I given to taste this fruit of temptation; the Gierosławskis had no such traditions and I inherited no such bad blood on my mother's side, only at the Imperial, on that day when we re-treated from the bolted doors of the Dickstein building, because a gleiss had settled on it during the night and frozen its way through all the aulas; lectures were cancelled, and we went our different ways, one lot here, another lot there – and Fryderyk Weltz was inviting everyone to a poker game. Now you'll think to yourself: well, how come, a stranger's word with no strings attached, I must have invited myself. Yet individuals exist for whom there are no strangers in this world.

'Fredek was a man with humanity in his embrace. You know such characters, miss? Before he comes across you, he's already your friend, heartiness pours out of him as from a vat full of holes, it's enough to draw near, show yourself, it's easy. Always he greets you with open arms, hollering loudly from afar, the more people around about the louder, with a broad smile, as he laughs from deep inside his belly, his guts; generally, such people are of strapping build, in any case of ample corpulence, with round face, thick pasty lips, long, flipper-like paws. Fredek had no athlete's grip, but apart from that – it was as I say. He was not yet twenty, yet you could already see in him the beloved uncle and ribald grandpa. Often, we are mistaken as to the nature of persons of this type, often we say: the life and soul of the party. I did not realise straightaway what was genuine in Fredek and what was fake. He laughed too loudly. Opened his arms too wide. Shook your hand too energetically. You see, miss, I am able to recognise shame in all its guises, including this.

'He swept me up like he swept up the many – those silent students who stood aloof, unknown to other students. On us he fed his hearti-ness, fed his shame. Who would he have been if he couldn't have been the jovial friend of every lost soul at the University? The next lost soul. Wholeheartedly then – to a game of cards. In the beginning, the play was a social occasion: you go to drink vodka, go to eat fish broth, go to play cards – it means the same: to meet up, sit for a few hours with a common excuse, in a smoke-filled annexe, dark cellar, in some attic where a cold draught sucks and icicles grow from the shutters like bean-pods, to sit and chatter. It's why you study; knowledge can be acquired in a thousand ways, but such acquaintances who are to accompany you throughout life on career paths and set up careers for one another, they for you and you for them, through the same student connections, such acquaintances – are acquired only like this. And no one tried to persuade me, just so you're in no doubt, miss, I was not *drawn into it*. They played, so I watched. They played, so I worked out how I would play in place of this man or that. They played, and so in the end I too began to play.

'Gambling was commonplace amongst the students, but the majority were penniless toffs like me. The sums were not large and we played none too seriously. The trouble was, Jelena, the trouble was, that I tended to win. But! Even that was not what decided it. You can't go on winning forever, I knew that, eventually I'd get scorched and withdraw. Because I was winning, however, and they all saw that I was winning – moreover they knew I studied mathematics and made a fetish out of it, a little jokingly, a little seriously – it was only natural I should land in games with higher stakes, amongst the hardened kartyozhniks, Fryderyk introduced me. And when I won with them, I won serious money. And what did I do with this money? Listen carefully, miss, because this is where the bad habit starts. If only I'd drunk my way through it! Squandered it on devushkas! I'd have been duly shaken by pangs of conscience, and my thirst would have been quenched. Instead, I poured fuel on the fire. The first large pot, I remember it, one hundred and sixteen roubles – what did I do? I sent my mother to a renowned doctor, bought her medicines. Made gifts of sweets and toys to the children in my lodging-house. You see, miss, from what the habit started? I grew addicted to their joy, not even to their gratitude, but to the joy in their eyes, to that warm satisfaction in the heart when we perform a selfless deed with such ease.

'You smile ironically. What a primitive excuse! But I am not claiming at all that this was why I played; when I play, there are no other motives apart from the play. I am merely telling you my journey. From flea-ridden student dens, via the backrooms of cafés and private salons, to the table of the Kind Prince. Fredek saw how much I was winning and one evening escorted me to the prince of Warsaw gamesters – as to whether he was really so high-born, it's possible; judging by outward appearances, his manners and speech, he could be just as much a count as I am. You bump into him on the street and think: he has aged well. A silver-haired gentleman with Roman nose, Vilnius lilt and pleasant smile. The minimal ante: two hundred roubles. But Fredek could not have known that I'd kept only enough from what I'd won to sit down to the deal the following evening. So now I was to borrow and run up debts. And yes, yes, naturally, on the first night with the Kind Prince I lost everything, to the last kopeck staked on credit.

'What does good sense dictate? Pay back the debt, there's no way how, yet up till now there'd been only wins – the simplest thing therefore is to win it back. You will say, miss, that's not at all sensible. Generally speaking, gambling isn't sensible and most human endeavours have little in common with reason – it's hard to recall a single sensible thing I've done since boarding this train – but since I was already playing, why should this particular gaming evening be a mistake? Of course, I then lost again and fell into debts twice as deep, but this is not what it's about. I took the money put aside for my mother's medicines; I lost. Pawned my father's belongings; I lost. Took what was earmarked for tuition fees and rent; I lost. Pawned my gold watch and my better clothes; I lost. Now please ask me, why.

'Yet there is no "why". This is the deceit of all stories like this: we look back – into memory – and make connections between events that occurred one after the other: I did that for such-and-such reasons, and this for such-and-such, even if I knew not then what I know now. Lies! When I sit down to play, there is nothing apart from the play. No external reasons; all those fairy tales about the joy of the beneficiaries – that was a stage along the road, but not the motive for playing. Just as you live not, miss, for the granite angels on your tomb – they're a posthumous ornament, outside of life. Whilst life – what of it, one is born, lives, dies. What kind of reason, devil take it, can be given here? You understand, miss? It is not I who plays. Not I who ever plays. *The game plays itself*.

'I come again to the Kind Prince, a Saturday evening, lots of guests, the upper crust; sometimes he organised receptions ahead of longer poker nights, and also when he introduced important personages from Warsaw society, gentlemen in frock coats, ladies in opera toilettes. The lackey didn't even admit me into the corridor – I already told you, I'd pawned my better togs with the shylocks. But how shall I win back my losses, when I cannot play for such stakes? How to win back my money, when I no longer have anything to stake? Enter Fredek with a handsome damsel on his arm. He noticed me, seemed concerned, heartfelt sympathy smeared over his gob, *c'est tragique*, old man, wait here a moment, we'll get help straightaway. He winks at me, slaps me on the back with his shovel-like paw, and dives into the salons. I wait a quarter of an hour, another quarter, their voices and music are right behind the wall; the merciful lackey brings me bread and pâté, I eat quickly with eyes glued to the parquet. Suddenly I hear footsteps – Fredek was bringing the Kind Prince. The prince is distraught, how can I help, dear friend, he puts his arm round me, reaches for his pocketbook. Take from him the red ten-rouble banknote? But this is no help, it's the next millstone around my neck, after all I didn't want to be indebted to him, I hadn't come to beg. Yet he is thrusting diengi into my pocket. Then I understood. I raise not my eyes, turn not my head, merely ask politely how I may settle my debt, whether some help for me can be found. The Kind Prince sighs heavily. A promissory note is a promissory note, the debt must be paid, at the Last Judgement too they'll add up our "debit" and "credit", Benedykt Gierosławski knows better than most the cold immovability of arithmetic. Of course, out of whose pocket the money comes is of no great significance, a rouble is just like its brother, so long as it ends up in the pocket it should, so that the columns balance. Maybe Benedykt knows someone with a relish for gaming and a few hundred to squander in pleasant company? So then I ask: what per cent? He says: seven. I say: fifteen. Ten is agreed. Fredek slapped me on the back.

'I left the prince's house with anger and hatred in my heart. They quickly paled. You have to understand the nature of shame; Fryderyk Weltz's false heartiness was as sincere as it could be – not because he loudly proclaimed his friendship in order to draw a man into the Kind Prince's web, but the reverse: the Kind Prince had singled him out to exploit for himself, because Fredek with that heartiness of his, which took people by force, was like flypaper to lonely souls. You see the correlation, miss? Knowledge of the mechanism of human hearts can be just as lethal as familiarity with the chemistry of cyanide and arsenic compounds.

'Whereas I was no tout and tempter, it would have taken me years to redeem the promissory notes from that ten per cent of other people's misfortune. Whatever little I wrested from my debt to the Kind Prince, I at once fell back into even greater debit. And so – the play went on. Win once, lose twice, play on, so long as there's a table somewhere, cards and a few willing players, whether it be for five kopecks or fifty roubles, whatever the stake and risk grasped in sweaty palms – the play went on. Did I not wish to break the habit, free myself? But of course I did! Until the play began.

'I had to invent a means, design for myself a trap, otherwise the Kind Prince would have devoured me sooner or later along with my soul and boots. The whole point is not to sit down to play at all. To make play impossible, turn it into non-play. How to deprive gambling of its significance, how to erase every stake? Please follow me with eyes wide open, it's a treacherous path, you have to watch carefully for signs and twists. How to turn play into non-play. And, as I've already told you, miss, removing the motives for playing solves nothing: play has no motives. Playing is for the sake of playing. The game is played because it's played. But this basic principle – with time I saw it more and more clearly – is not confined to gambling, not confined to what we usually call bad habits; unless we all consist solely of bad habits. Gambling, however, makes it more obvious, thrusts it before our eyes; you can no longer lie to yourself that it's you who casts the final rouble on the table when you know you ought not, when you'd planned to get up and walk away, when you wished not to cast it – yet cast it you do. After such painful experiences, it is very hard to persist in the lie.

'So, it remains to nullify the very idea of play. Remove the gamble from the gamble. Logic shows two methods of how to do it: either by replacing every possibility in the play with certainty – then the game would no longer be a game, just as the risings and settings of the Sun are not random events on which you can bet; or by reducing all stakes in the play to zero – then the game would no longer be a game, just as music devoid of sounds is no longer music, but silence. The first method might be good for crystal-gazers. The second also seemed impractical. You always play for something after all. Even when it's not about money, when money is of no importance – we play for the satisfaction of victory, humiliation of the opponent, a better sense of self, the respect of people, our reputation, our own good opinion of ourselves. However, money usually serves as the material measure of those non-material wares.

'So how to nullify it, strike it out? Follow close behind me, miss, and don't look back! But perhaps you already see?'

'Suicide?'

'Nothing of the sort! Whatever for! Suicide, my dear Jelena, suicide is nothing more than the next game, the next blind dealing of the cards – you're not going to tell me, miss, that you know with total certainty what awaits you after death, or if anything awaits you at all – maybe you believe, maybe hope, like one hopes for the ace of spades – but nothing more – to escape from former games into another game, what kind of solution is that, really – and then there's the stake, the very highest – so were it possible, I would have been an habitual suicide!'

'How then?'

'Whom will you not tempt with material wares? Not the rich man: to him it will always be too little, there are no perfect rich men, those from whom a richer cannot be made; this end of the scale opens onto infinity. At the other end, there is a limit: he who lives in absolute poverty is free not only from the terror of indigence – for he has already reached that extremum – but also from the need to make himself rich: *because he lives in absolute poverty*. Do you, Jelena –

'So that's it. That's it. The only possible liberation. And not on the scale of material riches – but those more important ones: satisfaction, respect, gratification, honour, all the riches of the spirit. Then, even though you've sat down to play: whether you have a higher card, or a lower card, whether the stake on the table is merely symbolic, pile of gold and sentence of shame, there is no difference – it's all like juggling the letters of an unfamiliar alphabet, like constellations in the sky, the shape of a cloud above the forest: empty and to you totally indifferent. Play washed clean of play. There is no play. Play not – perform only hand movements devoid of meaning and content, replace objects with objects, transfer papers from place to place.

'But, it transpires, there is nothing harder than reaching rock bottom. Did you ever swim, miss, in the deep part of a lake? The water resists the body, forces it upwards. Great effort is required, great strength of will, constant work and iron consistency in order to achieve the bottom. You have to tear out in turn everything that drags you upwards, any hopes, any bright aspirations, everything that elevates us in our own eyes, every tiniest germ of respect for our own self, every embryo of the qualities which one day might prove precious enough for us again to have something to play for – tear it all out!'

Miss Muklanowicz looked on with tremulous attention, leaning forward with lips half-parted; lips chapped in her dry breath, for she had forgotten to moisten them, forgotten to swallow the saliva.

'You were saying, sir, that not – but this is suicide!'

'On the contrary: it's freedom, freedom from the habit.'

'I don't believe you, Benedykt, it's some kind of monstrous lie, I've heard nothing more abominable in all my life!'

Shrug the shoulders.

'Besides, it's an obvious impossibility in itself, it's not possible to achieve such a state, though you've supposedly done so? How did you succeed?'

'I did not succeed.'

'Pardon?'

'This story has no punchline, it is not yet concluded, I am still living through it. Trying to tear myself out, trying. Sometimes it's down, sometimes up.' Demonstrate with the hand. 'I thrash about just above the bedrock, like a moth beneath a flame, always an inch from ultimate debasement, arising again to a fresh habit, as hot blood returns to the veins, roubles to the pocketbook, and the nerves itch, excitement re-animates shame, then again painfully breaking my soul and wrenching from it hope after hope, in order to stop however at the last moment. You've seen with your own eyes on this journey, miss, many a cycle of redemptive downfall and rebirth to sin. That which is torn out at once grows back – and fastest of all pride, fastest of all that liver of the soul bleeding with shame. And so, I swing between unlicht and light, a Black Prometheus.'

Took-took-took-TOOK, took-took-took-TOOK, took-took-took-TOOK.

'I don't believe you, sir, don't believe you.'

Laugh hoarsely; the throat feels dry from long peroration.

'It's nice, however, to encounter from time to time such an innocent little soul.'

Jelena threw back her head as if slapped on the cheek.

'So now it's come to insults!'

Laugh.

'Who else would take the mention of innocence as an insult – if not the truly innocent?'

'Oh, would she? Would she? Would she indeed?' Miss Muklanowicz was almost bereft of speech. Having set aside her glass, she took a moment to catch breath; reached into her sleeve, but not finding there her handkerchief, pressed the lacy cuff to her temple as if it were a cold compress. 'So,' she whispered and then, in the blinking of an eye, as if a kind of mental filter had been lifted from her, as if the blue spotlight had turned from her, she became a different person, Jelena Muklanowicz was replaced by Jelena Muklanowicz, the same neat outfit, the same pale complexion and charcoaled brow, but someone else was inhabiting the interior: someone older, someone cold-tempered, sedate, someone accustomed to the freedom of a strong, healthy body. Jelena dropped her hand, it sank loosely onto the bed. She crossed one leg over the other, smoothing down the narrow skirt with her left hand; in the course of this movement, she peeked without smiling from under her lashes, from under heavy eyelids. 'Pour me another,' she said calmly, in a croaky, deeper voice.

Stand up, open the drinks cabinet, top up both shot-glasses, no longer diluting the contents.

Miss Muklanowicz raised her left hand without spilling a drop; in an energetic movement, she upturned the glass and knocked back the cognac in a single swig.

'Another.'

Refill the glass.

She drank it just as swiftly.

'Sit down.'

She glanced at her reflection in the black windowpane. Touched her cheek, slightly raising her brow in clinical wonder. Without averting her head, she stretched her right arm up and towards the door, wrist and fingers drooping loosely; she was looking in one direction, pointing in another – it was the gesture of an opera diva, a prima donna stretched in her pose between scenic figures.

'Put out the light.'

Rotate the dimmer knob. Twilight descended. Fumble in the gloom for the chair. Beyond the window, along the line of the horizon, streaks were moving of the sky's dark colours – dark, yet brighter than the coarse-grained grey shrouding the expanses of Asia from east to west, from west to east. No lights, no fires or distant reflections; maybe a golden Moon would sail out over the plains, starlit lantern of the Orient.

Sit down groping in the dark. Within the compartment, only motionless shadows remained, and amongst them, at arm's length – Jelena's shadow. The ruby glinted; so this shadow relates to her neck, and that one – to her head, in these shadows – Jelena's eyes. And here – her mouth.

She was breathing deeply.

'I was born into a tanner's family in Powiśle. My parents passed away when I was ten, the year the gleissen entered Warsaw. The September Winter took also my siblings, sisters and brothers, uncle and aunt on my mother's side, and all their kin. Before my birth, my father had been a master craftsman at Gerlach's factory on Tamka Street; they shot off his leg in Grzybowski Square. He went back to tanning and they had to move out of the rented tenement in the Old Town. A week later, as I came into the world, in May nineteen-oh-five, the factory and slaughterhouse workers attacked the brothels with knives and axes, the whores and pimps had to flee for their lives, away from Warsaw, some driven as far as the forests. A girl with a headwound hid at my maternal uncle's; she recovered and then remained with us, she used to clean for a well-to-do family in Wilanów, carry laundry, Mariolka Belcik. After the first winter of Winter, she it was who looked after me; from then on, she brought me up.

'There was one year, several long months, when we were left with no roof over our heads. We thought to go to the provinces, so long as it was away from the Warsaw frost. Have you noticed, sir, how in the age of the gleissen, fewer homeless are seen on Warsaw streets? We begged, amongst other things. I still have scars on my body from those nights spent suffering on the ice in gateways. Mariolka was taken into service by a doctor and his wife, then I slept in the kitchen, it was warm. In the end they threw us out: the wife's gold earrings vanished and upon whom did suspicion fall? I was already fourteen. It was December, a week to Christmas, the Ice hung on trees and between rooftops, the black antichrist had settled on the Royal Castle, crows dropped from the sky frozen to the bone. Mariolka dragged me straight to Mariensztat, to the new skyscraper, huge neon sign on the ground floor at the front, but we entered from the back, the watchman recognised her. We wait till the owner appears – a man called Grisha Buntz, and so we entered the "Tropical", except that I still didn't understand, only when Mariolka pressed something into the hollow of his hand and whispered in his ear, and he laughed loudly and gave her a confidential squeeze… Yes, with those earrings she bought the favour of her old keeper; now, he had a nightspot for better-born gentlemen and would palm off on the well-heeled suckers not fob-watches taken from pickpockets, but diamond stuff, the shiny shoplifter. That's how I began work in the "Tropical".

'Mariolka always protected me. She at once put Buntz in his place: no work for me with the clients, only behind the scenes – I mended the girls' costumes, tidied up after closing-time, sometimes helped in the kitchen. Buntz at least did not run a brothel there, the venue was tip-top, crystal, stained-glass, plumes and dancers in sequins, shampan-skoye and Astrakhan caviar. But, of course, a lady companion would at once sit down beside a lonely gentleman, each one selected by Grisha himself; whilst above the venue, on the first, second and third floors, Grisha had several apartments artfully divided with separate doors, so that couples didn't have to go outside into the frost. I learned of this not immediately and not directly.

'And how? I pried. Pried and eavesdropped, busied myself with it even when busy with something else; and whenever there was a moment free from work, all the more so: eye to a crack, half-open door, window vent, from behind a heavy curtain, through smoked glass and even a keyhole – I spied on real life. Amongst Buntz's people were various crooked types, and also Jasio Brzóz, pickpocket and picklock, who taught us for amusement how to open locks as well as cat-burglar tricks. However, no one notices a scraggy girl in maid's outfit; we are as anonymous as gendarmes in their uniforms. There, people live; but here, we soak up that life, it leaves its stamp on us, remains within us. They experience their love dramas at dancing parties, brawls and scandals beneath the electric lights before the eyes of counts and princes; we dream about them. Into whom then does it sink the deeper?

'On one such occasion, Mr Buntz caught me in a compromising position, observing from behind a palm-tree an upper-class couple clasped in amorous embrace by the back stairs of the "Tropical". He grabbed me by the hair, dragged me into his office, summoning also Mariolka. He'll beat me up, I think to myself. But no. He ordered me to take off my pinafore, let down my hair, stand on tiptoe and spin around in a circle on the carpet in front of his desk; and he made this gesture, this movement of the hand with his cigarette holder in Mariolka's direction, as if showing her some proof, surrendering to some kind of wager, or casting off long-stifled distaste. Mariolka understood, I did not;

they didn't tell me to leave, but their whole conversation was like that gesture, just hints and insinuations, they were haggling over something, Mariolka never explained to me – meaning she lied, never explained truthfully.

'As a result of that haggling, Grisha began to send me for French lessons, lessons in how to write and speak correctly, dancing and piano-playing; I had no talent for the latter. I hasten to dispel your suspicions: the intention was not so obvious, Mr Buntz was not interested in the next young lady to sell as the kept woman of some financier or lord of the manor. Let us say, he receives clients. The gentlemen sit in armchairs in his office, a maid brings food and drinks, they pull out their papers, light cigarettes, poke at their abacuses. But here Grisha Buntz's young niece bursts into the room in her domestic dishabille, a scatter-brained girl, agh uncle, I've cut my finger, oy, really, let's take a look, there there, you'll forgive me gentlemen, my ward, but of course, what a ravishing child, so you won't hold it against me gentlemen, but of course not, *ce que femme veut, Dieu le veut* – because it's all done with a smile, a giggle, rolling an eye at the big fish and winding locks around a healthy finger. Or else: Buntz pays a visit to the salons, he, a square-jawed mug with loutish accent and scar on his forehead; but who should he take along: a woman of easy virtue with a kissy mouth and threadbare repu-tation? He will take a sickly underage girl who'll tell the old ladies with disarming coyness in Polish and in French of her family misfortunes, of horrific illnesses and the kindness of Mr Buntz, who may be boorish on the surface but who has a heart – a heart of gold! I had several different stories prepared. The ladies were greatly touched. Grisha would mutter something under his breath; there, indeed, he was genuinely overawed.

'It didn't take much for me to understand it from my own nature, which is nevertheless no small matter, comprehending your own nature, finding the right word to describe yourself, and I found this one: fibber. It wasn't because I was good at telling lies – though I was good at telling lies – but because I liked telling lies. You spoke of the gambling habit. This too is a habit and also a gamble: will it or will it not come out. Grisha was very satisfied with me and failed for a long time to take in the danger threatening him; even had he noticed, it was already too late. How many people drift through their entire lives in mediocrity, their work no more than work, a means of earning their keep; they've chosen it neither according to their own liking nor ac-cording to their own abilities, nor according to the satisfaction it gives them, but because it pays better than others, or is simply the only one that pays at all, since outside work too – what? because they can imitate a cockerel's voice extraordinarily skilfully? or knock back more beer than any other drunkard in the precinct? To be truly good at something

– this is an exceptional feeling, because it's accessible to so few, exceptional, because it makes you exceptional and defines your whole life. You were no one – now you are someone, namely what your gift makes you. So I tell fibs.

'It began from the fact that I lied more than I needed. First of all, we would establish the precise details of my stories; then, seeing that I took it in my stride, Buntz gave up his strict control. I was careful to the extent that it was necessary to maintain consistency in my lies. But you can always add something to a lie, always stretch the details. After all, it wasn't that I had to constantly stick to one story. In this too lay the unusualness of Grisha Buntz's position, that he operated on the boundary between different worlds that usually never crossed paths; therefore, I had contact with people who could never have contact with each other – what better field for a fibber to show off her talents? And in this too, I took care not to exaggerate my lies, to know the measure of truth, that is, of what sounds like truth, because that's how adults always recognise children's lies: because children exaggerate. But lies should be built up from minute crumbs of truth, added patiently one to another; better still if they're built up not by you, but by the person deceived, that is, when he deceives himself – when you allow him to *assume* the story you have prepared for him. Then he will defend such a lie to the bitter end.

'This is how it's done. You meet a stranger. You want to persuade him you are someone other than you are. You don't try to persuade: you throw him crumbs. Clues hidden in your conduct, in your speech, in the cadence of a sentence, in the way you hold your head, in your glance, and perhaps in the avoidance of a glance, how you move, how you relate to other people; if possible, in your clothes; if possible, in the conduct of your accomplices. Words must come at the very end, words have merely to confirm the knowledge already obvious from elsewhere. Besides, first of all you should deny everything, let him be curious and inquire of himself.'

'You describe, miss, the art of seduction.'

'Lies and more lies, whichever way you look at it. I am good at it – it comes to me so easily, almost without the participation of thought, so naturally... So, here's another riddle, Benedykt, sir: lying from nature. Lying from the depths of the soul! Whoever, wherever, whenever – and I'm already hinting at secrets, lowering my gaze, or staring him fierily straight in the eye, collapsing my voice; enter Grisha with a crony, and I'm covered in red blushes, or holding back tears with difficulty, or trembling nervously, or suddenly silent, or theatrically joyful, or mortally pale from terror. Why? Some plan? Has Buntz ordered me? Perhaps one of his clients? No. I lie because I want to, because I enjoy it, because I am able. Why do great safebreakers return to their trade, risking death behind bars, though they could peacefully see out their old age as men of leisure? Because only in this one thing are they exceptional, at this the best: unpicking safes.

'So, it was exactly like this with the affair of Shtabs-Kapitan Dmitry Sevastyanovitch Alla. He came to the "Tropical" not very often, usually in the company of fellow officers, besides, I didn't even know him by name, just another handsome Russian in uniform. But whether we'd passed once in the foyer, or he'd picked up my dropped glove in the entrance, or given me a light – I remember not the time and place – there was a moment, there was a meeting and there was a reaction on my part: a lie. I still said nothing, I lied wordlessly. Alla believed.

'I knew because he pursued me afterwards with his gaze, sought my eyes. When I was walking down the street with Mr Buntz, he bowed and stopped so as to enter conversation with Grisha, but he was looking at me – I said nothing the whole time, staring at the ground, fingers pressed into the sleeve of Grisha's coat. Had the captain noticed? Definitely. Then a waiter comes up to me and says a Russian in uniform is looking for me, according to the description: does such a young woman work here, is she perhaps the owner's mistress? What to say, he asks. But tell the truth! The rest Dmitry told himself.

'I know not if he were waiting for me, or if it were by chance – I step out one morning from the skyscraper, and the captain alights at that very moment from a droshky. Where are you heading, miss, we'll drive you there, but please, please. And off we go. I am scared. Mumble awkward words in French. The captain is in earnest. Is that dreadful Buntz holding you prisoner? Has he some sort of receipts for you? What about your parents? Can I help you? I deny it, of course. Mr Buntz has a heart of gold. Leave me alone, please! And I leap out of that droshky. Poor Dmitry was firmly convinced that God had placed an innocent girl in his path, suffering at the hands of an old voluptuary. An honourable necessity – and what satisfaction for a noble soul! – to rescue a defenceless woman from evil. What harm had Dmitry done me? Why did I do it? But you spoke correctly; there is no "why", there are no motives for playing beyond the play.

'Thus I toyed with lies and truth. How many more Dmitry Sevastyanovitches were there? The angels would know, if they'd counted; I did not. I failed to take it to heart when some angels vanished over the horizon; new ones would always appear. Besides, Alla also disappeared somewhere for long weeks, maybe some order took him outside Warsaw. Before that he was still sending fiery missives, entreaties and oaths on garrison notepaper. I made no reply to any letter. Until I was coming down one evening from the upstairs rooms – for I already had my own rooms on the first floor, together with Mariolka – and I see the older waiter making panicky signs at me. What's going on? Get you to the governor, miss, says he, a frightful row about you. Behind the scenes, outside the door to Buntz's office, the staff stand eavesdropping. I shoo them away. Listen myself. Shouts in Russian, my name, Grisha's voice and another voice I don't recognise, but something touched me and I enter. Buntz was behind his fortress desk, all red in the face, pinned to his armchair as if by an invisible hundredweight boulder; and leaning over the desk was Captain Alla waving a revolver and pounding his fist on the desktop. Collect your things, miss, he cries at the sight of me, an end to this rat's reign, chief rat of the whole robber gang, today you shall walk free! Grisha only stares at me, but stares in such a way that his eyes are almost bursting from the strain, inflated like a toad he grasps for air through his teeth, jaws clenched to forestall an eruption of fury; I knew Buntz's furies – once, having uncovered a traitor, he seized an ornamental palm along with its pot and pommelled the deserter for so long until all that remained in his hand was bare stalk, and on the head of the beaten man – a pile of soil and clay shards; another time, Grisha tried to throw someone out of a window, but the poor wretch flew not far enough and landed on the remains of the shattered pane and slashed his guts hideously; and yet another time, Grisha chased the saucy cook's boy two junctions down the street with a pestle in his hand, until he choked on his own breath – but now he only sits and stares, stares, stares, whilst I feel my legs giving way under me, and not because of the Nagant revolver in the captain's hand, but because of that stare from the silent Grisha Buntz.

'So Alla is shouting, Buntz saying nothing, both of them to me, and so this, Benedykt, sir, this was the moment to choose between truth and lies: between truth – for the pimp, thief and undoubted rogue; and lies – for the noble officer, who had hastened unasked to rescue a woebegone stranger. What to say? To whom to turn? Which story to choose? Yet no time was given me to decide, so I could weigh up the odds, reasons and consequences, good and evil, no, I was taken by surprise, had to react without reflection – without reflection, which means spontaneously, from out of my own nature, because when we're given time, reason and logic answer on our behalf, but suddenly, taken without warning – then it's the heart that shall answer. I wring my hands, fall at Dmitry's feet. He'll kill us both, I sob, he won't let it pass, be gone! The captain pulls the trigger, Buntz grabs the bust of Napoleon, crash, crack, shriek, and Dmitry Sevastyanovitch slides onto the Persian carpet with a smashed skull. I raise my head. Pinned in his armchair behind the desk, his face redder still, Grisha Buntz is clasping his chest, blood spurting between fingers. You, he roars, you serpent in my bosom, this is how you thank me, sending your lover so he can ruin me, shoot me on the spot, kill me in my own home, right here! I try to swear on bended knee, but he just keeps on with his own thing, frothing at the mouth, allows no word in edgeways, listens not. You! You, she-devil! You hatched a plot against me, he sent his okhrannik brother-in-law, the secret police crawled all over my club – Grisha stretches a trembling hand, brandishes some kind of papers thrown on the desk – blackmail, he screams, through blackmail they tried to strip me of a lifetime's earnings, oh, that'll be the day, rabid dogs, biting the hand that feeds them, such people should be shot without mercy – and he grabs the Nagant. If only Dmitry's revolver hadn't fallen on the desk! And had fallen instead on the floor! Good fortune, misfortune, good fortune, sometimes I dream it that way, other times this, because would I have had it in me – what? enough resolve? terror? calm? – to lift it, aim, fire, it wouldn't have been me who'd be indicted but the dead captain, everything would have fallen into place, definitely, most likely, probably, perhaps; but it fell onto the desk! It fell onto the desk but before Buntz managed to seize it in his trembling paw, I was already in the corridor and calling to Mariolka Belcik; we fled empty-handed, just as fate hit us, cloaks thrown over our dresses, running out into the frost, into the first sleigh and away from Warsaw – the morning of the fifteenth it was, Tuesday a week ago, when I escaped from Warsaw.'

Took-took-took-TOOK, took-took-took-TOOK, took-took-took-TOOK.

True or false? Night flooded the compartment, pouring from wall to wall, to the beat of steel wheels, to the rhythm of the words and breathing of Miss Muklanowicz. The devushka breathes as if a great weight were crushing her chest. See not her face, don't even look; more answers would be got from the finger-touch of a hand reaching across the compartment – but obviously, it's not done. Straighten on the chair. Miss Muklanowicz shifts on the bedding, the material of her skirt rustles. True or false? Across the flat, wide sky of Asia drift streaks of innumerable shades of gloom – or maybe it's the earth – or maybe the realm of still another element; streaks of darkness darker than darkness, and contours darker than those, and clouds of the greatest of all darknesses.

'I am no gambler. No gaming habit rules me. I kept losing in order to realise the lie. Let me introduce myself: Benedykt Gierosławski, thief. This is the story.

'True, I was no stranger to cards, too bad I didn't get a taste for that petty gaming amongst students; it was then I also began to smoke tobacco and learned the thirst for alcohol. But gambler was I never. Instead, I had to gain the reputation of gambler. I lost money in order to gain money. Poverty, Jelena, poverty is the one genuine bad habit that

affected me. Maybe if I'd had no memory of a pampered childhood…
It made such a life all the more unbearable. Pauperdom consumes a
man like a fatal disease, destroys what is best in him, fits him for base
pleasures, low aspirations, grinds him into the ground. I say: bad habit
– for in this is the similarity, that with time it gets harder and harder
to wrench oneself free, filth attracts filth, want attracts want, sickness
sickness, wretchedness wretchedness – in the kingdom of matter and
in the kingdom of spirit. *We grow accustomed to it.* He's a fool who believes the romantics and high priests: poverty ennobles not, straightens
not the paths to eternal life. On the contrary: it poisons us with envy,
jealousy, bitterness towards the world and people, so that we no longer
perceive anything good in them, wake up and go to bed with a grimace
on our face, with tightened lips; and such are our dreams also, and such
our waking phantoms, and even our love is such, impoverished. When
I boarded the Deluxe carriage… A different Sun shines above the heads
of the rich, different air nourishes them, a different pneuma drives their
souls.

'After my father was exiled to Siberia, my mother's health took a turn
for the worse. As if the desire to live seeping from her drew with it a tide
of vital forces from her organism, leaving behind a void. Just as dust
and vermin collect in the dark corners of an abandoned house, and
mice breed – so my mother was filled with illness after illness. And I'd
like to be able to say that what I did, I did for money for her treatment,
but it's not true: it was merely one more symptom of pauperdom. As
soon as Julia mentioned the sum – ten thousand roubles – I knew what
I would say. Yes. Yes, I am ready.

'The whole thing was possible solely because we'd known each other
since childhood, our families knew each other, her parents knew mine,
they knew me, perhaps we'd already been betrothed then in their jokes;
we were related, but distantly, the Church would give permission, you'd
find even closer affinities in our genealogical trees. Julia's family was
rich but already well aware of the young lady's character and keeping
her on a tight leash, not allowing her access to her fortune; all the cash
was to go to her dowry and into the hands of her husband, when Julia
was given away in marriage. Julia was therefore imprisoned under
threat of pauperdom; I was already pauperdom's slave. We came together like two magnets attracting within a single force field.

'As soon as it was settled with Julia, I began gambling more and more
intensively, joining the company of very serious players staking high
sums at poker and blizzarder, until I hit the Kind Prince's table, where I
witnessed rounds with turnovers of thousands of roubles. At the same
time, I was paying visits to Julia in the presence of her family, agreeing
to rendezvouses and invitations to dinner; once I even repaired there

for a festive supper with my mother when she rose from her sickbed. Julia was very favourably inclined towards me, making no secret of our mutual affection, so they quickly began to talk of betrothal and I was asked many times about my intentions – the most honest, I assured them – but can you guarantee, Benedykt, that you are able to support a wife – but I can't change the way I feel, and can I be blamed for a father who followed in the footsteps of insurrectionists and paid with his fortune, I cannot – but the young lady has a generous dowry guaranteed. Now concrete sums were mentioned. And so it came to our engagement and everyone in town heard that Benedykt Gierosławski was marrying twenty-five thousand roubles; the shylocks suddenly became considerably more generous and new credit opened before me.

'Of which I effortlessly took advantage. By then I was already playing exclusively at the Kind Prince's. He rented rooms in Kalka's apartment block on Marszałkowska Street, where the most hardened gamblers of Warsaw society played in the evenings and long into the night; legends circulated about fortunes squandered and won, about the players and their follies, allegedly a colonel from the Citadel, coming out of Kalka's, shot himself straightaway in the head, since he'd lost the funds he'd embezzled from the Imperial Treasury; another unfortunate, Director of the Christian Grocery Company in Chrzanów, had a stroke right there at the table and has suffered ever since from paralysis in his right side (as a result of which he's forced to hold his cards in his left hand and his shuffling and dealing are hopeless); whilst some winner for a change, whose name gossip does not recall, went so weak in the head after recovering his farm and lucrative slaughterhouse that, opening the window, he began to shower fistfuls of three- and ten-rouble notes down onto Marszałkowska, and people broke their legs on the ice trying to lay hands on that rain of money; a legend also circulated about another Russian from the garrison, it seems a major, who after exhausting his pledge and credit offered to give his creditor satisfaction according to the rules of revolver lottery, that is, spinning the revolver's cylinder with a cartridge inserted in a single chamber and firing blindly into his own temple, which is why the game is called "Russian roulette". So you see, miss, there was no joking at that table. I went there three or four times a week, always on Saturdays, staying until dawn on Sunday and sometimes even to midday. It was about losing as much as possible.

'Losing, but not to anyone. Obviously: it was essential for me to lose consistently and already for a longer time, so as to raise no suspicions post factum. But in the end one great loss had to come, the obvious and inevitable sequel to a long chain of losses amounting to tens, hundreds of roubles. It was a winter morning, the servants had drawn back the curtains; outside the windows a white Warsaw was awaking, the tall streetlamps had been extinguished, grey smoke hung over the table like the ghost of a soul escaping from a body, the lackey brought coffee, the Kind Prince dealt the cards, I glanced at them, but now they were the least important thing, I staked a thousand, then a second thousand, then raised the stake to four, and so in our bidding we exceeded twenty thousand, me and Fredek Weltz, the prince vouched for him, I staked my dowry, we signed the promissory notes, and in the end Fredek put down a pair of kings and won the lot. I thanked them, said my good-byes, picked up my overcoat and went out into the frost. They watched me from the window, maybe they expected that I too wished to shoot myself in the head – I had no weapon – maybe that I would walk under a gleiss; you must have seen those suicides, miss, the hiberniks hew them out later with hammers. I could scarcely stop myself bursting into laughter at the winter Sun.

'We had calculated that it would take no longer than a month. Everything went according to plan. I had lost at the city's most infamous table, the news spread like lightning, by evening all interested parties knew that Benedykt Gierosławski had squandered his betrothed's entire dowry on poker at the Kind Prince's. The scandal gathered momentum of its own accord. Julia's family naturally forced the breaking-off of the engagement – but that only uncovered new hotbeds of shame, because her husband *manqué* would certainly end up in jail, having drawn up promissory notes without funds to cover them. Already a public dis-grace, into which Julia's family will be dragged directly. Julia began to entreat her father to save her from such stigma; even so, she would have to leave Warsaw. In the end – after three weeks, just as we had calculated – Julia's pater paid off my creditors, depriving his daughter at the same time of her whole marriage portion. Me, however, he struck with his cane in the middle of Ujazdów Avenue. I was walking along in my halo of shame like martyrs for God in their nimbus of saintliness; only one thing, after all, was left me to sell: my shame. On the follow-ing Sunday, after mass, we were to share out the sum with Fredek: ten thousand for me, ten for Julia, five for Fredek.

'They did not come. Neither Fredek nor Julia appeared. In vain I looked out for them in the nave of the agreed church and then hung about in the snow like a fool till the bells rang for high mass. And despite this, I still wished not to believe it. My first thought: go to Julia. But the ultimate perfidy of her plan had been revealed: now there was no way I could reach Julia, I myself had cut off very successfully any access to her; they even intercept letters, chase me away from under windows, my might-have-been father-in-law batters me afresh. Second thought: go to Fredek. He appeared at no lectures, visited no friends. I called on his mother, she knew nothing. What to do? I lurked in the shadow of a gate on Marszałkowska, the windows are lit up at Kalka's above the Sokół cinema, the play is on for hundreds and thousands of roubles – because what will Fredek Weltz do with his sudden fortune? – he's the real gambler, the genuine addict, he won't be able to restrain himself, besides the plan was that he should show himself here and there with a bulging pocketbook, as if he'd received the twenty-five thousand – but if he really had received them? I smoke a cigarette, let my legs freeze, strain my eyes. Fryderyk may enter from the street, perhaps at the back, perhaps by the side staircase, perhaps with spectators to the Sokół, but he could have been sitting and playing there already since yesterday. And so, in the end, I see the shadow of his profile against the window-pane – he's got to his feet, is stretching his limbs; so, there's a break between deals. I charge across the street, up the stairs, to the top-floor rooms, the Kind Prince's servant recognises me, whether he's been ordered not to admit me I have no idea, I wait not, barge my way in, Fredek is there – horror-struck at my invasion. Before the Kind Prince could intervene, I had dragged Weltz into the adjoining room and shut the door. "Where's is my cut?" He is enraged: I did as agreed, kept five thousand for myself, the rest is with Julia, after all she squared it with you. And with an insinuating little smile he embraces me cordially: Oh! Has the lady Julia cheated her betrothed? This I could not bear, his triumphant insolence, I break free, move away from Fredek, but he has smelt a victim, attacks with his sticky heart-warming sincerity, assaults me with venomous joviality, will offer consolation! It required all my strength, all my fury coiled into a tight spring to cast him off, to shove away the massive hulk. Shove, and at once the impetus carries Fryderyk to the half-open window, where the low sill undercuts his centre of gravity; the fellow attempts still to grab hold of the curtains, the curtains remain in his hands, cocooned in white curtains he falls from on high onto the icy cobbles, dies under those curtains.'

'What, and they didn't do you for murder?'

'You too dodged the executioner. If you've been telling the truth.'

'But how does the story end? Who cheated: Fryderyk or Julia?'

'No more was found on him than those few thousand.'

'So it was her. And what next?'

'Next?'

'There surely was a next?'

'Well, I tried to recover my share. I imagined Fredek's misfortune would have at least this benefit: Julia will believe I'm capable of anything, take fright, hand over what is mine. But I was unable even to talk to her. After much persuasion, I convinced the cook to smuggle in a note to the young mistress. Julia did not reply.

'I won't be summoning her to court, she knew that. I have to keep silent because otherwise I'd be accusing myself. Did she not calculate thus? But! She underestimated my conversance with shame. I went to them on Sunday, at dinnertime. No scene would they make in front of guests. Her father ran out into the hall – I needed only a moment for him to hear my words, for him to understand what I had to say.'

'Agh! You destroyed her, sir, in front of her family!'

'All the more reason for them to keep the thing secret, a hundredfold disgrace. But she, but Julia, oh, she shall taste that shame for which she paid me not – so I thought – for the rest of her life, she must suffer shame for those twenty thousand.'

'Revenge!'

'Yes.'

'In the end, though, you made it up with Julia.'

'What makes you think that?'

'A station, we are coming into a station.'

The Express was trying to make up time. Nazyvayevskaya had been left behind a few hours earlier; according to the *Putevoditel*, the next longer-planned stop was Omsk: it must be Omsk. The lights drew gradually closer; a cold glow was accumulating in the night as liquid darkness loomed grey within the compartment. Miss Muklanowicz emerged from it like a shape immersed in clarifying water: the outline of her figure – her waistline, her head – hand resting on the window frame – slender fingers pressed against the glass pane – her ring – the whiteness of her blouse, black velvet of the choker – her parted lips – eyes wide open. She was staring defiantly. The train was braking; she rocked to and fro, bolt upright, without averting her gaze. True or false, now it's again time for the devushka to throw her card on the table.

She raised her chin.

'You watch me, sir, and think: the chit of a girl is boasting with her morbid lies.

'But it is precisely this innocent chit of a girl that is the lie, coldly premeditated from the start.'

'Jelena, really –'

She pursed her lips.

'There is no Jelena. We alighted from the sleigh in Praga outside the Terespol Railway Station, already frozen, petrified; Mariolka, having counted her money, discovered it was barely enough for the cheapest ticket out of Warsaw, and then we would have to find lodgings with strangers. Neither of us has relatives outside the city; I have no relatives at all. Hiding in Warsaw was out of the question: Buntz's people would seek us out, the whole demi-monde confesses everything to him. In the third-class buffet, we bought hot milk; we sit in a corner, and think. I had to tell her everything, it took me more than an hour; it was the only time the thought entered my head that Mariolka might actually turn her back on me, leave and walk away; were she to fall in the end at Buntz's feet, were she somehow to buy herself anew into his favours, bah, were she to drag me to him by the hair and hurl me before him as a sacrifice, she would then be safe; she would not have to run away at all. She could have turned her back on me: this was the moment to do it.

'We were espied by Jasio Brzóz. What was he doing at the station? Jasio belonged to one of those gangs that clean out goods wagons on the Terespol Line sidings at night, strip the plush upholstery from first-class carriages, rip out the fixtures and furnishings from the compartments. At once he came over, seized us by the arm, what you still doing here, word has followed you – we know, we also want out of Grisha's face – but forget about Grisha! Grisha is in the clutches of a sawbones, lost to the world! Word, however, has reached the brawns, the police are chasing everyone, the Okhrana has issued a warrant for you both, they'll be looking out at every station! We went pale as chalk. What had Buntz been screaming? That Captain Alla had a brother-in-law in the Okhrana? Well, his kith and kin, that brother-in-law won't let go of Dmitry's death, and when Grisha regains consciousness, then he'll crush me with it all the more, I ran away after all; and no doubt Dmitry told that brother-in-law everything about me. It was not enough to escape from Warsaw – we had to flee the Kingdom. But on what papers? Ours were still at the "Tropical", even so they'd only be a hindrance. Procuring new ones would take several days, and who'd do it anyway, every pro in town is the crony of a crony of Grisha Buntz, and for what sort of diengi, and where were we supposed to wait for those papers? Jasio too has a conflict of loyalties, scratches his throat, casts a furtive glance, better you leave now, I've not seen you, honest to God, don't sit in the third class, they'll look there first.

'We crossed to the first-class buffet, luckily our clothes didn't give us away. We'll wait till nightfall, we think, jump onto any train. But we know this has little chance of success, we need a miracle; we're sinking to the seabed in the whale's belly. And then the miracle: two ladies sitting at the table behind are squabbling over some travel documents, because one of the them, the elder, had to return home specially to fetch them, but at once the rest of their family appears and the quarrel breaks off, since there's confusion again with their bags, tears, kisses, snivelling babes – and so between one overheard word and another, we learn the following: a certain Jelena Muklanowicz is travelling to Siberia in the company of her aunt, to a sanatorium of the Ice, in order to freeze the tubercular nidus in her left lung; she is about to board the train to Moscow, and from there embark on her journey directly to the other end of the world on the Trans-Siberian Express; Jelena and her aunt have places in first class, purchased a long time ago, and here are the tickets, nearly forgotten by a hair's breadth. 'Was it necessary to spell out the whole plan? We merely exchanged glances, Mariolka didn't even blink. There could be no question of choice, of decision – we were dazzled by its self-evidence. With the remainder of our money, we purchased two first-class reservations to the nearest station – so as to be able to board in their carriage. All we had to do was observe in exactly which compartment they were travelling – but with such a noisy family around them they couldn't hide themselves from us.

'As soon as the train moved, we knock on the door of their *compartiment*. The aunt opens up. In her shawl, Mariolka was carrying a stone lifted from the railway track. The aunt gets it on the forehead. We storm in, I block the door with my back. The young lady squeals, but the steam engine also squeals and whistles and wheezes, besides Mariolka now stuffs her mouth: you saw, sir: how Belcik is of peasant build, no less, a woman with mighty hands. They struggled there for a while, Mariolka wrapped the girl's shawl around her neck, I seized the other end, and we throttled her in a trice. Then the aunt; after all, she was still breathing. You understand, sir, time was of the essence, time before the conductor appears. We rummage through their luggage, clothes, handbags – where are the tickets, their papers – here they are. Hide the bodies – under the seats, cover them in blankets; that is, I lay down and covered them up, as I had a fever, too weak to sit upright; the plaid rug encompassed everything. The conductor knocks. Mariolka explains the circumstances in a whisper, shows him the papers, Miss Muklanowicz is seriously ill, on her way to a marvellous clinic of the Siberian Ice, would he be so kind as to make sure no one disturbs us on our journey – the Lord God shall reward you, my good man – and she presses a rouble into his hand. So we locked the compartment. Tore the clothes off the corpses. Measured them quickly. Different sizes – we'll have to flog them in Moscow and buy a wardrobe befitting a young noble-born and her companion. We divided at once all the valuables. Then I found a little leather-bound notebook, Jelena's diary. What she wrote in there! – I knew not whether to laugh or cry – the foolish phantasies of a sickly girl who knows not the world. And yet I read on with flushed cheeks, as if it were an exotic romance: devoured her soul along with those phantasies. Their lordships! Elegant gentlemen, ladies clad in diamonds! The more I fixed my eyes on them, the more I lived their lives in sleep, in dream, more vividly, more deeply, longer than they – now I shall be a lady higher than a lady, an innocent maid whiter than white lilies, Jelena Muklanowicz more real than Jelena Muklanowicz.

'We waited for the black night and such wasteland, wilderness beyond the tracks so that no one would see us pushing the bodies out of the window – it's possible to do it, Benedykt, sir, two women can cope, truly – and so that no one would find those bodies. We cast them into dark woods, the train was travelling through primeval forest, they surely rolled at once down the embankment and into the under-growth where animals picked them up. Even if someone should find the chewed rotten carcasses, no one will recognise the faceless naked women, and besides were they to associate them with missing persons, then it'd be with us – and not with Jelena Muklanowicz and her aunt, because they are on their way to Siberia.

'We feared only that someone might be waiting for them in Moscow; but no. Everything went smoothly. The first night in the Transsib, however, took a toll on our nerves. You saw me, sir, it was by no means the face-powder that made me so pale, I really thought it was us they were after. Mariolka decided to stay in the compartment as far as she could, feigning womanly complaints, so as not to betray her lack of manners and unbecoming diction, besides she knows no languages. But I have an alibi, I am sick, consumption is devouring me, I'm free to do anything, a capricious girl in the shadow of untimely death; can she not amuse herself with crimes and their detection, can she not boast of morbid stories to whet the curiosity of a man, stories of murder, black-mail and an adventurous past? Hah!'

The train stood at Omsk station. In the semi-darkness between lamps outside the window, human figures drifted past, solitary voices carried through the night, the station bell rattled occasionally; other-wise, silence reigned, no wheels clattered, no engines roared, no whistle sounded from the locomotive. Whoever had to alight, had alighted; whoever had to board, had boarded; the remaining Deluxe passengers were sleeping soundly. Once someone came down the corridor. Avert not the gaze for a moment from the young woman's face – she had to have some name – Miss Jelena Muklanowicz. She finished her tale and smiled slightly.

True or false?

The cold electric light, mingling half-and-half with cold shadow, flowed down her pale cheeks and over the white neck, soaked into lace and ruches, trickled in parallel streaks along the folds of smooth fabric, pouring into a shallow residue upon her lap, where the devushka had modestly folded her slender hands. Think of the shadow-marks sur-rounding Tesla, of that self-reflection in the mirror. Jelena's image was free instead of the least distortion, lines of brightness and dark were in harmony, just as movement and lack of movement were in harmony, everything was neat and tidy, regular, obvious. The train was resting at a station, and so the rhythmic rocking had ceased; she sat calmly, bolt upright, staring with unblinking eyes, her head half-turned, chin raised, as if posing not even for a photograph but for a painting, a portrait from the brush of an old master.

Reach for the cognac. At this moment, it was possible to pour full glasses. The devushka did not avail herself. Knock back one glass; then, with a (twisted) smile, also hers. She said nothing, waited. The longer the silence lasted, the greater the stakes accumulating on the table. Undo the collar. Maybe simply get up and leave – no, it's not her compartment – ask her to leave – but how, nothing springs to mind, no word, no gesture – she was victorious, tilting her chin a few degrees; the combination of slender fingers on the windowpane and leather boot on the carpet had paralysed her interlocutor.

No one knows the rules of the game, yet the game is played.

Clear the throat.

'Dreams are but shadows, Jelena, have faith in God.' In a low whisper now, hushed in the night-time stillness, a husky whisper. 'Everything we tell here, we tell from our own memory, in other words, one way or another, it has as much in common with truth as Myth has with History. I am not going to pretend, that… Well, all right, Zeytsoff started it, it's contagious, indeed I should not have mixed murch with alcohol. Agh, I have not admitted to you, miss…! Please don't look like that, I am not drunk. I wanted –

'Dreams are but shadows, have faith in God. Does it not seem to you, miss, that your whole childhood is one great dream – don't you remember it as you remember dreams? In snatches, pasted together in no order, but scene by scene without logical connection, in one I'm a bird, in the next a fish, in the next a human being, then again a bird, but the strangest thing – the strangest thing is that I'm not surprised, that it all somehow flows together without jarring, connects with itself, overlaps, without logic, none the less – one thing *emerges* from another, like a flower emerges from the seed, like a chick from the egg, like an adult from the child; so these scenes unfold according to mysterious rules, with gentle obviousness, in soothing stillness, under warm light – the dream – the childhood. And as such I shall attempt to tell it you.

'So here is a scene of which I could not have been witness, though in dreams we also see events at which we were not present and in which we do not dream our own presence: a foreign manor house, the alien garb of solemn men, on the table a large book and a cross upon which the gentlemen swear an oath, and amongst them my father. And when my father speaks, they all listen with great attention and nod and clap and cheer, and at the end my father raises his hands, and then such great emotion is shared by all – including myself, who am not there – that the recollection breaks off and something completely different follows –

'In which I am swimming in a river by a forest, whilst in the meadow, in a patch of sunlight as if in the stream of a golden waterfall, sit my mother and sister Emilka. Emilka is still just a baby, but we, my brother and I, by some miracle, are almost grown-up, we splash each other with water, shriek, as Emilka – romping in the grass, giggling unrestrainedly – grabs with chubby hands the sunrays tickling her face, and our mother in a big straw hat leans over her; both disintegrate meanwhile in this cascade of sunshine into streaks and particles of light, broken down into colours, iridescent – all I see are bright sprays of happiness. I call out to them, point to someone standing on the other bank, an indistinct silhouette, the black shadow of a silhouette; then, with an Indian wolf-howl, my brother pulls me under the water. Emilka is lost from my sight. There is no sense in this, no truth, and yet in the dream, in childhood, in my dream of childhood, the impression is very strong that this was the last time I saw my sister alive.

'An horrific night-time raid, with horses thundering along a highway, red kerosene lanterns flashing in the dark, banging at the door, huge hobnailed boots smiting the floorboards of the manor, cries of anger and cries of terror – I wake, soaked already in sweat, listen intently, quivering in trepidation. They are searching for someone, cursing someone; for whom the rage and clamour? Filip Gierosławski, where's Filip Gierosławski, tell us where he is! We know very well that you know! Why are they shouting in Russian – this is still not Warsaw. But it turns out they've driven to our manor in Wilkówka, yet are searching the Warsaw house: I look out onto the street, at factory fumes above rooftops and the first flush of dawn. They are looking for father, always and everywhere looking for father, there and here. A tsarist police carriage stands outside the gate; a moustachioed soldier, patting the horse on the neck, lifts his head and stares straight at me, glimpses a child's face at the window, extends his hand – wanting to greet me? to call out to me? threaten me with his finger? I leap back, terrified, falling over painfully. They are looking for father, always looking for father!

'But now we're at a church fair, in a crowd of people, amid the hubbub and music, amongst animals and peasant children covered in mud running barefoot – I, meanwhile, in my Sunday best, stay close to my pater's side, hand locked in his, so short I have to crane my neck to see if papa is smiling, or whether a stern expression grips his face; more often it's the latter. We walk from stall to stall, everyone bows to him, he stops to talk to this or that man, to the village voyt, to the parish priest; the reverend father strokes my head. I wonder how all these people know my father when he's never here, when we see him so rarely, did he call more often on strangers? For a very long time, I wonder how to ask him this, in the end of course I utter no word. Father bends down solicitously – would I like a lollipop? I nod. He bargains with the peasant. A man with his back to us is quarrelling loudly nearby, swearing dreadfully at the same time; father rebukes him openly to his face. That other man, a farmer with a cigarette on his lip, looks down on me with hatred, I remember no purer hatred on a person's face. I hide behind father. Father prods the farmer in the chest with his finger, hold your foul tongue in front of women and children, you're spreading depravation on a feast day. The more he rebuked him, the more the farmer hated me. I burst into tears. Father flew into a rage and dragged me back to my mother, pulling me by the ear. He bought no lollipop.

'A church secret whispered at the foot of Christ's cross – in a church, because here no one will eavesdrop, and you are such a big boy now, there are certain things you have to understand. Mother whispers these words to me as we kneel alone in an empty pew after the May Day holiday. A secret! I listen in earnest. Mother smiles to drive away any childish fears. One day you'll understand everything, says she, be proud of your father. But we live in an unkind world; this is not a kind world, people crucified God, Our Lord, people do much evil to one another, some tread on others and especially on those who have the courage to stand up for the downtrodden – like your father. Father is afraid of nothing, I whisper. Yes, your father is afraid of nothing. There are people who hate him for that, says she. I remember the farmer at the fair – they hate, hate. Mother leans over me. Should they ask you, should anyone whom you don't know ask – you will say nothing, all right? – because you have not seen him, we have not seen your father for months, since we moved to the city, we have not seen him. I understood that I was to lie. Mother suggested nothing to me; I solemnly crossed myself and, pressing hand to heart, swore from then on to bear false witness. She laughed quietly and kissed me on the forehead.

'A dream within a dream within a dream, Jelena, miss, and there is no way of separating them. In the evenings, when we lay in bed, my brother liked to tell me terrifying swashbuckling tales, which, so he claimed, really happened to our father: how he attacked tsarist convoys, thereby freeing Poles captured by the Russians, how he escaped from prison, how he stole gold from trains (allocating it, of course, to a good cause!), how, in their secret hideouts, he and other heroes were preparing a great uprising, amassing weapons and gunpowder, how he went as an envoy to the kings of Europe and the world, winning them over to Poland's cause. My brother made it up, or maybe he overheard it from adult conversations, or maybe he heard it already made up by other children; one way or another, I then dreamed about it. But maybe it happened in reality, and I dreamed of my brother's stories? I would see my father in a night-time pursuit on horseback – see him in a forest battle – see him on a street barricade – see him delivering orations beneath golden emblems – see him with rifle in hand – see him in a strange fantastical uniform with white-and-red regimental colours. I had to lie, no one would have believed me, they would have laughed at me, yes.

'And yet he would come, truly come, at night, when no one saw; steal in through a window, or through the cellar, or down from the roof, or by knocking quietly in the agreed way on the back door, and mother would open to him without turning on the light, wrapped in her black shawl. At once she would lead him deep inside the house, they'd disappear in the darkness. Had I seen? Could I see? Dreamt I that I saw? And the soldiers and gendarmes also did not cease their surprise intrusions, sometimes only one or two of them, sometimes courteously, sometimes with a lot of noise and menace. Once a fatty in too large a bowler accosted us on the street, and even offered us sweets: but if you, children, want to share a secret... your papa is in grave danger, if we don't find him in time... you don't want to create trouble for your mother now, do you? He dealt out visiting cards, small and large, to anyone at random, pressing the bonbons into our pockets. I also dreamed about this man. For a time, I feared all gentlemen in bowler hats – they will find papa and take him away.

'And yet he would come; were it one night, or several different nights, I must have run down from the first floor, spied on them, hidden in the shadow, since I remember: his swift silent step, the embrace with which he seized and lifted my mother into the air, I thought he wanted to squeeze the life out of her, she clung to his clothing, placed a finger over his lips; once she found a revolver with a long barrel stuck in his belt, he tore it from her straightaway. I saw too how he went away, in the dawn silence I heard their hurried whispers, addresses exchanged, names, days, hours. I listened carefully: these were secrets I had to keep; and yet, first of all, they had to be known in order for me not to betray them, for me to shroud them in lies – true?

'On another night, or maybe the same one, they swept in without knocking, forcing open the door, running all over the house, I must have vanished up the stairs and into bed before they noticed me. On yet another night... it couldn't have been the ground floor because we were asleep, my brother and I and Emilka, on the first floor, and yet it couldn't have been the first floor, because for what did father come in here, why flee in here? ... that night, I seem to remember, he came directly from a ball, in frock coat, with his close-trimmed beard and white bowtie. Did it make any sense? What, in God's name, would he be doing at a ball whilst hiding from the police? When they burst in with a shout – Filip Gierosławski, where's Filip Gierosławski! – he ran down the corridor to Emilka's room. What for? Mother was running in one direction, the maid in the other, a fat gendarme with a lantern in his hand jumped out from the back staircase. Doors opened and closed, mother turned back from the half-landing, the gendarme shrieked horribly loudly, bam, bam, bam, shots rang out, upon which still more shrieks came from downstairs and father appeared on the threshold of Emilka's room, revolver in hand. Bloodstains glistened on his ball attire. He saw mama, saw me – and so, I was there! and so, I did see it with my own eyes! – and he thrust me angrily aside. "Take him away!" Mother hoicked me into a bedroom. Father fled. In Emilka's room, they found the gendarme and Emilka, both shot.

'Jelena? Does it make any sense? It doesn't hold together! A dream, a dream, a nightmare. Why the hell am I telling you? Besides, were I actually drunk… O! Pardon me.'

A whistle heralded departure, the locomotive hissed, the carriages panted and jolted. The Express rolled out of Omsk station. Alternate patches of brightness and black flooded the windowpane as the carriage passed the next lamps; the intervals grew shorter and shorter, until at last black conquered for good as the carriage left behind the final lamp. Took-took-took-TOOK, took-took-took-TOOK, there was no rescue; the Asian night – a coil of inky fluid crawling hither and thither in the air – filled the interior of the compartment, settled on the carpet, pasted black crêpe over wallpaper and boiserie, spread across the bedding, wrapped a coal-black veil around Miss Muklanowicz, who throughout all this time hadn't even flinched (which was inhuman); she flinched now as the movement of the train snatched her from her pose. Whether she performed some gesture or merely smoothed down her skirt could not be seen – darkness drowned the whole compartment together with Miss Muklanowicz, darkness of darknesses, the very darkest.

'Jelena, you don't believe me, do you, miss?' Reach gropingly for the almost empty bottle of cognac. Glass clinked in the gloom. 'It's not the alcohol, I'm not drunk, it's that murch. Do you hear me?' The train was gathering speed. Raise the voice. 'I implore you, Jelena! You have won, I surrender. I would fall at your dainty feet, but… But. Dreams are but shadows, have faith in God; I'm unable to explain it, not for a moment did it occur to me that father wanted to kill Emilka, that it was anything other than a macabre accident, a death for which no one was to blame, therefore it cannot be explained, you see, miss, I'm trying, but what can I do, what can I do, I sputter without making sense; these are things that can in no way be told to another person. Why I did what I did – but maybe I didn't do it – how old was I then, six, seven, my God, how I try to imagine it now: etching that letter at night by candlelight, in awful dread that someone would come in and catch me, but no one caught me; addressing carefully the envelope in my childish Cyrillic script, tongue hanging out, bare toes curled tightly from emotion, blowing on the paper, wiping away the inkblots, checking every sentence and word a thousand times. 'Where is Filip Gierosławski?' On the reverse side, I even drew a little map. They caught him the following Sunday.

'But, of course, they could have caught him by chance, without my help; after all, they were getting closer and closer, what's the likelihood the letter ever reached where needed, that I remembered correctly the address on the visiting card of the Man in the Bowler Hat, the likelihood anyone believed in the anonymous denunciation presented in such ill-formed scribbles – judge for yourself, miss. Besides, many years have gone by – my father has not written to me once. I also have not written to him. I know not if he betrayed something to my mother, she never admitted it; however, if they told him at his interrogation, showed him the anonymous letter... might he have suspected? What do you think, miss? Jelena? Jelena? Jelena!'

True or false?

CHAPTER THE FIFTH

On the light and dark sides of a light and dark katzenjammer

Look into the barrel of the interferograph: light, light, light, light, light – as many truths and untruths as beads of sunlight, a vast number.

Touch gently the temples, where the morning hangover was drumming out its rhythm – woob-woob-woob-WOOB. In the night, in sleep, it had played along to the rhythm of the Express's wheels; on waking, a second train could be heard, an engine gathering momentum on the internal curvatures of the skull, from forehead to occiput. Bypassing the left temple, it leapt with a clatter over a joint in the rails of the brain: that was the fourth WOOB. A whole bottle of brandy had been consumed, after all – Miss Muklanowicz had stopped at three glasses – and then, after her departure, the gin had been opened. Zeytsoff's vodka should also not be discounted. No surprise then that now talking through the hat, which brought saliva to the tongue.

Put away the interferograph, heave the body out of the bedclothes. Rinse out the mouth over the miniature washbasin. An unshaven face with swollen nose and scab on the lip appeared in the looking glass. Reach for the toilet accoutrements, throw on the dressing gown. What hour is it? Without a watch, it was difficult to estimate even the time of day, when beyond the window such a leaden sky hung over dirty-green plains – sky as far as the eye could see, plains as far as the eye could see, Siberia. Just below the horizon, the vast expanse of steppe was delimited by a darker line of forest; the Transsib was about to re-enter the taiga. Across the backdrop of green – when staring like this, rubbing the eyes – moved a tiny black dot: a horse, a rider on horseback, a local inhabitant in animal skins with a long stick by his saddle. For a while he galloped parallel to the Magistral, then disappeared, as if swallowed by the earth. Peek in the *Putevoditel*. Tuesday, the twenty-second day of July (the ninth – according to the Russian calendar): if, therefore, they have not yet summoned everyone to dinner, it means the Express is somewhere between Tatarskaya and Tchulymskaya.

Lock the compartment and proceed to the bathrooms. The first was vacant. Twist the gilded tap fittings; water gushes into the marble bath. The bathroom had one small oval window; the milky pane swiftly grew misted, and so Asia receded entirely beyond the frontiers of the European world of Deluxe. Took-took, hwoop-hwoop, submerged to the neck. Since it's impossible to be truly cleansed, cleanse at least the body. Filth slips easily off the skin – whereas what lingers in the head…

The game could not have ended well – whichever way the coin had fallen, heads or tails, truth or lies – since a word once uttered remains with us, true or false: as long as we remember it, the absolute truth will be for us the fact that we uttered it. Is this not the essence upon which rests the phenomenon of Holy Confession? Sin doesn't count, but the word on sin. Not life, but the word on life. Not man, but on man. Not truth, but on truth. On what we have done. And on what we have left undone. On good, on evil, on anything that can be uttered. On, on, on.

After crossing the frontier of the Land of Ice, when Tesla's interferograph will show the two-valued logic of light, will some kind of visible change really occur? People will continue, after all, to lie without restraint. Nor will they suddenly acquire some miraculous ability to recognise words of truth.

Is there any sense therefore in asking about the 'real' Miss Muklanowicz? And yet it is impossible to banish this thought from the mind; it keeps returning like the intracranial train, lap after lap, and still again and again, though the temples are shot with pain, though an unpleasant taste rises in the mouth, and again:

Is she the Warsaw dodger, the tanner's daughter schooled by the blackguard Buntz, thief and murderess, who, with the tacit assistance of the equally artful Mariolka, makes Jelena Muklanowicz a lie? who enlies Jelena Muklanowicz? – or is she Jelena Muklanowicz, the impressionable girl with a surfeit of fantasy depressed by years of illness, who enlies Buntz's slyboots, a bloodthirsty imposter?

The Express has not yet reached Winter, the journey goes on, truth has not yet frozen – both devushkas are equally true.

Rinse in cold water till ice needles pierce the skin and a sobering shiver runs over the flesh. Wipe the misted mirror. Light and shade at least had calmed down, there was no trace of yesterday's penumbra. By what effects does a katzenjammer manifest itself after charging with teslectricity? Very possibly Doctor Tesla had never experienced it, enmurching himself day after day, always before the effect of the previous shock had worn off.

Attempts to shave pulled the scab off the lip. The lip will heal quickly; worse with the nose. The blade scraped the skin at the precisely applied angle; in the rocking carriage, it was important to display a truly artistic fluency, the instinct of a virtuoso violinist. It'll succeed – or not succeed, and then there'll be blood on the skin.

Begin to hum, razor to cheek, a lively dance tune. Wherefore this sudden onrush of good humour? There is no reason for it, all reasons are against. Perhaps only Miss Muklanowicz – for two days of shared journey still lie ahead – ha, what a reason! Wash the face. A crooked, unpleasant smile appeared on the lips. Miss Muklanowicz, both Misses Muklanowicz, the older and the younger. What springs from memory is neither truth nor untruth. (The intracranial train leapt from track to track.) The body was heavily enmurched at the time. Memory of the past – the past in memory – a different memory, a different past – so what kind of lie, truer than truth, is contained in the second encoded letter?

Hurriedly tie the dressing gown. Espy Mr Tchushin approaching down the corridor from the opposite direction. Retreat, so as to let him pass before the bathrooms. He went red as a beetroot, grunted by way of apology, his eyes fleeing from the battered face. Swallow the shame – it was a physiological act; something rushed from the head down the whole length of the spine to the very feet: a kind of burning-hot poison from which the muscles stiffen and tendons tighten, and acid swamps the innards.

No time to hide in the compartment – a provodnik appeared from the passageway side, not fat Sergey, but the provodnik of another Deluxe car.

'Your lordship!' he cried, raising his hand. He ran up. In his hand – a bumaga folded into a tiny square. Stare as he presents it on his open palm as if on a letter tray. 'The young lady was very insistent that as soon as possible –'

'What's the time? Miss Muklanowicz is at breakfast?'

'Ah, no, kind sir, Miss Filipov from number eight, second carriage.'

After delivering the letter, he bowed. Seize his hand.

'What's this?

'What?'

'Where did you get it?' Snarl at the provodnik, jerking him once, twice, so much so the uniformed fellow, highly offended, stood his ground before the passenger and wrenched free his arm. Stepping aside, he straightened the fabric of his coloured tunic, brushed the braiding.

'That ring.' Point with the finger. 'Show me!'

Tentatively, he extended his hand, curled into a fist. A bloodstone engraved with the Korab coat of arms flashed before the eyes.

'I promise your lordship –'

'Where did you get it?'

'Found it.'

'Where?'

He shrugged his shoulders.

'On the platform at the end of the passenger cars. It were lying there. In a crack in the ironwork.'

Laugh. The provodnik cast a sullen glance, convinced the mockery was directed at him. Signal in order to detain him. Unlock the compartment all the swifter and locate the pocketbook.

'I'll give you ten.'

The provodnik reflected deeply.

'But if the natchalnik finds out –'

'Fifteen.'

In the end, the ring was bought for eighteen roubles. Polish it with a chamois and slip it onto the finger. It fitted just as well as three days earlier. Who was to be seen now in the looking glass – knotting his tie, chin held high above the stiff collar, standing erect? Count Gyero-Saski with his black-and-blue mug.

First thing before going amongst people: smash all mirrors.

Second thing: never tell the same lie twice, or the same truth. It's impossible to re-enter that same river, impossible to re-enter that same person. But who will understand this? Apart from Jelena Muklanowicz – no one. They all pretend to hail from the same past, bah, even quarrel over this past: it wasn't like that! I remember better! Hard to find a greater stupidity. Take the crumpled timetable out of a drawer. On it was scribbled the second missive to father – from the murched-through memory.

```
ZCZQPQAMKEDJWROXUUZX
IBJUYKBVJJMMWTYDPXNB
TWJPWUPGRSPTGEKNKMUX
TIVSLRGZCRSLGDRKNKEA
WKZIZFBXVSEMSIZFSEDL
KJCQPCFDEXQRKXOEXEIZ
CUELTMDHABBTWULJMTQI
VWOZBEBLTAXNCOBLIZNJ
MKWYWNCOKKXYVBXOWEGE
WTKWOPKXSUZJLVUEZZKA
WFWDCZQMAMODYZNFDIUE
EM
```

Transcribe it onto a clean sheet of paper. The method of ciphering should be assumed to be identical to that in the first missive. But seeking a regular pattern proved not so easy – KNK, KNK, what else? An interval of twenty-one letters – a password consisting of three, seven or twenty-one characters. The missive therefore has to be broken down into thirty-one alphabets… It makes no sense. Something is going undetected here, something must be escaping the misdirected attention. Other repetitions…?

But maybe it's an ordinary hangover, a side effect – maybe deciphering this is impossible without a charge of teslectricity in the body, without a flow of murch through the brain. Things need to be endarkened inside the head, only then –

Enough!

The Express passed through Kozhurla station without stopping. The firmament had brightened somewhat; the palette of light streaming onto the earth more befitted summertime, a dash of yellow, a dash of azure, here and there blinding white – columns of light piercing invisible clouds. Even the sound of the train's wheels was different, softer, duller, more drawn out, dwook-dwook-dwook-DWOOK, dwook-dwook-dwook-DWOOK. Open the window, stick out the head. Wind ruffled the hair. Look towards the rear of the train. It was tilting slightly towards the nearside; behind it could be seen the line stretching as far as the horizon. Watch as slides of a divine photoplasticon rotate in the heavens and a pillar of dazzling sunlight falls directly onto the tracks, as if angels were training their searchlights upon that very spot; coloured rainbows dance along the tracks, whilst glints of celadon green, violet, pink, purple take wing, and flickering ribbons spread like the *aurora borealis* not across the northern twilight but along the wooden sleepers of the Transsib. Dwook-dwook-dwook-DWOOK. The train runs already on rails of coldiron; these are the forelands of Hither Winter, today or tomorrow the Kingdom of Ice shall be entered. Feel mechanically for the interferograph inside the jacket pocket, for the Grossmeister behind the belt under the waistcoat. A different reflex prompts the fingers, nervously rotating the Korab ring first in one and then the opposite direction. Twist the ring, utter a wish. Shut the window. Oh munificent djinn, deliver me from this accursed train! With or without Jelena Muklanowicz. Someone knocked.

Open the door. Zeytsoff.

'Good day.'

'Ah yes, yes, greetings, what d'you want?'

He was slightly perplexed by the unceremonious response. He ran his fingers through his hair, less matted than on the previous day, presenting himself entirely tidily in contrast to the normal state of Filimon Romanovitch Zeytsoff; he had even donned a new suit, light beige with red stripes, sorely lacking admittedly in taste – but clean, and there was no sign of the ex-convict's drinking-bout of the previous day; he stared with sober eye, no longer bloodshot, head held upright. Except that he at once became mightily confused and stood in the doorway clasping his elbows and casting his eyes around as if he'd forgotten why he'd knocked on the door in the first place.

'Well, speak up! Because – by the way, what time do you make it?'

Zeytsoff took out his watch.

'After eleven.'

'That is, not long till dinner. Yes? How may I help?'

He scratched the wounds on his frostbitten fingers and suddenly raised his eyes.

'I have a favour to ask of you, Venyedikt Filipovitch. May I come in? Forgive me, it's hard to collect my thoughts out here in the corridor... Besides, I owe you an apology, yes, an apology at the very start. And for what? For what I told you yesterday; I know nothing of your father after all, you have to believe me in this, that had I known –'

'Come in, come in. What's it really about? I don't understand. Why should you care about my pater?'

'Well because today, already at breakfast, thank you, today they're all gossiping about it; not that I excel in such company and myself take part in these conversations, hah-hah, you know how it is: once a katorzhnik, then a pariah for the rest of your life; but I prick up my ears all the more, and what had been forgotten from yestereve came back to me when I heard their tales, Frau Blutfeld's especially, who told such a story about your father –'

'Ah! So, Frau Blutfeld was telling father's story! Now the whole train knows, it can't be otherwise. Go on, go on.'

'Father Frost, such was the name, Father Frost. Talks to gleissen, mind you, and whatever he whispers to them, gleissen will carry out; such is Winter's system descending upon Earth, and as such shall the Ice flow through lands and peoples according to your father's word, but now you're travelling to Sybir for what?'

'For what?'

'Well, here I must offer my apologies, don't be angry, Venyedikt Filipovitch, you won't be angry, will you? – I can see after all that you're a good man.'

'But why shouldn't I be angry, for Christ's sake!'

'Oy, oy! Already wrathful, the ardent soul.' Zeytsoff wheezed, winced, glanced nervously out of the window. At the same time, he slumped onto the bedding, anything to get farther away, and began scratching again at his scars. 'For, you see, had I not told yesterday what I told about Abraham, about History, about Ottepyelniks and Lyednyaks, and above all about Berdyaeff... But they heard, one repeats it to another, all at sixes and sevens, and it so emerges, mind you, that you and I were conversing, not that I was doing the telling but that we were conversing

– and who said exactly what, no one remembers. And now it turns out that you were telling me your plans.'

'What?'

'Meaning: what you're travelling there for.'

'Wait a moment, Zeytsoff, slow down, this ghastly katzenjammer is obviously still cramping me, for I'm understanding nothing of your ramblings; you dance around like a Jew around a pig. Pull yourself together and say it outright: what plans?'

'Well, to befrost History.'

'To what?'

'The son is travelling from the outside world to Father Frost with news of how to change the course of History, frozen under the Ice: this way or that way. Well. It came out.' He sighed plaintively. 'Will you forgive me, Venyedikt Filipovitch?'

Stare at him in silence.

'Oy, you're angry, I can see, angry.'

'It's a kind of curse, you know.'

'Eh?'

'No day passes in this dammed Express when I don't go to bed as one man and wake up as another.'

'Bah, people change,' Zeytsoff nodded.

'That's not the point. Ah well, never mind…! Tell me, what sort of favour.'

'But you haven't forgiven me yet!'

'What's this forgiveness to you! How come a stranger's single word weighs so heavily on your conscience! Obsessionist of mercy!'

Zeytsoff stared solemnly.

'Evidently, you still haven't realised the harm I've unwittingly done you. Whilst forgiveness – forgiveness is the foremost thing; without forgiveness there is no life, no happiness in life, there can be no happiness, for how do you imagine it: enjoying your pleasures, rejoicing in your joys, when you know someone holds a righteous grudge against you, since he has suffered and still suffers because of you? Therefore, what kind of joy is it – like you're feasting in the presence of paupers dying of hunger, from whose mouths you've taken food; no ambrosia will then be sweet to you. Everything begins with forgiveness, because if you store up hatred instead in your heart, or even the slightest antipathy towards another, can you rejoice sincerely in the littlest thing? And you see it most, of course, in the biggest matters: like when a man has sworn revenge on his mortal enemy – the years go by, he's raised children and grandchildren, gained people's respect, toiled for his fortune; yet does it please him, will he prepare for death in peace, will he gaze smiling upon the face of God? no, because in life he was unable to smell the flowers of the field without his brow puckering instantly, without his lips twist-ing and a dark cloud overshadowing his countenance: the very thought of his enemy's possible happiness has destroyed his own. Therefore, it's important to practise forgiveness beginning with the small things. For it's a question of practice, like the art of riding a horse or proficiency with a rifle – you don't point to a man on the boulevard and say to him: shoot a sparrow from a hundred feet. He won't shoot. The same with the commandment to love your neighbour. A great – the greatest! – mistake is when you adopt it like an imperial ukase: from Tuesday we shall ride on the right side of the road, from Wednesday we shall forgive. Yet so often priests speak in this manner; educators, them-selves badly educated, speak in this manner to children. We should be trained in forgiveness like sportsmen train their bodies in strenuous disciplines, for years, arduously, in pain, from lapse to lapse, without hurling themselves at once at the record-breaking dumbbells, but be-ginning with the smallest loads: forgive rudeness, forgive indolence, ask for forgiveness for a bad word uttered unintentionally. In this way, you'll develop muscles to move mountains of forgiveness that crush millions of the untrained.

'I beg you, Venyedikt Filipovitch: forgive me.'

The eyes dropped involuntarily; the hand rested on the waistcoat. Vazoff – but what was his Christian name? Yury? Had he had time to reply before he died? Blood had flooded his mouth; he spoke, but nothing was heard.

Shake the head.

'You must have a very high opinion of people, Filimon Romanovitch. Many, bah, the majority, bah, almost all have no trouble whatsoever in leading happy lives in unforgiveness.'

'That's what you think. That's what you think.'

'Well, all right.' Bend over, clasp him by the knee. 'I forgive you, I forgive you.'

'You imagine: what's so hard in pronouncing the word – anything can be said; that's what you imagine.'

'Let it rest now. What sort of favour?'

He took a deep breath – and, exhaling, ejected from his lungs the air fusty with evil thoughts, expelled the excrement of his soul, his undi-gested fears.

'Well yes, well yes. You'll send me packing, may well send me packing, but ask I must, though, as you see, it's hard to muster the audacity.' He lowered his eyes. 'Tell me: remember what I told you about Atchukhoff, about the reparation of the world according to God's Commandments, about the revolution of the spirit – remember?'

'You told me, I remember.'

'And so… And so, my request is this: when at last you speak to your father, whisper also a word for this.'

It was unclear at first what he meant.

'For what?'

'For such a path of History – I plead only for this – so as to give Russia a chance, so that people will have a chance to stand free before good and evil, and then the Kingdom of God, if it comes about, when it comes about –'

'You're out of your mind!'

'Oy.'

'Or else you've been drinking since early morning. You've just apologised for them spinning false gossip about me and my pater out of your words – yet now you say you believe in this gossip?!'

'Gossip is gossip, Venyedikt Filipovitch, I'm not saying it was your intention and for this reason you're travelling to Baikal – but since they're now arguing about it openly, and since you've not denied it with regard to your father, may I not ask? Should you not wish to, you won't grant it. But what harm does it do you? And so, you will converse with your father, whilst he, so you say, talks to gleissen, about what we don't know, and whether Father Frost really does control the Frost we also don't know, but what's the harm in my asking, what's the harm in his putting in a word for a good cause, well, Gospodin Yeroslavsky, it's no trouble after all, and if because of you Russia's time really would turn at last towards the age of the spirit –'

'You have believed it!' Clutch the head. 'What is this! What madness! You know it's all lies, and yet you believe!'

Zeytsoff bit his moustache.

'It's not for me to judge, your lordship, what truth is to you, when we've barely made acquaintance on this journey. Maybe the gossip is mistaken; maybe it was mistaken to start with, but having heard it, with time you make it true; or maybe it was true from the beginning. I did not beg forgiveness for lying – bah, surely the injury is greater to you, if the gossip be true. No law states that Frau Blutfeld can never be right.'

'Not for you to judge.' Repeat it dryly. Take out a cigarette, light up. Strike the tabletop with the heavy ashtray. Zeytsoff wiped an eye irritated by the smoke. Cross one leg over the other, flick off the ash. 'So, all right! I shall tell you how it is! For what am I travelling to the Baikal Land? For two thousand roubles. One thousand before, the other after. They paid me, so I'm on my way. The Ministry of Winter hired me. I am travelling to talk to Father Frost on behalf of Rappacki. There you have it, and there you have your controller of History. You wish to know more? I have no deuced belief in Berdyaeff's puffed-up metaphysics, nor do I give a damn about any of it: were imperial Winter to pay me another thousand, then I'd urge papa to bring back even Ivan the Terrible. Well, and? Eh?'

Filimon Romanovitch Zeytsoff rose reluctantly to his feet. Turning around in order to depart, he became entangled in the narrow compartment, legs with legs, and when the carriage rocked violently, he was forced to bend over and lean an outstretched arm against the wall; bent over, he whispered at close quarters: 'To forgive is the most important, begin from this, from forgiveness.' Then he bludgeoned his way towards the door. Even tried to bow, but again with little success in the confined space. He retreated backwards, almost colliding with someone in the corridor.

Rub the brow with a sweaty hand. Woob-woob-woob-WOOB, all the result of a ghastly hangover; why get so worked up? the drunken sot had already lost it long ago, babbling this, babbling that, whilst whoever takes the words of a fool to heart is himself a fool. *Begin from this, from forgiveness.* Supposedly for what? and forgive whom? And he whispered it with such mellifluous pity in his voice, such sobbing in his breast, as if urging a condemned man by the guillotine to convert. A fanatical drunk. Besides, he surely exaggerated those tales of Frau Blutfeld, as he did all others. Who could have heard that conversation yesterday over vodka? Miss Muklanowicz. Towards the end, also Doctor Konyeshin and whoever else approached from the billiard table. Dushin perhaps, but he remained in the wings. Was anyone sitting closer? Remember not. Frau Blutfeld must have got her version second or thirdhand; never, admittedly, a barrier to her –

'May I? Benedykt, sir?' Knock-knock.

Take a peek. Speak of the devil.

'Come in, please.'

Jelena left the door slightly ajar behind her.

'I heard raised voices, thought you must be up.'

'A fair deduction. I could, of course, be the rare case of a somnambulant ventriloquist; that would be a hard nut for Sherlock Holmes to crack.'

'Why so peevish?'

'Nothing. A hangover.'

'Ah.'

Today she was wearing a black silk blouse and matching black skirt; instead of the velvet choker with the ruby, her neck was adorned by a double string of white pearls falling onto a jabot of black tulle. Whilst this blackness, together with the corset most likely pinching the damsel's slender waist tighter still, and the rim of black mascara framing the hazel-brown eyes, and the heavy lipstick – only served to underline the pallor of Jelena's skin and frailty of her body. Think: she is not sick, but how adroitly she slips on the lie of sickness – without uttering a word.

Avert the eyes.

'Apologies for what in the night –'

'Why so! After all, we knew in advance, did we not? After all, you made it clear beforehand.'

'What?'

'That we would lie.'

'So, you were lying.'

'*Naturellement!*'

But she was smiling ironically at the same time, her little finger touching the corner of her lips as she winked.

Blow smoke towards the ceiling.

'You, miss, will never fold.'

'Mm-hmm?'

'All right, what's it about now? Please don't torment me regarding breakfast: I overslept. Has Mr Fessar been making a nuisance of himself?'

'Mr Fessar is parading around in a ridiculous fez, bandage underneath; he hasn't breathed a word. Instead, a question about you came from the prince's table; the steward had quizzed the Blutfelds, so there's more fresh gossip. What is it Prince Blutsky-Osey has against you, Benedykt, sir?'

'If I only knew. Contempt, nothing more. *À propos* the gossip, Zeytsoff was talking to me here as if my conversation yesterday with him and what you, miss, blabbed so blithely then about my father –'

'Yes, alas. You've become a gleissen ambassador or something of the sort.'

Gaze at her horror-struck. Miss Muklanowicz shrugged her shoulders, smiling airily.

'More convenient to choose the lies for yourself, don't you think?'

Shake the head.

'It will all pass, pass, pass.'

'I daresay. In the meantime, we need to take care of that Lyednyak agent who has designs on you, surely you've not forgotten? If you want to reach Irkutsk alive.'

'You mean Zeytsoff? That I shouldn't have allowed him into my compartment?'

'I don't think it was Zeytsoff.'

'Yesterday you swore it was! If not he, then no one!'

'But last night, in Omsk, a new passenger joined the Deluxe carriages in place of a certain von Prut from the second car, also with a ticket purchased to Irkutsk. I made his acquaintance at breakfast. You see, sir, we hadn't thought of this! Fogel did not claim after all that this agent had boarded the train at the same time as we. For him, it's more handy even to board for a short time, kill and escape.'

'So, you have a new suspect?' Sigh. 'Who then?'

'Mr Porfiry Pocięgło, a Siberian industrialist by all accounts, and yet, it transpires, Polish by blood and confession, so no doubt he'll be wanting to talk to you. It's about this I'm come now: please wait for my signal and, God forbid, never meet him in private. For we ought to somehow arrange things so that one of us engages him in conversation whilst the other checks his compartment.'

'I am beginning to understand, miss, the things you leave unsaid. "Check" means break in. And since you're a specialist at break-ins, I have to entertain Mr Pocięgło in a public place.'

'Except that I implore you to wait for my signal.'

'Oh, fear not, I shall wait.'

Miss Muklanowicz made to leave. Rise to the feet, bow theatrically. The devushka curtsied. In the doorway, she glanced over her shoulder, wrinkling her nose.

'What cologne do you wear, Benedykt?'

'Erm, to tell the truth, I don't recall the brand. Why?'

'Nothing. It reminds me of someone. I told you: smells stay inside me.'

And she vanished into her compartment.

Catch a glimpse in the corridor of the provodnik Sergey. Beckon to him, and request a jug of tea from the carriage samovar. Light another cigarette, lower the window. The papers were whispering from their place on the escritoire, loose pages rustling, scrawled with wrongly guessed deciphering. Pick up the copies of both missives to father. Beneath the first, the decoded content had been noted; the second was covered in graphs seeking imaginary regularities in the code. Of course, the voice taunting from behind the left ear is surely correct, the ironic angel on the left who proclaimed it gibberish from the start, not code, fabrication, not memory; there is no second missive from a second past, only empty froth spat from the enmurched mind of a mathematician.

But a different voice was also making itself heard, the voice from the right side. Second missive, second past, memory versus tangible proof... Despite everything, it would be some salvation! Fragments of the first missive, whole phrases-slogans-commands – THAW TO THE DNIEPER, DEFEND THE GLEISSEN, JAPAN YES, RUSSIA UNDER THE ICE, ALIVE – flared up in the thoughts in unexpected moments, disturbing the peace of mind, prompting angry grimaces and nervous reactions. Were the future to take shape in line with this particular past, were it to freeze like this, then perhaps Zeytsoff is not entirely in error, perhaps Frau Blutfeld's gossip hits home not far from the truth: the Pilsudchiks give orders to father, because he gives orders to gleissen. Or at least has some influence over them. Whilst the son in turn – or so they all think – has some influence over the father. So therefore – therefore, are they right? So, Lyednyaks are correct to have designs on the life of the son? So, there is method in the follies of the Martsynians? So, Fogel's fears are genuine?

The controller of History? Ridiculous! Begin afresh the cryptanalysis, slurping hot tea. The head was as heavy as a tar-filled balloon, move it this way, move it that, a black wave slops around inside jolting the skull from shoulder to shoulder. Safest therefore to sit bolt upright, to not move at all. Spot the victim of a katzenjammer by his stiff neck and dignified rotations of his pate. The cryptanalysis proceeded all the more laboriously, for attention strayed every moment towards the missive already deciphered. Had not its sense been misinterpreted; were not meanings being ascribed to it taken from other people's fears? Commissioner Preiss never said precisely what the Irkutsk delegation of the Ministry of Winter wanted. Will they incite the son against the father? Blackmail him? Try to persuade him? Do Baikal tchinovniks also share the belief of Berdyaevian Ottepyelniks and Lyednyaks in the Ice's influence on History? 'Father Frost'…! For pity's sake.

One other thing happened before dinner. On the way to dinner, in the passageway leading into the restaurant car, a head-on collision was narrowly avoided by moving away from the door – with Captain Privyezhensky. The captain stopped dead in his tracks, flabbergasted for a split second, even blinking hesitantly; regaining at once his self-assurance, he slapped his hand over the pocket of his uniform and moved forward with head held high, looking somewhere to the side, at the air, at the carriage wall, as if the passageway were empty and he trod paying no heed to his path – wherein no one stood in his way. Make no move. He had to stop. He snorted under his moustache, still looking to the side. 'Count Frost…,' he began to mock. Utter slowly: 'Count Frost is on his way to dinner,' having undone the jacket and undoing the waistcoat buttons, and feeling for the angular bundle behind the belt. Had the captain seen that movement of the hand? Seen the fat signet ring on the pinkie? He snorted a second time. 'Out-t of my sight-t, m-miserable clown,' he snarled and withdrew into the corridor. Enter the restaurant car without looking back. The heart was pounding like a steam engine gathering speed. Mwooch-mwooch-mwooch-MWOOCH. Woob-woob-woob-WOOB. Dwook-dwook-dwook-DWOOK. Lean, staggering, against an empty chair. Princess Blutskaya-Osey was summoning with a wave, calling across the whole length of the car. Dinner. Everyone was watching. Survive six paces before the sickly sweet, doggish smile spreads over the snout. But the snout had been smashed and those watching – everyone – saw only a twisted grimace of arrogant derision. Benedykt, Count Gyero-Saski-Frost took his seat at the table of the prince and princess.

On the dreams of Princess Blutskaya

'*Pourquoi?* And sortilege under the Black Auroras?'

'On that – Mr Pocięgło knows best.'

'Come, come, not everyone lets such superstitions go to their head.'

The princess was piqued, incensed. The prince meanwhile guffawed in malicious merriment – he was consistent, however, in uttering no word.

'Were my spouse not in such in a hurry,' said the princess, ostentatiously not looking in his direction, 'we would be staying longer in the Land of the Gleissen, I could have seen for myself. Do these Auroras appear at particular times of year? According to the calendar? When?'

Mr Pocięgło swallowed a morsel of meat, sipped his red wine.

'Mm-hmm. Your Highness, I see, has devoted considerably more attention to this, so it is rather I who might learn something from Your Highness…'

'Don't pretend, young man, you've lived there since childhood, you know them best. I wager that were I to light you a blackwicke –'

'So, has it reached even Saint Petersburg?' Mr Pocięgło shook his head. 'Fashion, it'll pass in the end, like everything else that depends on taste and not practical benefit.'

'And what d'you think, Gospodin Yeroslavsky?'

'It's all black to me.' Mutter without raising the head from the plate.

Had none of them really not perceived it? The penumbra swimming around Porfiry Pocięgło's silhouette, though many times weaker than Tesla's, could not have escaped their notice. Pocięgło's eyes were set deep in the bony orbits of his eye sockets, which had sharp, clearly defined rims, and he only had to lower his eyelids, or turn his head towards the light, or lean over the table – and already sputters of unlicht were gathering neath his brows, settling on the high cheekbones, clouding the blue pupils in black haze. It was most evident on his face, but the folds of his Sybirak clothes, the creases of his suit, were similarly unlichted; even the metal buttons shone with murky glints. Porfiry Pocięgło was returning to Irkutsk after barely a week's sojourn in Omsk; he was thirty-three years old, thirty of which had been spent on the shores of

Baikal, and thirteen of those already in the Land of the Gleissen. He was clearly one of those locals of whom Zeytsoff spoke on the previous day with drunken emphasis: scorched through by the Ice, they carry Winter within them, and recognise one another unerringly even when far removed from it: 'gleisseniks'. They had not simply grown accustomed to the frost, like hiberniks, but also to Winter's non-material effects; a first generation was already growing up after all, conceived and born in the shadow of gleissen.

Princess Blutskaya very quickly elicited Pocięgło's date of birth, Zodiac sign, parents' Christian names, favourite colour and gemstone, what patron saints he worshipped and what dreams he had most recently dreamed. The prince took no part in the conversation, muttering only caustic, senile remarks to Dushin, seated on his other side. The privy councillor was watching for the both of them: now the one, now the other guest at the prince's table with the double intensity of his snake-like eyes. Avoid his gaze, engage in no conversation, fearing that a single word might provoke the prince to a fresh outburst; the prince himself was trying hard to look in the opposite direction and gave the general impression of being eternally disgusted by his dinner-table companions. He slurped louder than usual, moving his jaw like a ladle on rubber hinges.

'I'm too used to it,' Mr Pocięgło was saying. 'Certainly, I wouldn't notice them at all were it not for the dazzling brightness of the cupolas of the Christ the Saviour Sobor beside the Angara. When a strong Aurora rises, the Cathedral illuminates half the city; at night the glow can be seen as far away as Zimny Nikolayevsk.'

'But the omens, the sortilege, and the dreams, the dreams beneath the Auroras, Porfiry Danielyevitch, that's what I am asking about. Tell me, please!'

'Come, come. It would be better to inquire of the Buryat shamans. I know not, I've never even laid out the tarot. No one plays dice or cards, if that's what Your Illustriousness is asking. Father Rózga warns in every other sermon against faith in early-morning dreams. We are to be on our guard whenever the Tchornoye Siyaniye hangs in the sky.' Pocięgło wiped his mouth with his serviette, sat up straight, as the noctaureole flickered around his hair. 'A person gets used to it, as I said, fails to notice such things in fact, lives with them every day. Only when he leaves Winter for a few days... Here, now, everywhere, such a beautiful summer.' He looked out at the leaden sky above the grey plain; maybe to him that scenery really did seem unutterably enchanting. Frightening then to imagine the beauty of the landscapes in the Land of the Gleissen. 'More subtle differences exist. Your Illustriousness is genuinely interested in all this?'

'I was even thinking of sending someone from the Society with the specific aim of researching it, writing it down, publicising it in Europe.'

'Society?'

'The Theosophical Society of Saint Petersburg.' The princess leaned across the table, the chain of her pince-nez dangling above the gravy boat. 'I am its honorary president.'

'Ah.' Porfiry glanced to one side, clearly seeking deliverance. Thrust the nose into a fried brain in the pancakes. Pocięgło sighed, stroked his thick beard. 'People behave... like people. Whereas here, or so it seems to me, they are more, mm-hmm, dislocated.'

'How do you mean?'

'Ye-es, I see, it's hard to describe. Largely insignificant things. In the Land of the Gleissen... Your Illustriousness meets a stranger and knows at once that he's lately experienced disappointment in love – but how does Your Illustriousness know? For he has not yet managed to say anything. It's not written on his forehead. Differences of this type.' Pocięgło sat up straight on his chair, crossed his bony arms over his chest. 'All right, I shall tell it from my own experience. The day before yesterday in Omsk I got up in the middle of the night, stepped outside onto the balcony and for several minutes cried out to the Moon. Words that made no sense, wolfish syllables. My neighbours woke up. Why had I done it? I know not. There was no rhyme or reason. I wasn't raving, I was calm.'

'You were howling at the Moon?'

'What I'm saying is that on Baikal's shores, things like that don't happen.'

The princess chuckled.

'You have no madmen there?'

'Indeed, I've heard of no cases of madness. But this is not what it's about: madness, lycanthropy, these are specific conditions. I speak of insignificant things, those that seep between words.'

'Crimes of passion? From great love? From jealousy? They never happen?'

'People steal mightily. Fights, robberies, frauds, we have more than enough Chinamen and vagabonds, as well as a restless peasantry constantly coming and going, there's been such a tradition, if it please Your Illustriousness, since the days of the oprichnina, since Kiselyoff, just as long as it's beyond the Urals. And where do the muzhiks stop and stay? Time was when they travelled as far as Yakutsk, capital of the Wild East and centre of the goldrush, but now – there's a new Siberian Eldorado, the one on Baikal's shores. Half the world, two dozen languages on the streets of Irkutsk. And another thing which surprises them – whereas I'm surprised they're surprised – namely, that people know not each other's tongues, yet they always somehow understand. You won't comprehend the words, but the intention behind them always seems obvious. Or something of the sort –'

Prince Blutsky-Osey rose from the table.

'We thank you,' he muttered. 'Ahem, yes, indeed, we thank you warmly and go now to take our nap; my dear, I shan't beg of you.'

The princess likewise rose to her feet, everyone rose to their feet. The stewards bustled around the table. Push back the chair. Miss Muklanowicz was sending discreet signals. Turn to Pocięgło.

'Are you, sir –'.

'Are you, sir –'.

He laughed whole-heartedly.

'Closer and closer to Winter!'

The princess reached over the table with her stick.

'You, you, young man,' she brandished it like a fencing foil, 'Count or non-Count of many names, you I won't let go; Porfiry Danielyevitch will have to forgive us, because I am kidnapping you, let's go, come on, I have kidnapped you, well, get a move on!'

Spread the arms in helplessness. Miss Muklanowicz must have seen the encounter. Porfiry Pocięgło bowed politely. Circumnavigate the table and offer an arm to the shrivelled old lady.

An odour of musty fabric and herbal medicaments hung about her, not even especially pungent, but sufficiently unpleasant to prompt the head, when taking in air, to instinctively turn away. She marched ahead with indefatigable energy: she had but one rhythm in her gait, one rhythm in her speech, one – in her breathing. Hear it distinctly, being now at such close quarters: hhr, hhrrr, hhr, hhrrr. The stick was for resisting sudden jolts of the train. A steward went ahead opening and holding open the doors.

She stopped only beyond the saloon, in the parlour car. Beside the great marble fireplace, the one-eyed gentleman, Miss Muklanowicz's neighbour, stood smoking a cigar. Princess Blutskaya levelled her stick at him. 'You!' The gentleman was put out, glared with his glass eye, glared intensely, bowed his head stiffly and walked out. The princess nodded to the steward. He moved up a chair. In more or less this same place, three days earlier, she had conducted her séance with the black-wicke; the round table was still there, tucked behind the upright piano. Glance around for the other chairs – they stood in a row by the gallery door.

'My husband...,' the princess began and broke off in order to catch breath, hhr, hhrrr. Look again at those chairs. But she had already caught breath and caught hold of the hand, tugging at the jacket sleeve, clawing her bony fingers into the wrist, so that the body leans – willy nilly – towards the old lady, collapses in a lackey-like pose: bent at the waist like a scraping loyal servant, ear to the lips of her ladyship.

'… says you're a crafty scoundrel, besides it's enough to take one look at your phizog, why grin so, young man?'

'Pardon me, I didn't wish –'

'And these lies about your birth, oh, and the ring too – she shifted the pressure from wrist to finger – perhaps you'll try to tell me it's your family coat of arms?'

'No.'

'A charlatan, says my lord prince, and I have to agree with him, charlatan, yes, but now you shan't escape me! now you shall listen to me! now the truth!'

She exhaled senile breath. Were air to possess colour, then that air would be black; she'd be breathing out blackness, that is, unlicht distilled into gas. Shut the eyes and turn the head, as if to move the ear closer to the lips of Princess Blutskaya, but in fact solely to be freed of her breath. Stare to one side as she speaks, stare through the eyelashes at the greenish grey of the taiga sailing past beyond the windows of the Express. Try hard to restrain the facial muscles, over quick to smile imploringly, so that they might remain in neutral symmetry, but when the words are heard – *now the truth!* – it was as if teslectrical flow surged through the body, tugging at the reins of every bodily nerve. Truth! Watchword of ill omen, warning sign, weapon in hand, armour over the heart to protect the soul; there shall be talk of – truth.

'For why have you been avoiding us all this time? Why refusing our invitations? Why running away from the councillor?'

'I was not running away.'

'Oh! Not running away! He was running away, and knows very well he was running away, he lies, not nice, not nice. I was asking Porfiry Danielyevitch before you sat down to dinner, I ask everyone here who knows those parts, anyone who might have heard of him: is there such a man in the Land of the Gleissen as Father Frost, *le Père du Gel*, confessor of gleissen, like you say, your father?'

'And so?'

'Porfiry Danielyevitch said he wasn't interested. But can I believe you? I cannot. A charlatan. Besides, Rasputin is a charlatan too, you are all charlatans. Only the Ice is genuine, only in the Ice is there salvation, from cold to cold, for out of cold wast thou taken, and unto cold shalt thou return, whosoever be nearest to death, the more distinctly he feels the frost swelling in his bones, you see old people – muffled, swaddled in warm sunlight in five feather quilts and furs… What? Why do you look like that?'

Turn the head back towards the window.

'Your Illustriousness knows the teachings of Saint Martsyn.'

She tightened the grip of her sharp talons.

'I know them! You know them! At court, not only Rasputin after all – but! but! How come it touched me at once? How come I recognised you on the first day? In this way, the true God speaks to us, for it's hard for Him to speak louder, in clear revelations. When you stepped then into the unlicht, when dazzling brightness poured from you as you stood in the sunlit doorway, angel of glintz, I feared my heart would leap out of my breast, and believed again I was dreaming – sometimes I doze off in the middle of the day, for an hour, a minute, then wake and know not why, where, when, for how long, what has happened, except that the sudden dream lingers inside me – and so when you stepped into the unlicht and the furnace of cold fire opened within you, I saw you take out the lightning bolt of ice with your red hand, your hand in the tide of warmthless white, oh my God, it all touched me at once. Since then, I dream of you day and night.'

'Your Highness –'

'At first, I understood not. But now! now the truth! You yourself have prophesied from the unlicht! Son of Frost!'

'Don't believe me, Your Highness. Don't believe yourself. It's all –'

'But they are coming true! Of this do I speak! Listen to me now! When we were stopped in Yekaterinburg – I awoke in the middle of the night; my dream was terrible, heart beating like a hammer, I dreamed naturally of you. But then I draw back the curtain and what do I see, I see you, under silver snow, by a dark wall. Oh, how it stabbed me here, below the breast, I merely glanced, and yet already. The prince swore at me horribly but I knew, and Zahary Feofilovitch convinced me; I sent him after you immediately with his men. And what? It had come true! You shan't tell me, surely, it was foolish superstition – dreams – dreams, cards, all manner of sortilege – the closer to the Land of the Gleissen, all the more so. How else is God to reach understanding with us?'

'Not everything that's true comes only from God.'

Thinking, however, about something else. Princess Blutskaya belongs to the court Martsynians, as perhaps does Privy Councillor Dushin, or maybe he merely obeys her like a faithful dog, it amounts to the same thing – for it was not due to the prince's intention but the princess's that the Blutskys' strongmen had hastened to the rescue in Yekaterinburg. And what happens next: the princess seeks contact, Dushin is more and more insistent – yet did they not see who also came out against the local Martsynians in Yekaterinburg? did they not recognise Pyelka? But how were they meant to know each other, a raw youth from Buy and a *grand dame* from Saint Petersburg? What are the hierarchies betwixt Martsynians? what factions and divisions? what orders circulate amongst them? Because Pyelka knew; the princess knew not. Did she not send Dushin to interrogate the boy as soon as the councillor made her aware of the disturbance in the city? So Dushin goes to Pyelka in the middle of the night, wakes him, drags him from the compartment and outside onto the observation platform to talk in secret about secret matters, and then – what happened? what did Pyelka say? what did Dushin say to Pyelka? how did Pyelka react? Did they fight? Could the princess have given Dushin such an order: "Throw Pyelka off the train"? She herself, after all, doesn't have to admit the whole truth now, a senile manner of speech does not signify senile decay of the mind. Bah, so all her wittering about dreams, intuitions, sortilege, is most certainly no more than a smokescreen. She dreamed, indeed! But not along the same lines as Pyelka and the Yekaterinburg Martsynians, yet the princess could well have learned about Father Frost and the new idea of Rappacki's people, oh, just by hosting the Minister of Winter to dinner. Moreover, she knows Rasputin; she may be initiated into the Martsynians' highest mysteries. It's impossible to get anything out of the provodniks and stewards; Dushin had browbeaten them more effectively than if they'd been bribed by a dozen merchants of the calibre of Fessar.

In what lie should the princess now believe? What lie would be safest? She'll dream something the other way and be ready to send Dushin and the retinue to remove the 'charlatan'.

'What does Your Highness want from me?'

'It's you, you.'

'I?'

She glanced to left and right and again to the left, at the steward standing erect by the passageway to the saloon, his eyes lowered directly in front of him: he watches yet watches not, listens yet listens not – listens nevertheless. The princess grabbed the arm higher up, neath the elbow, and pulled until the ear came close indeed to her corpselike lips; she was breathing now into the auricle itself, hhr, hhrrr.

'The emperor has lost his mind,' she whispered.

'Oh?'

'His Imperial Exaltedness wants to wage war on the gleissen. Listen to me now!' She pulled harder still; the back of the chair had to be grabbed, so as not to lose balance at the next lurch of the carriage and land with the entire weight on top of the princess. 'When, in the dead of night, the nightmare descends on him, he rings and shouts and raises half the court to its feet, orders ministers and generals to be brought before him, drags the prime minister out of bed, convenes secret councils. In the Winter Palace he has vast halls where half the world is sketched out on the parquet, two continents with their dependencies, the whole Russian Empire; there His Sovereign Majesty the Emperor stays up for hours – stays up for hours as the chimeras begin tormenting his brain, and moves lines across the Empire: here Winter, here Summer, expanses free of Winter, here cities under the Ice where gleissen have settled, there rivers caked in ice floes, fronts of the Frost; how far have its waves spread out of Siberia? how much of his absolute power over the land is still intact, the rest appropriated by gleissen? – for when he looks at it like this, sees it like this in his delirium, it's as if he's having to suffer an invasion of his own country. So whenever tidings came of a new Russian city where a gleiss had frozen up out of the ground, His Imperial Exaltedness would shut himself in his rooms for days and weeks on end, frightened, his nerves frayed, and neither Aleksandra Fyodorovna nor his doctors were able to entice him out; and when gleissen froze up out of the ground in Saint Petersburg itself and ice shackled the Neva and a nest of living icespikes hung from the black networks above Palace Square from the Aleksandrian Column to Voznesensky Prospect, oh, had you but seen him then, he ordered the gleissen to be shot at with rifles and cannon, ordered fires to be lit underneath the gleissen; officers from the General Staff and the Admiralty came flocking to him, but they were also unable to appeal to his reason, until some Prussian professor prescribed His Exaltedness Nikolay Aleksandrovitch sedatives, and the poor wretch fell asleep. But it's impossible to stand guard over the emperor, impossible to control every design and command of the autocrat. Everyone's afraid that he'll proclaim in the end an Ukase Against the Ice, try to drive the gleissen out by force; the army obeys him, though what can human might do against the inhuman Frost, yet disaster, I tell you, disaster will come of it one way or another. Whilst the war was still on with Japan, our emperor had enough sense to accept the argument that one enemy had to be dealt with first – but now, you see, we have a ceasefire and most likely peace, the Yellow Empire has been repulsed, who knows by what His Exaltedness will be seized, by what he has already been seized. Hhr, hhrrr. The least we can do – is to warn the gleissen, since there's nothing else. Your father... tell him! without fail!' Momentarily winded and hoarse, she caught breath. Again, she had to lower her voice to a whisper. 'Venyedikt Filipovitch. Defend the gleissen. While the Ice exists, Russia exists. There are heretics who twist Martsyn's words for their own petty ends, but the truth is one. I have had dreams. Russia is the Ice, the Ice is Russia. Defend the gleissen!'

Was she expecting maybe the swearing of a solemn oath? Wrench free of her clutches; she lacked the strength to grasp the arm again. Take a step back.

'I said Your Highness should not believe me.'

'What, will you now say, perhaps, that you are not the son of Father Frost?'

Shake the head.

'Those Martsynians in Yekaterinburg – what think you, Your Highness, why did they try to kill me? They fear the same as Your Highness – and that is precisely the reason why they won't let me reach my father alive.'

'When I am telling you: I have had dreams! And as soon as I saw you – at once – I knew – I know! It's in your power to reverse fate, to keep Russia under the Ice. You believe not, but I believe in you.'

Look away. Why not swear, in fact, to do what she wants? It would be very sensible, very safe, a good lie. Out of shame? Before whom?

'Your Princessly Highness deigns to speak nonsense. For how did my father come to be in this Siberia amongst gleissen? You and your people sent him into exile for rebelling against the emperor. And as to this deformed mug – you see, Your Highness? – why should your fine captain punch me yesterday in full view of everyone? Because I am a Pole. Give me one reason, Your Highness, one reason why I should desire the salvation of Russia, one!'

Princess Blutskaya brandished the stick from her chair. Leap back. Imagine for a second that she'll stand up and begin chasing around the ballroom with that stick, breathing forth her black stench, ruckling through her crooked teeth, on her stiff legs, in the ducklike waddle of her diseased hips and bent spine, one bony hand threatening revenge, the other raised above her head waving her club like a witch's wand – but no, she waved but once and sank back into her chair, resigned.

'All right,' she wheezed. 'I had dreams and know what I know, even if you know not about yourself, but… All right. May Saint Martsyn speak for me instead.'

'I spit on Martsyn.'

She stared as if at a madman.

'What's come over you, young man? Why behave like this?'

Burst into bitter laughter, so loud it echoed around the room.

'Why do you all want me to lie incessantly?! I am no Martsynian! I am no count! I know not your politics! Care not about Russia! Nor Poland for that matter! Have not seen my father since childhood! I spit on it all! Ice or no Ice, so long as I come out of it alive and with the money!'

Perceive that it's no longer laughter, but something very different in fact from laughter, nearer to hysterical sobbing, that voice emanating in brief spurts from the dry throat. Hands tremble all the while, flapping in equally hysterical gesticulation, hands tremble, whereas a leg jumps up and down on the parquet, tap-tap – wait a bit longer and the nervous attack will engulf the whole body; this demented force, usually well concealed behind the hesitant twisted smile, makes a bid for freedom. Glance around in panic. One hand caught hold of the collar, the other began to feel for the Grossmeister. A shrill cackle pushed up from the diaphragm, ready to burst at once through the teeth. Sway on the heels. The carriage shook; fly on top of the princess. She stretched out her stick – not to repel, but to hook onto an arm and pull down all the more powerfully. Collapse onto the knees. The bony hand of Princess Blutskaya locked onto the neck above the unbuttoned stand-up collar and scurried upwards, into the hair; the princess pressed the limp head deposited in her lap into her black dress.

'Shh, shh, quiet.' She stroked the pomaded locks. 'There, there, little son, there, there, mama Katya understands everything, no need to say anything, mama Katya knows you better than anyone, you can cry your eyes out, you can confess, Katya will take it with her to the grave. You think you'll surprise old Katya with something, think you'll shock her, push her off by telling her some horrible truth – there is no such truth. No need to feel ashamed, I know you better than anyone, four such sons have I had; and to whom did they come running to cry their eyes out, to me, to me. Shh.'

'They want to ki-ill me. I won't get through a-live.'

'No one shall kill you, you'll find a way, you'll see.'

'I s-sold myself to them. For a thousand roubles.'

'You shall ask forgiveness.'

'Forgiveness? Of whom?'

'You shall give back the money.'

'I shall.'

'You see. Relief already.'

Kiss her hand (the wrinkled skin covered in brown spots gave off a scent of old wood).

'Thank you.'

'You have family?'

'No. A father. No.'

'No one close by you? I see. That's the hardest.'

'I'm sorry.'

'Marry, my child.'

'Upon whom could I inflict such harm – not upon a woman I love.'

'But why judge yourself so harshly? You're all so ready to plunge at once into hell, each swears he's the worst man on Earth, youth, it's youth. Truly evil people are few and far between!'

'Evil?' Burst out laughing. 'When there is no me at all. There is no me, no me, I exist not.'

'Shh, shh.'

Calm down. Regularity returned to the breath, hands were restored to the control of conscious thought: motionless when thinking not of motion, closing and opening the fists when thinking of order and strength. Raise the eyelids. Green echoes of the taiga were reflected inside the empty carriage, which were also to some extent calming. Glance in the other direction – but there stands the steward, the steward who'd been forgotten for a moment, erect, his face expressionless, eyes unblinking; he watches yet watches not, listens yet listens not – listens nevertheless. Jump to the feet.

Princess Blutskaya was gazing melancholically, exhausted.

'I am very sorry.' Bow. 'I find no justification. Your Highness is right to hold me in contempt, nor is Your Highness's venerable spouse mistaken. Allow me –'

'You were asking about one thing.'

'Pardon?'

'One thing, in order to preserve Russia.' She found her handkerchief, wiped her slavering lips. 'You see, that's it.'

'What?'

'Forgiveness.'

Thrown into confusion.

'No right of mine to forgive in the name –'

'Not yours. But only the living can ask the living for forgiveness. History knows no mercy, History forgives not. Gospodin Yeroslavsky.'

She raised her arm. Kiss her hand, this time in a more formal gesture. She rapped twice with her stick on the parquet. The steward opened the door. Exit into the saloon.

Mademoiselle Christine Filipov leapt up from the ottoman.

'I've been waiting for you, sir, waiting and waiting!' she whispered, highly agitated, grabbing and embracing the arm in panic and pulling it towards her and across the saloon. 'He is no longer breathing! That Cerberus wouldn't let me in, yet every minute –'

'What are you –'

'The provodnik delivered no letter? Why, agh, why did you not come?!'

Reach into jacket pocket – it was there, unopened.

'I forgot.'

'You forgot?! Forgot?!'

'I have a headache. A terrible katzenjammer. What's the matter?'

'Nikola is dead.'

On death in the past tense

'He's dead.'

Bend over Doctor Tesla's body, pressing the interferograph into an eye. Light – light – light – light – light – light – light.

'Dead, Miss Filipov, but perhaps alive.'

She tittered a trifle hysterically.

'You're a fine pair!'

Glance at her suspiciously.

'What d'you mean?'

'For the love of God, sir, save him!'

'He did tell you, miss.'

Her lips trembled.

'You promised me! And so? Instead of dissuading him, you yourself have succumbed!'

'Soon you'll be saying that it was my fault; that it was I who killed him.'

In every respect, however, it was admirable how well Mademoiselle Filipov was bearing up in the circumstances. Whoever Doctor Tesla was to her – father, distant relative, lover – he was after all the only person close to her on this journey through an alien and wondrous land, amongst strangers, in the Transsib, in the midst of the Asiatic wilderness, en route to still greater isolation. Now she was alone. Can she count on the okhranniks? Functionaries of the tsarist political police; who knows what their real orders are: meant to protect the doctor, they have failed to protect him – what will they do? She was alone. She sat opposite on the edge of the bedcovers, tugging nervously at the sleeve of her organdie dress, plucking at her plait of fair hair, and leaning every other moment over Nikola, as if still waiting only for him to awake and raise his eyelids.

Doctor Tesla lay at rest on his bed, on the counterpane embroidered in scarlet thread, pillow under his head, head turned towards the window, beyond which the dreary green of the endless taiga sailed by, as the Express rode away from the last centres of civilisation before it crossed the true border between Siberia and Winter, dwook-dwook-dwook-DWOOK; whilst with every leap of the carriage, Tesla's body leapt too, and his long arms, laid against the sides of his body, slipped off the counterpane, his hands concealed in their impeccably white cotton gloves. The cuff of his left shirt sleeve was drawn up, exposing above the white glove the red hoop of an impression: here Tesla had wound the coldiron cable of the dynamo-machine. The machine remained on the table, its cable spilling onto the carpet, coiling like a snake, the crank swinging to and fro. The metallic elements were already dry; the hoar had vanished from furniture and walls.

Mademoiselle Filipov's account was brief and to the point. Christine had got talking to someone after breakfast – she returns to the compartment and discovers frost, unlicht; Tesla is turning the crank, black sparks fly off his skin and hair, a drawn-out moan emanates from his mouth, but still he stands there, still he turns the crank – the young woman grabs hold of him, tears him from the machine, sits him down on the bedcovers – he is already deathly cold – losing consciousness – his heart beats slower and slower; after a few hours it ceases to beat altogether.

Remembering the case of Ünal Fessar, take her not at her word. The eyepiece of the interferograph served as a coffin mirror. Move it close to Tesla's lips. No sign of breath appeared on the glass. He is dead.

'Has it happened to him before?'

'What?'

'Dying.'

'How can you jest so?'

'Well, both of us are jesting. "Save him, sir!" Arise, Lazarus!'

'Yet you said yourself: dead, but perhaps alive.'

Tap the chin pensively with the metal barrel.

'He has not frozen, if you follow my meaning. But several milliard other corpses from outside the Land of the Gleissen could say the same of themselves. Which is to say,' – smile beneath the moustache – 'corpses speak not, but –'

Mademoiselle Filipov burst into tears.

How quickly the roles are reversed: now it's time to embrace the weeping woman, hug her, whisper words of comfort, stroke her hair, rock her until she forgets, shh, shh, shh. She sniffed, screwing her hands into soft little fists, a baby's helplessness.

'I th-thought that you, sir – b-because you too – and he said of you –'

'What did he say?'

'That you'd u-un-understand!'

What to expect of a child? 'Mama, my doggie's broken, mend my doggie!' And she shoves the dead animal under the nose, not the slightest shadow of doubt appearing in the child's wide-open eyes – this is what grown-ups are for, to bring the world to order.

She calmed down.

'He's dead,' she repeated quietly.

'Perhaps I should fetch Doctor Konyeshin…'

'I begged him not to travel. A black cloud has hung over this journey from the very start.'

'He insisted.'

'Yes. He had to do all the experiments himself, it was always like that. At first, he wanted to travel there straightaway and carry out the experiments on the spot. I implored him to stay in Prague.' She found her handkerchief, blew her nose, apologised. 'You know, sir, that they accused Nikola of conjuring up the gleissen?'

'I beg your pardon?'

'Yes, yes, they've been slandering him again in the press. After Pierpont Morgan refused him funds, Nikola had to shut down his tower at Wardenclyffe, back in nineteen-oh-three or four. The whole affair with Morgan… Nikola would never have had all this trouble, had he not been so blind to certain obvious things in his dealings with people; but his mind always raced towards what was not obvious, to what no one else envisaged he would. That's how he won people over, that's how he alienated them. Why he never got married… He's blind to people; blind, deaf and insensitive. To Morgan too he probably spoke as if to a lover of science, and not to a cunning financier. And so, he lost Wardenclyffe.' Doctor Tesla's arm slid off the bedcovers, Mademoiselle Filipov picked it up again and placed it on the counterpane with great tenderness. 'But because he's been predicting for years that he would liberate the magnetic energy of the Earth, would be able to bring down Zeppelins from the sky and sink battleships with an invisible force, provoke earthquakes wherever he wished… You know how melodramatic he can be. And after the initial reports from Russia, that was exactly how it seemed: as if in the midst of the wilderness on the far side of the planet, an invisible energy had exploded; I read the articles in the old newspapers. Whilst Nikola was still being pulled down by that affair in Colorado, which dragged on…' She fell silent.

'Yes?'

Christine shook her head, rousing herself from the dangerous musings to which she'd succumbed. Whilst she speaks, everything's fine, let her speak, may she concentrate on her own words, for this is the beginning of all mourning rituals – remembrance of the dead.

'In July eighteen ninety-nine, in his laboratory in Colorado Springs, when he was working on registering the electrical pulse of the Earth, if I'm putting it correctly – he received a signal from the cosmos, repeated strings of numbers. Remember there were as yet no radio transmitters on Earth. Nikola reckoned the signal came from Mars. Straightaway he publicised it in the press…' She gazed with a gentle smile at the inventor's lifeless face. 'He never doubted himself, thereby harming himself all the more. My mother told me…'

'Yes?'

'And when he received that order from the tsar, initially only to do armaments research, for only in the spring of last year did he get a definite contract against the gleissen – it was with difficulty that we persuaded him to keep it secret. He was dreadfully afraid someone might again beat him to it and secure the patents ahead of him; if only you knew, sir, how many nerves that cost him! He met with engineers from Sibirkhozheto; it was only they, it seems, who persuaded him. You know the superstition? That in the Land of the Gleissen, there's no means of inventing anything genuinely new, all crucial discoveries in coldiron matters have been made elsewhere; those engineers told him that they travel specially to Vladivostock, or to Tomsk, in order to open their minds. As soon as they light upon an idea, they travel back, because the calculations themselves, the rational work, comes exceptionally easily on Baikal's shores – but whatever you don't have already stored in your mind beforehand, you won't force into your thoughts in gleissen country for love or money. And what inspires greater fear in Nikola than the possibility that he'll become like other people, think like they think, perceive only obvious things that have already been perceived? Perhaps then there'd be more of a normal human being about him – but less of the genius. You should know, sir, that Nikola is superstitious, he believes in all those –'

'One moment, Christine, what are you talking about? He used to pump himself with this murch precisely in order to clear his mind, he told me so himself.'

'You must have misunderstood him. In order to work late at night, or when he had to hurry with the construction of his prototypes, then of course; but for new thoughts and this little bit of madness –'

'What?'

Jump to the feet. Leap to the table, grab hold of the crank and the coldiron cable, spin the dynamo. Murch crept along the wire, pale unlicht flickered inside the machine, trrrrrrrr, a burning chill penetrated the palm, the forearm.

'What are you doing?! Throw it down!'

She tore out the cable, stopping the crank with her other hand, terrified, furious.

Step back.

'Memory, for the sake of memory.' Mutter under the breath. 'He was not inquiring about such effects, not about those, he didn't know himself, he was experimenting.'

'Benedykt, sir!'

Put away the interferograph.

'A man who lives on memory… You were saying, miss, that he converses with non-existent people, that he mistakes imagination for reality? Today at dinner the industrialist from Irkutsk was describing the local peculiarities: and so, in the Land of the Gleissen, there are no madmen.'

Miss Filipov frowned.

'Are you feeling all right –'

'There are no madmen! Don't you understand? It was not for this that Nikola was frequenting the carriage containing his arsenal of Summer! Here, he had his dynamo-machine, but there – without showing me, he fastened a cable to black salt, reset a hidden apparatus, drew out a tungetitum looking glass – there he has a flow-generator designed to do the work in reverse! Dear God, he told me openly after all: how to kill gleissen – well, here's how: not by flooding them with still greater quantities of murch, but by sucking all murch out of them! Just as electrical current, whether it flows to cathode or anode, is always current; so too Tesla's flow has two directions: more murch – less murch. You understand? This is the ticket to madness, the ticket to revelatory ideas never thought of by anyone before, the miracle machine of poets and inventors – Kotarbiński's logic pump! The same flow, except that it's reversed! The arsenal of Summer: that which neither is nor isn't, neither truth nor falsehood, neither yea nor nay', glance at the mortal remains of Nikola Tesla, 'neither alive nor dead, Mademoiselle Filipov, neither alive nor dead! The next station stop! Is when? Where? What's the time?'

Her hands were trembling. She took out from a drawer her own copy of the *Putevoditel* and leafed through it nervously.

'I've no idea how late we're running,' she moaned. 'Novonikolayevsk? Maybe you saw, sir, what the last station –'

'Hang on.'

Rush out into the corridor. The provodnik's compartment was located at the far end of the carriage, before the bathrooms. Find him with buttered fingers and a sausage stuck between his teeth. The man almost choked. In answer to the urgent question, he pointed first to a small clock standing above the samovar, then to a timetable pinned to the door and covered in handwritten red-ink insertions in sprawling fancy Cyrillic. Shove the nose close to the paper in order to read. Novonikolayevsk, an hour-long stop in twenty-eight minutes time. Twenty-seven. Time is running out. Run back to Tesla's compartment.

Grab hold of the doctor's arm (the skin was cold as ice), and wrench it. Mademoiselle Filipov cried out softly.

'What are you doing?!'

'These corpses, damn it, are heavy.' Puff and pant. 'My dear, go and treat yourself at once to some smelling-salts because I shall require your assistance, and your hand, and your clear head.'

'But –'

'In half an hour's time, Nikola must be in his goods wagon. I shall attempt to perform a miracle.' Take a few deep breaths, sit down at the foot of the dead man's bed, wipe the brow, 'now... now we must think of how to carry this out. Who will transport him. And how. So as not to provoke a flurry at the station and draw crowds to the arsenal of Summer; Doctor Tesla would never forgive me. I suggest that you, miss, as soon as the train comes to a halt, should knock on that wagon and bring those two agents here, they know you better than me, they'll obey you; then quickly –'

Christine Filipov disassembled the crank from the dynamo-machine and, leaning over the empty bed, struck the wall with its wooden handle, woop, woop, woop, three times, again and again.

Glance at her questioningly. She laid aside the crank. The door opened and Pavel Vladimirovitch Fogel burst into the compartment, Nagant in hand.

'Docto –'

'Put away the heavy artillery!' Growl at the silver-haired okhrannik as he stood stock-still, transfixed by Tesla's corpse, with the weapon dangerously aimed, his finger poised on the trigger, staring fixedly like a bird.

'Something happened to him?' he asked feebly.

'The doctor is dead,' announced Christine Filipov. 'As soon as the train stops in Novonikolayevsk, we have to transfer Nikola to the goods wagon. You are to fetch Oleg.'

'Dead?'

'Put it away!'

He put away the revolver. Placing his tsviker on his nose, he approached Tesla's body. Carefully he took the corpse's wrist. For a while he appeared to be measuring the pulse, gazing at the same time with expressionless eyes at the teslectric dynamo standing under the window.

'Yes,' he muttered, and slowly crossed himself with bureaucratic scrupulousness. 'We shall have to send a telegram. Will you testify, miss, that it was an accident? That there was no way we could have prevented it?'

'We still don't know.'

'What?'

'Whether it'll be necessary to testify.' Christine avoided eye contact, winding her plait around her fingers. 'Mr Gierosławski will explain.'

Stand up, take the elderly policeman by the arm.

'You have to organise a trunk, as large as possible, empty of course, so that the doctor's body will fit inside easily. We'll transport him in the trunk.'

Fogel adjusted the eyeglasses, frowning.

'What for?'

'You shall see. What have you to lose? Now that he's dead, no worse harm can come to you. Now get going, time is running out! A trunk, a large one!'

He left, looking back again from the doorway at the Serb stretched out on the scarlet counterpane – at the long legs protruding beyond the bed, the hand in its white glove slipping gradually towards the carpet, the loosened scarf around his neck revealing the blood-tinged bruises, and the white lock falling from the black hair combed to both sides of the parting, onto the arching temple – Fogel stood gaping until the door was shut in his face.

'Will he obey me?'

The spirit had drained again from Christine Filipov; she sat slumped against the wall under the window, her forehead glued to the cold windowpane.

'Maybe. I imagine so. He should do.'

'I thought he was travelling in the service van behind the tender.'

'He moved here in Vazoff's place. They left the compartments empty as far as Irkutsk.'

'Ah!'

Vazoff and that other one, his skull split open by Vazoff – forget his name – two guardian angels assigned from the beginning to protect Nikola Tesla, had been bought seats in Deluxe, and indeed, following their deaths, the compartments had remained empty, two single berths either side of Nikola Tesla and Christine Filipov's compartment – that would be logical. And Fogel had moved into one of them, doubtless with the provodnik's knowledge. Nonetheless he possessed no ticket, was not a fully fledged passenger; he appeared at no meals, very likely never left the compartment. (Except for the night-time visitations to neighbouring carriages meant to intimidate any passengers crossing his path.) He was keeping an eye on Tesla.

'You really hope… to… Nikola…'

'We have not yet reached the lands of Ice, Christine, there is still room for lies, even the greatest.'

Light a cigarette. It would be somewhat disconcerting to have everything suddenly explained, and in an order agreeable to the mind – were it not for the awareness that this is by no means the first such perfect explanation; whereas every foregoing one has swiftly proved false, or at least incomplete. Ultimately, we are dealing with a new domain of knowledge, a new science – the science of unlicht, of teslectricity, of the physical foundations of logic – we are therefore also travelling, during this journey into the heart of Winter, through successive epochs of the history of science, theory replaces theory, hypothesis supplants hypothesis.

... And so, Nikola Tesla had reversed the direction of flow in his generator and hence when the coldiron barrel was seized, murch flowed not into the body but was sucked out of it, and the body became demurched. Remember: the salt crystal – one of not many in the jar – was not black to begin with. Remember: that the whole incident had been forgotten, from the grasping of the cable to its releasing. Now Doctor Tesla's words made sense. The arsenal of Summer. To kill gleissen. Every organism, every biological structure possesses not only a defined electrical charge, but also a teslectrical one: it is a receptacle of murch. In their natural state on Earth, organisms remain incompletely filled. (Probably, the maximum capacity of a given structure could somehow be calculated, as could the degree of its enmurchment. Insofar as a maximum exists. For did not Nikola mention a limitless influx of teslectricity...?) Summer is the realm of true lies and lying truths. Winter, on the other hand, admits of nothing between truth and falsehood. Gleissen, children of Winter, live in a great inundation of murch. Just as it is possible to pump murch out of a gleiss, so too murch can be pumped out of any other organism, as much murch as that organism carries within it. Will a completely demurched – "defrozen" – man still go on living? that is, will it be possible to say anything at all about him with absolute certainty: that he lives, that he lives not, that he is, that he is not? will all assertions about him be equally true-and-untrue, and will all attributes of being-and-non-being pertain to him in equal measure? Had Nikola Tesla carried out these experiments on people? or on animals? No doubt he's reckoning that for gleissen, the Kotarbiński pump will prove to be an instrument of doom.

... The body, therefore, had been demurched, whilst to the seeing eye a dearth or surfeit of murch appears as one and the same: as those small light phenomena, light and unlicht, shadow and glintz. Whether a magnet is applied with the south or north pole – the force is the same; whether electrical current flows in this or in that direction – the force is the same. But direct pressure on the organism and mind, this will already differ with the dearth or surfeit of murch.

... Now everything slots into place in the head dangerously smoothly, everything fits together: because there's also the Pilsudchiks' second missive wrung from 'false' memory, as well as those suspiciously easy illuminations and deductions of the previous day, and the tales told in the night... Demurched. The logic of soletruth and solefalsehood had been pumped out. With time, the effects vanish, levels of murch even out to the local average for Summer. Or Winter, where the average murch is significantly higher – hence the predictions of Zeytsoff and Pocięgło: it's another country, people acquire different habits, thought patterns change, other laws hold sway, God-the-Autocrat has switched the points.

Rest the palm on the casing of Tesla's dynamo-machine. No longer even cold. Think first whether not to turn the crank and admurch the self for the sake of healthy balance. But almost half a day had already elapsed, no difference was visible even in the mirror. Besides – was it really desirable: admurching? more Frost?

Drag out the sac de voyage from under the table, pack into it the dynamo-machine, the cable, the crank. The little key was nowhere to be found; no point in searching the pockets of a corpse. The cubby was luckily unlocked. Shove in the heavy bag; it rattled against the wooden floor. Miss Filipov suddenly raised her head as if roused unexpectedly; perhaps she really did wake up, having dropped off with her cheek pressed into the windowpane, a red imprint left on her skin. She blinked for a moment amazed, regaining her bearings in the new situation: Nikola's mortal remains lay on the bed whilst a strange man was bustling about the compartment. People swell in sleep; heavy with slumber, they turn slack softened faces, rounder fuller countenances, towards the light. Fair-haired Christine now seemed like a blossoming little girl with cherubic mouth and big eyes, the azure of stained glass. Even the hesitant movement of her hand, a gesture cut off midway, spoke likewise of childish vulnerability and lostness. She had slept – also a form of escape.

Prise the cigarette from the lips, let down the window, flick ash to the wind. Cool air blew the black curtains over the dead man's bed. Mademoiselle Filipov took a few deep breaths.

'Will you go back?' Inquire quietly.

'Yes.' She gulped. 'First to Prague, I have to take care of his assistant Czito; then to America.'

'What will become of that wagon? And its contents? The machines and all the rest?'

'Everything belongs to the tsar.'

'Does anyone understand them?'

Christine glanced at the dead inventor.

'Nikola himself didn't understand them, no one does; not even the engineers from Zimny Nikolayevsk. Otherwise, we could go and ask. Or read it in books, don't you think?'

'My concern is… will someone be continuing Doctor Tesla's experiments? taking up the work, making use of his discoveries?'

Christine raised her eyes.

Make rapid signs of the cross.

'God forbid! Don't look at me like that, please! I'm not asking for that reason, truly! Besides, I have no idea what it's all about!'

She covered her mouth with her hand.

'Yet I almost believed you! That you know what you're doing. That when we transfer him there... that, as Nikola said, you had intuited something more and –'

'Resurrection.'

'What?'

Inhale the cigarette smoke.

'I shall state it out loud to see if I myself burst out laughing. Resurrection from the dead, voskresheniye, the raising from the tomb, the resurrection of the body.'

She leaned across the width of the compartment and adjusted the scarf on Doctor Tesla's neck.

'It seems I troubled you unnecessarily, sir, I should have informed the provodnik and had them put Nikola's body in a coffin, not have it desecrated in trunks, I'm sorry, I know my conduct is blameworthy, you see, I'm no longer crying, I am sorry. None of it makes sense.' She stood up. 'If you'll allow me, sir –'

'Are you showing me the door? I'm in no hurry to go anywhere.'

Sit down comfortably on a chair.

'What do we need for resurrection to happen? Not a corpse. You will sit yourself down, I shall tell it out loud, and you will note whether it makes sense to torment ourselves with the trunk. Ye-es. For resurrection to happen – not a corpse. Needed is a living body and the memory of at least one witness that the living man had at one time been a corpse.

'Because, you see, there is only the present: the present Benedykt Gierosławski, the present Christine Filipov, present cigarette, present train, present body of Nikola Tesla. Their pasts and futures – these are frozen to the present in a variety of possible manifestations. For yesterday's Christine Filipov exists not, and neither does tomorrow's Christine Filipov.

'But: our minds belong also to the present, as do their notions of the future and their memory of the past. Because it's so hard, however, to catch memory in the act of lying, and because any notion of the morrow is always subject to strict verification, we regard memory as certain, and as likewise certain the past imprinted in memory. But, Christine, this is a delusion of the present-day mind! Has it never befallen you that you remembered some past event clearly and distinctly, yet other witnesses remembered it completely differently? Were they lying? Nothing of the kind. A million roads lead to the present, and a million roads run out of it. Do you play chess? How often does it happen that, having glanced at the pieces on the chessboard, you know with total certainty what the arrangement was a move earlier and what it will be – a move later? How often is it possible to reconstruct from the current layout a single, exclusive former layout?

'How rare are moments in the dominions of Summer when what is possible tallies completely with what is necessary!

'Mr Zeytsoff would avail himself of surer knowledge, but we all know the stories of biblical resurrections. How did Jesus raise from the dead? One of the rulers of the synagogue comes wringing his hands to Jesus and kisses his garment, Master, my little daughter lieth at the point of death, dying in the house, my family bewails the maid cut down before she bloomed, but I believe it be in thy power to restore her from the dead, should thou but wish it, should it be thy will? Jesus goes to the dead girl's house, amongst the mourners; why do ye weep, he asks – now pay attention, Christine – why do ye weep, for the child is dead, they say, and they all know that she is dead. But no, says Jesus, she is not dead, but sleepeth. And he entereth in where the damsel lies, leans over her, Maid, I say unto thee, arise, he whispers. And the maid arises. Imagine the family's amazement. He had raised her from the dead! What had he done! A miracle! From the jaws of death, he tore a maid already sunken into death: she was dead and now she lives. But no, Jesus says – now she lives, but before she was only sleeping. But tell it to no man, I charge you. You remember it wrongly; behold you have her before you breathing. Do you understand, miss? What He did – could He change the past, when there is no past? For in the end there is only the deceptive memory of witnesses. What counts is the present state – only the present daughter of Jairus exists – whilst the past freezes in our eyes in the way we can most easily embrace it with our reason, the easiest of all possible pasts. "She was only sleeping".

The Express jerked, ending the application of the breaks, and the body of Nikola Tesla slipped off the bed together with the counterpane. Grasp it in both hands, dropping the cigarette end on the carpet. The door opened; Mr Fogel thrust in his silver head. 'We have a trunk, I am going to fetch Oleg.' The Novonikolayevsk station building and a row of goods wagons on a siding drifted past outside the window.

Mademoiselle Filipov blew her nose.

'*What* you say, sir – I believe not, neither do I understand it. But *how* you say it – Mr Gierosławski – he used to speak in that same manner,' she switched again to English, 'or is my memory playing tricks on me, so I could hear him once more, his manner of speaking, his manner of thinking, exactly the same – this I trust.'

'Where is that trunk?'

There then followed the next instalment of the deathly comedy or battle in the confined space of a Deluxe Trans-Siberian Express carriage with a lifeless, torpid corpse. For as soon as the train came to a halt, a commotion arose in the corridor and in the passageways; the compartment door had to be kept closed and casual busybodies listened out for. The trunk purloined or redeemed by Pavel Vladimirovitch (perhaps simply a trunk emptied of the luggage of the dead okhrannik) was waiting in the compartment to the right; when Fogel returned with Oleg, they transferred the empty box to Tesla's compartment, thereby blocking the corridor for a good minute, as it transpired in the course of the operation that even a double *compartiment* could not accommodate a large travelling chest, four living people and one corpse – Mademoiselle Filipov was therefore the first to excuse herself and escape onto the stone- and gravel-strewn platform at Novonikolayevsk (formerly the Ob Resettlement Camp). The remaining threesome set about packing Nikola Tesla into the trunk. The window looking onto the single-storey station building also had to be shut and covered, since by now, prompted by the arrival of the Transsib, half the one-horse town had gathered, and a veritable fairground hubbub prevailed; both station doors stood wide open under their steep pediments, clerks and other parasites sat at low windows, whilst hawkers and postal agents bustled about on the platform and between the tracks, as well as indigenes with Asiatic faces in European dress or leather tribal costumes; meanwhile, in a small garden to the right behind a white painted fence, semi-wild mongrel dogs were yammering, drowning out even the dreadful clunks of a rusty draisine that was trundling along the other track with a troika of railway officials on board dressed in ceremonial uniform. In addition, the locomotive had not calmed down in the least or fallen silent; whistling, wheezing and shrilling, steel against steel, it jolted the whole train time and again for some reason, an inch forward, an inch back, but it was enough to make a gawping man lose balance and fall onto the trunk and into the arms of the corpse, face downwards. Close the window. The shindy on the station died down, whereas in the compartment it grew instantly hot, unbearably stuffy and sultry. The inventor's body had not yet begun to smell, praise God. But it didn't take much for Oleg – being of corpulent build – to at once start panting; his visage turned pale, beads of sweat appeared on the muscular forehead, and already his eyes were rolling upwards and revealing the whites, as his knees buckled under him – he let go of the trunk lid, the carriage jerked, Oleg had fainted. But because he'd let go of the lid, he fell luckily not onto the corpse but onto the trunk. The okhrannik had to be revived. Time was running out. Reopen the window without drawing back the curtains. Again, the sobakas were howling, the steam engine roaring, people shouting. Mr Fogel was endeavouring to flip Oleg onto his back so he could slap his face, but the task proved beyond the strength of the silver-haired policeman;

except that Oleg rolled over at an angle on the convex lid, legs splayed to either side, his bonce struck the tabletop, and shag spilled from his pockets along with copper and silver coins. Seize Oleg by the collar. His hands dropped to the carpet, his legs were splayed even further; so now, on the iron-shod coffin of Nikola Tesla, were piled the okrannik's enormous buttocks, left hemisphere, right hemisphere, water balloons straining the black cheviot cloth; with every shudder of the train, successive waves and convulsions passed over them, and when Pavel Vladimirovitch Fogel, irritated beyond human patience, took to slapping them, striking rhythmically first the left hemisphere, then the right hemisphere, Oleg Ivanovitch gradually regained consciousness, bouncing up and down unbecomingly on that trunk, whacking it and battering the furniture in the compartment until he'd gouged long marks in the wardrobe door, smashed the ashtray knocked onto the floor, whacking, whacking like a man possessed. 'Enough to waken the dead!' Fogel cried in righteous indignation, brandishing his right arm above his head. Impossible not to laugh at the whole scene.

Lug the trunk the length of the Transsib along the gravel platform; willing porters appeared at once – dismiss them with a curse. The revived Oleg hoisted the chest at the front, old Fogel assisted from the rear. Mademoiselle Filipov hurried ahead to warn Stepan. Keeping in step with them was tricky, the trunk rocked dangerously; feel Tesla's body tossing and turning inside, the long limbs and birdlike head. The burden had to be transported as soon as possible before one of the passengers, some acquaintance from the Deluxe carriages, caught on; trip with mincing steps, half-running. Precisely such haste – on the other hand – could give everything away.

As if the Ob River were the natural boundary of the weather front, the sky over Novonikolayevsk suddenly lost its gloomy leaden hue and filled with dazzling sunshine, releasing onto the station, onto its white building, white fence, white gravel, white sand – an avalanche of blinding light. There were points, directions of looking, where whiteness multiplied by whiteness burned out all colour, shape and scale from an image. Espy then in that infinite depth, holes in the fabric of material reality, nubs of torrid nothingness – here, here, there, linked by webs of reflections, by threads of sunlight – above the station roof, beyond the garden, in the clouds over Novonikolayevsk, on the carriage windowpane, in the vista of the railway line. Chmookhh, chmookhh, chmooff, thus the solid mass of a locomotive moving slowly along the siding loomed out of white nothingness. Narrow the eyes, gaze straight at it beside the shoulder of the panting Oleg – first its solid mass, then, after a slight delay, sucked into the whiteness, long coldiron rainbows, arches and bubbles of flickering colour enveloping the steam engine like the sails of a four-mast galleon bellied out by the wind; and the more the parovoz distanced itself from the solar hole, the more it was overlain by iridescent rainbows, until it drew level with the last carriage of the Transsib and then unfurled its full rigging of watercolour wraiths, ten, twenty, thirty metres above its chimney, and in equally widespread wings either side: a heavy coal-powered machine in the full glory of dazzling butterfly lights. This was a locomotive forged wholly of cold-iron. A locomotive designed wholly for coldiron: not a copy of old engines but a truly new engine. Gaze for the first time upon the technology of the epoch of the Ice on such a scale. Its aesthetics had been foreshadowed by the Grossmeister – but this was no simple tool which could be held in the hand; this was a *locomotive*. Paper-thin wheels with spidery spokes revolved on either side of the black caterpillar, every one twice the height of the caterpillar; the engine's roof, curved like an insect's scaly abdomen, appeared to hang on the axles of those wheels. The chimney sprouted not from the middle of the black grub's brow – but unwound parabolically out of its left temple, the beast's sole surviving horn. Grey smoke flared from it, beginning at two-thirds of its height, shooting up not in a single trail, but fanning out in a broad banner beyond the chimney-shaft. The engine's asymmetry was visible in every element, even the windows were drawn aslant its face so that they resembled the single squint-eye of a wolf; one moment the panes were reflecting back bright reflections, the next they appeared totally transparent, only to cloud over in the blinking of an eye with inky blots, and a blinking later – with kaleidoscopes of colour. This had to be that renowned ice-epoch glass seen in Warsaw only as an exclusive adornment, that frostoglaze: impossible to break, possible only to melt. The lanterns were two, the right-hand one larger and higher-placed. The tongue of the deflector protruded over the track a good three arshins ahead of the kholodvoz, an openwork *traîne* preceding the armoured bride. Above the snake-coiled deflector, above lanterns and windows, the double-headed Romanoff eagle gleamed icily. Meanwhile, on the starboard side, on a shield shaped like a pectoral fin, beyond a curved ladder and a door into the driver's cabin that resembled fish gills, on the black scaling, in bone-coloured paint, were inscribed the number and name of the engine:

В-Сиб 5Х-3 паровозъ "Чёрный Соболь"

'What is it?'

'They are reattaching us; from the Ob onwards, the Transsib is serviced by Baikal locomotives,' replied Fogel. 'Ooph, better get a move on, Venyedikt Filipovitch.'

'So now you're trying to frighten me? A Lyednyak agent is going to shoot me in full view of everyone?'

'In full view of everyone, ooph, no, he won't, but – yes, we are in full view of everyone!'

It was true, the arrival of the Black Sable had attracted about a hundred passengers onto this side of the train; whoever had not alighted was sticking their head out of a window. Happily, the last second-class sleeper had already been passed. Glance over the shoulder. One man on the platform was not looking at the coldiron parovoz: a lean, upright figure in a fez, cane in hand. In response to a glance, Ünal Tayyib Fessar saluted with his cigar.

Thrust the trunk inside the wagon with Stepan's help. Fogel was last to climb in. Bolt the door after him and brush the dirt off the hands.

Having swung around, fall under the silent gaze of the agents and of Mademoiselle Filipov.

'Yes?'

Christine folded her arms over her chest.

'We are waiting.'

Refrain, with difficulty, from biting the nails.

'All right. You, Pavel Vladimirovitch, Oleg Ivanovitch, take him out and lay him over here. And you, Stepan, I shall ask you to open that chest where Doctor Tesla keeps the machine that he was working on yesterday morning when I visited you here. I also need the cable for it. And any construction diagrams… ah, well, that's what I thought. Which chest is it?'

'This one.'

'You have keys to the padlocks?'

'To these? Nah. But the doctor never opened them either. Here, look, see, he drilled holes, like wood knots, then stopped them with rubber bungs. He came every day and stuck these wires in and let that stuff into himself, tphoo, I'm telling your lordship, I knew this were how it would end, and I implored him, but what can you do, what can you do, you have to obey authority, and so I watched the man poison himself with this diabolical filth – what does your lordship intend to do?'

'Attach him to the filth. How is it switched on?'

Prise the stoppers out of the wooden boards. Stepan dragged a serviceman's grip from under a straw mattress and drew out a bunch of keys. He took a moment to sift through them, glancing about suspiciously. Wait. Mademoiselle Filipov moaned, urging him to hurry. Heaving a sigh, Stepan opened the chest with the salt jars and extracted the cables. The one with the vice at the end (the okhrannik pressed its jaws into the crystals) and the one with the barrel – but which was to go in on the right-hand side, and which on the left? Memory prompted now one image, now the reverse. Stare inquiringly at the old agent. He stepped aside, shielding his face with the bunch of keys.

'And so?' Miss Filipov urged. 'What now? Have you any idea what you're doing?'

Stand holding the cables before the sealed chest with its printed label *Tesla Tungetitum Company*.

'Well, either way, it will be resurrection *à l'improviste*.' Insert the cables into the apertures and mechanical sockets concealed behind the apertures. 'Fifty-fifty. How is it switched on?' Feel already, however, the shudder of the stirring mechanism; showers of dust and shavings poured off the chest. The main switch had to be located in one of these sockets. No smoke was visible. What powered this generator? Did it remain connected to an external source of electricity? Comparison of its dimensions with the three large flow-generators taking up most of the wagon showed that it was more a kind of miniature prototype.

Spit into the palm, then place it on the trigger, onto the naked barrel.

… Drop to the floor.

'Good.' Slide onto the floorboards, brushing the jacket against the rough timber of the chest. 'Good. Please could someone… Better I do it. In a moment.'

'You've done it again!' cried Miss Filipov. 'Fallen into the same bad habit as Nikola! My God, why did you throw him into the trunk, why tussle with his remains, to think that I could have believed you, that you, sir, could have – that what they say of you – a "lying bastard" – is all true!'

'It cannot all be true.' Mutter, raising the hand before the eyes. Black flecks flickered on the surface of the skin, or maybe just below the epidermis; sometimes, when the limb goes numb, white-and-pink mandalas form inside the palm, but it looked now as if living corpuscles of shadow and living corpuscles of glintz were warring there. Stare with the left eye, stare with the right eye. Semi-darkness prevailed inside the wagon; light fell through small grated windows, partially obscured anyway by stacks of crates. Millions of dust particles were rising in the air, all swirling and shimmering gold, and all casting their shadows; it was unbelievable, yet they could be seen with clinical accuracy, each one separately, black flecks, white flecks, golden flecks; the whole interior of the wagon was broken into kaleidoscopic splinters of colour. A kaleidoscope, yes, that's the right association – because they go on spinning, remain in cosmic motion, so it wouldn't have taken much for them to spring into a totally different configuration and hey presto, there'd no longer be a wagon, no longer be wooden boards, no longer people, no longer a corpse.

No longer a corpse. Look up. The three Okhrana agents stood

around about with solemn countenances, Oleg with a yellow handkerchief in his fist, Stepan with the keys clutched to his breast, Pavel with a
hand shoved under his jacket, a hand on the butt of the Nagant, iconic
figures, each in his allotted place – Pavel in the middle, Stepan on his
right, Oleg on his left – each attribute – weapon, keys, handkerchief –
each role ordained by God, a trinity of tchinovniks of the tsarist order.

'Glass.' Give instructions. 'Silicon. Stones. As a last resort, metal.
Find something that we can lay underneath him.'

'What for?' Christine snorted.

'For insulation. Otherwise murch will seep out of the wooden
boards, come up out of the floor. I am about to stand up. Someone keep
a check on the time, please, we have to return to Deluxe ten minutes
before departure. Undo his waistcoat and shirt over his breast. Is there
water here? Anything to drink? What's the matter? I am about to stand
up.'

'You have light in your hair.' Oleg indicated with his handkerchief.
'It's pouring from your eyebrows, Venyedikt Filipovitch.'

'What? Hoar?'

'Lights, little sparks, fireflies.'

Run a hand over the head. Bright glintzen formed around the closed
fist, over the knuckles and between fingers. Press the eyelids tightly shut.
Blinding red burst beneath them. Jerk the head backwards, banging the
occiput against the wood, once, twice, thrice, harder and harder still.
Mademoiselle Filipov came running, grabbed the collar and plucked at
an arm. Stand up awkwardly.

'What on earth are you playing at?' she whispered, clearly terrified.
'What's possessed you?'

Shrug the shoulders.

'I know not. My sincerest apologies. Now it may happen to me that…
Well, it may seem strange. I'm unable to describe it.'

She bit her lip.

'He used to say the same! And then…'

'Then he went to the other machine, yes?'

They laid Tesla on three tin cases, creating a kind of catafalque; his
feet stuck out beyond it, he was too tall, meaning too long. Seize hold
carefully of the insulation and lift the cable. (The bending movement,
however, proved too sudden; the head began to spin.) Place the barrel
on the inventor's exposed breast, press on the coldiron with his open
palm, crooking the corpse's thumb onto the trigger. Make sure the
mechanism is fully cocked, and withdraw to the chests.

The sealed flow-generator was running with a low whirr. The
Kotarbiński pump was drawing the teslectricity out of Nikola's body
and into the jar of salt crystals.

'He repeated it every day, did he not? Christine?'

With difficulty, she tore her eyes from Nikola.

'Yes.'

'In the morning he would demurch himself and in the afternoon bemurch.'

'Yes, I think so. Are you trying now to do it – the other way around? To draw out of him what he injected? Yes?'

'Dead men are not restored to life by removing a bullet. You can't cure someone who's already dead.'

The three okhranniks stood over the doctor's mortal remains, looking on in silence. Oleg continued to clasp his handkerchief (occasionally mopping his brow), Stepan to rotate the keys in his fingers, Pavel to mechanically hold his hand under the flap of his jacket.

'Did he ever tell you, miss, why he did it?' Ask softly. 'Especially now, on this journey, he must have been conspicuous. The teslectric dynamo he had to hand in the compartment, but he would come here to the pump, to the arsenal. That was why you were so upset, yes? He could no longer conceal it like he'd concealed it in his own laboratory. Tell me, please. Did he ever explain it? Why like this? One thing for breakfast, the other for dinner.'

'Before the Urals, when I noticed it was stronger than he, we quarrelled and...', she broke off. 'He called it, *pardon pour le mot*, an enema for the mind. He said that the best ideas occur to him before midday. And then he jots them down. And that he must... must... must...'

She choked on a dry sob. Feel again the urge to embrace her, comfort, console – but she quickly retreated into a corner behind the large cylinder of the flow-generator, burying her face in her handkerchief. The okhranniks, after all, were watching.

Tesla's body appeared to be just as dead as a minute before, more dead even than on its bed in the Deluxe carriage, because now, with palm pressed against naked breast, it was resting in a distinctly unnatural mannequin-like pose on the tin catafalque, as if modelled within a casket by an embalmer.

Approach, stand over Tesla. Is it an optical illusion, or are those in fact sparks of shadow – murchflies – collecting already on Tesla's eyelashes? Pass a hand above his face. Should an organism grow warmer after murch is pumped out, since an immurched object undergoes cooling?

Oleg wheezed protractedly, wiping his forehead and fanning himself with the handkerchief; again, the unwholesome pallor of his visage was visible.

'Stand back.' Give them orders. 'Don't look.'

'What? Why?'

'This is not a public matter. Such things are performed under cover of darkness, in silence, underground, behind a rock, when no one is watching.' When no one is watching – think: when there's no continuity between past and present; behind the veil of Maybe. Only in Winter, only at the very heart of the Ice, within the solid masses of icecradles; only there does there exist solely that which exists, and not exist solely that which exists not. 'Get out.'

The trinity of okhranniks glanced at one another.

'Get out! Have a smoke, stretch your legs, I'll summon you. Well, get going!'

Mr Fogel nodded and grabbed the door bolt. Sunlight poured into the wagon. Retreat into shadow. They departed slowly, looking over their shoulders, Stepan last. They left the door open a hand's width, a crack allowing torrents of warm radiance to stream into the cellar-like semi-dark.

Walk across to the corner behind the flow-generator, to Mademoiselle Filipov. She was sitting on an iron crate with a plaid rug thrown over it, resting her temple against the casing of the generator.

Crouch on the next chest.

'Have you considered the possibility, Christine' – ask without pre-amble – 'that it only looks like an accident, that it was meant to look like an accident?'

At first, she comprehended not; comprehending, she tightened her lips.

'I saw it with my own eyes. He alone did it with that infernal machine.'

'Think, please. He it was who designed these mechanisms, he who built them, no one knows them better than he. He'd been applying them to himself for months, if not years. Like with the electric dynamos earlier on – he was passing thunderbolts through himself; you told me yourself, miss, he held lightning shafts in his hands, illuminated light-bulbs with his touch, conducted destructive forces through soil, air and flesh, never suffering as a result of his own mistake or miscalculation. So why now? When a Lyednyak assassin lies in wait and tsarist agents have to guard him round the clock. Pure chance?'

'I saw!'

'What you saw, miss, was the final effect. Would Nikola have known at once if someone had crept into the compartment in your absence and switched over the power calibrator in the mechanism of the dynamo-machine, some cog increasing the pressure of the teslec-tric flow? Almost anything proves lethal when administered in too large a dose.'

'We can check! Look inside the dynamo!'

Shake the head.

'Now? When we left it unattended in an open cupboard, an open sac? Did you lock the compartment?'

'But who could have done it? Who knew at all about Nikola's habits!'

'Who indeed?'

Mademoiselle Filipov opened wide her eyes.

'You, sir!'

'True. Who else?'

'No one! Only you! I told no one but you!'

'And the okhranniks? And Doctor Tesla himself – who else did he speak to? And the people from the Prague laboratory – might not Lyednyaks have paid a visit there? Moreover, how do you know that I have not told someone in turn?'

'Have you?'

'That's not what it's about.' Rub the moustache in irritation. 'You are not listening. It's not about how it was and how it was not, but how it *could have been*. You see, the sun is shining, it is summer, the sky is blue, we are still standing in Novonikolayevsk, the Ice lies far beyond the horizon.'

She sniffed, blew into her handkerchief, which she'd screwed into a rag.

'I fail to understand what you're aiming at, Benedykt.'

'I implore you for a moment's attention. How the situation looks now: there's no way of ascertaining whether Nikola Tesla perished in an accident, or whether he was murdered. All circumstances fit both pasts. Even Doctor Tesla would be unable to judge which one was true. They have killed him and not killed him. It is in your power, Christine, which history shall freeze: murder or accident.'

Something began to sink in. Against her will, she leaned forward, lowering her voice.

'You wish me to spread the word that he was killed?'

'Spreading the word is out of the question for the time being, but, yes, such a past would, mm-hmm, be wiser.'

'I am to lie?'

'Nothing of the kind! Lie? Why no! One is true and the other is true, or at least both are true to the same extent. You say "A" – you will tell the truth; you say "not-A" – and you will also tell the truth.' Button up the jacket, cross one leg over the other. 'So how shall it be? Meaning, how was it?'

'But – why?'

'Why would murder be wiser for you? Is it not obvious, considering the doctor's contract with the tsar and his obligations, which on arrival in Irkutsk –'

'Why is it so important to you, sir?' Christine frowned. 'What will you profit by it, when they say that…' She audibly drew in air, covering her mouth with the handkerchief. 'Father Frost! What they were saying at breakfast about your father – that you're travelling to negotiate the fate of Russia with gleissen – that –'

The sound of spitting and a loud cough interrupted her mid-thought. Peer out from behind the flow-generator. Doctor Tesla was sitting on the tin cases, one hand massaging his chest, the other raising to his mouth the beaker of water prepared by Oleg.

'Christine,' instruct quietly, 'you won't scream or do anything foolish –'

She leapt to her feet. Catching sight of Nikola, she uttered a long, drawn-out moan. Tesla raised his head, smiled. She fell upon him, almost knocking the beaker out of his hand; he clasped her to him, hugged her, kissed her hand. Mademoiselle Filipov again burst into tears. Tesla stared at the young woman, confused. Step across to the door, slide back the bolt. Pavel Vladimirovitch was standing barely a few feet away; he glanced around at once. Nod to him. He stamped on his cigarette butt, then summoned Oleg and Stepan.

Unfasten both cables from the pump; the machine sneezed, whistled, wheezed and fell silent. Stuff the bungs back into the boards of the casing, wind up the leads, arrange them in the chest with the jars. A lump of salt in the clamping ring of the coldiron barrel was black as coal. Wipe the hands on the trousers – cold moisture had collected on the cables despite the thick insulation.

The agents stood around Tesla; their helplessly drooping arms and flabby, buttery countenances said all that was to be said.

Tesla drank up the rest of the water.

'My throat's gone dry,' he croaked.

He squinted deep into the beaker and chuckled flutily. It made a nightmarish impression: Nikola Tesla does not conduct himself in this way.

'I know not,' said Pavel.

'He breathes,' said Stepan.

'He lives,' said Oleg.

Tesla stood the beaker gently on the tin surface. Christine Filipov sat on his knees. He whispered something in her ear. She played with the buttons as she did up the old man's shirt.

'We shall have to write a report,' said Pavel.

'Because he lives, yet ceased to live,' said Stepan.

'Because he lives,' said Oleg.

'I checked his pulse. He had no pulse. He was not breathing.'

'You could have made a mistake.'

'You are not a physician.'

'You were upset.'
'I was, that's true, I was.'
'He lives.'
Laugh neath the moustache. They watched. Spread wide the arms.
'He was only sleeping.'

On the necessity of controlling History by hand

A heraldic symbol of a tiger clutching in its jaws an animal similar to a weasel was engraved on the silver lid of his cigarette case.

'The Ussuriysk tiger,' said Porfiry Pocięgło, offering a cigarette. 'It's supposed to have lived at one time in the vicinity of Irkutsk; Buryat hunters retell the tales of their grandfathers' grandfathers. And the Siberian sable; the first fortunes were made trading in its skins.'

'It's the seal of your house?'

Pocięgło burst out laughing.

'The coat of arms of Irkutsk, my dear man, the coat of arms of Irkutsk! The tiger and sable.'

'You, sir, so I understand, are a Sybirak by birth, your father came to Baikal – when? after the January Uprising?'

He took out his visiting card. It was printed in Cyrillic with addresses in Irkutsk and Saint Petersburg and proclaimed Pocięgło P.D. to be Director of the Siberian Metallurgical and Mining Company Kossowski and Boulangier, neath the twin crests of Irtkutsk and Sibirkhozheto.

Light a cigarette. Mr Pocięgło nodded to the steward to open a window in the saloon car. The maltchik began tussling with the shiny mechanism of the ceiling skylight. Pocięgło sighed and pointed towards the front of the train. Shrug the shoulders. As on every evening, at least half the Deluxe passengers were gathered in the smoking room and by the billiard table; in such circumstances, it was hard to talk at any length in private, someone would immediately latch on, interlocutors coming together and dispersing, rebounding off one another like – like billiard balls. And Jelena Muklanowicz had to be given at least half an hour. She had already left, given her signal and left.

Move to the parlour car. Encounter there, in turn, Frau Blutfeld; she shone in such company, hooked on the arm of the tall prosecutor, without abandoning the upright piano, where Monsieur Verousse was rapping out mournful melodies and making eyes all the while at the black-haired widow. Gertrud Blutfeld, my God, out of the frying pan and into the fire. Had she noticed? She had not noticed. Pull Porfiry as quickly as possible into the gallery. Breathe more deeply only once its door had been closed. The industrialist looked on in amusement.

'Social claustrophobia,' announce with a sour smile. Look around. No one, only Zeytsoff snoring quietly on a stool in the corner. The twin glass panels on either side of the iron dividing-wall before the observation platform stood ajar; wind swept in unconstrained. Stop by the iron wall itself, still before the torrential onrush but already in the movement of fresh, cool air; the puffed-out smoke swirled within it in spirals and cockades. Staring from here, with the eye right up against the glass, it was possible to see ahead – on the flanks of the speeding Express, against the backdrop of the taiga's washed-out greens and yellows, neath a long banner of smoke – the coloured wings of coldiron Auroras whipping arshins and arshins high off the icy body of the Black Sable (which itself was invisible).

Tuck the little card into the pocket.

'I am impressed. The Siberian Coldiron Industrial Company has shaken my right hand, I will show it to my grandchildren.'

Pocięgło burst into laughter for a second time; he laughed naturally and with great ease, prompting the desire to laugh with him.

'Ours is but one voice on the Sibirkhozheto board. I don't make a habit of drinking vodka with Pobedonostseff, if that's what you were imagining. Besides, in the Metallurgical and Mining Company itself, I own only minority shares. But it's typical you made the assumption in advance that I'm either an exile myself, or that my parent was exiled. I have never set foot in the former Kingdom – does everyone there really have such an image of Siberia?'

'Well, things have changed a bit following the coldiron boom, I know that many people leave to make money...'

'Even now,' Pocięgło glanced around for an ashtray and flicked cigarette ash out of the window, 'even now you say it, sir, in such a tone...'

'What tone?'

'As if there were something unseemly about it. But please, don't pull a face, yes, yes, I've already heard about your father, exiled for anti-tsarist misdeeds, le Père du Gel, how could I not hear; so, just imagine, sir, what strange emotions this arouses amongst exiles themselves. We try to hire them first and foremost, men with sentences of forced settlement or deportation, who on release don't receive permission to return to Poland – which is always at the beginning, mm-hmm, awkward.'

'If the whole of Siberia is a prison for Poles, who are those growing fat on this prison?'

His look was grave.

'And who are those that were born in the prison? Listen, my father was an engineer, brought to Irkutsk by Sawicki at the time of the goldrush; it had to do with graphite boilers, some Frenchman had discovered seams of graphite there and so Sawicki's gold-bearing fields on the Angara became twice as valuable. Father then brought his betrothed from the Annexed Lands; they were married here, that is, in Irkutsk, in Father Szwernicki's church. In eighteen seventy-nine the church burned down, and five years later a brick basilica was erected on its site, dedicated to the Assumption of the Blessed Virgin Mary, thanks to the efforts and fortune of Michał Kossowski; in this church I was baptised, Kossowski himself held me in his arms. When the great Russian railway projects got off the ground, the Transsib and the Chinese Eastern Railway, a second life began for the Baikal Country; Kossowski and Edgar Boulangier founded their Company, a worldwide concern with headquarters in Saint Petersburg and branches in Irkutsk, Tomsk and Paris. Despite the Company's name, it's also involved in commerce, and builds river ports. At first, it indeed profited mainly from mining, from copper and nickel extraction. Everything changed with the arrival of the Ice. I worked in the beginning for the Butiny brothers when they moved from Nikolayevsk to Irkutsk. But after the first Frost, we set up our own company. And when the tsar issued an ukase on monopolies and Pobedonostseff established Sibirkhozheto, that Company made lavish offers to many firms like ours. We agreed. Mr Kossowski was no longer alive, Boulangier had died already in the last century. I joined the board of directors and we set up our Company headquarters in Zimny Nikolayevsk. Since nineteen thirteen we have increased our turnover more than tenfold. At this moment, Mr Gierosławski, six point three per cent of global exports of coldiron goes through the Metallurgical and Mining Company. We hold the patents on sixteen coolbonds of coldiron, including the nickel coolbond, the Tomsk number one. And on tungetitum conductors. And you speak to me of prisons? Of escaping? Of killing guards perhaps?' Mr Porfiry Pocięgło screwed his hand into a bony fist and, no, did not brandish it, but held it before the eyes in a stony gesture, one second, two seconds, a long moment of silent immobility under the sign of a punch, and only then snapped with wolfish joy: 'We shall buy up that prison!'

'*Autres temps, autres moeurs,* if it's possible now to simply buy such things, then indeed, it's clearly not worth fighting for them. And all the more so, dying for them.'

'Oh! It's as if I hear those people! Lucre, Satan's doing, we must reject him and all his works!' The coldindustrialist burst out laughing, a smidgeon of his irony already aimed at himself. He flung the cigarette out of the window, took out the next. Sunlight flashed in the tiger's eye on the silver case. Mr Pocięgło rotated it this way and that, catching glints of light, his own reflection, a reflection of the gallery interior. He raised

his eyes. 'At the prince's table, I somehow failed to notice it, but now –
you, sir, are one of us! A gleissenik if ever there was!'

Wave this aside in irritation.

'An optical illusion.'

'You don't say!'

'An optical illusion, Porfiry, sir! In reality, it's precisely the reverse –'

'A pox on your illusions! Stand here in the sunlight. And now look at
yourself, oh, a born gleissenik, even your eyes, oh, even your eyes don't
flee from the sun, the pupils aren't –'

The ballroom door opened, piano sounds and a babble of female
voices floated in; turn on the heels with the back to the Sun.

In the doorway stood Ünal Tayyib Fessar in a fez tilted at a rakish
angle, a half-empty glass in his hand.

'Here!' he shouted. 'Ah, here's where he's given me the slip, the honourable Mr Frost, the lost innocent – if you've never seen a guiltless
mug, then take a look – is he not the shining angel? – *piç* – *sherrefseez*
– allow me to embrace the poor mite – come to the arms of the bloody
cutthroat!'

He was drunk. He tripped on the threshold. From under the fez, a
white strip of bandage peeped out, and from under the bandage – a red
gash. The train was not rocking unduly at that moment, yet the Turk
walked like a sailor aboard a ship tossed by a squall: striding with feet
wide apart, on bowed legs, his torso thrust forward, hand and glass
extended far to the side as his additional centre of balance. A fresh stain
was visible on his sky-blue frock coat.

'He knows nothing! Has heard of nothing!' he cried. 'Oh, the holy
fool knows not Kossowski and Boulangier either, no indeed – is not
conveying ice machines here in a sealed carriage – who would have
suspected him of collusion with the secret police, with the prince, with
God knows whom – he knows no one, knows nothing, nothing!'

The symmetrical silhouette of Doctor Konyeshin appeared in the
doorway behind Fessar's shoulders. He was making signs: helpless,
angry, warning, helpless.

Pocięgło stepped up briskly, took the glass from the Turk's hand and
hurled it through the window; a stream of alcohol splashed against the
half-open pane.

'You're beginning again!' he barked. 'Must you get so hammered?'

Fessar's jaws gaped open in something akin to a smile.

'At home under the gleissen, a man won't get drunk like this, he has
to make the most of it whilst he can.' Fessar snapped his jowls together
like a wooden knocker. 'Then I shall apologise, ah yes, apologise in
abject fashion.' Here he actually doubled up in a genuine Russian bow,
head to the ground, that is, to the floor, to the smooth parquet, and

because he at once lost balance in that grotesque parting of his legs, he steadied himself with an arm, raising the other – similarly straightened – behind his back. 'But in the meantime, agh, in the meantime, drunk as a filthy dog, I can pay my fitting respects to the c-c-c-count, no one has so bamboozled me in business in my entire life, my very deepest respects!' And from his steadied position, bent rigid, he charged forward in a bullish attack, losing the fez, his dishevelled frock coat flapping.

Leap aside with no trouble.

He rammed his mahogany nut into the iron wall, the sound was like a bell clanging. Porfiry shuddered as if struck himself.

'*Rahim Allah,*' Mr Fessar still squealed, then collapsed.

Doctor Konyeshin summoned the stewards. Picked up the fez, brushed it off, leant over the Turk. Felt the skull with his fingers; and having felt it, shrugged his shoulders. The stewards lifted the businessman in a well-practised hold, one on the right, one on the left; a third goes ahead, opens the door, apologises to the passengers. The doctor placed the fez on the Turk's lifelessly lolling head and closed the door behind them.

'He gets alcoholic fits when Allah's not watching,' muttered Mr Pocięgło, 'but, it's true, such excesses never happened to him in the Land of the Gleissen. Does he often –'

'He seemed to me to be a man with feet planted firmly on the ground.' Cast the cigarette stub to the wind.

Pocięgło, yet again, took out his cigarette case. This time he offered it also to the doctor.

'And that?' Porfiry drew a finger around his head. 'From where?'

Smile modestly.

'My doing, not wishing to boast.'

Doctor Konyeshin hiccoughed, amused. Exhaling smoke, he squinted in the glare of the evening sun. Even the wrinkles around his eyelids composed themselves in mirrored formation.

'He wished not to tell me when I asked. Some kind of high financial games, as I see it. You, gentlemen, are competitors, *n'est-ce pas*? Yet here, he sees a Pole hand-in-glove with a Pole... You were promising him something, Benedykt?'

'I? God forbid! He convinced himself.'

'Of what namely?'

'Oh, some moony hogwash. That they'd discovered a method to freely cultivate coldiron and that I knew something about it.'

Mr Pocięgło froze with the half-closed cigarette case in his raised hand.

'And what do you know about it?'

'Oh Christ!' Kick the steel doorframe. 'Another one! It must be some sort of curse! I have no idea! There is nothing to know! I know nothing at all!'

'Holy fool,' muttered the doctor.

Grit the teeth. They were watching attentively now, very discourteously, without averting their gazes for long seconds, not even pretending this was a fleeting exchange of glances like in a conversation, like in company; no, they were staring as if at a bizarre specimen, an exotic animal chased into a corner – what will it do next, what will it surprise them with, how amuse them? hence the curiosity, the hint of a smile, the *soupçon* of sympathy on the countenances stooping over the stupid animal – that whole theatre.

Shame flowed through all organs of the body – a hot sticky phlegm. What words should a liar use in order to overturn his reputation? Ought he to admit that he lies? Even if he is not lying? But neither is he telling the truth – he knows not the truth. The hand was trembling, involuntarily reaching for the interferograph. How to disengage from this? How to become frozen? Lower the eyes, avert the head. Bring on the Ice! The Ice! The Ice!

'Gospodin Yeroslavsky,' said the symmetrical doctor, 'is travelling to his father in Winter, an intimate of gleissen, mind, their trusty dyak from the human race. Are you acquainted, Porfiry Danielyevitch, with the Berdyaevian creed? With the exegeses of Lyednyak and Ottepyelnik mystics? Yesterday we heard from the mouths of Benedykt and that katorzhnik over there, a whole conception of the rule of History through the rule of the icers. You know it? You hail from their city, you must know it. What do you say? Why is Mr Yeroslavsky really travelling to his father?' He put a finger to his lips, emphasising even more the symmetry, since he placed it exactly in the middle. 'As one Pole to another. What were you saying between yourselves? Already on day one, the count, whilst he was still a count, told us clearly his attitude to Russia and the Russian people. If I believed in these Berdyaevian idealisms, should I not... as a loyal subject of His Imperial Exaltedness... be treating you as our captain did?'

Attempt to laugh dismissively; it failed.

'People can believe what they like!' Shout, by now a nervous wreck. 'Either way, it remains arrant nonsense. What Zeytsoff was saying about History – how God communicates with man through History – that from its course, from the succession of its various configurations, it is possible to interpret Divine thought and purpose... Well, this can only be valid if the world is ruled by two-valued logic – if this History really *exists*, that is, if there exists a single and concrete past of our present. For if three-valued logic remains valid for past and future, then there are as many Histories as stars in the sky, more even, a different one for every person, and a different one for that person in different moments of his memory; as changeable as the tsar's designs. And you will read as much sense and order from it as you will from the autocrat's successive ukases, that is, nothing at all, since such History is ruled by random association, nightmare, nocturnal terror.'

'Yet you say, sir, that in the Land of the Gleissen –'

'Yes.'

'That the Ice –'

'Yes. The past must freeze, then it becomes History.' Raise the eyes. The others were staring through grey smoke, their facial features smeared by red sunlight; they dissolved into pink jelly. Step aside towards the lowered panel, enter the wind. A breath in, a breath out, a breath in. 'It must freeze. There is as much History as there is Ice.'

'Whilst your father – your father converses with gleissen.'

'So they say.'

'And yet you still fail to grasp what position this puts you in?' Doctor Konyeshin glanced at Pocięgło as if seeking a witness to the unbelievable obtuseness of his interlocutor. 'It doesn't matter how much of this is true; what's important is that they firmly believe in it – Lyednyaks, Ottepyelniks, defenders of the old order, as well as anarchists, socialists –'

'Well, I don't suppose hardened Marxists will fret over me: they believe History is on their side anyway; the only thing is not to stand in its way, and it will do its own thing. Why should they through Father Frost –'

'And you think, sir, that amongst Russian Marxists, there are none that believe at the same time in Berdyaeff's theories? Yet these are the staunchest Ottepyelniks, beware their sort, they will do anything to destroy the Ice and drive out the gleissen. It's a wonder you ever left Warsaw!'

'Evidently, I was protected. As I now recall...' Pull a wry face. 'Well, but now I can recall whatever suits me.'

'You will go, and whisper a word in your father's ear... A Pole! Son of an anti-tsarist conspirator! It might suit the purpose of some Ottepyelniks – but Lyednyaks! That you should still walk amongst the living! A miracle, no less!' The symmetrical doctor, no longer with any trace of amusement, instead distinctly ruffled, was puffing thick smoke and tugging at his whiskers, now a fiery red. 'How do you imagine it – after all, here in the train they all know and they will all know there on the spot, in Irkutsk, as soon as you set foot on the soil of the Ice; half are disembarking there. They will give you no peace!'

'Why worry so much about me, at most they'll stab me to death in some dark alley, what's it to you?'

'Ah yes, they already tried before, in Yekaterinburg. My dear young fellow, you are riding to your death!'

Mr Pocięgło flicked ash mechanically out of the window. Lost in contemplation, he pressed a knuckle against the sharp rim of his eye socket; the eyelid rose above the white which was goggling like a bird's, a glintz flashed beneath his brow.

'Looking at it from the other point of view,' he said, 'since they wish to kill you, then from the other point of view – this is power! Do I understand correctly? You, sir, speak to your father, your father, himself clearly incoherent in thought and will, speaks to gleissen, the gleissen freeze History. War or peace, autocracy or anarchy, Russia or Poland, revolution or no revolution – yes? Benedykt, sir? Is there any mightier power imaginable to man on Earth than the ability to control History?'

THAW TO THE DNIEPER – RUSSIA UNDER THE ICE – THE PARTY ORDERS – SPRING OF NATIONS. Bite the nails.

Porfiry threw out the cigarette stub. Moving one hand over his piqué waistcoat as if searching blindly for a watch or tobacco pouch, he reached across from the sunlit side with his other, embracing and drawing towards him in a gesture of great confidence and cordiality.

'They will come to you, bow from the waist, yes, from the waist, lay at your feet every kind of gift, urge you, offer bribes, implore you, threaten you, yes, they will certainly also threaten, but give too, they will give anything in exchange for the power over History!'

'What are you drooling into his ear!' growled the symmetrical doctor from the other side of the gold-and-carmine deluge. 'What inciting him to! That he should look to his own interest in all this? That – what? he should put History up for auction? A businessman's soul!'

'And you, Doctor,' ask him, 'you know, do you, how History ought to be?'

'Yeh, the Kingdom of Poland from sea to sea, and the Russian Empire reduced to dust,' smirked Doctor Konyeshin.

Shake Porfiry's hand off the shoulder.

'But my question is serious. Berdyaeff believes that the gleissen have distorted the course of History. So, is it enough to push back Winter, and History will be as it should? Or should History in fact be fine-tuned… by hand?'

'If only some means existed,' Doctor Konyeshin mused, closing his eyes and warming his face in the glowing sunlight. 'If only some scientific method existed for recognising what has to be, not what may be, but what ought to be –'

'God's thoughts.'

'What do we still need God for! History is not a communiqué from God – or only to the same extent as constellations in the sky, chemical formulae, or the composition of the intestines and liver in an organism. So, were a scientific method to exist, as exists for diagnosing from the look of the intestines which organism is affected by disease, and which presents a picture of health and biological correctness – were such a method to exist for diagnosing diseased or healthy History, then, yes, you would be able, sir, to straighten out distorted History, that is, cure it; and this would be the sole valid use of the power to rein it in by hand.'

'Our doctor is an atheist,' stated Porfiry Pocięgło, unsurprised.

'That's not what I said. I simply don't need God for anything in History.'

'So, this is why I say: the doctor is an atheist,' Pocięgło repeated.

'Or the Martsynians are right.' Speak slowly, 'and History was already perverted long ago because the world is in the sway of Evil and the true God has yet to come, He who shall heal what is sick in the world, in other words History itself, cure History above all else, He, not people.'

'He?' Porfiry raised an eyebrow. 'You mean the Ice? Gleissen?'

Touch the swollen lip with the tongue.

'In order to look at History as a gleiss does – to be frozen in this way, that is, bemurched, flooded with murch to the point where the rock-hard Frost –'

'With – what?'

'Not that which is possible, but that which has to be – which is being done – the truth –'

'Are you feeling all right?' Pocięgło drew near again, leant over, moved his mouth close to the ear. 'You are standing in the sunlight,' he whispered. 'Careful, for the doctor too will notice eventually, you burn with unlicht like an old coldmill hand.'

'Be gone!' Shriek out. 'Get lost! Tempters! I will not lie!'

Shove aside Porfiry and leap towards the iron dividing-wall. Fall out onto the observation platform, slam the door and press the back into the cold metal. Were they trying to bang on the door, force it open? Feel it not at all, even if they were. All sounds from the carriage interior remained behind that sluice gate; whereas outside, there was only the roar of the Black Sable, whistle of the wind and hypnotic rhythm of coldiron struck by warm steel: dwook-dwook-dwook-DWOOK. Breathe out with a full chest. The rhythm wound its way from the wheels through the suspension and undercarriage, through the walls and doors, and into the flesh, into blood and into bones, and into the skull, driving that locomotive of the brain, which had already been almost forgotten: dwook-dwook-dwook-DWOOK, think-think-think-THINK!

Time to sober up. The acrid smack of terror still stung the tongue and palate (the smack of terror, or perhaps of telestrical flow). Admit for the first time with total conviction the possibility that everything had been true from the beginning: the gleissen freeze History – pater converses with gleissen – the Ministry of Winter wishes to steer the father through the son – steer the gleissen – steer History. Lyednyaks and Ottepyelniks, Poles and Russians, socialists and Martsynians, the Okhrana and the Pilsudtchiks, Tesla and Sibirkhozheto, these and those, those and these, they all try to win over to their own side, and when they fail to win over, they kill so that the son can't be won over to other factions.

This is fear talking – but what sayeth reason? It's time to think with a clear head. A plume of grey smoke was spreading in the sky above the Express – crane the neck and glimpse between carriage and carriage, where a river of smoke could be seen racing across the evening firmament; straight ahead, however, along the full length of the train, auroras and rainbows fuelled by the fires of the setting sun stunned the eyes, as did ghostly arcs of cold colour sparking off the edges of the black locomotive; half the horizon had vanished behind the blaze of these shimmering flares. The Trans-Siberian Express tore through the taiga in a roar of swirling air and thunder of hundreds of tons of steel, yet it seemed as if drawn by a team of butterflies, a great cloud of brightly coloured babotchkas preceding, surrounding and overwhelming the engine itself.

With a clear head. If the Ice is forcing on the world the logic of Aristotle, and History, that is, the continuity of truth between past, present and future, exists solely there under the Ice, whereas the chaos of millions of possible pasts and futures prevails in the three-valued world of Summer – if this be the case, then the gleissen have not perverted History at all: the gleissen are establishing History, the only true one, the only possible one. Whilst everything outside of the Ice – is non-History, another frost delusion on an historic scale.

If, on the other hand, Nikolay Berdyaeff is right and History was being realised in truth before the appearance of the gleissen, and gleissen have frozen it in the most literal sense possible, that is, stopped it in its tracks – if those Lyednyaks and Ottepyelniks are right and Russia's survival in her present form depends on the preservation of the Ice – what implication for History has the difference between the logic of Winter and the logic of Summer? This is no delusion after all. Doctor Tesla has been building machines. He pumps murch. Tungetitum teslectrical fields are changing the nature of light.

... In what way, therefore, is a world based on 'maybe' more valid than a world based on truth? In what way is the History of what exists not, truer than the History of what exists? Uncertainty more certain than certainty. Untruth truer than truth! God on the side of lies! The History of the world like that night-time tale confessed on a train to a stranger by a stranger – God leaning forward in the twilight with a perverse smile, an indistinct shape against the backdrop of the darkness of darknesses – travelling is a magical time – His words refuting His words – History – true or false? true or false...?

It cannot be so!

Spit to one side, wind snatches away the spittle. All hope rests with Nikola Tesla, hope that he lives, that he has ousted death from the present into one of his pasts, that the demurched Tesla-of-many-possibilities will reach Irkutsk, assemble his machines, and pass teslectrical flow through the gleissen; all hope rests with the Serbian genius – he will make History the object of experimental science, connect History to electrodes, switch the points, whee-eee, black shafts of lightning will fire off and we will see whose come out on top.

Step up to the barrier, lean heavily on the balustrade. Sleepers flashed by below the inter-carriage coupling, merging in a geometric wave. Only one more day to go, morning after next: Irkutsk. What to do then? Go to the address given by Preiss, notify the Ministry of Winter, submit to being bait for catching father? But what if some Lyednyak informer, a disciple of Martsyn from Rasputin's faction, what if someone sees and gives the sign? it won't take much in a city like this at the end of the world, where hordes of Chinamen, Siberian savages, erstwhile katorzhniks and all manner of earthly scum throng the streets, it won't take much – a ten-rouble note or flagon of khanshin, no more – for a dagger to be thrust neath the rib; you have your thousand roubles, now go play blizzarder with Iscariot in hell.

Flee perhaps? When? how? Alight at a station before Irkutsk? melt away into Siberia? it's possible, the money saved from the commissioner's pool and won off Fessar would easily suffice; no one asks for papers here, it's possible to live for years beyond the reach of the state, to swap identities with some fugitive or other. Or later acquire a ticket *incognito* in the second-class sleepers to Vladivostock, whence ships sail to all ports of the world – hadn't that been the original plan anyway? – Cape Province, the Antipodes, the West Indies, America.

'Allow me, Venyedikt Filipovitch.'

Standing alongside, Zeytsoff clutched at the rail with his hand of few fingers, as the Express swerved on a slight kink in the track.

'Have they gone?'

'Beg pardon?'

'The doctor and Mr Pocięgło. Did they wake you?'

'Don't know... yes... I only...' But why is he so confused again, why clutching at his beard, scratching at his matted black hair, why crushing and crumpling again the material of his suit, leaving oily streaks? 'Allow me to...'

'Well, Filimon Romanovitch, you've been harkening to inanity upon inanity, a rare occurence.'

'I... I believe they were by no means inanities.' He scratched his scar nervously. 'You remember, your lordship, what I begged for this morning.'

Straighten the back.

'If you mean to torture me afresh with –'

'No, no!' Letting go of the rail, he twisted his hands. 'I have precisely the opposite request: should you remember... forget it.'

'What?'

'Forget it, it was wrong of me to ask.' He averted his eyes. 'I was inciting you to evil, forget it.'

Stare at him for a long while. He squirmed and scowled neath the gaze as if roasted.

'I'm totally unable to comprehend you, Zeytsoff. You weren't drinking just now, by any chance?'

'It is not as you think, Venyedikt Filipovitch. I heard what you three were saying, and rethought the whole thing. Bad that I came out with such a request, and worse still were you to satisfy it, were you able to satisfy it.'

Wave helplessly.

'Why should I give toss! Leave off with your requests, your Kingdoms of God and deep-souled confessions. Begone!'

Only now did he feel the sharp spur; he sprang up with eyes ablaze, brows knitted.

'Gospodin Yeroslavsky! That's not what you think!'

'And what do I think?'

'What were they inciting you to? – what did you say that you'd do when you at last meet your father – what use will you make of the power over History? You listen, you ask, you shout, you take offence – but what's your opinion? Your most honest opinion?

'Tell me: do you really believe History is the work of people? That had someone behaved differently in his time from how he did behave, Rome would not have fallen, or the Middle Ages never have died, or the Bastille not crumbled? Or now: that someone will do something and revolution will change the face of Russia, the face of the world; or do nothing – and everything will remain as before. Does History really arise from this? Is that what you think?

'Or is History rather a picture of necessities unconnected with anyone's actions: Rome fell, the dark ages set in, after them came another Roman era, after that another age of reason – just as an even number follows an uneven, which follows an even?

'Venyedikt Filipovitch! So, tell me honestly: in which History dost thou believe?'

He was staring straight into the eyes, without witnesses, his face free of ironic sneers, signs and grimaces. This is how he ensnared in the trap of honesty: for had there been a third party, had there been the slightest hint of mockery in his speech or gesture – then that external compact would have been entered at once, turning the whole conversation into the next parlour game. And so – there is only man and man, and what is possible to express in the speech of men.

'This is what I believe, Zeytsoff: It is not History that creates people, but people that create History.'

The ex-katorzhnik shook his head. Having retreated a step along the balustrade, he bent over halfway. Think: the next to partake in the kow-towing theatre. And indeed, his tangled mane almost reached the iron plates of the observation platform.

'Forgive me,' he said in a loud voice, very distinctly.

Then he seized with both hands beneath the knees. Grab hold of the handrail – he seized and pulled – river of smoke in the sky – straightening suddenly, he thrust upwards – sky, taiga, steel, embankment, earth – release the rail before something snaps in the twisted wrist – embankment, earth, roar and whistle of wind in the ears – fly through the air, somersaulting, legs first. No time even to shout. A whip – a pliant bough – lashed the back. Crash onto grass and sand; and roll farther away. Pain flared in the bruised, mangled body. Come to rest at last on gravel and stones; they tore the face, pierced the neck, dug holes in the clothes and skin. Heave one side onto an elbow. A knocked-out tooth slithered onto the beard along with saliva. The roar gradually subsided – subsided because the train was receding, the last carriage of the Trans-Siberian Express disappearing in the prospect of the cutting dug out of the taiga as a railway embankment. The lamp marking the end of the train blazed still, yet already only the cold glare of the Black Sable's aurora shone above the trees – but the cloud of coloured butter-flies was fading too and paled against the darkening horizon. Dwook, dwook, dwoo-ook, silence. Spit out a second tooth and glance in the opposite direction. In the distance, against a backdrop of red sun, a small silhouette was moving of a man on horseback with a wooden bowstave by his saddle. Sit up slowly; the broken fingers protruded at odd angles. A frosty cold was coming off the glistening rails. The first stars of the Asian night twinkled low in the sky. One, a second, a third, a fifth, the constellation of the Hunter. The coldiron rainbows had died down. Animals were calling in the forest thickets. Shivers shook the battered body. Reach for the Grossmeister.

CHAPTER THE SIXTH

On the dreams of Benedykt Gierosławski

The train will come off the track. Draw back the tail of the scorpion. The train will come off the track, derail, a bloodbath. How often do trains run on the Trans-Siberian Magistral? The passenger train departs from Saint Petersburg several times a week – but what about goods trains? local trains? military transports? On the left track? right track? Lean back against a pine trunk, raise the straightened arm, wrap a finger around the coiled-snake tail – the middle finger, the only entirely functional one of the right hand. Bright-blue shimmers flitted above the rails. The train will come off the track; even if the tungetitum bullet, as it strikes the coldiron, causes no additional damage, an explosion of ice will ensue, as in Yekaterinburg, and the tracks will be covered in a coating of solid ice. The ice won't warp the rails themselves – that's why they're made here of coldiron; no frost daunts them – but a barrier will arise, at which a train will have to stop. Or at least slow down. Then it will be possible to get in. Then the driver will spot the European beside the line, apply the brakes, and take him on board. Except that – the train will come off the track. Bah, but weren't coldiron steam engines designed precisely to break up such obstacles on the line, as railway icebreakers? It will most probably drive past, gathering speed, and not even feel the obstruction. Only the crystal shot-glasses in Deluxe will ring more audibly. However – if it comes off the track? Touch with the tongue a bleeding hole in the gum. Goods train or passenger, local or Express – a bloodbath. It will be said that it was a gleiss, that a gleiss froze up here out of the ground. One way or the other – they'll pick up the European. Because otherwise – what? Die in the midst of the wildness? Impossible to know even how far to the next station. Yurga had been passed, but then – what did it say in the *Putevoditel*? No memory of that. Twenty, thirty versts between subsequent stops in the taiga. The knee twinges like hell with every step, something had snapped there in the tendons, the bones, the muscles, heralding a torturous ramble lasting many days. If some bear doesn't devour a chap on the first night. Pull the trigger. Clack-ck, the scorpion's pincers struck with a soft rattle.

Was it damaged? Break the Grossmeister in two, peek into the calyces of the bullet chambers. Empty – the shot had been fired from an empty chamber. Had the cylinder been twisted back after firing in Yekaterinburg? Could it perchance have twisted itself back? Reassemble the revolver cursing loudly, dolefully, and tuck it behind the belt, under the waistcoat. Wipe the nose with the sleeve (the blood had stopped oozing). Look back towards the west – a quarter of the Sun's disc was hidden behind forest. The Sun could still be gazed upon directly – insofar as anything at all could be gazed upon directly and without trembling. The left eyelid was slowly swelling, wrapping itself under the brow into a Mongolian fold, from which blood also seeped, flooding the eye. Blink every now and then. An owl was hooting from a branch overhead, tu-whit-tu-whoo. Shudder. Long shadows of trees stretched along the railway cutting like signpost blades pointing: east, east, east. Shake the head. There was no way of recalling the last page of the *Putevoditel*. And even had there been – with no knowledge of the current position on the line, all Transsib timetables and maps were as nothing. Take out a three-kopeck copper coin. Heads, the two-headed eagle – means back towards Moscow; tails – to the east. Toss the coin. It lands tails up.

Ten paces and already a need to stop, to catch the breath. Break a young birch tree gnawed by some animal, it will be a cane for support. Step onto the railway tracks; here at least the path is even. Quickly adjust the marching rhythm in time with the sleepers; the cane strikes timber every other pace: chwap-chwap-took, chwap-chwap-took. The fingers refused to curl around the stick, they were hurting badly – press them against the thumb of the other hand, they hurt even more but, oh, now comes the relief: greater pain, therefore lesser pain. Tug at one finger, a second, stripped of skin by the signet ring. Most however were probably just dislocated – pull on the index finger, pull on the right thumb. A golden-red squirrel hopped onto the bough of an elm tree, leaned out over the tracks, crooking its head. Try to whistle, but merely spit blood. A third tooth was loose. Chwap-chwap-took. Light a bonfire perhaps? Would a train then stop? A great bonfire on the tracks. Feel in the pockets for matches. There are none, are none. Swear softly (now there's only melancholy in the voice). Pain shoots in the knee, flares in the backbone. Chwapoo-chwap.

He had thrown off the train, taken hold of and thrown off the train like a sack of oats! And so, Miss Muklanowicz had been right! He had wanted to kill! The Lyednyak agent! Filimon Romanovitch Zeytsoff, a curse on all his clan! *Forgive me...!* Oh, that forgiveness will be coming out of his ears, he'll be gathering up Christian mercy off the paving stones, along with his guts.

Reason began at once, however, to generate doubts. Had he really

JACEK DUKAJ

wished to kill? Had he really taken orders from Lyednyaks? It seemed otherwise. Most likely, Zeytsoff knew not himself what he'd do before he did it. No hard bone has he in him, a man soft to the core; instead of a spine, all he has left is groaning cord and alcohol glass. What was he truly concerned about when he asked about History? First, he requests that father be persuaded of the Kingdom of God on Earth; then – no, the reverse, since for Zeytsoff everything has changed again. Neither socialist, nor anarchist, nor Tolstoyan, he himself converts and reverts between breakfast and supper, that is, between bottleful and bottleful. Had he received a different answer to that question, would he have renounced his murderous design? Through his sleep he heard the conversation with Konyeshin and Pocięgło; God knows what he fancied... For if he allows the son to persuade Father Frost of this or that strategy for the gleissen, what's supposed to happen to History...? Handing to a man the power over man's History – was that what had so horrified him?

But what's so horrifying in that?

He was drunk, that's clear, befuddled, and was sleeping there sozzled until a new phantom embraced him and Filimon Romanovitch surrendered to the phantom, just as he had surrendered throughout his life to revelations in dreams and to monumental ideas; no need to pay good money to men like him, it's enough to whisper a big word in their ear – they will kill, begging forgiveness of their victim from the bottom of their hearts.

Chwap-chwap-took. Took-took – impossible to walk any farther, it's time to rest. Just a few more steps to that forest glade... Descend, limping, from the tracks and sit down on the decayed trunk of an uprooted cedar – cedar, stone pine, a twenty-metre giant, which falling had cut a deep crater in the wilderness, shrouded over now in spiderwebs of damp shadow and besieged by clouds of insects. How far had been walked? – half a verst? maybe a verst? The sun was no longer visible above the crowns of the trees, night was already descending. Take out a handkerchief; blow the clotted blood from the nose, bind rigidly the three swollen fingers of the left hand. What a miracle that the larger bones had survived, that the neck was not twisted and that no branch had pierced a lung. Tiny midges, so small they were invisible in the evening twilight, were crawling into the ears, into the eyes, behind the collar, into the mouth. Spit, snorting loudly. The saliva was now clean, there was no red phlegm.

Rummage through the pockets. Indelible pencil, cigarettes, pocketbook, loose change, a three-rouble bill crumpled to dross, and what's this? – Miss Filipov's note. Also, a comb, a toothpick. The red chamois case with the interferograph. Take out the barrel. It's unscathed, the glass not even cracked. Think at once of fire. Of knocking the lenses out of the clamping ring, setting light to the touchwood, throwing it onto a pile of dry twigs... But only in the morning, when the sun returns. Need to collect a lot of this wood; it's unknown when a train might approach, the bonfire has to burn for hours. But should a wind blow up, carry the sparks... Had it rained here recently? Come to the senses, open the eyes, draw in air. It smelled succulently of all the scents and odours of living forest undergrowth. Together with the warm fragrances, however, the accursed midges also invaded the nostrils – spit, blow and snort for a good minute. Until answered by the loud snorting of a horse.

It emerged from behind white birches, veering from the railway embankment into the crater: thus it revealed itself in the clearing, first a pale shadow, indistinct in the grey semi-darkness, then a head, neck, stick, rider. A stocky chestnut, shaggy, with a man on its back. They stop and stand still, the man stares, the beast stares, peering with great bulging orbs. Sit upright on the pine trunk, clutch the cane tighter. The rider leaned forward, lowering his stick. Dozens of fringes hung from his leather garb, cords strung with figurines and pebbles rattling with the local's every move. His narrow eyes watched with calm curiosity. Seams of black scars traversed his chubby cheeks. Also, something was dangling from the short crosspiece at the end of his stick – the corpse of a bird.

The horse snorted and pawed the soil with its hoof. Shove the fingers in the gob and start gurgling abominably, inflating the cheeks and rolling the eyes, until the echo resounded through the taiga and momentarily silenced the surrounding wildlife.

The savage said something softly and jumped down from his horse. Supported by his stick, he marched towards the stone pine. Now it was evident he's a cripple: he clearly limps, his left leg is shorter, he has to support himself. On his head he wore a pointed felt cap, whilst his loose felt cloak was adorned with red, green and yellow appliqués, sewn on without rhyme or reason, patches upon patches. From his neck hung more braided fringes, collections of primitive wooden, stone and iron figurines strung on a leather thong, some resembling the ragdolls botched together by poor children from scraps and twigs. Having approached, he thrust his stick into the ground (the bird hung with head facing down) and patted himself three times on the belly. He reeked of animal fats; his long black hair fell onto his shoulders and back, tangled in knots, tied with colourful ribbons. His slanting eyes seemed to gaze cheerily enough – the folds of taut skin around the eye sockets allowing no other expression.

Hunched over, bent forward birdlike, he watched for a long time, clicking his tongue and grunting under his breath. Then he hit out from the left side. Duck clumsily, but no, it was not a blow: left hand, right hand, left again; with rapid jerks the savage was tearing down invisible curtains from the air all around. Was he driving away midges? Cease shaking on the tree trunk, sit upright, whilst he, humming gruffly to himself, performs a series of resolute movements – around the head, along the length of the arms, in front of the chest, brushing with filthy hands the even-filthier jacket and shirt, along the trouser legs, then again from the face all the way down. It grew completely dark; above the forest clearing, in the spaces between treetops, silver stars were shining, dense abatis of zodiac constellations. Glance at the hand with its signet ring pressed onto the birch cane – understand only now what the savage is doing. Why he stopped, peered, dismounted. Doctor Tesla's machine, the Kotarbiński pump... Mr Pocięgło had seen, now the Asiatic saw too: the pure strong penumbra, the mingling of light and unlicht – the seal of gleisseniks. Shadow from the stars spread neath the outstretched hand as a white blaze, as a sharp negative of the night. Sit erect, without stirring, regretting only the lack of a mirror. To look into it now, to see from the outside a noctaureole at dusk! Is it light? Does it gleam? Look along the ground, along the bark of the decayed trunk, over the nearby bushes. Is it really brighter? Look at the fabric of the suit, at the skin of the hand, at the shoes. For what had the savage seen? Whom had he seen? The Sun had set, it was the end of the day, high time for the next lie about Benedykt Gierosławski. So here we go: it's Wednesday, twenty-third day of July, enter Ye-Ro-Sha-Ski, the Siberian demon. Burst into frenzied laughter. The lame-leg chuckled in response and gave the daemon a friendly pat on the shoulder.

Having apparently concluded the ritual of cleansing from unlicht, he applied himself to setting up camp. He led the horse behind the stone pine, quickly gathered wood and made even quicker work of laying a fire: a few kicks in the soft ground, some stones, leaves; from a blanket he unwrapped an iron tripod and small cauldron, took out matches from under his fringes, spat and sprinkled something onto the hearth, and at once: a bright hypnotic fire leaps up on the dry stalks, crackling and hissing. The grinning cripple smacked his lips in satisfaction. From a leather waterskin, he splashed water into the cauldron. Having flung down the baggage from the horse's back, he fumbled about in a sackcloth and dug out a metal tin; from this he shook into the cauldron lumps of compressed Chinese tea, throwing one onto the fire. A drink! Swallow the saliva. The savage was only now gathering momentum. From another tin, he magicked a whole dispensary: this type of herb, that type of herb, leaves and tiny flowerets and seed clusters and dried fruits and a dozen bunches of mummified plant remains and God knows what else; he rummaged and sifted, raising to his eyes, sniffing and even licking. Aha, one of their native medicos, a quack, that is. He sees a man is battered, wants to cure him, kind soul. God shall reward him. He boiled the tea, poured it into a tin beaker. Proffered it with a smile. Bare the teeth.

Sss, hot! Put the beaker aside on the trunk. The native indicated with a vigorous gesture: drink, drink. Shrug the shoulders. Lay the birch cane across the thighs and wrap the beaker in a jacket flap; raise it in this way to the mouth. Dead midges floated in the dark beverage. The lame-leg grinned broadly; he likewise had missing teeth. Slurp the steaming liquid. It trickled through the body in a hot stream, the change in temperature felt in the internal organs as each sip made its way down. Now morbid shivers shook the body again. How quickly darkness fell in the taiga! how swiftly a tide of moist chill swept over the earth! As if the seasons changed with the going down of the Sun: summer – autumn – winter. Despite the razor-sharp starlight, vision no longer reached farther than a few feet beyond the primitive fire; a mist had arisen. Tu-whit-tu-whoo, ts-rrv, ts-rveee, tlee-eek, birds of the night were talking to one another from the forest depths. The lame-leg patted himself on the belly and cast onto the fire the next batch of herbs. Drink the hot tchay – cowering, shivering in the chill.

He pulled out a drum. On its taut skin were painted schematic figures, or maybe landscapes, or maybe maps, or maybe animal skeletons. Hiccoughing, yawning, smacking his lips, closing his eyes, the savage began to beat the drum. Lightly at first, quite tenderly, not even with his whole palm but with fingertips, as if he were stroking it, rousing it from sleep – pam-pwam, pam-pwak. The mist came in waves and the taiga rustled whenever the wind blew; the trail of smoke from the campfire hung low, spreading almost horizontally now, directly onto the pine trunk. Cough, dispelling the smell of burning from before the face. Bam-bwam, bam-bwag, the cripple was pounding harder with a thick club made of bone, humming something at the same time under his breath, teeth clenched; his shorter leg jumped up and down to the rhythm. Swallow the remains of the tea; it had indeed had a warming effect. As if he'd added rum. Shift position on the trunk, so as to avoid the smoke. Bam-bwam! Bam-bwag! The savage drums with all his might, and begins moreover to yelp and moan, answered by the forest beasts. Was that a wolf howling? Look around helplessly in the dark. Smoke continued to smite the eyes. What was this Mongol up to? Perhaps he really had trusted to the night-time impression – because what does an uncivilised Siberian customarily do when he encounters a demon? try to drive it away? appease it? kill it? exorcise it by pagan methods? With a broad grin on a face that resembles a loaf of wheaten bread.

Stand up, leaning on the birch cane, and walk around the smoke and fire. BOOM-BWAM! BAM-BWAG! Everything quakes and vibrates from the sound; shivers pass not through the chilled flesh but through the surrounding world; ripples are visible in the leaping flames, on the trail of smoke, ripples on the surface of the mist – only the drummer himself is no longer visible. Was he hiding in the mist? Yet – BOOM-BWAM! – he was drumming close by, close to the ear. Prod about with the cane, wheeling around, circumnavigating the fire. Till it was needful to stop, shake the head, wipe the watering eyes – what is this, what's happening, what kind of ritual, why loiter around the flames, three, four times, where's the rotten trunk, where the shaman, where his belongings, where the horse and the railway track? The hand reaches into the mist; the mist parts before the hand. The hand retreats – the mist returns, namely the darkness. Whence therefore the light, how does it happen that I see the hand at all? The source of light, yes, the campfire! I approach, bend over – but it's no longer a campfire, it's a pillar of radiance, an upstanding column of light, one end driven deep into the earth, the other deep into the sky; I craned my neck – a column, or maybe a tree, here are its roots, and there its branches and fruit, namely the stars. With a slow underwater movement, I stretched out my arm towards it, outwards and upwards; I reached for the stars. Slippery, chilly, slightly smarting to the touch, they leapt off the skin as if galvanised. I burst into laughter. The light of the tree carried my laughter across the plain. Squinting, I cast my eyes over the starry firmament. White blades of grass – each more than a metre high, each one of the million individually visible, nimble sabres with distinct sharp edges – spread in gentle waves from horizon to horizon. A herd of antlered animals – elk? deer? no, reindeer – was swimming in that sea of grasses, half-immersed, whilst every reindeer was also visible and countable, every coat glistening as if strewn with silver dust, sprinkled with spring water. I walked around the tree of light. On the other side stood huntsmen's tents – tents, bivouacs, low constructions on wooden poles, covered in bark and skins. White smoke was emerging from their openings. I set off at a slow pace – yet I'd hardly managed to transfer the cane from hand to hand when I found myself already beside them. I entered the first. They turned from the stove to look at me. Semi-darkness prevailed, a snowstorm howled outside the windows, dirty clouds hung over Warsaw; whilst something clogged the chimney and smoke reached the ceiling, fouling the already foul glow of gas lamps. Father was kneeling and rummaging in the hearth with a long poker. Knocked against the bricks and doors of the grate, the iron seemed to emit no sound. I touched my ears. Had I gone deaf? Mother was saying something to father, waving a handkerchief in the air. I went up to the window. It was Warsaw, but I was unable to identify the street or even the district. Right bank? Left bank? The configuration of roofs and streetlamps appeared utterly foreign, and yet – it was Warsaw. I went up to another window. Something was blocking the view. A closed shutter? I pressed my cheek to the pane. A needle of frost pierced the bone neath my eye, penetrated to my brain, struck my skull from below and burst there under the cupola into an ice-blossom, a snowflake-bush whose side-shoots sprang from my ears. That mass outside the window was a gleiss, frozen into the façade and walls of the building. It had entered the chimney; was that why the apartment was so full of smoke? A fair-haired young woman appeared in the doorway in a red jerkin, dragging Mama by the hand. They went out. I broke free from the windowpane, leaving behind on it half my ear, and went after them. In the parlour, Bolek, Uncle Bogasz and Zygmunt were sitting at a table. Mother and the young woman sat down on empty chairs. Bolek adjusted the spectacles on his nose and reached for matches. A tall blackwicke stood in the middle of the empty tabletop. No! What on earth do you think you're doing! Dear God! Scattering snow on the carpet, I leapt to the table, grabbed the nearest person by the hand, tugged at her – the young woman tore away as if scalded, glanced at me, at her arm, at me, opened her eyes, rolled them upwards, revealing the whites, and then collapsed fainting. We kept watch by her bed as she battled the fever. On the second night, one of her hands began to go black, ulcers appeared, the pus-filled spots began to weep. She raved in delirium. I watched her closely from a distance, from a corner beneath a portrait of the Gierosławski ancestors. Shiny from sweat, her skin pallid, her hair tucked into a tight cap, so that only a rectangle of smooth complexion gleamed within the surround of white linen – who was she? of whom did she remind me? In the beginning, I thought: Julia, well yes, Julia, of course, she was altered, but it was Julia, none other – what have I done now, sweet Julia, wake up, look at me, I didn't want to, I didn't want to! – but then I peered at mother, peered at father, how they had aged, how many years had flown by, and understood: that the young woman suffering in sickness was Emilia. On the fourth night, the infection entered her shoulder, her chest. The doctors threw up their hands. A priest came. Everyone went out (I stayed), Emilka was confessing her sins (which I did not hear, icicles had nailed up my ears). At dawn, my desperate father brought the last salvation. Bwoom-bwam, a shaman entered, hobbling along a trail of smoke and mist, and from the threshold at once turned his gaze upon me; he tilted his staff like a spear and, jabbing with it, advanced step by step, shoving me aside; the bird's corpse dangling from its crosspiece swung before my face, I retreated in disgust, farther, farther, farther away from them, from Emilia, from my mother, from father, farther away – until the floor of the Warsaw apartment completely gave way under my feet, and I fell, bwoom-bwam. My back struck hard earth; air was forced from my lungs. Whatever then re-entered them was not air, or rather it was different air: an earthy, gravelly mass inhaled by grinding it in the lungs into sand, as the lungs rotated in the chest like heavy quernstones – stony breath in, stony breath out. I sat up. The birch cane remained in my hand. It was a bright day, the black shadow of the sun hung in the black sky, a jagged disk, from which crooked rays leapt in zigzags over the whole grassy plain. This time, no pillar of light, nor of unlicht, stood in its midst. I rose to my feet. A wind blew up and rust spilled from the iron blades of grass. Nearby, at the lakeside, herdsmen were watering reindeer. Out of the reindeers' heads, instead of antlers, grew the white skeletons of other animals: dogs, fishes, eagles, rats, also of little children. I went up to the herdsmen. All were one-legged, one-armed, one-eyed. I inquired the way home. They answered me in a tongue that singed half my face, tore off my other ear and knocked out my teeth. I tried to drink water from the lake, but it was hotter than the tars of hell, boiling and bubbling and exploding in black blisters. Out of the lake flowed a wide river, straining towards its source in reversed waves. At its backmouth, I caught sight of a two-legged, two-armed silhouette. I went up to him, supporting myself on the cane. The Man in the Bowler Hat leant over me, handing me a visiting card. On one side was printed an address, whilst on the verso – in white ink, was written the name of Gustaw Gierosławski. I was reminded that my great-grandfather had been called Gustaw; he perished allegedly in the January Uprising. I tucked the card into a pocket. The Man in the Bowler Hat stroked my hair. Now I noticed that he had a hole in his chest, a bloody crater scorched by a high-calibre bullet; and that all of his clothing was in some way spoiled: shoes full of holes, trousers unpicked along the seams, waistcoat with no buttons, even an angular orifice carved out of his geometrically rounded headgear. I marched along the river. A few versts farther on, the next Man in a Bowler Hat was waiting. He handed me a visiting card. On the back he jotted down the name of Lise Grüntz. I remembered that this was the name of one of my mother's great aunts – was she not the one who poisoned her husband and fled to America with the family jewels? I walked on. The visiting cards of the Men in Bowler Hats differed only in the name on the verso. Jerzy Bertrand Gierosławski. Maria Gierosławska. Juliusz Watzel. Antoni Wilk. Grzegorz Bogasz. The river flowed into dense iron weeds, I floundered in rust, had to walk at the very edge, steadying myself with the cane on the slope above the water. Izydor Hertz. Wacław Salomon Gierosławski. Bolesław Gierosławski. In the forest thickets, I lost all sense of direction, only one direction counted: downstream, that is, upstream, against the current of the waters. In the meantime, night had fallen, black stars had spread like inkblots over the icy surface of the sky. Eulagia Gierosławska. Filip Gierosławski. Faster and faster I walked, though my strength was also ebbing faster and faster; the quernstones of my lungs were seizing up mid-revolution, the air in my mouth bristling with granite tombstones. Benedykt Gierosławski. I screamed. The Man in the Bowler Hat also handed me a sweet. I threw it in the river. He pulled out another visiting card. I dashed between trees. Raked with my cane in barbed-wire coils of spruce and fir. The underbrush was already so dense that I had to force my way step by step through iron vegetation, as if wading through snowdrifts; in a moment I shall drop down breathless. All the time, however, in the middle of the night, between the steel needles and leaves, a bright light kept flashing ahead of me, a light, a tiny light, a firefly – closer, farther away, closer, farther away, closer, closer, beyond that trunk, beyond the branch, at arm's length – an electrical beam, a man in an afterglow of cold fire, in a bushy crown of thorny sparks, upon the tangled roots of thunderbolts – Nikola Tesla gave me his hand, clasped me to him, embraced me, hugged me. Bursting into relieved laughter, I returned his embrace. He spun around and, with a theatrical gesture, showed me the way. We stepped into the golden luxury of the Trans-Siberian Express.

On the angels of shame and shamelessness

But what if it's not a dream?
'... wake him up.'
'Are you sure?'
'He ought not to, but there you are, I am leaving the thermometer.'
'Thank you, doctor.'
'C'est mon devoir, ma chérie.'
And Doctor Konyeshin floats away into the brightness of the morn. Cool bedsheets cover the cheek, silk against skin. A stirring of air brings the fragrance of jasmine scent. A bird is singing. Why can't the clatter of wheels on rails be heard? Silence, peace, warmth.
But what if it's not a dream?
Rosy blotches of sunlit radiance dance on the surface of the eyelids. Open the eyes.

Miss Jelena Muklanowicz was leaning over the bedcovers with white gauze in her hand, a string of milky pearls swaying against a backdrop of black tulle, tick-tock – reach out and stop the pendulum.

Jelena smiled teasingly, touching her upper lip with the tip of her tongue.

'Ah, at last he's had a good sleep!'

'If only you knew, miss, what dreams I've had…!'

'Tell us, tell us.'

'I dreamed Zeytsoff threw me off the train and –'

'Zeytsoff! That inveterate drunkard! Him!' She flipped the gauze like a riding crop. 'How could I have been so foolish!'

Turn over on the bedcovers, pulling the pillow higher.

'Wait a moment, it's coming back to me – are we standing at a station? – what time is it – what's happ–'

'You're awake!' cried Mademoiselle Filipov, closing the compartment door behind her.

Switch to German.

'I kiss the hands of my angels, maidens of mercy, but could you be so kind as to –'

'Is it true, sir, that you fought with Mr Pocięgło?' Christine asked, holding her breath.

'What? No! Excuse me, but now I really must –'

'You're not going anywhere, sir, until I permit it,' commanded Miss Muklanowicz and took out the thermometer. 'Open wide, aa-aa.'

Run the fingers over the bandages on the neck and face, over the whole left cheek neath thick adhesive plasters. Three fingers had been immobilised by improvised splints. Finger the ribcage. Also bandaged. Feel under the pyjamas the huge bulk of a tight dressing on the left knee, preventing any bending of the leg.

Shift the mercury thermometer to the corner of the mouth.

'So, I guess I didn't dream it after all. Doctor Tesla – it was night – in the taiga –'

'But what did you imagine?' Mademoiselle Christine sat down at the foot of the bed, tucking the blanket under her skirt. Sun from the window fell directly on her face, she squinted; her fair hair, released from its plait, shone golden in a spectral halo as if borne on that breeze of sunlit radiance. 'That Nikola would leave you there – after you'd saved his life twice? He declared he would not return without you.'

'So, it was Doctor Tesla… Still, that shaman…' Search for wounds to the forehead from the metal leaves.

Jelena Muklanowicz measured a spoonful of yellow powder into a glass of water.

'So, there was a shaman too. In this dream? Only please be careful, don't bite through the thermometer!'

Try to retell the whole story, but the gibberish made less and less sense with every sentence until, listening in amazement to the words uttered, lapse into silence mid-flow.

The devushkas looked on with great interest. Flee with the eyes to the ceiling, the wall.

'Why did you not ask him to take you to the nearest station?' inquired Miss Muklanowicz.

'And in what language do you suppose?'

'In Russian, of course. You say he had matches, Chinese tea, didn't come directly out of the taiga. Surely he understood some Russian, at least a few words.'

'I didn't think of it.'

'Mm-hmm, sounds indeed like a dream.'

A dream, a dream, but had there not been prior warning? Mr Pocięgło as well as someone else before him had plainly said: give no credence to dreams, beware of dreams and sortilege, any kind of fortune-telling, the closer to the Homeland of the Gleissen, all the more so.

But it had been no ordinary dream, God only knows what that savage had sprinkled in the tchay, what had been inhaled in the smoke, and that drum, that accursed drum –

'Aa-aa, drink up, oh, very good. Mm-hmm, but it's no more than a slight fever. Everything will be all right, Benedykt, sir. Doctor Konyeshin said you must have a proper sleep, rest up, and he'll check again that no infection appears, but even so you have something for which to thank the Mother of God, and as to that drunken sot, I shall –'

'No!' Seize Miss Muklanowicz's hand, still holding the thermometer. 'Leave him be. I shall settle it myself.' Sit back, take a breath. A bitter taste of medicaments still clung to the mouth. Swallow the saliva. 'Above all I should thank Nikola Tesla. By what miracle he managed to –'

'Nothing of the kind!' Christine Filipov bridled. 'You have no idea! How wrong you are! It's her, her you have to thank! If only you'd seen what she did – just wait till you hear Madame Blutfeld's version – Mademoiselle Muklanowicz fought like a lioness, all but sprang at Prince Blutsky digging in her nails, Dushin had to pull her off by force, if only you'd seen!'

Jelena was waving the gauze, eyes lowered, her face bright crimson from black hairline to black jabot.

Christine smiled broadly. She will relate the thing twice over so as not to miss any detail. And so, in accordance with her words, a picture took shape in the mind of those events: Jelena returns from searching

Porfiry Pocięgło's compartment – where's Mr Gierosławski, he stayed behind in the gallery – she goes to the gallery, no Mr Gierosławski, no sign of him either on the observation platform – so what's her first thought: Pocięgło! Mr Gierosławski was to keep company with him only in public, but what does he do, he runs off at the first opportunity to be on their own, and see, there's no Benedykt Gierosławski – she asks the stewards, asks the provodniks, there's no Benedykt Gierosławski – she catches up with Pocięgło, Pocięgło points to Konyeshin, but the doctor says he returned to the saloon earlier, leaving behind Messrs Pocięgło and Gierosławski, the latter went out onto the platform – dear God, so the story of Pyelka repeats itself! – he killed him! killed him and threw the body off the train! but maybe he only threw him off, pushed him off, and Mr Gierosławski is still alive! lying there and dying with broken bones! – already it's a sensation, a scandal, there's pandemonium in Deluxe, the crew are running back and forth as if possessed – and her second thought: who has the power to stop the train, who can issue orders to the natchalnik of the Trans-Siberian Express? – only Prince Blutsky-Osey, who had shown unusual interest in Mr Gierosławski, had cross-examined him, invited him to his table – Miss Muklanowicz then runs to the prince and keeps imploring, trying to persuade him, threatening and shouting and weeping and moaning – until the princess compels her spouse to give the order to the natchalnik – and the train stops, diverts onto the first siding reached, stands in the middle of the taiga whilst search parties make their way back, Doctor Tesla leading the first.

'The whole Express is at a standstill because of me?!'

'He's not fully come round yet,' Miss Muklanowicz murmured to the American.

Turn on the bed so as to look out of the window. No station, no platform, not even a railwayman's shed – forest, forest, forest. The travellers wander amongst the trees, children buffet one another with green stalks, Jules Verousse is picking a bunch of wild flowers for the handsome widow, the Amur prosecutor is returning from the woods with a basketful of mushrooms.

Glance in despair at Miss Muklanowicz, at Miss Filipov. They were sitting politely, their lips primmed, and only from their furtively exchanged glances was it possible to surmise what amusement the whole situation was affording them, how they gloated over man's confusion. Even their arms were arranged similarly, straight down the line of the bodice with hands held in the lap; even their heads were inclined the same way: a little forward, a little to the right. Jelena: black silk trimmed with lace, black high-waisted narrow skirt, black liner around the hazel eyes, black hair in a tight bun; she hadn't changed her clothes overnight, had she slept at all? Christine: ecru batiste bodice, wide gigot sleeves, pleats, green amazon skirt, limpid blue of eyes, face illuminated like a stained-glass window. Angel on the right side, angel on the left – whichever way the gaze turns, they are watching, watching, watching.

'How can I show my face now!'

Jelena smacked her lips loudly.

'You're so very ashamed, Benedykt, when there's nothing to be ashamed of, and so very sure of yourself when it least becomes you.' Again, seemingly without looking at her, she directed her words at the young American. 'Perhaps you can appeal to his reason. An intelligent man, or so it seems. Yet he's bred such terrors within him, it's beyond human comprehension. He says he exists not. Says he's ruled by shame. The great logician! How can anyone be ashamed of anything, when they exist not?'

Pull the quilt to the chin. Where to hide, where to flee? Thrust the head under the pillow? A sick man at the mercy of the healthy is stripped first and foremost of his right to shame. They had besieged the bed like – like – not like angels; like hyenas, hyenas of mercy.

'From the very beginning, miss, you've been trying to convert me to shamelessness.'

'Would to God I had succeeded.'

Turn the back ostentatiously on Jelena, focusing on Mademoiselle Filipov, seeking her eyes and her attention.

'No doubt, miss, you've heard it more than once from persons enjoying great esteem and authority when they're asked for some maxim, according to which a man might safely steer himself through life, that is, a recipe for life, short, simple and understandable: "Behave in such and such a way, so that you never have to feel ashamed of your behaviour". You've heard it, true?'

'Hard to find greater humbug! What we're ashamed of and what we're not ashamed of – one person differs from the next thanks precisely to this, because not everyone is ashamed of the same thing, not to the same degree, not in the same situation, not in relation to the same people. It's what makes me what I am – my shame.

'And now, miss, picture to yourself an individual unashamed of any of his deeds. The possibilities are twofold: either he is the greatest shameless profligate the earth has ever spawned and ashamed of absolutely nothing, or he has behaved from the very start in accordance with a perpetual feeling of shame: the child who is ashamed of the same things as a grown man, the grown man who feels shame like a child, the old man with the shame of a young man, the young man with the shame of an old man on his deathbed. Picture him, miss. Who is he? Who is he?'

Christine glanced inquiringly at Jelena.

Miss Muklanowicz folded her arms over her chest, pouting.

'Oh, yes? Yes? "The greatest shameless profligate the earth has ever spawned"! And what sort of invective is that, I ask myself! It's a compliment! The highest happiness and goal of human life! To be shameless, free of shame, yes!

'So, he exists not, and yet is ashamed! He wished not to say it – so I shall say it: he exists not *because* he is ashamed. My shame begins where my "I" ends; "I" marks the boundary of my shame. For indeed, a man completely in thrall to shame is a man who exists not. He is like a leaf tossed by the wind in all directions, not according to his own will, but to the will of the wind, to random nudges of the elements. Flotsam carried on the waves.

'Man exists only when, and only insofar as, he acts against shame. More than this: not "against" shame, because then shame would continue to hold sway over him – but *irrespective of* shame, that is, without paying any attention to its prescriptions, without remembering it, never and in no situation acknowledging it.

'People that remain instead in the power of shame, non-existent people – how many of them do we meet every day!

'One feeling accurately distinguishes man from the semblance of man: boredom. The meeting between one person and another is never boring: something authentic touches something authentic, a mystery touches a mystery, a riddle solves a riddle. But how many people do you know, Christine, like that? You've frequented the salons, so you've seen hundreds of those puppets frozen between decorum and necessity. They don't have to come to Siberia – born in the Ice, they shall die in the Ice, gleissen have already frozen through their souls.'

Sit upright, resting the pillow against the wall by the window. Wrenched into position to give support, the bandaged leg was resisting; a signal of protest shot from the knee. Utter a prolonged hiss.

'It hurts?' Jelena was alarmed, her tone and pose changing in a flash. 'This powder –'

'That was to make you sleep, the doctor said –'

'I've lain in bed long enough.' Massage the leg. 'Pain, yes, dear ladies, so there's pain in the body, you stab it with a pin, cut through the skin, fracture it, cripple it – the body will let you know at once. But pain in the soul... Here Jelena may be right, it's a kind of enslavement. Sometimes it seems to me –

'Imagine yourself suspended on a web of steel threads stretched between thousands of people, your family, friends, neighbours, "the folk you look up to", whilst every thread ends in a barbed hook implanted in muscle, in bone... And now – now try to move against other people's movements and you'll fracture your spine, try to say something against other people's throats and tongues and you'll tear out your own tongue, so now defy Shame!'

Mademoiselle Filipov no longer listened in amusement, no longer exchanged impish glances with the Varsovienne. For all these arguments were directed at Christine, as if she'd become the *ad hoc* court for whose verdict the sides were waiting – it all merely confused and saddened her.

'Bu-ut – but why do you both speak of it as if it were a nasty ailment, as if it were a curse? Even you, sir, you too. Shame – implying it would be better, were there no such thing. How then would we recognise that we were doing wrong? For how? – shall I steal and not be ashamed? shall I tell lies, and nothing, not even a blush?

'I'm sorry, I...,' she said in English before returning to German. 'Perhaps I don't understand, most likely I don't understand. These are metaphors, you're trying to say something behind the words, yes – but... shame is a good thing! Shame is good, shame is needed, thanks to shame men live alongside one another in brotherliness and not like hungry, greedy wolves. Just think about it!'

'Benedykt defends it, that's not right either: says his shame distinguishes him from other people. But no! It's quite the reverse! Were one man to be ashamed of this and another – of that, how could we live together at all? How could we converse at all? Jelena – the meeting between mystery and mystery, yes; but how would they be able to meet at all?

'And why do these steel threads run outside of you? Who made you surrender your shame into the hands of others? And so, if no one is watching, no cold hook will tug at your soul when you inflict harm on an innocent person?'

'Someone is always watching, even when no one is watching.' Mutter. Jelena pressed her nail to her lips.

'So, Christine, have you never had occasion to be ashamed of a good deed?'

Mademoiselle Filipov raised her head high.

'No.'

'Oh! Really?'

Mademoiselle Filipov tightened her lips.

'But if you are ashamed only in relation to yourself,' Jelena probed, 'it follows that you yourself are the sole source of good and evil, yes? You say to yourself: this is good – and it will be good. And on the following day, say it is bad – and it will be bad. Yes?'

'All goodness comes from God.'

'From God! Oh! And so, God has told you what to be ashamed of?'

'You're laughing at me.'

'Why d'you think that? Am I laughing? Is Mr Gierosławski laughing? What are you so ashamed of? Your convictions?'

'I am not ashamed!'

'So how was it then with God?'

'Well, there's the Ten Commandments for instance!'

'And did He impart them to you personally?'

'The Bible!'

'But who told you they were genuine?'

'You do not believe in God.'

'Did I say such a thing? I am merely endeavouring to find the ends, that is, the beginnings, of your threads of shame, who tugs at your hooks; tell me honestly, after all there's nothing to be ashamed of. Who then?'

'Holy Writ tells the truth!'

'Who?'

'God is watching, when no one is watching!'

'Who?'

'They committed the original sin, and only afterwards knew shame!'

'Who?'

'And the little children, who are guiltless.'

'Who?'

'Papa,' Christine spoke softly and lowered her eyes. 'Nanny. My governess.'

'Thank you.' Jelena removed the nail from her lips.

Christine wiped away her tears with the sleeve of her blouse.

'You ought to be ashamed of yourself.' Whisper to Miss Muklanowicz.

'What, in front of you perhaps?'

'But who caused that delightful blush but a moment ago?'

'Don't imagine too much, sir, everyone has moments of weakness.'

'Of which they're later ashamed.'

She stood up, leant over Christine and swept back the hair from her face, skimming the plump girlish cheek with her palm. Miss Filipov nestled up to Jelena. Cease to comprehend a thing. Jelena was kissing Christine on the crown of her head; the American laughed quietly. During the night, when they were awaiting the return of the search parties – had they waited together? of what had they talked? what had Jelena told Christine, what had Christine told Jelena? Women make friendships differently, strike up acquaintances in a different way; entanglement starts much earlier and is much stronger (they confess to each other their innermost secrets, which no man would ever betray to brother or wife) but at the same time it's much more complicated, for never is it mere friendship: threads of rivalry, envy, pity enter the tangle

– the soft wool of cruelty, the linen fetters binding possessor and possessed. Miss Muklanowicz led the American out of the compartment, seized her hands, whispered something in her ear; the other nodded… They were laughing. Comprehend nothing at all.

Having returned, Jelena leaned against the door. She lifted her head and looked down from on high; who stares like that? – the tanner's daughter, the ward of Grisha Buntz, Jelena Muklanowicz more real than Jelena Muklanowicz.

'Christine will keep the secret,' she said. 'Now you will sleep. For three, four hours before the natchalnik and the prince interrogate you. The natchalnik will have to draw up a special report, the situation is exceptional, you realise; we've dropped out of the timetable, military transports are sent from the Japanese front and to the front via the Transsib, Myerzhoff's supply trains, we have to wait for the next free passage, until the afternoon; the telegraph cable runs somewhere near here. We have to decide on a version, they'll ask about Zeytsoff's motives. You will sleep, sir, and I will set to work. He's lying in his compartment drunk as a skunk, I bribed the provodnik, I know.'

'Zeytsoff is harmless.'

'*Pardon?*'

'It's not Zeytsoff we're looking for.'

'He threw you off the train! Yes or no? Tried to kill you!'

'Oh Christ. Be so kind as to sit down, miss, we're not going to shout like this.'

She frowned. Point to the chair by the escritoire.

'Have you forgotten already?' Whisper. 'I shan't make the same mistake twice. Remember how it was with Fogel? Train at a standstill, silence, walls like blotting-paper, no one asleep…'

She sat down.

'Fogel was speaking in Russian – but who apart from us understands Polish?'

Lay a hand on the side wall of the compartment.

'Your aunt, your Auntie. What? Did you imagine that when you plied me with mind-numbing powder, all the screws in my head would spring out of place and I'd suddenly lose my tongue?'

Jelena Muklanowicz rolled her eyes.

'I sense you've again thought up some dreadful theory that will turn everything on its head.'

'Tell me first what you found in Pocięgło's compartment.'

'Nothing.' A butterfly flew in through the open window and began to dance around Jelena's head; she shooed it away with an impatient wave. 'Nothing to suggest he's any more than the next Sibirkhozheto industrialist. He has some sort of papers sewn into the lining of his fur coat.'

'Papers?'

'Banknotes perhaps. After all, I couldn't unpick it, he'd realise. What are you getting at?'

'Quiet! I am telling you, miss, that the Lyednyak agent is not Zeytsoff. And now you're telling me it's not Pocięgło either.'

'I don't know whether it's not Pocięgło. There's no proof for, no proof against.' She tapped her forehead. 'Sherlock Holmes is at work. For me, Porfiry Pocięgło remains the prime suspect. Besides, this halt suits him. But Christine is keeping a close watch on Doctor Tesla, she won't let him go anywhere now without one of the okhranniks. In the search for you in the taiga, four of the prince's men went with him, only then did she relent.'

Wipe the eyes; the lids again began to weigh heavily.

'Dushin too?'

'What? No. Why?'

'You know that Princess Blutskaya is a court Martsynian? A diehard Lyednyak to boot. She knows Rasputin.'

The devushka pressed her fingers to her temple.

'In which case... that clears her.'

'Beg pardon?'

'She had the perfect opportunity. Doctor Tesla strides off into the wilderness in the middle of the night in search of you. And disappears without trace, you disappear without trace. There is no Nikola Tesla, no Benedykt Gierosławski. Yet what does she do? She forces the prince to stop the train in order to rescue you. Her people, the prince's people, carried you back alive. So, it's not the princess, someone else is Fogel's agent.'

'You assume that the princess knows anything at all about Doctor Tesla, about his arsenal, about his contact with the Tsar. I agree she's no agent – but had she known... she wouldn't have hesitated. It was she who sent Dushin after me in Yekaterinburg. And then sent him most likely to Pyelka.' Press a thumb into the eyeball till red suns burst into flame on the pupil. 'What I can't make head or tail of is this: Pyelka is a Martsynian, the princess is a Martsynian, the killers in Yekaterinburg were Martsynians; yet they tear each other apart without so much as a by-your-leave, whilst each tells a different cock-and-bull story about Father Frost. Even if they don't know one another – what could the princess have in common with a fellow like Mefody Karpovitch Pyelka? – even though it's one faith.'

Jelena adjusted the quilt that was slipping onto the carpet.

'Here logic lets you down, true?'

'Mm-hmm?'

'You want to find reason in religious wars. Is it any different with

Christians? One God, one Holy Writ, one voice of good and evil – yet how much blood has been spilled?'

Press harder, the suns flare into an intense black.

'There is no problem before which you will force me to surrender my reason. Every act of folly, so long as it happens in the world, has to take place according to the world's rules. When I acknowledge that I have no right to ask "why?", I might as well shoot myself in the head.'

'*Vive la raison*. So – why?'

The black sun pulsed to the rhythm of the blood: darkening, undarkening, darkening.

'I understand why Martsynians in the Perm guberniya received orders regarding me: some tchinovnik in the Ministry of Winter, a devotee of Martsyn, found out that Ottepyelniks were sending the son to Father Frost, himself a Pole and a rebel, and so the Lyednyak faction of Martsynians had to react, Lyednyaks in general had to react. But Pyelka? Was he an Ottepyelnik Martsynian? He tried to protect me, did protect me. Why? Likewise, the princess – but the princess saw it in her dreams. Whereas Pyelka?'

'You have loyal followers, sir, amongst Martsynians,' Miss Muklanowicz muttered, 'ready to lay down their lives for you. Very nice. But what shall we say to the prince?'

'We could write it out as a matrix with vertical columns and horizontal rows: Martsynians – non-Martsynians; Lyednyaks – Ottepyelniks. And every possible combination betwixt them. Hence there are at least four different images of History. Do you see, Jelena? Whoever wishes for some kind of History, believes in some kind of History, has surrendered to some kind of History – such will be the goal he imposes on Father Frost and his son. They cannot kill History, but they can kill me. They cannot rescue History, but they can rescue me.' Squeeze the eyelids. The head slumps lifeless onto the pillow. Fly into the black well of the sun. 'Do you see, Jelena, do you see? They cannot control History, but they can bind *Le Père du Gel* and *Le Fils du Gel* in their power and through them –'

'What will we say to the prince? What will you say? Why did Zeytsoff throw you off the train?'

'Let Zeytsoff be. He threw no one off.'

'Well, who was it then? Pocięgło nevertheless? Or perhaps the Turk? He also had a go at you, there are witnesses. There's no shortage of candidates when you stop and think, because Captain Privyezhensky also… Soon half of Deluxe will be wanting to kill Benedykt Gierosławski.'

'Not Benedykt Gierosławski. The lie about Benedykt Gierosławski. Some stuffed hollow-man from the prophecies of Saint Martsyn. Hungarian count. Enemy of Sibirkhozheto. Son of Frost.'

'Oh really. Yet who wears an heraldic signet ring on his pinkie? You said, sir, you'd flung it away.'

'I did fling it away. It came back.'

'What, in a baked fish's belly perhaps?'

Grope over the fingers.

'Where's it gone?'

'I hid it with the rest of your things. Yes, fear not, that revolver too. Auntie and Doctor Konyeshin took care of you in the night, they had to undress you, put you in pyjamas…'

Raise an eyelid. The black afterimages drifted away for a moment. Miss Muklanowicz's corseted figure sat bolt upright in the shafts of morning sun; the butterfly perched on the shelf above her head.

'You took… There was a letter…'

'And when I'd read it, Christine told me everything.'

'It's not…'

'That he died. And lives.' She grinned broadly. 'Now you'll try to persuade me that Martsynians are killing each other over you for no reason.'

'He was only sleeping…'

Miss Muklanowicz cocked a snook.

Try to grab her hand, pull her over, and breathe the truth straight into her ear – black sun darkened the eyes, the black well sucked blood from the head. It is warm, silent, peaceful, birds are singing.

'All lies.'

Feel the devushka's cool hand on the forehead.

'Auntie will watch over you now, I too have to catch up on sleep, or I'll look like a ghost. They're organising a dance for this evening. Should the prince ask, say we don't know one another, that we met on this journey.'

'B-but –'

She moved her hand over the mouth, smothering the words. Touch the pad of her finger with the tip of the tongue.

She leaned over the bed.

'Where's your shame, Mr Gierosławski!' she whispered.

'No one is watching, *mon ange sans honte*…'

'*Je regarde.*'

'*Qui êtes-vous?*'

'*Un rêve, naturellement. Nous sommes dans l'Été.*'

All lies.

On the Siberian madnesses

'I fell off.'

'Fell off!'

'Fell off.'

'I'll have him fall off…! They'll be picking him up all the way to Vladivostock!'

'Why so worked up,' Princess Blutskaya was trying to pacify her spouse, 'you'll get indigestion again, make yourself ill because of him.'

Prince Blutsky-Osey was puffing, blowing, grinding his teeth, tottering around the compartment from wall to wall, shaking his head, clutching now at his chest, now at his denture, since it was this, the metal orthodontic sculpture, that was grinding away. Fear that with his next outburst, the old man might spit it out along with his words and saliva; violently expelled, the denture could knock out an eye, break the nose, for the distance was not great, an arshin, half an arshin, whenever the prince came too close, gathering speed with his short footsteps within the confined space, whenever he came too close, leant over, exploded in fresh anger, whilst the reptilian denture bounced in his gob to left and right as if on rubber pegs.

'Fell off! Drunk, eh?'

'No.'

'See? See?' the prince grew heated. 'For once he's told the truth!'

'Of course, I am exceedingly obliged to Your Princely Highness for stopping the train on my behalf, I know not how to thank you and beg pardon that all this trouble and confusion has landed on your head because of me, Your Highness, if only I could somehow –'

'Jests!' roared the prince. 'Now he makes me the butt of his jests!' He snatched up the princess's cane and raised it in a clumsy attempt at a blow, but caught it on a fancy bracket on the high shelf above the bed and staggered over, almost falling.

'Councillor!' cried the princess; cried and began to cough. 'Zahary Feofilovitch, be so kind as to take the prince for a breath of fresh air, a preprandial will do him good.'

Dusin thrust in his head from the corridor, through the open door. The prince flung the cane on the floor and strode out of the compartment. Dusin glanced inquiringly at the princess. She dismissed him with a wave of her lace handkerchief.

Pick up the cane and hand it to the old lady.

'*Merci*. You must forgive my husband, again you brazenly lie to his face, he's not accustomed to it.'

'Your Highness, may I sit? My leg –'

347

'You may stand, you may stand. Don't imagine Rappacki's stamp gives you a licence to tell lies. You see, when Doctor Nikola Tesla and our people were searching for you in forest by the railway tracks, Pavel Vladimirovitch Fogel, a former tchinovnik of the Third Department of the Emperor's Own Chancery, acting now at the behest of the Okhrana, came to us here; came with Mademoiselle Christine Filipov, and they told us about Tesla's work and the great threat hanging over him, and how you had saved his life, and that your life too is in danger from those same assassins. Thanks to whom, so they told us, you had vanished from the train, the murdered body deliberately removed from sight. Khh, khh. Be so kind as to pour me some tchay from that little pot – *merci bien.*

'So, the prince was greatly perturbed by this and only then ceased to reproach me for insisting on stopping the Express. I too was perturbed and began to ask myself: did I indeed do right? I am rescuing you for the second time. And thinking to myself: my dream has come true. I was right, it was in your power to save Russia – had you let Doctor Tesla die. Tesla, who is conveying in this very train, alongside ourselves, his armoury arrayed against the gleissen, so say Mr Fogel and Mademoiselle Christine. So, my dream revealed the truth, except that I understood it amiss. Well, young man, tell me, because I'm tired of all this talk – am I right?'

The Blutskys' compartment was no roomier than other double compartments. The princess was sitting on a made bed piled high with bolsters, pillows and cushions, buffeted on both sides by softnesses and roundnesses, as if on a throne of down and plush; she sank into it, buried. Try to stand at a fitting distance, but how far is it possible to flee in a railway compartment? – stand over the princess, gazing down from above, stooping involuntarily in a hunched bow whenever she raised her shrivelled, wrinkled little face, whenever she glanced blinking from under her lace cap. Smiling, not smiling, old biddy, babushka, mother of mothers.

'Your Highness wants me to tell her who threw me off, because she's seeking an ally against her own husband.'

She almost choked on the hot tchay.

'Khhrrkk, you really do do everything amiss; has no one ever taught you when to lie and when to tell the truth?'

'The prince does not believe at all in the emperor's madness, *c'est invraisemblable.* The prince is travelling to treat with the Japanese, so as to bring the emperor peace on the eastern front and a free hand against the gleissen. But you accompany him on this journey in order to thwart his work, ruin the negotiations and, at the first opportunity, violate that peace. You can barely walk unaided, yet in the name of your

Martsynian faith, you won't let go: whilst there's war with Japan, there's peace for gleissen.'

The princess raised her head higher still, now almost straightening her back; her mouth dropped wide open, probably no longer in her control – a thread of saliva hung from the corner of her pale lips.

'Khhrr, khh, madman, this is madness, yes, yes.'

'His Imperial Exaltedness's...'

'Not the emperor's; yours. Tell me: in what lunacy must a man dwell in order to expect not only the worst of his neighbours but also describe to them the evil openly and without shame?'

'Lunacy?! Had you known about Tesla before the search parties set off, what order would you have given your people? Eh? What order?'

The old lady whacked her cane on the floor; the carpet deadened the thud.

'Silence!' she hissed. 'Enough! *De quoi parlez-vous*! Control yourself! Again, hysteria has got the better of you! It's improper!'

'Proper, improper.' Answer her calmly, 'I know not and care not. Order your thugs to beat me up, if honest words so offend you. But why talk to you at all? Why come here? Out of politeness? Gratitude? My respects to His Highness; he, it seems, is a genuinely good man, him I thank. You – no longer. There will be no truce, no pact between us, but should you envisage the reverse because of it: to destroy me with your own word, or hand me over to the mercy of night-time killers – the choice is yours, mother mine. The Ice be with you.'

Exit into the corridor. In the distance, one or two compartments farther on, stood the provodnik, the natchalnik of the train, an old steward, as well as a silver-bearded servant dressed in the prince's livery. The natchalnik bowed at once, pressing hand to heart through his sumptuous uniform. How much had they heard? Hasten after him, limping, towards the provodnik's duty room. The prince and princess were travelling in Deluxe carriage number one, immediately behind the saloon car. Stop for a moment, feigning problems with the knee, and glance underfoot. Dark bloodstains remained on the carpet runner, no longer so distinct, though not immune to detection. All the windows were open; sunlight streamed in together with warm air redolent of the forest. The natchalnik pushed open the door to the duty room. Monsieur Verousse peeked out from his compartment, opened wide his eyes and jumped as if stabbed in the butt by a pin. '... me absolutely readers Paris France history world absolutely Siberia journey absolutely brigands and now rescue adventure you tell I write down write down absolutely!' 'Later, sir, if you'll forgive me.' Escape into the duty room.

The natchalnik was writing his report with the unction worthy of a scribe of the Holy Synod, all the more so since the train was stationary, the table no longer shaking; a man could dip his nib into the inkwell with total pomp, and guide his penholder with all the artistry of official calligraphy – who knows whose eyes will examine the report, who knows what will determine any decision about his position; maybe his job will be saved precisely by that neat and even script, or threatened by a single careless inkblot or slovenly letter betraying the insubordinate character of the railway official, who knows. To watch the natchalnik sweating thus over his report to his superiors, to look into his concentrating eyes, into his soldierly soul, into the religious devotion with which he pieced together word upon word for Authority – was to understand more about Russia than would be gleaned from long study of her politics.

He saw the papers stamped by the Ministry of Winter, inquired therefore with obsequious urbanity, apologising for asking, apologising almost for apologising. Repeat the brief, simple tale of falling off the observation platform – the head was reeling, and why was it reeling, well it was like this, I was gazing up at the sky, at the smoke, at the coldiron rainbows, a patent fool, yes, that's me – while the natchalnik translated it into officialese. Stare out of the window at the tall trees of the taiga, at the different greens of spreading pine and spruce, at the white bark of birches growing more sparsely beside the tracks, sunlit clearings between white and white, green and green, so that the strolling passengers, entering the forest between trees and disappearing behind one, two, three trunks, were unable to perceive when and if they'd entered, there being no boundary line, no beginning to the taiga – except that its vast oceanic mass stretching from horizon to horizon was clearly visible, and a deep echoing boom issued from the tree ocean whenever a sudden wind blew over Asia and a roar awoke in the wilderness, a great protracted roar, a wave of living sound, shshshshshhh, till the curtains and drapes ruffled in the windows of the Deluxe carriages, the papers rose from under the natchalnik's clumsy hand, and he glanced up frowning over pen and inkwell, rebuking disobedient nature with his official glare. Yes, the head had been reeling, I was gazing up, a patent fool – that's me. A young stag emerged from between the birch trees and pricked up its ears, turning his head towards the flickering glows of the Black Sable… Think of the Princess Blutskaya.

The old harridan was terrifying. The last miasmas of the sleeping draught had passed from the blood, the night-time weakness had departed as well as the hangover from smoke-induced hallucinations; keenness of judgement had returned. Princess Blutskaya! How to argue with someone who had become her own oracle, who measures everything by her own dreams, by her own intuition, according to some internal image visible to no one else? Yet it often occurs that elderly people acquire such belief in their own authority, and cling to it for their own sakes: patriarchs of dynasties, shrivelled old biddies, holy soothsayers. With such people, there's no way to reach understanding. They listen to you like you listen to a barking dog or babbling child. They speak, but in reality speak always to themselves. To the outside, to others, they merely utter commands – commands in the form of commands, commands in the form of subtle manipulations, commands in the form of wordless lies. You'll never convince them that their behaviour is evil. It's rather they who are used to judging what's good and what's evil.

... Yesterday, the princess saved life and made trustful supplications, today she'll no doubt exploit the first opportunity to take life away. Because of a dream, a nightmare, a premonition – clack! she's flipped the points, and so good and evil, truth and falsehood have switched places. She was inveighing against the autocrat – but who is she? She is shaped by the same lunacy. So how to converse with someone like this? With a genuine autarch, there is no conversation: there is only submission or refusal to submit. Abraham asked of God no causes, motives, reasons; questions made no sense.

In everyday life, we think not in such categories – had a truly evil person ever been encountered even once? or a truly good? – Princess Blutskaya, however, seemed the closest to that evil we know from the Bible, she, not Zeytsoff, not Privyezhensky, not the Kind Prince or the merciless shylocks, not Martsyn's cutthroats or the okhranniks obeying orders, but that dreadful old harridan, that impressionable old biddy, racked by illness, ruckling into her handkerchief.

Exit into the corridor, no sign of the Fleming. Stop by a window, take out a cigarette. The natchalnik offered a light. The second-class sleeper travellers were playing ball amidst the stone pines at the edge of the taiga. From the compartment beyond the prince's, the Frenchwoman leant out, the one with the neatly dressed children and distinguished-looking husband; greet her with a flourish. She gave an icy stare and called to her son. It was all so unbelievably, fabulously quiet, so peaceful and bright; even the narrow corridor seemed somehow more spacious. The Trans-Siberian Express stood at the height of day on a forgotten siding in the taiga. Wild birds and real live butterflies were perched on the cold carapace of the Black Sable, forest melodies warbled above the engine... Move out of the way, as the little boy came running to his mother with a book under his arm. Glimpse through the stream of sunlight: *Michel Strogoff, le Courrier du Tsar* by Jules Verne, volume two. The worn copy had clearly been read and re-read; the kid must have found it in the Deluxe library. Flick off the ash and hobble towards the saloon car.

Incredibly, it was empty – not a single living soul, everyone had been lured outside into the sunshine. The bookcases stood at the back, behind the billiard table and radio receiver. Slide the stiffly bandaged fingers over the spines of tomes bound in brown leather, embossed with the emblem of the Trans-Siberian Railway. Adventure stories were shelved lower down – such as Arnould Galopin's novel *Le Docteur Oméga. Aventures fantastiques de trois Français dans la planète Mars* – whilst higher up were more serious books. Mm-hmm, a geographical atlas, no, an illustrated history of the Romanoffs, no, tales from the days of the Siberian goldrush, no, poetry of the steppe, definitely not, a guide to 'Siberia New and Old', mm-hmm. Sit down in an armchair with the book resting on the knees.

As a scholarly compendium, its composition and choice of topics was far too chaotic, leaping from curiosity to curiosity; a thing designed precisely for the blasé passengers of Deluxe. Leaf through the overlong introduction. Begin with the historical part. First concrete evidence of travellers to Siberia: the Novgorod Chronicles, *De itinere Fratrum Minorum ad Tartaros* by Benedictus Polonus, Marco Polo's *Description of the World*. Chapter CCXIX of the *Description* bears the title 'Here the Province of Darkness is described'. In other words, Siberia, where *night always reigns and neither sun nor moon nor stars appear, and it is always dark like with us in the twilight.* The indigenous peoples, knowing not the world beyond darkness, have no king of their own, are subject to no foreign ruler and live like beasts. They have, however, *a vast quantity of valuable peltry. And the people who are on their borders, already living in the Light, purchase all those furs from them.* What was it about the Province of Darkness? Had the Venetian ventured so far north he'd chanced upon the polar night? Or maybe he heard only rumours of it?

… But in the chronicles of Old Rus, they also write of the 'Province of Darkness'. In the Laurentian Chronicle, 1096: merchants from Novgorod cross the 'Great Stone' and trek towards the lower Ob. In 1114: *old men still went on foot to Yugra and the Samoyeds.* The Novgorod Chronicles retell merchants' accounts from before the time of Ivan the Terrible: in the Province of Darkness live one-eyed people, and under the earth – people without heads, hunters. There they hunt for mammoths. Inserted alongside is a primitive engraving portraying a layered cross-section of the universe: on top – trees, the sun, and immediately underneath a line indicating ground level; but below this begin darker and brighter strata of the underground world, plains and rivers and earthen paths along which, between the roots of plants and layers of permafrost, run mammoths and one-eyed men, one-armed huntsmen with spears and bows, chasing after one another, men after mammoths, mammoths after men. The cigarette slipped between the fingers. Lean over the book. Under the earth, of course, no sun burns, under the earth there reigns eternal gloom.

... The seventeenth-century map of Jodocus Hondius, undersigned: *Tartaria*, shows the mythical Bargu Campestria, steppes stretching as far as the polar circle, and beyond these the rivers of the Apocalypse, Gog and Magog, the province of Ung under the sceptre of Prester John, as well as the province of Mungul, wherein live the Tatars. Karakorum, or the capital of the Mongol khans, was located within the Arctic Circle. Lower down: Cataio and the Great Wall and *Xuntien or Quinsay, or the city that is the seat of the Chinese emperors.* Think, picking up the fag-end from the rug and placing it in an ashtray: the fantasies of ignoramuses. Fantasies about lands that exist not – in other words: History written by men of Summer. That which exists not. That to which values of truth or untruth cannot be ascribed. Where is this Ung, where the polar Karakorum? Nowhere. But Hondius's map also doesn't show Siberia *Anno Domini* 1924. Where is the Province of Darkness? Indeed, are these not things just as impossible as a move made by a pawn, contrary to the rules, in a game of backwards chess? Backwards, that is, going back to the seventeenth, thirteenth or tenth century, to epochs preceding the birth of Christ, to centuries prehistoric. Starting out from a directly experienced given present, which pasts do we recognise as false, which – as possible, and which – as true?

... What are the rules of the game of History? Are they determined by the physics of the human world? Or perhaps more modestly – by mathematics? Or perhaps only by logic?

... Open the next chapter. In 1574, the Stroganoffs receive from Ivan the Terrible a million desyatinas of land beyond the Urals. In 1579, Yermak Timofeyevitch, a Cossack ataman and bloodthirsty brigand from the Volga, with the tsar's death sentence hanging over him, leads his army beyond the Urals, a thousand savage plunderers, amongst them Polish adventurers, noblemen gone rogue – and it is they who discover, they who conquer Siberia; such was the Cortez of this golden America of the East: the Don Cossack; and he behaved just like Cortez, eventually bringing artillery to the wilderness against the indigenous inhabitants, borne across the taiga on rafts. In these accounts, written in the wake of Yermak's expeditions, come mentions of the 'woolly elephants' encountered by Yermak in Siberia – or merely described to him by the Tunguses, it wasn't clear.

... End of the seventeenth century, a Dutch merchant Evert Ysbrants Ides, now bankrupt, entreats the tsar to send him on a trade mission to China, begging him for credit on goods from state warehouses. The tsar agrees, Ides travels across Siberia to China and returns having made a fortune. Ides's clerk, a certain Adam Brand from Lübeck, publishes in

1688 in Hamburg a memoir of this journey: *Beschreibung der chinesisch-en Reise.* The book creates a furore and in 1704 Ides publishes his own version in the Netherlands: *Driejaarige Reize naar China.* From this comes the earliest information on the Tunguses and their beliefs. *They were formerly a War-like Nation governed by its own Princes, inhabiting a very large Country. But they have of late years been conquered by the Victorious Arms of the* Czars of Muscovy, *unto whom they pay a yearly Tribute. As to their Persons, they are very lusty and well proportion'd, their Cloaths being nothing but the Skins of Beasts, with the Furrs on the outside of divers Colours, neither Sex being to be distinguish'd by the least difference in the Habits. They take a particular pride to have their Cheeks stitch'd (whilst they are young) with black Thread through and through, some crossways, some in imitation of a Square, or any other figure they like best. This unaccountable piece of Pride, as painful as it is, (as causing great Swellings in their Faces) they look upon as Badges of Honour. As to the excruciating Pain that this should cause, the Gracious Reader may judge for himself.* Adjust the bandage on the cheek. The Gracious Reader may judge. That shaman indeed had very regular scars upon his face. In any case, at night, they looked like scars. Shaman, shaman. Skim impatiently through the pages, moistening the thumb. *Some miles upwards from hence,* wrote Ides, *live several Tunguses, amongst which is also their famed* Schaman *or* Diabolical Artist. *The reports which passed concerning this Cheat made me very desirous to see him. Wherefore in order to gratify my curiosity I went to those Parts, to visit him in his Habitation. I found him a tall old Man, that had twelve Wives, and was not ashamed of the Art he pretended to: he shewed me his* Conjuring Habit, *and the other Tools which he used. First I saw his Coat, made of join-ed iron-work, consisting of all manner of representations of Birds, Fishes, Ravens, Owls &c, besides several Beasts and Birds Claws, and Bills, Saws, Hammers, Knives, Sabirs, and the images of several Beasts, &c, so that all the parts of this Diabolical Robe being fixed together by joints, might at pleasure be taken to pieces. He had also Iron Stockings for his Feet and Legs, suitable to his Robe, and two great Bears Claws over his Hands. His head was likewise adorned, with such like Images, and fixed to his Forehead were two Iron Bucks-Horns.* Brand: We examin'd and touch'd his Habit in the greatest of Wonder. *Then, appearing in it, he beats a Drum in a very doleful manner, at which the Standers by break out into most dreadful Lamentations and Outcries, pretending that they see certain Spectres in the figures of Ravens and other strange Birds. At the Sound of the Drum, they all begin howling like Dogs.*

At the Sound of the Drum. Raise the head above the stream of sunlight. This was the dream; everything had been dreamed. What was the sequence? First the rider's shadow against the western sky, the silhouette of a native on horseback; then the sitting down on the tree trunk, the dozing off – and then the dreaming? A native on horseback. And what was dreamed later still – that dream within the dream. With the smoke, with the drum, the tea and the shaman's herbs.

How could that which had been dreamed then in delirium, be read about only now…! Yet the whole thing could be seen from a different perspective, from the only valid perspective: from the present. Book in the hands, but dream in the head: the dream exists not, for the dream is only *remembered*. And the memory of it belongs to this same present in which the Tungus sorcerers are being read about. But here, so close to Winter… How had Mr Pocięgło put it? Thought agrees with thought. There is less and less room between truth and falsehood.

Nonetheless, this still doesn't explain the Province of Darkness, the mammoths, the whole underground world of Siberia. Nowadays it's called 'geology'. Nowadays it's not shamans who trace the Ways of the Mammoths on reindeer skins or flat stones, but tsarist cartographers at the Mining Institute in Saint Petersburg on Bristol board from topographical projections. The Siberian Coldiron Industrial Company is hunting miraculous spoils throughout the underground world; one zolotnik of pure coldiron is worth nearly a pound of ordinary iron in Vladivostock. Whilst auroras of unlicht swell above the city of tiger and sable, glows from the Byzantine cupolas of the tungetitum tserkoff, for it was and is the Province of Darkness…

Madness.

Stand up, twist the shoulders till something tweaks in the small of the back. A bird with decurved bill crouching on a branch crooked its head, staring straight into the eye, intrigued. Rest the forearm on the lowered window. The bird was gazing down from above, tilting so much it almost fell off its perch. A brief thought flashed through the mind: a whole twenty-four hours had gone by – the last traces of the penumbra must surely have left the body – do animals perceive teslectric disturbances? birds, cats? are they sensitive to them? Be that as it may, cats are definitely creatures of Summer. Blow into the half-cupped palm. Nothing.

Below the windows, puffing and panting and clasping the belly spilling from his uniform, Sergey was hurriedly tottering towards the rear of the train.

'Hey! Has something happened? Are we leaving perhaps?'

'The honourable Mr Fessar, ooph, has deigned to go berserk.'

Lean out. The siding curved here in a slight arc so that the more distant carriages could be seen at a sharper angle on the inner side; as well as very clearly – the persons gathered at the far end of the train to where Sergey was heading. Narrow the eyes. They were standing by the drawn-back door of a goods wagon, yes, of course: Doctor Tesla's wagon. Privy Councillor Dushin, the two elderly okhranniks and a man in Prince Blutsky's livery (with a double-barrelled shotgun slung over his shoulder). From the far side, circling around the end of the final carriage, Miss Filipov came running towards them, hitching up her skirt. They were engaged in heated discussion, gesticulating in all directions, at the interior of the wagon and at the taiga. Sergey soon joined them and also took to waving his arms. Looming out of the shadows, Doctor Konyeshin and Tesla stood in the doorway, Konyeshin with his physician's bag under his arm.

Exit from the saloon car, descend the stairs to the ground and hobble towards the preoccupied disputants.

Stepan was the first to glance around. He put a finger to his mouth, grabbed an arm, pulling aside between the wagons. Wrench free.

'What's this? You're letting people inside? What's Konyeshin looking for in there?'

The silver-haired okhrannik threw up his arms.

'Oy, disaster's struck, disaster! Oleg's lying lifeless with a lump the size of a walnut; the doctor says he could've smashed his brain.'

'What? Who?'

'The damned Turk! Broke in, clubbed Oleg on the nob with that cane of his and laid hands on Doctor Tesla's apparatuses. Oy, we'll have to file a report, carry the can before the natchalstvo.'

'Did you apprehend him?'

'How could we! He got away.'

'Got away?' Bridle up. 'But where could he get to away to here?'

'Well, there,' Stepan waved a hand at the horizon, 'into the taiga.'

'What?' Stare into the monumental wilderness; the gaze floundered amongst the tree trunks. 'Pickled again?'

'No, sober, they say.'

'So, what now? He'll return on foot to Europe?'

The okhrannik shrugged his shoulders.

'He's off his rocker, that's for sure.'

Approach the wagon door, peek inside. Oleg had regained consciousness and was sitting on a tin crate clasping his head and emitting the occasional soft groan; the symmetrical doctor was peering into his eyes. Nikola Tesla and Pavel Vladimirovitch Fogel were bustling around the chests disembowelled by the burglar, affixing temporary guards, covering the innards of the machines with blankets and boards; like gore from a living animal, buckets of bright sawdust spilled onto the floor from the slashed casings and claddings. Ünal Fessar must also have smashed at least one jar of murch crystals; cakes of ink-impregnated salt, glistening coal, lay scattered in the sawdust; Doctor Konyeshin trampled over them, they shattered under his heels. The housing of the Kotarbiński pump had likewise been smashed; obscenely twisted bundles of wires, some sort of black tubes, some sort of coldiron coils, the machine's whole unwieldy anatomy jutted out into the sunlight.

Someone was standing behind the back. Glance around. Dushin, he always stands behind the back.

'I thought you were supposed to be taking the prince for a walk.'

He nodded.

'It was us who spotted him.'

'You mean, you and the prince? The Turk was inside, right? He left the door open or what?'

'He was shrieking.'

'What?'

'Shrieking,' said Dushin. 'Now listen, as to this matter with Her Princely Highness –'

'But! Wait a moment! You're saying, that… Wait a moment. You knew whose wagon it was.'

'I know what Mademoiselle Filipov told Their Highnesses during the night. Doctor Tesla is conveying machines commissioned by His Imperial Exaltedness.'

'So, you hear someone shrieking inside… Was he calling for help?'

'He was shrieking in Turkish. I summoned our people, sent His Highness away, drew back the door – he sprang out like a jack-in-the-box, leapt over my head and rushed straight ahead, one, two, fell head over heels, and that was as much as we saw of him.'

'Drunk.'

Dushin shook his head.

'Yesterday, he spent half the day plying that daft journalist with tipple, but today, not very long ago, Mademoiselle Filipov spoke to him and she says Mr Fessar –'

'Was sober, yes.' Glance again at the exposed Kotarbiński pump, over which Doctor Tesla was wringing his hands. 'I think I understand. Tell me, you managed to catch a glimpse at least of his silhouette as he ran off, you must have turned towards him, a natural human reflex – his back, the running figure, for a few seconds, true?'

'Because what?'

'Did you notice anything about him – anything odd?'

Dushin crossed himself discreetly.

'You know very well. You're Frost's flesh and blood, for you Martsyn's word. Did not Her Highness speak to you of this? Remember, however, that Martsynians are not all the same. But – the American brings extermination to the gleissen, it can't end like this.'

'Like what? Don't give me that mumbo jumbo fit only for Rasputin's salons. Besides you're too late, it so happens the princess has undergone a change, now she wishes for my dead body, the sooner the better.'

Dushin shook his head again.

'You don't understand old people,'

'I understand perfectly.' Heave a sigh neath the moustache. 'I'm pleased to have had the opportunity to exchange a private word. You can tell her that I remain, come what may, in the service of the Ministry of Winter and have no intention of doing anything against the emperor. And if anything should happen to Doctor Tesla, I shall write everything to Rappacki. He's likely to read a letter from the Son of Frost, is he not? So better whisper in her ear what's needed, before she embarks on fresh stupidity.'

He tightened his lips.

'Twice she saved you.'

'She'll tell you herself, it was a mistake.'

'Saint Martsyn shall –'

'Be fucked in hell by a gleiss. Skedaddle, leave me be! The greater the lies you try to talk into me, the more my head spins. Pray I shan't believe in them.'

Step aside as Doctor Konyeshin jumped to the ground. Furiously, Tesla flung after him Ünal Fessar's cane. Grab it before it lands amongst the chattering passengers. Monsieur Verousse, meanwhile, had joined them with the handsome widow at his side, as had a couple from the second-class sleepers as well as the Imperial Navy captain from Deluxe; more travellers arrived, a small crowd formed.

'… five hours at most,' Sergey repeated, wiping the sweat from his forehead. 'There's no other possibility! You have to understand, your lordships. This is the Trans-Siberian Express, things like this don't happen, we'll all lose our positions because of it. Never mind half the passengers have escaped into the forest – five hours, no more, but the track will likely be free even quicker.'

'Competition, nothing else, my dear, he wanted to learn his competitors' secrets, they caught him and he lost his head.'

'Toss a coin, heads or tails, Sibirkhozheto always comes out on top.'

'Either way,' said the symmetrical doctor, 'here we have a burglary, the destruction of personal property, an assault on an imperial official, who knows whether not with murderous intent – had the blow fallen slightly differently, the poor fellow might not have survived; this is a job for tchinovniks of the law.'

'The doctor is right! Send for the gendarmes!'

'Gendarmes, where from?! The tarantass has only just returned from the transport-providing village, we'll telegraph from the station when we can.'

Squeeze through to Christine Filipov, Fessar's massive cane proving very helpful.

'You spoke to him today, is it true?'

'You're out of bed. Are you feeling all right? The bandage has slipped onto your chin.'

'To Mr Fessar. About what?'

'Clearly, news has spread about Nikola. He asked if he's the Doctor Tesla. His deepest respects and so on.'

'Had he spoken earlier to Councillor Dushin? To anyone else? It seems he tried to get something out of Verousse yesterday.'

'How should I know? A-ah, forgive me, sir, I'm falling asleep on my feet.'

She turned away and walked back to the Deluxe carriage. The prince's guards bowed respectfully as she passed.

The crowd by the goods wagons had swelled in the meantime to several dozen.

'... who to complain to? The thing's outrageous! First some idiot falls off and we all stop, then this madman! I have a ticket for a ship from Vladivostock, who'll reimburse me?!'

'And he was such a nice polite gentleman, that Mr Fessar, truly!'

'... not right a man to the mercy of bears even a criminal but know not know what happened how come one day at table bread and wine the next perish in dark wilderness we travel on and he wounded perhaps gone crazy who knows railman says five or four hours but how long with whistle who'll help search this and that and this direction I first we'll find him!'

'Well said, we'll drink to that!'

Sergey clutched at his head. He began to beg, moan, swear; hardly anyone listened, for a new diversion had fired the imaginations of the Transsib passengers: they summoned their companions, sorted themselves into groups like picnic parties, an excited youngling came running with binoculars, someone had hoofed it to the natchalnik to fetch whistles. Gentlemen took out their watches and checked the hour, comparing in so doing the native time zones according to the shorter hands. A Jew from the second-class sleepers appeared with a dog on a lead, a bandy-legged mutt of obscure provenance, and at once someone began shouting about the fugitive's clothes, the scent, the scent, the animal should pick up the scent, let it go after the scent! Whistles were handed out. The natchalnik arrived, but no one was listening now. Frau Blutfeld escorted the stewards, carrying baskets of sandwiches; people stuffed the proviant into pockets. A Tatar from second class sold two old compasses for five roubles a piece. Monsieur Verousse, having kissed the widow's hand, ran to his compartment to fetch notebook and pencil, brandishing a huge picnic basket clearly still full of un-consumed victuals. High-spirited children tried to climb into Tesla's wagon; he pulled the massive door shut with a crash. The one-eyed gentleman, Miss Muklanowicz's neighbour from Deluxe, marched off into the taiga on his own, shotgun in hand and bandolier over shoulder. As if on cue, further expeditions set off into the wilds. The natchalnik was waving his cap, shouting after them the agreed signals – one long: return; three short: he's been found – but any agreement was out of the question. Sergey sat looking dejected on the coldiron track chewing on his moustache. Guards in the prince's livery, laying aside their long-barrelled rifles, spat coarse tobacco into the blackberry bushes. Spruce and birch rustled above the passenger cars, their doors thrown wide open, and over the shimmering Black Sable; birch branches spread in arching zigzags, as if a nervous painter had sketched them with brush bobbing up and down on the paper. A rosy butterfly danced above the natchalnik's bald head, shiny from sweat, and eventually alighted upon it; children pointed their fingers at it. Pure whiteness flapped in the background: wind had blown out the curtains in the Deluxe carriage windows. It would fit the Gallic painters, one of those impressionists of the Mediterranean sun who blurs the contours of limestone belfries, olive groves, sailing boats on the horizon. A small painting, a rectangle ten inches by seven, yellow, green, azure and black (black onyx to portray the coldiron of the steam engine). And its title: *Summer in the Taiga*. Or: *The Taiga in Summer*. Surrounded by a thick, unwieldy dark-wood frame. *Vacationers, Asia and Engine*.

Engineer White-Gessling watched the passengers hiving off into the forest with unwholesome fascination.

'When bears really do live here.'

'You don't say?'

'And God knows what other wild beasts. They've all gone crazy!'

'Indeed. Perhaps it's their last opportunity before Winter.' Hobble after Doctor Konyeshin and Herr Blutfeld. 'Eh, hang on, wait for the cripple! Gentlemen! I'm coming with you!'

On the great significance of a brief difference of opinion between Doctor Konyeshin and Herr Blutfeld

Birds were singing in the taiga; in the churchlike stillness between trees, light fell from green stained-glass windows onto untamed paths, onto bushes heavy with unfamiliar fruit, onto grass strewn with unfamiliar blooms, onto men in elegant suits strolling at a leisurely pace from sunny clearing to sunny clearing.

'Yesterday evening. Yurga, Tutalskaya. Now a horse-drawn carriage has arrived, it seems, from the direction of Litvinovo, if I heard the natchalnik correctly. No settlements in between, only this transport-providing Stolypin village; unless there's some huntsman, or gold prospector in his open-pit mine. The stupid jackass can keep running north till he drops into the Arctic Ocean. Or some bog, more likely.

'Really, sir, I'd advise you not to strain that knee; with a smidgeon of luck, if you rest the leg, it'll be as right as rain in a week or two.'

'You can see, Doctor, that it's Herr Blutfeld who can't keep up.'

'But should something happen, who will carry you back? Those two charming damsels who were nursing you – would never forgive me. In my fifth decade now, I still find it a fascinating phenomenon, this character trait, I know not what to call it even – honey that attracts women. You've always had such success, yes?'

Burst into laughter.

'Thank you, Doctor, thank you, I'll remember this, you've amused me no end.'

'A well-brought-up son from a well-to-do family with pure heart and unblemished reputation – no, they won't even look. But just let some rake or adventurer, some infamous scoundrel wanted by the law across three uyezds, arrive in town – and the flame lights up at once in the young women's eyes, fervent whispers circulate in the salons. Why should he be such a magnet for them? Why does what is respectable, stable and dependable only disgust them? Because, you see, it's boring, that's what they say: boring.'

'All down to French romances.'

Doctor Konyeshin scowled.

'For many years I was happily married.'

'I can believe it.'

The doctor craned his neck as though gazing intently at the treetops. Walk in silence, brushing aside stalks with the Turk's cane. In a northerly direction, easy therefore to take bearings from moss on the trunks; mark the moss with horizontal notches, leaving a green deposit on the cane. The doctor touched instead the bark of passed trees with his fingertips without even leaning on them, but as if checking they really did stand there where he saw them, a birch, another birch, elm, spruce, maple, as well as those unfamiliar monstrosities of Asiatic dendrology, taller even than cedars; those he touched twice.

'That young American, Filipov... is she the daughter of the old engineer? Granddaughter perhaps?'

'I don't know.'

'She seemed too innocent to me... Mm-hmm.' Lost in thought, the symmetrical doctor tugged at his ginger sideburns. 'Sometimes it's hard to tell.'

'What d'you mean?'

'Above a certain age difference, when a man gets involved honestly, when he unites with a woman, if you understand me, young man, if you're capable of understanding it at all... then he no longer sees only the woman. Then, there's is a kind of ambiguity in it, a double vision, the imposing of images upon images,' he demonstrated with his hands on a level with his face, 'like in those glass toys: you look with the left eye and you see a young lover, you look with the right and you see the daughter you never had.'

'Because she's both one and the other.'

'Yes. No.' In his irritation, Konyeshin kicked at an anthill and sprang back. 'Ah, since we've already left Deluxe...

'The experience of fatherhood, Benedykt, the experience of fatherhood – that a man becomes a father – cannot be compared to the experience of motherhood. A mother becomes a mother gradually, in a process lasting many months, a woman grows into the idea and role as the child grows inside her. A father, on the other hand, becomes a father all of a sudden, in the space of a day, an hour, a single moment. It drops on him like a sharp guillotine-blade separating the time of non-fatherhood from the time of fatherhood. Only when he takes the child in his arms for the first time does he "believe" in its reality. Or, worse still, when he learns some day: "You have a son", "You have a daughter". Without the intermediary stages. For men, there is no state of blessedness. No male pregnancy. Men experience no fatherhood in their own bodies. It's impossible to prepare oneself.'

'But a mother always knows she's a mother; a father can never be certain he's a father. He may suspect. May believe. May pretend, that is, decide: this one shall be my son, this one my daughter – even if before this, she was someone completely different; it's an act of mind, not biology. To the end of his days, he will remain a provisional father, a would-be father, something between a real parent and a non-parent. A mother however is tangibly, unshakably sure, like the ground over which we tread.'

'Hah, yet it's evident, sir, you have absolutely no knowledge of women! A moment's conversation is enough to be convinced that it is they who inhabit the world between truth and falsehood. We men are the hapless sons of Aristotle.'

Laugh.

'Why "hapless"?'

'Well, isn't it obvious! He who is capable only of lying or of telling the

362

truth stands no chance when confronted by someone who freely denies both falsehood and truth at one and the same time. How many times, sir, have you been at loggerheads with the fair sex? How many times did she acknowledge you were right? Bah, how many times in the end did you not even know for what she was arguing?'

Strike a birch trunk with the cane till slivers of white bark shoot off all around.

'I know what you want!' Snarl at him. 'Some Curer of the Past! Quack of Human History!'

Konyeshin paused, slowing his breath.

'I am trying to warn you, sir,' he said calmly. 'One good can come out of this, as I already told you; and that will be if and when you indeed find a means of curing History. You should take this responsibility upon yourself, judge according to your own understanding. And not sell yourself to the Pocięgłos, not hire yourself out like a mindless performer: whatever kind of History they purchase, such will be the History you wheedle out of Father Frost. All the more reason, therefore, not to let yourself be captivated for nothing! Not to let yourself be entrapped by an artful strumpet, for the sake of her beautiful eyes, for the sake of a tender word or chivalric pity, till in the end you no longer know what you want, what she wants, what you yourself think and what she's insinuated between her words, what is good, what bad, what is truth, what is falsehood – History like a woman's whim.'

'You think Miss Muklanowicz –'

'All needless distractions! Temptations of the world of the senses, which you should reject as soon as possible! That which is gratuitous and non-necessary – the life you have experienced, sir, though you could have experienced a different one – what does it matter?'

Beyond an old cedar, the ground fell away into a shallow gully. Descend the gentle slope gradually, leaning on the cane.

'You, sir, are trying to persuade me of your own obsessions!' Raise the voice, without looking back at the symmetrical doctor hastening behind. 'By what am I to recognise "healthy History"? Is the History frozen beneath the Ice – healthy? Perhaps the free History of Summer – is healthier? Bah, does any tangible difference exist at all between the world of many truths and the world of soletruth? We are men of empiricism, you and I, so tell me: how am I to measure, on a naturalist's instruments, the end of one logic and the beginning of another?

'I may put forward hypotheses, concoct theories, search for phenomena connected with this or that physical influence, light phenomena, for instance, about which, I can assure you, Doctor Tesla has many curious things to tell; he's even constructed special optical instruments for this, I can at last investigate various effects caused by tungetitum.

Yet by what can I know that these are not new physical manifestations, not cases that expose the imperfection of our hitherto descriptions of nature – but rather the results of a change in the logic that confines us?

'How can I know that logic is at all a measurable force, bringing direct pressure to bear on matter or on influences on matter, like gravity, electricity; and is it possible, having transcended the boundary between Summer and Winter, between the logic of Gierosławski and the logic of Aristotle, to take readings of the ebb and flow of this force on some ingenious logometer? After all, I might just as well say that every form of frost favours two-valued logic, because each thing, once frozen, is more concrete, certain and uniform; the column of mercury therefore demonstrates the power of Classical logic – and would you not call this argumentation primitive, sir, would it not be a brazen abuse of the authority of science?

'Yet on the other hand – look at it, Doctor, together with me – on the other hand, logic is simply a language for describing reality, the criterion for the correctness of propositions expressed in this language, and now please tell me: after moving to an exotic unfamiliar country amongst strangers with different customs – and you, Doctor, are a well-travelled man – so, finding yourself in a faraway foreign country, when you sit down to write a letter to your family and come to give an account of this new reality, of what you see outside the window, what people you meet, how they behave, what kind of holidays and habits they have, what order prevails amongst them, in their homes, on the streets and in their heads, when you attempt to capture in words the spirit of this land, but faithfully, but honestly, uncensored consciously or unconsciously, do you not then find your own old language – the language of a different soil – very recalcitrant, inadequate, cumbersome and not up to the task?'

Doctor Konyeshin caught up on the ever-disappearing and -reappearing path, adjusting his step to the step of the cripple, and glancing attentively from under his slanting brow, now at the uneven ground beneath his feet, now at the surrounding forest, now to his side; that was when he squinted the most.

'I see, sir, you have given it considerable thought.'

'They don't allow me to think of anything else.'

'You're a mathematician, that's what you said, yes? – a mathematician, you deal in absolutes; even when asking about logic, you ask according to a logic adopted a priori, Yea, yea, Nay, nay. Boundary, to find the boundary! Measuring devices! A clear, explicit criterion! Such is your "scientific method". But I am a practitioner of knowledge gleaned from the thousand-year experience of other practitioners, a hesitant thoughtful practitioner, corrupted by the prejudices and imperfections of the senses; I dirty my hands in stinking wounds, poke around blindly in slippery entrails. I have no need to count every pustule on a patient's body to decide whether he has smallpox. From how many droplets does a downpour start and drizzle end?

'I see the symptoms and name the disease. Having begun from the world of ideas, as that katorzhnik Zeytsoff rightly said, because that's where everything begins, hence already in ideas: what was certain is uncertain; what was single is multiple; what was necessary is subject to free choice. Rights! Religions! Hierarchies! Systems of government! Social orders! You can see, sir, what is happening in the world, you are not blind after all. That they throw bombs in the streets and fire guns at ministers is but a faint echo.

'Besides, you too have called a spade a spade. Yes, History can exist only under the Ice: there is no History when there exists no past. When everyone is left in his own Now, with no guarantee of continuity between what was, what is and what will be – this is what we get: war, chaos, destruction, discord and hatred, confusion of all values, disintegration of all systems – people who believe in nothing, or, worse still, believe in so many things at once they themselves don't know what they believe – states that undermine their own legitimacy – nations that deny their own nationality and paint their faces with the foreign – rulers who fear to rule and long to serve, that is, be ruled – subjects who long to be suzerains of kings: ignorant peasants, undereducated youths, illiterate factory workers and unscrupulous tub-thumpers who wish to impose laws on their betters, so as to overturn all order and set the wicked above the virtuous, fools above the wise, the poor above the rich, the lazy above the hardworking, the dull-witted above the talented, the ordinary above the extraordinary, lies above truth!'

Laugh once again.

'The difference between us then is that you, Doctor, want to erect constructs of iron certainty, monuments to sacred necessity upon uncertain hazy foundations, whereas I seek a certain foolproof means of grasping uncertainty.'

'You make light of it, sir!'

'Whereas you – one shudders to think!'

The symmetrical doctor waved in irritation.

'Maybe Captain Privyezhensky was right about you... but maybe not. Maybe not, maybe I've been struck by a one-in-a-million chance, a meeting on a journey, an accident: that my word shall indeed have some bearing on History! that I shall touch History with my naked palm, like flesh to flesh! And you wonder at me?'

The gully led down into a hollow, in the midst of which the taiga slightly thinned; only old giants stood there with their spreading boughs. Glades of light, thrown open neath the eyes of a clear sky, were overgrown with densely matted spiky bushes, a type of small tree with tangled cleft branches. On some, between the thorns and leaves, unripe fruit could be seen, miniature plums. The doctor tore off a few, bit into them, spat them out.

'But they'd make good jam,' he muttered, 'delicious.'

Below an oak bough, beyond a pool of sunlight, hung a wasp or hornet nest; the insects were circling low above the earth. Herr Blutfeld aimed a swipe, trying to drive one away, but knocked off a dry branch, which showered him in wood dust and grey pine needles. They flew into his hair, down the back of his collar, whereupon he came bounding up, brushing more prickly particles off his clothes. The doctor smiled (symmetrically). Bears could indeed pay a surprise visit – to the wasps, or bees – don't bears have a taste for wild honey? The ones in Russian fairy tales certainly do.

A branch snapped behind the oak, undergrowth rustled, something began shuffling noisily. Stop still, raise the cane involuntarily; the heart leapt at twice its normal pace. Exchange glances with Doctor Konyeshin. The doctor assumed a questioning air.

In a theatrical gesture, he put his hand to his mouth and called out:

'Mr Fessar! Mr Fessar, please make yourself known!'

Bite the lips. It's all very well having a cane, but realistically – a man won't get very far with a leg like this. Lean back against a pine tree. Maybe better to take out the Grossmeister at once –

'Mr Fessar!'

'Quiet there, it's not him!' someone shouted out of the thicket.

Breathe a sigh of relief, wade through the undergrowth, skirting at a distance the branch with the nest. The doctor coughed and hiccupped from behind, amused.

A few arshins beyond the oak, beneath three birch trees, inclined like dominos tumbling on top of one another, stood the tsarist naval officer from Deluxe car number two, dispatched – according to Gertrud Blutfeld – across Asia and assigned to the new warship at Nikolayevsk. He stood wreathed in a dark cloud of flies and lesser insects, revolver in hand. He stepped back three paces. Spot then the carcass: a stag or something akin to a stag, but significantly smaller, without antlers, already horribly mangled, its neck twisted above the spine, torso torn open, innards spewing out all around, stinking to high heaven.

'I overheard it eating,' said the captain. 'I crept up, it fled. A lynx, or so I believe.'

Konyeshin and Blutfeld stood alongside. The military man introduced himself: a captain of the second rank, Dietmar Klausovitch

Nasboldt, an officer on Winter's cruiser *The Vengeance of Vladimir Monomakh*, my respects. He put away his revolver, shook hands.

'You were alone, Captain?'

'No, there were three more, somehow we got separated.'

'With that dog?'

'Indeed, it'll lead the quickest to fresh carrion.'

Prod the carcass with the cane. The flies started buzzing afresh, erupting in a black flare three or four arshins above the meat. Nudge the stag's head, and again harder; it rolls over on its soft neck, offering no resistance, like jelly. Sniff, and sweet odour pours into the throat, sticks to the tongue and palette; swallow the saliva mired in nauseous sweetness. Open wide the mouth, the flies buzz about; stand over the chewed guts, reach down. The palm tightens around the dirty yellowish hair just below the animal's head, which is dead, dead, dead; twist the head, this way, that way, like a limp wet doll, two fangs jutting out of its upper jaw; kick the buck's front legs, then higher, for the sake of symmetry, and now let it look upward with its black eye –

Doctor Konyeshin grabbed the jacket, tugged, pulled away.

'Whatever are you doing, for the love of God, playing with carrion!'

Vomit. Konyeshin barely managed to leap back. Bent double, supported by the cane, cast up the stomach's liquid contents onto the forest floor. The doctor, shaking his head, fumbled in his pocket for a handkerchief.

Herr Blutfeld was hopping up and down nearby, panting and covered in sweat, his visage purple from the strain, shaking the mouldy wood dust from his sleeve.

'Ye-es,' Captain Nasboldt muttered under his breath, 'so I shall leave you to it, gentlemen.'

The symmetrical doctor proffered a second handkerchief.

'Wipe your hands, lest you catch some abomination.'

Curse, having injured again the swollen finger.

The doctor sighed, sniffed, tugged on a sideburn and sighed again.

'Let's move away from here.'

Clear the throat.

'Some brook... I would rinse my mouth.'

'Maybe we'll have a bite to eat, it should be about the right time. Herr Blutfeld, I saw, has been abundantly provided for by his wife.'

Herr Blutfeld patted the pockets of his loose-fitting jacket and shook the haversack slung over his shoulder.

The doctor was the first to cross to the other side of the thicket, brushing apart the tall stalks and treading on huge fungi from which rose a pungent stench; his trouser legs were soiled in green and brown.

At the foot of the northern slope of the hollow, in the shade of an overhanging rock, stretched a heap of white boulders, as if some cyclops of the taiga had crushed a marble wall. From on high, from above the upper rim of the hillside, a narrow stream was trickling over the boulders.

Walk up to it, wash the hands. Herr Blutfeld took advantage of the opportunity as soon as he could and sat down on a nearby boulder; head tilted into the shade, he fanned himself with his hat. Stoop down low, leaning on the cane, so as to catch the stream of water directly in the mouth. It kept changing direction, jumping over the uneven stones – splashing into the eyes, spattering the chin, drenching the bandage, shirt and tie, leaping only at the last moment onto the tongue. The spraying droplets tickled the oddly sensitive skin.

'Well, it's as though He were at your beck and call,' Doctor Konyeshin was settling scores, seating himself comfortably beside Blutfeld. 'God is in a good mood today, Benedykt, fulfilling all your wishes. He saved you from a broken neck, halted the train, let you get away with only a few bruises and sprains; take a seat, please, which do you prefer, herring or caviar? ... and now He even favours you in matters so trivial.' The doctor laughed in his doctorly way, such that Herr Blutfeld stopped eating for a moment. 'Maybe it's time to return the compliment, don't you think?'

Unwrap the thick butterschnitte. A beetle was wandering over a boulder. Squash it with the cane, the insect carapace stuck to the wood; wipe it off with the serviette in which the bread had been wrapped. The symmetrical doctor watched these manipulations, barely concealing his amusement.

Thrust the cane into the moist earth between the feet.

'You should let it rest, sir. After all, you said yourself that you have no need of God in History. These be cheap ploys. Am I to promise you – what? that I shall persuade my father of the History of which you approve? Necessary History, no less! Look at it closely: God is God, be it people or gleissen, no matter, everything is contained within His knowledge and design. Therefore, any attempt whatsoever at war with History, at changing its course, even at straightening it out – will be a struggle against God. Maybe Berdyaeff is right, maybe he's wrong... I already asked about this, I shall ask in a different way: is self-defence against History morally permissible? Eh? Eat, doctor, and stop talking nonsense.'

Herr Blutfeld instead needed no prompting; his jaws were already at work with the power of a mining crusher, rack-rack, as breadcrumbs and whole chunks of meat and lettuce spilled from between slavering lips. Since he could not swallow at the speed of his bite – the gullet works slower than the teeth – he was stuffing in the rest with his fist, as if driving a bung into a barrel, with screwed-up fist and heel of his open palm, drooling and shoving the grub into his gob, until he no longer turned purple but red-blue and blue-black from moustache to brushy brows and to the line of his dark hair, thick and heavily pomaded. Expect the surfeit of food crammed into his throat to sprout from his ears, as though from a meat grinder, from ears and nose, in long spirals of slimy mince. Rack-rack, as he wiped saliva from his beard with his sleeve.

Avert the gaze. Eat slowly, holding the bread with two hands, in all six healthy fingers. The bandage was getting in the way; tear it from the cheek.

'When I treat people,' muttered the symmetrical doctor between morsel and morsel, staring ahead of him into green leaves and green shade, 'when I insert into their veins an artificial chemical, devised by the human mind to alleviate the diseases and natural indispositions of the age – am I then working against God? For I am opposing the natural order, the brutish plan of life and death. I am damaging nature's clocks. "Self-defence against biology". Is that morally permissible, mm-hmm?

'Man is guided by his reason – that's what makes him man. We used to live in forests, in the wilds,' he encompassed the surrounding taiga in a sweeping gesture, 'in an unchanged world, in a garden designed not by man; now we live in vast cities, in tall buildings made of materials not given to us by nature, in unnatural warmth, in unnatural light. We used to live in the freedom of family and kingdom; now we live or-ganised according to rational projects, in unnatural systems concocted by man. We used to live from the work of the body; now we live from the work of the mind, at least some of us do. Tell me, young man: we lived for whole epochs and millennia in the natural element of History, things happened that had to happen; later we sometimes looked back and described them, yet the tide of History pressed onwards and con-tinues to press onwards unbridled – but why, from now on, should we not *live in History designed by man*?'

Chew on his words to an even rhythm; sometimes the doctor's thought floundered uncracked between the teeth, and then the chewing process ground to a halt.

'Precisely for this reason: because scientific progress is the motor of History.' Pick out a morsel with a fingernail. 'Is it possible to antici-pate inventions not yet invented? Possible to include powers of science as yet unknown to science in theories of history? That's a logical con-tradiction, doctor: anticipation of such progress is synonymous with progress itself – having described in advance in suitable detail the dis-covery of electricity, by this very act you make the discovery. And so, no description of History can exist that goes beyond the present, no definite theory of History, according to which we might be able to plan it; and no such rational activity will determine which History is good for us, and which is bad.'

The symmetrical doctor screwed up his left eye, breaking the symmetry.

'If knowledge of what is good, of what is morally permissible, comes not from reason – where does it come from?' He sighed, stretched his limbs, and unpacked another sandwich. 'Mm-hmm, this ham is first-class, aah, and we can breathe green air, oh, this is healthy and natural, exercise and nourishment, mm-hmm, so imagine that the Son of God comes to us here from out of the trees, but, mind you, the Son of God as in Holy Writ, which means who – look: some uneducated savage, miserably clad, in sandals, skins, sackcloth robes, let him even speak in tongues – yet what does he know? does he know machines, does he know trains, does he know the forces of electricity and chemistry, does he know everything we know, and still more: how matter is built out of atoms, where the earth and sun hang in the universe amid the stars, how diseases are transmitted; does he know the microscopic world of germs, can he fly aeroplanes, drive automobiles; does he know everything that it's possible to know? Bah, this is what Jesus's humanity is based on, on limitation – limitation, the opposite of absolutes: incompleteness, defectiveness, ignorance. Above all, ignorance – the first difference between God and man; the enclosure of a finite mind within the "here and now".

'How easy it is to accept the bodily humanity of Christ! That he bled, that he suffered, that he was too weak to lift his cross, that he ate, drank and sweated. But when it comes to the mind… His vacillations in the Garden of Gethsemane, moments of doubt, fits of violent emotion even – well, indeed. But did the Lord Jesus ever *make a mistake*? In the most trivial, most earthly matter? For how can this be – Christ an ignoramus? Yet were he to confront any educated European at the turn of the twentieth century, he would emerge as a fool; as a savage full of superstition.

'But because he performed miracles… because he called on anti-rational truths… You see, Benedykt? Look at him closely, sir! Think! Of whom does he remind you? Do you see what, whom you defend? – the god of Russia's madnesses, emperor of insanity, parasite of the elements – do you see, who wields sway over History?'

'Rasputin.'

'Yes!'

At this, a sudden outburst broke out behind the symmetrical doctor, to his left. Glance up: Herr Blutfeld was spitting out the uneaten core of an apple.

'Wisdom!' he growled, snarling and spitting.

Watch in amazement. Doctor Konyeshin rose to his feet, stunned. Then he was brushing his suit, staring at Blutfeld from under his red brows.

Herr Blutfeld wiped his face with a handkerchief, after which he blew his nose loudly, energetically.

'Wisdom!' he wheezed and raised his eyes to the doctor. 'What are you talking about? Wisdom is not knowledge! What was he called that Greek jester? – Socrates – what a curse, two thousand years and again the same thing, and now we also have machines, machines, MACHINES!' He choked and took a long while to catch breath, massaging his chest with his fingers and whistling through his nose. 'Wisdom! They've seen microbes, so they think they know what's good and what's evil! Who taught you? Frenchmen, no doubt! Britishers! They make no distinction: wisdom – discrimination – knowledge. It's all letters and figures! Tphoo! And they pull faces in disgust: for the most important teachings of the past, teachings that open up a path to salvation, can come from the mouth of an uneducated simpleton! He knows not the good, because he has no brains, no brains, no BRAINS! Tphoo!'

He spat, red in the face. Reminiscent of Mitschka Fidelberg in Herszfeld's restaurant. The likeness was truly disturbing. Blutfeld – Fidelberg, Fidelberg – Blutfeld. And how he spoke, how he flared up when speaking.

'What are you talking about? About the machine of History, about Divine intentions, yet how – always seeking order and certainty, the greater the better, Mr Count-not-a-Count is appalled at even the slightest "maybe", whilst the doctor wants a world arranged by man according to what has to be – Winter is good, because it permits nothing outside truth and falsehood, Summer is evil, because nothing in it is certain – is this what I'm hearing from you, or not? – so I, ooph, dammit, I shall state the opposite! State the non-obvious!

'Summer is good, Winter is evil! Good is uncertainty, evil the certainty of truth and falsehood! Chaos is good, order is evil! Good the lack of History, broken History, myriads of jumbled pasts and futures, this is good! Evil the one History. History is evil! Evil, evil, EVIL!

'Evil the law written to the misery of millions, evil the necessary holy dominion founded on the suffering of peoples, evil the mathematical order of fetters and prisons. Oh, if only there could exist orders of innocence and governments of doubt! But herein lies the tragedy: that every History is built on Truth – do you see it, you must see it! – every History enclosed in the Ice shackles first and foremost man within it: Truth depends not on me, Truth is located outside of me. Redundant then is God, and redundant too man. Reason, order and History will beget the most terrible tyrannies with which neither the madness of Rasputin, nor the crimes of one or other lunatic, even the emperor, the tsar-god, nor the oppression of senseless disorganised evil, will bear any comparison.

'A man who is free – that's what I say. A man who is free, free in his uncertainty – a man who is free, man minus History – a man who is free, man between truth and falsehood – man, man, soul above the angels, MAN! The individual in his own right, you, he and he, and I, I, I!'

He wanted to say more, tetchy, puffed up, still wanted to shout, but it took him too long to compose his next sentence; he seized it like a circus weightlifter throwing a spectacular barbell onto his ribcage – chest, breath in, shoulders, bulging cheeks, teeth gritted; he leans forward, stuffed to the ears with ready questions – pfook, he'll shoot –

Too slow; Doctor Konyeshin was a more agile athlete of the word.

'Such men have I seen!' he growled, his fiery whiskers bristling to left and right. 'Free, individual men, he and he and I and you and every free anarchist with his own History and own bomb under his arm! I gathered up legs and hands and little children's bodies after your fireworks of freedom there on Kreshtchatik! When freedom swept through Kieff, and all that was left was red haze over the streets. Chaos is good? Confusion is good? Neither God, nor tsar? So, get you gone into the forest, go guzzle roots in Siberia! Go on! Join the packs of wolves driven by wolfish greed, one against the other, for when such craving takes hold, who or what shall restrain him, the free man? – go for the throat! the throat! Knowing neither security nor prosperity, they won't rally for the sake of any great deed or create any great thing, won't build cities, won't develop science or defend civilisation, but when the enemy himself appears backed by a powerful order, what remains to them? – to flee with their tails between their legs. But – they're at liberty! But – they're free! But – he and he and he and the next holy idiot, the high-handed Polish noble in his manor, the bourgeois guzzler gorged on sweet ideas!!'

He spun on his heel and marched off into the taiga.

Struggle to the feet willy-nilly and hobble after him. Herr Blutfeld dallied behind gathering up the remnants of the food; then he came running and began panting afresh.

He had run out of steam, however. Glance at him: again, he scarcely watched his step, as an expression of lubberly bliss washed over his countenance.

Attempt to engage him. 'I didn't think you were listening, sir, to those stupid conversations of ours. I hope we didn't offend you unintentionally, the doctor's fever is sure to pass soon.'

Herr Blutfeld was masticating in silence behind his lips; in this way, he gathered his words. Hop across the little brook, approach the side of the valley – still too steep; veer towards the north-east, clamber over a tree trunk blocking the way out of the hollow... lose all hope; only then did Herr Blutfeld rediscover the tongue in his gob.

'Well, I wasn't talking nonsense, wasn't talking nonsense. Do you know the anecdote about the Jew who sets off on a long journey on business? Negotiations drag on, so he goes to send a telegram his wife. So that she won't be anxious, since he has to stay on a few more days; it's a question of bigger profits, back as soon as I can, hope you are well, Itzhak. He is given a blank form to complete; the postal clerk explains that the price is calculated according to the number of words. Itzhak writes his message, adds up the words, adds up the cost of the telegram – and then begins to figure out what he can delete as superfluous, unnecessary. "Itzhak" – well, his wife knows it's from Itzhak, who else? "hope you are well" – obviously, why would he not wish his own spouse to be well? "Back as soon as I can" – well, that's self-explanatory; should he be unable to come back, then he won't come back. And so on, word after word, until eventually he's struck out the entire message: all self-evident platitudes.

'So, you see, it's the same with me. Not because I'm a miser – but because I lose heart. It's enough to think for a moment of what I intend to say, before I say it. I hardly ever butt into conversations, don't even object to the greatest inanities being uttered in my presence. The greater they are, the less sense in opposing them, because then the platitudes I'd have to recite in opposition would be all the more glaring. I keep my mouth shut, sit in a corner, hold my tongue. It's of no importance if others discern the banality of my words – I see it all too clearly myself. And this, you understand, this, with time, turns into a kind of general disheartenment, laziness in relation to people. I say this, therefore they say that, therefore I this, therefore they that, therefore I, therefore they, and so on and so forth, for as long as you want – what's the point of starting this torture at all? I sit in a corner, hold my tongue.'

'We have heard, sir, how you hold your tongue.'

'I know others don't behave in this way, it's not normal. So, I'm not going to recite here, ooph, any banalities and platitudes. There's no way you'd have guessed by yourself.'

'But this explanation of yours – I would have guessed, wouldn't I?

Herr Blutfeld shut his mouth, held his tongue.

Held his tongue – and then those sounds were heard coming from the forest to the left, from behind a thicket of coniferous bushes: snarling and smacking and coarse chomping. Stop still, raise the cane, barring Herr Blutfeld's path. Survey the wilderness. The gully, the hollow, the route out onto the flat – were anyone to enter the gully, they'd surely have to pass this way – from south to north – was this where the lynx, shooed away by Captain Nasboldt, had run? Hand the cane to Blutfeld; he clasped it in dumb amazement. Unbutton slowly the waistcoat, take out from behind belt the bundle containing the Grossmeister. Listen – unravelling the cloths and checking the cartridge in the chamber – to the snarling of the feasting animal.

Herr Blutfeld saw the weapon and paled. Put a stiffly bandaged finger to the lips. Grasp the Grossmeister in both hands, hobble into the bushes.

It must have heard noise in the undergrowth: it growled once loudly and fell silent. Creep out from under a double-trunked stone pine. The beast sprang back from the body of Ünal Fessar and bared its fangs. Hanging from them were red ribbons of flesh; it had bitten deep into the Turk's thigh. Raise the Grossmeister. Branches shook behind the back; Herr Blutfeld must have shaken the trunk of the mangled tree – he emerged from behind the stone pine and miniature birches, brandishing the cane. The lynx hissed and bolted.

Blutfeld leaned over Fessar. Staring into the glassy eyes, he crossed himself slowly.

Put away the Grossmeister.

'Doctor, sir! Doctor Konyeshin! Over here!'

Take back the cane and kneel beside the corpse. Fessar lay on his back, with the chewed leg tucked up unnaturally and his arms flung wide to the sides, as if he were trying, in post-mortem spasm, to dig his nails into the soil. Apart from the wound gouged out by the scavenger, the blood on his bald head was conspicuous: a carmine glaze coated the skull, trickling in smooth streaks of sugar-icing over the temples and forehead and into the open eyes. The heart beat faster; lick the lips from emotion. Touch this enamel with a fingertip – sticky, warm, moist. Wipe the finger on Fessar's shirt. Behind the Turk's head a burdock-like weed was growing; tear off its largest leaf. Slap the leaf over the knee to straighten it, then lay it on the dead man's chest: vertically, perpendicular to the breastbone, parallel to the sunrays penetrating through the double crown of the stone pine. Close the left eye. And now: one side of the leaf, other side of the leaf, gaze and compare: light, shadow, light – is there agreement and harmony on both sides of the divide? or chaotic glintzish dancing and constant ferment on the dividing line between sunlight and obscurity, like in a devil's cauldron? Oh, there can be no doubt, Ünal Tayyib Fessar had well and truly drained himself of murch in Tesla's wagon, it was a miracle he'd been able to stand on his feet, that he'd escaped from the arsenal of Summer still as a man –

'Move back, sir! I can't leave you alone for a moment… Whatever is it that so draws you to dead things!'

Stand up, leaning on the cane, and step aside from the corpse without a word.

Konyeshin took out a railway whistle and blew a series of terrifying blasts into the taiga, startling the birds from nearby trees and forcing Herr Blutfeld to put his hands over his ears. Then the doctor leaned over the unfortunate Fessar.

'Ugh, horrible, horrible. Let me take a closer look… Nothing here. It certainly wasn't this leg that bled him to death. Mm-hmmm.'

Skirt around the businessman's resting place, raking aside the forest undergrowth with the cane. Herr Blutfeld made himself comfortable in the fork of the stone pine, opened his haversack, hogged what he had not managed to dispatch beforehand. Doctor Konyeshin, for the second time in two days, fingered the skull of Ünal Fessar, this time twisting the head with grim expression, his hands completely smeared in blood. Trudge through the ferns and dwarf bird cherry. Captain Dietmar Klausovitch Nasboldt appeared, and with him some spindly youngling from the second-class sleepers, who at once turned green and leant against a trunk, breathing frantically. Wade into mud; one boot became stuck. Jules Verousse appeared, and the hunter with the glass eye; the glass-eyed man also took out a whistle and blew protract-edly. The siren of the Black Sable responded from afar. Half the Express would soon come flocking. Venture deeper into the thicket, ignoring the shooting pains in the swollen knee. Herr Blutfeld was distributing the rest of the proviant. Verousse and one of the prodigal brothers were discussing incoherently cases of fatal *delirium* as they bit into smoked bacon. Lose sight of them, walking in spirals beyond the first ring of trees, overturning with the cane every stone as well as a bough lying loose on the ground. Think fleetingly of the lynx: if it had drunk its fill of such strongly demurched blood, stuffed itself full of demurched flesh – yet is not teslectricity, both negative and positive, diffused in soil? A scavenger, a beast of prey, prowls here now, but also something between beast and not beast, between lynx and not lynx. Is it hereditary? No. But if such animals were to be bred, always ensuring that the moment of conception takes place in torrid demurchment of male and female, in the first, second and third generations, in the tenth and hundredth – a non-necessary evolution – the evolution of a Fauna of Falsehood, Darwin cheated by Satan – the Kingdom of Kotarbiński's Animals – the Natural History of Maybe… Doctor Konyeshin was calling for a stretcher to be improvised from birch branches, for someone to run for the stewards, to fetch the natchalnik. Turn over a large pebble, glistening still with droplets of water, trapped between the roots of a hornbeam. On the edge of the pebble there remained a long streak of blood. Circumvent at a distance the double-crowned stone pine and the loud company assembled beyond it, and hobble back to the train.

On Winter

Dwook-dwook-dwook-DWOOK. Mariinsk, Suslovo, Averionovka, Tyazhin, Tisyul, Siberia sped by beyond the window of the hurtling Express. At the sunset hour, on the eastern horizon, a rift of warm red radiance appeared above the taiga, like a mirrored reflection of the evening glow. Stand in the compartment and watch through the windowpane as the line of smouldering embers swells on the horizon ahead of the locomotive; against this backdrop, the coal-black silhouette of the Black Sable sometimes came into view on bends, its coldiron rainbows acquiring a sepia sheen, as if singed and made sooty at the edges. Low in the east loomed a third-quarter Moon: a golden coin-face similar to a five-rouble piece, except that instead of the bearded profile of Nikolay the Second it showed the sliced-in-half visage of a livid striga – here a sunken eye, a crooked ear, a fang, the lunar seas. It brought to mind a negative of Doctor Tesla's karmagraph burned onto a matt tungetitum plate. Dusk was gradually descending upon Siberia and reflections of the compartment interior were beginning to appear in the window, now fading before images of forest and steppe still illuminated by sun, now more distinct than these – reflections of the compartment, the figure of a man, his pale face. Draw close to the pane, narrow the eyes. Bruises and red streaks remained, not only the puffy lip but also the whole right cheek, lacerated by sharp stones, maybe also by branches – with the regularity of a deliberately designed pattern, vertical strokes, horizontal strokes. Touch it carefully: hot, swollen, painful to the touch. Wash it in cold water, glancing into the gilded mirror above the basin. How to shave? There is no way. The face would look even more like that of a shady troublemaker, the caricature of a blackguard born and bred. Slip the bloodstone signet ring back onto a healthy finger; take from the wardrobe the cane with the dolphin-shaped handle. Fessar's handy, more hefty cane had had to be deposited with the natchalnik; it had been stamped and sealed in the Turk's compartment along with the rest of the dead man's luggage. They'd already telegraphed ahead to Irkutsk for representatives of Ünal Fessar's trading house to be waiting at the station. Twirl the cane between the fingers – it slips through, for the fingers are stiff as wood, several still bandaged. Think: whichever way the dolphin-snout points, such will be the choice. And only then glance at the feet. The handle was indicating the door. But perhaps… Look away from the mirror. Deception! For already a different thought, a fresh wager, what is this? – touch the forehead – what weakness, feverish delirium and internal trembling, what fluttering of the spirit swiftly manifesting itself also externally: to sit down, or not to sit down, look out of the window, no, go to bed, no, set to work on Teitelbaum's papers, or not set to work, fall asleep, though there'll be no falling asleep, and therefore go out, or not go out, go out, not go out, go out – stand by the door, listening intently. Woop, woop, heart, dull headache, black pulse neath the cranium, its footfall as it closes in, has closed in – Shame. Yet it had been forgotten! People had been clung to! Smoothly executed words and gestures and deeds had been succumbed to, out of sheer momentum, out of sheer stupidity. But it was enough for that momentum to be lost just once, and for a few hours to lapse in the seclusion of the locked compartment, knocked off stride, with empty time for the imagination. And it had returned – shame or not shame, it has no other name, yet how better to label its visible symptoms in the world of matter? Pick up the cane. Now every movement will be a new decision, a new battle. Put on the knitted Jaeger vest, white dress shirt with pleated bib, black trousers of English wool, black patent leather shoes. The fingers shake when tying the laces, all except the bandaged ones, and when tying the soft wide cravat with silver stars. Comb the hair with water and pomade, smoothing it back from the forehead. Slip on the waistcoat and frock coat. Fasten the stiff collar, a good two vershoks high; the collar claws into the bruised skin. Cufflinks still need adjusting. Handkerchiefs. Cigarettes. Matches. Go back: unbutton the waistcoat, insert behind the belt the Grossmeister. Clothes brush, spittoon, *eau de Cologne*, what else, no, it's time to go – stand motionless. Stand, twirling the cane between the fingers, the dolphin does not fall; standing like this till the end of the world. On the eastern horizon, already dark, a yellow line is swelling like the outline of an amber wall slowly rising out of the taiga backwoods. To go out, not to go out, to go out, no. The hand reaches for the doorhandle, presses down; turn on the heels and hobble out into the corridor. Whilst locking the compartment door, catch an echo of the music, carried this far from the parlour car, despite the clatter of the train hurtling at full speed. So, the dancing had already commenced, dwook-dwook-dwook-DWOOK.

Gospodin Tchushin was standing in the short corridor before the entrance to the parlour car, puffing on a cigar by an open window, beads of sweat on his face, collar undone. He glanced around – will he flare up again at the very sight? bespatter again with the spittle of shame? – he glanced around and opened wide his mouth, lips ingratiatingly oozing butter.

'Venyedikt Filipovitch, so it's you, alive and well! But what bad luck with Mr Fessar, d'you know what they're saying?'

'What?'

'That this train of ours – is like a ship at sea, you understand, you've been rescued from the belly of the whale.'

'What?'

'Jonah, you'll see for yourself,' Tchushin laughed, 'Jonah! Jonah!' And only after a long pause, when he received no answer in word or expression, did he reflect and shut up.

It would have been better had he spoken. Anything at all, so long as he went on swimming in his own stream of words, talking away, unthinking – but since he'd shut up, one thought or another must surely have begun circulating inside his head, as he rushed to describe himself to himself in language of the second kind – is he not a buffoon? a great durak? a society ape? – well, he was chagrined at himself, his mug blushed redder than ever, whilst a cold draught ruffled his hair; poor Tchushin was incapable of averting his gaze. Had the response had been one of laughter, it would have given him a chance to make a second escape into ribald chortling and coarse mumbling – and thereby extricate himself from the trap; he could have done something, changed the subject. But no – stand likewise and merely stare. Jonah! Tchushin began feeling with a trembling hand neath his frock coat – what was he searching for, handkerchief, pocketbook, watch? He was already slightly tipsy, but that was no justification. After all, there'd be no turning on the heels now and fleeing back to the compartment! Since leaving it had been achieved! No better could be expected of the other passengers, and more likely worse; Aleksey Tchushin is a harmless cretin, blabs whatever vodka flushes out on his tongue. Jonah! Bite the lips, step forward, striking the cane against Tchushin's knees. The Russian leapt back as if scalded and –

The door opened into the parlour car, into the room with the fireplace, releasing loud music and merry voices onto the outside. Zeytsoff appeared in the company of Captain Privyezhensky. Filimon Romanovitch strode energetically in front, jostling his way through ahead of the military man in gala uniform; but one step farther and the picture was reversed: the captain, one hand gripping the ex-katorzhnik by the elbow, the other by the collar, is pushing and pulling and jerking Zeytsoff through the door and passageway between the carriages, into the corridor and saloon car, with his final step bestowing on Filimon Romanovitch a heavy blow to the small of his back, whereupon Zeytsoff pressed against the boiserie as though hacked down, like a straight tree trunk felled on its side. Thus, he collapsed against the wall, hiding his head under arm, and only an agonised prayerful lament could be heard from under that arm.

Captain Privyezhensky turned from him in contempt.

'And you as well!' he declared in a loud voice, raising his white-gloved hand and aiming a finger like the barrel of a Nagant. 'So I don't have to see you there either, Count Ice, tphoo, get out of my sight!'

Everything would have gone differently, fates and lives been turned around – had it not been for Aleksey Tchushin. Who stood watching with florid mug, eyes agog, cigar in trembling paw.

Smile – and even without a mirror now, realise into what grimace of arrogant disdain and evil mockery the battered, swollen, lacerated physiognomy had twisted.

Captain Privyezhensky clenched his white fist.

'O, the rabid dog now bares his teeth, o!'

'Get lost!'

'Because I won't touch a cripple? Believe me, you're still a healthy specimen!'

There was no doubting the captain's intentions and fists: should this young bull choose to hurl himself, there'd be no time to reach for the Grossmeister, to disentangle it, take aim.

'Never have I expected any better of Russian officers,' say hoarsely from a dry larynx. 'Well, go on, show us what they taught you at the imperial academies!'

Privyezhensky raised his fist but failed to move from the spot. Beads of perspiration, thick drops, stood out on his forehead, glistening from the burning lamp fixtures and gilded ornaments of Deluxe.

'Rat's spawn!'

'Well, come on!'

'You!' He wheezed, taking a long time to catch breath. 'Polacks! He stands there moaning that he's defeated, such is his superiority over the stronger man, such his rat's honour! And they buried you with honour and without!'

He drew himself up, saluted with a sneer and marched off into the ballroom without even closing the door behind him.

Hobble after him.

Zeytsoff grabbed the arm and hung on to it.

'What d'you want?' Snarl at him. Cough, swallow the saliva. Drink, a drink was needed, to rinse it from the throat.

'Venyedikt Filipovitch, I owe you my thanks, owe you,' whispered the katorzhnik, 'yes, owe you gratitude, God bless you, I thank you.' And without taking a step backwards himself (so it was essential to retreat as far as the large radio apparatus), he bent forward in a sudden bow, almost prostrating himself on the floor, once, twice; something slipped from his pocket, but he didn't retrieve it, only cozied up again, grabbed the elbow and whispered in the ear, feverishly excited: 'I had thought: he will do as he said, he the fickle youngling, as they flip him over, both onto the other side and then onto a third, if not the doctor and Gospodin Pocięgło, then other jackals of History, they'll bribe him, talk him round, one way or another, against God, against the true History, for I grasped only then how the doctor had clearly named the terrible thing, when he was trying to persuade you of it there: despite their best intentions, dear to God – it is not the task of men to make History! not the task of men! But now, what do I see: would such a mercenary ma-lapert eager to sell his soul stand up in defence of poor Zeytsoff, bah, his own abuser, would he shield him from just punishment? Well, no! And yet it is proved again that God could not have arranged it better! Everything is –'

'Or maybe I simply don't wish it to be known *why* you threw me off the train, eh?'

He didn't even flinch. Nodded his shaggy bonce, joyful, beaming.

'Yes, yes, I have known it: to forgive but not look in the eye. Truly, almsgiving burdens not the bestowed, but the bestower. Didn't I speak to you of this? A man must practise it, practise it! Throw a beggar a quarter-kopeck piece and don't run away, but stop, bear it, harken to his thanks! That takes real courage!'

'Be gone!'

Step into the room with the hearth, into music and bright dazzling light, into the hubbub of voices, against the flow of dancing couples. Contrary to the initial impression and prior assumptions, there were by no means many of them: the vast majority of first-class Transsib pas-sengers were men, businessmen and representatives of various Siberian professions, whilst there were no more than a dozen women eligible as partners. Glance around quickly: no Miss Muklanowicz or her mighty-handed auntie. Were they not heard leaving their compartment? Lean on the cane and the doorframe as the carriage lurched more violently. In addition to all wall lamps, a branching chandelier blazed in cold flames of crystal and silver, it most of all – a chandelier suspended especially for the occasion from the convex roof of the parlour car. It swayed to the rhythm of travel, seemingly to the rhythm of the music. Monsieur Jules Verousse was playing, watched over by Frau Blutfeld, who sat beside him and fed him delicacies from a glass *bonbonnière* standing on the piano; one of the Deluxe provodniks was accompanying him on the violin. The spindly Fleming, his mouth full of sweets, peeked every so often over his shoulder at the handsome widow spun on the parquet by ever different partners; he alone, the pianist, would not dance with her here. On his other side, betwixt fiddler and fireplace, sat Prince and Princess Blutsky, he dozing, she curled up shrunken in her armchair, a diminutive figure roasted into it like meat in a tin – should she move hand or head, her skin will crack and bones pierce through the scorched surface. So, she moves not, sits motionless, as if she too were sleeping; but she does not sleep: twinkling light from the chandelier is reflected in the old lady's moist, wide-open eyes. She sees everything. Bow to her at once from the threshold. She gave no sign of recognition. Except that Councillor Dushin, standing behind the prince's chair, laid his hand on her shoulder; that was the sign.

The width of the carriage prevented, of course, the organisation of anything remotely resembling a genuine evening dance, let alone a ball. Knocking into one another again and again, the couples glided in two irregular lines from the entrance to the fireplace; farther away, as well as in the gallery, stood those who were not dancing, resting or merely watching the dancers. Several of the men wore tailcoats; striking was Dietmar Klausovitch in the dress attire of an Imperial Navy officer, his greying beard trimmed to a sharp wedge, a noble scar across the bridge of his nose. Whilst the women treated this Trans-Siberian dance, naturally, as an excuse to show off the best of what they had in their trunks and travelling jewellery cases; eyes were dazzled by the diamonds alone, sparkling with the reflected brilliance of the chandelier. The French woman, dancing with her husband, was conspicuous: in her Poiret gown, target of the princess's sharp tongue, narrow, flowing, trailing, made of silk satin or lamé, worn without corset, open at the back in a deep décolletage, slit down the side of the leg, the waistline oddly dropped; such a gown seemed obscenely... indefinite here. And also, that eccentric Monsieur Antoine haircut, which Frau Blutfeld had grouched about from the start... Evidently, they really had come with their children directly from Paris.

A slow polka was being danced, or maybe a *Schottische*. Manage to hobble along the carriage wall between the couples without waiting for an interval. Captain Privyezhensky was standing in a corner by the open door to the gallery talking to one of the prodigal brothers, Captain Nasboldt and the tall prosecutor. Stop on the opposite side to him and the upright piano, to the fireplace and, seated by the fireplace, the princess. A steward appeared with drinks. Shampanskoye! Look out of a window with glass to the lips. On the dark horizon ahead of the Express, the long glowing streak of red and yellow embers was swelling, brighter than the cold half-moon. The train was speeding straight into that wall. Sip the shampanskoye, it tickles the nose; sneeze. Behind the back – applause, whistling and laughter; Verousse had finished playing, and now they were urging him to play something called the 'Cake Walk'.

'Ooph, I must get my breath back. So, you're on your feet again, I was having pangs of conscience.' Porfiry Pocięgło snatched two glasses from the tray, emptied both, and huffed into his folded hands. 'Because we left you there, for you won't pull the wool over my eyes: you did not fall off of your own accord, I don't believe in such wonders. You have to tell me, sir, what kind of roguery it is. Ooph. Gunshots in Yekaterinburg, and now it transpires that someone has been rifling through my things! Why? Because I was talking to you!'

'And you're talking again.'

He burst out laughing.

'That's true, I myself court disaster.'

'Jonah, what?'

'A-ah, I heard, I heard. You're on friendly terms with that American, true? Doctor Tesla? The prince has loaned his own people to protect Tesla's wagon of machines.'

'Do you want to end like Fessar?'

'What?'

'He was asking –'

'The same questions, well yes.'

'You have no idea even, how hard it is to hide a secret that exists not.'

'Oh, I take you at your word, sir, you're not familiar with any secret coldiron technology.'

Verousse struck up a lively tune; the passengers began to clap in time to the rhythm.

Pocięgło drew closer and raised his voice.

'But you won't deny your father! Here, there's no longer anything to hide.'

'You told the princess that you'd heard nothing of him.'

'We-ell, no one writes about Filip Gierosławski in *The Siberian Herald* or *Irkutsk News*. Also, I failed to make the connection immediately; and I would be lying, after all, were I to say I recall the name. On the other hand, the Martsynian legends... You see, sir, all these wild hiberniks are a highly dubious bunch...' He took out his business card and, deep in thought, spun it between his fingers, resting a shoulder on the sculpted window frame. His reflection was visible in the glass pane, fluid, transparent, black-and-white; Porfiry Pocięgło appeared in it as if depicted in charcoal and whitewash, in unlicht and glintz. 'True, it's hard to walk along a pavement in Zimny Nikolayevsk without bumping into a hibernik; my brother-in-law, not to look any further, runs naked with his dogs through the snow on the creamy frost. But *le Père du Gel*... This already stinks to high heaven of Martsyn.'

Bridle.

Mr Pocięgło pulled a sour face.

'We hire them to work in the coldmills, on the production of cold-iron coolbonds. These most hardened hiberniks are either originally Martsynians or become infected with Martsyn sooner or later. You, sir, have a misguided notion of it. In Europe, even in European Winter,' he waved his arms incoherently, 'it's all words, words, words. Salon mysticism and the princess's theosophical societies. But in the Land of the Gleissen – in the Land of the Gleissen, peasants gather their wives, children, dogs, all their animals and, having gorged on ice and moonshine, having stripped naked, with naught but a holy icon on their chests, they crawl like this into an icecradle, into the throats of the icers. It comes in waves, there's supposedly calm, then suddenly you hear: a quarter of a village has committed self-glaciation. What has happened?' He shrugged his shoulders. 'It's not madness. In this there is calm as well as that silent obtuse peasant resolve; more like a religion.'

'Like at the time of the Great Schism.'

'Quite. Russians probably have it in their blood. And authority, how do you imagine authority reacts? No differently from before. Governor Schultz has proclaimed laws against all Martsynian practices. Anyone caught within the borders of the Irkutsk Governorate General gets five years' incarceration, and not here, but in the Orenburg fortress or the southern Caucasus.

'So it was only in the night, when they went searching for you, that I put two and two together. And, mm-hmm, how to tell you...'

'They take him for a Martsynian, that's clear.'

'Benedykt, sir,' he said softly, gently, 'there's a warrant out for his arrest. By all accounts, he has drawn entire villages after him into the Ice. Schultz must have put a price on his head.'

'How much?'

Mr Pocięgło stared oddly.

'I don't know.'

'What is it?' Press a finger to the windowpane. 'Do you see? There, on the horizon.'

'Ah, that. The taiga's ablaze.'

No longer a line, no longer a wall, but a strip of land encircling the Trans-Siberian Railway, a path of fire – a golden half-girdle separated from the starry firmament by a black girdle: fumes from the forest conflagration obscuring the night sky. It must have stretched a good fifty or so versts in order to engulf the whole expanse of horizon. According to the books read, fires in the taiga can be so voracious, spread over such vast distances, that they can be traced with a finger on the surface of a globe. At that moment, very little was yet visible beyond the bewitching play of colours in the dark, but should the Transsib really cut through those fields of flame...

'I hope we shall see one another in Irkutsk. Perhaps then you'll be able to tell me the whole story.' Mr Pocięgło parted at last with his business card. 'And should fate prove unfavourable... We endeavour to take care of newly arrived compatriots.'

'Thank you.'

He moved off into the gallery. Turn away from the window. The steward obligingly proffered the tray; grab a second glass of shampanskoye. An arrest warrant – whole villages into the Ice – Father Frost. No wonder various smitten Pyelkas are ready to sacrifice their lives to defend his son. One and the same faith, yet from this one faith some Martsynians deduce a great threat to Russia and in short to the world, whilst others – a duty of veneration. Take two Poles and you'll hear three types of politics; but take two Russians – you'll see three roads to God.

Laughing couples flashed by at arm's length, the carriage rocked underfoot. At this rate, even the shampanskoye will intoxicate before midnight. Cast the eyes around the room as the tongue tingles in the mouth. No sign of her. Maybe she won't come at all, has changed her mind. To return, rap on her door? Dolled up in a pink frock, a little girl ran past along the wall, squealing loudly. And knocked the dolphin cane out of the hand; it rolled towards the gallery.

Another man's hand was faster.

'Merci, merci beaucoup.'

'De rien. Comment vous portez-vous?'

'Ah, mon jambe? Cela ne vaut pas la peine d'en parler.'

'I have not yet had the pleasure –'

'Madame Blutfeld, I think, already introduced us in her own way.' Smile. 'Prosecutor, sir...'

'Razbyesoff Pyotr Leontinovitch.'

He nodded stiffly. Realise at once, since his handshake is likewise brief and resolute, that he's the next military man amongst the Deluxe passengers, and that it's no surprise he's drawn to Privyezhensky and Nasboldt. And indeed, a few minutes of social chit-chat and two glasses of shampanskoye later, he confirmed it himself: a retired lieutenant colonel of artillery, currently in the civil service in the rank of court councillor, prosecutor in the Kamtchatka circuit. On his way via Vladivostock precisely to Petropavlovsk-Kamtchatsky, to where he's been transferred from the department in Blagoveshtchensk.

'Kamtchatka and the Tchukotka Peninsula, my dear sir, will now become, once we sign God willing the peace with the Japanese, the key to peace in our internal politics, bah, the key to all Siberia.'

'Really?' Mutter, attempting unsuccessfully to peer over the prosecutor's shoulder and into the gallery. The aim was difficult to accomplish since Pyotr Leontinovitch stood a good five vershoks taller. Yet despite his height, he was not in the habit of bending over in order to talk to a shorter interlocutor; his spine curved not at all, permitting movements of the head only, but the head also the prosecutor held bolt upright. Thus, he peered down from under half-closed eyelids, over the black moustache and chin with its ugly gash – there was something predatory and avian about him. Vulture? Eagle? Turkey-cock? His tonsure-like bald patch merged with the high forehead; above his bushy eyebrows, he shone in the reflected light of chandelier and lamps. Vulture.

'Were you not in contact perhaps with Oblastniks, Venyedikt Filipovitch?'

'With whom? I think not.'

'You should realise as a matter of urgency that any support for their designs will be treated, well alas, I must tell you plainly, as a crime of treason.'

'But what are you talking about, sir! I know no Oblastniks.'

The prosecutor turned his eyes towards Mr Pocięgło dancing with the handsome widow.

'When Harriman builds his Around-the-World Railroad, Eastern Siberia will become a very close neighbour of the United States of America. If war with the Japanese Empire no longer stands in the way, what can delay construction? You understand me surely. The Ice is not moving in all directions of the world with the same velocity. Now, were it possible to induce the gleissen to veer more to the east... across the Bering Strait... to Alaska, to Canada, to the Indians and cowboys... to shackle the golden prairies in Winter...'

Sigh out loud.

'And I was hoping we'd already come too close to the Land of the Gleissen! How much more of this nonsense must I listen to! All it takes is a word or a word left unsaid for them to come up with – lies, lies, lies.'

Razbyesoff smiled good-naturedly. In a fatherly gesture, he laid his hand on the shoulder; brush it not off. He was at least fifty years old, no doubt a father himself; sense no falsity in these reflexes of his.

'Forgive me. A prosecutor's soul.' Now he stooped forward so as to be heard above the music, above the dancing and clatter of the train; but he also bent stiffly, unnaturally, having to put aside his glass and lean against the window. 'You harbour no ill-will, I trust? Likewise, you can't blame Monsieur Verousse for wanting to write an article about you. First, His Princely Highness drives you from his table, just an ordinary social misunderstanding, I wager, but then you ruin Her Highness's spiritualist séance, then there's the notorious street brawl in Yekaterinburg, there were dead bodies after all, then we hear about Father Frost, then Monsieur Fessar attacks you in revenge for some underhand business practices, then you fall off the train, yet that very same prince stops the train for your sake, and then we find Monsieur Fessar dead. Truly, this dancing party – it seems like a wake for Fessar, or something to fill time instead of a wake, wouldn't you say, sir?'

'Well, all right, I follow, I am an agent of the Kaiser or a mesmerist in the pay of Rasputin?'

The prosecutor laughed again and gave the arm a squeeze.

'You are a young man out of his depth, fallen amongst people of power and money who are accustomed to dealing with other people of power and money, a young man intelligent enough to know how to exploit their habits, which is not to say that you wish to exploit them for any particular purpose, you have no clue even for what – as I say, you are out of your depth – yet you cannot restrain yourself. It's a kind of compulsion.'

'Have we come sufficiently close to the Land of the Gleissen, Venyedikt Filipovitch?'

'*Excusez-moi*, I must exchange a few words with Doctor Tesla.'

Catch a glimpse of the Serb's face neath Razbyesoff's arm; it moved across in the deep perspective of the gallery above the faces of passengers standing in the doorway to the fireplace room, watching the dancers and clapping to the rhythm; the inventor was taller than any of them. Trip briskly towards the gallery, placing the empty glass on the sculpted windowsill, forcing a passage through with the aid of the cane. Captain Privyezhensky fortunately had his back turned at that moment.

Find Doctor Tesla by the middle window of the three great gallery windows, on the left side of the train; he stood eating an apple, juice trickling down his bony chin and onto the white foulard scarf wrapped high around his neck above the whiter-still bowtie. In one corner of the gallery, the stewards had hung baskets of victuals on coloured ribbons; naturally, all the children of the Deluxe passengers came running in, choosing from the wicker nests crystallised fruits and pastries, sugared almonds and chocolate delicacies. The little girl and three boys frolicked behind the backs of the men standing in the doorway, clumsily mimicking the dance steps. Verousse and the provodnik were playing a tango.

Stop beside Tesla.

'Asia is burning,' he said pointing through the window with the apple.

'It's hot in here.'

'Were you dancing?'

'No.'

'You're very flushed, sir.'

'And stuffy.'

'Christine is enjoying herself.'

'So I saw.'

'The Fleming's playing is not bad. Once Paderewski tried to teach me, ah, your compatriot besides, the lion's mane, I remember those concerts, the ladies used to faint.'

'On your shirtfront, Doctor –'

'Oh, thank you.'

Between men who owe each other their lives – debtor and debtor, saviour and saviour – what further conversation can there be? what more can be expressed in language of the second kind? Nothing.

Stare at the conflagration in the taiga, a beautiful spectacle of faraway devastation.

Lights and shades undulated over Tesla's skin and tailcoat in irregular ebbs and flows, as if the radiance from an additional source fell upon him alone, revolving around him on a drunken ellipse.

'The colour of your eyes –'

'Mm-hmm?'

'It seemed to me.'

'I had darker ones, but they've grown lighter over the years from intensive brainwork.'

He still passes teslectricity through himself; this was to be expected, not even a close encounter with death would restrain him. Does Miss Filipov know? She would not be dancing there, delighted, if she knew. Nikola no longer does it in the compartment; he goes no doubt to the goods wagon, even to immurch himself after dinner. Besides, he spent half the day there after Fessar's break-in.

'Tomorrow after breakfast, all right?'

'Pardon?'

'You will drop by, sir, to let a little murch.' Doctor Tesla threw away the apple-core, wiped his white gloves. 'Just a little bit...' He twisted his index finger against his temple. 'What's the word – inspiration? a creative vein? madness? foolhardiness? For to give birth to a genuinely new idea, *mon ami*, is the only task worthy of man and the sole purpose of human life.'

Press the forehead into the cold pane.

'I have been wondering about this. To let murch... A bit yes, a bit no – because you see, Doctor, it's not like in your optical toy, the interferograph: either a string of beads, and then it's Summer, or two dots, and then it's Winter. Maybe on light itself, it has that effect. Maybe light changes suddenly when a certain limit is reached in the concentration, in the pressure of the murch. But here... there are degrees. Less Summer, more Winter. You pump in a little murch, then a bit more – and we shall be like those hiberniks in the cities of the gleissen – and a bit more

– like the gleisseniks in Siberia – and more – like the Martsynian self-glaciators – and still more, more, more, black crystal after black crystal – how much is needed in order to see the world as gleissen see it?'

'As your father sees it?'

Stare at the distant fires, stare not at the doctor. Two reflections in a dark pane: extend the lines of their gazes – and where do they intersect: on the glass, or out there, over Asia? Stereometry, the science of the soul.

'He has frozen.'

'So you've been telling us.'

'So they tell me.'

'And you are travelling to him...'

'For what?' Laugh. 'A young man out of his depth. But it's true, true, we are already so close to the Land of the Gleissen... For what am I going to him? Doctor, sir...'

'Yes?'

'Your machines... That murch pump, the weaponry against the gleissen... In Irkutsk, first you will have to conduct experiments – experiments on people...'

'You're surely not thinking of yourself –'

'No! Him. To demurch him, to draw the Ice out of him.' Shut the eyes, pressing the cheeks into the windowpane. 'Pump it all out of him, the entire soletruth, the whole of Winter. Is it still possible to save him at all? They won't allow me; the emperor's people want to exploit him, while you too, Doctor, are working for Nikolay the Second and I can't demand from you –'

'Of course, I shall help you, my friend.'

He proffered an apple. Munch in silence, juice flowing onto the chin. Dwook-dwook-dwook-DWOOK, a fast waltz now playing. The Moon was rising above the fires, the Moon was illuminating the two reflections in the wide pane, an imperial gold coin above the silver lock on Nikola Tesla's temple.

A breathless Christine came running up, caught Nikola by the hands, whirled him around this way, that way, and then began dragging the old man onto the dance floor.

Turn towards her, watching not without sympathy.

'And you, sir!' she cried. 'Why are you standing there! She's waiting for you! Ah, your leg, well yes, the ill-fated leg, the no-good damaged leg, and that mishap; who made you throw yourself off the train?' She burst into laughter and spun away in the arms of Captain Nasboldt. Dietmar Klausovitch exchanged glances with the good-humouredly concerned Tesla. Pouting, Mademoiselle Filipov began to play with the glittering decorations and buttons on the sea wolf's chest.

Enter the fireplace room. There was a pause in the dancing. Miss Muklanowicz was standing behind the piano. Turned in half-profile, she was talking to Frau Blutfeld over the head of Monsieur Verousse, who was savouring his wine. Push a way through between the passengers, tapping the cane. This time, Miss Muklanowicz had chosen a totally different gown: pale-blue crêpe marocain, lavishly gathered from the waist down, with dark-blue appliqués; the bodice instead was high, supporting the bust in a daring décolletage, and above it only the black choker against her white neck, for her shoulders too were bare, discounting the *cache-nez* light as a veil. For the first time, the *devushka* had let down her hair, it fell in a black wave onto her shawl and shoulders. Only the painting of her eyes and lips was the same: Gypsy kohl and juniper carmine.

Was it illness that gave her complexion its alabaster tone? Or everything together – the hair and the *maquillage*, the gown and her inscrutable smile – all of which emanated directly from the febrile imagination of a tanner's daughter from Powiśle...?

The straight back and pinched shoulder blades, however, and the very way she holds her shoulders square to the torso – these suggest a young lady moulded from childhood by corsets. But this too may be a lie, of course, acted out over time by conscious effort of will in order to inflict upon herself the painful pose. Genuine damsel, fraudulent damsel – there's no way of knowing.

'*Mademoiselle, puis-je vous inviter?*'

You could contemplate this moment for a hundred years, yet never see the least sign of confusion on Miss Muklanowicz's countenance.

'You know how to dance, Benedykt, sir?'

'Not exactly.'

She raised her brow.

Laugh.

'Hasn't it worked out admirably? My leg.' Slap the thigh. 'Let's dance – for once in my life I need not worry: no one will realise that I know not how to dance.'

'Except your poor partner.'

'Fear not, miss, I'll be trampling on my own feet.'

'Oh, in that case – the pleasure is all mine.'

She held out her hand in its lacy glove.

'Monsieur Verousse!'

The journalist put aside his glass, sighing theatrically.

'*Souvent femme varie, bien fol qui s'y fie.*'

He struck the first chords, the provodnik drew his bow.

Throw the cane behind the piano, glance questioningly at Miss Muklanowicz.

'The korobotchka? Lead on, falconer!'

The Russian melody met with applause from the passengers. At once the couples formed a double row: a few steps back, a few steps forward, it's hard to go wrong in such an organised dance. Miss Muklanowicz spun around along with the remaining ladies, three paces back, clap the hands, return again, take the partner's hand; face to face now with her, breath to breath – but already she's spinning again on the spot, and stand now before a different partner. Korobotchka! Cross paths with Jelena, she laughs mockingly. The chandelier rocked overhead, the carriage rocked underfoot, the leg was hurting.

Eventually, the dancers stood again before the same partner as at the beginning. Miss Muklanowicz curtsied, adjusted her shawl and laughed again.

'I thought you'd be pleased! It's enough to do what the others do. And you also had no opportunity to trample on anyone's feet.'

'You planned it, miss!'

'How was I to know you couldn't dance?'

Bow towards her, kiss her hand.

'Maybe the cripple's waltz...'

She whispered something to Verousse. Standing erect, she raised her arms. Embrace her hesitatingly. She corrected the position of the hands on her back, blew a black lock off her face and gave a roguish wink.

'Benedykt, sir, hold on for dear life.'

One, two, three. Pass after the first rotation in front of Prince and Princess Blutsky and then towards the gallery, glancing over Jelena's shoulder. Were they watching? They were watching. Everyone was watching, but – it was a dance! Anyone who dances, for as long as he dances – remains a slave to the dance, what is not allowed is allowed, what is improper is proper, what is unforgivable is forgiven; isn't this what the dance serves first and foremost?

'You are laughing, sir.'

'I am dancing with a beautiful woman, am I meant to be sad?'

'*Oh là là*, when did you learn to pay compliments?'

'I fell on my head; radical changes happen after to the psyche.'

'What?' The music and clatter and hubbub of voices were already too much, the damsel moved cheek to cheek, and the fragrance of her jasmine scent entered the nostrils like warm incense.

'I fell on my head!'

She moved away in rotation, laughing.

'So that's the end of the compliments!'

The leg was hurting more and more.

Thinking, by the second lap of the carriage, less about the rhythm of this tight improvised waltz – the waltz is a mathematical dance, it's enough to count the steps and rotations – and more about that smile of hers, more about the young woman's dainty hand locked in a hand half its size again, about the soft hair spilling every third step over the hand pressed into the back of her bodice, about the rapid breath powerfully lifting her tightly strapped breasts, about the lips, always remaining half-parted now, her white teeth gleaming in between, half-parted and wide open whenever she audibly draws in air – the waltz flowed on and on; lose count of how many laps of the room, the old prince and princess, Jules Verousse wildly attacking the keys, the applauding spectators, the yellow seam of fire flashing across the black surfaces of the windows – it all glides past in the cold silver glare of the swinging chandelier, like images in a photoplasticon wound faster and faster so that in order to keep the very balance, focus is required on the closest image: the devushka's dark eyes, the devushka's complexion hotly flushed, her mouth poised as if to cry out. From under the velvet choker with its ruby stone, two rivulets of sweat trickled down between her breasts.

Stop by the wall.

'Forgive me, miss, my leg can't take any more for the time being, perhaps –'

'Yes, yes, by all means.'

Walk through to the gallery, but here too the throng is dense, the atmosphere hot and stuffy; at once the laughing faces turn from all sides, a steward bounds up... Jelena drinks a glass of some dark beverage, fans herself with the shawl.

'You shall keep an eye on me so I don't fall off.'

Jelena laughs breathlessly.

Push open the iron door, step out onto the observation platform; offer the damsel a hand, she steps gingerly over the threshold in her ballroom slippers. Kick the door shut, the music and human voices subside; instead: dwook-dwook-dwook-DWOOK and the roar of the engine, and the prolonged whistle of the wind in the darknesses of night.

Leaning on the balustrade on the southern, right-hand side of the platform, Jelena inhales deeply. She wraps the *cache-nez* around her shoulders and upper arms, so that rays from the quarter-moon illuminate only the white triangle of her décolleté and her slender face in its icon-like frame of raven hair. Too sharp now the contrast between shine and shade, no longer the soft gentle beauty of plump devushkas and well-fed ladies – now all the angular features come to light, all the asymmetries and disproportionalities, every single bone neath the taut, transparent skin.

Take out the cigarettes, light up, stare through the smoke.

The brownish-yellow river of fire, overlaid by the crests of red spark-storms, stretches behind Miss Muklanowicz's back; the northern horizon is uniformly black.

'We are passing it by, however. It is passing us by.'

She looks over her shoulder. For a long while, she is silent, mesmerised by the spectacle of the great conflagration.

'Thank you, my head was spinning a little in there. I'm sorry.'

'You and Doctor Tesla.'

She looks inquiringly.

Shrug the shoulders, flick off the ash.

'Dancing, such things as dancing – they are also means.'

'Of what?'

'Of saying things that cannot be expressed in any language comprehensible to more than one person.'

Will she resort to mockery? No. Resting her elbows on the handrail, leaning slightly back, she opens and closes her mouth, unable to decide on any word.

'I…'

'Shame, true? Say nothing, miss, I can see. I prefer such word, though it's obviously not shame. He averts his gaze, blushes, stammers, loses his self-assurance, shuffles his feet, flees before another's eyes – this is shame. But what am I describing here? A man's behaviour. Yet how am I to describe what no one sees, no one hears, no one else experiences?' Curl the hand into a fist and beat the chest, then strike the frock coat with the splayed fingers as if trying to pluck out, through fabric and bone, the beating heart. 'There is no language! There is no language!' Scratch the shirtfront and cravat with the nails. 'You probably saved my life, I ought to fall on my knees and thank you, but I shan't do it, I shan't do anything of the sort; I owe you honesty, so I shall keep silent.' Raise the fingers twisted into claws before the eyes, with a fleeting smile on the swollen lips. 'Or we will dance.'

Miss Muklanowicz trembles. She wraps herself more tightly into the dark-claret *cache-nez*.

'I feared this.'

'This?'

'This.'

'Ah, this!'

'This, this.'

'This, well yes, this, this, this…' Having reached its limit, the speech of men devours itself, consumes all sense and meaning; nothing remains but to turn the thing into a joke.

Smile. Jelena sees the ugly, crooked smile and sticks out her tongue.

'You, however, are courting disaster.'

Take a drag of tobacco.

'I know, I had no need to traipse into the taiga after Fessar.'

'Christine told me that Dushin came to them and tried to prohibit Doctor Tesla any contact with you.'

'Mr Pocięgło has realised someone was ferreting through his things.'

'Mr Pocięgło is an extremely observant bourgeois.'

'That prosecutor from Kamtchatka seems to think he's an Oblastnik.'

'And what's that? An imperial office? A new sect?'

'And my father has another sentence hanging over him, evidently he's been leading Siberian peasants to death in the Ice.'

'Don't believe it, they always say the worst things.'

'Someone there cracked open Fessar's nut.'

'So, you don't believe the Turk was the Lyednyak agent.'

'No, impossible.'

'All the same – that Zeytsoff...'

Embrace her around waist, pull her close, kiss her. She tastes of sweet wine.

Leaning again on the balustrade, Jelena enfolds herself in the *cachenez* as though in a peasant shawl, tying it over her head and crossing hands on her breasts.

'In your place, sir, I wouldn't let him out of my sight.'

'Zeytsoff was lying sozzled in his compartment; I made sure he didn't go into the forest.'

'The prince's men?'

'Dushin?'

'The agent? No! But if the princess commanded him to throw Pyelka off...'

'Of that I'm not sure either.'

'We're running out of time. Either Fogel was talking nonsense, or the agent has only one day left to destroy the machines, kill Tesla, and maybe kill you as well.'

'So, I should stay in the compartment?'

'I invite you to mine, if you get bored.'

Jelena pulls off her right glove and places two fingers on her tongue, inside her mouth. Then she clenches her teeth. Tearing the hand from off her red lips, she proffers it with a gracious gesture, with an expression neither serious nor mocking, her eyes twinkling.

Bend forward in a formal bow and lick the warm blood off the dainty fingers, to the last drop, to the drops still blossoming on the open wounds. A long shudder passes through the devushka.

Take off the frock coat, throw it over her shoulders. A rush of air lifts the empty sleeves above the balustrade.

'It might be wiser, however, to stay in the restaurant car, or saloon.

It's not exactly difficult to pick the lock and break into the compartment, and before you know it – whack-thwack; nobody saw anything,
nobody heard.'

'You should place a chair against the door, push its back up under
the lock.'

'I am thinking, however, of Irkutsk. Here, in the train – is half the
battle. But in the city? If only there'd be one single agent! If only just
Lyednyaks! You hear what they say about me. Even Doctor Konyeshin
almost lost it. Should they wish to kill me, they'll kill me.'

'I don't think so.'

Laugh.

'You don't think so? Don't think so?' Cast the cigarette stub to
the wind. 'What a comfort you are! Maybe, however, you have some
argument?'

Miss Muklanowicz crooks her fingers and draws her nails over the
bodice of her gown. A four-pronged red trace remains on her breast, a
fresh gash left by the touch of something wild, inhuman.

Gazing still at this fourfold scratch on her white skin when, close
by, right here, neath a flap of the English frock coat, above the drop of
blood on the devushka's heart, there lands a silver starlet, a tiny crystal
of snow. At once it melts, vanishes.

Glance at the sky above the anti-smoke shield. Yet it is not smoke
but cloud that obscures the stars and from time to time even the
golden half-disc of the Moon, constantly fading, constantly reignit-
ing. In those bright intervals, the mother of all strigas illuminates the
desolate expanses, the forested plains of boundless Asia, to the north
of the Trans-Siberian line and to the south, as far as the band of flame,
crowns of ash above it. Cloud, Moon, cloud, Moon – whilst the Express
speeds ahead, into the tunnel of brightness carved out by the squint-
eyed headlamps of the Black Sable – Moon, cloud, Moon – straight
into Winter. For suddenly, in the next illuminated gap between clouds,
as upon the raising of an operatic stage curtain, there is: whiteness,
whiteness, whiteness, fields of whiteness; this is snow, but snow already
hardened, congealed on trees and in clearings, on marshes and rivers,
on railway embankments, on wooden huts and half-dilapidated shelters passed in the blinking of an eye, snow solidified into ice. When
had it happened? There is no frontier, but should some frontier exist,
then the train had left it behind long ago. All around, there is now only
whiteness and snow and ice.

'Es ist so.'

Dark-blue breath mist flees from in front of the face, along with
the words evaporating in a whistle of cold air; whilst more and more

numerous snowflakes, blown up by the wind, quickly escape the eyes. Slip the hands into the trouser pockets.

'Ha! I dreamed of Winter.'

Miss Muklanowicz enfolds herself in her shawl, leaving only a narrow slit for eyes; from the inside, she pulls the frock coat over her pale-blue gown, hugging her shoulders underneath.

Pressing the gathers of her skirt into the spiral bars of the balustrade, she stares from the platform at the icefields to the south. Dwook-dwook-dwook-DWOOK, a few more minutes and the whole of Siberian nature is locked beneath sculptures of ice – there's no longer any green, no silhouette even of a tree, whilst the very configuration of long swathes of taiga lies hidden neath a thick coat of permafrost. No surprise then that the conflagrations of Summer do not enter Winter – no fire bites into this frozen weald. It's possible to guess at the life arrested there in the frost, all that can be seen are more or less fantastical formations of white: waves, crests, billows, walls, towers and crags, ridges and fountains, castles and hives, gleissen and gleissen.

Images from inside the parlour car, from the fireplace room, are projected – like on a cinematograph screen – onto the nearest formations springing up beside the tracks, as the Express races past in a roar of biting wind, for in there the dance goes on, music plays, long-fingered Monsieur Verousse thumps on the keys like one possessed, the bearded provodnik wields his bow, couples whirl; gentlemen in tails or long frock coats cut according to the immutable fashion of icebound Europe, ladies in creations of lace and diamond, above them the silver-and-crystal chandelier – everything is projected in images of shine and shade, gliding smoothly over the concavities and convexities of the ice sculptures, pageants of men and women in the Deluxe car, dancing, dancing.

Miss Muklanowicz coughs dryly, eyes fixed. Stand behind her, peer over her shoulder. The damsel coughs through the shawl, breathes through the shawl, speaks through the shawl.

I dreamed of winter, I ran in the row,
Behind the column, under sky and snow.
People beside me marched two by two,
Women, old men and children too.

Laugh briefly, blowing from the damsel the hazy clouds of this laughter, which swiftly disperse.

Since, however, the lands of Summer have been forsaken, thoughts adhere a little better to thoughts, words cling a little more powerfully to words.

I glanced at the faces: some seem to me known,
And baulked: for all were like unto stone.
One stepped out from the right-hand side;
A woman veiled, though still bright-eyed.
Her face Transfigured in the Lord's own wake;
She drowned her gaze in the Albanian Lake;
Curiously she stares, her lids flinch not,
As if she saw in that deep-blue grot
A far reflection of her own fair face
Tending by the lake the roses' grace.

Miss Muklanowicz turns her head without turning around, her eye flashes beneath her veil. Maybe she smiles, maybe not; a hoar frost is forming on the shawl that hides her face.

To thee she spoke with childlike smile:
'My parents to another wish me wed,
But I, the swallow, would be fled;
I know of all your erstwhile friends,
To graves and tombs my footstep wends;
I'll find them yet in woods and churches,
Ask trees and herbs, extend my searches.
Of you the strangest things they know
Where you once went, what did below.'

It's cold and growing ever colder. Embrace the devushka through the frock coat cleaving awkwardly to her gown; she withdraws from the handrail, nestles into the embrace, seeking also warmth. The streak of conflagration – like a whip of flame lashing across the white infinity, like the shedding of hot blood on pristine canvas – grows ever narrower and narrower, farther and farther away, receding to the horizon and vanishing at last behind the ice statues. There remain the half-moon, the stars between clouds, and thousands of snow-sparks spraying loosely off both sides of the carriage.

And the glow of the Black Sable ahead, in the east, more distinct now – coldiron lunar rainbows bounce off mirrors of ice. The driver pulls the siren lever, and the butterfly engine's protracted whistle reverberates across the landscape of Winter.

Yes, when this landscape is closely observed, mighty upheavals of pure ice may be perceived here and there that seem not to depend on any geological features hidden underneath – massive autonomous stacks, monumental nests of Ice scattered over hundreds of versts of frozen taiga: icecradles? Perhaps this is they, perhaps not; the train does not slacken, and they're already left behind.

But there are irregularities in the landscape caused by the railway line itself. Just like cities and other centres of population, so here, in this wasteland, it's the Transsib that attracts gleissen. Already a fourth, already a fifth icer emerges first from the trackside in the yellow gleam of the Black Sable's headlamps, in the azure haloes of its cold-iron auroras; catch it like this for a second, two seconds, in a fleeting glimpse, devouring the image with watery eyes: a gleiss astraddle dozens of frost-strings – a gleiss thrust arshins high towards Moon and stars – a gleiss stretched out in its glacial march along the embankment – a gleiss shooting out hundreds of stalagmite needles from under the earth, a gleiss outspread in a mighty mandala laced in stitches of frost, a thunderbolt of Ice split into a million white and black threads like a petrified electrical discharge leaping in a great arc from the north side of the railway to the south... At once it scampers back and vanishes completely in the darkness behind the train. Gleissen freeze their way across the line this close, piercing almost the very tracks of the Siberian Magistral with thousand-pood icicles.

The Express plunged under a long overhang and arctic shadow passed over the carriages and observation platform, a frost lasting seconds, as painful as the smack of a wet riding crop; squeeze the devushka tighter still. She shivers; shiver together with her, resting the head on her shoulder, breathing hazy words into the shawl that totally conceals her face – maybe into the pale cheek, maybe into the frozen ear, maybe into the hot red mouth.

Recalling suddenly all my faults,
The wasted moments, reckless bolts,
I felt my heart so sorely riven,
Unworthy of her, and bliss and heaven.

And with every word, with every breath and shiver, ride ever deeper into the Land of the Gleissen, as the Frost rides deeper into Man.

CHAPTER THE SEVENTH

On the sculpting of smoke

'Tsushima, nineteen-oh-five. Other are the wars of Summer. On the third day of October of the previous year, we had sailed from Libava to relieve Port Arthur with twenty-eight craft, seven battleships. Then, on our way from the Baltic Sea to Vladivostock, we were joined by another dozen or so vessels. The whole of this Second Pacific Squadron was commanded by Vice Admiral Zinovy Rozhestvensky. It was the greatest naval expedition in the history of modern warfare. The Japanese had attacked in January, storming the First Squadron without warning in Port Arthur, Vladivostock and Tchemulpo; you should know that they consider a prior declaration of war to be a foolish European eccentricity. In April, His Imperial Exaltedness created the Second Squadron to assist the First, and to protect the army in Manchuria, where upward of half a million of our soldiers were fighting; but already by August, the Japanese had dealt a crushing blow to the Far Eastern Fleet and laid siege to Port Arthur. It became clear that the Second Squadron was coming to face the Japanese unaided. All battleworthy Russian vessels were assembled, except those blockaded by treaties in the Black Sea. As repairs and the building of new ships accelerated, in no way could sufficient experienced sailors be found for the crews. Peasants were therefore conscripted, as well as common and political criminals who were chased onto the decks from prison, whilst cadets from the Saint Petersburg Naval Cadet Corps were promoted prematurely as young officers. By this means, I landed straight from school as a freshly minted *garde-marine* on the battleship *Oslyabya*, the flagship of Rear Admiral Dmitry von Fölkersahm, Rozhestvensky's second in command. I was seventeen years old when I set sail that October morning on my around-the-world voyage as part of the Russian Empire's mightiest armada, en route to the greatest armoured battle in the history of the seas.'

Captain Nasboldt raised his crystal goblet and took a sip of mulled wine; in the light of the oily flames, the potion in the crystal looked like thick, dark-red blood. A precious stone in the ring encircling the officer's finger was of similar hue; lower the eyelids a fraction more, peering through the eyelashes and through cobwebs of sleep, and see the stone throbbing, flickering, overflowing like a huge drop of liver blood from its black metal casing. The band itself, worn by this captain of the second rank, was of pure coldiron.

Dietmar Klausovitch Nasboldt rested his hand with its wine cup on the arm of his chair. A steward loomed out of the semi-dark behind his back with a carafe poised to pour, but Nasboldt, without turning his head, straightened his index finger over the goblet and the steward withdrew. All the drinking cups and glasses stocked by Deluxe were wider at the base and had taller stems than in regular sets. Now the Express was maintaining an even speed, braking almost not at all, swerving on hardly any bends. And indeed, the gentle rocking of the carriage had a soporific effect; Mr Pocięgło was already asleep, Engineer White-Gessling's eyelids clung together… The rocking of the carriage, yes, but also the captain's voice itself now rising, now falling… children have their lullabies, and so do grown-ups. A good tale tastes like a good tobacco or good whisky; it should unrushed, the storyteller unhurried; it's not about getting to the point as quickly as possible, grabbing the plot by the scruff, learning the fates of characters, meanings and mysteries, no, not about that at all. We listen, fall asleep, wake up, return to the tale, fall asleep again, wake up again, whilst the story flows and ebbs like tides – now we're immersed in one unreality, now in another; the spell works, we've been removed from time and place. In the flurry of city life, it's harder to succumb. But here, closeted for days on end with other listener-storytellers on a journey… It sufficed for Captain Nasboldt to raise his hand and utter the first sentence. No one interrupts, no one persuades him to return to previous topics, no one poses impatient questions. The phrase must be allowed to sound itself out. Likewise, silences punctuating the officer's lines form part of the tale. Likewise, sleep. As well as the darkness all around, and the cold whiteness gleaming out of it, and this fire, and Mr Pocięgło's snoring. Prosecutor Razbyesoff and Doctor Konyeshin were listening most attentively, puffing at the English cigarettes offered them by the engineer. But they too were spellbound.

Adjust the plaid blanket on the knees. Of all the passengers left in the room after the dance, sit closest to the fireplace. Waves of heat beat off the grate and swelled the muscles in the left leg and left hand, soon causing half the body to feel like rubber pumped with alcohol. Shift in the chair to a semi-recumbent position. The eye then fled from the grate, from the flames, but since no lights were burning apart from the fire and a single lamp by the passageway into the saloon car, the gaze was left to grope in the dark over the ceiling (the cold glittering chandelier), over the men's faces around the hearth (soft, rotund, flushed), over the moonlit white world outside the windows – so long as the

still-conscious eye had something to fix on. At first, the ice phantasmagoria flashing past against the backdrop of more ice had been observed,
along with the other passengers, standing with the nose pressed to the
windowpane, vodka glass to lips, after the lights were extinguished in
the parlour car. The same monotonous landscape, however, that op-
presses any traveller crossing Siberia – steppe, taiga, sky, earth, for
hours on end – soon oppressed them here: whiteness and whiteness
and whiteness and whiteness, like a clinically white hell. How much can
a man take. Everything in moderation. It's a type of pathological mania;
such insanity is treated after all in hospitals: building block upon building block, with dull stare and stuck-out tongue, day after day for twenty
years. This is exactly how God created Asia.

Ice rolled past in angular waves outside the windows of the Deluxe
carriage (sometimes a gleiss would flicker), whilst inside, in the fireplace room, the amber glints of flames drenched everything in warm
wax, furniture as well as people, so that even the edges and peaks
and triangular friezes of the boiserie appeared half-molten. Captain
Nasboldt had no need to raise his voice; his words fell soft as snowflakes
onto the skin, onto the tongue, into the ears. From where they flowed in
unsullied streamlets to the brain.

'Afterwards I tried to grasp it mentally, formulate it according to cause
and effect, truth and untruth. Idle inquiries! We had scarcely entered
the Danish Straits, bah, it was earlier, for whilst we were still lying off
Kronstadt, Reval and Libava, we were constantly practising alarms
and night-time watches and anti-torpedo blockades in anticipation of
a covert Japanese attack, but when we entered the straits – we got so
muddled in our manoeuvres during artillery exercises that the *Oslyabya*
ran into the destroyer *Bystry*, smashing her bows, yet immediately afterwards information came from the listening-post in Copenhagen
that Japanese torpedo-boats really had been spotted, namely fishing
cutters with camouflaged rocket launchers, submarines, balloons lowering mines from the sky into the Squadron's path. Lies, fantasy? On
this occasion, navy intelligence and the Okhrana had received half a
million roubles, so maybe they invented it all – but maybe not, maybe
not. Reports were already coming in from our own vessels: of unknown
torpedo-boats under the lights of fishing cutters, of schooners without
ensigns, of dark silhouettes in the night. Rozhestvensky ordered the
guns to be trained on all passing ships and fired at any vessel cutting
across the Squadron's course in defiance of warnings. Thus, we came
through the straits firing at ships with neutral ensigns. On the following
day the auxiliary ship Kamtchatka lost her bearings; only in the evening
did she appeal for help, reporting that she was fleeing in a zigzag course
from eight unknown torpedo-boats. Rozhestvensky declared full battle

alert. The middle of the night, Dogger Bank, pitch dark, everyone expecting an attack. Well, and then there's a flare, shadows on the water – we switch on the searchlights. I myself was on duty at the stern telescope, straining my eyes, heart pounding, God save us. We watch: two larger vessels, a host of smaller ones; we check the profile, count the smokestacks, Pyotr says this, Ivan that, Grisha something else, but already the report goes out: two torpedo-boats attacking the flagship and a whole fleet determined to push us off-course. All searchlights in the Squadron came on and the cannonade began: shafts of light in the darkness, flames from barrels, a terrible roar, the panic-stricken search for shapes on the waves – suddenly something looms out of the night, a few seconds, and a torpedo-burst will rip you to shreds. Then it transpired that they were merely trawlers and fishing cutters. We also managed to blast a smokestack off the cruiser *Aurora*, almost killing the ship's priest at the same time. A week later, we're bunkering coal in Vigo Bay, when a wire comes from Saint Petersburg. Russia and Great Britain are on the brink of war; we had shot and destroyed five trawlers belonging to the British fishermen's union on the anniversary of the Battle of Trafalgar, killing fishermen and fleeing the scene of the crime without rendering aid. Crowds are marching through London demanding that the Royal Navy be sent with orders to sink our armada. But at once the matter gets even more complicated, because the enraged fishermen present firm evidence of a Russian torpedo-boat destroyer circling them till morning without reacting to the shouts and pleas of the drowning men. Yet no destroyer was sailing with us at the time! So, what then? Had Japanese warships really taken us by surprise amidst the English fishing boats? There was an inquiry by an international commission, yet do you imagine, gentlemen, it led to anything? Who attacked us? Had anyone attacked us at all? Had we seen the Japanese or not seen them? Yet I had been there myself, I myself was watching! Had I therefore seen what I saw? – or had I imagined that I saw what I'd not seen? – or do I only now remember what I didn't see, as well as what I saw, what was not, as well as what was? With whom were we fighting that battle? Had a battle taken place at all? Such is war without the Ice, a false lying whore.

'We crossed the equator – no one knew when; the strength of the Atlantic currents had been calculated erroneously, mistakes were made in the hour and geographical latitude. There were constant problems with bunkering coal, the German company HAPAG no longer wished to honour its contracts, Japanese and British diplomacy had closed the ports to us, forcing neutrality on successive countries; thanks only to Rozhestvensky's determination, we reached Madagascar. There we were joined by lighter cruisers which had sailed through the Mediterranean and Suez Canal, and it was there, in Nossi-Bé, that news reached us of the capitulation of Port Arthur, and also of the revolutionary riots in Russia and of Bloody Sunday. So on the one hand, from the military point of view, the expedition made no sense; on the other, however, from the political standpoint, it was one of the emperor's last-ditch efforts, a chance for peace within the country as well as with Japan; because only with some suitably weighty success in our pan of the scales, would it be possible to sit down and conclude a reasonable treaty with the Japanese, and then, following the extinguishing of this conflagration – to send troops from the front to quell the conflagrations in Russia herself. We conducted exercises firing at targets. Out of several thousand shells, not one hit the mark. Vice Admiral Rozhestvensky sent a wire to Saint Petersburg asking to be relieved of his duties on grounds of poor health. The Admiralty refused, agreeing to the transfer of command only in Vladivostock. Rozhestvensky then set reaching Vladivostock as soon as possible as his main objective. Thus we sailed across the Indian Ocean in a single hop from Madagascar to Indochina. That was some voyage…! What else can I say, pain and torture: the sailors were on the point of mutiny, Rozhestvensky quickly filled the prison ship, there was no fresh water, no food, no clothes even, men's boots fell apart, the stokers were working in hemp moccasins, we sailed non-stop, constantly overloaded with coal, since Rozhestvensky was petrified we would be without fuel; with such a draught, the ships lost speed of two or three knots, the *Oslyabya*'s armoured belts were totally hidden below water, yet despite this we had to keep loading coal from freighters, I tell you, gentlemen, pain and torture – but then when we saw the British faces in Singapore, when the whole Squadron filed through the strait after our lonely voyage across the ocean…! I understood how legends of the high seas are born.

'Rozhestvensky resolved to reach Vladivostock by the shortest route, that is, between the Korean Peninsula and Japan. We entered those waters in battle array with orders to maintain wireless silence. At any moment we expected an attack from the whole Japanese fleet. Again, there began the search for foreign vessels and submarines, the vigilance and fear. During the night, we kept up communications by shining Morse signals onto clouds in the sky with searchlights. On the *Oslyabya*, the mood was exceptionally foul; von Fölkersahm, struck down by a serious apoplectic fit, had not been commanding for a long while, then on the evening of the tenth of May, he finally gave up the ghost. But Rozhestvensky refused to have the admiral's flag taken down from our ship! The officers said it was so as not to destroy the Squadron's morale. Von Fölkersahm was therefore laid in a coffin below deck, and the *Oslyabya* continued to sail as a flagship. Mark my words, gentlemen, note how from an initial falsehood flow all subsequent frauds – and how they destroy the underpinnings of the universe, like cracks spreading over ice from a single blow; and only that initial thunderbolt from Zeus, which splits the ice, only that thunderbolt goes unheard.

'When everything falls apart, what can be relied upon? We were set to enter the Korea Strait on Friday the thirteenth of May, thus Rozhestvensky ordered first a day of senseless exercises so as to avoid a battle on that unlucky date. The priests scrupulously blessed the guns on all vessels. We sailed in three, then two-line columns; the day was grey, foggy, clouds covering the sky. During the night the airwaves had been abuzz with Japanese communication signals, we knew their fleet was close. At dawn, the first enemy cruiser appeared; it summoned others, they sailed parallel to the Squadron, but we were forbidden to shoot. In the end, people couldn't restrain themselves, it seems one of the artillerymen on the *Oslyabya* fired the first shot, it's hard to say, since the whole cannonade began immediately; once we even hit something – after all, the men were gunning for a fight, yes, yes. At noon, the main Japanese forces appeared, armoured flagships in formation cutting across our path. They were faster than our motley crew of mixed-class vessels laden with coal and overgrown with seaweed; they were faster, and could choose and impose the position and distance for the exchange of fire as well as the angular course, the line columns' angle of approach. Rozhestvensky tried to outmanoeuvre them, without success, and only broke up his own battle array. You must know, Messieurs, that according to the old naval tactics of Summer, in clashes between armoured ships, a ship's position relative to another can have more bearing on the encounter than the power of its guns and strength of its armour. A vessel exposed to full broadsides, but capable only of responding with front artillery, is condemned in advance to destruction. And so, the first manoeuvre is simple: cross in front of the bows of the armada, cutting across its course at an angle of ninety degrees. A Japanese squadron, faster than ours, sailed back and forth ahead of our bows, shelling us from six miles away with concentrated fire, for it was clear immediately they'd received orders to aim first at our flagships, starting with the nearest – and which flagship lay like a sitting duck in direct line of fire? The *Oslyabya*! Flying the dead man's ensign on the mast, we were anchored to the spot, knocked from the line, because when Rozhestvensky on his Prince Suvorov tried to come out at the head of the column, he almost caused a mass collision: the *Suvorov* had obstructed the path of *Emperor Aleksandr*, the *Aleksandr* – of the *Borodino*, the *Borodino* – of the *Oryol*, whilst we, that is, the *Oslyabya*, came between them at the head of a second group of ironclads. We stood at anchor, hoisted black cannonballs on the yards, as the array split to the sides. The Japanese bombarded us mercilessly, both flagships, but ours most of all; I then escaped death by a miracle, when a man two steps away from me was swept off the deck and flying shrapnel brushed my skin like a broom made of razorblades. The navigation bridge on the bows was in flames, our anchor torn away. The worst was that we were hit twice on the port side where a hole had been blown through the armoured plating and hull, just above the waterline, large enough for a troika to drive through without any problem, and we began to list more and more, there being no way of patching the hole, the swell was too high; the *Oslyabya* tried nevertheless to retreat from the barrage, but nothing came of it as an ever greater trim dragged us down, so far down the hawseholes disappeared. The gun turret had been shot off the bows, electricity went down throughout the ship, the combat bridge was on fire, coal dust hung in the air and settled on everything in a vile, caustic, blinding, sticky gunge, rivets and pins leapt out of the metal in their dozens, armoured plates peeled off us like dried-up scabs – the commander ordered us to abandon ship, the *Oslyabya* keeled over and went to the bottom.

'I saw it floating on the waves, fifty or so arshins from me, as I swam towards the destroyers rescuing survivors – Rear Admiral von Fölkersahm's coffin. We were picked up by the *Buyny*; half of the *Oslyabya*'s crew, however, drowned. The Japs did not cease their bombardment; besides, they were no longer even visible on the horizon – fog, smoke, grey sky, grey sea – whilst they'd painted their hulls and quarterdecks in dark olive-green, so it was impossible to make out who was firing at us, who murdering us, the *Buyny* was hit, the *Bravy* was hit; we fled into the fog, as long as it was farther from the battle. Only rumbles resounding over the waters of the strait, only flashpoints piercing that suspension of greyness, told us of the progress of combat. Captain Kolomiytseff was searching for the squadron of lighter cruisers, I've no idea if we were roaming about lost, or whether the captain wished to bring some kind of order first to the *Buyny* – more than two hundred shipwrecked men had to be accommodated on board. I squeezed my way onto the bridge, flimsily bandaged, one eye streaming with blood, chilled to the bone, to eavesdrop on the officers. They knew little more than I. An order had been issued to follow the light forces on their port beam – but where were the light forces grouping? Who was in command? Was Rozhestvensky still alive? There was no battle plan; no plan had reached the captain. The officers were trying to interpret anything they could from old orders – when those orders no longer fitted the situation. We'd barely entered the array behind the cruisers, when Kolomiytseff pulled the *Buyny* out of it. We saw a great whirlwind of smoke like an upturned pyramid of black cloud in the sky, whilst below it, beneath its apex – red flames. It was the *Suvorov*, Vice Admiral Rozhestvensky's flagship, burning, already half-sunk. The officers protested that there was no room on deck; the captain gave the order to approach the battleship and take the crew on board. We sailed in under fire. The *Suvorov* was being covered by Japanese artillery; they were pummelling it to smithereens, but on our own deck it was like at a march-past, hundreds of men standing and gawping – were a shell to hit, it'd be butchery. Lifeboats – there were no lifeboats; on the *Buyny* all were wrecked, on the *Suvorov* all wrecked or aflame. What to do? Kolomiytseff gives the order to draw closer still – but the swell is already too high and the fire on the *Suvorov* like an open blast furnace, whilst the Japanese shoot better and better – he gives the order to draw closer and transfer the men from broadside to broadside. So, they slung over the officers and wounded from the *Suvorov* until eventually the *Buyny* herself was hit; shrapnel sliced in two a cook rescued from the *Oslyabya*. Heavily submerged, we sailed away from the sinking battleship. I was summoned to the officers' cabins, ordered by the first officer to take care of the staff officers from the flagship. I enter their mess, now a hospital ward… and who should be lying on the couch under a porthole? Vice Admiral Zinovy Rozhestvensky.

'Wounded in the head, wounded in the back, wounded in the hip and foot; whilst the medics dress his wounds, I repeat the first officer's question: hoist the flag of the Commander of the Second Squadron on the *Buyny*? No! He's no longer in a fit state to command, have Nebogatoff take command! I return to the bridge – Nebogatoff knows nothing about it, cannot know, because there's no way of communicating with him. What to do? A long evening off the Tsushima Archipelago, officers whispering over the vice admiral's bed, I run to and fro, bearing questions, questions, questions and questions: but no answers. How many of the Squadron's vessels have been saved? Where are the rest? Where are the Japanese? What are the orders? What is the battle plan? What to do, what to do? The *Buyny* is chasing after Rear Admiral Enqvist's group, but with damaged propeller it'll be hard to catch up. And now it's dusk, growing dark, the visibility is getting worse and worse, the swell is bad, there's fog and no wind, whilst more and more dreadful communiqués explode over the heads of the gentlemen officers like deadly bursts of shrapnel. The *Borodino* is heavily shot-up, the *Borodino* is taking on water, the *Borodino* is burning! The *Oryol* is torn asunder, the *Aleksandr* is sinking, has sunk! No one was rescued, eight hundred men went to the bottom. Communications were poor anyway; the Squadron had fallen outside the range of wireless stations. Rozhestvensky kept repeating: Vladivostock, to Vladivostock. But what are Nebogatoff's orders? Had the admiral's order reached the *Nikolay Pervy*? Before darkness fell completely, however, we had joined the formation behind Enqvist alongside the surviving ironclads. Nebogatoff raised the navigation signals – and, yes indeed, forward to Vladivostock. We'd been waiting for the battle plan, none came. No one dared ask Rozhestvensky anything. During the night, the Japs would have to cease their fire – but in the night, their torpedo-boats would take us on.

'So again: the menace of the dark ocean, the search for shadows on the water, the staring through telescopes into the gloom. This time we tried not to get lost and to stick with the main forces – some must have got separated from Enqvist in the dark and drawn close to the ironclads; they, likewise terrified, took our torpedo-boat destroyers for Japanese torpedo- boats and we began to shoot at one another. Upon which Nebogatoff speeded up, so we were immediately left behind; the array was broken. A total blackout was decreed. Thus we held out in fear until dawn, drifting for hours after our boilers broke down, lost in the darkness. But the nerves that night, I shall never forget. No one knew anything, so everyone imagined everything. On the *Buyny*, the engines gave up one after another; had a torpedo-boat assailed us then, we'd have got no farther than a mile. I ran from one high-ranking officer to the next and each dispatched me with a different question, a different fear, a different version. Whilst on deck and below deck, an even denser confusion of fears and ghastly notions hung over the officers emanating from the minds of hundreds of sailors. Midnight came and went, the night reached its climax; we were sure the Japs had torpedoed all our ships apart from the *Buyny*, which had so thoroughly lost her way in those alien waters that even the enemy couldn't find her. I shall not describe to you, gentlemen, the atmosphere that night, the dreadful trembling in a million uncertainties, the swelling of black imaginations – agh, if only they'd finally attack us, torpedo us, sink us! Let it be decided now, now! But no. And what it had come to in the meantime… Rozhestvensky and the staff officers proposed landing on the shore, sinking the ship and surrendering to the Japanese; the staff officers pulled a white bedsheet from under the admiral and went with it to Kolomiytseff. Kolomiytseff was incensed, tore up the sheet and flung it overboard. But at dawn, he already had to wireless for help, the *Buyny* was breaking up, the admiral and senior staff had to be transferred to other craft. We were found by the cruiser *Dmitry Donskoy* accompanied by two torpedo-boat destroyers, the *Bedovy* and the *Grozny*; we moved to the *Bedovy*. The destroyers headed full steam for Vladivostock, but the *Dmitry Donskoy* stayed behind to escort the *Buyny*. Later I learned that it was the *Dmitry Donskoy* that sank the *Buyny* – the Japanese had appeared on the horizon, there was no time, a single well-aimed salvo destroyed

Captain Kolomiytseff's ship. Whilst Rozhestvensky, it transpired, had chosen the *Bedovy* because he knew its commander, Captain Baranoff. This Baranoff was incapable of refusing him a thing. At once a white flag was made ready and we were on course for Dagelet Island. The *Grozny*, however, was still with us, and her commander in turn was a Pole, a certain Andrzejewski. Venyedikt Filipovitch is smiling – well yes, no surprises then how the story continued. Baranoff approaches the Japs with guns immobilised, Andrzejewski asks what's going on, Rozhestvensky orders him to hop it to Vladivostock and himself hoists the capitulation signals on the *Bedovy* and requests help for the seriously wounded – but what does Captain Andrzejewski do? He disregards the order, turns back and fires all his guns at the Japanese. The vice admiral's nerves nearly brought on a heart attack. We are surrendering, yet this Pole is attacking – and the Japs are shooting at both of us just the same. Ask me now, gentlemen, what I prayed for then: for them to send us to the bottom, or for them to take us prisoner alive and whole? Come on, I shall answer honestly, may my father curse me if I tell a lie: both for this, and for that.'

'And God heard you?'

'Am I not sitting here before you! Rozhestvensky surrendered, we went to a Japanese camp.'

'And what about the *Grozny*,' asked Doctor Konyeshin, 'what happened to the Polish captain?'

'He brought his ship safely to Vladivostock. Only three or four vessels made it, his amongst them. Admittedly, Captain Andrzejewski emerged with serious injuries after a disastrous attack on the destroyer's bridge.' Nasboldt swirled the wine around in the goblet, lowering his eyes towards the red whirlpool. 'What more is there to say... you see, gentlemen: such are the wars of Summer.

'But now war will be waged differently. I betray no secrets, since Mr Pocięgło here and the engineer, working in Zimny Nikolayevsk, know only too well themselves what the transports of highest-grade coldiron from Sibirkhozheto are for, and whose orders get priority. I swore to myself that I would do everything I could, according to my modest abilities and talents, to erase that ignominy, and I don't mean just the Tsushima catastrophe. First of all, I took care of production matters there for the Admiralty – now Winter has to be won no longer in the Land of the Gleissen, but at sea. Much has changed since nineteen-oh-five. At once, the English built the first dreadnought – such speed, manoeuvrability, long-range guns, uniform parameters, armour. And everyone began to copy them, as they adapted to the new combat conditions. Everyone, so Russia could at most equalise her chances. But since the advent of Winter, since the discovery of tungetitum and coldiron, we have a natural advantage. Coldiron dreadnoughts are at least ten knots faster than the dreadnoughts of Summer. Their armour, thinner after all and lighter, nevertheless withstands strikes from the heaviest of missiles. Cannons designed in Tomsk and built from Irkutsk coolbonds, with barrels cast in Zimny Nikolayevsk, reach beyond the range of the grandest naval gunnery of Summer. Tungetitum bombs, should they now prove themselves in practice on manoeuvres, will sink the most solidly constructed vessels in combat, dragging them into the depths with a million-tonne ballast of ice.

'However, artillery, armour, technologies – it's not these that will alter the face of war in Winter. His Imperial Exaltedness is looking to the future, the Admiralty is planning for years ahead, whilst Russia – Russia can wait for whole generations, centuries and longer if needed. The Ice is pushing across Asia, the gleissen are spreading, Winter is consolidating – slowly, at an unquantifiable rate, and according to laws unknown to professors in Saint Petersburg, but however long it takes, the wave will eventually reach the limits of the continent, when the Ice,' Dietmar Klausovitch embraced in a wide gesture the white landscapes beyond the windows, 'when the Ice will descend to the seas. I do not say that the oceans will freeze at once, certainly nothing of the kind will happen – but how different will be sea battles under the skies of Winter! We fire – and we know at whom we fire. If we hit, then we hit; if not – then not. We sail here and here, and nowhere else. The orders are such and such. He who must triumph, will triumph; he who must lose, will lose. Non-necessity gives way to necessity, falsehood to truth. Nothing but Sybirak fairy tales, no more than a Baikal legend? No! These are plans, these are strategies.

'So, this is my assignment, this is why I'm travelling to the Pacific, such is my profession and my foremost dream: wars which are icy clean, geometrically beautiful and follow a mathematically inevitable course. Once we learn this, once we master the tactics of Winter, what shall stand in the way of the Empire? who shall threaten Russia? She will triumph, because she won't be able not to triumph.'

And having raised a silent toast, Captain Nasboldt quickly swallowed the rest of his wine.

'All wars have looked like this since the beginning of the world,' observed Prosecutor Razbyesoff with some amusement. 'Chaos, uncertainty and jumble of falsehood and truth – man has fought no other battles.'

'Mm-hmm, but communications, without communications, how can it be without communications?' Mr Pocięgło yawned, roused from sleep. 'An even greater muddle, I would imagine.'

'Why "without communications"?' Adjust the plaid on the knees and move back from the fireplace till the chair pressed against the prosecutor's chair.

'Venyedikt Filipovitch is not *au courant*,' smiled the symmetrical doctor. 'Maybe Nikola Tesla will explain to you. Have you tried picking up any broadcasts on that contraption in the saloon car? During my first sojourn in Siberia, when was it? at least ten years ago, they were only just experimenting with wired and wireless telegraph. Wireless never worked well in Transbaikal. Even now there are problems with the cables. But radio – you might as well forget it.'

'They say it's because of the Black Auroras,' muttered Pyotr Leontinovitch. 'That they cause interference. But there's always this hum in the ether, Aurora or no Aurora. From Blagoveshtchensk, mail goes via the Transsib and horse couriers, but eastwards only by cable, to Nikolayevsk Amursky and Vladivostock, because towards the Land of the Gleissen, only Nertchinsk is relatively reliable.'

Pluck at the moustache.

'This means, if I understand you correctly, that in Irkutsk there are no telephones, there's no telegraph…?'

'And the captain too may be disappointed as to his whole plan,' Doctor Konyeshin interjected, increasingly amused, 'when no ship goes out to sea, quarantined and locked in port due to the White Plague. After all it's a disease endemic to Winter, unknown in the lands of Summer. Even those who've been saved – imagine, captain, commanding a squadron of battleships crewed by men left in the power of diverse nervous manias, recurrent eccentricities, obsessive movements and speech.'

'You, Doctor, shall cure them,' muttered Dietmar Klausovitch.

'Ha! That is the question!' Unsticking a cigarette from his lower lip, Konyeshin held up his index finger straight as a knife between his whiskers, on a level with his mouth. 'Ought we to be curing from Winter? Ought we rather to be curing from Summer? Everything that enemies of the Ice take to be evil and perverted –'

'The next friend of the Ice,' the prosecutor bristled neath his moustache, flicking ash from his cigarette end into a ceramic ashtray proffered by the steward.

Take out the cigarette case.

'You know Doctor Konyeshin, sir?' Ask in an undertone.

'No, why?'

'Only now does he mention that he's lived before in Siberia. This, mm-hmm, fascination of his with Winter…' Light a cigarette. 'Just as Martsynians surrender to the Ice for mystical reasons, so Doctor Konyeshin has succumbed to the pure idea of the Ice. If you follow what I mean.'

Pyotr Leontinovitch leaned over the arm of his chair.

'He was trying to persuade you.'

'What?'

'He was trying to persuade you, was he not?' Razbyesoff waved his free hand. 'All of them… like wooers, like bribers, I've been watching and wondering: whom will the young man admit, whom will he choose? Has he any idea that he's choosing?'

'You, sir, are the next… whoremaster of History.'

He took no offence. He narrowed his eyes, rolling the vulturine head on its straight neck.

'History, well yes, I heard, I heard, *tel père, tel fils*. But why? Because you attract them. As a light attracts moths, worse, as a victim attracts malefactors, such a man is easily recognised, and they will recognise him sooner than any. They seize their opportunities. We are already in the heart of Winter – save yourself, sir!'

'Save…?'

He leant over deeper still, his backbone about to crack.

'It's not what others – but what you want to do with History!'

'I?' Laugh through the smoke, catching the breath with open mouth under a wave of heat. 'I want nothing.'

'What does that mean? Have you no desires? Don't you want to see a better, more perfect world? Everyone wants it. Even criminals – bah, they most of all; believe me, sir, never have I heard so many schemes for universal happiness or high-minded dreams of paradise on Earth as from murderers and other criminals of passion, and the filthier their crime, the more surely they reach for lofty words in their later confessions, as if in that ultimate downfall, cast to the bottom of the deepest darkest well, they could look only upwards, as if only one image remained before their eyes: the sky, the stars, the expanse of angels. That katorzhnik wino who unbosomed himself here to you of his sorrows – tell me, what did he talk about if not the salvation of mankind? Ha!'

'They who have fallen to the bottom, know upon what they stand.'

'You laugh, sir. Is it a laughing matter? You know not what you want – so how can you know who you are? And laugh please, do laugh – I watch and it breaks my heart. I am not saying Doctor Konyeshin is right. But, for the sake of the One God in Three Persons, you can't fritter away your whole life in Summer!'

'Once upon a time, people prepared themselves for this Winter as though for death, that is, without fear and with calm self-confidence, and this is how it still is in our provinces, in the villages; the simple Russian people are born and die in Winter, the peasant, the peasant's son, son of the peasant's son, who could never hope for any life other than the only one obvious from birth: in back-breaking labour bending him to the soil, in misery, in grinding poverty, in suffering, in nothing but hopelessness. But city folk like us, educated men – we were blessed by being born in Summer, whilst this Summer lasts longer and longer with every passing generation; now it's not only childhood, not only raw youth, but later years too, the twenty-year-old man, the twenty-five-year-old man, attending this or that school, circumnavigating the world at his parents' expense, imbibing the nectar of love from this or that flower, without having either chosen a profession and steady career or bound himself for life to a woman in accord with the sacraments or having erected his own house – who is he? Behold, the butterfly of the field, the glimmering firefly, the bright rainbow. But sooner or later Winter closes in, he is felled by the Frost, and suddenly: who am I? what's happened? whence these brats, are they mine? and this woman by whose side I wake every dawn – did I chose such a one? and this toil, to which I must drag myself morn after morn in heartfelt hatred of its every act – my life? It wasn't meant to be like this! It wasn't meant to be like this! And so, it is they, they, the children of Summer, felled by the Frost, who take up bricks at night in their drunken paws in order to smash the skull of their well-to-do neighbour, without enough tenacity even to ransack his coffers. It wasn't meant to be like this!'

Drop the eyes under the vulture's predatory gaze onto the plaid blanket and parquet floor shimmering in the reflected light of the flames, and onto the dancing, flickering flames themselves.

'Why tell me such things, Prosecutor?'

'You may take me for an old fuddy-duddy… But I have lived long enough in the lands of the Ice. Beware! In the Land of the Gleissen, sudden conversions or changes of heart don't happen, I have never heard of hardened scoundrels falling flat on their faces before the icons, or of noble souls discovering only here a taste for crime and squalor. Whoever comes here as this or that, as such he will most certainly remain.'

Unless he has at hand the Kotarbiński pump – the peevish thought occurred.

Nod to the steward. He held out the ashtray. Nod a second time – a glass of vodka.

'You have gazed with your prosecutor's eye, pierced right through the suspect with your stare, known in a flash everything that there is to know about him, and what he himself knows not about himself, this too, quickest of all.'

'Mr Yeroslatsky –'

'Gierosławski, my name is Benedykt Gierosławski.'

'*Oh, je vous demande pardon, je n'avais aucune intention de vous offenser.* Please believe me, Benedykt, sir, there's no ill intent in my

advice. First in the army, now in the service of the law – these are professions where the butcher's eye pays off, the eye of a butcher of men. I
look once, twice, and I know and decide: send that one with this order,
this one with that order, that one's a coward, he'll scarper at the first
rumble, whereas this one's courageous, shove him under fire and he'll
carry out any order. And it's the same with investigations and trials: am
I to believe him? could he steal? could he kill? The butcher walks up,
takes a thorough look, feels with his fingers: this one'll make a good
saddle of meat, that one needs fattening up, this one's for sale, that one
for breeding. You will say, sir, that every man is different and men are
not cattle, man is a mystery. In novels dreamt up in big cities, one in a
thousand, one in two thousand, maybe. But in life?

'I'm betraying wisdom gleaned over many years: people resemble
one another. Bad people are like bad people, good people like good
people, cowards like cowards, the noble-minded like the noble-minded,
liars like liars, truth-tellers like truth-tellers, murderers like murderers,
and fools like fools – especially here, in the land of the Ice.'

'And whom do I resemble?'

Pyotr Leontinovitch Razbyesoff exhaled a thick coil of tobacco
smoke and, placing his hand within it, performed a twisting gesture,
sculpting it with his fingers over and over again. In the end, he was
left empty-handed with a semi-dispersed grey cloud, and a melancholy
smile neath his moustache.

Sip the warm vodka, clear the throat.

'So you're not going to persuade me of the gleissen, not going to tell
me what I am to whisper in my father's ear... Aren't you tempted? You
said yourself: everyone has some notion of a better world, everyone
longs for something. What is your dream?'

'No.'

'But why? And yet you're trying to convince me!'

'How can I convince you, when you've no opinion of your own?'

'You're afraid to take responsibility!'

'Were you really my son...'

'Then what?'

'Are you trying to get drunk?'

Wave to the steward for a second and third glass.

'"Trying"? As if it were possible not to succeed?'

'Go to bed.'

Empty the glass in one. Razbyesoff caught the raised arm.

'Go to bed, dream it all away, thus the soul sweats out its sickness;
and when you rise in the morning, refreshed and invigorated, have a
wash and a shave and look at yourself in the mirror – and you'll know
who you are, what you want, and what you have to say to your father.'

Crush the cigarette into the empty glass.

'Yes. Quite right. I have my insh-shtructions after all. A courier will come. Trust not the Old Man. Alive!'

He helped to the feet, supporting under the elbow and catching the toppling chair, whilst the steward bent to retrieve the blanket fallen dangerously close to the grate. The Express wasn't even being tossed from side to side, wasn't braking, wasn't jerking – lean against the wall, however, with every step, against the doorframe, against the cast-iron handle. Glance back from the threshold of the inter-car passageway, through semi-darkness and semi-shadow, towards the bright hearth beneath the coldiron canopy of the fireplace. The engineer was snoring loudly with head thrown back and mouth wide open, Doctor Konyeshin and Captain Nasboldt were discussing in undertones, gloomy smiles on fleetingly illuminated countenances, whilst Porfiry Pocięgło was offering the prosecutor a cigar from his silver case. Banks of white looming outside the windows flashed above the passengers, as the golden half-moon momentarily pierced the clouds. Shake the head. A drunken delusion, Pyotr Leontinovitch Razbyesoff in no way resembles him. Totter towards the compartment, brushing the shoulder against the boiserie and trailing the stiff leg.

In the corridor, outside his compartment, stood the solitary figure of Prince Blutsky-Osey clad in a thick dressing-gown embroidered in red, coat of arms and initials over his heart, in hair net and black moustache bandage. Hands thrust into his pockets, the prince was staring out of the window, scowling and squinting in the manner typical of myopes. He was whistling or humming something under his breath, but the staggering in the narrow corridor made too much of a clatter; the prince glanced around at once and stopped whistling, so the tune remained unheard.

Press flat against the carriage wall.

'Exsh-ushe me.'

He withdrew.

Attempt to pass him avoiding eye and bodily contact, but whether the train swerved more violently for once, or whether a balloon of mercury sloshed across inside the head, dragging with it the torso and legs and arms in defiance of any sense of balance – collide with the prince, slamming the forearm at the last moment, praise God, into the door of the compartment.

'Exshsh.' It was hot, all the windows were shut, a man could suffocate in here. Grapple one-handed with the buttoned collar, bent in an awkward position. 'M'excuser.'

The prince winced, retreated another step and rapped on the adjacent compartment. At once, Councillor Dushin stuck out his head.

The prince whispered something to him, motioning urgently. The councillor threw a frock coat over his pyjamas and stepped out into the corridor – the next man to proffer assistance: he seized under the arm, stood to one side, led the way, left leg, right leg. Having reached the compartment by this method and collapsed onto the bedcovers (Dushin had opened the door with a key extracted from his coat pocket), only then did the asphyxiated mind awake to faint wonderment. The prince – not so long ago wishing to bestow a good hiding, now seemed a nice old boy, short of offering a sugarplum. Dushin – why not one of the provodniks, or a steward? Feel for a glass of water placed on the escritoire. Dushin – because they'd been chatting with Tesla's okhranniks, and had believed Fogel. The secret agent would kill the Son of Frost in the dead of night in an empty corridor of Deluxe. Hah! Now the prince will protect him in defiance of his spouse. A friend of Nikola Tesla is a friend of the tsar, an enemy of gleissen. Hop, skip and a jump, and everything's upside down. Where's that glass? The hand slumped, brushing the papers onto the carpet. Pale reflections of ice cast cold blinks around the inside of the compartment. Had the councillor shut the door? Where's the key? Where the cane? Sit down, undo the frock coat and shoes. Ooph, Mother of God, what heat.

A knock at the door.

'Who the devil!'

The knocking continues.

'The master's not at home. Clear off!'

No good, the blighter knocks and knocks. Who gives a toss, let him stand there and tear his knuckles. Struggle to unbutton the shirt cuffs, assisting the hapless fingers by way of the teeth.

Dushin had not, however, closed the door. It fell slowly ajar, and into the icy glow drifted the shadow of a tall silhouette.

Blood rushed to the head; breath stopped in the lungs. He has come! To kill! Wrest the Grossmeister out of the belt – it slips from the hands, flies under the escritoire. Drop to the floor with a crash, toppling the stool and precipitating the glass onto the head. Seize hold of the glass, groping in the dark, aiming with all might at the door. It exploded on the doorframe like a thundering grenade, raining splinters all around. The shadow leapt back into the corridor as the thrust-back door crashed against the wardrobe.

Crawl out from under the tabletop, unwinding the cloths from the Grossmeister.

'… *putain de merde*, that should throw glass, *mon oeil, sacrebleu…*'

'Monsieur Verousse…?'

The beanpole journalist peered cautiously into the compartment.

With one hand clutching his cheek, in the other holding out the dolphin cane.

'... behind piano my apologies you'll allow sir found thought you'd gone to compartment request this conversation apologies sir *bonne nuit, bonne nuit, bonne nuit!*'

Whereupon he delicately placed the cane beyond the threshold and fled.

Standing upright at last on the legs, hurriedly close the door.

And so, freezing will be like this, no two ways about it: as a coward. Chuckle. Recognise the great wisdom: cowards are like cowards! Switch on the light. Movement in the mirror – white dickey, crooked necktie, obnoxious physiognomy, black revolver held in the fist. Place the feet wide apart and aim the Grossmeister into the looking glass, closing the left eye and sticking out the tongue. Freeze! Bang, bang, Russian roulette – he upon whom the blow falls, he shall enter the Land of the Gleissen: Hungarian count, Piłsudski fighter, crazed mathematician, Son of Frost, foe of Martsynians, ally of Martsynians, Rappacki's dog, habitual gambler, bluffer and liar, friend of Nikola Tesla, traitor and coward and great hero, steward of History, the man who exists not, and yet –

Pook-pook.

'Who goes there? Declare yourself! For I'll sshh-shoot!'

'Benedykt, sir? Is everything all right? We heard loud noises. Nothing's happened? Benedykt?'

'Oh, nothing, nothing – exsh-ushe me a hundredfold, let Mariolka get back to sleep, that is, I meant Auntie Urszula, I'll be quiet now, Auntie, quieter, quite-quite quiet, shush. Goodnight, Jelena, miss!'

'Mm-hmm, goodnight.'

She went.

Stoop to pick up the rags to the Grossmeister and hiss with pain. Hop across on the sound leg to the stool, and sit down. A splinter of glass had cut through the sock and skin, piercing the heel. No way to grasp it with the fingernails, especially as they're chewed to the quick; a pair of tweezers or some kind of needle would have come in handy. Locate the mangled Waterman, the nib ought to suit – that is, the narrow spike re-maining of the nib, the rest being stuck still in Yury's neck. But perhaps better to disinfect it first. Reach for the drinks cabinet. What was left? – a miniature vodka, it'll do nicely. Pour some out. And the rest down the hatch, why waste it. Proceed to the operation of gouging out the glass from the heel. Dwook-dwook-dwook-DWOOK, hunched on the stool, leg drawn up crosswise almost to the chin, the knee again diabolically painful, the deformed pen poised like a shaman's lancet... jab, jab –

Pook-pook.

Jab!

'Ouch, bugger it, God damn it!'

Fly off the stool, banging the head on the bed.

'Open up, sir.'

'Pocięgło…?'

'If you please.' And again: pook-pook, pook-pook.

March on all fours towards the door, scanning the carpet ashine with glass shards, trailing the left leg behind like a lame dog. Having reached the handle, swivel round on the backside, twisting the limb in order to wrench the gold-filled Eyedropper from the heel.

Mr Porfiry Pocięgło stood in the doorway and in the doorway stood rooted to the floor.

'Wha d'ya want?' mutter, studying the fantastical new shape assumed by the savaged carcass of the fountain pen.

'Indeed, it seems…' Pocięgło took out a handkerchief, wiped the sweat from his brow, blew his nose; umbriance remained nonetheless on his face. 'Not the best time…'

Level at him the scoliotic Waterman, once again with blood on its nib.

'Speak.'

Glancing swiftly down the corridor in both directions, Pocięgło heaved a sigh and crouched in the doorway, catching hold of the swaying door.

'I wished before Irkutsk, in private, mind you… Are you listening to me? Miss Jelena Muklanowicz –'

'Miss Muklanowicz!'

'Shush!' He was irritated. 'Keep your voice down!' he whispered. 'Oosh, you're drunk as a pig.'

'I won't shtand for shuch conduct. You insult me, sir!' Brandish the bloodied pen under the nose of the exasperated Pocięgło. 'I demand satisfaction, tha dis, sadistfaction.'

'You're about to throw up.'

'A fucking puking duel at – at – four, two metres apart, and let's see who'll puke over who – I shall puke farther! Come on! I can go farther, I the master-puker, there's none like me! I'll puke on you so much your own swine won't recognise you!'

Pocięgło thrust back the hand armed with the pen.

'Disgusting boor. And I thought I was addressing a gentleman about an affair of the heart.' He stood up. 'What she sees in you, sir, I really don't know. Tphoo!'

'Heeheehee.'

He tried to slam the door but couldn't, and walked away without a grand gesture.

Retreat on all fours. Fling a shoe at the door; it closed at the second attempt.

About an affair of the heart, that's a fine one. Taken a fancy to Jelena, has he, or what. Bind the heel with a cravat. Disgusting boor, why not, a splendid career to be made there, boorishness has a great future, the whole world stands open to boorishness; the refined, the shamefaced and the sensitive give in to it, since only a boor would stand firm and not give in; after the first blow of the cudgel, wisemen no longer intervene in arguments already lost, the noble-minded take pity on the boor's misfortunes, whilst the boor presses on, nothing ruffling the serenity of his boorish soul, for the boor knows no shame, blushes not, smiles not apologetically, fails to see even the sneers and smirks, never feels uneasy and awkward – precisely because he's a boor. What can stand in his way? There's no such power. Verily, boors shall inherit the Earth, riffraff shall mount the thrones of the world. Stick the head into the washbasin and bring up half a litre of acid and vodka into the porcelain bowl. Dwook-dwook-stook-stook, the opened miniature had rolled against the wall. Tilt back the little bottle and shake the remaining liquor into the gullet.

Ye-es. He's fallen in love, poor sod. Crawl on all fours into bed. A piece of paper had stuck to the knee. Gather up the scattered documents. What have we here, *The Problem of the Existence of the Future*, who gives a fig, the future exists not, nor does the past either; ah, and the second PPS missive, the cipher of parallel memory – tell me: true or false! And also, those scrawled pages – the letter to Julia! So long ago was she last written to! Completely forgotten.

Snatch up a pencil. Fingers are slimy, the pencil slips out. *Please forgive me for taking so much time to* – but why does this train shake so! – *that I must needs get drunk* – well, can't say that to her – *that I must needs stare into the eyes of death* – oh, how dramatic! – *in order to understand* – what? – *all my faults, The wasted moments, reckless bolts* – drunk, dear God, well, he gets drunk and writes verses! Poke the pencil inside an ear. *It seemed to me that I loved you, since the idea of it was too beautiful to reject* – what is more sublime than unhappy love? *I know all too well that after what happened you gave me no* – and yet how she smiled from under her fringe, how with her swift dainty hand she grabbed the wrist, the forearm, and pressed it to her, as if to attract and hold the attention, to compel more urgent heeding of her words and no missing of her devious snake-like wiles; but don't women understand the signs, don't they comprehend that it's not the overt kiss, not the pettings in a dark gateway, not the words crude and vulgar, but – only the fleeting glance, the smile behind a handkerchief, the brush of a fingertip, the hem of her dress falling on an admirer's trouser leg beneath a table –

... Like on that day when we stood neath a linden tree in the autumn rain, and you were saying something hurriedly, rubbing hand against hand, inhaling deep the rain-soaked air, till a thunderbolt struck above the meadow, then a second beyond the woods; courage Julka, I cried, let's escape from under this tree, before we too are struck! We ran along the boundary strip between fields and then a muddy lane to the Wągiels' barn. Then Julia shook the rain out of her hair, drops of water like glass beads, except that their hard patter fell unheard on the threshing floor – she shook her hair, bent forward, head low between her knees; on the arch of her back, at the very top, above the embroidery on her light dress but below the collar, through the wet fabric, the shapes showed through of the uppermost vertebrae of her spine, round buttons like buttons of skin fastened on the wrong side from within, as if by red fingers of cartilage and sinew reaching from the breast-bone, from lungs and heart. I stretched out my arm and laid my hand on those vertebrae, pressing my fingers into Julka's neck. Beneath them I could feel every tiny bone, every button. She glanced over her shoulder. I stepped back, confused. She stood in the barn doorway gazing at the stormy landscape; beyond the farmyard, the vista opened onto the whole valley bathed in drizzle, onto the lands of the estate and leasehold forest. She clapped her hands joyfully. 'All this will be mine!' I nodded in assent, accustomed since childhood to nod at all her plans. I stood behind her, looking at nothing beyond the maiden. My hands were shaking, and I had to hide them behind my back. The buttons of her backbone stood out neath the fabric more clearly than I could bear. How much I longed to *strip* her...

Other are the loves of Summer.

On foreseeing the future

A fierce snowstorm had bleared the shapes of the Kansk-Yeniseysk station buildings and daubed the whole platform and even the Trans-Siberian Express itself in streaks of white, so that on stepping off the lowest rung of the disembarkation stairs onto the freezing grey mud, all that could be seen were the two nearest carriages, a platform lantern as well as an old wooden warning sign hanging below it, and maybe also the solid mass of the coldiron steam engine illuminated in the distance by a blaze of iridescent rainbows, its intense black shimmering through the all-embracing white – this was all.

On the wooden sign, from under a thick coating of hoarfrost, a crooked inscription glowed red:

Лёдъ!

As if anyone still needed to be informed. The Kan and Yenisey rivers are under floating ice, clusters of icicles hang from trees, steam gushes from under engines and drifts over the earth in angular clouds. Fasten the new fur coat donned for the first time, pull the heavy shapka onto the head and hobble towards the back of the train. The cane slid from side to side on the permafrost coated in fresh slush and snow, there was no support. A smarting pain was smouldering in the knee, the brain pounding, the stomach clenching and unclenching in spasms that brought up into the throat a warm acidic taste, whilst the mutilated throat hurt of its own accord. The Deluxe carriages, heated to an un-bearable degree, had so dried the overnight air in the compartments that the traveller awoke at dawn with a Cossack boot-sole inserted from his palate to behind his tongue, a pumice stone in lieu of a tongue. A litre of water had been swallowed straight from the tap, and only then had a human voice emerged from the larynx. A voice, that is, yet another early-morning curse at the sight of the pesky mug revealed in the mirror. Sleep had descended as the face rested on the unfin-ished letter, and now below the eye was reflected, like a circus clown's makeup, the elongated triangle of a pencil-tip – the caricature of a tear. Yawn till the jaw creaks.

Eight in the morning local time; the Sun obeys astronomical summer, but here on earth – it is Winter. Crane the neck, trying to peer in passing inside Miss Muklanowicz's compartment, but the cur-tains are drawn. They're probably asleep, obviously they're asleep. Sleep should be sought likewise and would be – were it not for the insistent memory of Prosecutor Razbyesoff's words of the previous day, were it not for the dark katzenjammer which time and again –

Scrunch-scrunch – this is no echo in the snowstorm but a person ap-proaching from behind, hurrying step by step. Stand still, turn around. Dushin.

'Good morning.'

'Greetings, greetings.'

He also stood still.

Grit the teeth. There'll be no speaking first, even if it means standing like a post till the Express departs.

Councillor Dushin hastily buttoned his overcoat, turned up the collar, pulled his fox-fur shapka over his ears.

'You'll forgive me, sir. Whenever you leave the train from now on,

throughout the day until we arrive in Irkutsk – I shall be accompanying you.'

'Ah!' Blink, as snowflakes glue the eyelashes together. 'And what does
the princess say to that?'

'Their Highnesses –'

'Have fallen out.'

'The evening before the dance –'

'Over me.'

'Not wishing –'

'You couldn't keep your trap shut in front of the prince. He believed
that –'

'Now they're not –'

'Not talking to each other.'

Whose man in the end is Zahary Feofilovitch Dushin? Scrutinise
him through the swirling white. He stood with hands thrust into overcoat pockets, chin raised haughtily, his viperous stare burning through
the blizzard.

'And have you banished your Martsynian, Lyednyak fears?'

'His Highness gave orders, Dushin went. Her Highness gave orders,
Dushin went. Inquire not into Dushin's fears.'

Clear the throat.

'But perhaps it's all a pack of lies, perhaps the princess has ordered
you now – to follow me, to shove a knife into a kidney when I turn my
back on my guardian angel.'

'I am not lying!'

Was he lying? (Gaze now like Prosecutor Razbyesoff!) He was not
lying.

Stride towards Tesla's wagon, Dushin two paces behind.

Fogel opened up. Shielding his mouth from the frost with a
muffler, he extended his other hand, assisting entry. He also wanted
to assist Dushin – but shake the head: 'Wait outside!' The silver-haired
okhrannik gave an odd look and slammed the door in the councillor's face. Then he reset the pince-nez on his nose, polishing it with a
handkerchief.

Take a look around.

'Is Doctor Tesla here?'

Fogel pointed to some blankets strung slantwise across the wagon
from the casing of a large flow-generator to a pile of tin crates. Draw
back the heavy fabric with the cane. It was a kind of vestibule improvised
to maintain warmth in the farthest section of the wagon, wherein lay
the guards' bedding, a samovar and now also a massive cast-iron stove
whose chimney-pipe led out through a high upper window made airtight with tar-soaked rags. The floorboards were covered in a thick layer

of old straw mattresses, holey skins, sacks of tow; stomp over them as over a quaggy peatbog. Nikola Tesla, clad in a huge unhooked black fur coat and bowler hat, was sitting on a stool by the stove; hunched over, he was making notes in a little leather-bound book. On the bedding, neath blankets and a soot-stained sheepskin, Oleg was snoring. Meanwhile over the puffing, purring samovar leant Mademoiselle Filipov; and she it was who first looked up with a greeting.

And on closer inspection, pursed her lips and wrung her hands.

'Benedykt, sir, have you any idea what you look like? you were supposed to stay in bed, you obviously can't be as well as Doctor Konyeshin said, all that dancing, you shouldn't have, oh, and you're still limping, what on earth are you doing to yourself?'

Kiss her warm little hand.

'Can they understand us?' Ask in French.

'Who?'

'Our chancery knights.'

'No. They don't know –'

'But they're able to understand what's most important,' remarked Tesla, raising his eyes from the notebook. 'If what people say about the Land of the Gleissen is true.'

Hobble over to the inventor, grasp him by the arm; the smooth fur of his coat slipped from the gloved hand.

'Do you remember our conversation?' Whisper to him. 'When we were watching the fire in the taiga?'

'Yes.' He looked down, sucking in his dry cheeks. 'No need to ask.'

'Good. The Kotarbiński pump – Fessar damaged it, I saw.'

'The pump… ah, that.' He glanced at Christine. 'I already repaired it yesterday.' He got to his feet and fired a shot into the air with his white-cotton fingers. 'I am about to serve up.'

They had moved the pump from the front of the wagon; it now stood on a chest by the samovar. It sufficed for Tesla to throw off the sackcloth.

'I was curious to know before.' Mutter, pulling off the gloves, whilst the doctor inserted the black cables into the machine and injected warm lubricant between the unreeling metal parts. 'What actually drives it, I see no –'

'Think, young man, think! When I work the crank and convert the mechanical energy into murch, then in the opposite –'

'True, the power comes from telestrical batteries. But are they any more efficient than steam or oil-fired engines?'

He shrugged his shoulders.

'They're still only prototypes, I make this calculation, that calculation, we shall see. More convenient, I grant. Well, be my guest.'

Grab hold of the coldiron barrel with the naked hand, Nikola Tesla pressed on the trigger.

… at Miss Filipov, who was watching with no hint of fear on her bright face, whereupon sugar blushes had been charmingly baked by the frost, with no hint of anger or reproach, but with a morbid intensity, a kind of ironic satisfaction, her eyes narrowed and unblinking. She tapped the chest with her heel and blew into her knitted woolly gloves. Hard to believe she won't hold out, won't erupt in disgust and bitter recriminations, won't run out sulking. No, otherwise: she'll throw herself with clenched fists at Nikola, at the machine, ripping out the cables and trampling them underfoot. No, otherwise: she'll grab hold of the coldiron wire herself, stand before Tesla, let him now unmurch her too, let him shoot! Or otherwise still: she'll break down suddenly and all irony will fly from her, and Christine will burst into tears, stamping on the sacks and rags in childish frustration. No, otherwise, otherwise:

She took a handkerchief from her sleeve.

'Please mop yourself, sir.'

'*Merci bien.*'

Wipe the chin, where saliva, oozing in the meantime from the limply gaping mouth, had collected.

'You're staying?' Christine asked Tesla.

He declined to answer, bending with puckered brow over his pump, which had begun again in its whirring racket to splutter and whistle unpleasantly; he merely raised his hand. Mademoiselle Filipov understood.

'Well then… in that case Benedykt…'

'I'm very sorry, miss.'

'Sorry for what?'

She buttoned her coat, adjusted her stole and, having instructed Mr Fogel to mind the samovar, departed; the pushed-back door scraped at once.

'What's she so upset about?' Ask disorientated. Where the gloves? Left pocket, right pocket; find them wedged behind the chain of the flow-generator. How to pull them painlessly over the bruised mangled fingers? Impossible. 'Khshsh. She was afraid some new disaster would happen, but now…?'

'I talked to her during the night,' Doctor Tesla said softly, still in French, without turning around. Fogel was rattling the teapot lid, Oleg moaning protractedly in his sleep. Nikola glanced at the okhranniks. 'She drank too much, we sat for a long time, in the end I told her everything.'

'Meaning…?'

'Everything, my dull-witted friend, that plan of yours hatched from the apple.'

'My – what?'

'Go now!'

Breathe deeper, once, twice. The boots sunk into a straw and sawdust mattress caked in mud; the train was stationary yet the entire goods wagon swayed side to side neath the flabby legs. Emerge from the vestibule curtained off by blankets and only then remember the cane; turn back. Doctor Tesla didn't even glance up; he had already disconnected the transformer and was attaching a kind of measuring device, rigged from a thermometer and glass flask overgrown with some spongy abomination, to the machine's tungetitum entrails, which had been pulled onto the outside.

The wagon door remained pushed back; descend gingerly with the help of Dushin. Mademoiselle Filipov was standing beside him, smiling radiantly at the privy councillor.

Grab her by the elbow.

'You shouldn't be talking to him, miss!' whisper vehemently.

'Ay! I shan't say a thing, I am not stupid.'

Dushin did not move from the spot; he watched in silence, hands back in pockets, with that sullen stare peculiar to Dushin.

'Let's go!' Drag the devushka away into the blizzard. The knee was aching, the head spinning, white, white, much too much white: where was up, where was down, what to stick the cane into – was that a cloud or heavy snowdrift? In the end it was Christine who provided support and orientation, the first to put down a foot. 'I'm sorry.'

'We have to discuss it later,' whispered the devushka, pressing her flushed face into the collar of her fur coat. 'In private. I'll help you with everything in Irkutsk.'

'Help – with what?'

'With saving your father! Isn't it for this that you imbibe that poison? In order to think up a means, in order to, as Nikola puts it, churn up your brain, pull the rabbit out of the hat – true? – in order to think up a means of saving your pater. For this!'

'No. Yes. No.' Stand still. 'I can't, give me a moment...' Lean heavily on the cane thrust into the permafrost and succumb to a loud bout of coughing; the throat and lungs couldn't cope with the cold air. 'Is he listening?'

She looked back.

'I can't see him.'

'Keep your voice down. All this... cannot be told in this way. I begged Nikola, but...' Pull the shapka over the eyes. 'We talk like this because talking is easy, this is said, that is said, as the moment prompts a person, and maybe at the time he really does believe in his own words, but – how is it possible at all to speak of the future? how is it possible to say "I shall behave in this way," "I shall do this and that"?'

'You are afraid!'

'Hah!'

'Don't you want to rescue your father from the Frost?'

'We're not even in Irkutsk yet! And you demand of me, miss, that I should foresee the future, prophesy from the snow.'

She puffed out her cheek.

'Mr Zeytsoff can do it!'

'What?'

'Prophesy from the snow. It's called cryomancy. He showed me. You place a hand in a bowl of water, but flat, with the palm open, oh, like this, holding it on the very surface, and then expose the bowl to the frost – and watch as the water freezes around the hand. From the embroidered patterns in the paper-thin ice between their fingers, you can read people's fortunes.'

'You believe in this sortilege, in horoscopes and tarot cards? True, I saw you at the princess's séance. It's nothing but a fraud of the present-day mind! Should I wish to hoodwink myself in this way – what could be simpler? Take the ill-starred Mr Fessar. When we found him, khhrr, with his head smashed open, if you'll excuse the expression, with blood pouring off him as if he'd been wrapped in red muslin, daubed in red gloss paint – I had seen him exactly like that twice before and thought to myself then with total certainty: blood, killed, lifeless, dead.'

'You had seen…?'

'A prophecy, you'll say, an omen, khhrr.' Continue faster and faster despite the frozen nose and claw in the throat. 'But upon this hangs the delusion to which everyone succumbs who believes that past and future exist, who believes that yesterday's Ünal Fessar and tomorrow's Benedykt Gierosławski exist. Whereas all that exists is present-day memory of the past, as well as present-day notions of the future! Therefore, because I recall now that Mr Fessar died in the way he died, khhrr, I also recall now my previous images of his death, those particular images and not others – and so there arises in my mind, out of the combination of two non-existent pasts, a prophecy come true.

'When you read a horoscope, miss, when you hear a prophecy, the future foretold in it does not yet exist; and when things happen remembered from a former prophecy, that prophecy no longer exists – only your memory of it. The whole charlatanry of Doctor Freud hinges on this very fallacy: we do not interpret memories of the past, khhrr, khhrr, but affix to our present-day interpretation a past that suits us.' Burst into coughing once and for all. Retrieve from a pocket Mademoiselle

Filipov's handkerchief, apply it to the mouth, breathing now through the fabric, through the glove and through the hand. 'I am not claiming that it's, khhrr, lies, that we are lying. These are things beyond truth and falsehood. Let's go, lest the train should again depart without me; they won't spot us in this blizzard, khhrrr.'

'Don't say more.'

'Beyond truth and falsehood – the past, the future. Anyone who tells or writes of the future is fantasising, whilst anyone who tells or writes of the past, that is, about people, things, countries that exist not, creates a similar fantasy. Every memory of the past is true only insofar as it doesn't contradict the present. Khhkrrr. Pray look behind you, miss: do you see our footprints in the snow? And so, I would be lying, were I to say that a minute ago we were standing there, and not there. And that is as much as exists, all that exists, khhrrrrr, of the past. Whilst beyond it, or in addition to it – you see – nothing, only whiteness, whiteness, whiteness, nothing certain behind us, nothing certain ahead of us. So don't be seduced, don't be beguiled by what exists not. Send Zeytsoff packing. Trust none of them: fortune tellers, strategists, detectives, planners, historians. Every historical novel is a fantasy. Khhrrrrr.

'Look meanwhile at the mechanisms typical of human memory. This contraption,' whack the shapka with the cane, 'functions according to its own laws, which are like no other laws. As I say, we never see the past as it was; we see it through the filter of our later experiences. You remember a childhood friend and would bet your right arm he was a boisterous joyful child – because that's how you know him many years later; but maybe in those days he hid in corners and fled red-cheeked at any harsh word? You won't know, khhrr; the past exists not. You re-member a former event, oh, say your first rendezvous with a lover – and not the meeting with the stranger he then was, but rather the man who you've been clasping to your heart for years. That's why so many swear that their love was love at first sight: because the first sight as remem-bered already carries within it all the pleasures and endearments that came later. You won't know the truth; truth about the past exists not. Khhrr! For lately you've experienced some occasion that repeats itself – a funeral, an illness, a journey – in this or that weather, in one or other mood, in these or those material accidents… It was already like that in the past! Khhrrr! You've been persuaded by signs and symbols. But this is only a jar in the machinery of your memory. Have you never had the impression, some presentiment at the limits of certainty – that our life, that is, our memory of it, consists of a series of constantly reverberating echoes; events recall events, words – words, feelings – feelings, people – people, objects – objects, in a continually repeated pattern organising the entire past? These are images of deception, illusions of what exists not, endlessly reflected inside the skull.'

'And yet,' Mademoiselle Christine mused, tilting her pretty head as sticky snow settled on her blond hair, 'and yet, there must be ways of knowing, I can imagine what Nikola would do at once: take it and write it down, record the exact words of the prophecy together with the date and hour; and when it came later to verification, not memory but paper proof, a material tangible thing, would testify to the past.

'And why can't you plan the future according to your own designs – this is beyond my comprehension. After all, the future never works out for anyone exactly as planned – but this is no reason to live solely for today, solely in the present moment, is it?'

'You, miss, are trying to wrest from me some heroic oath: that I shall take a stand against okhranniks, tchinovniks and Martsynians, against the gleissen, that I shall unfreeze my father and remove him from Siberia. But how can I give the word on behalf of a man I know not?'

'You mean, on behalf of whom?'

'Of Benedykt Gierosławski, who exists not!'

She bridled.

'You, sir, are an even greater maverick than Jelena was saying!'

Out of whiteness loomed the elongated shape of the passenger car. Lights were burning in the windows, a row of bright rectangles marking the boundary of the snowstorm.

Brush the icy flakes off the moustache and stubble.

'How can I know if any Benedykt Gierosławski will exist in future remotely like the one overcome yesterday by desperation – like the one remembered from yesterday – eh?'

'Aa-ah, so that's why you shoot yourself with that black current of Nikola's? "Dead, but perhaps alive." What? Not wishing to, but perhaps wishing. Afraid, but perhaps not afraid!' She jabbed with her index finger. Feel it even through the fur coat; she jabbed still harder, then struck with her open palm in a cack-handed attempt at a blow, almost slipping over; grab the devushka by her stole, embrace her around the waist. She stamped vigorously on the foot.

'Ookhhrr!'

'You take me for a foolish child! Yet I understand everything! I know what you did then to Nikola! But why did you not also resurrect the Turk? The "ill-starred Mr Fessar"!'

Clear the throat.

'By God and in truth, it never occurred to me. But with smashed head… in front of so many witnesses… and he was already strongly demurched… You think, miss, that I somehow directed it, that – that I *planned* that Nikola should come back to life? It was the toss of a coin.'

She snorted disdainfully.

'But you'll not toss a coin for your own father?'

So, shame had to be swallowed coming from her as well! Had to burn before her as well; had to sink under ice before the angel of shame!

'But what am I doing now!' Shriek through the blizzard, a cloud of hot breath flaring before the face, white mist, black mist, frost. 'What am I doing now! What!'

Mademoiselle Filipov recoiled, terrified, her mouth hanging open and her arms instinctively spread wide.

'Whom would you have me be!' Yell, brandishing the cane. 'A miracle worker! Hero! None such exists, he exists not, is not! Khhrrrrr!' The heavy shapka slipped from the head. Kick it into the snow neath a wheel of the train. Someone was standing on the staircase with light from the Deluxe carriage behind his back, a silhouette in a long great-coat. Shake the cane in all directions, at him likewise. 'I shall not lie!' Scream hoarsely in Russian and in Polish. 'No lies! One truth! Without me! Khhrr!' Keel over at last and drop to the ground, banging the shoulder-blade against the high permafrost.

Oh, what relief to lie like that motionless in the snow, in warm fur, under a sky of soothing white, as wondrously cold flakes settle on the inflamed skin, khhrr, khhrr, and flow in tiny rivulets onto the lips, as they drop straight between the lips, melting already in the cloud of dark breath mist – straight out of the whiteness above the peering-down countenances of Captain Privyezhensky, Privy Councillor Dushin and Mademoiselle Filipov.

'You're not hurt, miss?'

'We were just talking loudly.'

'So I saw. Drunk?'

'No!'

'He was in the wagon with Doctor Tesla's machines. Nothing should surprise you, Captain, I'm recalling what Mr Fessar of blessed memory was up to yesterday; it's just as well for us that this one's not run off into the taiga.'

'So, you're telling me, sir, that with these madmen, the American doctor passes shocks of current through their grey matter and then they –'

'I have no idea. But – you can see for yourself, Captain.'

Unmelted snow fell onto the tongue. It tasted of the most sublime spring water.

Captain Privyezhensky landed a kick below the ribs (the fur damp-ened the impact), spat and walked away, scrunch-scrunch.

Khhrr, khhrr, laugh lying winded on the ice, laugh standing up, as Dushin and the bemused devushka restore the body to the vertical, laugh, as the sullen councillor plants the snow-covered shapka on the bonce and guides to the Deluxe steps and into the carriage.

'As for you, miss,' he was still giving Mademoiselle Filipov advice, 'in Siberia, you ought never to set foot outdoors with a bare head, even if the frost seems of the lightest, you could forfeit your life.'

She merely nodded silently.

Chuckle, dragged by Dushin along the corridor and bundled into the compartment.

'Thank you, my good fellow,' call out, fumbling for a rouble piece in the pocket, 'and don't forget, my good fellow, to close the door behind you!'

This time he slammed it shut.

Collapse onto the bed still in the fur coat, in shapka, in boots, and fall asleep.

Glintzen danced on the walls of the compartment, on the window enveloped in white, as the train passed the massive hulks of trackside gleissen, dwook-dwook-dwook-DWOOK; later, glintzen remained only neath the eyelids, caused by a reversal of red spots. Telestrical flow tickled the veins and unmurched the dreams.

On the temperature at which truth freezes

Prosecutor Razbyesoff raised his vulture's brows, laid aside his knife and fork, took from an inside pocket a pair of wire-rim eyeglasses, painstakingly wiped the lenses and placed them on his vulture's nose. Having thus placed them, he leaned back in his chair, not with neck and shoulders but with his whole spine, and only then looked up over the table and dinner plates, clear chicken soup with vermicelli, stuffed duck, *pommes soufflées* and cold salad, and steaming gravy.

'Gospodin Gierosławski,' he stated, 'I withdraw what I said; I discerned it not, but you, sir, are already a gleissenik.'

'Shillushun,' swallow a meatball, 'it's an illusion –'

'Put your hand over the candle!'

He seized the hand below the cuff and drew it over the flame. Turn it on its side to prevent the finger bandages catching fire. The flame brushed the skin and for a brief moment – for the blinking of an eye, but Razbyesoff blinked not – it flickered blackly, sinking into its own negative, that is into the light-eating flame of a blackwicke.

Pyotr Leontonovitch let go.

'You were living here?'

'What?'

'In Siberia. In the Land of the Gleissen.'

'Not at all!'

'I have seen such darknings,' the prosecutor said deliberately, 'amongst former kholodniks, katorzhniks working for Sibirkhozheto, vagabonds from the shores of the Tunguska river.'

'I know, Mr Pocięgło mentioned it. But as for me... You can ask Doctor Tesla, it's temporary.'

Razbyesoff put away his eyeglasses.

'No need to explain to me, I am not interrogating you.'

'I wouldn't want you to take me for a liar, sir.'

Razbyesoff shook his head.

'So, you're travelling to your father.'

Dig the fork into the salad.

'Also not true. The Ministry of Winter has paid me, that's why I'm come. But now... I no longer know myself.'

Pyotr Leontinovitch smiled under his moustache.

'Fathers and sons, a Russian affair.'

'Mm-hmm?'

He wiped his lips with a handkerchief.

'Take this Zeytsoff here,' he pointed with his eyes to the ex-katorzhnik who, as usual, was dining alone, in a corner, at a separate table provided by the window. 'What was it he was saying? Travelling from birth father to spiritual father in order to save the latter with the former's money, himself a prodigal son – is that not his story? What other nation on Earth discovers a man's identity in his father's name? Venyedikt Filipovitch. Only peoples of the Book – Jews, Moslems. Because it's a sacred thing. In every earthly fatherhood is reflected the relationship of God the Father to the Son of Man, of God to men. Hence the father – but why not the mother, out of whose flesh new flesh is born? Have you read, sir, *The Brothers Karamazov*? Is it a tale about sons, or rather about fathers?'

A spice seed had lodged in a gum cavity left by a knocked-out tooth. Poke around in the gob with a toothpick.

'Mm-hmm, but you were right: I really have no idea why I boarded this train, and no idea what I'll do when I alight from it. All smoke and illusions of Summer. That I am his son... of this too, I really was reminded only of late. Earlier... I had no father in actual fact. No, otherwise: I had a father, but amongst his chief traits, apart from the virtues and shortcomings of his character, he also possessed this one: non-existence. But that's the thing – try to imagine them both alongside: the existing man and the non-existing man. How shall you distinguish one from the other? You shan't. Do you understand?' The restaurant car gave a jolt; the toothpick stabbed the soft gum. 'Damn it. Excuse me.'

'I shan't pretend that I understand you in this.' The prosecutor touched the tip of his nose with his finger, a gesture realised instead of another gesture, the unrealised one. 'But I cannot resist the connection… Before I was transferred to the artillery, I served as a young officer in the Caucasus, following the uprising of Alibek-Haji, at a time of ruthless Abrek activity. There, the wars of the local mountain peoples never cease; they fight amongst themselves and fight the Empire. Something exists in the very culture of these wild peoples – a shared characteristic that I detect neath their various lesser and greater eccentricities, things we can in no way accommodate in our heads… And so, these are peoples whose men go off to war in every generation and the majority never return. Who brings up the sons? Mothers as well as the fatherly ideals, that is, the non-existent fathers. But, take note, young man, these very sons will later depart themselves to perish for the lost cause, leaving behind their own sons, so that they become – the non-existent fathers. Et cetera, until non-existence itself becomes the ideal, meaning: upbringing through lack, which is not the same at all as no upbringing or upbringing by a woman without a man.'

'Therefore – therefore you are saying, sir, that it's a kind of historical necessity, that as the child of a non-existing father –'

'No!'

'Yet now they say: the Son of Frost, *le Fils du Gel*. Am I to consent to this? It's too easy, like donning a theatrical costume.'

'You're asking me?' Razbyesoff averted his eyes. 'I said: I shan't answer for you.'

'You know, it's precisely because you… because you…' Break the toothpick, push the dinnerplate away so violently that the glasses jingle on the tablecloth. 'Why I'm able to ask you at all – do you understand? You, sir, are perhaps the closest of all people to understanding.' Lean towards him across the table. He continued not to look, fleeing in his gaze to one side, outside the window, into the snowbound landscape. 'Listen, sir – I am not saying what I say, but maybe you will hear, maybe understand – listen, sir: *I exist not.*'

He cleared his throat.

'For it was passed on to you by your father? Or perhaps it's *à propos* of Dostoyevsky? For if there is no God – and here: if there is no man –'

'No! It's not a figure of speech. Can you see beyond the simple paradox of language? I exist not.'

The prosecutor pressed his palm to the windowpane, wiped the steamed-up surface.

'Who knows if you're not right, whether it's not the shortest path…'

'Path? To what?'

'First reject everything, both truth and falsehood, and only then –'

'No, no, no!' The head was spinning. 'But…' At last, he glanced over the flame of the decorative candle. Lower the eyes. Fold the serviette, stand up. 'Thank you.' Bow stiffly and quit the restaurant car as swiftly as possible. Razbyesoff called not from the table; besides, there'd have been no looking back.

Back in the compartment, the bed had been made and the carpet swept of glass shards. Check: the drinks cabinet had been replenished. Mustn't forget a few roubles for Sergey. Pour a cognac. The afternoon drabness heralded an early twilight, only the ubiquitous white deceived the eyes. Gaze through the shot-glass and through the liquid at the inside of the palm. Are those glintzen forming along the palmist's life and fate lines, or icy reflections splintering on the cut-glass rosettes? But the worst thing: the palm is shaking.

Flick on the electric light. No desire was there to sleep, since plenty of sleep had been had during the day. Take out the folder from the escritoire, fumble through the papers. The hand paused at the PPS-men's missive. SPRING OF NATIONS YES. THAW TO THE DNIEPER. PETERSBURG MOSCOW KIEFF CRIMEA NO. JAPAN YES. COURIER COMING. ALIVE. If this were not a prediction of the future, then what was it? But this second – prediction, which had not been deciphered – and the infinite number of parallel predictions, which had not been remembered – for which equally strong foundations were lacking in the present... The toss of a coin, of course, it's the toss of a coin. Step down from the train on arrival in Irkutsk and –

Glance in the mirror. Count Gyero-Saski, the Incredible Felitka Caoutchouc – this is easy, there's nothing easier, it'll come true of its own accord, with no effort and, to some extent, in spite of effort. But to do the opposite: to dismantle the falsehood, to peel away the lies, one after another like the skins off an onion... What will be left? Apart from tears in the eyes.

Jerk the lion's tail, pull down the window; frost swept into the compartment, dwook-dwook-dwook-DWOOK, frost, the clatter of rails and ringing gale whipped up by snow – until the whiteness brought on a fit of choking; rub the eyes, blink the sticky snowflakes off the lids – and catch sight in the far distance, above the ice-benumbed forest, of a soaring icecradle, a monumental stalagmite leaning in defiance of gravity – so this is it, already here, now, the Land of the Gleissen, yea, the heart of Winter. Pull from the finger, clenching the teeth, the signet ring with the Korab coat of arms and fling it with all might out of the window. It flew a good twenty arshins from the track, into deep snowdrifts.

Cough out the frost once the window is closed. The cognac helped. Returning to the mirror, ruffle the hair, already severely ruffled by the wind. On second thoughts, comb it onto the forehead and to the sides, this way, that way, and differently again – but still it altered nothing.

Hobble to the duty room.

'Is there a maltchik proficient with the razor?'

Sergey raised his head over his magazine.

'Razor?'

Press a banknote into his hand.

'Ah, the gentleman wants a shave!'

'When do we stop? Have him knock and wait outside the bathroom.'

'In a quarter of an hour, in Kuytun.'

The steward-cum-barber appeared on time, a minute before the train began to brake. Luckily, he also had scissors. Sit down on the edge of the bath, throw a towel around the shoulders. The train stopped with a shrill drawn-out whistle; the steward glanced inquiringly.

'Cut!'

'What style does your lordship require?'

'As close as you can. So long as it's quick. And then go over it with the razor, a baldhead it shall be.'

'As your lordship prefers. And the beard?'

'Leave the beard.'

His hands worked swiftly, running over the skull with the smooth blade, clipping the skin but once. Two impressive lumps were revealed in the process as well as extensive bruises, already well matured and diffused into cherry-violet stains, one at the front stretching from above the ear to the right temple. It looked very ugly.

'Your lordship is satisfied?'

'Couldn't be more delighted.' The train lurched. Grab hold of the washbasin; the Express was moving again. They're trying to make up for the delay. Shove a three-rouble note into the maltchik's pocket. 'When's the next longer stop?'

'In an hour, Your Esteemed Nobleness. We're to stop for forty-five minutes in Zima.'

'Where? We've been in Winter for ages.'

'The town called Winter, Old Zima, like the River Zima that flows into the Oka. Or flowed.'

Back in the compartment, down in one the rest of the cognac to the health of the mirror. The cravat! It's essential to be rid of all these stylish cravats, English neckties and shiny tiepins. What else? The cane? The cane, alas, is indispensable. Fur coat? It will be exchanged in Irkutsk for a cheap sheepskin; the sable overcoat ought also to be disposed of. Feel inside the pockets; the hand catches on a bulge behind the belt. What to do with the Grossmeister? Give it back to Tesla?

Next arises the question of money. Take out the diengi from the bumazhnik as well as the meagre bundle of notes from the bottom of the valise. Even with the winnings at blizzarder, the combined sum was too paltry to pay off the Ministry of Winter in one go. Whilst to drop by to say good-day and chuck their money on a desk would mean they'd never let the Son anywhere near Father Frost for all the tea in China, not to mention allowing the necessary freedom to unfreeze and kidnap him from Siberia. Hence lies – lies it had to be one way or another.

No! Lie once and it will freeze forever. Even silent acquiescence in the lie – how much evil this can cause! how distort a life! And this long before the Land of the Gleissen, still under the Summer Sun. Pass a hand over the smooth scalp, feeling for slight convexities and concavities in the cranium neath the skin, the phrenological map of character. Were it only possible through such deformation of the brainpan to remould the soul... This is the last moment; these are the last station-stops before the City of Ice. Since you know not who you are, be sure at least of who you are not. Thrust the bonce into the washbasin under a stream of cold water. Not at all in order to sober up for sharper thought and clearer mind – but in order to think of nothing else but this cold water, to arrest the unmurched imagination already leaping ahead to the next possibility and the next and the next, each one equally true. Need to hold out until Tesla again bemurches the trembling bruised grey matter.

Wait in the corridor by the door, clad in fur coat and shapka, cane in hand and cigarette in mouth, as the Express brakes; jump down onto the Zima platform, nearly tumbling over before the train comes to a halt. Snow had not fallen so thickly here, but the ground was covered in that same triple-layered grume: fresh fluff on top of half-frozen mud on top of solid ice. Tread over it as over spilling gravel; the undersoil slips away beneath the boots, the legs twist at the ankles.

Totter along, puffing and blowing. Zima, one of the last station-stops, barely two hundred and fifty versts from Irkutsk. Station building on coldiron skeleton, sawmill warehouses, barracks and sheds under frostoglaze lanterns. In the glare of the lanterns, the whole platform and carriages behind the Black Sable and entire surroundings seem as if enveloped in coldiron rainbows, as if enclosed under a dome of glimmering reflections, where sparks of snow spin neath the light and drop slowly to earth – within a glass globe filled with porcelain trinkets for childish amusement; whilst above it all, from above the station, leans the huge spidery mass of a gleiss. Rattle the door, once, twice, louder, a third time – Oleg opened up. 'Is Doctor Tesla there? Well, lend me a hand!' Spit out the cigarette under the wagon.

Tesla even showed no surprise. Apart from himself and Oleg, no one was there; Fogel had gone to fetch Prince Blutsky's men who'd promised to stand guard around the wagon whilst the train was stationary. Everyone was growing more and more nervous, the closer they drew to Irkutsk.

'Have you got that dynamo-machine here? Maybe it'll be quicker to simply switch the flow over in the pump. Please!'

Doctor Tesla stroked his cleanshaven lip with his bare hand. Unlichted afterimages crept over his parchment-pale skin.

'To plus?'

'Plus, yes, plus; more murch, Frost. Plus!'

Without moving from his seat, he pointed with a courteous gesture to the Kotarbiński pump.

Pull off the gloves, walk up to the machine. As per usual, two long coldiron cables ran out of it, one ending in barrel and trigger.

'Are they set up? May I? May I?'

The machine was ticking over with a subdued whirr.

Seize the barrel and quickly press the other hand down on the trigger without thinking.

... from the stiffened fingers.

Bend forward, raise the barrel so as to depress again the metal tongue.

... to stop trembling.

'Leave off, sir, you're already completely blue!'

'More.'

'You'll suck the murch out of half a jar. Look, my tea is freezing.'

'More!'

...helping to stand on the feet. The iced-over machine glistened ominously. Oleg handed back the shapka, which had rolled far away amongst the rags and sawdust. At first, however, it was impossible to lift the hands to plant it back on the bald head, they shook too much. Try to warm them by breathing on them – the breath was colder; a cloud of thick unlicht swam before the eyes. Burst into a bout of coughing. Nikola offered a mug of steaming tchay, boiling water straight from the samovar. Press the fingers onto the mug. Perceive then on the skin of the palm, an extensive pattern of white and red blotches, like a chessboard almost in its regularity. Saliva prickled the tongue and the whole inner mouth was teeming; to breathe through the nose was impossible, speaking had to be done by opening wide the lips and slowly, painstakingly articulating sounds and taking deep breaths between words. Gaze through the mist and shadow of breath. The noctaureole surrounding the Serbian inventor was conspicuous as never before, glintzen were sprouting from under his hands, black light streamed over his lean face; he resembled more a copperplate engraving of Nikola Tesla than the living Nikola Tesla.

He raised his bare hand.
'Yes, I will,' was the answer to him.
'Yes,' he confirmed.
'And as soon as possible.'
'A month, perhaps two.'
'Whenever.'
'All right,' he said in English.
'Through her.'
'Yours, if officially.'
'It doesn't matter.'
'Only the transport.'
'They've still not captured him.'
'Where.'
'Will manage.'
'Hah!'
'*Bien.*'

Drink up the cold tea, bow to Tesla and step out into the turquoise, pink and celadon blaze of frostoglaze lanterns. Oleg slammed the door with a crash. Nearby, between the wagons, stood a man dressed in Prince Blutsky's livery with a rifle by his side. He pressed his shapka to his knees; greet him cordially. Move along the line of carriages with a smile frozen from ear to ear. Fall over in the snow after a few paces. Contemplate in calm amazement the watercolour shades washing over the snow. The prince's man came running up, held out the cane, brushed the fur coat. Colours, colours, so many colours. Walk on slowly now, examining everything with the avid attention of children, madmen and the terminally ill. Turn even the head warily and gently, focusing the eyes like the heavy barrels of high-calibre guns. And so. Evening. Zima. Snow. A gleiss. A station. People. Carriage. Carriage. Carriage. Dushin. 'Must you keep running away from me like this…!' Breathless. 'You yourself court disaster, as God's my witness!' Greet him courteously like a long-lost comrade. He withdrew, frowning. Carriage. Carriage. Their rectangular windows: brightly lit openings in a wall of shadow behind lace curtains of snow. For the lamps are burning, of course, in the compartments, electric bulbs in white and red globes; and as soon as the eye turns towards the glare, it is blinded at once to the twilight all around, to the whole rest of the world immersed in this twilight and half-twilight, and so it leaps between windows as if between the pages of a book, a photograph album, from photo to photo, from *tableau* to *tableau*, the mesmerised eye. It sees: Frau Blutfeld bent over Herr Blutfeld, vigorously trying to persuade him of something to the accompaniment of sweeping gestures, caught in profile in this *tableau*, projected onto the steamed-up pane as a massive silhouette with prominent bosom and hair coiled in towering pyramid. Next image: Captain Nasboldt peering out of his closed window, arms behind back, sea-wolf's short pipe between teeth. Next: the children of the French couple pressing their pink faces against the glass pane, whilst behind them, in the backdrop – the protective shadows of their parents. A woman's hand looms from behind the half-drawn blind, a wrist adorned in a lace cuff, a long cigarette holder and cigarette, a trail of smoke, the fluid movement of the hand like the falling notes of a minuet. Prince Blutsky-Osey dozing with his nose in a book, his arm twisted unnaturally above his head, an old man frozen in all his helpless senility. Prosecutor Razbyesoff smoothing down on a hanger his prosecutor's uniform, back turned to the window image, so that the electric *tableau* shows only a broad, stiffly upright rear-view of the erstwhile lieutenant colonel of artillery; and there's nothing vulturous in the image, nothing false. Next a rich man and his servant bent over a table, over a chessboard, the servant pouring his master's coffee, the master moving his castle. The handsome widow mechanically combing her black locks, whilst the fingers of her other hand dance over her lower lip, around the half-smiling mouth. The two brothers sitting face to face in their compartment, motionless and silent, arms crossed over their chests like two dry mummies, two soulless profiles. Horsey-jawed Monsieur Verousse playing his typewriter as if it were a piano, one hand quickly turning a sheet of paper on the roller without looking. Stop dead on the spot, frozen, benumbed. Dushin approached, touched, shook, began to speak, louder and louder still. It was impossible to move, impossible to avert the gaze. 'Venyedikt Filipovitch! Venyedikt Filipovitch!' Stand for a very long while – for Dushin was screaming and tugging that much; in the end, it attracted the attention of Verousse, who glanced up from his typewriter. Snow was falling in between, three arshins of wind and snow before the illuminated windowpane, falling on the face and eyelids – but the eye didn't blink. Verousse likewise blinked not. Take a stride backwards, a second, a third; the muddy grume crunched under the soles, a fifth, a tenth, whilst curtains of opalescent snowstorm were drawn across the eyes, shutting out the golden *tableau* of the compartment, the whole of Deluxe car number one, the elongated shape of the train and massive bulk of the black coldiron superbug parovoz beneath its butterfly-wing Auroras.

'Mr Dushin.' Say with a frosty gasp. 'Run and warn Doctor Tesla – Verousse – not-Verousse – he's the one about to blow up his wagon.'

On the power of contempt

Miss Jelena Muklanowicz adjusted the pince-nez on the hawk nose of Pavel Vladimirovitch Fogel. The silver-haired okhrannik transferred the Nagant from one hand to the other, wiped the inside of his palm on his coat-tail and gave a nod. The provodnik turned the key in the door to Jules Verousse's compartment, pushed down on the handle, and Fogel burst in.

'Not here!'

'I told you so!' Snarl in irritation. 'I realised after a single look; I gave myself away; he knows that we know. He's taken his bomb and gone to blow up Tesla's arsenal.'

'So, what are we waiting for? Depart as soon as possible,' interjected Miss Muklanowicz.

The natchalnik of the Express took out his pocket-watch and glanced at the face.

'Twenty-five minutes.'

Peer through the window.

'He's gone into the snowstorm, no hope in hell we'll find him now. We have to guard Tesla and his machines, it's the only way.'

Fogel set off down the corridor towards the door of Tesla's wagon.

Jelena turned on her heel. 'Wait here, Benedykt, sir, I'll get my coat!'

Extricate the Grossmeister – before she comes back – from under the unhooked shuba, unwrap the revolver from its oilcloth, check the tungetitum bullets in the flower-stem cylinder, adjust slightly the snake-like trigger. The natchalnik stared at it in confusion, twice opening his mouth and twice swallowing the unuttered words. In the end he merely crossed himself with a gloomy expression.

Mechanically rub the butt-end against the back of the other hand. Miss Muklanowicz came running.

'Here I am,' she whispered, panting heavily, 'let's go... I wasn't ex-pecting... you'd wait... for a woman...'

'You wanted an adventure, miss.'

'But one... in which she might even get... killed...!'

'Indeed. This is what distinguishes an adventure from imagining an adventure.' Point to the passageway. 'Please.'

She looked again at the Grossmeister – great dark eyes in small pale face – and went ahead.

Step down onto the platform. Fasten the shuba. Cane in left hand, Grossmeister in right, ice underfoot. From the direction of the station, a uniformed railway official came running together with the local police sergeant and two constables carrying rifles. Jelena was looking all around, pressing her face into her downy sable collar. Suspended above the tracks, the gleiss straddled the Express, coal and firewood warehouses, sidings and locomotives. The pulsating glare of frostoglaze lanterns painted the icer in waves of watercolour: pale green, marine blue, insipid orange, burnt yellow. Even the falling snow, bah, the very air itself – shimmered with these same colours.

'And if it's not Verousse?'

Rap the cane into the permafrost.

'Having doubts? The Sherlock Holmeses are proliferating like wildfire.'

'You jest, sir!' she snorted in exasperation.

'The typewriter, Jelena. You should make deductions according not only to what exists but also to what exists not. I'm going to Tesla, you shall come with me or not come with me, pray decide now which Jelena Muklanowicz is entering the land of the Ice.'

She gave an odd stare.

'Again, you look somehow different, sir. The shadows under your eyes – I heard how afterwards, in the night, they had to carry you back –'

'Are you coming or not?'

She thrust her hands deeper into her pockets.

'You think, sir, I'll be scared.'

'I do entertain such hope, that's true.'

She released a long breath from her lungs; the cloud of vapour unfurled before her like a silken fan. Once it had vanished, she was already staring differently and a different grimace was freezing her face. Miss Muklanowicz stood up straight, raised her head. Wait in silence; knowing, after all, how hard it is, how painful – and how shameful, when people watch, when even one person watches. However, we're not talking here about ordinary fear. It's a different type of terror. Even those unable to express it in language of the second kind through any artifice, sense in that moment an overpowering impression of *non-existence*. Wait humbly as the snowstorm roared in the ears.

Breathing out for a second time, Miss Muklanowicz stood on tiptoe and quickly pecked the frozen, unshaven cheek.

'Thank you.'

Walking along the length of the train, she rushed ahead every so often and stopped, glancing impatiently over her shoulder; make no attempt, however, to hurry, fearing an accident with the Grossmeister, should another somersault happen on the permafrost. Besides, the snowstorm was thickening; apart from the smeary glows of lights above the earth, not much penetrated the swirling clouds. People were running hither and thither, as their broken shouts, the blasts of whistles, slamming of carriage doors, crunch of trampled ice, were borne on the wind. The Grossmeister hand was already raised when a figure fell out of the rainbow snow – but it was a soldier, a policeman, a shaggy railwayman, one of the prince's men or Captain Nasboldt, he too had a revolver poised to shoot. He smiled, apologised, bowed to the young lady, and ran on.

'A crowd is gathering again,' she panted. 'And then it'll turn out –'

'What?'

'He might simply have taken fright and fled; sometimes it's not hard to be scared of Benedykt Gierosławski.'

'The typewriter, Jelena. You yourself described his method to me the other night over cognac. For whom were we seeking? A passenger who'd bought a ticket at the last minute, because only at the last minute did the Lyednyaks realise they'd been compromised and decide to place one more agent in the Transsib. So it was Zeytsoff, so it was Pocięgło, the next suspects. But – when was it, miss, that you bought your own ticket? you and Mariolka Belcik, when did you buy them, eh? You didn't!' Shake the head in dull amazement. 'You laid it all out before me, but I didn't understand it; however, you didn't understand it either. Travelling is a magic time, Jelena. We are what strangers see us to be. By what means can you verify the genuineness of Benedykt Gierosławski? By what means can I verify the genuineness of Jelena Muklanowicz? I can't. The same applies to the identity of every one of the travellers. Most passports lack even detailed descriptions. Therefore, what does the agent do? He looks out in the Deluxe passengers for a solitary man, one who certainly has no old acquaintances amongst the other travellers to Siberia, and –'

'So, Jules Verousse is not Jules Verousse.'

'I have no idea what he's called. The real Verousse was probably devoured long ago by wolves. This Not-Verousse – I bet you is no foreigner at all. He talks so chaotically not because he knows no Russian or German, but because Russian is his native tongue. I told you: make deductions also according to what exists not.'

Pass a group of passengers from the second-class sleepers gazing curiously at the platform, that is, at the small fragment they could perceive from their carriage steps, from whence they had not ventured far: two pot-bellied bearded merchants, a muzhik with a dog, an old woman wrapped in three shawls so that only her Mongolian eyes could be seen between the folds of red fabric, a scrawny Orthodox priest. They'd no sooner been spotted than they redirected their attention, shouting out violent questions moreover and pointing with their fingers: look, big black revolver, look, young krasavitsa at his side, look, he's limping, the troublemaker who dines with princes and richlings, it's him, it must be to do with him, tphoo!

439

Flee as fast as possible into the snow, almost overtaking Miss Muklanowicz.

'The first question, khhrrr, which we should have asked ourselves is: why didn't the affair erupt after I smashed Fessar's head?'

'He made no complaint.'

'But I don't mean the poor Turk! In whose compartment did we leave a pool of blood on the carpet?'

'Agh! The typewriter!'

'He unlocks his compartment, enters, sees: and so, during his absence someone had bloodied the floor. And what khhrrr, would a normal person do then? He'd run to the provodnik, the natchalnik, raise a hue and cry. But what does Monsieur Verousse do?'

Miss Muklanowicz was already initiated into the logical routines of Doctor Watson; she listened with joyful tensity, earnest and excited, so that no space within her was left for fear; frost or no frost, rosy flushes would still have rouged her pale cheeks. She answered half-breathing, swallowing the wind and snow.

'Nothing.'

'Nothing! Now look further at the non-existent things. What was it this famous journalist was writing on his typewriter? Where are his reportages, interviews, traveller's letters, tales from wild Siberia? He was banging out pure nonsense on those sheets of paper, literal chaos and thousands of repetitions of the same character, nothing more. And why was he doing it?'

'Wait a minute… Don't tell me, Benedykt, let me work it out for myself!' She bit her lips. 'He's not Verousse, yes. Therefore… Hah! He cannot type!'

'He cannot.'

'But everything can be heard through these walls, and he had to keep up appearances. Therefore – every evening he thumped conscientiously on the keys. Yes? Yes?'

'No doubt he'd have abandoned that Verousse typewriter at once, had he been able to foresee it. At first, however, he was trying to write something, copy out sentences perhaps from a book – but what it must have sounded like! He realised he'd betray himself very quickly like that, so then he was banging on the keys just in order to make a fast sound: track-track-track, as if he were playing the piano. Because he can play the piano – and when I saw him through the window, *playing on a typewriter*… Understand?' Strike the shapka with the dolphin cane till the white fluff spilled off – 'All obviousnesses froze together in their places, as if a gleiss had trampled on my head.'

The gleiss, which Jelena instinctively spun around to look at, hung over the tracks at the height of the station building. Its main bulk – a

vast star-shape of dark ice piled eight or nine arshins above the carriages – remained invisible; all that could be seen through the blizzard
and radiant glares of lamps were the outlines of two thread-like limbs.
Limbs, or maybe pillars, or maybe roots, or maybe perpendicular geological waves, threads of glacial slime distended and cracking over
hours, over days. Maybe it's not matter at all that shifts from place to
place but only the unearthly frost itself, the temperature gradient, congealing everything in its path into a fourth state of matter: a gleiss. The
hoarfrost on the windowpane – it too roams according to –

Whack the big shapka again with the cane.

'And the next obviousness: he discovers blood, keeps quiet about it –
but what's going on? All night he did nothing but painstakingly search
his compartment, inch by inch; I bet my right arm that's what he did.
What did he find?'

'What could he find? We threw away…' She stood stock-still, almost
stumbling over from the realisation; instinctively, she reached with her
gloved hand to the tightly wound hair. 'My hairpin!'

'Your hairpin. He found a woman's hairpin – with a black hair. So,
what did he assume? Whom did he start to suspect? We were still, after
all, far back in Summer. Try to remember, miss, the exact beginning
of his affection for the lonely widow. Who has long black hair and is
travelling two compartments away from him.'

'Jesus Christ!'

'You were saved by the positioning of the carriages. Do you think
he hasn't killed anyone here yet? Hah! Pray remember the Lyednyaks'
target: Tesla, Tesla's arsenal, the defence of the Ice, defence of Russia's
status quo. Whatever plan he had beforehand, then after my falling
off the train, just as Mademoiselle Filipov was opening her heart to
the prince and princess and the prince started loaning his own men
to help the okhranniks – this Not-Verousse had to quickly construct
a new plan. Remember, miss – two memories are more truthful than
one – remember how he began, already on the previous day, to work on
Fessar; events weren't supposed to take the course they did, he'd wanted
to make an entirely different use of Fessar –'

'What are you saying?'

'When you sent me to distract Mr Pocięgło, Fessar bursts in on us,
into the gallery, well and truly drunk, and babbles about the machines
locked in Tesla's wagon, about my alleged business contracts with Tesla,
with Pocięgło, with God knows whom – yet all to do with these machines. How did he get this into his head? Who pointed him in that
direction? I ask around later – and what do I hear? That on that very afternoon Fessar got Verousse drunk! Who poisoned whom, Jelena, who
poisoned whom? They were seen in company quaffing firewater, but

Not-Verousse can easily simulate mental obfuscation with that salad-talk of his, so people thought what they thought. But in reality, who has the stronger head: a Mohammedan unaccustomed to alcohol or an ageing Russky? And the next day, at the first opportunity, the poor fool breaks into Tesla's wagon. Had Dushin and the prince not been walking past at that moment, who knows how it would have ended. After all, the Turk had already made a public scene, and then his remains would have been found at the explosion site – Not-Verousse needed nothing more: he'd have blown up Tesla's arsenal in a trice, the matter would have taken care of itself and no suspicion would have fallen on the Flemish journalist. But he was too late, and the Turk ran off into the taiga alive. So, what does the crafty agent do then? Remember, miss! Which past fits? Or was it otherwise? He, he was the first to call for an expedition into the forest to save the madman! He it was who dragged people there! Because he had to hunt him down privately, before Fessar returned to his senses and returned to the Express and began to tell everyone how the famous journalist had talked him into it. And so Not-Verousse himself set out after him as fast as he could, stopping first at his compartment, however, to leave the already prepared bomb; and luck was on his side, or perhaps one determining factor sufficed: we were going for a walk, a picnic, whereas he alone was genuinely looking for the Turk – and he found him, and smashed his head in with a stone. Then he immediately appears again at the crime scene wringing his hands, scratching an account of it into his reporter's notebook, khhrrr, muttering words of wisdom from the Tower of Babel. So, he killed; killed and is killing.' Cough – too many words, the frosty air again irritates the throat. 'And Doctor Tesla's accident? It could indeed have been an accident, I admit – but it could also have been the hand of Not-Verousse. And last night? He stole after a drunken man, supposedly to return his cane – but if I'd been lying there immersed in sleepy delirium, do you imagine, miss, I'd ever have awoken to see the light of day? Hah!'

She pressed her tongue into her cheek, bowed her head.

'But if despite this… You said yourself: murderers are created. And that such deductions are never proven true, that nothing can be said about the past with total certainty, it's all blurry, ambiguous, unstable. For a puzzle may be put together like this in a book, but not in real life, not in the world of "maybe", between truth and falsehood. And if you had not glimpsed him just now through the compartment window –'

Extract from under the shuba the metal barrel of the interferograph, remove the red chamois case.

'Take a peek. Well, go on, I am requesting you.'

She clasped the instrument gingerly between leather-gloved fingers, stroking the white ivory rings. She turned towards the glow of a frostoglaze lantern bleared by snow, towards the aureoles of cold azure; towards these she directed the interferograph, there being no sun. Holding the eyepiece to one eye, she narrowed the other.

'And what do you see?'

'A light, little lights, two points, one above the other, like two small eyes, they're twinkling, a blue imp –'

'Two.'

'Two. Oh! Ice, Benedykt, sir –'

Raise the Grossmeister. He came out of the blizzard from behind Miss Muklanowicz. Gazing into the interferograph, she failed to notice him till he was right beside her – lower the revolver, again it was not Not-Verousse – the fellow was right beside her and shoved her from his path, hurling the devushka onto snow and ice; she flew with a muffled cry as he raised a long sharp glistening skewer above his head: an icicle shaped like a dagger, a spear. No time was there to re-aim the Grossmeister, time only to glimpse the man's bare feet and naked torso neath his torn rubashka, and think blankly: in Zima they were waiting, from cold to cold, in Zima they killed, Holy Martsyn, help us –'

He plunged the dagger into the heart.

Collapse to the ground. The Martsynian dropped down behind the blow. The icicle had not pierced the thick fur. He sat astraddle, trapping beneath his knees both the hand with the cane and hand with the revolver. The heavy shapka slipped from the head; the bare occiput struck sharp permafrost.

The icicleman glanced and hesitated.

'Venyedikt Filipovitch Gierosławski?' he wheezed.

'Yes!' Snarl through gritted teeth.

He took a swing and thrust the icicle into an eye.

Jerk the head to the left. The icicle slid down the cheekbone and crashed to the ground; icy splinters lodged in the skin, ripping open anew the recent wounds.

The Martsynian flung aside the blunt shaft of the icicle and took to throttling. Fiery-cold paws pressed down on the neck, thumbs sank into the chin, into the larynx; losing breath, the body writhed in panic as he pinned it to the ground like a cemetery slab: right arm, left arm, chest – crucified, nailed. Above the Martsynian's head, livid and red from old and new frostbites, shone the rainbow colours of an invisible frostoglaze lantern, outlining the sectarian's broad-shouldered frame in a radiant nimbus worthy of a saint on an iconostasis – he had, after all, no evil expression on his face, he murdered with no grimace of anger, hatred or fear, rather of bitterness, of some desperate grief –

The nimbus dimmed, become shrouded – as the black spyglass splattered across the Martsynian's temple. With a moan he keeled onto his side and covered his bleeding eye with his hand; thus he lay in the snow, moaning.

Roll around on the ice, wheezing, spitting and weeping, biting the air; what Miss Muklanowicz did next was therefore unseen. By the time the breath had been caught and a sitting position assumed, she was standing at the very limit of the circle of visibility, gazing intently into the blizzard, in the direction of the lantern and monumental limb of the gleiss. All that remained of the Martsynian were the shattered icicle and a winding trail of blood drops swiftly buried by watery whiteness.

Retrieve the cane and the Grossmeister, stand shakily on the legs. From the depths of the coloured snowstorm, from the direction of the goods wagons, panic-stricken cries rang out, doors slammed. Somewhere in the blizzard, to the north, south, west or east, rifle shots were being fired. The station bell began to toll. A low shape leapt out from between the wheels of the Express: a dog, the dog of that peasant from the second-class sleepers, its neck-rope trailing over the ground. Raise the eyes. A shadow loomed in the dark carriage window, the face of man or monster glued to the frosted pane at an impossible angle. Step back involuntarily. The bell tolled and tolled. People came running from beyond the range of the visible world, someone chasing someone, someone running away from someone else. Wipe the face with the furry sleeve. Miss Muklanowicz was pointing to something with her out-stretched arm, the other hand pulling up her sable collar, her black eyes above it staring urgently. There! Look! The snow-front opened for a moment, revealing Councillor Dushin, Captain Privyezhensky and a Cossack in a tall hat holding a Berdan rifle to his eye; the Cossack's greatcoat had a bloody hole below the armpit. The bell ceased tolling. Jelena lowered her arm. From under the hoof of the gleiss, out of the frostoglaze aureole, came Not-Verousse in his dishevelled sheepskin, a pair of wooden shoe-trees in his hand. Depress the serpent's tail. A thunderbolt pierced the ears with knives of ice – frost stung the hand, frost filled the lungs, frost gored the heart. Fall to the knees.

Missed. Missed, of course – instead of hitting the Lyednyak agent, the bullet had strayed to one side, into the gleiss. That thunderclap still echoing dully inside the skull – was the rumble of splitting ice: the gleiss crashing onto the station, onto the railway tracks, onto carriages and wagons, masses of black glacial matter descending onto Zima.

Kneel with head hung over the chest, pinned to the frozen earth at this odd angle by a javelin of frost; and hear, for a long while afterwards, only aftershocks of that missed shot, feel only the ground trembling and the cold wind, its fiery sting on the bloodied cheek.

Impossible to breathe with frozen lungs – the first inhalation is so painful, shriek at the top of the voice; but no word emerges, only the hollow sound of air passing through a larynx nipped by frost. Had anyone heard – in that thunderclap – in the whistle of the Black Sable's siren – in the cacophony of dozens of other shrieks? – no one had heard. Until soft warmth penetrates the palm frozen fast to the viper-butt of the Grossmeister, the warmth, touch of another's body; rip apart the eyelids sewn together by hoar, and look down at that doggie in its noose licking the armed hand. The sobaka lifts its head, reveals its broad tongue. Move the right hand in a spontaneous reflex to stroke it, burying the fingers in matted hair – ice cracks on the furry coat-sleeve, shards of fine permafrost shower down, azure and violet in the lanterns' glow. The dog leaps away, looks warily about. Thrust the dolphin cane into the snow piled before the knees and rise to the feet; black breath mist settles on the snow like tiny grains of soot. Stand up straight. Where's Miss Muklanowicz? What's happened to Jelena?

The blizzard had as though abated for that short interval and the Trans-Siberian Express was visible, from the elliptical plates and curling chimney of the coldiron paravoz to the final carriage. The gleiss had broken in two, fallen onto the tracks in front of the Black Sable and onto the east wing of the station building, crushing sheds and warehouses. Torn-up tree trunks, ten arshins in length and stripped of their bark, lay scattered about; one such trunk, like a telegraph pole driven into the ground, juts out a few paces from the track where Miss Muklanowicz had stood. The platform and earth around the station are covered in a thick carpet of steam, steam or some kind of dense gas, billowing in white waves; it spreads gradually from broken fragments of the gleiss, from its armoured star-shape split asunder on the coldiron trusses of the station, seeps out of severed frost-strings, bubbles out of shattered limbs, evaporates from the icer's shot-through pillar. Rushing to the scene of disaster, people wade through the steam as if through morning mist, as if through the miasmas of a swamp. Light from those station lanterns still standing and burning imbues the steam with iridescent tints. Stare through half-closed eyes and see people pouring from the image together with the diffusing dye – they flounder in this dye, the dye clings to them, as they disintegrate into primary colours. Someone is forever falling over, crying out, cut to the marrow by frost, shrouded by the whitish carpet of aerial suspension.

Where is Miss Muklanowicz? Glance in the other direction. Two Cossacks, a policeman and a man in the prince's livery are levelling their rifles at Not-Verousse, their backs pressed against Doctor Tesla's wagon – Not-Verousse stands barely ten arshins away, with a shoe-tree raised in his hand poised to fling – Dushin and Fogel are running towards him from behind the wagon – at the Lyednyak's feet, a dead Cossack lies in the snow – and by the bolted door of the arsenal of Summer

445

lies a second corpse: Oleg with head shot through – whilst behind Not-Verousse's back, from the direction of the ruptured shank of the gleiss, across the carpet of iridescent vapour, steals Miss Muklanowicz, unkempt black hair scattered over her sable overcoat, mosaics of frosto-glaze glints on the side of her face white as ivory, a tusk of black ice readied in her gloved hand. With tightened lips, her great eyes wide open, with trembling hand, and yet – smiling; and yet – with tongue thrust out between teeth, head held high, a twinkle in her eye.

Jelena! What are you doing! For God's sake! What's got into you! He's about to...! Run! Choke on the unbreathed breath; breath lodges in the larynx like a bone in the throat. Jelena! The permafrost will surely scrunch beneath her feet; besides, she's about to stumble over something in the icer's misty fumes and the Lyednyak will glance around, must glance around. Hold the breath so as not to scream. Dushin and Fogel rush out of the shadow behind the wagon and Not-Verousse hollers in warning, raises the shoe-tree still higher; they stand as if anchored to the spot. Jelena, meanwhile, draws closer and closer to the bomber. The Black Sable's double siren resounds along with a clatter of iron as all the carriages ram into one another and the locomotive spouts grimy steam under its coldiron auroras, as it shunts the whole train backwards, away from the dark mass of ice, away from the wrecked body of the gleiss obstructing the track. More terrified passengers jump onto the Zima platform. The heavily bolted wagon bearing the arsenal of Summer passes slowly behind the backs of the guards. Not-Verousse takes a step forward. Now everyone is yelling. Then, from the discreet windows and narrow slits in the walls of Tesla's wagon, sheaves of unlicht shoot out, cutting across frostglazed Zima with horizontal and oblique slashes of dark and with splotches of glintz burned out behind snowdrifts and behind figures blocking the unlicht. The scene of confrontation mutates at once into a theatre of shadows and counter-shadows; objects, people, the landscape, fluctuating with every heartbeat, turning into their own negative – and the negative of the negative – and again the reverse – and again – light-unlicht-light-unlicht-light-unlicht. There's no way to maintain orientation; the head spins at the very sight.

Not-Verousse curses, spits and –

Miss Muklanowicz makes a run for it –

Stretch out the arm and flex the ice-benumbed finger on the trigger of the Grossmeister. Thunderbolt. Frost. Ice.

This time, try to keep standing.

The bomb exploded beforehand, but the goods wagon, thrown into the air, froze with wheels half an arshin above the rails, leaning to one side. A quarter of its length was transformed into a star-shape of barbed ice and scattered shreds: an explosion frozen within a hundredth of a second – statue of an explosion. Longer needles, discharged rounds of ice, jut out of the chaotic sculpture to the height of a cedar tree; those not facing upwards were stuck everywhere into the ground. They had bored through the Cossack, bored through Dushin. Fogel hangs suspended in the air with a leg caught in jaws of ice. A large chunk of teslectric machine, a coldiron ring twisted into a coil, had frozen into the torso of one of the constables; the constable dangled in the evening twilight above the ice panopticon, raised on icespikes the height of the station roof: a symbolic figure, the guardian angel of a battle splayed across the sky, that is, man fused with ice and machine.

Bereft of feeling, the right hand slumps onto the shuba and cane; the cane had frozen into the earth between the feet, as if it had put down roots deep into mammoth country. Stand motionless like the next ice sculpture; even the eyelids – frozen to the skin of the eye sockets – could not be lowered, a desirable thing when staring directly into the muzzle of a loaded gun. For the tungetitum bullet had not struck the wagon and rails where only glacial matter was ricocheting; it had been targeted at the ground in front of Not-Verousse, but away from Miss Muklanowicz, who was on the other side of the assassin: to freeze him without wounding her – to strike at the epicentre of the Ice at a distance safe for her, fatal for him – that had been the aim. And of course, at the last moment, the hand had jerked to one side. No harm had come to her, she picks herself up from the snow – but neither had much been done to the lanky agent of Ice: the permafrost had immobilised the Lyednyak up to his knees, so he won't escape, but all those needles and pins from the frost-explosion had passed him by, and he broke loose at once from the clamp of frozen earth ejected in streams by the crater on the platform, freed his hands, smashed the arc of gravel shooting up in his path, leaned forward and picked up the Cossack's rifle – now he aims surely and calmly like a member of an execution squad, he won't miss, not he, barrel levelled at the centre of the chest as if the target were painted on the snow-sprinkled fur – there'd have been a cry, but the lungs and mouth are maimed by frost, there'd have been fear, but frost had gone to the brain, he won't miss, not he, eye, hand, his thought is steady, he'll shoot straight at the heart, warrior of the Ice.

He fires. A movement to the left – someone jumped – who? Collapse together in the snow. Pain, but it's old pain, familiar pain: frost in the chest. And yet he fired, he'd hit someone, whom had he hit? The hands are frozen like heavy logs, to the right lies the loaded coldiron revolver, to the left – the cane; with unfeeling hands, roll over the body of a man, resting his head on the fur coat flaps tucked neath the thighs. Captain Privyezhensky bared his bloodied teeth. Another shot rang out. Look up. Not-Verousse keeled over backwards and fell onto his back, his long legs still imprisoned in the ice shackles. Leaning out of a hole in the wagon wall, Stepan fired a second and a third time, finishing off the Lyednyak; then the Nagant slipped from the old okhrannik's hand as the whole wagon containing Tesla's arsenal turned on its side, knocked off the plinth of the ice-bound explosion by the carriages still shunted by the Black Sable. The catastrophe was not yet over, and its subsequent acts followed one after another with avalanchine inevitability; it seemed never-ending, that nothing would ever stop it. What next, who next...? Captain Privyezhensky was spitting out the final drops of his life onto the iced-encrusted fur, a grimace of immeasurable contempt contorting his mouth neath the evenly clipped moustache. On his tsarist officer's uniform under the unbuttoned greatcoat, in the light of the last surviving frostoglaze lantern of Zima, a stain was spreading – pink, then black, then dark plum. He tried to raise his hand – but merely squeezed his palm into a fist. Gaze into his eyes without blinking, from under frozen eyelids; gaze coldly, the face also frozen, despite the Shame burning within. He sought that gaze, for that gaze he died; it was the ultimate triumph of Nikolay Petrovitch Privyezhensky.

Without blinking or averting the eyes, as the first scream of breath welled in the depths of the cold breast, in fire and ice – stare into the Russian soul: what greater contempt hath man than this, that he lay down his life for one he holds in contempt?

On the unrealised

At night, lights dimmed and the temple pressed against the black windowpane whilst in the corridor a gendarme counts out loud the dead by forename and patronymic, a devushka sobs somewhere farther away in Deluxe and a fine trickle of blood seeps from under the dressing below the eye: Contempt is one of the faces of shame.

Contempt is one of the faces of shame, like envy is one of the faces of admiration, and jealousy – of love. Nestle tighter into the thick blankets. A glass of hot tea was scalding the skin on the hand, it felt good. Sniff. A cold – the first thing that appears on coming in from the frost. Beyond the window of the compartment, the Siberian night drifted past. Dwook-dwook-dwook-DWOOK. In a few hours' time, still before dawn or at dawn, the train will arrive in Irkutsk. The compartment door remained ajar, swinging now at a wider, now at a lesser angle, whilst every so often, in the brightly lit corridor beyond, uniformed and non-uniformed figures walked past, pausing to peer inside the compartment. Cease to pay them attention. Were it not for Tesla's guarantee and the ministerial papers... But the mind of a Russian tchinovnik in the Land of the Ice knows no intermediary states; uncertain and half-true statements slip from his mind like wet soap between the fingers. Since he's neither a prestupnik nor a terrorist – went the sergeant's reasoning – then he's our man, and what he does, he does on official orders. They even returned the Grossmeister. Stuff it back behind the belt, swaddled in its oilcloth and rags; without the lump of coldiron pressed to the belly, the body had felt mutilated, incomplete, like after an operation to remove a pound of gut. Doctor Tesla, having extricated himself from the overturned wagon, breathed no word concerning the Grossmeister when the sergeant inquired before his eyes about the ice revolver. Afterwards it transpired that four people had perished on the station beneath the collapsed gleiss, amongst them a saintly cripple who sold pious images to travellers. But who had demolished the gleiss? Who had impaled those people with a sudden rush of ice? Mademoiselle Filipov presented documents from His Imperial Exaltedness's Own Chancery that put the secrecy and security of Doctor Tesla's machines above all other rights; well, and luckily there was the body of a genuine terrorist, and also a second bomb which was soon discovered under the snow, an undetonated charge of dynamite concealed in a wooden shoe-tree. Six hours it took to clear the rails and shunt the Express onto an empty track. The goods wagons were to remain behind at the station in Zima, but detaining the Express passengers longer, especially those in Deluxe, lay outside the jurisdiction of the local constables and gendarmes, for even the regional ispravnik could not be reached at short notice. Nikola Tesla stayed therefore in Zima with his arsenal guarded by the two injured okhranniks and half the town's forces of law and order. He reassured everyone he'd be arriving in Irkutsk within a few days. Most of his apparatuses were reparable; the assault would cost him two to three weeks' additional work. There was no opportunity to speak with him at the time in private. Two to three weeks – which means that even with the most auspicious star configuration, there'll be no setting out from Irkutsk for Kezhma sooner than October. Meanwhile it's no longer Rappacki's tchinovniks that should be feared, but first and foremost those fanatics sent by Rasputin. After all, the Martsynian in Yekaterinburg had forewarned that they'd be waiting, that an ukase had been passed in the sect, and that the faithful had been alerted in cities along the Transsib route. And after the events in Yekaterinburg, no solitary excursions had been undertaken, no more than a dash from the Deluxe carriages to the goods wagon and back – but that too had been in full view of everyone, and so safe. Until the blizzards began. On entering the Land of the Gleissen, the blizzards had begun and fate had twice been tempted: once in Kansk Yeniseysk with Christine Filipov, and once in Zima with

Jelena Muklanowicz. Had Christine found herself in place of Jelena… But – who knows? After all, Mademoiselle Filipov really is an unknown quantity. Just like Captain Privyezhensky was an unknown quantity. Swallow the hot tea; it entered the supercooled organs like acid a log of wood. The right hand no longer trembled so visibly, the frostbite pain was bearable, feeling was returning quicker to the fingers. Maybe the second time, it really is easier. Maybe the hundredth time, there's no suffering at all. The thousandth time – maybe then, there's already a brutal pleasure in it, salvation in the mortification of the body. This is how the journey of every Martsynian doubtless begins, the journey doubtless taken by Father Frost. Mm-hmm. If only it could be turned into a favourable circumstance… It was obvious that they would find, catch up and hunt down – and caught up they had. They are waiting also in Irkutsk, as surely as two and two make four, and in the land of Ice doubly surely. How to convince the Martsynians? Convert them with what? *In the Land of the Gleissen, sudden conversions or changes of heart do not happen. Whoever comes here as this or that, as such he will most certainly remain.* Were entry into Irkutsk, however, to be made as someone else, that is, not as Benedykt Gierosławski – were he to hide – mask – deny… No! The thought floated away as soon as it occurred, already entirely unrealistic. The frost sat deep in the bones. Beyond the windowpane, whenever the door swung to, darkening the compartment, pale ramparts of snow loomed, the icy landscapes of the Baikal Country steeped for upward of thirteen years in eternal winter; but sometimes – whenever the door was positioned differently – there also appeared the ruffled visage of Benedykt Gierosławski. The gendarme was reciting the next name. Twist the face in the window into a grimace, which was anything but a smile.

Contempt is one of the faces of shame, maybe the most honest. If it's possible at all to know anything certain about another person, then it is precisely now, precisely here in the Kingdom of the Ice. But how much of this can be expressed in the language of the second kind?

The model: Captain Nikolay Petrovitch Privyezhensky. Young, ambitious, not at all cynical, not yet disenchanted, he entered the service with sincere heart and open mind, having sworn allegiance from the depths of his soul and of his own freewill to the majesty of the Emperor of All the Russias. But that same sincerity and simplicity, when confronted by the iniquities of Saint Petersburg, forbade him to keep silent and obey with impassive countenance and muted conscience every filthy, foolish, ignominious command or whim. The more he wished to believe in the emperor and in Russia, the more the gall rose within him; the tighter he defended his own innocence, the thicker the breastplates of pride, conceit, contempt he had to forge every day, every night. With what shame – pure, ardent, paralysing shame, like an electric shock – must he have burned in his service at court, what impotent energies must he have imprisoned in his soul, beneath his armour! Until someone recognised, fortunately for him, his unbearable suffering, borne somehow till then, suffering by no means so very different from Zeytsoff's; recognised it and dispatched the captain with all haste, as far as could be from Saint Petersburg and Petersburg affairs, before it led to some tragedy.

... So this Captain Privyezhensky boards the Trans-Siberian Express and at once, on the second day of his journey, finds himself conversing with foreigners about Russia and the tsarist system, as seen through foreign eyes and according to foreign systems. Naturally, first the gall rises in his throat: to disparage further and ridicule the feckless earthly tsar, who had so lamentably failed to live up to the captain's beautiful ideal. Shame! Shame! Shame! What other force would have impelled him to make that scandalous speech, what else would have enabled him to disclose so bald-facedly to strangers such immoral tales from the monarch's private life? But behold – who else was slandering and demeaning the emperor and the motherland in his presence? Not a Russian; bah, a Pole! Nikolay Petrovitch Privyezhensky would not have been himself, had he not taken this as deliberate *lèse-majesté*, and all the more so, since he himself had been bellyaching about Russia only a moment before – here, a dependency exists of direct proportions: each word of his own amplifies the indecency of similar words uttered by the foreigner. For in his heart of hearts, Captain Privyezhensky feels that he has sinned against his ideal, turned his back on his Tsar-God, since whatever the tsar shall say, whatever he shall do and command, he still is by his deeds and commands the undisputed ideal – because he is tsar. And so, from then onwards, throughout his whole Transsib journey, the captain is motivated by one force, one principle, one inner muscle: shame, shame, all-powerful shame.

... Until he rides into the Land of the Gleissen, and the Frost congeals his overboiled soul.

... Nikolay Petrovitch Privyezhensky and Filimon Romanovitch Zeytsoff – they alight at different stations, yet their journey is one and the same.

Suck through the teeth the remains of the rum tea; the tongue touched a hole in the gums. Pain: man seeks physical pain in order to divert the mind from non-physical torments – in order to stifle them – to redeem them in a tying arrangement. For here's the diabolic gamble: he who withstands pain, earns not the right to relief, but the right to the pain. Put aside the empty tea glass and reach under the blanket with the left hand for the right arm. Squeeze the muscles, push the thumb under

the elbow, scrape the nails down the skin of the forearm, over the subcutaneous bulges of the wrist. The frostbitten limb responded to the touch
with scorching bursts of fire, whilst it was impossible to foresee when
the flame might shoot along the bone to the shoulder, and when not,
even when the same place was touched again and again. The right-hand
fingers were already moving ably, that is, the ones which had previously
been able and healthy; they merely trembled slightly. The point was,
however, that firing from the Grossmeister – and twice in a row – had
been done entirely without knowing if the organism would bear the
experience more easily; or if it would bear it at all. It could have meant
death. Now it's clear that it could not have meant death, yet – the shots
were fired without such certainty, and besides, totally without thinking.
In any case, no such thoughts could be recalled. Only the movement
of the hand, the sudden jerk, the thunderclap and the freezing. Here's
the heroic gamble: you leap blindly into battle and live to tell the tale,
because you survived. Hah! Turn now towards the black windowpane
so as to pull a mocking face, scoffing in the reflection at such tastelessly
sublime thoughts – stare instead at the reflection's pale eyes and purse
the lips, raising higher the bald head, bruised and disfigured. So you've
given alms – now look the beggar in the eye! You've found it in you to
do a good deed, a courageous one – mock it not in front of yourself, but
stand by the truth: It was I who did it!

I? – Who?

Bow the head, flagging and slumping on the bed into the wall by the
window. Mel-mel-melt-ing.

The door swung open and with a discreet rustle of her dress Miss
Muklanowicz entered the semi-dark of the compartment. She stopped,
glanced around, uttered no word. Sat down on the chair opposite the
bed, right arm resting on the escritoire; inclining her head, she peeped
under the blankets – pulled in the meantime over the aching skull in
imitation of a monkish cowl. The door lurched open once more, so
forceful had been Jelena's thrust, and fell to with a muffled clatter,
cutting off the gendarme's mournful litany drifting in from the corridor. It also cut off the faint electric glow shining in – and almost total
darkness descended upon the compartment; any radiance came now
from the white nocturnal world beyond the window, able to pick out
just enough of the nearest shapes for the black outline of the young
woman's silhouette to be discerned against the dull black surface of the
wall.

And so long minutes went by, a quarter of an hour maybe, when
it seemed the devushka might say something, ask, burst into tears or
laughter, or start chattering about anything at all – but nothing. She came
in, sat down and continued to sit. Dwook-dwook-dwook-DWOOK.

How long could she sit like that? all night? What did she want, why had she come? *Jamais couard n'aura belle amie et les grands diseurs ne sont pas les grands faiseurs*, as Not-Verousse might have said – may he feast with the worms! But the night of three days ago now came back, a night of long true-and-false tales – sitting, just as now, by the dark window opposite the young woman. And so, the word is the deed, the word demands more courage than the bodily gesture, that is, the empty movement of matter.

But maybe she'd already been bracing herself, many a time in fact, to say something she was unable to say, for which there are no words in the speech of men – but that hesitation too was invisible in the dark. Maybe she closed her eyes, fell asleep. Maybe she was merely sitting and listening to her own and the other breath, counting the echoes of her heart. Maybe looking out of the window. Maybe biting her lips and wringing her hands. Dwook-dwook-dwook-DWOOK. Invisible.

Stretch out an arm from under the blanket, reach towards her – alas, she won't see this either, the almost-touch, the almost-caress, sees not what was not done, what died in the attempt at a deed.

But with that came the end to the luxury of darkness: the half-moon emerged from behind clouds and cast a silver sheen over the icy land-scape; it grew lighter in the compartment, and then everything froze, just like that: the devushka sitting on her chair, one hand drooping, a little helpless, a little disheartened, the other propping up her chin, the index finger pointing straight upwards, pressing into the pale cheek, her dark eyes staring straight ahead, very grave, but with the upper lip trembling slightly, ever so slightly, as if hinting at a secret smile known only to her and to him whom she watched.

Slide from under the cowl of plaid blankets, straightening the back instinctively and raising a cold right hand – but this intention too froze halfway, unrealised.

And so, there was no getting up, no grabbing her by the waist, no leaping to the feet to kiss her passionately. No pressing of the mouth onto hers, no swallowing of her hot breath, no tasting of her saliva laced with sugar and spice; no clasping with the lips of her soft chapped lip, her tremulous little tongue, the humming-bird flitting in her breath from cheek to palate. There was no kissing of Miss Muklanowicz, no.

And neither did she dig her nails into the frockcoat, waistcoat and shirt, scratch or caress the chest, throat, nape of neck, face, or stroke the smooth skull; nor did she embrace the heavy head inflamed by post-glacial fevers, nor smother it in kisses, giggling, from bruise to bruise, tugging drolly at the ears when the body broke free of her awkward embrace, dropping at last on its knees, forehead buried in the tight-fit-ting dress smooth over corset below a modest *décolletage*. She laughed not from throaty depths as she traced her fingers voluptuously over the clean-shaven skin, tickling it above the ears and burying her nails neath the occipital bone.

No. She sits and stares, not even blinking, face to face, silence to silence, only her breath gets gradually shallower and shallower, less and less regular.

So, there was no reaching up from those bended knees to the hem of her dress, no slipping of a hand under the fabric, onto the slender ankle in its silk stocking, no squeezing of the taut fetlock above the high English heel of her boot – in response to which she pulled not the ears, turned not towards her the countenance half-hidden in bandages, eyes wide open to eyes, questioning, frightened, thrilled with delight. Nor was there any creeping of the cold palm over silk, up the quivering calf as far as her knee, without pausing there for a moment whilst she parted not her lips, emitted no subdued titter-cum-sigh; nor above the knee, as far as the suspender and boundary of the silk, beyond which the palm trespassed not onto the narrow strip of bare flesh of Miss Muklanowicz's thigh. To which she uttered no word, froze not in doe-like stillness, fingertips bitten to the quick.

No. There she sits, gazing fixedly, unable to wrench away her eyes. This is no duel of shame, as between chance rivals: who shall be first to advert their gaze? No one wants to advert their gaze, sitting in stifling silence on either side of the narrow compartment, at arm's length, frozen in the moment before reaching out, arrested a second before. No one knows the rules of the game, yet the game is played. It's the last night after all, maybe Jelena won't be seen again, and certainly not in such an atmosphere of sinless temporality as the Trans-Siberian Express – never again shall this Benedykt Gierosławski encounter this Jelena Muklanowicz. Is she thinking the same? Evidently, she is – here, in the Land of the Ice, where presentiments are closer to presentiments, phantasies to phantasies, truths to truths, here precisely, only here could there be such a night. Wrap the shoulders in the plaids, cross the legs, clench the fists. Jelena's hand, the drooping disheartened one, strays blindly over the coral buttons below the neckline of her dress.

There'll be no ripping off of those little buttons by tugging at the fabric or grappling with the baleen stays underneath, for there was no heavy panting and the devushka did not erupt in rippling laughter, did not sweep up the material of her own accord, loosening the hooks and eyes, slipping the sleeves off her shoulders, the whole dress off her bodice, slower and slower, in order eventually not to stop, suddenly gripped by uncertainty, the dark batiste crushed in her clenched little fists, a look of inquiry in still wider eyes. Luck, which won't happen, did not rock the carriage as the Express hurtled (did not hurtle) downhill, and there was no tumbling and losing of balance, together with the devushka caught up in her dress, onto the bed thickly strewn with blankets and freshly cleaned fur. Jelena did not laugh, again in playful mischievous mood; laughed not and gagged not on her hiccupping giggles, since there was no kissing of every dainty finger in turn and then all the way up her bare arm to the cleavage above the white petticoat, to the line of her black velvet choker with its ruby star, when she, unable almost to catch breath from all that giddy cackling, did not grab the bald crown and start pulling in childish abandon first the ears, then the nose, then the chin, then the skin on the unshaven cheeks, snatching off the bandages already half-torn from before – since there was no coating in saliva, like an excited pet dog, her petite, icily pale breasts crosscut by pink corset-marks, no catching between the teeth the red button of her left breast benumbed into a hard coral bead, a raisin, not thawed in the mouth by all the puffing and snorting and rolling of the moist tongue back and forth, at which she did not grab the pillow poking out from under the blankets and thump the raisin-lover on the back, and did not cover herself with it, hiding her flushed face and smothering her chortles and moans. The hand did not touch the second raisin. Nor did the right hand return to the silk below the knee, silk above the knee, silken skin of the thigh beneath the silk. Nor did the broken, frozen fingers slide under her calico lingerie, demarcating a new frontline with a deliberate caress every half inch, as if trying to probe with the fingertips neath her outer skin the movements of some little agent of Winter, a slippery lump of permafrost that kept escaping and swimming upwards, seeking greater warmth within the devushka's body. But to nobble that speck! Squash it with the fingers! – then she would melt immediately and absolutely in the hot embrace, dissolve neath kiss and caress like a peak of whipped cream – no. And nor did she pull the body towards her, under the pillow, nor crush with her thighs the hand trailing the ice spy right up to the very source of the fever, nor reach with her free hand for skirt and petticoat, gathering them up and lifting them above the white suspenders; nor did she whisper in so doing, in the suffocating dark beneath the pillow redolent of jasmine and cloves, immodest words gleaned from French romances – to which she received no reply in other French words – and upon whose utterance she did not part her legs, thereby releasing the crippled hand, which did not eventually overtake and apprehend the little agent of Winter on the outermost promontory of burning skin, between finger and finger, delicately, gently, with the vicious tenderness of a hunter – at which she did not cry out mutely, clenching her fists, in order not to relax at once afterwards all her quivering muscles in one deep long-drawn-out inhalation, mel-mel-melt-ing –

This is already too much for Jelena Muklanowicz; she takes flight in her eyes and thoughts, springs up from her chair, knocking a cup and saucer off the tabletop, and with her sudden movement disturbs the air permeated with the fragrance of her jasmine scent. Try to spring up too, roused all of a sudden as if from hypnosis – yet still reasoning and moving at the speed of sleep, as if submerged in amber honey. Open the mouth and relish the fragrance; it entered the lungs, went to the head. Associations are sealed gradually, with geological inevitability. That fragrance. That fragrance! Had she not spoken truth? Imaginary taste of the locust – indistinguishable in memory from experienced tastes. From then on, jasmine would always trigger vivid memories of that night of frantic love in the Trans-Siberian Express, all the more vivid with time, all the more real.

Legs wobbling, her shaky little hand groping in the dark for support, Miss Muklanowicz staggers towards the exit. Breathless, flushed all over, she presses down on the fancy doorhandle. An undisciplined lock escapes from her hitherto immaculate coiffure, first one, then a second, then a third; she reaches for them, adjusts them, nervously running her hand through her hair. Stepping hurriedly into the bright corridor, she almost stumbles on the threshold. Under the electric light, she shields her eyes and face shiny from sweat; her red lips, still half-parted as if in anticipation of a timid kiss, she can no longer shield. She walks away with head hung low, tracing her drooping hand along the smooth boiserie of the Deluxe carriage.

Anyone seeing her now would have been in no doubt as to what had transpired behind the closed door of Mr Gierosławski's compartment. And after all, they would have been right.

Despite the murches and unlichts, despite all the powers of reason turned against the Ice: the unrealised is more real than the realised.

PART III

The Ways of the Mammoths

'Let us suppose that every truth is indeed eternal, but not every truth has existed since time immemorial. If something is true at a given moment, then it is true for all time counting from that moment. Truth does not perish, nor turn into falsehood with time, just as falsehood does not turn into truth. If something exists at a given moment, then it will continue from then on to exist for all time. But not everything which will be true one day, was always true in the past, not every proposition which is truthful today was so yesterday, or which was truthful yesterday was so the day before. There are some propositions which become truthful at a certain moment, there are propositions which are made into truths, whose truthfulness is created.'

CHAPTER THE EIGHTH

On the City of Ice

On the thirtieth day of June 1908, reckoning by the Gregorian calendar, in the early morning, close to the Podkamennaya Tunguska river in central Siberia – there was an explosion, a hurricane, an earthquake and a pillar of fire and smoke, that's how it began.

Coloured auroras, unlike any other auroras, had already been observed in the sky for several days. The locals spoke of animals having bad dreams, which prevented their cattle from sleeping peacefully at night. The summer was warm.

What came flying in came from the south or south-east. Witnesses say it left behind a long trail of dust across the firmament. They remembered the trajectory – from the south towards Kezhma – and how it changed direction: veering seventy degrees to the east, then after three hundred versts veering one hundred and twenty degrees to the west, another three hundred versts, and only then hitting the ground. A tower of smoke rose twenty versts into the sky. There are hosts of witnesses, since people witnessed it even a hundred Russian miles away, within the Arctic Circle: some were deafened by the thunderbolt, whilst the undeafened heard the subsequent crashes and then a long-drawn-out, rhythmic rumbling. Those living a little nearer were flung to the ground; many were struck hard at the time. At the Vanavara trading post, sixty versts away, the shock wave catapulted passers-by three, four arshins into the air, and swept up the tents of local tribes along with their people; reindeer flew up above the Earth, fracturing legs and spines.

The forests were alight.

There followed some of the brightest nights in history, since pedestrians on the streets of Königsberg, Odessa and London could read newspapers at midnight without artificial lighting. Red, white and violet auroras illuminated the heavens. Sunsets were of an uncanny beauty.

Superstitious folk ascribed these phenomena to an inauspicious conjunction of the planets and mysterious astrological synergies. More scientifically minded folk spoke of the earth passing through a cloud of cosmic dust, likewise of a volcanic explosion, recalling similar sights from a quarter of a century ago, when Krakatoa erupted.

So much for the outside world; in Siberia instead, people spoke of an insidious attack by the Japanese. Since for the time being no Siberian account had percolated to Europe and no one knew the real causes of the empyrean phenomena. Only one official report has survived from those days, namely from Yeniseysk, from where the local natchalnik of police, a certain Solonin, informed the governor general that: *On the seventeenth day of June at seven in the morning above Kezhma village on the Angara river coming from the south in a northerly direction, in fine weather, high in the firmament, an aerolite of huge proportions came flying, emitting sounds similar to bursts of artillery fire, and vanished.* The report made its way via the local branch of the Russian Geological Society to the Irkutsk Magnetic-Meteorological Observatory. And there the matter stalled for almost a year.

In the spring of 1909, rumours began to filter from the north of new meteorological phenomena, namely of unrelenting winter and unimaginably cruel frosts still shackling central Siberia, despite the calendar change of seasons. And then, also for the first time, an eye-witness account reached the Empire's scientific institutions of a gleiss. A correspondent by name of Nikolsky wrote to the director of the Observatory, Voznesensky, A.V.: *Guided by directions from the forest workers, escorted by a hired huntsman, I travelled some eighty versts to the north and north-east of the village of Malyshevko where, on the third day, during a very cold dawn, on a field of snow, we caught sight of a strange formation of dark ice. This formation (I attach a sketch) appeared to be upheld on an invisible skeleton of rock. We tried to approach but our horses refused to obey. To which I attribute our salvation, since that strange ice seems to radiate such intense cold that no man or beast would walk away from it alive, which I demonstrated to myself with such improvised experiments as the following: first, I threw at it a bottle full of water, but the water froze even in the air at the place of its shattering, i.e., very quickly; second, I walked up as close as I could, into the wind that blew a soft icy dust off the glassy ice-mass, which proved unwise in the extreme since, struck by a heftier gust, I felt the frost painfully bite the skin of my face (still smarting after a week). I measured the size of the formation from a distance, estimating the height at twelve, and the width and length at five-and-twenty arshins. We spent the night there, aiming to commence our return journey the next morning, and it was then I noticed another thing – that during the night the whole shape of the ice-mass must have shifted position according to the lie of the land (stones, inclines, trees and so on). This I do not understand, so I am describing and reporting it all the more scrupulously.*

The speed of the Ice encroachment was such that by the first calendar winter, it had already swept up Kezhma, and by the second reached

Baikal, driving gleissen onto the streets of Irkutsk some five hundred days after the Impact. In the metropolis of then more than 70,000 inhabitants, according to the latest census, only 1,190 of the 18,187 buildings were not built of wood. The city of tiger and sable had a long and inglorious history of conflagrations; the June fires of 1879 had destroyed well-nigh three-quarters of structures. In the Winter of the Gleissen, the disaster was repeated – to protect themselves from the inhuman frosts, people exploited any source of warmth, no longer mindful of the danger from flames, and when the conflagration flared up, leaping from wooden shack to wooden shack, there was no means to stop it: all water had frozen to stone. The fire reduced nearly the whole of old Irkutsk to ash and slag – following the night-time inferno, all that stood in the morning above the black plain were the silhouettes of gleissen glistening with icy sweat. According to estimates of the Chancellery of the Irkutsk General Governorate, six hundred inhabitants were burned alive. Losses were reckoned at seventy million roubles.

It was certain, however, that the city would be rebuilt, just as it had been rebuilt before, and again new architecture would alter its aspect entirely. For six months already, expeditions of European scholars of different ilks had been descending on Baikal via the Transsib. Tungetitum, purchased from the Tunguses and from huntsmen, was transported to laboratories in Saint Petersburg, Königsberg, Vienna, Paris. After the fire, when piles of debris were excavated from the conflagration sites over which gleissen had passed, the first coldiron coolbonds, as yet very impure, were discovered and described. On the shores of Baikal, on Konny Island on the Angara river, as well as to the north of the city on the road to Aleksandrovsk and Usolye, huge nests of gleissen had frozen up out of the ground; likewise, to the north, the greatest and most permanent icecradle yet known to man had crept out of the earth. In the summer of 1911, the first experimental coldmill, designed by Krupp, was built in its vicinity. Governor General Timofey Makarovitch Schultz, promoted at breakneck tempo by Nikolay II, swiftly established there an industrial town named, following Novonikolayevsk founded eighteen years previously on the Ob river, Zimny Nikolayevsk.

In 1912, the Year of the Gleissen, the Ice bites into Europe and, confronted by the confusion and hunger disasters caused by frozen crops, confronted by a second war with Japan which has just broken out – revolutionary, anarchist and nationalist-independence movements are again on the rise; whilst in Irkutsk – in Irkutsk, steelworks and coldmills, factories and plants of the new technologies are flourishing; capital pours in from every corner of the world, as well as common people seeking work or other opportunities to make money. Irkutsk, however, has its own revolutionary tradition. Many exiled Decembrists and Petrashevists settled in the city, influencing its middle-class culture. Rebellion and subversive attitudes towards power arise here somehow more often and more easily. In 1883, a leader of the Irkutsk nationalists publicly slaps Governor General Anutchin in the face; from then on, Baikal governors avoid appearing before the people. Since 1890, a committee of the Russian Social Democratic Labour Party has been functioning in Irkutsk. In 1902, Feliks Edmundovitch Dzerzhinsky organises a revolt of forced labour workers in the distilleries of Aleksandrovsk. In 1905, during the First Revolution, strikes and demonstrations by workers and officials gather so much momentum they are joined by part of the army and the Cossacks, luring over even the natchalnik of the garrison. (After that the Okhrana arrests the entire local RSDLP.) At the time of the Second Revolution, a plan is promptly hatched for workers' soviets to take control of Zimny Nikolayevsk; gatherers of tungetitum and trackers of mammoths come together in societies and cooperatives. In reaction, in 1913, by virtue of an ukase issued by the tsar at the instigation of Stolypin, Aleksandr Aleksandrovitch Pobedonostseff (a relative of the renowned Konstantin Pobedonostseff, Ober-Procurator of the Most Holy Synod of the Russian Orthodox Church and former tutor to the emperor) establishes the Sibirskoye Kholod-Zhelezopromyshlennoye Tovarishtchestvo, the Siberian Coldiron Industrial Company, which has controlled ever since the market in raw materials of the Ice and products of the ice technologies. De facto it is Sibirkhozheto that wields power in the city, for although the mayor of Irkutsk of more than twenty years' standing remains the Pole Bolesław Szostakiewicz, and the general governorate is administered by Timofey Schultz, bolstered in his post by the tsar's conferring the title of count and the honorary double-barrelled surname, it has never yet happened that they would decide on any crucial matter against the will of Pobedonostseff. Not only Zimny Nikolayevsk, but also Irkutsk itself, rebuilt following the fire, has emerged in accordance with the plans and business interests of Sibirkhozheto. Irkutsk is the City of Ice, the City of Coldiron, as can be seen at first glance.

The Trans-Siberian Express rolled in under the roofs of the Muravyoff Station halls in the early morning of the twenty-fifth day of July. Watching from a window in the second-class sleeper car, it was impossible to make out anything of the building – there, ahead, above the tangle of railway tracks, hovered a radiant fata morgana, a kaleidoscopic coil of suns, rainbows, fires, angelic lights. Only when the train had come to a halt inside were the halls visible from within, and a picture of the building arose in the mind. In this way, Irkutsk introduced itself to visiting guests. For behold, the entire Muravyoff Station stood upon fine coldiron skeletons like spiders' legs, whilst whatever empty spaces were left between the coldiron in walls and ceilings were filled with giant panels of frostoglaze. Look out in curiosity through the steamed-up panes, pushing along with other sleeper passengers towards the carriage door piled high with luggage, concealing the face at the same time behind the thick sheepskin's threefold collar lest any agent, spy or other informer positioned on the platform to ambush the Son of Frost should notice and perchance recognise his face in the window. Perchance, or rather by some miracle, since all measures had been taken, enabled by the actual truth, to eschew recognition. For truth now offered the best protection: it was not expensive furs, rings and perfume and silk ties that told the truth about Benedykt Gierosławski; besides, there were fewer of those wealthy types, men of fashion and aristocrats from Deluxe, and they're the ones who attract most attention. The very same Benedykt who'd walked the streets of Warsaw ought now to step down onto the soil of the Ice; at least not one making a lie of the old Benedykt. Ergo – a simple heavy sheepskin, purchased here in the train from an Armenian, to whom the new fur coat and stylish overcoat were sold at a loss; ergo – sackcloth bags and shapeless bundles in lieu of trunks and sacs de voyage; ergo – a wounded snout, unshaven, dark, and not the smooth face of a Petersburg fop. Even amongst the second-class passengers, the image was not the most advantageous. But – who knows, maybe the tsar's men and Martsyn's followers had received a truthful description, the one from Warsaw? A deep shapka hid the clean-shaven skull. Sweat still flowed whilst in the throng, in the scrum in the stuffy corridor of the last second-class sleeper, though each breath was already congealing in the air into thick mist and sharp frost carving through the throat like a shard of mirror – but on jumping down onto the stone platform and dragging the luggage towards the gothic arches of the station gates, the body immediately shook from cold neath sheepskin, sweaters, vests. Huge thermometric clocks with copper faces and spirit measuring-bulbs (mercury freezes in the Land of the Ice) showed twenty-two degrees below zero centigrade. The clocks hung on either side of a coldiron tympanum, under which flowed the stream of travellers. Apart from the main platform, where stood the engines and carriages of the Transsib and Northern Cold Line, there were two further passenger platforms beneath the frosto-glaze roof. Think, now tugging at the bundles, now pausing to catch breath in the arctic air, that it's true what they say; then gawp, coughing, at the architecture of the station halls like the latest Siberian bumpkin. It's true what they say: Irkutsk is the capital of Siberia. Russian coldiron art nouveau had endowed the roofs with the shape of three huge leaves, still wrapped at ground level almost vertically, but up above, high above the trains, overlapping like scales. The smooth incline and whole slanting construction – it seemed right to assume – were designed so that snow might slip off easily and ice not accumulate on the frosto-glaze panels, allowing the sky to be observed through clear rainbow prisms, and the sunlight to peer into the halls' interior. Yet even so, someone must have had to clamber up the coldiron ribs, moulded into the shapes of the stalks and veins of those leaves, someone must have stomped over the angelic palaces in workaday clodhoppers, to smash with pickaxes the permafrost gradually covering the indestructible, un-crackable frostglaze – celestial cleaners, proletariat of shovel and rainbow... Grab again the bags and bundles. Were it not for the sheep-skin, a porter would surely have come running. Shout? Wave? It would have taken a cannon blast to be noticed in this din and tumult; yet this was the point, not to be noticed by anyone. See how most people's faces are wrapped in scarves, how they breathe through the scarves; follow their example all the sooner. Who shall recognise a man robbed of his face? Make it through to the waiting room. Along one wall Chinamen, Jews, Mongols, a dozen representatives of other Asiatic nations, had laid out their stalls; Russian hawkers, judging by the visible parts of their physiognomy, were the decided minority. Against a second wall stood the gendarmes, repeatedly beckoning to someone with a hand-sign and demanding they uncover their visage as well as show their papers; they were accompanied by three Cossacks armed with sabres. Turn to the right, pulling the bags, so long as it was far from them. By the door to the booking office lay a wolf, or a dog that looked like a wolf; a native child, a little Buryat or Yakut girl, was feeding it out of her hand. Behind the booking office, on the black coldiron wall above the timetable, the misshapen contours of an elephant had been drawn in a few white strokes of lime or chalk. Someone must have climbed on a very high ladder. Shuffle still closer with the luggage. Probably a mammoth. Some of the local vendors had larger and smaller mammoth figures laid out on skins – made very likely of mammoth ivory. Others – on closer inspection – were offering blackwickes, a great profusion of blackwickes, fat and slender, long and short, straight or carved into shapes of undoubtedly magical import. Here, blackwickes are dirt cheap. Many of the new arrivals stopped by these primitive stalls and purchased without lengthy haggling: a blackwicke, an amulet, a little bag of mysterious Chinese or Tibetan ingredients, a pair of frostoglaze spectacles... Notice now those people who conceal, above the lower part of their face wrapped in a scarf or other rag, its upper part behind wide bulging eyeglasses, goggles as big as tablespoons. For behold, a uniformed railway official too, on walking out of the station, takes out a shimmering rainbow pince-nez and fixes it atop his nose. Ha! Now no one will recognise him! Yank the weighty baggage, panting heavily, towards the open boxes of the purveyors of frostoglaze spectacles and acquire, without exchanging a word, a pair of oculars that can be put on at once. Everything was suddenly injected with colour, as if someone had removed a thick dark veil from a brightly coloured painting. No object was any longer only white and no object any longer only black, whilst many naturally coloured things changed hue with every movement of the head, every twitch of the eyes; and this happened not in sudden jumps like with blinking, but in keeping with the movements of murch, with the flow of oil: colours combined, merged, mixed, flooded and dislodged each another, squeezing out of shape like juice pressed out of fruit. Glance at the travellers. Colours, colours, colours. Glance at the sky above the transparent roof. Colours, colours. Glance at the hands, at the feet, at the mud on the flooring underfoot. Colours. Close by, a slant-eyed pedlar of blackwickes was urging to buy with waves of his hand and in sing-song broken Russian. Grab the bundles. Another hand, wearing a two-fingered glove, grabbed the heaviest. Raise the head. It was a young boy, teeth bared in a snaggle-toothed grin, his porter's tin badge pinned to his jacket. And so, all the wealthier passengers from the Express had already been serviced and driven away. Heave a sigh of relief. The maltchik, without extinguishing his grin, was prattling away in Russian, having introduced himself as Vasily and telling wonders about his Uncle Klyatchko, who was the honestest, cheapest, reliablest and jammiest izvoztchik this side of Baikal. At once a second porter came running up and the two of them made off with all the luggage. Exit down the blue marble staircase into the square outside the station. Coloured sour cream hung in the air, drifting in vast streams that filled the square, streets and spaces between buildings to the height of the second storey. The rainbow light of the nearest street lanterns, burning here evidently night and day, scarcely penetrated the milky suspension. People walked into and out of it like underwater shapes looming and disappearing in clouds of silt above a riverbed; hurrying sleighs sped across the square, leaving a wake of slow-whirling eddies and vanishing into the cream. How did they find their bearings, by what miracle not lose their way? The noise of the street traffic was nothing to go by, it came from all directions. Gazing still from the steps of the Muravyoff Station, all that could be seen above islands of roofs (also coloured white since completely snowclad) were two twin tserkoff cupolas, far away, yet seeming all the more monumental in that cloud-locked distance, and also, farther away still, a solitary tower, so high that its summit was lost in the dark cumulus. Board the sleigh onto which Vasily had loaded the luggage, settle comfortably neath plaid rug and reindeer skin. Agh, one more thing was visible up above – one and a second and a third – spin around on the seat, glancing back at the

Classical-style wing of the Muravyoff Station crowned by its huge statue of Count Nikolay Muravyoff-Amursky – and a fourth and a fifth. On wooden masts ten arshins high, like on the poles of some ghostly flags, everywhere around, above the station, above the square, above the city – hung old corpses. Gutted carcasses of black-haired men, fastened by their twisted-back arms like wings, bedecked with pounds of ivory and iron amulets, ropes, fringes, chains, but moreover naked, naked, exposed to the very bone to public view. Ice had congealed them in statuesque poses, they do not hang – but look more as if they stood on those poles like pagan incarnations of Saint Simeon Stylites. Shudder. Whilst out of the depths of the city, from the heart of the metropolis, out of the swirling white colour, comes a constant muffled bass rumbling, the slow pulse of the mammoths. Wind the scarf tighter around the neck, pull the shapka down lower. In this way, Irkutsk introduced itself to visiting guests.

Where to, your lordship, asks Klyatchko, twisting around on his driver's box and glancing over his shoulder, as a tear of filthy greyness flows off the fabric of his threadbare greatcoat and onto his bearded mug under the fur shapka, and rivulets of pink, white and red flow off these onto Klyatchko's collars and sleeves. Where to? Feel the gums with the tongue. Perhaps you know, my good man, some hotel, inn, boarding house with rooms at human prices, but not too seedy? At which Klyatchko bared his teeth amid his shaggy beard, revealing that even his snaggle-toothed grin was identical to Vasily's. Family! Weak teeth and sharp tongues run in the blood! For he had already cracked the whip and jerked at the reins; the sleigh moved off and its heavy harness bells began to jingle, as Klyatchko intones: Your lordship's lucky to find a man who knows the city like his own drawers, that is, to the last godforsaken hole, but being of kind heart, he'll not take you to some thuggish den but a cheap hotel, entirely respectable, where his brother-in-law works to boot, so he can vouch for it; besides it were a costly and famous guesthouse in its time, only fell into disrepute and the wrong clientele just like the whole of Uysky district and erstwhile Glazkovo suburb, when in recent years the Chinks began to settle in droves on the left bank, along with landless peasants from Stolypin's Siberian villages driven out by eternal winter. Aye, aye, your lordship, all this evil thanks to foreign strays and ice devils, may the Lord God send them to hell. Well, let's be off!

Ask him about the frostoglaze spectacles. He says they're against snow blindness and in case of the Tchornoye Siyaniye. Ask him about the carcasses on the masts. Ah, sir, that's the business of the Buryat shamans hired by Pobedonostseff and the city hall. Klyatchko emits a spitting sound, crossing himself with one hand, pointing his whip with the other at the coldiron finger of the Sibirkhozheto Tower jutting into the sky above the city. Press him further: but what are they for, these desecrated dead bodies hanging in the sky, an affront to God and man. They're keeping watch, he says, so no enemy shall steal along the Ways of the Mammoths. Meaning that the mammoth drawn on the station wall is intended to ward off the same? The fellow crosses himself again, invoking the name of the Saviour. They painted it, he says, as a sign of war on their brothers, so that the gentlemen can make more roubles on the underground riches. And this drum, this drum whose rumble gets ever more intense – what is it? That's – the gleissen.

Old Irkutsk had arisen on the right bank of the Angara; the Uysky district, which shot up after the Great Fire, lies on the left bank, to the north of the Irkut river and Kaya mountain. You're supposed to turn onto Shelekhoff Bridge, but everyone rides over the ice; the river has not thawed for fourteen years. In truth, it's hard to discern even the Angara's shoreline. Highways and streets run across the ice no different from those in the city. And the one we're driving down now is the most important, explains Klyatchko, whose mouth never shuts despite the frost, though maybe for him it's really not so painful. This is Glavnaya Street running from the Angara, the Box and the statue of His Sovereign Majesty Emperor Aleksandr III along the whole of right-bank Irkutsk – and that's Amurskaya Street, and that's Tikhvinskaya Square, off which leads Tikhvinskaya Street, where stands the old tserkoff with its copy of the miracle-working icon, to which pilgrims flock from all over Siberia, saved by God's will from the fires, which is more than can be said for the great Kazan Sobor, about which your lordship must have heard; you haven't heard? How people forget, how swiftly passes the matter of this world! Look there, oh, farther in the distance, where in its place the coldindustrialists have erected their Sobor of Christ the Saviour, even bigger, look, look! Klyatchko waves his whip in all directions in the fog, through which nothing of what he tells is visible. Visible instead are tiny glimmers of penumbra on his shapka, on the back of his neck when he rotates his head, on the sleeve of his greatcoat; tiny glimmers, yet highly conspicuous – but maybe it's just the frostglaze that exaggerates them? Stare at him above the lenses. Now they're even more conspicuous. Inquire of Klyatchko: Have you lived here long? Ah, sir, I hail from the Baikal Kray, a Siberian born and bred! Examine him closely through the oculars. It is as Pocięgło said, half of them are gleisseniks.

As the sleigh drives across the Angara ice, a wind blowing down the river's wide corridor probably from Baikal itself disperses the frosty vapours, and it becomes possible to glance a little farther to north and south, at the old railway bridge, recently been traversed in the Transsib onto the eastern bank – at the new Grigory Shelekhoff Bridge, made purely of coldiron, visible almost exclusively as rainbows, shimmering radiances and celestial glows, so fine-wrought and lacelike is its structure devoid of spans, girders and pillars – at the fantastical formations of an icecradle or maybe gigantic nest of gleissen towering above Konny Island, outgrowth upon outgrowth, like the ruins of the Snow Queen's crystal palace amid a white-hued plain of ice; but since the fog is now rent asunder, the bracing sun of a summer morn streams down upon everything, sparking silver will-o-the-wisps in ice and snow and setting alight coldiron glints on the bridge. Also visible on the Angara is the city traffic; clusters and streams of pedestrians drift back and forth, scores of sleighs glide past harnessed for the most part to one or two horses, like Klyatchko's, but there are also troikas, as well as heavy sleds pulled by teams of four or six, loaded high with stacks of goods to trade, baskets of coal, piles of wood; and all furnished, apart from the bells, with frostglaze lamps, one at the rear and one at the front. So that even in fog, if it's not too dense, double stars can be seen flashing by in the swirling flurries of white, swinging to and fro, twinkling in kaleidoscopes of colour – and heard the constant jingle-jangle of their bells.

Entering left-bank Irkutsk, returning to the wintry damp unruffled by wind, there is a noticeable change in the sleigh bells' tone: their voices carry differently through fog. Some sounds it stifles, others it brings closer to the ear – like that soporific drumming, drawn out in time like the wail of a slowing gramophone record. So what's going on, is some gleiss sat on the Uysky district? Klyatchko, turning onto a wide prospekt, points with his whip to the south-east. Like the old station and ruins of Innokentyevskovo from before the Fire, so he says, here a Way of the Mammoths comes closest. For no icer has passed through The Devil's Hand for over a year. Prrr! He stops the sleigh. What Devil's Hand? Here we are, the fellow laughs, jumping off his box and already seizing hold of the luggage, here's your promised hotel, after you! Frostoglaze lanterns shine on either side of the inn sign depicting a clawed paw covered in black hair. The blackness of the paw flows in greasy blisters onto the white-and-grey façade of the brick building, whilst the white and the grey drip in turn onto the snow; the fog, instead, faithfully repeats the colours of the lanterns, as does the prospect long and wide. Shut the eyes for a moment. Even if there is no room, there will be room, jabbers Klyatchko, I will install your lordship in the hotel. Exhale from the lungs a cloud of warm steam and step inside The Devil's Hand.

The landlord recites the services, the prices and luxuries included in them (such as running water and bathrooms on every floor, as well as bedding free of bugs). Klyatchko brought in the luggage; thrust him a handsome tip. It's time to finally shake off the prodigal habits of Count Gyero-Saski – pay in advance therefore for a room for only two nights with single-rouble notes unwrapped from the meagre bundle. Cough through the glove. Explain in a croaky voice – a chap is exhausted after a long journey; we'll deal with the paperwork once I've slept it off. A large Chinaman lifts all the bags and bundles at once with no effort. The landlord leads the way to the second floor, where it's already warm; undo the sheepskin, take off the shapka. They stare at the black-and-blue bonce. But those papers, says the proprietor, tomorrow morning at the latest. He opens the room, hands over the key. But why, to change the subject, such an unwelcoming name? why The Devil's Hand? Aha, because a famous English sorcerer stayed here in his time, by name of Crowley; he came in order to know the gleissen, to address them through his intellectual magick, he even talked to the honourable Aleksandr Aleksandrovitch Pobedonosteff; but one day, he went climbing in the Hamar-Daban mountains, into the icecradle, and never returned; downstairs we have a table with his chess set, where he used to play long games with Father Platon from Christ the Saviour Sobor, the future exarch. We also have his photograph, that is, Crowley's, where he stares into the camera with black fire. And should you require food out of hours, let us know in advance. And add no logs to the stove yourself, because we'll put it on the bill. Sleep well, sleep and forget.

They went.

Sleep and forget – forget what exactly? Sit down limply on the high bed with its faded counterpane and adornment of five pillows, one on top of the other, smaller atop the larger. Waves of heat drifted from the corner, from a large porcelain tile stove painted in flowers and animals. Massage instinctively the right shoulder. On the wall opposite hung a small dark icon, on a table by the window stood two half-burned blackwickes. But the windowpanes were of frostoglaze, and even after removing the spectacles, the whole world outside the window seemed blurred like colours running into one another on the palette of a drunken artist; the whole world, that is, the fog and those few roofs discernible in the fog, and the wide canvas of the sky, and against it the black tibia of the Sibirkhozheto Tower, and the tungetitum cupolas of Christ the Saviour Sobor. The drums were beating.

Strain the ears. Drums were beating and music playing. The district was indeed not the most salubrious; it's still not midday, Friday after all, a working day, yet raucous tunes and singing and drunken shouts penetrate from the neighbouring building despite thick walls and tightly sealed windows. Tavern or no tavern, the party is in full swing, nothing but echoes of brawl and fistfight can be expected. To the sounds of mouth organ and gusli, the fellers bawl out vulgar chastushki, splitting their sides with laughter after each one.

Frenchie groped them, Fritz repelled them,
Chinky fed with venomous herbs,
Lech took slight before the gleissen
Shat on them with icy turds!

Undress, wash in not very cold water in the basin. Transferring the belongings from bags to wardrobe, discover an old Bible, signed by a family named Foytseff. Open it at random and stab the forefinger into a verse.

Job, naturally. Chapter thirty-seven, verse ten. *By the breath of God ice is given.*

Recall at once the biblical sermon delivered by Zeytsoff. For shall a world frozen in soletruth and solefalsehood be closer to God? *Yea, yea, Nay, nay. For whatsoever is more than these cometh from evil.* Braids of mist above the roofs coiled back momentarily and in the far distance, on the banks of the Angara, the ovoid shape of a gleiss glistened in the sunlight. Yea, yea.

Rasputin is the tsar's bedeared,
The monk took the premier by the beard,
At Martsyn's feet poor Struve kneels,
Beneath the Baikal ice he reels!

The fact is, tiredness and lack of sleep were truly taking their toll. Not a wink had been slept since Zima Station. Count out and roll together all the banknotes and, in accordance with old habits, stuff them along with the documents into the bumazhnik and behind the headboard of the bed. Extract from amongst the papers Alfred Taitelbaum's letter of recommendation. In a day's time, two days' time – there'll be a need to stand before the tchinovniks of the Ministry of Winter and state loud and clear: yes and yes. (No and no.) But better to benefit first from the knowledge and advice of a friendly local – someone not encountered in the Trans-Siberian Express, who has not heard of the Son of Frost and knows not the lies about Benedykt Gierosławski. To pick his brains on the people, on the government departments, on the work of Sibirkhozheto, maybe the Ministry's design will turn out to be too obvious; maybe it'll be possible to simply sit out Rappacki's plan. Maybe it'll be easy to wriggle out of it and, who knows, let this one problem resolve itself on its own. Before even Doctor Tesla arrives with his machines – before he sets the machines in motion – before he tests them on the gleissen – and before a means has been devised for transporting his pumps and teslectric motors to –

The blood doth melt, the eye doth bleed,
The will to live deserts before
The man who's glimpsed in mortal need
Pobedonostseff's ghastly maw!

Draw the heavy chintz curtains, which did nothing to deaden the tavern noises or slow drumbeat; but at least the icy-cold light, the glare of the sun filtered through fog ceased pouring inside the room. Slip the Grossmeister under a pillow. The straw mattress scratched beneath the sheet. Writhe back and forth on the creaky bed. Realise only after a while why sleep refused to come, what sustenance it lacked: the rhythmic clickety-clack of the train wheels. The sound had been so habituated to, it was as if a whole lifetime had been spent on the move – as if that journey in the comforts of Deluxe had really been a whole past life, real to the extent it was clearly remembered.

But there it was – the destination had been reached.

They howled, they drank, they danced and clucked,
A mammoth too they shagged and fucked,
Roublies three they got for that –
Buryat, Tungus and Yakut!

On a night in the cemetery and rising from the grave in the morning

A voice and a second voice.
'Venyedikt Filipovitch Yeroslavsky.'
'Asleep.'
'Yes, asleep.'
The dream of Warsaw returns like a wave of water reflected off a bank: for they've entered, they've stopped by the bed, they gawp and natter. Sink into the depths, shielding the head beneath the wave. Beneath the wave, beneath pillow, beneath quilt, curled in a ball of hot flesh, in the warmed-up bedclothes – sleep and forget... Whilst they stand bent over the dream and stubbornly whisper something. Then follows the shaking-up of the dream and everything is inundated by black, suffocating hallucination, of which nothing is remembered except just that – darkness in the head and a feeling of suffocation.

Woken by frost. The chilled body shudders, limbs tremble and shivers convulse the torso till the last remnants of sleep are shaken from the head and the eyes open: darkness.

Darkness – hardness – coldness – silence – stench of chemicals – rough wood neath the fingertips – impossible to move – encased in a confined space – bang, bang, bang, leg, hand, head, there's nothing for it but to thump on the wood – from every angle – the body's encased in a coffin!

A panic-stricken scream is born in the throat, or lower down, in the chest, or lower still, somewhere in the very guts. Yet no sound will emerge from a larynx clenched in animal spasm.

Thrash about between the rough-sawn boards, clawing in vain with the fingers and short chewed nails at any potential cracks, at places to hook onto, in order to tear apart, force open, smash the coffin. All that is gained is that the whole casket begins to shake and toss, hammering on the ground. At which hot sweat pours over the skin: ergo, there has been no burial! ergo, this is no grave!

Writhe about with redoubled energy. Brace the feet in their wool-knit socks and push on the boards of the coffin lid with the knees – whereupon thin lines of light appear between them, longitudinal streaks of yellow radiance, almost blinding at first.

Press against them, pummelling with the fist.

'Quiet there!' someone shouts in Russian and slaps the lid three times.

'Open up!' rattle in a throat full of cold saliva.

'Quiet, I say!'

Listen intently, petrified. At shuffling, slamming, scraping – most likely of a door – footsteps, distant voices, a dog's howl and brief yelp as someone hit it, kicked it. No sound of tavern music, no beating of the drum. This is not The Devil's Hand. They had doped with some chemical, kidnapped, transported in a coffin, heaven knows where to.

Well, had they really wished to kill –

'He's awake.'

'I heard, I heard.'

'Are they come?'

'Aha. And frost like God ordered.'

'So where?'

'Well, the grave's dug, it's waiting.'

'Lev Ignatyevitch, they said –'

'But let's get on with it! It has to be filled and burned level before dawn.'

'So don't stand there like a gleiss, grab your pliers.'

They set to work on the coffin. Wood shavings rained into the eyes. Close the eyes. When they opened again, the lid had already been removed, and two Martsynians were standing to one side neath a solitary kerosene lamp, arms folded, watching with interest.

They gave no help. Climb out of the coffin alone, almost dropping to the ground. Stand up, leaning against the uneven wall of a rough-timber shed.

'H-hand me s-something, for God's s-sake, I'll freeze in just my drawers!'

They glanced at one another, sharing the same contempt. He's cold! They were in linen breeches and single sweaters, not very thick; except on their heads, they had fur shapkas.

'As you wish. Find it for yourself, all right; what does it matter, you'll all turn to ice in the end. Only make it quick!'

Glance around the shed. In here they kept tools – spades, pickaxes, wheelbarrows, buckets, some sort of demijohns and baskets, ropes and sacks – kept materials for making coffins, like unpainted boards; kept coffins already assembled and prepared. With a flick of his chin, the elder Martsynovian pointed to two lying by the door. Walk over. Here lay the remains of an elderly man in an old formal suit and the remains of a peasant with mutilated head, clad in blood-soaked rags. Both were pressing their hands onto Latin crosses held on their breasts. Shudder – but whether from disgust or from cold, this could no longer be read from the bodily reflexes. Turn the back on the gravediggers; they whispered croakily between themselves.

Try to collect the thoughts shattered by frantic shivering, as the numbed fingers rip the frozen clothes off the corpses. Grave already dug! Everyone entering into the ice! These are Martsynians, Irkutsk Martsynians, beloved children of the gleissen; they have captured, kidnapped and won't let go alive – do they know about Yekaterinburg, know about Pyelka? – what do they know? what do they want? – to kill – to bury in cold earth, to freeze. No one shall help, no miracle come to save the day; self-salvation shall come through cunning alone and – and – and through lying, there's no other way out, but to lie.

The shivering intensifies, the galloping resonance of fear grinds the bones, splits open the skull, knocks the last well-honed thoughts from the brain; all that remains is a protracted plaintive moan.

Will they believe that it's a mistake? That this is not Benedykt Gierosławski?

Or at least that he's not the Son of Frost? That it's all – a fiction dreamt up by Rappacki and his people, a Siberian fairy tale, a courtly legend?

That Gierosławski had naught to do with the death of the Yekaterinburg Martsynians? That he has no desire to unfreeze Russia, is no enemy of gleissen? That he has no plans for them? Should they wish it – then any oath can be sworn by all that's holy, Saint Martsyn's icon kissed, the tsar's portrait knelt down before...

But all this is words and empty gestures; it's a well-known fact that in the face of death, everyone says what is demanded of him. Why should they swallow it? – swallow it they won't. They have to be told something where they can see profit for themselves by resigning their murderous aims; they have to be given some great, bedazzling, glorious lie. These are Lyednyak Martsynians, Rasputin's own, defenders of gleissen, defenders of Russia in the Ice... Do they know about Tesla, about the emperor's crazy designs, about machines for waging war on the icers?

That's it! Hand over Tesla! Yes!

And the tighter the body was wrapped in the corpses' garb, the more warmly swaddled in the bloody rags and overtight suit, permeated by the stench of old age, the deeper the bad throbbing cut into the flesh and into the mind, and the stronger the grip immobilising the jaws; bite the lips in terror and desperation. Whilst the Martsynians neath the crooked lamp – they watched.

The door swung open, a ringing frost swept inside from the dark night, and another Martsynian stuck in his head.

'All are gathered! Deliver him up'

They seized the crippled body under the arms, dragged it to the door. Exit into the cemetery.

Knowledge acquired later revealed that this was the oldest burial ground in Irkutsk, transformed into a Christian holy place from still earlier pagan fields of death. Orthodox Christians were buried here, Catholics too, Protestants also had their graves, whilst next door lay a Jewish cemetery; further away, the bones of Buryats and Tunguses languished beneath the open sky. The hillside fell away towards the west, towards the night-time frostoglaze illuminations and coldiron auroras of the city shrouded in dense fog; the fog didn't reach these altitudes, or reached them already soft and rarefied. And so out of its bluish seductiveness loomed waves of crosses, snow-covered tombstones, rows of graves under a rugged carapace of ice. To north and south stretched similar heights crowned by ridges of frozen birchwood. This one they call Jerusalem Hill. It was also later revealed that the gravediggers' shed stood on the foundations of a burned-down tserkoff. A single dilapidated wall had survived, a slanting ruin. Beneath its tarry wing, the rest of the Martsynians were waiting, a group of a dozen or so men, none thickly dressed, one hibernik even half-naked, his livid torso exposed to the sharp frost, but wearing an ushanka with the earflaps pulled over his bearded countenance. At once they began to shout amongst themselves, releasing cloudlets of steam from their mouths, very dark in the light of the ghostly crescent moon; shouting, they set off down the slope towards the freshly dug grave, around which burned naphtha bonfires. Follow them down, the icy gravediggers continuing to drag without a word.

Collapse onto the knees between the fires, facing into the pit where black water had collected, covering the bottom. The pyres were burning on heaps of earth scooped from below; beyond the smoke and sparks, spade-shafts thrust into the hard ground still protruded.

They were watching. There was no need to lift the eyes and look into their faces, flushed from the nearby embers; everything was perfectly visible in the mind. How they stare at the kneeling man, his whole body atremble between the frost and the heat, clad in the abominable garb of corpses, too large and too tight, his nut covered in purple bruises now pressed into the mud, gasping raucously for breath, at such a Son of Frost – what can this Son of Frost say unto them, so they might turn their backs even momentarily on the commandments of their icy faith, with what falsehood shall this caricature wean them from the sacred soletruth?

Soundless neath the cold skull, audible in the frozen larynx, that one mournful prolonged groan swelled on a string of vibrating phlegm.

'From cold to cold; for out of cold wast thou taken, and unto cold shalt thou return, frigid be the Lord God, from cold to cold –' intoned a silver-bearded peasant in a bass voice, crossing himself vigorously and kissing his coldiron medallion.

'From cold to cold!'

'People in fervour –'

'He shall freeze!'

'Burning desires –'

'He shall freeze!'

'Fiery sins –'

'He shall freeze!'

'Stirred-up blood –'

'He shall freeze!'

'Inflamed souls –'

'He shall freeze!'

'Infernal tongues –'

'He shall freeze!'

'The world in flames –'

'He shall freeze!'

'Life reduced to ashes –'

'He shall freeze!'

'The Word of Martsyn!'

'The Word! Christ our God, Christ our Saviour, have mercy upon us, to the Ice we look, by the Ice we live, in the Ice we believe, into the Ice we go.'

'Amen.'

'You see, brothers, man and even the best man, living in this world,

475

chooses not between good and evil, but merely between evil and evil, and the greatest good in his mortal life comes when he has power to turn from the evil of reason unto the evil of the heart, from evil for his own gain unto evil for the gain of mankind, for the gain of the world, yes. Look ye: the lord from the Great Russian Heartland, Venyedikt Filipovitch Yeroslavsky, proclaimed son of Batyushka Moroz. Look: it is he.'

'He.'

'Our fathers have spoken: this instrument of Ottepyelnik evil, this instrument comes to convert his begetter to the undoing of the gleissen, on orders from the ministry of the Ice's enemies, at the instigation of courtiers and sordid traitors who hate the motherland. Yes?'

'Yes, yes, yes!'

'Behold the evil before us: to shed the blood of a defenceless man. Well, as our brother Yerofey says: afore we take him upon our consciences, we are to put him to Martsyn's test, as it is written in the prophecies: frozen in sacred ground, he shall rise again on the thirteenth day of the Ice, alive, taken from the earth. But wherefore doth brother Yerofey demand this test of the grave? What revelation does he expect? Eh?'

Raise the eyes. All were gazing at the Martsynian standing to one side on the left, at the top end of the oblong pit. Recognise him from the crookedly darned rubashka and ancient frostbites, from the red wound on temple and cheek, from the eye swollen by splinters from the smashed interferograph.

And everything became clear and obvious: for so quickly had they discovered the hotel chosen by chance and where no name even had yet been entered in the guestbook – for they'd worked it all out – the icicleman, this madman from Old Zima – had not fled blindly into the snowstorm, no, but had taken the Express to Irkutsk, hidden somewhere on the train and let nothing escape his eye; he had followed all the way from the station or caught up with Klyatchko afterwards and wrung the address out of him – and so sneaked into The Devil's Hand, leading his comrades there at night, brother-gravediggers with their caravan sled, the coffin ready prepared – the angel from the dream had come to rest, had recognised him: 'Venyedikt Filipovitch Yeroslavsky'. Everything became clear and obvious – apart from one thing: what was it that Miss Muklanowicz had said to him on the Zima platform?

'The word from Saint Petersburg resonates differently in the land of Ice,' proclaimed the icicleman, peering over the fire with his single living eye. 'You know full well, it has been so many a time.'

'What sayst thou, brother Yerofey?' asked the silver-bearded one. 'Are we to bury him in the frozen soil?'

'Let him say!' cried the one-eyed Martsynian, pointing through the smoke with his outstretched arm.

Stagger up from knees. Tug at the sleeve of the formal jacket, twist the tie, shift the weight from ailing foot to healthy foot on the loamy brink of the pit, both feet squeezed into overtight shoes.

'Benedykt...' They heard not. Clear the throat and repeat louder. 'Benedykt Filipowicz Gierosławski, yes.'

Clench the fists, so as to stem the shivers. As if fired from a whip, the roused wave has to bounce off a man at some point, discharge itself at the extremities of his limbs.

In that moment, the scene, that outburst, at Princess Blutskaya's feet in the parlour car of Deluxe came back.

'Do what they told you!' Shriek in despair into the sepulchral night. 'It's nothing to me! Khrr! Neither your Martsyn! Nor your God! I spit on both!'

Choke on the words, wishing truly to spit; cough with gathering momentum, almost tumbling head first, bent double, into the dank grave.

They moved not, spoke not. One or the other glanced at Yerofey. Yerofey stood still and waited.

'My father,' declare after a pause, already calmer, eyes averted, 'is some freak of the Ice, I know not my father, I have no father. And now the aim is: to unfreeze him, take him away from here, away from the gleissen. Not the Ice, not politics, Histories, religions, not Russia, neither the things that are God's nor the things that are Caesar's. Father. This much only. That's all. That's it.' Stare boss-eyed into the interior of the grave. 'Am I to enter? Shall you bury me alive?' Sniff. 'Damned Martsyn. Out of fear. Khrr. Well, what? Am I to enter? Eh? So be it, I'm jumping in, be my guest.'

This torrent of words might have flowed on longer still, but first the old man with the silver beard, then the other Martsynians – turned their backs, stomped away, dispersed into the foggy murk of the dawn. Gawp after them shaken to the core, arms crossed over the chest, blowing into the upturned collar of the corpse's jacket. They didn't even look around. Leaving behind their spades and glowing pyres – till the latter burned themselves out.

The last standing was one-eyed Yerofey, the would-be murderer of Zima. Stare at him blankly, whilst from between the quivering lips, wails of resentment cascaded forth:

'So tell me, tell me, what was that supposed to be, to intimidate, yes, to intimidate, some sort of game or something, so he'd fall in out of pure terror, huh, khrr, so they'd laugh at him dancing over his grave, that's what it was about, night-time, the kidnapping, the cemetery, even having to force his way out of a coffin, so his heart was ready to burst, and look, the pit's been dug, into the pit you go, to intimidate, yes, to intimidate?!'

Yerofey shook his head.

'So, what then?!' scream, leaping up to him through the azure flame. 'What then?! I'm supposed to utter a few words – and that's enough? What am I, an idiot?!' yelling the head off. 'What's it about?! Not this after all! I could have said anything! What theatre! Yet if I had! Said this, said that, terrified. The stupidity of it! What I did say – was that the truth?! Supposedly the truth?! Not for this reason have you let me go! Not why!'

At which Yerofey simply pressed his clenched fist to his breast and uttered a single phrase, quietly but firmly:

'It has frozen.'

Later, later, later... Sitting in the lounge of The Devil's Hand under the photograph of Aleister Crowley in its frame of thickened frosto-glaze, drinking hot tchay laced with rum, as outside the windows the summer Sun rose above the Irkutsk fogs. A sleepy garçon brought breakfast. The first sleighbells were jingling in the street, as the urban traffic began in the Uysky rayon; Saturday, the twenty-sixth/thirteenth day of July 1924, and the City of Ice awakes to the working day as the night shift of coldiron and tungetitum proletariat wends its way home from Zimny Nikolayevsk. On the table with the chessboard, where pieces of Crowley's unfinished game still lay, someone had placed an ashtray with an unquenched fag-end. It gave the impression that the Englishman had only just left the table, would return in a moment and finish smoking his cigarette. Try to eat something, yet blowing the nose and coughing up phlegm were taking longer. The hands shook, the feet were bobbing up and down, jolted by the spasms of frozen muscles. First it had been necessary to dash upstairs to the room, change the clothes and also retrieve the dolphin-head cane: it was more or less impossible to stand on the left leg. Despite having completed the greater part of the journey from Jerusalem Hill to the west bank of the Angara – along Laninskaya Street and under the giant triumphal arch towering over the Moscow Highway – in Yerofey's sleigh, the damaged knee swollen afresh refused obedience, bah, the whole battered limb refused obedience. That trembling, which had begun already in the sealed coffin, could not be snuffed out to the end: if not shivering, then it was a nervous tick, if not a tick, then cramp, if not cramp, then strange convulsions of the head, and if not convulsions, then again shivering. Yerofey had loaned a reindeer skin; wrapped in the skin and a plaid blanket extracted from under some sacks, the ride got underway. The Martsynian spoke no word; but at least he didn't behave boorishly, and even bowed politely. Had they really spared their victim? What will they say to the fathers of their sect, what report to Rasputin? And what if fresh orders should be forthcoming? But maybe there are more of them – not only Rasputin's faction and Pyelka's, but many like them who dread the effect of the Son of Frost on History, and many like them who will defend everything that comes from Father Frost – so maybe the next fanatics will pounce any moment and try to bury alive? Clench the jaws so the teeth ring not in their chattering. What an odd compulsion, what a surreal situation: they had kidnapped, placed in a coffin, tried to murder, yet now the victim rides alongside his would-be murderer and even lacks the nerve to sling it back in his face; even accepts gratefully the filthy blanket, almost thanking him out loud. But the Martsynian is not ashamed, not ashamed of anything – and herein lies the problem with people of faith, with vassals of the absolute, divine or human, that whilst they carry out its orders, they do no evil, whatsoever those orders might be. They'll strangle your children and then invite you warmly to supper, and be astonished when you fail to turn up. Behold the man *living in the truth*. And one other thing, about which Yerofey was not asked, because such things cannot be asked: why did he request a test and audience for an unbeliever condemned by their Martsynian superiors, an unbeliever who a day earlier had himself tried to kill? What on earth had come to pass? But Yerofey said nothing to the end. He drove across the river, set down his passenger, cast a furtive glance. 'Godspeed.' Hobble away without a word. The hand now shakes as the tea glass is raised. Splinters from the coffin-boards remain embedded in the fingers. Go to the police commissariat? He had said nothing, because he knew full well that the Son of Frost would not go.

Impossible to swallow the bread roll, even when dunked in hot milk; the clenched throat had no wish to open. On the other side of Crowley's table, a fat Armenian sat down to eat, still wearing his bulging frosto-glaze specs. Having lapped up his black coffee, he unfolded the latest issue of the bilingual *Angara Courier*. On the first page was something about Poles – take a peek, crooking the head stork-like – about Poles, but it also called them 'Yapontchiks'; a few days before, someone had blown up the Cold Line, the railway to Kezhma, and suspicion had fallen on 'Polish terrorists'. The gendarmes and Cossacks on Muravyoff Station sprang to mind. So, it was not because of Not-Verousse's bomb; here other struggles were afoot, for which the business of Tesla and the gleissen was merely a minor sideshow. The Armenian rolled his milky-coloured glasses over the newspaper. Swivel in the chair, instinctively averting the gaze – aside, upwards, to the picture hanging above the chess game.

In this photograph, enlarged to portrait-size dimensions, a smooth-shaven man in double-breasted suit stood before the hotel's façade, in those days under a different signboard, whilst in the background and to the right, above the grey mist that blurred most of the picture, coal-black columns hung in the sky. Crowley had a muscular face with the mouth ironically contorted, which was distinctly in contrast to the ice-encrusted elevation of the building and snow lying around about, since his skin, teeth between lips, and especially his eyes – had all come out in the photograph in various intensities of black; dark also was the cloud-let spreading above the Englishman's head: his unlichted breath. How long had Crowley stayed here? How quickly had he evolved into such an inveterate gleissenik? The landlord said that Crowley was wont to walk into icecradles. Was some natural method of immurchment con-cealed here – natural, that is, possible without the aid of Doctor Tesla's machines or without spending long years in the Land of the Gleissen? Of becoming charged with teslectricity through association with gleis-sen, so that even the flickering umbriance, the infernal blackness on and around the body, and the angelic glintz can't escape the camera's eye? In which case, gleissen must be true receptacles of murch – and indeed, does not their ice often appear dark like shimmering glass filled with ink? Aleister Crowley found a method to drink it straight from the source. He stands in the frost with uncovered head, a mocking smirk on his thick lips. Does he feel the cold? Does he shiver in the fog? Does he freeze? He had already frozen, that's the point. Shake suddenly all atremble; the dropped teaspoon clanged on a plate. After all, they had sounded the warning note – Pocięgło, Razbyesoff, Zeytsoff – the warning note: it's another world, other laws pertain here; were they but limited to the physical realms…!

It has frozen. Yerofey in no way explained the matter, it went without saying. Whether the truth was uttered or lies – whether those thoughts on father's behalf were truly honest, or merely a shudder of desperation – the night, the cemetery, the fires, the moon, the prepared grave – it was uttered – and it has frozen.

How many times do we stop in amazement, hearing the words enun-ciated out loud by our own selves, especially in debates political and religious or conversations about feelings: it has been expressed, so now the opinion is known; it has been expressed, so now it's known whom to hate, whom to like. Enter the quarrel – and you shall know your own mind. Leap into the mortal fray – and you shall know your own heart. Or at least be a high-stakes gambler. Or better still: peer into your grave, into the black water. Whatever you shall know of yourself, in Summer you shall know it but momentarily and at once lose certainty of that knowledge; but in the lands of the Ice, it's not possible to know anything which is not totally true or totally false.

It has frozen. Can, by this means, something that was not true suddenly become true, so that it will then remain true for all eternity? There are some propositions which become truthful at a certain moment, there are propositions which are made into truths, whose truthfulness is created. But even Kotarbiński had in mind exclusively past facts. It is not possible to freeze man in this way, that is, freeze also that which this man has not yet done. Not possible in the literal sense to create truthfulness, like a handcrafted object is created, a foetus in the womb, a mathematical formula or a magnetic charge in the body. Even murch-bearing machines, even gleissen do not do this. Blow the nose, pour rum down the clenched throat. The Armenian removed his glasses; he had the eyes of a young child, and was watching with childlike audacity. Avert once again the gaze. A grey ribbon of cigarette smoke hovered over Crowley's chessboard. He went out and never returned; went on an expedition to see gleissen and never returned; entered the icecradle and never returned. Shake the head. It is not possible to impose truthfulness by any physical act!

Later, later Tadeusz Korzyński's finger was also remembered.

On the charms of family life

'Oneiromancy is rife in the lands of the Ice!' Father Rózga thundered from the pulpit. 'Just look, my dears, at those dreamslaves who lose their way in their waking hours, like a man loses his way in a nightmare, doing out of dreamy conviction anything to which the dream induces him – but why, but what for, but did he really want to do it – yet the dreamer won't say; for sometimes it seems to him that he himself is not in his own dream at all, that the dream leads him, the dreamer who exists not, from mysterious scene to mysterious scene by some inner power of its own. Do we not know such dreams? We know such dreams! My sisters, brothers! Oneiromancists and soothsayers of every hue prey on our weakness! Look at those already ruled by dreams: have the dreamslaves attained happiness by it? It is not dreams that foretell their future, but the lived future that resembles their dreams! First, they lose awareness of the effects of their own actions: children go hungry at home and frost pervades their hovel not because a husband wanders from hostelry to hostelry the whole livelong day and refrains from honest work – but because a crippled dog ran across his path, because a star flashed at him from the sky and the shadow of a gleiss fell to the north. Later, they cease to see the sense and significance of any action at all, for whatever they do, or don't do, the dream will sweep them up in its current just the same, life will drift by all around them, and what must happen will happen. And so firmly do they believe in this that no one shall dissuade them! You know them – answer in your own spirits: be they Christians? how can one or other victim of oneiromancy obey Our Lord's commandments? Shall dreamslaves, after death, enter through Peter's gates? No, they shan't, and you know full well why not: in the dream world there is no good and evil, there is no truth and falsehood, there is no sin and there is no salvation! A Christian – a Catholic – a Pole – is not he who waits for revelations and necessities and succumbs to those that act for him, think for him, live for him – but he who acts for himself and knows why he acts, who lives and knows wherefore he lives, who chooses and chooses for himself, even in defiance of those necessities, and when he sins, it is he who sins and it is his own sin, coming from his own living soul, honest sin consciously sinned! They who sit and wait on a wayside stone shall not gain the Kingdom of Heaven; the Kingdom of Heaven is for those that walk, that run, that take aim at the goal; and even when they drop in pain and flay their legs before the ones resting unexhausted on the verge – it never enters their heads to step down from the road and give up. And even if they walk that road in the wrong direction, this one thing shall be counted still in their favour: that they did go, go, go! Do not believe therefore the soothsayers – especially those that prophesy truly!'

Such were the sermons delivered by Father Rózga to Polish million-aires in the Church of the Assumption of the Blessed Virgin Mary, the basilica of the Roman Catholic parish of Siberia, the largest parish in the world.

Listen to the priest with no great attention, looking out from behind a pillar for the figure, described by the beggars, of Mr Wojsław Wielicki – said to be a strapping fellow, two arshins and twelve vershoks tall, with impressive paunch grasped tightly by a corset neath his stylish frock coat, light-coloured beard divided in two, and all the more con-spicuous by virtue of his wearing on a finger of his left hand a large tungetitum ring set with a diamond that once belonged to a tsarina. And it was all true: he was easily spotted as soon as they stood for communion, amongst the gentlemen in the pews nearest the altar: height, beard, belly, ring – everything matched to the letter. Move along hugging the wall so as not to lose him from sight; people made way for the limping, coughing man leaning on a cane. Wojsław Wielicki took his seat immediately behind the pew of Mayor Szostakiewicz and Mr Ignacy Sobieszczański. Beside him sat two women of Balzacian age and three small children, probably between three and seven years old. Towards the end of the mass, Wielicki lost patience and glanced several times at the watch discreetly drawn from his waistcoat. He hurried to the exit without waiting to the end of the chants. Hobble after him.

Find him beside a sleigh on Tikhvinskaya Street; he was talking animatedly to the driver and issuing instructions to two servants, who at once turned on their heels and rushed off to carry out his orders. Wojsław Wielicki had fastened his squirrel-fur coat and was just pulling a pair of buff-coloured gloves the size of large loaves onto his hands, when he was caught up with. The faithful had begun to leave the neogothic church in small groups; the beggars raised their chorus of wails. From the crossroads to the bank of the Angara was a beggar's paradise: the Spasskaya Tserkoff, the Cathedral of the Epiphany as well as the Polish Church. It crossed the mind that Wielicki might shoo away the seeming beggar; better then to shove the envelope under his nose before uttering a word.

He glanced up unsurprised.

'You're from whom?'

'From Warsaw, you'll see when you read it, sir, from Alfred, khrr, Teitelbaum.'

Even if the name meant nothing to him, he showed no sign. He fixed a pince-nez on his nose and took out the letter. By Irkutsk standards, the temperature wasn't low, nothing to write home about: not even fifteen below zero; cloudlets of unlichted breath were flowing off Wielicki's patriarchal beard with a second's delay – without frostoglazes over the eyes, the lambent glintzen on the folds of Wielicki's fur coat were clearly visible.

'Ah, so you're Benedykt Gierosławski.'

Straighten warily.

'Khrr, you know me from somewhere, khrr, you've heard, yes?'

'Alfred writes that you're his bosom pal!'

He folded the letter, blinked from behind the eyeglasses.

'Direct from the Congress Kingdom, you say. But – but you are looking a bit frail!'

'I wanted... whether I might... the fact is the tchinovniks from the Ministry –'

'We know this, we know. Fear not, sir, Wielicki won't allow a compatriot to perish. Are you quite sure there's nothing wrong with you?'

Cough again; stepping into the frost from the warm interior, it was hard to control the irritated throat.

'I had an accident en route, in the Transsib, khrr, so you see...' whack the cane.

He clutched at his head.

'So you arrived with that bombed train! And you say nothing of it! Where have you been staying?'

'At The Devil's, khrr, Hand.'

The wealthiest of the faithful were boarding their sleighs stationed along the length of the street; a crush and confusion ensued, and then

Wojsław's children came running up to him in their dwarf-size furs, sprinkled in fresh snow, under shapkas disproportionately large for their small heads, so that only their little noses and chubby faces were discernible in the summer-winter sunlight; he grabbed one, gave a leg up to another and picked up the third. Step aside to let the ladies pass; the cane slid over the ice, the left knee gave way like rubber, and the body lost balance.

'But, for the love of God, why not admit it, sir, I can see you're unwell, shaking with fever, barely able to stand on your feet.'

'I was frozen to the core, yesterday in the night, khhrrr, yes. Mr Wielicki, sir –'

'Allow me – Benedykt Gierosławski, my wife. Halinka, look at Mr Gierosławski, am I not right?'

'But really, I am –'

'Nonsense!' And he nodded to the driver. 'As soon as Trifon returns from Zimny, send him to The Devil's Hand for Mr Gierosławski's things. Children, children, don't lick ice, haven't I told you before! Keep them out of mischief, Marta, thank you. Come on, sir, get in. You shall regale us with all that's happening in the Old Country, and that whole terrorist adventure as well, did you know, my dears, that Mr Gierosławski is a famous Warsaw mathematician, come to us on the Thursday Express, the one blown up by a bomb. Why won't you get in, my dear man!'

'My name is Benedykt Gierosławski, khhrrr, son of Filip.' State it slowly, very distinctly, over and above the drivers' cries, horses' snorts and the nearby drumming of the shamans. 'A warrant is out here for my father's arrest; he was exiled in nineteen-oh-seven, now he consorts with gleissen. The Ministry of Winter has me under the muzzle. There'll be trouble.'

'There'll be trouble! You, sir, won't live to see trouble, unless you land as soon as possible under a warm quilt! Look at him – just arrived and at once a toughie in a pickle! Kindly get in and stop putting on airs, old fellow, for it's not every day that such visits happen to us at the end of the world!'

And so, in this way, began the sojourn under the roof of Mr and Mrs Wielicki.

Only when the image in the hallway mirror of their house had been checked were any last suspicions dispelled as to the sincerity of Wojsław Wielicki's motives, for it was an image of penury and despair – to the old wounds, bruises and scabs had been added a most unhealthy-looking red flush, a shine of cold sweat on the forehead and unpleasant gleam in the dark-ringed eyes, an unmistakable sign of illness. Coughing long and often, which echoed soggily deep in the chest. And when the outer clothing was removed, the battered skull and fingers in their stiff bandages were unveiled too. Wherefrom, Benedykt, sir? Well, from the accidents in the train. In Wielicki's women, they unleashed the worst protective instincts.

Mr Wojsław Wielicki owned a two-storey townhouse in the post-fire southern district on the right bank of the Angara, on Tsvetistaya Street, off Zamorskaya; the windows overlooked the Angara ice and the southernmost tip of Konny Island, and gazing from the corner rooms it was possible to see in the far distance above the fog the cadaver masts of Innokentyevsky Village and the housing settlements of railway workers. Like every well-to-do inhabitant of Irkutsk, Wielicki kept emergency accommodation in readiness for his family: a floor in a small manor house beyond the Uysky rayon, beyond the Kaya river. There they had a second pantry, second wardrobes: a couple of servants maintained the empty apartment ready to receive the family; all their servants had been trained in the art of swift removal. When the city was rebuilt, explained Wielicki, we still didn't know the routes of the Ways of the Mammoths.

Of the three women in the house – his wife, his sister and his mother – the most vocal and most demanding of attention was the eldest, who seemed on the first day to be the true head of the family and ruler of the roost, as was often the custom besides in the past century, when a widowed mother or grandmother, in the absence of men in their prime away at work, at war, in exile or on some other of life's expeditions, kept the whole family and family estate together with an iron hand. On the second day, however, it became evident that the youngest of the three, Marta Wielicka, in reality made all crucial household decisions and that her quiet word prevailed over the colourful emotional outbursts of her mother. On the third and fourth days, in fact until the seventh, nothing became evident, since they were spent lying plunged in feverish hallucinations whilst the two doctors hired by Wielicki, one Polish, the other German, argued over the bed as to whether it was pneumonia, or an infection of some other internal organ, or maybe the beginning of the White Plague. The following week, when the bed had been risen from and it was possible to wander about the house, eat meals at the Wielicki family table, play with the children and spend afternoons with the women and evenings with Wojsław in his corner study with its great frostoglaze windows and panoramic views onto ice and more ice and fog – the following week, the quietest truth became clear: not the ruler, but the real mistress of the house at Tsvetistaya number seventeen was Halina Wielicka *de domo* Gurgała, for she was the one in possession of the heart of Wojsław Wielicki.

The children – a little boy, a little girl and a little boy – took everyone for a ride, figuratively and literally. Often Wielicki could be seen

charging out of his study (even when entertaining clients after dusk or
on holy days), shouting resoundingly and stamping at an elephantine
gallop on the parquet floor, accompanied by the squeals and giggles
of a son or daughter or two little darlings at once, as he bore them out
on his wide shoulders or under his arm; once he even seized the collar
of the youngest, Piotr Paweł, in his teeth and transported him in this
way, thereby expressing his great indignation at how the sprogs were
interfering with his work, to which no one in the house of course gave
any credence. He could be seen napping after Sunday lunch on the
chaise longue in the drawing room, his heavy arm slipping onto the
floor along with newspaper, his spherical belly protruding from under
his frock coat despite it being so tightly strapped, whilst onto that enchanted mountain climbed Michasia, biting her stuck-out tongue, only
to choke on her own laughter once Wojsław awoke to find his daughter
comfortably installed on the equator; then she would bounce up and
down like on an inflatable ball, whilst Wojsław emitted droll sounds.
Or, he would pretend to be still asleep and only snore all the louder,
causing his bushy whiskers and shaggy beard to undulate and his belly
to quake, as a result of which the little girl would rise and fall in time to
her father's inhalations and exhalations, finally falling flat on her face
and shoving her fists into his beard so as not to be thrown off, so frenzied was that rodeo.

Remark to Halina that perhaps her children are growing up
dreadfully spoiled by too much freedom. In stark contrast to the rig-
orous upbringing in good bourgeois or noble homes of the Congress
Kingdom.

She was amazed.

'Spoiled? Benedykt, we do not spoil them, we love them.'

'Precisely, that as well.'

She gave an odd glance.

Mrs Halina Wielicka, a woman of unexceptional beauty but exceptional delicacy and warmth, set the rhythm of domestic life in the
absence of her husband, that is, for the greater part of the day, when
Wojsław was visiting the coldmills and factories of Zimny Nikolayevsk
or spending time in his warehouses by the railway station. Halina rarely
issued instructions even to the servants (and if she did, she did it with
a strange shyness, almost in a whisper). In truth, however, she had no
need to give orders because everyone perfectly knew their place and
duties and the whole house was organised according to Halina's plan.
One day after breakfast, as the body recovered from its fever, she visited
the sickbed with an armful of books and magazines, offering to read
to the patient for a while; then afterwards, a member of the household would drop by every day at that same hour, under this or another

pretext, in order to provide company – had she enjoined them to do so? The betting was she never uttered a word.

She brought a few old Sienkiewiczes and Dickenses, two romances by Helena Mniszkówna, the coalmining epic by Zabrzycki-Balut, crime stories by Marczyński and Wilk, a travel adventure by Ferdynand Antoni Ossendowski, five novels by Wacław Sieroszewski printed here in Irkutsk, including his famous *Hoarfrost*, from which was learnt the history of the Great Fire and founding of Zimny Nikolayevsk. Also, several issues of the illustrated weekly *Over Lands and Seas* containing travel novels by Karl May: *In the Balkan Gorges* and *Christmas*. Recent Polish literature was to be found in the reactivated *Homeland* published in Saint Petersburg, which included fragments from Żeromski's *That Will be the Day* as well as *Folks from Summer and Winter* by a certain Maria Dąbrowska.

More edifying was the daily press, European and Siberian. The Trans-Siberian Express brought newspapers from Saint Petersburg and Moscow with a week's delay; the Wielickis subscribed there to *Russian News, Russian Word* and *Stock Exchange News*, but also to *Siberian Life* from Tomsk. The European Russian press contained more or less censored information about Western politics and world events: on the controversial initiative to appoint an Atlantic Court of Justice, suggested by the president of the United States, James Cox; on waves of demonstrations in the industrial cities of Germany and Great Britain provoked by wage reductions and redundancies; on the butchery in Ireland; on the freezing of the third Balkan war; and even information from China: on the latest plot of the National People's Party against the emperor, for which two hundred and sixty people were allegedly condemned to death and publicly executed in the course of a single day.

In the Siberian press, they wrote instead about local peculiarities. In *The Baikal Voice*, a banker named Suslikoff had placed the following notice: whosoever had dreamed during the night of the seventh to the eighth of July of the current year of lilies blooming out of gas installations as well as of rust on the skin is kindly requested to make contact at such and such an address between such and such hours; a reward of about five roubles or more is envisaged. Alongside this, a notification from the Irkutsk Circle of Christian Socialists: Comrades Elanty A.S. and Pavlikoff G.G. have been shown to be traitors or provocateurs sent with the intention of comprising the CCS from the start, and incited by Plekhanoff's Northern Mensheviks, which we hereby make known to all. Whilst again, a certain Mr and Mrs Tolek, a communist couple from Tomsk, have been exposed as provocateurs of the Okhrana. But was their marriage itself a provocation? *Mrs*

Tolek, totally committed to the revolution, was unable to get over her husband's treachery and in a fit of melancholia took her own life with the aid of a steel crochet hook. The next page includes a Chinese bone-straightener's advertisement, and under it a plug for a miraculous salve to protect against frostbite. There are also cultural announcements. The First Public Discussion Club invites guests to its building for an ethnographic evening devoted to excavation finds on the terrain of the Military Hospital in Znamenskoye and from Glazkovo, where the earliest graves and Stone Age cult objects in Russia have been found; Professor Bazoff K.Yu. will deliver a lecture; admission free. Next: a large notice, occupying two columns, of the opening of a *salon offering blackapothecary services at number four, Peter the Great Prospect, open day and night.* Inquire of Marta Wielicka what these might be: 'blackapothecary services'. Well, in the Land of the Gleissen, a rather potent branch of pharmaceutics had developed in the past few years based on potions, pills and tinctures containing powdered tungetitum. This new chemistry had not been endorsed by any medical authority and opinions were divided as to the efficacity of the remedies, which didn't prevent black apothecaries from making fortunes on gullible people seeking wonder cures for cancer, the White Plague or infertility.

Published in Irkutsk, the journal *New Siberia*, although in Russian, revealed itself on second glance to be edited almost exclusively by Poles, and on third glance – to be the tribune of Oblastnik politics. It became clear at last what prosecutor Razbyesoff had been talking about in the train. In an article entitled *Why the United Free States of Siberia Must Arise*, a certain Pawłowski (undersigned as a professor at Tomsk University) laid out why it was essential to *establish the independence of the Siberian colonies from the imperial might of the Great Russian Heartland*. The 'Great Russian Heartland' appeared to mean European Russia. Pawłowski (a 'Siberian patriot', whatever that implied) described the balance of trade and investment in the Siberian provinces as well as the blatantly unjust structure of the Empire's budgetary expenditure. Oblastniks had been demanding the 'decolonisation of Siberia' for a long time; the idea had taken many forms, beginning with the conceptions of the Land and Liberty movement and semi-autonomy for the 'Siberian colonies' in relation to European Russia, through the envisaged regional state of Svobodoslaviye to which even Count Muravyoff-Amurski was allegedly sympathetic (maybe seeing himself as its first president), to a federation of native-people states under the control of a 'Siberian senate'. There were socialist versions. There were Polish independence versions (the Polish Siberian uprising of 1833 led by Father Sierociński and Doctor Szokalski was meant to inspire a general revolt across Siberia). Of course, all this was History in the versions and interpretations of the authors of *New Siberia*.

New Siberia also printed comprehensive reportage on the progress of the construction of the Alaskan Tunnel. And made space too for a sugary account of the opening of two refuges for people who had been 'iced out' (that is, upon whose homes gleissen had settled), refuges erected *far away from the tracts of the mammoths* by Mr Harriman's philanthropic foundation. All manifest propaganda, almost too transparent.

The Siberian Herald was the semi-official voice of the Russian authorities, easily recognisable from the very style of the articles. The largest Irkutsk firms, all the Zimny Nikolayevsk tycoons advertised here. The Thyssen consortium informed of the creation of the Joint-Stock Company Thyssen & Tikholeff with headquarters in Irkutsk, of Thyssen's sixty-per-cent share and twenty-per-cent input from securities freely available on the market, which current investors were being encouraged to buy; the Company is being set up with the aim of exploiting *primordial deposits of natural coldiron*. In turn, the Azoff Metallurgical Company invites tenders for the construction of a *coldmill specialising in the extraction of gleissen blood destined for industrial processes*; undersigned on behalf of the board of directors: St. Siemaszko, T. Handke. The Česka Banka announces a sumptuous opening for its Irkutsk branch headquarters. The Union of Catholic Tailors of Siberia invites readers to an 'anti-Paris' fashion show, Diegtyevskaya Street 22. At the New Irkutsk Theatre, a French farce was playing entitled *Who Brings Flowers*, but was stopped immediately after the first night by demand of the tsarist censorship; editor Vishny waxes lyrical on the moral decline of decadent Europe and the rotting of the Empire's healthy social tissue due to the moral pestilences of the degenerate West.

The Irkutsk News, for a change, was a typical afternoon paper, full of reports of scandals in the higher and lower echelons, of the fresh criminal exploits of notorious prestupniks, of extraordinary and abominable events overseas, and also stories of sudden enrichment and even swifter bankruptcy. Whole columns were devoted to social gossip as well as to the weirdest accounts of so-called occasions, in other words receptions held in the palaces of Irkutsk Croesuses, balls at the governor general's residence, theatrical premieres, weddings, funerals and judicial trials. These accounts were frequently undersigned by eccentric pseudonyms or simply initials, whilst the proportion of information contained in them was represented thus: one part on the occasion itself and nine parts – on a meticulous description of the apparel and coiffures of the ladies taking part. Maybe similar papers in the Kingdom looked no different – there, however, they were not the reading of choice; only in times of sickness, only when immobilised in bed, do you achieve such a state of intellectual desiccation that you'll read the stupidest paper from cover to cover, including the small advertisements, and then study the cartoons.

Read also in *The News* about the trial of Wienemann's gang. Wienemann was a metallurgical engineer originally from Prussia, who, during an expedition to a northern magpiery, was lost in the icy wastes to the magpies and Tunguses accompanying him, only to reappear six months later on Baikal's shores with one frozen-bitten hand and one glaciated eye frozen to his brain. He claimed that he was able to peer with this eye directly into the Underground World and see the frozen water veins of the Ice and meadows of the mammoths, and for a goodly reward would show the coldiron companies new riches; this skill he allegedly acquired *whilst living in the natural state amongst gleissen*. None of the coldiron moguls was hoodwinked by Wienemann's fairy tales; always in Irkutsk, however, you'll find men naïve when it comes to money, seeking easy and profitable investments. How great was the amazement when one, then another and then a third of those who had paid Wienemann returned overjoyed, having indeed found deposits in the places he'd indicated. Larger and larger concerns purchased maps and grid references from Wienemann. He was brought down by his own greed; he should have fled earlier. In the end, however, the Irkutsk Chief of Police put two and two together and made the connection between the Wienemann case and recent reports of prospectors and private geologists disappearing rather too frequently without trace. The bandits were caught torturing their next victim in order to extract the secret of his find. The ice-eyed engineer had been abetting them as effective camouflage – for people were quick to believe that he really did gaze below the earth with his icicled orb; the miracle in plain sight had shut the mouths of unbelievers. Only afterwards did someone bring news from Prussia that Wienemann, indeed a man with a technical education, had been sought for years in his home country for bigamy as well as trading in stolen purebred dogs.

The News published a daily map of Irkutsk with vectors plotted of gleiss relocations; similar information had been printed in *The Warsaw Courier*, though in far less detail and not day by day, and above all: heavily veiled for fear of censorship from the Minister of Winter. Here in Irkutsk, for understandable reasons, there was greater freedom. In *The News*, street lists were inserted of icebound buildings, as well as 'shaman horoscopes', that is, prophecies of the Buryat glashatays relating to gleiss movements in forthcoming days. Those 'heralds' beating their drums before the gleissen – as Wojsław Wielicki explained with a mocking guffaw – were no shamans, but random local hiberniks hired by the mayor to warn people in the fog. It happens that a gleiss freezes out somewhere straight up from under the surface of the ground for no rhyme or reason; thus the glashatays have already saved more than one sleepy townsman. Of course, should a glacius come up vertically in the middle of a cellar, there is nothing you can do. That's why whoever in Irkutsk is richer, lives higher. The Wielickis lived on the third storey of their townhouse, ten arshins above the street. Whilst Aleksandr Aleksandrovitch Pobedonostseff resided at the very pinnacle of the Sibirkhozheto Tower, in the sky above Irkutsk.

In Warsaw, people had no such problems. But these were completely different Winter cities: on the streets of Warsaw, no more than five gleissen had ever been counted at any one time, but here, in the City of Ice and its environs, from Lake Baikal to Zimny Nikolayevsk and Aleksandrovsk, no fewer than one hundred icers had always been wandering over the earth simultaneously since records began. The Ways of the Mammoths, Wojsław sighed and puffed thick smoke from his pipe. The illustrated Saturday supplement to *The Irkutsk News* also ran geological lotteries; for gleissen-nests and icecradles located far from the Ways, odds were paid of two hundred to one, two hundred and forty to one. The drawing of lots for the allocation of land and loans took place in Omsk and the results were delivered in sealed envelopes by the Transsib.

Much was also written (in a tone of excited sensationalism) about the blowing up by Yapontchiks of the Cold Line to Kezhma. These 'Yapontchiks', as already learned, were not native subjects of Emperor Hirohito, but Poles of the Japanese Legion. Readers were reminded on this occasion of the old arrest warrant for the treasonous state prestupnik Józef Piłsudski: fifty-seven years old; height: two arshins, six vershoks; face: concealed behind dark growth; eyes: grey; hair: dark blond; sideburns: light blond, sparse; mouth: regular; teeth: not all present; distinguishing marks: eyebrows meeting above the nose, wart at the tip of right ear. The reward for handing him over was seven thousand roubles. And five hundred for any 'Yapontchik' or other Polish fugitive caught carrying arms.

Poles in Irtkutsk were strongly divided in their opinions on Piłsudski's methods, political aims and alliance with the Japanese Empire.

'It's disastrous for business, Benedykt, sir, hard to say just how disastrous,' Wielicki shook his head, settling down in the corner study to his evening pipe. Take a seat in an armchair drawn up to the stove; the white lacey coverlet under the cheek still smelt of forest herbs, while Wojsław's tobacco – uncoiling in a long ribbon in the air – of hot resin. A single naphtha lamp burned under a Japanese paper shade; the house, like most in Irkutsk, was electrified, but frequent breakdowns in the network and cuts to the flow of current meant that people relied more on oil. Thus, despite the late hour, it seemed lighter outside on the street, neath the straggly clouds of white snow carried by the Baikal wind up the icy corridor of the Angara, over Konny Island and the left-bank districts, than in the dim study. Down below, on the ice, in the milky-grey fog, the sleighs' double stars flickered as they moved back and forth across the river. And since all this was now observed through frostoglaze windowpanes, the colours of the snow, the colours of the sky, the colours of sleigh and city lights could now be seen without squinting and without dreamy torpor – how the colours run into one another, wash through one another, exchange places. The gale chased away the clouds and out came the Siberian stars above Irkutsk, silver-coloured against the black-coloured sky. Memory returned of the shaman's smoke: inky constellations and a geometrically angular sun... The huge diamond flashed on Wojsław Wielicki's finger.

'Disastrous, disastrous. It's enough that they've cut off my supplies from the magpieries and mines in the north – well, what were we to do, suddenly close the coldmills and halt the factories? – and as to our contractors – it doesn't bear thinking. We've had to wangle something, beg and beseech, pay our middlemen through the nose so they'll dig up the reserves of coldiron ore before our competitors get there – eh, what can I say, dear fellow, they've done us great harm.'

The scene outside the church on Tikhvinskaya came back, and before it, inside the church, when he couldn't sit still and kept glancing at his pocket-watch.

'But have they repaired them?'

'The tracks? Why no! Piłsudski knew where to blow them up – some bridge before Kezhma has totally collapsed, it won't be quickly repaired.'

'So, you think that these struggles make no sense, that, as Porfiry Pocięgło says, the oppressor has to be bought, not fought.'

Wielecki toyed for a while with a frostoglaze paperknife, seeking the right words in the cloud of perfumed smoke.

'I understand perfectly why they do what they do. Yapontchiks and others like them. Piłsudski calculates according to the iron logic of military strategy: ally yourself with the enemy of your enemy. The more the war with Japan shakes the Russian Empire, the greater the chance that a repetition of nineteen twelve will succeed. And it's even of no great importance whether the Japanese emperor later keeps his word, because Japanese armies will never invade Europe. So why are Pilsudtchiks now blowing up coldiron railways in Siberia and damaging Irkutsk industry?'

'To disrupt the peace negotiations between Russia and Japan.'

'Precisely, the logic of this policy is indisputable. My God, do you imagine, sir, that in nineteen twelve, you'd have come across any Pole here not praying for the success of such uprisings and revolutions and the downfall of autocracy? Well, maybe some fanatical loyalists. But the majority, but we, I myself, those like me, no matter if wealthy or not so wealthy – oh, I'd have given my right arm!' And he actually spun the narrow knife around and dug the rainbow blade for a moment into his wrist. 'Except that History, Benedykt, since you so like to talk about History, except that History presents us with no such choices: sacrifice this and that, and you'll gain your fatherland as a reward. This is precisely the greatest difficulty. How many of them reach for their rifles because armed struggle brings the greatest chance of success, how many – because they're incapable of envisaging any other victory than the restoration of Poland *by force of arms*?'

'That's similar to what Pocięgło was saying. Capital not guns.'

'Do I detect a reproach?' Wojsław laughed good-naturedly. 'I detect a reproach!'

'No, not at all, I don't urge anyone –'.

'You don't urge! But you begrudge!' Mr Wielicki scratched his beard with the paperknife. 'Were you ever in America? No, you weren't. I sailed there a few years ago at the invitation of business partners, to the United States, to San Francisco. Take a look, sir, at their history from our perspective. People from different countries, from different state power structures, outcast in effect from their own polity or unable to find a place for themselves in their country of birth – settle on new soil, create a new state and now have a new fatherland. So, have they carried off a victory, or been defeated? Have they gained independence 'by force of arms' or, on the contrary: have they renounced it? Are they patriots or traitors?'

'But isn't this what *The New Siberia* writes? You talk like an Oblastnik, Wojsław, sir. We've been robbed of Poland, so let us create – buy up – the United Free States of Siberia!'

'No. Pocięgło is not so far removed from Piłsudski in this, except that Piłsudski stands for a country that no longer exists, whilst Porfiry Pocięgło – for a country that has not yet come into being. I, on the other hand, am trying to tell you something else, mm-hmm, I'll try again. Look at it closely, sir. Those who fight for Poland, what are they fighting for? For a name, geography, language, a Polish currency – or for something that such things serve, for a higher good of which they're merely the means, the symbol? Eh? What, in this case, should a reasonable man do, when he realises that in the given circumstances another means is efficacious, whilst the old is – in short, harmful?'

Impossible to tear the eyes from the diamond in Wojsław Wielicki's ring; the stone had caught the light of the naphtha lamp, was flashing in sharp reflections around the room full of soft half-glows and half-shadows.

'Kh-hmm, but what is that higher good?'

The door fell ajar and Halina entered the study.

'Excuse me. My dear, could you look in on the little ones, Michasia won't sleep, she's giving Masha a hard time.'

Wojsław roused his huge bulk from behind the desk.

'Coming, coming, *mon cœur*, I was just having a chat with Benedykt; you'll forgive me, sir.'

The diamond captured the last light as Wojsław withdrew his hand from the doorframe; it was at once extinguished in the shadows of the corridor, where the whole of Wielicki disappeared, his beard, his powerful stride and his voice.

Whilst the history of Wojsław's ring was as follows:

Won at cards from Yekaterina the Second by a lieutenant in her life-guards, it passed by way of an obscure succession of owners into the hands of Gustav Ojdeenk, an Amsterdam jeweller who in 1914 opened his Diamond House in Irkutsk; this diamond, however, came originally from the collection of the Great Moguls, plundered in 1739 from the treasury in Delhi by Nader Shah. Gustav Ojdeenk wore it on his finger as the specific emblem and trademark of his firm. Geologists dispatched in the Year of the Gleissen to the Podkamennaya Tunguska river, whilst gathering tungetitum and searching for natural ore deposits under the Ice, chanced upon deposits of graphite (which was no longer graphite) as well as diamonds (which were still diamonds). And as soon as people were persuaded that diamonds existed not only in the Urals, they began to be sought on a par with tungetitum. Wojsław Wielicki, who in those days was managing a textile warehouse on his father's behalf with no immediate prospects for his own business, believed the Yakut tales he heard in the homes of hunter friends about the diamond riches strewn around sources of the Vilyuy river and, having borrowed money at perilously high risk, financed an expedition and also hired a Lithuanian geologist with experience of Africa. The expedition returned six months later with specimens of two- and three-carat diamonds and maps of potential deposits. Wojsław went straight to Gustav Ojdeenk, to whom he proposed the sale of his maps and geologist's knowledge in exchange for shares in the diamond company, since he himself no longer possessed any active funds, only debts. After complex negotiations, when no expense was spared on vodka and caviar, the gentlemen reached an agreement, of which one of the more unusual clauses stated that should the said company, during the first three years of its activity, discover a stone at least half the size of the diamond gracing the finger of Mijnheer Ojdeenk, ownership of the diamond would pass to Mr Wielicki.

Four years later, Wojsław Wielicki sold his remaining shares in the firm Vilyuy Diamonds for a six-figure sum, in order to launch his own wholesale company dealing in ice ores.

A riddle: could he have not succeeded? At what moment did Mr Wielicki *freeze*: the hearty wealthy man, the diamond fatty, the head of a happy family?

Search for falsehood in the everyday life of the Wielicki family, falsehood between Wojsław and Halina, between Halina and her mother-in-law, between Halina and her sister-in-law, for lies cast somewhere in their midst. Impossible to hit upon any such thing. Unhappy families are all alike; every happy family is happy in its own way. Especially to someone watching from outside. Zeytsoff would have been mawkishly touched. Study them patiently. Asked if happy, they'll say what everyone says: oh, so many worries, so many cares, the children constantly sickening for something, coming in from the frost every day into the heated air and going back out, and Wojsław so rarely at home, toiling from dawn to dusk, especially nowadays when so many coldmills and manufactories are at a standstill, and he can think only about how to resume supplies of his priceless raw material, and on top of all this there's the constant unease about the war with Japan and rumours of the White Plague… It was obvious that they were happy, that this is what happiness consists in. Contemplate these images in dumb amazement.

Were the Wielickis some kind of exceptional people, good people at least? Not by a long chalk! Of the elder Mrs Wielicka, for instance, few would say otherwise than 'a grasping old hag'. In the course of half an evening she managed to consider out loud the health of her closest relatives, counting the expected bequests according to a succession of demises and legacies – but why won't they die any quicker: Uncle Grodkiewicz already does nothing but sleep and drink and sleep, and Cousin Huśba has twice clawed his way back from gangrene by some miracle, couldn't God take them a bit quicker unto Himself? They can't all expect to go on living to the end of their days…!

Happiness did not stem therefore from their personal characteristics. Did not depend on individual elements, but on the arrangement in which they found themselves, namely the family. May not bad people be happy? They may. Happiness experienced here on earth has nothing to do with the good and evil done in this life. Were the world constructed in accordance with the philosophy of Prince Blutsky, such that man receives happiness as a reward for his acts of goodness already in the kingdom of the flesh, people would follow the Ten Commandments like a well-trained dog follows its master's commands – likewise receiving an immediate reward for obedience. When doing good means doing the right thing, profitably and practically, then evil becomes a sign of nobility of soul.

Observe the Wielickis therefore with cool fascination, a bit like the fascination of a child spying on the life of ants or of a sclerotic old curmudgeon gazing uncomprehendingly at the chaotic games of children.

Only when old Mrs Wielicka, pausing to take breath for a moment after her long stream of words, asked with concern why it is that Mr Gierosławski doesn't say anything, why he just sits and keeps silent, does he really feel better, perhaps the cupping-glasses should be put back – notice only then that indeed, throughout the entire evening, no word had passed the lips. Might this be Herr Blutfeld's complex? Why speak, when all is banal; before a man opens his mouth, he's already ashamed of the platitudes he is about to utter. But no, it was not about this. The change was greater, affecting not only talkativeness and taciturnity. It's true that illness polarises character. Maybe the fever had not been so very grave, not so very long-lasting (though were it not for the Wielickis' care, it could have ended in death), yet departing from it had made the character a little quieter, calmer, slower in words and gestures, a little older. Now it was obvious. As if, along with the heavy sweats, along with the black fever drawn out under the cupping-glasses onto the surface of the skin, the poison of mental fever – that internal vacillation between Benedykt Gierosławski and Benedykt Gierosławski which had condemned during the journey in the Trans-Siberian Express to successive false games, losses of face and self-immolation in shame – had likewise been sweated out. Hence the fever had departed: *a cooling had taken place.* Perhaps an adaptation to the surroundings, a kind of domestication process in the Land of the Gleissen: the murch had been levelled with the outside, in other words the body was now swollen with this murch like blotting paper dipped in an inkwell – not for a few hours after a quick shot from the teslectric machine, or an injection from the jar of salt crystals, but permanently, profoundly, to the very core of human nature. How to recognise a gleissenik: was it solely by the flickering umbriance? Doctor Konyeshin had been told correctly: you will not describe the truth of a new land in the language of the old. Words had to be wrung out, thoughts forced from brains. What Father Rózga was demanding in his sermon. Some of the very oldest gleisseniks, probably those of weaker mind and weaker will, slip into a form of chronic *déjà vu*: they live according to their own dreams, according to symbols interpreted every day from the world, because everything for them becomes an omen and sign of the inevitable. Between truth and falsehood, no place remains for them even to toss a coin. Chinese medics, Tibetan charlatans, and lamas concoct and sell herbal potions which destroy the memory of a dream even before waking; imbibed prophylactically, since dreamslaves obviously no longer wish to drink them. All manner of sortilege – cards, dice, frost embroidery, animal footprints in the snow – are a stronger or weaker sign of the inevitable. Betting games based on these therefore make little sense; no one in the Land of the Gleissen has ever rolled five sixes and got a royal flush. If medical knowledge, such as Zygmunt was taught by his Warsaw professors, correctly reflects reality and the brain of *Homo sapiens* really is a kind of drum made up of semi-random electrical short-circuits, in which our thoughts revolve and combine with one another via mini lightning bolts – then it comes as no surprise that in the countries of the Ice, abject people remain abject, the courageous remain courageous, the talkative remain talkative, and that no one becomes wiser than he was, and, as Nikola Tesla said, it's impossible to conceive here of anything new; there's no way in the shadow of gleissen to slide into revolutionary thought. Just as isotherm and isobar maps are drawn by joining points of equal temperature or equal pressure by means of isolines, so too an isoalethic map can be drawn, on which we will see fronts of inhuman highs of murch descending in wide terraces from a peak above the Podkamennaya Tunguska river, most likely overlapping to a large extent with thermal fronts; and so, just as a man immersed in icy water will himself eventually freeze through, reaching the temperature of the water, so too the man living under a record pressure of murch – becomes saturated with it, absorbs it, assimilates. There is nothing unusual in this; in each of two communicating vessels, the heights of the water levels balance out. This is physics. Except it has a new object of study: this black, unlichted force, this electricity of soletruth and solefalsehood. Soon institutes, professorial chairs and universities will arise dedicated to black physics; its laws will be written down, its equations specified. These equations will require time of exposure to be divided by body mass and an alethic factor – and then it will be possible to read off a chart the day, hour and minute when fever departed from the soul. This is mathematics.

    … For had there been any desire to be changed? Had there been any such thought at all: to talk less, to do less, to be less – in order to be *all the more*? The change had even gone unnoticed, until other people pointed their fingers. No intention had there been of changing and no knowledge of its meaning. But since it had happened, there was no intention either of going back. As such it had frozen.

    Needless to say, at every opportunity, they were bursting with questions about Warsaw: how are things in the Old Country, what news from Europe, what's life like, what are people wearing, what are they saying, how do they think? Feel on such occasions the temptation of which Jelena Muklanowicz so often spoke: to confabulate, to tell fantastical tales or made-up anecdotes – not for personal benefit, not for any purpose; but because it was possible and because they'd believe it. It was tempting to lie. There is no creativity in truth; to tell the truth is to reproduce, copy, repeat across the world – what satisfaction can be had from a senseless newspaper-like account? Words are spoken, that's all. But – to lie…! To lie is to add something from the self, to build into their image of the world creatures of an individual mind, to call into being non-existent people, objects, events. Oh, how perfectly Miss Muklanowicz had been understood…!

Remember – already opening the mouth in answer to Marta Wielicka's question and having in mind a dozen Warsaw fictions – the first day in the Trans-Siberian Express and that deceptive ease with which lies, even the smallest, even those born not of words but of silence, entangle a person, control, take possession of him, till that which exists not grows mightier than that which exists and it is no longer possible to express any truth at all, for nothing certain, nothing permanent remains of the speaker that could be faithfully rendered in words of the speech of men.

Sigh protractedly. 'Ah, Marta, I was about to lie to you hideously. Don't you believe me, miss, for I won't tell the truth, only my dreams of Warsaw. Have you a wish for fairy tales?'

Tell tales happily to the children instead. They imbibed the fantastical lies with open mouths; the more fantastical and terrifying, the redder the flushes on their chubby cheeks. Discover in this an unexpected satisfaction: the fabulist…! Afterwards they insisted on these weird tales, sat around on the floor; Michasia would climb onto the knees and sometimes fall asleep like that, especially in the drawing room in front of the fireplace with its softly blazing fire, a wintry storm roaring outside the windows; the little girl would fall asleep like that, whilst the boys tugged at the trouser legs – go on, go on, what happens next. Innocent lies, obvious lies flowed in a steady stream: about monstrous crablike doctors who walk backwards, talk from behind and live in reverse, and who are able to undo any illness and overturn any misfortune, but no one has yet managed to catch them and force them to do it, because how to tie down someone who's been retreating throughout their life from moment to moment; about the ghosts of Cossacks blown up on the streets of Warsaw, roaming now on their spectral horses through the night-time blizzards, and only like this can they be seen, like this be heard in Powiśle, Wola, Praga – whips whistling in the whistling wind, black silhouettes against the dark backdrop of the night, a rifle-shot fired at midnight; about the ice Cinderella, a Jewish orphan, who froze to death after being thrown out of her home by relatives, until a gleiss came down Nalewki Street and froze into the ground along with the girl, and now she appears, encapsulated in ice, whenever some lost child wanders at night through the back alleys of the city – the frozeling stretches towards it her silver icicles, opens her crib of billowing snow and calls with a crunching of ice: come-come-come; about the underground mathematicians, calculating from below the geological horoscopes of the people living above, just like we read horoscopes from the stars – they, in contrast, calculate our destiny from our footfalls, trace the constellations, the black zodiac of the city's foundations, whilst to them every grave is a bright star, every pool of blood seeping into the soil a glittering nebula – and how a valiant rebel fighter, escaping along the underground passageways of the Citadel, descended into the realm of the geomathematicians and learnt from them how to calculate the future and then worked out the dates of his enemies' deaths, worked out the fates of his friends and family, and stepped out of the grave in order to stave off unavoidable disasters, and yet his every, mathematically sure stride upon the earth was changing the geometry of the underground prophecies...

Did the Wielickis cast some spell, a strange mesmeric enchantment? – for during that time all necessities of the outside world were forgotten, as if the world beyond Tsvetistaya number seventeen existed not in reality; even what was seen from it through the frostoglaze panes was merely a deceptive illusion of jumbled-up colours, an image of the next terrifying fairy tale, maybe dreamed, maybe remembered from childhood notions. In here – warmth, quiet, the ticking of grandfather clocks, muffled voices of servants behind walls, sometimes the patter of tiny feet and squealing laughter, sometimes a screechy opera coming from the gramophone, the smell of naphtha, freshly baked cakes and brewed tea; but out there – the howling of the gale, multi-hued whiteness, fantastical cityscapes of ice, the soaring rainbows of the openwork bridge over the river of compacted ice, the cylindrical towers of the cryofortress on the river-locked island, the caravans of fireflies moving in fog undulating with all the colours of frostoglaze, the wooden masts with their corpses protruding above the fog, and higher still above the fog – erect as a gallows, the caricature of the Eiffel Tower wreathed in cloud of eternal darkness; and looming out of this fog, like sharkfins out of ocean waves – the stalagmite backs of gleissen. Stand by the window, hands behind back, almost touching the pane so that the breath slightly mists it, stand thus and gaze at the white-hued panorama of the City of Ice. In here – the house; out there – a gruesome Russian fairy tale. For a magic line had been crossed, a protective circle had been entered, where no Martsynians, Petersburg agents, terrorists and custodians of History had access. They remained on the outside. Here, inside the house, they were unreal. There was nothing to fear. Inside the house, even the heart beats more freely, in time to the ticking of the old time-keepers, to the creaking of parquet neath the coalman's feet. The hands, wherein children's fingers nestle, forget the shape of fists, unfreeze from the revolver butt; the language of tea-time conversation will utter no threat of brutal murder. Polite table manners and a warm smile will save humanity from the greatest wars and crimes.

Initiated into the ordinary daily life of the happy brood simply by dwelling under this roof. One week spent still in sickness, but two, three – eating already at their table, living already amongst them, partaking in their joys and cares, even if enjoying only the rights of guest. But the greatest changes occurred in moments that evaded description in the language of the second kind, when in fact nothing happens, no one says anything, oh, like that Thursday evening sitting at the table in the parlour – fumbling with the spoon in cold cheese borsch; Wojsław sits alongside glancing through back issues of newspapers likewise in silence, the cat sleeps on a chest by the window, old Mrs Wielicka dozes over her prayerbook in an armchair neath a green landscape painting, the electric lamps flicker, the clock ticks: say nothing, do nothing, yet feel the freezing into this family with every second – fiddling mechanically in the bowl with the remains of the borsch.

Maciuś came running in.

'I can touch my nose with my tongue!'

'Ee-ee, impossible.'

'Look! Can you see! Look!'

And standing proudly with head raised high, Maciuś strains with all his might, almost bringing out beads of sweat on his forehead, so as to reach the tip of his nose with his stretched-out tongue.

'Indeed!'

'Did you see? I can do it!'

'What about touching the ear with the tongue? Or the nose with the ear?'

'Aaa, how…?'

'Well, can you?'

He frowned in great intellectual effort, trying to picture these anatomical excesses, whilst such deep cogitation did strange things his freckled face, as his stuck-out tongue, snub nose and knitted brows did not cease twitching for a moment; he seemed to approach his future career as mimetic athlete with great seriousness.

'Ee-ee, impossible.' He pronounced at last.

'And if I do it – do I win?'

'You won't do it!'

'And if I do?'

He glanced suspiciously.

'Nose to ear?'

'Nose to ear.'

'Mm-hmm.'

'So, come here. Well closer. Closer.' Leaning further over him, touch his ear with the nose. 'There.'

Maciuś was offended.

'Pa-paa, Uncle Benedykt is cheating!'

Wielicki chuckled behind the table, rubbing his pince-nez with a chamois cloth.

'The first thing, Mr Maciej Wielicki, that you have to learn in business,' he said at last, twisting his moustache, 'is always to specify the terms of a contract.'

'I shan't be doing any business,' Maciuś announced. 'I shall fly aerwopwanes!'

'What?'

The maid asked Wielicki to come to the door; he went out, still chuckling.

'Aerwo-pwanes, frrrrr!' droned Maciuś, running around the room in circles with his arms outstretched until his head began spinning and he flopped onto his backside in a corner by the jardinière. 'Frrr, frr! Brrr, frrr!' He stuck out his tongue, touching nose, chin, nose with it until his head spun even more and he collapsed in a heap. Opening his eyes, he peered up from under the jardinière. 'Oh, poor little worm! Doesn't he feel sick hanging upside down? How about putting the worm in an aerwo-pwane –'

Wielicki returned. Perceive at once how his mien is totally different, much more solemn.

'Who was that?'

Wojsław Wielicki extended his diamond hand, wherein lay an official letter folded in two.

'A messenger from the Ministry of Winter, I had to sign for it. It's for you, Benedykt. You have to report to them tomorrow at ten.'

On ministerial mammoths and the cartography of the Underground World

The delegation of the Ministry of Winter was situated in the building of the Irkutsk Customs House, near the Magpie Bazaar, opposite the East Siberian branch of the Imperial Russian Geographical Society, which had moved from the other end of Glavnaya Street, from the Angara embankment, where the governor general's Sibiryakovsky Palace was replaced following the Great Fire by the Citadel, a box-like structure sprawled over the neighbouring plots and resembling a clumsily hewn boulder. Were it not for the fog and massive edifice of Christ the Saviour Sobor, the towers of the Citadel would have been visible from the Bazaar.

In a side-street by the Customs House two gleissen hung suspended between roofs, whilst a third was freezing up out of the pavement. In the customs bookkeeping offices and the ministerial chancelleries, frostglaze panes were trembling to the slow rhythm of the glashatays' huge drums. A janitor in bulging spectacles, wherein white was infused with blue, stood outside the gate holding a lamp above his head, waving it to and fro and turning back sleighs riding past the Customs House. On driving up, glimpse first through the fog this lamplight wheeling in a semi-arc; and only then did the colonnades, cornices, turrets and steep roofs of the six-storey building loom out of the grey-hued suspension. As is customary in the architecture of the Ice, the bottom storey was designed very high, at least ten arshins above the ground – passing through the gate was like entering a mediaeval castle. The courtyard swarmed with sleighs and horses and reindeer, and there was also a team of dogs; all that was missing was a bear on a chain.

The crush and activity came as no surprise; after moving from Kyakhta to Irkutsk, the Customs House now collected the excise duty on all Far Eastern goods making their way further west, in other words on the greater part of everything that passed through the ports of Vladivostock and Nikolayevsk-on-Amur: wool and cotton from England, flour, machinery and weapons from San Francisco, furniture, sugar, wine and industrial products from Germany, tea from China. The tea alone raised forty million roubles a year (until the outbreak of war). Relieved of duty were goods destined for the Siberian market, foodstuffs in particular – which only opened up new paths to crookedness and increased the bureaucracy. The customs officials occupied four storeys of the capacious edifice; the Irkutsk delegation of the Ministry of Winter was located on the two uppermost floors.

Standing on the mud-caked tiles of the entrance hall, it was already ten minutes to ten. On skins spread in a corner near the door sat an elderly Buryat with scars instead of eyes, staring blindly and grinning; two Cossacks in frostglaze goggles stood guard beside him, the grey colour of their coats seeping into the walls, off which a limy white flowed onto people's faces. Remove the frostglaze spectacles. The Buryat looked up and grinned more broadly. On the opposite wall hung old wartime posters, on which caricatures of Russian soldiers and sailors (moustachioed peasants with fair wheaten complexions and muscles like large loaves seething under rough stripy shirts) were trampling into the ground or pushing into the sea caricatures of Japanese soldiers and sailors (rat-like creatures, a third of the size, with eyes like commas). The Wielickis had described how at the height of military operations, all Irkutsk was covered in posters warning of Japanese spies; police patrols were constantly searching the Chinese quarter, checking documents, looking for yellow-skins amongst yellow-skins. Before the first war with Russia, the Japanese Empire had flooded Siberia with masses of immigrants, who found work as lackeys or governesses in well-to-do homes, as shoemakers, tailors, cooks, hairdressers, or prostitutes in temples of pleasure. With the outbreak of war, they all vanished, having garnered God knows what information. The Japanese Empire had been planning for years and years in advance, in this respect very like the Russian Empire. Notorious was the tale of a doughty Japanese officer who embarked on a solitary expedition on horseback from Vladivostock to Saint Petersburg: captivated by the heroism of this feat, Russians showered him with honours along his entire route without concealing any state secrets – only later did the expedition prove to be one of the most audacious and fruitful spying operations. It's important therefore to be alert. Yellow spies lie in wait everywhere!

Climb the stairs, tapping briskly with the cane. The edifice – like most flagship buildings in Irkutsk – had been raised from Baikal marble, a coarse-crystalline variety in shades of white, pink and azure. In a niche on a half-landing stood a statue of Peter the Great frozen out of iced sandstone; the stone steamed in the chill air, as if recently doused in boiling water. There exist these iced-through ores, thoroughly gleissed substances, Wojsław Wielicki had explained, which reverse the processes of heat, as though tungetitum itself distorts them: if you take a hammer and strike against iron – you warm the iron; but when you whack tungetitum with a hammer – you cool the tungetitum. A similar thing happens with certain coldirons. He'd been shown the Grossmeister and its black cartridges. Wojsław stroked his beard. May I offer you a piece of advice, Benedykt, sir? Why of course, I'd been counting precisely on advice from the start, nothing more.

Mull over in the mind, whilst mounting the stairs to the fifth floor, snatched memories of the night-time conference in Mr Wielicki's study; for as soon as the summons arrived from the Ministry, Wielicki had sent for lawyer Kuzmentsoff. Wojsław was full of assurances of his total confidence in Kuzmentsoff, both in business and private affairs. Through acquaintances at the Bar and in the Irkutsk Duma as well as amongst lawyers advising Sibirkhozheto, Kuzmentsoff had insight into Siberian politics at the highest level. Besides, he was often at the home of Governor General Schultz-Zimovy, who valued his knowledge of international affairs – in his youth Kuzmentsoff had travelled throughout

Europe, to the East Indies and to the Antipodes, and even visited the open cities of China. Now he was an old man with a silver beard no less imposing than Wojsław's and a mane of hair the colour of pepper-speckled flour. Outdoors on the street, he was invariably accompanied by a hale and hearty servant who supported him neath the arm so that the old man wouldn't tumble on the slippery ice; over parquet floors, however, the lawyer moved with scathing vigour.

'You took money from them,' he said, having made himself comfortable by the stove. Thick penumbra settled on the back of the armchair, in place of shadow and in spite of shadow. 'A thousand roubles, yes? You signed a receipt, yes? As well as some statement of your obligations? Have you got the document?'

'They gave me none.'

'But according to your understanding, Venyedikt Filipovitch – what have you pledged to do?'

'I am to talk to my father.'

'Talk?'

'Talk.'

'His father,' interjected Wielicki, who had been mincing all the while, preoccupied, from one black window to another black window, 'is a significant figure, at any rate to those who believe in the higher meanings of the Ice; tell him, Benedykt.'

He was told.

'So, you are asking,' Kuzmentsoff took a pinch of snuff and sneezed so hard it grew dark in the study, 'one, whose word in the Ministry of Winter has had you brought here; two, what are the intentions of that figure with regard to yourself and your pater; three, do they believe here in Berdyaeff, and does that decision-maker believe in him; four, what has this to do with Ottepyelnik policy and the plans of Doctor Tesla – yes, yes?'

'And five, Modest Pavlovitch: can I –'

'... resign from it now, yes.'

'Because if –'

'From the Lyednyaks.'

'What is more –'

'Sibirkhozheto against Tesla.'

'Or Pobedonostseff, or Rappacki. You can't –'

'... History –'

'... the gleissen –'

'... should they be destroyed by melting. Yes.'

Kuzmentsoff took another pinch of tungetitum snuff and pronounced gloomily:

'A hanging matter.'

Nod in mute assent. The questions had been formulated and put into words; only the obvious things remained. Murch was pulsating in the soft shadows cast by the naphtha lamp, in the nocturnal swelling behind Wielicki's back. Stand there for a few minutes in silence equal to their silence – yes, no, yes, no; Herr Blutfeld, had he been born in the Land of the Gleissen, would have uttered not a single word to his dying day.

On taking his leave, lawyer Kuzmentsoff vowed to find out as soon as he could what and how, and strongly advised in the meantime to make no new promises to Winter, certainly not sign anything, and say as little as possible, only prick up the ears and keep the eyes peeled. The director general is one Zygfryd Ingmarovitch Ormuta, but he has been living in dreams for months; everything is run by the tchinovniks, sometimes one takes charge, sometimes another. 'Should you need me – here's my card.'

Money was the first thing that sprang to mind on entering the petitions chamber of the delegation of Winter. The tchinovnik asked for the name. Benedykt Filipovitch Gierosławski. He checked in his ledger. Transfer discreetly, clasping the cane under the armpit, the thousand-rouble bundle from the bumazhnik to the jacket pocket. The tchinovnik wrote out the pass. Next floor up, left-hand corridor, to the very end and then ask for Plenipotentiary Commissioner Schembuch. Almost as soon as the back was turned, however, he leaped up from his desk and disappeared through the back exit. Oho.

Schembuch was in another meeting; the secretary, a dandified fatso with Tatar features and faintish glintzen stretching down below his double chin like white bibs, indicated a waiting bench by the wall. Take off the sheepskin. Sounds of angry conversation in Russian, Buryat and Chinese drifted in from the corridor. After a while, the secretary went out, leaving the door ajar.

On the bare plaster of the left wall, a portrait of Nikolay the Second hung askew. Walk over to it, adjust it to the upright position. A Mongolian dressed in a leather overcoat, wrapped in a scarf like a boa constrictor, crossed the threshold and stood still, unsure what to do, crumpling some papers in his hands; under his arm he held the white skull of a dog or wolf. He said something in his mumbly tongue. Reply that the secretary had gone out. The Mongolian pointed to the door behind the empty desk. Reply that he's in a meeting. The Mongolian blinked, sneezed and went away, leaving behind the stench of animal fat. Having straightened the portrait of the tsar, wipe off the dust. The tsar stared reproachfully at the opposite wall, where a portrait of Minister Rappacki hung skewed in the other direction.

Compared to the Warsaw offices of Winter, the interiors of its Irkutsk headquarters were not very impressive. Notice everywhere piles of document folders stacked against walls, streaks of dirt on flooring-blocks, solidified drips hanging from the high ceiling; even cracks in the plaster and holes in the stucco. Every other moment someone's raised voice cut through the clerical silence, like those of the wranglers in the corridor. The muffled barking of dogs came up from the courtyard. Bwroomm, bwroomm, the glashatays were pounding on their drums in the fog; panes were rattling. Outside the window, the sky was flooding the snow-covered roofs of Irkutsk with its azure light. A barebones in frost-oglaze pince-nez entered the room.

'Gospodin Gierosławski!' He stretched out his hands. 'Do come in, come in!'

He seized an arm and pulled through a side-door, across the vestibule of an office whence emanated the clicking of abacuses and creaking of parquet, and then through an empty secretariat to a high-windowed study that opened onto Glavnaya Street and the massive twin piles of Christ the Saviour Sobor. A lustreless blackness was streaming off the mighty Byzantine cupolas onto rivers of fog flowing between buildings; stare long enough and see a city drowning in infernal tar.

The skinny man was dressed in a freshly ironed clerk's uniform decorated with orders, his fair hair combed in a Napoleonic fringe. When he removed his pince-nez, it transpired he had youthful, lively eyes – he couldn't have been much older. The Armenian from The Devil's Hand came to mind; there was something in the eyes of gleisseniks, or rather in the contrast between their eyes and their faces: as if they aged at different rates, faces faster, eyes slower.

The barebones smiled broadly, opening his gob wide unbecomingly; he was missing several teeth, others were completely blackened. Dark breath came off his tongue in snatched cloudlets.

'We were afraid you'd never appear! When news reached us of that accident with the bomb – Bozhe moy, terrorists here, terrorists there, what times we live in – yet you made it safely! But we were waiting, waiting, and everyone was already convinced something bad must have befallen you.'

'I was ill.'

'Quite, so we heard. Have a seat, please.'

Glance around the cluttered room.

'Can I offer you something?' He took ice lollies out of his pocket. Then, out of the desk, a bag of mallow caramels. Then a box of Fay's Bad Soden Mineral Lozenges (very healthy!). Then a pouch of shag, a tin of sunflower seeds. He also extracted from the safe a box of cigars and lifted the lid invitingly. Select one, unwind the wrapper. He offered a cutter and a light. 'You see, it's even of no consequence that you're late: whilst the Cold Line remains closed, we have to wait anyway. It's important not to waste time once Kezhma reopens.'

Inhale the smoke.

'I know nothing.'

'I beg your pardon?'

'In Warsaw they told me nothing. They gave me a ticket and money...' Whip out the thousand roubles with a swift movement and lay them on the table swamped with papers. 'You may regard me as having broken my contract –'

'What are you saying!' he bridled. 'Come off it! We're very glad you've taken the trouble to come to us.' He blinked, stared intently. 'What did they tell you?'

'Who?'

Biting on his cigar, he leapt to an office cupboard, flung open the upper door, tore out from above his head a roll of documents and charts and began brandishing them in a kind of bibliophobic fury, unwinding and rewinding, until he found a particular yellowed canvas, which he then spread out with a tobacco-filled wheeze on top of the clerical mess on his oakwood desk. He beckoned urgently. Stand beside him. He slapped the map with the flat of his hand.

'Take a look.'

'What is it?'

'The Ways of the Mammoths. Do you see? Here, here and here, and there, and here.' He stabbed with his dirty fingernail at places marked with little crosses and described in squiggly Cyrillic. 'Reports of sightings of Filip Filipovitch Gierosławski. According to time – watch how I move my finger – this is how Father Frost relocates along the Ways of the Mammoths. You see the most recent date?'

'I know nothing.'

He ground his teeth (as many as were left).

'A Pole, well of course. You're concerned about your father – you want to obtain an amnesty on paper? They can arrange it for you, the governor general will sign. But what good will come of an amnesty for a block of ice? They shan't tell you – but I shall tell all. Here, read this.'

He wrested a document with an official seal from the file, stuffed it into the hand.

Turn towards the window.

... on the saddle of the valley, as he descended at night, and thus we saw him also at dawn: six by eight, on his icy march, over earth, trees and icicles. First thermometer: minus forty-one point seven. Second thermometer: minus forty-six point two. Third thermometer: minus sixty-four point zero. Recognisable features: a hand, outline of face (left

profile), a footprint (scale one to four). He was freezing along a vein to the north-east.

'What are they describing here?'

'Your father.'

Cough up black smoke.

'What did you imagine?' Schembuch moved the ashtray from the windowsill to the table and laid aside his hardly-begun cigar. 'That we were holding him somewhere in a ministerial prison? Or that you'd be able to just go, oh, and visit Father Frost in some secret Martsynian house or vagabond camp? That you'd sit around a cosy hearth and talk the thing through over a bottle of moonshine? God Almighty, they told you nothing! You've gone pale, sit down. Do you imagine "Father Frost" is purely some Martsynian calling, some sectarian name? This is what you imagined!' He was so moved he sat down himself on a stool drawn up to the table. He rested his elbow on the map, bouncing off the official missives; he didn't even spare them a glance. 'Care for a drink?' he inquired softly.

'I knew he was frozen, meaning bemurched, you see, that the Ice had congealed him – a "freak of the Ice". But – this – is something else – this is – gleissen –'

'Ye-e-es.'

Raise the eyes.

'Is he alive?' Ask after a moment; whilst in the head – like the ring of a glass bell – echoes the high-pitched voice of Commissioner Preiss: *Is Filip Filipovitch Gierosławski alive! Is he alive!* Bwroomm, bwroomm.

'This is how the matter looks. The Ways of the Mammoths...,' the flaxen-haired barebones pointed with his eyes to an ivory figurine in the showcase by the door, where behind (ordinary) glass stood various ethnographic exhibits, some of a strange primitive beauty, made of nephrite, jasper, agate, onyx and above all white ivory, yellow ivory. 'Mammoth, that is "mamantu" in the Eskimo tongue, means: "one that lives underground". You have surely heard, sir, how bodies and plants are preserved in our permafrost for years and centuries and eons. Sometimes we get such instances here, for example in Znamenskoye or near Kaysk: a man digs the foundations for a new house, melts the soil, and then what does he pull to the surface out of the mud? A fresh corpse, as if buried yesterday – some warrior in skins with a spear, from before the time of Yermak. Or an animal: today's, yesterday's. Well, and there are animals you'll find only underground: mammoths. Ask any local here. Under the sky he won't ever have seen them, but in the Underground World – on the contrary; that's where the mammoths live. You won't come across them in the taiga, running amongst the trees, or on the grassy plains. You can only *dig them up*. Understand?

A mammoth is therefore an underground beast, it grazes beneath the earth, roams beneath the earth in great herds; people can hear these roamings – the ground shakes and a long low roar emanates from under the stones. Some people say it's beasts of the Middle World – bears, reindeer, pike – after death, after crossing to the Lower World, they become mammoths. Others tell whole legends about mammoths being banished there by humans in company with the gods. Especially the shamans – those who see miracles everywhere: from our domesticated Tunguses I have heard – take note – that a mammoth is a "fish with antlers".

'And so gleissen freeze up out of the ground, out of the permafrost. The first glaciometric maps were sketched before the great fire in Irkutsk, at the dawn of the coldiron industry. Now, we receive almost exclusively transcripts from the Sibirkhozheto Atlas of the Ice, though they are cruelly censored; Pobedonostseff awards funds to universities and research institutes, and here – oh, the Geographical Society is practically a branch of Sibirkhozheto. For the most important thing is to be able to predict the translocations of gleissen, in order to know the underground channels of these flows of the Ice. Distinct regularities exist, after all, within cities and outside cities, but here we can observe them best; geological pathways exist, some sort of thermoducts in the permafrost, along which gleissen freeze, in order to emerge, here or there, onto the surface – usually not far from precisely such an underground way. The coldiron extraction corporations and coldmill companies would give a fortune for a complete, accurately drawn glaciometric map of Siberia.'

'The Grochowski Map.'

'Indeed. In the meantime, professors, soothsayers, charlatans, anyone who can boast of having made a prognosis that's materialised, are wracking their brains over it. Our coldindustrialists don't necessarily hail from the most enlightened circles, as you've no doubt had occasion to see for yourself. A shaman or two squirming in clouds of sacred smoke to the sound of a drum is enough to persuade them of a profit-making method.'

'Do they come true? Their predictions. The shamans.'

He shrugged his shoulders.

'Sometimes yes, sometimes no. Shamans can be useful, I shan't deny it, I myself make use of their services. The fact is you'll more often encounter a gleiss in places where fresh mammoths have been dug up. But they're dug up precisely in those places, because they've been so well-preserved in the permafrost, in solid ice, whilst gleissen are walking ice. Shamans claim that during a trance the spirit leaves them and directly enters the Lower World, where it sees the wanderings of the mammoths

– that's how shamans know the movements of gleissen. Ask, however, a Tungus or Yakut – and he'll say the opposite, just to spite the Buryat. You have to be careful how you manoeuvre between them so as not to accidently inflame some new-old feud. These things weren't explained to you? If you go with the Buryats, mark their every word about gleissen and the Ice. "Mülheŋ" – is the Buryat word for "Ice". We have a theological war here amongst the savages, take heed, a kind of schism on the scale of yurt and drunken tundra. Already in eighteen fifty-one upward of thirty thousand men were taken from the Buryats and turned into Cossacks; they served loyally, serve still, they're a useful people. Except that, well, whichever way you look at it, they're uncivilised savages, pagan tribesmen. "Buryat" – in Mongolian means "traitor". But why are they working for Sibirkhozheto? The difference lies, as I say, in their beliefs.'

'Spirit rules over matter.'

'That's sometimes the case, so I've heard, though I don't frequent spiritual seances. To Buryats, gleissen appear namely as newcomers from the Upper World: whatever came flying in in nineteen-oh-eight flew in from the sky. But Tunguses and Yakuts say the reverse: gleissen are children of the Underground World. First, they claim, the deviltry struck in the north, whilst north somehow gets confused in their heads with the Lower World, perhaps because it's coldest there. Second, gleissen freeze up after all from under the ground. Children of the eternal permafrost. Abassylar, that is spirits of the Lower World, underground shadows, the monstrous flocks grazing there on meadows of iron... What?'

'Nothing. It's a good cigar.'

'Such is their belief, Venyedikt Filipovitch. Just as Martsynians descry in the gleissen the Ice Antichrist, or whatever it is they're eventually waiting for – so Yakuts fear the coming of the chief gleiss-abassy, one Arson-Duolai, the Belly of the Earth, the Underground Dragon. Once upon a time they chased all abassylar from the Middle World, now they see them returning. So, what do Buryats do when faced with this? Instead of helping drive them away again, they serve Sibirkhozheto, which only grows fat on gleissen. Hence the spiritual war between Buryats and the Yakuts and Tunguses. Pobedonostseff flew into a rage and dug in his heels but in the end had to agree, and so they erected everywhere these masts with corpses. This, you see, is the barrage against the souls of hostile shamans who persecute Buryats, and against abassylar spirits.'

'You really –'

'Of course not! This is not what it's about! But until the masts were put up, the Buryat shamans had no wish at all to peer into the Ways of the

Mammoths and the coldiron industrialists were giving Pobedonostseff no peace, for they were forfeiting millions daily because of it, losing in unfair competition, and so on and so forth until he relented. So, you see how it is.'

'But as to my father –'

'Precisely! There's no other method of finding him other than to follow the Ways of the Mammoths. But what good would even the Grochowski Map be to me, if I don't know which Ways Filip Gierosławski follows, or what his habits are? For even were I to count only the most frequented Ways, look, here they are, drawn with triple lines – they stretch for tens of thousands of versts!'

'Those reports –'

'You see the date of the most recent. Colonel Geist of the gendarmerie – he's the head of the Okhrana for Irkutsk – sends us to the police. The Chief of Police in turn – sends us back to the Okhrana. We even thought of hiring some local sleuths, trackers from the north, Tunguses. But then engineer Di Pietro arrived with his story and we decided against. This is a special case: it's not about sketching the Ways as such, a gleiss is a gleiss, you won't tell one from another, they will freeze together, unfreeze again into two, three, four – which is which? It's all the same. But Father Frost is singular, separate, specific. So what's left to us? The map and this collection of dates and coordinates. You're a mathematician, yes? Yes. So, this shall be our first request to you, as well as your first obvious task, if you are to see your father at all: take these figures and calculate for us the Ways of the Mammoths. Well. Imagine it's an equation you have to solve – because you must solve it – these figures and the Ways of the Mammoths – the cold equation – of your father. Work it out.'

He pressed some crudely folded papers into the hand. Glance at them with an air that evidently bespoke not the highest intelligence, bah, that probably bespoke rather pathological stupefaction, since the lanky official, clearly troubled, turned to the cupboard and quickly drew out a water carafe from behind the porcelain teacups; he cast his eyes around for a glass.

Crush the papers in the sweaty hands. *Six by eight, on his icy march, over earth, trees and icicles.* Even if the thought had already occurred that he had fled somewhere into Siberia's vast primeval woods from the arrest warrant, and would have to be sought outside the knowledge of the Ministry of Winter – it had not been supposed that the Ministry itself would remain so helpless. *And when you talk to him, well, then it will be all right.* When we lose faith in the power of institutions – what will remain? In truth, only the shamans.

'So, how much has he frozen?'

'Pardon?' Schembuch crouched by a cabinet in the corner, found a tin mug, tossed it aside, found a porcelain one.

'They measured his temperature. In this report –'

'Ah! I know not, it's not the way to test it.'

'They even took three measurements.'

'Three rotary thermometers – since the strength of a gleiss is not measured by the temperature of its ice, for the temperature of every gleiss is always the same, nor by the temperature taken at a single distance from it, since it depends on the difference in ambient temperature, and that may be different here, different there, and different again somewhere else. Measured instead is the temperature gradient calculated from the increases at distances of three, six and nine arshins from the gleiss, best along the path of its march, from its front. Can it be in a liqueur glass?'

'But my father is not a gleiss!'

'But they weren't to know that.'

Thrust suddenly open, the door slammed noisily; a bulldoggish old man burst in buttoned to the neck in the uniform of a superior tchinovnik. Noticing the fair-haired clerk straightening up with carafe in hand, he stood with arms akimbo.

'So, this is how it is!' he wheezed. 'This is what you get up to as soon as my back is turned! Do you imagine I shan't note it down? Just you wait!'

'Note it down then, the soul is free. Gospodin Gierosławski –'

'Whose case is this? Whose responsibility here, eh?!'

The barebones shrugged his shoulders.

Shift the eyes from one to the other. The more the bulldog puffed and blew, sulked and swelled with fury, the more the flaxen-haired black-a-tooth calmed down, fell silent, as if he'd lost interest in the whole incident; eventually he gave an odd start, put aside the carafe and turned his back, staring out of the window at the sky-tinted cupolas of the Sobor.

'Come with me,' commanded the older tchinovnik. 'Get a move on, bring your things. Commissioner Plenipotentiary Schembuch Ivan Dragutinovitch. Why did you not report to us as instructed?'

'I was waiting in the secretariat, I thought –'

'That long?'

Tuck the papers under the sheepskin. Schembuch – the real Schembuch – led the way back through the secretariat, vestibule and other secretariat, to his office. Here the windows likewise looked onto the monumental cathedral. The fat Tatar was leaning over two work tables evenly spread with official documents. Schembuch shooed him away with a wave of the hand. He pointed to the chair earmarked for suppliants. Sit down. Standing behind his desk, he opened a thick clerical portfolio and folded his arms across his chest.

'Ten twenty-eight,' he said glancing at the longcase clock. 'I've lost a good quarter of an hour thanks to you, before I even set eyes on you, and before that I lost whole weeks.'

'I was ill.'

'In which case, one comes along and lodges the form certifying one's illness!' Schembuch roared across the desk.

'But the Cold Line is at a standstill, therefore –'

'And what business is it of yours, that line or any other?! Your bounden duty is to come, register your arrival, and await orders!'

'I am not –'

'You shan't leave Irkutsk without permission. Show me your passport. Come on, hand it over!' He unfolded the paper, glanced, snorted and flung the document into a drawer, closing it with a shove of the knee; the boom resounded like a cannon, inkwells jumped on the desktop and a pen landed on the floor. 'Mikhail will issue you with a temporary residence permit. And you shall report here regularly and await word, understood? Understood?'

'Yes.'

'Where are you – ah, with your compatriot on Tsvetistaya. Well, all right, stay there. Fine.' He sunk into his chair. 'My brain is splitting.' He took out a crystal jar containing a dark liquid and applied a few drops to the huge tongue lolling onto his beard. 'Ugh!' He shuddered all over. 'Fine. Now tell me. What do you know of Filip Filipovitch? Where is it that he roves? What do you know of his Martsynians?'

'Nothing. Pardon me, Your Esteemed Nobleness, but could you tell me for what exactly I am needed? In Warsaw, they told me I have to talk to him, to my father, that is; but when you now tell me I should wait, and I have no idea even for how long, then I...' Break off gradually, slipping at last into total silence; for Schembuch did not interrupt or react at all, merely went on sitting behind his desk, bulldoggish, paws held together flatwise in front of him and rabid eyes levelled at the suppliant's chair. Bwroomm, bwroommm, the windowpanes trembled. Clasp the knees with the hands.

'For a complete idiot!' Schembuch suddenly shrieked without any warning, without altering his posture, only opening his maw so wide that his dewlap shook like a turkey wattle. 'For a total fool, no doubt! What! How dare he! Barefaced shiteater! Get out! Whore's spawn! And yet still he jokes! Begone! Begone!' He spat black saliva; murch swelled neath his skin in blotchy mosaics of darker blood.

Stand up slowly, pressing against the chest the sheepskin wrapped around the cane, around the hands holding the papers.

'I have returned the money.' Say it, pausing for breath at every word. 'Arrest me, if you wish. I am returning to Europe by the first express. Goodbye.'

About turn and quit the office of Commissioner Schembuch. Realise at once, having crossed the threshold, that, obviously, there would be no returning to the Kingdom – staying was needful, in order to save father. Sit down heavily on the bench before the secretary's desk. There would be no leaving, least of all on the Express: without a passport, even buying a ticket would be impossible. Stuck now in this Irkutsk. What to do: tuck the tail between the legs, crawl back in there, apologise to Schembuch? The hot phlegm of Shame had ascended already to the throat, higher, had flooded the mouth, higher, was now oozing from under the tightly closed eyelids. Not even the rumbling of the glashatays' drums was audible, only the clangour of blood.

'... too long.'

'Beg pardon?' Open the eyes.

The Tatar leaned across his desk confidentially, glintzen flowing down onto his white shirt-front.

'Never fear,' he whispered gently, 'he can't do anything to you; Schultz already knows everything, he called off a visit to Pobedonostseff, sent the Cossacks, now he must negotiate.'

'What? With whom?'

The fatty chuckled thinly.

'With gleissen.'

Another din was heard emanating from the commissioner's office and the secretary cowered over his papers. Question him one more time and then again, but he would say no more, only handed over the document permitting a three-month sojourn in the Irkutsk Governorate, having delicately impressed upon it a large stamp. He raised not his eyes. Put away the pass together with the lanky tchinovnik's papers, mutter something by way of thanks and walk out without glancing back.

Thus ended the first visit to the Irkutsk delegation of the Ministry of Winter. Settle down, having returned home, to pore over the maps of the Ways of the Mammoths and the copies of the ministerial reports. The children had gone with Halina to the skating rink near Zvyozdotchka on the Irkut river; Marta was sleeping off her migraine of the night before, whilst old Mrs Wielicka was sitting downstairs in the kitchen. The valet brought *café au lait* and cold crumble left from the previous evening. Over coffee and cake, seated at a freshly waxed heavy oak table, in white light streaming through frostoglaze half-encrusted with snow – venture onto the Ways of the Mammoths.

The principal map, a reprint from the Sibirkhozheto Glaciometric Atlas (*Map of the Ice 1923*) stamped as having been approved for internal ministerial use, covered the whole of the Irkutsk Governorate General, lands stretching to the Arctic Ocean in the north and Chinese border in the south, as well as part of the Amur Governorate General to the east. The place of impact of the Ice beside the Podkamennaya Tunguska river was indicated with a five-pointed star. The map was described by a threefold legend: one, representing the Ways of the Mammoths themselves; two, the geocryological fronts; and three, the uncovered deposits of iced-through minerals.

... The Ways of the Mammoths cut across Asia like a network of subcutaneous water veins, in whose arrangement, despite the map being examined from a distance as well as close-up and through a magnifying glass, no fundamental regularities were detected. Perhaps it's easier for geologists to perceive order; maybe dependences exist here on rock formations, on the type of subsoil, on the history of the earth's crust. There were expanses hundreds of versts wide and hundreds of versts long, which no Way dissected; and there were areas – like precisely the Baikal country – where the dense jumble of thicker and thinner lines was indecipherable without the magnifying glass. In some places, the Ways ran parallel; elsewhere they intersected like city streets; in this, therefore, they were unlike rivers. Make, however, certain observations. No centre existed to this network; the place of impact of the Ice, located amidst great white blotches, was definitely not singled out in the network's structure. Not always, but very often, the Ways of the Mammoths ran in tandem with the currents of nearby rivers. No Way ran under Lake Baikal.

... Here, however, a certain reflection occurred immediately: the map does not show reality as it is, but merely represents human knowledge of it – yet how were people supposed to measure the subglacial movements of gleissen? It's obvious that the lake is a white blot. Similarly, the great wastes and backwoods of the Central Siberian Plateau – no one sees how often gleissen freeze up there out of the ground, or whether they freeze up at all; the carcasses of mammoths spat out by the earth are devoured by beasts of prey and scavengers before any Tungus or Yakut or other huntsman alights upon them. Whether the Ways intersect, or not, you won't learn from a two-dimensional map: it won't show the third dimension, depth. The same principle should be applied to towns and cities. Irkutsk, Nizhneudinsk, Krasnoyarsk, Ust-Kut, Yakutsk, Chita, Blagoveshtchensk, Khabarovsk – all under the Ice, all sawn up by the Ways of the Mammoths. Yet it's hard to assume that for centuries people founded their settlements in places of mysterious geological phenomena. So, do gleissen descend on human anthills because the Ways of the Mammoths lead them there, or because they simply take a fancy to nesting in those spots? How to distinguish – between a Way as a way and a Way as a line on a map drawn by a human hand?

... Let us say that Mr Wells's Martians observe like this the wanderings of men, without seeing at all the material basis of human civilisation, without seeing the earth's geographical formations. With time, however, would they not deduce the shape of our road networks and railway lines? Would they not discover by this method the boundaries of countries and seas, the positions of mountain ranges? Would they not recreate the frontiers between states? Yet how could they differentiate a political boundary from a physical boundary? Both one and the other restrain the migrations of *Homo sapiens*. Maybe gleissen move along the Ways of the Mammoths only when it suits them; when, however, they head for a destination where no Way leads, they simply leave them. Whilst the Sibirkhozheto and Ministry of Winter cartographers scrupulously join up points on their maps of reported freezings-out, according to time, frequency and strength measured by the three thermometers, and then every such dotted line becomes for them a Way of the Mammoths, even though no elephant corpse has ever been dug up beside it.

... But here bold assumptions have already been made: that gleissen think, that they set themselves goals, that they possess consciousness, that they are something more than manifestations of the mindless element that is inhuman Frost, rising up above the surface of the earth like waves rise up on stormy waters.

... Geocryological fronts marked the progress of the permafrost. This was a particular meteorology of rock. Irkutsk, for instance, was situated between the isotherm for the year 1909 and the isotherm for 1910. Why were geothermal fronts not marked instead? Would it not have been possible to detect the Ways of the Mammoths by taking measurements of the temperature of the permafrost? Find a clean sheet of paper and make a note of this question as point number 1. And point number 2: since the permafrost is increasing along with the expansion of the Ice (permafrost is evidently one aspect of the Ice), do new Ways of the Mammoths arise in lands swallowed up by it? After all, the *Map of the Ice 1923* showed Ways also beyond the line for 1908. The problem is that the oldest isotherms, those from before the establishment of Sibirkhozheto and the first research expeditions financed by it of geocryologists, were drawn in very light, broken lines: reliable information for demarcating the then boundaries of the everlasting permafrost was simply lacking. It was known which cities stood at that time on the permafrost, and which did not; and nothing more, in fact. On the other hand, between the most recent isotherms, Sibirkhozheto's cartographer had dared to suggest in dotted lines only a few supposed Ways. In the map's legend, a reference had been inserted by hand to Professor Hertz's memorandum. Flip over the document. Professor Hertz had put forward the thesis, namely, that in prehistoric times, Siberia and Asia in general had repeatedly experienced 'ebbs' and 'flows' of the permafrost: there had allegedly been periods when no less than the entire continent was in the grip of underground frost. The implication was obvious: these Ways of the Mammoths existed already then – now they were merely *opening up.*

... Every deposit of coldiron or other iced-through minerals recorded on the map had its legal owner, an owner with exclusive rights to its exploitation. (That is, only those already reported in the newspapers were noted.) Separate smaller maps were devoted to the hard-coal basin on the Angara north of Irkutsk, to the mica mines west of Baikal, to the great basin of coldiron ores to the south-west of Ust-Kut, as well as to the goldfields in the Stanovoy Highlands up and down the Vitim river belonging to the Lena Gold Mining Company, Lenzoto. Near Bodaybo was located the only gold-fluff mine, the most valuable metal ore in the world: gold iced-through to the density of whipped cream and with the specific gravity of Irkutsk fog.

... Temporary opencast mines and magpieries were not marked on the maps, even though nearly all tungetitum and most 'natural' ice ores came from them. But there were rather too many of these places and such maps remained current for no longer than a season. Whilst the majority of extractive companies and magpie partnerships probably never made this information public. It is therefore very difficult to assess the correlation between the course of the Ways of the Mammoths and the location of coldiron deposits. It was not the case that gleissen sat 'especially' on the minerals. So, the whole idea of coldmills at Zimny Nikolayevsk stemmed from the need for artificial, industrial icing-through of 'warm' ores. Sibirkhozheto nevertheless sent hosts of geologists regularly to search for seams of 'natural' coldiron. The area around every icecradle was scrupulously investigated; at the site of a longstanding nest of gleissen, bore-holes were dug and the permafrost was blown up with dynamite.

... From the reports of such geological expeditions come descriptions of three of the seven encounters with Father Frost recorded in the dossiers of the Ministry of Winter. Separate out the relevant papers, arrange the extracts according to date and make a note – as point number 3 – of all the coordinates:

61°57'N 101°16'E – 17 June 1919
61°55'N 99°07'E – 8 February 1921
54°41'N 102°50'E – 17–18 October 1921
60°39'N 100°33'E – 4–7 January 1922
67°32'N 109°22'E – 28 March 1922
61°57'N 101°16'E – 3 December 1923
56°44'N 110°11'E – 17, 19 April 1924

... Sketch, by running a pencil over the map like the tchinovnik of Winter his dirty finger, a shape similar to a skewed letter K, with one lower limb resting above the Oka river and line of the Trans-Siberian Railway, the other lower limb – stuck into the Stanovoy Highlands on the northern edge of Lake Baikal, and an upper limb – reaching towards the diamond-bearing Vilyuy. Meanwhile, between the arms of the letter outspread towards the east, close to their point of intersection, was located the place of Impact, the epicentre of the Ice on the Podkammenaya Tunguska river. In fact, four of the encounters with Father Frost – the first, second, fourth and sixth – had taken place no farther than 250 versts to the west of the epicentre. It was a relatively small area consisting in a couple of dozen square versts situated 200 versts to the north-west of Kezhma, to the west of the Vanavara trading-post.

... Minds failing to distinguish between premises and implications would quickly conclude that Father Frost is present in precisely this region most often. Whereas the interdependency is the reverse: the areas surrounding the point of Impact – not the lands closest to it, but how far men are able to get in Winter – are visited exceptionally frequently by the various scientific expeditions, industrial geologists and ultimately magpies collecting tungetitum; hence in these areas it is simply easier to make observations.

... Usually, their descriptions were confined to brief notes in travel diaries. On such and such a day, in this or that place, we caught sight of ice which we took initially to be a fragment of a gleiss freezing up out of the ground, then we perceived a man there. A couple of huntsmen testified to the delegation of Winter that *this ice man made a hostile movement at the sight of them*. Geologists from the Müller and Sons Extractive Company, having fallen asleep one evening by their naphtha fire, noticed at dawn *a glacial figure crouching in their midst, which leaned over the fire as if trying to melt itself, with hands and icicles outstretched towards it*. A Russian married to a Yukagir woman was hurrying with a sick child along the frozen Vilyuy to a lama healer; they passed a *man in the ice, marching up to his knees in the frozen river*.

... Most attention was paid in the Ministry of Winter to the account of an engineer named Di Pietro, who encountered Father Frost in the Stanovoy Highlands in April of this year. On the seventeenth day of April, heading from the expedition camp to the designated measuring point, he was walking through a ravine between mountains under the overhang of a high precipice. It was then that he noticed in the shadow, *a frozen man, beneath large icicles*, his hand and leg sunk into the ice incrustation flowing down the wall of the precipice. Driven by scientific curiosity, he tried to approach him and take a closer look; at once, however – writes Di Pietro – *I felt such a cold frost that I was forced to retreat*. As he had been taught to proceed with gleissen, he took out the thermometer and rotated it at nine and at six arshins; he did not get as close as three. What was it that attracted his attention and why did he not think this was simply the next poor wretch frozen beneath the Siberian ice? It was just that this man was naked, standing upright and not lying down, and moreover had open eyes, which *seemed to stare at me through the ice and firn entirely consciously, though without moving*. A day and a half later, as he was returning along this same ravine from taking measurements elsewhere, he no longer noticed Father Frost. When he came out higher up, however, he saw a flash of ice at the top of the precipice and took out his field glasses. *This man of ice* – he writes – *loomed as far as his chest out of the rock behind the overhang, his hands clinging to gigantic icicles*. Thus engineer Di Pietro concludes that *Father Frost travels in the same manner as gleissen along the Ways of the Mammoths*.

... So much for the hard facts. Most of the information about Father Frost, however, sprang from rumours, legends and Martsynian accounts circulating first amongst the sectarians, then – amongst the hibernik workers, and heard eventually in hostelries and shelters and beside campfires in the taiga along with other Siberian fairy tales. That he walked in and out of an icecradle. That he had *broken in gleissen*. That he *speaks all the languages of the frost*. That he lives off snow and icicles. That the glaciuses had adopted him. That he is the first apostle of the Antichrist of the Ice. That he had received as his reward *eternal life in ice*, since *that which is once immersed in the tungetitum permafrost, shall never die or be corrupted*. Dozens of fictions were doing the rounds – stories originating from a friend of a friend of a friend – about errant huntsmen and magpies, whose lives had been saved by Father Frost in exchange for swearing a never closely defined *oath of allegiance to the Ice*. This or that hibernik vowed that it was precisely from Batyushka Moroz that he'd received the gift of extraordinary resistance to cold. As to the charges, on the basis of which the warrant for Filip Gierosławski had been issued, these dated already from 1918, when father, following his reprieve, indeed joined some Martsynian movements, albeit in those days legal; Martsyn himself was still alive at the time, they say he met with father. Father was linked to several collective ice murders and two mass self-glaciations in 1919. There were no direct proofs (all potential witnesses had descended into the Ice); there was, however, strong circumstantial evidence, including the testimony of a gendarme who had conversed with father in one of those villages two days before the self-glaciation; also attached was a copy of a statement from a hibernik of Czech origin, who claimed that Filip Gierosławski had admitted to him that he'd led people into both those glaciations, and even boasted of it as an *act of service to the gleissen*. Finally, horror of horrors, pinned to the file was the testimony of a Buryat shaman, one Ürig Kut. He stated solemnly that he saw those acts of voluntary and non-voluntary glaciation with the eyes of his soul, which was wandering at the time along the Ways of the Mammoths, and that he had seen people descending into the Underworld chased by a man bearing an exact resemblance to the European shown to him in a photograph. Dear God, what obscurantism!

… Point number 4. Add up quickly the distances on the *Map of the Ice* and the times of observation, dividing the number of versts by the number of days and hours. The places of the fourth and fifth encounters were separated by more than 700 versts, which father covered in eighty days. This gave a minimum velocity of 390 metres per hour, in other words many times faster than the velocity of gleissen calculated on the Ways of the Mammoths, not to mention on the surface. What did this prove? That father was not a gleiss…? Hah!

Stand facing the white-hued landscape outside the window and light a cigarette. On what was the flaxen-haired black-a-tooth counting when he handed over all these documents? Even were a place and time to be calculated for the meeting with father, they shan't be betrayed to any tchinovnik out of pure gratitude. Bah, but is there anything here to be calculated at all? Is it possible to calculate a man's behaviour and predict from this calculation his movements, as if he were a wind-up mechanism? The most that can be spoken of is probability: as he had been seen four times by the Podkammenaya Tunguska river, this is where it is incumbent to go and await his manifestation.

But on the other hand – let us look if only at a map of Wojsław Wielicki's translocations (were someone to compile it from similar scraps of knowledge). Home, work, work, work, home, and so on; thus it is with any man, most likely. We create patterns of behaviour, life freezes into a predictable model like a star of hoarfrost; who can honestly say of himself that he is *incalculable*?

Without appreciating them, without seeing or feeling them, we all nevertheless move along the underground Ways of the Mammoths – in our daily cycle, weekly cycle, annual cycle, but above all on the scale of a lifetime, that is, from birth to death. Only then do the cartographers of History come along and draw maps of those Ways according to our deeds, words and journeys. The secret networks of flows in the Underground World do not determine a man's choices, but attract them rather onto the easiest, most frequently trodden paths. He attended these schools, got married, worked, sired children, died. Maybe fought in a war. Maybe amassed a fortune. Maybe travelled the world. Maybe committed a crime. (Already the lines are individual, interrupted.) At any rate, there remain only individual observations, the remembrance of facts scattered in time and space: the date of his marriage, the day of his sentencing, hazy photographs of his family home, beneath a tree, before a church, hazy memories of fragments of scenes from his final years – what more can possibly be recorded in the language of men? When the trajectories of a life are drawn between these dots suspended in a non-existent past – what shape shall arise? what subcutaneous structure be revealed?

Wojsław returned from his work well after dusk. Brief him as swiftly as possible on the ministerial affair. He sent for lawyer Kuzmentsoff with a polite inquiry. No sooner had the door to Wielicki's study closed behind the valet (brandy for the master, a shot of slivovitz for his new guest) when old Kuzmentsoff came straight to the point.

'Schembuch, yes?' He stroked his beard. 'Schembuch is Krushtchoff's man, and Krushtchoff is the Lyednyak opposition to Rappacki.'

'So, it was Lyednyaks that had me brought here?'

'No. The order came from Ormuta.'

'Ormuta is a dreamslave, you said so yourself.'

'At the time, he still lived awake. Patience, young man, I am explaining the political anatomy. Whose man was Ormuta? Ormuta was the man of Governor General Schultz-Zimovy.'

'They used to go stag hunting together,' muttered Wojsław, swallowing the alcohol.

Release air from the lungs.

'So that's why Schembuch told me to wait! Ormuta is a somnambulist and now they've no idea what to do with me! Nor what to do with my father. What a confusion of functions at the delegation – as if they'd split into two separate ministries, one working against the other. They were almost jumping at each other's throats before my very eyes. What kind of tchinovniks are they, upon my word!'

Kuzmentsoff, warmed by the slivovitz, chortled good-naturedly; a fine ruddy complexion radiated above his silver stubble.

'Tchinovniks, yes? But this is Asia, this is Siberia, this is the Ice! How much did you comprehend of that whole visit? The positions of tchinovniks, Venyedikt Filipovitch, like the positions of functionaries at court, are for the most part inherited. This doesn't mean to say they pass automatically according to bloodline; however, it is considerably harder for an outsider to obtain them: those who deal them out are themselves dependent on other tchinovniks. Yes? Whilst a man who's once taken his seat in the tchinovnik's chair is assured of success and prosperity to his dying day; unless, of course, he turns out to be an exceptional fool or the devil gets under his skin, but then nothing can be done about that.'

'You speak of corruption, Modest Pavlovitch, backhanders for unlawful privileges.'

'Not at all! Maybe that's how it is with the English – but look at it as a Russian. What decisions does a tchinovnik take upon himself, what choices does he witness in the name of the state and His Sovereign Majesty the Emperor with his pen and official stamp? Far more often, it befalls him to decide between possibilities, each equally valid and logical; whichever he should choose not, he will be within the law. He does not have to break it, and so everything depends on his inclination and pleasure. Yes? And the beneficiaries of such decisions know this perfectly well: he could have granted someone else's request, he granted ours. Will they forget him? No, they won't – other tchinovniks wouldn't be so well-disposed to them afterwards. And years later, when that tchinovnik retires from his position... Or even during his time of service, though not to him, but to his family, his friends, his relatives... All entirely legal: a position, a contract, business connections, joint investments... If not the beneficiary himself, then someone who owes him a favour. And all this accumulates, proliferates of its own accord, from generation to generation, since as I said, state positions and functions are for the most part inherited, yes? Thus, we have whole tchinovnik families, little empires of opulence, connections, privileges amassed over a century or more, and often webs of affinities too, since they marry amongst themselves. No one has any interest in overthrowing this constellation as long as every participant carries away a large profit, whereas a fellow knocking at the system from outside might as well bang his bare head against a marble wall.'

'So why this internal war within the Irkutsk delegation of Winter?'

'Because, you see, here, in the Land of the Gleissen, it's harder –'

'Ah! Those equally logical and equally valid choices –'

'Yes. It's clear they are –'

'Inevitable.'

'And the tchinovniks are –'

'Getting smaller.'

'Freezing.'

Worms of Summer, rotten vermin of a world melting between truth and falsehood. What remains for them to do in a world totally flooded with murch, a world ensnared in the Ice? There's as much tchinovnik power as there is Kotarbiński logic.

'All tchinovniks are Ottepyelniks at heart.' Utter it quietly.

'Well, maybe not Ottepyelniks, but you're right, there's no love lost between them and Winter.' Putting aside his empty glass, Kuzmentsoff reached for his snuffbox, scooped some snuff onto his long finger-nail, inhaled it into his hairy nostrils, and massaged his nose. 'And here is revealed the first cause of confusion. The Ministry of Winter was created to subdue the Ice, yes? To organise life in Winter. Piotr Rappacki was appointed head, a Stolypin-style democrat, whom they now take to be an Ottepyelnik, because he declared himself for the constitution. But then Sibirkhozheto was created to derive profits from the Ice, yes? The more gleissen sit on the deposits, the greater the income for Pobedonostseff. And as long as neither side has any real influence over the Ice, such contradictions prevent nothing; but I asked around people in the governor general's chancellery, and what should come to light? Mind you, these are mostly my own conjectures, since, obviously, they didn't tell me directly, but – this is exactly how it has frozen.

'And so, in mid-June, a letter arrives from His Imperial Exaltedness's Own Chancellery to Governor General Schultz-Zimovy with orders to prepare accommodation, people and resources to facilitate new scientific work in Irkutsk on the gleissen; the deadline is one month, detailed instructions and requirements are in the annex. Schultz passes on the order to the Geographical Society and the Imperial Academy, but he is curious, naturally, not to mention puzzled, that the Emperor of All the Russias is intervening on behalf of some scientist; there are plenty of engineers here, after all, at least fifty pre-Ice scientific institutions already standing in our city. Schultz writes to his informers at court. They reply that –'

'Nikola Tesla and his arsenal of Summer.'

'Exactly so. Now try to follow the reasoning of Governor Schultz: on his left he has the Ministry of Winter, on his right Sibirkhozheto, and above him the emperor, who has clearly declared outright war on the gleissen. Schultz cannot oppose the wishes of His Most Serene Majesty! Yes? Yes. But the destruction of the Ice and collapse of the entire industrial might of Siberia – this too he cannot allow. I know him, he is not a man to sit with arms folded and watch this gold-bearing kingdom revert to a land of convicts and deportees forsaken by God, tsar and people. So, he thought up, amongst other things, this tactic: to come to an understanding with the gleissen.'

Kuzmentsoff sneezed resoundingly, praised the Lord and wiped his nose.

'How shall you talk to a gleiss? You shan't. But here on his desk the governor has an arrest warrant for the heretic prestupnik and Martsynian, the Polish convict Filip Yeroslavsky, Father Frost, who – so it states in black and white – talks to gleissen. But where is this Father Frost? How to reach him?

'Have you understood?'

Sit up straight.

'You know the governor general, Modest Pavlovitch, yes? From the time he arrived here. You know as what – as what sort of man he has frozen. Tell me: is he a man of honour?'

The old lawyer lifted his chin, gazing from neath heavy eyelids.

'Yes.'

'Are you thinking of negotiating with him, Benedykt, sir?' Wojsław asked. 'Because if you try meeting him behind the backs of the tchinovniks of Winter, it won't be such a –'

'I don't know, that's not what I'm worried about.'

'What then?'

'Doctor Tesla. I'd completely forgotten about him. By now, he should have reached Irkutsk. With his machines, with everything. Schembuch's secretary mentioned that Schultz had already had the Cossacks sent somewhere.'

'To protect the doctor?'

'But from what Modest Pavlovitch says, it's clear for all to see, that Count Schultz-Zimovy is a Lyednyak of the first water, that is, of the first ice-floe, if not from heartfelt conviction, then from political calculation. Nothing would delight him more than if everything were to remain just as is it is – frozen. I am asking whether he is a man of honour, or – whether he'd be capable of hiring an agent and murderer to remove the threat before it even arrives in his city?'

Wielicki struck his breast till it rumbled.

'So that terrorist with the bomb – is this what you're saying? – is supposed to have blown up the train on Schultz's orders?'

'I am looking at the circumstances. The Lyednyaks had their agent there in the employ of the Okhrana. But he gave himself away already before departure. And immediately a second agent is sent. But why send a second, if you'd not learned of the compromising of the first? But who could have known of it? Who has such informers in the Okhrana? And did Schultz himself have to hire the man? It was enough for him to slip the information to the Lyednyaks. The devil knows whether that agent had any idea who he was working for. But also – and take note of this too – he attacked openly, and where? In Zima, on the borders of the Irkutsk Governorate. Coincidence, probably, the chance convergence of various circumstances. Thanks to this, however, he could rely on the jurisdiction of his paymaster; he would detonate his bomb, kill Tesla, destroy the machines, then calmly hand himself over and await the justice of Count Schultz.'

Kuzmentsoff shook his head.

'He's not that sort of man, not that sort of man.'

'Your word, Modest Pavlovitch, is as true as the cold.'

Proof of the governor's character: Wielicki vouches for Kuzmentsoff, who vouches for Schultz. A month ago, the very thought would have been laughable. But today, but here – the reasoning has the power of a mathematical equation, C equals B, B equals A, *ergo* C equals A: *He's not that sort of man.*

'... rightly so, because Schultz inevitably defends Lyednyak principles and must, must side with Pobedonostseff, yes? Just as no director of Sibirkhozheto can be an Ottepyelnik, so too the governor of the Land of the Gleissen cannot wish for the melting of the Ice. And here, young man, lies the second cause of confusion.' Kuzmentsoff sighed deeply, raising a wave of silver on his chin. With hands interlocked on the waistcoat over his belly, he assumed the pose of a careworn sage. 'For let us say you were to negotiate, through your father, some truce with the gleissen, some geographical pact: the Ice up to here and no farther; this much Winter, that much Summer; from here onwards Thaw.'

Avert the eyes. PETERSBURG – MOSCOW – KIEFF – CRIMEA –

'Let us say that everything went according to the governor general's plan,' lawyer Kuzmentsoff continued. 'What then happens? One, Spring in Europe. Yes? Two – oh, but two is an enormous question, the biggest: in this Spring, do only earth and nature unfreeze – or something more, in line with the ideas of Berdyaeff and his like? For if so, then a single comma, a single accent in this agreement of yours with the gleissen – and monarchies will collapse, revolutions erupt, states fall into ruin and wars stalk continents from Danzig to Vladivostock, from Königsberg to Odessa, from Kamtchatka to Peking. Yes? Yes?'

Cover the face with a hand.

'Wojsław Christoforovitch, be sure to keep an eye on him.'

'I'm used to watching my investments,' Wojsław laughed.

Peep at him between the fingers. Why did he suddenly consider it necessary to recall the four-hundred-rouble loan?

'What then is my advice to you?' Kuzmentsoff sighed heavily. 'You've already said yourself what you ought to do: leave as soon as possible. You have no passport, yes, but this is Siberia, here forgotten people lose themselves in the taiga in their hundreds. I don't wish to know the details; Gospodin Wielicki will no doubt explain what and how.

And don't travel back to the Vistula Land, for it's also Winter; sail to America, to the Antipodes perhaps.'

'No.'

Kuzmentsoff raised his bushy brow.

Remove the hand from the face.

'I shall defreeze my father, he'll be the one to escape.'

Mr Wielicki pressed his fist to his breast.

The old lawyer was highly dissatisfied, shaking his head still in the doorway. 'Well, why did he tell me, why…?'

Suppose that Wojsław too would resent it. But he was being silently consumed in the meantime by another matter.

'The venom of mistrust circulates within you, sir,' he said, hesitating in the hallway, his face already turned towards his bedroom. 'It's frozen into you once and for all.'

'Are you annoyed with me for casting a shadow on the governor?'

'You don't know him; it seemed logical, I would probably have thought the same. But,' Wojsław waved his hand above his head, catching the words that flew off his tongue, 'but it came to you so easily, so quickly, so naturally…'

'What exactly are you trying to say?'

Wielicki let the air out through his nose.

'You are a suspicious man, Benedykt. You do not trust people, you expect only evil from them, and most likely also from yourself.' He rubbed his great pawlike hands, rotated the diamond ring on his stubby finger. 'You need someone to deliver you from this evil.'

On old and new friends known and unknown

'Don't like the look of it,' muttered Tchingis Shtchekelnikoff, feeling for his bayonet. 'Put them oculars on. It's as dark as up Pobedonostseff's arse.'

Blackwickes were burning in all the windows, doorways and vents of the Physical Observatory of the Imperial Academy of Sciences building. In the night-time cloudscape of the city centre, narrow glintzen flashed only intermittently obscuring the intense darkness, as workmen and porters and what looked like a whole squad of soldiers as well as the flurried employees of the Observatory itself were crossing between the sources of unlight, bustling around the gateway and courtyard. Farther away from the street and square, beyond the reach of the unlight, a few onlookers had gathered; almost all passers-by stopped, however, and sleighs distinctly slowed down. Outside the main gate, on wide sled-runners, wrapped in rags and straw, covered in snow, lay the huge cylinders of the flow-generators. Amongst them stood the Cossacks, their Asiatic faces concealed by wide frostoglaze goggles, rifles in hands.

Seen through frostoglazes, the unlicht was less blinding. Walk between the sleigh and the Cossacks, amongst their blurry grey silhouettes. Colourless patches drifted out of shadow into shadow – until one of the patches sprang out, grabbed the arm, cried in amazement and withdrew.

'Gospodin Gierosławski!'

'Hush, Stepan, hush!'

The old okhrannik led the way through the main entrance of the Physical Observatory's new building. Here too Cossacks were stationed, smoking cigarettes and chewing shag. Unlicht was seeping through from outside and from under side-windows, but bright electric lamps were blazing inside, whilst in the constant battle between light and unlicht, like whirls of milky tar soup, more snatches of wall, ceiling, floor tiles, monumental coldiron pillars and mammoth furniture – now loomed, now sank back into greyness, into darkness, into underground gloom.

Unfasten the sheepskin, remove the shapka and spectacles. Breath hung in the frosty air. Nod to Stepan. In his case too, murch had got well and truly under his skin, no need to say anything out loud; he bowed his head and scurried into the gloom.

Cast the eyes around the great entrance-hall, muddied now and cluttered. A globe studded with coloured spangles hung from the ceiling. One wall of the Observatory foyer (first storey seven arshins high) was covered in a gigantic fresco depicting a Siberian landscape in summer, waves of white and green forest and an azure sky looking like an upturned lake.

Tchingis Shtchekelnikoff gave it one glance and coughed up noisily.

'Can't stand birch trees, especially in summer. So white – like them birds had shat all over 'em.'

'The aesthete extraordinaire.'

Walking the streets of Irkutsk, the ears of a European unaccustomed to the culture of the Empire will shrivel and die, so obscene and peppered with swearwords is the speech of the inhabitants of eastern Russia; and Shtchekelnikoff was no exception. A square-shaped fellow with square paws and a rectangular broken nose hanging above the square bone of his chin, his body crammed into an old soldier's blouse under a double-faced sheepskin, in knee-high felt boots trimmed with leather – all he possessed of the civilised man was that he was clean-shaven and spat not on carpets. When Mr Wielicki introduced him as a trusty and resourceful chap, yet with a valiant heart, who had played his part in the Dutchmen's early diamond expeditions, he seemed at once the image of some bloodthirsty killer who, thanks to his heinous deeds, had deservedly ended up in Siberia, banished from the Great Russian Heartland to beyond the Urals for the rest of his life. But he was a native Siberian, born allegedly in the Zheltuga Republic on the Chinese Amur. As to his crimes – committed or uncommitted, well, he had most likely inherited criminal blood. Marta Wielicka readily shared Tchingis's story. Thus it was that until the sixties and seventies of the previous century, attempts to settle Siberia with a Russian population had gone so slowly and arduously that the administrative authorities seized at various non-regulatory means of achieving this goal; amongst other measures, Governor Muravyoff-Amursky, notorious for his unconventional initiatives, devised an original method to improve the statistics for 'voluntary' resettlement by several thousand: he rounded up all villainesses and streetwalkers from across eastern Siberia, drafted in an identical number of convicts, liberated those men from the remainder of their sentences and then married the well-matched couples with his own hands and dispatched them to places of 'settlement'. Tchingis Shtchekelnikoff was the child of one such Amur marriage. Hard to say whether his father's worse character traits triumphed in him, or those of his mother. He never introduced himself with a patronymic. Never offered his hand. Never bowed. Never blinked (the saurian intensity of his stare was the most unnerving thing about him). He wore huge, bulging frostoglaze spectacles in ivory frames, and picked at his square fingernails with the long bayonet.

Mr Wielicki was highly perturbed by the letters that started arriving at Tsvetistaya number seventeen already on the day after the first visit to the Ministry of Winter. Not all were addressed to 'Gierosławski B.F.'; some were inscribed thus: *For the attention of the Son of Frost, Young Master of Winter, to be delivered into his own hands*, or, worse still: *For Him*. Also, certain personages, total strangers to Wojsław, came knocking on his door at odd times of day and interrogated his people. Someone hurled through a window a stone wrapped in a piece of paper that contained threats. Announce, in the light of this, the return to The Devil's Hand, so as not to endanger the Wielicki family. But neither Wojsław nor indeed Halina would hear a word of it.

Impossible that the crump in the Ministry of Winter would pass off without echoing throughout the City of Ice. Especially when, to all and sundry, the following truth had already frozen: the son of Batyushka Moroz is come to Irkutsk. That hurled stone also destroyed the magic protective shield until then separating the Wielicki household from the rest of the world. And suddenly, all the fears experienced in the Express returned: that every person in Irkutsk must be either a declared enemy or some cunning agent – that they'll hunt down, kill – shoot – plunge a knife under the ribs – as soon as a foot is set on the Irkutsk cobbles. Already on the first night, had they not in fact kidnapped in a coffin, not tried to bury alive in a grave? Just give them an opportunity – and they'll tear to shreds. Recall that febrile trembling of body and soul – prompted by the very idea of such threats, by fear, by the thought of future fear – back then in the days of cowardice.

Mr Wielicki, ever far-sighted, took on workers from his wholesale warehouse on overtime, three strapping toughs in crudely patched greatcoats, swathed in felt rags from top to toe, so that only the white-hued hemispheres of their goggles protruded, insect-like, from amidst the coils of material. Exuding black steam, they guarded the house from the backyard and from the street, from the river and from the side of the alley between the houses, day and night. Whenever the Wielicki family came out to board their sleigh, the toughs would bow to the masters and smile through their scarves at the children, hiding their great bonebreaker clubs shamefacedly behind their backs.

Whomever they scared away, they scared away; not everyone, however. Two days later, after dusk, a loud crash and clatter reverberated through the house on Tsvetistaya Street. The piece of paper scrawled with obscenities, wrapped around a lump of ice that broke a window on the first floor, turned out this time to be a page torn from *The Irkutsk News*. Grzegorz, the valet, brought it to Wojsław in the kitchen and showed it to him smoothed out. The article, accompanied by an indistinct copy of a photograph of Nikola Tesla standing proudly with hands locked on the needle-ends of lightning rods, in the bristling aureole of a million-volt discharge, was entitled: *Doctor of Thunder Arrives in Irkutsk!*, complete with fat exclamation mark, and yes, fancy underlining. Send a man to buy the latest newspapers. Tesla's arrival had been noted in all the dailies. *The Baikal Voice* had reproduced a different photograph of Tesla, above the caption *The Sorcerer in his Laboratory in Colorado Springs*, calmly sitting reading a book beneath white serpents of electrical discharges, thick as tree trunks and several arshins long; this made no small impression. Some journalists were speculating about miraculous machines for producing and treating coldiron, ordered from the inventor by Sibirkhozheto; others, however, had rightly intuited the hand of the emperor and more complex intentions. Browse through the press nervously. None of the hacks had sniffed out the precise details; most worrying, nevertheless, was the very fact that anyone should exist at all who would associate the name of Nikola Tesla with that of Benedykt Gierosławski. Who knew they travelled on the same Express? Had the leak come from the Ministry of Winter – one faction spreading rumours against the other? Or perhaps the Serb had himself let something slip, egged on by someone else. He is prone to such megalomaniac urges, has the nerve to create theatrical effects, as Mademoiselle Filipov might have said. Yet he can also be paranoically secretive and not poke his nose outside of his laboratories for weeks.

Question: as what kind of man will Nikola Tesla freeze – has Nikola Tesla frozen?

People change – until they cease to change.

But he; he sucks truth and falsehood out of himself every day before breakfast, by the bucketful, by the demijohn, into poods of black salt, into gallons of murch. Had he promised help? What of it – pumping himself to the limit, terrified by a vision of intellectual Frost, he is capable at one and the same time of both keeping and not keeping his word, at one and the same time of holding his tongue and turning traitor, of helping Ottepyelniks and helping Lyednyaks, of serving the tsar and serving Pobedonostseff, of simultaneously saving Father Frost and delivering him into the hands of Schultz, equally sincerely, intelligently and logically.

Hence the early-morning visit, at a time of day before the second teslectric ritual.

With his basilisk's eye, Shtchekelnikoff was sizing up the Cossacks puffing at their cigarettes by the coal basket against the opposite wall (he was capable of fixing his angry, unrelenting stare on a stranger for hours at a time) and failed to notice when, out of the depths of the foyer, from beneath a staircase arch, there emerged the tall figure of Nikola Tesla. Stepan was trying to keep up with the Serb's long strides, followed in turn by a second silver-haired four-eyes hot on his heels. Tesla shooed them away with a motion of his white-gloved hand and deftly avoided Tchingis. He was dressed in an elegant single-breasted suit with a black spread-collar fur coat thrown over his shoulders. Pomade glistened on the hair symmetrically combed either side of his central parting, flashing with glintzen and black sparks. In his wake he left a coaly afterimage, like a trail of astral projections extinguishing gradually in succession; the palest lingered still on the stairs, stepping slowly onto the tiled floor of the foyer and only raising their head, delighted, at the sight of the unexpected guest.

'Benedykt.'

'Doctor.'

He smiled broadly. Squeeze his hand.

'And so.'

'Yes.'

He peered closely with warm affection, leaning forward half-protectively.

'You've been ill.'

'I look bad.'

'Already better.'

'But.'

'Yes. And over your eyes.'

'Eyes?'

He touched a lower lid with his cottoned finger.

'The organ that absorbs rays of unlicht...'

'Ah!'

And so, he himself was now demurched, no doubt about it.

The square figure of Tchingis crept out from behind the doctor, spat and felt for the bayonet.

Tesla watched good-naturedly.

'And this man – who's he?' he asked, speaking still in German.

'Don't like the look of it,' Shtchekelnikoff repeated under his breath, casting a furtive glance at the bony Serb.

'What's wrong with him?' Tesla was curious.

'He's fine, fine. Just extremely mistrustful.'

'Uh?'

Scratch the chin under thick growth.

'The greatest mistruster and malcontent found this side of Baikal.'

'What do you need him for?'

'Bah! And whose idea was it, these blackwickes?'

Tesla was escorting with his eyes the next tin crate being carried in from the darkness of the street by a party of four breathless porters.

'Well yes. Both Stepan and this local officer they've sent us are terrified of spies and journalists; can you imagine – they'll photograph the emperor's machines and thus create a scandal or some political crisis.'

'We must talk in private.'

'I know.'

'The machines.'

'Mm-hmm. What "machines"?'

Ye-es, demurched to the level of childlike dissociation.

'Everything depends on the state in which they've survived.'

'Not bad. The majority.'

'How long will it take?'

Tesla adjusted the fur coat on his shoulders, shoved his handkerchief deeper into the pocket and then spun around on his heel to face Shtchekelnikoff, who was more than a head shorter than he.

'He's eavesdropping,' Tesla declared, astounded by the insolence of the rectangular cutthroat.

'They're all watching.' State it with a certain amusement. 'You see: Stepan and that other grey one there, they're waiting for you –'

'Mm-hmm, time, time, yes, today we're to start burning the well. In which case, I invite you to the New Arkadiya! Christine will be pleased.

And once I'm installed here – drop by as soon as possible. I'll show you... Besides... But good, good to see you, sir! Ah,' he leaped from one association to another, 'I will tell you what –'

'Today I'm booked for dinner, maybe tomorrow.'

'Tomorrow definitely!'

Burst into a laugh.

'Definitely.'

He held out his hand a second time.

'They ought not to see us together here,' he whispered seizing gloved hand with gloved hand.

'There's nought you can do, Doctor.' Sigh. 'It has frozen.'

He nodded.

Raise the cane.

'Shtchekelnikoff!'

Tchingis planted the frostoglazes on his nose.

'Saw you, Gospodin Yer-Gyer-Gierosławski, how he took fright? I know Gypsies, no good ever came from Gypsies. Count the money in yer pockets! See what an 'ardened gleissenik he be – an' he only just arrived. It's a dark business, I'm atellin' ya. Uh, may a gleiss fuck 'em.'

'Fucked by a gleiss, jaw bound in ice. He that asks the road, snuffs it in the cold. Frigid whore – guilty mother; hot whore – blames her father.' Similar sayings and street wisdom could always be relied upon from the mouth of Tchingis Shtchekelnikoff, served up in his rich unholy tongue. Marta Wielicka never admitted him above the ground floor; the stairs had to be descended from the Wielickis' apartment, whilst he waited in the lofty hall below. This was also where he was seen off. Without offering his hand, without nodding his head, without muttering a word, he would turn his back and thrust his great cubic fists into the pockets of his double-faced sheepskin. Discover him one morning, on descending to the lower kitchen, in the company of two of Wielicki's toughs – the troika sat at the table, grinding mugs of moonshine in their huge mitts and staring sullenly in front of them. The only difference being that the toughs had not shaved.

If truth be told, and the higher echelons of society and new arrivals from the Great Russian Heartland discounted, then almost no smooth-cheeked men were to be seen here: by shaving, a man destroys the natural lubrication of his skin, which then makes it easier for the frost to bite him. Look in the mirror. The beard had managed to regrow, though not yet to its Warsaw dimensions; the fringe too had grown back. Summon the valet to cut off the hairy mop and then remove the bristles. What has frozen, has frozen.

The scars on the cheeks were covered in new growth, only one was visible, the longest, running beneath the very eye. Press the skin.

From what had this stigma actually been acquired? From falling off the Express? From the iron leaves of the Underground World? From the icicle wielded by the Martsynian Yerofey? Look again in the mirror once the razor had done its thing – bare skull, black beard-growth disfiguring the facial features, the gaze of a consumptive from under black brows. Now, amongst the Ministry of Winter papers was an old photograph of father taken for the prison records when he arrived as a katorzhnik, dated autumn 1907: Filip Gierosławski, aged twenty-nine, Rasputinian beard, hair closely cropped in the convict style, dressed in crumpled jacket and old shirt. Throw off the clothes. Still more weight had been lost during the illness; it was possible now to count the ribs and finger the bones. Stand in profile, stand with the back to the mirror, looking over the shoulder. Thinking: it doesn't take much, the body is like a house of cards – one touch, one puff, and it falls to pieces. The Ice – whatever ill they say of it, offers some way out. Who can tell how a man's mind distorts after ten years of hard labour in forest work gangs and mining squads? Zeytsoff's epiphany was after all nothing unusual. All prophets and Gnostics hail from the desert, from the great secluded places. In the wildernesses of Palestine they see burning bushes and fiery angels; in Siberia – apostles of ice.

Don the last remaining suit (the excesses of the Transsib had cost at least half the wardrobe purchased with the Judas roubles). Mm-hmm, maybe it might be wiser to start calculating father's Ways of the Mammoths from the other end, that is, not from the frosty revelations but from the time of his katorga, from the early years of his exile and what brought him in those days to Martsyn, in what direction he was going, that he reached where he reached – and where he'll go next – and whereto runs the thin, broken line of his Way – so as to overtake him upon it and meet him there.

But a best suit was indispensable – various illustrious figures from Irkutsk society and finance were invited to the dinners given by Mr and Mrs Wielicki, bah, from government circles as well, Germes Danilovitch Futyakoff for instance, member of the city duma, who, it was predicted, was soon to replace Bolesław Szostakiewicz as mayor. Futyakoff always arrived an hour earlier; he and Wojsław would shut themselves in Wojsław's study, from which the councillor would emerge flushed and animated. 'Gospodin Futyakoff,' Wojsław let it be known in half-whispers leaning across the table, 'is a very honest thief.' He said it light-heartedly and with a smile; but enough time had been spent in the Land of the Gleissen for the importance of these words to be grasped like a shot. A equals B, B equals C, C equals D, *ergo* Germes Danilovitch Futyakoff is an honest thief. And next: Pierre Ivanovitch Schotcha, from a family connected to the Swabian Hohenzollerns via some Rumanian mésalliance, a young man of frail build and androgynous beauty nonchalantly consuming his food half a bite at a time. 'A notorious womaniser and morphine addict, a born idler' says Wojsław. And whom do we have here – why, whom? None other than Mr Porfiry Pocięgło, director of the Siberian Metallurgical and Mining Company Kossowski and Boulangier. 'A genius with a fiery heart.' Next: Bittan von Asenhoff, one of Irkutsk's old Croesuses, an industrialist from before the coldiron era, now so satiated with riches that he clutches for amusement at more and more different affairs and business interests; co-owner of brothels and organiser of infamous sleigh rides on the Angara. 'An unhappy victor.' Next. Andrey Jusche, a young banker, recently married to a niece of Rabbi Israel ben Kohen. 'A well-brought-up coward.' Mr Saturnin Grzywaczewski, deputy director of Krupp, a keen huntsman who rushes off into the taiga at any opportunity; his left arm's not fully functional – an encounter with a bear left him with a huge scar visible beneath his shirt cuff. 'A hardworking egoist.' Mr Jeż Wólka-Wólkiewicz, correspondent of the Saint Petersburg *Homeland* and *Illustrated Weekly*. 'An avowed Pilsudtchik, angry at the whole world. You should know that under a pseudonym, Jeż also edits *The Free Pole*.' Et cetera, et cetera; all of them fierce gleisseniks with murch lodged under their skin and sharp penumbra trailing over their faces, hair and apparel.

Reiterate in thought, every time the eyes travel the length of the table, Wojsław's characterisations as if they were labels assigning titles or inalienable distinctions to the guests. How can this be – exclaims the educated European, well-read in his Freuds and Bergsons – how can this be, since a man is not a measurable object, a lump of matter definable in terms of scales and qualities: that this one is such and such, but that one there – is like this, not otherwise, and the one over there – is exactly such. How can this be? Locking a man in words – bah! stating the truth about him in a couple of words – impossible! There are no cowards and there are no heroes, no noble and ignoble, no saints and sinners. A person's truth cannot be stated in any speech of men! And yet here, they say: a born idler – and this is the truth! An honest thief – the truth! A hardworking egoist – the truth! And when you try to lie – you will lie in total certainty of the lie.

Pass the tongue over the roof of the mouth, observing them secretly above the dinner plates, searching for that taste and sensation remembered from the train after a session in Tesla's wagon. So, does such a place truly exist – such a time – in the Ice, under the absolute power of the Frost, when alethemeters reach the extreme of their scale, when murch crystalises in the veins and teslectricity shoots from the fingertips in black lightning bolts – such a place, such a time, when language of the second kind becomes identical to language of the first kind and it is possible to express what is impossible to express?

Dream of nothing else from the time of the first dinner party other than to overhear, amid the convivial hubbub of the banquet, some word whispered by Mr Wielicki in the ear of another guest – a word about Benedykt Gierosławski.

'… *est-ce possible? C'est à peine croyable.*'

'*Nullement*, I succumbed to temptation and went there myself, he's one of those Chinese doctors. See these fingers, sir– I was unable to straighten them at all. *Alors*, you lie down on a hard mattress, not of the cleanest, mind, whilst the Chinaman inserts the tungetitum needles into your body. It's called the Art of Zhen-jiu. Shown to be particularly beneficial for rheumatism and age-related ailments. The doctor lights some kind of incense sticks, applies the burning embers to the needles, and a soothing coldness spreads through your muscles…'

'I've also heard of Chinese doctors preparing opium mixtures based on tungetitum,' said Pierre Schotcha. 'Maybe you've had occasion to try this too?'

'No, you know how it is, somehow it didn't happen.'

'So now you see, ladies, what's so extraordinary about black opium stupors – for a dreamslave needs nothing, rather the reverse: they pour herbal remedies into him to pull him back to the waking side – but black opium, ah!' The young man sank into reverie and, in his reverie, thrust a whole potato onto his fork and popped it into his mouth. 'Mmm, black opium, it acts quite differently.'

'You indulge?'

'As Mr Grzywaczewski so nicely put it, "somehow it didn't happen".'

'But you know someone who does?'

'And here's the next obstacle. I do, or rather I used to know two connoisseurs of oriental medicine who claimed that one way or another they'd come into possession of this powder. Naturally curious about its properties, I made them swear they'd give me an honest account at once of all their dreams and experiences, together: the pleasant and the unpleasant. But later it never came to a meeting: they both vanished without trace, swallowed by our frosty fog, mm-hmm.'

'It's all a prank of these Chinese gangs,' growled Germes Danilovitch. 'These triads, or whatever they call them. White Lotus! Doctor Sun's Children! The Society of Righteous and Harmonious Fists! Who gives them such names? They're a scourge on our lives, first this Chinaman then that Chinaman – there you have it, try telling one ant from another ant. And of course, they don't speak Russian. And we only learn things when some filth again sprawls out from them across the city, or we suddenly uncover firearms in their shops and houses.'

'You fear perhaps a Chinese revolution, gentlemen?' Editor Wólka-Wólkiewicz burst out laughing.

'Eh, my dear fellow, a Chinaman will never believe in any social-isms; they're too family-minded a people to give up property amassed over generations or place the wisdom of the crowd above the wisdom of their elders. Every year a hundred new industrial plants spring up in their empire, each worth a million yuan. I know what I'm talking about, I do business with them. You'll build many a mighty concern on Chinese cunning! Whereas they're resistant as a nation to high-flown ideas – they have only one idea: pragmatism. Have you read Confucius, sir? Some nations, like the Poles, if our hosts will excuse me, were able to live in freedom on the blessings of a land flowing in milk and honey, and for this reason have never learned the discipline and single-mind-edness necessary for great-power enterprises, whereas other nations, such as the Chinese, have had to organise themselves since their dawn into the vast work of regulating rivers, in order to survive at all, thus you have the Great Wall, thus you have an empire that's lasted four thousand years.'

'Maybe I'm mistaken,' said Andrey Jusche, 'or maybe not mistaken, and if not mistaken, then the situation is that the anti-Manchu revolu-tionary party is simply waiting for an opportunity to move against the emperor, and since there are no gleissen as yet in the south of China that's where the peasant uprisings are spreading, where Doctor Sun is rallying his troops, and since there is no Ice in Hong Kong, then –'

'You'll forgive me, sir,' groaned von Asenhoff, 'but my head is aching from all this; my brain swells and trickles down my nose whenever I hear about the Ice and History. All gammon, gentlemen, Martsynian gammon and spinach!'

'How could you, sir, really!' Mrs Grzywaczewska bridled, and cast a startled glance towards this end of the table.

Von Asenhoff banged on the tablecloth with his open palm.

'As if I cared! Just like in the house of a hanged man you don't mention gravitation? Mr Gierosławski will forgive me. And if he won't forgive me, then I don't wish to know him, for what for?' He laughed again. 'I wish to add a soupçon of cheekiness to this duck, *nota bene* exquisite duck, I kiss your hands, Halinka; a soupçon of cheek today. What do you say, honourable sir?'

'I think the same.' Answer whilst cutting Michasia's meat. 'That it's gammon.'

'Ay-ay-ay, but why d'you have to agree with me straightaway? You ought to be sulking, sir, out of delicacy for your offended feelings, hurling abuse at me, or at least slinging cutlery at the glassware and slamming the door. Oh!'

'In which case I should probably stay out of the city, and shut myself in my room like Pobedonostseff in his tower.'

'Hah and do you know, sir, why Pobedonostseff never ventures out into the light? Wait – it's a fresh rumour. Now, allegedly, he's so consumed by the French disease he can't bear the sight of his own image and –'

'Herr Bittan!' The infuriated Wielicki roared from the other end of the table.

'As I say,' continued von Asenhoff, 'the duck is exquisite, exquisite.'

It should be added that Bittan von Asenhoff had the appearance of a distinguished elderly gentleman of patrician charm, hair lightly sprinkled with silver snow, elegant suit of English wool, a monocle attached to his lapel and a diamond pin in his silk foulard. He came to the Wielickis' dinners alone, having been widowed still in the previous century.

The wife of Andrey Jusche was a bosom friend of Wojsław's wife; they gossiped uninterruptedly across the table, scarcely eating anything at all. No memory had been retained, incidently, of women in the Kingdom being so tightly squeezed into corsets as here in Irkutsk. They talked of love affairs, recently opened shops, love affairs, children, love affairs, migraines caused by the Black Auroras, love affairs, the price of ball-gown fabrics, love affairs, love affairs and love affairs. Gleisseniks are extremely amorous folk: this thought occurred, as Michasia's chair was pushed aside and the little girl ran to her father's knee. What is it about the concentration of murch that triggers in people affections of the heart? After all, this is a form of madness and provokes sudden change in a person's nature; it's not meant to happen here.

If, however, the opposite is true, if all the poets are wrong, the Romantics mistaken – and love is not in any way an exceptional state, but rather the natural basis of the truth about man, from which he merely departs, losing himself in a world betwixt 'yea' and 'nay'... A loving person is simpler and more truthful than a person who loves not. Complications and uncertainties increase together with the distancing from love. Zeytsoff would doubtless subscribe to this. It can be verified at least from the parish registers of marriages and baptisms in the governorate general. Madness is existence without feelings, disease is the absence of passion, perversion is the life left empty after love. Whoever loves, regains health. Feeling speaks in the language of dogmatic certainties; whilst out of dry reasoning, devoid of passion and desire, comes every kind of uncertainty, every kind of half-truth and half-falsity. See how Michasia nestles into Wojsław's waistcoat; as such the child will freeze in the child's truth; whilst you will find no soletruth in a child torn from its parent.

Move to a vacated chair on the right of Editor Wólka-Wólkiewicz.

'I heard you knew Filip Gierosławski, sir?'

Disconcerted, his first reflex was to bristle angrily.

'From whom did you hear it?'

'So, you did know him! Did you meet him here?'

He turned to face, propping his silver head on his arm thrust amongst the crockery and glasses.

'Dear boy, you trick an old man into reminiscing over wine, too cruel a game.' He chuckled hoarsely. 'First of all, it wasn't that... but, but, how much do you know in fact about his underground work?'

'Nothing.'

'Nothing? Nothing. Mm-hmm. Well, first of all, it wasn't that we came together as some kind of political brothers, foot soldiers of the same idea.'

He motioned to the servant-girl indicating his goblet; deftly avoiding the children outstretched on the carpet, who were tying a large decorative bow around the loudly mewling cat, she filled it to the brim with red-berry wine. Mr Wólka-Wólkiewicz took a prolonged slurp, heaved a sigh, and nodded to come closer still. Move up together with the chair. Jeż crossed one leg over the other, adjusted the bowtie beneath his prominent Adam's apple, puffed and blew.

'Ye-es. When I talk to young people nowadays, or when I have to expound something to them in a polemic in a newspaper column, I see how difficult it is to show them our past in all its movement, changeability, fluidity and indecisiveness. All the more so here, under the Ice, where everything seems so certain and everlasting. What a curse! How to explain that you were once someone different from whom you are now? How to speak honestly in the name of a man who exists not?'

'How to justify youthful mistakes.'

'No, that's the point, my boy, they weren't mistakes. You assume that in those days there were better solutions missed due to stupidity or flaws in character. But does the child reason like the adult reasons? Is it the child's mistake that he thinks like a child? Were they our mistakes because we thought as we thought?

'Take nineteen-oh-five. Earlier even, nineteen-oh-four, when the PPS began to break up on account of the first Japanese war. Now when you hear: "Piłsudski", you think: "terrorist", "fighter blowing up trains", "Japanese partisan", "Siberian warlord". But for many years, he was Poland's first socialist, an underground activist of the PPS, pursued by every tsarist police organisation for publishing *The Worker*, which agitated for proletarian revolution, and was incarcerated for it. Admittedly, not much was heard of him in those days. Or earlier still:

would he seriously have embarked on revolutionary activity at all, had he not been exiled to Sybir – as an innocent man – in that People's Will trial about the assassination of Tsar Aleksandr? Surely, he wouldn't have been a conspirator, had they not sentenced him in the first place to five years for a conspiracy that never was! Thus, by chance, falsehood comes true. Summer!'

'But what has this got to do with my pater?'

'Because with him it's no different! Perhaps you imagine he was a socialist out of inborn conviction? There are times when an idea enters people like a microbe transmitted in fluids, like common influenza – Piłsudski or Brzozowski, one source of ideas – there's no way to protect yourself from infection; the only question is how quickly you'll recover. And in those days, we were all suffering from socialism.'

Suddenly, he cast a nervous glance from over his goblet.

'And you, sir, beg pardon I ask point-blank, how stand you politically?'

'And I answer point-blank, that politically I sit on the fence.'

'Ah, so that's the fashion now in the Congress Kingdom!'

'No, sir. In the Congress Kingdom, there is Winter.'

He snorted.

'In the Congress Kingdom, there is Winter, but what do we have here? The Party of Sitting on the Fence has no glorious past in the history of Poland. Do you imagine, sir, that if you keep silent on political matters, it's not politics? It's also politics, except of the most foolish possible kind!' he growled, slightly annoyed. 'In my generation you'll not find so many naïve greenhorns. Filip Gierosławski was a hot-blooded man. Unable to sit still for long in any one place. All the less so on a fence, hah. Socialist ideas had probably evaporated from his head long before the first war with Japan. No, I didn't know him in those days. He told me a bit about it. It seems he never joined the PPS. But in nineteen-oh-five he clearly already favoured the "old guard"; the split ran along the division between proletarian revolution and national uprising. Piłsudski chose the Combat Organisation and fighting soldiers. Filip never confided to me many details of his activities; ex-katorzhniks who remain in exile tend to become very discreet in such matters, hah, names, places, dates, no, I won't give you any.'

'Nor am I asking for them.' The tomcat adorned in its bow rubbed against the trouser leg. Grab it by the back, lift it up. It wound itself into a ball on the lap, twisting so its belly was uppermost. Scratch it with the left hand, feeding tasty morsels from the table into its mouth with the right. It licked its lips in feline satisfaction and narrowed its eyes, not without suspicion: he's feeding me, fine, but maybe he'll stop feeding me, maybe he'll suddenly run amuck, who knows what a human is capable of. 'When they released him in nineteen seventeen –'

'Yes, I met him then at Wierczyński's. Wierczyński kept a house here in Irkutsk to help convicts.' Without averting his eyes, Jeż redirected his gaze to another place or rather another time: he stared into the past. 'Filip looked very haggard, very haggard indeed. After all, he's not a man of powerful build, and katorga always enfeebles people, they grow stunted, waste away. And I remember most of all how he took offence at the proposed donations, proffered out of pity. After ten years of hard labour, he still stood erect, held his head high, shook hands like a free man, spoke in a bright clear voice; dressed in rags, haggard in body, he bore himself like a nobleman. I remember it well, Benedykt, sir. Your father makes an impression on people, doesn't fade from the memory like any old familiar or unfamiliar. You met Filip Gierosławski and you knew whom you'd met. In this he was indeed like Piłsudski, if not the Dragon-Slayer.

'I thought to help Filip – most likely because he didn't want help. I asked him to write his story; would have paid him by the word. After all, I recognised the name, had read some of his things, he had a sharp pen, maybe not the lightest, but sharp, sharp.'

'And so, did he write it?'

Mr Wólka-Wólkiewicz screwed up his badgerlike face, emblazoned by the white brush of his moustache.

'He visited me in my editorial office. I was publishing at that time *The Siberian Pole*. He promised me ten pages entitled *How I Became a Revolutionary*; and perhaps he would have written more articles. But he became acquainted at once with these people and those people...' Jeż winced again.

'With whom? Pilsudtchiks? Martsynians perhaps?'

The old editor glanced away, hastily hiding his embarrassment behind angry irritation.

'I understand it all, sir, a son looking for his father, the separation of many years, a family tragedy et cetera, but when you start asking me about –'

'Names, places, dates.'

'Maybe when *dementia* dissects me in my old age – but by then, thank God, I will have at last forgotten those dangerous secrets.'

Now, this is the thought that sooner or later enters all their heads: the son of a conspirator wanted by the Empire, brought here at the instigation and expense of the Empire, yet not in shackles – to whom does he really owe his loyalty? It's of no great concern to the Polish coldiron industrialists and bourgeoisie, but men the likes of Wólka-Wólkiewicz are constantly on their guard.

'But surely you can point to people who knew my father in those days, who were not involved in any political, illegal doings; there must have been such people.'

'We-ell, of course. But how would I know them?'

'Where did he live? How did he support himself?'

'Agh, true!' Jeż cleared his throat, gargled with the fruit wine, again cleared his throat. 'Yes, he stayed briefly at Wierczyński's. Found lodgings in Irkutsk... But what on earth are you doing, sir, with that cat!'

'Ouch, the brute never stops guzzling. Found lodgings...?'

'With some shoemaker, I believe they'd been in the same work gang, the shoemaker got five years for smuggling or receiving stolen goods, wait a moment, such a coarse name – Kutzba? Hutzpa? Wutzba? Wutzba! Henryk Wutzba!'

Henryk Wutzba, shoemaker, nineteen seventeen.

Where in Irkutsk does this man have his shoemaker's workshop? Inquire of Tchingis Shtchekelnikoff when driving next day to the New Arkadiya. Tchingis knew not. He promised to make inquiries; the idea was to go straight there on the following morning.

The New Arkadiya, built on the site of the nineteenth-century Arkadiya, maintained its tradition as being the most expensive hotel in Irkutsk; Nikola Tesla was not accustomed to put up in others. His Imperial Majesty's Own Chancellery, or whoever was covering Tesla's expenses, had evidently not set any financial limits to such questions; maybe they dared not refuse him after the incidents in the Transsib. He was living in a six-room apartment on the top floor, the eighth. From the windows stretched a view over fogs, roofs and fogs. The rumbling of the Buryat drums could barely be heard. Room service had laid a table for four. As entry was made, the startled young ladies leaped to their feet: Christine and Jelena.

Stand stock still on the spot, half-paralysed.

Miss Muklanowicz blushed charmingly, lowering her eyes and pinching her lips. With reddened cheeks she smiles at her own memory, blushes at her own memory – and already the recollection of what was unrealised during the last night in the Transsib is more important than everything that was realised.

Mademoiselle Christine covered her mouth with the luxuriant cuff of her blouse. 'I shall go and fetch Nikola.'

Stand and stare. Jelena approached slowly, step by tiny step. Take her hand, raise it to the lips. She instinctively clenched it into a fist.

'Benedykt, sir.'

'You were meant –'

'But the trains –'

'... to the sanatorium –'

'... he blew them up –'

'True, so you're waiting.'

'Waiting.'

She smiled frankly. Kiss again the knuckles of her thin, slender fingers, one, two, three, four.

'You should at least have sent a note.'

'What for?'

'So I'd know!'

'And what would you have done?'

There's a rhythm to it – to this raillery, to the maidenly banter – a melody.

'You don't wish to set eyes on me now, do you.'

'Yet we're seeing each other. But! Let me look at you, sir.' Without releasing her hand, she turned away from the window. 'Must you cut your hair like that? With that beard as well – you look like a katorzhnik on the run. Is it just my impression, or have you grown even leaner?'

'I was ill.'

'Your leg?'

'No, the frost.' Assume a stern expression. 'Martsynians tried to bury me alive.'

'You don't say!' Half-embracing the waist, she pulled closer to the window, beyond which the greyness of the clouds dripped onto the snow-covered rooftops, and the whiteness of rooftops trickled down shadowy facades. 'Have you already spoken to him?' she asked in a softer tone, as her moist breath skimmed the cheek and neck.

'He walks now along the Ways of the Mammoths, speaks the ice tongues.'

'But you and Doctor Tesla –'

'Please don't tell –'

'Anyone, I know. Except that –'

'What?'

She breathed out words in strange haste. 'I've been wondering. Whether you'd thought of it. For a moment at least. Coldly. That is... For if not – if you really do talk to him and he with gleissen and they unfreeze History, how we imagined it –'

'Jelena, we've already –'

'I know he's your father and –'

'You want –'

'... is it *worth* unfreezing him?'

'You talk politics!'

'Fatherland, politics, History, but – what would you sacrifice? Remember Zeytsoff?' she whispered. 'Abraham and Isaac? So, you see, it's not whether the father is to sacrifice the son, but whether the son –'

'Whatever's come over you, Jelena?!'

She broke off.

'Nothing, nothing.'

Observe her carefully during supper. She had dressed her hair differently, tied back the raven locks into a Greek knot, which gave her an air of demurity. The velvet choker with its ruby had been replaced by the dense lace of a black *collarette*. She wore no lipstick. Beneath her fine, morbidly pale skin, faint blotches of murch were forming along the blue lines of her veins; under her eyelashes, pinpoints of glintzen shone like droplets of fresh snow. Before the mind's eye arose the scene on Old Zima Station, the moment when the devushka had overstepped the boundary. For as whom precisely had Jelena Muklanowicz frozen, this virtuoso of lies indistinguishable from truth? Saying something in French to Doctor Tesla, she mechanically moved the salt cellar to the edge of the table. Respond with an aggressive reorganisation of the battery of carafes. She watched, amazed. These be the games of Summer, bereft under the Ice of the least importance and sense.

Naturally, in freezing, she must have changed – from all possible Jelenas into the one true Jelena.

Bah, but was it needful for this to journey into the heart of Winter, to patiently imbibe murch? Travelling is a magical time, it's true; but every journey will end sometime.

'You've stopped biting your nails,' remarked Mademoiselle Christine, as the hand poured sour cream onto her plate.

Glance at the fingers all the quicker. Indeed, no onychophagia had been succumbed to for several weeks.

As both young women had been initiated into the secret business, the unconstrained conversation over coffee in the corner sitting room naturally turned to the plan to unfreeze father and remove him from Siberia.

'... and we were about to leave that out-of-the-way little town. In the usual course of events, we wouldn't have spent so much time there, but the opportunity was exceptional: a wounded gleiss, a killed gleiss – is this possible at all? I wanted at least to see what would happen to that toppled Ice.'

'And what?'

'Nothing, it went on freezing from place to place, but because Benedykt had hacked off a leg, struck it down from on high, the glacius simply made its way over the surface of the ground, across the railway tracks and then down, into the permafrost. Anyway. Next day I go there in the morning, and what sight greets me? A silent crowd standing both on the tracks and alongside the tracks, at the place where the platform goes into a freight junction and our wagon was waiting on a siding; they were standing everywhere around. A hundred people, probably more. What, Christine?'

'*En effet*, an uncanny panorama. For you have to imagine, Benedykt, sir, the complete picture: a pale sunrise, it's only just stopped snowing, white all around, the station ruins buried under snow, on the horizon a gleiss, two gleissen, and the people standing about, peasants, village women, old and young, all standing in total silence. It's so quiet that the snow crackles under your feet like crushed walnuts. And only cloudlets of steaming breath above the people, puff, puff, like dark shadows on the snow. Ah, what a *tableau!*'

'They wouldn't have let us go.' Tesla marvelled. 'Only when that local policeman ran for the priest, and the priest blessed the wagons and even went inside and recited prayers, did they withdraw.'

'At least in the city there's no danger of a crowd of superstitious peasants.'

'Compared to Pobednostseff and the whole Sibirkhozheto… I prefer peasants any day.' The doctor laughed joylessly. 'The Okhrana people even want to mount darkbulb searchlights around the Observatory, so that no one can shoot from a distance or throw a bomb through a window, or even approach without a large glintz.'

'Have you had such threats?'

'Hah!' Tesla leaped to his feet and disappeared behind the study door; he returned with a grey envelope. He took out a small slip of paper. 'You will see whether it's a threat.'

The Brotherhood of War against the Apocalypse invites Nikola Tesla to cooperate in the greatest work of humanity. Signed: Khavroff E.G. And underneath, a coat of arms or a kind of stylised emblem: a flower on a skull. We shall rise from the dead!

'Is there an address? What man is he, this Khavroff?'

'Of all these strange letters, this was the strangest,' sighed Mademoiselle Filipov, gazing absent-mindedly over her cup of hot chocolate at the white-hued city, at the cavalcades of sleigh-lamps submerged in fog. 'But we've also received letters of friendship from the local Socialist Revolutionaries and from some sect called to terrible self-mutilation. Show them to Stepan? They'd move us to the Cossack barracks, God knows where.'

'Various madcaps and shady individuals also write to me. Mine host has hired some toughs; also, I'm accompanied everywhere by this antithug. But there's no choice, is there, other than to do your own thing as soon as possible; unless you tuck your tail between your legs and run away. However, you have signed a contract. With the emperor!'

'Will you be leaving, Benedykt, on the first train to Kezhma? Together with Jelenka?'

'No, I don't think so.' Glance at Miss Muklanowicz, who had likewise averted her eyes towards the Irkutsk evening. 'The Ministry took my passport. The imperial tchinovniks are wrestling with Schultz as well as with Pobedonostseff. Hard to say what twist it'll all take. In the meantime, no one has a clue where to find Batyushka Moroz.'

Mademoiselle Christine put aside her cup and reached across the table proffering a solicitous handclasp.

'Benedykt, sir, what on earth will you do? how will you save him? how unfreeze him and get him out of Siberia?'

'If truth be told, these delays suit me. The doctor spoke of two months. But it has to be tested first, it's not been tried in any way yet, right?'

Tesla shook his head.

'That's what we're here for.'

'Which means,' Jelena drew her nails over her lower lip as if examining in her reverie the shape of her own mouth, 'which means how is Benedykt intending to put it into practice? Let's say they find him. Well, and delegate you to go to the place. But obviously not alone. But you, I understand, have to take with you the doctor's relevant machinery, which could consist of several bulky loads – how bulky?'

'The pump,' muttered Doctor Tesla, 'and the cables, and the engine for the pump, or batteries, or –'

'A crank – can't it be done with a crank? Like your dynamo generator?'

'Maybe it can. This also has to be tried and tested: what pressure of murch is necessary, at what rate it should be drawn from the human body, what physical dependence links murch to temperature, mm-hmm.' The old inventor produced a pen from his pocket and began to note something down on the back of the invitation from the Brotherhood of the War against the Apocalypse, lolling on the teak chair with his long legs stretched before him. 'Since for now we know a few limited *exempli*, but not the rule, all this lies ahead of me, that's what we're here for. I wrote the first textbook on electrical engineering and I shall write –'

'What?'

'The first textbook on black physics!'

The young women exchanged knowing glances; Christine raised her eyes to the ceiling. Stir the teaspoon in the coffee cup. Tesla stared for a long while into snowy space, then suddenly switched his gaze to Mademoiselle Filipov.

'I told you to do something with those earrings!' he growled peevishly.

Christine automatically pressed her palm to her ear, lowering her head so that her fair locks fell over half her face.

Miss Muklanowicz sucked air in with a hiss.

'Well, and so,' she resumed aloud, 'let it be with a small pump, a handheld one – but how to get it past the eyes of the Ministry of Winter? Benedykt, sir? How then will you demurch your father there on the spot? How smuggle him back? They won't let you! They'll arrest you!'

'I know.' Reply quietly. 'I have to think it through carefully.'

'You have no plan as yet, is that right?'

'Benedykt doesn't believe in the future at all.'

'Here, fortunately, it's easier to realise the most complex of strategies.'

'But first you have to devise them!' cried Tesla. 'First, you have to hit upon an unthought thought, create something out of nothing! You know how hard it is, *mon ami*. The most difficult of all!'

Avert not the eyes from the Serb's intense stare.

'Where?'

'Here,' he indicated the study.

'Now?'

He spread wide his arms.

'My machines are your machines,' he announced in English.

Stand up. Miss Muklanowicz groaned theatrically. Clear the throat, smooth down the overly loose waistcoat and jacket. Nikola Tesla hurried ahead.

In the study, he had the blinds drawn, electric lamps burning; he'd also lit the naphtha lamp on the broad walnut desk. In its soft light, his tall black-suited silhouette grew blurry at the edges like a warmed-up wax figurine. Only the long-fingered hands in their white gloves stood out like two dazzling blots, attracting the gaze like a conjurer's hands on stage; the eyes followed them involuntarily under the spotlights – as they seized the handle of a great wooden suitcase, as they heaved it onto the surface of the desk, as they unhooked the clasps and raised the lid, revealing the ceramic-steel-tungetitum bowels of the mechanism. Under the lid were coiled spirals of cable. Tesla unwound a few arshins and fitted it skilfully into the clamping-ring of an electric wall lamp, the only one that was not blazing, stripped of its globe and lightbulb. Having returned to the desk, he guided a second cable into a jar of grey crystals standing on the shelf above the lamp; the third cable he presented on his white palm: this was the one that ended in the firing pin and trigger.

'All right? Is it already working? All right?'

Tesla put his left hand inside the suitcase. It began to clang.

He smiled perversely.

'I have to bleed myself of murch here several times a day, otherwise I'd most likely get intellectual constipation. You know, after that accident, I installed safety valves, in order to –'

Catch hold of the coldiron.

... Jelena's voice.

'Like two alcoholics! For the love of God!'

Lean against the edge of the desk; the study lights pulsed overhead in a bewildering rhythm.

Breathing through the mouth, scrutinise Miss Muklanowicz.

'Well what?' she was angry. 'Now what's got into your head?' She stood in the doorway, arms akimbo.

Stumble, after taking the first step, onto the carpet; prop up the body in the kneeling position. Seize, still reeling, the young woman by the arm and drag her towards the desk. She was too taken aback to resist. Doctor Tesla raised his bushy eyebrows. Grab the cable by its insulation and hand the gleaming firing pin to Jelena. Still aghast – in mute terror, like an astonished spellbound child – she grabbed it in both hands.

Then she stood motionless, breathing slowly; only her eyeballs moved, following invisible sights. The crystals in the jar darkened at a rate imperceptible to humans – evidently, there's no means of measuring demurchment except unlicht phenomena or subjective impression. But since everyone here, in their own way, deviates from the teslectric norm in the other direction, how it is possible to tell which flickering glintz on the devushka's garments comes from the difference in potentials for better and which – for worse? Were a thermometer to be placed in the mouth of the person being demurched – or the conductivity of their skin measured locally...

Possibilities again drifted through the mind in swirling streams – it was impossible to keep pace with the frenzy of outlandish images.

Shake the head.

'You think this is wise?' Tesla muttered, wrenching some thingummy in the suitcase pump.

'No. Yes. The devil knows.' Bite the lip. 'Have to toss a coin.'

Mademoiselle Christine entered and uttered a piercing cry. Jelena shuddered and let go of the cable. Doctor Tesla turned off the machine.

Spring to the damsel's aid as she loses balance. But instead of trusting to the helpful shoulder, she wriggled free and fled to the window, clinging to the heavy fabric of the curtains.

'Cold-blooded cad!' she yelled, hurling some bibelot snatched from the etagere.

Duck to avoid it. The porcelain burst against the wall.

Bare the teeth and begin creeping up to the young lady on bended knees, crooking the arms at the elbow in a grotesque pantomime.

She flung the next object. Missed. And burst into a giggle.

Hop towards her on the left foot, hop on the right, and then take a running leap.

She squealed and hid behind the desk.

'Children, children!' cried Nikola Tesla, waving his long limbs above the unclosed suitcase. 'What are you up to!'

'When I catch you, I shall devourrrr you!'

'Catch and devour me!' she wrung her hands.

'When I catch you, I shall rrrreckon your virtue!'

'Reckon my virtue!' She frowned. 'What's that supposed to mean?'

Run around the furniture from the other side. She bounded behind the doctor – but became entangled in the unwound cable and fell flat on her face. She tried to stand up, saw she wouldn't manage it and instead grabbed, uttering a Red Indian war whoop, these legs as they came charging towards her – collapse like so on the carpet beside her, almost knocking over the jar of crystals gorged with teslectricity.

The devushka rolled onto her side. Catch her without difficulty, as the narrow skirt restricted her movements.

'So, what next, you won't escape me now.'

'Ay!'

'Not nice, not nice.'

'What's not nice? To creep up on me like this!' She blew out shadowy breath to confirm it.

'Almost a month in the city and she gives no sign. Very not nice!'

'But maybe I really didn't wish to set eyes on the young man.'

'Hah! Because the police are after you, they've found Jelena Muklanowicz and are hunting down the imposter; you, miss, will go into hiding and not to any Ice sanatorium.'

'That's right!' She pouted. 'I flash by in snowstorms and enter through back windows! Whoever has seen me and not handed me in, five years of Siberia!'

Press forehead against her forehead. The scent of jasmine drenched the nostrils.

'What is it you do all day?' inquire of her softly.

She sighed.

'I draw. I've even started painting. Ice landscapes – white and more white. I'm also trying my hand at portraits. We attend the Polish salons, visit Sobieszczański's mansion, go for walks in the Commissariat Garden.'

'Heart-throbs are throwing their coldiron fortunes at your feet.'

'Jealous!' she was delighted. 'Oh dear, now poor Benedykt will be following me every day in the fog –'

'Grrr!'

'And just so you know! Porfiry Pocięgło, for instance!'

'What?'

'He comes every day,' she whispered, 'brings fresh flowers, gifts for me and for Auntie, invites us to dinner, to dancing parties, skating, the opera.'

Is she lying or telling the truth?

Impossible to tell.

Burst into a joyful laugh and smack a kiss on her little nose.

'Perhaps we should order the staff to throw them out.' A leather court shoe belonging to Mademoiselle Christine landed right by Jelena's head. 'The frost will soon bring them to their senses. That machine of yours makes people do unseemly things.'

'It will pass,' said Doctor Tesla distractedly and lit a cigarette, after which he began talking to himself in an unknown language.

But sure enough – once stood on the pavement outside the hotel, pulling on the gloves and waving the cane at a passing sleigh, the pulse of the body and pulse of the thoughts calmed down after only three swigs of frosty air (minus thirty-eight according to the New Arkadiya's thermometer). Ye-es. Jelena Muklanowicz. Nikola Tesla. Father. Governor Schultz. His Imperial Exaltedness Nikolay the Second. Józef Piłsudski. Porfiry Pocięgło.

'Oblastnik. Harriman. America! Khhrrr.'

Sizing up the beefy doorman with his malevolent stare, Tchingis turned his head at the sound of the words, took a good look, frowning all the more; clearly, he had noticed a difference in the gleissenik penumbra, since he let out a burst of black steam through his nose and spat vigorously.

'It's all right, Shtchekelnikoff.' Cough out the words. 'Authority persecutes, women lie and enemies threaten. But alive!'

A sleigh drew up. The evening wind blowing off the Angara cast clouds of spiralling snow onto the street; they cut through the fog like Siberian djinns, like dancing ifrits of cold.

Tchingis Shtchekelnikoff pulled his Cossack papakha deeper over his eyes.

'Don't like the look of it.'

On the peculiar glory of the Atra Aurora

The press had been delivered from the Kingdom and from Galicia. Read before breakfast in *Time* newspaper an impassioned political polemic on the new autonomy laws recognised by Emperor Franz Ferdinand, as well as an extensive article on the great Iconoclastic Masses staged by Mr Stanisław Przybyszewski in the Cracow Meadow Park; the spectacles scandalise the public flocking in crowds and drive women to fainting fits and hysteria. In addition, in politics – things of the greatest importance to politicians. *The Sejm, Lwów. Deputy Ścielibogóski had lodged an interpellation demanding tighter controls on railway bookshops and their displays due to the unacceptable spread of pornography.*

Next, in *The Warsaw Courier*, they wrote in half-mocking, half-sensational tones about a certain August Fądzela, from near Zhitomir, a Magnet-Man who attracts any form of iron by virtue of some invisible power. Hammers and anvils stick to his torso. An indistinct drawing had even been inserted showing what looked like a sickle and a bunch of keys and the slug of a clothes iron hanging from above a man's belly button. Think: maybe this is fakery, maybe fakery and fairground trickery, yet maybe not, perhaps people exist in whom magnetic energy swells beyond measure, but over which they have no control themselves and for which neither they nor their parents deserve any credit. Perhaps therefore similar differences appear between people in other physical spheres, including in black physics, that is, on teslectrical scales. Some people come into the world preternaturally resistant to murch and dislodge it from their organism; others absorb it preternaturally easily. The temperature of their bodies is always a fraction of a degree lower (or higher). They freeze more easily (or indeed with greater difficulty). Without realising on what their otherness really depends, we nevertheless identify them, at least some of us do, according to some sixth sense or instinct shaped by our life experience, even by working in courtrooms like Prosecutor Pyotr Leontinovitch Razbyesoff.

'A messenger came with a letter for you. You asked for the sleigh?' Wojsław Wielicki inquired after reciting his pre-breakfast prayer.

'Yes, perhaps I'll learn something about my father.'

'Be careful,' advised Marta Wielicka. 'The Black Auroras are out.'

'Is that dangerous?'

Wojsław drew a sinusoidal wave in the air with his spoon.

'People react differently.'

'Tshlightishnight,' Maciuś smacked his lips.

'He who talks with his mouth full, prophecies ill.'

'It's light in the night!'

Walk across to the window and look out over the city and the Angara. The day was exceptionally gloomy, there was a dark aura, clouds had to be covering the whole sky. (The forecast from the Irkutsk meteorological station stated in *The News: Mainly cloudy, intermittent snowfall, winds moderate, conditions unchanged, settled.*) But look more closely – these were not clouds and the sun was shining brightly above the roofs and fog. From the northern horizon, across the firmament, waves of unlicht were swelling as they arranged themselves into vertical ridges in slow but rhythmic pleats and dilations. Press the fingers into the wrist. One, two, three, four, waiting for over a hundred heartbeats; in such lazy ebbs and flows, the Tchornoye Siyaniye was superimposed on itself in consistent amplitudes and extinguished in reversed phases. In moments of upcast wave, the ridges of unlicht became sufficiently clear for it to appear as if someone had suspended parallel blocks of graphite over the land, had placed there instead of clouds giant boulders of coal as high as mountains, each one geometrically hewn. Imagine it must be an illusion caused by the frostoglaze. Outside on the street, however, with the frostoglazes still in the hand, as the head was lifted towards the Auroras – their unlicht struck the eyes with dark-blinding intensity; almost lose the balance, fumbling around in search of support, as black tar streamed from under the eyelids.

Until Shtchekelnikoff offered his assistance into the sleigh.

'It's for this you have to wear them glazes! Ain't some clever-clogs told ya that? Fools of a feather flock together!'

Glance, having come to a junction – once sight had been restored – in the direction indicated by the lines of shadow, towards the north-west, and there, above the rainbow-coloured fog – catch sight of a second sun blazing radiantly above the City of Ice. As the sleigh turned onto Amurskaya Street, it was possible to look almost directly into that scalding fire, fulminating from on high in dazzling lightshows and cas-cades. The flame that had burst from the belly and through the pink hand during Princess Blutskaya's séance in the Express sprang to mind. Three more junctions – and see how the bonfire in the sky splits in two. It was the twin Byzantine cupolas of Christ the Saviour Sobor.

'Someun's following us,' muttered Tchingis Shtchekelnikoff.

'What?'

He glanced over his shoulder into the fog clogging the vista of the street wherein dozens of sleigh-lanterns flickered, pale and indistinct in daylight hours, as they drifted between the high aureoles of frostoglaze streetlamps that were never extinguished.

'Bin riding behind us since Tsvetistaya.' With his two-fingered mitt, Shtchekelnikoff pointed to some dot in the milky suspension.

'You mean you can tell those lights apart? remember which is which?'

'Cos what?'

The shoulders would have been shrugged had it not been for the heavy, overlarge fur coat (on loan from Wielicki in another of his attacks of uncompromising hospitality).

'Nothing. But what can we do about it? Hole up in some alley?'

Shtchekelnikoff shrugged his square shoulders without difficulty.

'I thought pr'aps the gentleman'ud prefer not to lead 'em to where the gentleman's a-driving.'

'For the love of God, we're going to a shoemaker's!'

'Nothing does all day but swings his hammer, gob fulla nails; mean sons of bitches them cobblers.'

This was a dubious addition to knowledge – the suspicions of a man who in his heart of hearts suspects everyone and everything.

The shoemaker's workshop under its signboard 'Wutzba's Made-to-Measure' was located in the basement of a proletarian tenement on one of the dark streets of the Pepelishtche district, close to the right-bank narrow-gauge railway connecting Irkutsk to Zimny Nikolayevsk known as the Marmeladobahn, because of the inhuman jams in its passenger carriages transporting workers to and from the coldmills, foundries and manufactories of the industrial town. Pepelishtche was situated at the intersection of some larger Ways of the Mammoths (echoes of the glashatays' drums could be heard everywhere) and was an area distinguished furthermore by but one feature, namely the low cost of real estate and tenant rents. That Wutzba was obliged to work in a room situated below ground was proof of penury verging on the suicidal.

Shtchekelnikoff entered first, kicking the snow off his boots outside the doorway. The stairs were covered in ice. Lean on the cane and bricks jutting out of the wall.

In the spacious workshop (it seemed to occupy the entire basement), apart from two stoves, four coal braziers were burning; the air was dark and bitter from the smoke. Even the smoke, however, was unable to kill the tell-tale smell of leather and boot-making glue. Cough once and twice. Tchingis pointed to two figures in aprons on the left side where naphtha lamps illuminated the cobblers' workplaces. The client's path was enclosed on both sides by piles of ancient footwear, worn out, taken apart, stripped down to the original components, as well as leather and felt as yet unworked, and also unfinished high Cossack boots, shoes in rare gargantuan sizes, ankle boots, knee boots and felt boots.

A silver-haired shoemaker rose from the lasts, wiped his hands on a rag, turned up the lamp flame and bowed briefly.

'At your lordships' service!'

'Henryk Wutzba?'

'Beg pardon?'

'You're Wutzba?' inquire of him in Polish, unfastening the fur coat. 'I'm after the owner, Henryk Wutzba.'

'Ah, fellow countrymen!'

'Countrymen-Polishmen, make nice shoesies for 'em!' A younger cobbler scanned his response, furiously whacking his shoemaker's last; he possessed handsome Gypsy features, unsuccessfully conceal-ing a harelip neath an abundant moustache. Glintzen swelled under his sleeves and cap cocked at an angle.

The silver-haired one kicked a stool in his direction and turned back with a broad smile.

'Should I take measurements?'

'Henryk Wutzba.'

'You're here on private business, gentlemen? Wutzba, may he rest in peace – it's already three, four years since he chanced to pass away.'

Cast a meaningful glance at Shtchekelnikoff; this much Polish he understood. Again, he shrugged his shoulders, saying nothing.

'His signboard's still here.'

'That's right. People get used to things. Once something's sunk in their heads, it's hard to bash it out.'

'But you knew this Wutzba? How did you take over the workshop?'

'From Meister Henryk's widow. I often used to help when he was behind with work, so –'

'Then maybe you remember a man who lived here on and off in nineteen seventeen. Filip Gierosławski. You've a room upstairs for lodgers?'

'Ah! Maybe I saw him once or twice.'

'Wutzba spoke to you of him?'

'A nobleman they say back from his katorga, yes?' The shoemaker blinked, massaging his forehead. 'So, it's him you're after, eh? I know nothing of what's become of him.'

'That's right!' cried the younger cobbler. 'What've fine gentlemen's doings got to do with us? Sit down, Meister. We have to make shoes!' He whacked his hammer in a rage. 'Shoes, shoes, shoes!'

'Hold your trap when I'm a-talking to customers!'

'You can hear they aren't come to order boots! The lord of the manor cares only for the lord of the manor, the lord of the manor tramples on the common people. For that he's got to have tough heavy boots – we'll rustle up armoured-plated soles for our honourable customers here, so they can trample on us all the more powerfully and comfortably. Sit down, Meister. To work! We have to make shoes!'

'You gone out of your mind with that hammer? Do your revolutionising inside your own brain, such revolution you can have – your bonce, your blood. Bozhe moy, and to think such dandiprats set about bashing other people's skulls into shape – all right, you'll hammer out a new people and new lords of the manor: square, triangular, semicircular, pinked edges, smooth corners and that's about it – people all shaped on a single last, everyone alike – and then you'll have your one-size-fits-all paradise!'

'And so that you know! Paradise! For no hammerer will have to jump to, so as to polish another hammerer's boots, and nor will any old shite in a hundred-rouble fur coat force a master craftsman to stand to attention, in case the gracious do-gooder deigns to throw him the last kopeck of his rotten charity! Here you have the one-size-fits-all political interest! For if not, then you, the master craftsman, will always find someone to kowtow to, who's been hammered into shape on a different better last, licking the floor at his feet.'

The shoemeister clasped his head in his hands.

'So that's the splinter shoved deep up your arse! Eating into your soul basted with guts: that there be superior folk on earth as you have to took up to. This is the nail of your revolution: hammer them into the soil, so they stand above you no more! This is what your revolution comes out of – out of shame! Out of ambitions brewed and fermented in the poison of your soul! Instead of you turning into lords of the manor and standing over the people, you fucking reduce all to your lowest low!'

'Horror, horror, horror!' cried the younger man and flung a half-made shoe as high as the smoke-stained vault. 'Turning into lords! But what difference does it make who stands over whom with his whip of bundled roubles, when there's still those as stand and those as kneel! Bah, were it only possible for them ambitions to be realised...! This is why left-o-lution is necessary, for even if you sewed a million shoes, you'd never crawl out of this dark hole, or sewed even a million million, they'd never let you into their salons as a result. Right-o-lution props up the government! Born a cobbler, die a cobbler. It has frozen!'

'Excuse me.' Interrupt him. 'Perhaps you can tell me at least, my good man, where I might find this widow of Wutzba?'

'She's a cook in the Jewish inn at Olkhon Station,' the meister flung out, turning back at once to the journeyman. 'A million shoes! And you've got your eye on salons where they admit you for sewing shoes? All right, so have it!' He kicked one and then a second and a third boot-carcase. 'Wa-la! We'll set up our own cobblers' salons right away! Bring on the cobblers' whores, pour out the cobbler's vodka, proclaim the one-size-fits-all cobblers' paradise. There'll be equality, brutality and squalidity!'

Rush out hurriedly onto the street, slithering up the stairs; echoes of the shoemaker's blind fury failed to reach beyond the basement. Breathe clean, frosty air into the lungs. Still slightly dazed, exchange glances with Tchingis.

'What got into them?'

He shrugged his shoulders.

'The auroras.'

Drive to Tesla's, to the Physical Observatory of the Imperial Academy of Sciences.

A heavy cloud of unlicht covered half the district – unlichted houses, unlichted ice and snows, unlichted street with few pedestrians, in rainbow-tinted spectacles, glintzen shimmering behind their backs like angel-wings; gendarmes, likewise unlichted, concealed in one or other gateway. Pull up before the main entrance, prompting from the sleigh a long bright flare pierced from its sides to the inside by further of shafts unlicht. Not blackwickes, not black torches, but real unlicht bonfires and search-beams must have been set ablaze around the Observatory.

The guard had evidently been instructed to admit Gospodin Gierosławski with no questions asked. Tchingis Shtchekelnikoff remained in the monumental entrance hall neath the globe and frescoes of Summer; having rolled a cigarette, he scowled askance now at the janitor, now at the guards, now at the sunlit landscapes spread over the bright limewashed wall.

Doctor Tesla had occupied some of the Observatory's storerooms (adapted as laboratories) as well as the cellars of the edifice's north wing. 'The fact is they have no proper cellars here,' he was saying, as he strode briskly down a side corridor, buttoned to the neck in his working overcoat; the rap of his heavy stick thermometer, resounding on the parquet floor with his every other step, bounced off the high ceiling. 'The whole Observatory was built, or rebuilt, only a few years ago; they erected everything on the permafrost, on a coldiron skeleton, without creating any deeper foundations. Instead in this other part of the building, the old brick cellars still remain from the former that was razed to the ground.'

He pushed open a door. A moustachioed Cossack armed with sabre and Nagant revolver was dozing on a stool in a corner of the antechamber. Tesla gave him a friendly nod and opened a second door. A stone staircase led below into darkness black as ink.

'Bloody hell,' Tesla cursed in English, 'the current's snuffed it again. We can't rely on the electricity here, that's the biggest problem.'

'Do you think it's because of the Auroras?'

'Something kept breaking down before too. Mind your head, this was built for Lilliputians.'

Having lit a second naphtha lamp from the Cossack's lamp, he took a step down.

'Things have been breaking down for them here since the beginning, that is, since nineteen ten. Immediately after our arrival, I visited the local electricity station. The usable transmission range of the alternating current is little greater at times than the range of the direct current. Black despair, my friend. If for no other, this is sufficient reason in itself for a showdown with the Ice.'

Count the steps. The staircase was spiral. Forty-seven, forty-eight. Step down onto the uneven floor of a dungeon. Dungeon – for there was no other way to conceive of these basements. Unplastered brick walls, low vaults supported by chipped arches between pillars, and amongst the pillars – charcoal braziers. Naphtha lamps hang on hooks driven into the bricks, their soft cinnamon-coloured light making the interior seem even more ruined and antique, in short ancient. Only the rats and chained shackles were missing. And the human bones.

Instead, the rhythmic echo of a diabolical racket could be heard coming from the depths of the dark casemates.

'Khmm, at least there's plenty of surface space.'

The other extremity of the dungeons could not be seen. Tesla set down the lamp on a crate by the staircase and began moving along a bunch of cables falling from the ceiling of the stairwell onto the floor covered in crushed rubble, sand and sawdust.

'These are also no good?'

'We've connected them to the Observatory generator. I have to take the current for my flow-generators from there. Otherwise, it'll probably mean switching to steam-powered engines. Or...'

From the naphtha semi-gloom emerged the muscular figures of workmen, first one, then a second, then a third – five of them stood leaning over a wooden construction sunk into the ground; farther away loomed the cetacean bulks of two flow-generators and other cold-iron machines belonging to Doctor Tesla; cables branched out in all directions, separated into clusters on a wooden framework cobbled to-gether from rough boards; from the ceiling, meanwhile, and around the pillars, lamps with concave steel mirrors hung on iron brackets and ferrules. Behind a small improvised table deeper within, on a barrel covered in folded blankets, sat Mademoiselle Filipov in an unhooked sheepskin and woollen scarf wrapped around her neck, leafing through some kind of mathematical atlas, into which a silver-haired elderly gen-tleman in lenticular lenses peered over her shoulder, chewing on a blue pencil with what remained of his teeth.

The rhythmic clatter, metallic clanging and muffled shouts of the workmen as they counted up to three reverberated all around – at the count of three they let go the ropes and winches in order at the count of one to pull and wind all over again. A fifth worker stood beside a bucket suspended on a smaller compound pulley.

Step closer. The wooden construction encircled a pit dug out of the cellar floor; in the gloom behind the flow-generators towered slag heaps of excavated material. Peer inside the trench. Five, six arshins below the surface, two men stripped to their shirts were at work, jabbing at the permafrost with a coldiron spike, with which the massive rammer raised and lowered by the four Siberian Herculeses was armed. The uneven walls of the pit, hollowed out roughly into a ring shape, glis-tened in the milky-blue naphtha glow.

Nikola Tesla walked over to Christine, checked something in the documents. Cinnamon-hued glintzen were moving over the folds of his greatcoat exceptionally energetically. No doubt here, in the Observatory, he demurches himself at will.

Kiss the ink-smeared hand of Mademoiselle Filipov. She introduced the silver-haired gentleman. 'Professor Kliment Rufinovitch Yurkat.' Press the frail hand. The professor smiled shyly. He was an old gleissenik; murch had discoloured his skin like fluid internal bruises.

'I had thought, Doctor, that you'd begin experiments straightaway on gleissen.' Address Tesla in German. 'And on people.'

Tesla thrust the stick thermometer into the ground, pulled off his white gloves and began to rub his skin with a greasy ointment from an aluminium tin.

'That too. Patience, young man. We've only just begun organising ourselves in the storerooms upstairs. The governor is to send me some condemned hiberniks. The prospect of such experiments fills me with no great enthusiasm. I'd rather –'

'On yourself, yes. They write today in the papers that the Cold Line will be up and running again in six weeks.'

'Total solutions are always better than partial solutions; general laws – better than laws of exceptions. You get to know the fundamental patterns, and from these you easily deduce detailed specifications.' Pulling on his gloves again, he drew near the pit. A kibble-full of fresh rubble had just been extracted. Doctor Tesla rummaged in it with his stick and only then allowed the worker to dump the output on the slag pile. 'They gave me several places to choose from, several buildings. Why do you think, sir, I decided on this?'

Sometimes it seemed that murch flowed between people here in their very words, so obvious was the answer once the question had been posed.

'A Way of the Mammoths runs here.'

'Right beneath our feet.' He rapped on the floor with the stick. 'A duct of the third magnitude according to the estimate of Pobedonostseff's geocryologists. Every step we check the temperature, the geological composition, the colour of the ice and pressure of the teslectric flow. We shall dig until we reach it. And then –'

'You'll connect the murch pump directly do the Ways of the Mammoths.'

He moved his head, indicating neither 'yes' nor 'no'.

'Here, more possibilities are opening up. For the time being, I prefer not to decide.'

The diggers changed shift; a fresh twosome jumped into the pit to replace the tired workmen. Having scrambled to the surface, these two seized their bottles and gulped massive swigs. The sweat from their drenched shirts turned to steam.

'Aren't they freezing down there?'

'These are phenomena of the Siberian ice. Ask the professor, it's his field. Kliment Rufinovitch? What's the temperature?'

'Four point seven, it stays constant.' The old man thrust his notebook under his arm, wiped his spectacles with his sleeve and pointed with the chewed pencil to a folded ladder against the pit wall. 'I'm going down to take a measurement; we shall see if anything has changed. What said Pavel Pavlovitch?' he asked Tesla.

'Nothing doing, he's afraid everything will collapse on his head.'

Glance at him inquiringly.

'We were thinking of speeding up the work by using small explosive charges on the rock strata,' sighed Nikola Tesla. 'The professor says he employed this method in Yakutsk.'

'Though not underneath a standing building,' admitted the professor.

'Wouldn't it be wiser to melt the ground?'

Kliment Rufinovitch smiled under his moustache.

'Well, that's the surest means of bringing the whole edifice crashing down on your head. Easier to control the power of an explosion stage by stage than a fire inside the earth. But that's beside the question. You see this ice?'

'Which ice?'

The silver-haired professor stood by the compound pulley and pointed to the opposite wall of the pit, some four arshins below the surface.

'See how in this cross-section, veins and columns and whole walls of ice run through the soil? How its colour changes? How under the sand and gravel we have these slanting strands of shales, and there again a milky-white vein, which shines so brightly – that's flowery ice crystal.'

He tramped over to the waste heap and returned with a sizeable lump of ice-infested clay. He showed it: on the straight side, itself seemingly hewn from a geometric mould, starlets of crystal, sparkling buds of ice had formed into a mosaic.

'There is ice and ice. Do you imagine, sir, that we are dealing here with frozen water? I could show you places where water bursts out of the glaciated earth in geysers at minus sixty degrees. Or again, when you dig foundations through the permafrost, you wait for the helocrene to freeze and forge only ice. New watercourses are created in the earth, new ice barriers that redirect the water runoff. The ice itself boards the walls. Same here: at four degrees, anything may suffice to open a new sluice-gate to the water and we'd have a genuine well – flooded to freezing point. We'd have to forge again from the beginning.'

'At four degrees?'

'Hah!' Kliment Rufinovitch was fired up. 'In the thirties of the past century, the Russo-American Company commissioned research in Yakutsk into the depth of the permafrost. The merchant Shergin began to dig a shaft in the courtyard of his house; he proceeded as we have done, checking the strata and measuring the temperature. After he'd dug down ten or so arshins, the Company stopped giving him money because there'd been no change: four degrees below zero and four degrees below zero. But Shergin was bent on it and paid out of his own pocket; the deeper he went, the more expensive it got. Forty, fifty arshins. Sixty. Seventy. Constantly four degrees. The poor fellow was ruined and still had not reached anything.'

'How deep did he go?'

'One hundred and seventy-three arshins. And all the time four degrees below zero. Anyone who visits Yakutsk can go and take a look at that pit.' The professor held up a chip of ice to the light. 'You see, this is a veritable philosopher's stone, a solid mystery. In any place on earth, at any depth, irrespective of the surface temperature – four degrees below zero. Workers in the Sibirkhozheto mines really live in the underground galleries, because even in the severest frosts the temperature there never alters at all: four and four.'

'Mm-hmm, and on the Ways of the Mammoths?'

'That's just it! That's the challenge! To get a glimpse of a gleiss under the earth, that is measure it in cross-section, moving along a Way, before it freezes out onto the surface as black ice – to examine it earlier, underground, under the earth, surrounded by granites, sandstones and quartzes, spanning temperature gradients not in air but in shales, clays, limestones!

'Everything is recorded in the permafrost. What do we know of it apart from the fact that it's been here for millions of years? Maybe gleissen once stalked the earth and the permafrost is all that now remains of them – an underground, million-year-old icecradle. Or maybe the permafrost is in itself neutral physical phenomenon, a dead medium, which only when struck by a suitable material, with suitable force – as in nineteen-oh-eight – begins to resonate and surge; waves rise up out of it like waves on the sea – and so gleissen "are born"...?'

Mademoiselle Filipov rolled up the documents and whispering something in the ear of the stooping Tesla, hurried towards the exit with the rolls under her arm.

The professor called to the workmen. They stopped their hammering and grabbed hold of the ladder. Puffing and blowing, he descended into the depths of the pit.

'An original. Has he been "hunting" gleissen for long?'

'From the very beginning,' said Nikola Tesla. 'But why so gloomy? It seems I shall have to thoroughly demurch you again in order to resurrect your smile.' He seized the arm and pulled it a distance of two pillars farther. 'I have not forgotten, Benedykt, about your father. You have set your mind on the one method, and maybe it will actually come to this, that we dispatch you into Siberia with a murch pump adapted for field use in the hope you can smuggle it past the eye of the Ministry of Winter and apply it somehow to your father by stealth. But it's not a path with much prospect of success, you have to admit. Fear not, I shall keep going in this direction as well; please drop by in a few days' time, once we've set to work in the laboratory upstairs. In the meantime, permit me to cast around for other solutions. Please trust me. This,' he pointed with the stick to the pit, 'I wanted to show you, because should it be totally successful... then no artillery, no weaponry at all may be necessary against the gleissen, nor will we have to separately defreeze Father Frost. Give me time, sir, to test certain hypotheses. Tomorrow I'm travelling to Baikal, where, so I have heard, certain biologists are making bore-holes in the ice core to a depth of fifty or so arshins; they say it's possible to see the roots of the Olkhon icecradle in the ice of the lake. Professor Yurkat says that in the Technological Institute in Tomsk, German scientists are measuring the mushiness and distribution of the permafrost according to changes in electrical resistance, using vertical soundings; I've rustled up a teslectrometer with salt battery and –'

'An icecradle on Olkhon Island?'

'Yes. You –'

'So could I –'

'Ah! With great pleasure!'

'Tomorrow –'

'First thing in the morning.'

Professor Yurkat extricated himself from the trench. 'Ooph!' He took out his notebook, licked his pencil. 'Four point seven, spot on.'

On the way back to the stairs, however, Doctor Tesla stopped every few paces, swinging the stick thermometer from above his head and driving it into the hard ground, and then interpreting after a lengthy pause the readings on the horizontal dial.

'Everyone keeps telling me to be on my guard,' he said in answer to a question. 'In case some glacius should suddenly freeze up out of the ground here before the staircase –'

'A fatal trap.'

'C'est la vie sur les Routes des Mammoths.'

Drive next to supper in the restaurant of the Hotel Warszawski, where an appointment time had been made with Porfiry Pocięgło; to the invitation sent yesterday, he had briefly replied stating the place and hour. It proved, however, to be a waste of time.

The restaurant was not situated, of course, on the ground floor. From the high-storey location, through double frostoglaze panels, a hazy boulevard as well as the colonnade of the city baths were visible looming out of the fog. A gleiss hung between the already extinguished chimneys of a neighbouring building. Fine snow was falling, whilst the whole image of the city, a fusion of alternating colours, further softened by the lighted candles adorning the tables, seemed to resemble a moving illustration to a Hans Christian Andersen fairy tale. Sit down at the reserved table. The elderly waiter, a grey-bearded Greek dressed in tails, came hurrying with the wine list; he served up an envelope on a platter. Extract the familiar visiting card belonging to Porfiry Pocięgło. *Please forgive me, a sudden change in circumstances, let's move the business to tomorrow*; he had scribbled the words on the verso. But tomorrow is the trip to Lake Baikal! Order, out of spite, three hearty courses and a bottle of Californian Zinfandel, Sonoma Valley 1919, straight from San Francisco via Vladivostock. Think, breaking a lump of bread, of father, who in nineteen nineteen was already walking the Ways of the Mammoths. Well, all right, so he gets his pardon, but the verdict of permanent settlement precludes his return to Europe – yet why should he go back north, amongst gleissen? Did he genuinely believe in that mystical mumbo-jumbo of Martsyn? Judging from Wólka-Wólkiewicz's account, father had fallen more into political company at that time; besides, hadn't his katorga cured him of even a little of politics?

Barely had the Neapolitan soup been negotiated, when it grew dark in the restaurant as of a December twilight. A rustle passed through the room; one or two guests shouted vociferously for blackwickes. Glance out over the city. In the sky, the Tchornoye Siyaniye was growing blacker from east to west – now it no longer consisted of flickering glimmers of unlicht, of streaks of dark colour, but patches of monolithic darkness, like holes in the firmament out of which gushed liquid coal. Tungetitum jewellery shone increasingly intensely. On the exposed coldiron elements of buildings, vehicles, lampposts, on the coldiron and tungetitum advertising boards of department stores, banks and insurance companies, long rainbow-like braids were splitting off, infiltrating the fog and colouring it peacock-blue and coral-red. Even the penumbras of gleisseniks dining in the Hotel Warszawski swelled unhealthily. The waiters went along the windows, placing rows of blackwickes on the sills. Having drawn the heavy drapes, they lit the blackwickes. Glintzen from their veiled unlicht illuminated the room. It was hard to comprehend the laws of black physics. Would it not have sufficed to cut off the unlicht itself coming from the Auroras? How does one lot of unlicht differ from another? Is it true that unlicht waves, unlike light waves, do not amplify or extinguish, but – *force out each other*? Though in fact, they are not waves at all, not here, not in the Land of the Ice. The first question of black physics comes back: can emptiness, lack – the lack of light – in other words what exists not, affect that which exists? Can non-being oust being? The red wine, kindled by a dazzling glintz, was painting the tablecloth and plates in raspberry watercolour. Raise the glass before the eyes. A gentleman with grizzled hair dressed in an out-moded nineteenth-century double-breasted suit, frostoglaze monocle in eye, was approaching from a table three windows away, nervously crushing a white serviette in his fingers. Oho! Did Shtchekelnikoff now have to be taken to restaurants as well? Clasp discreetly the steak knife.

'Mr Gierosławski?'

'Do we know one another?'

'No. But – may I?'

'I am expecting someone.'

'My apologies, sir.' An ashen penumbra undulated around about him like smoke around a flame. His white-hued eye stared through the monocle with wild rapacity. 'No mistaking the likeness – you, sir, are that son of his.'

'You knew Filip Gierosławski?'

'If you'll allow me, sir – Ignacy Chruściński.'

Stand up, squeeze his hand.

'Benedykt Gierosławski.'

'I remain in your father's debt. When you have time,' he took out a visiting card – 'please get in touch. At the moment I'm with a client.' He glanced over his shoulder.

Chruściński & Sons, Spiritus Vodka Stores, Tumanny Prospekt 2.

'And so, you suddenly – recognised me?'

'You see, sir,' he took in the glintz-filled room with a sweep of his hand and serviette, 'such strange things are now afoot.' He bowed his head. 'In the meantime, please beware of Piłsudski.'

'I beg your pardon...?'

'He's coming for you.'

Put away his card together with Pocięgło's.

Such strange things are now afoot. Now – this means under the Auroras? Outside the Warszawski, the street had been transformed into a tunnel of unlicht, in which thick fog billowed in greyish surges, and sleigh lamps and street lanterns flickered feebly within the fog. Blackwickes were burning behind all the windowpanes on either side of the street. In the sky over Irkutsk hung a great mountain of onyx. Even a glashatay's drum behind the edifice of the baths was beating faster than usual.

Board a sleigh, snuggle under the skins. Frost stung the cheeks flushed with alcohol.

'Why are they burning blackwickes, eh?'

'Gospodin Gierosławski, don't look,' growled Tchingis Shtchekelnikoff.

'What?'

'Gospodin Gierosławski, get them bleedin' glazes on. It ain't healthy like that.'

'But why blackwickes?'

'You ever seen them shadows from the Black Auroras?'

Raise a gloved hand above the knees. A pale glintz was cast onto the uneven folds of sheepskin. At first it merely trembled at the edges, twisting to no particular rhythm and swelling outwardly, like any normal glintz. But a few frosty exhalations passed – and disturbing meanings grew discernible in its shape and metamorphoses of its shape, a suspicious correspondence between the image and the thought. And this profile of a face – whose was it? – already it was sensed, already it was known. And that cloven bush of thunderbolts. And that rectangular banknote. The revolver. Again, the face.

'Dreamslaves say this is how it begins.'

'What?'

'Necessity.' He grabbed hold of the hand and brutally pulled it down, quenching the glintz. 'Meaning, the motherfuckin' truth.'

Drive through the City of Ice immersed in fog and unnatural darknesses, under the afternoon Sun, under the meteorological phenomenon of murch. Even the gleissen were the colour of ash (in the frostoglazes, colour trickled off them into the snow and steamed into the sky). Turn to look at the Sibirkhozheto Tower. Its pinnacle, the uppermost storey housing Pobedonostseff's apartments, was completely invisible, swallowed by the Tchornoye Siyaniye. The Kingdom of Darkness. Returning images from the dream sent shivers down the spine: the sky of the Underground World transformed into its negative, the negative Sun with its crooked rays, the reversed light and shadow, radiance and gloom, day and night, life and death, being and non-being. The dead freezing their bones full of holes by the unlicht of black fires.

But of course – today's remembrance of the remembrance of the dream has as much in common with truth as next year's horoscope.

Depart the following morning from the Muravyoff Railway Station with Doctor Tesla, Stepan and Tchingis. The train to Baikal followed the route of the Trans-Siberian Magistral, as from the time the lake froze over, the Transsib no longer crosses it by ferry to Mysovaya but on tracks laid on the ice. For the same reason, settlements near to where the Angara river flows out of Baikal had lost importance – Listvyanka, Grubaya Guba and Port Baikal, which was no longer a port. Whilst the Circum-Baikal Line (the costliest stretch of railway in the world) had remained closed for years. The Krugobaikalka had been created precisely to avoid the necessity of painstakingly transporting the rolling stock of the Express across the lake by ship – but Baikal lies amid steep mountains, between cliffs many arshins tall overgrown with taiga, in an extended rift valley between daunting rock formations; so, building a railway along its shore required miracles of engineering ingenuity with which only the Alaskan Railroad would come to be compared. Nearly forty tunnels were dug, twenty high galleries were constructed. One tenth of the Circum-Baikal Line runs inside rock; the result was such that following the encroachment of the Ice, the Line became a mortal danger: a single gleiss inside a tunnel or on top of a gallery could cause a catastrophe, and these glaciuses were freezing back and forth across the mountains again and again. Coldiron rails were laid therefore on the Baikal ice; at Olkhon Station, a few versts from Khuzhir, the tracks branched out in five directions. Olkhon Station was not located on Olkhon Island – it had been erected likewise on the ice, at the most opportune spot from an engineering point of view. From there, it was also not far to the Olkhon icecradle, where teams of academicians and specialists from Sibirkhozheto companies were constantly travelling. At Olkhon Station began the route of the Cold Line to Kezhma – wherefrom it probably acquired its name, since the first few hundred versts ran across the Baikal ice. This was the true parting of the Siberian ways. It was enough to glance along the rainbows of the coldiron rails: to the south-west – Irkutsk, to the north – Nizhneangarsk and Kezhma, to the east – Verkhneudinsk and Chita, to the north-east – Ust-Barguzin, to the west – Sarma.

Except that, alighting onto the icebound platform after a journey lasting seven hours, it was impossible to see even the end of the outstretched arm – such a furious blizzard was raging across the white plain, such dense snowcloud standing in a horizontal vortex before the wooden sheds of the station. There was no fog to speak of; the famous Baikal gales – the kharakhaykha, verkhovik, kultuk, barguzine – descending suddenly from the mountains to the waterside and managing in unforeseen attacks to overturn whole fleets of fishing boats or sink ferries, had driven away any hint of fog – but in the time of the Ice and the glacial revolutions taking place in the atmosphere, these same gales covered the frozen lake with an almost constant veil of ferocious snowstorm, day and night, come lesser frost or greater frost, come storm or clear sky; one way or another, the face was lashed by a freezing sticky paste as white squalls pummelled it in waves from every direction;

impossible to know which way to turn in order to catch breath; such wind increases the actual degree of frost two or three times. Step down onto the ice and at once regret it. Despite the scarf thickly wound about the face and large frostglaze goggles resting on the nose, despite Mr Wielicki's fur coat and squirrel-skin shapka – the frost cut in a flash to the bone.

Leap back onto the carriage steps, seize the arm of Nikola Tesla.

'Let's agree on a time!' yell through the whistling blizzard. 'Here! Where! Hour!'

'This inn! For you! Six o'clock!'

'Six!'

'Evening!'

'Don't know! To wait!'

'Today! Yes!'

'To wait!'

Run towards the station building; Tchingis Shtchekelnikoff quickly rushed ahead. Lose all sense of direction after a few steps as the train vanished behind the back into the snowcloud – as to where the island was, where the west shore of the lake, where the railway line north.

The station natchalnik pointed the way to Elias Letkikh's inn. His instructions relied on two certainties: that a man is able to distinguish left from right, and that he won't walk through a wall. Between the Olkhon Station buildings and around about them, several fences two arshins high had been knocked together from narrow stakes, solid enough to stop a man on foot, but offering no resistance to the wind and piling snowdrifts. The natchalnik took the liberty, whilst still in the doorway, of relating a malicious anecdote about some travellers who, having alighted to stretch their legs or because they had to change trains, at once lost their way in the blizzard and, having wandered onto the icy-white plain, died somewhere out on Baikal, frozen rock-solid; only then did it occur to someone to erect these directional fences.

And so, stumbling over lumps of snow-ridden frozen ground and groping with the outstretched hand over the ice-encrusted stakes, the lanterns of Letkikh's inn were reached – which took all of five minutes, no more; Letkikh had built not far beyond the station sheds, beside the tracks. The whole provisional architecture of Olkhon Station seemed designed so that the buildings fronted onto one of the tracks.

A maid appeared at once in the vestibule and, bowing from the waist, led the way to the inn lounge. On the floor above and in the annex were rooms bookable for up to ten hours or for a whole day to travellers awaiting trains, now mostly empty most likely because of the closure of the Cold Line. By the fireplace in the lounge, an old man in shabby clerical uniform was dozing; in a corner, a bearded vagabond chewed black bread. Brush the snow off the shuba, stamp it off the boots. The proprietor himself materialised, wearing sidelocks, in frayed black frock coat stretched over thick sweater; moreover, his pink chubby-cheeked countenance made him the living image of the traditional Jewish tavern keeper. A room for your lordships? Two rooms? Half price! The very best! And hot dinner, buttered mashed potato, cabbage soup swimming with meat, stuffed pancakes in lots of fat! Sit by the stove, ask for mulled wine, fish soup and Baikal salmon in pastry. There had been no Baikal salmon for a long time; instead, there was red gorbusha caviar, very cheap, straight from the Korean transports. Into the jovial talk on the methods of how this or that dish should be prepared, it was easy to introduce the person of the cook – maybe the old widow Wutzba still helps in the kitchen? Letkikh narrowed his eyes suspiciously, frowned, clutched at his beard. Mrs Wutzba, you say, Your Esteemed Nobleness? Mrs Wutzba? Eventually, a coin thrust into his pocket persuaded him.

A perspiring, downtrodden woman in a peasant's headscarf tightly enveloping her tiny head came shuffling from behind the scenes, dragging in her wake unlichted steam and a bouquet of nauseating kitchen odours. She stopped beside the table, red hands pressed together as if in prayer, and not for anything would she sit down; Shtchekelnikoff had to plant her on a bench almost by force. Then she lowered her eyes onto those clasped hands, not to raise them again till the end.

Extracting anything from her beyond simple confirmation or denial in answer to a factual question demanded enormous effort. It might have been supposed that the very sound of Polish would make her more trusting; but no. Remove the shapka and sit down before her with the fur coat unhooked; she didn't lift her eyes yet must have seen with whom she spoke – not the slightest sign of recognition was discernible in her, however. Confess therefore openly: a relative come from the home country in search of a former convict, help me, good woman. Reach for the bumazhnik, slap on the tabletop a rouble, another rouble. But Mrs Wutzba was an odd flower: she clammed up all the more, withered on the stalk, shrunk into herself, and so sat petrified on the edge of the bench as though some ispravnik were interrogating her on the circumstance of a plot again the tsar, and not a man begging for inconsequential memories in exchange for good money. Till the sweat stood out on her forehead neath the white headscarf, till the murch swelled on her wrinkled cheeks and oozed from under her eyes, so that the woman seemed still more sick, exhausted and unhappy. What was going on here? Maybe the Hebrew Letkikh had said something to frighten her! Maybe Shtchekelnikoff's mean squint puts her off – dismiss Tchingis from the table. Still, Mrs Wutzba as befits Mrs Wutzba grunts in monosyllables, then again stony silence. Question her louder and louder, repeating the questions and banging the fist on the table. Did her late husband own a shoemaker's workshop in nineteen seventeen and eighteen in Pepelishtche? Did a man live there at that time by name of Gierosławski? And exactly – from when until when? What did he do? What things did he say? Did he pay Henryk? Where did he get his diengi? How well did they know each other? Where did he move to? Did he leave altogether? Where to? When? Did guests come to visit him? What guests?

Pose a question that she cannot answer with a simple 'yes' meekly shaking her head, and she'll shut up lost in thought with her mouth hanging open and not respond not at all.

'Mr Gierosławski,' she murmured slowly, 'if that were what he were called, for I don't know, don't remember, maybe such a man did lodge there, yes, yes, since you say so, sir. All right? All right?'

It was enough to drive any man to desperation and despair. Just how obtuse and dim-witted the Polish peasantry can be, had been forgotten; too long had been spent in towns, too much time amongst the peers and city riff-raff – totally different from the rural riff-raff and particularly in Warsaw where any crafty dodger, so long as he's left to his crooked bourgeois milieu, will outsmart with his innate and well-schooled cunning five provincial petty noblemen, as well as the lord of the manor and his steward into the bargain. While this babushka – does anyone threaten her? has she anything to fear? is she suffering any torture?

'But do you remember, or not?' Now almost howling. 'Tell me the truth, accursed woman, I won't hurt you!'

'Yes, yes, yes, forgive me, sir!'

Grab hold of her and stop her in mid-action, since she was already wanting to throw herself on her knees and embrace the legs.

'I remember, I remember,' she kept repeating, 'everything, as you wish.'

Chase her away ere anger intervenes and causes real harm to the innocent soul. Out of breath, red in the face, remove the fur coat and fling it after the shapka. The Jew tiptoed stealthily in with the mulled wine and soup. The codger by the fireplace awoke and called for vodka. Wiping the saliva from his beard, he resumed his tale, interrupted for sleep or within sleep, of fishermen drowned in Baikal by the holy gales, men to whom the singing of the sands had foretold an afterlife of hell, and who now appear beneath the lake's surface in order to come out amongst people by the light of the Moon or Black Auroras – but how? this is how: trapped in angular, geometrical blocks of ice, the fishermen and every other unfortunate drowned Siberian drifted along the Ways of the Mammoths to the Holy Sea, that is, to Baikal, just as all Siberia flows into Baikal, but for the Angara which flows out – except that the Angara flows out no more, shackled by the frost to the lake bed; and so with every month, more and more unresurrected corpses surge and knock against each other with an icy roar beneath the white coat of the mighty pack ice; ever more crowded is it for them in the ice, and ever stronger the pressure pushing them upward from the dark depths, from the Underground World, so that whoever wanders outdoors on a rare clear night and gazes luckily or unluckily at the vast expanse of frozen Baikal may hear and see the crack and sudden hollow rumble of the glaciated mass, like a salvo of underwater cannon and, Hospodi pomiluy, see a corpse in its milky half-transparent sculpture catapulted towards the stars from under the pack ice, such as I have seen – so said the codger to the fire.

Shtchekelnikoff returned.

'She's a-spying on us,' he whispered, hunched conspiratorially over his bowl. 'Eavesdropping, watching our every move from behind the door, through the slit.'

Merely stare sullenly.

'The whole time,' he drawled with satisfaction, 'and afterwards, after she left.'

'Who?'

'Am I to go find her?'

'Go.'

He lapped up the fish soup, sat a while longer, smoked a cigarette, considered for a moment and departed.

Poke the gap in the teeth with a toothpick. Questioning the past – so why be surprised when it turns out there is no past? But let's suppose the woman blabs back and forth – so what? how does it help to map father's future Ways? Isn't too much being expected of the Ice? Mr Korzyński's finger! For it is supposedly possible here to create truthfulness and destroy untruthfulness – just like the soletrue murderer was created in the Express – so too the true father shall be created…?

Shtchekelnikoff returned.

'Come.'

'What? Where to?'

'Grab the shuba and come, we'll talk by the stable, she's slipped away for a second out of sight of the Jew and her mother.'

'What?'

Hurry after Tchingis, pulling on the coat. Step out briefly into frost and snow; turn at once under a deep lean-to, in the shadow of a corner, between a kind of outbuilding and what looked like stables, in the opposite direction to the railway tracks; there, in a nook behind a woodpile, stood a swarthy black-haired young girl thickly wrapped in shawls and scarves, blowing darkly into her hands and coughing up from time to time a rippling glintz.

'Liva Henrykovna Wutzba,' announced Tchingis, almost smiling, 'Gospodin Venyedikt Filipovitch Gierosławski.'

'Daughter of Henryk Wutzba? The shoemaker from Pepelishtche?'

'Yes. You're looking for your father, sir?'

'Am I causing trouble, miss? Exposing you to danger? Is there some secret? So that you hide like this, whilst your mother –'

'Agh, no.' She was embarrassed. 'You don't understand...'

'What?'

'My mother...,' Livushka wrapped the shawls and scarves around her all the tighter so that only her dark eyes flashed between the fabrics; but the eyes faded when she averted her gaze. 'Do you imagine, sir, that we toil in the Jew's kitchen, in a cold lice-ridden inn at the end of the world, in the midst of an icy desert – because this was what we pictured in our womanish stupidity?' Suddenly she burst into tears. 'We would probably have starved, frozen to death in the cellars! Bozhe moy! How vile people are! Uncle Stefan, the one that took over the workshop from father, seized it from us and threw us onto the street – and mother, my mother, my poor mother...' She paused for breath. 'You don't understand, sir – for it's possible to fall sick from poverty itself, possible to lose your mind from poverty. Mother is a different woman now. You imagine, sir, that a person is afraid of something, of someone – of this, that, something else. But now she's constantly afraid, you saw for yourself, she finds solace only in exhaustion and pain and in praying for strength to bear that suffering; then she's happy, after the day's exhausting drudgery, when of an evening she can offer up to God her sufferings and woes, then a feeble smile appears on her face – Jesus Christ! I can't! Can't!'

'Shhh, hush now, calm down.' Sometimes, in a foreign country, the sound of the native tongue is enough to open the floodgates.

She wiped her eyes with her sleeve.

'Your father's a good man, that's what I wanted to say, sir, your father taught me to read and write, gave me books, sat by my bed at night, told me the history of Poland... Your father – that I haven't frozen like my mother – is all thanks to Mr Gierosławski. So, if I could somehow...'

'He was living with you.'

'Yes.'

'When did he move out?'

'In nineteen eighteen already. It lasted not quite a year, yes.' She sniffed. 'I missed him terribly and kept pestering my parents: when's Uncle Filip coming back, where's he gone –'

'And where had he gone?'

'I don't know if he didn't go to the magpieries. Papa mentioned something… Mr Gierosławski worked, I think, for some ice company…'

'Yes?'

'I don't know, maybe I've muddled it up.'

'He paid you for his lodging?'

'I think so. He'd go off for days at a time, return late, I know, because I was waiting. For him to tell me a bedtime story – oh, such stories he told – Benedykt, sir, I envy you those tales. Later he was absent for longer and longer – for a day, two, a week.'

'Guests came to visit him?'

'Well, yes, yes, but I can't remember – some gentlemen – I don't know.'

'But when he moved out –'

'His woman will tell you, sir.'

'Beg pardon?'

'Well, he must have moved to hers, no? Did he get married? Mr Gierosławski?'

'Do you know her name?'

'Ah!' She put a hand to her mouth hidden behind the scarf. 'I used to see them in church or on the street. A tall statuesque woman, vivacious, laughing, with a long flaxen plait and skin covered in sunny freckles… And – wait! wait! – she works in that Rappaport's Fashion House opposite the New Theatre! Last month, when my Maciek – because you see, sir, I am engaged to Mr Maciej Liszka, I've no intention of wasting my life like my mother in this accursed damp shack,' she kicked the wall, 'of rotting to death in poverty, of being so poor I go crazy – no! Although I'd – although I'd – I don't know what I'd – I ca-aa-an't any longer!'

'Shush, shush.' Embrace Livushka, hold her tight; she nestled her head in the fur, trembling.

'Such wonderful stories,' she sobbed and raised her tear-stained dark eyes. It was quite clear whence this torrent of memories, and what the devushka now saw – whom she now saw – whose face.

'The landlord treats you well?' Place a fatherly kiss on her forehead.

'The landlord's the landlord,' she shrugged her shoulders, already straightening her back and recovering her breath.

Ferret in the pocketbook for two ten-rouble coins, and then another, and also a few rouble notes. Press them into the devushka's fist.

'Please. Get away from here and take your mother with you. Your fiancé will help you, yes? Please don't wait, you shouldn't wait, a person can get used to anything.'

She quickly hid the money under her shawl.

'Thank you, thank you, your lordship.'

'Don't thank me, it's also a kind of payment.'

She seized the hand onto which no glove had been pulled, seized the bare hand and pressed it to her lips under the damp fabric, spun on her heels and fled.

'She's a-fooled ya,' growled Tchingis. 'Anyone can switch on them tears, it's good for business.'

'You know that's not true.' Stare out from under the lean-to at the snowstorm over the frozen lake. 'It's about charity, Shtchekelnikoff, and being able to look the beneficiary in the eye. Get it?'

There was a brief lull in the storm when the white curtains were drawn aside, when the hoary veil fell away and sharp horizons appeared under the afternoon Sun and Black Aurora. And there, to the north-west, on the far shore of the ice sheet, against the backdrop of the scarps and cliffs of Izhymey and Khoboy, below the line of the Primorsky mountains – shone a dazzling mass of diamond crystal, shimmering and intensely beautiful: the great icecradle of Olkhon.

Nikola Tesla appeared at six in the evening as agreed; six, because the train left for Irkutsk at a quarter past. Baikal at this time of day was whiter still – perhaps something had obscured the Tchornoye Siyaniye, cut off the torrents of unlicht, and so the whiteness blazed all the more vividly, electrifying with bright sparks the snow and ice and frozen dust being propelled onto the plain in horizontal waves. Put on the frosto-glaze spectacles – not against the Auroras, but to protect against the arctic dazzle. Tesla's sleigh stopped outside Elias Letkikh's inn. Quickly take a seat. Hidden under a heavy cowl, the izvoztchik cracked his whip. Look back over the tail of the sleigh. The rickety wooden house – a structure without foundations laid on quoins – seemed to tremble and sway in the wind like a drunkard; were it not for the gale, the creak and moan of its warped planks would surely have been heard. In a crooked window neath a crooked eave of the crooked roof, a pale smudge flashed – a woman's face – Wutzba's widow? Wutzba's daughter? The gale spun around and Letkikh's inn swung in the opposite direction.

Once in the train, Tesla produced a notebook and pencil.

'Did you learn anything useful, Doctor?'

'Interesting – oh, without a doubt. They've still not bored down as far as water!'

On Olkhon Island, independently of the camp of the Sibirkhozheto engineers, stood the camp of Benedykt Dybowski-Bajkalski's natural-ists, who were investigating not the icecradle but the lake itself. Such total glaciation lasting so many years was threatening to utterly destroy Baikal's unique fauna – the Baikal seals had already perished irretriev-ably; perhaps only crustaceans and deep-sea fish still survive. Old Dybowski himself used to travel to Governor General Schultz with projects for constructing artificially heated airhole-aquariums. This was too costly an attraction, however. In the meantime, the Geographical Society and the Lwów Academy were financing biocryological research: narrow shafts were being bored in the ice by the pipe method in order to take soundings of the ice depth and penetrate the secrets of the life beneath.

'It is not so, always and necessarily, that nought degrees Celsius means the transformation of water into the solid state. In this case, we need to take into consideration pressure. Since the higher the pressure, the lower the temperature required to form ice. And, as you surely know, pressure in the ocean depths is considerably greater: on every square metre stands a column of water with its entire mass, which gets heavier and heavier the lower we descend, because there is more water on top of us. Once we've accepted, therefore, some constant temperature for the permafrost – let's suppose Professor Yurkat's four to five degrees – then it is easy to calculate the threshold depth below which the frost proves too weak to congeal water into ice.'

'But cannot the same be said of the soil? What was Yurkat saying? They went down a hundred and seventy or so arshins and still the permafrost was measuring four degrees.'

'Exactly so, Benedykt, exactly so! And these limnologists here have also encountered a puzzle: they bore and bore, yet still there is ice. Bah, it's worse than in the case of the permafrost, because here the temperature drops along with the depth!'

'Too crowded for the dead…'

'What?'

'Nothing, nothing. It has only just occurred to me… May I?' Light a cigarette. 'Only an hypothesis – may I?'

Tesla closed his notebook and leaned across the compartment.

'When did you last pump yourself? The day before yesterday? You must visit me more often. Every day! But go ahead, my friend, go ahead.'

Gaze through the smoke, narrowing the eyes, at the white landscape beyond the window of the train as it hurtled across the ice. The calm rhythm of wheels on coldiron – dwook-dwook-dwook-DWOOK – put the mind in a state of hypnotic relaxation. Speak slower and think slower – but with a kind of measured fixity of purpose typical of mechanical processes, of the inertia of solid masses: for every word and every thought is not only possible and right, but right and necessary.

'When you were speaking, sir, of your black physics textbook… The first thing is to derive the formulae for linking teslectricity, murch and tungetitum with the forces of magnetism and electricity, with light, with temperature.'

'Yes, yes, that's exactly –'

'It's probably due to the Black Aurora – like when that drunkard at the inn was telling his hallucination – a man sees strange symbolism, irrefutable truths not only in glintzen, but in every sentence, if you understand me, Doctor. Hundreds of rivers flow in here, and only the Angara flows out – though in fact, it no longer flows out. Have you seen Sibirkhozheto's atlases and the Ways of the Mammoths around Baikal? The lake appears as a blank spot; the most they've marked is that gleissen persistently freeze through the tunnels of the Circum-Baikal Railway. So please think of this lake, Doctor, as a natural reservoir of Siberia, a water filter. Septic tank of the gleissen. I currently live in the home of a man whose foundry processes coldiron and tungetium ores; like it or not, I hear this and that. There are still rivers that are not yet fully frozen as well as rivers shackled to their beds. On a small number of them, Lenzoto still carries on its extractive works; gold is rinsed out from beneath the pack ice, that is, out of masses of soil industrially sifted in hot tanks. And from some of those bore-holes comes so-called sandy tungetitum: Lenzoto sells to its middlemen light tungetitum rinsed out of the output left when gold has been extracted. So you see, sir, if some chemical or physical dependency exists, some natural process whereby tungetitum affects temperature –'

'Ah! At the bottom of Baikal!'

'At the bottom of Baikal, under the ice. Carried with the water until the Baikal watershed froze –'

'Tons of pure tungetitum.'

'What reactions are taking place there? Under such pressure – in the darknesses –'

'Neath the roots of the icecradle.'

'How deep is Baikal?'

Well into the night, the train left behind Port Baikal and Listvyanka and flew past the verst-wide Angara Gates. The snowstorm had abated and an unlichted sky was visible above the scramble of white dust, a black hole between the stars. Put on the frostoglaze spectacles, removed when boarding the train. Doctor Tesla for his part had drawn the blind – a pale glintz danced on the carriage floor and on the boots of the dozing Stepan.

'I had intended to use those bore-holes of theirs to take measurements, so as to collect composite information for my teslectrical tables.' Tesla crossed one leg over the other, tapping the pencil on the cover of his notebook; the white of his gloves flowed onto his trouser legs whilst the legs' dark grey seeped into the wood of his seat. 'Soil is not such an homogeneous medium, too many variables have to be considered, I discussed it for a long time with Professor Yurkat. But here – we have pure ice. To begin with, I will lower a murch-absorbent probe. Then, I shall have to dig several shafts spaced at greater distances from one another. At the central point, I shall set in motion a tungetitum generator and examine the propagation of murch.' He opened the notebook and began to sketch something. 'How are teslectrical waves diffused in ice, in the earth's crust? What is the frequency of the planet's teslectrical pulse? For when I possess this knowledge…' He went on writing, muttering something under his breath in his native tongue.

The glintz on the compartment floor fawned at his feet, springing aside at the old inventor's every move.

The deadline for reporting to the Ministry of Winter fell on the following day. The mood had been foul since early morning. The very act of waking augured no good: sleep had been curtailed by the intensifying roar of the glashatays' drums. A gleiss was approaching from the Angara; if by tomorrow it hadn't turned a corner or frozen back down into the ground, Tsvetistaya seventeen would have to be abandoned. At breakfast, Michasia was dreadfully fretful; it ended with her knocking the butter dish off the table, blubbering and giving the nursery maid the slip. The butter dish landed on the trousers of the only remaining decent dark suit. 'Well, with my figure, I have nothing to lend,' Wojsław laughed, 'but perhaps Grzegorz will find something in his room. You'll have to book an appointment with the tailor.' 'I'm about to drop into the fashion house, they must stock gentlemen's wear and accessories.' Before that, however, the Magpie Bazaar had to be negotiated in order to register in the delegation of Winter. Travel in the stained trousers, cleansed after a fashion with potato flour and spiritus vodka. A great octopus-maw spewing out black ink gaped over Irkutsk; torrents of unlicht were inundating the city streets, ruffling the fog; the morning sun was unable to properly break through. Shadowy glintz-like rainbows blossomed in the sky. A monumental icer stood in the fog on Amurskaya Street. Try to drive around it; a traffic jam ensued. The scene at the junction of Marszałkowska and Jerusalem Avenue arose in the mind's eye, the naphtha flames beneath the glacial medusa. Everything flickered nervously, fierily on the frostoglazes. There are certain images (a gleiss above the middle of a street) whose very composition confers rightness and weight; like a draughtsman's eye and hand invariably aim towards the centre of a circle and an equilateral triangle is more proper than a scalene. Or maybe the Tchornoye Siyanye had already affected the mind. 'He's a-driving behind us,' muttered Shtchekelnikoff, 'following since we left home.' Don't even ask. A column of infantry was marching off the Shelekhoff Bridge. The Empire, so they say, is transferring troops from the Japanese front to Kamtchatka in order to build the Alaska Tunnel; some detachments, however, were evidently being sent west – maybe these soldiers were stuck in Irkutsk not by chance, but on account of the increased activity of the Japanese Legion? Besides, the war poster had already been torn off the foyer wall of the Customs House. Seated in Commissioner Schembuch's secretariat (the fat Mikhail had again vanished somewhere), it was impossible not to notice in turn the portrait of the tsar on the wall opposite – did someone deliberately keep it hung at an angle? Get up, walk over and put it straight? Sit with the shuba on the knees, hiding the greasy stains. A silver-haired moustachioed dignitary entered, stopped in the middle of the chamber, farted loudly, bowed deeply before the image of Nikolay the Second Aleksandrovitch and sat down on the bench beneath it. Glance at him discreetly (which was not easy given that one face was aimed straight at the other, like the portrait of the tsar aimed at the portrait of the minister). The tchinovnik sat stiffly upright as if he'd swallowed a stick, his occiput resting against the wall and his poorly shaven chin thrust upwards, staring ahead of him with bulging eyes. There was no way to interpret this game of glances. Is it a look of anger, of accusation? Is the greyhead looking down 'from on high' in contempt? In disgust? Resentment? About what? Adjust the shuba on the knees, arranging it wider. Does he see the stains? Not see? He sees. Take flight with the eyes. He sat motionless, as the penumbra seeped from behind his back onto the white plasterwork like foam trickling off fermenting beer. Is he breathing at all? He certainly isn't blinking. Swallow the saliva, sensing, despite all efforts and oaths made in the soul, a hot blush beginning to crawl out onto the visage, a red blossom of shame. 'I've been waiting a good quarter of an hour, the commissioner must have gone off somewhere again.' State this raising the voice every second word. The greyhead did not react. More and more bizarre ideas began erupting in the head – maybe he really isn't breathing because, silently somehow, he's had a heart attack? and so the supplicant sits now opposite a stiffening corpse? and talks to a corpse? exchanges glances with the venerable corpse? A vision arose of a vast waiting room in an Imperial Department wherein sit, bench after bench, silent and motionless, living and dead supplicants, as well as those slowly expiring in anticipation of the tchinovnik's favour. And when a corpse's turn comes, the janitors bear him in, rigid in his sitting position, before the countenance of the department head, his proxy or some other clerk, since the tchinovnik ritual introduced by Prussian bureaucrats in service of the tsar has to be satisfied, and no one may insult the authority of the Department. The Tatar secretary entered. At the sight of the moustachioed greybeard, he paled slightly. Bowing to him politely, he sat down at his desk and buried his face in papers. Attempt to catch his eye, signal to him with the eyes, discreetly convey an inquiring expression – but he didn't lift his head even once. The situation became still more complicated. The greasy, revolting stains must surely be visible under the coat. The cheeks were aglow. Suddenly the old man rose from the bench. Almost leap to the feet. He approached, extended his hand. Stand up instinctively and squeeze it with the right hand, clumsily pressing on the coat with the left. 'Congratulations,' he said out loud, with emphasis. Thank him blankly. He nodded, grabbed some documents from the table without looking at them and marched out. 'Who was that?' ask in bewilderment. 'Director General Zygfryd Ingmarovitch Ormuta,' Mikhail replied in an undertone. Heave a sigh. And they say there are no madmen in the Land of the Gleissen…!

In Rappaport's Fashion House, head first to the men's department. Purchase without needless ado (with Wielicki's money after all) two raw-silk lightweight suits, moderately well-fitting and of a dirty-brown colour, cheap nevertheless because ready-to-wear, as well as one pair of loose-fitting black trousers. Having changed at once in the fitting room, make inquiries of the salesclerk, who gave directions to the fourth floor, to where a modiste's signboard hung. If Wutzba's daughter be not lying, then the woman is called Leokadia Gwóźdź. Mrs Gwóźdź – a married woman or widow. On the stairs, Shtchekelnikoff drew close and whispered in the ear: 'Don't give 'er no money.' 'Should I feel so inclined, I'll give my whole purse.' 'Oo-oo, fetid heart.' 'Get lost.' 'Ta, easy to spend someun else's dough,' he sneered. The cheeks were aglow.

In the 'Elegant Lady' Emporium, amid the mirror-lined aisles in which mannequins adorned in the latest chic were inspecting themselves; amid the semicircular wardrobes full of evening creations sparkling with novelty, copied from Viennese fashion magazines; amid racks laden with fur coats glittering as if with fresh dew as well as overcoats, pelisses, stoles, muffs and fur-trimmed capes; beneath high shelves from which coloured fabrics spumed, chiffons, chenilles, batiks, taffetas, damasks, organdies, crêpes de chine, crêpe marocain, muslins, as soft to the very gaze as a childhood dream; from one display of headwear to another, from fanciful hats to those cut in the Russian-shapka style – wandering thus from beautiful temptation to more beautiful temptations, women floated over marble floors laid with coir carpet-runners, but never alone: in groups of two or three, or leaning on the arm of a gentleman. These were the uppermost echelons of elegance.

From inside a deep alcove bathed in honey light came the next onslaught on the senses. The crystal treasure-houses of the perfumery presented expensive fragrances in elaborate frostoglaze flacons that interwove the bright rainbow-sheens of parrots with rainbows of seductive aromas. It was enough even for a chap with a half-blocked nose to walk past the first stand in order to succumb to its spell, enough to read the tags on the coldiron plates neath the flower-basket emblem of Ed. Pinaud: *Paquita Lily, Jasmin de France, Violette Princesse, Persian*

Amandia, Blue Nymphia, Bouquet Marie-Louise... Is not the sense of smell – the sense that reacts to the invisible, inaudible, untouchable – closest to the extra-material world?

At once the imagination conjured a picture of Miss Wutzba in the timid company of her not-very-affluent wooer strolling through the Fashion House on their one free afternoon of the week or even month, in order to feast their eyes at least on the beautiful sights, to rub shoulders with a higher form of life, admire the elegant gentlemen and stylish ladies, twice the age of that teenage girl – since it's for them after all that fashion is created, for mature women, over thirty, that is, the womanly ideal: the compleat woman, the consummate woman and not an immature devushka or half-woman, quarter-woman. *La passion se porte vieux.* But at least for the time being it was possible to breathe the air of opulence – to inhale into the lungs those perfumed miasmas of luxury...

'Mrs Gwóźdź?'

'Over there.'

Recognise her by the blond plait and freckles. A Junoesque woman of Balzacian age with prominent bosom and broad powerful hands. She was not wearing a wedding ring.

Wait till she walks away from a customer; then approach and politely state the name.

She instinctively looked out of the window at the glintz in the street. 'I thought as much.'

'Pardon?'

'I dreamed I was in the cemetery.' She took a deep breath, shook her head, tightened her lips. 'Wait a moment, I'll ask leave of the clerk.'

She reappeared after few minutes dressed already in an overcoat with rather faded otter collar and a fur toque.

She ran quickly down the stairs, pulling on her gloves.

'Don't stand there like that, sir, or they'll start blabbing again.'

'Is that so bad?'

Ostentatiously take her by the arm.

She burst into vehement laughter, suddenly revealing her teeth, almost all still white and straight.

'You're welcome!' She inclined her head, offering her rounded cheek. 'A wench kissed at dawn, brings happiness all morn.'

Out on the street, she led the way, turning at once towards Glavnaya Street and the buildings of the Geographical Society and Customs House visible through the fog, in the direction just come.

'Benedykt?' She was making sure, having taken her frostoglaze spectacles out of her handbag and placed them on her nose. She paused to rub her face with a kind of salve; then wrapped herself in a white scarf embellished with many long tassels that flowed down her coat as far as the waist.

'He told you, ma'am?'

'He told me he had children. How did you find out about me?'

Tell her.

'But why so surprised? After all, he could have written home.'

'About me?' Vow that she smiled again under her scarf.

The bad mood of the morning swiftly returned.

'You know my mother died only a year ago, a year and three months.'

'And do you think she knew?'

'No. He never wrote.'

'Then she surely didn't die because of me. For me, she existed not.'

'For my father too, she probably existed not.'

'Agh! And now you've come here to – what? to throw it all in his face? And make of it an abomination! Pshaw!'

'You admit, ma'am, you knew he was married.'

She was silent a long while. She changed the rhythm of her breathing and when she spoke again, also changed her tone.

'We are not going to talk like this, young man.' She did not tear away her arm, but it could be felt how she considered it; eventually, she let the arm go limp. 'You shan't make me ashamed of my sincere feeling. I loved Filip. Love him. Loved him.'

Put on the frostoglazes.

'Sorry.'

'For what exactly? You're ashamed on my behalf!'

Stare into the white-hued fog.

'How did you meet?'

'Filip is physically strong. You must know that better than anyone. I have never known a stronger man. My father, who for a quarter of century ran the Mining Directorate on the Amur river, says you can tell a man's strength from the misfortunes that befall him. Whoever is pliable, weak and feeble has no problem swimming with the current and the wind, and adapts to any circumstances; but whoever is tough will resist, and the harder he stands his ground, the harder life will push back against him. In the end, he feels as though the whole world has crushed him out of pure malice: give in, give in, give in! Everything else has caved in, been watered down, surrendered – yet here a single barb sticks out and stabs to the side. So, the world's weight makes for that barb: to break it, rip it out, destroy it. There exist such human barbs – didn't you know, Benedykt? That they stab. That they always stab everyone. Such toughguts may be sincerely admired and sincerely loved, but they cannot in any way be lived with.'

'You went your separate ways.'

'Yes.' The scarf on her face turned grey from her unlichted breath. 'But – how we met! We met, because he beat up my cousin and then carried him home to us to dress his wounds.'

'I can believe it.' Burst into a fit of coughing; frost was entering the throat, swelling in the chest. Raise the collar of the fur coat, concealing the mouth and nose. 'He was living then at the Wutzbas, yes? When did you last hear from him?'

'He left in the spring of nineteen nineteen. Then – there were rumours, tall tales. Once the Okhrana descended on us, and also kept asking if I had any news from him.'

'He never wrote.'

'No.' She laughed hoarsely. 'He never wrote.'

'Did he tell you why, khrr, why he did it?'

Come out onto Glavnaya and turn eastward, leaving behind the Bazaar, the Customs House, the Geographical Society and the governor general's Festung.

The longer a person walked the streets of the City of Ice, the stranger the impression growing inside him: that he was walking alone. That there was no one on those streets other than himself; even were someone to leave home on foot, he'd be swallowed up at once by the fog. Other pedestrians were seen extremely rarely, that is, only when they were nearly collided with and avoided at the last moment. The sound of their footsteps, their voices, the noise of street traffic – everything floundered in that moist cottonwool. Lanterned sleighs sped by on the left in a jingle of bells, in a river of sky-coloured fumes. The sky was the colour of sky, because really it was the colour of the Black Aurora, yet in the frostoglazes it came pouring back like the yolk of a broken egg sucked back into its shell.

'This beaten-up cousin,' she said, 'works in Zimny Nikolayevsk in the coldmills, has comrades amongst the hiberniks, a fraternity of firm believers. It's from them I hear these rumours. Father Frost, salvation or annihilation of the world, Ambassador of the Underground World.'

'You don't believe it.'

'He never told me too much about his past, but I know he was sentenced for political reasons, for his armed exploits. Yes?'

'But what has this to do with –'

'For I thought for a long time that he was done with it, cured at any rate, that he'd sweated it out of himself, that he'd settled down – a family man who loves his family shakes off his utopian ambitions, which are the privilege of youth. But then I realised –'

'The barb.'

'In the spring of that year, immediately following the sensation of the Dumb Ballooner, when Filip stopped returning from work at night and

I discovered only from my cousin via his friends at Horczyński Ores that some men were visiting him there in Nikolayevsk after dusk, that Józef Piłsudski was supposedly passing through Nikolayevsk with his Siberian Riflemen, it was then that –'

'Hang on!' Grasp Leokadia by the elbow. 'My father worked at Horczyński Ores?'

She turned her head. Stare through the frostoglazes into frostoglazes, colours scrambling on the corneas.

'You didn't know, sir?' she was miffed, astounded. 'Filip is a trained geologist! What was he to do here? They were only too pleased to take him, Horczyński didn't even ask for diploma certificates.'

'So why did he spend so much time in that cold hovel with the shoemakers?'

'Whereas I ask his own son: why is Filip Gierosławski as he is? Perhaps his son will sooner answer me that! Why can't he live normally like other people, why must he constantly chase after his own tail, rushing from adventure to adventure, from one life impossibility to another, always driving himself into a corner, so that in the end all one can do is grit one's teeth and count on some miracle saving him! Why!'

Clear the throat.

'But you wanted him like that, ma'am.'

She removed her spectacles for a moment to dab her eyes (it being very unwise to weep in such frost) and wipe her nose in a handkerchief.

'I know I'm no hero. I wasn't born to be, nor dreamt of being the companion of a legend. What are you, sir?'

'By profession? A mathematician.'

'A mathematician. So, will you necessarily take a wife who's fluent in numbers? No. Your wife will marry Benedykt Gierosławski, her fiancé, and not Benedykt Gierosławski, the mathematician. We look at people only from our one point of view, each from their own; it's God who can see a person from all points of view at the same time, as well as from above, and from below, hah, and also from within.'

'And so, Leokadia, ma'am, looking at him from your point of view –'

'For he loved me!' She caught her breath. The colours of her dark coat streamed off her into the fog; minute by minute, Mrs Gwóźdź was becoming more and more the colour of the fog and almost transparent. Hold her tightly by the arm. She walked quickly, staring ahead of her. 'Am I to sink into vulgar words? Before his son? It's improper. Why do you ask, sir? Have you ever known true passion? Eh? So how do you tell it to other people? How explain it?'

'Such things are untellable.' Mutter. 'Such things are unthinkable.'

'Yes! Yes!' She burst into a throaty laugh from below the diaphragm, as if she suddenly felt great relief from something. 'May you one day find such love from a woman, such passion devouring your soul – the true desire of a strong person that consumes you unconditionally – not because you desire, but because you are desired –'

'An honest sensualist is closer to God.'

'Indeed, but what's that to me.'

Ahead, a Buryat drum was beating louder and louder. These were already the outskirts of the city beyond Laninskaya Street; the walk had lasted more than half an hour. Wait a moment for the fog to clear of lights and fall silent of harness bells, then run across to the other side of the steep street. A small plate loomed out of the fog. Third Soldatskaya Street.

Leokadia Gwóźdź glanced behind her.

'Some scoundrel is crawling after us,' she remarked in a tone of distracted surprise.

'Ah! That's my scoundrel.'

'You make a habit of collecting shady individuals?'

'All sorts wish me ill. Whereas the good Shtchekelnikoff wishes ill to everything that lives.'

'Haven't you thought of adopting strategies healthier to the spirit? Love your enemies.'

'It's easier to love them and show compassion when I think, khrr, what Shtchekelnikoff might execute upon them with his knife.'

'Would that everyone had his own Shtchekelnikoff!' She chuckled thickly. 'The Kingdom of God would immediately come about on Earth.'

'All in good time. For the time being, Messrs Smith and Wesson sell the most exquisite fine revolvers.'

She snorted through her shawl, prompting a watery glintz.

'You must be the foremost attraction in all the salons!'

'In the salons I think too much, khrr, forget the tongue in my gob and pass for a cretin.'

Come out, conversing in this way, onto a dirt road, that is, a glaciated mud track between fields of white-hued snow, twisting at once directly eastwards and higher still, because it was leading up the slope of Jerusalem Hill. Recognise it – like through a dream, like in sleep – that track and that hill.

Hurry along; now it was Leokadia Gwóźdź who had to keep pace up the steep slope. She hadn't commented on the way; where it led was all too familiar. Recognise the neighbouring hills standing out above the sea of fog with their birch spinneys also covered in snow; recognise the uneven rows of crosses, Latin and Orthodox, inclined at angles above the icebound graves; recognise too the ruins of the burned tserkoff and the gravediggers' shed. Here, the fog hung low above the earth. Wade through it like through those gaseous fumes spewed from the gleiss on Old Zima Station – the white-hued suspension grew more blurred with every step. The Tchornoye Siyaniye was flooding the cemetery with grey unlicht; glintzen spilling off the crosses were almost invisible against the white snow.

Lower the collar so as to draw the icy air directly into the lungs, maybe it'll restore the senses; but no, it didn't help. Wander amongst the graves, trampling on the hard crunchy névé, black breath steaming on the lips. Gradually, in the frostoglazes, the whole penumbra took on sharp poisonous colours, sucked out from God knows where; there was no coldiron here whose rainbow it could have stolen from. Instead, there was a burning September Sun in the sky as well as two stars of cold fire shining above the city: the tungetitum cupolas of Christ the Saviour Sobor like the eyes of a vengeful archangel – and for this reason, all the cemetery crosses now had the colour of the Sun, that is, shone with a white glow, whiter than ice. The black sky had drenched the path with unlicht.

Leokadia Gwóźdź seized the hand. Stop still before a tiny, low, Latin cross. Someone had been tending the grave – not long ago the slab had been cleared of frozen debris; it sufficed to brush off the snow.

In Loving Memory of
Emilia Darya Gwóźdź
Entered this world on the ninth day of
January in the Year of Our Lord 1919
An innocent soul taken by God to be amongst the Angels
on the twenty-seventh day of February 1919
Who shall count the tears
For a life that never was?

Mrs Gwóźdź fell on her knees and crossed herself. White-and-blue rivers swam in the mother's frostoglazes. Avert the eyes. This mound – these crosses – the shed over there – the pit dug here… The grave in which the living body had been destined to be buried alive lay not far off, some five arshins from the spot. Today, a fresh headstone already stood upon it.

Leokadia recited no prayers – she was telling her daughter something in that melodious voice in which people address babies. The cross shone fierily. Follow with the eyes the glintz coming off the tserkoff wall – a half-naked man with a spade stepped out into the unlicht, turned his head, peered with his single eye. He bowed stiffly. Touch the edge of the shapka with the gloved hand. Yerofey smiled imperceptibly under his scar and beat his livid torso with a clenched fist. Curl the gloved hand into a ball and strike the chest.

It was a time of strange Black Auroras, and many things done in their unlicht were more akin to deeds conjured in a dream, necessary within the dream.

On the last kopeck

'As a sales assistant for instance, or office auxiliary, or bookkeeper in some accounting department.'

'But Benedykt, my dear fellow! For goodness' sake! No one is throwing you out!' Wojsław Wielicki even went so far as to grab in emotion at his heart (admittedly on the wrong side of his body). 'Really, it's a pleasure to host you! The children love you! Ever so much! The ladies too – because they have someone to talk to. Don't they say so – that you are the perfect listener – is it not so?'

'Since I have so little to say.'

'Benedykt, sir! If you're worried about those few hundred...'

'I must earn my keep.' Repeat it with stubborn insistence. 'I must pay off my debts.'

'But do I ask about deadlines! Demand repayment! No!'

'You, sir, are too hospitable, I can't say a bad word. Yet what? – a month, another month, who knows when Schembuch will let me go – and I'm meant to live here as some hanger-on, like a moribund old aunt sponging off her family? But I shan't go to Winter and demand a post in the ministry! I was thinking therefore of the coldiron companies – every second name I hear is Polish – you know them all, sir.'

Swallow the rest of the infusion, put aside the cup. Glance instinctively in so doing at the fingernails: not because they're bitten (since they're not), but because they're entirely wan and livid without even a pink half-moon showing underneath. This was one of the visible effects of a low-murch diet in the high-murch environment of the Land of the Gleissen. There was also the constant impression that the penumbra coming off the body and clothing differed from the penumbras of gleisseniks: same intensity in the perversion of light, opposite vector. People, however, paid it no attention.

'I'm not referring even to Porfiry Pocięgło, that would indeed be tactless – but how about Horczyński...?'

Wielicki waved this aside as if shooing away a fly.

'Wherever did you hear of Grandad Horczyński? Horczyński had to sell out to Krupp a long time ago in exchange for Harbin debts secured against his company, he got only sixteen per cent, poor soul.' Wielicki patted his belly, tugged at his beard and peered searchingly, as if examining his interlocutor afresh with the clear suspicion of being swindled.

Maybe he'll see it. Such was the thought – avert not the eyes, however, answering him directly gaze to gaze, raising the head and pinching the lips. Maybe he'll recognise it; after all, what has frozen cannot suddenly change shape.

But no – for how was Mr Wielicki to know the arcana of black physics?

He let the air out of his lungs.

'Perfect timing!' He clapped his hands. 'A man must have an occupation; a man must feel value in his own hands. Unable to earn himself, he's dependant on another's kindness, living like a kept woman – you are right, sir!' He seized his watch chain, glanced at the bulbous ticker. I'll send Tryfon, Mr Zweigros will have time to give an answer. So get ready, Benedykt, we're going!'

'Now? I've only just got back.'

'And where have you been absconding to lately at dawn, my fine fellow? Breakfasting somewhere in town? Or maybe Benedykt Gierosławski has already cooed and wooed himself a krasavitsa, eh? In which case, I'd sooner understand his evening sorties, hee-hee. You won't be the first to be shot here by Amor.'

It was the thirteenth day of September, the Feast of Saint John Chrysostom, a Saturday, morning-time following a late breakfast in the Wielicki household. Icy rays from the summer Sun lit up the fluid stained-frostoglaze panels of the tall dining-room windows. The gleiss had frozen back into the Angara, thereby lifting everyone's spirits on Tsvetistaya. During the night, Maciuś had lost a milk tooth and received from his father in exchange a heavy half-imperial – he was shining it now in his eyes, standing by the window and catching golden sunbeams through the frostoglaze. At the same time, he opened wide his mouth, twisting his tongue into his cheek; he stopped fumbling in the gum only when a new person entered the room – the old famulus Grzegorz, the maid, the cook, the nurse, Tryfon – whereupon Maciuś turned the polished coin towards them and tickled their faces with a firefly. 'I got money!' he declared. 'Ready money!'

Accompany Wielicki to the café Vittel – situated in a side street off Glavnaya, on the third floor of a magnificent secessionist apartment building, above the signboard of the New York Germania Bank, entrance from the annexe. Pass on the stairs a paunchy half-Asiatic, hurriedly pulling a shuba onto his back. 'What, running away?' Wielicki inquired. 'Where are you off to in such a hurry?' The other merely snorted and galloped downstairs. 'Uzhetsky,' Wojsław explained. 'Chinese on his mother's side, but an Orthodox Old Believer, making big money on brick tea, worth half a million alive.' Understand what sort of company was about to be entered.

Before Wielicki had time to hand his fur coat to the cloakroom attendant, he was waylaid by a young Semite with a plastered-down black forelock, wound up with nervous energy; he'd evidently caught sight of Wielicki through the glass door of the vestibule.

The man waylaid him and began with no introduction:

'Seven thousand poods of impure devilite in three days' time on the siding at Innokentyevskoye One, forty per cent payable in advance, my man is taking Schtorts and Gorubyeff's bills of exchange, the endorsement of Bruhe and Co., Fishenstein just gave me twenty-six and a half, two and a half times the capacity of Pietrycki's rolling stock, so what do you say, Mr Wielicki?'

'He gave, so why didn't you take?'

'Who says I didn't take? Am I sick in the head not to take when they give? I took it! But I'm asking what you'll say, because I know you've got a taste for Fishenstein's blood?'

'But where's the gesheft, Mr Rybka?'

'There's always gesheft!' Twitching with excitement, the overwrought young man pulled Wielicki aside, heaven knows what for, since he made no effort to lower his voice. 'I can have the next five thousand poods for this coming Saturday and sell them then for twenty-seven or even eight. But –'

'But by this coming Saturday, Schultz will have had time to announce the re-opening of the Cold Line ten times over.'

'So, I'd sell them to you today for twenty-five – well, may God punish me for my stupidity – twenty-four thousand seven hundred, and you'll be laughing in Fishenstein's face, a green worm devouring Fishenstein.'

'You are selling me someone else's risk, Mr Rybka.' Wielicki extricated himself from Rybka's grasp with difficulty and pushed open the door into the main room. 'Today I buy your coming-week's ores, but on Monday I read in *The Herald* about the opening of the Kezhma Line, and then everyone will be laughing in my face.'

'Repeat that to me in a week's time when you won't find semi-pure devilite anywhere for under thirty!'

'Upon my word, Mr Rybka, for all I know you're financing Piłsudski?'

'What? How d'you mean? Who?'

Enter the room. Wielicki made at once for a table located neath a gigantic gilt-framed mirror.

'Where's Walduś?' he inquired of two sad-looking fair-haired men in crumpled suits.

'With Zweigros. Have you read this? An affront to God!'

'What's that you've got?'

The blond man on the right slapped a newspaper spread out between the tchay and the bowl of nuts and dried fruit.

'Whether they sign the peace or don't sign the peace, the war tax is to be maintained for at least a year owing, I quote, to the necessity of restoring the Empire's military potential.'

'Where did you get that? Ah! Not yet official.'

'I'm going to Pyedushtchik,' announced the blond man on the left gloomily. 'To offer my head on a plate. If Pobedonostseff nails the Holey Palace in another deal exclusively to Thyssen, I'm selling up. May a gleiss mow me down, I'm selling up!'

'But there, you're going to sell up…!' Wojsław snorted, making himself comfortable with a wheeze in the neighbouring chair and signalling to the elderly waiter. 'Were you to sell up, you'd be doing it during a shamans' strike. How much have you made on the Warsaw trams, fifty thousand? Waiter, a samovar please!'

'You sold coldiron for the Warsaw tram tracks?' Interrupt him. 'But who has the contract there for plumbing?'

'Huh?'

'For how did it look in cities taken earlier by the Ice? Didn't they change the pipes?'

'Mr Benedykt Gierosławski,' Wielicki completed the formalities. 'Recently arrived from Warsaw. Listen, Uzhetsky was flying out of here as if scalded – is it because of that tax?'

'The latest quotations from Europe, Hamburg and the rest of the money markets; Bankverein shares have plummeted into the gutter at forty-five Kronen and fifty Heller.'

'Show me!'

'The rouble stands at two hundred and sixteen Kronen and a trickle.'

'And since you pass for such a great speculator, who'd think it's all in four-per-cent covered bonds and government securities.'

'Spoken by the specialist in fortune loss.'

The melancholy fair-haired pair were the brothers Gawron, sons of Jakub Gawron from Łódź, a peasant's son who made a fortune on sweatshop machinery and educated his sons in European schools; having choked on a plum stone, he departed this world of drudgery and lucre at the age of forty-four, leaving his sons Jan and Janusz more than three hundred thousand roubles in hard cash plus several invest-ments in Łódź. The incident with the plum happened in nineteen ten. By nineteen thirteen, the brothers had managed to squander most of their fortune. Having squandered their father's, they set about making their own, and Irkutsk in the age of coldiron seemed to them the best place to do it. In this they were not mistaken. Meanwhile Janusz had got married and fathered a daughter and a son – a new generation of Gawrons was growing up. Perhaps the whole cycle would repeat itself.

Over tea and petit fours, over coffee and fruit in hot pastry, here at Vittel's, this was where Mr Wielicki discussed his semi-serious, coffee-table deals. The aforementioned Fishenstein approached the table for a moment, an imposing figure with silver beard and silver sidelocks, dressed in black frock coat and leaning on a walking stick as thick as a flagpole, and with an atrophied left eye that had been gouged out and replaced in its concave socket by a frostoglaze ball with tungetitum pupil – whenever he directed the ball in his half-blind stare at some object, it caused the colours and glintzen to fluctuate in the inhuman eyepiece. Wojsław stood up and they greeted one another courteously with the respect customary amongst stolid businessmen. A digressive conversation was struck up in Polish, Russian and Yiddish, in which – as became clear when it neared its end – they were discussing who would cast his vote for what project at the next Sibirkhozheto board meeting, and in particular what licences for iced-through minerals would be granted to whom. The Gawron brothers pricked up their ears. Neither Wielicki nor Fishenstein had a seat amongst the directors and shareholders of Sibirkhozheto; both nevertheless exerted some influence on the votes of the sitting members. Understand that this is how politics is conducted in Irkutsk, what is meant by the voice of the people and what is its translation into the decrees of power: not through the duma or politics from the bottom up, but through the voice of money.

When Wielicki moved away, escorting Fishenstein to the exit, the Gawrons willingly explained first one thing and then another, embellishing their explications with moaning complaints. Sibirkhozheto could vote how it liked; in practice, it was Pobedonostseff who decided matters affecting the exploitation rights to the gleissen-nests in Zimny Nikolayevsk, as he did throughout Siberia. The longest-lasting and deepest nests were situated in the so-called Holey Palace, whose transmutation capabilities were estimated to well exceed five million poods per annum. Thyssen's coldmill consortium in partnership with the Belkoff-Zhiltsoff company had received the majority of contracts from the Russian War Ministry, including all coldiron contracts for building the warships of the Winter Pacific Fleet.

'It's one thing to grind us down with taxes,' grumbled Jan.

'That's what taxes are for, to grind down honest people,' echoed Janusz.

'But it's a different thing, for as long as they maintain these military priorities, we won't elbow our way into the coldmills.'

'Again, prices of natural deposits are going through the roof.'

'Magpies and geologist-prospectors will strike out into the taiga.'

'Court cases will block land ownership.'

'The number of bandits will increase.'

'Everyone will be stealing, stealing.'

'And bribing the shamans.'

'Killing on the Ways of the Mammoths.'

'When steel-grade coldiron hits seven roubles a pood on the Harbin stock exchange, war will hot up anew in the Underground World.'

'Fishenstein is a wise man, he invests in real estate.'

'Whoever lost out in the land trade? There's no longer anywhere here even to bury the dead.'

'The cemetery business! There's a thought! They arrive in their thousands and what do they do? Die.'

'If only a good law could be passed by the city duma, so that city hall would pay for the poor devils.'

'Fear not, fear not, we'll get the parish priests and soft-hearted wives of our high officials to write to the newspapers. Who'll raise his hand against Christian charity? Eh?'

Remind them then of the Irkutsk gravediggers, who evidently govern themselves beautifully.

'Not so, Benedykt, sir. The Jerusalem Cemetery was closed already in the nineteenth century; now only Catholics in fact are buried there. Well, open or closed, a graveyard must have watchful diggers on guard, in order to enter in the burial records every freezing-out of a gleiss from under the ground. Then it's essential to follow the gleiss's path, collect a dead person's remains and return them to the grave – we've had quite a few of these second half-burials; in Irkutsk you'll find a fair-sized cemetery next to every tserkoff, and there are a lot of tserkoffs. Because, you see, the stuff treading the city streets inside an icer is not only water, that is, ice, but also various random scraps which its frost has picked up from the earth. Including bits of human remains once buried neath a cross, should a gleiss happen to have walked over them. Would you wish to see your mother of holy memory, may she rest in peace, dragged over the roofs and pavements of the city? Well, that's why we pay the gravediggers.'

Look around the room. The Saturday antemeridian hour meant that for the time being, the number of guests could be counted on the fingers of one hand. It seemed the majority really were Poles. Also, not a single woman was in evidence.

Under a sunny landscape painting opposite sat a red-haired misery-guts in the pose of Sienkiewicz's hero Longinus Podbipięty, only with an oddly small head fixed on his long arched neck, at this moment however – drooping low, as his nose was in a tankard of beer. Yet his eyes, neath angrily puckered brows, were following every movement in the café; nor was anything likely to escape the carrot-top's ears, a sign of his heightened attention being the red flash in his pupils and the grasp of his huge paws – born to wield an axe – around the half-empty tankard.

'That's Mr Lewera, our local scribbler,' whispered Wielicki, having sat down again to the steaming tchay. 'I advise you not to approach him.'

'Why so? Does he bite?'

'When he reads something good, but not his own.' He laughed under his moustache. 'And under any circumstances, do not mention Wacław Sieroszewski or any of his works in Lewera's presence. Lewera will never forgive him to the end of his days. Imagine, sir, he had decided in his own mind he'd become the bard of the New Siberia, but whatever he tries to write, Sieroszewski always beats him to it by six months.'

Two tables away, a bearded, broad-shouldered man in ornate rubashka, colourfully embroidered in a cross-stitch pattern, was sipping coffee. A certain Gorubsky, the only Russian present. Whilst at the table beyond him, under the clock, sat Doctor of Laws Zenon Myśliwski, Mr Zweigros's secretary.

'He will stand by the door and greet everyone,' Wojsław continued in an undertone. 'Introduce yourself politely and watch whether he offers his hand; if he offers it, that's good, you can go in. Find a seat somewhere by the wall, and then sit and listen until we break our last kopeck. After that, you can talk about a position.'

Rub the back of the left hand, still tingling under the skin.

'I was hoping you'd recommend me to someone – maybe someone from Krupp.'

'Oy, that's exactly what I am doing! Once you step inside – no better recommendation will be needed, inquire and ask boldly.' He cleared his throat thickly. 'The proper thing would be, were I myself to –'

'Why no! Really!'

'No, no, I have dozens of posts in the firm in which I could try you. But, you see, the times are such, were it not for Piłsudski, who knows – but now I have to lay people off for several weeks. Therefore –'

'You put me to shame, Wojsław, sir.'

'No, no, no,' he waved his handkerchief, smiling in embarrassment. Having lapped up his tchay, he peeked at his watch. 'Half eleven, they'll be assembling.'

It was true, more guests were gradually arriving; one went in, a second, a third. They all knew one another; first they moved from table to table, exchanging words of greeting, only then finding a place and snapping their fingers at the waiter.

The fur trader Kozheltsoff came running up for a moment in search of someone. At the sight of Gorubsky, however, he reddened and began to shake feverishly; leaning with both hands on his silver-topped cane, he spat out crude invective in theatrical whispers.

'What's the matter with him?' inquire of the others.

'Kozheltsoff and Gorubsky were the best of cronies and jointly held a healthy slice of the trade in state furs.'

'State?'

'Yes, because of the yasak tax exacted from the indigenous peoples. But Kozheltsoff took a fancy to the daughter of Feliks Gniewajłło; the poor fellow fell hopelessly in love. Greetings, greetings, Porfiry, sir!'

Porfiry Pocięgło sat down at the table.

'It happened, if I'm not mistaken,' continued Wielicki 'in nineteen-oh-seven – all ancient history now.'

'And so, this Gorubsky was also making up to her?'

'No, no. It was just that Mr Feliks Gniewajłło was a proud nobleman and had no intention of giving away his daughter to a caesaropapist. Well, so Kozheltsoff switched to the Roman rite. For, you see, this was after Nikolay Aleksandrovitch's Edict of Toleration, so he had the right to convert; soon afterwards, Stolypin again fenced off the religions. But – the thing was done; Kozheltsoff became a Roman Catholic, the husband of a Polish woman, and quickly began to Polonise. This got Gorubsky's goat. He tried to reason with him one way or another, brought Orthodox priests, deacons, scholars to talk him out of it, bah, even tried to make Miss Gniewajłło appear loathsome to his crony – all to no avail. They squabbled like savages. The more Catholic Kozheltsoff became, the more Gorubsky became Orthodox. The more Polish Kozheltsoff became, the more Gorubsky became Russian. And so it was in everything. Kozheltsoff buys up cattle, so Gorubsky immediately sells cattle, even at his own loss. Kozheltsoff is an Ottepyelnik, so Gorubsky is a diehard Lyednyak. With time, they surely would have been reconciled and somehow made peace, but in the meantime the Ice has encroached and – it has frozen.'

Pocięgło nodded in assent. All were all observing the row nicely brewing between Kozheltsoff and Gorubsky.

'What about that land, promised me a year ago!' sputtered Kozheltsoff in Polish without, however, giving the syllables their full length.

'Don't you speak the language anymore?' Gorubsky scoffed in Russian, without even raising his head from his coffee.

'If you'd at least made a profit on it!'

'Don't worry your head, my profit, my money.'

'Bloody revisionist, you're all dogs in the manger, make no money, won't let others!'

'So go, go, do what you want – so long as it's not in my lifetime.

Nor my children's! Go shut yourself in some khutor in the midst of the taiga, like them Skoptsy or other warped sectarians, in seclusion, where you won't offend anyone with your iniquity, and butcher yourselves there, copulate with swine, fire your stoves with roubles and icons – or whatever the most fervent progressives are planning there now for the world.'

Kozheltsoff was already as bright red as a Chinese lantern; his crop of hair, shaven at the back and sides in the Sarmatian style, really did seem to fume with smoky penumbra.

'You, mister, are fuck, thug and phoney!'

'Mister? Mister, you say?' croaked Gorubsky. 'Now you want to turn me into a Polish gentleman?'

The company around the table could barely stifle their mirth.

'Perhaps someone should calm them down. They're about to hurl themselves at each other.'

'Not at all, Benedykt, mere harmless banter.'

'Somehow it smacks too much of politics.'

'Kozheltsoff has frozen as the great democrat,' muttered Jan Gawron; placing a lump of sugar under his tongue, he gulped his tchay and immediately changed the subject. 'You were saying something about pipes – it may well be true. The Tungus Coldiron Industrial Company sold on the strength of its Saint Petersburg contract four hundred thousand poods of high-carbon coldiron. But there's always haggling with city councils or whoever actually controls public procurements – you have to liberally grease their palms, suck up to the tchinovniks. It seems various owners of apartment buildings or the water companies will start replacing the pipes without a decree. Mm-hmm. The Warsaw pipes – why bring them up?'

'Because pipes burst in the walls and water freezes in the taps.'

Mr Pocięgło moved aside the samovar and leaned across the table.

'My apologies for yesterday, Benedykt, business matters. What is it you wished –'

Wince.

'Not here, not now.'

There was a deafening crash. It was a milk-glass panel splitting on the door; Kozheltsoff had slammed it with such fury as he ran out. Gorubsky merely sprawled wider on the Empire-style sofa and called for vodka.

'Why did he come here at all?'

'Precisely for that, no doubt.'

Bite into a chocolate rusk.

'Do such stories happen often?'

'What stories?'

'Stories of Polonised Russians.'

Pocięgło opened his silver cigarette case engraved with the tiger and sable coat of arms and offered it around to everyone; they lit up. Also have a smoke.

'Mr Benedykt Gierosławski, as a Kingdomite, sees only one argument between Poles and Russians.' Porfiry inhaled, crossed one leg over the other, sighed. 'I recall your amazement, sir, in the Transsib. You dwell in Romantic falsehoods! Do you imagine, sir, that the Poles are a divinely ordained nation itself incapable of oppression and blood-sucking? Yet here in Siberia – the native peoples remember the Polish lord, Jan Krzyżanowski, who in the seventeenth century decimated the Tunguses with fire and sword, ruling according to the worst traditions of rogues like Łaszcz and Stadnicki, so that he provoked a veritable re-bellion of the local population in Okhotsk.'

'They remember?'

'It's the memory of a nation, not of people. Do we not like to remind the Germans of Grunwald?' Porfiry blew tobacco smoke provocatively over the table. 'I tell you that had History taken a different turn, we would be ruling the Russians from the Grand Duchy of Muscovy to the Black Sea, and Russians would now be lamenting their wretched griev-ances before portraits of the King of Poland and Lithuania, whining about official Polonisation and denationalisation, whilst their careerists would be outvying one another to convert to the Catholic faith and dress in Polish robes.'

'You daydream, sir.'

'On the contrary! Siberia is the best proof. In History there are always entanglements, particular events and objective conditions that distort the picture and are impossible to change, so it's difficult to take this man and that man or this nation and that nation – and compare: this one is more talented, this one less talented, this one knew how to help himself, this one did not, these are material for Empire-building, whereas these rock a quarter of the globe merely by chance. But if ever, at any time in any place, there is a testing ground of History, an empty field untouched by History yet hard for everyone, containing hidden opportunities for success for the able and strong-willed and inevitable punishment for the foolish and idle – then Siberia is that testing ground.

'And look how it is now: something out of nothing. There was nothing here, neither culture nor industry, nor people to create it. Still a century, half a century ago, you'd have travelled through the oblast and not met a single literate person. Upon whom, then, was it possible to build, whom was the Empire's power even to exploit, when what was needed was an intelligent, educated individual able to make his own decisions? But precisely such men were banished here for political reasons! In the beginning, therefore, all functions of state and private power, for which there were no volunteers in Siberia, were carried out by exiles. And amongst the exiles, after Russians themselves, the most numerous were Poles. But their sentences came to an end and they often stayed and settled here without the judicial compulsion to settle; they married or brought their wives; the next generations grew up; meanwhile new settlers arrived from the home country after work or the opportunity to enrich themselves, now of their own free will – for profit! And how they enriched themselves! And how they built! Something out of nothing – so you see what Poland might have been like, had History played with us fairly.

'Look: Mr Ignacy Sobieszczański, upward of thirty thousand million roubles, the foremost salon in Irkutsk, scores of mines from the Yenisey to the Amur, a seat at the right hand of Pobedonostseff, president of the Coal Convention, vice-president of the Siberian State Council for Fuel. Yet when he came here after the First Revolution in nineteen-oh-five, all he had in his pocket was his engineering degree certificate from the Saint Petersburg Institute. He decided to make a career for himself, and so he clambered up mountains and over summits, roamed along rivers and dug in the soil, till he hit upon seams of iron, copper, coal, wolfram. Now he himself employs mostly Poles. Have you been to his manor? *Master Thaddeus* vivant!

'Look: Mr Kazimierz Nowak, a man who married into the Koziełł-Poklewski family. They say that the Poles made Siberia drunk – the Koziełł-Poklewskis conquered the Russians with vodka. Stop at the most outlying trading-post or remote lodge in the taiga – and you'll find "Mr Poklewski" and "Mrs Poklewska" on the table. Warehouses in Tyumen, distilleries in Padun, and here in Irkutsk the Aleksandrovsky distilleries, factories producing candles and blackwickes, acids and phosphorous. It was they who developed river steam navigation beyond the Urals. And erected so many Catholic churches, so many Polish schools, orphanages and soup kitchens and almshouses…!

'Engineer Szymanowski from the Debalcewo Mechanical Factory, worth a million two hundred; Mr Wicowski from the New Bank of Irkutsk, two million; Messrs Becki and Wartysz, shares in coal, oil and Spasowicz shoes, half a million and more; Engineer Reszke from the Northern Mammoth Company, shares in half a dozen coldmills, twenty million annual turnover from tungetitum alone; Mr Masjemłow, trans-Pacific export-import business and colonial goods stores, after the opening of the Around-the-World Railroad he'll be worth at least six million; Mr Otręba, king of the Irtkutsk Salt Refinery, despite even the concentration of gleissen there, he'll be worth a million four hundred on the salt manufactories in Usolye.

'But we all live here like maggots in the alien organism of the State – yet just imagine, sir, a State built from our own might and for our own might! Would you not wish for such History?'

This was not the reason for coming here, not the intention, nor was this thought uppermost in the mind – but the teslectric flow was too strong; feel that vibration organically, the tremble coming from every cell in the fingers knocking rapidly on the tabletop and reaching every one of the brain's nerve cells, from which tiny thunderbolts shoot black as murch neath the skull, tossing out from this lottery-drum more images of non-necessary possibilities, neither true nor false.

'No!' Growl in reply. 'I do not wish for such History!'

'Oho!'

'Polish might instead of Russian might! Or, if you prefer, Siberian might – since you, sir, are an Oblastnik and want to build a Siberian state here, not so?'

'Yes!'

'Yet what difference does it make, who wields power over whom and what language the tchinovniks speak? Again, there'll be gendarmes pursuing anti-Siberian rebels in the night and again there'll be Baikal uprisings steeped in blood. Don't tell me that it'll be otherwise; you've already dreamed it and consented to it in your dream of might – I can see – it has frozen.'

'And you would wish things to be – how? without authority? without law? You, sir, are an anarchist!'

Remember at once the quarrel in the taiga between Doctor Konyeshin and Herr Blutfeld. Shake the head in irritation.

'No! There has to be order and a force to defend us against those who would enslave us. But there cannot be any state, any power dictating good and evil from earthly thrones – nothing that exists can stand above man.'

Porfiry Pocięgło broke into a hearty laugh.

'Your head's in the clouds! The scholar logician! A state and yet no state! Power and yet no power! Freedom and yet no freedom! Marvellous! When you've devised a way of realising such paradoxes, let me know without fail, I shan't omit to make use of the prescription!'

Porfiry drank up his tchay, excused himself and headed for the conveniences. Calm down, cool down quickly. In the main room of the café, more guests had assembled, no longer sitting down even, exchanging greetings and gossip in small groups. Altogether there were more than forty of them, corpulent well-dressed gentlemen with gold and tungetitum rings on their fingers, diamonds and gold-fluff, in a show of wealth which in Europe would have seemed indecent and simply vulgar. A hubbub of Polish voices filled the café. Stub out the cigarette. The clock

stood at ten minutes to twelve. Think: a dose of murch now, the teslectric dynamo now, would come in handy – to freeze for this hour, or two.
For if something weird again enters the head at the wrong moment –

Pocięgło returned. Leap to the feet and collar him again in private,
against the wall between the pictures.

'Somehow there was no opportunity,' begin in a muffled voice with
the eyes directed at a watercolour panorama of Baikal, 'and yet I should
have done it a long time ago: I wanted to apologise for my conduct that
night in the Trans-Siberian Express.' And only when having said it was
it possible to turn the eyes towards Porfiry.

He stared oddly from under those arched hawk-like brows; flickers
of glintzen gleamed in his azure eyes. If shame were being concealed,
then it was not beneath a mask of indifference – Pocięgło must surely
be wondering now whence this anger, wherefore this ominous hostile
mien on the countenance of Benedykt Gierosławski.

'Yes?'

'I'm asking for forgiveness. I want no ill feeling between us.'

'I harbour no ill feeling,' he said cautiously.

'I want no ill feeling, for I must ask for another thing, important to
me. You are a frequent visitor to Miss Jelena Muklanowicz.'

'Ah!'

'You asked me about it then, you remember, an affair of the heart
and so on.' Attempt to untangle the mimed gestures from the face, but
it seems without success. Withstand at least Pocięgło's stare without
flinching. 'Will you – will you – will you give me your word of honour
that – with regard to Miss Muklanowicz – that you think of her – that
your intentions – are only of the most serious?'

He hesitated.

'And if I give it?'

'Then I give you my blessing. But if not, or if some lie should freeze
here –'

'So why don't you yourself... Well, yes, le Fils du Gel, c'est très fâcheux.
Are you minded to wait? Till when? She is leaving Irkutsk, and you –'

'So how will it be?'

He pressed a clenched fist to his heart.

Nod the head.

'It's a diabolical pact,' he said after a while. 'Not because it's a pact
over a woman, although – one woman two men, the devil's always med-
dling. But you well know, sir, that I desire nothing so much as Thaw
and change, the liberation of Siberia. And after the Thaw – after the
Thaw there'll be a new world and new truths. So, you make a pact over
a woman – and you already know of what you won't persuade your
father. Is it seemly – to sell History for a woman's charme?'

'You have been living too long, sir, in the Land of the Gleissen. In Summer, we also know honour.'

Again, he gave an odd glance.

'You nevertheless surprise me, Mr Gierosławski. There's a kind of madness in this, that is, mystery.' Under his stern gaze, he was suppressing a laugh, with which he intended to defuse the situation. 'Was this what you wanted to talk to me about in the Warsaw Hotel?'

'No.'

Midday struck.

Midday struck and they all suddenly rose from their tables. The head waiter together with Mr Myśliwski took up position by the double doors that led within; the head waiter pressed on a doorhandle and bowed low from the waist. Beyond the doors a red curtain was undulating; he thrust his arm into the material and drew it aside, indicating the way. The guests approached one by one, exchanging a few words with Myśliwski and disappearing between the carmine folds. In went the Gawron brothers, in went Mr Pocięgło, in went Mr Wielicki. Notice Editor Wólka-Wólkiewicz walking through the door following a brief chinwag with the doctor of laws. Soon no one was left in the room apart from the merchant Gorubsky and scribbler Lewera. Lick the lips, pass the palm over the stubble growing back on the cranium (now the skin on the head was tingling) and approach with a determined step. 'Yes?' Mr Myśliwski smiled encouragingly. 'Benedykt Gierosławski.' 'Benedykt Gierosławski,' he repeated, as though he had to hear the name from his own mouth. Was it incumbent to say something more? Was it necessary on the first occasion to pass a test? According to what criteria did Myśliwski separate those who enter from those who cannot? The ritual was obligatory; the tradition was obligatory. But Mr Wielicki had given no instructions! *Introduce yourself politely and watch whether he offers his hand.* Meanwhile the doorkeeper stood in silence, making no gesture, clearly waiting for something. Bow again? Click the heels? Hold out the right hand? Say something – absolutely. But what? That brought here by Wojsław Wielicki? That the son of Father Frost? That don't know what to say? Maybe what was needed was simply to ask. Wielicki should have forewarned! Stand like a stone statue staring ahead with an obstinacy that was hardly friendly, seeming even to hold the breath, whilst only teslectric flow, a stream of scalding negative murch crept under the surface of the flesh, in the veins and along the nerves. Tlicktlock, tlick-tlock, clacked the amused clock. The head waiter pretended not to be watching the scene before him, half-turned away with an arm in the red drapery. The compulsion rose with every second – that internal force which comes after all from outside of man and has nothing in common with man – an impersonal force stretching the muscles of the face, opening wide the mouth doglike, kindling fires neath the skin. About to smile apologetically; shame is about to take possession. Stand like a statue. Mr Myśliwski lifted his open hand. React only after a moment, seizing and squeezing it violently. The head waiter gestured invitingly. Step into the soft redness.

Beyond the red curtain was a narrow spiral staircase leading to the floor above and at their top another set of doors, propped wide open, and only beyond them – the spacious clubroom mapping more or less onto the dimensions of the coffee house below. The central space was taken by a table shaped like a letter T, at which members of the club were seated. In the middle of the crosswise arm of the T, against the backdrop of windows looking onto Glavnaya Street, sat an elderly gentleman disfigured by numerous frostbite wounds, with a hearing trumpet attached to his ear – Mr Zweigros no doubt. Notice there also Messrs Pocięgło, Grzywaczewski and Sobieszczański. A dozen or so people occupied the chairs, ottomans and benches spaced around the walls between pots of azalea, araucaria and rhododendron. Live indoor plants – no small luxury in the City of Ice. Sit down beside a white bloom, next to Wólka-Wólkiewicz. Tempted to ask him a question at once, but the old editor, removing his pen from the pages of his notebook, pressed it to his lips, enjoining silence. Indeed, no one was saying anything; outside the windows could be heard the whistle of an icy gale and the echo of the glashatays' drums carried through the fog. Glance at the wall above the head where a portrait hung of a man in seventeenth- or eighteenth-century dress. The room in general was embellished by many pictures, portraits as well as representations of Siberian nature, or genre scenes painted against its background. Read off the engraved brass plates on the frames of the nearest paintings: Joachim Leśniewski, Ferdynand Burski, Leopold Niemirowski, Henryk Nowakowski, Stanisław Wroński. Maybe they were recognised artists or maybe equivalents of Lewera in the realm of the brush; a lack of knowledge here to judge. Make no attempt to guess the identity of the persons portrayed. Read also, without craning the neck, a brass plate on the wall to the right: *Lord of the Mammoths – Karol Bohdanowicz – 1864–1922 – His coal, His cold iron*. A greying stocky man looked down from the portrait, with short neck, massive head stuck firmly on shoulders, receding brow, clipped moustache and pointed beard above a stiff white collar and black cravat.

Mr Myśliwski closed the doors. Everyone stood up, Mr Zweigros recited a prayer. A loud 'We beseech Thee, O Lord' and 'Amen' resounded throughout the room. They sat down. Only Mr Zweigros remained on his feet, leaning on the tabletop with his bony fist. In a few short words he thanked everyone for coming, announced the tragic death of one of the club members and asked for generous donations to the Father Szerwnicki Philanthropic Society (this month the chief cause was saving the Polish Library, frozen-through by a gleiss), whereupon he handed the floor to the chairman of the convention, Mr Ignacy Sobieszczański. Engineer Sobieszczański read out from a sheet of paper three proposed resolutions for the club to adopt; these concerned, amongst other things, various articles slandering Mayor Szostakiewicz as well as the dissociation of the 'Polish industrial circles of Siberia' from the activities of Piłsudski's Yapontchiks. This provoked a rather sharp exchange of opinions between several club members. Wólka-Wólkiewicz assiduously took notes.

Whilst further points were being discussed at the table, uninhibited thought tore itself from the present and flew back to the moment not long ago outside the downstairs doors. If that were a test – upon what had it depended? in what way had the test been passed? By doing nothing, by saying nothing, by loitering before Myśliwski like a lifeless doll. Had the correct reaction in fact been the lack of reaction, that is, the failure to react? Not a word, but the lack of word? Not a gesture, but the lack of gesture? The unrealised – is more important than the realised. But what is this unrealised meant to betoken? If a man who pleaded not, bowed not, asked no questions, was allowed to enter – then were those who pleaded and urged driven away? Maybe this was beside the point. Mr Myśliwski had gazed with the eye of judgement boring into the soul – an old gleissenik – a doctor of laws and working solicitor experienced in the diseases of human character, character, which in the land of the Ice is a quantity as certain and measurable as the temperature of an organism or the spatial dimensions of a material object. It was impossible not to be reminded of Prosecutor Pyotr Leontinovitch Razbyesoff. 'Fairy tales!' shout in spirit. How does he manage it? A minute, two minutes, no words, he gazes – and then already he knows? has already known the person? Fairy tales! Moreover, flows of teslectricity could still be felt in the body demurched at dawn by the Kotarbiński pump. Had the reverse been so: had the body been bemurched, had it frozen – well, maybe then Myśliwski would have had something to watch in the man before him. But now, in the ungluing of Benedykt Gierosławski from Benedykt Gierosławski? Whom exactly had he seen? Whom had he allowed to cross the threshold? Scratch nervously at the back of the hand.

Having voted on the resolutions proposed by Engineer Sobieszczański in his function as chairman, the club members proceeded to discuss the main item of the convention, namely their positions on the mining law reform in the guberniyas of the Ice, proposed by Prime Minister Struve. Thus far, the principle binding in the Empire had been that ownership

of land also encompassed all of its natural resources, whilst lands belonging to the state (in other words, to Romanoff Russia but not to
the Romanoffs personally) remained open for mining. This was now
about to change. Pyotr Struve intended to nationalise the Ways of the
Mammoths. At this point, a regular debate flared up around the table
with the usual fist-banging on the tabletop, shouting at one another and
ringing on a glass to calm the most inflamed – which had little effect.
Of the men sitting by the walls, some approached the club members
and whispered something in their ears; papers were circulating. The
club was of one mind in its opposition to Struve's proposal, whereas
radical divergences of opinion arose as to the methods by which the
project should be opposed. Since it struck at all coldiron industrialists alike, irrespective of their nationality, the faction led by Porfiry
Pocięgło was pressing for the exploitation of this opportunity to build
a common secessionist front striving to declare the economic independence at least of Siberia. The loyalist faction had no wish to hear such
'provocations against the tsar'. The Polonocentric faction, via the lips of
Ignacy Sobieszczański, was tabling questions on Polish independence
in the context of Siberian independence – would the chances of the
former increase or diminish thanks to the latter? and according to what
geopolitical plans might it be calculated? Finally, there were numerous
more cautious voices amongst the club members, largely of the older
generation, who doubted the feasibility of introducing any kind of pro-
founder change under the Ice. 'But do we really want to get rid of the
Ice?' they asked, fearful of the threat from the Japanese Empire should
the tsar's armies abandon Siberia. Who shall defend us then, Piłsudski's
ragamuffins? Pocięgło banged on the table with a frostoglaze ashtray:
'The state! The state!'

Others were smoking – light a cigarette.

'They won't admit it,' remarked Editor Wólka-Wólkiewicz acrimoniously, tugging in his fury at the bowtie caught high on his Adam's apple.
'Bourgeois hypocrites! I could point the finger, sir, at those who gave
money to Piłsudski and the old Polish Socialist Party. Now that they've
lost hundreds of thousands due to the closure of Kezhma, none will
admit it.'

'How come the greatest capitalists pay socialists?'

'Of course! Who else? Not the paupers who can't afford their own
bread. But you won't finance mass armed struggle by robbing trains.'

'But where's the logic? They're paying for their own ruin!'

'You live in his house and still can't tell the caricature of a bourgeois
from the real bourgeois! The majority are good people, Benedykt, sir.'

'Beg pardon?'

'What bad thing could you say of your host? Does he not have a kind heart? Does he not like people? But he has money. Why should he not invest in the struggle to straighten out History in the name of universal justice? Is he not pained by inequality, not embarrassed by his own wealth confronted by another's penury?'

Glance at Mr Wielicki, who was energetically perorating about something at that moment, as rainbow sunlight flashed in the diamond once belonging to Mijnheer Ojdeenk.

'He...?'

'I am not saying that Mr Wielicki – but precisely such people, people like him. Do you imagine, sir, that once a man has made money, he'll no longer be what he was before but suddenly, by dint of some magic spell, take on reactionary anti-human views? The ability to make money has nothing to do with political taste. They exploit without knowing they exploit, sincerely believing in such a world order. Of course, still greater hypocrites, having enriched themselves, may act out of stupid petty fear despite their heartfelt convictions, especially if they put their faith in the latest caricatures of socialism, the various Leninist and Trotskyist visions of class terror – but stupidity, dishonesty and hypocrisy rarely go hand in hand with a personality predestined to succeed in business. You'll find more constitutional democrats and Struvist socialists amongst Russia's recent millionaires than amongst the small landowners and old petty bourgeoisie, not to mention the superstitious uneducated peasantry. Just ask yourself, how many parsimonious yet pious Jews invest – not in popular philanthropy, but in social movements! Why? Because they are good people.'

He too was wanting to smoke; offer him a light.

'The second circumstance, Benedykt, is that Piłsudski is no longer fighting for proletarian revolution, but for Poland. As to the PPS... Besides, the situation in the socialist party has grown very confused in recent years. Again, they're quarrelling over assets snatched following the scission; after twenty years of arguing over a print shop and a pile of books, the arbitration of the International Socialist Bureau brought them next to nothing. Perhaps you read the underground pamphlets or the Cracow press? The 'Young Faction' has firmly seized the reins in the former Kingdom and in Galicia. The Revolutionary Faction has no clear idea of how to position itself between them and Piłsudski. Whilst Piłsudski is no longer even trying to create a new party here, he just waits for opportunities to make use of the military forces. So long as the Frost retains its grip on everything from the Pacific to the Oder, however, there's little difference between one vain hope and another vain hope.'

Inhale the smoke, deep in thought. Mm-hmm. That no less a schism existed in the PPS than amongst the Martsynians – had not been considered. From which political faction indeed was that earless PPS-man in Warsaw? Perhaps he wasn't a Piłsudtchik at all; and perhaps that's precisely why their people can't reach Father Frost, because Piłsudski blocks access here on the spot, intercepts their messengers. They're feuding amongst themselves.

'But tell me, Editor sir, which faction of the PPS might wish for the following kind of Thaw: in the west as far as the Dnieper, no farther, the whole of Russia under the Ice, but Japan free. According to Schultz's model: leave the gleissen here in peace, don't break up the Ice? Whose policy would that be?'

'And since when have there existed policies of Thaw? As though we could decide about such matters...!' he bridled and immediately explained. 'They come to you with this, huh? Father Frost and his little son, well, yes.' His badger's whiskers bristled. 'Mm-hmm, there've been articles on it in *The Worker*, in *The Tribune* and I believe also in *The Free Pole* – but considered only on the same basis, you understand, as any other direction in the development of events, such as the death of a tsar, war in the Balkans, revolution in the West, or the fratricidal madness of Willy, Nicky and Ferdinand. So here, the "Young Ones" differ in their hopes from the "Old Guard" and Piłsudski.

'The former count on total Thaw, that is, in Russia first and foremost, for in this way a workers' revolution would ignite the whole Empire – but that it should happen in the Polish lands would be as occasion arose, and that an independent Poland might be born out of it is for them the secondary issue.

'The latter assess their political chances differently: first, their aim is not to liberate only the Russian partition but Poland in its entirety, hence Thaw would not in itself suddenly change the politics of the Habsburgs and Hohenzollerns; second, there's no guarantee that a Russia moving forward in History would enter Revolution and a form of socialism eager to grant freedom to the enslaved nations of the Empire, and not grow for example into an even mightier Empire, because it would be modern, organised along Bismarckian lines. The state! Do you understand, sir? The state outlives everything else.'

'Yes.'

'And with this argumentation, Piłsudski eventually convinced Perl and comrades in the Revolutionary Faction, in the Combat Organisation, and in the Rifles back home.'

'And so Józef Piłsudski has turned out to be a Lyednyak.' Heave a sigh. 'He's defending the Russia of the Ice, or have I got it wrong?'

'Come, come, don't be so facetious, dear boy.' The little editor was overcome by irritation. 'He is a man who at least has a concrete plan and has not ceased trying for years to realise it. He knows what he wants, knows how to achieve it, and does everything he can to get it. Of how many of our basement politicos and coffee house ideologues could you say the same, sir? How many believe at all that Poland is something we can build, create, gain by force of arms, attain with our own hands and not thanks to the favourable dispensations of fate, to an auspicious configuration of the stars, to some fluky war between the Triple Alliance and the Entente, or thanks to the caprice of foreign powers into whose good graces we have to insinuate ourselves at any cost – or thanks simply to some magical force of History? Eh? But do people understand him? Value him? Hah!' He snorted fierily and shifting his cigarette to the other corner of his mouth, sat hunched over his notebook.

After upwards of an hour, the position on the question of the mining law was voted on; Pocięgło lost, and victory was carried by the option favouring a symbolic protest, sending a letter with instructions to the councillors in Saint Petersburg and waiting to see how the situation developed. But it transpired at once that Porfiry had no intention of laying down arms; this was merely the overture to the real battle he was about to wage over a matter brought before the club on his private initiative. And so Pocięgło had obtained information from his own people (most likely commercial agents in America) that Harriman's competitor on Wall Street, the American steel and copper tycoon John Pierpont Morgan, had dispatched a delegation by sea via San Francisco and Vladivostock with the explicit intention of blocking work on the Alaskan Tunnel and Around-the-World Railroad – such a transportation line connecting Alaska and America to Siberia would have cost J.P. Morgan a fortune in contractual and stock-exchange losses as well as monopolies on raw materials. Buying off US Steel from Carnegie twenty years earlier, Morgan had paid a quarter of a billion dollars; today the concern was worth more than all Russia's resources put together – these were already spheres wherein money rules politics and not the other way around. (Prick up the ears.) The Around-the-World Railroad, however, was an enterprise crucial to the triumph of the Oblastnik idea. For purely economic reasons, the Railroad had the support of Pobedonostseff, whilst Schultz-Zimovy was also pleased, naturally, to see the greater independence of his general governorate from European Russia. It was different with the emperor and nobles and generally amongst Lyednyaks from the Great Russian Heartland. Precedents were well known of backhanders worth millions of roubles changing the course of Russian politics. Morgan could afford such a bribe. He had no need to buy over hosts of tchinovniks and court councillors; it was enough for him to be assured of Rasputin's goodwill. (Whatever rules the tsar – nightmares and a Samurai sword – there is no logic above the divine whim of the autocrat.) Mr Pocięgło argued very seriously that pure calculation of profits required the coldiron industrialists to undertake every effort to prevent J.P. Morgan's mission from establishing contact with the Martsynians, as well as to protect the construction of the Tunnel. Asked what specific actions he had in mind, he replied that these would be the responsibility of a secret committee appointed for this purpose by the club. 'Shame!' shouted one and then another. 'Whom do you take us for, some sort of bandits! God shall judge you!' And so on, and so on; it went on for a long time although Pocięgło was unable to supply any more particulars, and the dispute remained on the level of invectives and generalised appeals for decency, Christian virtues and the like. A vote was taken and Pocięgło's proposal passed in a ratio of three to one with a large number of abstentions. Pocięgło stood up, bowed and thanked everyone. 'Ask yourself, sir, how many of them have shares in Harriman's Railroad,' whispered Editor Wólka-Wólkiewicz.

Mr Zweigros hoisted himself out of his chair and raised a glass of red wine in a toast to business success and Polish wealth in Siberia. They drank to it. Standing, all members of the club reached under the serviettes folded on the side-plates to their right, and grasped in the fingers of both hands some small coins. A protracted ring reverberated like the sound of crushed porcelain. The convention had come to an end.

The unofficial part of the meeting commenced, probably more important than the official, as usually happens in politics. They all gathered in little groups and circles of close-knit acquaintances; the room filled with the hubbub of free conversation. Cast about for Mr Grzywaczewski, who had vanished somewhere in the throng, not being the tallest in stature. Notice only then that someone was standing close by and observing with a friendly smile. Who? Turn around. Engineer Reszke from the Northern Mammoth Company.

'Excuse me.'

'I –'

'Permit me –'

'Benedykt Gierosławski.'

'Yes, yes. Reszke, Romuald Reszke. Might we –'

'What can I do for you?'

'I hope you won't take it amiss, sir. It so happened that I exchanged a few words about you with Mr Wojsław Wielicki. Well, all right, I admit it,' he lowered his eye, 'I was asking about you. We have been interested from the very beginning in the doings of Doctor Tesla. You, so I hear, are a good friend of his…' Suddenly, he changed the subject. 'Have you spoken already to the governor?'

'No.'

'I think you'll find him a very reasonable man, and the solution proposed by him – the only right one in our situation. The quicker it's decided, the better. It has come to my ears that, in the meantime, you are seeking a position here, and –'

Understand what Reszke is aiming at in his roundabout way: how to bribe without uttering aloud an improper word. Understand: they will all lose a lot – entire fortunes – when the Ice retreats. Wielicki will lose too. So, this is his investment: the gratitude of the Son of Frost! If only they could, they'd blow up Tesla and his machines!

Ah, no! They're 'good people'! Suppress an acrimonious snigger. For there's no Tchingis Shtchekelnikoff, no one to protect from the devouring poison of suspicion as he absorbs into his body; it's already re-infecting the soul. Seek with the eyes the jovial countenance of Wielicki. *Does he not have a kind heart? Does he not like people?*

'... with Doctor Tesla?'

'*Plaît-il?*'

'At a time and in a place convenient to him, it goes without saying. You see, sir, we have been trying to contact him, our man was at his hotel and in the Observatory, but –'

Take a deeper breath.

'There's no point, Engineer. Surely, you've had dealings with scientists like Tesla. There are no riches for which he'd give up his discoveries and fame as inventor, as the father of black physics. Forgive me, sir.'

Steer a path between the club members to reach Grzywaczewski.

On the second blinking of his eye, he recognised who it was.

'Benedykt... sir.'

Squeeze his hand, the healthy right one; he had a grip like a vice.

'I heard you knew Filip Gierosławski.'

'I beg your pardon...?'

'Ah, in that case I apologise.'

Mr Saturnin Grzywaczewski dismissed his previous interlocutor with a motion of the head and detached himself from his group, walking away to an inside corner of the table.

'Mr Wielicki told me. If I might be of any help,' he took out a visiting card, 'please don't hesitate.'

Ye-es, every second coldiron industrialist wants to buy dirt-cheap the gratitude of the Son of Frost. What would be simpler than to let them? To ask for a loan – he'll give it without a murmur, a thousand, two thousand, three, what's it to him?

Give a start as if licked by living fire. Clench the fists; the skin had almost stopped stinging. Damned Myśliwski, doctor of laws and judge-cum-executioner.

'I'm looking for regular work.' Speak emphatically, almost theatrically. 'A permanent post.'

Director Grzywaczewski, the 'hardworking egoist' (penumbra like a black aureole), merely nodded.

'What qualifications do you have? Have you ever worked in the mining industry, in metallurgy, in commerce perhaps?'

'No.'

'You know languages?'

'Russian and German. I can get by in French. Cope with the Classical languages in written form.'

'What exactly did you do in the Kingdom?'

'Mathematical logic.' Cross the arms over the chest, clucking at the same time. 'Experimental logic. I'm afraid nothing of practical use in trade or industry.'

'Experimental logic, you say. In other words, you're an egghead. Wait a moment, I have an idea.' Leaning over the table, he jotted down a few words on the back of his card. 'Report on Monday to our countinghouse in Zimny Nikolayevsk with this, they'll direct you to Doctor Wolfke. We shall see if you're fit for purpose. Then we can discuss terms.'

'Thank you very much. But on what salary –'

'Should Wolfke find you useful, we can talk about it. Later, later.'

'All right, sir.'

He grunted something else encouraging and walked away.

Think at that moment, for no apparent reason, of Julia. Why, in Warsaw, had the idea of permanent paid work remained so inconceivable that a position had never even been seriously sought? There was a crisis, true, everyone was looking for work, a dozen similar emaciated students knocking daily on doors everywhere – and yet. Mr Korzyński and those like him would surely have helped for the sake of father's memory. Had a chap really applied himself, had he but tried... Here in Siberia, as Pocięgło was saying, they even appoint educated people from amongst the exiles. But that's not what it's about. Unclench the fists, lay the hands flat on the tabletop; the little white card fell onto the mahogany. Blue nails, bricklike pattern of pink blotches under the skin... The murch, pumped off by the litre into the crystals, also explains nothing in the final analysis – for what explanation can there be? One gets to know the world, gets to know a language for describing the world, but does not get to know oneself. Something is done, so we speculate: why was it done? And even if the speculation turns out to be true – it can in no way be put into words, for these are not things that can be put into words in the language of the second kind. At most, Mr Pocięgło or Mr Myśliwski may be asked – they'll express without inhibition their judgement on the stranger; and so, for a moment, Benedykt

Gierosławski will see himself from outside. Benedykt Gierosławski, who is such and such, because he behaved in such and such a way; bah, before he even behaved in any way at all.

There was a ringing of glass. Mr Wólka-Wólkiewicz had stumbled over a chair. Making the most of the opportunity to get drunk for free, the journal editor had already assailed the drinks table and managed, despite the early hour, to drain into himself a respectable dose of alcohol – his nose shone, his ruddy cheeks were baking, sweat stood out above his silvery brows, whilst the stiff bristles of his moustache trembled unceasingly like insects' eyestalks.

'I see you too have clinched some deal,' he muttered, casting a squint-eyed glance at Director Grzywaczewski's visiting card. 'It's infectious, you know, this atmosphere, this energy,' he waved his glass – wine splashed over his cuff but he failed to notice, 'this impetus; the world revolves faster here, days flit by faster, hour eats into hour, a man chases from dawn to dusk and not in the least because he's hurrying to work, not because he's hungry or poor, but because there's always one more rouble to be made, always some opportunity, some profit in sight – and already you can see the spark in his eyes, fresh strength in his muscles; they can rush like this day and night, from rouble to rouble, the predators of the market. Do you imagine, sir, I don't feel it – I also feel it, though younger men obviously feel it a hundred times stronger. When they're making money, they're livelier; when they let money slip through their hands, life drains from them. It's possessed you too, huh?'

'Maybe. A little.'

'Will you set up your own firm?'

Wince mockingly, but mockery fell at once from the face. Sit down at the table, brushing the elbow against a side-plate covered in a serviette; clearly, the place was reserved for a member of the club who had not shown up at the convention.

Own firm... Scrape mechanically between the knuckles. No time to build a business from scratch; better to buy shares in an existing one. Someone has to take care, after all, of the transport of equipment and proviant to the outlying magpieries, beyond Kezhma. So this would have been the ideal cover. But where to find the capital? Isn't it better to hire people as a one-off? No point in building a hammer factory to bang in a dozen nails.

'You want to go into coldiron?' asked Wólka-Wólkiewicz.

'Mm-hmm? No, no. I'd first have to look around, investigate the conditions...'

What an idiotic idea! Setting up a business! A man never possessed in life his own four walls, yet here he's suddenly dreaming of shares, capital investments, enterprises! A fresh bout of insanity – evidently, the murch levels in the brain had not yet evened out.

Wólka-Wólkiewicz raised his near-empty glass in a half-derisory toast. 'To the birth of our next capitalist here.'

'Yeh, a capitalist with no capital.'

'Capital? Marx knew nothing of people! Look, ephh, look at the Jews: they arrive here without a groschen to their name and twenty years later, half the city shops belong to them. Capital ebbs and flows – whilst men have frozen either with a head for money, or not.'

Move the palm over the surface of the table. The thumb reached the coin lying neath the serviette. Draw it off the plate, toss it in the hand. It was a copper kopeck from the previous century with the two-headed eagle on the reverse, small and light. In addition, a groove had been filed across its diameter, between the heads of the bird, so that the two halves were joined by only a thin strip of metal. Clasp it in the fingers. A child could have broken it.

On what cannot be felt

Posing here as a model already for the third time.

'But can you not keep still, Benedykt, sir!'

'I am keeping still.'

The stool was uncomfortable. When Miss Muklanowicz had been visited for the first time at Kirytchkina's boarding house, the young woman was all smeared in charcoal – dainty black fingers, a streak under the eye, a blotch on the nose, till the hand reached of its own accord for a handkerchief. Jelena had begun with bold sweeping sketches on large pieces of cardboard. She also had an easel, which came in useful when she tried her hand at portraits – of auntie, the maid, Mademoiselle Filipov, Mr Pocięgło. Pocięgło had presented her with a full set of artist's accessories, including eight-by-ten-inch stretched canvases, a large palette and box of oil paints. Jelena drew in the corner room, taking advantage of the sunlight whitened by ice and snow; the stool was positioned between windows. More comfortable upright chairs and armchairs had proved too low, as Miss Muklanowicz had to have the model's face at a suitable height; only this heavy pinewood stool was fit for purpose.

The door to the sitting room, where Aunt Urszula lay gently snoring, stood open in order to uphold decorum. Speak in undertones so as not to wake her. Immediately to the right, a spitting distance or breath away, was the frostoglaze surface of the windowpane, flooded by every discoloration of white; Jelena had to be squinted at with the left eye.

When painting, she wore a sarafan that was too big for her, purchased most likely from the maid; now it was wholly covered in splodges of charcoal and oil paint. Twist the head, twitch by twitch, so as to capture Jelena's half-profile in that enchanting state of forgetfulness, when she was totally engrossed in her picture-making: tongue thrust out, lip bitten, frowning drolly, head inclined this way or that till the black locks fell onto her forehead, onto her eyes, onto her flushed rosy cheeks. Then she would blow angrily, pushing back the hair; or she'd forget herself still further and reach for it with her hand, so that flecks of smudged maquillage arose on the devushka's face, like a flowering meadow bright with colour.

'Well, all right, but wasn't he in that case a bigamist?'

'No, he and Leokadia Gwóźdź were cohabiting.'

'Nevertheless – what an unfeeling heart! You'll forgive me, Benedykt, but – his wife was dying at the time in Warsaw! Yes? Knowing the meanness of human nature as I do, it's a wonder no "well-wisher" wrote to her about it, out of pure malice.'

'An unmarried woman with a child – do you imagine, miss, they ever ventured anywhere here in society? Maybe in the Russian provinces, they'd have got away with it, but in Irkutsk? They kept it to themselves, it's unlikely anyone ever knew about Mrs Gwóźdź and her baby daughter.'

'Head straight! So therefore – so therefore you think it's because of that, because of the child's death. Agh! She was your own sister after all, your little half-sister – but what was she called, the one he's supposed to have shot?'

'Emilia, Emilka.'

'Again, you moved.' She strode over, grabbed the elbow and wrist, arranged them this way, arranged them that way, bent her head, screwed up her eyes, sucked in her cheek, no, it still wasn't right.

'Ow! You're twisting my arm.'

She turned over the hand, examined it closely.

'Well, you see, you scratch and scratch, maybe you should go to a doctor, it looks like some kind of eczema –'

'It's hard to stop when –'

'Ointment. Or wear cotton gloves.'

'Mm-hmm. Like Doctor Tesla.'

'Oh, that way! And please hold it there for a moment! I have perfect light for the profile and shoulder.'

The forms of houses, fogs and gleissen swam on the frostoglaze. Kirytchkina's boarding house was located in the southern part of old Irkutsk, in Gretchesky Pereulok, not far from Innokentyevskoye Village. The skeleton-like finger of Sibirkhozheto Tower divided as usual the cityscape of the metropolis into two, but from here Christ the Saviour Sobor could not be seen. The bronze bells, however, were pealing audibly enough. No snow was falling, the bright sky was clear and cloudless, smooth azure-blue, whilst the Sun stood high above the fog; the Tchorniye Siyaniye had completely died out. It was one of those rare days when Irkutsk, viewed from on high, opened before the human eye a broad panorama worthy of a fresco or indeed a monumental painting. Notice, already on the way from the Church of Our Lady of the Assumption to the Commissariat Garden, sitting in the sleigh beside Aunt Urszula, the extraordinary peace, stillness and lack of Sunday traffic, which contributed also to the atmosphere: the winds had subsided, clouds had evaporated from the sky, even the fog had thinned and sunk low into the streets between houses. For the first time it was possible to admire the coloured shutters of the Irkutsk cottages, blue, green, yellow, adorned in various frostlike patterns, carved in fanciful symmetries as well as clumsier geometries. The air was marvellously transparent as happens on fine frosty days; the farthest shape on the horizon stood out sharp and distinct. The pale light of frostoglaze streetlamps and rainbows refracted on coldiron did nothing to ruffle the image, only outlined it in thicker contours of shadow, so that every object, every silhouette appeared surrounded by a ribbon of precious material – like on a huge movable icon. The drums too had abated and street vendors no longer rent their throats, whilst no words were exchanged in the sleigh – only the sleigh-bells rang out as before on the horse's harness. Jingle-jangle. Glide across the white-hued icon of the City of Ice…

The Intendantsky Garden had been established on the bank of the Ushakovka river more than half a century before; later it was utterly devastated twice, and only several years after the Great Fire did the idea take shape in the Irkutsk city duma to revive it and restore its function as a place intended for the townsfolk to commune with nature, irrespective of the cost; this was extraordinarily important in the time of the Ice and perpetual winter cutting off the metropolis from the natural world. Amongst the project's funders were most of the prominent coldiron industrialists; their names and the titles of firms and companies adorned in pure tungetitum the marble plaques erected at the entrance to the Garden, that is, by the temperature-adjustment chamber where an entry fee was collected to the tune of two and a half roubles per person, one rouble for a child. The charges served as a tool of social filtration, for no working family could afford such expense for the pleasure of a short walk in the warm; besides, the upkeep of the Garden was devouring a vast fortune year on year. Blowers pumping warm air under the frostoglaze worked non-stop, powered by diesel engines. At night, when the Garden was closed to the public, hiberniks hired by the dozen crawled over the gigantic greenhouse construction scraping off icy accretions and searching for the tiniest cracks. The construction stood on a lacework coldiron skeleton representing the same architectural style as the Muravyoff Station, since it had been conceived in the mind of the same architect. Rubetsky K.I. had imagined the Garden covered in roofing-panels like the vast upturned calyces of rainbow-coloured lilies. In time of sunshine, like today, light from the sky, split on the frostoglaze into soft seven-coloured beams, falls directly onto streams, footbridges, shrubberies, flowering meadows, ponds and fountains, onto white-painted benches and summer houses, onto ladies and gentlemen strolling along the sandy walkways, onto small children romping on the green sward dressed in stockings and frills *à la* Little Lord Fauntleroy, in sailor suits and *canotier* straw boaters. A theatre of summer takes place, where the lie of dress, behaviour and word is obligatory. From under the furs and stoles left in the adjustment chamber, ladies reveal bright-coloured dresses with silk petticoats, English light suits, and kimono-style asymmetrically cut high bodices, and this all neath a spring parasol, as if it offered any real protection, clasped in a white-gloved hand, from the sweltering sun. Gentlemen in unbuttoned three-piece summer suits lie with their bowlers and homburgs, slender canes and clean patent-leather shoes with pointed toes. The rumble of heating engines rolls around the Garden in a monotonous rhythm; as such beats the mechanical heart of the greenery. Through the rainbows of the undulating roof can be seen the surrounding thicket of corpse masts – they do not, however, deter gleissen. Every time an icer traverses the Garden, the grass has to be resown, the trees regrafted, the idyllic landscape reconstructed flower by flower – all of it a lie. The streams flow neither out of nor into the Ushakovka; they circulate in peculiar loops, assisted by hidden contraptions, separated by insulation lining from the permafrost – lies, lies. Walks are taken at a slow dignified pace, sitting from time to time on a bench, pausing by a picturesque brook. Friends and strangers alike are bowed to politely. Empty courtesies are exchanged – no word at all about business, no reminder of icebound real life, nor mention God forbid of any family or health worries! For here – it is Summer. Here – a warm cosy falsehood is thrown around the shoulders like a muslin *cachenez*. What would the bourgeoisie be if robbed of its right to lie about itself? Neither aristocracy nor proletariat; neither life in spirit nor life in matter. At least once a week, therefore, it's incumbent to go for a walk neath the bourgeois sun, in the best light-coloured suit with an extravagantly dressed woman on the arm. Once under the orders of Miss Muklanowicz – how many weeks ago was it? – in church at Mass, seated under her eye, she will no longer let go and in her resolute flirting demands to be accompanied to the Intendantsky Garden. Where an hour or two is spent in the heated air, willingly consenting to that compromise with truth. Aunt Urszula remains at a suitable distance; it's possible to speak freely with Miss Muklanowicz, all the more freely since it's once again a stroll through a Urals meadow, a rainbow conversation in the Kotarbiński Express – possible to speak the most honest adamantine truth – she won't recognise it – true or false? – as she pauses on the alabaster footbridge under a heat vent leading from the industrial engines, exposing her baked cheek to the caress of the breeze, her eyelids half-lowered –

'How is it with your dreams, Benedykt?'

Twist around on the stool.

'Dreams?'

'Haven't they been warning you? They warn me endlessly. And the priest was saying again today in his sermon.'

'I don't dream.'

'Everyone dreams.'

'Not everyone remembers his dreams.'

'Perhaps you're taking those Chinese herbs at bedtime?'

'Something really momentous has to happen for me to remember a dream afterwards.'

'Ah, for you dream of the past! But,' she scratched above her eyebrow with the paintbrush handle, 'you don't believe in the past. Don't believe that you exist, correct? So how can you dream?'

'In dream, Jelena, in dream I exist.'

'I don't understand.'

'What don't you understand? *A man dreams that he exists.* Others dream like this all their lives.'

'Hah! So, what does the non-existent man dream of?'

'Precisely of this.' Adjust the position on the stool, tensing and slackening the muscles. Dreaming, for example, goes like this... Imagine, miss, a type of illness: mental obesity. That you are, and are more. That you devour, suck into your own existence more and more, stage by stage, beyond all healthy limits. For first of all, you are the very source of your senses, a receding point behind the eyes, behind the ears, under the skin. In the head, in the brain. But then you consume the rest of your body, torso, limbs: you are not in your head, but are the head; you are also the legs, also the fingers; the nail peeling off the thumb – is likewise you. Is it healthy? You go on getting fatter: not only your body, for if the fingernail, then also the objects surrounding you, the matter closest to you, the air you inhale, exhale, the air all around you. More.

Your house. The earth over which you tread. The boundary between bodily matter and body-affecting matter is erased and disappears: this is you, and this is also you, maybe a little less – but you, you, you. And so, you absorb further realms of matter, unable to restrain yourself. Have you seen genuine guzzlers? How they eat?

'One's existence is a type of addictive disease.'

Miss Muklanowicz watched gravely from over the easel.

'If you'd only stop poisoning yourself, sir, with that teslectricity...!' she sighed following a long pause.

'Aye-aye-aye, poisoning but not really poisoning!'

'But I can see how it affects you when you come straight from Tesla's.'

'Like how?'

'Head still!'

'Wait a minute, I'm still freezing.'

'You thought you'd tempt me – once someone's had a taste, they're hooked forever, huh?'

'But what exactly have you got against it? You've been listening too much to Mademoiselle Filipov, well no wonder.'

'Dear God, can you be surprised! It's dangerous! No one knows what effect it has, what it does to the human body; even Doctor Tesla!'

'So how do you know that it's dangerous?'

'How you annoy me with your clever talk!'

'I'm sorry.'

'He almost died of it!'

'It's possible to overdose on anything, even oxygen, with fatal results.'

'...'

'I'm sorry.'

'But what for, what for, tell me, what for!'

'Because then you are someone more.'

'I beg your pardon?'

'No, no I can't.'

'Try, Benedykt, sir.'

'You are who you are, think what you think, feel what you feel. But if you're to go beyond, if you're to conduct thought that no one has ever conducted before – like a pendulum nudged from its state of rest – you have to knock yourself out of yourself. Be at the same time both yourself and someone other than yourself.'

'En-lie yourself.'

'En-lie. Perhaps. The point is that... The more we freeze, the less we can. The more... true we are, the less we feel, the less we think; we are lesser – narrower – more insular people.'

'And you want, Benedykt –'

'To think what has never been thought before.'

'To feel what has never been felt before.' Wiping her forehead with the sleeve of her linen blouse, Miss Muklanowicz laughed hesitantly. 'But that's absurd!'

'Do you really believe, miss, that the feelings of which you yourself are capable are all possible feelings?'

'So, what others are there?'

'Am I to utter a word for which you have no words? Try describing sadness to a man who's never heard of sadness.'

'He doesn't laugh. Wants to weep. The world is ugly. He moves without energy. Dispirited.'

'You're describing behaviour.'

'Yes.' She mused for a moment. 'As you, sir, put it in the train…

How can the heart itself express?
Another understand what you confess?
Will he understand what you live by?
A spoken thought can only lie!

Spring up from the stool, grab hold of an ear, reach for the window-pane and begin to violently lick the frostoglaze; the other arm jumped up and down in the joints like an enraged snake, waving the outspread hand all around; the left leg was kicking the right; make moaning, meowing noises and roll the eyes.

Miss Muklanowicz was miffed.

'Madness.'

'This – this – this is your feeling now.' Gasp between the licks and moans, 'but what do I feel?'

'Dirt on your tongue. Stop it, sir, what tomfoolery, you'll wake Auntie.'

Disengage from the windowpane. Spit into the spitting-box, straighten the frock coat.

Miss Muklanowicz was wiping her hands on a cloth, having stepped back from the easel.

'Anyway, what is it you're trying to persuade me of? That this black current turns a man's brain topsy-turvy?'

'But you don't remember, Jelena? What you felt? How you behaved? Who you were?'

She shrugged her shoulders.

'There are other ways of going beyond yourself. Alcohol, for instance.'

'Alcohol is a sick substitute. It exchanges one prison for another, Frost for Frost.' Draw close to her. 'Have you finished?'

She hesitated.

'I said I wasn't going to show…'

'But I am beg-ging you.'

Peep over the top of the easel.

The daub was dreadfully bad.

'What a likeness!'

Her face lit up.

'You really think so, Benedykt?'

'I can make out two eyes, two ears and even a nose.'

She hurled the paintbrush into a corner.

'Since you keep constantly moving and twisting and turning and waving your arms! Every time I look, I see a different shape – so how am I to portray a good likeness?'

'But how portray scenes that are fantastical, invented?'

Rest afterwards in the little sitting room at a high tabletop made of sandalwood. Sunday was the maid's day off, so Miss Muklanowicz herself brought in the samovar and tea service, and would not allow any help. From the colonial goods store in the building next door, she had tins of various green, red and black teas, and Chinese spice mixes with strange short names which sounded doubly exotic when pronounced by Jelena. The scent of herbal tchay wafted throughout the rooms, a colourful trail almost visible as it floated in the air above the carpets, chests-of-drawers, ottomans, Dutch porcelain stoves, sideboards and jardinières, above the snoring Aunt Urszula. Auntie woke for a moment, smacked her lips and wrapped herself tighter in her shawl only to slip back into slumber.

The icicles outside the window sparkled with an azure tint.

On the windowsill, alongside Russian editions of adventures stories by Thomas Mayne Reid, lay several fat tomes: Russian-Italian dictionaries, an Italian grammar, anthologies of Italian poetry. Miss Muklanowicz had been given them by Porfiry Pocięgło; she was minded to start learning Italian in order to 'kill time'. Not long ago, a branch of the Berlitz School, the Universal Institute of Foreign Languages for Ladies and Gentlemen, had opened in Irkutsk. 'A language that feels like water!' she enthused, then opened a volume at random and read out a few sentences without the slightest inkling of their meaning. 'How it flows, how it froths, how it bubbles, how it undulates!'

Before sitting down, she did not change out of the stained sarafan, only washed her hands. Wielding a bone-handled knife, she sliced the bird-cherry bread and smeared it with arctic-berry preserve.

'A real housekeeper.'

'Mr Pocięgło told me before church how you'd been trying to per-suade him to marry me.'

Choke.

'No. That is… It wasn't like that. Maybe he…' Lap up the tea. 'I, after all – will be leaving – or – what with my father – I've no idea what will become of me. So... In order to behave honestly...'

'Which means how?'

'I apologise, miss, please don't be angry.'

'What is it today with all your apologising...!'

'In truth I should no longer be calling on you at all.'

Lost in thought, she licked the berry jam off her fingers.

'But why, Benek, why?' she asked softly.

Lower the voice likewise.

'Now again you ask me about things for which there are no words.'

She drew in air with a hiss.

'You have fallen in love, sir, no shame in that.' She sought the hand above the table. Press the palm after a second of indecision, onto the devushka's cold hand. The thumb wandered from her wrist along the bone line between the dainty knuckles. Here a subcutaneous vein pulsed to the rhythm of Jelena's heartbeat. Pause the thumb on the vein. The highest and hardest form of bodily honesty...

'I shall try.' Whisper it, raising the eyes to the devushka's concentrated face, her left profile illuminated by icy radiance; the radiance settled on the young woman, on the tabletop, on the samovar, bounced off the gleaming blade of the knife. Sunbeams reflected off the panorama of the white city fell into the sitting room, filtered through kaleidoscopic frostoglaze; the whiteness had thousands of vivid shades, whiteness sunk into fabrics, into wood, into flesh; whiteness governed the moment – white were the thoughts and white the words and white the voice.

'I shall try; a try shall be made. *Alors*. Has love been fallen into? How to tell the truth? Jelena, this is how it is when the inner language is translated into the speech of men. How does a man know he's in love? For such is the word in the speech of men when there are flowers, kisses, trysts, passionate declarations, billets-doux, clandestine glances in prenuptial confessions and romantic situations, in a woman and a man's first flushes in the madness of youth. You see, miss? Behaviours, behaviours. Since this is his behaviour – he must be in love. But not the other way around, not if we start from the feeling – for how will you translate it, how explain it? You won't explain it. He was punched in the mug, turned around and walked away – therefore a coward. But how do we know whether he's a coward? Because he behaved like a coward.' Blink, blinded by the light. 'Is a man in love because he behaves like a man in love? How to compare one man's soul with that of another? There is no such measure, no such weighing scale. Manifested only are movements of matter: bodily gestures, sounds emanating from the mouth, the fantastical forms of hoarfrost. But because we live in this language from childhood and know no other, we get the idea into our heads and sincerely believe that since the movement of matter is similar, so too the movement of the soul is the same, called the same – that it's not the hoarfrost – that this shape means something, that it exists in and of itself. Cowardice. Courage. Hatred. Love. My God, do you really believe, miss, that the feelings of which you yourself are capable are all possible feelings?!'

She gradually released her palm from the grasp, moved it along the knife, along the sharp blade and down the smooth handle.

'So, what others are there?' She asked, barely audibly.

Drop on the knees before her, thrust the index finger into the mouth and bite into the flesh, then, having kissed the hem of her paint-soiled dress, make a triple mark on the young woman's lips in warm blood. She shuddered. Seize with the other hand the devushka's leg above the ankle, lock the palm around it like an iron fetter. Count to ten, feeling the teslectrical flow swell in the body. Tighten the grip each time she opens her mouth to say something, until she no longer tries to speak. Stare in silence without blinking, laying down gaze upon gaze. And Jelena slowly, very slowly nodded her head. *Voilà!* Beat the fist into the parquet floor with a joyful smile till the skin flays off the hand. Then sit down again on the chair to finish the Chinese tea.

Miss Muklanowicz removed a heavy volume from the windowsill; opened it without looking. Only when she paused her nail on a line of verse selected blindly did she raise the book towards the white and read in a sing-song voice:

'*Qualsivoglia.*'

Savour the word on her tongue: like water, like a wave, like froth.

'*Qualsivoglia.*'

On gleissen blood

On the first working day at Krupp, a quarter of the coldmills in Zimny Nikolayevsk came to a standstill as the hiberniks' strike shook the ice industry.

It began with Mr Wielicki being exercised again about honour and refusing to hear any offer to return the money he'd had to spend from his own pocket in order to pay the bonebreakers engaged in protecting his house. And then there was Shtchekelnikoff; all these taken together were now into their second month. But were these fellows still necessary? Was someone still likely to throw stones at the windows or believers in conspiracy theories of the Ice to attack in the street?

People will begin to laugh at the man with a strong-arm brute in tow, the scaredy-pants oddity.

Descend the stairs with Mr Wielicki on the Monday morning, bantering in this way, to the ground-floor vestibule, and discover there the heavies assisted by Shtchekelnikoff pinning a screaming muzhik to the ground, suspiciously lightly clothed, from which his hibernik nature was at once clear. 'To Batyushka Moroz!' he screamed. 'Before it's too late!' he screamed. 'Cocksucking heathens!' he screamed. 'Let go!' With their cedarwood rods, they showered him with blows on the spine and rump. Wielicki restrained the zealots. It transpired that the captured hibernik had tried to steal in through the coach-house as the sleigh was being brought out. Perceive the flash of a medallion on the man's livid breast, in the opening of his shirt, as they were about to throw him outside the gate. Ask him if he professes Martsyn's faith. He spat only blood. Ask him: 'Too late for what?'

Now, this story had been unfolding since lunchtime on the previous day, when Governor General Schultz-Zimovy had again unexpectedly rejected an invitation from Aleksandr Aleksandrovitch Pobedonostseff, and moreover had refused to see his Angel; instead, he had received at the Citadel 'some four Americans'. Events then quickly gathered pace, for already by Sunday evening, a written instruction came from the governor general's chancellery ordering the intensification of operations against the ice sects, and in the frosty night of Sunday to Monday, the army accompanied by gendarmes was deployed throughout Irkutsk and Zimny Nikolayevsk, arresting dozens of hiberniks and non-hiberniks, all suspected of professing the Martsynian faith. Wielicki himself was clearly annoyed by it and began cross-examining the muzhik; the man muttered something indolently about heated coldmills and disturbances in Innokentyevskoye Two, but it was obvious that he knew little more and fear of arrest had simply got the better of him, and this was why, frightened out of his wits after a night of panic, he had knocked at the door of the Son of Frost. Maybe more of his type would surface. Wielicki ordered the bonebreakers to close the gate and waved to Tchingis Shtchekelnikoff, declaring that he too was going straight to Zimny Nikolayevsk. Drive to the Northern Station.

The Marmeladobahn ran every quarter of an hour in the morning, but on working days two double-decker trains departed at six o'clock in order to accommodate all the workers heading to Nikolayevsk for the day shift. On the covered platform, where stood the compartment coaches, in which the directors and engineers and whole fraternity of non-proletarian Nikolayevsk travelled, Wielicki encountered scores of acquaintances similarly alarmed. Glimpse Director Grzywaczewski surrounded by his colleagues; before the train left,

Saturnin Grzywaczewski had time to dispatch three errand-boys with instructions. All the gentlemen in fur coats and fashionable sheepskins, in ushankas with earflaps and large spectacles, kept glancing at the long open platform where hundreds and thousands of Irkutsk workers were gathered, men and women, five different confessions, a dozen indigenous Siberian peoples, three races. The frostoglazes rendered interpretation of the gentlemen's gazes impossible. On the snow-covered dial of the station thermometer, a snakelike arrow pointed to minus thirty-eight degrees Celsius.

In the train, Wojsław Wielicki, inhaling large drags of a cigarette made from Manchurian tobacco till red sparks flew into his shuba and widely parted beard, repeated aloud to himself the ever-more-novel theories heard from other travellers. Since it seemed obvious at once that those 'Americans' lunching with Schultz were J.P. Morgan's people sent on their mission to bring down Harriman and his Around-the-World Railroad to Russia, endeavour now with Wielicki to square the governor's actions with Morgan's plan. Which appeared logically unworkable – for Morgan's plan as presented by Mr Pocięgło to the Last Kopeck Club convention rested on a contrary strategy, namely an alliance with Rasputin, who was supposed to persuade the emperor to halt construction of the Alaskan Tunnel. How to reconcile this then with Schultz's sudden action to arrest the Martsynians?

'But why assume they persuaded Schultz of anything?' Make this observation, raising the voice above the hubbub prevailing in the long compartment. 'Pocięgło said himself, did he not, that greater independence and closer relations between Siberia and America were also to the governor's taste.'

'That's the temptation of all governors of Siberia,' admitted Wielicki, 'since the very first, Prince Gagarin of Tobolsk. Porfiry always bores us with these tales. The Tsardom of Siberia existed already under Yekaterina the Second, a coin was struck with its coat of arms; it was a Russian colony no different from the British Crown's American colony. It wouldn't have taken much for the Irkutsk city council to appoint its own Siberian government under the authority of hereditary tsar-governors. In Saint Petersburg they remember it well. Whomever they send and put in office here… This country is moving east of its own accord,' he indicated with a sweep of his hand and cigarette, 'towards the Pacific, towards Japan, towards America. They are right to be afraid.'

'So, the Yanks were simply unsuccessful; Schultz saw through them. After all, they're Ottepyelniks whichever way you look at it. Nothing would delight Morgan more than total Thaw and the collapse of the coldiron industry. Schultz knows what threatens him.'

'Except why arrest them immediately? Rasputin is also a Lyednyak.'

'With whom are these Yankee saboteurs meant to be conspiring?' interjected a young clerk in frostoglaze pince-nez, tearing his eyes away from his morning paper, 'Well, first of all with that inventor hired by His Imperial Exaltedness to kill the gleissen.'

Give a snort.

'Well, then Pierpont Morgan will be spitting into his own beard, because Doctor Tesla would sooner treat with the devil than anyone recommended by Morgan. There's been a sharp wedge driven between them for years; Morgan more or less absconded with the capital from Tesla's firm, forcing him into bankruptcy.'

'Their sole chance then,' Mr Wielicki calculated, 'is to frighten His Exaltedness Nikolay Aleksandrovitch with Oblastnik secession, with the dangerous self-sufficiency of upstart local rulers at the other end of the Empire. For as soon as the railway is built under the Bering Strait, it will turn governors' heads. Nothing is more terrifying to an autocrat than the self-sufficiency of his subjects.'

'And Schultz doesn't know this? Schultz knows. And knows that Morgan has enough cash to eventually reach, one way or another, the imperial ear.'

There had been no time that day to call on Tesla and grasp the Kotarbiński pump. The organism was still running on minus murch after yesterday's siphoning-off – teslectric flow was felt on the palate and neath the skin of the hand; nevertheless, with every hour, the freezing process grew faster and faster.

Remember the Ice's mathematics of psychology: character A, therefore character B, therefore character C. Moreover, they all – slaves to the soletruth about man – realise it equally well themselves, even if they're unable to capture the phenomenon within any neat theory.

'But it's happening entirely logically; think about it, gentlemen. For what could Schultz do to reassure Nikolay Aleksandrovitch in advance of his fidelity and loyal subservience?' Straighten the fingers one by one. 'Arrest the sectarians. Send the Okhrana after the Oblastniks. Tighten the screw on democrats and socialists. Want to bet? Mr Pocięgło and Editor Wółkiewicz have also had official guests today for sure. *New Siberia* – is closed. The Okhrana is doing the rounds of prominent Ottepyelnik homes. Whilst in the afternoon papers, we shall read of a new offensive against Piłsudski's Yapontchiks.'

'True, true,' nodded the clerk as snowy white and boiserie brown spun in his pince-nez. Scrolling back through the newspaper in the opposite direction, he slapped the paper with the back of his hand. 'See what signals the tchinovniks are giving us!'

A spying affair. From our reporters in Aleksandrovsk: The joint-stock company 'Tungusia' recently employed in its offices a Jew by name of

Kohler, a locksmith by trade, a highly intelligent individual of good appearance. It came to the general attention that this Kohler, despite his meagre salary, was enjoying a life of plenty and supporting a wife and child. On Friday last, a police agent travelled to Aleksandrovsk and, having summoned the gendarmerie to intervene, arrested Kohler. During a police raid carried out in his apartment, many journals and brochures were collected. Kohler had come to Aleksandrovsk from Königsberg and, so they say, was engaged in espionage.

A throng of workers was surging on the platform in Zimny Nikolayevsk. They should have been drifting out at once from under the station roof into the snow-packed streets of the industrial town and the workers' hamlet appended to its eastern side, known as Innokentyevskoye Two; instead, they stood huddled under clouds of human breath mist, buzzing with a kind of bitter restless energy. Through a sky woven in smoke and coldiron rainbows, as well as sastrugi left by the sluggish snowstorm, came wave upon wave of infernal wailing, of sirens summoning the workers to the coldmills, manufactories, foundries, freezeries and icecradle plants – yet they continued to stand. Workers alighting from the Marmeladobahn mingled with them; upon merging with the greater crowd, the lesser at once acquired the properties of the greater: the movement, the angry hubbub, the yelling and scraping of feet. The gentlemen directors did not hang about, did not pause to look – they retreated from the platform as fast as they could, leaping to the far side of the tracks, under the wings of the auroras spreading over spidery cranes and reloading belts.

'In Harbin, coldiron is about to hit a record high,' sighed Wojsław Wielicki, wrapping his thick scarf around his face. 'And why am I not pleased?'

'Let's sooner walk,' growled Tchingis Shtchekelnikoff, looming suddenly alongside. 'Don't like the look of it. A hundred blokes, devil provokes. Where's them Cossacks when you need 'em!'

The countinghouse of Friedrich Krupp Frierteisen AG was located on the fourth floor of the Five O'Clock Tower, which was roughly equivalent to the twentieth in high-rise buildings of Summer. Innokentyevskoye Two consisted of hovels and low slum dwellings – but the eyes had never seen so many skyscrapers before as here, in Zimny Nikolayevsk. Building on a concentration of the Ways of the Mammoths, people were condemned to tall architecture, whilst the use of coldiron steel had enabled the raising of the heaviest structures on light slender pillars, totally indiscernible in the snowstorm. Know all the reasons and know what to expect; yet the sight of classic townhouses suspended in the air sixty arshins above ground, often with frostglaze rotunda galleries, turrets and Byzantine cupolas, with spiral staircases and elevator tubes underneath, was astonishing – the whole architectonic mishmash was visible through curtains of snow and itself lavishly snow-covered and ice-encrusted, hung with icicles, encased in a cladding of butterfly sheens. The buildings loomed without warning one after another whenever the wind changed direction or the hoar-frost drapery fell away momentarily – a tower on the left, a tower on the right, tower upon tower, yet in reality one vast edifice made half of Baikal ice-marble and half of frostglaze, of which the ten or so lower storeys had been wiped clean like a chalk sketch from a school black-board: as far as the duster had reached in the schoolboy's hand, it had vanished. However, the sky-high levels thus rescued also vanished with every step, as colour drained from them on the goggle lenses, and the omnipresent white seeped into its place. It would have been impossible to tell one tower from another; good that Shtchekelnikoff was there to show the way.

This whole terrain – that is, the centre of Zimny Nikolayevsk orien-tated according to the Holey Palace and neighbouring industrial nests, as well as the railway track with its warehouses and appendages – rather gave the impression of one great construction site or epicentre of el-emental catastrophe, now being half-heartedly restored to order. The earth was torn up in irregular trenches and pits, here and there mine-shafts gaped covered by tarpaulins stretched on steel frames. Naphtha bonfires were burning. Ice-encrusted planks guided pedestrians from one crippled building to the next crippled building, from icecradle to icecradle, by roundabout routes; whenever a gleiss passed through, the planks were relocated, creating a different route. And because about two dozen gleissen were always on the move here, the street map of Zimny Nikolayevsk looked like a graphic jigsaw-puzzle, or a field where two opponents kept rearranging each other's pick-up sticks.

The transportation of industrial output and commodities to and from the Marmeladobahn took place not on the ground but in the air, along coldiron wires strung in the sky. Their tangled network of cords remained invisible even on rare sunny days, let alone on one like today. Stand aghast, as a bunch of black lines suddenly leaps out of the fluffy mist overhead and trundles, jangling like glass, towards the gantries above the railway track. Perceive then, staring into the wind, several more such bulks drifting slowly above Zimny Nikolayevsk, appar-ently in defiance of the laws of physics: a thousand poods of ironware levitating higher than factory halls, machines, sheds, mineshafts, fires, gleissen and people. Learn later that a gleiss had never been observed here more than fifty arshins above the surface of the earth; had they begun to rebuild Irkutsk a few years after they did, the whole city would doubtless be hanging in the air on skeletons of coldiron.

Half a dozen men were waiting for the lift under the Five O'Clock Tower. Shtchekelnikoff pointed to the stairs. Shake the head. Gazing directly upwards, the great black rectangle of the tower's 'underbelly' could be seen. Even from there, however, the openwork side pillars were indiscernible. Craning the neck, take in the perimeter of the structure's 'foundations'. The Sibirkhozheto Tower had been designed and erected immediately after the Winter of the Gleissen but before the European Year of the Gleissen, when much was still unknown about coldiron, hence it was modelled a bit on the Eiffel Tower and seemed, despite everything, so massive; whereas the Clock Towers – as was ascertained with incredulity – stood on legs slimmer than an ordinary lamppost. Travelling up in the rattling, clattering lift (the wind drove streams of white dust inside), it was impossible to control an irrational shudder: but what if it should all suddenly come tumbling down? The men crammed into the lift exchanged glum jokes about the army pacifying the coldmills on the orders of the governor general, and about Feliks Dzierżyński returning to Irkutsk for the next revolt of the proletariat. Someone mentioned Rasputin, someone else – Martsyn. Alight from the lift and climb another four storeys up a staircase made of granite polished to mirror finish. On the half-landings, great white cacti were growing in large flowerpots. Beyond the panoramic windows, a green snowstorm was raging. Turn to the left on reaching the fourth floor and join the throng of clients standing outside the door to the offices of Friedrich Krupp Frierteisen AG. Tchingis Shtchekelnikoff rolled his eyes gloomily. 'I got my stick.' He had his stick. 'Hit out. I'll do the apologies.'

Friedrich Krupp Frierteisen AG. In 1909, Gustav Krupp von Bohlen und Halbach had taken over the management of the concern. One of his most successful moves had been the swift decision to engage the firm in the research and development of coldiron technologies. Gustav was not a Krupp by birth; he was made to marry the sixteen-year-old heiress to the Krupp fortune so that he could take over the reins when her father, Friedrich Alfred Krupp, committed suicide following a scandal involving young men brought from Capri for his carnal enjoyment; the Kaiser meanwhile gave the marriage his blessing and anointed the new generalissimo of German steel with the name of Krupp.

Many similar stories had been heard from Mr Wielicki already on the previous evening. The naturalness with which Wielicki crossed the line from the role of cordial host to confrere in the fraternity of Money Men was truly disheartening. A job had been sought in order to pay off the debts; no private business interests, however, were being launched! But clearly Doctor Myśliwski and the members of the Last Kopeck Club knew better. Wólka-Wólkiewicz had frozen as an angry newspaper editor and tippler, whilst Benedykt Gierosławski... Benedykt Gierosławski had access to the Kotarbiński pump. It was warm inside the tower, in the crush outside the countinghouse – stiflingly hot and stuffy. Force a way through at last to the door, unhook the shuba, unwind the scarf, pull off the shapka, tuck the eyeglasses into a pocket. In the polished granite appeared the image of a weedy, bearded man with narrow skull covered in dark stubble. Adjust the necktie and stiff collar: a whiter-than-white vatermörder. Head up! It's possible to learn anything – including the art of making money.

'First of all, Benedykt, you have to accept that money is made', Wielicki had sermonised. 'Wealth is created not through robbing the poor, or through the flow of riches from hand to hand. Were we to increase our affluence only by taking away someone else's fortune – so there'd be more here and less there – then we'd have been getting poorer from generation to generation since the beginning of the world, because the volume of goods would be the same and the number of people amongst whom it had to be shared – ever greater. But God has ordained things otherwise: so that he who has the gumption and the will and the strength, the desire to work, he shall create something out of nothing, thereby enriching himself and humanity. Apart from the instinct to reproduce, the Lord has given us the instinct to enrich.'

Yet no intention was there to live and work here a day longer than was needful to unfreeze father and remove him from Siberia. Great and incomprehensible is the power of mirrors.

Gustav Krupp von Bohlen und Halbach (aquiline nose, clipped moustache, bulging forehead) peered down from a greyish sepia photograph hanging in the inner hall of the countinghouse above the desk of the chief clerk. Under the photograph was written: *12. Oktober 1922*; it was a souvenir of the chairman's visit to the Land of the Gleissen. Around Gustav stood ten or so men in shubas or fur-lined overcoats: the natchalstvo of the company's Irtkutsk branch. For the occasion of the photograph, all had removed their spectacles and some also their shapkas. Herr Direktor was distinguishable from the others only by his clear face and bright eyes; the others had been burned out on the film, their countenances discoloured, in oily penumbra. Second on Herr Gustav's right stood Saturnin Grzywaczewski. In the background loomed the twisted massif of the Holey Palace and the outlines of the soaring Clock Towers.

Elbow through to the desktop, show the clerk Director Grzywaczewski's visiting card. The clerk – a typical specimen of a new breed of Siberian, a peculiar mix of Mongolian and European features – read the card, tapped his teeth with his *porte-plume*, glanced at the clock and summoned an errand-boy.

'I don't suppose you'll be waiting till evening.'

'No. What's the problem?'

'Doctor Wolfke is in the Workshops today. Here.' He returned Grzywaczewski's card. 'Show it, should they not wish to let you in.'

'Who?'

'In case you're Thyssen's or Belkoff-Zhiltsoff's spy.'

'You're not suggesting…!'

'Go, go. I've no time for you now, you can see what a veritable Hades it's been all morning.' Without getting up from behind his ledgers, abacuses, accounts and greater still piles of loose documents, he encompassed with hand and pen the entire countinghouse abuzz with human voices, full of human traffic. Clients were almost trampling on one other in the surge towards doors and offices and desks raised on pedestals half an arshin above the floor, from where they were chased unsuccessfully by bookkeepers and company skinflints; fists were propelled into motion, papers flew up, papers were stamped underfoot, banknotes carelessly thrust into paws flew up, banknotes were stamped underfoot, until this man or that fell on his knees to retrieve them from under snow-soaked boots, so greedy fingers too were stamped underfoot; money hung in the air. 'What's a-brewing, what's a-brewing, everyone fooling, idiots ruling. Six coldmills at a standstill! Go, go.'

Push the way back through, Shtchekelnikoff jabbing people with his stick. The errand-boy turned out to be a teenage Buryat in tight-fitting jacket. Pulling on a hooded sheepskin coat, he charged down the stairs. Forced to run in order to keep up. Instead of waiting for the lift – the boy wrenched open a coldiron door; and return was made into the world of frost and snow. Descend the ice-compacted stairs, clinging on for dear life to the cold handrail with every step. Blurred fragments of the panorama of Zimny Nikolayevsk emerged between veils of blizzard: the Holey Palace, the Clock Towers, the cranes and gleissen and coldmills and open icecradles and factory roofs, as well as the smoke and fires, pale rainbows and chaos of the lilliputian houses in Innokentyevskoye Two. The errand-boy paused for a moment in order to point with outstretched arm towards a smaller box-like structure built onto the side of a larger box, about a verst to the east of the Holey Palace. That's where we're going.

In the Workshops attached to Coldmill Number Two belonging to Friedrich Krupp Frierteisen AG, Doctor Mieczysław Wolfke was bleeding gleissen. The corpulent middle-aged gentleman with bulldoggish face, small moustache and crop of hair shaved high at the sides was standing with head uncovered on a rickety ladder held by two Asiatic helpers and delivering instructions down a tin tube to a team of hiberniks, who, twenty arshins further on, in a passageway leading to the main hall of the coldmill, were manipulating a heavy coldiron apparatus suspended above an intricate system of pulleys, winches and counterweights; the other ends of the long jibs that they were wielding, more like pikes or lances, were lost in clouds of milky steam emanating from the side of the tortured gleiss.

When an attempt was made to approach and peek into the hiberniks' unlighted faces, the way was barred by a man in a shapka with bear's ears. Try to reason with him once and twice, but he merely shook his head. Recognise him later as Busytchkin G.F., Doctor Wolfke's assistant since their time together at the Polytechnic in Karlsruhe. Busytchkin was a mute.

Before running away, the errand-boy pointed to the Workshop offices opposite the coldmill; in the Workshops, it was colder than outside, but the offices were heated. Unfasten the shuba, lay the palms on the stove. Indescribable mayhem prevailed on the tables and hundreds of shelves; scattered everywhere were parts of coldiron mechanisms, plenty of frostoglaze blown into various shapes, burettes, ampoules, beakers, cannulas, condensers, evaporators, desiccators, retrifiers, hydrometers, dozens of thermometers, as well as books and scientific journals; between the windows – both those facing outdoors and those facing into the hall of the Workshops – hung white charts densely scrawled over in black chalk. Remove the frostoglaze spectacles; white and black returned to their places. Schematic diagrams of some kind of mechanisms had been sketched on the charts; there were also a lot of numbers compared in columns, and equations expanded and reduced with no clear final solution, with substitutions of unknown symbols; on the other hand, the mathematics appeared relatively straightforward, definite integrals and liminal sequences. On a chart by the stove, it seemed thermal balances were being calculated; pieces of paper showing beautifully calligraphed results of temperature measurements had been drawing-pinned to the frame – they fluctuated between one and three degrees.

From the point of view of content, the books likewise presented a picture of irrational chaos: written in five languages, on every subject under the sun, sometimes only a single volume of a multi-volume edition – and amongst the latter, a Polish title stood out: volume one of the *Great Illustrated Universal Encyclopaedia* ('Passed by the censor'). Flick through starting from the back cover. A, A, A, A.

> **Ambition**, derives from the Latin *ambire* = to go around, and means the desire to elevate oneself, since in Ancient Rome candidates competing for political offices used to go around the city's citizens collecting votes. (*See* Ambitus)

How to recognise ambition in man? Only by the movement of matter. The greater the movement amongst people, the keener the ambition in the soul. As we grow colder, we knock against people less and less and lose in ambition. Such is the measure of momentum from the domain of the first kind converted into language of the second kind.

Next. There are entries too for mathematical terms.

Algorithm (*Algorismus*), a calculation, or rather a method of calculation, a set of signs used in a given calculation; hence we may speak of an algorithm for proportion, an algorithm for differential calculus. The expression derives from the name of the mathematician al-Khwarizmi (*see* Algebra) whose work is entitled in Latin translation: *Algoritmi* (i.e., al-Khwarizmi) *de numero Indorum*, and begins with the words: So saith Algoritmi. With time the author's name was forgotten, and the word Algoritmi began to be regarded as the genitive of a Latin word *Algoritmus*, *Algorismus*. In this way the name of the author became the name of the thing. In particular, a. can also mean the same as arithmetic. For example, the earliest exposition on arithmetic in the Polish language, by the Roman Catholic priest Tomasz Kłos (1538), is entitled '*Algorithmus*, that is, Science of Number'.

A red-haired man with a large photographic camera under his arm burst into the office.

'What do you want?' he wheezed.

'We're here to see Doctor Wolfke on the recommendation of Director Grzywaczewski.'

'We were promised exclusivity for a week! They can strike if they want, we shan't be giving up a single hour!'

He spoke in heavily accented Russian. Introduced himself as Henrik Iertheim. When he removed his frostoglaze goggles and malakhay fur hat with animal tail, a nightmarish visage was revealed above the ginger beard: gashes, frostbites, patches of skin discoloured by murch, holes in the flesh reaching almost to the bone. Here was a veteran of black physics, on the frontline of Ice science since its very inception, that is, since the Winter of the Gleissen – the first to measure their frost, the first to let their blood. Which he didn't fail to omit from his immediate eulogy of himself; it wasn't easy to reassure him that the visit was merely about a job.

'I cut my eyeteeth on this!' he bellowed, warming up some milk with butter and garlic in a frostoglaze laboratory flask on a Bunsen burner. 'When we built the first experimental coldmills, there was no town here, just fallow ice fields and a load of gleissen. The first controlled transmutations took place under a felt tent, barely shielding us from the gales. Men froze before my very eyes. One Buryat's arm froze so hard that his hand fell off like a lump of clay; we keep it in the coldmill, you can take a look, sir, khrr, khrr, as a warning.'

Put aside the *Encyclopaedia*, gather up a pile of stained brochures and perch on the edge of the low table.

'Why such a mess?'

'What were you expecting? This is the centre of Zimny Nikolayevsk, a coldmill with an output of a quarter of a million poods, a crossroads on the Ways of the Mammoths – every moment we have to lug everything to the tower and back.'

Leaf through a back number of *Leiden Communication* which contained an article on improvements in the construction of the 'cascade cryomachine'. Spot at the end, neath a group photograph of the team of fifty or so men, Iertheim's name. Which of these stern bearded men in black suits was Iertheim? The photograph did not show the colour of their hair.

Recognise instead with no difficulty the rounded countenance of Doctor Wolfke.

'That's exactly why,' said Iertheim, espying the topic of the article being read. 'When we published the initial results, Doctor Wolfke abandoned optics and returned to low-temperature physics. In Leiden, under Kamerlingh Onnes, he had researched the cryogenics of liquid helium. Krupp outbid Zeiss for him.'

'Liquid helium?'

'Gleissen blood!' Iertheim wheezed, which sounded more like a curse or a Viking war cry, whereupon he gulped down the hot milk from the flask.

Having wiped his mouth and moustache, he approached and held out his hand. Shake his savaged right hand – two fingers of which were missing. Despite this, his grip was worthy of a lumberjack's; he seized and wouldn't let go, seized and pulled, breaking by sheer force the stereometry of gazes between stranger and stranger.

'The Geographical Society?'

'No.'

'The Tomsk Institute.'

'No.'

'You're not a physicist?'

'A mathematician.'

'Well, we still have a long way to go in finding a good quantitative theory.' He bared his jagged dentition and finally let go the hand. 'Have you worked on statistical analysis?'

Without waiting for an answer, he reached up to the highest shelf of an improvised bookcase and removed the thickest folder from a pile of others. Having untied the tapes with his inept stubby fingers, he took out two files of papers scribbled over profusely in red ink. Assume at first glance some kind of mosaic patterns or map orientations.

'This is ours,' he laid it out, 'and this one's from Tomsk. Have a look.'

'Mm-hmm?'

'The coin toss as laboratory experiment (double-headed eagle or tails?);

```
OPOPOPOPOPOPOPPOPOPOPOPOPOPOPOPOPOPOPPOPOP
OPOPOPOPOPOPOOPOPOOPOPOPPOPOPOPOPOPOPOPO
POPPOPOPOPOPOPOPOPOPOPOPOPOPPOPOPOPOPOPOPO
POPOPOPOPOPOPOOPOPOOPOPOPOPOPOPOPOPOPOPO
POPOPOPOPOPOPOPOPOPOPOPOPOPOPOPOPOPOPOPO
POPOPPPOPOPOPOPOPOPOPOPOPOPOPOPOPOPOPOPO
POPOPOPOPOPOPOPOPOPOPOPOPOOPOPOPOPOPOPOP
OPOPPOPOPOPOPOPOPOPOPOPOPOPOPOPOPOPOOPOP
OPOPOPOPOPOPOPOPOPOPOPOPPOPOPOPOPOPOPOPOP
```

'So?'

'Don't you see anything unusual? But look at the Tomsk results.'

```
OPOPPOPPOOOPOPPOPOOOPOOOOPPOPOPPPOOPOPO
OOOOOPOOOPOOPOOOOOOPPPPPPPPPOPPPPOPPOP
OPOOPOOOPOPPPPPOPPPPOPOOPPPPOPOPOPPOOO
OOOPOPOPOPPPOOOOOPOOOPPPOPPOPPOPOOOPOPPPO
PPPPPPPPOPOOPPOPOOOPPOOPPPOOOOPPPOOOOOP
OOOPPPPPPOPOOPOOPPPOOPOPOOOOPOOOOPOOPP
PPOPOOOOOPOOPOOOOPPOOPOPOPOOPOOOOPOPPOP
OOOPPPOPPPOPOOPOPOPOPOPPPOOPOOOOOOPPOOP
POOPPPOPOOOPOOOOPOPPPOPPOOPOOPOOPOOPPP
```

'Greater irregularity. At least at first glance. Is the difference constant? Even several experiments prove nothing; after all, it's probability theory.'

'Here,' Iertheim shook the folder, 'we have results from a dozen other places. They need to be properly elaborated statistically, according to the geographical coordinates, isotherms and Ways of the Mammoths.'

'Under the Ice they show less variation, are more ordered, are more – how to put it – unambiguous. Yes?'

He glanced suspiciously from under his bushy brow.

'You've not taken much interest in the cryogenics of tungetitum, eh?'

Put aside the papers.

'No, Henrik, sir, I'm here for another reason. Seeking a position, yes. But – a few years ago Krupp bought up Horczyński – my father used to work there, Filip Gierosławski, a geologist. So… Maybe you met him?'

Iertheim smacked his forehead with his palm.

'Gierosławski, why of course!' he cried with visible relief.

'So, you did know him!'

He averted his eyes as if reaching back into the past, whilst ostensibly gazing out into the hall (where Doctor Wolke had already climbed down off his ladder and was now looking into the eyepiece of a telescope-like gadget, routed by a coldiron pipe towards the gleiss).

'And then the angel of the Lord said unto her, Behold thou art with child, and shalt bear a son, and thou shalt call his name Ishmael; because the Lord hath heard thy affliction. And he will be a wild man; his hand will be against every man, and every man's hand against him; and he shall dwell in the presence of his brethren.'

Blasts of wind blew outside the window.

Scratch the back of the hand.

'My pater…' Speak in order to break the awkward silence.

'Our hiberniks remember him sometimes by his Martsynian name; he always hung around more with the workers. But I call him Ishmael.'

Iertheim sat down on a crate below a chart, took out his pipe and tobacco pouch, filled the pipe, lit it and began to puff out smoke irradiated by unlicht. Under his unhooked sheepskin, he also wore a white bekesha tightly strapped with leather thongs. Observe the way Iertheim now holds his head atop his spine, like on a vertical mast, and how he leans back and regards his interlocutor from this leaning position – every bit like Razbyesoff.

'Man,' said the mangled redhead, releasing from his nose a slow stream of smoke, 'in order to live amongst other men, must acquire certain social skills. The skill of leaving truth unsaid: you meet a friend, you don't say good-day by telling him he's a swine, even though he is a swine; you greet a lady, you don't tell her she's ugly, even though she is ugly. The skill of employing conventional phrases: "Nice to make your acquaintance, sir" – when in fact you still don't know him, so what's so nice about it? The skill of accepting universal evil: even the best people sometimes do wrong out of thoughtlessness, disinterestedly, in insignificant everyday things, at the same time as they do great good in the most important – you have to take one along with the other: churlishness, bragging, obstreperousness, quarrelsomeness, envy and selfishness; saints too go to heaven with these. A genteel man shuts his eyes to them, does not call them by name, lives alongside them, does not apply the Ten Commandments to minutiae where the Bible is silent.'

'There are different types of lying; you speak, sir, of lying.'

'It's not possible to live without lying. That is, it is possible, but like Dostoyevsky's Idiot or like your pater, like Ishmael: making life intolerable for himself and for his neighbours, until in the end he becomes like that wild man: his hand against every man, and every man's hand against him. Being of weaker will, such a man grows quickly embittered, shuts himself within himself and flees into the wilderness. But your father did not flee; all the more did he arouse anger and provoke discord.

'There was the case, for instance, immediately after the purchase of Horczyński Ores, of the night-caretaker Fiedojczuk. A prikaz came from the natchalstvo to shed five people, for why duplicate jobs. Everyone liked Fiedojczuk, a cordial man, never a nicer fellow, with four little mites, and a capital joker into the bargain. But Filip Gierosławski, as soon as he learns of Fiedojczuk's dishonesty, informs higher authority that the caretaker's taking home the firm's coal – so Fiedojczuk's out on his ear; they even brought a criminal case against him.

'Or of another member of Horczyński's geological team, Engineer Pavlushko, who used to sell obscene pictures from his desk drawer here in Zimny Nikolayevsk. On one occasion, Mr Filip Gierosławski burned all that pornography. Guess whom people backed: Pavlushko of the lewd drawings, or Ishmael?

'Or the case of the cartographic archive – this I know at second hand, from people in the firm's Geological Department. Horczyński Ores were closing their offices and Krupp was taking over all their materials; Krupp also bought the data gathered by Horczyński's magpies and geologists. Not all of them, however, managed to commit it to paper before the transaction was concluded. Some of them were up north at the time; they kept the archive in their heads. When they came back, they were dismissed. The honest, lawful and decent thing would have been to admit to Krupp also this unwritten knowledge – but who does it? Only Ishmael. And since, in so doing, he drew the attention of the natchalstvo to the other dismissed men – you can imagine, sir, how grateful they were to him. And then, as a reward, he was even reinstated: it seemed obvious, he bought his way back in.

'But does Ishmael pay heed to how people see him? No. He always knows better when he's done wrong. You won't shame Ishmael.'

'They hated him.'

'Break-time.'

Glance around following Iertheim's gaze: Doctor Wolfke had called a break, the hiberniks had torn themselves from the machinery, the wound in the gleiss's hump was freezing fast; the rest of the company – Wolfke, Busytchkin, the man with the notebook, the man with the darkbulb spotlight – were returning to the heated rooms.

Iertheim dived behind the stove and rattled around in the ironware – it transpired that they kept an old samovar there; the Dutchman turned up the flame, produced some frozen brick tchay. The company burst in, immediately slamming the door and stuffing the gap above the threshold with rags. They made themselves at home in the mayhem, breathing blackly, blowing into their palms, coughing and calling for boiling water. Doctor Wolfke sat down by the stove where he kept his books on shelves. He grabbed a large tome, leafed through the pages and wheezed in resignation. Only then did he raise his eyes and notice the unannounced guests. Beneath a pressure temperature chart for gases, Shtchekelnikoff was cleaning his nails with a half-cubit blade. Doctor Wolfke opened wide his eyes. Make the introductions all the quicker.

'The directors have sent us a mathematician,' declared Mijnheer Iertheim, handing Wolfke his tea; at the same time, he winked. 'One of your compatriots.'

'My dear Henrik!' groaned Wolfke and automatically slipped into Polish. 'A mathematician, who needs a mathematician! I asked for glassblowers from Amsterdam and metallurgical chemists – and they send me a mathematician!'

Wolfke's pronunciation was curious: 'mathematithan', 'Amthterdam', 'glath'.

'Someone with a head on his shoulders has to finally put together the results of the measurements. *Door meten tot weten!*' Iertheim croaked. 'We're drowning in it all. The report for Berlin awaits us at the end of the year. Who's going to write it – you, sir? Mr Busytchkin? Mrs Pfetzer perhaps?'

Doctor Wolfke waved his hand in irritation.

'I haven't time, haven't time! As if I hadn't got enough on my mind! Have you heard,' he waved again in the direction of the hall, 'that if this drags on, our hiberniks will walk out too, they've already forewarned me: solidarity of the Martsynian brotherhood, loyalty to the Ice creed, and such like.'

'You're surprised? You ought not to be surprised.'

(Learn afterwards that Mieczysław Wolfke is a prominent freemason, Grand Master of the National Grand Lodge of Poland.)

'But the work, my dears, the work's still underway! Have you checked the air-tightness of the coal chamber?'

'The manometer has frozen.'

Doctor Wolfke drew out a handkerchief, looking like it was cut from a quarter of a tablecloth, and cleared his nose, which had turned very red, into the linen sheet.

'Everything is freezing.'

'Everything ith freething.' Either he was suffering, in addition to a cold, from a serious case of pharyngitis and laryngitis, or he was born with a speech impediment. The intention had been to walk up to him now with a fervent plea, show him the letter of recommendation, argue the point briskly, but the mouth refused to open. Scratch the back of the hand. The windows were fogging up. Wipe the frostoglaze with the naked hand; chill water vapour remained on the skin. In the Workshop hall, the hiberniks had made themselves at home on packing crates and barrels of naphtha (the whole coldiron machinery, stretching towards the gleiss and into the deep interior of the coldmill, moved back and forth on rails, and every time after the passage of a glacius, it had to be de-iced by melting). Six men, half of them with bare heads, half in fur shapkas, with light jackets on their backs or literally a single shirt or sweater pulled over their bodies – were sitting, chatting, chewing thick slices of bread and swigging from a bottle of ice-cold liquor.

Fasten the fur coat, venture out into the frost of the coldmill. Sit down beside the hiberniks on an upturned wheelbarrow – only then did they look up.

Neither shapka nor frostoglazes had been put on. The grey-bearded, broad-shouldered old man in leather apron, the one sitting nearest, re-alised at once. No clear memory was there of the face of the muzhik in the ushanka squatting opposite, but of the old greybeard – yes. And also, when he spoke – that voice of his, in which he had sung the litany of Saint Martsyn above the open grave – it was he, him.

'Gospodin Yeroslavsky.'

The rest fell silent, turned their eyes.

'Venyedikt Filipovitch Yeroslavsky,' the old man repeated and swallowed the last morsel of bread, brushing his hands. 'You were looking for us?'

'I hit upon father's Ways.'

He stared for a long while. The hibernik workers listened in silence. Clouds of black vapour rose off them into the unlighted air.

'As you said, as such it has frozen,' he said.

'Yes. No.' The skin tingled in the frost. But show restraint. Slide the hands deep into the sleeves. 'It is freezing.'

'Has anyone been bothering you?'

'Anyone?'

'Heretics, renegades.'

'No.'

'Just as well.'

'It looks like I'll be working here.'

They exchanged glances.

'Ah!'

'Tell me, good people. Do you obey the father from the Great Russian Heartland – or does he obey you?'

The greybeard bent his head forward.

'What I recognise, I repeat, but whether he obeys – is up to him.'

'Rasputin's word has power to change a lot here. You know that all these night-time arrests – are due to Schultz-Zimovy's fear of the fear of Batyushka Tsar. Envoys have arrived from a gentleman in America; they will seek audience at the court of His Imperial Exaltedness. They will inveigh against Siberia. The governor must prove his loyalty in time. First under the knife are the Oblastniks, yet this you know.'

'But if men be not in solidarity with men in adversity, the lords-and-masters will gobble us up and get away with it effortlessly.'

The hiberniks grunted in assent.

'So, ponder this one thing: whether by this solidarity of yours, you strengthen the Ice, or whether by this means, you hasten Thaw. What does Schultz-Zimovy stand for, and what – the Oblastniks? What would your Saint Martsyn say? Eh?'

They were confused.

'You don't believe in Martsyn,' muttered the greybeard.

'Is truth any less truth coming from the mouth of a doubter?'

To this they no longer had an answer. When Doctor Wolfke returned, they rose without a word and resumed their work, grabbing the cold-iron machinery, re-entering the industrial frost. Stop at the boundary of the breathable air; shadowy vapour seeped through the scarf wound as high as the spectacles; the shapka was retrieved. Even so, it was hard to stand still for more than a few minutes; forced to visit the fire braziers stationed at intervals in the corners of the Workshop – retreat to the stove room where Mijnheer Iertheim was still smoking his tobacco.

A coldmill of Krupp's type – in contrast to a Barnes or Zhiltsoff coldmill – operates in an open system, hence its greater exposure to the frost. Snoop on the transmutation process through a hole in the wall separating the Workshops from the coldmill's main hall, where a gleiss had spiked out of the ground. Electric lights were reflected off the glistening mass of black ice – waves of penumbra and pale glintz swam over the smooth coats of the icers compacted into one gigantic cryosculpture, whilst the nest was surrounded, veiled, wreathed in coldiron trusswork, cranes, chains and gantries, machines the size of houses and machines bigger than houses. Here, the gleissen were dwarfed by the manmade machines; whereas man – the distant silhouette of one or other hibernik attending to the coldmill's flow of ore – was but an insignificant speck in processes of magisterial scale and truly glacial tempo. Rainbow-lit arms of openwork cranes moved with theatrical grandeur. Steam from liquified air, liberated again into gas, swirled in misty clouds like billows of whipped cream, the red eyes of orientation lamps imparting to it a bloody tint. Observed through frostoglazes, the scene looked in one moment like a picture of the nethermost hell, yet in another – like the heavens above the cloudbanks, immaculate, drenched in cold colour. Somewhere in there, coal fires were burning and drop-hammers ramming. Unseen through the hole, all that could be heard from the coldmill was the hollow after-boom: amplified and extended in time, a mechanical echo of the glashatays' drums.

The hole, like most mutilations to the architecture of Zimny Nikolayevsk, had appeared as a result of the glaciuses' repeated freezings from place to place; on such a concentration of the Ways of the Mammoths, it wasn't worth carrying out constant repairs. In the very beginning, that is, immediately after Irkutsk's Great Fire, when no maps yet existed of the Underground World, it was decided to encapsulate a vast icecradle with contiguous nests of gleissen, thereby constructing an industrial moloch worthy of the Ruhr Basin: with covered halls scores of arshins high and iron cupolas hundreds wide. Subsequent repairs and reconstructions, however, were halted very quickly, and additional supports added only when needed to prevent the edifice collapsing; gleissen were freezing unconstrainedly from place to place. In this way arose the Holey Palace, Zimny Nikolayevsk's snow-black monument with its crippled architecture unlike any other architecture in the world. The map of the Ways of the Mammoths is reflected here on the earth's surface in the pathological network of maimed buildings.

A coldmill of the Krupp type operates in an open system, which means that the ores get frozen through by gleissen outside of the nest, at ground level. More invasive methods are also more costly, since they require digging underneath and around the nest, as well as the construction over it of hermetically sealed coldiron machinery, including for reliably transporting thousands of poods of excavated output in extremely low temperatures. But there can never be any guarantee of how long a given nest will stay in one place. True, the great icecradle of Zimny Nikolayevsk remains for the time being a conspicuous concentration of glacial nests – the only one in the world – but who would give his right arm that in a week's time, it would all not freeze back down under the earth and the whole industrial town be but a useless relict of its former glory, like those defunct little mining towns in America when their veins of gold run out? For indeed, nothing definite is known about the Ice.

A businessman strives to secure his investments. Krupp and Krupp's competitors had set, as their main goal, making the production of coldiron and its derivatives independent of the presence of gleissen; thus far they had not succeeded; however, Doctor Wolfke's research, as well as that of scientists working for other concerns, was aiming precisely in this direction. Even the Saint Petersburg Mining Institute and the Imperial Russian Geographical Society, serving directly or indirectly the same interests, were seeking answers to those questions. What physical and chemical processes take place within the 'organisms' of gleissen? In what does the 'life' of the Ice consist? What change in the frozen-through matter is responsible for the change in its physical and chemical properties? On what energetic processes do these transmutations rely? In other words: what exactly is the Ice?

Doctor Wolfke's hiberniks were piercing gleissen with tungetitum lances and catching their blood in vacuum cryostats made of frosto-glaze – it was helium. Helium, the solar element, for it had been first detected in the spectroscopic spectrum of the Sun, is a noble gas, that is to say, one indifferent to any chemical temptations: it enters into no compounds easily discoverable or researchable by humans. Professor Heike Kamerlingh Onnes of the Cryophysics Laboratory in Leiden, who in his experiments to liquefy helium used great quantities of it, had to buy monazite sand wholesale via Amsterdam (he had a brother well placed in the trade). The Ice struck on 30 June 1908; Kamerlingh Onnes liquefied helium ten days later. The boiling point of helium, the temperature at which it changes into a gas, registers less than five degrees on the Kelvin scale. The attainment of such frost by the Dutch scientists required a complex system of compressors and expanders reducing the temperature lower and lower by stages – liquefying oxygen, nitrogen and air, then hydrogen, and eventually helium. It was an incredibly time- and energy-consuming process that allowed the low temperatures to be sustained only briefly, and any break in the hermetic seal would have caused a sudden warming of the substances. Whereas, inside gleissen, the liquid helium flowed freely in unconstrained streams.

Contemplate how such extremes of frost may be measured at all. An ordinary thermometer indicates variations in temperature through the changes in volume of a standard substance, for example, mercury or alcohol. The temperature charts drawn in the office beside Krupp's Workshops included not at all the Celsius scale, where zero represents the freezing point of water at standard atmospheric pressure, but the absolute scale of Lord Kelvin, where zero is absolute zero: lower than this, no temperature exists, just as no time exists before the dawn of time.

'But what does it mean in that case?' Return to the stove corner for a mug of hot tea. 'Two point two degrees, one point eight. If at the end there is absolute zero, or a total lack of heat – then what is this? How to measure abstractions?'

'True, for a very long time we had only an empty mathematical model,' Iertheim admitted, releasing aromatic smoke from the corner of his mouth. 'Since temperature is a measure of the extension or expansion of matter, and a liquid is more expanded than a solid body and a gas more expanded than a liquid, then the limit of a gas's expansion is the limit of its temperature. We take a certain volume of air and –'

'We cool it down, then we measure the change in volume, that is, pressure, we work out the dependency, we substitute zero pressure –'

'Yes.'

'Can a gas have negative pressure? It can't. Mm-hmm.'

'Hence absolute zero in temperature. The equation shows the limit to be minus two hundred and seventy-three degrees on the Celsius scale.'

'And that's how you measure it? By the pressure of the gas?'

'Well, closer to absolute zero, the method falls short. Electric thermometers are also not the most accurate; electrical conductivity at low temperatures is yet another enigma. The point is, Mr Gierosławski, that really close to absolute zero –'

'In the heart of a gleiss.'

'Bah!' Mijnheer Iertheim took his feet off the chair, surveyed the graphs hung on the wall between the external windows, grabbed whatever he could lay hands on, a long dirty pipette, and pointed with it, like with a conductor's baton, to a ruler nailed vertically alongside a window frame. At one quarter of the ruler's height (and it was more than an arshin in length), a blue arrow had been pasted. At the bottom loomed a large zero, rounded like an egg, carved into the wood. 'These are our best assessments of the latest measurements.'

'A quarter of a degree?'

'Pshaw! This whole board represents one hundredth of a Kelvin,' the Dutchman broke into a laugh.

Swallow a swig of hot tea and assume an astonished expression.

'And how does zero point zero zero three degrees supposedly differ from zero point zero zero two?'

'Imagine, sir, a gas on the molecular level. You breathe air into a glass container.' He blew smoke into a frostoglaze flask, plugging it swiftly with his pipe-wielding hand; behind the glass, dark-blue eddies swirled around, quickly discolouring to yellow. 'What's happening? Myriads of particles fall out of one volume into another. Phew!' He brandished the pipette above his head. 'They rush wherever they can. What is the volume of the lungs to the volume of the flask?'

'Suppose we blow into a vacuum?'

'Let's say.'

'The greater the space, the lower the pressure.' Rub the knuckles against the unshaven cheek. 'The lower the pressure, the lower the temperature. But heat is energy – where does this energy escape to?'

'So here you've discovered the First Law of Thermodynamics. But how to gauge the pressure?' Iertheim pressed a wide cork into the flask that he'd used for his milk. 'I am placing on the container an airtight weight. What pushes it from below?'

'The striking of those particles.'

'I place a weight twice as heavy. It sinks lower. The volume shrinks, the pressure increases, the temperature increases. I have warmed up the air.'

'It's a measure of the movement of the molecules. The sum of their energy, of the momentum with which they hit that weight.'

'But only in part.' He tapped thrice on the flask with the pipette; it rang like a celebrant's bell. 'For here we come to the Second Law. Work, movement, translates into heat as it ought – but heat turns into work always with loss of energy. Were I to raise my imaginary weight to the height of a weight twice as light by heating the air in the container, I would have to expend more energy in the flame than I'd spent on applying pressure to the air. This difference, this absconding energy, dear sir – is entropy.

'Just look at this mess here.' He described a circle roundabout him with his glass baton. 'To bring our workroom to such a state, energy was needed to move each object from its original place in the orderly arrangement to whatever other place. But, to restore order again now, the energy required to move the objects to whatever other place is no longer enough. At best, the mess will remain as it is, but will most likely grow. Entropy increases.

'When I melt ice, entropy increases: I had an ice crystal, now I have a freely flowing liquid. When I evaporate the liquid, entropy increases: I had a fluid organised in accordance with the surface of a vessel, now I have a cloud of particles flitting wherever.

'Do you perceive the dependence?'

'The colder it is, the lower the entropy.'

'Which means, according to Messrs Nernst and Planck, that at a temperature of absolute zero, the entropy of every system is zero.' Mijnheer Iertheim jabbed the mouthpiece of his pipe into a frostbite scar above his eye, tapping in his pensiveness on the naked bone. 'In our Laboratory we have a Roentgen lamp for X-raying coldiron,' he remarked; then, still muttering something under his moustache, he made a sluggish attempt to do battle with the local entropy: one shelf, a second shelf, a cupboard, a box of papers, a heap of files, a third shelf; eventually, he found a sort of album inserted under the shorter leg of a vacuum-pump stand. With his three-fingered hand, he rummaged through the dark plates. 'This one.' He took it out, held it up to the light. 'Brass, a day after alloying.'

Narrow the eyes.

'I don't see anything.'

'Well, yes.' He was confused. 'The thing is… Somewhere here, there were some drawings.' In the end he found a scrap of paper torn from an old page of *The Irkutsk News*, in the wide margin of which someone had drawn patterns in pencil. 'This is what the molecular structure of brass looks like a day after alloying.'

[PUBLISHER TO INSERT DIAGRAM (an irregular pattern, p. 577)]

'And like this – after several months.'

[PUBLISHER TO INSERT DIAGRAM (an entirely regular pattern, p. 577)]

'The copper and zinc atoms have arranged themselves in perfect order. The alloy *has cooled down*.' He stood up straight, stiffly raising his head. 'So now guess, sir, what all X-rays of coldiron coolbonds show?'

'This ideal order.'

'That's it! The atoms stand to attention as though on drill – within the tiniest filing, within the thinnest string – like inside a crystal.'

Glance automatically at the ruler representing the one-hundredth part of a degree.

'Therefore, it's not only about taking energy away from the particles, about stopping them in their movement.'

'No. Absolute zero is reached through –'

'The ordering, unambiguousness, soletruth of matter, Yea, yay, Nay, nay.'

Wasn't this already known? Hadn't it been experienced on the journey in the Transsib? What else is Winter if not the binding of chaotic, unpredictable, ambiguous matter within the mathematical order of ideas? What else is Summer if not the Kingdom of Entropy?

'When only thousandths of a degree separate us from zero,' said Iertheim, 'no energy of movement makes a difference – since nothing should be moving – not the energy of particle vibrations – since the particles should not be vibrating – nor even the order of their atomic structure – since this is already absolute. The process of ordering takes place at a significantly deeper level.'

Murch was tingling beneath the skull.

'If, however, we no longer measure temperature here according to changes in pressure, how do we know whether this cold energy of Order and Disorder, of Truth and Falsehood – won't allow us to descend into states beyond the mathematical model, that is, below minus two hundred and seventy-three degrees Celsius?'

During subsequent breaks taken advantage of by Doctor Wolfke's team to warm themselves, Mijnheer Iertheim permitted a peek into one of the thermoscopes mounted on the railed conveyors between the Workshops and the coldmill, away from which the punctured gleiss was moving. Bend forward carefully, having already removed the frostoglazes, over the circular viewfinder in its coldiron surround. This was one of three lateral thermoscopes screwed into permanent position at an angular tilt; it served to observe an experiment being conducted on the gleissen blood in conditions of Frost, that is, in an apparatus inserted into the side of the glacius like the shaft of the Roman spear or finger of Doubting Thomas thrust into the side of the Crucified Christ.

The apparatus consisted of two frostoglaze measuring vessels, one placed inside the other. In both, there was gleissen blood, whilst the smaller vessel was suspended above the larger without any direct contact between them, its base located two vershoks above the level of the blood in the lower container, whilst its upper lip reached high above that container's lip. In this experiment, they were measuring the rate of spontaneous flow of helium at a temperature close to one degree Kelvin. In the eyepiece, a drop of the icer's blood could clearly be seen forming at the bottom of the upper vessel. Pure helium – atom upon atom upon atom upon atom – was crawling, impelled by a mysterious energy, up the inside walls of the upper vessel, sliding over its edge and crawling down its outer walls, dripping into the lower. The movement of the helium ceased when the levels of liquid equalised. How did the gleissen blood in one container 'know' that it was to begin to climb? What mysterious force lifted it in defiance of gravity? What order had the helium particles attained in this movement, if not the stony lifelessness of crystalline structures? It almost looked as if one of the simplest elements in its most primitive form had suddenly acquired under the Ice the properties of a living organism. The more frozen – the more alive. Here was the black-physical physiology of gleissen.

The experiment was measuring the rate of their blood flow, because it had emerged from initial observations that this remained constant, irrespective of differences in the position of the measuring vessels or of other conditions; data were also being collected in order to work out a formula for the velocity of gleissen freezing from place to place on the surface of the earth and along the Ways of the Mammoths.

In Krupp's Cryophysics Laboratory, other phenomena had also been observed, eagerly reported besides in *Annalen der Physik*. Gleissen blood was a substance devoid of viscosity, or at any rate having a viscosity a million times less than the viscosity of helium in Summer. In addition, the narrower the cracks it flowed through, the further its viscosity dropped. Similarly, the thermal conductivity of the helium inside gleissen rose a million times. From Thyssen's laboratories, moreover, they were reporting the impossibility of calculating the specific heat capacity of gleissen blood in the region of 2.2°K, at the point of its greatest density; here, the apparatus was giving absurd results.

However, according to Mijnheer Iertheim, the black physicists' greatest success to date was their description of an effect from which they expected to work out the laws responsible for the strangest properties of tungetitum and coldiron, that is, their counterheatability. Tungetitum (and also to an extent the majority of coldiron coldbonds), having received a portion of energy – whether in the form of electrical current, magnetic force, kinetic energy or simply heat – instead of warming up, reduces its own temperature without however releasing the lost energy onto the outside in any other measurable way. Formulae exist describing the proportionality of these changes; Doctor Tesla must have known about the results of such experiments, but the physicists were clearly unaware of the results of his work on teslectricity or of the operating principles of his murch-bearing machines. Investigations were moving here in the direction of black optics, that is, of measuring the energy of unlicht.

Comprehend at once that the factor missing from their theory is murch: the energy of logic, the carrier of the Frost. Tesla's discoveries could have been mentioned to Iertheim or to Doctor Wolfke himself – this would certainly have guaranteed a job with Krupp. Fail in time, however, to even pull a wry face at the thought: this was the role of an industrial spy and, in short, a traitor. It was hardly surprising that Nikola had barricaded himself inside the Imperial Observatory and would sooner have accepted invitations from charlatans or some other Brotherhood of the Apocalypse than from the black physicists of the coldiron consortiums. No science exists that is totally uninvolved politically or economically; even higher mathematics exerts an influence on the face of the world, on the course of History. And so, there are left-wing equations and right-wing equations, progressive equations and conservative equations, Ottepyelnik equations and Lyednyak equations. Behind Tesla stood the Tsar-God autocratically demanding the expulsion of gleissen from his dominions; behind the black physicists – the forces of money sprung up on the Ice.

Caught once again midway between the Ice and Thaw, that is, between the hammer and the anvil of History.

Utter no word about Tesla. God willing, they shall learn nothing at all of this acquaintance.

As to the experiment revealing the basis for counterthermism, it was as follows: a glass receptacle with a vertical cross-section similar to the Greek letter Ω, that is, with a narrow neck, was semi-immersed, the other way up, in a reservoir containing gleissen blood. At the start of the experiment, the levels of helium in the receptacle and the reservoir were equal. Within the helium inside the receptacle was a heating device. And so, after the heater was switched on, the level of helium in the receptacle rose: instead of evaporating into a gas, which would have pushed the liquid down, the liquid helium swelled. *The gleissen blood, when heated, had reduced its own temperature.*

The experiments over which Wolfke had been toiling that day were related in turn to the superconductivity of coldiron. In Summer, the phenomenon of superconductivity was observed exclusively at very low temperatures; whereas here, certain coldiron coolbonds were exhibiting zero electrical resistance also at temperatures above zero Celsius. This opened the door to totally new technologies, beginning with frictionless magnetic bearings and ultraprecise gyroscopes. Patents with obvious military applications.

Iertheim and Wolfke were complaining about the requirement to send frequent detailed reports to Berlin; Berlin, on the other hand, sent them plans for a whole series of experiments to be performed in Zimny Nikolayevsk. 'Let them employ trained monkeys!' Wolfke grumbled over lunch, also consumed in the office by the Workshops, in haste and amidst the mayhem. Since his youth, Mieczysław Wolfke had been intrigued by the concept of interplanetary flight and would rather have devoted his time to the purely engineering applications of coldiron, such as designs for large constant-current cells. No less rigour was suffered, however, by the Belkoff-Zhiltsoff scientists, led by academicians at the Tomsk Technological Institute. Myths about the fruitlessness of intellectual work in the Land of the Ice were more widespread than Nikola Tesla thought.

Assist Busytchkin and Iertheim in the afternoon with the cataloguing of coldiron specimens, which, after the prolonged freezing-through process, were returning to the Laboratory in the tower for detailed measurements to be made of their physicochemical properties as well as for X-rays to be taken.

Tchingis Shtchekelnikoff never took his eye off the hiberniks. He came by during the next tea break and announced gloomily: 'Don't like the look of it, Mr G. Why not on strike?' 'Most aren't striking at all.' 'But keen even to work. Beware the worker as don't laze about! Quick to work – trouble will lurk.' There you have it, Russian folk wisdom.

Strive to prove the personal suitability. Demonstrate initiative by tidying the papers strewn across tables and shelves; it was, however, a Herculean task. Wolfke, peering into the stove room, said nothing; later, he only asked if German were familiar – all the firm's documentation was conducted in this language. Reply that the place of birth, the place of upbringing, had been in Prussia.

After four o'clock, a moustachioed gendarme strode into the

Workshops with an instruction to finish all non-essential work in the coldmills for the day; civilians were to return to the tower. Wolfke looked as if he might make a scene over this so-called 'non-essential work'; but no, he merely waved his hand and trumpeted into his handkerchief.

The Krupp Laboratory was situated on the seventh storey of the Five O'Clock Tower, and consisted of something akin to an irregularly shaped mansard built under peaked attics and clad in panels of light coldiron and frozen-through glass. The laboratory occupied the entire floor and was no less cluttered than the office by the Workshops. Metal cupboards dotted here and there divided the space. The stairwell reached higher still, onto the roof – everyday, an hour before sunrise and an hour before dusk, de-frosters would climb up there to chip off fresh accretions of glazed matter and brush away the snow. At the base of the towers, between the pillars, red warning fires were lit at this time. As the upward journey was made in the company of Busytchin and Shtchekelnikoff, laden with heavy cases filled with metal specimens, factory hands were already preparing the braziers. From the Laboratory itself, of course, their flames could not be seen. Yet a moment later – the coat barely removed and hands warmed by the stove – four hiberniks came marching up the stairs in huge hobnailed boots; they climbed onto the roof, and a hollow whoop-dwoop-whoop began to resound. The electric lamps flickered – now blazing brightly, now almost fading – but not thanks to that whooping racket; in the Land of the Gleissen, they always behaved like that. Observe closely Mijnheer Iertheim, who, despite the noise, was bantering merrily with the tchay-wallah as she watered the rickety pot plants below the windows. Shtchekelnikoff, kicked out by Doctor Wolfke, still managed, before descending to the lift lobby, to deliver his Cassandrine prophecy about the Dutchman: 'Friendly, hah, when such a one befriends a stranger, he's surely got a knife ahind his back!' Attempt to see inside the ugly engineer, before he stomps away to his corner behind a cupboard, through the eyes of Mr Wielicki, through the eyes of Mr Myśliwski. What kind of man is he? What's the truth about him? Light was flickering, the penumbra around Iertheim shimmering; he rotated his hideous face in shadow and in brightness, first this way, then that, from right-hand memory – came the powerful clasp of his hand, from left-hand memory – poisonous suspicion. Feel completely lost, as when confronted by the next anonymous companion on the Trans-Siberian journey. Scratch the hand, though it no longer tingles at all.

By evening, the snowstorm had distinctly abated, and since the Sun had not yet sunk, a fine view stretched from the heights of the Clock Tower over the greater part of Zimny Nikolayevsk and the first shacks of Innokentyevskoye Two. Gaze through the panoramic window of the

Laboratory towards the Holey Palace, towards the north-west. Then, as white névé flowed over the geometrical shapes of the coldmills, and industrial browns and blacks spilled from engines, smokestacks and warehouses onto fields of snow and ice – an image blossomed forth, as on a stained-glass window in a church, illuminated by radiances whose source lay behind the stained-glass; fire – beneath the colours, light – beneath the earth. Factory chimneys, slag heaps, soaring waggons, processions of workers, railway depots, mighty cranes, coal trucks harnessed to reindeer, trusswork, poles, overhead wires, lamps and lanterns, roofs of industrial plants, plant gates, factories being built, factories in motion, bricklayers on factory building sites, working factories, factory chimneys – refulgent, dazzling, holy, holy, holy.

From that distance, the disturbances around the railway tracks remained almost wholly imperceptible. Catch sight once, when colour ebbed from the glass pane, of a bright-blue column of infantry armed with Berdan rifles disappearing behind the star-shaped spine of a gleiss. The striking workers must have blockaded the Marmeladobahn, and this could no longer be tolerated. Captain Nasboldt's account of Tsushima flashed in the true-and-false memory. Here, in the heart of Winter, what chance has a spontaneous anti-state revolt during the war of mathematical necessities?

Light a cigarette. Doctor Wolfke, having stopped alongside, was wiping his nose. Three, four sirens wailed protractedly. Human ants were wending their way in the snow amongst the monuments of Frost and greater still monuments of Industry.

'I sometimes think so too,' said Wolfke, staring at the scene. ('I thumtimes think tho too.')

'Ten years.'

'Yes. So, what world of ice technologies shall our grandchildren see?'

Brush off the ash, wipe the palm.

'The whole Earth under the Ice.'

'Oy, so you too, sir, are backing Thaw!'

'Beg pardon?'

'All of us Poles here have mixed feelings.' He wiped the frostoglaze with his handkerchief, stared at the discoloured reflection of the Laboratory's interior. 'Henrik told me about your father. Excuse me, I had no time even to welcome you.'

Wave the hand angrily, leaving in the air a tobacco exclamation mark.

'A political matter, I was held by the Ministry of Winter. That's why I am intruding on you. And there's one thing I can promise you, sir: whilst the Son of Frost is working here, Krupp will have no shortage of hiberniks to labour in its coldmills.'

Ten or so bursts of flame flashed on the Marmeladobahn station. No sound reached the tower from there, and that light also sped, leaving no lasting trace. Watch absentmindedly, flicking ash into the hollow of the hand, red from the imprints of the fingernails.

Doctor Wolfke gave a lengthy grunt and held out his hand.

'So welcome to Krupp's Cryophysics Laboratory.'

'Sixty?'

'Fifty.'

'Fifty-five?'

'Fifty. Then we shall see.'

'Everything here is obscenely expensive.'

'Fifty roubles, dear chap, no more, such is the salary for assistants, and no mediation from Engineer Iertheim will alter it.'

'And what about patents?'

'You're reckoning on inventions?'

'Various strange ideas revolve in my head.'

'So better haggle with the management.'

Squeeze his hand.

'Fifty.'

'It has frozen.'

'It has frozen.'

After a second display of lightbursts, the crowd of ants scattered from behind the carriages towards Innokentyevskoye: miniscule people on the snow, leaving in their wake spots of red, which spread at once on the frostglaze into the next stained-glass flower. The sight was very beautiful, all the more so when still in motion – with white-hued shadows on sky-hued earth, as twilight fell over Zimny Nikolayevsk and the long shadow of the Holey Palace indicated the Seventh Hour. This was how the tsar's army dispersed a workers' protest.

Hard Frost reigned supreme.

On death in the present tense

Modest Pavlovitch Kuzmentsoff, calling on the Wielickis for afternoon tea, shared the latest news from governmental circles, that is, from the corridors of the governor general's palace and Citadel. And so, Schultz-Zimovy's daughter, Anna Timofeyevna, was to be engaged to a certain Gerushin from an old landowning family from the Olonets Governorate; to mark the occasion, a great ball was to be held, to which His Illustriousness would invite all the more influential families in the Baikal Kray. Marta and Hanna Wielicka began imploring the elderly lawyer to whisper a word where necessary and do them the enormous pleasure of reserving such an invitation for the Wielicki household. The lawyer stroked his silver beard, helped himself to the sweetmeats generously pushed his way and purred contentedly, gratified by the attention afforded him and the impression this information had provoked. The master of the house, however, cared little for balls and aristocratic connections; he began questioning Kuzmentsoff about matters of an economic or governmental nature, especially about the governor general's new policy of repression: was he intending to maintain such terror for long? Any social unrest was bad for business. J.P. Morgan's deputation had already left Irkutsk, heading on the Trans-Siberian Express for the Great Russian Heartland. The lawyer informed him that they allegedly had plenipotentiary rights granted by the White House, signed by President Cox himself. This came as no surprise, given that the US Treasury Department was in debt to Morgan to the tune of billions of dollars. A different piece of news was more to Wojsław's liking: Prince Blutsky-Osey had handled things well during the peace negotiations in Hong Kong with the Japanese – so well that his mission had ceased to be a secret in fact, and people were already speaking openly of talks between Nikolay the Second and Emperor Hirohito; the government newspapers would be writing about it before long. In honour of this, Wielicki downed a glass of madeira.

Sit down on the chaise longue next to the august old gentleman's armchair (Michasia immediately scrambled onto the knees) and quiz him regarding the well-known matter – had he not heard anything new? maybe Schembuch had received other instructions in the meantime? what was happening with Ormuta? when will some tchinovnik finally apply the stamp and hand back the passport? what are they saying on the Sibirkhozheto board about Schultz's idea of dialogue with the gleissen? are they saying anything at all?

Gospodin Kuzmentsoff sighed so deeply that glintzen sparkled on his moustache and beard.

'It's a political matter and won't be unravelled by methods other than political. Yes? Hence legal manoeuvres, procedural tricks, tchinovnik connexions, bribes and favours will be of no avail. With respect to you, a political decision has to be made, with respect to you all, you, Father Frost, the Ice and History. Until they decide what use to make of you and what use you're fit for anyway, that is, what you stand for here yourself – they won't let you go, Venyedikt Filipovitch, even if the train to Kezhma were to restart tomorrow morning.'

'But as soon as I openly declare myself for anything here, I shall at once make enemies. There's no possibility, is there, that I would stand for something or someone and not at the same time be against someone else.'

'Agh, the delusions of youth!' the old gentleman chortled jovially. 'Do you still persist in the hope that you'll go through life as everyone's friend, making an enemy of no one, yes? Capital!'

'At least they regard me now as useful, both one side and the other. But should I say anything in support of Thaw – the Lyednyaks will set their dogs on me; should I say anything in support of the Ice – the Ottepyelniks will lay their bait.'

'I have never known a man worthy of respect who had not mortal enemies.' Kuzmentsoff sipped his café au lait, smacked his lips, wiped his moustache. 'You wish to extricate your father from the Ice, yes? You wish to get away from Irkutsk, yes? Well, so you have to freeze in one or other political shape, only then will the matter get underway; someone – this one or that – will declare himself for you with force and conviction, and break the stalemate.'

'But what if I'm unable to freeze like that? If all these notions of yours are equally alien and unsavoury to me?'

Modest Pavlovitch threw up his arms.

'Bah! It's your life, your father; it's up to you.'

Michasia had fallen well and truly asleep. Carry her cautiously to bed, summoning Masha. The thought that there was no choice but to stand on one side or the other, to declare support for this or that History – Zeytsoff had not been mistaken: in the final reckoning of deeds and their effects, it will be the choice of History – this thought would not have been so unpalatable, were it not for the awareness that here, under the Ice, it was not possible to freeze in falsehood. Pace around the room, scratching the hand and forearm, until nightfall and long after; the parquet floor creaked under the feet in the silent apartment. Freezing as an Ottepyelnik – means becoming an Ottepyelnik. As a Lyednyak – becoming a Lyednyak. As a Pilsudtchik – a Pilsudtchik. As a bourgeois – a bourgeois. As a socialist – a socialist. And as a cynical blackguard with no ideals – then no one shall be in any doubt: a blackguard! An end to the Kotarbiński pump, an end to the morning demurchment, after which a million colourful temptations spin around in the head and everything is so wonderfully fluid, open, possible but non-necessary – unrealised – warm – childlike…

Since early that morning, great confusion had prevailed in Krupp's Cryophysics Laboratory, whilst the source of the commotion and turmoil had been the mute Busytchkin. Hardly had the desk been sat down at (the morning sun was streaming through the pure frostoglaze) and the nib sharpened when Mr Busytchkin came running over, waving his arms in panic and clutching at his cravat as if in a chaotic attempt to throttle himself. In the traditional fashion, a visit had been paid before dawn to the New Arkadiya and the murch pumped out till the tongue in the gob grew numb and fingers turned blue – so now, there was no way of telling what was so upsetting Busytchkin: dozens of phantasies strange and gruesome swept through the mind at the sight of the miniscule chemist's agitation. Doctor Wolfke had not yet appeared, Engineer Iertheim was most likely in the Workshops, whilst the remaining employees had buried themselves somewhere out of sight. The desk was groaning under piles of disorderly reports of thousands of experiments carried out by the Cryophysics Laboratory of Friedrich Krupp Frierteisen AG as well as copies of articles published by competitor laboratories; the Kaiser-Wilhelm-Gesellschaft für schwarze Physik, jointly funded by Krupp, had been demanding for months a full report from Doctor Wolfke and this thankless task had now landed on the shoulders of his new assistant. Tear off a corner of ink-stained page from the rough draft of the report and push it in Busytchkin's direction. HELP, he jotted down, MY GARDEN HAS FROZEN.

Busytchkin, as it transpired, was conducting a research project of his own on the borderline between black chemistry and black biology, namely cultivating various species of grass, flower and vegetable in large laboratory trays filled with tungetitum soil. He kept the trays high up on the tops of iron cupboards, in order not to occupy space in the Laboratory; some of the trays were fully shielded from light, others – placed near windows. All the plants, however, certainly required watering and warmth. Anyway, on entering the seventh storey of the tower that morning, still ahead of the brigade of ice-stompers, Busytchkin had discovered the Laboratory under frost, with hoar-covered windows and cold stoves. He lit the stoves at once and hurried to rescue his plantation. The heavy containers had to be carefully lifted down from the high cupboards; Busytchkin bent over each one, inserted thermometers into the soil around the plants, laid specimens under the microscope, almost puffing and blowing on the little frozen leaves and stalks. 'An accident?' ask him. CARETAKER CRETIN LOST HIS HEAD!!! Should he wish to grab an honest job, here was an opening for Shtchekelnikoff; being a coal-wallah surely requires no great qualifications. He'll make a man of himself yet! But then have second thoughts: an old gleissenik; as he has frozen, so he has frozen – with his suspiciousness, with the sullen grimace on his square mug, with his knife.

As fresh teslectric flow was still buzzing neath the cranium, however, the warped and non-necessary ideas did not end on this one thing. 'Perhaps you were also cultivating edible plants, Mr Busytchkin?' Busytchkin pointed to a tray containing ginseng. CHINESE DOCTORS, I HAVE HEARD, CURE VARIOUS COMPLAINTS OF THE ICE WITH THE BLACK ROOT OF GINSENG. Which means, what complaints? Whilst lifting some large ceramic flowerpots, two new variations on this theme were immediately born: first, would it not perchance be possible to find a cure for the White Plague by means of this method, and how much would the secret of such a medicament go for on the market in Harbin; and second, the Chinese surely cultivate no differently their black opium, upon whose marvels Pierre Schotcha had waxed so lyrically at the Wielickis' dinner party. For might it actually be a simple mixture, just powdered tungetitum sprinkled into ordinary laudanum? Don't the poppies have to grow first in the soil of the Ice, and only then is the black juice harvested from the poppy-heads? The raw-silk jacket-sleeve had become soiled; feel the spark of a third idea, like the glint of polished amber, as the smudge is rubbed off with a spittle-moistened finger: what if this entire White Plague, which it had befallen Doctor Konyeshin to combat in the Pacific Fleet, is no more than an ordinary microbial disease spread by microbes gorged on tungetitum, grown on tungetitum? Had some Pasteur been found who could isolate these Ice bacteria and examine them under a microscope? Maybe the whole problem of treating the White Plague stems from the fact that its bacilli do not reproduce, poison or die like the bacilli of Summer; they are governed purely by the biology and medicine of Winter, that is, of the greatest possible cold and soletruth, the lowest possible entropy – maybe these sailors and inhabitants of Vladivostock are suffering from *order*?

Busytchkin did not calm down until midday. Doctor Wolfke arrived with Iertheim, their experimenter-assistants returned with bags of tungetitum receipted by the chief bookkeeper for fresh experiments (Wolfke locked the bags in a giant armoured safe behind his desk), Mrs Pfetzer appeared with an armful of maps – as Busytchkin tottered from one person to another wringing his hands, rolling his eyes and wordlessly demanding human justice, namely the sacking of the coal-wallah and hiring of a conscientious caretaker to look after the Laboratory, day and night.

Venture during the afternoon break, slurping from a clay mug the hot broth distributed at this time of day by the tchay-wallah, into the labyrinthine depths of the Cryophysics Laboratory, in order to get acquainted with other momentous works of Doctor Wolfke and company. Passing under charts of the coldmill reservations, near to the stove, and having glanced around carefully first, nab with the left hand one of Busytchkin's immature plants, a potato shoot together with its buried tuber. Plunge the potato into the suit pocket; then, pausing behind some cupboards, wrap it in a handkerchief. No one saw, because no one was watching.

Engineer Iertheim – the like of whose face gives children nightmares – lay stretched out, dozing on a laboratory bench, amidst a highly complex apparatus seemingly for measuring electric current, since it was equipped with many clock-face scales and was humming softly, yet so low the hair stood up on the back of the neck. In the tangle of cables, clipped together any old how, lay wires, ingots, plates and rings of tungetitum and of coldiron coolbonds. An entire fortune thrown on the scrapheap, treasures fallen on fallow ground. Turn back and bring Iertheim some of the broth. Awoken, he muttered half-hearted thanks.

Sit down on a stool beside him.

'I have an idea.'

He yawned.

'Congratulations, congratulations.'

'Wait. I have an idea: we shall make a fortune on tungetitum.'

'Aha. And that means who?'

'Can I count on your word of honour? Listen to me, sir. For I may be mistaken.' Slurp the broth. Reach for a handkerchief to wipe the moustache; but the hand struck the stolen potato – so merely scratch nervously. 'Listen to me, sir. The magpies collect the tungetitum that they can reach, but they can reach only the tungetitum that lies outside isotherms deadly to man, hence the desperate fight for business and the cutthroat prices and the chasing after rumours. For whole mountains of tungetitum lie at the epicentre of the Ice, where no human has yet set foot – not so?'

'Where it crashed, there it lies.' Mijnheer Iertheim reached mechanically for a small tungetitum hammer and tapped lightly with it on a thermometric anvil; the dials of the apparatuses fluctuated. 'Some Swedish black physicist recently wrote in *Studien über Thermometrie* on the following hypothesis: that the whole of Winter and the Ice stem only from the fact that a massive quantity of tungetitum from outer space, drunk somehow on helium straight from the sun, crashed in Siberia. Imagine what energy there was in that impact. Whilst the tungetitum, as tungetitum will, turned all that energy into Frost. There you have both Winter and the gleissen.'

'Listen to me, sir! The point is that man has no access to up to ninety per cent of the tungetitum resources. Unless.'

'Unless what?'

'Exactly. One of two things: either we inject the hiberniks with some kind of blackchemical antidote to give them even greater resistance to the cold, or – Thaw.'

Iertheim tapped the hammer against the exposed bone on his temple.

'Thaw! What are you talking about!'

'Think about it! When the ice dissolves away and Summer takes over – these minerals won't suddenly evaporate from the Earth's surface! They will remain where they landed. There'll be no gleissen to freeze the coldiron, but there'll be tungetitum – up to here!' Brandish the mug below the chin. 'And whosoever in the age of Thaw is first to lay his paw upon it, he shall be tsar of Sibirkhozheto!'

Iertheim was clearly disconcerted.

'If you're looking at the market value of the raw material, then you're right. But such an exchange would be like asking an engineer if he'd prefer a goldmine to the technologies of steel production. What kind of transaction is that, I ask you! And how come such an idea has entered your head at all?' He cast a swift glance. 'What, do you wish to go and incite Filip in favour of Thaw, that is, in favour of the death of the gleissen?'

Wave the arms.

'No, no!' Bite the tongue. Spilling the beans about Tesla's arsenal, after all, was out of the question. 'You know that the emperor –'

'The emperor!' Mijnheer Iertheim snorted. 'If you really think, sir, that they'll allow any move here against the Ice or destruction of the coldiron industry, then you're a child.' He surveyed the mess on the table, leaned over the edge of the tabletop and squinted towards the wastepaper bin. 'Somewhere here I had a newspaper... Nikola Tesla, the great inventor, arrived not long ago in Irkutsk. What? You've not heard? And do you know why they've not yet driven him out? There was a photograph of him there that explained a lot. Wizard! Lord of Lightning! An old man living in former glory and tricking gullible Russian tchinovniks into paying off debts he'd acquired in America. Few in Zimny Nikolayevsk see him as anything other than a theatrical charlatan.'

Recall Engineer Reszke from the Northern Mammoth Company, but again say nothing.

'Thaw!' Iertheim was now well and truly awake. 'Hah! You've also been listening to all that? The emperor angry with Winter, Winter in retreat!' He snorted again and struck himself with the hammer above his eye. 'Get it out of your head, sir.'

'In that case we have to make the hiberniks even more resistant to frost –'

'Look,' he interrupted. 'Over there, for example, is: a fridge.' He pointed to an oblong steel chest with its entrails hanging out, a scaffold of wires and spindles that took up half its capacity. 'We introduce a current, the engine keeps turning over, the mechanical friction on the coldiron coolbonds causes a drop in the internal temperature. In the walls we install frostglaze vacuum insulators and thus maintain the frost for weeks, for years. We began with tungetitum rings, but gradually we've reduced to cheaper and cheaper coolbonds. Have you any conception, sir, what a fortune Krupp shall make on this, once we accommodate the prototype within the price range affordable to our good townsfolk?

'Or this.' With the little hammer, he touched an invisible string stretched between two claw grips; only when it trembled did it release a thin rainbow, and the eye perceived an image of taut thread. 'Hoartin fibre. Also already patented left, right and centre. Lighter-than-light aeroplanes shall be made from it, armoured shirts and suits; upon it shall hang the architecture of the new Babylon. The gentlemen from the Kaiser-Wilhelm-Gesellschaft have already sent us great plans for new cities, new machines, new railway lines in the sky. And what they have not sent – we can but imagine. Those battleships and guns, for which the emperor ordered coldiron from here, will have to be scrapped within a few years.

'Pay a visit one day to Doctor Wolfke, perhaps he'll show you his new toy: the icevisor.' Iertheim laid his palms flat together. 'Two frostoglaze surfaces, the lower with a coldiron mesh sunk into it, the upper transparent. Between them a suspension with tungetitum particles. You see, sir, how coloured images run over frostoglaze. On the icevisor, they will fluctuate and arrange themselves according to applied voltages. That is, if he succeeds.' Mijnheer Iertheim grabbed his mug, knocked back the remains of the broth. 'He says he has to leave. But Krupp won't let him go.'

'Mm-hmm, I was trying to find out what happens here with employees' ideas, and –'

The unsightly Dutchman gave a friendly clap on the shoulder.

'Never fear, young man, I shan't betray anything to anyone.'

But why not, in point of fact? Tchingis Shtchekelnikoff was right, something doesn't add up; the mathematics of character in Iertheim's equations leaves great unknowns, or rather their right-hand side simply does not equate to the left-hand side.

'Will you be staying longer this evening, sir? I'll think it over and we'll discuss it further. Something is itching to tell me there's money to be made.'

Mijnheer Iertheim gestured invitingly.

Return to the report for the Kaiser-Wilhelm-Gesellschaft. Stealthily transfer the ice-spud to a pocket of the shuba. Spy and eavesdrop on Mr Busytchkin to see if he notices the theft. Doctor Wolfke arrived in the afternoon and politely gave his mute assistant a thorough dressing-down: this was not Busytchkin's main work, not for tungetitum cultivation would Wolfke have to carry the can before the board of directors. For Busytchkin was responsible for the research on cryocarbon. Iced carbon, which comes from deposits frozen through by gleissen (extracted mainly from the Tcheremkhovo mines), is characterised by the fact that when cast into a flame – it extinguishes it in the blinking of an eye and, in an explosion of unlicht, burns out in ferocious frost. The first conundrum faced by black chemistry relates to the molecular structure of cryocarbon and other ice and coldiron materials. Since a coolbond of carbon coldiron, such as high-carbon steel drawn through the coldmills, for example, is something other than – a coolbond of pure coldiron, Fe/gl, and cryocarbon, C/gl. In Tomsk, Saint Petersburg and Berlin, 'Black Mendeleyeff periodic tables' have already been devised for the ice chemistry, still awaiting however confirmation or falsification. Does ice transmutation take place in fact on the molecular level? Is a single atom of cryocarbon still cryocarbon? Is it therefore a property of every individual atom – like electromagnetic charge, mass or valency? So, on this most fundamental level, there exists a certain characteristic of this matter connected with its wave-particle nature, energy and state of arrangement, which manifests itself only when insight has been gained into the matter modified according to this very characteristic: we did not know we were living in Summer, until Winter took over. If this be true, then not only would there exist a different biology of helium, but also a different biology of iced carbon: organic chemistry built upon compounds of C/gl – ice carbohydrates, fats and proteins – ice flora and fauna – ice people. Had Mr Busytchkin collected blood from the hiberniks? Had he burned it in a spectroscope? Tested it in chemical reactions? Feel shame now at the display of enthusiasm in front of Iertheim. It's hardly surprising the idea failed to move him: for years here, they had no doubt been rummaging around in the guts of hiberniks and figuring out how to make man more resistant to frost. Jot down on a scrap of paper: *point number 5: The Way of Greed – did he set off into the Frost in search of tungetitum?* Father always sided after all with the hiberniks, with the Martsynians; everyone confirms it. He worked for Horczyński, then for Krupp, knew what the race was all about. In nineteen eleven, his convict labour gang was assigned to one of the first expeditions into the Ice; Commissioner Preiss said that the majority of them died – they went as far as no magpie has ever gone since; the isotherms besides are shifting, the Ice is advancing. What did they see then? What did they find? Did they reach the place of Impact? Who else survived from that expedition? Documents need to be unearthed at the Ministry of Winter. For perhaps in reality, the simplest Way is the true Way: he went off into the Frost because he was seduced by mountains of tungetitum; he had nothing to lose, everything to gain.

Stay well into the night – the roof-crawlers did their hammering and departed, twilight descended, lamps were extinguished in more outlying corners of the Laboratory. Send word to Shtchekelnikoff asking him not to wait, but he insists on waiting – stay until all are gone apart from

Iertheim. Stow the papers and tools under the tabletop. Ascertain, not without amusement, the colour of the fingers, blackish navy-blue from the ink. Need to procure some oversleeves; such a waste of a good jacket. Mijnheer Iertheim emerged from the labyrinth of cupboards, dressed already in his malakhay hat and spectacles, in his antiquated Turkish-style fur-lined coat. Wave to him, grab the shuba. Walking downstairs to the lifts, wind the scarf around the neck, thrust hands into gloves. Shtchekelnikoff roused himself, got to his feet. At that moment, the lift cage was still at the bottom. Stop by the window behind the shaft door, breathe on the snow-hued surface. Moonbows were sprouting from the roofs of the Holey Palace, as Zimny Nikolayevsk floated below in lakes of stars. The unsightly engineer stopped alongside, wrested a flagon from under his arm and took a deep swig. Glance over the top of the lenses. He held it up: it was milk. Shake the head.

'So how goes it with our young millionaire's zeal?' he croaked in German, clearing his throat. 'Or has it cooled?'

'You owe him a debt of gratitude, sir,' murmur through the scarf.

'What? No!'

He knew very well, however, who was being referred to.

Perhaps it was the Ice, or perhaps –

'You recognised me at once, sir. That is, you recognised him. I didn't ask for your help, for any mediation with Doctor Wolfke.'

He laughed hoarsely.

'I have a kind heart!'

'You've thought a lot about Ishmael.' The lift cage came up. Shtchekelnikoff wrenched open the doors, first one, then the other. Step into the frost; the metalwork clanged with every footfall. The Dutchman entered, closed the cage, switched the lever. The lift began to move. 'I have learned...' Raise the voice above the rhythmic rattle. 'They are two sides of the same coin: shame and contempt, gratitude and hatred.' Avert the gaze towards the panorama of the industrial town brimming with dark colours. 'These currents drag us across the boundaries of good and evil: the noblest intentions beget the foulest deeds, the blackest desires prompt acts of angelic compassion.'

'Soon you'll be speaking against morality, very fashionable now in Europe, in Summer.'

'Morality belongs to the speech of men, built upon words, deeds, movements of matter; whereas our deepest feelings and motives are often indescribable even to ourselves.'

The lift hit the ground. Again, Shtchekelnikoff was the first to step out. Head towards the Marmeladobahn station along a path of unevenly laid planks. The path was so narrow there was room for only two pedestrians to walk shoulder to shoulder; whenever someone emerged out of the fog from the opposite direction, they had to stop or step to the right. The Marmeladobahn platform was, of course, invisible – finding the right direction depended on the Clock Towers. The topography of Zimny Nikolayevsk was not as yet so familiar. Glance up at the sky. Lights were burning in Thyssen's Tower; in the Midday Tower, people in Pobedonostseff's Surveillance Department were also hard at work.

Slacken the pace so as not to leave the Dutchman behind.

'You were saying, sir, that he was impossible to live with, that everyone hated him –you too?'

Engineer Iertheim ruminated for a long time behind his scarf, under his black-hued spectacles.

'How easily you pass judgement in these matters!'

'For I have learned to separate the truth of words from the truth of the reality they tell.' Scrabble under the shuba, walking along, for the cigarette case; it was empty. 'What we say, what is possible to express, is a certain sign of the truth, but never the truth.'

'Never?'

'Never.'

Through his scarf, he let out clouds of dense, unlichted breath mist.

'I am dying.'

'...'

'Cancer is devouring me, Benedykt. They say that under the Ice, such diseases come to a halt. But also, no one here has ever been cured of ailments acquired aforehand. I've been thinking of going to that sanatorium up north… Maybe I'll go. I am not saying it so you'll sympathise with me. I want you to see the thing on the scale I do. We measure life's problems according to the worst tragedies with which fate affects us. Carefree children, whose greatest worry is a broken toy – cry their eyes out, hardly surprisingly, over spilt soup; to them, that soup is worth almost half a toy. But when a man senses in his own innards the claws of Death – in terms of how many financial problems can he measure Death? what setbacks to his ambition? how many troubles at work? how many lost loves – this one lost life of his own? Nothing but platitudes, platitudes, platitudes, *jongeheer*.'

Take a seat in the directors' carriage. Iertheim, yawning so much that his scarf slipped from his beard, sprawled on the bench opposite. Staring out of the dirty window, he filled his pipe.

'I regret time past, regret the unrealised, really regret them.' He puffed at his pipe. 'Regret the loss of a friend.'

'Friend? But you scarcely knew him!'

'I am not saying I knew him. Coming across a friend in this world, Benedykt, is harder than finding a good wife.'

'But you didn't even like him! If I understand your words correctly

– understand who Ishmael is to you – Ishmael, to whom people feel an instinctive dislike, who repels like a reversed magnet. Though not a friend!'

Other passengers looked round, a Jew with sidelocks peered sternly over his newspaper, a uniformed tchinovnik frowned. Mijnheer Iertheim pressed a crippled finger to his lips.

The locomotive's whistle announced departure.

'Have you never met a man whom you hate at first sight?' inquired the Dutchman softly. 'He's done you no wrong, you've had no time to quarrel in word or deed, yet already, already you're sure you'll find any excuse to bite each other like rabid dogs.'

'Mm-hmm, that's true, such cases do happen –'

'He's your enemy before any act of hostility occurs. Bah, he was your enemy before you set eyes on one another for the first time, before you'd heard of one another. And this hostility is not in the least towards his convictions, opinions, nationality, religion – but precisely towards his person, only towards his person. Do you understand?' Iertheim let out tobacco smoke. 'This precedes deeds, precedes realised actions. Every man has hundreds of bitter enemies whom he's never met and who'll never know anything about him. Every man has hundreds of friends whose lives are fated never to cross his own. That we occasionally do meet them, however, that chance – like with that series of coin tosses – sometimes throws us close together, is a separate thing. As a consequence, we can then behave in this or that manner, take up the acquaintance or turn our back on it, realise the friendship or deny it – but this in no way alters the fact that a man has met a friend. Even if he failed to utter a kind word to him. Even if he delivered him into the hands of executioners.'

'You will ask why –'

'No. I won't ask.'

'At the time, I was on graveyard shift; I had to call at the Workshops at around two in the morning, in order to calibrate the steel rods supporting the experiment apparatuses according to how the gleiss was shifting. So, I enter and see through the window a light on in the office. Who's sitting there at this time of night? I listen in: Polish, it seems. I take a peek: Mr Filip Gierosławski and some suspicious-looking types: unshaven mugs, vagabond rags; all I did was assume a surprised expression, and already first one and then another reaches under his lapel and pulls out a weapon. I made myself scarce. Then a week or two later, I see Filip Gierosławski again in the Workshops at night. What's he doing there, I ask, what's a geologist doing in a Cryophysics Workshop? I remember the caretaker Fiedojczuk, poor devil; it was hard not to remember him. I went and filed a report.

'Next day, I hear first thing in the morning that Filip had not reported for work. He was to be fired – but news came that it was because the gendarmes had gone there, to Horczyński's old offices, along with the Okhrana people with papers for Filip Gierosławski's arrest.

'I had no idea he'd been a convict, a state criminal, I didn't know.'

'When was it?'

'Sometime in the spring of nineteen nineteen.' He puffed on his pipe.

'In March? April?'

'And where were Horczyński's offices located?'

'Mm-hmm, I don't recall the address. Is it important?'

'Maybe some trace of the pater remains there.'

He nodded.

'Tomorrow I'll give you the address and write a letter of recommendation in case of need.'

Alighting on the platform in Irkutsk, he extended a three-fingered hand, still naked and ungloved. Shake it without hesitation, that is, without any thought at all; shake it because that's how the characters have frozen on both sides of the equation.

Obtain leave to finish work earlier on the following day; a meeting had been fixed with Mr Pocięgło in order to hold that long-postponed conversation. The invitation was to his place, to his home; he had an apartment in Theatre Lane, close to the residence of Major General Kuliga. Pass on the stairs some uniformed officials in regulation greatcoats: an assessor and a supervisor. Shtchekelnikoff saw them off with a glance like a loaded shotgun. 'Alone, so they ain't arrested him,' he said. 'Meaning: left him in peace. Beware of such a bird!' 'He's a wealthy man, wealthy and well-connected.' Whereupon Shtchekelnikoff merely crossed himself, once, twice and thrice.

An ancient footman led the way to the study. Porfiry wore a bright-yellow satin waistcoat buttoned over a fresh shirt; a valet was tying his cravat and inserting tungetitum cufflinks into the cuffs – slowly and clumsily, as Director Pocięgło was constantly interrupting him, bending over his desk, grabbing a pen, rustling newspapers, holding up to the light official documents and hurling curses at their white-and-inky face like Hamlet addressing poor Yorick's skull. On entering and removing the shapka and frostoglazes, find Pocięgło in just such a pose, holding up a multi-page letter prolifically stamped with mighty seals, and squinting out of his angular eye sockets at the valet bent double and diagonally across him.

'Will you get them in at last!'

'But your lordship won't allow!' The valet held the second cufflink between his teeth.

'Damn your clumsy fat fingers! Ah, Mr Gierosławski! All hell's hanging over us, Benedykt, no two ways about it: I have to hurry to the Citadel, bow and scrape to the company there and line the tchinovniks' pocketbooks.'

'Ten minutes?'

'Ten minutes, ten minutes.' He glanced at his watch. 'Be off!' He rapped the servant on the back with the papers and sent him packing. 'Well, let's get on with it. Miss Muklanowicz?'

'No, not Jelena.' Cast around for a place to sit, but the study had no suitable furniture. And the host was on his feet. Speak therefore standing up, still in the shuba, shapka in one hand, frostoglazes in the other. 'Please don't contradict me, sir, till you've heard me out. You have people in America. You have people in Harriman's firm; you must have. You must have an agreement with Harriman; like him you depend on the link between Siberia and America promised by the Around-the-World Railroad. It's a revolutionary matter, without Thaw you'll end up like every Oblastnik before you; Schultz has already tightened the screw. So, I imagine you also have emergency strategies: flight east across the Pacific. Contracted people already in place, both here and over there, transport, plans. That's what I imagine. Otherwise... it wouldn't add up. Therefore – therefore –'

'Yes?'

'Money? I can't offer sums that would mean anything to you, sir. You have no obligation towards me –'

Mr Pocięgło slammed the papers down on the desk, leapt to the door, tugged at the handle and peered into the corridor. No one.

'Let's go,' he said dryly.

He did up his frock coat; once on the threshold, the footman handed him his shuba and sable ushanka with its earflaps. On the stairs, Porfiry spent a long time winding his scarf, embroidered in frost-fern motifs. Allow Shtchekelnikoff to go on ahead. Mr Pocięgło paused by the gateway in a recess sheltered from the snow and wind; the reindeer harnessed to the waiting sleigh were jangling their bells, the rocking sleigh-lamps flickered. Fog stifled the crunch of passing footsteps.

'You and your pater, yes?'

'Two people.'

'But he'll be a normal human being, as I understand it.'

'That is, unfrozen.'

'Unfrozen.' Pocięgło clicked his tongue in a long-drawn-out manner; glintzen flashed neath his eyebrows. 'Unfrozen.'

'He will board the ship along with other people. Otherwise – the whole thing would make no sense. Unfrozen, Porfiry.'

'Papers?'

'Without papers. False ones, if you can.'

'You're asking a lot.'

'I know. And –'

'Jelena Muklanowicz –'

'No, I'm not trading Jelena for father.' Snarl abruptly. Pull on the shapka and goggles, signal to Shtchekelnikoff. 'Name your price, sir.'

'All right. Since for your sake, we have to take such a political risk…' He tapped the ice with his cane. 'The price is political. Besides, you know the price. I already expressed it in the Transsib; in any case, we discussed it at Vittel's.'

Give a hollow cough.

'I have no idea whether he will obey me. No idea whether the gleissen will obey him. Whether they'll harken to him at all, once he's unfrozen. How to carry it out: let him speak first to them; and then pluck him from the Ice? As Father Frost or not Father Frost. Have even less idea if History obeys gleissen. And even if it does… History – moves at a pace still slower than glacial masses. Years may go by, months at least, before it becomes clear whether or not I've fulfilled my obligation. We cannot wait in the port.'

'Take off your glasses. You shall give me your word.'

Raise the frostoglazes onto the forehead.

'The word of Benedykt Gierosławski: your History in return for safe flight with father.'

Porfiry tapped the ice for a second time with the coldiron ferrule of his cane.

'It has frozen.'

He turned away, jumped into his sleigh, whistled to the driver; the driver cracked his whip and the team of reindeer began to jangle and clatter, pulling away and vanishing into the fog.

March hurriedly to the address given by Engineer Iertheim (the frosts were getting more ferocious with every day), turning over in the mind, to the rhythm of loud panting, a single persistent thought: was this not deceit?

Realise that from the very start, despite all the heartfelt intentions and oaths to having told the truth, everyone is being deceived. The point is not that the word just given to Porfiry Pocięgło will be intentionally broken – because no. But maybe such an intention is about to arise; maybe everything is about to turn on its head – truth instead of truth – and some enormous lie, equally sincere, will take shape.

It has frozen – yet is unfrozen every morning under the Kotarbiński pump in Tesla's hotel room. The word has been given and maybe it will be kept – but maybe not. *Maybe not.* In Summer, no deception would be perceived in this, since in Summer there's no way of telling with certainty the soletruth about anyone, and every inhabitant of Summer well knows it. But here – they look and see: a gleissenik. They look and see: ah, that sort of man! C, therefore D, therefore E, therefore F; 2 + 2 = 4.

Deception is not realised in any action; the deception is in the *potentiality*. Even if the same truth is upheld to the very end – deception will have been committed, because that truth *might potentially* not have been upheld, it *might potentially* have been denied. It might still be denied. Doctor Tesla's machines are waiting.

Shtchekelnikoff kept glancing over his shoulder as if he really were able to make out something in the creamy fog. Urge him on with gestures, so as not to waste breath. The airways were freezing; frost forced its way through the scarf and into the half-open mouth. Images in fluid colours rumpled the shapes of the fog and shapes of the solid masses of buildings, and the lights from their high windows and from streetlamps; bearings are easily lost in such a city, though no gleissenik ever loses his bearings. Pause, wait patiently for Shtchekelnikoff. Regret having been so stingy: a sleigh should have been hired. Pedestrians were moving at their characteristic half-trot, swaying from side to side on legs almost rigid, gingerly placing their short steps. Sometimes their scrunching footfalls could be heard first, crushing lumps of névé and ice, before strangely hued human contours loomed out of the rainbow coils.

Horczyński's old offices were located in a former preparatory school by a crossroads to the south of the bend in the Angara, near the district of Znamenskoye. The solid brick building had survived the Great Fire; next to nothing had been done since apart from installing a new roof. The low architecture dating from before the time of the Ice meant that Horczyński had been paying a symbolic rent for not the worst location. He sought a groschen wherever he could. Nowadays the two lower storeys seemed to be leased to no one; when the watchman – a grandad so frozen-through from every angle that he had red scars upon white – was asked, he merely shrugged his shoulders. Think: perhaps a deaf-mute as well; but Shtchekelnikoff muttered a word in his ear, whereupon the grandad invited him to the stove in the ground-floor chamber and unwound the rags from his head, revealing something more than his scarred cheeks, namely one blind eye, its lid frozen to a pus-encrusted scab, and an ear that looked like a shred of flannel drooping over his silver stubble. Shtchekelnikoff offered him some shag, the best letter of recommendation, as it turned out. The grandad returned the compliment by extracting a bottle of moonshine from behind the pallet laid on the stove. Indicate to Tchingis to do the honours. They each took a swig and then another. The grandad opened wide his toothless gums and began to spin a mawkish Russian tale about the wealth and downfall of golden master August Rajmundovitch Horczyński from the Great Russian Heartland. Outside the windows, battered by powerful gusts, wind was howling off the Angara and Ushakovka. Glintzen danced in the old man's gob like glow-worms in a mouldering tree hollow. Ask him if any of Horczyński's old employees remain here. Not likely! All blown away! Ask him, in that case, if he remembers where Mr Horczyński's people had their offices. How could he not remember! Of course he remembers! Ask him if he recalls a certain geologist, Engineer Gierosławski, who looked like this and that. Well, yes, there was such a man. Will you show us where he worked? Is anything left at all of Horczyński and the Ores? That I know not, declares the grandad, they only sat upstairs where them chanceries and offices are rented now by the arshin. If anything were left, they'd surely have brought it down. Flash a silver rouble before his eyes. The watchman extracted a bunch of keys from under his sheepskin. You gentlemen take the lamps, everywhere up there is dark, cold and dread. Shtchekelnikoff lit two old top-handled naphtha lanterns; a waxy yellow glow crept around the watchman's junk-room. Cold, dark and dread, went the horror-grandpa's fearful refrain, d'you hear, your lordships, d'you hear? Prick up your ears! (Bwroomm, bwroommm, bwroomm, bwroommm.) Never far away! Seventeen times has an icer passed through the school since then. At night, when I lays me head down on the stove, I hear 'em through the vibrating tiles: the tramp of wild mammoths neath the cellars.

Mount the stairs. The watchman opened a door into a corridor. Everywhere lay snowy permafrost and dark ice. Warped, cracked furniture, doors forced out of buckled frames, parquet floors undulating and shattered, as if the passage of a wave had lifted the blocks from underneath; and on top of all this, lesser equipment frozen into the weirdest configurations – whatever things the trembling naphtha light fell upon it reanimated in a sculpted glacial tunnel, as in the intestine of the icecradle in Mr Korzyński's story which had absorbed and digested in ice a thousand objects, the work of human hands, fruit of human life. The corridor was low and narrow; the glazed matter had been accumulating for years in layers, growing like a salt dripstone. Catch the sleeve on a twisted icicle – like the claw of some saurian toe thrust out of the wall. No choice but to lean against these walls; the boots slid apart, the feet slithered lopsidedly as something snapped and broke under them with a hollow scrape – iced bones. Grandad showed the way. On a triple hanger frozen into the ceiling hung laboratory aprons congealed together in the shape of a cross. A desk swollen with petrified snow had crawled to the threshold of an office and there given up the ghost. A carpet pierced through by stalagmites had braced itself and fired its wavy hump at a doorknob covered in ice hard as granite; it had failed to reach its target and ice had lopped off its tongue. Two office bookcases had collapsed in unison, spraying each other with volumes of deeds that froze between them in a double-decker stream, underneath – the black leather of heavy bindings, on top – the froth of pages exposed. A clock with zodiac face had sunk into a rift in the wall; Taurus, Aries and Pisces were still sticking out; one hand pointed towards a smashed window, beyond which a cloud of rainbow fog was slowly coiling around a frostoglaze streetlamp. The watchman opened another door. In a windowless stockroom at the end of the corridor, geometric pyramids of packets bound in green twine lay frozen. Each packet consisted of half a pood of paper scorched by the frost. Grandad shone the light closer, brushing the hoar off one, two, three cardboard covers, and spotted the stamp in Cyrillic letters. 'Horczyński Ores.'

Set about unshackling the stacks of paper. Out of a broken candelabra arm, Shtchekelnikoff fashioned for himself a temporary pickaxe with which he pounded the archival deposits. He hacked at a rate of six reams every fifteen minutes. The watchman dragged in a charcoal brazier. Defrost over this the more promising documents. The pages went limp like dollops of under-baked dough; the thick gloves precluded more delicate operations, but to take them off – the fingers would quickly go numb from touching the icy bumaga. Grandad obligingly held up a light, glancing at the same time over his shoulder. And so, in this way, the bookkeeping diaries of the deceased industrial enterprise were read.

Encounter the name 'Gierosławski' for the first time in a geological report dated July nineteen eighteen. It was a copy of the reply to a memorandum of some kind addressed to the company directors by Engineer F. Gierosławski. A reply that had come back negative. Lay aside the document so that it freezes again with date and signature uppermost. Not long after this, Shtchekelnikoff dug out a file of original manuscripts from the Ores' magpie division. Defrost the documents in reverse date order; years and months melted away neath the glove into a warm formless pulp. Nineteen eighteen, May: Engineer Gierosławski returned from an expedition to the Nikolayevsky Works in the Nizhneudinsk uyezd of the Irkutsk Governorate; the mineralogical tables are full of percentage comparisons of siderite (dense ores of over thirty per cent, underlined in Engineer Gierosławski's own hand) – they mention flints, oxidised ores, sulphurs, porphyritic groundmasses. The next report: on the likelihood that they had found gold. Quartz, calcite, siderite, pyrite, glitterstones. Research trips around Baikal. Then again nothing: thick volumes of sterile bookkeeping and delivery contracts. Even implication in a civil lawsuit against *intimidation of the local workforce* (it concerned shaman terror on the Ways of the Mammoths).

After two or three hours, Shtchekelnikoff dug out a folder of internal correspondence between the director of the Ores' Geological Department, a certain Kalousek, and Chairman Horczyński. The upper and lower fragments of the pages were thoroughly iced-through, disintegrating to a hoary mud when defrosted, so there was no way of deciphering the dates or signatures on these letters. Doubt sometimes that it really was Kalousek still writing, or if he were quoting the pater, or perhaps this was the hand of the pater himself. No memory had been retained of the style of the pater's handwriting. Besides, having read hurriedly through the thawing manuscripts with the head in a cloud of charcoal smoke – the contents of a third letter had already frozen the mind; after this, every other letter dissolved to pulp and flew in a mucky stream into the fire.

Kalousek, or perhaps father, wrote about plans to extract untapped seams of tungetitum from deep Winter by employing hiberniks *fattened on frost*. The 'engineer' (Gierosławski?) was proposing to conduct experiments on volunteers *motivated by religious beliefs*, whom the experiments were designed to make resistant to frost, thus enabling excursions of ten days or more beyond the Last Isotherm. Unpeel one page from another; on the reverse sides, the handwriting was illegible. The next page contained a hand-drawn sketch of an apparatus similar to a hypodermic needle or piston-action enema syringe. Below it was an anatomical diagram of the blood circulation in a hand or leg or perhaps even the digestive system – try to invoke unsuccessfully memories of analogous drawings in Zygmunt's textbooks – a diagram provided with a legend that included the terms *tungeccinum, frosted vein, iceduct*. The skin burned under the scarf; stifle with difficulty a cough in the accelerating breath. Unstick page after page with the aid of a charred splinter. (Bwroomm, bwroommm, bwroomm, bwroommm.) Chairman Horczyński: the current position of the firm does not allow involvement in such costly and time-consuming ventures. Although we value the good intentions and initiative of our employees, et cetera, et cetera. Return to that drawing – it had to be preserved at all costs! Already, it was disintegrating into fibres, strands, a soppy pancake; ink vanishing like melted snow. Throw the page onto ice far away from the fire. To no avail: what was read, what was glimpsed, what was experienced – exists not, has no right to exist otherwise than in memory. There shall be no material proof; the whole past is a kingdom of probability; the Ice reaches not beyond the here and now. Maybe father wrote it, maybe not, maybe he existed, maybe not.

Bwroomm, bwroommm, croop-droop, Shtchekelnikoff forged away, the horror-grandpa held up a lamp: Kalousek or Not-Kalousek begs access to the orographic analyses made by Karol Bohdanowicz, deposited in the Sibirkhozheto archives; there is no reply. Engineer F.G. had devoted six working days to an inspection of Irkutsk's defunct sewerage system. Here's the request for approval of plans for a hydrographic expedition to the north of the Baikal watershed. Here's a reply to another letter which is not in the folder: in connection with the foregone sale of the enterprise and its incorporation into the Krupp concern, all funds assigned to meteorological and geological research led by Engineer Gierosławski are to be frozen. 'Meteorological?' Kalousek – this Kalousek absolutely had to be found, talked to. An estimate of costs signed by – oh, the signature was preserved, onto the ice with it! – by Filip Gierosławski, in a sharp slanting flourish. The list comprises: six teams of reindeer, provisions for men and animals, remuneration for the locals, including rates for the Tungus trackers and guides along the Ways of the Mammoths, as well as very expensive drilling equipment, pipe drills, several-score arshins of specially treated coldiron, ebonite thermometers in metal casings, folding Savinoff soil thermometers seven arshins long, dynamite (two chests), gold-prospecting and magpie equipment, three insulated yurts, a dozen cylinders of naphtha… The estimate had been crossed out and the deletion initialled by a certain 'H.K'. Kalousek? Maybe in a subsequent letter –

The movement of a dark shape ruffled the shadows at the far end of the corridor and a silhouette loomed from amongst the sculptures of dirty ice. Spring back startled, letting a file slip into the glowing embers – it was a corpulent bewhiskered man in unhooked fur coat, rattling a cane from side to side, thrusting a flabbergasted face into the pool of yellow light. 'What's this? I imagined vagrants or thieves. Gentlemen, for the love of God…!' 'I am about, about to lock up,' the grandad hastened to assure him. Inquire of Shtchekelnikoff: 'How much more?' He indicated with the candelabra axe: at least ten packages. Tchingis will be sent back tomorrow to bring out the rest, un-defrosted; maybe more shall be discovered about father's fate at Horczyński Ores. Another roublie in the grandad's hand and he won't object. Shove the few pages rescued from the heat into their cardboard folder and descend with the booty under the arm down the dark stairs and into a street filled with rainbow-hued fog; the legs hastened of their own accord to the rhythm of feverish thoughts – charging almost, the head set bullishly against the world, hands curled into furry fists –

He sprang out of the fog like the spirit of a drowned man from the depths of a bog, extending at once a filthy arm and staring with naked eyes out of a red countenance, whilst the colours of his skin flowed off his skin onto his vagabond garb, and the colours of his garb flowed off his garb into to the surrounding mist, and the colour of the mist flowed from the mist onto his skin: spirit, ghost, cold wraith. He seized the elbow and gasped (and he spoke in Polish):

'He is the daemon of the Ice! Flee! He has devoured your father! He will devour Poland! Trust not the Old Man! No –'

Thwack! The fog struck him a blow across the back of the neck with a crooked cosh and the wraith sank to the ground, that is, to the ice, before he had completed his warnings. Leap back against a wall. Again, the thick bulbous gloves fumble to unhook the shuba and reach the bundle beneath containing the Grossmeister – before a second ghost, emerging from the fog behind the cosh, thoroughly devaporates and assumes the colours of solid matter, and with solid matter shatters the other's skull. This one: wool-knit and frostoglaze mask neath bearskin shapka, shinel with lapels, above-the-knee military boots with leather laces, a thickset fellow spitting unlichty breath through the mask, ferocious glintz in his wake against the rainbow fog.

He advanced one step and then another – flee, but the legs won't flee, shoot instead. The Grossmeister was entangled in its rags. He advanced a third step, but then a square paw flashed somewhere on a level with his ear and he spouted blood from under his chin like a pig being stuck and sank to the ground, that is, to the ice, like a stuck pig. Pwook, the cast-iron cosh hit the ground with a clatter. Shtchekelnikoff wiped his bayonet against his boot-top, blade shimmering like a butterfly.

'Gives up the ghost under a post, won't escape the devil's host. Get yer arse out of here, honoured sir, I got to clear up afore the clown freezes to the ground.'

'But!'

'Well, what you waiting for!'

'And the other?'

'Eh him, he's breathing. What should I do, polish him off?'

'Who the hell is he?'

'You don't know 'em, my good sir? I said they was a-following us. Well, be off, be off. Wait in there – see them lights? Some den or hostelry. Sit yerself down over a vodka, keep where folks can see ya. I'll be there soon as I'm done. Well!'

Trot towards the azure-tinted windows of the drinking hole. Notice the lack of folder containing the Horczyński archive documents only when brushing off the snow in the porchway: dropped, it remained somewhere by the corpse. Go back for it? – not on your life! Sit down by the stove in the farthermost corner, knock back one glass, then a second. Only when gripping tightly the neck of a carafe of Nikolayevka did the hand stop shaking. Shtchekelnikoff was right, it has a calming effect: the hubbub of human voices and that fug peculiar to Russian drinking dens, the impression of confined space and neighbourly intimacy even when the room is half-empty and the door stands wide open. But in here the heated interior remains sealed against the blizzards and frost outside; only through tiny windows in the low walls can the snow-packed fog be glimpsed. The ceiling hangs low, lower even than the Asiatic sky. Man clings to man.

Effort was required to divert the thoughts from the attack. A third glass melted the ice in the bones. Oo-ookh. Sprawled on a bench, close the eyes. And so – and so – and so it seems father's Mammoth Ways have been followed all along. Shudder to think how closely on his trail. A few more months working at Krupp's and an identical plan to his would surely have been devised, down to the last detail, for extracting tungetitum out of the heart of Winter. One advantage arises from the deception: father had no Kotarbiński pump at his disposal, it wasn't easy for him to descend onto the less obvious paths. He had to reach everything through arduous toil, in stages, supposition by supposition, experiment by experiment, along the narrow path of logical necessities. Had he really injected hiberniks with some black chemistry? Had any of the coldiron concerns already taken up such research? How to find out? This, after all, would be their most closely guarded secret.

... So, on the other hand. What had this meteorology to do with? Geology, hydrography, meteorology. Perhaps something apropos of the Baikal hypothesis: the dead drifting under the Baikal ice, the drifting tungetitum – yet how does it drift when everything here is already frozen? Mm-hmm, but had *everything* in fact frozen? What had Professor Yurkat said about the difficulties of digging a well through the permafrost...? And Busytchkin's experiments – let's think for a moment – if tungetitum really is an element, then it doesn't lose its properties following combustion, oxidisation, dissolution, synthesis or any other chemical treatment of its compounds – in the end, it is always again an atom and atom of tungetitum. The case may be similar with all molecules of coldiron. Let's take those vast conflagrations in the taiga, those deluges of fire and smoke travelling thousands of versts across Siberia – such an elemental wall had been witnessed. Although, admittedly, before the borders of the Land of the Gleissen. But it is all still in circulation, retracing its steps, not escaping into outer space; meteorology, hydrography and geology create a closed circuit. After the Impact, did not the forests there burn? And the Great Fire of Irkutsk? Now, however, it seems to be happening on an even larger scale. Remember the industrial smog over Zimny Nikolayevsk. And the Tchornoye Siyaniye – a Black Aurora is also subject after all to the laws of atmospheric mechanics. In German black physics journals, certain hypotheses have appeared: about unlicht induced by electromagnetic energy, or by electrical discharges on volatile compounds of tungetitum escaping into the sky above the Land of the Gleissen. Of course, not knowing Doctor Tesla's work, they are unaware that not only unlicht is awakened in this way. Then the populace hides behind its frostoglazes, the Shtchekelnikoffs of this world spit over their shoulders, and Father Rózga fulminates from his pulpit about satanic delusions. For how to live every day in these mighty glintzen, in the wild unlicht beating out of the firmament with the force of electrical storms, how to live in a perpetual prophetic séance? And here again – people burn black-wickes, smoke tungetitum tobacco, swallow blackapothecary powders, inhale black opium; they live amidst coldiron, on coldiron, in coldiron. It enters into their organisms; they realise it not, contemplate it not, yet it enters into them. The sewers! Smile inwardly. Oh, that's what he was investigating! Because, after all, the leftovers are excreted, and flow together with other impurities into the soil and enter the network of watercourses – if those are not already frozen. Centres of population are natural collectors of tungetitum. The dream induced by the sha-man's smoke sprang to mind. Coldiron makes its way along black rivers into the Underground World.

... But the Ways of Filip Gierosławski lead farther still. Deceive here with the aid of the Kotarbiński pump, yet father had a fundamental advantage stemming from his participation in that expedition which came so close to the place of Impact, like no other since. Certain things he took for granted; he didn't have to make assumptions, didn't have to formulate hypotheses. After ten years he is pardoned with a prikaz allowing him to settle in Siberia. He does not write home. He lodges with a cobbler-comrade in an ice-ridden hole. Hires himself out to a coldiron company. Sires a bastard. Fraternises with Martsynians, with hiberniks from the coldmills. Enters a conspiracy with Pilsudtchiks – or the Pilsudtchiks conspire with him. Plans geological research into the runoffs of tungetitum, human trials of black biology. But. His newborn daughter dies. Iertheim has the Okhrana sent after him. And father runs away. Where to? Northwards immediately? Not many months later, tales are circulating here about Batyushka Moroz. They say he leads whole villages to self-glaciation. Wanders for years as a pilgrim across the lands of the Ice, constantly returning to the Podkamennaya Tunguska river, as is evident from the Ministry of Winter reports. He converses with gleissen.

... But! But! If he really does converse with gleissen – if someone had *persuaded* him so to do – driven to despair, to desperation following the second death of Emilka, hounded by a fresh police manhunt, in fear of a return to katorga – if someone: Martsyn, Martsynians, Piłsudski, PPS-men from the Revolutionary Faction or from the 'Young Ones' – had persuaded him to enter the Ways of the Mammoths and convince the gleissen of such and such a History – if... *then why had History not changed?* Five years had gone by. The Ice is advancing across the world, just as it was advancing. Martsyn's disciples are suffering oppression, just as they were suffering. There's still no sign of Poland on the horizon. The tsar sits firmly in the saddle. Bah, for the tsar things are even better: peace with Japan will free up the army, he'll let Struve underpin the economy with costly reforms. So? Did father's plan fail? The gleissen not obey him? Do they have their own, different plans? Or maybe, after descending to the Underground World, father changed his mind?

… Isn't it precisely for this reason that PPS-men in Warsaw send him coded letters via his dubious son?

'It is he, none other!'

Shudder, suddenly awoken. Who was it who'd sat down opposite? who was it leaning over the tabletop and belching hot, boozy breath straight into the face? The one and only irreplaceable Filimon Romanovitch Zeytsoff!

'I'm sitting and watching and thinking to myself: him, not him, him, not him – but it is him, he! Excepting the beard and whatever you've done to your hair, and the gloomy ice shadow hanging over you; I had to make sure. And it's not even the season for Black Auroras!'

'Drop it, Zeytsoff.' Sigh. 'I'm not in the mood.'

He'd already clung, no point in protesting.

'Drowning his cares in vodka, for what else does a man drop by at a drinkery, for what else; in the land of happiness and justice, such refuges yawn with emptiness. And even more so in the Land of the Gleissen, where a drunk, and the greatest drunk at that, never quite forgets or denies for what he drinks – to numb himself to feeling, to sorrow, to painful despair, and maybe also to make his brothers-in-sin less hideous in his own eyes in times of intoxication, just as we ourselves like ourselves better at such times – how amusing we are! how charming! Who could resist us? – no krasavitsa, for sure. Ah, water of Satan! Water of falsehood! Fire in the guts against the frost! But the frozen bonce forgets not, forgets not!'

Uttering a groan, he poured himself a full glass, gulped back the vodka into his throat as if it were lemonade and shouted for a fresh bottle.

'Well, Filimon Romanovitch, that's enough, that's enough, what is it you again can't forget? I didn't expect to see you again; you were to take your master Atchukhoff away from here at once, no?'

'Sergey Andreyevitch – indeed!' He broke off. 'Yes, I see it, the finger of God – you have to come with me!'

'What?'

'I told him about you, about Father Frost, he was asking questions. I shall introduce you – make haste! There's no time. Haven't I said? He's dying!'

'He's dying, and you're sitting here getting drunk?'

'A worm, I know, a miserable worm. Make haste!'

And he began tugging at the arm, at the collar, taking by the elbow and dragging away, wresting the carafe out of the hands – until a heavy geometric paw landed on his shoulder, and sat Zeytsoff down like a chastened dog.

'Nice way you pester the fuck out of a quiet drinker?'

Wave the hand.

'Leave him be. An old acquaintance.'

Shtchekelnikoff slapped his papakha hat onto the table.

'Well just look at him! An acquaintance!' Now it was Shtchekelnikoff who grabbed and dragged. Withdraw behind the stove. Zeytsoff stuck out his head from behind the tiles. Shtchekelnikoff leaned into the ear. 'What was them goings-on this evening! You sure, Gospodin Gierosławski, you don't know that un on the street?'

'How could I know him! Mug behind mask, spoke no word, and judging by his posture, then –'

'Not him!' hissed Tchingis. 'That un's still living!'

'What then?'

'He knew what were about to hit him. Mm-hmm.' Shtchekelnikoff scratched his Adam's apple. 'Prattling summat afore I gave chase.'

'You talked to him?'

'Mm-hmm. Said he'd bin to Tsvetistaya. The lads sent him packing. Said he were sending letters. You got them?'

Make a doubtful face.

'There were a few, various idiocies.'

'And that he couldn't do otherwise, for one or other of them Yapontchiks was always a-crawling after ya for weeks.'

'Meaning the one you killed –'

'Exactly. Some sort of Polish infighting, huh?'

Shtchekelnikoff's eyes wandered over the ceiling. Glower at him. There's one form of suspicion from which the master of suspicion won't protect: from himself. After all, Tchingis Shtchekelnikoff is in the pay of Wojsław Wielicki; his loyalty is to Wojsław Wielicki. Loyalty! It's true that life in the Baikal Kray is dirt cheap and Tchingis is a barbarian by blood and experience – but unlikely that he risks his neck for those few roubles of reward, committing murder on the streets concealed only by the fog? What is it that binds Tchingis to Wielicki? What precise instructions has he received? How much does he know? Remember the conversation with Wojsław about Piłsudski and his terrorists. Wojsław may be a good man, but good men also have their interests. Who knows what secret plan he's hatched out of the goodness of his heart?

'Mm-hmm. For you was lost from sight for a moment, and he already thought to lay hands on ya in the fog. Afore that Yapontchik realised.'

'Factional war in the Polish Socialist Party, as far as I can see. Politics, my good Shtchekelnikoff.'

For here, in Siberia, the PPS is run by Piłsudski's Yapontchiks. And this is how they imagine things: whoever has access to Filip Gierosławski, has access to History. Whilst Józef Piłsudski... *He has devoured your father! He will devour Poland! Trust not our Old Man!* TRUST NOT OUR OLD MAN – COURIER COMING – ALIVE. The letter won't get through. The messenger won't get through. Perhaps the son will get through. THE PARTY ORDERS TIME FOR COMPENSATION YES RUSSIA UNDER THE ICE – ALL MEANS YES – ATTENTION: YOUNG ONES AND OTTEPYELNIKS AGAINST WINTER. If editor Wółka be not mistaken, the authors of this coded letter are the 'old' faction of the PPS, believers in Piłsudski's notion that Russia itself should not be thawed, but not believers in Piłsudski himself, and clearly distrusting him. They're afraid he'll – do what? Is Piłsudski really a Lyednyak? He has sent people to spy on the Son of Frost, keep an eye on him – maybe to check he's not an agent of the Okhrana, or some sort of provocateur, but surely to also isolate him completely from the PPS-men in the Kingdom and the 'young ones'. Does he know that the 'old guard' no longer trust him either? Were he to discover the content of that letter to father... Bah, were he to suspect that the Son had received such a letter to deliver...! He has his own plans as to History! In the final analysis – was it not Piłsudski who sent father onto the Ways of the Mammoths? *He is the daemon of the Ice! Flee!*

Clear the throat, spitting out the smack of vodka, coughing up alcoholic fumes. A warning had been received once before: in the Hotel Warszawski, at the time of the Black Auroras, from the Polish owner of the Spiritus Vodka Stores. Piłsudski hovers over the Baikal Kray like the shadow of an invisible wraith, another colossal obscure figure unlichted against the sky. *He's coming for you.* Shudder.

'Well, how's it to be, Mr Thinking?'

'With what?'

'With him?'

Spin around to regard the impatiently fidgeting Zeytsoff.

'Such day awaits us, Shtchekelnikoff. We shall pay our respects at the deathbed.'

Sergey Andreyevitch Atchukhoff was dying very decidedly, very concretely, dying with death's brutal certainty – no one could be in any doubt that Atchukhoff was dying, least of all himself. As he had disowned the earthly Church and the earthly Church had disowned him, no priest was keeping vigil in the final hour beside Atchukhoff; there were no lighted candles, holy oils or propitiatory prayers. The humble apartment on the low first floor was filled with odours of naphtha and medicaments. The stove with its blocked flue was emitting black smoke; the landlady, a babushka bent double and almost blind, bustled around it clanging cast iron and muttering in a bizarre language of profanity or prayer, it was impossible to tell which. Atchukhoff's bed, wedged between the stove and the window, was nevertheless wide enough to leave room for a chair. Two chairs had been placed there, one behind the other, and two black-suited gentlemen with worn-out wizened faces, drooping lips and swollen eyes were seated upon them, their backs painfully upright, feet drawn up underneath them, hands folded on pressed-together knees. Zeytsoff said they were Tolstoyan brothers arrived from Tomsk; one was recording the words of the dying Atchukhoff in a notebook, the other merely smoking cigarette after cigarette. They too had tried to persuade Atchukhoff to leave Siberia, but Sergey Andreyevitch remained adamant. Once he'd lost this hope also, Zeytsoff, unable to witness any longer the death of his second father, had embarked on his tour of the drinkeries of Irkutsk. For why, namely, had Atchukhoff rejected proposals to leave the Land of the Gleissen when an entirely legal opportunity had presented itself? Did he hold it against Filimon Romanovitch for prostrating himself before the 'emperor of the flesh'? Did he want to die? His answers were unclear. Every moment, his monologues were interrupted by a cruel suffocating cough that rent his chest; Atchukhoff whispered and wheezed rather than spoke. The Tolstoyans, still as stiff as the tchinovniks of Winter, would lean over him, catching his words and preverbal gasps; Atchukhoff would raise a broad bony peasant hand above the quilt – and they would grasp hold of it, squeeze it and lay it down again; he would spring up from the pillows, jolted by a cough or an uttered truth – and they would lay him down again; he would ask for water – and they would give water. Then he would remain silent; silent and dying. The grizzly beard, tangled in knots, collected drops of saliva and bloodied phlegm. Beads of oily sweat shone on his crudely sculptured, almost boorish countenance. Approach any nearer and apart from the odour of chemicals, naphtha and burning wood, there was the all-pervasive fetor of disease and old age and bodily filth.

On this day, prior to his death, Atchukhoff was of lucid mind and still seeing consciously. He'd had long periods, however, days and even weeks, when it had been impossible to separate his hallucinations from his rational speech. At first, Zeytsoff had been writing everything down himself; then he began omitting questions of dubious content; eventually, he stopped taking notes at all. Squinting towards the bed illuminated by frostoglaze radiance, he recounted in whispers some of the madder hallucinations of Sergey Andreyevitch Atchukhoff.

Allegedly, as the Tchornoye Siyaniye was spreading murch outside the window, a black angel appeared to him in the sky above the city – wings of raven-black feathers, coal-black robe, Gypsy hair, face astream with murch – an onyx sword in his hand, surrounded by a powerful penumbra, and proclaimed that Irkutsk would be destroyed. The wrath of God, saith the angel, is turning on cities founded on sin, flourishing on sin and venerating sin – whilst there is no greater crime in the eyes of the One God than man's usurpation of the Creator's power. Yahweh is a Jealous and Avenging God, and I am his clenched right hand, saith the angel. Man cannot know truth – God alone knows truth; man believes. Man cannot make History – God makes History; man experiences it. Man cannot act consciously against God's designs – that is, he can; but then he is sinning, sinning, sinning!

The master had also summoned to his bedside his deceased relatives, whispered Zeytsoff, likewise summoned living yet absent relatives; worse still, they came in response to the dying man's invocation, or at least Atchukhoff behaved as if they'd come: he babbled to them, smiled at them, listened silently to their words, stroked the heads of invisible children and shook the hands of friends of his youth. Then again, he was convulsed by attacks of coughing or breathlessness that made him livid and red by turns, and sank back from exhaustion into a shallow sleep, barely distinguishable from death. No one dared wake him – till he woke of his own accord after a quarter of an hour, an hour or a day, and again addressed his guests, visible or invisible, in speech sober or plainly lunatic or a fluid combination of both, so that you had no way of knowing if what you'd heard from his lips was brain fever, or words of holy wisdom; wrap him in ice, in ice, maybe the truth will freeze.

'... who believe that by this means, they reach understanding with God. Khrrrkrrr! But I ask you, my friends, would not God know what lies in a man's heart before he expresses it to Him in prayer, out loud or in thought? It's not that kind of conversation! Krrrrkhrrr! Not that kind!

'Not in this therefore the power and meaning of prayer! We converse with God not in words and hymns and ritual gestures, for all these be the tools of Falsehood – khrrrkhrrr – I tell you, the tools of Falsehood! No, my friends, we converse with God only through Truth, in other words, through what is incapable of lying: through our own selves, that is, through our own life and through our own death. This is man's only conversation with God: that a man is as he is, that he has lived as he has lived, that he has behaved, khrrrkhrrr, as he has behaved. In this same way God speaks to us, not in the voices of usurpers who ascribe

His authority to themselves and amongst whom an honest man is powerless to discern Truth – but through His deed, that is, through Creation, in the voice of the world, in the voice of reality, which is the first and last instance of Truth. Therefore, khrrrkhrrr, and remember this well, therefore the purest prayer of God is the Truth of science, or the language of the material world, which sustains the human body in being.

'But what of the world of spirit, you ask. Such is the reason for prayer, as it seems to me. Khhrrr. For there are prayers for patience, prayers for courage, prayers for a cheerful heart, for the strength to forgive, for endurance in face of suffering, endurance in face of wrongs and injustice. But he who treats them like witches' incantations, sins through superstition and faith in foolish magic: I shall say or think the prescribed words, kneel or kiss a golden idol – and God will grant me the grace for which I plead. How can a man soil his spirit with such barter and hocus-pocus! Krrrkhrrr! It's all false! All lies! Lies! Krrrrkhrrr!

'How then do we pray? But think, brothers mine, do we not recite in our daily lives diverse prayers of the body? In order to muster energy and build up our limbs, we perform fast powerful movements that quicken the blood in our muscles. In order to arrest the chemistry of anger, we clench fists and teeth, bite lips. In order to restore balance between passion and reason, we slacken our breath, slow the heartbeat. Is anyone surprised, khhrrr, by these or other gymnastic rituals practised by athletes? Surprised by a military drill? By the exercises of boxers and wrestlers?

'This, however, is the difference between them: that prayers of the spirit are unseen and no one is in a position to teach them to anyone else. Yet it is not hard, is it, to recognise the true people of prayer – krrrkhrrr! – just as you can easily recognise proficient athletes and gymnasts. The athlete of the body controls his body and builds its strength; the athlete of the spirit controls his feelings, his fears and desires, his heart and mind, and trains their power. A man of strong body fears less for that body, khhrrr, is therefore calmer and more honest in situations requiring courage. A man of strong spirit does not lie, even if it leads to his persecution in the world of matter, because no pressure from matter can alter his Truth.

'Yet beware, my dears, for evil prayers exist just the same: prayers to envy, to rage, to black desires, to hatred. Krrrkhrrr! How often do we say them without knowing what we do! Stubbornly repeating an angry thought, mumbling a litany of curses against our neighbour, stammering in our evil make-believe, prompting dreams of harm and humiliation to others, learning to rejoice at their misfortune, learning to triumph from their defeat. Krrrkhrrr! Khhrrr! We know not that we pray, and yet we pray – and for what do we pray – to whom do we pray – to Satan, Satan, Satan! Krrrrrrrrrr!'

Exhausted, he flopped back onto the pillows and clearly lost consciousness. One of the men in black suits extended his hand to ascertain whether Sergey Andreyevitch still breathed. He breathed. The landlady rattled her poker – everyone shuddered as if suddenly released from some shamanic spell. Withdraw into the hallway.

Zeytsoff in the meantime had brewed coffee, of abominable quality, however, stinking like a sodden footwrap; he forced the cups into people's hands, only Shtchekelnikoff resisted. Tchingis had been watching Sergey Andreyevitch Atchukhoff sprawled on his deathbed from the threshold, and, wonder of wonders, had so far uttered no censorious remarks or sour wisecracks. Only a moment ago, he had hacked a man to death; he went first to wash his hands, but now, half-concealed beyond the doorframe, he was observing Atchukhoff with calm fascination.

'How long has this been going on?'

Zeytsoff told in a whisper of long months of dying in torment. Before Filimon Romanovitch had arrived with the tsar's document and his parent's money, Atchukhoff had been cooped up in some lice-ridden little room in a shelter for folk made homeless by the passage of gleissen through their houses, banishing the doctors sent by his friends and praying for hours on end.

'Be it true what they says?' Shtchekelnikoff began when Zeytsoff withdrew for a moment. 'That it gives 'em great pleasure?'

'You mean religious ecstasy?'

The felon shook his head in distaste.

'Folk oughta know restraint in their debauchery.'

Swallow a snigger along with the loathsome coffee. Where does it come from that a man willingly snorts with brazen laughter at such scenes of mortal tragedy? Atchukhoff is dying – is it funny? No. And yet there's something in this whole situation to which the only healthy response seems a burst of coarse humour. Does some nation exist that has a custom of telling jokes at funerals?

But maybe it's only the fault of the teslectric flow in the brain…?

Night is already falling, curiosity has been satisfied, it's time to go home. Enough death for one day.

'My good Shtchekelnikoff, just then in the street, on the snow, did you by any chance notice a folder –'

Zeytsoff came bounding back and snatched the coffee cup out of the hand.

'He's woken up!'

The Tolstoyan gentlemen, surrendering to the pleas of Filimon

Romanovitch, relinquished their chairs. Sit down on the one further from the bedhead, struggling to suppress the foolish smile and nervous twitches.

Sergey Andreyevitch was watching attentively from beneath heavy eyelids.

Search with the eyes for Zeytsoff – Zeytsoff had fled.

Clear the throat.

'Pardon me –'

He raised his hand off the bedclothes.

'What are you doing here?'

'Agh. Mr Zeytsoff –'

'I know you.'

'No, no. Benedykt Gierosławski. Mr Zeytsoff was saying –'

'I have seen you before,' he croaked slowly, pausing with belaboured deliberation after every syllable. 'I remember faces, remember people.'

Had his hallucinations finally blended with reality?

'Memory,' mumble in response, 'is Satan's tool.'

'Ah!' His smile revealed what remained of his teeth. 'Very good. Come closer, my son. They won't hear.'

'To me, it may also seem that I remember different things. What's the sense in asking about the truth of what exists not?'

'The past exists not? Oy, then I am not really dying! Khhrrr.' He laughed. 'Filimon described you well.'

'Yes?'

'How can I die – without a past? How can I be saved – without a past? How can you live without a past?'

Spring to the feet. The old man, however, suddenly showed the energy of a young buck: he grabbed the sleeve and held it firm. Was it right to tussle with a man who stood over his grave? Sit down again.

'Zeytsoff already tried to persuade me,' hiss at him. 'Does he imagine you'll convince me? What? – that if a dying man requests it, I shall consent to anything? It's some kind of trap, eh? This is how he planned it! Blackmail! I don't give a damn about your History, with the Kingdom of God thrown in!'

He was more and more amused.

'Khhrrr. For you, khrrr, believe not in History, khrrr, at all. And yet – don't you see? – if there is no History, there is no God. Christianity is the Truth about History. Take away History from Christianity – and what is left? Nothing! Nothing! Krrrr! There exists no God of Summer – in Summer, there are only suppositions, schools of speculation, parliaments of false gods, and prophets' discussion circles. True salvation is possible only under the Ice; true Christianity – only under the Ice; true good and evil – under the Ice.

'For if there is no History – there is no man! Krrr. If you cannot tell the truth about the past, what truth shall you utter about any of your deeds? Every action, every choice is born out of the past into the future. Not for one little moment in the great drama of life, stretching from birth to death, not for one flicker of a candle flame – shall you do good or evil. Only he who exists in History can possess free will. How shall you judge the murderer when the well-remembered murder, the murder that has come and gone and lingers not in your eyes – is no longer a real, sure murder? If there is no History, then there is no man – there is only the twinkling of chemical molecules, khrrr, and a formula for matter captured in the present.'

'I don't deny it.'

'You don't deny it.'

'I shall let you into a secret.' Chuckle shamefacedly, then lean over Sergey Andreyevitch Atchukhoff until the fetor of disease and old age and sweaty unclean flesh strikes the nostrils. Princess Blutskaya at least used perfume. Open wide the mouth. 'I exist not.'

'Agh!' He was saddened.

'Yes, yes.' Nod in childish satisfaction, as if delighted at a cunning prank played on an adult.

(Maybe it's only the fault of the teslectric flow in the brain, or maybe the vodka in the veins.)

'How unhappy you must be...' He clenched his fingers. 'Has anyone heard of deeper despair? What greater darkness of soul could there be, and what graver blasphemy? My son! Even the suicide, the reprobate, pays tribute to the Creator with his crime: in destroying His creation, he kneels before Him and recognises his smallness in relation to the One, Who Is. Suicides care not for life, since they care so much for themselves. But you, krrr, you care not for yourself! Never has there been such a total nihilist. Khhrrrrrr!'

He gagged on blood-tinged slobber. Pass him a handkerchief. His left hand shook so violently he was unable to wipe his mouth. Help him.

'Khrrr, khhrrr, you were thinking, khhrrr, that I'd beg you to put in a word with Father Frost and have you swear. Krrr. No.' He signalled with the handkerchief to come nearer. 'People suppose that before death, Sophia and some higher Gnosis descend upon a person, but in reality, it's hard to collect the thoughts on even the simplest of matters, everything hurts so much. Hee-hee. And so, here's my foolish wisdom for you: Go and get drunk. Go and make merry with your comrades. Climb to the top of a high mountain. Go hunt in the taiga, confront a wild beast. Find yourself a devushka soft and delectable in heart and body. Take up a political cause against everyone else. Eat like a glutton.

Always spare a moment to gaze into the starry sky, at snow sparkling on a branch, to stroke a dog, comfort a child. Spend all your wages on everyday material things: the best clothes made from fabrics most agreeable to the touch, furniture most pleasant to the eye, trinkets that delight the palm. If you have two dishes to choose from – choose the one you've not yet tried. If you have two cities to choose from – choose the one where you've not yet been. If you have to choose a life – choose the one you've not yet lived.'

'Is this a prayer for existence? It's a prayer for the flesh!'

Strength deserted him.

'Krrrkhrrr. But do also as you have remembered.'

Hours of the grimmest hallucinations now followed, when the pain became too much for Sergey Andreyevitch to bear, and he ceased to be in control of his bodily reflexes, and also of the sounds he emitted. Doze now in a corner, resting a temple against the flaky wall, since Zeytsoff's terrible coffee had been of no help (vodka had excited the brain, vodka had stirred up the thoughts, now vodka lulls to sleep). Until a fresh scream, a cry entangled in coughing and bloody hoarseness, interrupts the half-sleep – and again the eyes turn to the scene of agony, such as never yet immortalised on any canvas extolling holy martyrdom. Atchukhoff, once a powerful heavyset man, reduced now to a coarse-boned skeleton, was thrashing about on his befouled bed, spitting out blood and phlegm and every kind of abomination. The landlady would brutally roll him over on the bedclothes and wrap him in the plaids, immobilising him whenever he tried to break free and scratch at everything around him. Water was administered to him, some kind of medicaments in the water; whereupon he was seized by choking fits.

Zeytsoff disappeared for a moment and returned with a bottle of 'Mrs Poklewska'. He took a few nips, soon not even trying to conceal it. He needed three hefty swigs in order to enter at all and gaze upon Sergey Andreyevitch in this state. The eyes of the ex-katorzhnik immediately grew moist, his hands shook, and a plaintive moan escaped from his throat. He was feeling sorry for his master, for the world, for himself.

'What is there for me now, eh, O, God, for what do I go on living, foolish man, when everything around me turns to misery and greater pain – to save ignorant peasants, I shan't save them, to save Russia, I shan't save her, to save at least one good man, no, no, everything always brings the reverse – what use to the world such a man as Zeytsoff Filimon Romanovitch, nothing but a laughing stock.'

'Don't you have some honest work here?'

'Work! Did I ever need my own dough in order to swill'

'When you sober up, call on Krupp in the Clock Towers, their

Laboratory is seeking a reliable caretaker – you, sir, are an educated man after all, you'll make a good impression, and they'll take an ex-convict.' 'What do I want with work, when my father is dying! God!' And snap – back to the 'Poklewska'.

Shtchekelnikoff appeared once or twice in the doorway: let's get out of here. Shake the head in reply. Staying to the end. Zeytsoff was right, it won't be long now, Atchukhoff will die this night; it has frozen.

He, meanwhile, was spluttering incomprehensible confessions, crying out in anger inflamed by God knows what, to people visible and invisible, casting a misty eye at the wall, ceiling, window, holding conversations on matters long gone, on former sins, on individuals from the past – true past or false past, there was no way of telling; he was dying fired up, in feverish excitement, which means in uncertainty. He called for his mother. Called for his brothers. Called for certain women unbeknown to Zeytsoff. Called for God. They came or came not; conclusions could be drawn only from the insistence with which he repeated the summons. The whole room reeked already of urine and excrement and stale blood.

He called also for Benedykt Gierosławski – alternating with Filip Gierosławski. To them he spoke in turn of some Black Labyrinth under a sky of Black Auroras, on a field of black ice. Light, he wheezed, is not governed here by the laws of light, and the eye sees things which it sees not, that is, Truth captured in matter. Truth, he wheezed, takes the form of a perfect sphere and it's possible to touch it. The labyrinth on the plain of ruination is there to lose those who perceive not Truth. Six went, he wheezed, none returned. Gleissen, he wheezed, gleissen flowed like a river. The Sun rose black as coal and we hid under iron from living glintzen. Ice sculptures told us the history of the world: whoever caught a glimpse of himself, sank neath the earth. We had no need to eat and no need to drink and no need to breathe; it was impossible to die. Mammoths, he wheezed, mammoths, mammoths, mammoths point the way.

The crisis came at dawn. He fell asleep for a little while. The Tolstoyan gentlemen placed the Gospels in his hands. When he awoke, terrified, he drew the book to his lips, but not with the intention of giving it a devout kiss; he merely covered his face with it like a child, peeking out with bloodshot eye from under its boards. Death was already near – Atchukhoff was able to wring from himself nothing but a boyish whisper. Who? Who? What? What does he want? Where? What? What? Burning with fever, he dissolved into questions that were simpler still, shorter, increasingly generalised, aimless, like a chemical compound decomposing into its elements. What? What? What? He kicked off the bedsheets and plaids; a bare leg, discoloured by black veins of murch, scarred by numerous frostbites and God knows what maladies, thumped rhythmically on the footboard, as the bed shook and bounced. Sergey Andreyevitch, in his state of heightened emotion, was no longer able to catch breath; with his last words, he coughed out from his lungs what remained of air and blood. Hear you not? Feel you not the earth quaking? Mammoths, the mammoths have come for me! I am sink-sink-sinking. He sank.

The Tolstoyans made the sign of the cross over him, closed his eyelids. The landlady stoked the stove. Stand up. Filimon Romanovitch Zeytsoff, drunk as a swine, was kneeling by the bed and whimpering loudly, pressing his cheek to the dead man's hand. Walk over and take one last look at Sergey Atchukhoff. He was unrecognisable, so much had his facial features changed when the soul departed the body. Lean on the high bedframe, as the head begins to spin. Feel the need to say something elevated, to utter words of great import – yet at the same time the certainty, undimmed by alcohol, that such utterance would surely result in clownish imbecility bringing nothing but shame for months and years to come, if not to life's end. Unsteady on the feet, as though stunned by this death and this stench – can death be inhaled into the lungs like opium fumes? – open the mouth and –

Shtchekelnikoff led out into the street. The frost, the early-morning brightness and city coming to life restored the senses. The Sun was just emerging from behind the base of the Sibirkhozheto Tower. Search in a cloudless sky for the roofs and turrets of the gubernatorial Citadel and its unlichty clocks. The glintz against black background indicated eight o'clock. Time to travel to Zimny Nikolayevsk, to work. Shtchekelnikoff, however, was waving in the opposite direction to the Marmeladobahn, towards the cupolas of Christ the Saviour Sobor.

Tchingis purchased a blackwicke and at once vanished into the nave. Pause in the west porch. The footsteps of the square-shaped ruffian resonated with a brief echo in the seemingly deserted basilica. And for whom was he come to pray: for the Pilsudtchik whom he knifed in the night, or for Sergey Andreyevitch Atchukhoff? This time, a guttural snigger burst from between the clenched teeth. Edge into the deep interior of the great cathedral, sliding the glove along a wall, head pressed forward as though marching into a blizzard, in an easterly direction, that is, into the shining darkness. The entire nave as far as the iconostasis was filled with alternating streams of unlicht and light. For not only the cupolas funded by the Irkutsk coldindustrialists, but also most of the furniture and ornaments inside had been crafted from priceless tungetitum, from many-hued coolbonds of coldiron, incrusted with gold. Unlicht from countless blackwickes, falling onto the tungetitum, bounced off it in a fiery blaze; this then flowed into the twilight zones wherein it dissolved like drops of milk in ink, whilst other light, pure sunlight, beat through the windows – but the windows were also open to unlicht and lead directly into infernal black abysses: the mirrors hanging symmetrically between the icons. Unlicht from the blackwickes reflected off them back and forth – and whoever walked through the vast empty space from west door to royal gates projected monstrous glintzen, reaching from the flagstones to the high vault, onto all parts of the basilica, onto a thousand icons and countless faces of God and saints immortalised upon them.

Move all the swifter to one side, cower on a bench by the wall. A bad acidic taste was gathering in the mouth and there was nothing with which to spit it out, all saliva having seemingly dried up. From every direction, the dark eyes of heavenly figures gazed down, wide open in expressions of sorrowful wonder. Christ Pantocrator on the main tier of the iconostasis held up his hand in blessing, fingers crossed in a gesture of restraint or of invitation to the onlooker, not easy to tell at this distance. The icon of the Saviour the Great High Priest in the Great Deesis – God on a coldiron throne, with kings, beasts and gleissen at his feet – as well as the Mandylion at the bottom had been executed in tungetitum techniques with coatings of gold-fluff. Spot mirrors directed onto them torrents of unlicht at sharp angles, out of which the Saviour loomed in a paralysing fire of tungetitum dawn, in a cloud of coldiron rainbows, outlined in gold, in haloes of divine white. Hard to imagine more striking symbolism of the architecture of light. Bury the face in the hands.

Was Atchukhoff right? Be this despair? Bite the tongue. But Sergey Andreyevitch had looked at it from the other side: it's not possible to believe in the existence of God without believing in the existence of man. Being and History – History, or the truth about Being in the past – make up the fundamentals of all religion and morality. And when looked at closely, also the basis of a person's character. Reason may advance a million arguments for non-existence, but the very fact that people do not walk down a street randomly insulting, hitting, shooting whomsoever crosses their path – shows that reason here is not enough. Every uttered word, every gesture and physiological grimace and every act of conventional behaviour – attests to the mighty power of History.

But even if it were honestly desired – how can a man begin to exist from a simple decision? how is it possible to make a sovereign choice to cross from non-being into being?

This is the prerogative of gods, not of men: godheads call into existence, men are created.

An incomparably easier task: is to believe in personal existence. But how to force the self to believe? Like belief in God, belief in man's existence is either spontaneous or not at all. Shall such a one be found who has heard the theological arguments and – yes, you've convinced me, I want to believe, snap, *et voilà* – has believed? Why, it's absurd!

Cough into the gloves. A cold bitter taste was gumming up the gullet. Images of God and the saints gazed down through curtains of unlicht and light. Someone walked past in the distance through the kliros, glintzen flared on the mirrors, and for a moment the interior of Christ the Saviour Sobor was filled with a new architecture of antidarkness; images of the Last Supper above the royal gates of the iconostasis shone with gold-fluff and liturgical colours: red, light blue, green and gold. Avert the head, lean against the cold wall. They believe, not because someone convinced them but because that is how they have frozen. No one in the Land of the Gleissen has lost faith, and no one has gained new faith. The only things that can be relied upon here are the Kotarbiński pump and the opportune toss of a coin. Whilst monumental basilicas seem to take the shape of water frozen within them. Oy, there had been no need to enter this tserkoff – had anyone in Irkutsk ever seen an Orthodox believer in the Church of the Assumption of the Blessed Virgin Mary? No one drives them away with torch and cudgel – yet none even approach, paralysed by obvious Truth and Falsehood. The provodniks of the Transsib spoke aright: in the lands of the Ice, there cannot be two creeds equally truthful. If Orthodoxy be true – then Roman Catholicism is not; if Roman Catholicism be true – Orthodoxy is not. Enough had been heard from both Russians and non-Russians. A Pole – uh-huh, therefore a heretic! They are in no doubt as to the true history of Christ's legacy. History itself reveals the truth: the First Rome fell because it strayed into the Catholic heresy; the Second Rome, that is, Constantinople, the same; it fell a few years after it tried to reunite with the Latin blasphemy. The Third Rome, Moscow, has remained. The line of inheritance is clear-cut and plain to see: Kievan Rus receives Christianity from Byzantium; Sofiya Paleolog, niece of the last Byzantine emperor, marries Tsar Ivan the Third, bringing with her to Moscow the treasure trove of Christian wisdom, the great library of Constantinople; Russia adopts from Constantinople the double-headed eagle coat of arms; the cities of mediaeval Rus arise according to the architectural model of Constantinople, which had arisen in turn, commissioned by Constantine, in imitation of the First City, Jerusalem. There can be no denying it – this is the true Christianity. No one here is forced by violent means to renounce their heresy, because they know that it's impossible – you have frozen as a heretic – but at the same time they're in no doubt that you're cursed in your apostasy and proceeding straight down the path of damnation along with all the priests, bishops, cathedrals and riches of the False Rome, farther with every step from the light of Divine soletruth, into the unlicht, into the broiling darkness reeking of iron, under the black Sun of the Underground World –

Awake for a moment, but the head at once slumps back onto the chest. Is the Sobor heated? Unlichty breath mist oozes slowly from the mouth like blood bled from a vein. Dancing glintzen illuminate more frescos on the opposite wall. The entrails turn inside out, the organism rises in revolt. Maybe it's the vodka and then the noxious coffee imbibed on an empty stomach, maybe the fetor of death absorbed deep into the lungs, or maybe the allergy of Truth itself to Falsehood, of Falsehood to Truth – recall Gorubsky's bestial aversion to Kozheltsoff and Kozheltsoff's to Gorubsky – there had been no need, no need to enter this tserkoff! Double up and spew onto the flagstones of the Sobor. Glintzen pause on the icons; the saints peer down in wonder; a deacon, stopping mid-step, peers down in shock. Slide onto the knees and wipe the mouth with the scarf; a trembling hand instinctively pulls the frostoglazes over the eyes. Black and white, gold and silver, shadow and light merge into one another, images of saints suddenly sinking into deeper contrasts, into wells of perspective, whilst the deacon dissolves into an icon-like figure; his eyes grow immense, his black brows stretch, his nose becomes leaner, his face elongates and swells with bright-yellow pigment, the riza over his sheepskin glitters with gold-fluff. Smile in apology, whilst Shame, the steadfast friend, is already warming the innards, breast and cheeks. In Summer, it had been possible to hide neath a spectrum of uncertainty and even forget the very question, but in the Ice – in the Ice, it's clear what sort of God looks down from on high upon man. There are no faithful – there are only those who know Truth and those who have recognised it not. The deacon approaches, leans forward, offers a radiant hand with unnaturally long, slender fingers. Brush it feebly aside and, staggering along the wall, rush out of the tserkoff into the street. Whosoever departs in the Ice from the true faith does so out of clear belief in Falsehood; there are no stray sheep. Whosoever commits evil overtly opposes God. And whosoever dies in the Ice dies the true death.

On black physics, on the Un-State, on the fine art of saying farewell and the reason for authority figures

On the twenty-fourth day of January, the Cold Line restarted. By the restored bridge, as proclaimed by the newspapers, a fortified military post had been established; further campaigns were expected from

Piłsudski's Yapontchiks. An extension to the compulsory war tax was confirmed officially, whereas the situation on the coldiron and tungetitum market settled down, and the governor general loosened the fetters a little: the majority of Martsynians were released whilst the ringleaders of the strikes and disturbances were mostly kept in prison, the censor's office allowed *The Siberian Herald* to publish articles covering the events and a delegation of Oblastnik industrialists paid a visit to the Citadel. Porfiry Pocięgło was not amongst them. Then Pocięgło was travelling again on business throughout Siberia, no doubt taking advantage of the opportunity to distribute the independence movement's secret correspondence and meet fellow conspirators. He sent a card giving the name and Vladivostock address where fugitives awaiting safe passage across the Pacific were to report; and also, the address of his Harbin broker in case of trouble along the way. Two sets of false papers would be provided before departure from Irkutsk.

Learn, like every good subject of the Empire, to detect the peristaltic movements of History by reading between the lines of censored articles. *As they inform us from Yeniseysk, a man was murdered there who had stolen a large number of rounds of ammunition from a customs office. In connection with this murder, the police uncovered a widely ramified conspiracy involving members of a clandestine club. At the premises of this club was found a large quantity of masks, ritual implements, rounds of ammunition, daggers and other weapons. A large number of people were arrested. Several of them made very significant witness statements.*

In the meantime, however, despite the good rail connection with Kezhma, no sign had come from the Ministry of Winter regarding a decision in the personal case. Neither the governor general's people nor Schembuch, nor Ormuta, nor even that flaxen-haired tchinovnik, nor anyone sent by them had appeared with new instructions, or inquired about father; evidently, they were totally uninterested in Batyushka Moroz. And yet, know this to be untrue. Promise in spirit that on the next visit to the delegation – hard facts would be demanded. That the blacktoothed barebones shall be sought and found. Questions will be put about those initial expeditions into Winter, about father's participation, about Atchukhoff. Surely a list of participants, as well as reports, records, must have been preserved; the imperial bureaucracy would not have let the case drop without a cupboardful of papers and papers about papers. Surely, they've also got more on Father Frost. From those maps and copies thrust into the paw by the flaxen-haired tchinovnik, it's impossible to draw any helpful conclusion. Beyond Kezhma lies the Deadly Isotherm – is that in fact where father went? – but in the beginning, it had been possible to go farther; there must be magpies who remember it. But how to find them? After all, this is what their work depends on – they don't sit endlessly in Irkutsk, but roam for months and months around the Siberia of the gleissen. Well, perhaps now they'll spend more time in the city.

For the Baikal winter frosts had closed in; frosts, and with them milk-jelly fogs: at minus fifty, minus sixty degrees Celsius, moisture in the air curdled into a dense suspension that could be cut with a knife. Shtchekelnikoff went outside before dawn and demonstrated how to slice it; knife down, knife to the side, blade flat so as to draw a wider line – thus he outlined a metre square in the standing fog. The figure hung in the motionless air. The frost was intensifying, and it seemed that the power of the Ice was already so mighty that it had even begun to stretch back into the past: glance over the shoulder and see a tunnel carved out of the fog by the movement of the body, the shape of this body five, ten, twenty paces ago preserved on permanent display – the frozen past. People, animals, sleighs, all moving objects were reflected in the standing fog by a series of holes looking like tangible shadows of what no longer exists. It was possible to see with the very eyes and almost finger the existence from a few minutes ago, a quarter of an hour ago, an hour ago (if the wind coming off the Angara were weak). Minus fifty, minus sixty.

Anyone who did not absolutely have to go out sat at home on the stove bench. The stoves roared like damaged samovars. Steam condensed on frostoglaze windowpanes, whilst fountains of colour flowed out of this moisture; frostoglaze never froze over with hoar. Outside the windows, roofs of houses and spines of gleissen sailed by above streams of sky-blue fog drifting very slowly. But here – beside the naphtha lamp and cupful of finest tchay, in the plush, heated semi-gloom – write letters to Poland.

First of all, therefore, to Zygmunt, with a postal order for thirty roubles. Are the creditors banging heavily at the door? Stuck here in this Siberia. Then to Alfred. Stuck here in this Siberia, heartfelt thanks for the recommendation to Mr Wielicki, he certainly saved the life of the undersigned. The theoretical studies lie neglected, but logical engineering is being practised instead such as you've never dreamed of. How's the doctorate going at Lwów University? Has anything interesting cropped up in mathematical logic apropos of Kotarbiński's theories? Do send some new articles with which to disagree, before the brain completely dries up.

Write also to Bolek, reminding him after so many years. What's new with him? Is he well or what? How's he doing? How many churches has he already built? Married perhaps? Write, please, to this address in Irkutsk. A proper job has been found, a model citizen has emerged, all borrowed moneys will be returned, here's the first instalment. And perhaps fate shall decree that the American continent may also be visited – please send firm contact details where you can be found during the course of this year, next two years. Your loving brother, Benedykt.

After dusk, after a glass of cherry vodka, and a second, and a third – the time came to write to Julia. What's new – there's nothing new, except that a living is now being earned. Hah, you never imagined, did you, miss, that Benedykt Gierosławski would ever attend an honest place of work – how these journeys to exotic lands can change a man! (Plus the Kotarbiński pump, of course.) But what strange external reasons might not be sought, what justifications not found; though you cannot say that this is not also the truth about Benedykt Gierosławski. Why therefore, in Warsaw, were the lousy hole in Biernatowa's lodging house, the private lessons and jobs on the side, the begging from the shylocks, the card-playing – all so conceivable, but not a permanent position, not a normal humdrum future? Is such indeterminacy in time of immaturity, such colourful fluctuation in character really inevitable in Summer mathematically, biologically – like the chrysalis stage in the life of butterflies? Would everything have worked out differently, had it not been for you – had it not been for your warm, fleeting touch – for the fiery promises – great plans – all those unrealised futures? – your fault, Julia! your fault and you know it! That trust was placed in something which existed not!

Letters, letters, letters, with their formal greetings, stylish flourishes, written on vellum paper, thickly covered in kopeck stamps – are also one of the lesser rituals of bourgeois life, like quiet afternoon tea taken within the household circle, Sunday lunch, serious newspapers, the government paper over breakfast or the evening one over coffee at a gentlemen's club where, like at Vittel's, business is freely discussed alongside love affairs, politics and war.

Purchase a Patek Philippe pocket watch on a silver chain with the Irkutsk coat of arms engraved on the lid, it rests most agreeably in the palm. Standing now before a mirror in unbuttoned frock coat, with the gleaming silver half-bow hanging on one side of the waistcoat, below the navy-blue English cravat – think not at all about whom strangers will see, wonder not about whether such and such a detail fits the image, or what it may signify in their eyes and whether it be a lie, or not; freshly demurched, think not of it even under the penumbra shimmering in the looking glass.

Tesla had not been seen for several weeks. Regular use had been made of the Kotarbiński pump in his apartments in the New Arkadiya en route to the Marmeladobahn, but Tesla was no longer in the hotel at the time. Mademoiselle Filipov would say that Nikola practically never leaves the Observatory; spends his nights there and even eats his meals there. Again, he's stopped sleeping, talks to himself in many languages, walks around in a slight fever, releases through his brain kilomirks of murch and kilovolts of electrical current.

He sent a letter.

Dear B.G.

I am assuming you have not yet visited me in my new laboratory owing only to an excess of work. (And so, you too, sir, are now working on black physics!) Have your plans changed regarding THAT matter? I believe I am getting ever closer to solving our problem; please make no decisions, we will talk first. I am inviting you!

Your Devoted Friend
TGI

'TGI' stood for 'Tesla, the Great Inventor'.

Doctor Tesla had installed himself on the ground floor of the Physical Observatory of the Imperial Academy of Sciences, in storerooms at the rear. Coldiron cables as thick as a man's arm stretched in fibre insulation along corridors and stairways, hung from ceilings and in recesses hewn out of walls – down into the cellars, and into the excavated well-shaft where Nikola had 'connected himself to the Ways of the Mammoths'. Nikola – that is, his machines. Though there had never been much difference between them.

A gigantic tungetitum coil – a torus wound with hundreds of arshins of tungetitum wire – occupied the entire width of a storeroom. It had been moved to the very end of the long room, against a wall, because when the coil was working, no one could walk past it in safety. Coldiron capacitors as well as the large flow-generators had been placed at intervals in a line stretching back to the entrance. Nikola was using his flow-generators in controlled resonances to measure the impedance, reactance and induction power of the teslectric coil, as well as to determine their black-physical equivalents; most effective, however, were the experiments in which the coil acted as a murch-bearing system when connected to the Earth itself, that is, to the Ways of the Mammoths.

'I shall break into them yet!' cried Tesla and – in overcoat, gloves, goggles, sable shapka – jerked the lever of the machine, whilst hibernik labourers with Asiatic faces and thick umbriance shaded their eyes and fled from the laboratory as fast as they could. 'I shall find the frequency, may lightning strike me down!'

Gleissen-cold frost burst from the coil as dull lustreless rime crept over its winding and casing: this was air condensing and freezing.

Unlicht flowed from the machine in dense waves, casting glintzen so intense behind the smallest piece of equipment that it was impossible for a man to behold them without frostoglaze spectacles, even out of the corner of his eye. A low, ominous sound – a long-drawn-out drone that made the hair stand on end and the skin tingle – resounded throughout the building and far out into the street. (*The Baikal Voice* had published letters of complaint from local householders.)

Then the teslectric discharges began. Black shafts of lightning in bunches of a dozen, a hundred or a million, shot from the coil and clung for a few seconds to this or that object like leeches hungry for blood, wriggling, multiplying and dividing, faltering and straightening, before suddenly leaping elsewhere. At the same time, a crashing and crackling reverberated and a cold draught wafted through the laboratory. Several coal-black lightning bolts reached as far as the opposite wall of the storeroom, that is, a good forty arshins away. Which meant there was even less space to hide. Tesla had received a shock more than once. He made nothing of it.

'I don't even feel the cold,' he said. 'A man standing on the earth offers no resistance to murch.'

In a stockroom to one side, through a nearby door, Tesla had set up for himself a corner for more theoretical work that depended less on practical procedures; on the second floor of the building, he had a room furnished as a bedroom but almost never made use of it. Here, down below, immediately above the cellars and the Ways of the Mammoths, he also kept cages of mice and rats which he was subjecting to trials of demurching and immurching. A fair-haired Russian, his face profusely pitted with hideous pockmarks, was in charge of the documentation of these experiments: Sasha Pavlitch, a biologist recommended by Professor Yurkat who had previously worked on the phenomenon of dormant life in the permafrost.

This chamber was heated. Throwing off his overcoat, Nikola hurried to record the new results; he had no desk and occupied for his own needs a long laboratory bench pushed against the wall neath shelves housing a huge variety of different mechanisms and parts of mechanisms. Perceive there a handheld version of the Kotarbiński pump with crank, as well as a kettle full of holes. In a basket beyond this table lay stick thermometers as well as rods with bow-shaped antennae made of coldiron – murchometers, as it later transpired.

Sasha was in the process of feeding the mice; they squeaked softly. A cable reached into every cage, the coldiron wire clasping in a tight noose one limb of each rodent. The documentation lay in open trays on top of the cages, stacked vertically according to date: First Week Batch, Second Week Batch, Third Week Batch et cetera. Attached were photographs portraying the black-and-white bodies of animals frozen to the bone – and rodent entrails dissected posthumously. Pavlitch had marked and undersigned areas identified as centres of disease.

Tesla approached, peeking over the shoulder, a whole head higher.

'So yes, for the time being only mice and rats.'

'They were killed by teslectric flow?'

'Well, as with everything else, there are limits to the murch-load an organism can safely absorb. Or to the load an organism can be deprived of without danger to health. An immurched rat is killed by the side effect of overfilling its organism with murch: frost. A demurched rat – kh-hmm, here the cause is deeper. These blotches' – Tesla pointed with his white-cotton-gloved finger – 'these are the foci of an aggressive tumour.'

Seized by sudden terror.

'The Kotarbiński pump causes cancer?!'

'Now, now, there's no cause for alarm. We're already measuring it accurately enough: a living organism of this size can hold approximately seven hundred skotos. In any case, after pumping out seven hundred, the efficiency of the pump falls drastically. We may assume that the teslectrical capacity of the human body is several tens of times greater. The pump you are using in my hotel room does not exceed the intensity of one tenth of a nocta – so, for how many hours would you have to go on pumping? And we observed the cancerous effects only after total demurchment of the organism.'

Nikola Tesla was desperately trying to express the phenomena of black physics in concrete quantitative terms, to describe them by means of mathematical dependencies. The charts spread around the walls, full of dense calculations, columns of digits, crooked diagrams – very much resembled those in Krupp's cryophysical workshop. Tesla worked out most calculations in his head, and in his head constructed his machines; it was chiefly Sasha Pavlitch who scrawled on the charts, as well as one other assistant of Tesla, a certain Felix Jago, sent from the Saint Petersburg Institute on the recommendation of the Tsar's Own Chancellery: a distinguished-looking elderly engineer in monocle and bowtie, now counting in rubber gloves the black crystals and packing them into frostglaze jars, which were then closed and stamped with the seals of the Imperial Academy of Sciences.

Read off from the charts the symbols of Tesla's black physics. As the unit of murch charge, he had chosen the skoto, σ, defined as the teslectrical capacity of one gramme of hygroscopic $ZnCl_2$. Murch (W) flowing in time (t) is characterised by an intensity (Iw) measured in noctas, n. $Iw = \Delta W/\Delta t$. The pressure of the murch, also called the teslectric tension (Uw), that is, the 'force' measured in mirks, φ, with which the teslectric flow fills a carrier, depends on the intensity of the flow as well as on the carrier's teslectrical absorbency – which is different for different materials and structures. For here already, laws specific to teslectricity are manifesting themselves. Nikola was gabbling away beside a chart filled with several parallel strings of equations, different for each of the systems portrayed above them: a sphere, a cube, a tile so thin it was almost two-dimensional, a long cylinder. He gazed at them intently as if trying to burn through the chart with the stare of his deep-set eyes, now very dark as though welling with murch; the white lock fell onto his sharp cheekbone and he didn't even notice. Some 'structure constant' evidently exists, Q, which results not from an object's chemical composition, but solely from its structure, from its spatial form and the thermal processes taking place within it; and upon this constant depends the object's murch capacity, and also its absorbency and probably even the rate at which it generates murch. For – yes, yes, Benedykt – every solid body gradually collects murch within itself even in total teslectrical isolation, *from the very fact of its existence*. At the same time – and we are measuring this as accurately as we can – without consuming any energy.

'You're not talking I assume about *perpetuum mobile*!'

He winced.

'Often, I was accused of scientific naivety. *Perpetuum mobile*, hah! I have already patented several versions of the Faraday disc. Imagine, sir, a unipolar electromagnetic dynamo, where current is induced by the magnetic fields of the Earth. Taking a suitably large disc, or one that rotates suitably fast, or one made from material with a thousand times greater conductivity –'

'Electrical superconductors?'

'Yes. We would have a self-sustaining dynamo: generators drawing on the energy of the planet. Or from cosmic energies: take two such discs, one on the earth, the second suspended above it exposed to cosmic rays, and connect them on both sides to a capacitor. Or take cables so long so that one end is earthed and the other cast into outer space. Are these some kind of magic machines that break the laws of physics? No, simply fuel-less engines; they derive their energy from elsewhere.

'But we are dealing here with a different mechanism. At how many billion skotos should we estimate the murch charge of the Earth? The structure constant shows us which murch-bearing constructions are the most effective.'

Recall the cryophysical 'temperature of orderliness' and measure of entropy. Had Nikola, in his measurements of that constant, assigned to individual objects some objective measure of order, a scale of soletruth?

Do a geometry and stereometry exist that are more and less 'true'? Which shape presents greater order at even temperature: the sphere or the cube?

And man? How close to Truth is *Homo sapiens*?

Murch flows spontaneously along the line of teslectric tension, but does not flow in this way out of man, although he is perfectly susceptible, on the other hand, to immurchment from the air, from the earth and from water.

It's the same with ice – with the aid of Professor Yurkat, Tesla had already distinguished over a hundred types of ice, each behaving differently in teslectric flow.

'I suspect this has something to do with its molecular structure – how the water molecules arrange themselves during crystallisation. My hiberniks stay down there in the well and drive coldiron needles from glacial vein to glacial vein.' With the aid of serrated pliers, Tesla extracted the cork and poured mineral water into a glass. Bottles of it had been brought to him from the New Arkadiya. 'We've reached a point where, with constant pressure in the flow-generators, I am able to tell from the sound of the working machines the colour and contamination of the ice to which I've connected myself.'

'You're pumping murch out of the Ways of the Mammoths?'

He sipped the water.

'Well, I am pumping, but that's not the point. The flow-generators convert the murch into electrical current, so I am self-sufficient here. Only don't mistake it for a weapon against gleissen!'

'Truth to tell...'

'You were imagining that I intend to pump all murch out of the Ways of the Mammoths?'

'When you spoke of total solutions, I realised –'

'It'd be like scooping up the ocean with a teaspoon! My dear man!'

'How then?'

He listened intently for a while to the distant echo of a glashatay's drum, some association had suddenly diverted his thoughts from the conversation; a good minute of waiting was needed, and only then did he blink and return to the topic as if nothing had happened.

'The idea occurred to me already in the nineties of the past century. Of course, you are right, Benedykt, I knew nothing then of teslectricity and the Ice; no one could have known. I was working on a worldwide wireless telegraph system. The way the whole thing unfolded with Marconi is another matter: whereas my idea – how can I make it most intelligible to you... Imagine a balloon filled with water to the point where the rubber is taut. In the balloon there's an aperture with a tube and piston – you push down on the piston, water is forced into the balloon and the balloon expands. Install in various places more of these pistons – and they will rise and fall in time to the rhythm of your injections. And now exchange the balloon for the Earth, the waves of water for the Earth's electrical currents, and the pistons – for transmitting and receiving stations. The waves transmit information, but the waves also transmit energy – something people still think too little about. Imagine again that I provoke an explosion in this water – a wave passes through the balloon – I discern its frequency and pump the piston in accordance with it, constantly increasing the amplitude – after a given time, the balloon must burst. *In the same way, the Earth will burst.*

'You wish to destroy the planet, sir?' Laugh. 'You'll get rid of the gleissen, true, but somehow I'm not convinced this was what the tsar had in mind.'

Tesla rotated his glass slowly, staring at the ways the water flowed within.

'One afternoon in those days, I walked together with a friend from my laboratory on East Houston Street, near Wall Street, into the basement of one of those multi-storey skyscrapers. Renovations were going on at the time, the building was empty, uninhabited. I had the mechanical oscillator in a suitcase.' He indicated with his other hand how small it was. 'I clamped it firmly to one of the steel girders of the building. Finetuned the frequency of the oscillator's vibrations until the girder generated a resonance. After a few minutes, the whole edifice was shaking as if in a fever; other high-rise buildings in the neighbourhood were also trembling; the whole district appeared as if struck by an earthquake. Dust and dirt arose in the basement, we could already hear the fire-truck sirens – I seized a sledgehammer and smashed the oscillator. We walked away with our lives at the last minute. Ye-es. With the help of that mini-oscillator, I would have toppled Brooklyn Bridge in less than an hour.

'The Earth vibrates at a frequency of one hour and forty-nine minutes. Let's say we detonate a ton of dynamite precisely at such intervals, thereby intensifying the wave every time it returns. After a finite amount of time, the Earth must crumble; you surely don't doubt that, Benedykt, sir.'

'But you don't wish to split the Earth asunder.' No longer laughing.

'Of that you can be sure.' He drew his white palm over his Gypsy nose; a glintz sparkled in his dark eye. 'But there also exists a resonant frequency for the teslectric flow inside the Ways of the Mammoths. It must exist.'

'Whence the certainty?'

'Have you forgotten, sir, from what it all began? From an impact!'

Pour some water into another glass.

'And this is what you're testing on the tungetitum coil?'

'I shall then build an unlicht hammer, which will smash all the Ice. At least...' He sighed and sat down on the edge of the massive laboratory bench. 'Not long ago I was asleep and... Be not so surprised, sir, I do sleep, I do sleep.'

'You had a dream –'

'Yes. That one day, in this way, I shall bring down the entire City of Ice. Do not underestimate, sir, premonitions of the future! I always had a talent for clairvoyance; I once saved a man from death in a railway disaster thanks to a similar revelation.' He became lost in thought. 'My mother's death – I also saw it first in the clouds.'

'Everyone here warns of the snares of oneiromancy. Have you seen the dreamslaves?'

'*Excusez-moi.*'

He strode over to a cupboard, took out a small bottle, tipped something onto his white glove – he was about to wash down some tablets. Avert the eyes. Sasha Pavlitch was watching from over his microscope at the far end of the room, intrigued. Wink at him. Sasha blushed and hunched his shoulders over the eyepiece.

Stroll past tables along the walls. In contrast to the mess in the Krupp Laboratories, ideal order prevailed here. And yet this was the ground floor, right above the Ways of the Mammoths. Maybe they had been lucky and the gleissen had spared them for the time being. Or maybe it was the hand of Mademoiselle Christine. Pass by a tungetitum looking glass with a burned-in pattern similar to a pentagram; flip instinctively the pans of an apothecary scales; flick once or twice the switch of a darkbulb under a red lampshade (the stockroom was plunged momentarily into dirty-blue, as if inundated by an ocean wave), peep inside a ball lined with mirrors –

'Don't touch!' yelled Tesla, terrified.

Step back.

He came running up and disconnected something at the base of the stand with the ball. Several thickish cables wrapped in anti-murch insulation reached inside. A long arm made of frostoglaze with some sort of optical mechanisms attached stuck out horizontally from the ball. At intervals underneath lay a dozen measuring gauges with clock faces.

'A teslectric bomb or what?'

'Ooph. *Je vous demande pardon.* He glanced around at Engineer Jago and lowered his voice. 'Not a bomb; in actual fact – an unlicht lamp, but...' He drew closer still; his posture suggested a shamefaced confidence. 'A good thirty years ago, I constructed the first Death Ray Devices. Those lamps were able within a split second to disintegrate zirconium and diamond. Look, sir, the structure of such a light gun is very simple: a sphere lined on the inside with reflective material, a bit like in a Leyden jar, and a lump of highly polished carbon or zirconium or ruby connected to an energy source. The light is reflected inside and concentrates in avalanches on the stone. Puff, it evaporates! Or we use zinc plates and release the accumulated impulse of light onto the outside – what a weapon! Had I had the appropriate funds to work on it on a suitably larger scale – who'd still be conducting wars, when a beam faster than the eye can see could reduce whole armies to ash at distances of hundreds of miles?

'No one, alas, was interested in the invention. Here, however, I have an opportunity to test the unlicht version of the Death Ray in action. As the stone for concentrating the unlicht, I am using cryocarbon or pure tungetitum. The unlicht ray thus obtained strikes a temperature so low I've not so far succeeded in measuring it accurately.'

Examine the ball with its glass beak, ferociously scratching the back of the hand.

'It freezes but doesn't destroy?'

'I've no idea yet what it might be good for in practice – I don't have too much time for these experiments. I meant to concentrate on the T coil and the resonance of murch in the Ways of the Mammoths; this last, as I say, ought to be the chief object of my research – in the back courtyard, I am building a prototype of the tungetitor – but now it transpires that some kind of political machinations again stand in the way of my work. Apparently, the local governor, what's his name –'

'Schultz.'

'Very possibly. This Schultz sends malicious notes to Saint Petersburg about how I'm frittering away a national fortune on my private experiments, whilst Pobedonostseff throws obstacles in my path at every opportunity; we're finding it harder and harder to acquire pure tungetitum, whereas I need sixty poods for the tungetitor core alone – in a word, I have to give a demonstration in order to pacify the tsar.' He pointed to Engineer Jago with a discreet movement of the head. 'Hence the Battle Pump as well as all its handheld variants – you see, my friend, I am thinking of you – I've convinced them that these are smaller guns against the gleissen, and that I must test their effectiveness on organisms in the Frost. A *quid pro quo*; I don't imagine the tsar and his people supporters will be able to drive away gleissen with these and make the Ice retreat – in the best-case scenario, the gleissen would descend back down onto the Ways of the Mammoths – and what then? are they going to sink well after well and construct Battle Pumps every other verst? But the Ice will remain as it was. No, no, *mon ami*, it has to be disposed of at its source, so to speak.

'But, in order for them to give me time and a free hand, I have to produce some impressive theatre for them. This is what the life of an inventor and innovator looks like: no one understands his ideas, because if they did, they'd have invented everything sooner themselves; therefore, the true innovator has to win allies through his charisma, acquire trust based on his future successes or – or put simply: through deception, dazzling flair, brilliant bluff. I've had enough practice over the years.'

Fishing them out from behind a table with his long arm, he revealed diagrams and drawings of this Battle Pump sketched on cardboard. The construction as a whole was indeed imposing – the figure of a man added at the bottom for comparison looked like an ant. They resembled the illustrations to Wells' *War of the Worlds*: machines higher than houses on thin spidery tripods. All that was lacking in this sketch was an actual gleiss melting under the impact of the Pump.

'But there is a benefit to this constraint: black-biological experiments.' Nikola waved in the direction of the cages of rats and mice. 'Since the greatest difficulty lies, of course, in whom can I defreeze here with the murch pump? – icified corpses, chilled animals, in the best case hibernik katorzhniks – but not anyone or anything remotely approaching the state in which *le Père du Gel* finds himself. Let us say then that I give you a portable pump such as this, tested on these unfortunates, but you, sir, when applying it in the best faith to your father, could bring about his death, I don't know, provoke some kind of thermal shock or cause some other unforeseen effect.' He returned to his corner and poured himself more water. 'So, the question is this: what to do in order to gain certainty.'

'Reason says... Some other Father Frost should be used in the experiments.'

'That's right.' Tesla raised his glass of water in a toast. 'First of all, we have to learn how to freeze people, only then can we safely unfreeze them.'

Look away.

'You ask me, sir, how my pater became this – this – this –'

'You don't know how.'

'I am pursuing him to precisely that spot on the Ways of the Mammoths.' Glance at the cages of rats slowly freezing after total bemurchment; hoar covered their furry coats, saliva turned to ice in their muzzles. 'Might I exchange a word with Professor Yurkat?'

'He's gone for a week or two to Tomsk University.'

'Ah.' Scratch the wrist. Feel the teslectric flow, having come straight from the New Arkadiya – the sucking of murch into the organism – distinctly like the movement of this cold water down the gullet. Or maybe it was merely autosuggestion following Tesla's words. 'When do you intend, sir, to get going with the experiments on people? Did they supply those condemned men?'

'I would really prefer to know more before I start risking human life. Therefore, I'm telling you: please refrain for the time being from any thought of rescue expeditions and secret defreezing of your father somewhere near the Arctic Circle. If I succeed, Tsar Nikolay will get what he wanted and the Ice will disappear from the earth altogether – faster than anyone supposed.'

'Meaning you'll drive out Winter, kill the gleissen.'

'That's the idea.'

'So how can we be sure *le Père du Gel* will survive such a Thaw?'

Nikola Tesla became confused, spread wide his arms, dropped his head onto his white shirtfront, stood hunched over, adjusted the scarf neath his chin, muttered something under his breath in an unfamiliar language and again spread wide his long arms. Only in such moments was it evident just how old he was, how exhausted: the wrinkles, the shadows under his eyes – not in the least penumbrous, the fine skin stretched over sharp bones. Normally, all this went unnoticed: Tesla was in absolute control of his body; his mind, wound up into a state of eternal restlessness, never allowed it to pause, stop or be destroyed.

'You have a father unique amongst men,' he said, 'and this is the price: fear and confusion and uncertainty.' He put aside his glass. 'Do you want some ointment for your hands?'

The appointment in the delegation of the Ministry of Winter was not till five o'clock, whilst Miss Muklanowicz was due to depart only in the evening. Pay a visit first to the Polish Library.

The research questions had been written down on a piece of paper and inserted into the bumazhnik. The most recent, the ninth, concerned the Dumb Ballooner, according to whose sighting Mrs Gwóźdź had accurately pinpointed the precise month. The librarian, an elderly gentleman shuffling about with the aid of a stick and with white film over his left eye, confirmed that of course, they had annual runs of all periodicals published in the Baikal Kray, including the Irkutsk daily press. Request the year 1919. He led the way through to a store at the back and pointed with his stick to a metal box. Well, you can see for yourself, sir, what goes on here.

The Polish Library, despite the latest generous grant from the Last Kopeck Club, had not managed to extricate itself from a state of permanent disaster: it had fallen victim to gleissen freezing through its stacks and reading rooms with a regularity worthy of a moneylender or Chinese curse. Moves to ever more costly locations, ever farther from the Ways of the Mammoths, had not helped; fourth floors and basement security guards also had not helped. For the fifth time in only three years, the entire collection had had to be hurriedly evacuated. Now, they weren't even trying to find a new building – once an icer had moved on, they cleaned up and dried out the rooms and unpacked everything again. Most of the furniture, however, was fit for nothing but kindling; new items were no longer purchased, whilst the book collections remained in piled-up chests and crates, creating labyrinths in the empty spaces, similar to those constructed by the coldiron shelving units and cupboards in the Krupp Laboratories. People crept around the Library like worms in the entrails of a sleeping monster. Every other moment – often right beneath the feet – a creaking and scraping resounded that made the hairs stand on end at the back of the neck: the parquet blocks, warped by the passage of a glacius, were straightening themselves out. Grey plaster dropped from the ceilings in large flakes.

Retrieve the annual runs, bound in large tomes each weighing half a pood, and lug them to a window table in the main reading room, not far from the librarian's desk. The old man pushed across the daily log. Press a three-rouble note into the donations box.

Sit down at the table and open a tome.

The story begins in 1882, when Engineer Salomon August Andrée took part in the first scientific expedition to Spitsbergen. He was obsessed at the time with the idea of conquering the North Pole by means of an aerostat, that is, in the basket of a hydrogen balloon. Salomon Andrée worked in the Swedish patents office, was a member of Stockholm's city council and a propagator of women's emancipation as a result of industrial progress, whilst he was renowned in the scientific world for his publications on phenomena – yes, yes – of thermal conductivity. In 1896 he constructed an aerostat, the *Örnen* (or *Eagle*), a veritable miracle of contemporary technology; for his enterprise he won the patronage of the Royal Swedish Academy of Sciences and subsidies from the King's personal coffers as well as from Alfred Nobel. On the eleventh day of July 1911, with Messrs Andrée, Frænkel and Strindberg on board, the *Eagle* took off from Spitsbergen. In the gondola were also cages containing homing pigeons, by means of which Andrée intended to send out information about the progress of the expedition. The last communication from the *Eagle* received on Spitsbergen was dated 13 July, 12.30 p.m. *All goes well on board. This is the third message sent by pigeon. Andrée.*

... The search for the balloon and its crew continues until today. The Swedes spare neither money nor effort. For many years the campaign was led by Andrée's brother, Ernest. In February 1900, initial rumours circulated around the world of the discovery of the *Eagle*'s hull in Siberia. Assistance was offered by Prince Kropotkin, resident at the time in Great Britain and a member of the Royal Geographical

Society. He drew up a map marking the site of the catastrophe near the sources of a Yenisey tributary. For years hunters, gold-diggers and Tunguses collected various metal, wooden and canvas relics, demanding the promised rewards. Ernest Andrée disqualified successive finds by means of telegraph messages. Then, after the arrival of the Ice, telegraph communication became impossible. Further rumours, legends and myths, increasingly fantastical, circulated throughout Siberia. Amongst the Tunguses, the tale lived on about the landing of a 'flying boat' on Togo Mar mountain. In 1918, Togo Mar together with Yakutsk, the Aldan mountains, the Dzhugdzhur range and the coastline of the Sea of Okhotsk were already long under the Ice. Then, by the Olyokma river at the foot of the Stanovoy Highlands, gold prospectors hired by Lenzoto encountered a man whom the press later christened the Dumb Ballooner.

... He did not speak, that was the first thing. He possessed the physiognomy of a European, which was clearly revealed only when they shaved off his beard of many years' growth. He was already very old and ravaged; he lacked all his toes, both ears, many fingers, as well as all his teeth, and the frost had also claimed his left eye. They found him without clothes or baggage apart from a few animal skins badly sewn together. Hence the hypothesis that he had lived for years amongst the locals. He reacted not to the Russian language and appeared not to understand at all what was said to him, or what was communicated through gestures and expressions – which by then was already very odd in the Land of the Gleissen. For many years, katorzhniks had not been branded as they had in former times with the letters KAT on their faces, on their palms – thus in the beginning, the Lenzoto people did not rule out that he could have been a fugitive convict; but no. Soon people remembered about the *Eagle*. A Swedish geologist, who worked somewhere on the Lena river, was sent for. Meanwhile the Ballooner was held at a camp beside the Olyokma, in a room off a small warehouse. He was examined by a doctor who declared him to be a hibernik, no two ways about it, unusually resistant to frost: some parts of his body were totally insensitive to touch, so frozen was the metabolism within them. And yet the old man was walking about, breathing, eating, excreting, his heart was beating (though very slowly). Trackers were sent out to trace back his footsteps – but all traces ended after a few versts.

... They held him in this warehouse for one week less a day; on the seventh morning, someone entered the room with breakfast and it transpired that the Ballooner was no longer there. He had not gone out – the windows were barred, heavily nailed shut besides, whilst the door was kept bolted and padlocked from the outside. The larch-wood flooring in the warehouse was in ruins, the boards smashed and broken loose; yet the Ballooner could not have dug his way out from under the warehouse by this method, since the ground was frozen rock hard. The idea that a gleiss could have risen up out of the Ways of the Mammoths and kidnapped him also made no sense: a glacius would have had insufficient time to freeze out and freeze back in again during the night; not to mention that everyone in the camp would have noticed a sudden drop in temperature, whilst half the furniture in the warehouse would have split or suffered in some other visible way. This second, stowage area of the warehouse, where the Ballooner had been allowed free range, was thoroughly searched. No trace of him was discovered there; the only peculiarity noted was that some supply chests had been completely demolished – in an article in *The Irkutsk News*, a journalist spun fantastical speculations linked to the fact that these chests were coated in coldiron and were well soldered, whilst the Ballooner possessed no tools for ripping open sheet coldiron. Had he destroyed them by sheer willpower?

... *The News* published the only photograph taken of the Ballooner; someone in the Olyokma camp possessed an old camera used for geological documentation. In this photograph – coarse-grained and not very clear, but reproduced to the dimensions of at least half a column – two men in hooded sheepskins and frostglaze goggles were supporting by the elbows on either side a poor wretch considerably shorter than they, skeletally thin and almost naked. It was hard to claim anything with certainty, just as it was to state anything about the details of his appearance: the men stood against a backdrop of icy-white slopes and snow-covered taiga, but in place of the Dumb Ballooner a black hole yawned in the photograph; a patch of dense umbriance hovered there, whilst instead of the Ballooner's facial features, instead of eyes, hair – only sparks of a glintz flashed in the blackness imprinted on the film, like constellations in a night sky.

... This story reached Baikal in the spring of 1919; articles were compiled on the basis of second- and third-hand accounts. Beneath the most expansive, published in *The News*, appeared the signature of one 'AGG'. Make a note of these initials.

Glance again at the list of questions. Answers to all won't be found in books, but what exactly, for example, had father been seeking in the orographic works of Bohdanowicz? No helpful hard facts had been found in the archives hewn out of the rime by Shtchekelnikoff in Horczyński's old offices, certainly nothing that might enable father's Ways of the Mammoths to be calculated. Still no inkling was there of what had come over him, so that he suddenly set off on his solitary pilgrimage into Winter – or of where exactly he went – and by what black-physical method he froze into Batyushka Moroz.

The librarian, now more obliging, pulled out of the chests a dozen or so volumes classified in the scientific section. As was quickly realised, the Sibirkhozheto maps of the Ways of the Mammoths, as well as the geology of Siberia in general, depended to a large extent on the discoveries and work of a troika of Poles: Aleksander Czekanowski, Jan Czerski and Karol Bohdanowicz. Czekanowski (exiled following the January Uprising of 1863) had compiled the oldest map of the Irkutsk Governorate, with special attention paid to the Baikal Kray; before this, people had still relied on such old and imprecise cartographical notes as those of Daniel Gottlieb Messerschmidt from the 1723 expedition ordered by Peter the Great. Here came the first surprise: Czekanowski's map, along with all copies, scientific elaborations et cetera, had been suppressed by the tsarist censorship. Czekanowski had also ventured to the Tunguska river, to the Tchulakan. His paleontological notes include the first studies of fossilised mammoths. At Ust-Baley on the Angara, he uncovered a giant underground museum of Jurassic flora and fauna. In 1875, he received a gold medal for his now-secret map at a geographical exhibition in Paris, and the Russian Geographical Society secured an amnesty for him and release from deportation. Less than a year later, Czekanowski committed suicide for unknown reasons.

... He had a pupil, Jan Czerski (also a post-January exile, except that he was younger). Czerski had specialised from the beginning in the geology of Baikal. He received an award from the University of Bologna for his map of the lake and surrounding mountains. Verify the facts: censored by both Rappacki and Pobedonostseff, all copies of the map had been withdrawn from public circulation. What was going on!? Mutter a curse. Czerski had lived in Irkutsk. On behalf of the Siberian Division of the Russian Geographical Society, he conducted research on the Lower Tunguska. He ventured further; based on his maps of the Indigirka and Kolyma rivers, large deposits were discovered of coal, zinc and gold. He collected mineral samples and animal fossils. Look for any references to mammoths. In the Katunga valley he dug up prehistoric human remains. At the Saint Petersburg Academy of Sciences, he worked for years on the osteology of Quaternary mammals based on a collection of tens of thousands of bones excavated in Siberia. He died in 1892 during his next expedition.

... Karol Bohdanowicz was a geologist by training, not by exile. At the time of the building of the Trans-Siberian Railway, he was leading one of the research parties seeking fossil riches along its route. In 1893–1894, for the first time, he studied Lake Baikal. Surely, he must have compiled maps; surely must have had at his disposal the maps of Czekanowski and Czerski. The *editio castigata* of his paper 'Materials on the Geology and Minerals Found in the Irkutsk Governorate', held by the Library, did not include them. When questioned, the librarian explained that recent scientific works in this field, like the majority of new editions of older publications, were in fact *editiones expurgatae*, meticulously purged by Rappacki's people, and often by Pobedonostseff himself, of any information and knowledge that might put the reader on the scent of Sibirkhozheto's commercial secrets. Merely shake the head. On the one hand – they're not going from private house to private house censoring the collections of every single person interested in the geology of Siberia. On the other – these are institutions, their activities can rarely be measured according to normal logic; a tchinovnik carries out the instructions of higher authority not because he sees any sense in them, but because they are the instructions of higher authority. Lawyer Kuzmentsoff would no doubt have put it still more forcefully: try not to guess, young man, the reasons behind the decisions of tsarist officials, it will drive you mad. Scratch the skin. There are always reasons!

... News of the Ice finds Bohdanowicz in the Caucasus at the time of the quest for crude oil deposits. Moving to Baikal, he sets about systematic work. Irkutsk is fresh from the Great Fire, from the Winter of the Gleissen. Initial expeditions to the place of Impact return from the north with sensational news. Bohdanowicz had always been on good terms with the indigenous peoples of Siberia and had written in his time outspoken letters in defence of the Tchuktchi. But here, in addition, there appears Aleksander Czerski, son of Jan, a pupil of Benedykt Dybowski. Czerski junior and Bohdanowicz collaborate from 1911 to 1917, or at least between these dates works undersigned by both names appear in their bibliographies. In 1914, they publish 'On Coldiron Ore and the Possibility of Finding Iced-Through Ores on the Ways of the Mammoths.' This is probably the first time that the 'Ways of the Mammoths' are mentioned in an academic work; find no earlier citations. Nowhere is this set out directly, but it seems that Bohdanowicz was the discoverer of the Ways. More or less at this same time, Aleksander Czerski publishes his *Buryat Diaries*. The Polish Library does not have them in its collections. Imagine how on one frosty day in 1913, a fateful meeting with far-reaching consequences takes place between Czerski, Bohdanowicz and a Buryat shaman. Maybe the idea was born after reading the works of Czerski senior on the mammoths unearthed in Siberia.

... Bohdanowicz and Czerski publish less and less, from the beginning of 1917 Bohdanowicz falls totally silent – and yet he was still working intensively, as can be read about in the contemporary Irkutsk press. Amongst other things, he mounts an expedition to the Last Isotherm. He is paid by the East Siberian Division of the Imperial Russian Geographical Society, in other words de facto by Sibirkhozheto.

In August 1922, he perishes in a failed attempt to blow up an icecradle in the Barguzinsky mountains. The official investigation ended abruptly: an accident; but the controversies surrounding it may be inferred from the tone of contemporary articles.

... In January 1923, an arrest warrant is issued for Aleksandr Ivanovitch Tchersky. The list of charges includes unspecified political crimes, the theft of commercial secrets (Sibirkhozheto's?) as well as membership of a religious sect outlawed by the state.

... In February 1923, the second shaman strike breaks out. The war on the Ways of the Mammoths escalates. The abattises of corpse masts surrounding the City of Ice get thicker. And shortly afterwards – shortly afterwards, His Imperial Exaltedness Nikolay the Second engages Nikola Tesla.

Stretch the limbs on the uncomfortable scoliotic chair. Floorboards shoot up beneath the feet. No hope should be cherished that any truth whatsoever shall be gleaned about the past from these scraps of History. Obviously, political and commercial battles are being waged here at the highest levels independently of the peripeteias of Filip Gierosławski. Cast back mentally to the conversation with the flaxen-haired tchinovnik in the Ministry of Winter. He has to be cornered and questioned – what exactly was he expecting from the Son of Frost? It's hardly surprising he handed over that copy of Sibirkhozheto's *Map of the Ice* so furtively, since they themselves are censoring even partial, already censored maps. But maybe it's not them? Maybe a different faction? Or maybe they target only partial, specialised maps – maybe the danger comes from these? Ultimately, the coldiron companies are working on their own maps; neither Rappacki nor Pobedonostseff have access to their libraries; such enterprises have archives in Berlin, in Königsberg, in Vienna, in New York, they hire their own geologists – like Filip Gierosławski.

Take another look at the chronology of activities of Czerski junior and Bohdanowicz. Assuming that some high-ranking person really did wish to be rid of them... Of what dangerous knowledge had they come into possession? Father was looking for Bohdanowicz's map already in 1918. Had he figured it out sooner than they themselves? Since Czerski and Bohdanowicz had definitely heard later of Batyushka Moroz. In 1921, in 1922. They must eventually have put two and two together. If –

The librarian proffered a handkerchief. Thank him and tie it around the left hand; wipe the drops of blood off the table and off the nails of the right. He wagged his finger in rebuke. Mind you don't stain the books.

If – if this transformation from man to iceman is not an individual, unrepeatable miracle that affected only Filip Gierosławski (and reason does not consent to miracles), then a general prescription must exist that determines the circumstances in which other people too are able to descend to the Ways of the Mammoths.

Hypothesis: Czerski and Bogdanowicz knew this prescription.

Who is most concerned to keep it secret?

Mm-hmm, of the highest-placed players we have basically five figures to consider: Governor General Schultz-Zimovy and Aleksandr Aleksandrovitch Pobedonostseff here in Irkutsk, as well as the tsar, Rasputin and Rappacki in the Great Russian Heartland. Schultz wants to use Father Frost in negotiations with the gleissen; Schultz should be crossed off the list. The tsar would not resort to such clandestine methods. War against the gleissen – yes; but murdering geologists and censoring maps? Rappacki – too little is known of his motives. Rasputin – well, what is there to say? Rasputin is a madman, yet the assertion may be risked that he'd be first to propagate the idea of similar self-gla-ciations and lead his Martsynian brothers along the path of Batyushka Moroz. There remains Pobedonostseff. He has a motive, he has the ca-pabilities, and he is on the spot. He sits at the top of that tower of his above Irkutsk in a cloud of unlicht and unscrupulously fights anything that threatens his Kingdom of Ice...

Where is Aleksander Czerski? Is he hiding from the Okhrana, most likely now on the other side of the world? And Bohdanowicz and Czerski's collaborators? Their Buryats? Is Pobedonostseff capable of censoring the whole of Siberian ethnography?

When asked, the librarian unearthed several valuable old printed books, amongst them the *editio princeps* of Adam Kamieński's *Diary of a Moscow Prison, its Towns and Places*: the first description, so he claimed, of Siberia in Polish. Taken prisoner by Russians in the mid-seventeenth century, Kamieński was exiled to Yakutiya, where he familiarised himself with the beliefs and customs of the Siberian peoples. Not long afterwards came the records of Siennicki, Lach and Piotrowski. Then, in his *Revelations of Siberia and Journeys Undergone there in the Years 1831, 1832, 1833, 1834*, Józef Kobyłecki writes of the Buryats and Tunguses. (All these authors were political exiles.) There is also, of course, Maurycy August Beniowski and his *Memoirs and Travels*, and for good measure – if you please, Słowacki's narrative poem *Anhelli*. It seems half the books on the Siberian lands and peoples were penned by Poles. The only existing dictionary of the Yakut language and culture was compiled by one Edward Piekarski, another exile. The final volume of this dictionary, signed 'Saint Petersburg, 1921', contains a lengthy chapter dedicated to the *tungetitum war waged by Yakuts and Buryats on the Ways of the Mammoths*. Notice on the penultimate page, however, the gigantic stamp of the Ministry of Winter's censorship office. Check the numbering of the pages: a total of eighteen missing. Here too they'd cut them out! And from a book that had already been printed, published, sold!

The librarian advised devoting attention rather to the ethnographical novels of Sieroszewski, since more truth can be smuggled into literature; the art of censoring fiction – that is, falsehood – is too subtle for tchinovnik minds.

Wacław Sieroszewski began his successful career as an ethnographer (his *Twelve Years in the Yakut Country* received the gold medal of the Russian Geographical Society), only to move gradually deeper and deeper into the field of literature. Where he also achieved great things, however. His penultimate novel, entitled *The Abassy Told Me*, describes the peripeteia of a young Polish exile, who, having enriched himself on the sable-pelt trade, forms a partnership with a hunter of Yakut blood to buy furs from the locals at considerably higher prices, thereby allowing the impoverished indigenous folk to extricate themselves at least from their indigence and build more solid structures to live in than felt yurts. Which then has the side effect – as a micro-economy in practice – that the hunters turn away from competition, whilst the hero enriches himself still further, gaining at the same time great respect amongst the Siberian tribes. So, when the Ice hits by the Podkamennaya Tunguska river, when fire destroys Irkutsk and the tungetitum and coldiron fever begins, our benefactor hero is ideally placed to set up a great magpie syndicate and pump millions of roubles out of Sibirkhozheto. In this way, however, he soon finds himself in the midst of a war waged between the Buryat, Tungus and Yakut shamans for control of the Ways of the Mammoths. First, he is robbed of his dreams: his spirit, during bodily repose, is abducted and subjected to various tortures. The hero turns for help to his partner, who brings an old Yakut shaman, a one-armed dwarf with a vendetta against American steel mills and Prussian arms manufactories. This sorcerer devil explains to the protagonist the nature of war. And so, there are two souls within a human being, the kut soul, which binds the world of matter, and the siur soul, which binds the world of the immaterial. Furthermore, the kut soul is made up of the iya-kut, the mother-soul, embedded in the body like a knot in timber, the buor-kut or earth-soul, encircling the body like a dog on a leash, and the salgyn-kut or air-soul, which leaves the body during sleep and –

Notice only after a long while that someone had paused by the table and was looking over the shoulder at the book. Glance up. Some miserable lout with Iertheim's hair colour, carroty red. Under his arm he had a pamphlet edition of Marx's *On the Asiatic Origin of Russian Despotism*. 'Any good?'

'I beg your pardon?'

'I'm asking if it's any good. Sieroszewski's novel.'

'Mm-hmm, I'm looking more for factual information, you know, than literary value...'

'But you're still reading it!' he retorted. 'So is it any good or not!'

Recognise him: Mr Lewera, 'our local scribbler,' the unhappy victim of Sieroszewski's talent.

'It's very good.' Gather up the notes. 'The man has God-given talent.' He nodded.

'I think so too.' He extended a shovel-like paw. 'Teodor Lewera.' Stand up, shake his right hand. 'So, what kind of information are you seeking?'

Describe in general terms the current curiosity about the role of local beliefs in the history of Polish Siberian geology, and also about the case of the Dumb Ballooner, as a mystery fascinating in itself that would of be interest to anyone. Take the receipts from the librarian meanwhile for the borrowed books, pay the required deposit. Inquire of him the editorial address of *The Irkutsk News*.

'I'll show you,' Lewera offered.

Shtchekelnikoff shoved the parcel of books tied with string under his armpit and cast an ominous glance at the writer, who was half a head taller. 'What now?' mutter on the way down the stairs. 'Too many of them redheads crawling after ya.' 'And what've you got against redheads?' 'Nobody likes 'em, and out of such hatred grow mighty tough cads.' 'I was afraid you had some real cause to suspect Mr Lewera!' 'Well, I ain't pulled me knife on him.'

In the sleigh, he sat beside the driver. When Teodor Lewera seated himself in the back on the left-hand side, Shtchekelnikoff glanced over his shoulder at him once and twice.

The izvoztchik cracked his whip and the horses moved off in the fog; the equipage left behind a carved-out tunnel in the rainbow-hued suspension. Coldiron fixtures and iced-through materials visible on the upper storeys of buildings were unfurling woolly aureoles around about, fleeting afterimages of light diffracted into colours and dazzling brightnesses – and this even before the frostoglaze spectacles had been donned. It looked as if the Black Auroras were again awaking above the City of Ice, though no unlichty projections were as yet discernible in the afternoon sky.

'Where are these editorial offices?'

'Just here, on this street, a few junctions further on.'

'Thank you.'

'My pleasure, I meant to call on them anyway this week, to extract a few overdue payments.' Lewera wrapped himself tighter in his squirrel skins and peered over his frostoglazes. 'You'll forgive me, sir, but I know of course who you are, that is, I've heard, seen –'

'At Vittel's.'

'Yes. I make a point of memorising, collecting such things: faces, names, gossip.'

'You knew my father.'

'No, I had not the pleasure. He didn't move in those circles. I would have known if… He never showed up in cafés, in salons, in clubs.'

'And what about Aleksander Czerski – did you hear anything? what can have become of him now?'

He frowned.

'I've heard – heard, that you're working for Krupp. But that didn't help Czerski. He was taken on by Thyssen, yet six months later – a prestupnik.'

'The Ministry of Winter –'

'Sir, I obviously have no idea who, why, how, what for – but I've been observing the Irkutsk scene for a good ten years or more and believe I can predict certain things by looking at the shape of the process alone, without knowing the internal intricacies; in the same way, you look down from above at couples moving across a dance floor – from their movements, you can easily tell what dance it is, without seeing the separate steps taken by every foot, bah, without hearing the melody.'

'They're trying to implicate me in some kind of political provocation, is what you're saying.'

He pointed with his head to the square shoulders of Tchingis Shtchetelnikoff.

'And who's he? Your lightning conductor. You know very well what I'm talking about. Better take to heart this advice: do what you have to do as soon as you can, and get out of their sight before they see in you the next Czerski. You've come to see your father, yes? So, get on with it!'

Feeling annoyed. How far can a man be threatened! Is this really the truth about Benedykt Gierosławski that everyone sees here: victim of the father's fate?

'And are you advising out of the kindness of your heart, not banking perchance on the gratitude of the Son of Frost, like all the others, huh?' snarl peevishly. 'Hoping he'll strike some deal with the gleissen and, having struck it, suddenly remember the kind-hearted scribbler and reverse History so as to make a new Sienkiewicz out of Teodor Lewera, eh?'

Force out these last words into the frost and fog and at once take fright that he'll now surely erupt: he erupted – into laughter.

'The unlucky prince! No one sees little Benedykt, everyone sees the son of a great father!' He wriggled from under his skins and thumped the back with his gloved paw, unable to wipe the smug grin from his face; grab the tailboard of the sleigh so as not to fly forward. Lewera snorted unlichty breath; the white hue of the mist flowed over his furs, whilst the black of the fur reached up to his eyes. 'Should someone appear friendly, you, poor fellow, at once suspect hidden self-interest in friendship with the Son of Frost; and should someone be an enemy – then he's an enemy on account of the pater figure.' He laughed. 'Perhaps you've already been doing the rounds of the drinkeries in disguise, *incognito*, getting to know the devushkas under a fictitious name? What? It's not yet come to that, eh? Poor you!'

He adjusted the scarf on his face, crossing his long arms over his furry chest.

'Anyway – one man alone is immune to Faustian temptation: the true artist. The creator!'

Oho – was the first thought – the scribbler has been egged on unnecessarily. Now he'll puff himself up, talk a load of nonsense, try to pull the wool over these eyes with bardic solemnity and declaim his tear-jerking platitudes.

'Because think about it, sir,' Mr Lewera went on, 'what has the Devil got to offer him?'

'Well, precisely success,' mutter in reply, 'achievement, fame.'

'But what do achievement and fame have to do with success? Is it about an author being praised to the skies and patrons showering him with gold for a work which, as he himself can see more plainly than any, represents no value whatsoever? Ye-es, the Devil may sell such success to a creator – but what creator shall surrender his soul in exchange for something he knows will be Falsehood, a flimsy counterfeit of true success?'

'Mm-hmm, so let them praise him for a truly great work – can't the Devil sell him one of those?'

'He can. But how will it differ from ordinary plagiarism? The author will take the credit for magnificence not created by himself, only with the guarantee that no mortal shall ever recognise the fraud. He himself, however, the creator – or rather not the creator – he will know that he is not the creator of the masterpiece. So, what has he bought? Again, he has merely exchanged his non-material soul for material commonplace goods and an ashy aftertaste in the mouth: awareness of Falsehood.'

'But could not the Devil enable the man to write such a masterwork himself?'

'You mean – but what should Satan do? Cast a spell on him so that words fly off his pen without his knowledge?'

'No. Simply...'

'Yes?'

JACEK DUKAJ

'Enable him to genuinely – genuinely have that masterpiece within him.'

'That is, replace the man who was incapable of writing it with a man who is capable – replace his life, memory, experience, character – yes? Do you imagine, sir, anyone would ask the Devil for help in such a suicidal pact: take this poor unfortunate standing here before you together with his soul and put another man in his place, only with the same name and face – who is he? An idiot, nothing more.'

'Why, it's as if you'd have to change the whole man…'

'For how else? Were art a spall of chance… But it is the fruit of order! When I write such and such a sentence, and not another, it's not because a fly has just flown over my head or I drilled in my ear, but because it emerges out of all my previous sentences, whilst those sentences taken together – emerge out of my preceding thoughts, and those thoughts – out of my whole life that has led up to them. Every genuine work of art is an image of History – the history of its creator, the history of the world that gave birth to him. Under the Ice, you have no daubsters like those proliferating, so I hear, in the west of Europe; from whose paintings you can't tell if they've been created by a rational man with prior intentions, or by some half-blind madman laying hands for the first time on brush and oils. Here you don't get blabla-ists and absurdist-Dadaists and versemonger-balls-ups and ballet masters possessed by Dionysus. No!'

The editorial offices of *The Irkutsk News* were pulsating with life. The day's issue had already gone to press, but this clearly did little to diminish the traffic and hubbub reigning in rooms and corridors. Editors smeared in ink, compositors with grease on their hands and clothes, errand-boys bearing armfuls of freshly printed newspapers and great sheets of machine copy were running here and there, as were couriers in sheepskin coats and frostoglaze shapkas, their goggles sewn into the thick facemasks which they declined to remove even indoors as they dashed straight back out into the frost; women in addition were chasing them away, a caretaker or janitor yelling over their heads – so it felt as if genuine crowds were sweeping down the narrow corridors of *The News*. Such work tempo and pulse rate of human interaction recalled the countinghouse of Friedrich Krupp Frierteissen AG. Typewriters clattered, doors slammed, paper rustled. The necessity to employ a large number of youngsters as messengers was understandable, given the uselessness in the Land of the Gleissen of telegraph, telephone and radio. Encountering nevertheless such hordes at this time of day meant that crossing from the stairs to the far end of the floor, to the offices of the senior editors, would have taken a good quarter of an hour and cost several minor bruises – had it not been for the formidable stances of Messrs Lewera and Shtchekelnikoff in clearing the way. One of the whippersnappers rushing with typescript in hand clashed head-on with the writer, who grabbed him by the collar and lifting him in the air removed him an arshin behind and to one side; thereupon Shtchekelnikoff seized the kicking maltchik and likewise relocated him at arm's length by a more brutal method. Strike a path in this manner across the territory of the Irkutsk press.

Mr Lewera went a separate way to settle his own affairs. Knock on the door of Editor Grigory Grigoryevitch Avksenteyeff, whom the red-haired penman had identified as the AGG who'd undersigned the article on the Dumb Ballooner. Knock once, twice and thrice; to no avail. In fact, knocking might have gone on till kingdom come: out here the editorial clamour, but in there – poke the head inside – in there, five men furiously slamming down cards on a desk piled high with paper, in clouds of tobacco smoke, seated on bales of old newspapers, heartily sipping grape wine from a single bottle, whilst steam from chipped samovars hums and puffs neath a misted window and a red parrot squawks in a wire cage suspended from the ceiling. Think that Lewera must have got it mixed up; think this must be the haunt of the company slackers. Yet one word leads to another – do have a seat, my good fellow, shut the door, take your coat off and sit down – and then it transpires that these are the publisher, the senior editor, two section chiefs and bald-as-your-knee Grigory Grigoryevitch Avksenteyeff, the gilded pen of Sensation and Scandal; these very gentlemen, after closing the day's issue, are indulging in lowlier pastimes. Whilst the paper – the paper for the next day now takes care of itself. 'What sort of editors-in-chief would we be if we only had to come to work to ensure the paper goes to press on time! But first things first – who let you in, huh?' 'I forced my way in.' 'You'll have a drop to get warm?' 'God bless you, gentlemen.' 'Well, Misha, you deal. And for you – what's your name? – for you to get still warmer, a round of blizzarder won't do any harm. What?' 'So, how much to enter?' 'So, a roublie.' 'So, let's go.'

The game was played. At first, the stakes were indeed raised by a roublie, but already into the third round, the stakes had risen to fifteen roubles, and the hand was even favourably cold, without a single fiery-red card – and almost forty roubles were swept up. The editors wailed in lament. 'Ah, what bird is this! Come to pluck our feathers!' 'He'll confess, Wiehermayer sent him.' 'And to think we let ourselves be hoodwinked!' 'No, no!' Bridle up. 'Not true at all, pure chance. Because I'm looking for Grigory Grigoryevitch' (shuffle the cards meanwhile for the next deal), 'with regard to a former article.' 'You don't say!' 'Article, article!' screeched the parrot. Avksenteyeff proffered a cigarette. Before it came to the checking after the bidding, he had remembered the

whole affair of the Dumb Ballooner and what he had written about
him five and a half years before. He swallowed his wine, took a sip of
tea and thrust a spruce lozenge onto his tongue. 'Well, there was a lot
about it at the time, indeed there was, quite a sensation for a week or
two, then of course something else took its place – but what is it you
intend to find out? has that wild man popped up again? or maybe some
Swedes are only now applying to see him? It'd be worth scraping together an article!' 'No, nothing of the kind. Just one detail from that former
article, perhaps you recall: what was in those chests the Ballooner destroyed in the Olyokma storeroom, from where he escaped by some
miraculous means?' 'God only knows, for I surely don't!' 'But be so kind
as to check in your notebooks from those years, in those old materials,
you must have jotted down something else, not everything reaches the
columns!' 'Columns!' squawked the parrot. 'Columns!' Lost in thought,
Avksenteyeff sucked noisily on the lozenge. Try to persuade him: 'Well,
it won't hurt you to take a few steps. You see, I'm losing a fortune to you.'
He got up and went.

The game was played. Now a better card turned up, now a worse.
Remove the shuba, undo the frock coat, loosen the collar and cravat.
One of the editors dashed out for a moment to borrow more cash.
Add up furtively how much money was left: thirty roubles plus small
change, but this included what was already in play, for only a solitary
chervonets remained in the bumazhnik. Slam it down on the desktop
– where's the sense in keeping one lonely coin in the pocketbook?
A cold hand came, a hot hand came, again a cold; thirty reduced to
twenty-five. 'A forrrtune!' screeched the parrot. 'A forrrtune!' Grigory
Grigoryevitch returned and showed a sheet of paper with handwritten
notes: in the smashed chests were supplies of blackwickes. 'But what
sort, tungetitum or cryocarbon?' 'All I know is what's written here,
take it.' 'Spasibo.' Well, it wouldn't have been fitting to make excuses
and beat the retreat, how rude it would have been when Avksenteyeff
had been so obliging – no choice but to play on. The game was played.
Raise the eyes no longer towards the editors; the gaze was glued to
the cards. The publisher kicked up a fuss over some cards marked
with blood; pull a glove onto the scratched hand. They magicked up
a fresh pack. From the next deal, receive only figures of Summer;
the hand quickly cast two roubles onto the pile. 'Trrruth! Trrruth!'
Shudder. The pocket watch – peek at the pocket watch – how much
will they give for such a brand-new, silver-plated timekeeper – peek
at the watch and glimpse the hour. Teslectrical flow courses below
the skin in a searing stream – the very touch of the cold metal turns
the thoughts upside down, breaks chains of associations. They're
waiting in the Ministry of Winter. On the table lies what remains

of the savings, it's time to stop bidding, make the excuses and leave, it's so obvious, so undoubtedly reasonable and right – see it being done, hear what's being said to them, hear them as they murmur their goodbyes… 'You'll forgive me, gentlemen, I've sat too long, business is slipping away.' Scoop up the final monies, the fur coat, scarf and shapka, and rush out into the corridor.

Shtchekelnikoff was reading the latest issue of *The News*, hot off the press. 'It's a-written here that holy confession makes Catholics' guts function better. What d'you say to that, Mr G?' 'I wasn't aware you could read.' 'He as reads too much grows daftly trusting of people, p'raps you've noticed?' 'Where's Mr Lewera?' 'Flogged some bookkeeper with a typewriter, they flung 'im down the stairs. Are we going?' 'Going, going.' Take a deep breath. 'These hacks, my good Shtchekelnikoff, are nothing but a bunch of bloodsuckers.' 'Bah!'

In the Customs House building it was again Entropy Day, since the gangs of masons, booked long ago to rescue the vast edifice, had finally reported for work; they were to insert new supports under the roof and ceilings, straighten the walls and refresh the plaster. For this reason, some tchinovniks had had to abandon their desks. But – worse still: when an attempt was made to sneak past Schembuch's Mikhail by way of a side door, in order to waylay the flaxen-haired barebones in his office, it transpired that it was no one's office at all. So, someone had been making use of it in his own time? For, you see, repairs were most likely underway then in a different place and he'd moved from there to here for a week or two. 'Well, perhaps you can tell me at least who he might be?' Describe him as best as could be done, down to the Napoleonic lock on his forehead. 'He must be an important figure around here!' The clerk seated there raised his eyes to the ceiling, winced, scratched his chin, tugged at his moustache… Understand, given the present state of demurchment, only after a good minute of this theatre, the man's obvious intention and reach for the bumazhnik. The tchinovnik ceased manifesting symptoms of dementia as soon as he spied six roubles. 'If my memory serves me correctly,' he said in a sing-song voice, 'that'll be Commissioner Uriah.' 'Where might I find him?' 'For that you need to inquire in Administration.'

Wander over to Administration. Five roubles. 'Commissioner Frantishek Markovitch Uriah? It tallies. We have the stamped papers, oh: in the first week of October, he returned to his post in the governor general's chancellery.' 'So where should I look for him?' 'In the Citadel, your lordship, in the Citadel.' 'But have a look in those papers, maybe you've an address for him somewhere in Irkutsk.' 'You wish to know the private address of a high-ranking gubernatorial functionary?' the official raised an eyebrow. 'How much?' inquire with a sigh. He showed it. It was time to stop bidding or there'd be no cash left even to travel to work on the Marmeladobahn.

Trudge back to Schembuch's secretariat, avoiding the piles of rubble on the parquet floors and clouds of plaster flying off the walls. No one here will assist a supplicant in anything for free, such is the culture of the state and man, visible even in matters so trivial; besides, in what matters is he to be visible? – a person of common birth and modest fortune has to do only with these, not with matters affecting reasons of state, not with questions of war or the throne. According to this measure, then, we distinguish one State from another State: according to the expression of the fellow at the entrance to a government department, according to the bending of backs and inclining of necks, according to the intensity of gazes between supplicant and bureaucrat.

Sit down neath the skew-whiff portrait of Minister Rappacki.

'Perhaps you'll rubberstamp me and then I'll go away, eh?' accost Mikhail. The Tatar bridled.

'There has to be order! You have to wait!'

'Tell me at least whether you've heard if anything's shifted in my case. What? Does Commissioner Schembuch intend to keep me like this on a leash for long?'

The secretary assumed an expression of amazement.

'But how am I to know what higher authority thinks or doesn't think?' After a while he took pity. 'Have you been following your case? Where've you been so far?'

It was hard to know where it was supposedly needful to go. To Count Schultz? To Pobedonostseff? Inquire about the gubernatorial chancellery. Oh, it's a mighty department, not any old office. The Main Directorate of Eastern Siberia had under its control also the Yeniseysk Governorate as well as the Yakutsk and Transbaikal Oblast; now it operates under the banner of the Chancellery of the Irkutsk Governorate General, but is no less important.

'They are saying everything hangs on a political decision. That is, up there, above Schembuch's head.'

'Well, what is it you want?' the Tatar was so amazed his little eyes grew rounded. 'As soon as word comes from on high, the stamp will be affixed. There has been no word – so you have to wait.'

Wait, what else could be done. A supplicant entered, a second, a third, a fourth; one Schembuch even received. In the corridor, the masons were hammering at the walls, their rhythmless racket drowning out the never faraway drums of the glashatays. A gleiss had been spotted below in the street, behind the building of the East Siberian Department of the Imperial Russian Geographical Society.

These constant repairs, hurriedly erected props, wedges, pillars, the continual state of semi-removal… As though the entropy extruded by the Ice had found an outlet only on the level of office chaos. Maybe that's how it goes, from atomic structures upwards: a lump of metal freezes faster than a man, a man faster than the State.

Well, what of it, when a man is still no match for the power of the State? The longer the wait, the greater the sense of being a forgotten trifle in the bureaucratic abyss, a miserable worm neath the under-sole of the Moloch. Over time, even the timid Mikhail with his jovial uncle's physiognomy, even he had acquired ominous features. Yet were it a department of Summer in the fullness of its tchinovnik potency, unshaken by threats of glaciation, it would be even worse! Thus a new nightmarish image is born in Schembuch's waiting room: of the intestinal system of the Empire, of its most vital entrails, wherein digestive juices and masticated food and hot blood itself roam from city to city, from governorate to governorate, from authority to authority – a system encompassing Asia from Vladivostock to the Urals and Europe as far west as Warsaw – offices, chancelleries, bookkeeping departments, delegations and departments, branches and commissions, registries and archives, directorates and institutions, as its organs – the paper, the stamp, the tchinovnik – entering a ministerial vein in Irkutsk and emerging in Saint Petersburg, entering in Saint Petersburg and emerging in Odessa – circulate, digest and rule.

Is it really true, as Doctor Konyeshin and Mr Pocięgło would have it, that until the end of time, man is the hands of the State? Is there really no deliverance? *If only there could exist orders of innocence and governments of doubt!* Would Herr Blutfield be such a foolish utopian? What liberty can there be between futureless anarchy and Commissioner Schembuch's waiting room?

Thrust the hands into the coat pocket so as to smother the unwholesome reflexes. On the ceiling above Mikhail's desk, a jagged crack is beginning to open, a long fissure spreading across the entire secretariat. Need to flee in thought from this theatre of horror. The most effective means: harness the mind to logical work.

A crack, so a crack. Mm-hmm, for how, in actual fact, does a gleiss freeze through a wall? How can a solid body pass through a solid body so that these buildings are still standing despite everything, so that pavements, from under which glaciuses have surfaced, do not crumble to gravel and dust? A gleiss does not bludgeon with its ice-mass like a battering-ram – that would reduce everything in its path to rubble. It *freezes through*. Bah, does that ice-armour really belong to the gleiss's 'body' at all?

… Gleissen blood seeps through everything, relocating the helium at near-absolute-zero temperatures through soil, rock and walls by mysterious means, like water through a sieve, except that it does this despite even gravity, despite the laws of white physics – molecular matter animated by the Frost. And apart from the helium – what else? Ah yes, the temperature gradient. This too you won't stem by means of any material barrier. So, the ice is solely a consequence of the gleiss's entry into the terrestrial environment, which is alien to its physiology: around about a gleiss, air condenses and freezes.

... Here's what happens: streams of liquid helium flow, the Frost moves, the glaciated mass increases on one side, melts and evaporates on the other. Is this not the model being constructed by physicists at the Kaiser-Wilhelm-Gesellschaft für schwarze Physik based on the re-search of Doctor Wolfke and his people? Written up at Krupp in those reports of conclusions to numerous experiments meant to support or overthrow such hypotheses? For we see no gleissen as such – we see them exclusively 'imprisoned' in forms imposed by environmental disparities.

... Whilst these cracks, infiltrations, fissures, vertical deflections and sometimes total ruins, like in the Holey Palace – are the results of multiple through-freezings by gleissen that have 'impurities' locked in their ice: grains of sand, pebbles, veins of ice mixed with substances with higher melting curves, or even shreds crushed out of coffins, as Mr Gawron described. The impurities remain stuck in walls and ceil-ings like tea leaves in a strainer. From which it may be inferred that a gleiss recently frozen out from under the ground is more threaten-ing to human architecture than a gleiss descending along icicles from subcelestial heights; gleissen are lighter in dry weather than in rain or snowfall; cleaner in the countryside than in industrial towns.

... And since, when freezing through, a gleiss deposits such material traces, it is possible, according to these traces, to recreate on a micro-scopic level its exact route throughout the entire underground world. Were the appropriate equipment and budget readily available, it would be possible to compile a complete map of the Ways of the Mammoths.

Wake up. A door had slammed, an angry tchinovnik had shouted.

'But does he know at all that I'm sitting here waiting…?!'

'He knows, he knows, there's no possibility he doesn't know.'

'I had to excuse myself from work in order to loiter outside his door for hours in vain, I'm losing money, you'll return it to me, huh?'

'Don't talk money, take my advice, don't talk money.'

Open the pocket watch.

'I have an appointment, I can't wait until dusk –'

'These are the office hours!' Mikhail raised his stubby finger. 'A de-partment's not a brothel, the client's not the boss!'

Four o'clock was fast approaching.

'At least give me paper and a pen and ink.'

Lay the stiff card on the knee. Mikhail leant again over his work. Official worm, client worm, all living in one vast body, feeding the one vast body.

The workmen hammered away till the portrait of His Imperial Exaltedness Nikolay the Second Aleksandrovitch leapt up and down on the wall. Outside the window, a luminous cloud hung over Christ the Saviour Sobor, a misty ice cap covered the tungetitum cupolas, now the colour of fog. Indecent words must have been muttered in fury neath the breath, since Mikhail cast a sideways glance once or twice from over his inkwell and stamps. *A state and yet no state! Power and yet no power! Freedom and yet no freedom!*

How to solve it, dammit? how to cut through the diabolical knot?

Having adjusted the bandage on the hand, dip the pen into the inkwell.

Apoliteia, or the Un-State

In what way can that which does not exist govern that which exists?

I ask myself this question as a subject of governments manifested in matter, an individual engulfed by the visible, tangible State omnipresent through its hundreds of thousands of functionaries.

What is the State? The State is the power structure of nations, by means of which some people govern other people. Furthermore, the number of rulers is small, and the number of governed large, so that in visual terms the structure is shaped like a pyramid or an upturned tree.

The structure always appears the same whether we take a monarchy answerable only to God like the Russian Empire, for example, or a universal democracy like the United States of America. In this structure we always find ourselves dependent on the will of a personage seated higher up, unless we be the emperor himself or the president.

For the State is by definition a system of oppression and bondage and the subordination of man to man. And should anyone claim that the will of an electorate expressed once every few years in a democracy makes any difference, then I shall answer that it makes no difference at all to the structure: the question is not who rules, but the fact that he rules.

The Polish state has not existed for a century and a half – three other states have shackled us in their structures of power. Not only do we suffer oppression, this is also the oppression of a different culture, alien to us spiritually and morally. They say that we forfeited our State precisely because of the squabbling and anarchic customs of our ancient nobility. I prefer to see in this rather a symptom of the trait I regard as Poles' positive side: a symptom of the desire to liberate man from the State. Indeed, it is hard to point to a nation equally in the thrall of this idea.

How may man be liberated from the State? Neither democracy (as stated above) nor anarchy opens the way. Why not anarchy? – after all Mikhail Aleksandrovitch Bakunin puts forward very similar postulates. Well, for the reason that describing a creditable utopia on paper is insufficient; it also has to be mobilised and defended in real life. But in the world as it is, a community deprived of the right to own land, whereupon it could live in peace, and possessing no army sufficiently strong to defend it on such land from its neighbours, is bound to fall victim to those neighbours' armies along with all its anarchic ideas, after which it will be incorporated by force into the structures of those foreign States. Therefore, no forms of socialism will bring a solution either, because it's not enough that their designs have been approved for constructing a great socialist State – this would be impossible, even in the ideal Marxist sense, whilst a single non-socialist State remained on Earth, against which the collectives of totally free individuals, liberated from exploitation and falsehood, would have to organise themselves afresh, willingly or unwillingly, into classes, strata and castes.

So here then is the task: how to defend people and land against States without creating one's own State?

The role of state structures and executors of power would have to be filled by the Non-State, the Non-Existing State. Without tchinovniks, commissioners, tax collectors, police superintendents and government ministers, without councillors and judges. Collective decisions, political choices, economic reforms and internal laws would come about not because this or that government – elected in this or that way, powerful because of this or that compulsion – had imposed them, but because they couldn't not come about. In the kingdom of nature there is no State: a caterpillar transforms into a butterfly not because some insect king or parliament has decreed the transformation and forced it to happen, but because it is the natural solution, the necessary and only possible one.

As the world gradually becomes covered by the Ice, so the gap closes between what is possible and what is necessary. The greater the Frost, the lesser the role of tchinovniks and all manner of executors of power. Eventually, the tsar himself in the Winter Palace will understand that he's become entirely superfluous, for he no longer gives any orders that he might not give, and has no freedom of choice to decide between two possibilities: one is always good, the other always bad; he sees in advance this preordained good and evil, thereby ordering only what is necessary (even if he sincerely desires this necessity). It is not the tsar that governs – what governs is the thing non-existent in matter: necessity, that is, Truth.

The State disappears in face of necessity, the State is the earthly substitute for soletruth and has no right to exist in the Ice.

The future of this world is apoliteia, where man is not subordinate to the will of another man, but directly to History, and where that which does not exist governs that which exists.

Four fifty-three. Fold the manuscript into eight and tuck it into a pocket of the frock coat. Snatch from Mikhail's desk the bumaga extending the right to stay in the Governorate General of Irkutsk, prepared and waiting for its stamp, and knock on the door to the Commissioner's office; then enter at once without waiting for the summons.

'What?!' roared Schembuch.

'This!' wave the bumaga.

'Yeroslavsky! Out!'

'You will stamp it!'

'Yeroslavsky!! Get lost!'

'The stamp!'

'Well, get on with it then! Now out, out, out!!'

Retreat back into the secretariat, politely closing the door.

'You heard?'

Mikhail pressed down gently on the enormous stamp and added his initials.

'God will punish you,' he whispered, almost with tears in his eyes.

Run down the stairs of the delegation of Winter and Customs House, overtaking dozens of tchinovniks likewise hurrying towards the exit, lost almost in the clerical throng. And acknowledge in spirit – that Mikhail was right: it was a type of sacrilege.

Miss Jelena Muklanowicz's train was due to leave the Muravyoff Station at six o'clock sharp. Gendarmes accompanied by Cossacks were checking tickets, not allowing anyone onto the platform apart from the travellers; the kopeck platform tickets counted for nothing. Observe even more men under arms than remembered from previous visits to the station. Every so often, from the space in front of the ticket windows, not far from the daubed fresco of the mammoth, some poor creature came running, hurriedly muffling his face; every so often, the gendarmes dragged there the next victim, stripping him on the way of scarf and frostglazes. Encamped along the opposite wall, the vendors of Irkutsk curiosities watched with downcast expressions, touting for customers as if with less enthusiasm than usual. Had Schultz devised some new form of repression? Or maybe the police had received a tip-off about Yapontchiks or Leninist communists or other terrorists? Shtchekelnikoff was ostentatiously admiring the rainbow architecture of the station-hall roof, whistling under his breath. Who gives a fig about them?

As those gathered to see Jelena off could not enter the platform, let alone the carriage, everyone had stopped here in the hall. In the moment of approach, Miss Muklanowicz was exchanging a few quiet words in private with Porfiry Pocięgło. Mademoiselle Filipov, leaning in a rather unseemly fashion against the wall below the mammoth, was eying them with a suspicious mien; she had removed her frostglazes and was toying with them mechanically, so that her eyes and puckered brow were clearly visible. The devushka's breath escaped through her scarf in short misty bursts.

Greet her hastily.

'Ooph, I was afraid I wouldn't make it, damned bureaucracy, *pardon pour le mot*. Has Nikola not come? No doubt he's forgotten. Where's Aunt Urszula?'

'Already in the compartment with the luggage. Have you spoken to her lately?'

'Mm-hmm, I don't recall –'

'To Jelena!'

'But what's the matter?'

Mademoiselle Christine stared intently, fixing her solemn gaze for a long time without blinking; children are able to stare like this, as are young women in that state of amazement-cum-terror-cum-disillusionment when their eyes grow large and rounded, and a lip trembles, and a little vein throbs rapidly on their neck.

'How can you play so with someone's heart?' she accused, exhaling. 'You cruel brutes are well-matched! You're as bad as each other!'

'But what –'

'After all – why's she going? Terminally ill! And you!' She choked and put the frostoglazes back on. 'Is this how you arranged things, or what?'

'For God's sake, Christine, what are you –'

'Better not contradict me, sir!' She stamped her foot. 'Jelena told me how between you, you disposed of her like – like – like a package of shares!'

'But... Porfiry... Has she...'

Mademoiselle Christine suddenly seized the arm and pulled it towards her, towards the mammoth wall, standing on tip-toes and brushing fur shapka against fur shapka.

'I shall whisk away Mr Pocięgło, give you time, and you shall talk to her!'

She gave no pause for response; rushed up to them immediately, seized Pocięgło by the elbow and hauled him towards the indigenous stalls whilst he glanced around baffled. Miss Muklanowicz watched them go with a look of astonishment – she too had removed her frostoglazes.

Also remove the spectacles. Bow in greeting.

'Benedykt, sir!'

'Jelena!'

That same smile, the smile still familiar after all from the Trans-Siberian Express.

She nodded, intertwining her hands under her breasts.

'And so.'

'Yes.' Adjust the gloves. 'Now it really is the end of our journey.'

She allowed the silence to drain away in drips of several seconds.

'She worries about me,' she said after a long pause, glancing at the American. 'Unnecessarily.'

'Mm-hmm, there's always danger of some kind. What if Piłsudski sees fit to blow up the Northern Cold Line again?'

'Surely they won't derail a passenger train carrying innocent souls?'

'True, under the Ice there's less likelihood of an accident overturning a strategic plan,' mutter in reply. 'Yet I well remember the number of times in the Trans-Siberian Express when I escaped death by a hair's breadth: a little chance event, a coincidence, a split second here, a split second there – and I'd no longer be alive. Nor you either.'

She turned her eyes from Pocięgło and Mademoiselle Filipov.

'That's how you remember it?' she was astonished. 'As little chance events?'

'And you – how?'

She hesitated.

'Well, you said yourself that no truth exists about the past...'

Raise an eyebrow.

'I said that?'

'Did you?'

'Did we travel together at all on the Trans-Siberian Express?'

A slight impish smile began to quiver on Miss Muklanowicz's lips.

'Did we?'

'Was there a bomb attack?'

'Was there?'

'Were there murders and investigations and secret agents and a battle under a gleiss –'

'Were there?'

'How do I know you, miss?'

'How do you know me, sir?'

Heave a sigh.

'You know, but if we agree on such memories, this is certainly how they'll freeze.'

'Better then not to agree.' She released a long shadow in her breath mist. 'Don't tell me what you remember.' She winked mischievously. 'Let it remain thus – melted, half-true. All right?'

Understand only then. Not even that shadow or the umbriance dancing behind Miss Muklanowicz's back prompted the realisation – but the shine in her eye and her head held high, the devushka's defiant pose like in that former moment, in that icon of memory, as she stretched out her arm and, half-turning towards the darkness outside the compartment window, ordered the light to be switched off, the fraudster-murderess.

'You went to the Arkadiya in order to demurch.'

She did not reply.

'So that's why Christine is in such a state of nerves!' laugh hesitantly. 'Yet making such a tragedy of it!'

'I wanted to try it for the last time.' She lowered her eyes. 'Before I freeze forever.'

'Really, you should have told me. Or Doctor Tesla, he surely wouldn't have begrudged you a small hand pump, Auntie need know nothing…'

'Ye-es.'

Something here doesn't fit, a hidden parameter is skewing the equation, the right side of character doesn't equate to the left…

And again, revelation comes too late: not as the crowning of a sequence of logical inferences, but through sudden association with the words of Mijnheer Iertheim. *They say that under the Ice, such diseases come to a halt. But also, no one here has ever been cured of ailments acquired aforehand. I've been thinking of going to that sanatorium up north…*

'That is…,' begin to stutter, struck by this knowledge as though by a stray bullet. 'Jelena, miss – I of course – oh Jesus, that was not what I meant – does Christine think you want to commit suicide?!'

She shrugged her shoulders.

'They're small doses, no? A person immediately freezes back again. How far can the disease advance, one day, two days?'

Smack the head with the fist.

'Fool, fool, fool! I wasn't thinking at all! You have to believe me, miss!'

'But Benedykt, it's nothing to speak of.'

Bite the tongue.

Jelena Muklanowicz took a deeper breath, adjusting the scarf over her grey squirrel coat.

'And what will you do now?'

'You already know,' reply grimly. 'I have to rescue father.'

'But what will you do with your own life?'

'Who can plan his own self!'

'But – were it not for this affair with your pater, what would you do?'

'Bah! I'd probably go on moaning to the Warsaw shylocks to give me another rouble.'

She shook her head.

'You can't carry on like this, Benedykt, no, no, no.'

'Not everyone is the Incredible Felitka Caoutchouc!' Break into an awkward laugh. 'What of it… It's all one big makeshift. I live in a corner of the house of a kind man, although he's also probably banking on the gratitude of the Son of Frost. I found a job as if I'd found a rouble on the street. I'm awaiting the political verdicts; the prikaz may come any day, either way. Even you, miss…' Sense the irritation rising. 'It's not that I think to myself: I want this and this – and the world's my oyster! I am trying – trying to stick to the truth – but –'

No awareness was there of the arms gesticulating till Jelena grabbed hold of one and checked it in mid-air.

'May you finally let be those machines of Doctor Tesla,' she said softly but decidedly.

Feel a flush of shame spreading from chest to neck; avert the eyes.

She came a half a step closer.

'When will we see each other again?' she whispered. 'Most likely never. This is farewell, Benedykt, genuine farewell. Not "goodbye, till tomorrow", but – last words, last image, last touch.' She squeezed the hand still firmer. 'Do you understand? Such a Jelena Muklanowicz you shall keep within you to the end of your days, khk, and with such a Benedykt Gierosławski I shall remain until death. Everything we might have ever said to one another, everything we might have done for one another, the whole unrealised future – is reduced to this moment, to these few minutes. For you – I am departing and shall be as if I'd died, even if I don't die; this is the end, it is closed, it happened and perished in the past, and won't return – and so – do you see? – there's also no longer the least reason to be ashamed. This is farewell, what is there to be ashamed of at the end of time? There will be no consequences. Everything is permitted.'

'Everything is permitted.'

'Yes.'

Fling the glove clumsily off the other hand. Frost pierced the skin. Raise the palm towards Jelena's face. Before the fingers had time to compose themselves in any kind of gesture, Jelena had already turned and inclined her head and lightly nestled her exposed cheek – also frozen in red blotches, her scarf moist from breath mist – into that cold naked palm.

She released the arm from her grasp. Avert not the eyes, but the stereometry of the soul itself had already framed the moment to fit the soletruth; rest the head to one side, neither staring nor blinking, laying it on the thin, bitterly cold fingers of Jelena Muklanowicz. She slipped her thumb under the muffler, made her way along the moustache, pressed on the lips – until the teeth parted; thus she reached the tongue, the breath, the saliva, the source of warmth escaping from the body in unlichty gasps. Repeat her movements – she opened her mouth, and seized the cold thumb between her little teeth.

Enter now with Jelena – in the fetters of a symmetrical stereometry of lovers – into a type of resonance strung upon gazes, bodies, breaths, upon the warmth and murch flowing between bodies. The Muravyoff Station, the travellers, hawkers, porters, gendarmes and Cossacks, everything excluded from that resonance slipped beyond the bounds of consciousness – they were things as remote and utterly stripped of meaning as the movements of constellations across the sky.

For here – pulse responded to pulse, eye to eye, subcutaneous nerve to subcutaneous nerve, glintz to glintz, unarticulated thought to unarticulated thought, tongue to tongue, blood to blood, warmth to warmth. And indeed, the impression was had that in this way – that is, without words – Jelena was told all those untellable things, and that in this way too – in that resonance of silence – the demurched Jelena was expressing under the Ice all her inexpressibles, all those possible and unrealised Jelena Muklanowiczes and all their fears, longings, shameful thoughts and desires – half-true, half-false – and all their probable but equally non-necessary pasts, amongst them both the childhood of sickly Jelenka-from-a-good-home and the fraudulent youth of the artful tanner's daughter, and a million other stories that equally fit the soletruth of the present moment; all the possible and still untrue

futures, amongst them the one in which Jelena dies swiftly from re-
crudescent consumption, and the one in which she marries Porfiry
Pocięgło, and the one in which Jelena is sentenced for a bestial murder,
and the one in which –

'... to say farewell!'

It snapped.

Squeezing together the eyelids, turn on the heel and march away
from Jelena Muklanowicz, deaf to the cries of Pocięgło, without glancing back until the exit onto the steps outside the station was reached;
release only then the tightly held breath. This is the end, the farewells
have been said, it is closed. It has frozen. Lick the blood off the bitten
thumb, tasting Jelena for the last time. Pull on the glove, don the frostoglazes. Dirt-coloured mists stood on the square and at the outlets of
streets like limestone rockfaces out of which passing equipages had
hewn dark adits in the form of reindeer and sleighs. Rainbows from
frostoglaze streetlamps were spewing onto the front elevations of taller
houses. A morbidly overcast sky was curdling above the City of Ice into
a lumpy mud-coloured pulp. Against this backdrop, the darkness surrounding the skeletal Sibirkhozheto Tower was swelling like an abscess,
a vast puffball, a nest of putrefaction. Red-tinted icicles hung from the
corpses on the high masts. The hands on the thermometric clock stood
at minus forty-eight Celsius, on the chronometer beside it – at five fifty.
She must already be boarding; the train's about to depart. It has frozen,
it has frozen, it has frozen.

'Shtchekelnikoff, hail a sleigh.'

'Best wait for t'other filly.'

'Hail, khhrrr, a sleigh!'

He gave a clap on the back.

'Lost yer heart to one, Mr G, naught to be done: you'll lose it to
others. Like with vodka. Or the murderin' game. First time and no
going back: leaves an 'ole in the heart.' As proof, he walloped his chest
with his square fist. 'Means hunger, Mr G, hunger.'

Cough croakily.

'You have a wife?'

He nodded his brick-shaped nut.

'Wife, not wife, enough she's a woman. Bloke without a woman soon
goes berserk. But woman without a bloke – the devil's work.'

Evidently, not even Tchingis Shtchekelnikoff had been spared the
amatory necessity of the Land of the Gleissen. It doesn't bear thinking
to what vagaries of character a man like Shtchekelnikoff might sink in
Summer.

Porfiry Pocięgło, bowing from afar, departed in his own sleigh.
With a silent gesture, invite Mademoiselle Filipov. The New Arkadiya,

admittedly, is not on the way to Tsvetistaya but also did not involve a detour to the other end of town.

Expect for a moment that Christine, still offended, would refuse; but no.

'A great act of thoughtlessness on my part.' Admit it as soon as the sleigh moved off. 'You are right. I shouldn't have.'

She gave no answer. Impossible to read her expression – under her enormous shapka, under her frostoglazes, under her wound-around scarf.

'You could at least have told me, when I come of a morning to the hotel –'

'I really no longer know what to think of you, sir. It had seemed that you cared for Jelena!'

'I no longer know, khhrrr, what to think of myself.'

'Oo-oo, a buffoon, not a man.'

Stare straight ahead at the driver's fog-hued back and at Shtchekelnikoff.

'This is how you think. This is how you see. *D'accord.*'

She sniffed.

'So now you take offence, please do, see if I care! All for the devil's gratification!' She shuddered. 'Confounded city, confounded gleissen, confounded frost! Khkhhh!'

Stretch out an arm to embrace her, but she thrust it aside.

'It must be hard for you, Christine, and all the more so now; I give you my word I shall visit, and not just for a minute to use the pump, but whenever –'

'I can no longer sleep because of it! They'll kill him in the end, you'll see!'

'What?'

'Do you imagine they've given up, now that we're in Irkutsk? Last month there were two attempts, this month already three. We also had a night-time visitation from a terrorist of the SR Combat Organisation, who, khk, offered us assistance in the name of the Berdyaevans in his party, how terrifying was that.'

'But – Nikola mentioned nothing to me!'

'He knows nothing!' Christine exclaimed. 'And that's how it shall remain, do you understand? Stepan is dealing with the Okhrana and the Cossacks. Better still if Nikola no longer sticks his nose out of the Laboratory. He sees no world beyond his Battle Pump, khhh, and great tungetitor. It's always the same with him.'

'But – who?'

'Martsynians mainly, hired thugs whom they've incited. Governor Schultz locked them up, which calmed things down a bit; but now it's happening again. Stepan calls it: dilettantism. But a week ago they caught students from some imperialist party there with a bomb, khhh, which could have blown up the whole Observatory. But when Nikola appears with this demonstration – I'm afraid to even think. I'd prefer them to believe, khhh, that it's true it's nothing but charlatanry and merely a method for extracting money in order to pay off his debts, and that they would hound him out in disgrace. Because when those cold-iron millionaires, or Pobedonostseff himself, or Schultz even – when after this demonstration, Benedykt, they believe that Nikola really does have the power to drive the gleissen from the tsar's lands... khhh...'

She was breathing heavily, umbriance casting shadows over her scarf. All colours of fog were brimming in her spectacles in kaleidoscopic streams. Was she crying?

'Maybe were I to have a word with him... About acting more cautiously...' But in truth, no clue was had as to how. 'Maybe it would be better to turn directly to the tsar for greater protection...' Well, yes, but in order for the tsar to believe that there was anything to protect, Tesla had first to stage his gleissocidal theatre. A no-win situation. 'Why don't you tell him of these dangers?'

'What for? What's the point? He'd only have more things on his mind and his work would progress more slowly, he'd pay a higher price in nerves – Nikola is no longer a spring chicken, Benedykt – and won't change his plans anyway. Now that he's set his heart on this black physics, khk, everything's already – already frozen, "it has frozen", as they say here. Don't even bother, sir, no one can persuade the great Nikola Tesla if he's reasoned the thing out in a different way.' Mademoiselle Christine turned her head and drawing a gloved hand out of her muff, aimed it accusingly. 'You, sir! Are just the same! Did you ever take someone's good advice only because you trusted the person giving it? And not because of your own rational calculations? Well?'

'Khhrrr. You say that as if it were a good thing. Meaning, such credulity.'

'Credulity? Credulity?' She pressed her hand into the fur on her breast. 'Do you have any friends at all, sir? And what about in your family – well yes, your father, mother – khhrrr – how can you live like this – without any authority figures?'

Shrug the shoulders, a gesture certainly not easily visible beneath the thick shuba.

'But what sort of man seeks an authority figure? Eh? What sort of man needs an authority for anything in life?'

'Doesn't know how to behave – better to rely on someone wiser.'

'And this wiser man became wiser not through being guided by his own reason, but through similarly relying on the reasoning of others?

Mm-hmm? And how may a man recognise who possesses wisdom when he possesses it not himself?'

'You have to trust generally accepted opinions, khhh, after all there are people universally recognised as authorities.'

'There are. But again: how will you distinguish a genuine authority from a false authority, that is, true wisdom from the semblance of wisdom? If you are able to do that – why do you also need authority figures?'

Mademoiselle Christine was coughing quietly. For a long time, she adjusted her frostoglazes, tightly concealing her whole face behind her glove. See into the interlocutor's thought in a rare surge of certainty as to soletruth: Miss Filipov had returned, no mistake, to that conversation in the Express in the midst of the taiga, to the interrogations about the shame of religious belief to which she'd been unintentionally subjected along with Jelena. Does she still think she's being ridiculed? Does she feel resentful? Bear a grudge?

'Are there not matters where reason proves helpless?' she said at last, barely audible above the jingle of sleighbells and grating of ice under the runners. 'Matters of good and evil, of ethical importance? These things you cannot calculate.'

'Undoubtedly.'

'What then? Unable to help yourself by the power of your own reason, you surrender altogether and become – what? a nihilist? an amoral beast?'

'But now you're talking pure faith, religion!'

'So you really don't believe in God!'

In the vista of Amurskaya Street, above the night-tinged stacks of fog, the great cupolas of Christ the Saviour Sobor shone in a blaze of white fire. The gaze sped hastily from them, prompted by animal instinct as when the hand recoils from a flame. *How can a man soil his spirit with such barter and hocus-pocus? It's all false! All lies!*

'In God – I believe. On the other hand, I don't much believe in what people say about God.'

On the Brotherhood of War against the Apocalypse

Drawn by eight reindeer, in a tall coldiron sleigh on spidery runners, in black fur coat and sable shapka, in frostoglaze goggles covering his eyes and half his face and brimming with sky and snow and Sun and every colour of the rainbow, in a flickering penumbra, leaving tarry afterimages in his wake, with his white hand on the handle of the murch battery, in a cloud of carbon vapour – Nikola Tesla rides over the congealed ice of the Angara to the site of gleissocide, to the foot of the three-storey teslectric machine.

Stand on the right bank of the Angara, on the square beneath the statue of Emperor Aleksandr the Third, where a scenic boulevard ran along the embankment, once offering a beautiful view over Konny Island, the wide Angara itself, bridges and left-bank Irkutsk; today wind and snowstorm had shut off the more distant vistas, the gaze reaching little beyond the gleiss freezing its way off the island onto the ice, and beyond the construction taller than the gleiss and erected above it at the end of the promontory. Tesla had chosen this particular gleiss and this particular spot because firstly, although situated in the city centre, it was at a safe distance from houses and streets; and secondly because it gave onlookers the opportunity to observe the whole experiment, and this after all was what it was primarily about.

On the statue square, despite the frost and blizzard, a substantial crowd had gathered. Squeeze to the very front with the aid of Shtchekelnikoff, to the edge of the ice-encrusted escarpment. Some spectators had telescopes and binoculars; the idea of bringing these had not occurred. On the other hand, everyone was wearing large frostoglaze spectacles, either close-fitting goggles like those of the Serbian inventor or flat glasses similarly covering the eyes and half the visage. As Tesla rode across the Angara in his sleigh, hired as if from some wintry oriental fairy tale, a hundred reflective rainbow kaleidoscopes were turned towards him, following his every move and slightest gesture. He had not shown himself previously at all; today he was stepping onto Irkutsk's public stage, it was his debut in the City of Ice. Magnesium powder flashed under the small tents stationed at intervals on platforms set up for the cameras of the Baikal press. Ladies swathed in white, in furs, capes, pelisses, under snow-sprinkled hoods, leaned out of sleighs parked along the street. Men hoisted toddlers tightly swaddled in muddy sheepskins onto their shoulders; the children stared through smaller, child-sized frostoglazes. In the crackling frost, very little gossip and very little conversation were exchanged, yet that characteristic rustle of gasps, stirs and sighs could be heard rippling through the crowd in waves. Unlichty clouds of breath mist rose above the throng. It was Sunday, the ninth of November, an hour after the morning church services. Doctor Tesla was launching his War on Winter.

First of all, before even alighting from his sleigh, he pressed on the battery handle. He must have been exceptionally strongly demurched; such an effect had never been witnessed before – standing up, he did not take his hand off the battery and the murch suddenly discharged into him in one fell swoop, the pure flow passing from his arm through his torso, head and all his limbs, spilling over his black fur coat, upon which every single hair stood on end needle-like and fired a minor telestric lightning-bolt: Nikola Tesla disembarked from the sleigh like a live smoking torch of unlicht, lighting every step with dazzling glintzen. In his other white palm he held a cane made of a special coldiron alloy and crowned by a knob of twenty-four-carat tungetitum. This knob now shone more brightly than the cupolas of Christ the Saviour Sobor, as pulsating seven-coloured rainbows streamed uninterruptedly off the coldiron. The reindeer harnessed to the sleigh took fright and sprang back as far as they could from the strange man. Shafts of black lightning lasting seconds leaped from man to sleigh, to the driver, to the animals, to the Battle Pump, to the gleiss itself. Tesla walked erect under his tall sable shapka, taking long strides, without leaning on the cane, wielding it more like a sceptre. In the frostoglazes, white and black swam around him like bubbles of underwater gases. The snow had the colour of Tesla, the ice had the colour of Tesla, the gleiss had the colour of Tesla.

… The inventor ascended the stairs of the Battle Pump. Glintzen flared on its coldiron components, a million antishadow sparks.

Nikola raised his hand and began to wave the cane. The crowd cheered. Magnesium powder flashed.

'Whore's sores…!' sighed Shtchekelnikoff, clearly rapt as well.

On the open platform at the summit of the Battle Pump stood an iron chair mounted behind a skeletal desk equipped with half a dozen levers and dials. Tesla sat down in the chair and pulled the first lever. The muffled rattle of an oil-fired engine reached as far as the Aleksandr the Third monument; dark smoke began to emerge from inside the Pump, snatched away at once, however, by the wind off the Angara.

Tesla pulled the second lever. A coldiron arm ending in a massive claw-like rammer dropped onto the back of the gleiss, penetrating the glacius by a good half-arshin. Along this arm, like veins wreathed around the skeleton of an anatomical model, writhed thick cables wrapped in murch insulation.

Tesla pulled the third lever. A piercing whistle blared as from a radio receiver tuned beyond the range of a station's frequency, only ten times shriller, and so loud that people pressed their hands to ears and bowed their heads in a single reflex. The whistle gradually subsided, however – the Pump was working to a regular rhythm – Nikola controlling its operation with his hands on the gears – small teslectrical discharges leaping over Pump and man and gleiss; they remained motionless, only a dense umbriance danced around them as off a cryocarbon stove. Will it collapse or not collapse, will he break it or not break it, will he unfreeze it or not unfreeze it – people stood and stared, clenching their fists and biting their lips, as they might stare at wrestlers petrified in an immobile yet fatal hold, all tension concentrated in motionlessness and expectation. Waiting for the first signal, first sign of weakness, first blood.

'But you know very well, sir.'

'Mm-hmm?'

'He wouldn't have appeared publicly had he not been totally sure.' The Polish-speaking man, short of stature, declined to even turn his head, eyes fixed likewise intently on the Pump, Tesla and the gleiss. He stood close by and his words, uttered in an undertone with strong eastern lilt, were clearly audible. His countenance was tightly concealed by malakhay hat, frostoglazes and scarf; the copious beard-growth and prominent nose could only be imagined. 'Tell him that when it comes to a question of life and death, we will always provide a safe escape route out of the Empire. And for his krasavitsa, the American, and for you too, Mr Gierosławski.'

'Khrrr. And there's some kind of bargain in this?'

'That Mr Tesla won't be testing his strength against the Ice in the lands of Russia herself, that is, beyond the Dnieper. To the west of the Dnieper – be our guest. And here too, in Siberia – he has a free hand. But not in old European Russia. And that he won't hand over his arsenals to anyone else, until the time comes. Besides, you know better than any.'

'You think he'll get cold feet.'

'The tsar would have to come down here himself in order to protect him with his person. But this too would certainly not deter Sibirkhozheto. There, do you see? – in that sleigh behind the monument, if I'm not mistaken, Pobedonostseff's Angel has deigned to come in person. After today's demonstration – let Mr Tesla be a fearless madman, but that's not the point; it's enough that he'll give them a fright. When the opportunity arises, you will make him see reason. Then you will give the sign from your window overlooking the river: leave a lighted lamp burning after dusk, replacing it at midnight with a blackwicke. On the following day, someone will report to you. The machines and any documentation must be destroyed. Repeat.'

'To the Dnieper, no farther, destroy the machines and notes, lamp in the window onto the Angara till midnight, from midnight a blackwicke.'

'Good. If they get him earlier, they'll destroy everything themselves. If anything should… You they may not suspect.'

'Why not? He is my friend.'

'So we've heard, so we've heard. But you are now a doctrinaire Lyednyak, not so? You've had your fill of tsardom's ever more powerful state, huh? Well, this can also be a way. To noble hearts, a country's misfortune and humiliation are the source of patriotism; character is forged in misfortune. In this we see the peculiar nature of Muscovite bondage: it's not enough for them to flog with the knout, they also have to make the flogged man kiss the instrument of his torture; it's not enough to fell an adversary, they also have to aim a blow at the conquered man's face. And he who does not accept the blow in all humility, is indeed unworthy of a better fate. Carry on in this vein, my son; they will see truth when it has frozen.'

'Wait! My interest is not in escaping – I am going to my father – wait! – it was you after all who sent him onto the Ways of the Mammoths – only give me –'

But he had already retreated amongst the people, melted into the crowd. Spin around and survey the throng to no avail; he was half a head shorter and had vanished without trace.

Curse under the moustache. Were they really so afraid of agents of the Okhrana? Were they really keeping constant track of the movements? Of late, Tchingis had mentioned nothing of the kind, but – who can tell whether he saw someone or saw him not; now too, throughout that whole conversation, he hadn't even flinched.

'Did you see him, Shtchekelnikoff?'

'A chum of yours? Better get out of here, Mr G, anyone in the crush can shove in the knife, no way to defend ourselves. Ju-u-st you-ou-ou wait, you twisted crapface, a-trampling on folks, a-forcing yer way through, half-cocked son of a bitch!' and he began to scuffle with some brazen petty thief.

Grit the teeth. They must have been keeping track, there's no other explanation; the death of the thug with the iron cosh hadn't put them off in the least. Impossible it was to resist looking behind as well as to the sides, and overhead at the townhouses and along the windows. But in the frostoglaze panes all you'll see is milk-jelly fog.

You are now a doctrinaire Lyednyak, not so? Well, thank God, probably not after all! That day, despite it being Sunday, the usual daily visit had been paid to the New Arkadiya to pump off the murch constantly flowing afresh into the brain.

But precisely such reactions had been calculated in, when the *Apoliteia* was handed over to Editor Wólkiewicz for publication.

It cannot be said he was enchanted by the text. He read it, pulled an astonished face, pulled a sour face, pulled an amused face. Poured himself a dram of herb liqueur, knocked it back and flicked up the corners of his moustache.

'And you wish, sir, that I should take – this metaphysical manifesto, and do what?'

'Print it at once in *The Free Pole*.'

'And "at once" too!' the old editor growled in angry irritation.

'That's right. And the most important thing – do you see, sir, on the final page, at the bottom?'

'"Benedykt Filipovitch Gierosławski". Like that, including patronymic? But!' Only then did Mr Wólka-Wólkiewicz grasp the matter in its entirety. 'I'm not releasing it under your own name! Don't you know these things always reach the Okhrana and the Third Department? All branches of the Empire's political police study these little news-sheets of ours assiduously!'

'That's precisely my idea.'

'Your idea!' He began to smoke a fat cigarette hand-rolled from Manchurian tobacco. 'It's not as if you write anything specific here… But this is foolish bravado, you're asking for trouble! They'll come after you, ask by what means your article found its way into an anti-state publication – and what shall you say?' He sucked in smoke till his cheeks swelled. 'Shall you recant?'

'No. I shan't hand you in, if that's what's gnawing at you. If the Okhrana had a prikaz to find fault with you, they'd have found fault long ago, after all everyone here knows you well.' Tug at the beard, striving to put into words for Wólka-Wólkiewicz truth that has not yet fully frozen. 'You see, I have to swiftly earn myself some political enemies.'

He finished smoking his cigarette in silence – which took a few minutes, but once fallen silent, he said nothing more; merely pulled eloquent faces: of fear, helplessness, full of horror, even angrier still.

Yet print it he did, and now, if you please, appear the yapontchiks, for this is the truth they see and none other; soon, no doubt, will come the summons to the Ministry of Internal Affairs, or maybe the tchinovniks themselves will take the trouble to pay another home visit –

The crowd seethed noisily; magnesium powder hissed. No one was clapping – everyone wore thick padded gloves – instead there began a loud stamping of feet. Return the gaze to the gleiss pierced by the fang of the Battle Pump. Doctor Tesla stood on the platform, white left palm on one of the levers, white right palm holding up the blazing cane, umbriance fuming off his black fur shapka – whilst the gleiss before him sweats milky blood. Streams of mist – maybe still liquid, maybe already dense gas – drifted gradually over ice, icicles, frost-strings, monumental stalagmites. Guess that this is the helium escaping from the glacius. 'Devilspunk,' Shtchekelnikoff concluded with satisfaction. The crowd cheered. Man had defeated monster. (Man, that is, man's machines.)

What kind of blackchemical process, however, had taken place within the gleiss? What changed after the teslectric flow had been pumped out?

Back at the Observatory, after returning from the Angara, Tesla expounded his theory (because of course he had a theory) on this topic.

'And so, Messieurs, there exist certain states of Frost for whose maintenance not only low temperature is necessary, but also a full charge of murch.'

Such states were familiar enough. Bite the tongue for the umpteenth time. To tell or not to tell Nikola about the cryophysical experiments of Doctor Wolfke and other scientists in Zimny Nikolayevsk? Eventually, the majority of these discoveries will appear in miscellaneous physics periodicals; Tesla surely follows these researches, he can draw his own conclusions...

Before the mind was made up, Tesla had gone out to the tungetitor.

Which worked out well, since Sasha Pavlitch remained alone in the laboratory.

Greet him.

'No Engineer Jago?'

'Doctor Tesla set him to work on the tungetitor, the dress rehearsal's been going on since morning, do you hear? That rumble.'

'Ah, indeed. And Professor Yurkat?'

'He'll be down soon. Did you want something from the professor?'

'The truth is...' Reach into the inside pocket of the jacket, take out the egg-shaped bundle. Sasha watched inquiringly. Unwind the handkerchief to reveal the rotten potato. Point to the cages of rats and mice. 'I have a request to you, an idea in fact for an experiment. Could you separate out a few specimens and somehow give them this to eat? And only then demurch them? I would like to compare results.'

Pavlitch put on his pince-nez (which aged him by a good ten years) and bent over the potato.

'What is it?'

'A potato.'

'I can see that.'

'A potato, and yet not a potato. That is, a black-biological variety.'

'Aha!'

'But,' place a finger on the lips, 'quiet, shush, I can't admit where I got it. I'm interested only in –'

Pavlitch picked up the potato with laboratory tongs.

'What's in it? Tungetitum?'

'That's what I think. It grew in tungetitum soil. Unless the very presence of this element in the earth somehow alters the structure of the plant.'

He laid the potato on a metal tray.

'Will you allow me to slice off a sample and examine it under the microscope?'

'So long as there's enough for the rats.'

'Well, it's certainly too little to feed several regularly.' Sasha sat on the high stool and pensively wiped his pince-nez. 'You know, Venyedikt Filipovitch, there have already been a few cases.'

'What cases?'

'Of tungetitum poisoning. In people. An acquaintance, who works here at the Holy Trinity Hospital, mentioned to me serial poisonings, though none at all in Zimny Nikolayevsk. Then it transpired they were most likely Fyodorovians.'

'Holy Mother of God, another sect…?'

'No, no. Well, unless we substitute religion for science – then they're a sect. Mm-hmm. They apparently died of it.' He massaged his neck. 'I'll call on him today, find out the details, maybe he'll say something useful.' He glanced at the clock. 'Someone must have kept the professor; all sorts have been coming since morning because of the demonstration… Forgive me, sir.'

He went out.

Sit down at a bench close to the prototype of the Black Lamp of the Death Ray. The mechanism had recently been dismantled; the smooth interior of the open sphere reflected light like polished diamond. Again, the palms were itching, and it was also itching beneath the skull. Curse in resignation and reach for the chamois gloves purchased ereyesterday in Rappaport's, when a trip had been made to the Fashion House to question Mrs Gwóźdź about further details of father's secret biography. But after pulling on the gloves, the itching did not cease. Begin playing with a tin of butterfly screws. The animals in the cages squeaked nervously. A rhythmic rumble could indeed be heard, causing rings to form on the liquids in measuring flasks, and glass and metal to resonate. Open the pocket watch. WoobooMMM! – twenty-seven seconds – WoobooMMM! – twenty-seven seconds – WoobooMMM! Nikola Tesla is rousing waves on the Ways of the Mammoths. It'll be interesting to see if the shamans complain to Pobedonostseff. Start to chuckle. The tin slipped from the hands and the screws scattered on the floor. Bend to pick them up – and freeze just like that, with the fingers outspread, in that strange hunch-backed pose. What was it they'd said about sortilege in the Land of the Gleissen? About card games? No one here has ever rolled five sixes and got a royal flush. The screws lay in regular columns as if arranged by a ruler.

Dig out from the pocketbook a half-rouble coin and begin to toss it on the benchtop with the clumsy gloved fingers. Double-headed eagle, eagle-head, eagle-head, EEEEEEEE, after eight throws tails appear, but – but! WoobooMMM! Gather up the screws. Eight eagle-heads in a row

– this is not regularity, it's the fluctuation of chaos, the crest of a wave of entropy. The skin on the hands burned as if doused in acid.

Sasha Pavlitch appeared with Professor Yurkat; Engineer Jago came in immediately after. Ask the professor to step aside.

'I have a question. Do you remember, professor, what you told me in the cellar? About watercourses under the ice and the permafrost?'

'What was it I said?'

'The problem is the following. The rivers have frozen, yes? Frozen to the bottom. The majority at any rate. Here, in the Baikal watershed. Am I right? And the one river flowing out of Baikal has certainly frozen to the bottom: the Angara. But you assert, sir, that the permafrost has a constant temperature, those few degrees below Celsius, and that irrespective of the isotherm on the surface, watercourses often flow in the earth under pressure, so that a man digging a well without due care could be drenched in the twinkling of an eye and freeze in pure ice – yes?'

Kliment Rufinovitch blinked; murch had collected in the creases of his skin.

'We-e-ll, roughly speaking –'

'Therefore, were I to find an up-to-date hydrographic map of the Baikal Kray, I would see a thousand living underground runoffs bringing water into the lake. Am I right?'

'A thousand? Hydrographic maps –'

'I know. But – that's how it ought to look, true? So perhaps you can solve this paradox for me, professor: where, devil take it, does this whole permafrost runoff from Baikal go if not into the Angara?'

The old man began to puff and blow.

'Meaning, you're suggesting, meaning, that what? – that somehow – that it does not run off?'

'Meaning, I'm suggesting that the hydrology of the permafrost under the Ice is governed by different laws and that these maps would look entirely unlike the hydrography of Summer. I am suggesting that, since the ice on top of the lake does not rise up and the railway line still runs across it, as it has run, then Baikal relinquishes at least the same volume of water via underground rivers.'

'But this makes no sense!' The grizzle-nob adjusted the thick lenses on his nose, took a deeper breath, cleared his throat. 'First and foremost, my dear fellow, the underground hydrology in the lands of the Ice is very scanty. Here, even before the Winter of the Gleissen, during the time of ordinary winters, the permafrost walls up groundwater. Read Middendorff, sir. Had you but seen the taiga in summer, those thousands of versts of sodden ground, swamps, peatbogs, marshes, alases, then you wouldn't say such things. The Yenisey, the Lena, the

Ob or even the Yukon on the far side of the Bering Strait – these are colossal surface rivers versts and versts wide. And yet, judging by the precipitation here, we have almost desert climates. Whilst at the same time – soggy green taiga proliferating across half the continent. Why? Well, because about seventy to eighty per cent of precipitation sinks into unfrozen soil, but here with us it's the reverse: ninety per cent goes into open rivers, travels over the permafrost as if along conduits laid immediately below the topsoil. Understand? Not enough of this water remains in order to develop a proper system of underground watercourses. Moreover, Baikal lies between rocks of very low permeability, of low capillarity and porosity. Don't you think you, sir, that under such pressure, it wouldn't have drained away underground already before?'

'But are you aware, professor, how the rock structure changes after the passage of a gleiss? After multiple passages? The structure of the rock and of these permanently frozen grounds which are normally impervious? Have you seen, sir, how marble edifices foolishly erected above the Ways of the Mammoths come crashing down?'

The grizzled cryogeologist began waving his arms in irritation.

'The Ways of the Mammoths! You can't work like this! First study the thing in depth, then tell me your theories! Whatever are you dreaming of? That the underground wanderings of gleissen somehow soften the rock and frozen-through earth, and because of this an entirely new hydrography of Siberia is unfolding along the Ways of the Mammoths? No doubt also reaching from Baikal upstream, against the runoffs of the whole watershed? Hah!'

Nod the head, whilst continuing to see things completely differently. And so, tungetitum water flows along the Ways of the Mammoths, lifted from the bed of the sacred lake where the dead sleep. And since the natural direction of thrust of fluids and ice is upwards, these watercourses eventually emerge on the surface. Perhaps there are thermal springs here, hot sulphur baths, volcanic valleys giving off geological warmth? Recall mention of such a spa in the bay of Khakusy; there must be other similar places. Oases of black flora and fauna, where not one sole potato but an entire system of vegetation grows up out of the tungetitum soil, drawing tungetitum juices into its tissues; and animals eat this, animals absorb it into their blood, and if some fortunate-or-unfortunate wanderer should stray there... Ye-es.

'What do you know about ice, young man?' Professor Yurkat was perorating in peevish excitement. 'What do you know about water? These be great mysteries of science! Near Oymyakon, for instance, they have a miracle: minus ten degrees Celsius and the river freezes; but then it drops to minus fifty – and splosh, the ice has melted and the current is flowing as smoothly as under a June sun. So explain that, sir, and then set to work on the hydrology of gleissen…!'

Arrive back at number seventeen Tsvetistaya Street before the Wielickis return from church. The valet handed over a letter delivered in the absence by a special messenger. A bad premonition at once seized the imagination. Rip open the envelope with one foot still imprisoned in the bootjack, half the boot already off. As if a bolt of unlicht had shot into the spine. It was an invitation for the second (that is, fifteenth) of November to the palace of Governor General Timofey Makarovitch Schultz-Zimovy on the occasion of the engagement of his daughter Anna to Pavel Nestorovitch Gerushin. Complete with the count's handwritten signature: Monsieur Benedykt Filipovitch Gierosławski *est invité, pas de cadeaux, R.S.V.P.* Well, this was unexpected!

Turn around in the bedroom doorway and call back the servant. Had this messenger also brought a letter for Mr and Mrs Wielicki? The servant affirmed it. So at least appearances will be maintained; they could delude themselves that it really was Lawyer Kuzmentsoff who'd wangled the invitations. Sit down at once to write a note of thanks and confirm the attendance. An errand-boy was just being dispatched when the Wielickis appeared. Announce to them at once the surprise. Wojsław read the invitation and showed it to his wife. The women began squealing with delight and smothering everyone with kisses, whomsoever was at hand. Their joy infected the children, who, not yet divested of their sheepskins, ran riot throughout the whole apartment strewing mud and snow over the polished parquet floors, so that Misha and the cooks had to hunt them down. Not five minutes had elapsed, however, before the mood reversed completely and the ladies began wringing their hands and raising tearful eyes towards Wojsław. Whoever saw such a thing, barely a week's notice, no time to properly prepare, what are we to appear in at the gubernatorial palace! Gowns, new gowns have to be ordered forthwith from the Chinese tailors and fitted at extraordinary speed! Wojsław grumbled something into his beard, clutching at his pocket in a theatrical gesture with his diamond hand. The invitation was to Wojsław and his wife as well as to Marta. 'I'll go bankrupt,' he muttered, 'this obscene fashion will be the ruin of me, so help me God!' (Piotruś in the meantime had climbed onto his back and was pulling at his ears.) The women were no longer listening, busily devising their sumptuous creations. Bah, even planning a new tailcoat for poor Wojsław. 'It won't do otherwise! And Mr Gierosławski – Benedykt too has nothing to wear,' they concluded with satisfaction. 'Tomorrow evening both shall be measured! No ifs and buts!' Wojsław took Piotr Paweł under his arm and retreated into his study. Observe these domestic scenes with the tomcat sat on the knees; it was licking in earnest the new gloves that smelled of leather. It had not even occurred to anyone to inquire why Modest Pavlovitch should have added to the invitation list, at the very last minute, the Wielickis' guest. Somehow it didn't bother them, they didn't perceive it as odd – it fitted them – the equations added up. Listen to them in melancholy amusement.

'You have to let her know, Benedykt, as soon as possible,' Marta Wielicka suddenly recollected.

'Who?'

'Who you intend to go with. The mysterious young lady you've been seeing –'

'She's left.'

'Oh. Who then?'

Get up before sunrise and venture into the dark starless night, driving in the two-horse sleigh through fog that had curdled into limy suspension, in such biting frost that scarf and skin and beard and breath froze together, and the mouth had to be slapped open every so often. The frostoglaze streetlamps shone green, the spines of gleissen awash with summery colours. The sound of the glashatays' drums carried above the City of Ice.

Unlock Nikola Tesla's apartment with his spare key, switch on the light. The New Arkadiya was still asleep. The intention was to go first to his study and demurch, but from behind the connecting door came sounds of movement and French words uttered in a rippling voice. Pause. Why not? It would give her pleasure. After all, she'd been promised. Knock vigorously, once, twice.

Mademoiselle Filipov opened the door, already dressed in a morning skirt of light crêpe de Chine, in a long gilet over pleated chemisette, her golden braids interwoven, coffee cup in hand. At the breakfast table sat old Stepan. Greet him wordlessly through the door.

'Christine, miss, may I for a moment?'

She stepped over the threshold, pulled the door to. Brushed the lumps of snow off the fur coat with her left hand. Remove the shapka and spectacles. Warm air swelled in the larynx; cough, blow the nose. She waited, sipping coffee, watching curiously from under her lashes.

'I fall at your feet, Christine, at your feet. Khhrrr. Have you heard about the engagement party for His Excellency's daughter? It would do you good to take a break from your worries, from the Stepans and Cossacks and police superintendents; you're always the first to dance, I remember well. Therefore,' sweeping the shapka before the knees, 'if Nikola has no objection, I wanted to invite you... What?'

She smiled sweetly until dimples appeared on her chubby cheeks.

'Oh, with pleasure! So long as you swear, Benedykt, that you'll never take any more of this black teslectricity.'

Laugh hesitantly.

'But seriously speaking –'

'Yes or no?' And she reached for the doorknob.

'But –'

'Yes or no?'

Cast the eyes about helplessly.

'I demurched only yesterday, how can I swear a genuine oath, when –'

'Yes or no.'

'I have to bemurch myself in order to be sure! Besides – swearing on the future…!'

'Oh well, that's a pity. So, toss a coin. *Pile ou face?*'

'Why are you doing this, miss?' Feel the irritation mounting.

She continued to smile over the coffee cup pressed to her lips.

'Why am I doing it? There's no edict, sir, stating you have to appear at the governor general's party with me. So why is it a problem? As Benedykt Gierosławski decides, so shall he act.'

'But –'

'But Benedykt Gierosławski is already beginning to understand that he won't be able to act in accordance with his own decision.'

Pull a wry face.

'There are – there are good addictions. Things, actions, connections, to which we have willingly enslaved ourselves. You understand this, miss, you are not Jelena.' Look away at this point, somewhere above and to the side of the devushka, at the stucco ceiling, at the chandelier. 'You understand the necessity… of shame.'

'La, la, la!' she flapped her hand. 'You can hold forth like this, sir, to Jelena. But I am a stupid girl, to me you have to talk straight. Yes or no.'

Shrug the shoulders, slap the thigh with the shapka.

'Yes.'

'*Bien*. When is this engagement?'

'The fifteenth, on Saturday.'

Krshshtook! The dropped cup shattered to pieces.

'And you tell me only now?!'

In Krupp's Cryophysical Laboratory, Doctor Wolfke was entertaining metallurgists from the consortium's industrial division; they were discussing spectrographic charts and various samples of coldiron coolbonds. Sit down to work on the papers, listening in to their conversation, occasionally raising the head. Take off the gloves to better grip the pen; every touch smarted. Thinking: today it's still nothing, but tomorrow, the day after tomorrow, in a week's time – a man will freeze, sooner or later he will freeze. Begin to plan already how to circumvent the promise given to Mademoiselle Filipov. Murch was stinging the palette.

Tungetitum-coloured fog swelled around the Holey Palace; from the heights of the mansard of the Clock Tower, Zimny Nikolayevsk seemed like the caldera of a frost-volcano slowly belching out black vapour from white magma.

As Wolfke and the metallurgists moved away to the far end of the Laboratory to switch on the Roentgen lamp, creep over – as if to the cupboards housing documentation on earlier experiments – to the table where the metallurgists had spread out their cases of metal samples. Slip into the pocket several plates marked as standard low-carbon cool-bonds (the Tomsk numbers one, two and three), and also comparative samples of unchilled-through ore. No one was watching. Transfer them at the first opportunity to the fur coat.

Less trouble was had in acquiring the results of research into these coolbonds, descriptions of their molecular structure and tables of their superconductivity. Simply copy all the information onto separate sheets of paper and then hide them with the samples. Funny: because Krupp's property was not being stolen for the sake of competitors, but with an eye only to personal profit, no feeling was there of being a thief; the deed was somehow pure, justified, the instinct to grow rich of which Mr Wielicki had spoken propelling to subsequent necessities. An animal hunts, man grows rich. Was Krupp made any poorer by it? Soon all this knowledge would be public anyway. Had money been filched from his pocket? No; those billets cost little. The money had yet *to be made*. So, what sort of theft was it? You divide information in half and have not half-and-half information, but two pieces of information equally good. Behold the new mathematics of the economy of knowledge! Combined with that instinct to grow rich, mobilised in the general population, would it not lead swiftly to a world of universal prosperity and well-being in keeping with Wojsław Wielicki's principles of a biblical bourgeoisie? See clearly this inevitability, just as relentlessly obvious as the imminent materialisation of apoliteia.

Moreover, such excitement as now – in practising black physics on the side – had never been felt before, not even when hundreds of roubles were won at blizzarder. Such childlike joy! Understand Nikola Tesla a little better. All great discoverers and inventors suffer from a certain inborn infantilism, they almost 'pray' for it, as Atchukhoff might have said. Refrain with difficulty from grinning at the frostoglaze reflection, from rubbing the hands in satisfaction. (Murch would have shot under the skin in bolts of shadow.)

In order to acquire, however, further black-biological plants to feed Pavlitch's rats, Zeytsoff had to be brought into the plan, since it was impossible to climb up to the cupboard-tops unnoticed and unearth the tungetitum vegetables from the trays whilst people were still at work in the Laboratory. Depart before Iertheim, so as not to arouse suspicion, and wait in the corridor a floor below until Tchingis gives the sign that the Dutchman has left; then return and knock in the agreed fashion. Zeytsoff gave entry. Hasten to the trays without a word so as to complete the job before the brigade of de-icers arrives, and pack eight well-developed plants into a sack concealed neath the shuba, one from each tray, smoothing over the holes left in the soil. Busytchkin will surely notice in the end, but, with God's help, it'll be too late then for any investigation. Slip from the Laboratory, ordering Zeytsoff to stoke the stoves well. He nodded sullenly.

And, yes, it was undoubtedly theft – but perpetrated not for anyone's profit, but in pursuit of a father frozen on the Ways of the Mammoths.

The Spiritus Vodka Stores owned by Chruściński & Sons on Tumanny Prospekt closed their doors long after dusk. Pull up in a sleigh hired outside the Marmeladobahn station and send Shtchekelnikoff to inquire if Mr Izydor Chruściński were on the premises; he was not, but expected after seven to deal with some bookkeeping matters. Announce the intended visit through Tchingis and head to Tesla's Observatory. Glintzen had settled on the fog in graceful arabesques, whilst the tunnel carved out within it by the sleigh drowned in red, blood-tinged rainbows. Slap the mouth and turn to look at Christ the Saviour Sobor. 'Don't you have the impression, Shtchekelnikoff, that the Tchornoye Siyaniye lingers still over the city, yet somehow invisibly, without shedding much unlicht?' 'You reckon?' He peered over his frostoglazes. 'Their work again, damn mongrels, all should be impaled.' 'Who?' 'Them deuced aboriginal sorcerers, who else?' 'Khrrr. Because they influence the Aurora?' 'Well, let's see if they does or doesn't. Impaling never did no harm.'

Open the pocket watch, whilst hurrying across the entrance hall neath the fresco of summer; held against body warmth, the watch performed well. The tailor was booked to come to Tsvetistaya at half-past eight in the evening, since Mr Wielicki could not promise to be home earlier; so there was time.

At the foot of the staircase before the entrance to the Observatory's inner corridors, a dozen or so men had gathered, some carrying their distinctive camera bags; notice amongst them Avksenteyeff. Two hefty Cossacks barred their way. Sneak past to one side before the journalists could get their bearings. Maybe Grigory Grigoryevitch had no time to recognise the man slipping past. It lay in Tesla's nature to keep them waiting for a few hours and then appear with some fantastical announcement to the press. Think, whilst extracting the sack of black-biological vegetables from under the arm: the horses have bolted. No one now drives this troika, and certainly not Nikola, and not Christine, whatever she imagines. But maybe the yapontchiks' proposal should be put to her; maybe things really are reaching a point where saving the lives of the inventor and Mademoiselle Filipov will be all that matters. Who knows if it wouldn't also save father's life, were Nikola to mobilise already this winter his Murch Hammer for smashing the Ice on the Ways of the Mammoths. Of the two evils, preserving the Ice in Siberia and Thaw in Europe would seem to be the safer scenario. In other words, the missive had prophesied well: THAW TO THE DNIEPER – PETERSBURG MOSCOW KIEFF CRIMEA NO – JAPAN YES – RUSSIA UNDER THE ICE. DEFEND THE GLEISSEN! Although, admittedly, word had been given to Mr Pocięgło promising something totally contrary…

Sasha Pavlitch together with Engineer Jago and another of Tesla's assistants were grappling with the great tungetitum mirror. After removing the pure tungetitum sheet, Tesla was intending to bombard it with bundles of concentrated light, studying the reflected light or changes in the sheet itself; and then repeat the same experiment with unlicht.

'He spent half the day pumping back and forth,' said Sasha, heaving a sigh, 'and then suddenly he feels like studying the properties of unlicht. He speaks of Maxwell, Einstein, some Planck and Bohr, talks to himself about rays of negative probability, all of it interspersed with Goethe. Ooph! You know him better than I, don't you, Gospodin Gierosławski? What can it mean?'

'He's devised new experiments, it's a longstanding complaint of his to leap like this from idea to idea. Especially now, when he's demurched, he's easily distracted.'

'No, no.' Pavlitch glanced at Engineer Jago and pointed to a corner behind the rat cages. Follow him there, shedding the fur coat on the way and removing the shapka. 'Venyedikt Filipovitch, this morning, it wasn't yet nine, a high-ranking tchinovnik from the governor general's chancellery came to us here in our laboratory on the personal instructions of Count Schultz, with a military escort, with Cossacks; then they interrogated us, each of us separately –'

'This tchinovnik. Lean of body? Fair hair? Rotten teeth?'

'Yes, well yes.'

'What was his name? Not Uriah?'

'You know him?'

'He didn't introduce himself.' Hand Pavlitch the sack; he peeked inside and hid it under a bench. Remove the frostoglazes; and the contours and colours of people and objects froze in their places. 'And what did he want from you?'

'He spoke for long time with Tesla, they went out into the courtyard to inspect the tungetitor prototype.'

Prick up the ears: the Murch Hammer was silent.

'And?'

'And he said he'd organise living quarters for us all here, that is, here, in the Observatory; that the governor general is bringing the whole property under government control on the strength of some emergency law; that it would be better for us not to leave the building without someone from the Okhrana. And furthermore, that both the governor general and His Sovereign Majesty himself are most interested in our work.'

'Mm-hmm.'

'And in the afternoon...'

'Yes?'

Sasha bit his nails.

'Men were prowling around in the unlicht with tungetitum torches and marking out the ground around the Observatory. With them were one blindman, one without a hand, one cripple and one pierced with iron. They were beating drums, as if pulling a gleiss on a leash.'

'They're erecting corpse masts.'

'What's the matter, Venyedikt Filipovitch?'

'It's for your protection.'

'But – from whom?'

Is he really so naïve? Glance into the clear bright eyes under brows resembling clumps of thistle. He blinked not, staring candidly. What age was he – under thirty, still young – but nevertheless older. So why does he look upon the higher-born like upon a guardian sent from heaven? Whence this instant familiarity, whence this tone of tacit understanding? As if he'd known a chap for a long time. And he also agreed willingly to help with the rat experiment with no questions asked.

So, are there indeed friends to be had in the world before they've ever been met, before they've ever been heard of?

'How did you end up here?'

'The professor invited me, I have family near Baikal, so travel often from Tomsk, and I my university job's only from the spring term...'

A poor fellow wrested from his books and scientific abstractions cast suddenly neath the flails of Siberian politics – hardly surprising he's struggling to get the hang of things.

Take a hard look, however. For was not a certain Benedykt Gierosławski dragged by force from his logical abstractions in Warsaw: what clue had he about anything when he boarded the Trans-Siberian Express?

Feel genuine sympathy for the obliging lad, terrified beyond the bounds of his imagination.

'They told you rightly: don't go anywhere outside. It will no longer be safe for you in the city; for anyone close to Doctor Tesla.'

'You go outside.'

'And have you seen the bonebreaker with whom I keep company? Exactly.'

'But – how come? why so? who?'

'And what are you working on here? On the destruction of the Ice. So, do you think the mighty powers in the Baikal Kray will leap for joy when one day their money factory – melts?'

His mouth dropped open.

'They will oppose the emperor?!'

Wave the hand dismissively.

'This year the emperor sees things this way, next year he'll see them differently, and perhaps in the meantime Rasputin's interests will change too, who can tell, logic doesn't stretch that far. But when all hell hits the gleissen, the bird will have flown, so there'll be no more golden eggs, Amen.'

'Which means,' he bit a second finger, 'that the price of coldiron must rise sharply after yesterday's test of the Battle Pump.' He glanced around at Tesla's desk. 'Whoever's first to acquire knowledge of the doctor's discovery shall make a fortune on the Harbin stock exchange.'

Molodyets! Yet Sasha Pavlitch gained on closer acquaintance. Does he also avail himself of the Kotarbiński pump after working hours? No strong enmurchments typical of gleisseniks had been detected on him. A bookworm, hah…!

'Indeed, he will, he will. Unless!' Raise the finger.

'Unless…' He frowned. 'Unless…' A third nail of Sasha's strayed into his mouth. 'Unless the technology of the ice transmutations is discovered in time!'

Pat him on the shoulder.

'Pity you're a biologist, for I'd foresee a great future before you in industry and commerce.'

Sasha smiled under blushing cheeks, which only further emphasised the pockmarks on his skin.

'When little has interested me since school apart from nature and wildlife; as such I have frozen.'

'Just wait, brother, we shall see after Thaw.'

'All right, but time is running out, I have to –'

'Ah! Venyedikt Filipovitch, I inquired about those tungetitum poisonings.'

'And?'

'I remembered correctly; they were Fyodorovians. Which came to light when Mr Fishenstein paid for their treatment. A big figure amongst the Fyodorovians, at any rate he's their chief sponsor.'

'How do you know this?'

'Didn't I say what I work on at the university? On life in the permafrost, on the reanimation of plants and small animals extracted from ice. The Fyodorovians have long been pestering us; sometimes they pay for equipment and expeditions, but then they print the results of our research in their own publications, somehow weirdly distorted. They produce pamphlets that lie around in every bookshop and café here, in every tobacco shop, maybe you've seen, sir, they're free to take. Mr Fishenstein is a rich man.'

'But these poisonings – what more do you know? Fishenstein paid up and they were cured – or what?'

Sasha shook his head.

'Rodion says they all pegged it. At the hospital they did their best to the last, but nothing was to be done. None regained consciousness. A dozen tough blokes, and all of them in the space of one week; a dozen, or maybe more. A tragedy! *Congelationes, thromoangiitis obliterans, embolia et collapsus.*'

'*Il semble étonnant*, but what does it mean? Frostbite and total collapse, yes?'

'Hypothermia, huge problems with circulation, something like much accelerated Buerger's disease; obstructions arise, body tissue atrophies, cold as stone.'

'All of them, you say. Well, this we have no way of knowing.'

'But I'm telling you that Rodion –'

'Logic, Mr Pavlitch! Working backwards from effects to causes, you fail to see all the causes that could have led to totally different effects. Why would they take to hospital those others who took the stuff with no harm to their health?' Don the spectacles and shapka. 'Fishenstein, yes. They lie around everywhere free to take, you say? Feed them regularly, Sasha, and pump them with teslectricity till they freeze. Or freeze not. Well, till we meet again!'

Leave by a back door into the alleyway leading from the storerooms. Shtchekelnikoff ran ahead into the unlicht in search of a sleigh.

Following his initial greeting, Mr Izydor Chruściński took a long hard gaze, with and without the frostglaze monocle over his eye, until a number of thoughts entered the head – one, that here in his person was met the next butcher of the soul boring into a man's entire soletruth with his sharp stare; two, that Chruściński had guessed from the umbriance that it came not from the immurchment characteristic of all inhabitants of the Land of the Gleissen but from mechanical demurchment, contrary to nature; and finally, three, that the Tchorniye Siyaniye was again having some minor effect, deceiving Chruściński with the false symmetries of a glintz.

One thing was right: the body was still heavily demurched, since all these assumptions turned out to be wrong.

'Forgive me for tarnishing you with such a stare,' he said, sitting down, 'but today you remind me of him even more. When I saw him for the last time, he also had a thick beard. But he never shaved his head down to the scalp. And also, just like you standing there now – do have a seat, do have a seat! – he looked down at everyone from on high, whether standing or sitting or lying, he looked down. You'll have a drop?'

In the room to the rear of the Stores – decently furnished even with leather armchairs, naphtha lamps neath gilded shades and a far-from-ugly landscape painting – three of the four walls were lined with bottle racks. Chruściński and Sons did not trade in the best-tasting or highest-priced liquors; here, however, alongside the viler spiritus vodka and ordinary wines, lay bottles with labels of entirely noble brands. Izydor Chruściński poured a glass of absinthe each.

Savour the absinthe on the tip of the tongue, heavily sweetened and watered down. *He looked down at everyone from on high* – had not Jelena Muklanowicz gone on repeatedly about arrogance? But – what arrogance, for crying out loud?! How was it possible to look down at people when they had the power, with a single glance, to kindle the red blush of shame, to reduce the soul to ashes through shame? Such an equation of character has no right to balance!

Push away the shot glass.

'Of precisely what nature was your acquaintance?' Ask him directly. 'You mentioned, sir, a debt of gratitude…'

'Of what nature.' Chruściński sat up straight behind his desk, passed a blotchy frostbite-scarred hand over his spotted waistcoat and smoothly shaven chin, removed the monocle from his eye socket, and began tapping with it on the desktop recently purged of documents. 'My elder son, Radosław… You see, sir, that signboard "Sons" – is a charm, it casts a spell over the future. Jan, all right, but Radosław – he was seventeen years old; in nineteen fifteen he got ten years for anti-state conspiracy. Your father… Were it not for your father, Radosław would not have survived his first year of katorga. He was put in his work gang, Filip took him under his wing, kept up his spirits, taught him the convict life.' Chruściński jerked his head higher. 'So, you can imagine, sir, I wanted to thank him when he appeared in Irkutsk.'

'He took nothing.'

'No.' Izydor Chruściński smiled dryly. 'I thought he'd give me a talking-to.' He sighed. 'So, when I saw you under the Black Aurora... A son for a son, is that not divine justice?'

'You warned me against Piłsudski.'

Chruściński knocked back the remainder of his undiluted absinthe.

'He is the daemon of the Ice!' he whispered croakily. 'Flee from him, sir!'

'You know each other?'

'What do you think made Radosław throw away his life? Here,' he gesticulated expansively along the bottle racks, 'here they would meet at night, discuss their operations, do their politics. And then Filip...'

'What?'

Chruściński clenched his fist.

'For he hooked him too! Accursed comrade Wiktor! He attracts them like a magnet – get too close and you'll never break free. It has frozen! And where is Filip Gierosławski now? Siberian ice!'

'In other words, if I understand you correctly – you're sure it was Piłsudski who sent my father onto the Ways of the Mammoths?'

Chruściński took a deep breath, crossed his arms over his chest.

'It stands to reason, I wasn't there at the time,' he said more calmly now. 'But I have eyes and ears, I have my wits. I know that the day before Filip came to me, Filip had spoken with him at his own place, somewhere in Zimny Nikolayevsk. Immediately after that, the police began following him around Irkutsk. He bursts in here after dusk, so tightly wrapped in a scarf no scrap of face was visible below his frosto-glazes, and lays down the diengi for five bottles of sazhayevka. And by next day, he was probably already on the trail – that was all we saw of him.'

'Sazhayevka?'

'For the road.' Izydor pointed to a row of bottles located high up to the left. 'Ten roubles thirty kopecks, an expensive comestible, he could have chosen something cheaper.'

Stand up, take a bottle off the rack. On the label was sketched a panorama of Irkutsk with the Sibirkhozheto Tower in the middle; its corona of darkness radiated out into black letters spelling the name of the liquor.

Сажа

Байкальская настойка

Taken down from the high rack, the bottle's contents were shaken up. In the transparent liquid, probably pure vodka, swam petals of black snow, coalblack sootflakes.

'People drink this stuff? Doesn't it harm them?'

'Vodka always harms when not consumed in moderation, Mr Gierosławski.'

'The tungetitum in it.'

'That's why it's so dear. People drink vodka with gold, with powdered bone, so why should they not drink it with tungetitum? In blackapothecary syrups, you have still thicker chunks.'

Shake the sazhayevka once again. The black particles gyrated slowly.

'I understand why you harbour a grudge against Piłsudski –'

'Grudge!'

'But – the daemon of the Ice?'

'Think you, sir, that he honestly desires Thaw? Hah! He beguiled first one lot and then another with political arguments in his letters, in missives sent into Summer from afar, from a safe distance, so that no one could doubt the character of their author. But I saw through him: his is a Lyednyak soul; he has to melt Poland in order to restore her independence; but as he would only take her under his own command, he himself would quickly freeze the whole country under his autocracy.' Again, Mr Chruściński clenched his fist. 'Time and again I stood face to face with this man and realised the truth about him. Such men appear more frequently here than they do in the home country; there's something in the Russian soil that makes it easier to break with the falsehoods and uncertainties of the material world, and grab straight at the idea, at Truth, at God's beard. And whosoever has heard a voice from God, even if he be but a swineherd, stands up at once before the crowd without shame and declares himself the legitimate tsar, denouncing the anointed tsar as a usurper – and more often than not the crowd will believe him.'

'Why should it not believe him?' Mutter, squinting at the sazhayevka. 'Truth is truth, whosoever has touched it. When God addresses man and commands him even to kill his own son, man asks not whether God is free to command, only seizes his knife.' Put aside the drink. 'It seems to me, Izydor, that those geologists who discover the prehistory of the Ways of the Mammoths in the oldest layers of the permafrost have got it right. In Russia, it was always... *colder*, if you understand me; Russians have always lived closer to Truth. That's why there are so many pretenders to the throne, divine madmen, prophets, so many cruel sects, such ferocity on the road to heaven. In Summer, all becomes blurred, uncertainty adds to uncertainty, we judge more often from the semblances of matter. But here...'

'They're a Lyednyak people, you're saying.'

Sit down, light a cigarette. Mr Chruściński declined, pouring himself another absinthe. Glance at the watch.

'Are you in touch with them now?'

He frowned.

'You're thinking of talking to the yapontchiks?'

'How can you know what Piłsudski wants of me?'

He slammed his open palm on the desktop.

'For God's sake, do not enter any bargains with them!'

'Izydor, sir…' Soften the tone to one of gentle persuasion. 'I have to find my father. If Piłsudski really did send him into the Ice… whom am I to ask, if not him?'

Chruściński looked away. A tide of trembling shadow from the naphtha lamp infused with gleissenik umbriance drenched the noble profile of the spiritus merchant; a wave spread this way, a wave spread that way, now he seemed angry, then a second later – overwhelmed by sorrow.

'People say… Things didn't go as he wished. News broke that the Son of Frost had come to Irkutsk, and immediately afterwards – that Ziuk had arrived specially from Harbin. No doubt he wants to see you.' He chewed over something for a long time in silence. At last, he asked: 'Am I to send word?'

Nod the head, slowly stubbing out the cigarette in an ashtray.

Rise to the feet in order to say goodbye, reach for the pocketbook.

'Ten roubles, thirty kopecks.'

Mr Chruściński pulled an offended face and resolutely thrust forward two bottles of sazhayevka, brushing aside the hand offering the banknote.

Take a step back, calculate for a second time the whole amount due, even the small change, and lay the diengi on the bottle rack.

'So this is how it is,' muttered Chruściński. 'This is how it is.'

On Tumanny Prospekt, a printer's and second-hand bookshop was still open; take a peek inside, trotting hurriedly across the street in the frost, but they had no Fyodorovian pamphlets. Driving onto Tsvetistaya Street, notice through frostoglaze rainbows the signboard of a Jewish tobacconist; stop the sleigh. The Orthodox salesman pointed to a small pile lying beside jars of sweets. There were three issues of an ephemeron entitled *Resurrection*. On the cover of the most recent was a drawing portraying a scene apparently taken from the illustrations to Jules Verne's fantasies: some kind of gigantic machines stretching their iron limbs into the depths of the ice and raising human corpses, tens, hundreds of corpses, beneath bunches of rays blazing from above. The pamphlets, as the reader was informed directly below the title, were published by the Irkutsk Brotherhood of War against the Apocalypse. Pick up one copy of each, using the occasion to purchase a box of cigarette tubes with tungetitum filters.

At Tsvetistaya seventeen, the Chinese master tailor was already manhandling Wojsław Wielicki with scissors and needle; Wielicki's deep roars and growls could be heard emanating from the more distant rooms together with the Chinaman's prattle. Halina and Marta, forced to express an opinion forthwith on this or that colour, on this or that style taken from a fashion magazine, had spread themselves in the drawing room with samples of expensive fabrics. It was just possible to sneak into the bedroom, take off the coat and hide the documents containing the result tables of the coldiron experiments, as well as the metal plates, two bottles of sazhayevka and the Fyodorovian pamphlets.

As the elderly Chinaman unravelled his tape measure around the body and prodded neath the shirt with his stubby fingers, Wojsław, having recovered his breath after his own torturous experiences, lit a pipe and blurted out as if from nowhere:

'Modest Pavlovitch says that your invitation was Pobedonostseff's doing.'

'Pobedonostseff's? I thought they were at daggers drawn. Why would Schultz invite someone to his daughter's engagement at the behest of his enemy?'

'Uh, your enemy isn't always who it seems to be; both have Lyedynak interests.' Wielicki smiled through a cloud of tobacco smoke; then waved his hand with its pipe and diamond ring and, abracadabra, his smile had vanished. 'Modest Pavlovitch says that you're now a political player; a controversial figure and a radical. Whom am I fostering under my roof?'

'The Son of Frost, didn't you know?'

This sounded fiercer than intended. He was joking after all. (Was he joking?) Agh, a powerful shot of freezing murch would have come in handy now... The palms were burning cruelly under the gloves, but just then the tailor ordered the arms to be raised; standing there like a fool, it wasn't easy to answer Wielicki, even with a knowing grin. It was only day two – but if freezing is to be like this...

Finally send the Chinaman packing with a curse and shut the bedroom door. Outside the windows, there was nothing but monumental darkness and, in the darkness, fog washed with the colours of streetlamp rainbows, whilst inside – man and man's thoughts. It's the time of day when the tiniest thing provokes irrational irritation, when the world scours the senses like a bone scraper, when it's hard to occupy body or mind; objects are picked up and put down without as much as a glance, walls or furniture rubbed against as if by an agitated cat, the enclosed space paced up and down. The time of day, the time of night, when weariness still prompts not sleep, yet nothing has to be done, nothing even has to be pretended to be done, removed from amongst people. Nothing is necessary; everything is possible. What to do, what to do? The hands clench and open; the whole body would be scratched of skin, scratched naked. Peasants at such times get drunk or beat their womenfolk or commit some great life-affecting stupidity. A woman tidies the house (or gets drunk). Hide the bottles of sazhayevka in the top drawer of the chest of drawers. Having set a lamp on the bedside cabinet and lain on the bed, open *Resurrection*. Hosts of the resurrected were marching through a Factory of Immortality, along a boulevard neath fantastical machines, behind which a tall figure sat on a pulpit throne looking, in this grey-and-white drawing, in the light of the naphtha lamp – very like Doctor Tesla. The chief editor of *Resurrection* was a certain Edmund Gerontyevitch Khavroff. On every page, in a ghastly pastoral frieze at its foot, flowers were growing out of human skulls. *We shall rise from the dead! We shall be resurrected!* Behold, the bedtime reading.

This Nikolay Fyodoroff had been possessed by an idea, but not as a man of the West is possessed: for the latter will force himself, throw himself vehemently into the cause, and either achieve the intended goal (with all guns blazing) or fail (with all guns blazing), whereupon he will return to life. Fyodoroff's idea came as Russian ideas come: silently, as a whisper from deep inside the skull, speaking first to the soul, then to the mind, but with such force, with such certainty of rightness and truth that nothing could sever Fyodoroff from life, for the idea at once engulfed the whole of that life, the whole world, the whole of History, as well as the one small man Fyodoroff. Just as the earlimost authors of the letopisi, chroniclers of the misty distant past of Rus, created their greatest works through lifelong joint effort in isolation, so too Fyodoroff, consumed by his idea, had no thought of declaring himself before people; if he publicised anything during his lifetime, it was under a pseudonym. He existed not separate from his idea; the idea spoke through him. He lived the ascetic life of a monk, that is, in seclusion, in poverty, amongst books. Born a bastard son of Prince Pavel Gagarin, he spent his life on a monthly salary of seventeen roubles as an official of the lowest rank in the Library of the Rumyantseff Museum and in the Moscow Archives of the Ministry of Foreign Affairs. Seventy-four years he lived – during which time he read all the books available in the libraries (the idea grew) and filled tens of thousands of pages with his writing, expounding the details of his Project. Only after its author's death was the Project praised by Solovyoff, Tolstoy, Dostoyevsky, by Russia's greatest intellects. For Fyodoroff had been planning, namely, the engineering of immortality; his idea was the conquest of death – but not only future death, but every death that had ever happened in the abyss of History. Fyodoroff had drawn up a detailed prescription for the resurrection of all mankind beginning with Adam and Eve.

... And yet he had based himself on geology and hydrology. *Energy derived from air currents and transposed to various layers of the Earth shall provoke in them regular tremors, replacing today's destructive earthquakes, which nevertheless enable the flow of waters gathering particles of the dust of the dead. Science concerned with the infinitesimal movements of molecules, which can be perceived only by the sharpened hearing of sons of man equipped with the subtlest organs of sight and hearing, shall not be seeking precious stones or particles of noble metals, since the seekers shall not be humanists to whom everything parental, paternal, is alien, but sons who have come of age; they shall seek the molecules that made up the beings who gave them life. The waters carrying the dust of the dead from inside the Earth shall become obedient to the collective will of the sons and daughters of man and begin to react under the influence of light rays, which shall no longer be blinding, just as thermal rays shall no longer be cold and insensitive; chemical rays shall acquire the ability to select, that is, under their influence, related elements shall be united, and alien elements detached.* The detailedness of his technological projects becomes greater the farther Fyodoroff and his successors reach into the technologies of the future. As a limit exists to the perceptions of the human senses, the sons of man will not be engaged directly in operations on the molecules of their fathers, but minute machines built by the sons, or even machines built by machines built by the machines built by the sons. For the internal structure of the particles originating in the dust of dead humans is accessible only to microscopic animalcules invisible to our eyes, and this on condition they are equipped with such microscopes as would expand their field of vision to the extent that our microscopes expand our field of vision. Here *Resurrection* includes an article on these automated worms illustrated by sketches of micromachines so small they are visible only to other micromachines. Fyodoroff's worms take the form of geometric figures with dozens of tiny twiglike limbs, vaguely resembling the drawings of microbes in Zygmunt's atlases, and a little – the radio-controlled automatons described in Doctor Tesla's patents and rejected by the US Navy.

... Possessed by this idea, Fyodoroff reflects on subsequent problems standing in the way of universal resurrection. Settle down in a more comfortable position under the lamp; the thing was fascinating, as other people's obsessions often are at first glance. How to retrieve all the particles that once composed the bodies of our ancestors? After all, they had been *dispersed in the space of the Solar System, and perhaps also in other worlds. The problem of resurrection therefore has a telluro-solar and even a telluro-cosmic character.* Furthermore, the monumental mathematics of the Project also does not escape Fyodoroff's attention: if we take, at a single given moment in History, all the people who ever lived, without even taking into consideration future generations, there is no way we shall accommodate them all on a single earth. Therefore, a logical consequence of the Project of Universal Resurrection is the necessity to go beyond earth, to master the cosmic abysses and discover other heavenly bodies. *The duty to resurrect also requires such discovery, because without conquest of the celestial space, the simultaneous coexistence of generations is impossible, although, on the other hand, total mastery of the celestial space is impossible without resurrection. Well, that's obvious! The whole universe will be a unification of innumerable worlds of boundless celestial spaces, a unification accomplished by thousands of thousands of resurrected generations swallowed by Earth in the course of endless centuries.* We have to emigrate beyond Earth, colonise celestial bodies, take possession of them and make star systems, galaxies, subject to ourselves.

... Whence the energy for this, what kind of technology shall enable it? In the penultimate issue of *Resurrection*, already on page three, a copy had been inserted of an old photograph of Nikola Tesla sitting beneath gigantic lightning-bolts of electrical discharge. Since the starting point for the technology of Resurrection shall be, according to Fyodoroff, *a lightning conductor raised in the air with the aid of an aerostat and acquiring storm energy not only for people to maintain their own lives, it goes without saying, but also to restore life to those who have lost it; but this is only the barely perceptible beginning to the regulation of the forces of nature.* 'Regulation' is the key word; 'regulation', 'order', 'power over matter'. *The entire life of the universe is an uninterrupted storm and tempest of varying degrees of intensity, because the force operating in the universe is not yet a force subjected to regulation. To study nature means to seek a means of discharging electrical energy and transforming it from a destructive into a regenerating, resurrective energy. Having united to control the meteorological process, in which solar energy is concentrated, the sons of man shall acquire the ability to transform the dust of their ancestors, excavated from the deep strata of Earth, not into nourishment for their descendants, but into the bodies of those to whom they once belonged.* Eventually, Earth itself will become an obedient machine in the hands of resurrectionists. *Research into electricity, and at the same time into the whole of nature, shall be set on firm ground only once we have contrived to bring Earth as a single body into various degrees of electrical induction and to perceive the influence provoked by it on other worlds. The unity of the meteorological and cosmic process creates the basis for extending regulation to the Solar System and to other planetary systems with the aim of regenerating and rationally mastering them.* Regulation

will embrace the whole of time – not only people living contemporane-
ously and so subject to this regulation, but also the whole of History
and the people who have passed with it – as well the whole of space –
not only Earth, but the entire cosmos. *The totality of worlds revived by
resurrected generations and remaining in close brotherly union shall itself
become a tool in resurrecting our own ancestors.*

... And so on. Turn up the lamp-wick. And so on and so forth. As
humanity will possess powers and faculties enabling it to realise such
undertakings, it will no longer be humanity in today's understanding of
the species or of mankind. It is not possible at one and the same time to
be both adult and child; not possible to be an angel and live the life of
a vagabond. *Restoring life to the dead shall* **create immortal, indestructible beings**, *because the re-creation of life from a being deprived of life
shall then become not only a possibility (as it always was) but a proven
reality.* Resurrectors and resurrected shall redirect their endeavours
towards other ideals. A human being fears death and does everything
to cling to life – but towards what does an immortal being now strive?
*Not only the functions of all organs but also morphology should become
the products of knowledge and agency, of work. We have to ensure that
microscopes, microphones, spectroscopes and similar become, in a natural
yet conscious way, the property of every human being, which means* **that
every person will have the capacity to recreate himself out of the most
elementary substances, gaining thereby the possibility of dwelling anywhere**. Thus, it will be a pancosmic civilisation of former humans who
exist not thanks to the body but despite the body, because they will be
able to alter it at will, to reconstruct it, to subtract or add this here, that
there. The boundary between bodily matter and non-bodily matter will
finally be obliterated: every particle will be able to be exploited by the
automated worms so as to recreate or create flesh. *The task of the human
race lies in transforming everything that is unconscious, that arises out
of itself, that is inborn – into a conscious, enlightened, real, universal,
personal resurrection.* The resurrection of bodies, understood literally
in this way, is important precisely because in the end, it will enable
humans to break free from the bondage of what is bodily into what is
spiritual. *Thanks only to the regulation of matter shall the spirit too gain
total victory over the flesh.*

... For the motivation and meaning behind the whole Project and
the essence of the idea that consumed Fyodoroff is the Truth of the
Christian religion, the Word of God. *Christ is the Resurrector and
Christianity, as the true religion, is the resurrection.* Biblical forecasts
taken from the Apocalypse do not amount to and cannot amount to
an absolute description of the future. As such, they would deprive man
of hope and free will. This, instead, is a *plan* presented to humanity

for realisation. All those who join it not Fyodorovians contemptuously call 'passive Christians', 'customers of religion', 'lazy Lazaruses'. Only Fyodorovians are 'active Christians'. They do not wait passively for the resurrection of bodies – they *work* so that the resurrection shall come about. Fighting against the Apocalypse, they are fulfilling God's design for History. They take the example of Christ as diligently as possible: they shall raise from the dead, as He raised from the dead. For *we shall all indeed be resurrected, but not all shall be changed. In a flash, in the twinkling of an eye, at the final trumpet (for a trumpet shall sound), the dead shall rise undefiled, but we shall be transfigured. Yes, my dear brethren, be firm and unwavering, always abounding in the Lord's work, knowing that your work is not in vain in the Lord.*

... Religion is bound up here directly with science, science is the tool of religion. No surprise then that they travel around universities and research institutes showering them with diengi for this or that study. A special impression had been made on them by cases of the 'spontaneous' resurrection of animals extracted from the permafrost. Ice, ice – this is already some kind of beginning. Khavroff himself writes in one of the pamphlets about experiments on terminally ill volunteers laid in cavities in the ice and removed a day or two later, once they had had time to freeze rock solid – will they arise or not? Or perhaps they failed to arise only because, despite everything, their disease had utterly got the better of them. (Do Fyodorovians realise that they merely repeat in their own way the rituals of the Martsynians?) Ice, ice – the lower the temperature, the more complete the freezing. They had even wondered already about experiments on gleissen. They had galvanised dead hiberniks. Gentlemen in thick shubas, with bare heads and solemn countenances above patriarchal beards, were photographed beside open graves forged out of ice; amongst them, propped against a wooden plank, stiff as an icicle, stood a corpse, likewise a gleissenik, that is, severely bemurched. *Ideal conservation of the body is the first step on the path to resurrecting bodies.* Extinguish the bedside lamp, press the thumbs on the eyelids. Does this not sound rather like Nernst's theorem of thermodynamics? As temperature approaches absolute zero, entropy approaches zero. In other words, if teslectrical flow really does reach beyond hitherto measures of temperature... Take off the gloves; the prickly feeling passed from hands to cheeks, to forehead. Is zero Kelvin indeed the point at which entropic processes are reversed? And on its other side, there in the Kingdom of Darkness, out of which only gleissen emerge, whatever is mixed shall be unmixed, that is, put in order, what is damaged shall be repaired, what is forgotten – remembered, what is falsified – put right, whilst the dead – shall they be resurrected?

Glance out of the window at the Angara, golden and flame-tinted from the colours of the crossing sleigh-lanterns, which swam on the frostoglaze into the shape of the frozen river; while the snow ran – into the sky; and the sky – into the rooftops; and the rooftops... Rub the eyes again. A day and a half without demurchment, and sureness of the soletruth already begins to gnaw at the mind. Sense in Fyodoroff's idea a rightness springing from its very totality, from its all-embracing receptiveness. So how will it be after a week, a month? Even conversion to Martsynianism could happen...! Laugh under the moustache. Dust of our fathers. A corpse removed from the grave, high-ranking Fyodorovians standing over it. Return to the pamphlets, relight the lamp. Find the editorial address, which is also that of the headquarters of the Brotherhood of War against the Apocalypse. Glavnaya 72, Floor IV. Well, well, a prestigious location. Copy down the address into the bumazhnik.

The editorial offices of *Resurrection* could afford such a prestigious location since this same apartment building also housed, as was observed on arrival there the following day after work, the countinghouses of Fishenstein's import-export company as well as the New Winter Bank (in which Fishenstein also owned the majority shares). Besides, the second floor also contained the offices of the Baikal branch of Lloyd's Insurance Brokers. Fishenstein was a fierce competitor of Wojsław Wielicki and Wielicki often mentioned him (especially after getting it into his head that some great industrialist would suddenly emerge out of the poor mathematician). 'Fishenstein is a Jew, but a strange Jew. First, because he doesn't mix with other Jews – but with Christians, all his partners are baptised men. Second, because he's extraordinarily profligate: how many unprofitable projects has he sunk capital into in advance! And I'm not talking here about philanthropy pleasing to God. And third, because he's a scholar of the Book, meaning he enjoys great respect amongst the rabbis and is the main funder of the Irkutsk Beth Hamedrash. The more he moves away from them, however, the more they value him. Did you ever see, sir, such a paradox!'

Evidently, greater ingenuity in doing sums as well as Razbyesoff's prosecutorial eye were needed in order to solve the equation of Fishenstein. It's curious what truth a pious Jew sees in Fyodoroff's idea. Or perhaps he's living consciously in falsehood? He wouldn't finance the Brotherhood of War against the Apocalypse so generously for the sake of a whim. It was quite another matter that he could afford it: rumours were circulating in Irkutsk about Fishenstein's false modesty, for he'd allegedly already amassed five fortunes and then lodged them outside Siberia, in Swiss and Italian banks, in German mines and in real estate (he apparently owned a district of rented apartment blocks in New York). Well, every rich man walks amongst people surrounded by an aureole of lies about riches ten times greater, especially a man of the tribe of Moses.

On Glavnaya Street stood a gleiss; the building had to be approached and entered by the rear door. The thought suddenly occurred that the block had been taken out of use: for on the roof too, a glacius had sprawled spiderlike. See only afterwards, on second glance, in the umbriant glow of evening shadows, the soletruth of its form: it was no glacius, but an architectural representation of a glacius, that is, a monstrous almighty sculpture splayed over the gables.

The door to the *Resurrection* office was locked. At that precise moment, however, a man emerged from the adjoining room with an armful of rust-eaten scrap-iron; he stopped, stared, rattled the iron and inquired: 'For the Brotherhood, gentlemen?'

One word led to another and it became apparent that he too was a Fyodorovian, Arsky Yakoff Yustinovitch, at your service. There'll no longer be anyone in the office today, but Edmund Gerontyevitch can be found at the firm where he holds the responsible position of deputy director – ah, oh, here, to the left of the stairs. Should the matter be sufficiently important.

As might have been expected, Deputy Director Khavroff had no inkling of an unannounced visitant at such a late hour. Quickly jot down two sentences and send him a note via the clerk. Khavroff – a gleissenik, a balding well-padded four-eyes of unimposing stature, dressed nevertheless in a double-breasted suit of the best English wool – appeared a minute later.

'Is it true?' he asked softly holding the piece of paper in his raised hand. 'That you can bring us Doctor Tesla?'

'I can introduce you and guarantee he'll hear you out with the greatest attention, yes.' Remove the frostoglazes and extend the hand. 'Benedykt Filipovitch Gierosławski.'

He squeezed it hastily. See clearly at once that he's not made the connection; his thoughts and eyes wandered off somewhere to the side.

'You say that you can. And in return, you'd like – what? our gratitude calculated in roubles?'

'You know what? I will leave it with you; you sleep on it, ask around, then we'll talk.' Head for the door.

A moment later Mr Khavroff burst into the corridor.

'Wait a moment! Wait a moment! Did you say – please forgive me – Gierosławski?'

Reply nothing, remembering the method of Doctor Myśliwski at the Last Kopeck Club; stand still in silence, weighing him up with a sharp, angry eye and repeating inwardly like an incantation: cold, cold, cold, cold.

Which probably caused him, without further hesitation – or Edmund Gerontyevitch had already also made the decision – to shout something to the clerks on his way out and lead back to the room out of which Arsky had carried the scrap metal. Yet this was no tradesman's store but a clubroom, attractively furnished with picturesque paintings and electric lamps, a Dauerbrand stove in the corner and tall windows with panes of ordinary glass. The panes shook to the rhythm of the glashatays' drums. Hang up the shuba, take a seat in a comfortable arm-chair. Mr Khavroff called for service. On the table lay plates left from afternoon tea, ashtrays and cups. The parquet near the stove shone wet.

'Truth to tell, we've thought for a long time of knocking at your door,' Khavroff wheezed. 'But, as I see, Mohammed has come to the moun-tain, hee-hee,' he laughed like a yapping lapdog. 'You know, Gospodin Yeroslavsky, I sent the doctor an invitation, thinking that he'd heard of us, must have heard; I know not if –'

'He's not heard. It's possible to read all kinds of terrible and threaten-ing things into such invitations.'

'Well yes. We consulted on this matter. Does it behove us, against the interests of our most prominent members, to –'

'Mr Fishenstein is one of those who'll defend the gleissen to his last breath, huh?'

'It was decided that once Doctor Tesla knows of his own accord, he'll come. He has not come.' A servant, having cleared the mess off the table, set up a samovar; Khavroff sat closer to it and began rearranging the little porcelain cups, sprinkling the dry tchay, choosing the lumps of sugar. Siberian tea-brewing ceremonies often took up entire business meetings; Wielicki used to claim that he clinched more deals over tea than he ever did over vodka. Edmund Gerontyevitch poured the first cups. 'Please. You obviously understand, sir, how much we depend on collaboration with the doctor, since things have worked out so fortu-itously by his coming to our city. That demonstration on the river, the melted gleiss – and that black electricity with which he treated the gleiss – they're talking of nothing else. Nikolay Fyodoroff, if you know his writings, sir, foresaw that –'

'You would like to use teslectricity in your experiments to resurrect people.'

Khavroff dropped his eyes to his saucer, slurped the hot tea; slight-ly red in the face, perhaps from the tea, or perhaps – perhaps he felt ashamed before the Son of Frost.

'You don't have to believe what we believe,' he said. 'I only ask for the possibility of testing a hypothesis. So little to ask in comparison with the ultimate goal: the restoration to life of every single human being. A year, a century, a millennium of blundering and set-backs and ridicule

– of what significance are they now? In comparison.' He slurped up the rest of his tea. 'When in the other scale-pan. As the alternative. If. Pshaw. More tea?'

Proceeding according to the principles of Siberian good manners, turn the empty Chinese cup upside down and place a lump of sugar on top.

'Forgive me, if I gave any pretext for such an impression. I am not laughing at you at all. Who knows, maybe you're right seeking solutions in teslectricity. Have a word with the doctor, you'll see for yourselves that he has an open mind.' A charman wiped up the puddle under the stove. Wait till he leaves with his rag. Nikola certainly has an open mind, maintains after all that he himself was restored to life thanks to de-murchment; infect him at the right moment with Fyodoroff's idea, and for a week he'll be thinking of nothing else. A week, maybe a month, maybe two with any luck, and if Khavroff *et consortes* prove sufficiently resourceful. And this should delay long enough the construction of the Baikal Murch Hammer and those dangerous experiments with wave resonance on the Ways of the Mammoths. Khavroff again proposed more tea; again refuse. 'In return, I'd like to ask a favour.'

'How can I help you?'

'Maybe Mr Fishenstein can help quicker.'

'If it's about financial –'

'No. It's about certain experiments, which, I believe, you have already carried out. I don't know who exactly, but I know Mr Fishenstein paid for the medical care of people that took part.'

'Ah.' Edmund Gerontyevitch sat up straight and adjusted his spectacles; umbriance began to bubble around his neck encased in its stiff collar.

'I am aware that these were not, could not have been, entirely legal undertakings; you are obliged to exercise discretion, Mr Fishenstein could be implicated in a very nasty affair, a man in his position can't afford to be so compromised. After all, you don't inform readers of *Resurrection* of everything. Digging up corpses from the permafrost, inserting terminally ill patients into the ice at their own request, gal-vanising mongrel dogs – you can somehow get away with. But collective poisoning with tungetitum crowned by death?'

'More tea?'

'Thank you.'

He poured it.

'Excuse me a minute, I'll go and ask.'

'Perhaps you can throw in a word for my man to be given something hot.'

'Of course.'

He went to ask, but it took longer than a minute and when he reappeared, it was not alone, and it was even not he who first crossed the threshold of the Brotherhood's lounge, but Abraham Fishenstein in his own monumental person, supporting himself on a heavy stick neath his storm of grey hair and hypnotic eye, which radiated shafts of frosto-glaze and tungetitum from under his fierce brow. Stand respectfully. He nodded slightly. The servant pushed up a chair for him. The Jew tucked back the tails of his black satin gaberdine, stooped, squeezed his beard with his left hand, hooked the walking stick over the furniture, and thus sat down; sit down opposite.

Glance questioningly at Khavroff. He gave no sign.

'Mr Fishenstein –'

'Easy,' drawled the millionaire in a low voice, 'easy.'

What's this, was he so exhausted he had to rest for a while in silence? He wasn't that old. Wasn't gasping for breath. He sat and stared with his healthy eye, as the still-life one filled the lounge with kaleidoscopes of colour. The thought occurred that under the Black Auroras, this tungetitum pupil of his must shine like a silver torch from beneath his raised eyelid or through his closed eyelid, which would then glow pink. Or maybe not, perhaps it sufficed to shield it from the unlicht by means of flesh, just as during Princess Blutskaya's séance in the Transsib the Grossmeister had been shielded. And at what might the Jew be staring with his magisterial, sacerdotal gaze, tugging idly at his sidelocks? At the Son of Frost, of course, the attraction of the salons.

'Gospodin Fishenstein, the matter stands as Gospodin Khavroff has no doubt told you: for your Brotherhood, the opportunity to win over Doctor Tesla, for me – scientific information about your experiments. My question therefore to you – is about that accident in which a dozen or so men died of tungetitum poisoning at the Holy Trinity Hospital.'

Abraham Fishenstein tapped with his stick.

'Easy, easy.' He nodded to Khavroff; Khavroff bent forward, whispered something in his ear. Fishenstein listened, chewing over the unspoken words. A flustered clerk rushed in with a document in his hand, pencil behind his ear; Khavroff snarled, furious at him. Mr Fishenstein raised his finger. Edmund Gerontyevitch left, the clerk left, the servant left, shutting the door behind him. Bwwroommm, bwwroommm beat the Buryat drums. The Jew cleared his throat and heaved a sigh. 'A youth knocks at a wiseman's door,' he intoned in his bass voice. 'Rebbe, he asks, I'm in love with two devushkas, which am I to take to wife? And which is in love with you, asks the rebbe. One says she's in love and the other says she's in love, replies the youth, but how can I tell if she's really in love? And which is the better cook, asks the rebbe. One's dreadful, replies the youth, the other's awful, but both swear they'll learn, only how can I tell if they'll learn? And which is faithful and obedient, asks the rebbe. Oy, rebbe, each is ready to jump into the fire and sees no world beyond me, but in ten years' time, twenty – how can I tell! The rebbe shook his head and said: Marry the uglier. But why the uglier, the youth was amazed. In response to which, the wiseman explains the principle of righteous happiness: either way you have to reject one, whilst the prettier will easily find another husband.'

It made no sense.

'It makes no sense.'

'Just imagine, honoured sir, how beautiful the world would be, were all people to behave according to this fine principle!' sighed Fishenstein. 'How beautifully business would be conducted! How we would all come into our fortunes by way of the straight path!'

'Ah! I give you my word that Mr Wielicki has nothing to do with my visit and never lets me into his commercial secrets; I am neither his crony nor his partner.'

'So you say.'

'So I say.'

The Jew blinked; rainbows flickered.

'And yet the luckless Fishenstein must take it on trust from you that Mr Wielicki won't think of unleashing against the inconvenient Hebrew wrongheaded prosecutions, like those in Stary Multan and Kishinyoff, and to whose hymn-sheet newspapers throughout the Empire will immediately be singing: horrific massacre of Christians, deicidal Yids butchering the Orthodox Christian populace, our good muzhiks poisoned near faraway Baikal, soon they'll be poisoning folk in our city and secretly offering burned human sacrifices, Hospodi pomiluy.'

'Jesus, no, Wielicki is not that kind of man, and I've not breathed a word to anyone, I swear to you on the Holy Cross!'

'You swear?' Fishenstein raised his hands above his head. 'You have al-ready sworn! It has frozen!' He dropped his arms, tapped with the stick. 'It's true, the Son of Frost is come to Abraham Fishenstein.' He grinned. 'Well, for what reason do you wish to know these things of which you ask?'

'I am looking for my father, Mr Fishenstein, I have to find out how he descended to the Ways of the Mammoths. These volunteers of yours – I am assuming you took only volunteers – in what form did they take the tungetitum? in what doses? was it orally? intravenously? at what temperature? Were they hiberniks? Did any survive? What course did their illness take?'

'Unfortunately, it ended in total disaster. Ye-es.' He swayed back and forth in his chair. 'Edmund Gerontyevitch will show you the notes.

You should know, sir, that I forbade suchlike experiments – where my money is involved, everything shall be done first on animals.'

'But does Fyodoroff write anywhere about animals? I don't recall them at the Last Judgement according to Saint John.'

Here Abraham Fishenstein again fell silent. Averted his rainbow gaze. Bwwroommm, bwwroommm, a dozen glashatays' rumbles were counted before the Jew reverted to words; yet then he no longer spoke in answer to or for the attention of another man – gnarly fingers clutching the stick, real eye and false eye hidden neath their lids, his shallow breath lost in his beard – he spoke alongside him.

'There was this madman living, by all accounts, in Irkutsk, Piegnar, Aleksey Piegnar, of European blood, his father neither one of ours nor a Russian. And what did he do? He dismembered human beings. Long years passed before it came to light, but when it did, folk gathered outside the prison, the authorities stood by, and Piegnar was torn apart in the street. That was how Piegnar met his end, for he even has no grave; nor will his dust descend speedily under the earth, so it was.

'Piegnar was wont to wander north as far as the white ocean, to the lands of low sun. It's a well-known thing: you venture alone into those regions and every sleepless night takes its toll on the mind – who has not gone crazy out there? Ay, old skippers sailing their trading vessels along the Polar Rim to Archangel and respectable merchants have become unhinged, not to mention hunters gone astray. Piegnar pitted himself against the blizzard, foolish man; lost animals, lost provisions. That he didn't die – well, later in Irkutsk, he confessed to a woman: there in the ice, under the snow, he discovered other poor wretches, a buried tent or yurt, frozen solid, with people inside. So that was how he survived, by eating corpses preserved in the ice, that was how.

'Later on, after he'd been rescued, he returned to Baikal, where madness began to rattle louder in his head. In his shack by the lakeshore, he kept frozen human limbs, quartered torsos and heads stored in ice. Sometimes he partook of them according to his fancy, admiring a charming sunset behind the summits, but at other times he used them for a different purpose: for fashioning ice goylems, that is, assembling new people, new Frankenstein's monsters, in frozen form. A solitary vagabond, a katorzhnik on the run, an anonymous destitute villager, as well as countless victims from Siberia's indigenous tribes, or whosoever happened to cross his path in the wastes of the Baikal mountains – he would quarter, dismember and reassemble; but in ways unseen before. Oykh – O, God! – what the court officials found later in the ice at his home: frozen corpses with four arms, frozen corpses with six legs, or rather two human trunks put together with the head at one end and three pairs of legs attached at shoulders and pelvises, or whole chains of human limbs fixed to the hinge joints of torsos, or wreaths of heads and necks, or children's tiny carcasses set upon the legs of huge muzhiks, or feminine parts laid between the abominable paws of Buryat men. Such were the blasphemous creations that Aleksey Piegnar fashioned for himself.

'And yet, in the course of the investigation, when they got around to asking, he claimed he was giving them new life, for he was an Artist of the Force, an Engineer of Flesh, Discoverer of White Harmonies. Then something immediately rattled in his head, and he claimed the opposite: that it wasn't he, that he wasn't Aleksey Piegnar at all. Never mind that everyone recognised him – he was not Piegnar. Who then? He was a Piegnar-like creature, new, with Piegnar's own head planted on him by other frozen-corpse artists, but not the man who was born Piegnar, not Piegnar! And when he came apart at the hands of the mob, a legend began to circulate shortly afterwards in Irkutsk based on the madman's own words: he had come apart, disintegrated, because he had not been sufficiently frozen; such was the legend.

'The hibernik volunteers who came to us when Mr Khavroff placed the advertisement – were honest Martsynians, or dreamslaves who'd already dreamed they'd eaten and drunk tungetitum at your Christian communion, but there were also two of Piegnar's Children, hiberniks white-red-and-livid from former and recent through-freezings, stunned by the Black Auroras, and swearing by all things holy that they were not humankind born of woman, but old patchworks put together by Piegnar, reanimated only now by the cadaverniks of the Okhrana and sent into the night with secret orders from the emperor – and, as proof, they pointed to frostbite scars where their limbs had been conjoined, and clamoured to be fed tungetitum and thereby rescued from death, that is, from disintegration, since only harder freezing would ensure survival in their new goylem form. Therefore, they ate the tungetitum and froze for all eternity. Forty days we waited and, on my insistence, another forty – none rose alive, no.

'Today I wonder: did we do any better than Aleksey Piegnar, eh? Khavroff was very angry, but I insisted they be taken to the doctors. If all are to be resurrected, does this mean that they didn't die at all? But how can they be resurrected if they haven't died? Doctors speak of people being resuscitated after an ice death lasting half an hour, even when the heart has stopped beating. How many drowned men do we hear of pulled from airholes – who at first show no sign of a pulse or breath or human warmth – of such men raised from the dead! Half an hour – or maybe half a day – or maybe half a month? Is that death or not?

'Animals. To animals, Yahweh hath already granted immortality.

For I have seen maybugs and mosquitos of the Siberian gnus extracted from ice more ancient than the mammoths, thousands and thousands of years old; seen them shaking moisture from their bodies, brushing off the frost, preening their wings – flying away towards the Sun of our own day. Somewhere between the worm and the human being, the mystery of death and resurrection lies hidden. From the human angle or animal, one way or another, we shall reach it, because reach it we must.'

He sighed, swayed back and forth, stood up.

Accompany him to the door.

'So you've nothing against Doctor Tesla?'

'Why would I have anything against him?'

'Because he is working on Thaw, he could cost you your entire fortune.'

'So long as he contributes to the Resurrection Project, so long as he assists us; besides, let him work on what he wants, what does it matter to this stupid Jew?'

No way was there to solve this equation; the soletruth of Abraham Fishenstein remained shrouded, B did not result from A and two plus two did not equal four.

Mr Khavroff must have perceived the confusion; he gave his assurance he'd see to it that all records on the progress of the fatal experiment were provided forthwith. Nod the head lost in thought.

'That eye,' inquire, already putting on the fur coat, 'forgive me, sir, if –'

'Eye? He lost it in the Winter of the Gleissen, scalded in the fire of Irkutsk.'

'Ah!'

Not the next day nor the day immediately following, but only on the Friday, on the Friday evening, or rather the Friday night, that is, the night rolling from Friday into Saturday, on the eve of the governor general's ball, only then was everything at last organised so that the graves of the Fyodorovian hiberniks poisoned with tungetitum could be safely visited. Shtchekelnikoff had mustered three clear-headed heavies capable of wielding axes, spades and crowbars; Yerofey, the Martsynian gravedigger, promised a deserted cemetery. There was, however, a hard milky frost; a viscid fog was immuring the streets and squares of Irkutsk, whilst walls of damp air encased the tunnel carved out by the sleigh, as it raced through the City of Ice after dusk; on these walls, streetlamps shone in smudges of colour, flowing in the frostoglaze spectacles onto the ground, the sky, the driver's back and silhouettes of the broad-shouldered ruffians wrapped in their skins neath skins neath furs, more like monsters out of some Buryat fairy tale. Bwwroommm,

bwwroommm, the sound of the warning drums carried far; the iz-voztchik was navigating by ear. Seven of the nineteen volunteers who'd taken part in the experiment were interred on Jerusalem Hill; some had died without being taken to hospital. Riding now into the cemetery, rise above the surface of the sea of fog – where earthbound constellations of cold will-o'-the-wisps hit the frostoglazes: naphtha flames burning on the Fyodorovians' graves. Alight onto the snow; sharp névé crunched beneath the heavy boots. Shtchekelnikoff egged on his workers, the only voice above the crackle of ice-infested soil. No snow fell, and the wind was tolerable. Despite the thick scarf, cold breath stabbed the throat like an icicle stiletto; try breathing through the corner of the mouth with the tongue wound around the teeth. Yakoff Yustinovitch Arsky signalled from the first grave, where Yerofey had already put out the flames and was tearing up the earth thawed by axe-blows. Arsky was to ensure that the Fyodorovians were reburied without detriment to their posthumous dignity. Suspect, however, that his presence was due chiefly to the curiosity aroused in Edmund Gerontyevitch; the hope of what might be uncovered had been kept from him, so he was suspicious of everything. Once Arsky tried to say something, to talk from over the grave – but he choked on the frost, battling long afterwards with a convulsive cough. Shtchekelnikoff took one of his workers and went to dig open the next grave. A crescent moon, considerably brighter than in Europe, hung low above the western horizon, beyond the Triumphal Gates, beyond the city and the Angara and the Uysky District, casting a golden sheen over the icy rooftops and gleissen spines protruding above the vanilla-jelly fog. Axes hacked into wood; the coffins here had been buried very close to the surface. The heavies rammed their spades between boards and prised up the lid; Arsky leaned over the pit with a lamp in his out-stretched hand, as inky-black shadows sputtered out of the grave. The corpse lay in its casket as if still alive, that is, it had frozen immediately after death and not decomposed, welded into its suit by the hoarfrost and with a large Latin cross held in its white hands; but this should have been expected – here prehistoric warriors are dug out from the perma-frost with mammoth meat still stuck between their teeth. Indicate with the hands: bury him again. Move on to the second grave. The stench of naphtha bored into the nostrils. Shtchekelnikoff, half-leaning on a cross torn out of the ground, was smoking a cigarette, unveiling and reconcealing along with every puff his bristly countenance. Seven had swallowed the tungetitum as a powder, in a blackapothecary tincture, measured in half-pounds, which was a very expensive dose (and of a greater order of magnitude than the amounts inserted into sazhayev-ka or inhaled from blackwickes). They drank their vodka and went to sleep. Seven ate bread with tungetitum baked into it, slicing off thick chunks to stuff their bellies; of these, two suffered the longest, probably the ones who in the unequal share-out ate the least. Five had relied on the nightlong inhalation of tungetitum from incense-burners; these were the first to die, suffocating and spitting black blood. Yerofey forced the lid of the second coffin. Another Fyodorovian – a corpse – as if still alive – asleep. Rebury it! Walk from flame to flame. The Fyodorovians had not tried to shock the poor tungetitum-infected wretches with teslectricity, or subject them to bemurchment – but then neither the Dumb Ballooner nor Aleister Crowley nor father knew the principles of Doctor Tesla's black electricity, they had no access to his machines. Spade – coffin – corpse – rebury. But then again, the other side of the coin was that – the white electricity had likewise been present in nature long before Faraday built the first dynamos and electric motors. And only a few people – such as that August Fądzela from Zhitomir – are born with white or black-physical properties pushed to extremes, since it's characteristic of any naturally occurring distribution that the majority collect in the middle of the scale: there are few dwarfs and few giants, many more people are neither short nor tall; there are few obvious cretins and few undoubted geniuses, many more petty squires from the sticks destined for mediocrity. Not like Crowley. Not like father. Spade – coffin – corpse – rebury. Yet shine the coin once more at the moon: how is it when run through in detail? A gleiss is frozen helium seeping arbitrarily through the narrowest of cracks, following lines of depression and upward incline. But man? Man is meat, bones, solid flesh, he won't seep through clay and sand onto the Ways of the Mammoths – here, a concrete animal organism, and here, geological formations. It cannot be! What kind of physics, what kind of biology would enable such a thing? No logic, no logic in it! Spade – coffin – corpse… there is no corpse. Yakoff Yustinovitch, leaning after his lamp, almost fell into the pit. Shtchekelnikoff had hoicked up the lid and opened the coffin, and the coffin was revealed to be empty. Arsky handed the lamp to Tchingis, who shone it lower. A frozen pulp remained: soil, splinters and chips of wood, scraps of black fabric. The lid is untouched, but the coffin-bottom exists not. Shtchekelnikoff lit a cigarette; the heavies exhaled thick unlichted murch mist. Moonlight was spreading over the graveyard, the snow, the fog and the City of Ice. Pick up the cross and read out the name of the Fyodorovian: Ivan Tikhonovitch Kopytkin. He had died, and only then descended onto the Ways of the Mammoths.

On the Daughter of Winter and beautiful devotchkas, on the war between spirit and matter and the difficult love for the body

'Day six.'

'What's that you're muttering?'

'I shall freeze.'

'You'll warm up once you start dancing.'

'But there I shall make my excuses. I am no dancer.'

'*Sans blague*, you danced with Jelena in the Express.'

'Ah, then I had a sore leg.'

Mademoiselle Filipov made a wry face, pouting and gazing reproachfully from under her snowbright lashes.

'You promised, Benedykt, you'd stop playing the madman!'

'I am not playing.' Swear with the white-gloved hand pressed to the silk revers of the tailcoat. 'I never play.'

She stabbed the chest with her folded fan as if with a stiletto.

'Why do you do this to me? Couldn't you at least today – like a normal man? You yourself invited me, yet now –'

Place a gallant kiss on her lace-cuffed hand.

'May lightning strike me dead and reduce me to cinders if a dozen dancing partners aren't found at once!'

She cast her eyes around the crystal gallery.

'But I don't know anyone…' she mumbled.

Yet in truth Christine Filipov looked spectacular – with her golden fair hair pinned aloft and clasped by a light silver tiara, her bosom raised high below bare shoulders and deep décolleté in the nineteenth-century fashion which had frozen here under the Ice, her waist tightly pinched by a gown of the noblest rustling silk. Blushing neath the rouge of her ballroom maquillage, she still resembled a chubby teenager who'd not quite blossomed into womanhood – a debutante at her first ball.

Couples spilled one after the other from underneath the gallery onto floor of the foyer, the ballroom and other thrown-open rooms, as Mademoiselle Filipov leaned down to observe them from above; in the backdrop, snow-covered taiga shone in the moonlight. The governor general's palace stood upon gubernatorial land some thirty versts from Irkutsk, on hundreds of spidery coldiron spans – suspended in the sky above the wilderness between clouds and stars, where no gleissen could reach the count and his guests. It was reached by driving up a serpentine incline that added half a verst to the distance, a slope so gentle that reindeer could pull their sleighs over the ice without difficulty. The palace was built largely of pure frostoglaze – the floor was of frostoglaze, as were the walls of at least the first storey. When all the lamps and candles were lit within, like now, the night-time taiga seemed to opalesce in kaleidoscopes of colour as far as the very horizon.

'And that – isn't that Princess Tatyana? And Count Schultz – will you recognise Count Schultz, Benedykt, sir?' whispered Mademoiselle Christine, discreetly pointing to this or that personage from behind her fan. 'Mr Pobedonostseff most likely won't appear, will he? But yesterday in the hotel, I heard that General Myerzoff had come to Irkutsk specially with his suite. *Il y a du monde ici!*'

'Well Siberia at least.'

Maybe as a result of the six-day fast – the next certainty of soletruth flashed through the mind, acute and blinding.

'You've never been to a ball in your life. When you moved in New York society… who was it as?'

Again, she blushed.

'Agh, so you too, sir, were placing bets, am I not right? In the train, like everyone else. "His daughter, granddaughter or lover?"' She took a deep breath, her breasts almost popping out of her décolletage. 'So, I shall tell you, sir, what the truth is –'

Catch her as swiftly as possible by her whale-boned waist and spin her around, placing a white finger on her lips and closing her mouth. Her eyes widened.

'Shhh!' Hiss at her. 'Don't tell me! None of those things. I don't want to know! Couldn't I have asked Nikola myself ages ago? But no! I shall resist it to the last drop of murch! No certainty about a woman, do you understand?'

'B-but,' she stammered, 'why ever not?'

'Doctor Konyeshin was right, it's a male complaint.'

'Whatever do you mean?'

'Truth.' Withdraw from the balustrade. 'Let's go, it's time to introduce you to society.'

'And you, sir, are going to do the introductions?' she pouted again, instinctively adjusting her evening gloves and folds of her gown, which trailed behind her over a modest bustle.

Offer her an arm.

'I even had visiting cards printed for the occasion. But no, it won't be me. Do you imagine, miss, I didn't thoroughly study their customs first?'

'A pity one can't learn to dance from scholarly books,' she sighed, descending the spiral staircase onto the frostoglaze floor, that is, onto the sky above the taiga.

'Were it possible to learn all such things from books, we would be what we read, Christine, and there'd be little difference between the written instructions for what a man ought to be and the living man. Allow me: Lawyer Modest Pavlovitch Kuzmentsoff, a friend of the court; Mademoiselle Christine Filipov.'

She curtsied neatly. The old man, dressed in tails and supported by a lackey in Count Schultz's household livery, placed a kiss on the young woman's hand.

'Charming, charming,' he muttered from the depths of his beard. 'Really, Venyedikt Filipovitch, you didn't do her justice, let me look at that smile, my child, ah, a little warmth still for my old bones…!'

Her cheeks blushed bright pink, which only enhanced her innocent charm.

The lawyer motioned with his stick to a swarthy young officer in the dress uniform of the guards paying his respects nearby to two heavy-weight salon witches, who were completely blocking the pathway of the remaining guests.

'I was thinking that there's no better person than our young warrior fresh from his training in England – well, come here, before you get swept away again – Lieutenant Andrey Avivovitch Rostotsky of the Preobrazhensky Regiment, Mademoiselle Christine Filipov, coming to us directly from America via Europe at the invitation of His Imperial Exaltedness, yes? – but you can tell him yourself, child – take care of the young lady, Andryushka – because I am inviting Gospodin Yeroslavsky to step to one side, ooph, wait a moment, wait a moment…' Assisted by two lackeys, he strode in dignified fashion towards an adjoining room. Cast Mademoiselle Filipov a knowing glance – had she noticed? She was already beaming coquettishly at Lieutenant Rostotsky, marvellous-ly abashed, whilst he, a handsome beast with pointed Spanish beard and whiter-than-white teeth, was enchanting her with English compli-ments, no doubt actually sincere.

Modest Pavlovitch sat down on the cushions of an ottoman beneath a collection of wolf snouts mounted on the frostoglaze wall; immedi-ately beyond the wall, a new stream of guests flowed past: black tails, white shirt-fronts, double-hued uniforms all sparkling with orders and sashes in different shades, the ladies' toilettes similarly variegated, gold, diamonds, gold, diamonds – the aristocracy and haute bourgeoise of Tsarist Siberia.

The lawyer tapped his stick on the floor – whilst far below his feet, above the cold-coloured wilderness, the wind was whipping up a kogel-mogel out of clouds of snow-dust, a single rotation of the spiral blizzard stretching over two versts.

'Were you in the gallery?'

'No sign of him there.'

'Wait then by the stairs. He's that kind of man –'

'Mm-hmm?'

'He'll stand in shadow, watch from above. In the gallery or behind a colonnade, so you'll catch a glimpse of him as he walks through the hall.'

'And the Angel?'

'The Angel hasn't yet come, they're to whisper in my ear when he arrives. Maybe he won't come at all, Pobedonostseff has sent his wishes with apologies.'

'Then why should they insist on my coming?'

'Pshaw! For a thousand reasons, for you mostly tragic. Should some-thing happen, God forbid' – he crossed himself, once, twice, thrice, finally kissing his ring – 'you have someone to guard your back, eh?'

'Here? At the governor general's ball?'

'Do you know how many Ottepyelniks are here at Count Schultz's express invitation? For I shan't mention the courtiers touched by Rasputin.'

'No one knows me.'

'That's how it seems to you, is it?' growled the old man and took a pinch of snuff. 'At least the tails sort of fit, but – you could have had a civilised haircut!'

'I did have a haircut.'

'Then you should have shaved off your beard! You look like – like –'

'Like what?'

'Some hermit snatched by force from his skete and dumped in a palace!' He sneezed, gasped, as his anger lost impetus. 'But maybe it's better this way, people expect something after all from the blood of Batyushka Moroz, yes? Only remember: There is no Gospodin Wielicki in any of this.'

Strike the chest with the fist.

'But should something happen,' address the lawyer in German, 'I've got a hefty revolver.'

Kuzmentsoff shielded his eyes with his hand.

'By the Saviour's wounds, whom have I let into the salons...'

Instead of lurking by the stairs, climb back up to the gallery and sit down in the farthest, most shadowy corner – such as was found in the gubernatorial glass palace only upstairs, where the floors and certain walls were lined with ordinary brick, since it would have been indecent in the extreme to make a house transparent on every level and at every cross-section.

As usually happens at such receptions – at least this was deemed to be the norm – more interesting things were going on all around the evening's main attraction than in the centre of everyone's attention, that is, in the great frostoglaze ballroom, modelled probably on Louis

XIV's Hall of Mirrors, beneath tungetitum chandeliers glowing fierily in the unlicht emanating from hooded blackwickes. Fifty arshins away, on the far side of the gallery, the musicians were getting ready, strumming and twanging on their tuned instruments; here, on the entrance side, people were converging and dispersing under the gallery – into six corridors and a dozen glass drawing rooms – relatives and acquaintances, friends and enemies, lovers and *hommes d'affaires*, Russians and Poles, Russians and Germans, Russians and French, Russians and subjects of the Austro-Hungarian emperor, Russians and those so high-born they acknowledge ultimately no nationality and no subjugation to any power: speaking the languages of the salons and loyal to houses to whom borders and politics and religions count for nothing. Prince Vasyl Orloff and the princesses, Grand Duke Dmitry Pavlovitch, Prinz Gregory of Oldenbourg and his princess, Grand Duke Nikolay Nikolayevitch, first cousin once removed to the tsar and banished from European Russia by Rasputin, General Myerzoff and his wife... Ladies handed over their *sorties de bal* and picked up their decorative dance cards, gentlemen fondled the white bowties at their throats... Count Schultz-Zimovy in full dress uniform – it had to be he – was greeting the distinguished guests in the narrow neck of the hall, standing against a backdrop of swirling snow.

Observe them closely, their reflections and prismatic figures overflowing from luxury to luxury on the frostoglaze walls and columns, and experience a strange feeling of detachment: God had clenched his fist and pushed Schultz's palace half a sense farther off. Stare inside the terrarium. Or rather, from inside the sealed terrarium – at them, living in freedom. Why, these were two entirely separate worlds in the most fundamental biblical sense, kept apart by a sheet of armoured glass between them. What is a poor mathematician and private teacher, son of a Polish exile, doing at Governor General Schultz-Zimovy's ball? Transport a Yakut from his native taiga to the court in Saint Petersburg and have him try to find his feet in such alien surroundings! And so, what to do – laugh at the whole thing? or rather tremble in fear? The worst thing was that the skin on the hands no longer burned at all.

Two couples traversed the gallery, a flustered valet darted across, then a young woman in a waft of carmine ribbons, a maid chasing her mistress's lapdog, then lackeys carrying chairs for the ladies; someone walked in and walked out, someone walked in and waved laughing over the balustrade, someone walked in and lit a cigar.

Beneath the tungetitum chandelier, performances by Yevgeny Vitting and Fritz Vogelstrom, apparently famous tenors, were announced.

'*Quel dommage.*'

'*Pardon?*' He glanced round, having removed the cigar from his mouth.

'*Le Père du Gel n'a pas pu venir.*' Stand up and approach him. Embrace the entire glass palace in a single sweep of the hand: 'Imagine such a *tableau* forever frozen in the purest ice: all your riches, all your puffed-up airs, overbearing orders and decorations, cloying women. A drop of History, History in a frozen drop.'

'Gospodin Gierosławski has sipped the wine of politics,' said Frantishek Markovitch Uriah and offered a cigar magicked from under his tails. 'His tongue's in a twist from the drunken allusions.'

'Why did you give me those secret maps and reports of Winter?'

'Well, why d'you think? So that you could find your father.'

'Aha.' Light the cigar. 'Find my father. And then – what?'

He smoothed the blond lock on his forehead; a glintz drifted over the pale countenance.

'A drop of History, you say.' He moved his cigar over the rainbow-coloured scene, as if measuring it up for a painting. 'You see Prince Folche there? Sucking up to His Excellency? Once upon a time, the prince possessed an estate of fifteen thousand souls and annual income of a million roubles. Now he begs around the manors and mansions of his relatives.'

'He fell into disfavour?'

'Disfavour?' Uriah snorted. 'The Ice set in, that's what. The prince had invested vast sums in enterprises which immediately after the introduction of coldiron technologies proved to be passé, and bankrupted him accordingly.'

'Ah. So, an Ottepyelnik.'

Uriah fixed his pince-nez on his nose and stared from close up in clinical amazement.

'Better sit down, Venyedikt Filipovitch, it may come as too big a shock to you. These people, the majority of them – well, to be frank: almost all these people, except perhaps a few highest-ranking officials elevated in government departments thanks to their own ambition, such as Timofey Makarovitch, all these people have no political opinions worthy of note, because they are simply stupid. I know it's an indisposition totally alien to your experience and hard for you to empathise with, but try: they are stupid, each as stupid as the next, stupid as a butcher's block. "Lyednyaks"! "Ottepyelniks"! This would mean they had understood something in those pea-brains of theirs to their own benefit: that this or that politics would be more worthwhile, History flowing in this or that direction. But listen for a moment to their banal conversations, to their idiotic discussions conducted with great solemnity. A child playing with a doll has a better idea of human anatomy than they of affairs beyond the salon world. Bored ladies meet to experience excitement at spiritualist evenings and theosophical lectures, and thus, because of fashion, Gospodin Gierosławski, because of fashion, they drift into Rasputin's circles, and now I hear that we have in Russia "court Martsynians". Hah! Or two squires, drunk as lords, dancing together with a bear, will spur on one another to even greater follies, and oh: they'll enter politics – but what's the political fashion nowadays? Democrats? Nationalists? Socialists? Liberals? Lyednyaks? Ottepyelniks? Well, there you have it! *Et voilà*! This is how it always was in Russia, and how it will be, since it has already frozen. And all the more so once they arrive here under the Ice – the truth about them,' here he began flicking his cigar from one distinguished figure to another, 'idiot! idiot! idiot!'

Let out a long stream of smoke over the tongue.

'What's happened?' inquire in an undertone.

His mouth was already open but he restrained himself at the last moment. He merely smiled and put away the tsviker.

'Please follow me. At ten paces, so as not to attract gossip. Well, Venyedikt Filipovitch, we will try to find a remedy for your misfortune.'

He descended calmly from the gallery and turned down a corridor to the left. Hurry after him at an even pace, the cigar helping to preserve a semblance of nonchalance. Wonder at what could have happened, without taking the eyes off the barebones's back; no doubt some daft illogical order had again descended on Schultz and his people and upset their political plans, thwarted their arrangements, destroyed their well-baked strategies. The frustrated Frantishek Markovitch now breathes bitterness against Saint Petersburg and everything Petersburgian. D is the result of C, which is the result of B. And where, in this mosaic of high imperial politics, is Father Frost…?

Uriah pointed to the entrance of a corner room that was not transparent, that is, with walls made of brick or wood separating it from the rest of the palace. Step inside; Uriah gave the order to wait patiently, withdrew from the threshold and gently closed the door. The external walls as well as the floor, not covered by any carpet, revealed a panorama saturated with the colours of the nocturnal taiga beneath the moon in its first quarter, a vast expanse of multihued ice and snow. Open the pocket watch. Seven minutes to nine. The first bars of music sounded in the depths of the palace. Search for an ashtray. Displayed in showcases and on the internal walls of this private study was a rich collection of mammoth ivories and blacktungets. Mijnheer Iertheim had once demonstrated one of the latter: a lump of tungetitum gathered by magpies from the surface of the soil, an early chip off the main mass that landed by the Podkammenaya river. This was the most precious form of tungetitum because its value was calculated not only according to weight, but according above all to shape and composition. Blacktungets resembling human or animal figures were regarded by Buryat shamans as powerful talismans. There also existed polymineralic kholodovniks: forms of tungetitum deposited as veins in quartz or granite, misshapen sandstone blacktungets and the like. Count Schultz's collection must have been worth upward of a hundred thousand roubles. Admire the exhibits, strolling slowly along the cupboards and glass stands. Several of the blacktungets made an exceptionally strong impression; it was hard to resist the belief that they hadn't been miraculously cast in tungetitum by some indigenous artist – in the shape of a woman in the blessed state, a mammoth, a kneeling man, a man with stag's antlers… They resembled the frozen patchwork goylems put together by the madman Piegnar. Shudder.

Sit down in an armchair in the corner, that is, in the air above the chasm. Cross the arms involuntarily over the chest in an instinctive movement to protect the body from the frost. Let us say that the plan succeeds and the governor general grants his protection, gives his blessing and the official document for an expedition into the heart of Winter together with guides and shamans, and that it's possible to smuggle in and apply on the spot the Kotarbiński pump, adjusted in the meantime by Tesla for use on people, and that the pater, defrosted in this way, doesn't die; let us say it all works out successfully – so how then to escape together with father the attention of the whole party, how to give the state-backed trackers the slip in the icefields of Siberia and safely reach Harbin or the ship in Vladivostock. Even if it's possible to strike a deal with the Yapontchiks, then all that will change is that father and son will find themselves in the hands of Piłsudski, and not of the governor general. God only knows which is worse.

Either way, even if it means open bondage, a decision needs to be made quickly, before Nikola moves to testing his Great Murch Hammer on Baikal – for then it really will be a pure lottery: spat out somewhere in the wilderness like the Dumb Ballooner, even if father survives Thaw itself, even if the resonance of the murch wave *does not shatter him*, as Nikola is predicting with his usual self-confidence for the entire Ice –

Leap to the feet, rush to the door, jerk the handle. Locked. Howl furiously.

How was it possible to be such an idiot! For the word given to Miss Filipov had been willingly kept – and so, as a result, the mind has frozen to stone; pound it with a hammer and not one fresh half-thought flakes off!

Locked, locked, and this the only door; Uriah had chosen the chamber well, no one shall see through the walls, whilst the gubernatorial palace possesses no windows, obviously, for what's the use of windows when there's an abyss below. Kick the spittoon; it resounded against the frostoglaze. Kick the leg of the sofa; hiss in pain.

He had locked the door and gone to inform Schultz. They'll wait till the ball finishes, then send in their thugs or their gendarmes even, arranged on some pretext; thus, the whole affair will come to an end. Cursing to left and right under the moustache, wrest the Grossmeister from the belt, unwrap the oilcloths. The black revolver shone coldly opalescent in the white hand.

Grind the teeth on the cigar. And so, it had been a mistake from the start, shouldn't have come here. What had happened – well, what had happened was that Schultz was no longer dependent on Father Frost; evidently, instructions had come saying that negotiations with the gleissen could no longer help him, bah, the very presence here of the Son of Frost compromises the governor; Lawyer Kuzmentsoff had sensed something, the invitation had come after all as a result of Pobedonostseff's machinations; something did not add up from the start, yet how can a man keep up with rotations of the cogwheels of State, how penetrate the thoughts of the Tsar-God – he won't penetrate them. Inspect the tungetitum bullet in the cylinder, draw back the scorpion-cock. Fire at the frostoglaze floor? (Far below, beneath the feet, the spiral of snowy mist was spinning above primeval forest.) At best, there'd be no falling out and breaking of the neck at once – equally certain was that freezing would happen within a few minutes. Fire at the door? But suppose Uriah had posted someone behind it? Well, maybe then at the wall. Gaze at the cupboards of exhibits, and at length an original idea rattled beneath the skull.

The frames, wire stands and candleholders were made of coldiron, of a high-carbon coolbond. Arrange them along the internal wall, in the place farthest from the door, having moved the furniture to the sides. Wedge the wires under the boiserie, knock the candelabra into the wall, hammering the chill metal with the butt-end of the Grossmeister. For nothing will come of freezing the wall itself; the wall has to be blown out, and this can only be done by frost having the force of matter, that is, ice. The blacktungets will serve as the main counter-thermal mass. On the other hand, if heat from the impact turns to frost in the counter-thermal material, how will this material behave under the impact of frost? Will it emit heat? Tungetitum, after all, radiates under unlicht. But how to calculate – according to what scale – such an anti-heat wave? Passing through the tungetitum, it would reverse at every atom: colder – warmer – colder – warmer – colder... Is this precisely what shattered the gleiss? But tungetitum never warms up, all the more so in frost. Maybe such unique coldiron coolbonds do exist, for instance, the nickel coolbond used to construct the Grossmeister – it has to smother the tungetitum's cold within the structure of the barrel... Try to rec-reate in memory the details of the events on Zima Station, the whole model of that frost-explosion. Where the bullet struck, how the frost spread over the coldiron rails. And what Doctor Wolfke had written in his conclusions to the experiments in the coldmill workshop. The con-densation and solidification of air... Engineer Iertheim's tungetitum hammer tapping on the thermometric anvils... Thermal superconduc-tivity... Gather the blacktungets into a single black pyramid; coldiron scaffolding strayed from it in labyrinthine twists across the wall, like an electrical circuit assembled from baroque fittings entangled in ivy. Withdrawing to the opposite corner, take aim with the Grossmeister. The whole installation, seen now with one eye along the lizard-barrel to the horned bead, resembled the altar of some pagan cult – but maybe the local savages themselves build such –

All of a sudden, the door was thrown open to reveal the most beauti-ful girl ever seen.

Freeze, having instinctively turned the gun on her as she entered. The devushka squealed and shielded her mouth with her hand, staring in childish amazement at the Grossmeister. Then she slowly redirected her gaze towards the construction of coldiron and blacktungets, and her eyes grew bigger still.

Lower the revolver. Her whiter-than-white gown, its neckline en-circled in a haze of sky-blue tulle, cooled by gold-fluff, hung suspended above the snowy abyss like an angelic cloudlet in a devotional picture. The devushka took a step forward, whilst her flounces, laces and pet-ticoats rustled as though a wind were blowing. She took a second step and a third. Stand rooted to the spot – whilst she, instead of running away, came closer still and touched the barrel of the Grossmeister with her outstretched finger. A silver-and-pearl necklace sparkled on her alabaster breasts with each hastening breath.

Remove the chewed cigar from the mouth, exhale a cloud of tobacco smoke.

The krasavitsa burst into ripples of laughter.

'Que c'est beau!'

A flower of unknown species, of purplish-violet hue, was pinned into her chestnut hair, flowing loose in the peasant style. The diamond stars chilled into her frostoglaze ear-studs flashed in alternation with the necklace. Suppress the defensive reflex: to raise the arm, shield the eyes.

In the doorway, fresh turmoil: Uriah accompanied by a gentleman covered in orders and decorations, two lackeys, as well as a crowd of people thronging from behind. The devushka sprang up like a startled bird, spun around on her toes, rushed to the door and accosted the dignitary whom she'd only just recognised. '*Oh, papa…*!' And embracing him around the neck, she began to whisper in his ear.

Hide the Grossmeister at once neath the tails and white piqué waistcoat.

Frantishek Markovitch eventually forced the rest of the company back into the corridor; there remained only Governor General Schultz-Zimovy himself and his servants, who quickly drew up an armchair for him, installing beside it incense burners, positioning within hand's reach a side table with crystal and frostglaze goblets, and pouring out liquor quicker than the master could click his fingers. With a sigh, the count sat down in the gothic chair, crossing his outstretched legs at the ankles; a lackey shoved beneath them an empire-style footstool.

Next, Schultz nodded his consent. Take a seat in the chair prepared by one of the servants at a suitable distance. Another ripped the cigar out of the hand. Sit straight as if nailed to a board, with the knees pressed together and the palms on the knees. The ill-concealed Grossmeister dug into the kidneys.

According to the mathematics of character in the Land of Truth (Wielicki, therefore Kuzmentsoff, therefore Schultz), the governor general of the Irkutsk Governorate was a successful man, that is, someone who had distinguished himself in the highest spheres of imperial Russia through his own person, since he had not been born on the heights (from which a man can at best only fall), but had climbed up single-handedly; unaccustomed to social success, but achieving success; not hungry for success, but hungry for something to which he could only now aspire thanks to his success. He hailed from an impoverished landowning family; the gubernatorial chair he'd received as the crowning glory of his military and ministerial career. Following the Winter of the Gleissen, however, the Irkutsk governor generalship had not proved to be an attractive reward for a court favourite, but a dangerous challenge and field of onerous work – in different circumstances, it would surely not have fallen to a person the likes of Timofey Makarovitch Schultz.

The count raised his hand, into which a handkerchief was immediately placed; he coughed into it, turning his head towards the stream of perfumed incense. His greying beard was trimmed in the Swedish fashion but with luxuriant grizzly side-whiskers. He was significantly bald; light from the naphtha lamps bounced off the high hairless pate. On his chest shone the Order of Saint Andrew the Apostle the First Called hanging on a heavy triple-chain collar adorned with medallions in red and blue, silver and blue and red and gold, as well as the figure of the crucified apostle on a Saint Andrew's cross set on a golden two-headed eagle incrusted with tungetitum. The eagle on the order's eight-pointed star was encircled by the inscription: *For faith and fealty.*

The count narrowed his eyes, glanced at the moon, glanced at the icebound taiga beneath his feet, glanced at the installation of coldiron and blacktungets and again lowered his lids.

'But you're not some Martsynian fanatic, eh?'

'No, Your Illustriousness.'

'Thank God for that.' He coughed once more and thrust the handkerchief back at the lackey. 'Forgive my daughter, she'd heard speak of the Son of Frost and, well, you can't restrain a woman's curiosity. She's still a child. But you,' he suddenly shot a swift glance, 'what about you, Venyedikt Filipovitch, am I right?'

'Yes, Your Illustriousness.'

'You give the impression of a definite person. Frantishek Markovitch says you are a mathematician. Which, I confess, I find no guarantee of great practicality when it comes to life matters. I was reading your, mm-hmm, *Apoliteia*...'

'Your Illustriousness reads such illegal rags?'

'But where else can one read anything interesting these days? Not in the newspapers blest by our right-thinking tchinovniks. Nothing will get past them that might disturb the minds of good Russians. If you want to know what sizzles deep in the Russian soul, then read the underground press. They collect it for me every week, an uncommonly edifying read.

'And so,' he inhaled the incense smoke into his lungs, 'and so you consider that our Most Gracious Lord as well as the prime minister and all our ministers and government departments, and I too, for example – shall be made redundant by the Ice?'

'Yes.'

He smiled under his moustache.

'Your Illustriousness can see for himself that His Sovereign Majesty the Emperor is also certain of it, from his dreams and intuitions if not from actual knowledge; therefore he is protecting himself, therefore he wants war on the gleissen.'

'Aleksandr Aleksandrovitch believes you are a Lyednyak.'

'Pobedonostseff?'

'On a second reading, however, I noticed you wrote the text in such a way that it's impossible to tell: do you really wish to see such an Un-State?'

'Forgive me, but what does it have to do with –'

He flinched; the first spark of irritation flashed in his eye.

'Perhaps I'll throw you to the Okhrana,' he said, 'or perhaps dispatch you to your parent with an amnesty, but whatever use I decide to make of you, I must first understand the instrument I hold in my hands, true?'

'Understand the man...'

'You said something?' he snarled.

'I am not a Lyednyak.' Speak sharply without looking him in the eye. 'Nor am I an Ottepyelnik.'

'But you believe in History under the Ice. So, who are you, eh?'

Who? Close the eyes for a moment before the mirrors and crystal goblets and the other man's eyes. The sixth day of Frost. Who?

'I am... a mathematician. A mathematician of History, *le Mathématicien de l'Histoire*.'

Count Schultz-Zimovy brought his fingertips together and rested his chin on his thumbs. Now he was staring partly from under his brow, from below the high forehead.

The servants moved out of the field of vision. Apart from the smoke drifting from the incense burners, nothing obscured the Siberian horizon, the clear starlit sky and below it the snow-laden blizzards revolving in slow, rainbow-coloured prominences. The gothic throne, the footstool, the hard chair, the incense burners – hovered above the Land of the Gleissen like words uttered in absolute silence.

'Three months,' said the governor general. 'Will you manage to reach an understanding with him in three months?'

'If I find him.'

'Mr Uriah gave you all the maps and pointers.'

'It's outdated. Your Excellency, the Ways of the Mammoths of Batyushka Moroz cannot be calculated in this way.'

'Why not?'

'Because there is more than one of them. At least three, maybe four.'

'Fathers of Frost?' he bridled.

'People who have descended onto the Ways of the Mammoths in the flesh.' Enumerate them on the stiffened fingers. 'The Dumb Ballooner. A certain Ivan Tikhonovitch Kopytkin, a poor hibernik from the Catholic Martsynians. Filip Filipovitch Gierosławski. Maybe Aleister Crowley. It's a black-physical process, not a divine miracle.'

'So, you're saying you won't succeed.'

'That I did not say. What became, Excellency, of Karol Bohdanovitch and Aleksander Czerski?'

He frowned.

'Of whom?'

'The geologists who first described the Ways of the Mammoths.'

'I'm not familiar with their case. Ask Frantishek Markovitch.'

'I suspect... Your Illustriousness will forgive me, I will speak honestly.'

'You will speak honestly, even when lying.'

Laugh with relief.

'That's true! Even when lying; especially when lying. But here... Your Illustriousness isn't devoting precious time to me at his daughter's engagement party for the sake of some whim of Mr Uriah's – but because he's been forced to by political necessity. Your Illustriousness can see that I'm not after Rappacki's dirty money; I am interested only in my father. Your Excellency is pressed for time, I am also pressed for time. Three months, yes. I'm guessing it's some ultimatum from Saint Petersburg, perhaps the work of Morgan's agents. The reasons at this moment are of no consequence. For the sword hangs over me too. Your Excellency knows of the emperor's contract with Doctor Tesla.'

He nodded.

'Doctor Tesla is my friend.' Continue without altering the tone or averting the eyes, now already very hard: 'But Doctor Tesla prophesies total Thaw and death to the Ice, and I believe he may succeed; for he's a man who's made a career of achieving through his own reason things which everyone before him regarded as impossible. Nothing and no one will stop him, for I don't imagine Your Illustriousness –'

'Say no more, it's the command of His Imperial Exaltedness. No hair shall fall from the doctor's head.'

'That's the thing. That's the thing, the dependency here is plain, mathematical. I shan't allow any harm to come to him either – but at the same time –'

'You have to rescue your father, yes.'

'And what for me is the only means of doing so? The emperor's word. He it is who will recall Tesla, he who will prevent Thaw and any other engineering against the Ice, and he who will then leave the Land of the Gleissen and you, Excellency, in peace. Before this, however, the gleissen must withdraw according to a political agreement, History has to be parcelled out. You have three months left; I – the time until Thaw. You see, we are after the same thing, we shall both profit by realising the one aim.'

The governor gradually breathed in the sweet incense, leaning over on his throne; the decorations on his uniform twisted out of shape.

'What I do see – what I do see is that you lie honestly,' he said and suddenly raised his hand as the mouth fell open in protest. 'I've had plenty to do in my time with born-and-bred Poles: the worst prevarications – yet honest to the marrow, since that pride of yours always remains, that stupid arrogance which you're incapable of discarding even in face of mortal danger, so that in Summer any fellow who knows how to bow and scrape to his clients easily swindles you. On the other hand, here in Winter, I would fill all offices in the Citadel with Poles, if I could. "Apoliteia", by all means!' He sat up straight in his chair. 'I'm offering you this agreement backed by my word: by the end of January nineteen twenty-five you will provide proof of an understanding reached with the gleissen; to this end, you will immediately receive all official permissions, men from the Blagoveshtchensky Regiment, money for necessary expenses within reasonable limits, as well as the suspension of all sentences against your father. If His Sovereign Majesty the Emperor is convinced as a result, then you have my gratitude. If not… well, what of it, the thing will already be beyond my control anyway.'

'Proof, proof.' Repeat the word under the moustache. 'What proof shall satisfy His Imperial Exaltedness? The Ice won't withdraw so quickly.'

'Are you sure?'

'I work for Krupp's cryophysicists, I know what speeds are possible in the Frost. Imagine, Excellency, History as a mountain glacier descending down a slope into a valley.'

The count kicked aside the footstool.

'In that case – nothing will come of it, *c'est la fin*.'

'Wait!' Begin in a thoughtless reflex, as they had not been itching, to scratch the hands through the cotton gloves. 'What kinds of proof hold up strongest in Winter? What will logically defend itself here even more effectively than the testimony of the senses?'

'Speak clearly!'

'Your Illustriousness reads Cicero? In Ancient Rome, the verdict of a trial was often decided by so-called "proof of character", that is, testimony to the upright character of the accused lodged by other upright Romans – even though a hundred material proofs testified against him. For what is more important, what is closer to Truth? Knife and flesh or spirit and idea?'

'Agh!' Count Schultz-Zimovy held out his hand, coughed into the proffered handkerchief, then tossed it behind him; the agile servant caught it in mid-air. 'I understand. You're right, you're right, that's how it has to be done. Someone who already enjoys the trust of Our Gracious Sovereign…' Again, he brought his hands together under his chin. 'It's even worked out well that now, at the ball – you will stay, I will summon you again – certainly I'll find someone suitable. Two grand dukes are here, but they… Mm-hmm.'

'Meanwhile, something else still requires agreement.' Moisten the lips with the tongue. 'The substance of this understanding with the gleissen. Excellency, do I have a free hand?'

'You must know from Doctor Tesla at least what will satisfy the emperor: the liberation of European Russia from under the Ice, especially the cities. Saint Petersburg without gleissen – this will already buy us a year, or two.'

'I know, ahem, of this shock to His Imperial Exaltedness, I heard, I heard.' The eyes fled to the moonlit snow-laden gales. 'But it's not just a question of temperature –'

'Are you asking if I believe in the theories of Nikolay Berdyaeff? Well, no, I do not believe in them. You may practise your mathematics of History as long as you leave the Ice intact, so as to both pacify the emperor and not harm industry in Irkutsk.'

Bite into the tongue. Although it's hard to conceive of under the Ice: the more left unsaid, the better. Why raise the topic at all? Besides, a governor general of the Russian Empire can't be asked, for example, whether he would sell to the Son of Frost a free Poland in exchange for safeguarding the coldiron wealth.

'You have still not explained,' said the count rising from his seat, from his Siberian throne, above the wilderness, 'how you intend to find your father, if not from calculations of the Ways of the Mammoths.'

Rise likewise to the feet.

'Karol Bohdanowicz and Jan Czerski, they surely knew the secret. Geological maps, scientific works and descriptions of indigenous beliefs have been censored. The stamp of the Ministry of Winter is upon them, but also of Sibirkhozheto.'

The count threw up his hands.

'Not mine the power over Rappacki and Pobedonostseff. You must settle the matter yourself with Aleksandr Aleksandrovitch. You're thinking of hiring local shamans? Of having them track Batyushka Moroz along the Ways of the Mammoths?'

'Another method is also possible: as soon as I work out, from the black-physical details, how those people descend to the Ways of the Mammoths, I shall send such a tracker after them...' Fall gradually silent, having discerned that Count Schultz had been intently contemplating for some time the altar of blacktungets in the corner of the study.

'You did that.'

Thrown into confusion.

'Mr Uriah ordered me to wait and –'

He narrowed his left eye.

'Very nice.'

He inquired the hour of a lackey, alerted his ears to the music drifting up from the innermost depths of the palace, and adjusted his cuffs and decorations.

'You will do me a favour,' he said, already turning towards the door. 'My Annushka wishes for one dance, you understand, before society, she's already entered the Son of Frost on her dance card.'

'B-but…! I don't know how…!'

'Come, come,' laughed the governor general as he made his way out preceded by his servants, the incense-burner carriers bringing up the *arrière-garde*, 'fear not, young man, Anna may be more pushful than befits a woman but she'll not harm you, hee-hee!'

The last lackey thrust the extinguished cigar back into the hand.

They left.

This time the door remained wide open. No one stood guard on the other side. A hubbub of music and human voices flowed along the palace's crystal corridors like sounds forced down the pipes of an organ.

A blood-curdling thought occurred, as the angular bundle containing the Grossmeister was shoved back behind the belt: that were it not for Mademoiselle Filipov's angry whim, were it not for this six-day fast, who knows into what fit of horror-filled fantasies Benedykt Gierosławski might have been driven – melted, trembling in every limb, like that Benedykt Gierosławski in the Trans-Siberian Express; would he not, in a panic-stricken reflex, have shot the first person standing in the doorway?

Step out quickly towards the rooms.

Herr Bittan von Asenhoff stood amid a group of disputants beside Lawyer Kuzmentsoff's armchair bending every moment towards the old man in ironic mannerisms of mien and body. Pierre Ivanovitch Schotcha was indulging in banter across the back of the chair with an Orthodox priest and a lady in a Chinese wig, which may have been a familiar fashion acceptable in the New World or in European Russia beyond the Ice, but here such coiffure gave an impression of impropriety, even vulgarity. Realising that it was impossible to approach and talk freely to Modest Pavlovitch, pause in a distracted pose by a glass wall, within earshot (the cigar again came to the rescue).

'No, no, the reverse, the complete opposite!' the priest was perorating, tugging at a button on the uniform of a portly old campaigner. 'Myerzoff could not have done such a thing; since when did cavalry storm fortifications on their own? For a week they'd been marching from Shandong under Japanese fire; were they to shed more of their own blood, chasing them blindly into the Zibo mountains? Where's that map, who's taken the map?'

'The colonel was whisked away to dance by his wife,' yawned Monsieur Schotcha.

'So, you do exactly what the general did!' the ecclesiastic was arguing to the hussar; the hussar merely twisted his long, pomaded moustache behind his ear and bit his lips, whilst the priest, hunched over, moved his finger over the soldier's ample chest, thereby drawing the tactics of Myerzoff's Bohal Campaign. 'First you give chase with cavalry, then you bring up the infantry and engineers and establish a front, squeezing the enemy into a worse and worse position till he has to retreat, and so you conquer the land; this is what military art consists in!'

'How well-versed you are, Father, in military arcana...!' warbled the lady.

'The captain's point,' said von Asenhoff, helping himself to a pinch of Kuzmentsoff's devilishly sharp snuff, 'as far as I understand it, is different. He's not denying at all the tactical expediency of the general's actions. A separate question, however, is a strategy heavily embroiled in politics. *N'est-ce pas?*'

'Let Myerzoff bleed twice as much, let him knock out the whole army in his triumph,' grumbled the captain, 'but destroying at the same time all of Hirohito's land forces; not like he did, allowing them to retreat in orderly fashion, so again we have no definite clear-cut victory, only pacts, ceasefires, negotiations, peace treaties fought at a desk with ink – which on paper reflect not the truth, but try merely to force this paper falsehood on the world.'

'They weren't fighting under the Ice,' muttered Modest Pavlovitch and sneezed.

'*À tes souhaits,*' the lady hastened with her wishes.

Von Asenhoff shook his head pitifully above the old lawyer.

'You're starting on your old theme again. How much can we take! I can't imagine the German or English *Hochgeborene* letting themselves be so hoodwinked by such mystical balderdash. Or even the French. Who has ever *seen* History? Who has measured, fingered, weighed it?'

'Monsieur Bittan surely won't deny that the gleissen have upset the world order,' interjected a pale-faced young man with a bored *devushka* hanging on his arm.

'And if I do deny it,' von Asenhoff rose to the bait, 'how will you prove, sir, that I'm wrong, eh?'

'Along the Ways of the Mammoths –'

'But has anyone *seen* the Ways of the Mammoths?'

'No one has seen truth, justice, the nation, love,' the priest wagged his finger.

'*Bien entendu!*'

'No one has seen speed, time and colour. No one has seen thoughts.'

'I see colour,' the lady mused. 'Oh, I have a lavender-coloured gown *par example.*'

'You do not see the colour lavender,' the priest asserted authoritatively. 'You see that your gown is lavender-coloured.'

The lady failed to understand. She pulled a sour face, then smiled coquettishly, but when this too made no impression, she raised her eyes to heaven.

'My sister's tea woman,' she began, as if precisely this thread of her conversation had been interrupted, 'has a Chinese mother, and she still goes to their idolaters and repeats the ancient beliefs of various Mongolian and Hindu lamas and sorcerers. What say you, Messieurs, to the fact that since time immemorial they speak of "veins of energy" embracing the globe from one sacred place to the next and along which flow human souls, and that according to such geography they divide up the world, and had divided it up long before anyone uttered a word about the Ways of the Mammoths – hah, what say you?'

One of Doctor Tesla's numerous projects sprang to mind, namely his project to industrially exploit the murch energy running along the Ways of the Mammoths. Maybe this mythological thread should be put to him? He used to admit himself that esoteric spiritual experiences were not alien to him. It would take him another few days to search for maps of the local indigenous religions and devise a structure for his teslectric power-plants in places sacred to Lamaism and Hinduism.

'Say what you will,' interrupted Pierre Schotcha, 'some strange force of attraction is at work on the Ways of the Mammoths. Though no one has ever seen them,' he nodded ironically to von Asenhoff. 'My acquaintances with a taste for more refined pleasures –'

'Opium eaters,' the lady whispered in a theatrical voice to the hussar.

'My acquaintances,' began Schotcha, 'have sampled once or twice the infamous black narcotic –'

'You told us they disappeared without trace,' von Asenhoff reminded him.

'Well, the trace is such that one of them who recently tasted the black poppy juice was found only after a whole day of searching by his servants, in dishabille and horribly wasted, lying on the ground, several junctions away from his house. And yet he'd forewarned his valets not to let him out of their sight. He must have wandered there like a dreamslave, poor fellow.'

'Aren't there enough folk getting up to odd things in states of intoxication?' sighed the priest. 'Instead of devoting themselves to God, they prefer to entrust their souls to illicit chemicals.'

'But what I wanted to say is this: for where they found him – was precisely above one of the Ways of the Mammoths. He was lying frozen to the ground with the skin torn off his arms and legs, completely unconscious.'

'Perhaps he'd also stumbled into a gleiss.'

'Well, that he would not have survived.'

'The colonel,' the captain twirled his moustache and took the lady by the arm, 'once had this altercation with gleissen…'

He continued his tale as he led out the overdressed lady in his cockerel's walk, chest thrust forward; the company hastened after him in the direction of the main hall and ballroom; only von Asenhoff sat down on a settee neath a portrait of a cheerless progenitor of Schultz in order to sniff, wistfully, a lace handkerchief belonging to one of the fairer sex.

Approach Kuzmentsoff's chair, a lackey offered a light; puff out a cloud of tobacco smoke. The lawyer raised an eyebrow inquiringly. Bending low to his ear, summarise the results of the conversation with the governor general.

'Which means you achieved what you set out to achieve, no?'

'I have no idea what's going on, Modest Pavlovitch. You have to help me with your knowledge and intuition.'

'Mm-hmm?' He peered from under his grey mane.

'Their plans were not like this. When Mr Uriah, in the Ministry of Winter, put me onto the trail of Father Frost, they had conceived of things entirely differently, aiming for different ends via different paths. Yet now – Uriah spits bitter venom and the count keeps repeating: "three months". Three months!'

'Therefore – things have changed. What's so strange in that? Separate the politics from the mathematics! After all, the world doesn't revolve around you, for neither good nor ill. You won't penetrate the causes of all events that affect you by way of reason. Not even most of them. This can only drive you crazy: stuffing the whole world into your head in order to take it apart on your own, like a Swiss watch, and having put it back together again, seeing why its cogs rotate, how they rotate, why it ticks. Yet this is what you'd like, isn't it?'

'I had thought that here at least, in the Land of the Ice...'

'What? You aspire to omniscience?' he snorted mockingly.

Shake the head.

'Tesla conducted successfully his demonstration of the Battle Pump. Pierpont Morgan's delegation travelled to the emperor and turned him against the Russo-American Company, the Around-the-World Railroad, and against Schultz. Schultz clamps down with repressions. Peace is signed with Japan. He didn't want to show it, but – three months! Modest Pavlovitch, can the emperor dismiss Count Schultz from the Irkutsk general governorateship?'

Lawyer Kuzmentsoff shifted uncomfortably in his chair. A lackey approached; the lawyer pushed him aside with his stick.

'The emperor can do anything,' he growled grumpily. 'The emperor is the emperor. Yes?'

'Yes. Yes.'

'You don't think, do you, that such an ultimatum, were His Exaltedness Nikolay Aleksandrovitch actually to issue it, would be made public knowledge? Should a letter arrive dismissing Timofey Makarovitch, then it will arrive at the very last hour and the count will depart with all honours, accolades and no doubt some new decoration.' The old man opened his snuffbox and offered it across; decline with a shake of the head. 'You imagine too much. Cool down, Venyedikt Filipovitch.'

'Isn't this what the gift of cognition depends upon?' mutter absent-mindedly. 'Upon certainty of the one and only soletruth amongst all possible truths.'

'Will you finally abandon this accursed mathematics!'

'Gospodin Yeroslavsky?'

Spin around.

'Anna Timofeyevna requests Your Esteemed Nobleness to join her in the ballroom,' announced a footman without lifting his eyes off the icebound taiga drenched in moonlight.

'Well, well, well,' gasped Kuzmentsoff and sneezed resoundingly.

Bittan von Asenhoff, sprawling inelegantly neath the gloomy portrait, watched from over the batiste handkerchief pressed to his lips. Blink. The footman was waiting in a half-bow. No way to avoid dancing with the governor general's daughter.

Hundreds of people in a colossal ballroom, lights iridescent on bodies, fabrics, jewellery, and instead of walls – the star-studded horizon of the Siberian night, and instead of floors – the white earth of the Siberian night, the air ashimmer with a thousand reflections of beauty, and she the most beautiful amongst them, the krasavitsa in lilac golden-white amid the other krasavitsas *en grandes toilettes*, who were gaping wide-eyed, holding their breath in the sudden silence – as the footsteps approached, the bow was taken and Mademoiselle Schultz invited to dance.

They sighed audibly. She curtsied, clasping the proffered hand, glove to glove. The fans quivered. The musicians struck up the opening bars of a melody. Not the slightest notion was had of what dance it was to be, of what step should be taken. Lead the count's daughter into the centre of the sky. The swish of her gown – its stacked petticoats and heaped lace towering like a springtime cloud – rustled in the head. Everyone was watching. Sweat trickled over the bare skull in a mean-dering stream, down the centre of the forehead and along the nose. Madness. The young woman smiled a greedy, capricious smile. Swallow the saliva. Everyone was watching.

'Le Fils du Gel,' she whispered.

'La Fille de l'Hiver.'

The dance commenced – was danced.

'You're not in the least cold.'

'So, it seems to you, miss. I've already frozen you.'

'What?'

'Fairy tales, Mademoiselle, fairy tales; please don't believe in them.'

'You kidnap people into the ice, lead them onto the Ways of the Mammoths, ride on the backs of gleissen.'

'At the stroke of midnight, you'll wake up in a block of ice neath Baikal.'

'You jest!'

'You've danced with the Son of Frost, all is lost.'

The dance was danced.

'You won't hurt Papa.'

'I? Hurt the count?'

'Don't harm him, I implore you.'

'But! The revolver was not for him. I have enemies.'

'Ah! But not Papa.'

'Your Papa is extremely generous to me.'

The dance was danced.

'Why close your eyes?'

'It turns out I'm afraid of heights.'

'So why look down?'

'So as not to tread on your feet.'

'With closed eyes, it must be still harder.'

'What can I say, my head reels dancing with you.'

'How funny you are!'

The dance was danced.

'You're already betrothed, true?'

'Yes, true, Papa has agreed, we've been kissed by maternal aunts, cousins, paternal aunts, if you'd only seen…! Did you not see?'

'And your betrothed won't bear a grudge?'

'He will!'

'Oy. Am I to flee?'

'You won't flee.'

'No?'

'No.'

'How do you know such things?!'

'You're cross with Annushka?'

'You like playing billiards with people's characters, huh? Truly, the Daughter of Winter!'

'You're angry, sir –'

'You even know no other world, no other people. Magnet to magnet, water versus fire, choleric versus sanguine, fear versus fear, pride versus jealousy –'

'And Pavel Nestorovitch versus the Son of Frost –'

'But you play such cruel games!'

'Don't hurt Pavel, I implore you.'

'Everyone is watching us, you told them in advance!'

'*Comme vous l'avez dit vous-même, monsieur: le Fils de Gel et la Fille de l'Hiver.*'

'*Excusez-moi.*'

Break loose. Steering a narrow path between dancing couples, cross behind the colonnades and into a side room. Sit down on a stool. The calves were still atremble. An obliging lackey proffered a tray. Gulp down a whole glass of some burning liquor without even registering the taste. The music flowed on, a kamarinskaya probably, the dancing continued; the couples could be seen after all through the frostoglaze walls, swimming over them in streams of colour, so that the outlines of beautiful ladies and handsome men seemed formed merely by chance. Seen just as perfectly therefore was the outline of an angry devushka approaching along the wall in a cascade of kaleidoscopic reconfigurations – Anna Timofeyevna – she swam closer – not Anna Timofeyevna; she entered, fired a shot with her fan, bit her lip. She wanted to come closer, but something suddenly stopped her in her tracks, as if she'd collided with another glass wall.

'It simply eludes me how you could possibly…' Gasping for breath, she merely cried out in wordless despair. Beneath her, the icy gale was gathering momentum, lifting clouds of rainbow mist off the frozen forest in a front several versts wide. 'The Great Son of Frost!' she snorted in contempt.

'They were showing me their finger, huh?'

Mademoiselle Filipov swore rather vulgarly in English, swirled around in a rustle of silk and returned to the swarthy Lieutenant Andryusha with his braided aiguillette, who was observing everything through the glass wall. She held out her hand in a gesture of invitation. They mingled with other dancers.

Icy wind was shattering the icicle-strung trees. Moonlight reflected off the stalagmitic spines of gleissen. The night of the governor general's ball was only just beginning.

When dancing with Jelena… Memories of the dance in the Trans-Siberian Express seemed more intimate now, more vivid and somehow more… *real*. In the current state of mind, no clear image could be evoked of the dance interrupted but a moment ago – as if in reality someone else had been dancing, as if even not this body had been dancing; in no way did this past wish to freeze.

A fat man in tailcoat constricting him like a fish bladder flopped onto a neighbouring stool. His peasant's face with its thousand furrows and dozen frostbite scars crumpled between one expression and the next in constant fits and starts, as if the man's physiognomy were announcing several vying inhabitants of his one inflated body, none of whom were able to gain lasting dominance in the miming war.

'Petrukhoff Ivan,' he introduced himself in the apparent conviction that the name itself explained everything, and at once extended a paw in greeting. 'You certainly gave that Schultz doll a spin, hee-hee! And to cast her off like that – it went to her heels – blushing so much you can smell the burning, hee-hee-hee!' He bent his flabby countenance in mockery-joy-horror-amazement.

'What do you want, Petrukhoff?'

'What do I want? I don't want anything! I'm come to lift a comrade's spirits.' Here he slapped the thigh straining from inside his smooth trouser leg. 'We, the people of ice, Petrukhoff and Yeroslavsky, must be on guard against them, and not fly into their sweet honey like flies into trapping-paper, into these sparkling spangles, flimsy fandangles.'

'"We"?'

He slapped his thigh for a second time.

'You and I, well you'll see for yourself, two outcasts, the looks they give us when they think we don't see –'

'You're mistaken, Petrukhoff, nothing unites us, in nothing are we alike.'

'No?' His physiognomy began to flutter between wheedling, mournful, angry and indifferent airs. 'Do you imagine they'd have let you into their crystal salons if chance hadn't forced them? For they hold their noses, avert their eyes and pretend they don't see, as rabble, hee-hee, rabble, I say, lick their sugar-coated daughters? With these here hands,' he clenched his lacerated hairy paws, 'with these here hands I did everything! For this here magpie pushed on for another verst or so into the deadly frost and discovered a tungetitum field the size of a cowshed – chance! The only way to get amongst them, the only way in: by chance. But a magpie with millions is still a magpie to them.' Petrukhoff whacked a fist into his chest devoid of decorations. 'It has frozen! Riffraff in the salons! Hee-hee-hee!'

Stand without uttering a word, making the most of the excuse when Mr and Mrs Wielicki appeared on the other side of the wall. The music fell silent, applause rang out, a hubbub of conversation arose, couples opalesced in kaleidoscopes of colour between the frostoglaze colonnades.

Wojsław was mopping pearly beads of sweat off his broad forehead.

'Ooph, it's killing me, killing me, I'm no longer a young buck like Benedykt, my love, have pity…'

'I had no idea you were such a splendid dancer!' Halina Wielicka was baring her heart meanwhile. 'And with what airs and graces!'

Smack a kiss on her hand.

'So perhaps you can explain how that's possible when I can't dance at all?'

'Why insist you can't, when you can?'

True or false? Shake the head, chewing on the moustache and doubtless presenting a very dull face. The past exists not, all memories that fit not the present must by definition be false, therefore if now able to dance...

But doesn't this affect most people in fact? Since it cannot be expressed, however, in language of the second kind – it remains forever locked in the private secrecy of the heart. Weak distillates of experiences, warped descriptions of presentiments and vague impressions seep instead onto the outside.

For something here does not add up. For we are not entirely the person whom we remember. For someone else also dwells inside us, an alien, with alien experience and memory. And in these brief moments when he gains the upper hand and takes control of the body, a deeper truth is revealed. We know what we shall see beyond the next hill, even though we've never set foot in this country. In a moment of sudden compulsion, after a lifetime spent sitting behind a clerk's desk, we grab hold of a rifle – having never held a rifle in our hand – and fire the perfect shot. We land in high society where they observe foreign manners of which we haven't and can't have the faintest clue, but then – the cutlery in the hands, the conversation around the table, the word and gesture and *savoir vivre*, for it turns out we're more smoothly versed in all this than even they. Had anyone taught us? had someone prompted us? we know it – but how? As kind-hearted fathers, docile husbands – suddenly we raise our fist against a child, against a woman, in a reflex natural to the hardened thug. We dance, even though we know not how to dance.

Something here does not add up. Life does not match life; past does not match present.

But how to render this experience in the speech of men?

The past exists not.

'Maybe he possesses inborn talent.' Wojsław Wielicki tucked away his handkerchief, stubbed out his smile, winked conspiratorially. 'You'll permit me, my love, a moment, ooph, a quick word with Benedykt.'

Retire behind a pillar.

'Get a move on, Benedykt, and jump into the sleigh!' Wielicki commanded at once. 'Whatever came over you to humiliate her publicly like that! Everyone can see what's brewing; some young officers are already egging on Anna Timofeyevna's betrothed. As if he needed any additional spurs! Don't be a fool, don't court disaster.'

'I can't. I can't, Wojsław, sir, I've just had a word with Schultz; he'll give me the papers for father, papers for myself, a whole agreement, that's why I'm waiting now –'

'So, you can make arrangements with him later! Later, later! Well, just think what you'll say now to Schultz, once his future son-in-law settles scores with your bones or, worse still, you lay a finger on his darling's husband-to-be. Get your arse out of here!'

Grit the teeth.

'I shan't run away.'

'Jesus Christ, by all that's holy! What of it, that they whisper you're the Son of Frost – today they have this attraction in the salons; next week they'll have a different one – anyway, you don't believe in these Siberian fairy tales –'

He broke off, having raised his eyes to the reflections swimming over the frostoglaze.

'Too late.'

Glance around. A band of dandified cavaliers, half in civilian dress, others in uniform, was approaching at a brisk pace, led by a young man red as a beetroot, thin as a rake, dressed in tailcoat crossed diagonally by the sash of some low-class decoration, and with a monocle pressed furiously into his eye socket, adding only to his foppish air.

'This is he?' murmur neath the moustache.

'Pavel Nestorovitch Gerushin.'

'Make yourself scarce.'

Wielicki bridled, angrily waving his hand, diamond flashing. After this slight hesitation, however, he retreated behind a pillar to join his wife, who was fanning herself nervously. Petrukhoff emerged from a side room; he stood against the wall with a large glass in his hand and a pious-joyous-malicious-gracious expression on his face, awaiting the piquant spectacle. Catch in the corner of the eye, on the opposite wall, as in a stained-glass window, the lilac contours of Mademoiselle Schultz: she gazes from afar at the carambole she herself has set in motion with that same greedy smile, just as angelically beautiful. Whilst from behind farther walls across the gubernatorial palace, the whole of Siberia's elite is also watching, no doubt – ladies, gentlemen, counts, princes, generals, millionaires and arch-millionaires.

Mr Gerushin came to a standstill, folded his arms behind his back, rocked on his heels and cleared his throat loudly.

'I insist…,' screeched his voice, and Pavel Nestorovitch turned even redder; he cleared his throat for a second time. 'I demand! I demand that you apologise to Anna Timofeyevna without delay. And… And leave… You have to…' He cleared his throat for the third time, 'Get out!'

Say nothing.

'But first of all, apologise!' Gerushin yelled breathlessly.

Say nothing.

Pavel Nestorovitch's companions whispered to him angrily behind his back. He adjusted the monocle, shuffled his feet.

'Thrash the bastard!' shouted an officer.

Gerushin clenched his fists, took a step forward –

Respond with a broad grin.

He leapt back.

Petrukhoff burst into a guffaw worthy of the taverns; the glass flew from his hand. He clasped his belly, continuing to guffaw as he slid halfway down the wall in convulsions of hilarity.

'But that's choice!' he squealed. 'Oh, I can't, I can't! The maid's found her knight! Hold me upright! The poodle's going to bite the calves of the Son of Frost! Bow-wow!'

Blood rushed to Gerushin's cheeks, the monocle dropped from his eye, the poor fellow shook as if in the grip of fever. A dozen iridescent reflections of him likewise turned bright red, even more glaring. The palace glowed with every shade of shame.

Colder, colder, cold, Frost. Run up to Petrukhoff, grab him by the lapels, shake him till the man finally loses balance and slumps, limbs dangling like shovels, onto the floor, that is, onto the moonlit front of icy gales.

'Was ever such riffraff let loose amongst the high-born!' roar at the top of the voice. 'As the boor sees, as the boor thinks, so shall he spit!'

Pavel Nestorovitch also leaped to and pulled Petrukhoff by the collar as he attempted to stand; Petrukhoff again lost balance and fell on all fours, tossing his head back and forth in shock, coat-tails dangling, tongue hanging out like a dog's, mug flying from grimace to grimace, as the former magpie melted utterly away.

Gerushin restored the ocular to his goggle-eye, bent forward, took aim and dealt Ivan a sweeping blow to his protruding buttocks – oy, he struck pretty solidly, for the fatso shot over the frostoglaze as if over ice, polishing the floor with his belly and shirt-front, continuing to windmill with his arms at the same time, whilst the farther he glided between the prismatic columns towards the ballroom, the more he howled and squealed; he caught his knee on some object and began to spin, travelling farther still; he lost a shoe; lost his neckerchief; eventually he careered into a vase of flowers and came to a halt.

Resounding laughter echoed throughout the palace, everyone was watching and everyone was laughing – Pavel Nestorovitch Gerushin loudest of all, and with such audible relief he put his hands together as if in prayer. His companions crowded around slapping him on the back and exchanging vulgar witticisms in several languages; feel also a wallop or two on the shoulder-blades. Retreat slowly behind a wall, maintaining a dry indifferent expression, and into the rooms. The cavaliers scattered in groups, highly amused. The lilac figure of Anna Timofeyevna vanished from the stained-glass window of shining frostoglaze.

The Wielickis looked on anxiously, yet strangely overawed.

'Ooph, Benedykt, why, you've a nerve, I thought my heart was about to leap from my chest, I must have a drink. It's worked out luckily for you, however, a miracle, a miracle that you wriggled out –'

'Not a miracle and not lucky, only mathematics, Wojsław, sir, cold mathematics.' The head was spinning slightly, a mild shudder passed through the muscles; lean on the doorframe. Discoloured, sequin-dotted images of the Son of Frost were swarming everywhere. Great and incomprehensible indeed be the power of mirrors. 'On one point you're right: we need a drink.'

Cast around for the lackey with the drinks tray. Instead of the lackey, Frantishek Markovitch Uriah loomed before the eyes. Introduce him to Wojsław; Uriah muttered something under his breath and indicated a corridor leading to the untransparent rooms. Apologise to the Wielickis.

'His Illustriousness himself asked me...' begin in conciliatory tone, catching up with the flaxen-haired barebones, who hadn't even glanced back to see if the Son of Frost were hastening in his wake.

'Their salon amusements,' he snarled, 'just one more stupidity.'

Pausing by the half-open door, however, he issued his final advice.

'But now – go in and give the impression of being the most dependable fellow under the sun.'

'Well, what can I do: as it has frozen, so it has frozen.'

'Were that so, you'd still be stuck in Schembuch's waiting room!'

Enter. Suspended against the sky over Siberia, Governor General Schultz-Zimovy turned around at the sound of footsteps. As did Prince Blutsky-Osey.

'Allow me, Your Highness, this is the man –'

'We've met before,' drawled the prince and then, in a toadlike movement of his mouth, adjusted the artificial jaw.

Bow to him – to the prince and also to the princess, who'd been espied dozing in an armchair in the corner.

'Congratulations to your Princely Highness on the signing of the peace treaty.'

The count quickly sensed the situation freezing.

'Gospodin Yeroslavsky will serve us solely as a go-between,' he assured the prince. 'Your Highness never had the opportunity, I presume, to meet his father?'

'No.'

'I had the pleasure of travelling with His Princely Highness on the Trans-Siberian Express.'

'The whole train was nearly blown up thanks to you!' muttered Prince Blutsky.

'You don't say, Your Highness! That wasn't how it was!'

If eyes could strike with physical impetus, half the palace would have shattered to dust neath the count's gaze.

'As I was saying,' he barked, 'because what is not in doubt is that Venyedikt Filipovitch's evidence cannot in any way be regarded as satisfactory for Our Most Serene Master, whilst it is also obvious that His Princely Highness won't be bothering to pursue Batyushka Moroz through the backwoods of the taiga; testimony shall be provided by a witness whom His Princely Highness deems fully trustworthy. The prince has agreed to remain as my guest until your return; he shall hear this man's account from his own mouth and hand the account in person to the tsar. For the prince enjoys the total confidence of His Imperial Exaltedness Nikolay Aleksandrovitch. Do you understand, Venyedikt Filipovitch?'

'Perfectly, Your Illustriousness.'

'Sacré nom de Dieu!' Prince Blutsky clicked his tongue angrily, waved his hand in irritation, and then stomped off without another word, working his short legs in rather sprightlier fashion than might be expected for a man of his years.

The count shattered the other half of the palace, wheezed through his nose and hurried after the prince. The lackeys thronged after him in the doorway. All that remained in the room was the sweet scent of incense.

Exhale in relief. It seemed to have gone well. Considering all the circumstances. Mm-hmm. Evidently, the count too is relying on it heavily. Had he received an ultimatum from the tsar regarding his dismissal, or not? The frostoglaze was very cold to the touch; the gloved hand left no warming trace. Blow into the wall. A mist of unlichted breath stole over the half-moon. Wojsław Wielicki is no doubt right: what was there to be won, had been won, there's no point in annoying them further, especially after that fatal dance with Anna Timofeyevna Schultz... Rest the forehead against the icy frostoglaze.

True or false? The past exists not, all memories that fit not the present must by definition be false; therefore, if now able to dance... On the other hand: it has frozen. (Is freezing.)

An insistent rhythmic knocking penetrated the thoughts. Princess Blutskaya was rapping the floor with her stick.

Perhaps she was summoning a lackey, perhaps Dushin's ghost; all the servants had rushed after the count. Draw near with caution. She raised her hand, extricating it from under the black lace; her entire gown was made of lace and had doubtless cost a few villages half a century ago. Kiss the wrinkled skin. The princess stank of herbs and old age even more than remembered (or the memory was weaker than how she'd stunk in reality).

'Gospodin Gierosławski,' she screeched as if, despite everything, she was amused.

'Yes, indeed, it is I, Your Highness, I, I, the very same.'

'Well come here then, you ne'er-do-well.'

Bend even lower than before in the train, in the parlour car.

She gave off a warm foul smell of bodily corruption.

'What's happened to you?'

'This scar below the eye –'

'Ee, scar.' She straightened her index finger and stabbed her nail into the tailcoat lapel. 'You, something's happened to you. I'm not blind, khhlrr.'

'And what was meant to happen? I've survived here somehow, although those Rasputinian Martsynians of yours tried to bury me alive in the permafrost.'

She seized the beard, gave a tug. Hiss from pain; break free, step aside.

'Witch!' mutter under the breath.

'Fool!'

'Damned Lyednyak!'

'Insolent brat!'

Laugh together with the princess.

She reached inside her archaic reticule, rummaged around for a handkerchief and wiped the drooping lips upon which sticky saliva had collected. Examine her with barely concealed disgust.

'But I shan't forgive Your Highness for Pyelka!'

'What, khhe, Pyelka!'

'These Martsynian games of yours –'

She waved her handkerchief.

'Pshaw! It has frozen!'

'So, Your Highness is no longer playing this game? And how are your dreams in the Land of the Gleissen? Neath the Black Auroras? Eh? The prince has signed a good peace treaty, now Your Highness won't be able to break it.'

'And you're so delighted for that reason, huh?'

Shrug the shoulders.

She began to chuckle into the handkerchief.

'And now tell me, little son, was I not right about you? Were my dreams of you wrong? Huh?'

The consternation could not be hidden.

'But I have not fulfilled any of Your Highness's designs!'

'No?'

'Bah, I saved the life of Doctor Tesla – have you forgotten? – of him who will soon smash the Ice.'

She nodded, clearly pleased with herself.

'No matter, khhr, no matter.' She shot a quick glance. 'But perhaps you have seen, dearie, the honourable Aleksandr Aleksandrovitch Pobedonostseff? Or his people?'

'No.'

'Krhhm, hhrmm.'

Her blotchy hand trembled on the stick; the other she pressed to lips which she could also no longer properly control; her body betrayed her on every front, everywhere emanating abominable old age and as-saulting the senses. Retreat another step to avoid the stench. But as to Princess Blutskaya-Osey herself, that being inhabiting the stinking sack of skin and bones, nothing ruffled her malicious joy; she had frozen in a grimace of evil satisfaction warping her soul.

Run from her, away from that room. An obscure fear beat in return-ing waves to the rhythm of the hurrying footsteps. What was she so pleased about? What had she seen, whom had she seen? A Lyednyak ready to defend the Ice and the gleissen? But it's not true! Not true!

Halina Wielicka was sitting neath some ornamental ferns in the company of the youthful Mrs Jusche – a creation of chiffon and *pail-lettes* beside a creation of taffeta and pearls. Enjoying a rest, sipping fruit wine from silver cups, they were running down their acquaintanc-es amongst the dancers visible through the wall.

Make the excuses, smack a farewell kiss on the lace-cuffed hand of Halina Wielicka.

'Forgive me, it'll be wisest if I forgo the rest of the evening, Wojsław –'

Mrs Wielicka failed to release the hand.

'And the young woman with whom you came, sir?' she whispered, turning discreetly from Mrs Jusche.

'You know Mademoiselle Filipov, don't you? Should you bump into her, please –'

'I don't believe it. You shan't do this, sir, you are not that sort of man.'

'What sort of man? What's it about now? Mademoiselle Christine has surely danced her fill. Modest Pavlovitch found her some ladies' man in uniform, they'll dance the night away –'

'To bring a young woman to a ball, perhaps the greatest she's been to in her life –'

'That's true. She hasn't –'

'To bring her,' Halina raised her voice, and Wojsław's habitually meek wife was witnessed for the first time in such state of irritation, 'in order to cast her at the first opportunity into the arms of a stranger – who does such a thing? Only a man devoid of sensitivity or totally inconsiderate of someone else's feelings, a callous monster.'

'But! I am not here for my own amusement, I have other things to settle, and Mademoiselle Filipov was perfectly well aware in advance.'

'What are you saying? None of that matters! You do not treat a woman in this way, all the more so at such a tender age.'

'No, no, no, madam, you're imagining it wrongly, there are no romantic overtones between me and Miss Filipov, no thought –'

'Benedykt! For pity's sake! *What does it matter*? You brought a young woman to a ball! If you do not *feel* it, sir, then at least *calculate* it! Well?'

Glance at Mrs Jusche, who was eavesdropping and no longer making any secret of it. Avert the eyes.

'Maybe... indeed... a certain impropriety...'

'Go to her, sir!'

Bah, but how to find one devushka at a vast gubernatorial ball? She could not be spotted amongst the dancers. Hundreds of liquid-coloured figures glittered on the prismatic frostoglaze, every other one could have been Christine Filipov. They had to be examined carefully in order to pick out the undispersed faces, to distinguish the irradiated image from its double, triple or quadruple deflection. Enter the gallery in the hope that from above, with a good view onto the whole dance floor, the devushka would be discovered more quickly. Nothing of the sort. Perceive instead how one couple and then a second slips away behind the colonnades and, as if on a random stroll, totally disappears from the frostoglaze floor, hiding in the private, untransparent rooms. So that's how it is!

There'd be no poking the nose into every chamber in the palace; how many floors were open to guests, two, three? No doubt another scrape would be gotten into, given the undoubted talent for this. Light a cigarette in the shadow brooding over the gallery. Grab a servant, recognisable only by his black bowtie and gold buttons, and request a glass of dry wine; maybe it'll rinse away the foul-smelling smack, still clinging to the palate, of the old woman's repulsive corporality. Down below, an interval in the music. A heavily decorated admiral, merry from drink and steaming with murch, was clapping his hands and tapping his feet, summoning the guests to join in a slow folk dance; some more distinguished-looking ladies rose to their feet from under the mirrors; boys in livery sprinkled showers of gold confetti from high balconies; rows of couples stepped onto the icebound taiga, into the current of the moonlit gale. The lackey brought the wine. Flashing a banknote before his eyes, describe in words worthy of a police report Mademoiselle

Filipov and the lieutenant of guards. Before the slow dance ended, the lackey had returned, signalling with his head to follow.

It was one of the upstairs smoking rooms, known as the Chinese Room, so the servant whispered as the money was handed to him before the closed door. The walls, though made of frostoglaze, were tightly sealed internally with silk hangings and protected by screens, which ensured the privacy of the chamber. Knock? Without much thought, inhale a puff of tobacco, press on the handle and peep inside. The lieutenant of guards and Mademoiselle Filipoff, enmeshed in each other's arms, failed to notice the intrusion of the uninvited guest. Freeze motionless for a second on the threshold. Semi-recumbent on a chaise longue upholstered in damask, neath a paper lantern that cast green shadow, against the backdrop of the starry Siberian horizon, the lovers were succumbing to sinful delights – no sound emanated from their mouths, for their mouths were welded together – no movement was there of bodies, for their bodies were interlocked – they had frozen. Visible were her dainty foot in its French slipper with golden bow, her calf in its bright pearly stocking, calf and knee and even a fragment of thigh, since she'd raised the leg obscenely, having extricated it from petticoats and frills, lace and skirts, in order to clasp and press ever closer, tighter, the cavalier in his white uniform. His hand was thrust brutally into her décolleté as he grasped, squeezed, kneaded, crushed her whole breast under the bodice – like a side of meat – since meat it is – flesh on flesh. Her maquillage was smeared, a moist red streak on her cheek coming off her lips – moisture below the lips, moisture on her neck – saliva – hers – his – the mingling secretions of flesh. The muscles of his legs and buttocks taut neath the tight-fitting trousers of his uniform. Her fingers clutching at his arm. His vein – coarse, bulging, bursting with blood – throbbing below his ear. His red neck. Hairy wrist. Naked shoulders squashed against the back of the chaise longue. Saliva. Tongue. Hand. Calf. Neck. Buttock. Breast. Meat. Meat. Rotten grey-green meat.

Beat a swift retreat, dropping the cigarette somewhere on the way. Rush back to the gallery. Mr Gerushin was coming from the opposite direction in the company of a matron so heavily powdered she was deathly pale, no doubt the governor general's wife; withdraw towards the musicians' balcony. The balcony was flanked by life-size statues sculpted out of some rare mineral, intensely iced-through, which emitted unlichty steam at room temperature and sweated black moisture. Hide behind the statues, sit down on a cold pedestal. The sculptures were uncommonly faithful copies of Greek or Roman figures; eclectic Russian Art Nouveau had congealed under the Ice facing the classicist pole. Every muscle or tendon was portrayed with anatomical precision; a naked shepherd shielded his eyes from a naked female archer; oily shadow smouldered out of them reaching as far as the ceiling. Only Priapus was absent. Avert the eyes. Aphrodite at that moment was clothed: a military jacket hung from her shoulders. Above the music, very loud here, could be heard the even louder gossip of the gentlemen gathered by the balustrade, mainly young bachelors. They were exchanging opinions about the devushkas espied from above on the frostoglaze parquet of the Siberian night.

'... a carthorse couldn't budge her.'

'But wait a moment, wait, and that lump in roses?'

'Tekla Petrovna? Wouldn't wish her on my worst enemy.'

'Milushyn, after downing a half-litre, was threatening to swoop on Reptoff's daughters.'

'Both at once? Hee-hee.'

'He'll ask for the hand of the one that won't send him packing.'

'Ambitious fellow. Myself, I'd... Ah, what sweet little does!'

'With their frothy little diddeys –'

'Oh, see how she wiggles her posterior!'

'... at the desperados around the princess! Trampling on each other's feet, bludgeoning one another to death, the penniless wet-weaks.'

'But His Illustriousness has trouble on his plate: look how the krasavitsa makes eyes, fishes for smiles, thrusts out her bosom.'

'If only she had something to thrust!'

'Unlike our Agafiya, who's seen off two husbands, eh?'

'Oh, don't you say a bad word about Agafiya!'

'When she takes breath, all candles bow down.'

'So, tell us about the winds coming from her other end.'

'Last year at the Heisses' salon –'

'Oh! And the elder Kuragina daughter?'

'Pyotr has a deep-seated need to atone. Pyotr has sinned greatly against women.'

'Atonement, mm-hmm. Two hundred roubles, plus shares in Kuragin's factory when the old boy kicks the bucket.'

'Crooked eyes and crooked teeth, but a straight road to riches.'

'And the horror also possesses the talent of unspeakable stupidity, look at her mother; Kuragin never let any devushka alone, you could create a whole squadron out of Kuragin's bastards, yet no inkling of suspicion ever dawned on that lump.'

'I feel a sudden surge of tenderness gripping me, my dears, I've fallen in love, you've found the ideal woman!'

'And what about Colonel Merutchkin's widow? Still fresh and probably still fertile.'

'Bah, yet pawned already twice over! Look at her dress!'

'That's a good prescription: calculate their worth according to the weight of gold-fluff on –'

'Clear off!'

'What?'

Furiously hurl the jacket pulled from Aphrodite at the first man.

'Out of my sight!' snarl at them, sensing an angry rush of fever, red fire swelling within, burning just as powerfully as Shame, but in fact the opposite of Shame. 'Animals! You should be rolling in dung, not living amongst men!'

'But what do you –'

The musicians struck a louder note; raise the voice higher still, clenching the fists.

'To butchers like you!' scream at them, now totally out of control. 'Meat! Meat! Meat!'

They stared as if at a madman. One or other muttered something under his breath, lowered his eyes. A good-looking fellow in cadet's uniform poked his neighbours with his elbow and they began to move off into a side gallery; one of them bumped into a sculpture of a javelin thrower, confusion arose; they turned their backs and hurriedly withdrew, the last man slinging a vulgar word over his shoulder.

Energy ebbed just as swiftly as it had flowed into the veins; lean on the handrail drained of strength. Down below they were dancing a trepak, the onlookers applauding. Trumpets and drums roared behind the ears. It was time to slip away, slip away! Close the eyes, but it helps not; tableaux of the ball were ingrained even more vividly on the eyelids, and the first was of Mademoiselle Filipov. For there the meat market went on, the abominable display, the waves of movement repeated to music: arm, leg, arm, leg, arm, leg, until thou art laid in earth, and then it's the maggots that move.

'Precisely why I don't usually attend.'

He stopped alongside, having emerged from behind the Greek nudes. A single order adorned his chest; the type and class of this distinction, however, were unfamiliar. The man was slender and comported himself in an official pose, so that he almost leaned over backwards, head held high. Stand up straight; he was taller by several vershoks. Face very pale, smooth-shaven, almost free of glintzen, a soft smile on his lips. The tungetitum Orthodox cross around his neck was dazzling to the eye against his white shirtfront.

'Ziel Arkady Hipolitovitch.' He bowed.

'Benedykt Gierosławski.' Remember at this point the visiting cards; find a card, hand it to Ziel. He didn't even glance.

'I know.' In a flowing balletic movement of his hand, he encompassed the entire ballroom below with the card. 'His son.'

'Well yes.' Now the flame was reversed, now it burned inwardly; Shame had returned. Bite into the cheek so as not to grin involuntarily, doglike, apologetically, ingratiatingly. 'I fear I have again made a scene. Really... I am not that kind of man; this is not how I have frozen. I hope.'

'Not the kind of man to openly call sin a sin, and virtue a virtue?' He put away the card and pointed to the left. Walk ahead; Arkady Hipolitovitch made room so as not to have to squeeze between the sculptures. 'My ears are ringing.' Return to the shadows of the gallery; Ziel stopped the lackey and requested a glass of water. 'Precisely why I don't usually attend. You rub shoulders with people and then it settles on you like rime blackened by foundry fumes, like dust off the street, like greasy filth.' Sipping the water, he peeped into a side room. Drunken gentlemen were throwing shot-glasses into a fireplace in the opposite wall. 'I am not talking here about bodily filth, you understand me, Benedykt Filipovitch.'

'Yes.'

'Purity, the hardest thing is to preserve purity. If we only lived in a world where communion was possible exclusively between souls...' He sighed. His voice too was soft, flowing in languid undulations, up and down; it had melody, rhythm. 'What is the higher ideal? Man minus body.'

'Have you read Fyodoroff?'

'Purity, brother, purity. I can see, after all, that you feel the same disgust, the same embarrassment, the burden.'

'I –'

'God so ordained that we are born into this world in a sack of dung, baptised in dung, consuming dung: in dung we flounder, with dung our senses become clogged, dung we pass on to others in expressions of love; dung is our happiness, dung our bliss.' He leaned forward anxiously. 'We should try at least to purify ourselves! It's not possible to step out of the body – but it is possible to –'

Lurch to one side, suddenly yanked from behind; lean against a prism-wall. Who now? Herr Bittan von Asenhoff was brazenly dragging towards the stairs, taunting Arkady Hipolitovitch with a mocking stare, whilst the latter merely watched the odd scene with a sad gentle air.

'I'm taking you with me,' declared von Asenhoff firmly.

'What do you want, for God's sake –'

'Aleksandr Aleksandrovitch will welcome you with hope,' Ziel was saying. 'I can disclose to you that Aleksandr Aleksandrovitch read your *Apoliteia* with great attention, and spoke fine words.'

'Who is he?' inquire of von Asenhoff, breathing shallowly and finally breaking free on the staircase of the Prussian's iron grip.

'Pobedonostseff's Angel. So, what now, do you still have work to do here? Because it seems to me you've caused enough mischief for one evening.'

'But what on earth are you up to?!'

He bared his teeth.

'I'm rescuing you, young man.' He snapped his fingers at the servants for them to bring the outer garments. 'Another moment and he'd have had you sitting on a white steed.'

'What?!'

Fireworks were shooting into the sky above the crystal palace as the descent began down the serpentine slope into the moonlit taiga aroar with windstorms, one sleigh, a second sleigh, a third sleigh, all filled with rollicking riotous company, and a fourth – now seated in the fourth sleigh under the bearskins with Bittan von Asenhoff and that portly captain of hussars. After the first sequence of fireworks, crackers were let off under the palace, but these were loaded with cryocarbon charges, so that they exploded in great flowers of unlicht; only once they'd passed through the palace's coldiron-and-frostoglaze structure did they burst into a thousand and one rivers of rainbow colour and glintz. On a lower loop of the descent, as the gubernatorial palace loomed on the left against the starry firmament, there was no need to twist around, more or less impossible anyway, as the body was immured in furs, skins, plaids, shawls and patchwork coverlets sewn from dozens of squirrel, hare and sable pelts. Depending on the angle and distance at which these freezeworks had shot through the palace, collages of unlicht and light were daubed across the sky, star-shapes devouring brightness, star-shapes sowing brightness; whilst some merged into others, or the others were outgrown by the first, until all eventually plummeted into the icebound taiga in a fine drizzle of sparks and antisparks. The stupefied reindeer shook their heads, noisily jangling their decorative bells. From out of the deep night, Siberia was extinguished and lit up by turns, like a land in God's dream at which He now gazes between fingers, now blocks from His very gaze and existence.

'He's after you, I saw,' croaked the now existing, now non-existing von Asenhoff through scarf and frost. 'He who is ready to sever the body's anchor, khhrr, to renounce the sins of the flesh.'

'To commit suicide?'

'No! Suicide is a sin! This is a man in the mould of Selivanoff, of the Khlysts and Skoptsy of centuries past. Khhrr. Under the Ice, the certainty of faith has returned to them; once more they are castrating.'

'Pobedonostseff –'

'Him – who knows. But Ziel, khhrr, khhrr – probably this is why they call him the Angel.' Von Asenhoff swiped his gloved hand through the cloud of unlichted breath mist back and forth, chop-chop, like a knife. 'Castration has made an angel of him!'

'You're saying, sir, he's a eunuch!'

'A whitewashed one! A castrate cleared by the tsar's stamp.' Chop-chop, he wielded his hand again. 'Balls and cock, the lot. They also burn off women's breasts, as far down as the bone.'

'Did you think, sir,' choke on the frost, 'I'd agree so they –'

'Bah! He did it to himself.'

'Khhrr.'

'Exactly – I have to find an antidote to this poison before you freeze.' Von Asenhoff emerged from the next spell of twilight with an ironic, acerbic grimace. 'My good deed for the month.'

The hussar broke into a deep resonating laugh.

The sleigh rode onto the river ice of the Angara or one of its branches or tributaries. After a couple of bends, the palace with its lights and unlichts, fireworks and freezeworks, rainbows and eclipses – was hidden behind escarpments of ice, behind ranks of frozen trees coated in a froth of sparkling snow. Along the river course – along the winter road – travelling was faster, it was the main highway; on the way to the ball too, the frozen Angara had been ridden. The drivers cracked their whips, a drunken bourgeois in the first sleigh hurled a bottle at the Moon, someone in the second tried to hurl one in turn at him, a gust of wind caught him, causing him to miss and hit a reindeer; the team of animals swerved to one side, swerved to the other, and wild slaloms commenced on the smooth white surface of the river; the gentlemen howled into the sky like wolves, quickly becoming hoarse; the only devushka kidnapped by the company from the ball squealed in her soprano voice; the bourgeois stood up from under his furs and leaned over the back of the sleigh, reaching the tail lantern and swapping it a moment later for a large reflective lamp with cryocarbon wick, so that the first and second teams drove suddenly into a vortex of shadows and glintzen, making the animals lose their bearings and the cavalcade scatter in five separate directions; instead of reindeer, crippled negatives of reindeer now ran over the black whiteness; instead of trees, grotesque iron weeds now stood in the taiga; the ice was transformed into incandescent darkness, into a torrent of carbon lava; men or their shadows made holey by glintzen like scorched-out paper-cuts bowed in the wind, crumbling as they rushed into the confetti of snow or soot; the sky brightened, the Moon darkened, the night turned inside out. The infernal cavalcade sped through the Land of Darkness.

Arrive in this manner at Pussy Court.

The house stood at the foot of a hill, well sheltered from gales blowing off the Angara, and since it was a long way from the Ways of the Mammoths, no one was too worried about the danger from beneath the ground. As the hill stretched one or two hundred arshins in a concave sickle-shape, so too did the row of buildings at its foot with the two-storeyed house at its centre. The sleigh pulled up at once in the carriage-house, which was festively lit, its doors flung open. On the approach, on the final bend in the road coming from the river, some muzhiks had been standing tightly wrapped in sheepskins, monkey-like creatures with flaming torches directing the guests in the taiga. More sleighs had arrived earlier, perhaps also from the governor general's ball, or directly from Irkutsk. A baby bear on a chain was prowling behind the carriage-house, rising on its hind paws whenever a fresh team of jingling reindeer fell out of the wilderness, screwing up its muzzle in disgust.

All the sleighs could not draw up at the same time; a small queue formed. The hussar stood up in his seat and yelled to someone on the verandah. Music could be heard coming from inside the mansion. Awakened dogs were barking in their kennels. Shrieking, squealing figures came running from an outbuilding at the back in coils of steam and began chasing one another and wallowing in the snow, men and women, stark naked as the Lord God created them; avert the eyes. In a clearing behind a woodshed, two gentlemen in expensive fur coats, clutching bulky casks in their left hands, took aim with their right into the taiga; shot after shot reverberated from their long-barrel revolvers. At what were they firing? Icicles?

Alight from the sleigh. Herr von Asenhoff led the way along the verandah towards the main door illuminated by torches and lanterns. Silhouettes of boisterous dancing guests flashed in the narrow windows; wild music, quite unlike the sedate melodies of the crystal palace, burst into the forest through the thick-beamed walls.

They are dancing... Herr Bittan surely isn't intending to insist on more dancing? Unravel the scarf, shake the snow from the shapka, pull off the gloves. True or false? The past exists not, all memories that fit not the present... On the third hand: after so many pumpings-off of murch, so many tosses of the coin...

'Marushka!' cooed the captain above the ear in his deep bass voice, spreading wide his arms. Into them fell a radiant devushka clad in an obscenely low-cut dress, brandishing a bottle of champagne. Boys in colourfully embroidered rubashkas helped the guests off with their coats; mugs of hot tea were served, glasses of rum and vodka. Scarcely had the nose cleared when a sweet scent made itself felt, a floral fragrance permeating the air.

A ginger cat rubbed against the trouser leg; move it aside with the boot.

'What is this place?' inquire of von Asenhoff, who was issuing orders to an older muzhik.

'Oh, Pussy Court, my retreat from the cares of the city. Feel yourself invited as my guest, my special personal guest.'

The hussar knocked back a glass of champagne, twirled the corners of his rimy moustache, grabbed the titillated krasavitsa, kissed her racily, pawed her pert little rump, then her bosoms, after which he burst into loud laughter.

'A brothel, my dear Mr Frost, the very best bordello east of the Urals!'

Von Asenhoff must have noticed the dubious expression, for he unceremoniously seized the tailcoat and dragged it deep inside the hallway, amongst the people. A woman in a red dress appeared on his other arm, her lips and lashes coated in gold-fluff, a purely Russian beauty with long wheaten plait wrapped over her shoulder. She planted a kiss on Bittan's cheek.

'You need to learn one lesson,' the Prussian patrician was saying, raising his voice above the hubbub. 'That man is also an animal, that woman is an animal, an animal born of her own animal tastes and lusts, a most beautiful animal. Katya, take care of the Baby Son of Frost.'

'Ce serait un grand plaisir pour moi.'

Recall the whores of Warsaw, their sour kisses, the secret grabbings and scrabblings in the shadows of dank annexes or drinking holes, those eternally unwashed pallid girls from whom the hands fled of their own accord during the filthy act, in a reflex of aesthetic revulsion and judicious repugnance at the bacilli, maggots and lice of which the devushkas were undoubtedly hotbeds, even if they weren't picked up off the street but through acquaintances in the lodging-house or precinct, daughters of washerwomen, daughters of tailors, daughters of roofers and stove-tilers; rarely the daughter of a gentleman lawyer or doctor met through giving private lessons or via a student chum – girls with whom it was never possible to go farther than a fleeting kiss or hug. The body had access to unclean pleasures only, the more degrading the easier. Close the eyes, avert the head, try to expel from the nostrils the loathsome odours – as long as the animal managed to do its thing: having conquered the body, to use and free it from animal possession. In order then to immediately forget, forget, forget.

Until remembered. Shame struck between the eyes, a six-pound hammer.

Retreat into the hall towards the door, raising the hands as a sign that no one should even approach.

'I know about all this perfectly well! The animal, yes! You don't have to convince me by making me visit a house of debauchery. I thank you graciously for your hospitality, von Asenhoff.'

'You will thank me in the morning.' Nodding to Katya, he whispered something in her ear. 'You surely don't imagine I'd surrender so easily to Mr Cockless. Do you intend to return home on foot, huh? Because I'm not lending my sleigh. So, calm down, forget the drama.'

Katya, markedly older than the other girls at Pussy Court, was watching with a shrewd smile, one that was a little sad, a little ironic, a little impatient. Seizing a serving-maid by the ear, she hissed some order. After which she gathered up her plait and pointed to a narrow corridor leading off to one side under the stairs.

Follow the krasavitsa willy-nilly, cursing von Asenhoff as well as that feeling of dissociation and bewilderment which had allowed the removal here like that of a passive child.

'Bittan says you desire purification,' she said as she opened the next door, keeping her voice low, likeable, closer to a melodious whisper, so that against his will a man pricks up his ears and leans towards carmine-and-gold Katya. 'He says it's youthful *Weltschmerz*. We have no herbs for that, but the banya works well. Please.'

Here the mansion was connected to that outbuilding where the banya was housed. Heat and damp prevailed already in the anteroom; Katya stopped on the threshold and chased into the passageway. Clapping her bare feet on the splashed floor, the bathhouse attendant tottered over: a robust ruddy-faced village woman in half-drenched shoddy blouse and skirt. Katya clicked her tongue and withdrew, shutting the door. It grew hotter still. Tailcoat, waistcoat, shirt, all the expensive clothing – was about to get well and truly soaked. The attendant applied herself to the cufflinks, to the buttons. Push her aside more brutally than intended. 'On my own!' Undress hurriedly, turning the back on her, wrapping the Grossmeister in the trousers, and enter a chamber full of tubs, pails, running hot and cold water, in order to ablute before entering the steam room. Encounter one couple completely engrossed in amorous games: the devushka senselessly entangled in wet transparent linen, and a fat man pink as a piglet pursuing her and laughing with a besom of birch twigs in his hand. The fatty was naked, the devushka half-naked; the steam did not cover them, nor did they cover their nakedness themselves; giggling uproariously, they rushed into the white coils of steam, thwack, thwack, thwack. Cleanse the body all the quicker, gritting the teeth. What barbaric customs, what shamelessness, befitting indeed only a whorehouse!

Yet in this enormous steam room, built on stones and more than a storey high, a man could lose himself, so densely clouded was the air with steam, whilst the temperature and damp and sticky closeness of the banya immediately did odd things to his mind, so that after only a few steps, he was walking through dark-blue coils as if through the boundless mists of an extraterrestrial land: his eyes spin, the world perceived through those eyes tells lies. He has to sit down, lower his eyelids, breathe evenly, calmly. This is the greatest virtue of such a bath-house: you see a thousand things in its steam, but no one sees you, hidden and blurred.

Feel after a minute, two minutes, the heavy dirty sweat already seeping from all the body's pores. A feeling so distinct, so acutely physi-cal – stemming without any doubt from the organism and not from the delusions of thought – that a vision was imagined of succulent maggots the size of slugs and tapeworm larvae, imbued with every kind of in-ternal impurity, pushing their way out through the orifices of the skin, streaming out in long drips of phlegm, sweated out and leaving this vessel of meat lighter, softer, whiter, *cleaner*. Even if he is not purified, a man certainly feels purified after a visit to a banya. Hear the rhythmic flogging of other bathers. It goes to the head. Grope for a pail of water, splash the face. Therefore – therefore – therefore Pobedonostseff's Angel is a Skopets castrated of his sex. But von Asenhoff is mistaken if he thinks that in this latest Siberian madness, on this seemingly neces-sary and infallible path to Russian salvation – anything whatsoever of Truth is perceived. It's clearly insane! How on earth could he make such an assumption?

Wipe the water and sweat from the brow, from the eyes. Flickering shapes were moving in the mist. Had frostoglaze lamps been lit here? The shades of naked people – beautiful and hideous – were wander-ing in the steam; the steam had affixed elephant trunks to them, bull horns, horse genitalia, frog feet, angel wings. Squeeze the eyelids to-gether again. All caused by the six-day fast. It has frozen. The coin is tossed this way or that, but in the end Benedykt Gierosławski clearly returns to Benedykt Gierosławski. For from what had Count Gyero-Saski and all those similar falsehoods sprung? From the expensive suits, clean shirt, fragrant perfume, ornamental ring, brilliantine in the hair, from the miasmas of luxury. Warsaw, Biernatowa's lodging-house, the shit-stained privy, the whole stinking louse-infested life fit only for spewing up – swish, the guillotine blade has cut off this truth. The past exists not! There is but the present moment. And *voilà*! There was dancing!

And yet – it's all a lie! It has frozen in the heart of Winter; this is no longer a trans-Siberian journey but the City of Ice, murch is making its pressure felt: it's no longer possible to be voluntarily contradictory. Swish. The guillotine severs absolutely, everything belongs either on the left side or on the right side. Body or spirit. This mortal life or existence outside time. Herr Blutfeld or Doctor Konyeshin. Summer or Winter. Man or God. Stinking putrid corpse decomposing in broiling heat beneath a million flies – or mathematics. The tyranny of human contingency – or apoliteia. Animal – or –

Flush off the remaining water. Only what business is it of Bittan von Asenhoff's that the Son of Frost should not become like unto an angel? There was no Shtchekelnikoff to take upon himself the burden of suspicion; the poison must be fully ingested. Yet it gets harder and harder; more and more often action is taken first, before dozens of possibilities for treachery and lies and shame are imagined. *You are a suspicious man, Benedykt.* Comparison surely prompted such an impression – for people here do not suspect. Suspicion is a state of uncertainty – whilst they have touched soletruth; murch flows in their veins, freezes their brains. Paradoxically, therefore, Tchingis Shtchekelnikoff is the ideal protective shield: he *knows* in advance that everyone is his enemy and wishes them the worst. With whom would he best find understanding: with one-eyed Yerofey, disciple of Saint Martsyn.

The last maggot crawled out of the body. Leave the steam room, staggering and drawing a light papery hand along the wall; wash again, this time in icy water; the attendant proffered a glass of vodka and a kimono; dress in miraculously soft, smooth silk, knock back the firewater; enter the cool transparent air of Pussy Court saturated with fragrances. An angel treads on Persian carpets.

All around the room, animals were surrendering to animal desires. Not all were concealed in private chambers behind closed doors. Beside a long table piled high with meats and cakes, gentlemen plastered in fat and wine were stuffing themselves with delicacy after delicacy, chucking whole handfuls or spoons of food across the tabletop, squashing expensive fruits imported from warmer climes down cleavages, pouring liquors of one colour or other into the girls' mouths and staining their elegant dresses. Cats strolled amongst the silver dishes. A banker and a councillor, one in a pince-nez, the other in a wig, otherwise naked, were licking caviar out of the hidden recesses of a sleeping whore's ample body, both panting and red-faced as if running a Sisyphean race; the tart snored as they burrowed their noses and tongues into her creases, cracks and hollows, overgrown by dark hair, later flooded and blackened with caviar. The cats watched from beneath a portrait of the Empress Yekaterina. In a chamber furnished in the Turkish style, on a floor strewn with hundreds of cushions, the captain of hussars was riding Marushka's protruding rump, her head and shoulders completely wedged and buried in the cushions, so that all that was exposed of the devushka in the wavering candlelight was her freckled back, thin quaking thighs and posterior already red from the buffets of the dashing trooper, as the captain thrust Marushka into a rhythm well-practised for gallops and charges, his torso thrown forwards, his sagging wrinkled buttocks flapping idiotically, till his moustache flew up to his bulging eye. The cats wandered amongst the cushions. A smooth-faced youth of barely lyceum age, divested of his breeches somewhere along the way, lay in turn with a krasavitsa stripped from the waist upwards – his feet resting on an étagère, his head on a chaise longue, one hand in a chamber pot of vomit, the other up the devotcha's skirt, her head craning towards him under his armpit; both lay asleep entwined in this impossible position, smeared in bodily excretions glistening like the mucus of snails. The cats licked it up.

Discover Herr Bittan von Asenhoff and his Katya in a corner sitting room on the ground floor. The aria 'Vesti la Giubba' wafted from a wind-up gramophone. Katya, legs tucked under her on a plush velvet ottoman beside the dignified Prussian, was warbling something in his ear. Von Asenhoff was smoking a long-stemmed coloured pipe with coral brick bowl, and staring from under dropped eyelids through the opposite window at the ice-clad taiga, at the white-hued gale raging above it, at the half-Moon resembling a puddle of dark-blue ink, and at the spine of a gleiss protruding above the trees, the same colour as the Moon. There was a smell of arak.

Stop still in the doorway, burying the bare feet deep in the carpet – for how else is a hot, no-longer-sweating angel to anchor himself to the earth against such extreme agitation, such disgust and holy wrath?

Bittan put a finger to his lips. With the pipe he performed an invitational gesture, already drowsy and languid. Sit down, having hesitated once and then twice, in an armchair between the windows, wrapping the long flaps of the kimono tightly around the legs, folding the arms over the chest. Katya didn't even glance up; dipping her finger in a glass of arak, she drew it over von Asenhoff's lips whenever he removed the mouthpiece from between them.

A cat yawned beside the ottoman.

The gramophone record ended. Bittan awoke, reached out with the pipe stem and paused the mechanism.

'Katya,' he crooned, 'our guest is lonely.'

Katya reached for the bell.

'No! I shall wait till morning and depart with the first man returning to Irkutsk.'

'That's not nice, not nice,' muttered the old nobleman. 'Such ingratitude, such contempt.'

'Contempt!' Give a snort.

'But of course. Whenever you eat, sir – you cover your mouth, avert your head. Whenever you get drunk – then it's in solitude, true?'

'Decency, it demands –'

'Decency!' He bridled. 'Is this how you lie to yourself? Because you've been taught so, trained so?'

'No,' reply more gently. 'I can't do otherwise.'

'I'll wager you chose for yourself, and no doubt in defiance even of your whole family – this mathematics, this logic. Yes?'

'I don't remember being any different.' Sit up straight. 'But memory, what is memory? It still doesn't mean that –'

'But out of love – what low animal thing have you ever done publicly, sir, prompted by amorous desire?'

'He is *pure* now,' said Katya softly and nestled closer to von Asenhoff.

'Such is love according to you…!' Burst into mocking laughter. 'Better that you tell me, sir, what you wanted from me when you dragged me to this lupanar.'

He shrugged his shoulders, puffed smoke.

'Nothing.'

Perceive at once this truth about his character. He is perhaps the only one of them all who with absolute certainty wants nothing from the Son of Frost, who has no plans or fears or hopes associated with him – for he doesn't care a hoot about History, doesn't care a hoot about the state, about religions, peoples, nations; Bittan von Asenhoff doesn't care a hoot about past and future: so fixated is he on himself and the pleasure to be relished at any given moment. His absolute egocentrism guarantees satanic disinterestedness. After all a saint doesn't do good because he calculates the profits, nor does a devil do evil in accordance with some cold strategic design – they do what they do because this is what is most dear to them.

'*Mauvais sang ne saurait mentir,*' mutter and shudder at the chill whiff of air coming off the window. 'It amuses you, sir; in giving them pleasure, you take them captive, collar the animal living within every man.'

Katya poured more arak. Von Asenhoff slowly licked the alcohol off her fingertips.

'What amuses me…,' he sighed, adjusting himself on the ottoman. 'At least you don't spit Catholic moralising at me. Russians, meanwhile, treat the body more as an object. On the one hand – we have Selivanoff, on the other – Danilo Filipovitch; yet their faith is the same. Except that here in this land, of course, it's taken to infernal extremes: either the complete truth, or a cursed lie, nothing in between; they chop off and burn their sex and desires, or they organise continual orgies for whole religious communities. The hardest thing,' he wagged his hand in front of his face, 'is to remain somewhere in between. But you, sir – you quickly slip to an extreme. Besides – you're a mathematician.'

Feel the hackles rise.

'Well, what of it that I'm a mathematician? No one has yet gelded himself because of numbers!'

He winced again, breathed smoke.

'Bor-ring,' he intoned, 'he's starting to get bor-ring. What are we going to do, Katya, with Monsieur Frosty, mm-hmm?'

'You wished to amuse yourself with me, sir, throw me to the animals and watch the beast crawl out of the Son of Frost!'

'He is *pure* now,' Katya repeated, her face for some reason sad, framed in gold and glintz like a stained-glass image.

Herr von Asenhoff, transferring the pipe to his left hand, embraced the krasavitsa with his right arm from behind her back and slipped his palm inside the bodice of her rose-red dress, in order to then extract from it, in a soft drowsy movement, a white breast and expose it to the naphtha-shaded moonlight, enfold it in a cradle of wizened fingers and twirl between them the breast's bright bud, rose-red like the dress.

'Amusement, amusement, amusement,' he crooned, 'but where's the pleasure for someone who already bought every kind of pleasure long ago? Will you eat a thousand more cakes? Drink one more bucket of champagne? Amass more diamonds and gold in your treasury? Build crystal palaces so others will be openly jealous – where's the satisfaction in that? Maybe the first time, or the second. But when you get so rich that no one threatens you any more in your riches, when they all envy you – what then? Competitors to be overcome – have been overcome. Enemies to be humiliated – have been humiliated. While the next million or two million – what difference does it make? All the pleasures that you can buy – because you can buy them, bring you no pleasure.

'I once dropped by this little haberdashery store, having parted company in the doorway of the Arkadiya Hotel with *une femme vénale*; I had not hired a droshky, rain was falling with a vengeance, I leapt under the awning, the bell jangled, a client came out – I went inside. It was a small shop, dark and snug, and behind the counter stood a sweet little devotchka, a plump baby bird barely out of childhood; she noticed the overcoat, frock coat, rings – her eyes grew enormous and she gulped. I smiled, bowed. She curtsied, returning the smile and revealing her dainty white teeth. The rain was lashing relentlessly, so what better than to chat up the young lady, I joked, winked. We chat away and it turns out that she's able not only to smile, what a nice surprise: she's feisty, sharp-witted, tells of her blind grandmother, who scratches the faces of all her interlocutors, and of an uncle with serious gout who was once driven so crazy by the pain he tried to chop off his foot; and this is their family shop, she works there in the afternoons as a sales assistant. Not once did I look around; the rain ceased, half an hour or more had passed in pleasant conversation.

'A week or two later, on a day when I was totally drained after some long financial negotiations, I was driving in that direction, espied the haberdasher's sign and immediately hit on an idea of how to improve my mood. I entered the shop. The devotchka stood behind the counter. Have you come to buy, sir? And already her eyes were laughing. Customers came and went, but we went on joking between ourselves. As I left, I threw a twenty-five-rouble note onto the counter. What's this for, the young woman frowns. For the time spent, I call from the doorway, and am gone. On my next visit, she wants to return the roubles, tries to stuff the note into my pocket – I writhe with laughter, adding the same amount again. A game therefore arises between us: I give according to whim, she acts all coy, and the more she acts coy, the more firmly I spurn the diengi. On this the game hinges – she no longer really cares about returning the money. I leave and pay; and the rest is *charme* and flirtation.

'The spring unfolded beautifully. Won't you close the shop earlier, there's no customers as it is, and now's the best hour to go for a walk around town. But I can't, Bittan, sir, my uncle relies on me. I draw out a rainbow-coloured banknote. It's in uncle's best interests; I will pay, pay even for a quarter of an hour. We both laugh. Irkutsk in springtime is magical indeed.

'From then on, I always pay in advance – before a conversation, before a walk, before time. An element of the game is also the size of the sum. If I suddenly draw out a lower-denomination note, the devotchka feigns great disappointment and her pretty little face is pained: why the devaluation? So, there's only one way to go: upwards, for more, and more. Longer conversations, longer walks, leading into ever higher social circles, so now I'm already bowing and raising my hat, whilst she, taken by the arm, is also introduced. To the theatre, if you please, for everyone goes to the theatre in the evening! At which she draws me swiftly aside and whispers she can't – but why – she has nothing in which to appear in society. So, I buy her an evening gown. Still she asks the price and makes a sour face; but by the fifth, seventh, twelfth occasion – shoes, jewellery, veils, gloves, whole exquisite outfits – she already looks only at their beauty. And I buy exclusively beautiful things, the most beautiful!

'For a walk, for dinner, for supper, for the theatre – when she kisses me, I pay her also for the kiss – when she surprises me with some invention of her own, I pay too for this inventiveness. I pay, and so therefore

I buy, and so therefore I demand, choose, judge; not because I insist, but because no purchase after all exists without such conditions, just as there's no light without colour, no sound without tone. Coiffures, dress creations have to please *me*; this and not another style of skirt; this and not another neckline. The devotchka's very behaviour – and she'd have capitulated if she wasn't up to the game – hold your head up high, smile, curtsey to this one, ignore that one, talk to this one, dance with him. And then later: fifty roubles if you flirt with the prosecutor; a hundred if you drive the deputy director's wifey into a paroxysm of jealousy; a hundred or more if you flash your knee before the eyes of that shrivelled-up grandad so that he's left speechless. Two hundred if all evening you'll be such and such a woman. A beautiful woman! The most beautiful! Four hundred, if all night.

'But here's the point, Monsieur Gierosławski, for had I walked into the ribbon shop and said to the innocent devushka: "I'll pay you a fortune if you'll be my whore for the night," then she'd have punched me in the face and run to the police. And from this stem the entire amusement and satisfaction: to buy the thing you cannot buy.'

'You simply seduced her, sir.'

'Did I seduce you, Katya?'

Katya fed him drops of arak on her fingers.

'You bought me, Herr Bittan.'

Swallowing a bad word, observe Katya however with renewed attention. Powder and gold maquillage hid her substantial wrinkles. She was a mature woman; she ought to have children, a family, a long future within the family. That sadness in her bright eyes – was no fleeting expression; such is the truth about Katya, the ribbon girl.

'When did it happen? Spring, you said. Before the Winter of the Gleissen, yes?'

'A year before.' He kissed Katya on her wrist. 'I bought her, and thus it has frozen.'

They indeed made a fascinating pair – in the same way as a man with a deadly cancerous growth is fascinating, or a child with two heads.

Shake it off.

'Amusement!' groan hoarsely, covering the eyes. 'Still you wish to play with me. Why not bed any strumpet from under a lamppost instead of corrupting an innocent maid? That's no longer animal lust, but common baseness!'

Von Asenhoff clicked his tongue in disappointment. Spitting out a long coil of smoke, he pinched Katya in the pale flesh of her breast; she dug her fingernail into his chin. He grinned under his breath.

'Those who know not and value not the pleasures of the flesh make the greatest fetish of the flesh,' he said laying down his pipe on the coffee table. 'And yet the flesh, though it makes pleasure possible, itself gives no pleasure. Were these purely bodily sins, as you imagine in your youthful idealism, sins from which a sharp knife and red-hot iron bring redemption – then the goatfuckers or disciples of Onan would indeed be right, for it's enough to aggravate the relevant nerve and that's all there is to it. But this is not how it is! What makes the difference: not the body but the consciousness within you of who's looking at you through the eyes of that body. So, this is the source of the greatest excitement upon which depends *la puissance d'Éros*: the encounter with the spirit controlling the body. Therefore, my fire is never kindled by even the youngest, most beautiful of whores with statuesque curves and lips of honey, if behind her eyes I see nothing but some untaught milkmaid, neither conscious of her own deeds nor able to put them into words. Instead, when I meet a woman of strong spirit, of awakened intellect launching a thousand fantasies with every second, my equal in her span of thoughts and desires... Monsieur Gierosławski, sometimes it doesn't even have to reach bodily intimacy, it's enough to look into her eyes. The greater the consciousness of *la presence d'Éros* behind a woman's eyes, the greater the pleasure to be had from her body.

'As you can see, sir,' he laughed, 'I am the greatest advocate of female emancipation!'

He clasped Katya to him and whispered something in her ear. Katya set aside the arak and slid from the ottoman onto the carpet, revealing bare feet neath the carmine-coloured dress. She did not fasten the bodice or pull up the straps. Dropping on all fours, she raised a golden stare out of solemn eyes that blinked not at all, wide open as if in deep hypnosis – for it was impossible to tear away and avert the gaze, once it had been let in. Her long plait fell the length of her arm, stroking the carpet, as Katya slunk across the room in slow, leopard-like movements. Her dress rustled; the cat purred.

'You won't find a girl at my Court unable to read and write or hold a conversation in various languages on art and politics,' Bittan von Asenhoff was saying. 'You won't find a girl devoid of her own unpredictable moods, incapable of scratching out your eyes in a moment of anger, or of slitting her wrists in desperation. Were it not for Katya, I wouldn't cope in this house of hetairas. But in return –'

Reaching the armchair, Katya stretched upward, tugged at the flaps of the kimono, her golden lips glistening with moisture as she drew her cool hand up and along the calves and thighs –

Leap to the feet and rush out into the corridor, into the hall and to the front door, by which a muzhik in a sheepskin coat was dozing; trip over the muzhik, run into the porch and from the porch out into the snow and ice. The icy air smote the skin and flooded the lungs like a burning liquid, like corrosive acid. Choked by a fit of coughing, sink to the knees.

Snow, unblemished white snow, its sparkling mirrorlike coating – ice, the purest ice – gather in handfuls the crust of the permafrost, rub it into the burning face, into the chest. Wind shook the icicled forest; on the horizon, the Moon was reflecting off the solid mass of a gleiss; shadows and lights from the upper windows of the Court flickered on the névé; in there, people were amusing themselves, drinking, fornicating, dancing… Eat the snow, drink the frost. True or false? True or false? The past exists not, all memories… On the fourth hand: the finger, the finger, Mr Korzyński's finger!

Feel the fur on the shoulders – von Asenhoff was wrapping them in a shuba and leading back into the warm interior. Give a start, break free for a moment – but in such a state, there was no resisting the Prussian's steel grip. The ice was melting in the mouth.

'Take for yourself the purest, whitest, most innocent,' von Asenhoff was whispering in breath redolent of tobacco and arak. 'I have no virgin for you, I have no angel. I have beautiful animals hungry for pleasure – and that which lies behind their eyes.'

On the Kingdom of Darkness

Ride in a rattling coldiron lift into the infernal blackness that hangs in the sky over Irkutsk.

'Don't look at him,' said Pobedonostseff's Angel. 'You won't see anything, but don't look anyway.'

'This is why he lives in darkness.'

'Why he lives.'

From the inside, the Sibirkhozheto Tower seems considerably smaller; not lower but narrower. The floors passed in jarring creaks – the fifty-second, the fifty-third, the fifty-fourth, where the Company offices are located – cover no more than half the area of the Krupp Laboratory in the Clock Tower. Aleksandr Aleksandrovitch Pobedonostseff's apartments make up the sixty-ninth and seventieth floors, but above these lies the latticework superstructure of the lift with a second wreath of darkbulb reflectors as well as the masts of the Magnetic-Meteorological Observatory (Sibirkhozheto sponsors research on the Black Auroras). From close up, the Sibirkhozheto Tower also gives the impression of being even more unwieldy and clumsily designed, botched together with blacksmithian flair: rivets the size of horses' heads, gigantic trusses, tee-bars and rods and metal sheets, coldiron to coldiron – possessing not a quarter of the architectonic subtlety and lightness of the Zimny Nikolayevsk towers and new Ice technologies designed by Mr Rubiecki.

Pass, at the height of the fifty-fifth floor, telescopic installations, spyglasses mounted on coldiron booms and limbs protruding from platforms on the outside of the tower. From here, police geologists trace the aboveground translocations of gleissen, in order to then consult the Buryat shamans on the official glacial prognoses to be published later in the bulletins of the Siberian Coldiron Industrial Company.

Above the fiftieth floor, twilight gathers pace with every arshin travelled into the sky. Plunge into shadow, enter the night. Below, in the City of Ice, the morning sun rebounds off snowy whiteness in thousands of sunshine-sparks, whilst fog flowing through the streets – streets that seem like papillary ridges on a thumb pressed into the Angara – pulses with luscious rainbow colour.

Remain silent as far as the sixty-sixth floor. By the sixty-seventh, it's impossible to hold out. Inquire in an undertone:

'Has he also severed himself from the body?'

'No.'

'Aha. I thought that was the reason why –'

'No.'

Unlicht alternating with glintzen floods the lift shaft; there's no way to read the Angel's smooth face.

Arrive at the sixty-ninth floor. The lift comes to a halt, the doors open, Mr Ziel enters first.

The antechambers and entire lower floor, since devoid of windows, are drowning in the porcelain dazzle of a glintz, caused by the immense gloom behind the walls. Walk through the short vestibule lined by mirrors where a servant with Mongolian features in dark livery takes the fur coats and shapkas, scarves and gloves. (The private staff of Chairman Pobedonostseff consists of Russified Buryats.) Ziel leads the way to a staircase. Animal skins cover a floor made of coldiron tiles; step on them warily, slipping and stumbling amidst the irregularities.

In a narrow chamber empty of furniture, two hefty Buryats in soldiers' blouses adorned with the Sibirkhozheto emblem draw back a velvet curtain from a wall. The wall in reality is one great frostoglaze window similar to the panoramic windows in the Clock Towers. One of the darkbulb reflectors is clearly directed inwards: a black froth of unlicht floods the chamber.

'Go.'

'Where to?'

'Go, go.'

This is their next cautionary measure. As the visitor crosses the room, the glintz of a walking silhouette dances on the opposite wall: the grotesque daub of a negative of darkness overflowing back and forth at the edges. The Buryats stare at it with great attention.

'Halt!'

One seizes the left arm, the other the right, as they shove their paws into the pockets, inside the collar, under the waistcoat, and extract the angular bundle. Having uncovered the Grossmeister, they jump back, blinded. Pobedonostseff's Angel utters a cry, lights flash against the backdrop of the window, glintzen leap jabbering over the walls. The revolver is aflame.

Close the curtain. A monochrome brightness returns. The Grossmeister dies down.

Ziel watches with a gloomy expression.

'But that you should deceive us so.'

'I forgot. I always carry it with me.' Unfold the arms. 'I also have enemies, by the very fact that I exist; after all, you well know it.'

Ziel kicks the Grossmeister towards the feet of the lurking Buryats.

'He wants to talk to you in private, yet you still pose the same threat to him unarmed.'

'I pose no threat to Aleksandr Aleksandrovitch!'

The Angel purses his bloodless lips, intertwines his long arms behind his back, bows his forehead.

'I know whom I saw at the governor general's ball, and I know whom I see now. But this revolver –'

'I forgot, for God's sake, I didn't think you'd search me!'

'Well exactly. And why is it made of tungetitum?'

'Not of tungetitum. It's a nickel coolbond with high anti-thermal properties, so that the shooter isn't killed on the spot by the frost. Because the bullets – because the bullets are made of tungetitum.'

'The bullets.' The Angel glances at one of the Buryats, who, clasping the Grossmeister with two fingers on the reptilian barrel, raises it to his eye. 'Yes, this is the weapon of the Son of Frost.' Gospodin Ziel draws himself up pathologically (won't his spine crack when arched back like that?), clears his throat and for a moment shuts his eyes. 'Please wait,' he blurts and quickly climbs into the darkness of the seventieth floor.

Remain with the two Buryats; one continues to wield the Grossmeister in his stretched-out hand like a dead snake. The chubby-cheeked countenances of the indigenes express no emotions interpretable to a white man. Speak to them perhaps, explain, walk over and perform a friendly gesture? The mathematics of character, algorithms of race leave no doubt: it's futile, these systems are built upon different axioms and cannot be used to convert one man to another. Stand motionless with an expression equally vacant. All that can be heard is the distant rattle of the lift and creak of elements in the tower's construction as they against each other.

The Angel descends from the darkness, makes a gesture of invitation with his hand. Enter the apartments of Pobedonostseff.

All the walls are made of frostoglaze; glaring unlicht pours forth from everywhere. Perceive Arkady Hipolitovitch and the furniture filling the apartments only as fragmentary glintzen. There are fixtures here, however, whose shape and function cannot be deduced by such means – hangers with a dozen arms? wire racks? revolving cages?

Unsymmetrical intersecting partitions divide the floor into four uneven areas; Ziel half-opens a curtain and withdraws to one side. His glintz extends bushy limbs over a partition wall, swells into a tuber the shape of a cow's head, burgeons with electric tentacles.

'Don't look,' he whispers.

'This light –'

'Him.'

Aleksandr Aleksandrovitch Pobedonostseff, whom no inhabitant of Irkutsk has seen with his own eyes, chairman of the Board of Directors of Sibirkhozheto and de facto ruler of the City of Ice, blazes with cold fire on a dais between mirrors of darkness, drenched in unlicht from the cryocarbon reflectors surrounding the tower – the negative outline of that blackness, the contours of ice embers; this much is visible of Aleksandr Aleksandrovitch. Shield the eyes with the forearm, and in this way draw near to the dais.

'You may put on your spectacles,' a metallic voice resounds from both right and left, till the body shudders, shaking the head and straining the eyes into the dark from under a shaft of brightness, to no avail. Nervously take out the frostoglazes and place them on the nose. The oculars disperse the concentrated glintz into rainbows and gently flowing kaleidoscopes, in which it is all the more impossible to decipher either a face or any form silhouetted within.

Stop before the dais and think: he has encrypted himself. It smells here of oil and mechanical lubricants, but also of ozone. The metallic reverberation – emanates from gramophone trumpets, horns mounted on either side; out of these come Pobedonostseff's words. Whoever looks, shan't see a man, only a tree of glintz; whoever listens, shan't hear a man, only a worn-out record. Only the content of his words remains, and that is very little. He has encrypted himself, he, the first gleissenik, the one who best knows the basic principle of the Land of the Gleissen; thusly he hides from the mathematics of character, so that no one can *solve* him. And so, despite years spent under the Ice, he remains for everyone, in the literal sense, *unpredictable*. Is not this the source of his power?

'Venyedikt Filipovitch Gierosławski,' he says from all around; and this time, any glancing to the sides is resisted.

'Aleksandr Aleksandrovitch Pobedonostseff.'

Something grates in the speaking trumpets, krkhhr, trtrtr, krkkkk – Pobedonostseff is laughing.

'You came to me with a revolver. Agh, agh! You want to kill me.'

'For what? For what would I want to kill you?'

Krkhhr, trtrtr, krkkkk.

'You have no reason, so you won't kill.'

'I have no reason.'

'On behalf of your friend, Nikolay Milutinovitch Tesla.'

'So, it's true you have designs on his life.'

'True.'

'You pay for his head.'

'True.'

'You already tried to murder him on his way to Siberia.'

'True.'

True, true, true, murch freezes every uncertainty; the crystal of truth grows bigger like ice structures under a microscope.

'You learned of the emperor's letter to the governor general and sent word to the Lyednyak courtiers, and they dispatched their special agent after Doctor Tesla, to kill him, to destroy his machines. Have you people also in the Third Department? How did you know the first agent's cover had been blown?'

'Agh, but even so you really have no reason; you gave yourself away in your *Apoliteia*, you also have no wish for Tesla's Thaw by machine. That he's your friend –'

'For life.'

'Then save him, send him packing.'

'My father –'

'Your father!' he roars out of the steel horns, as the ironwork on the dais clatters, creaks, clangs. 'Forget about him! Tell me about the Un-State, about the Kingdom of Ice!'

Pull off the spectacles for a moment, wipe the bridge of the nose. The eyes sting. Glancing thus to one side of the unlicht fire projected out of Pobedonostseff by the mirrors, a magnificent panorama of Irkutsk can be seen through the broad window behind his back, a metropolis in seven shades of white padded with milk-jelly fogs, iced by the star-shapes of gleissen, with its thousand ribbons of chimney smoke, thousand sequins of frostoglaze lamps. True, true – when he is not receiving guests, and he receives them very rarely, he surveys his city from up here, by day and by night, gazing always out of the gloom, surveys the city, counts the gleissen, calculates the profits, weaves his far-reaching plans.

'But what did you understand in fact of my *Apoliteia*?' Speak in an undertone, momentarily amazed at the bare-faced lack of deference. The moment passes. 'All those who believe in History frozen under the Ice, whether they be Lyednyaks or Ottepyelniks, always build upon the same picture: History was advancing as it should, until suddenly something blew, split, was chilled through, and so under the Ice we have a distortion of History instead of the right History. Some like it, others don't, but the diagnosis is one and the same. It has frozen. But I have lived here for several months and not yet succumbed to the Frost, at least in this I have courage to draw original conclusions from the reality. The Ice freezes everything in soletruth, the Ice reduces each thing to its necessary form or to its own negation, still identical however in form, just as the negative of an image equates to the positive. The Land of the Gleissen is the Land of Truth. And so, with the impact of the Frost in nineteen-oh-eight, no catastrophe and no deformation of History ensued – History under the Ice is how it should be. Berdyaeff correctly interpreted from matter how ideas move, but started from the mistaken assumption of seeing God behind every historical fact, of hearing the voice of heaven in the turn of the eras. Since it's hard to get our heads around this, hard to tear our thought away from what we've taken to be obvious, this is the most difficult. For since time immemorial we have lived precisely in the History of chance, of non-necessity, of uncertainty, of half-truths. Whatever the German philosophers dreamed up, these were only approximations of truth, crude speculations, and the forcing of distorted History into geometrical figures. Only here, under the Ice, will it be possible to formulate History within strict rules, to work out with mathematical precision the interdependencies of eras and the consequences of political systems, to infer ideas from ideas. Winter has distorted nothing; Winter has revealed History's soletruth. Without the Ice there is no History, and without History there is no God and no man – because the past exists not outside of the Ice. Non-State government, in which you have taken such interest, Aleksandr Aleksandrovitch, the direct authority of History – this is possible only under the Ice. In Summer instead – man rules, that is, chance, half-truth, half-falsehood, a billion unrealised possibilities. Here in Russia especially, where it has always been colder, you have always been instinctively looking out for the earthly viceroy of History; Russia is governed by the night-time whim of an autocrat, who is unto himself the measure of all Truth.'

Hidden in the embers of glintzen, the mechanism of Pobedonostseff's box throne creaks, scrapes, clatters, as the boss of Sibirkhozheto leans out on his dais above the mirrors, not far, yet rising above the blazing bonfire of unlicht.

'Agh, agh! Our Most Serene Lord is therefore right in sending Doctor Tesla to wage war on the gleissen.'

Surely there was mockery in this; the echo of the speaking horns drowns any nuances in tone.

Fold the arms behind the back, rest a foot on the edge of the dais.

'But you will fight against him, you will fight for the Kingdom of Ice.'

For a long time, nothing but steely silence emanates from the encircling trumpets. The coldiron tower trembles and creaks underfoot; wind whistles beyond the frostoglaze walls.

'When the Tchornoye Siyaniye blossoms in unlicht across the sky,' Pobedonostseff begins, enunciating his words slowly, 'it seems to me that it's no longer darkness from the reflectors encompassing me but the Atra Aurora itself flowing in inky waves through the top of the tower, I feel it on my skin, on my tongue, in my veins; I fall asleep in it and wake up in it. In my dreams, for which the doctors prescribe potions of Chinese herbs, in my dreams and in the mesmerising glintz of the city below, as if in a throw of dice cast by a shaman's hand – I see the future of Siberia, the future of the world, which shall be realised thanks to me. This is how I know the things that I know not; such is my sortilege machine for reading hidden knowledge: machine of the City of Ice and Fog.

'Have you ever thought how the world will look when the Ice eventually covers it from pole to pole, all continents, all states and all peoples? Lyednyaks and Ottepyelniks, Berdyaevians and unbelievers, Martsynians and legitimate Christians tell one another all sorts of tales and auguries. But I know, I see. There shall be no war with gleissen. I see people cohabitating with them. Gleissen underground and on the surface, and people – high above, in metropolises of rainbows, in strongholds shot into the sky on coldiron spans, in Alhambras suspended above the eternal snow. The Tchornoye Siyanye kindles blazes of unlicht across the firmament in every geographical latitude, day on day, night on night. No roads are there in the Kingdom of Ice except the Ways of the Mammoths, along which gleissen roam. People travel by train on soaring crystal rails strung in the sky; or in aerostats made of still lighter, through-frozen materials. The new ice technologies have opened the sky to us, led us out towards the stars. No one starves, no one suffers needlessly, the diseases of Summer have disappeared. In our frostoglaze greenhouses, under the unlicht, we cultivate types of corn and fruit resistant to every pestilence. Never do we lack heat or electrical current.

'Agh, do you think I don't know what Doctor Tesla is up to in his

Observatory? He is drawing energy directly from the Ways of the Mammoths. We shall have no need of hydroelectric power plants – all rivers will freeze; we won't have to burn coal or crude oil – all coal will turn to cryocarbon, and as for oil, the oil will freeze. We shall pump energy straight out of the earth, out of the Ways of the Mammoths. The planet will be our power plant, and every man will take whatever great force he wants from the Ice.

'But now, agh, agh, I have read your *Apoliteia* and glimpsed the spiritual foundations of this Kingdom of Darkness. For indeed, it shall be one Kingdom, one human organism: the State of Order and Justice, sanctioned by Truth, just as rigid and obvious as the rules of arithmetic. There will be no rebels, for who rebels against chemistry and physics, against multiplication tables and gravity? No revolts in the name of religion or ideology, for no dispute is there as to which faith and idea be true. The truth is one, the soletruth. History rules.'

Clear the throat.

'That is… impressive.'

'It is inevitable!' roars Pobedonostseff out of the steel trumpets.

'Well, unless Thaw comes.'

'So, you understand why Tesla has to be wrested from the Ice. One way or another.'

'I told you,' snarl in reply, 'Nikola is my friend!'

Move the left foot onto the dais, without knowing when, and stand there three armlengths away from the chairman of Sibirkhozheto concealed in his cocoon of glintz, behind the mirrors of darkness. A violent whistle and rattle of invisible mechanisms precedes a reconfiguration of light and shade – and the whole installation moves off towards the window, as shafts of unlight shoot straight back and murk thick as tar erupts in the face, sticking under the closed eyelids; feel its clammy touch on the skin.

Retreat, step down from the dais.

'Rest assured that I shall tell him everything!'

Krkhhr, trtrtr, krkkkk.

'Agh, tell him, tell him! You have heard it from me, he shall hear it from you – he'll perceive the truth and necessity, and leave.'

So, that's how his thinking went. Except, was it only truth being witnessed here? The twilight blinds, the phonic horns deafen.

'Agh, and you too should be on your guard,' Pobedonostseff crackles on. 'I'd like to see you at my side on the day the Kingdom is founded; a rare happiness to meet a brother in the idea. But in the meantime, you hobnob with Schultz, with Martsynians, you plan to go north into Winter in search of your father… as if you didn't know, after your

Apoliteia, that Ottepyelniks see in you all the more the embodiment of Frost: no longer just the son of Batyushka Moroz, but the foremost ideologue of the Ice. They'll also discover without fail that you've been talking to me.'

'To father,' repeat with emphasis, lowering the eyes. 'I have to go to father.'

'Father, what's father? A figure of ice. You won't help him, nor he you.'

Shake the head.

'You wish to help me? So please. What happened to Karol Bohdanowicz and Aleksander Czerski? Why censor the geological maps and works about local peoples?'

'Agh! Agh! You're asking for Company secrets!'

'A method exists, a rule exists. Who walks with the mammoths? But you have forbidden, erased, barricaded this knowledge. These are no accidents. Opening to the rabble the gates to the Ways of the Mammoths – would snatch the geological secrets from your hands, and you would lose millions, millions.'

'What fellow are you?' Aleksandr Aleksandrovitch growls, clanking his irons. 'I extend the hand of friendship, open before you the Kingdom of Darkness, yet you attack me with accusations, with venom!'

'Will you help or not?'

Again, a long note of metallic silence.

'What can I say, obstinate youngling… In nineteen sixteen, I secured from the ministry an ukase against the falsification of Siberian geography. Do you not know that indigenous shamans possess the power to distort the landscape, warp distances, bend straight lines on the earth and in the sky? No truth is there about Siberia in the cartography done with the aid of locals, on the land of locals, above the Ways of the Mammoths wherein wander the souls of their sorcerers. Have you examined old maps of Siberia, those from the time of Yermak? But since war flared amongst them here – there's been falsity upon falsity! The farther towards Summer, the worse. The Company geologists often returned from long marches during which no mountain remained in its place, and no river flowed as it ought.

'Prime Minster Struve's plan to modify the mining law is meant to prevent these frauds, at least in part. Siberia must be calculated! As to the number of versts, the number of poods of subterranean wealth! Geological piracy shall end! For I can see after all how this chaos suits various lesser coldiron firms, suits dishonest competition which extracts illicit priority patents from the Gubernatorial Office for State Property. Grochowski's map – ah, so you've heard of it – when they become a little more honest over their vodka, the Grokhovshtchik at once springs to mind: the mythical cartography of soletruth. Power over the world rests in the hands of a geodesist!'

'So, you've not tried sending your own people onto the Ways?'

'Agh! Don't do it!'

'You have tried! Aleister Crowley! His conversation with you – the icecradle tomb – was it an icecradle at all?'

'Don't do it! It can't be done –'

'What? What can't be done?' Very nearly step back onto the dais, shuffling the foot forward in the dark. 'He is alive? Not alive?'

'Go now. I shall be waiting for you, you have not en-lied your *Apoliteia*, I shall be waiting in the Kingdom – but now go.'

Is that weariness heard in his voice? Or not, as a wave of sound lined with sharp-edged sheet metal comes down the pipes.

'If you only could, you'd have filled the Ways of the Mammoths with your agents,' mumble into the beard. 'What is it that's needed to descend to the Ways, which the whole of Sibirkhozheto is unable to buy?'

'Go! Go! Go!'

Withdraw, having removed the spectacles, rubbing the eyes in the darkness. The voice of Aleksandr Aleksandrovitch Pobedonostseff grows weak. Maybe he really is weary… Those mood swings, that untimely laugh… Why does he hide in glintzen, in unlighted apparatus – maybe Herr Bittan and the rumours are correct: the boss of Sibirkhozheto is ill, mortally ill, and this is the final phase of some terrible malady; he can no longer even shift himself on his own, cannot stand on his own legs; moves only together with his box throne, talks in whispers through speaking horns, loses strength after half an hour of conversation. *They say that under the Ice, such diseases come to a halt. But also, no one here has ever been cured of ailments acquired aforehand.* He cannot recover, probably couldn't anyway – but so long as he's under the Ice, he won't die, since he's already frozen, or rather – his body has frozen. Consumption, a tumour – what other diseases does it affect? Certainly not every disease, for people still die here nevertheless, Atchukhoff died, Emilka died… How to recognise which acquired ailment depends on Lies, and which tells the Truth about man? Without doubt, old age and all the infirmities associated with old age belong to the natural order.

Well, is this the solution to the equation of Aleksandr Aleksandrovitch Pobedonostseff? Will he fight for the Kingdom of Darkness because of bodily weakness? Does matter indeed govern spirit?

Pause behind a partition, struck by an unsavoury thought. For were the freezing to be for once and for all, what soletruth would be glimpsed in memories of the past? Doesn't all this – including the *Apoliteia* and deepest current convictions, along with the political situation in Irkutsk and the relationships and interests connected with the place – constitute the mathematical expansion of that Warsaw afternoon when two tchinovniks from the Ministry of Winter woke a chap in the chill, bombarding their way into his lodgings and standing uninvited over his bed, grinding him into squalor, stench and indigence with their own tchinovnik power, with their black bowlers and snow-white vater-mörder collars, plunging him into the hottest Shame straight from his peaceful sleep? So, what now – will Pobedonostseff build his Kingdom of Darkness out of this...?

But how are political opinions supposedly born in man? After all, they're not sucked in with his mother's milk, not taught like algebra or geography. Instead, they are acquired in part, like culinary palate, taste in art or fondness for a given type of woman, from the conditions of his birth and upbringing, but in part – and is this not the greater part? – from the chance events of his own life. Was not a reflection of this truth observed in the case of poor Zeytsoff? He became a socialist, then an anarchist, and now a radical Christian – because he heard of his father's infamy and saw the destitution of the peasantry. But from what life events are democrats born? From what life events – monarchists? From what life events – Pilsudtchiks? By the time it'll be possible to calculate them with hundred-per-cent certainty, politics will have actually descended into a class of banal likes and dislikes: this lot prefer cigars, that lot pipe tobacco.

Pobedonostseff was right: under the authority of the Non-State, under the direct rule of History, any dispute about crucial political questions will cease to be possible. Instead, parties will emerge of supporters of this or that aesthetics, pressure groups of connoisseurs of meat or meat-free cuisine, parliamentary factions of admirers of the fair sex or gourmets of pederasty. Debate will be about colours, coiffures and rhymes. An eloquent good-looker with a top-notch tailor will become chancellor.

Only in the lift did Ziel return the Grossmeister.

'Spasibo.'

'His orders.' The Angel stood in the opposite corner of the coldiron cage facing outwards, so that a good arshin of empty space remained in the middle; and even on the descent from the subcelestial darkness, Pobedonostseff's Angel was no more than the shadow of a slender silhouette, arched unhealthily backwards. 'We are falling. Lighter, lighter, lighter. I love these moments.'

'Even less body.'

'Yes. When you –'

'Let's forget it.'

'You will try to forget, but you won't forget. The body crushes. The body pinches.'

'Let's forget it, on Saturday at the ball I was distraught.'

'God will summon you.'

The lift cage shook as it slowed.

'Pray, sir, that you won't live to see Thaw.' Light a cigarette. The Frost over Irkutsk had formed itself into horizontal flounces of white. Fall from the lake of tar into a sea of milk. Tuck the Grossmeister under the shuba. Thinking already about naught else: two days since the ball, the word given to Mademoiselle Filipov is no longer binding – why not go and pump off? Not to the New Arkadiya, but to Tesla's Observatory. Why not? After work.

After work, on the Marmeladobahn station, Editor Jeż Wólka-Wólkiewicz attached himself at once. He must have been waiting there, lurking – he fell out of the crowd of muffled figures devoid of countenances and coiled in breath mist, one more human fright steeped in tasselled umbriance, hanging already off the arm and cackling away neath the shapka before he was recognised as Jeż. There was just enough time to prevent a blow from Shtchekelnikoff's paw. Editor Wólkiewicz, however, paid him no attention.

'Benedykt, sir! What have you done! They're wringing my neck! Save me!'

Dive into the first nearby tavern. Unwinding the scarf and removing the spectacles, unfreeze the throat with hot tea. Editor Wólkiewicz clasped his glass in gloved hands but failed to lift it even to his mouth.

'Save me!' He suddenly raised his voice in order to penetrate the vodka-fuelled din. 'They've confiscated my machines. I've been kicked out of my premises. Terrible police types are thrusting themselves on me, Okhrana or not Okhrana, I'm well acquainted with the Irkutsk Okhrana after all –'

'You mean because of me?'

'Who else! Because of that damned *Apoliteia*! Holy Madonna of the Meadows! I've printed the most dangerous anti-tsarist pamphlets but there's never been a storm like this!'

He was quaking with anger – but directed at whom? He glanced now here, now there, tossing his head from side to side, his Adam's apple dancing below his chin like the rubber tube of a laboratory pump; he squeezed his hand around the glass, spattering the tea. Shtchekelnikoff, treating himself to a Shtchekelnikoff-style beverage, displayed a crooked grin over the editor's shoulder: here was the next illustration to Tchingis's black sayings, the Angry Coward. True? True.

'Odd that it's only now?'

'Most likely someone higher up read your article. I didn't have to publish it, didn't have to!' He slammed the glass on the tabletop; the remains of the tea splashed out. 'You, sir, persuaded me...'

'Well, I'm very sorry. I give you my word it wasn't I who denounced you, besides no one even asked me –'

'Spineless cads! Didn't even take a rouble for a cup of tea, everything had to be above board, official, and I even had to sign the summons to the prosecutor. If it doesn't die down soon, they'll arrest me, give me a trumped-up trial; I shall have to do time in my old age.'

'For the *Apoliteia*? Eee...'

'Of course not! They'll enter something else in the documents! Don't you know, sir, how it's done? I have no licence to publish *The Free Pole*! How could I have? The thing was legal insofar as Schultz tolerated all these folkish movements, circles promulgating this or that culture, townsmen's societies, Oblastnik parties. Only recently – that wave of arrests – my heart was in my mouth!' He gulped once and twice. 'And now they really have come for me. You see it, my God, yet you say nothing!'

'I didn't think it would produce such a result.' Rub the back of the hand against the beard, deep in thought. 'I can't even see whose work it could be, neither Schultz, nor Pobedonostseff –'

'Save me! Write me a letter of recommendation to the governor general, such things can be undone only from above, and quickly, quickly.'

'How can I recommend anyone to the governor...!' Break into laughter.

'Don't mock me, sir!' Wólka-Wólkiewicz was irritated. 'You have Schultz's ear.'

'From whence that nonsense?'

'Half the city knows you talked to him for a long time at the ball, and to Prince Blutsky too. Don't play the innocent with me, Mr Frost and State of Ice!'

Listen with a disagreeable sense of déjà vu. Was this the return of Count Gyero-Saski? The difference being that now it is freezing; now it is the truth.

Slurp the tea.

'Calm down. I will write the letter.' Reach for the business-card holder. 'Though I'll be very surprised if it helps.'

'For the bearer, please.'

'Huh?'

'I'm not that naïve, they won't admit me; I have more presentable friends.'

'Well, all right, pangs of conscience are pricking me, let it be as you wish, I'll write "regarding a matter that brooks no delay". You can also do something for me. No, no, nothing like that; I would simply like to know more about Abraham Fishenstein, especially about his past, what kind of man he be – I need more particulars.'

Jeż Wólka-Wólkiewicz peered over his frostoglazes.

'So, you did set about making money?'

'What? No. It's on a different matter: Fishenstein is a donor to the Brotherhood of War against the Apocalypse and I need to –'

'Now you're cosying up to Fyodorovians, eh?'

Encounter the Fyodorovian again at Tesla's. Drive to the Physical Observatory of the Imperial Academy of Sciences, stopping first at Tsvetistaya Street to pick up the metal laboratory samples as well as a bottle of sazhayevka. Above the cloud of darkness shrouding the Observatory building, masts strung with fresh corpses jutted into the evening sky; icicles had not yet managed to grow beneath them; glintzen spreading from the deceased men plotted the vertices of a pentagram in the sky. The Cossacks gave entrance. Pass Engineer Jago in the corridor coming from the storerooms; he pretends he doesn't see. Find the laboratory deserted. Hard to imagine a better opportunity. Quickly throw off the fur coat and shapka and extricate Tesla's unlicht bomb from behind the other prototypes and experimental installations, fortunately reassembled into one piece. Exchange the cryocarbon in the lamp's hearth for pure tungetitum. Check the cables. The oscillometers showed the voltage they ought. Stick a plate of tungetitum in front of the outlet beak of the reflective sphere. The test shot sparked on the plate a spot-glow more blinding than the cupola fires of Christ the Saviour Sobor. Take out the notebook. The hypothesis had been jotted down at a time when five separate theories had been rattling around the brain at once due to the shortage of unlicht; now it no longer sounded so convincing. Do the calculations: twenty shots fired per sample in order to affect an area greater than a pinhead, and eight samples: non-chilled-through ores, high-carbon steel, low-quality coldiron. There was still a quarter of an hour, if haste were made. Note the hour and minute, in case the effect should fade with time. Begin with base coldiron. Chshtik, chshtik popped the Death Ray Machine. In the moment of the shot, a rainbow of all existing and non-existing colours flooded the frostoglazes. Air must have dispersed the ray slightly, however, as the flakes of tungetitum in the vodka also glowed faintly. Remove the bottle of sazhayevka to a nearby bench.

Still having no idea what to do with it. The thinking went as follows: drink the tungetitum vodka and instead of habitually demurching, do the reverse: bemurch the body as much as it could take. Maybe the morning visit to Pobedonostseff had given the spirit a final spur, for at last it was openly acknowledged: what easier way to find father on the Ways of the Mammoths than to descend to the Ways after him? The idea thrown to Schultz as a deflection, and which had been gnawing at the mind for a long time, was only too obvious. That Pobedonostseff's people had not succeeded meant nothing: in the beginning, every new science functions haphazardly, gaining one success for every hundred failures; thus it was with the steam and internal combustion engines, with aeroplanes, with electromagnetism, thus it is with black physics. On the other hand, no exact formula was known, certain things were only speculation; and so, for the time being, the sole desire was to re-search the organism's reactions. Let us say: half a litre and two thousand skotos.

But perhaps it would be wiser and safer to experiment first on someone else. Interesting to know how Sasha Pavlitch's rats fed on Busytchin's potatoes are coping in the Frost. The rodents in their cages by the distant wall appeared to be healthy, but there was no way of knowing what batch these were; all those used in the experiment might have snuffed it.

Either way, it would be pointless to rely on calculating father's route along the Ways. Straightforward investigations had to be resorted to, based on matter, not on mathematics. The idea of sending a salgyn-kut soul after Father Frost was by no means the craziest. Another hope was linked to the forbidden hydrography of Baikal; Mr Uriah had promised to produce copies during the coming week of Karol Bohdanowicz's old maps. And also reports of the first tsarist expeditions into Winter, in-cluding the ill-fated expedition in which Filip Gierosławski and Sergey Atchukhoff took part.

The problem was that all this taken together did little to solve another, rather more crucial problem, namely: how to safely defreeze father, assuming that he is found. Here, there are no roundabout methods; half-means, half-conjectures merely enhance the danger. It is vital either to know the entire black-physical process that enables men to descend to the Ways of the Mammoths, or have access to at least one other such abassylian for live testing. Whilst finding the Dumb Ballooner, Kopytkin or Crowley is just as hard as finding father. And guzzling sazhayevka for this purpose makes little sense: a man turned into an abassy would have to be someone upon whom experiments could freely be carried out.

There's less and less time however. On the following day, Prince Blutsky-Osey was to introduce his trusty proxy; Frantishek Markovitch was coming with the estimated costs of the expedition and a reliable indigenous tracker; on the following day, a concrete plan had to begin to be realised. There was still no plan. Cold calculation prompted that it was high time to abandon the calculations and try more desperate methods.

At the sight of vodka, Sasha swiftly took out two graduated cylinders.

'No, no,' wave the hand, 'it's a scientific aid.'

'Ah, a "scientific aid"! But you mean to pursue science this evening? In company maybe?'

'Loneliness pricks the soul, eh?'

'Agh, Venyedikt Filipovitch, why pull the wool over your eyes – we're living as if in a fortress.'

'Where's Nikola?'

'That Khavroff of yours has taken up half his day, they've gone now into the courtyard, to the tungetitor. Do you hear? An interval in the rumbling. Why did you acquaint him with the Fyodorovians? They've completely ensnared him, now everything is lying neglected.'

Pat the pockmarked biologist on the shoulder.

'It'll pass, with him such fascinations always pass, sooner or later.' Light a cigarette; offer one to Sasha, he accepted with thanks. 'And the fact you're in a fortress, believe me, is your best way out at present. Pobedonostseff has it in for the doctor.'

Pavlitch raised his head, eyes sparkling, a glintz flowing over his cheeks.

'Exactly! Mademoiselle Filipov brought news that you were talking to the governor and to Aleksandr Aleksandrovitch's secretary.'

'Ah yes, Mademoiselle Filipov...'

'Exactly, exactly!' He grew so excited that his pitted skin erupted again in a brick-red rash. 'How was it at the ball, tell me!'

'What, did she not tell of how the Son of Frost roughed up the governor general's daughter?' Sigh through the smoke. 'A ball like any other ball, a vanity fair, bodies decked in flowers and lace and sprinkled in scent so they look less like bodies and stink less like bodies. How is it with our rats?'

He blinked.

'The rats.' He took an exercise book out of a drawer. 'Well, what can I say, the bad news is they all froze to the marrow. As you wished, I buried them in their cages by the well in the cellar. No extraordinary effects, so far. You can check, I fixed a cable to a murchometer on the wall.'

'And there's good news too, I assume.'

'There is. In the controlled pairs, not all specimens froze after the same length of time despite equal doses of teslectricity and equal portions of tungetitum potato.'

'Mm-hmm. But did it take longer than with rats fed on ordinary food?'

'Yes, decidedly. Up to a hundred and twenty per cent, see for yourself.' Skim through the numerical comparisons.

'The variation doesn't exceed twenty-four hours.'

'Yet nevertheless.'

'True.' Flick ash into a cuvette; raise the eyes to the ceiling blackened long ago by soot. 'Conclusions. Despite Doctor Tesla's original assumptions, every material object, in any case every living object, has a defined murch capacity. If we pump telestric flow into an organism above this capacity, the drop in temperature eventually causes a shutting-down of vital processes.'

'This was already more or less known.'

'Next. Pumping tungetitum with teslectricity prompts the translation of murch energy into kinetic energy, indirectly also into thermal energy. Tesla's engines work after all according to this principle, thanks to which we have current and light in here,' wave the cigarette, 'and all of it on energy drawn from the Ways of the Mammoths.'

'Therefore, an organism stuffed with tungetitum,' Sasha Pavlitch joined in, narrowing his eyes and spouting smoke from the corner of his mouth, 'when pumped with teslectricity, will remain above freezing point for longer, since processes will take place on the tungetitum inside him that partially neutralise the influence of the Frost.'

'Exactly so.' Stop the hand rubbing against the waistcoat. Ah, how five minutes on the Kotarbiński pump would come in handy right now...! 'And just think: organisms that rely totally on black biology would have an infinite murch capacity: their vital processes themselves would occur through the conversion of teslectrical flow into movement, heat, cell chemistry.'

WoobooMMM! A shudder passed through the building. WoobooMMM! A deep rumble irritating the inner ears. WoobooMMM!

'On the other hand,' Sasha was thinking aloud, 'any endothermic reaction would prompt a reduction in the organism's temperature.'

'So would they freeze or not?'

'And yet they'd be alive!'

'Frozen.'

'Perhaps. No. In some other way.'

He removed the pince-nez, massaged his nose. Stared with sincere curiosity and with equally sincere sympathy.

'You think he's alive also in that way?'

'Yes, Sasha, I think he's alive. I've been weighing it in my mind for some time. And since even rats –'

Nikola Tesla and Edmund Gerontyevitch Khavroff came dashing indoors, dusted in snow and billowing with unlighted breath mist, kicking the permafrost from their boots. Pavlitch leaped to his feet.

'No mud in here, gentlemen, I implore you, no mud!' They didn't even glance around. Khavroff, rushing in leaps and bounds and having swapped his frostoglazes for wire spectacles with lenticular lenses, caught sight at once of the bottle of sazhayevka and, rubbing his hands, applied himself to pulling out the stopper. Before there was time to fly over and protest, he had swilled a whopping great mouthful down his gullet. He exhaled, and his bald patch reddened in delight. 'Ugh, how the frost washes off you immediately.' 'It's soot, Edmund Gerontyevitch, watch what you're drinking.' 'Well, what of it? Should I pour you some?'

Tesla emerged from his corner with glasses and a bottle of Chivas Regal. There was no turning back.

'Engineer Jago has clocked out,' said the Serb mustering the glasses on the laboratory bench. 'The coast is clear.'

'What are we celebrating?' Heave a sigh.

Gospodin Khavroff, whose posture and flushed expression were not very directorial at that moment, seized and squeezed the right hand, feverishly excited in his convulsions of cordiality.

'Great triumph against the Apocalypse, Gospodin Yeroslavsky!'

'Huh?'

He gave a vodka-soaked snort.

'Don't pretend! Doctor Tesla has told me how you raised him from the dead.'

WoobooMMM!

Sasha stared wide-eyed, the pince-nez almost slipping off his nose.

Pull an irritated face.

'That was in Summer, in Summer! Such raising from the dead there...'

Nikola Tesla emptied his glass, straightened his back, raised his arm – already at near ceiling height – and froze in this thunderous pose, the jacket of his black suit pulled up, cravat askew, birdlike skull tilted towards his target, grey lock aslant the deep eye socket – awaiting the signal – WoobooMMM! – a moment – then he flung the glass with all his might.

It shattered on the tiling by the door into a thousand shards, which came to rest in regular rhomboid shapes: a stained-glass pattern in crystal, a diamond mandala.

'The Murch Hammer!' cried Tesla. 'Whoever possesses that knowledge will forge with it on waves of murch, miracles and resurrections and whatever arabesques of entropy he pleases!'

Then the boozing began.

Having more than enough glass within easy reach, they threw themselves into negentropic games – Khavroff and young Pavlitch included – smashing the vessels for greater and greater artistic effect, whilst the trick depended on anticipating the right moment between strokes of the Hammer, that is, the point at which the wave travelling in the teslectrical field of the Ways of the Mammoths descended in high amplitude to the local minimum, to the anti-entropic extremum. A symphony arose of booms and yells, not entirely conscious; the cadence went as follows: Hammer – burst of shattering glass – voice of joy or disappointment. Sasha grew so animated that he hurled his graduated cylinders with both hands – which resulted in a symmetrical image of a two-winged angel.

'You must flee as soon as possible,' whisper in Tesla's ear.

'Huh?'

'I've been talking to Pobedonostseff. The man is half-demented, he'll defend his kingdom at any cost even if he has to openly oppose the tsar, even if he has to slaughter all your Cossacks. You are not safe, flee now with your life. I can organise a painless escape for you, in secret from everyone, only say the word.'

'In other words, I would not only have to not fulfil my contract with the emperor, as if that weren't enough, but also surrender to the Ice and relinquish black physics to strangers?'

'You may not care about your own life, sir, but at least have regard for Christine!'

'If only she listened to me…!'

'For God's sake, this is no joke! The agent in the Trans-Siberian Express substituted for Monsieur Verousse – that was already Pobedonostseff's doing.'

'Didn't I tell you!' Gratified, Tesla raised a silent toast.

'Your mood has changed a lot, sir.' Speak without hiding the distaste. 'Have you pumped often of late?' Glance at the umbriance surrounding him, yet it seemed, at least here and in this light, not to differ especially from Tesla's usual (that is, unusual) umbriance.

'I don't have to. Drink, sir, and stop grumbling!' And he pressed a glass of whisky into the hand.

'Were Christine to see this… What's come over you?'

'I am carrying out an experiment!'

'Experiment?'

'Didn't they tell you that in Winter, there's no way to get properly drunk? Even before the advent of the Ice – Russians had stronger heads, more alcohol was always needed here. But the Hammer strikes in both directions! Drink!'

Sasha Pavlitch poured himself some sazhayevka.

'We're pursuing science!' he chortled.

WoobooMMM!

'See for yourself.' Tesla walked over to a black tile laid flat under the lamps. On the smooth matt surface were scattered brown sand and white grits. Tesla jerked the tile; the particles were thoroughly mixed. He waited a moment, then jerked it again – two-thirds of them separated off, dispersing to the left and right of an almost perpendicular line.

Recognise the tile as a tungetitum mirror.

'So, you've also given up experiments on the nature of unlicht?'

'Unlicht, unlicht, unlicht...' He performed some complicated gestures with his white palms, intended no doubt to convey equally complicated ideas. 'How to build hypotheses upon hypotheses? After all, we don't know everything about light itself.'

Having taken another swig and sat down on a high stool near the Unlicht Lamp (restored to its place), the inventor launched into a rambling lecture on his theories about unlicht. First and foremost, he dragged up his beloved Johann Wolfgang von Goethe. In a work of fifteen hundred pages entitled *Zur Farbenlehre* and published in 1810, the literary genius had proclaimed a revolutionary theory of optics to which he'd devoted years of experiments with prisms and which he considered to be the work of his lifetime. According to Newton and other classic theoreticians of optics, darkness is simply the absence of light; Goethe maintained instead that light and darkness are like the opposite poles of a magnet and that one affects the force of the other; colours, meanwhile, are not contained within white light ('split up' by a prism into a spectrum), but arise on the borderlines between darkness and light. Yellow and red, when light dampens darkness, and blue and violet when darkness dampens light. Darkness here means something which we now call unlicht – it directly affects the light. Stand at sunset against a clear background before a lighted candle, says Johann Wolfgang, and look over your shoulder at your shadow: you will see a strong blue. Light does not have to have the nature of a wave in order for man to perceive colours, spectra and rainbows; we can see this after all.

... Tesla raised other constructions upon more recent theories. If we take the crazy hypothesis that light in Summer is simultaneously both a particle, Einstein's *Lichtquant*, and a wave, a wave as it were of being, that is, the ebb and flow of the probability of the light particle's existence – then unlicht would be an analogous physical symptom of non-existence, that is, the impact of particles of the 'negative probability' of light; a stream of unlicht would be a *stream of the non-being of light*. Assume the mien of a doubting Thomas. Does this mean that there exist 'molecules of non-being'? But how can non-being exist? Being is that which exists; non-being that which exists not. Yet the same might be asked, Nikola observed, in the case of light interference: how can something which does not fully exist, since it exists only fragmentarily, only in probability – how can such a thing affect visible, tangible beings? Unlicht ousting light does not therefore constitute any new effect. Negative probability neutralises positive probability.

... Except what then are glintzen? Here, Tesla was already swinging his long limbs around like a windmill; summoned out loud, glintzen appeared on his suit in greater profusion, whilst murch stained his wizened skin. All breakdowns of the spectrum as well as experiments with foil screens, he continued to declaim, show that in principle it's again ordinary light. Evidently, when passing through solid matter – through that which exists in the absolute sense – unlicht again undergoes reversal in its probabilities. But does some change take place in the unlichted matter? If so – then it's on the submolecular level or simply on the level of murch energy, since Tesla had failed to detect anything definite. Nor did he define the relationship between the wavelength of light/glintz and the wavelength of unlicht – since again, they do not have to be waves at all.

'But light is also diffused in frequencies invisible to the human eye. That is, if they are frequencies...'

'The infrared,' belched Tesla.

'For instance. So how is it with unlicht?'

Nikola again spun his arms. Take this at first to be more mimed gibberish – but he was trying in fact to point to himself: at the glintzen, at the unlichtings.

'A man who is warm,' he said and fell silent for a moment, listening intently to the workings of his own organism; reassured that everything in there was functioning as it ought, he poured more C_2H_5OH fuel into the machinery and resumed: 'A man who is warm emits light by the very fact that he is warm, only we don't see it. On the other hand, a man with an imbalance of murch, *vide* a gleissenik, we-e-ll, what else does he radiate? Amuse yourself with prisms and you will see how light, passing through a different medium, changes its character. It may also be the case, dear boy, that escaping from within matter, such radiation, even if it's unlichty to start with, turns into glintz on the outer tissues. Only from these external layers can the liberated unlicht escape undisturbed. So, this is why we see, if I am not mistaken, such optical phenomena on inhabitants of the Land of the Gleissen.'

'And the Black Auroras? And the fact that glintzen constantly scramble, tremble and wobble like jelly? And the predictions made from them? Did you read, Doctor, what I brought you from Krupp's, these theories from Berlin? For there's some link here with the states of mind of a man irradiated by unlicht, of this I am sure.'

'Bah! Maybe that hypothesis of Born and Di Veloci about de Broglie waves being sudden increases in the probability of existence, is in itself false! As in Winter, so too in Summer!'

'And of what "negative probability" do you speak, sir? Mathematics clearly defines probability: from one, indicating a realised event or an event that is equally certain, to zero, indicating an event that has no chance of happening. How can the chance be less than zero? This means – what? not only that a given thing will not happen in any event, but in addition – well, what else? Can something "not be" and "not be more"? Is non-existence gradable? For God's sake, Nikola!'

'Drink, drink.'

WoobooMMM!

Mr Khavroff divested himself of jacket and waistcoat, untied his cravat, rolled up his sleeves: he applies himself to drinking as if to hard physical labour, or crushing stones. Sasha had already cast off his laboratory coat. A large hoard of liquor had obviously been stashed away in the workshop, for two bulging flagons of Siberian khanshin suddenly appeared out of nowhere. Watch all this with unconcealed amazement. No doubt the head was still too sober, no doubt the Murch Hammer had been bashing the brain for too short a while – but observed from the outside, the whole scene had the appearance of collective possession: an evil spirit had entered into them and was prompting their bodies, their minds. Crash-bang, they'll quaff themselves to death. What a weird sort of trance! In Warsaw, the drinking was different: from glass to glass, quarter-hour after quarter-hour, chum outdrinking chum, over a bite to eat, over conversation, where intoxication somehow crept up imperceptibly. But here: they drink in order to drink. Khavroff's call was a hollow pretext, something else could have served equally well as the signal. Pavlitch too was understandable insofar as in his current state of mind – imprisoned in a fortress, frightened, isolated, left to his own devices in the evenings and at night – any path to oblivion was good. But Tesla? With one spindly leg crossed over the other, bent stork-like on his stool, he savours the Scotch in long swigs, gazing with a benign smile at the deputy director and the biologist, who were pulling silly faces at the rats and mice.

Old Stepan entered the laboratory and at once fell head over heels in the doorway on the carpet of glass. Laugh along with the others. The okhrannik clambered about screeching curses. Just as all had been chortling, so now all threw themselves into assisting him, brushing shards of glass off his clothes, guiding him to the table, thrusting one glass and then another into his hand. Edmund Gerontyevitch, already fired up, pulled a broom from a cupboard and, highly amused, swept away the pile of crystal splinters; he at once began to sing (in his operatic baritone) as he worked, stretching the melody to fit a slower time signature, and so move the broom in sync with the rhythm of the striking Murch

Hammer. Having mastered his step and stroke, he swept the floor clean within six rumblings.

Sasha meanwhile, so pink in the face from cordial feeling that his love of neighbour erupted again in pockmarks and pimples, had sat down to what remained of the sazhayevka poured into measuring flasks and, having thrust these towards everyone, was making some vehement confession into Tesla's ear, tugging at his jacket tail and beating his skinny chest with his fist. Impossible to hear what he was saying.

Khavroff was dancing a waltz with the broom in his embrace; he knocked back a whole flask, licking the tungetitum off his lips.

'Well, Venyedikt Filipovitch, did any good come of your cemetery games?'

'Did Arski not tell you?'

'He told me, he told me.' Edmund Gerontyevitch rested his chin on the broom handle, and winked. 'You're looking for the path taken by Father Frost, eh?' He lapped up the last black flake with the tip of his tongue. 'Ate his fill of tungetitum and froze into the ground, eh?'

The whisky scratched at the gullet. Clear the throat.

'Ate his fill, drank his fill, immurched his fill.'

'And so? Now,' Khravroff flexed his limbs in awkward front-crawl movements without raising his chin off the broom, 'now, he's swimming underground, hee-hee.'

'Here's the sore point, dear sir, for a living man obviously can't walk along the Ways of the Mammoths.'

'Oh! Can't he?'

'For how? Man is not an earthworm.'

'No, that he's not.'

'But this will please you.' Give the broom a kick; Khavroff flew forwards. Prop him up by the shoulder. 'How does he roam the Ways of the Mammoths if he's no longer a living man? This is how: he dies and is resurrected.'

The Fyodorovian began to bark like a poodle, thoroughly amused.

'Dies and is resurrected!'

'Do you hear?' WoobooMMM! 'There, that's what flows along the Ways.' Place a glass in the middle of the black mirror strewn with sand and kasha. 'It separates what's jumbled up, assembles what's broken, refreshes what's rotten, sticks together what's torn apart, resuscitates what's dead.' Lean again towards Khavroff; he was listening now with lips half-parted. Grab him by the cheeks, ruffle his rounded bonce. 'He freezes not from place to place along the Ways as compacted flesh, breathing in his frozen state. No, no! He flows like helium – seeps through – presses onward like the permafrost – a fibre, a tiny bone, a clot of blood, a thread of skin – and when the wave rebounds, he reassembles into a whole, like one of Piegnar's goylems.' Laugh. 'Under the ground, on the ground. My father!' Laugh louder still. 'On a wave of murch, at temperatures below absolute zero – whether he lives, or lives not... He exists even more! Exists a hundred times more powerfully! Exists above everything!'

'And that Martsynian,' Khavroff gasped, drunkenly earnest, 'that –,' 'Kopytkin.'

'Ah yes, Kopytkin!'

'You remember him? What sort of man was he?'

'Ivan Tikhonovitch Kopytkin, insufferable boor, brute and savage.'

'But what differentiated him from the other volunteers? Arski told you, we dug through the graves of all of them – only Kopytkin had descended into the permafrost.'

'Oy, I wasn't so well acquainted with them. What differentiated him – an even greater churl and bumpkin.'

Let go of Khavroff.

'The rats will sooner tell me.' Snarl at him.

He straightened his back, raised his finger.

'Rats are clever animals!'

'What's this the rats will tell you?' asked Tesla, smoothing his cuffs and gloves with unmitigated pedantry.

'Why some freeze sooner than others,' Sasha hurried with an explanation and, lacking a stool, hoisted himself onto the benchtop and flopped down beside the Death Ray Machine.

Hurl a glass at the wall. It rebounded as though off rubber and returned to the hand, not even cracked.

'God created men unequal!' yell at the others. 'Some drink through fortunes, whilst others magnetise iron filings on their chest! The doctor will measure the structure constant of the soul! Who absorbs more murch, who exists more than others!'

'The Hercules Rat!' whispered Sasha. 'Soletruth Mouse!'

'Ahem, mm-hmm, ahem,' Tesla spent a long time clearing his throat until he at last took a sip of vodka and his speech was restored. 'Are you saying, *mon ami*, that there can be no physical, chemical or biological law for this, because in addition you have to freeze – out of soul?'

'Out of character.'

Deputy Director Khavroff frowned in great intellectual effort, whilst his brain weighed so heavily upon him that he again had to prop himself up, folded in two like a pocket-knife, against the broom.

'You, sir, try to fit man's character expressed in numbers into physical equations!' he finally articulated.

'And what's so strange in that?'

'Well, isn't it obvious! Physics, mathematics, the natural sciences, which use measurable values – they treat not of man. At most of his body, but not of man! No, no, no! For understanding man, you have literature, poetry, psychology, philosophy, religion, for understanding man, you have words, not numbers!'

'What's this for a new kind of dogmatics! And from the mouth of – of a disciple of Fyodoroff!'

'Dogmatics? Agh, you, sir,' he began spitting his syllables over the broom, 'you, sir, are a determinist, a Lamettriean, a clockmaker of the soul!'

'*Au contraire.* Can everything about the world outside of man really be explained in terms of simple Newtonian or clockmaker's mechanics? Had you, Director, read anything of the works of Planck, Einstein and Gross, then you would know, sir, that it can't. And yet this does not take morec-moclec-molecular physics out of the realm of number, does not take it into the realm of literature and poetry. Why should the human mind not be treated with similar rigour? Eh? You will see, sir, how someday a mathematics of the soul will arise in accordance with the electricity of the brain and of effects as yet unmeasurable by us, which will describe human character in a table system worthy of Mendeleyeff.' Catch the breath. 'Or you won't see. If we live to see it.' Pour another Scotch. 'Or if we be resurrected.'

Doctor Tesla applauded scarcely audibly in his cotton gloves.

'Well said, Benedictus!'

'Sometimes,' confide to him above the tungetitum mirror, 'sometimes, it seems to me I manage to express the inexpressible.' Nod the head in doleful solemnity. 'That's when I say the most ridiculous things. Oh, such foolish things! Masterpieces of stupidity! Meisterstücke of cretinism! Nonsense revelations, imbecilic strokes of genius!'

WoobooMMM!

Three bottles later, Stepan, having crept beneath some wired frames, chewed through the cables and gave himself such a shock from the electric current and teslectric flow that white-and-black sparks flew out of his glaciated sock as he was dragged from under the ironwork by the leg. Hardly had the old okhrannik been pulled out when the half-naked Khavroff crawled into the same spot, chasing after a mouse to which he'd not yet had time to confess his whole directorial life; convulsed by sobs, he called after it in his operatic bass – it fled, terrified. The rodents had dispersed throughout the laboratory, beneath benches, on benches, into the apparatuses. At first, Sasha pursued them; now he climbed atop a steel cupboard and hurled screws and cable-coils from there around the room whenever a beast poked out its nose or tail; sometimes Pavlitch hit one, sometimes not, in keeping with the strokes of the Hammer. The calmest of the drinkers was Doctor Tesla, who had simply fallen asleep, his face slumped onto the tungetitum mirror so that the dark and light particles stuck to him, some to his right cheek, others to his left – which could have meant something, but didn't have to. Unlichty breath emanated from his half-open mouth shrouding the mirror in mist.

Tear off a bunch of cables too, having extracted Stepan; then, sprawling comfortably on the floor with a round frostoglaze flask on the head and stick murchometer dangling from the neck, start on a fresh bottle of khanshin biting now into electricity, now teslectricity off the naked wires. The hammer struck clean through the temples. Shut the eyes alternately, catching the burned-out images with further mouthfuls, black, white, black, white. The vodka tasted better with murch; the teeth blossomed in lemon sugar from the current. Whoop – a screw bounced back and hit the heel. Put the hands together. Bushes of coaly hoarfrost were overgrowing the fingers, reaching the pale pink nails. Close and open the fists; bursts of barbed energy were climbing along veins and up nerves to the fingertips as well as towards the heart, towards the head. Whoop. Catch one of the rebounding nuts in flight and throw it back at Pavlitch. The biologist tumbled off his cupboard, killing a mouse and a rat. He rolled around on the cluttered floor waving his arms. Hide the bottle behind the back. 'The last!' moaned Sasha. Stretch out the palms before the eyes; a pale pink mosaic shone from under the skin, a papillary chessboard. Close the left eye. Sasha seized the hand.

'C-c-cold!' he hissed.

'Let go!'

He shook a mouse corpse off his sleeve.

'Also frozen, the popopopoor mite.'

'That's odd.'

'What?'

'With this eye,' poke an eyelid, 'I see only shadows, and with this one – only lights.'

'And me, with which do you see me?'

'Bwoo-bwoo-bwoo, bwoo-bwoo-bwoo,' Stepan was perorating nearby at his sock, having pulled it over his palm; the sock quacked back at him like a duck.

'Half and half,' mutter in reply, taking a swig from the bottle and bringing the skoto cable against a tooth. The jaw went stiff.

Sasha blinked, blinded by unlicht.

'After the mammoths, after the mammoths you want to –'

'Bwhere does he eat? Bwhere? The mwaps!'

'Fffreeze!' Pavlitch bit in earnest into the mouse's tail. 'I shan't allow it! I ffforbid it!'

'So many years. Eats it straight from the sssoil? Bwhere does it unfleeze?'

'No-no-no!'

'Bwoo-bwoo-bwoo!'

But why do they all splutter like this? Take a deeper gulp so as to purge the vocal chords.

'Abassylar,' articulate the words very distinctly, 'how do they live or not live or do whatever they do there – they have to guzzle tungetitum – no?' Embrace Sasha around the neck. 'You will shit it out, piss it out, sweat it out, breathe it out. The bababalloonist unfroze. No?'

Without understanding anyhing, Sasha nodded solemnly; the mouse swung like a pendulum under his chin.

'Therefore – therefore – therefore,' scratch the crown of the head with the cable. 'What was trying to be said... Sasha, Sasha!'

He spat out the corpse.

'To guzzle tungetitum! To freeze.' He hauled himself up on his legs, grabbed hold of the stick murchometer, and pulled. The round frosto-glaze flask fell off the head and shattered in a geometrical pattern of stained glass. 'Stand up! Stand up, I say!'

Stand up. Sasha fell down. Drag Sasha to his feet. Keel over again after a single step. Then Sasha helped with the standing up, after which he himself toppled onto all fours. Wind a cable around his neck and pull him to the vertical. He grabbed hold of the cable half an arshin above his blond crop of hair and in this fashion remained upright on his legs. Return to the floor meanwhile in order to retrieve the bottle. But Director Khavroff had already snatched it up; now he was pouring vodka into the muzzle of a rodent squeezed in his fist, drowning it clumsily. Shafts of electricity shot below his knees. A suffocating clasp suddenly put square black stars before the eyes – it was Sasha Pavlitch pulling on the stick. Maintaining his vertical position with his right hand on the cable looped under his chin, he tugged with his left at the murchometer. March in this way out into the corridor. WoobooMMM!

Blunder about in the Observatory's dark crannies, deserted at night, bumping into walls and crashing into furniture. Sasha led the way, pulling on the gallow-wire now this way, now that. Trip over the legs of the Cossack sleeping on a stool outside a doorway. Sasha retraced his steps. He began to count the doors out loud, whereupon he had to be quickly corrected, since he lost track of his numbers between three and four, between seven and six. Suddenly he stopped, having suspended himself by an iron door with grated window.

'All yours!' he croaked hoarsely and throttled with the murchmeter-stick against the door until rivets and rust scrubbled through the skin.

Peer into the shadowy interior, feebly lit by the glow from the corridor. It was a confined chamber with bare walls, evidently converted into a cell; aroused by the commotion, ragged figures rose from straw mattresses rubbing their eyes, unshaven mugs agape.

'All yours! Take your pick and freeze!'

'Who –'

'The emperor ordered! Katorzhniks, volunteers! Hah!' He hiccupped and hanged himself higher, standing on tiptoes. 'All yours!' he squealed.

Gaze at them with the eye of darkness, gaze at them with the eye of light. Emaciated, crushed, ground into the earth, even now they instinctively bend their spines and gaze from under brows, from below; and upon whomsoever the black-or-white stare rests, they lower their eyes and bare their gums ingratiatingly, doglike, toothless.

'Scum, not abassylar,' snort in indignation.

'Huh?'

'All would die.'

'So, whom –'

WoobooMMM!

'Ishmael!' Roar and break free from the stick, in order to drop to the knees and vomit over the trouser legs of Sasha Pavlitch dangling half an arshin above the floor. Carbonaceous murch flowed out along with the stomach juices.

'Ishmael!' wail, wiping the mouth.

Fall asleep there in Tesla's laboratory at the Observatory beside the torso of a small flow-generator, wrapped in someone else's fur coat, clutching the stick murchometer neath the armpit (the bruises remain). The Unlicht Hammer, the Murch Hammer, was thrashed right through the dreams, shattering them one after another. What was unusual, however, was that anything at all was remembered of those dreams, that they forced their way through to the waking side – which happened rarely even here in the Land of the Gleissen. But the Hammer had thrashed them deep into the soul. WoobooMMM! The katorzhniks locked in that storeroom, hastily turned into a prison, began to bite and consume one another – the monstrous bestial echoes of which penetrated to the outside. I moved aside Sasha Pavlitch hanging before the door, but lifting the iron bar was not enough; a key to the lock was also needed. I ran to the Cossack guard. The Cossack couldn't understand what I said to him: instead of words, a stream of cryocarbon flew out of my mouth. The soldier loaded his weapon and fired once and twice: head, chest. A fiery glare burst from the orifices. Plugging them with my hands, I returned to the cell. Sasha was already hanging three arshins above the floor, still dragging himself upwards. I peered through the grate. Only one katorzhnik remained inside, having bitten and torn to pieces his fellow prisoners. At first, I didn't recognise the spidery froglike silhouette crouched over the heap of severed limbs, skulls and trunks. I withdrew my hand from my forehead. A cyclopean beam of light illuminated the cell. The katorzhnik started, began to exert his seven limbs and, still splayed flat on the stones, turned to face the door. On this Piegnaresque patchwork of body-parts originating from at least a dozen persons, on the neck still not solidly frozen to it, swayed the head of Sergey Andreyevitch Atchukhoff. 'There is no man!' he rasped, as a corona of teslectrical lightning bolts reeled around him. 'There is no History, there is no man! Despair, despair, despair! Even the suicide! Go and get drunk! There is no man!' Another part of the goylem rebelled, however, reached for the back of its neck with a paw frozen to its left shoulder blade and tore off Atchukhoff's head; it unearthed a new noggin from the heap and set it in its place. This one was thoroughly soaked in blood and battered above the temple; I nevertheless recognised at once the rotund visage of Herr Blutfeld. '... evil, Winter is evil, Winter is evil, Winter is evil, evil, evil!' he droned grumpily. 'History is evil, History is evil, History is evil...' Affixed askew, however, Blutfeld's nut quickly slid off, slid off and rolled away into the gloom. The covenant of forelimbs re-seated Atchukhoff's skull on its neck-throne. 'There is no History, there is no man!' he howled afresh, glowering furiously. 'The mammoths, the mammoths! I am sink-sink-sinking.' Then he really did sink as the corpses and stones and soil parted beneath all his many legs and arms increasing and increasing in number (coalitions of body parts were arming themselves with ever-new limbs dug up from the battleground). I pressed against the door, striving to see into the Ways of the Mammoths as they opened in the prison. The permafrost was splitting to the accompaniment of roars and peals worthy of cannon fire. I covered my ears; then the Hammer struck. WoobooMMM! The Hammer, the Hammer, it has to be stopped before it's too late! Prototype or not, it can't be allowed to stir up such waves on the Dorogi! I ran out into the courtyard of the Observatory. The coldiron machine, similar to a well crane, was beating into the earth with a tungetitum rammer forged in the shape of a bust of Nikolay the Second Aleksandrovitch. Gleissen were kneeling before it all around. Nikola Tesla sat astride the spine of the largest glacius, raining down black lightning bolts with strokes of his long arms – raining them into the crater that the Tsar-Hammer had smashed out of the Ways of the Mammoths. Unlicht flared from the crater, in which a distorted glintz flashed only intermittently to reveal the outline of a human silhouette, its arm raised beseechingly, the profile of a suffering man. I threw myself into that darkness, guided by the light emanating from my heart and head, but already after a few paces I could feel the frost hardening around me in gelatinous waves, gnawing into my flesh, binding my body to the time of the gleissen. The next step, the next – whole hours went by. The gleissen turned around on their spidery stalagspikes, tilting towards me dark glistening medusas of ice. They extended after me icy tentacles swollen with murch. The emperor grinned from the Hammer like a lunatic, blazing like a comet on its downward arc and fading on the upward bound for the stars. Something flew from on high into the unlichted welter, not stars – but grey particles frozen in flight by Doctor Tesla's thunderbolts. Slowly, slowly, slowly, I lifted my eyes and with them the lance of light beaming from between them. It was Sasha Pavlitch – Sasha had pulled himself up on his noose above the height of the corpse masts; he loomed now against a black sky, swaying gently under a Moon in its first quarter, whilst rats and mice spilled off his left sleeve. Rats and mice, I thought, let father feed at least on these: warm blood, warm meat, living flesh. WoobooMMM! O Christ! WoobooMMM! The mammoths, the mammoths are coming for me, wooCooMMM; the earth quakes as they roam through it.

But before I managed to descend to the Kingdom of Darkness, Shtchekelnikoff appeared, smashed the Hammer, pissed into the crater of unlicht, spat on the gleissen and drove me home to Tsvetistaya. Sleep there now without dreams, in order to wake instead on the following day with a mammoth hangover.

On the delight of temptations repulsed

The Irkutsk News reports that a new aberration has afflicted the dreamslaves; the editors advise families to keep the unfortunates locked indoors and also to bind their hands and feet at night – for they are lured into the city, even in the hardest frost, whilst they pay no attention whatever to their own well-being. When questioned, they speak of a friend in need or similar nonsense. The newspaper no longer writes about it, but it's plain enough where they are lured in their waking, which is their dreaming, which is their waking. Visible from afar by their huge glintzen, they make their way namely to Tesla's Observatory; politely ask the Cossacks to admit them; and resist not when the Cossacks bind their limbs and hand them over to the gendarmes. Stepan would tell how since the time Nikola set the Hammer prototype in motion, close to two hundred had invaded the Observatory. Beggars and bankers, barbers and izvoztchiks, gentleman officers and paupers, teenage devotchkas and silver-haired matrons, Russians and Germans and Poles and Chinamen, even an Orthodox parish priest and his wife. All of them – slaves to necessity, serfs of soletruth. The thought occurred that lengthy demurchment has this distinct advantage at least: no dreaming. That is, until now.

Yesterday evening in a boarding house on Petropavlovskaya Street, a forty-year-old machine operator by name of Apollonius Ćwibut slit his throat. Mr Ćwibut had recently arrived in our city from Lvoff and complained horribly of dreams during the Black Auroras. The police are seeking the opinions of metropolitan Buryat sorcerers.

In *Russian News*, the paper of Moscow liberals, they write more about the politics of European Russia. The Hong Kong peace treaty had clearly been received in Russia as no mean triumph for the tsar. Octobrist Lyednyaks, of Yarkoff, Myerzhinsky and even old Gutchkoff, but also Milyukoff's Kadets, not to mention right-wing loyalists and Trudovik converts, all in the Duma passed unanimously a servile resolution of congratulations. The question of zemstvos in the western guberniyas, as Mitschka Fidelberg had rightly predicted, returned at once to the State Council, as did the long-postponed second tax reform from the Stolypin plan. Was the Ice letting go? Japan as well as British Hong Kong still belong, after all, to the dominion of Summer. And if the impulse is coming from there... Wipe the temples; the Murch Hammer was still pounding in them. Can History be carved up, so that half the world stands still, whilst the other half – despite this, advances freely? Freeze part of a man – and the whole man will die. However, principles of cause and effect do not suddenly cease to apply. Logic breaks down at the border between Summer and Winter, just as light breaks down at the border between different mediums; and yet the rays somehow cross the border. Bah, *Russian News*, in its editorial, also strikes an optimistic tone. Peace at last! Year in, year out, war devoured so much money that we've never yet felt the prosperity brought by the coldiron boom; now, and surely after the launch of the Alaska Line, the Russian Empire will enter a Golden Era (provided it be wisely governed).

Reach from the bed for *The Illustrated Weekly* folded on the bedside table amongst a pile of other recent magazines delivered from the Kingdom by the last Trans-Siberian Express, yesterday or ereyesterday. Two columns in the *Weekly* were devoted to an appeal from the Warsaw Society of Animal Lovers. Winter lasting many years had not only caused the extinction of rodents and driven all birdlife from Warsaw, but had also deprived the city and its inhabitants of any contact with animals, discounting utility horses which were treated nowadays more as biological engines. As if it weren't enough that street mongrels and cellar cats had died out – people, egoists overly fond of their comforts, had largely ceased to keep animals in their homes; rearing dogs had become especially burdensome. The Society is appealing for social efforts to be made to gather 'our little friends' afresh to the domestic hearth. To this end, the Society will import hundreds of kittens and puppies from the countryside in excellent physical condition – to be collected from the Society's headquarters in exchange for a symbolic sum and nominal pledge. In particular, families blessed with children ought to guarantee them the opportunity to have daily contact with living dogs and cats. As the twentieth century is to be the century of machines and impersonal pragmatism of money and technology, and as we live additionally in a metropolis covered in ice, cut off from nature – let us at least take care not to stifle within us those feelings inborn in man as a result of his dwelling alongside small defenceless life. Human nature does not change as quickly as civilisation (if it changes at all). Our fathers, grand-fathers and great-grandfathers – practised in this way tenderness and love, were raised in this way to adult affections and mature sensitivity, learned in this way to value every little drop of Life: from the touch of a trusty pointer's warm coat, from the joy of wonderfully awkward frisky kittens, from the trembling of a foal's nostrils caressed by a palm, from the quivering heart of a bird enclosed in the hollow of the hand. A person raised on ice, bricks and coldiron will never fully open his soul. Between this and the next generation, the ability to feel certain emo-tions will be lost; our sense of empathy will be blunted. Other people – people of ice – will lay us in our graves. They will have their romances, passions and sentimental attachments – yet already shrivelled, leaden, pallid. Our poetry, our dramas, our lives – these they won't fully un-derstand; to them we shall seem like overexcitable hysterics, irrational triflers. Humanity will be overwhelmed by spiritual blindness and deaf-ness. Varsovians, preserve dogs and cats!

Old Grzegorz brought a mug of pickled-cucumber water for the kat-zenjammer but failed on his way out to close the door behind him; the Wielickis' tomcat squeezed through the crack. Now it lay at the foot of the bed, stretched its limbs, yawned and blinked, slightly amazed. A cat may draw gout out of a man, but a hangover? The clock in the drawing room chimed half-past nine; the Hammer rumbled in the head. Swallow more sour water, abschmack replaced abschmack. A good move to have taken the morning off work for the meeting with Prince Blutsky and his man; at least at Krupp's, no laughing stock will be made of ap-pearing in such a state. Gather up the newspapers, stretch out on the pillows. The cat marched over the quilt in dignified strides, after which it tried to climb first onto the head (push it off) and then shoved its own head neath the chin and wrapped itself around the neck like a living fur collar. Detached by force, the cat scratched the cheek with its claw, incensed. To hell with all Societies of Animal Lovers! 'Open the soul', not likely! Hissing and baring its fangs, the brute prowled around the bed. Spring to the feet and chase it from the room, shutting the door.

Shuffle over to open the curtains. Whiteness gushed over the pupils. Rainbow fogs swirled outside the windows – a cruel snowstorm had been tormenting the city since dawn. Having hacked into the spittoon, press the forehead for a moment against the cold frostoglaze. Somehow, there has to be an awakening from this rumbling in the head, an arousing from stupor, spitting out of bitter tastes. Today so much may be decided… And there is no certainty at all as to whether the Ice is now needed. How great the longing for that feeling of lightness, strung out in thousands of possibilities, for that whirlwind in the brain: this thought, that thought, effortlessly outstripping one another, forging ahead in their dozens, they kidnap into a wild chase over the fields of the imagination… And for that exciting conviction constantly accompanying them: that so much is still possible, that almost any future is open; nothing is a-hundred-per-cent certain, yet everything somehow probable. Therefore – to demurch! To pump off the Frost! Roll the skull over the cold compress of frostoglaze. For why not? What forbids it? (Apart from conscious will.) And soon, the pump for unfreezing father will have to be fetched from Nikola anyway; then it will be possible to demurch at any time. Meanwhile, freeze all the more. After all, the sickness on arrival in Irkutsk had run a not dissimilar course. And how had things ended? By laying the hands on the Kotarbiński pump at the earliest opportunity. Except for this difference that then, freezing had been out of necessity, but now – now it's out of choice. Except for this difference – but what a difference! Move the head away from the window; from between the blizzards and streams of snow Konny Island emerged, the dark smooth surfaces of glaciuses, pale lights of sleighs on the Angara. Around the corpse masts a dense storm-cloud was spiralling. Try at once to catch the face's reflection in the glass, but quickly withdraw the gaze; this too was a curse of Summer: the power of mirrors. Instead, a red blotch remained on the windowpane: imprint of the sore neath the eye, of scratched-open old wounds. Rub it into a slanting streak. The blizzard turned pink. Blood flooded the City of Ice.

Sit down in the dining room to a late breakfast, having dressed slowly and tottered to the bathroom and back. Anything so long as it was warm… But: the porridge – was sour; coffee – sour; scrambled eggs – sour, sour.

Bewailing thus over a cottage-cheese butterschnitte, when Marta Wielicki entered the room.

'You don't like it?'

The sour expression grew fiercer still.

'My dear Marta,' reply in a hoarse voice, 'at this moment I couldn't swallow even ambrosia.'

'Well, there you have it!' She folded her arms across her bosom.

'He who spends the night wandering around filthy drinking dens and returns at some unearthly hour dead drunk, when the working day has already begun, to boot, gets what he deserves!'

'Drinking dens…!' Heave a sigh, but without the slightest wish for a quarrel. The tomcat appeared in the doorway; follow it with a gloomy stare. Sighing for a second time, pour herbal honey onto the cheese. 'At least the kids aren't galloping over my upper storey, thank God.'

'They're doing parish tasks with Masha and their mother. Aha, Benedykt, sir, you left orders not to be woken on pain of execution –'

'Did I?'

'Yes, yes. So, we did not wake you. A woman was here at the crack of dawn, Polish, wanting to see you. She said she was hurrying to work, so –'

'You spoke to her, Marta? She introduced herself?'

'Gwóźdź.'

'Gwóźdź?'

'Gwóźdź.'

Lick the sticky sweetness off the fingers; taste was being restored to the palate. Sit up straight at the table.

'What did she want?'

'I don't know, she didn't say.' Marta Wielicki sat down opposite, peering into the eyes. 'Oy, truly, you do look wretched. And you injured yourself somewhere as well?'

'No, it's only –'

'But we need some raw spirit. Wait a moment, wait.'

'What does this infernal cat want from me!' growl, thrusting it aside with the foot under the table.

'Bags beneath the eyes, oily vision, and these shadows like under the Black Auroras,' Marta continued, not without satisfaction, as she went to fetch the medicaments.

'Optical illusions, all illusions.'

But exactly what sort of cables had been bitten into when drinking the vodka? How much heavy teslectricity had entered the body? And what else had been done in the night in Tesla's Observatory when the vodka demons were already cavorting in the mind, so that all that remained in the memory were nonsensical dreams? Touch involuntarily the middle of the forehead with a honeyed finger.

Then the cat licked the finger.

In the Citadel – known as the Box on account of its clumsy architecture modelled on the shape of a chest – an alarm must have sounded; in any case, judging by the activity, overall excitement and number of soldiers in arms, a powerful order must have come not long before from the governor general's rooms. The good Shtchekelnikoff asserted, naturally, that he didn't like the look of it, after which he said no more, since the soldier stationed in the inner guardhouse had overheard his swearing and not let him out of his sight; besides, Tchingis was immediately detained on the first floor. The thought occurred that were they to relieve him of the quarter-arshin blade and his temper get the better of him, then maybe the rectangular ruffian might not step out of the gubernatorial fortress into the light of day for a long while to come. This time, out of caution, the Grossmeister had not been brought – such caution was to prove unnecessary.

Escorted to the Box's north-west tower and ordered to wait in the atrium. Every moment a flustered official or minion came running hither or thither; turn the back on them. From the narrow window, a vista opened onto Shelekhoff Bridge and Glazkovo, stretching as far as the outlet of Troitskaya Street onto the Angara, where during the Winter of the Gleissen the Tsarevitch Nikolay Aleksandrovitch pontoon bridge had frozen solid forever. The blizzard was blowing straight off Baikal, not directly therefore at the windowpanes, but its howl was audible even so; whilst placing a hand on the frame was enough to feel the sting of rabid frost on the skin. It must have been nearly fifty degrees below Celsius, and in the wind – colder still. A column of infantry hurrying towards the Citadel was already running up the foot of the hill so as to get inside as swiftly as possible: hunched white wraiths, not men. The Irkutsk barracks were located outside the city, far removed from the Ways of the Mammoths; the quarters in the Citadel permanently housed at most half a regiment. Meanwhile, so many troops had gathered that it looked as if the governor general were preparing to repel an assault. Units of various military formations sprang to mind, seen marching through Irkutsk for weeks, months, or soldiers in the city on days off; also, Wojsław Wielicki had often remarked on delays to the Transsib caused by Ministry of War transports – men were being withdrawn from the dissolved Japanese front and transferred to the Great Russian Heartland, but clearly, forces within the City of Ice were also being strengthened. Józef Piłsudski's Japanese Legion had got under their skin. Grin involuntarily under the moustache, smooth down the frock coat. The infantry detachment rushed inside; the gate was slammed shut. Borne on the mournful note of the gale, the slow pulse of the blizzard struck also through the windowpanes – the echo of the glashatays' drums? – the Murch Hammer? –

'Your Esteemed Nobleness.'

Escorted by a young non-commissioned officer to a room where beside a large fireplace, in which a huge blaze was crackling away, the governor general was conferring with his staff officers and tchinovniks: almost all wore uniform, several were armed. On a table beyond the fireplace, amidst maps and documents, dishes of cold food and empty glasses lay strewn. In a longer wall to the right, half a dozen doors kept opening and shutting – every moment someone fell in or fell out of them, errand-boys and orderlies with messages and commands. High on the wall below the ceiling hung a large portrait in tungetitum frame of Nikolay the Second Aleksandrovitch, shimmering gently under a black double-headed eagle.

Behind the fireplace screen, Prince Blutsky-Osey sat in a leather armchair. He was reading a newspaper, squinting birdlike behind oval eyeglasses.

The floor tiles, polished to look like porcelain, sharply reflected the sound of every step. Quicken the pace involuntarily, setting the feet down more firmly, to an even rhythm. The non-commissioned officer went ahead. Several uniformed men glanced around without interrupting their discussions. Flushed sweaty countenances, swirling moustaches and sideburns, decorations, frogging, shoulder straps, large paunches.

Never before had the feeling of being Polish been so strong.

'Aah, our Venyedikt Filipovitch, molodyets!'

The captain of hussars approached from the table, spreading wide his arms and flourishing his pelisse. Bow to him politely, but this failed to stop him: he grabbed hold of the body, clasped it in his embrace, breathing lewd ribaldries into the ear. 'Well, plainly, you've not recovered yet from our night out! not everyone's a born shagger! But Lidia's a marvel of a devotchka, eh? you sent her a pressie afterwards? Tut tut, but you must! It's only proper! You should!'

'So, you're acquainted too with Captain Frett,' the prince remarked sourly from his chair, folding the newspaper with an angry rustle.

'Your Highness.'

'Hee, hee, acquainted, acquainted!' The hussar, of all persons gathered there, appeared in the best mood; his ruddy cheeks and pink nose suggested he had either just returned from the frost or, despite the pre-noon hour, had already succeeded in knocking back more than one glassful.

'The captain,' continued the prince without raising his voice in the slightest so that it was necessary to walk over to him and the fireplace; a wave of heat struck the right ear, feeling like a dousing with boiling water. 'The captain, though I agree it doesn't look like it –'

'Your Highness is too kind!' laughed the moustachioed warrior.

'The captain enjoys my infinite trust. The captain...' Here Prince Blutsky half-closed his eyes, held his breath, shifted his jaw back and forth, and only then continued: '... is a man of honour and a man of duty. Understand?'

'Yes.'

He beckoned with an arthritic finger. Upon what depends this amazing power of theirs, whereby they magnify a thousandfold the implications of the slightest gesture until they're interpreted as living glintzen – the trembling of lips, a half-wink, a breath, a finger? It had seemed that he wanted to say something in private, in whispers, as his spouse was wont to do; but he merely narrowed his eyes, staring out from behind the lenticular lenses, in which reflections of tall flames flickered.

Having stared his fill, he waved his hand impatiently.

'A Pole, not a Pole – it has frozen.'

Withdraw.

An altercation had erupted in the meantime amongst the tchinovniks. The officials began to shout across the table, to hurl papers at one another; a silver-haired colonel joined in, someone knocked a tray, a vodka carafe, which then shattered on the floor tiles with a loud crash. 'Treason!' croaked a portly tchinovnik in the uniform of the Ministry of Winter. 'Treason! Treachery!' He was led from the room.

The prince rose from his chair and approached Count Schultz. He began to lecture him, wagging that crooked finger of his under the governor general's nose. Prick up the ears.

'... at the emperor's mercy. You have to learn diplomacy, my dear Count, the art of conversation and negotiation. Nothing in this world has yet been solved by violence.'

The governor general stared as if at a madman, but soon hid the unflattering thought reflected on his face beneath a neutral expression of courtesy; his umbriance altered not an iota.

'Your Highness deigns to be in error. Anything at all that has been resolved in world history has been resolved with the aid of fire, sword and gunpowder. Diplomacy comes to the rescue when power is lacking; it buys time, but solves not problems. Had we been able to drive the Japs into the ocean, Your Highness would not have had to go and treat with them.

'But enough of this. You know very well, Prince, I do not tolerate such thoughts in anyone.' He averted his eyes, applied his handkerchief for a moment to his mouth and caught sight of the colonel. 'I shall conduct a trial tomorrow morning, away with him to prison.'

Blood drained from the colonel's pasty face; he reeled, reached out to support himself on the table as if groping in the dark; to no purpose, since other hands were already propping him up, other hands unbuckling his sabre, other hands forcibly removing him from the room.

'But! Your Illustriousness!' he moaned. 'I only! Only to Your Illustriousness!'

'Away with him!'

Rebounding from his heart, the blood returned to his head. Burning-hot, his cherry-plum phizog shining with sweat, the colonel braced himself, broke free of the dozen arms holding him, rushed around the table – someone stuck a foot in his path, whereupon he tripped and crashed onto the tiles, leaving traces of saliva on the mirrorlike surface, his decorations jangling and grinding against it – even then, however, he did not stop: he trotted towards the governor general on all fours.

Grabbing him below the knees, he pressed his silver pate into them.

'I am a faithful dog! Whatever Your Illustriousness says! I implore you!'

Count Schultz-Zimovy kicked him in disgust.

'This minute dammit!'

He was dragged out like a dog.

Prince Blutsky-Osey watched through small pince-nez with cold attention, as if this were a demonstration of some new method for polishing floors.

'What's going on?' inquire under the breath of Captain Frett.

'So, what do you think, why does His Princely Highness keep me by his side?'

No glances were even exchanged; the tone of voice was enough, murch mingled with murch.

'Because you are a man of honour and a man of duty.' Mutter the words without irony.

The captain turned down the collar of his uniform.

'Did you hear about our adventures in Hong Kong? I was plucked from the regiment for the diplomatic mission and assigned to the prince. Here's where the samurai sword stopped.'

Out of one of the side-doors on the right barged Mr Uriah; there was no time to question the captain. Frantishek Markovitch, without so much as a greeting, gasping for breath, his flaxen hair uncombed, flung down a folder on top of the maps, after which he began to lay out documents from it on the table like cards for a game of patience.

'Here you have your certificate of trustworthiness, here your passport valid for three months, these are the papers for your father, here – his parole from the arrest warrants and criminal cases, here your permits for the military authorities in the Irkutsk Governorate, and here a credit note for the First Baikal Bank. Keep a record of everything on which you spend official cash.'

'I will.'

'Good. Sign here. And here. Good. Have you spoken to the count?'

'No.'

'Come.'

Count Schultz was standing by a window, reading a letter that had just been handed to him and inhaling smoke from the incense burners. Mr Uriah whispered something in his ear; the count lent forward as rainbow light from the snowstorm flitted over his bald patch; thus they whispered for some while until Schultz-Zimovy glanced at last over the shoulder of Frantishek Markovitch. Bow to him.

'It can easily be this way too,' grunted the governor general, 'this way too. What do you say?'

'But what's Your Illustriousness asking?' Fire the question without averting the gaze.

'Harken to him, the shameless Polack,' the count smiled.

'His Illustriousness would like to know how soon you can fulfil your task,' said Uriah.

'The contract was to the end of January and –'

'I know,' the count snapped. 'I am asking now for your frank opinion. How soon. Can you afford such audacity? Well!'

Framed by the snowstorm, his motionless umbriance as well as the murch in the wrinkles of his skin were all the more visible. The thought occurred that were his photograph to be taken now, no shades of grey or internal forms would survive on it, only an inky hole in the window of whiteout. What is the truth about Count Schultz-Zimovy? Well, this is it.

'I am unable to say. No sooner than three weeks. I told you, Excellency, a tracker has yet to be found for me who would safely descend to the Ways of the Mammoths and –'

'Three weeks,' sighed the governor; a moment longer, and he'd have lost interest. 'And you would still have to return... *Mais bon*.' He went back to reading the letter.

Frantishek Markovitch was dissatisfied with the course of the conversation. Pursing his lips, he packed his papers into the folder, tugging at its straps in irritation.

Seize him by the arm.

'The contract was to the end of January!'

'Never fear, sir, His Illustriousness will keep his word. Only it's a shame... Egh. You need a tracker, yes? Well then, come with me.' Without glancing around, he marched towards the door, almost colliding on the threshold with two officers still with snow on their brows and moustaches.

Hurriedly gather up the documents, thrust them under the frock coat. Captain Frett raised his glass across the table in a toast. 'Next time we'll be drinking with your father!' Nod to him courteously.

Mr Uriah ran down four flights of stairs and then turned off to the side of the entrance hall before an outside courtyard. Many wide doors and gates opened and closed here, if not onto the courtyard itself, then onto corridors and passages leading into it. The temperature had dropped to well below zero – breathe out cloudlets of unlicht and swallow icy saliva; walls of frozen-through granite gave off oily steam. It made sense to go back for the outer garments of fur left somewhere on the first floor along with Shtchekelnikoff. But the flaxen-haired black-a-tooth in only his uniform, once propelled into motion, made off on his long legs as if chased by a knout; the sentries opened doors without a word. In one case only was it necessary to retreat against a wall as a line of riflemen – wrapped in their regimental shubas, heads tightly bound like a pilgrimage of lepers, with knapsacks on their backs – trudged past in the middle of the walkway leading to the Citadel's coach-house and stables. Again, the instincts of a son of a subjugated people made themselves felt: stay glued to the stones, avert the gaze, melt with indifferent expression into the *nature morte*; maybe they won't notice, won't seize, won't throw into a dungeon, a lone Pole in the heart of a tsarist fortress – irrational instincts, but all the closer to the heart's truth.

Beyond the coach-house were quarters also for izvoztchiks, seemingly unused for a long time; now, around coal stoves, were encamped indigenous hunters and shamans. Moreover, they were not one single group, but two groups, a smaller and a larger, and it was obvious at once that they were divided, that is, united, by strong enmity. Stand by the first stove warming the hands. Frantishek Markovitch was talking to three figures clothed in thick sheepskins as they chewed smoked fat or some other filthy grease; whilst the rest, gathered by the opposite wall, bristled and turned away ostentatiously, pulling their hoods deeper over their heads and hiding under their pelts.

Uriah quickly rallied one of the troika and brought him to the stove. The indigene had a distinct limp. Between his sheepskins and turbans, all that could be seen were the small dark eyes in unlichted folds of skin, and a few tufts of black hair tied with faded ribbons.

He bowed, without however uncovering his head.

'*Garbus ni*?' he croaked (or something similar).

Uriah began to explain to him in broken Tungus.

'*Sami, Huta Ü-Nin*,' muttered the savage through his rags; glimmers of irony shone in his coal-black pupils, or perhaps it only seemed so – account in this way for the unaccountable sign from the algorithmics of another race.

'This is Tigry Etmatoff from the Second Tcharabus Tribe of the Nertchinsk ulus,' Frantishek Markovitch introduced him. 'The Upper Amur Goldmining Company used to hire hunters from his ulus when it finally succumbed to its greed for coldiron and tungetitum and sent its geologists west. Now we also make use of Tcharabus guides.'

'A shaman.'

'Your tracker along the Ways of the Mammoths.'

Shudder from cold.

Tigry conjured a small goatskin from under his coat and plopped a drop to each of the four winds for the local spirits.

'*Araky umynann⬚?*'

'Venyedikt Filipovitch will have a drink,' advised Frantishek Markovitch. 'They're terrible drunks, these indigenes of Winter, drink themselves to death, I tell you, the whole family gets so inebriated they turn to stone, fall asleep, the fire in the yurt goes out, and they freeze; well, if you don't drink to their health, they'll not believe you.'

Lift the goatskin to the lips. It was some kind of heavy moonshine with a sharp herbal tang. Twist the mouth as a man ought. Tigry chortled.

Hand back the skin and lean towards the shaman.

'You speak Russian? Ru-shun – understand?'

'*Ah⬚m sara lucza turannan öczem sara.*'

'His brothers speak a little. Anyway, out there under the Ice, you'll make yourselves understood somehow.' Frantishek Markovitch rubbed his hands. 'Well, he will guide you. You can inquire of our geologists, our Tigry has a good nose.'

'This wasn't exactly what I had in mind when I spoke of sending a tracker onto the Ways of the Mammoths... And why a Tungus?'

'You're going north, towards the Tunguska river, are you not? These are not lands of our Buryats. Do you want to get shot on your first encounter on the trail? But for you, this is doubly good, Tungus hearts have warmed towards Poles; Polish engineers building the Transsib have married Tungus women, there are these hunting partnerships –'

'But you yourself said that these religions of theirs... That to Buryats, gleissen have fallen from the Upper World, but Tunguses, Tunguses see in them abassylar, nightmarish spirits of the Underworld – not so?'

'That's exactly it,' Mr Uriah drew near confidentially and lowered his voice, but so that Tigry Etmatoff could nevertheless hear, 'I had to find Tunguses convinced, how to put it, of the opposite pole of their belief.'

'You mean some kind of Tungus Satanists...?'

Frantishek Markovitch shifted his weight from one leg to the other beside the stove, watching with concern.

'But you look as if you'd seen a ghost.' He glanced at the shaman and back again. 'Perhaps you've already met Tigry?'

'No, no.' Clear the throat; the taste of the herbal hooch had frozen to the tongue. 'An old dream, an illusion...' Laugh hesitantly. With warmed-up hand, wipe the blood from former wounds reopened by the cat, etched on the cheeks by the leaves of iron trees. 'It's only my past aligning with the present moment: one more prophecy for simple minds fulfilled. Dreams are but shadows, have faith in dreams.'

The dream, the past, white non-being. Snow was sticking to the spectacles, flying into the eyes – the city, the sky, the sleigh, Shtchekelnikoff and the driver, everything was being erased from existence. A real purga was raging over Irkutsk, no surprise then that even the locals took shelter in the Box. The howl of the wind stifled all other sounds – no other sounds existed. And as to colours – none existed save white. Even streetlamps and carriage lanterns penetrated with difficulty – not due to their colour, but to their whiteness, still more intensely white. God was leafing back through the book of the world to the very beginning, to before the time of creation, to the first, clean pages. Wrapped tightly in thick furs, the thought occurs: but what if this doesn't succeed? if he's never found? For it won't succeed. Won't succeed.

Alighting from the Marmeladobahn in Zimny Nikolayevsk, fastening again the shuba under the low platform roof, feel instinctively for the weight of the Grossmeister tucked in the belt. Yet the revolver had been left behind at Tsvetistaya Street. This brought to mind, however, the metal samples blitzed by the Unlicht Bomb – lying there with yesterday's clothes, most likely taken by the servants to be laundered. Return to Irkutsk? Any changes to the rota have to be checked; if Engineer Iertheim is on night shift tonight, it may be possible to swap with him. Mm-hmm.

Yesterday's path from the station to the Five O'Clock Tower had been blocked overnight by a gleiss, a roundabout route had to be taken; Shtchekelnikoff strode with upturned head, scanning the overhead goods tracks from the depths of his tightly laced hood. So he failed to notice the gendarmes stomping into the wind in single file from the Holey Palace. Only when he collided with the first did he step aside. They were dragging between them some unfortunate with tethered hands. And there were eight of them, a whole detachment.

In the laboratory, despite the early hour, all lights were burning. Snow had stuck to the frostglaze panels; Doctor Wolfke and his team were working as though in a bathysphere submerged in an ocean of milk. The stoves were roaring loudly, the samovar was puffing away and the tchay-wallah distributing aromatic boiling water; barely had the threshold been crossed, icy powder still being shaken off, when she came hurrying with a cup of tea.

'Spasibo. Tell me, where is Engineer Iertheim today –'

'Benedykt, sir!' Doctor Wolfke's voice rang out from behind the metal cupboards. 'We have to see each other, but now, at once!'

Remove only the shapka.

'Very sorry, Doctor, but, khhrrr, I did warn you yesterday that, due to official business, I had to –'

'You have official business!' Wolfke snorted, softening his consonants in the manner specific to him, and slammed a sealed bumaga on the desk.

Put aside the teacup, raise the letter to the eyes. It was a summons from the Irkutsk delegation of the Ministry of Winter issued to Benedykt Filipovitch Gierosławski, for today, supplied with all the legal niceties including the threat of a fine and arrest, undersigned by Commissioner Plenipotentiary Ivan Dragutinovitch Schembuch.

'They came here,' Doctor Wolfke said, wiping his bloated face with a handkerchief, 'they were looking for you, well nigh carried out a search, can you imagine?'

'Gendarmes? Did they take anyone with them?'

'This is all we need!' Wolfke folded the handkerchief and tugged at his moustache. 'And so, do you think they're after anyone else?'

'No, I don't know, no.'

'Is it a criminal case?'

'Politics unfortunately, Mieczysław, sir.' Stow away the summons along with Uriah's documents. 'I thought, khhrrr, I'd settled everything, and now something like this…' Slap the desktop with the shapka.

Doctor Wolfke leaned over the desk cluttered with books, notes and sheets of figures.

'If Krupp can assist in any way,' he said with concern, 'please don't hesitate, Director Grzywaczewski and I…'

'Thank you, thank you very much. But I fear it's not that kind of trouble. It will be resolved above even Krupp's head.'

'It starts with articles in the underground press and ends in a cold dungeon,' Wolfke sighed woefully. 'In the beginning, I held out no hope that you'd be of much use to us, but now I'm afraid that without you, we shall drown afresh in all this German bureaucracy. It's no easy task to find a man who both understands the nature of scientific work and is himself proficient in numbers, and also able at the same time to express himself in writing in the languages of the firm and the state, in addition to being a countryman who comes with the recommendation of brothers whom we trust absolutely.'

'But I did forewarn you it would only be for a time. One way or another, in a few weeks, I shall have to say goodbye.'

'You intend, in the middle of winter, to go in search your father as far as the Last Isotherm?'

'You know…?'

He blinked, trying to conceal his sympathy and, yes, his not-very-noble pity.

'Everyone knows.'

Murch, murch and more murch, it's harder and harder to mask what is obvious here between truth and falsehood what is obvious. Everyone knows. Nod the head.

'Please reconsider,' said Doctor Wolfke, slumping back in his chair. 'Nothing is a foregone conclusion. What other future do you have ahead of you? Do you remember, sir, what we spoke of on your first day?' He glanced out of the window and turned away at once from the total whiteout. 'Tomorrow's world belongs to the ice technologies. In the meantime, it may look a makeshift, but we both know very well that there is currently no more auspicious place on earth for earnest young minds. Well, maybe in Tomsk, where the Frost besides is less intense. Anyway, you must be aware: by seriously binding yourself now to Friedrich Krupp Frierteisen, you will be making the wisest decision of your life. And I need people here I could trust. Think about it, sir.'

And the worst was that he was right, and that this fitting and prosperous future could be seen equally plainly. Fulfilled people tell in old age of similar life 'chances', perceived only with the hindsight of decades as life's inevitabilities: what caused him to choose precisely such a career path, what gave him the idea for his profitable business, how he met his partners, what prompted the direction of his research leading to that momentous discovery – there are always such 'leaps to the side' from the original path, momentary stops on the road to his goal that stretch by strange coincidence into months, years, his whole life; whilst the former goal is no longer remembered. It could clearly be seen: work in the expanding moloch of Krupp, promotions within it and pay rises, and how the *homme d'affaires*, the money man, gains the upper hand over *le Mathématicien de l'Histoire*, as already intuited at the meeting of the Last Kopeck Club, but that intuition quickly changes into cold soletruth and such a life becomes from then on the only possible one: *Herr Werkführer, Herr Direktor*, shareholder of the firm, and eventually – the bearded bourgeois, well-fed, dressed in expensive suit, monocle in eye, bowler hat in hand, head held high above vatermörder collar; thus he is photographed before the façade of his palace, or maybe on the rooftop of his aerial villa in Irkutsk, patriarch of a Siberian dynasty: Benedykt Gierosławski, karmic brother of Gustav Krupp von Bohlen und Halbach.

Breathe a deep sigh, and a kind of electric vigour spurts into the lungs.

'No.'

Wolfke waved his hand in resignation.

'Go to them.'

'I'll be back as soon as I've settled the matter.' Put on the frostoglazes. 'Aha, who's on duty in the Workshops tonight? Henrik?'

'Yes.'

Leave the laboratory whistling (until the cough again grips the throat).

And so back to Irkutsk, this time to the Customs House. In the Marmaladobahn, the good Shtchekelnikoff advised affixing a bandage or plaster to the cheek: in the ambient warmth of household stoves, a wound thaws, as can be seen, and blood oozes in a stream into the beard. 'Well, what of it, I'm not bleeding to death.' 'Don't talk to authority dressed for the sacrifice!' 'Beg pardon?' 'Once struck, any man'll strike; once fucked, arse on a plate.' Remove a glove and run a spittle-wet finger over the cuts. What then? will the tchinovnik beast of prey scent gore and sink in at once his judicial claws?

Commissioner Schembuch's welcome in his office followed the usual Schembuch pattern, that is, with a thunderous roar, in response to which the Tatar secretary's eyes began to water and the poor fellow fled behind the door.

'Treason!' roared Ivan Dragutinovich, barely turning around from the stove. 'Now against Our Most Gracious Sovereign Lord, yes?! Yes?!' Whack, whack, he pounded the broad desktop with his fist to the rhythm of his words, so that inkwells and ornate pen-boxes leapt in the air. 'So, this is your slimy gratitude, this your crappy Polish honour, tphoo, tphoo, scrubby son of father's shit!'

'Hands off my pater!'

'Oh!' Schembuch assumed an expression of great umbrage. 'He barks, the dog!'

Move a chair from against the wall, sit down, light a cigarette. Wipe the cheek with the back of the hand. With the other, take out the papers received from Uriah, find a relevant document and wave it from afar at the commissioner.

'The power is no longer yours, Gospodin Schembuch. Appeal to the governor general, if you wish. You don't even have to return my passport. This is the last time I set foot in here. And should you send your uniformed boors again to my workplace, Lawyer Kuzmentsoff will start filing formal complaints against you personally, so you won't clean up your records for as long as you live.'

Schembuch flopped down on his throne. He loosened his collar, jerked at one, two, three drawers; having found what he wanted, he swallowed the drops, puffing and blowing.

'Yesterday he forced his way into the salons, today he threatens with his connections,' Schembuch muttered under his breath with murderously piercing gaze. 'Schultz...! Schultz remembers as much about you as his secretaries remind him for a minute. Who are you to Schultz? What do you imagine? The political game is between the highest-ranking players.'

'I know that.'

'You know? Show me those papers!'

Hide them neath the frock coat.

'Send me a letter, Lawyer Kuzmentsoff will reply.'

'Don't wipe your mug with Kuzmentsoff. Once we're done with you, no lawyer shall want to visit your cell.'

Rise to the feet.

'I'm merely wasting time on you. Since you lost the rough-and-tumble between the tchinovniks, you have to let the bile. Take it out on your secretary! Goodbye.'

'Sit down!'

Sit down.

'In order to return at all to Europe alive and before your hair turns grey,' the commissioner smiled sweetly, suddenly stretching his bulldog chops in a grimace foreign to them, 'you shall do as follows. You shall deposit with us all the documents you received stamped by the gubernatorial office. You shall make full statements in the presence of Colonel Geist and Councillor von Eck of your scheming with the traitor Schultz, and also describe your entire role in his anti-tsarist plan, that is, how you conspired to make a pact between him and the gleissen through Father Frost for control of the Kingdom of Siberia. Understood?'

Stare at him in dumb amazement.

'And if not,' Schembuch grinned, 'and if not, then wham-bam, you'll find yourself in prison, on charges punishable by death, and no Schultz-Zimovy will help you then.'

Raise the cigarette to the lips.

'Is this blackmail?'

'What do you think?'

'It is blackmail!' assert with unconcealed joy, while His Esteemed Nobleness Ivan Draguntinovitch Schembuch blinked in sudden consternation as if staring at a madman; even his umbriance withered somewhat.

Blackmail! What a relief! Feel a desire almost to grab the commissioner by the jowl and kiss him on both cheeks from heartfelt gratitude – for his having opened up such a prospect. Blackmail! Blackmail in the Land of Ice, icily pure and clear: the threat of death in return for an obvious lie. My God, real blackmail like out of a drama, like out of a fusty novel!

Blow tobacco smoke for the last time, then flick the fag-end in Schembuch's direction.

'For me prison. God be with you, my Ivan.'

Decline even to slam the door on leaving.

'It went well?' asked Shtchekelnikoff.

'Mm-hmm?'

'Since you're so overjoyed.'

'He promised me the death penalty. Life imprisonment at least.'

Tchingis paused on a landing of the marble staircase between floors. Having slumped his rectangular back against the wall beside the steaming statue, he began to laugh resoundingly, eventually clasping his belly and midriff.

'What?' mutter with teeth still bared, catching a drop of blood off the moustache with the tip of the tongue.

'N-nothing, Mr G,' he panted. 'Got that revolver of yours?'

'I'm about to collect it. Let's go, the day is slipping away.'

Drive to Tsvetistaya to fetch the Grossmeister and metal samples. Then return via the Marmaladobahn to Zimny Nikolayevsk, to the Krupp Laboratory. Mijnheer Iertheim was still not to be found at his workbench; coldiron gadgets and tungetitum electrical systems, braids of hoartin fibre finer than sunrays, and frostoglaze lightbulbs – all of it lay amidst the usual chaos; the previous week, another evacuation lasting several days had taken place in the Workshops (a gleiss almost froze its way into the laboratory) and the entropy in the tower had not yet fallen here to its normal state. Scribble the official reports sitting at the desk, beside a white window blocked with snow, under a naphtha lamp, under flickering electric lamps, to the sounds of the purring samovar and tinny rattle of some new apparatus being tested just then by Doctor Wolfke, as well as the whistle of the never-distant wind; scratch with the pen in the not entirely pleasant awareness that this was one of the last of such days, that this interlude was drawing inexorably to a close. Irkutsk, Nikolayevsk, Krupp – it was a particular stage in life, no doubt necessary. But now it was time to unfreeze from it.

Engineer Iertheim appeared after three o'clock, lugging a tin chest under his arm; he tidied himself for a moment, brushing off snow and warming himself by the stove. Take a small bottle of rum from a locker and pour a few drops into his tchay. He was grateful. He could barely hold the glass in his few-fingered hand, stiff with cold and disobedient. The chest he left in the doorway. 'Because it'll melt. I must throw it at once into containers.'

'What have you there?'

'Ice.' He drank the tea; pour neat rum into his glass. '*Dank u.* I was thinking I'd verify what you said about the second hydrological cycle of tungetitum compounds.'

'Did you inquire about those people?'

'That too. Oomph. Wait a moment. Assist me!'

Carry the chest between cupboards and racks to the engineer's work-place. He cast off his shuba and malakhay hat, unwound his scarf, then, in a sweeping gesture, wiped clean a fragment of the bench surface. From Busytchkin he had borrowed a dozen deep trays. Now he placed blocks of ice into them, icicles and partially compacted névé removed from the chest. One chunk was wholly black. Pass a finger over the lumpy mass.

'It's from soot, khhrrr, from chimneys. I crawled onto the roof of my apartment building. I shall arrange for our brigade of de-icers to chip a bit off the roof for me here too.'

Obvious.

'You will melt them, sir, evaporate off the water, burn the residue in a spectrograph, measure the chemical proportions and the tungetitum content.'

'Wait a minute, so that I make no mistake over which ice comes from where...' He had it noted down, but the piece of paper had got soaked; now he twisted his face and narrowed his eyes trying to inter-pret his descriptions of the ice forms, as his monstrous physiognomy assumed in these grimaces a noble regularity: meaning does not lurk in the casual ugliness of the body, all meaning comes from the spirit that gives rise to the body.

'And what did you learn, Henrik, sir?'

'Mm-hmm? Ah, well, so this Kalousek, whom you asked about, hang on, I also jotted it down – Hilo Kalousek worked for old Horczyński to the very end, which fits, Filip Gierosławski worked under him, there was some public squabble between them, but here I couldn't find out any details; your father, as you know, provoked squabbles and quarrels time and again, even fisticuffs, so that people no longer remember the thing itself but only echoes of similar previous events, just as you taste in the smack of your thousandth cigarette only an echo of previous tobacco pleasures; but it's clear that for Filip it was also an addiction. Leave that there, please, on top of the cupboards. And these two also.'

He heaved a sigh and, having reminded himself of the taste of tobacco, took out his pipe and tobacco pouch. 'Mmm, and when Horczyński Ores closed down, Kalousek really didn't find work with Krupp –'

'I told you I'd checked in the firm's papers.'

'... but did not leave Irkutsk. Yesterday at the club, I met a certain Mr Makartchuk, who is the junior partner in a lawyer's chambers, and we talked about wills –'

'Don't start that again, you still have a long life ahead of you.'

He lit his pipe, puffed, waved his hand in the smoke.

'What lies ahead of me is a different grief. Anyway, Makartchuk says that he is also the executor of the will of one living deceased, and that the Okhrana will surely be scaring away clients from their firm again. What "living deceased", I ask, whereupon Makartchuk mentions something about a geologist sought by the police, whereupon I at once think of your pater and, well, set about questioning Makartchuk.'

'So, say!'

Mijnheer Iertheim grinned under his red stubble.

'Hilo Kalousek, it transpires, left family here. A sister and niece at least. Makartchuk, as executor of Kalousek's will, takes care of an annuity paid them by an insurance company. The point is that this company has been receiving anonymous letters and, recently, also semi-official denunciations from the Third Department claiming that Kalousek faked his death on a northern expedition so as to avoid investigation in the case of, listen, "Polish geologists sought by arrest warrants for crimes against the state".'

Leap up.

'Did he mention names?'

Mijnheer Iertheim, for greater effect, first released the smoke from his nose.

'Aleksandr Ivanovitch Tcherski.'

Burst into laughter.

'I was right! The key to the Ways of the Mammoths lies in the secret hydrography of Baikal! What flows up somewhere here onto the surface out of the tungetitum waters and from secondary atmospheric circulation, perhaps already chemically changed, perhaps already biologically bounded – they knew the secret – Bohdanowicz, Czerski, my father, most likely also Crowley, and Kalousek – the formula, the method of the shamans, or perhaps only the cartography – the geographical coordinates of the Black Oasis! Do you think, sir, that some such thing really exists?' Grab him by the arm. 'You have to introduce me to her, his sister. She surely has a means of contacting Kalousek! And Kalousek shall lead me to Czerski and as I shall have at my disposal Karol Bohdanowicz's maps and the maps of the governor general –'

'Steady on, steady on!' laughed the Dutchman. 'I'm not going away.'

'But time's running short for me. Henrik, sir, in the coming week or two, I have to leave Irkutsk. Schultz is giving me equipment, money, people – and now, at last, a real chance has appeared, concrete information which I can seize upon and –'

'So, you are leaving.'

Let go of his arm.

'Yes.'

He nodded. With his left hand, he mechanically tapped the stop-pin of the laboratory clock back and forth.

'I shall try to help you, Benedykt,' he said averting his gaze, 'and yet –'

'Are you thinking of what I'll tell him about you.'

'No. That is… this is not what's most important.' For a moment he sucked on the mouthpiece of his pipe. The umbriance grew stronger. 'The way the prince negotiated peace with the Japanese, this is how you're meant to negotiate with gleissen, correct? A territorial treaty: whether the Ice will retreat, or not. But before you leave… You understand, sir, if in reality it means Thaw, then I…'

Obvious.

Cast the eyes over Engineer Iertheim's workbench swamped with half- and quarter-finished products of the ice technologies, over the disembowelled machinery and the sketches and cross-sections of various mechanisms covering the walls and cupboards, over charts of physical and chemical properties, photographs of gleissen nests and icecradles, and projected microscopic images of coldiron coolbonds. Pull out a half-stained sheet of paper from under an electric battery, and moisten a pencil with spittle. Iertheim peered over the shoulder at the diagram thus being sketched.

'A dynamo-machine,' he said.

'But here we insert tungetitum. Please pay attention to how I portray the motor winding.'

He blinked.

'I und-understand.'

Hand him the sheet of paper.

'You will not show it to anyone. You will build a generator like this for your own use only. Please charge yourself with frost from this dynamo every morning and evening. You'll recognise the limit yourself; you'll lose feeling because of the cold.'

'It works in Summer?'

'Yes.'

He hid the paper in his pocket.

'Don't worry, I shan't advertise it, after all I know you were contemplating inventions from the start –'

'Actually…' But something prevented denial – and this very refusal to rectify a false truth felt like an effusion of acidic crapulence, the return of the most abysmal katzenjammer. Quickly take a deeper breath. 'Henrik, sir, I have this favour to ask – you are on graveyard shift tonight and I'd like to swap with you, let's say: against the next night-time duty. Will you agree?'

He unfolded his arms.

'Gladly! In which case, I shall try this evening to speak again to Makartchuk.'

Filimon Romanovitch Zeytsoff appeared together with the gang of roof-crawlers. For a long time now, he'd been seen only sober. (Wonder whether to take this as a good or bad sign.) He was pleased to see the Dutchman had been replaced.

In his leather bag, along with a hunk of bread smeared with lard and onion, he no longer brought to the night shift a bottle of 'Mrs Poklewska', but large printed tomes. Doctor Wolfke's last assistant had barely left the seventh floor when he shyly produced them: anthologies of new metaphysical poetry, some sort of religious works, and to top it all *On the Glorious Work* by anti-Struvian Christian Marxists. It didn't bear thinking what sort of new Zeytsoff might arise following Atchukhoff's death out of all this spiritual manure.

'Mind you don't get involved again in any agitation,' issue him a warning. 'Now is the very worst moment for it.'

'Thus I've heard, thus I've heard: they lock away, let out, lock away. Egh, Winter.'

Outside the windows of the tower, the gale was roaring and moaning like a hundred cracked trumpets of Jericho; feel the vibration neath the feet as it passes through the whole coldiron structure, the beginning of resonance. Tesla would probably have measured the frequency at once, done his calculations, and shattered with his pocket apparatus the towers and the Holey Palace and the entire overhead rail network of Zimny Nikolayevsk. Press the forehead against the windowpane, shielding the eyes with the hands from the naphtha-and-electric glare – but it was hard to make out even the lights of other towers in the arctic snowstorm, in the winter twilight. Open the pocket watch. Two trips will have to be made across to the Workshops by the Palace, or maybe three, if Wolfke is late in the morning due to snowdrifts. Whack, whack, whack; the ice-breaker roof-crawlers were banging overhead.

Wait until they descend, then take out the bag containing the metal samples bombarded by the Death Ray.

'Listen, Zeytsoff, those books must be very boring, don't you happen to fall asleep sometimes?'

'No, no, it's totally –'

'What d'you say? For four hours, well, just until midnight? I should be quick.'

Zeytsoff scratched in his matted beard.

'But I won't tell lies, if they ask me.'

'If they ask, the whole thing will be over anyway. Only don't say anything unasked; it's the least you can do for me, huh?'

This was cruel – for how was he to get off the hook of gratitude, gratitude if only for this job, not to mention forgiveness for the attempt in the Trans-Siberian Express? Pierced through, he hung like a worm squirming on a needle.

He lowered his eyes, but it helped not, he was not freed; he pressed the open book to his thin breast, nodding.

'But you won't steal anything, will you, sir? What d'you mean to do?'

'X-ray a bit of old iron.' Rattle the bag. 'The machine is in another corner, you won't even hear.'

The only thing unthought of was what to do with the exposure plates, that is, with their absence, how to disguise the shortfall. True, in the chaos following the hasty removal from the Workshops, a few specimens had even had the right to go missing. But Doctor Wolfke's inventorisation could be made harder still, were all exposure plates to be transferred here from the coldmills... Pick up the bunch of keys to all Krupp's industrial workrooms on the way to calibrate the machines set up there for ice experiments.

It was already the middle of the night in truly wintry conditions; the snowstorm pounded from darkness to darkness, the gale slashed every scrap of skin left carelessly exposed. Walk almost gropingly, treading on boards laid on the permafrost, along the azimuth towards the Holey Palace and Krupp's Second Coldmill; heavy with sleep, Shtchekelnikoff passively followed one step at a time. Frostoglaze spectacles were now essential to protect the eyes from the razor-sharp wind. Snowflakes and frozen pellets of mud flew past like stains on Chinese paper illuminated from below; perceive, only when peeping over the top of the frostoglazes, what these bright glows be in the inky night: not snow itself but its englintzenment. Was the Tchornoye Siyaniye standing once again over Irkutsk?

The coldmills operated in three shifts around the clock; now too, therefore, thousands of people were at work in Zimny Nikolayevsk, yet a man might equally well have been marching across the snowfields of Antarctica: no single living soul as far as the eye could see, that is – in the whole world accessible to the senses, or at arm's reach around about. And even were someone to show up on the path – it would be a strawman, only seemingly human, swaddled from top to toe in skins and furs, plastered in snow, incapable of uttering an audible word – no, there are no people here.

The gleiss in the hall adjoining the coldmill was freezing in the shape of a cloven tongue uncoiling towards the earth, which, as had been learned, was a pretty sure sign (because statistically confirmed) that the glacius was about to descend below ground level. In the meantime, it hung suspended on a hundred black strings frozen to the roof and to a wall, through which part of its medusa-like bulk was also freezing. Switch on the searchlights by the entrance; shafts of electricity poured blots of liquid mercury over the icer's spine and stalagmite-legs. From behind it, from out of a hole, drifted the usual clamour of the operating coldmill and its attendant machines. Blow to its rhythm into the gloves, selecting the key to the laboratory from the bunch. Which probably took all of a minute but turned out in the end to be unnecessary, for the door was unlocked.

Trot over to the stove; someone must have forgotten again (the order was to light it always in the evenings before leaving). Then Shtchekelnikoff whisked a knife from under his sleeve and swooped like a minor avalanche into the corner behind the stove.

The squeals of a slaughtered piglet rang out. Leap to light a lamp, light it... With his forearm, Shtchekelnikoff had pinned to the wall a bluish-faced muzhik in torn shirt, and was readying his other hand to puncture him with the quarter-arshin bayonet – the muzhik's eyes had already sprung from his noggin, now the pupils were attempting to leap from his eyeballs, directed at one and the same time towards the knife and the rectangular pate of Shtchekelnikoff neath its hood and papakha; thus arose a majestic boss eye worthy of the brush of El Greco.

'Let him go, I know the fellow, he's, khhrrr, one of our hiberniks.'

'Killing you as a friendly favour makes it less of a complaint? Why were he a-lurking in wait?'

'Let him go.'

Indeed, the man was a dayshift worker, previously met in the brigade of that old silver-beard who had tried to bury alive in a grave on Jerusalem Hill. As soon as the scarf was unwound, the muzhik likewise recognised the face. At once, he began to moan disjointedly about great misfortunes, cruel fate and punishment of the heavens, such that there was no way of comprehending him – entirely as if he'd been spying on the customs of the Polish peasantry and copying them today theatrically; but clearly, peasants are the same everywhere. Only when Tchingis had to thrust the blade again under his nose did the Martsynian pluck up courage and compose his words according to rational thought.

And his thought went as follows: that the Son of Frost should flee from Nikolayevsk and Irkutsk forthwith, for Official Persons are coming after him and inquiring about him; the Martsynian meant to do exactly the same as soon as it grew light, that is, smuggle his way through to the Transsib line and take off with the first train somewhere into Siberia under a new name. But what had so terrified him? (Apart from Shtchekelnikoff now.) Well, come their evening knocking-off time, a large band of gendarmes had descended on them and questioned them about Martsynian affairs, about Father Frost, about the Son of Frost, about some traitorous political scheming – of which the muzhik hadn't the faintest clue – and when the old man also denied all knowledge, they beat him cruelly, and when other hiberniks were gripped by anger at the sight of it and three attacked the gendarmes with their fists, the latter bashed them with truncheons, so that one gave up the ghost on the spot, and the other two had to be taken to hospital. 'Extraordinary events!' the muzhik fidgeted nervously. Even a few weeks ago, when they threw anything that moved into prison, they hadn't beaten to death on the spot! 'Oy, deadly be the rage in the hearts of our lords and masters against Martsynians and, clearly, against the Son of Frost – may he flee, flee, flee!'

'Commissioner Schembuch has had a quiet word with Colonel Geist,' mutter cuttingly into the beard.

Shtchekelnikoff, however, looked uneasy. Having kicked the hibernik out of the door, he spent a long while cleaning the knife on his sleeve, lost in thought.

'You's made some powerful enemies, Mr G.'

'So what, such was the intention. Instead, I have an ally who's even more powerful. Tomorrow I'll say the word to whomever needed.'

Tchingis continued to shake his head.

'But they knew you'd find out.'

'Exactly: they tried to frighten me.'

'Why in't they come to Tsvetistaya?'

'Because I'd drag them through the courts, khhrrr, but here they can trample on the wretches to their hearts' content.'

He put away the knife.

'They're stitching up your sentence, Mr G.'

'All empty talk. You always imagine the worst –'

'Heed Tchingis's advice, live to see yer grandkin.'

Zeytsoff must have had supplies, however, of high-proof liquor stashed away somewhere in the tower, for on return from the second trip to the Workshops, he was discovered in his corner by the stove completely sozzled, nose and beard shoved between pages of the transcendental verses, exuding the perfume of spiritus vodka. Before lulling himself to sleep with the spirit, the crafty beast had re-hidden the bottle. Shake from cold throughout the entire ride in the Marmaladobahn, then by sleigh across Irkutsk under a purga so white that even the rising sun was invisible, teeth almost ringing, dreaming of a glass of rum or slivovitz.

The Lord God was begrudging. Run upstairs to the second floor, stamp off the snow in the doorway, still in shuba and shapka, bag over shoulder; and here already Marta Wielicka is calling and leading Leokadia Gwóźdź from the kitchen. 'Benedykt, you have a guest!' What was to be done: invite her into the drawing room; the maid brought coffee with freshly baked bread and honey.

'Mm-hmm, forgive me, ma'am,' mumble with the mouth full, having pounced on that pre-breakfast, 'I can barely stand upright after a night –'

'The Okhrana came to my home,' Mrs Gwóźdź said accusingly, glancing after the departing maid.

Sigh mournfully.

'I know, I know, Leokadia, ma'am, I've trodden on a few people's toes here, things will soon soften, but for a few days still –'

She banged an open palm on the tabletop, and her palms were like those of a coldmill worker; cups and saucers leapt in the air, the sugarbowl lid fell off, the naphtha lamp jingled.

'Benedykt, sir! I have not come to warn you! You are a man driven by crazy ideas and also oddly stubborn in your follies, and in fact not very unlike your father, I can see that now; I want you to get them off me once and for all! They're intruding on my family! Frightening people! Yesterday, worse still – they came to Rappaport, terrorised the management – I have lost my job!'

Imbibe hot coffee with the warm bread – waves of lifegiving warmth spread from inside the organism, sloth and drowsiness naturally followed; slump into a chair with an expression certainly not testifying to the sharpest of intellects.

'But what can I do – apologise, well, I apologise – one way or another I am leaving, so of itself it will –'

She leaned across the tabletop.

'What did you tell them, for God's sake! Those men who came with the Okhrana, they –'

'Mm-hmm?'

'They showed me the documents!' She clenched her fist. 'They want to exhume her!'

'Beg pardon?'

'Emilka, your sister!' she hissed. 'They want to dismantle the grave, dig up the coffin, open it… Over my dead body!' Again, she slammed her fist on the table.

Come to the senses.

'Wait a moment – exhume Emilka – wait a moment! – of course – why didn't I think of that? – Batyushka Moroz's own flesh and blood, bone of his bones – someone from the Brotherhood of War against the Apocalypse must have blabbed – to Schembuch? to Pobedonosteff? Leokadia!' Grab her by that clenched hand. 'Please try to remember! Did they introduce themselves somehow? Say at whose behest they act? Threaten with anyone's name?' Well, yes – well, indeed – well, obviously! But a little child, a baby – could she have? – she couldn't have – what is the structure constant of an abassy like that…?'

Mrs Gwóźdź stared in horror and for half a moment gave the

impression she would explode in uncontrollable rage; withdraw the hand even, step back from the table – she'll demolish the china, smash the lamp, overturn the furniture – but the moment defused into its contrary, and Leokadia's steam suddenly vented itself in the form of hollow laughter.

She waved her hand in resignation.

'People not made for life.'

'Well, I am very –'

Wielicki entered. Mrs Gwóźdź rose to her feet, curtsied; Wojsław kissed the proffered hand, and polite social chatter began. Switch off the ears. Who's making use here of the Okhrana? (A visit would have to be made that evening to Modest Pavlovitch in order to seek his advice.) Who has such power and ambition turned in this direction? Schembuch? Clearly, the thing is linked to the blackmail of the commissioner in the Ministry of Winter, but Schembuch is a lowly figure; he might arrange to meet Colonel Geist at the Arkadiya for dinner, but his word won't prompt the Okhrana into action. Who then? Who has the courage to confront the governor general? Only Pobedonostseff. Wince, another mistake in the equations, again something doesn't add up. After the meeting in the Sibirkhozheto Tower, Pobedonostseff would sooner protect the ideologue of the Ice State, and not –

'Benedykt, sir?'

'Yes, yes.'

Bid farewell to Mrs Gwóźdź. Wojsław Wielicki still stood in the hallway, tying a white foulard scarf under his beard. The sleepy voices of children reciting their morning prayers drifted from deep inside the apartment; downstairs, in the kitchen, a mixing-bowl thumped rhythmically; dawn had come and gone more than an hour ago, yet the windows, still plastered in snow, might just as well have been hermetically sealed; lamps were burning everywhere; the coal-wallah went from stove to stove clanging his scuttle and ash-pan. Wojsław finally wedged the foulard into his waistcoat, twisted the diamond ring on his finger and, lost in thought, patted the globe of his belly.

'Will you find time for me today? After work. Mm-hmm? We should sit down and talk over a few things.'

'What, for example?'

'Very sorry to have to say it, my dear fellow, you can't imagine how sorry... but I shall most likely have to ask you to find a place of your own. Of course, you will continue to be most welcome here! Most welcome! But –'

'Maybe the police paid you a visit because of me?'

'What? No! You see, Benedykt, it is one thing to help a fellow countryman, even in the worst of criminal plights, but quite another – for a businessman to affiliate himself with this or that political party. After all, everyone knows you are staying with me.'

Understand him perfectly. His confusion was sincere, his embarrassment sincere, but sincere too was the decisiveness of his request. Such is the man, Wojsław Wielicki, for in reducing his competitors to bankruptcy, he undersigns the final murderous contract, sighing melancholically and inquiring with concern after the bankrupt's health.

'In any case, sir, you cannot seriously take me for a Lyednyak.'

'Lyednyak?' He laughed. 'You examine yourself too rarely in a mirror, Benedykt! They see you according to other scales now in the city.'

'How supposedly? Well, tell me! I can't look at myself from the outside.'

He raised his eyebrows.

'Well, you are an Oblastnik and plotting against the Holy Emperor.'

'What on earth?!'

He laughed even more sonorously, thoroughly amused.

'Well? Not true?' He took out a handkerchief, wiped away his tears, blew his nose. 'How quickly things are changing since the governor general's ball! Almost as if a minor Thaw were already in the air. (Preserve us, Lord God!) In Harbin the prices of coldiron and tungetitum have risen by thirty per cent. Thirty per cent! Perhaps you know something about that too, eh?' He patted the shoulder in friendly fashion, lowered his eyes. 'Isn't your doing, is it, old chap?' And he laughed for a third time.

But truth was – as could clearly be seen – that Wojsław Wielicki himself did not consider it entirely a joke.

On the great designs, that is, on the power of man over future and past

Nikola Tesla adjusted his snowbright cuffs, pulled his gloves on tighter still, glanced over his right shoulder and left shoulder with a mysterious air and then produced with a conjuror's flourish a black pebble from a pocket of his tailcoat and placed it on the laboratory bench. It was a tungetitum revolver bullet. Pick it up in the fingers. П. P.M. 48. Tesla performed a second gesture – and rapped a second cartridge on the benchtop. П. P.M. 41.

'A-ha!' Murch welled on his face, he was that pleased with himself. 'Many happy returns of the day!' He winked. 'I asked Stepan nicely.'

'I –'

'No?'

'Quite right! But how did you know?'

'Christine told me.'

Clear the throat.

'Well, it's true…'

'So, how many years is it?'

Calculate mentally, subtracting date from date, amazed as always at this one simple calculation.

'Twenty-four.'

'Ah, *un Enfant du Siècle*!' Tesla smiled.

Clasp the cartridges in the hand.

'But what gave you the idea, sir –'

'What do you mean, you asked for them.'

'Asked?'

'The night before yesterday – don't you remember? When we'd already smashed the coathangers. Because you have to – how did you put it? – "just in case", oh. But I heard fear!' He raised a white finger. 'I heard fear!'

He spoke truth. Remember nothing of the kind; Nikola had quickly fallen asleep with his head on the tungetitum mirror, so how had it been possible to ask him for anything? And now he spoke truth.

Well, but then the Murch Hammer had been pounding without interruption, crushing every passing minute to rubble before it froze for good. So – a request had been made to Nikola Tesla for bullets for the Grossmeister – true or false?

'*Merci, merci beaucoup, mais…* mm-hmm, do you think I might need them?'

'You haven't disposed of that revolver.'

'No.' Glance at the door (the laboratory was deserted, everyone was awaiting the governor general in the main hall under the sequined globe and fresco of Summer), extract the bundle from behind the belt and unwrap the gun. The Grossmeister opalesced dully. Break it open and blow into the empty chambers. 'These agents of the Okhrana, sir, to whom you gave the ice weaponry…' Insert the bullets into the flower calyces. 'It wouldn't have been very effective against people, especially in the Express. Were you really afraid the gleissen themselves would make some defensive move against the arsenal of Summer?'

'Are you now certain they're incapable of thought or self-defence?'

'Let's not jest. After all, it wasn't for this that you ordered these revolvers.'

'It was an experimental series, before the Kotarbiński pumps, before any thought of tungetitors. Whilst in the process, a weapon against people emerged more powerful than ordinary…'

'A tungetitum bullet strikes ice – and what? Still more ice. Why precisely against gleissen –'

'And yet you shot one.'

Touch the cartridge inserted into the revolver with the fingertip.

'Doctor Wolfke hasn't researched it yet.'

'Researched what?'

'The behaviour of high-energy tungetitum in liquid helium, in gleissen blood. Just as there exist coldiron coolbonds with complete anti-thermal symmetry – this lock, chamber, barrel – so too there exist tungetitum compounds... Am I right? Below zero Kelvin... Perhaps that was your idea, sir, for destroying the Ways of the Mammoths?'

Slam the Grossmeister closed. Toss it up instinctively to the level of the eye, gaze along the length of the reptilian barrel. The horn was pointing at the centre of a chart of sacred ice geometries.

'Speaking of which, my dear doctor, did you finally measure those structure constants? Because I've almost forgotten.'

Tesla muttered something under his breath in a foreign language.

'*Pardon?*'

'It's well-known fact that people differ!' he growled. 'You measure electrical resistance on the bodies of one man and then another man, and with suitably sensitive apparatus you'll always get different results. But character? How to measure a man's character?'

'But you understand I must have this information before I set out after my father.' Tuck away the Grossmeister. 'I wander a thousand versts across the ice with the Kotarbiński pump, but then it transpires on the spot that father absorbs murch faster than the pump is able to extract it – what then? Worse still, if it's true that abassylar can continue to grow and mature there once they've descended to the Ways, as a child, for instance, then the teslectrical capacity constant derived from character –'

'The pump!' Tesla interrupted.

The obvious! It swept through the murch like an invisible lightning bolt.

'You've got it?'

'Tomorrow –'

'Where?'

'Please.'

From under a bench near his workstation neath the blackboards, he dragged out a wooden trunk chock-full of electrical debris, cables, lamps and burned winding; he raked this aside, revealing the tin surround of a small naphtha stove.

'Inside?'

'Below the reservoir.'

'The cables –'

'In spools..

'When it's fired up –'

'I've tested.'

'Ah! Brilliant! No one will notice, temperature above zero.'

'And not with a crank, but –'

'Steam.'

'Or from a murch battery. Look.'

The tramping of many feet in the corridor heralded the arrival of visiting dignitaries. Tesla kicked the trunk under the bench, drew himself up to his full height and again adjusted his cuffs. The thought returned, however, that perhaps it might be better to slip away unnoticed and not flaunt before Count Schultz-Zimovy the acquaintance with Doctor Tesla, who was after all a thorn in the count's side, whatever the count had claimed officially; to not stab him in the eyes with it – but before action could be taken in accord with this thought, the door opened and in marched Engineer Jago, doom-ridden as a hail cloud, and after him the old okhrannik Stepan and a whole group of Observatory functionaries, tchinovniks, Cossacks and also the indigenes in their filthy pelts; whilst in the midst of the group came Frantishek Markovitch Uriah in decidedly undress uniform.

'Important matters of state,' Sasha Pavlitch whispered to Doctor Tesla. 'The count is busy.'

Tesla began unbuttoning his tailcoat.

'I too am busy!' he growled angrily.

Commissioner Uriah caught sight of him over the grey head of the Observatory's garrulous director.

'Ah, our wizard!' he exclaimed and broke away from the intrusive retinue. Straining to give him a flagrantly artificial smile – a false smile – he shook the inventor's right hand so vigorously that old Tesla had to prop himself against the bench. 'My Buryats are asking why your drum is not beating today,' Frantishek Markovitch quizzed him further half seriously.

'I switched it off,' the doctor mumbled.

'But you haven't abandoned your research? The governor is immeasurably curious as to your progress.' Falsity in his voice, falsity in his mien, falsity in his bodily pose.

Seen from the other side, the truth was that in recent days, Tesla had been devoting himself almost entirely to the increasingly crazy ideas of the Fyodorovians (during the night they had resurrected mice under the Murch Hammer; Sasha vowed that for several seconds, that is, at the extremum of the negentropic wave, the rodents evinced signs of life) and had simply made no progress at all.

'We are most gratified by His Excellency's interest,' Engineer Jago bowed.

Mr Uriah looked him up and down, now with a serious look.

'Ye-es,' he sighed. 'I don't doubt it.' With a quick gesture, he dismissed the director, who was nagging him from behind his elbow. 'Gospodin Gierosławski, a word.' He strode off into the corner and laid his palms on the hot tiles of the stove.

'In fact, I have business to raise with you myself.'

'Oh?'

Briefly describe the events with the gendarmerie in Zimny Nikolayevsk and the Okhrana pursuit of the pater's friends in Irkutsk.

It can't be said he was visibly surprised.

'Stupid, they're all stupid,' he muttered, resting his high-domed forehead neath its flaxen locks against the stove. 'You see it after all, you must see it.' Then he fired a swift glance. 'You shall honour your contract with His Illustriousness, no matter how the die falls!'

'But speak clearly, Gospodin Uriah!' shoot in irritation, for it was impossible to understand why it was so hard to read the truth – as if someone had specially drawn a curtain of semi-falsity over the mind.

'Thaw in Europe, Winter in Siberia. You gave your word!'

'Word,' reply slowly.

'Remember: only Schultz in power can ensure your safety and that of your father. Tigry Etmatoff and his people are loyal to me – they'll be loyal to you. Understand? His Illustriousness may not believe in the freezing of History, but I...'

'But – what's going on? Who's sending the police after me everywhere?' Step closer still. 'Pobedonostseff?' whisper on the out-breath.

'Stupid, stupid, stupid,' Mr Uriah repeated softly to the stove. 'Had he not absolutely had to, the emperor would never have appointed a man like Schultz to the governor generalship, that is, someone resourceful, ambitious, independently thinking – a man of character!' Red flushes burned unhealthily on Uriah's cheeks; eventually, he unstuck himself from the stove. 'For the principle of government in autocratic states manifests itself most clearly in this: the one who remains safe despite wielding the power granted him by those above him, is the stupid one, Mr Gierosławski, the stupid one, because he's less of a threat to the autarch. Who lives in constant fear,' he whispered, 'of anyone to whom he's been forced to surrender even a fraction of his absolute power.'

Yet these treasonous words from the mouth of a tchinovnik in the governor general's chancellery were not at all surprising. Despite everything, more of that soletruth flowing in murch must have been touched than could be spat out in words – in language of the second kind – into the material world.

'So, you can see for yourself,' address him with a note of sarcasm in the voice, 'the power of History is the only way out. Not any one man or any human collective.' Pick up and let drop the poker; it clattered against the stove door. 'Does there exist an unjust gravity? Are there ignoble astronomies? Dishonest mathematics?'

'Yes, I know, Aleksandr Aleksandrovitch wrote the governor general a comprehensive letter... But at this moment,' Frantishek Markovitch turned to look at Tesla, 'at this moment, other matters demand attention.' He blew his nose, which sounded like a horse sighing. 'Will he listen, if you ask him?'

'About what?'

'Why do you imagine I've bothered to come here? To save his life.'

'So, His Illustriousness no longer answers to the emperor for Doctor Tesla's safety?'

Mr Uriah merely snorted.

'What can I do, one has to try, if only for peace of conscience. Do you often spend time with him?'

Think about the Kotarbiński pump hidden in the portable stove. Won't it be easier this way? (At last, an original thought in the frozen bonce!)

'Order your Tunguses and whomsoever needed in the Box to assemble the harnessed sleighs here, at the Observatory, with all the equipment.'

'You don't wish to show yourself at the Citadel?'

'And those maps you promised me –'

'Yes, all in good time, all in good time, in a day, in two days' time – if only you knew how much I have on my mind now!'

'It's important, otherwise I won't calculate where father –'

'Yes, yes, yes!' he snarled. 'Neither do I relish the idea of war and schism!' He exhaled. 'Forgive me. So, he won't listen to you, huh? Doctor Tesla! Allow me!'

On the train to work. It was already nearing two o'clock; the furious snowstorm was still raging, however, entrapping the body in a whirl of white lagging two feet in diameter. Impossible to comprehend what Tchingis Shtchekelnikoff had in mind when he suddenly shouted from behind the collar on the Marmaladobahn platform: 'He be following you!' Try questioning him only in the lift of the Clock Tower, but of course, he wasn't able to provide a concrete description. Perhaps the man had been suggested by the fleeting play of glintzen, the overpowering symbolism of necessity – for the windows, sealed tight by the eternal frost, were already shining with a pearly sheen, and even a slight glow never noticed before was coming off the walls. A great blacker-than-black Aurora must have been standing over the Land of Gleissen.

So Engineer Iertheim had also not removed his frostoglaze spectacles inside the Laboratory. It was impossible to read the expression in
his eyes and glances ran awry when he stated in all seriousness, summoning with a gesture from over the cupboards:

'Angels are watching over you, Benedykt.'

'You think so?'

He pressed a rolled-up scrap of paper into the palm.

'Tomorrow evening at eight. She remembers Filip Gierosławski, her
brother must have told her about his work. She'll talk to you.'

Read the address. A turning off Amurskaya Street, close to
Tsvetistaya.

'Thank you.'

He scratched the scars on his face with the scars on his fingers.

'You've heard the rumours?'

'What rumours?'

'What they write in the newspapers about dreamslaves going berserk.
Apparently, they're now forcing their way onto the Transsib. Like rats.
There's talk of war, but not with Japan.'

'It's because of the Auroras, Henrik, you said so yourself: under the
Auroras, it's always like this.'

'In Krupp's countinghouses,' he pointed to the floor with his thumb,
'there's been panic since early morn, Herr Direktor has ordered raw
materials to be bought up at any price.'

'Mm-hmm, they're uneasy too in the Citadel.' Light a cigarette, lapse
into musing. 'What are you thinking?'

'Pobedonostseff and Schultz have fallen foul of one another?'

'Mm-hmm. No, not that.'

'The Chinese?'

'I've also read of fresh anti-Manchu rebellions. But the Kuomintang
larks about mainly in the south, beyond the Ice. The Ice, the Ice is come
to stay, Henrik, what can change here?'

Leave before seven so as to reach Rappaport's before closing.
Leokadia Gwóźdź no longer worked there, but one way or another garments (several sizes too big, since they shrank in frost and damp) and
other accoutrements had to be bought for the journey into the heart
of Winter. Pack the body back into the sleigh with all the purchases,
bundles, bags and clumsiest of packaging containing the Siberian skis
(that is, skis bound in reindeer hide with hair smoothed specially in
the direction of travel, as the salesman demonstrated in transports of
professional joy).

Arrive at Tsvetistaya already after dark; even the rainbows from
frostoglaze streetlamps failed to penetrate the curtains of snow. White
arctic darkness, about which so much had been read in diaries of

travellers to northern lands, was roaring through the streets of the City of Ice; white darkness, smeared on the glazes into a kasha spiced with strange colours. But men grow inured to it and cease to pay it attention. Shape, movement – only these. The rest is irrelevant. Men see not what they see, but what the brain deciphers of violent daubs painted on their pupils.

Swirling snow – billowing seas – feathery cloud – coloured shadow – a five-legged, three-armed silhouette – a Piegnarian beast with icicle mane – a man leaping into the sleigh – a boy in light jacket with snow in his black hair, ice on his brows and lashes – who – him – Mefody Karpovitch Pyelka, alive.

'Gospodin Gierosławski! They're coming to arrest Your Esteemed Nobleness –'

This was as much as he managed to yell before Shtchekelnikoff locked him in a rectangular grip and dragged him from the sleigh. Both landed in a snowdrift. Jump to the feet, brushing aside the skis and heavy coil of hare coverlet; the lighter packages flew directly onto the street. The two of them were tousling somewhere in the snowstorm, indistinct shapes, a bear and a monkey. Call out once and twice. A light flashed in the gateway of the Wielicki residence. The bonebreakers come rushing to assist. They'll cudgel that Pyelka to death. Leap into the roaring purga.

Wind doesn't cover deep footprints so quickly. Totter after them – here, Tchingis had shoved Pyelka an arshin into a drift, here hauled him by a limb, here Pyelka still kicks out, tearing up the sludge-ice in all directions, and here – here Shtchekelnikoff throttles the sickly Martsynian, pinning him against a wall with forearm wedged neath his chin. He's about to pierce him with the blade, just as he tried to stab the coldmill worker; such be the Shtchekelnikoff custom.

Yank Tchingis by the arm – he doesn't even twitch.

'Inside!' Shout in his ear, pulling the scarf from the face.

'Look!' he pointed to the ground at Pyelka's foot, where lay a butcher's knife with characteristically wide blade, like in children's drawings of robber-ogres.

'Inside with him!'

Shtchekelnikoff shrugged his shoulders – which had the effect of allowing the liberated Pyelka to slip from the wall, choking in panic and massaging his neck.

The bonebreakers came shuffling up with lamps and sticks. Order them to unpack the merchandise from the sleigh. Then, grabbing Pyelka by the collar of his shoddy jacket, drag him into the hallway and up to the first floor. Shtchekelnikoff brought up the rear, rotating Pyelka's monstrous knife in his paw with the air of a disgusted connoisseur.

Push the quaking Martsynian into a room adjoining the kitchen, immediately locking one of the doors from the inside and stationing Tchingis by the other with instructions to admit no one. Cast off the shuba, shapka, gloves, scarves, chin-straps, top sweaters; remove the oculars, undo the shoes. Walking over to the stove, place the palms flat on the smooth hot tiles – the first thing a Siberian does on return, as if extending a hand in greeting to his home.

Unless he's a Martsynian hibernik and retreats instinctively into the corner farthest from the stove. (Coughing and croaking and suddenly thawing from his hair and summer clothing.)

Having blown the nose, push a chair in Pyelka's direction. He sat down awkwardly, uncomfortably, like a schoolboy brought before his headmaster's presence, on the very edge of his seat, legs pressed together, not knowing what to do with his hands (he crossed them over his chest, shoved them under his armpits, laid them on his knees, thrust them into pockets).

Notice now a filthy bandage protruding from under his left sleeve; a bandage also visible through a rent in the shoulder seam.

'You're injured?'

'Broke my arm then.' He coughed. 'Your Esteemed Nobleness must –'

'When? Agh.' Now that the frostoglazes had been removed, there was no protection against the glintzen bouncing off the walls and black-and-white window behind Pyelka's outline; Mefody Karpovitch's umbriance cut sharp into the eyes: yea and yea, nay and nay. 'As you jumped off the train, well yes. So, to whom who were you talking that night?'

He opened his mouth, closed it, opened it.

'He's no more, so I'll tell Your Lordship. Councillor Dushin came to warn me to flee, for Her Princessly Highness had learnt of me from her retainers and were about to send her people. So, I jumps off.'

'Princess Blutskaya saved my life then, so why should she... Ah, she's a Martsynian – so it was all about the Martsynian faith!'

'In Moscow, Her Highness's community and my community dwell in great enmity, blood between us, Truth between us.' He lowered his eyes. 'Rasputin strangled our batyushka with his own hands. But, Your Lordship, it ain't the time –'

'Wait! First it has to freeze! Why did Dushin – a confidant of the princess, and so by that same token also a Martsynian – but –'

'Mr Dushin were loyal to Their Highnesses, but our brother. He promised to help you too – what, he didn't help?'

It has frozen.

'All right.' Blow the nose a second time. 'So, what are they supposedly arresting me for?'

'For the murder of Governor Schultz.'

The handkerchief flew to the floor. Flop onto a stool by the stove.

'You are not lying.'

Pyelka crossed himself nervously and kissed his medallion.

'On my soul's salvation!'

'How came you by such knowledge?'

He bit his lip.

'But you won't betray me.'

'I won't, Pyelka, never fear.'

'Well. It were like this. When I arrived after Your Lordship, a good month back, where were I to turn? To my brothers, friends of friends. I still needed time to recover but sent word at once should anything involve Your Esteemed Nobleness – and everyone here hastening down Martsyn's path has heard of the Son of Frost – the news was to come to me and I'd throttle the hotheads' dangerous designs, so as they'd leave Your Esteemed Nobleness in peace. And then just today, the terrible news reaches me from our brother, who – but I beseech Your Lordship, tell no one – who is a servant in the household of Colonel Geist, and says, oy, what he says: there's been a bloody attempt on the life of His Illustriousness Count Schultz-Zimovy, for which they've already drawn up an initial charge against Venyedikt Filipovitch Gierosławski and decreed certain swift death. And if they ain't taken you yet in irons, it's probably only cos they're preparing huge gendarmerie actions across all Irkutsk. Which may save your life, sir: escape whilst you can!'

Wipe the forehead and only then notice the sweat stuck to the skin. Move away from the stove.

'When was this attempt?'

'Ah, when they ran back and forth raising the alarm – were how long ago? An hour?'

'Wait here.'

Go out to the drawing room. Having shouted for pen and paper, scrawl three sentences to the Honourable Modest Pavlovitch Kuzmentsoff and dispatch a servant on horseback, squeezing a rouble coin into his pocket so he'd race through the purga at breakneck speed.

Marta Wielicka was asking what was going on – Shtchekelnikoff was still standing in the corridor by the door, except that he'd hidden the nightmarish knife under his armpit. Kiss her dainty hand, showering her with apologies and begging her to knock when Wojsław returns from work; snatch some hot chocolate from the kitchen and return to Pyelka.

He didn't want chocolate; pour it into a single cup. He sat with livid countenance pressed into the cold windowpane, his black right eye staring sadly out at the white expanse, whilst his left roved around the room in a bulging squint.

Blow on the chocolate.

'Who are you anyway, Pyelka?' ask softly. 'Why pursue me across half the world, kill for my sake, risk your own neck?'

He strained his moist eyes wider still.

'What d'you mean? Your Esteemed Nobleness! Why!'

'Sincere faith, I understand, but –'

'Faith!' he exhaled and collapsed in a fit of coughing. For a long while he massaged his throat injured by the hand of Shtchekelnikoff.

Swallow the chocolate in tiny gulps reckoned in prime numbers, that is, one, two, three, five, seven, trying to measure every thought and gesture in time to the internal beat, so that no alien rhythm, having imposed itself on the body, might impose itself on the soul. Without tearing the eyes off Mefody. Squire and farmhand, beat constable and street urchin, Pole and Russian.

'Tell me truthfully, what is it that so matters to you?' Persist in gentle conversation. 'That is, to Martsynians? What is it you want? What are you waiting for?'

Amazement and consternation flowed through Pyelka from one expression to the next.

'And you, Catholics – what *matters* to you? What do you *want*? What are you *waiting* for?'

'So not faith, all right. What then?'

He was confused, looked away; but he could equally well have been trying to break free from coldiron wires.

'Cos you gentlemen are always the same…,' he muttered.

'How d'you mean, Mefody, how d'you mean?'

'Yacking away like womenfolk.' His shook his head. 'Well, so why don't Your Lordship escape?! They're arresting you!'

Wipe the chocolate from the moustache.

'You're a fine molodyets, Mefody, no woman, but you can say what's playing in your soul; it's the manly thing not to prattle about sentimental trifles, but to look inside yourself and clearly name this or that spirit driving you to perform great deeds. For as you rightly see, Mefody, the gentlemen masters more often possess the knack of sight and word, soul and intellect; whereas a peasant, even if he's hacked his neighbour to death, can in no way explain to a judge wherefore, for what and why he did it. Still less will he put into words wherefore he's spent his whole life labouring in the fields like his father and father's father; for in this life of his there is no "wherefore". Why, it has frozen.' Spread the sweet chocolate over the palette with the tip of the tongue; its taste and smooth mellow viscosity so left their magic mark on the tongue that the tone and rhythm of further utterance turned truly chocolatey, that is, runny, soft, low, sweet. 'On the other hand, the gentlemen masters… What think you, Mefody: what's it about, all this art, which they admire so much in their cities and manor houses, all these tales told in theatrical plays and books?'

'Seducing women to sin more easily,' he grunted.

'This too. But I'm not asking what art is for – but what's it about, what's it about? Well, about this: how a man does something great – a noble deed, an ignoble deed, an unexpected feat – something different which comes as if from outside of himself, and what consequences he then has to bear, and how he tries to tell himself and other people why he did what he did; and usually, he's unable to tell it in any speech of man – so this is what art is also for, it tells.'

'Can't say,' said Pyelka. 'I'm unlettered.'

'But we're in the land of the Ice; here even a muzhik, who's never glanced into a clean mirror in his life, can *calculate* himself on his fingers.' Put aside the cup. 'Tell me, Mefody: of whom are you so very ashamed?'

He pressed his temple into the pane, clenched his fists.

'My parents, of them.'

'Who are they?'

'Who?' he sighed. 'They walk already with the mammoths.'

'But shame pulls.'

'Shame pulls, sir, pulls, oy, how it pulls.'

'Of what?'

'Meanness, ruthless nastiness, their black hearts and my life, such shame afore God and men, such…' He almost gagged. Laid a fist on his breast, bowed his head. 'It pulls, chokes, rips apart like claws of fire, so it's nigh impossible to breathe, sometimes it's like that.'

'I know, Pyelka, I know. But I also know that we live not by the sins of our parents. Had we inherited everything from them along with the stamp of original sin, then after so many generations, Satan's kingdom would have arisen on Earth: every child would have added his own sins to the sins of the past. But it's the reverse, Pyelka, it's the reverse!'

'But it's because of me, for me and about me!' Mefody howled. 'For I live!'

'What was it you did?'

'I… Five years ago, five years ago, I were this raw youth chasing through the snow with the wolfdogs, a plague to mother and father, roaming in the forest, stealing food and skiving off work. We lived in Mratchnyetovo, this village on the forest edge, built under the free law of Prime Minister Stolypin, still before the gleissen; maybe a hundred versts from here.'

'It was Winter.'

'It were Winter and it were winter, and I, like a fool, went into the forest with them boys to lay traps, we wanted to sell skins, earn roubles, and this other maltchik brought a bottle of rotgut, and another brought... We all got blind drunk, I no longer remember, but we all got blind drunk and fell asleep there for the night; forty-below frosts came and fixed us in stone... They say, I were dead.'

'And what happened?'

'Well, in the night Batyushka Moroz paid a visit to Mratchnyetovo.'

'You already knew him.'

'No. Except that, Your Esteemed Nobleness, except that the Sunday previous, the ispravnik had stopped in the village and nailed a notice to the headman's wall promising a reward of a hundred roubles in gold to any handing him over to the authorities. With a large photograph.'

'Agh!'

'A hundred roubles in gold for a peasant! But he came at the time of greatest frost, that is, in frost, with frost, on frost. Totally naked he were, and walked like that through the blizzard. Old Goseff asks him what he's come for – and Father Frost says he's following the Black Sun, and to give him the sick; he'll cure what can be cured, freeze out them maladies.'

'He spoke?'

'He spoke. At that time. Yes.'

'In nineteen nineteen?'

'Yes. But you should know that he still weren't Father Frost in everything, like I know him today; and I remember not if he were even endowed with that name. Whilst people told me: that he walked, that he sat down, that he talked like a living man, that he even drank vodka – except it were all somehow slow and with odd movements, and that he creaked, and snow and ice flaked off him, and he were generally very cold, you couldna touch him nor keep him indoors, his icicles reached to the ground.'

'And then what? Tell me, Mefody.'

Pyelka moved his cheek across the frostoglaze pane like a cat fawning to – to the frost.

'Mother comes running in despair: save my child! Our babies have frozen to death! She falls at his feet, it's cold, she nearly dragged him there herself. Where dogs had led trappers – so he went.'

'And then what?'

'And I live, you see.'

'What did he do?'

'Oh, who's to tell! There was four of us, drunk and frozen; one of us they moved, set about freeing him with hammers; first an icified hand fell off, then his body burst – so they left him and sent for the priest. But then the women brought Batyushka Moroz. As we lay there neath the trees, on bare permafrost… first, he did something to us for a long time, poked about in the blood; they say he froze red icicles into our hearts… and then he took us and descended with us onto the Ways of the Mammoths.

'Three days my parents waited and prayed to the icons; on the fourth day, at dawn, he came out of the earth with me and Petya. They say we was entirely conscious; I remember it not. But you see, alive, alive and well and totally sound of mind. Only one thing was to stay with us till death: frost in the bones. For Petya it meant but a few days, for the hoar wouldna let go, though he spewed up ice and stones and soil, and dug out black clots from his flesh with a knife, and lay down in fire; but I –'

'You walked the Ways of the Mammoths, Pyelka.'

'I know not. They say I walked. So, I must have walked. I remember it not.'

'You remember it not, but – it has frozen.'

'It has. So after that: when, next day, the starostas and foremen descended on Mratchnyetovo with a whole crowd of ispravniks and began firing from afar at Batyushka Moroz, and when he, split open by bullets like crumbling clay, threw himself to the ground, gradually drifting away again onto the Ways of the Mammoths, little by little in the frost, they smashed and mowed him down with bayonets, sticks, scythes, every kind of old iron, and trampled on him with their horses, and ripped him apart with chains, Bozhe moy, and hurled stones at him; thus throughout the whole village and across the fallow fields and into the forest, until eventually he dived somehow under the earth, a torn shred.

'Then they paid my father and mother the hundred roubles in gold.'

'Agh.'

Mefody rubbed his face over the windowpane in a kind of trance-like frenzy, beating his breast with a clenched fist.

'Yet I live! I live! A hundred roubles for betraying my saviour! Upasi Hospod!'

'But he also survived, Father Frost, he too lives.'

Pyelka pursed his blue lips.

'A month went by maybe – but I were no longer there, my parents sent me away to grandparents near Vyshny Volotchyok – a month later, when he returned, the ispravniks was long gone and no one saw him beginning to freeze up at night out of a well; by morning he stood almost upright, but this time it were impossible to talk to him for he spoke no more in the words of men, and all I know is that those as got into their sleds forthwith come morning and left Mratchnyetovo kept their lives, for when the gendarmes arrived several days later, they found nought but frost and ice, ice, ice, warped snowbound cottages with wide-open doors, icicle-covered furniture, petrified cattle, neither living soul nor warm body. Only a great cross made of half-frozen pine trunks standing in the middle of the village.'

'He took them.'

'They went.'

'A whole village.'

'Justly, Your Lordship, justly for the evil done to him in return for good.'

'But you –'

'I, Your Lordship – I, Your Lordship – I –'

'Another man would still seek revenge.'

Mefody beat his skinny breast with passion.

'Me – it tugs at me, stings me, burns me. If only a word. But from whom? From him? Well, even were it to be he me, or I him – what is there to forgive! Your Esteemed Nobleness understands it? I understand not!' He clasped his head. 'I understand not! Nothing!'

'There is no forgiveness here, Pyelka. Only shame.'

It had frozen.

It was impossible, however, not to keep returning to the same bitter thought: what an Ishmaelian curse – a hundred roubles, a thousand roubles, sold by peasants to whom he brought only good, sold by his own son, betrayed by his work colleague, by a 'true friend' – what an Ishmaelian curse! Is it upon this that the 'structure constant' of character is based, for it turns people against it willy-nilly, arousing in them malice and anger and umbrage, steering hearts in the end towards overt betrayal by means of some secret magnetism? *And he will be a wild man; his hand will be against every man, and every man's hand against him; and he shall dwell in the presence of his brethren.* Ishmael, man of Truth, abassy-man, living teslectric dynamo, divine murch battery. *Such toughguts may be sincerely admired and sincerely loved, but they cannot in any way be lived with.* Difficult to say even whether their fate is worse in Summer, where they can only flail about between half-false-hoods, or here, in Winter, in the land of the absolute. Either way, they are people not made for life, not made for life…

'Look, Mefody –'

'Your Lordship has to listen to me, escape without delay –'

'Well –'

A knock at the door.

Step out into the corridor.

The valet was helping Wielicki off with his furs and scarf. Wojsław removed his spectacles so as to lift Michasia and kiss her, whilst she, ready for bed, came toddling up at once to Papa, dragging behind her a rag bear by name of Mr Fuffluck.

'Benedykt…,' he began over his daughter's head as she squealed into his beard that his cheek and nose were impossibly cold to touch.

'You'll permit me a word, sir, this instant, it's very urgent.'

He passed Michasia to the nanny.

'I just wanted you to…,' he gasped. 'For just as I was leaving the firm, extraordinary rumours reached us, whilst you've been mingling again today in government circles – not so?'

'I have a man here who says Schultz-Zimovy was murdered an hour or two ago. And take heed, he's telling the truth.'

Wojsław stiffened. The ice in his copious beard hadn't yet had time to melt; it sparkled brightly against a distinct umbriance, ornamenting Wielicki's silence with silver.

'On the other hand, I know that somewhere along the way it got broken into falsehood, for the fellow also tells me in this truth of his that they want, take heed, to arrest me for this murder; yet today, I haven't even been anywhere near the Citadel, I've only just returned from Krupp's.'

'What are you saying, sir!' Wojsław gagged.

'I am asking if your manor house –'

'Wait! We must first make sure! Modest Pavlovitch –'

'I've already written to him. Kuzmentsoff's truth is almost Schultz's truth.'

Wielicki, lost in thought, was slowly pulling off his boots on the wooden bootjack.

'And these rumours – what are they?'

'Ah, completely different,' he replied. 'That Count Schultz's sudden dismissal had come from the Winter Palace and that Prince Blutsky-Osey is to establish a new order here with the Imperial regiments.'

'Damn.'

'The Tchornoye Siyaniye, Benedykt, there's a bit of the dreamslave in us all, taking a sign of truth for truth, an omen for necessity fulfilled.' He removed his second boot. 'In a moment I'll send Trifon, there's no reason to panic unduly. Do you have any objects in your room on which the Okhrana could pin a case?'

'No… I don't.'

'And this fellow of yours?'

'Mm-hmm, you're right.'

Return to Pyelka. Thank him judiciously, that is, without pressing diengi into his paw or proposing any other reward. He nodded but continued to stare somewhere off to the side, embarrassed by the shameful memory (which itself burns with shame). 'You must go now, Mefody, you'll serve me best this way.' 'But flee! Flee!' 'Certainly, I have no intention of going to the wall for a crime I didn't commit.'

Lead him out of the room. Shtchekelnikoff peered suspiciously. One hand was still concealed, no doubt on the hilt of the bayonet. Indicate to him to return the butchering tool to the hibernik.

'What was that knife for?' question Pyelka in the doorway.

'Was I to know if I'd make it? And what if they'd already taken Your Lordship –'

'You meant to throw yourself at the gendarmes with this.'

'Whatever came first to hand.'

'The way you rushed out, gave chase – means it wasn't you following me earlier today.'

'I? No, Your Lordship, not I.'

Beyond the threshold, he again had a change of heart and endeavoured to turn back, gripped again by violent unease: 'I shan't as walk away till Your Lordship leaves safely!' so that he had to be conducted downstairs to the gate and let out with the aid of the stickwielders onto Tsvetistaya Street under the exit lamp, into the wind; he was snatched away, swallowed by the snowstorm.

The domestic clocks chimed half-past eight. Consume a hot supper of thick sour soup and crispy onion bread. Old Mrs Wielicka was embroidering on a tambour frame by the fireplace, glancing up from the fabric every other moment with her harridan eye: half her wrinkled physiognomy in the flickering firelight, half – in shadow and umbriant glow. The scratchface tomcat was warming itself at her feet.

'But you haven't dragged our Wojsław into any bad company, have you, young man?' she squeaked sweetly.

'No, ma'am, I haven't.'

'Into any political brawls, eh?'

'No, ma'am, I haven't.'

'Dear Wojsław has such a kind heart...'

'Very kind.'

It was hard to comprehend how the old lady imagined such a truth whereby Mr Wielicki would be forcibly persuaded to do anything against his convictions, bah, against the welfare of his family. For that the persuader would indeed have to be a world-famous mesmerist! (Or Aleister Crowley.)

At five minutes to nine, an errand-boy banged on Wielicki's door with a missive from one of his firm's employees. Namely, a train full of troops, presumably from the regiments recalled from the Japanese front, had just pulled into the Muravyoff Station; the soldiers had been debarked at lightning speed and formed into detachments, into three long units. Wielicki responded with instructions to recruit additional people to protect his warehouses.

Sit in the drawing room by the naphtha lamps and fires burning in both stove and hearth, trying to intervene in a conversation which fell apart, however, again and again of its own accord; the mood of anticipation was shared by all. Sitting with Wielicki were his sister Marta and wife Halina; here beat the heart of the household. The servants brought coffee and biscuits (which Wielicki alone munched, making up for the others by the fistful).

Before half-past ten, Lawyer Kuzmentsoff arrived at Tsvetistaya. Gasping for breath, covered in snow, red from frost, black from murch, led by the hand by the Wielickis' famulus, he first had to make himself comfortable in an armchair and swallow one and then a second dram of slivovitz before he returned to full consciousness and to his voice – by which time everyone had had their nerves stretched again.

'Khhrrrm! Yes. Umph! It's not for old duffers like me to go gallivanting around at night in steely frosts. They nearly didn't let me out of the Box at all –'

'You've come from the Citadel?'

'Quite so; you see, Venyedikt Filipovitch, I read the dreadful news received from you sooner than the chief of the mayor's chancellery, who was due at my house for a game of mahjong –'

'But what's happened! Will you tell us at last!'

'Well, I am telling you! No? I am telling you!' So saying, he again gasped for breath, and only a third shot of slivovitz restored his voice. 'Brrr! Praise the Lord, for ye know neither the day nor the office! This evening, in his own study, whilst poring over gubernatorial papers, the unfortunate Timofey Makarovitch Schultz was stabbed with his own paper knife!'

The women shrieked and crossed themselves. A tray slipped from the hands of old Grzegorz – they shrieked a second time. The awakened cat scampered away over the tray, rattling the metal and meowing shrilly.

Wielicki lit his pipe.

'To hell with them all.'

Old Mrs Wielicka was almost overcome by convulsions.

'Mama should go to bed.' Wojsław threw the words at her without even as much as a glance. Drawing up a stool to the lawyer's armchair, he leaned his body towards the august old man as far as his own, no-less-monumental figure allowed. 'Who killed him?'

'Ah, some cesspit rabble, the Okhrana nabbed them immediately, there were two of them, apparently anarchists or nihilists or communists, but nothing more definite is known at present. Now they're huddled around the bed of the dying man – his personal physician, an army of prominent civilian and military doctors, even Chinese and Buryat quacks. Whilst tinpot soldiers-in-arms race up and down the corridors like madmen; before the night's out, they'll be firing in their feverish excitement at any shadow-cum-glintz and shooting one another, no? Shooting one another.'

'But tell us, Modest Pavlovitch, how did it happen?' question him tenaciously. 'Was there some kind of plot? Had the arrest warrants arrived? For such are the rumours reaching us. And also, about Schultz's dismissal by the emperor, supposed to have just landed on his desk.'

Kuzmentsoff stroked his silver beard, casting a sanguine glance.

'Well, yes, you speak true. An order has come from the emperor, which I heard about from those people as if I'd seen it with my own eyes. An order to "undertake all necessary actions with the aim of suppressing Schultz's rebellion".'

'What rebellion?!' Wielicki bridled.

'Prince Blutsky-Osey would never agree to any secret assassination…,' mutter neath the moustache. 'But Geist and Schembuch, all those okhranniks and tchinovniks who hate Winter…'

'You think those assassins were sent to the governor general by the Okhrana?'

'Modest Pavlovitch, tell us from your own mouth the truth about Count Schultz – what sort of man he is: would he surrender cap in hand, were he sure of the injustice and dark machinations behind the dismissal? Modest Pavlovitch! The Tchornoye Siyaniye hangs over us. And what's obvious now: could it have been any different for Count Schultz?

The lawyer touched his temple with his gnarled hand.

'He's a strong man, a righteous man.'

'You see! To dismiss a corpse is easier and less dangerous. Especially here, in Siberia, five thousand versts from the Imperial palace.'

'Against His Most Serene Majesty, Schultz would never –'

'But is His Most Serene Majesty able to ward off that fear?'

Lawyer Kuzmentsoff shook his head blankly.

From his armchair, Mr Wielicki indicated towards the table with his pipe.

'Listen, Benedykt' he whispered, 'if this is Okhrana provocation, then really, something may also lie in store for Poles. God only knows whom Colonel Geist has pointed out.'

'Am I to pack my bags?'

'At least for the initial days, you understand, till everything calms down; then Modest Pavlovitch will send formal letters and explain the matter officially – right now any tussle with the soldiers could earn a bullet to the head. Why provoke Fortune?'

'You don't seem to see it, sir, entirely clearly,' hiss more sharply than intended. 'Schultz was my protector, it was Schulz who gave me and my pater free passports, he who thought to use me against the gleissen; he who brought me here in the first place, for God's sake! After Schultz's death, I'm carrion amongst wolves.'

'You think that's where the rumour came from about the arrest warrant…?'

The valet entered.

'Director Pocięgło for Mr Gierosławski.'

Wielicki puffed on his pipe inquiringly. Throw up the hands: a surprise visit.

Porfiry Pocięgło had no wish to enter the drawing room. He barely crossed the threshold on the second floor. Removed neither shapka nor frostoglazes; it was as much as he did to unfasten his shuba and take off his gloves. With those gloves, he was nervously slapping the palm of his hand.

He shook hands swiftly, threw blood straight from the doorway:

'They've butchered the governor.'

'We know.'

'You know?' he breathed out. 'Well, so you know. For, you see, his dismissal had come –'

'We know.'

Buttery kaleidoscopes churned in his frostoglazes.

'Benedykt, sir, please say it wasn't your doing.'

'What?'

'Thank God!' Only now did he remove his spectacles, smile feebly. Under the sparrow-hawk brows, glintzen shone like drops of molten silver. His unshaven face was heavily encrusted with scabs and pimples, overgrown with fresh beard, as if he'd arrived straight from the frostiest Siberian wastes. 'I came to warn you, but since you already… Have you packed? I can take you in my sleigh. The route via Harbin, admittedly, is impossible at the moment, likewise the Transsib, they'll be checking every passenger individually, but somehow –'

'So, there is a warrant out for me!'

'Good gracious, Benedykt, they gained admittance on your letter of recommendation!'

'What?!'

'On your visiting card, on your own handwritten recommendation to Governor General Schultz!'

Lean against a wall. The mammoths were galloping past beneath the foundations of the house, everything was shaking, one second, two; still unable to catch the balance. Pocięgło summoned a servant; sit down on the proffered stool.

'Schembuch,' whisper as blood returned to the brain.

'Pardon?'

'Schembuch, Geist. That such an Irkutsk non-entity should dare against the Governor General...'

Mr Pocięgło was clearly disconcerted.

'That is not in truth how it appears, my dear Benedykt.'

Focus the gaze on his unlichted frostbitten countenance, on his eyes emitting an odd impression of mingled shame and joy.

'But he's still breathing, yes?' inquire gently.

He nodded.

'Three punctures, a lot of blood, everyone's praying, God willing, he'll survive.'

'And you too are praying, you Oblastniks, secessionists, praying more fervently than any.'

His eyes fled towards a lamp; he shifted his weight from foot to foot, knocking the permafrost off his boots.

'What is this,' shout at him dully, 'that you always come running with your shame, with your pangs of conscience and wish to make amends – *post factum* – when you've already brought all the mischief to a head! Then it's – friends! Then it's – pour balm on the wound! But first – the wound caused by your own hand.'

'Yet you know very well, sir, that the gentlemen's agreement between us is entirely sincere on my part: you shall talk the gleissen into Thaw, as discussed – Summer here, Winter in Europe – and I shall smuggle you safely to America.'

'Sincere. But from the very beginning, from the time of the Last Kopeck Club meeting, or even before it, already on your Siberian travels, you were working just as sincerely for the triumph of the Oblastnik idea by a totally different route. Conspiracies, yes! Conspiracies as predictable as a Swiss watch – in the one and only time and place on earth where they are really possible: here, under the Ice! No need to nod, sir,' level the finger at him, 'I can see!'

Begin *counting*.

'The success of Prince Blutsky's peace treaty. And therefore! An end to sea blockades. And therefore! The renewal of Siberia's trade with America, resurrection of the Russo-American Company, return to building the Alaskan Tunnel. And therefore! A dramatic fall in steel prices on stock markets across the Pacific. Panic in the mind of J.P. Morgan and ruthless instructions to his agents in Moscow and Saint Petersburg, millions in bribes. And therefore! And therefore! The calculation of Porfiry Pocięgło and his Oblastniks: not to torpedo Morgan's mission at all – but to help him instead, help him as far as possible, by blackening the governor general in the eyes of the tsar.

'The mathematics of character! Algorithmics of History! Thriller of the Ice! As certain as two and two make four, like the deductions of Sherlock Holmes! You know not Count Schultz personally, but you know the count's soletruth. What will Schultz do, wrongly accused of treason by the tsar and toppled from his Siberian throne, banished from the kingdom of coldiron?'

'It's a toss-up,' he muttered.

'So, a carambole. But equally calculable in either variant. Such is the man! Driven against a wall, pushed into falsehood, into injustice – will he yield? or will he proclaim the independence of Siberia? And the Oblastniks will triumph!

'Only you had not considered, Porfiry, that the tsar would also safeguard himself. Schembuch, hah! Schembuch, Geist, exactly! It was not against Schultz, but against the tsar himself that the game was played! His orders have thrown the Ministry of Winter and the Third Department here into an ice conspiracy, he has embroiled me in political murder.' Bare the teeth grimly. 'In Irkutskian intrigues between this tchinovnik and that tchnovnik, I could have pitted one man against another – but what can I do against the Emperor of All the Russias?'

Mr Pocięgło looked down his nose.

'You used to talk so much about History. Well, so now you've been kicked by speeding History. It hurts? It cannot not hurt. Everything else will soften into a delusory mist – History alone remains the hard reality. So don't moan again like in the train. You have touched the naked matter of History!'

'And I held you to be a man of character!'

He snorted ironically.

'You overestimate my cunning. No such conspiracy exists, no such slanderous intrigue by means of which I could cause Count Schultz here, under the Ice, to en-lie himself, that is, become someone he isn't. I am not able to fabricate Truth at will, to fashion Truth out of Untruth according to whim. Had the thing contradicted the shape of the count's soul, then Prince Blutsky-Osey would have been first to spot it and tell the tsar that the Truth is such that there is no treason in the character of Governor General Schultz-Zimovy, that his loyalty is stronger than his ambition, and he would never seize Siberia from His Most Serene Lord and Master. And with that it would have ended, and Schultz himself well knew it. Meanwhile what was he doing? Locking up hundreds of freethinkers for any hint of suspicion of secessionist ideas, ordering Cossacks to shoot at ordinary working folk, paying servile tributes to

Saint Petersburg at every opportunity, and throwing his own people insufficiently palatable to the autocrat forthwith into prison.'

Recall the scene at the Citadel and Schultz's maltreatment before Prince Blutsky of the colonel with the too-honest tongue. Indeed, the Mathematics of Character – for in what way did that game differ from the game with Ivan Petrukhoff at the ball in the governor's palace?

In the Kingdom of Ideas, the mathematician will be the most practical of men.

'I would not have lied to the Club,' Porfiry continued. 'The idea occurred only later, after the Americans' visit to Schultz, when he reacted with those sudden arrests… And I had to disappear from sight at once so as not to give myself away. Whatever we could, we dealt with on paper, by letter, via foreign messengers.'

'But when you were making arrangements with me – it was already like this then – the police – it was because of orders from Saint Petersburg, no? What did you do then? – did you own up to a treasonous Oblastnik plot under the secret command of the governor general? You were lying, sir, you must have been lying!'

'But I was genuinely counting on your pact with the gleissen! I am still counting on it. Without Thaw in Siberia… who knows how far the push for independence can succeed at all. You see, the whole idea depends on the impetus not coming from the Ice, since from the Ice no new revolutionary impetus can come – but from far beyond Winter, from America, from the New York stock markets, from Morgan and the Emperor of Japan. Carambole, you say. Yes. Billiard ball strikes billiard ball – in this hemisphere, in that hemisphere, knock-knock-knock, and no one sees the hand of the billiard player, only the unexpected all-embracing movement. This is how History is made.

'If only the Ice would relent here for a year, two years, enough for one change to bounce deeper off a second and third, before it freezes afresh.'

'Forget about Thaw!' Laugh grimly. 'There will be no negotiations. I shall be glad to escape with my own life. Everything's gone to pot. So much for the great designs! Master of intrigue indeed. Pish!'

'Are you sure that –'

'How can I be!'

'Maybe if –'

'That Thaw!' A circular glintz flashed on the wall behind Director Pocięgło. Leap up almost from the stool. 'But! For goodness's sake! Tryfon!'

Tryfon appeared.

'Your Esteemed Nobleness wishes…?'

'Put your top clothes on chop-chop and hurry to the Physical Observatory of the Imperial Academy of Sciences, to Doctor Tesla. Tell him the governor general is inciting rebellion against the emperor and Doctor Tesla must flee at once, whilst Schultz lies lifeless and bleeding to death. That it's Mr Gierosławski who says so. Understood?'

'Understood, Your Esteemed Nobleness, understood.'

'Only make sure no one overhears!'

Porfiry Pocięgło lit a cigarette.

'You fear, sir, that he may yet survive,' he muttered bitterly. 'You are praying for the defeat of a free Siberia. And yet now, only the United Free States of Siberia will save you from the noose! Have you forgotten? Should Schultz die, then the tsarist tchinovniks will adjudge you his joint murderer, our Nikolay Aleksandrovitch is already taking care of it.'

'Should Schultz die – this is only half the trouble: the provisional war government will fall into the hands of Prince Blutsky, that is, back into the hands of the tsar, and Doctor Tesla will receive all the more state assistance, and so you may even live to see Thaw, awakened by Tesla's machinery, who knows.'

'A fat lot of good it will do me then…!' he bristled.

'But should Schultz survive and hold on to power, what's the first thing he'll do, after having taken an open stand against His Highness Nikolay Aleksandrovitch? What is the one single cause which despite the emperor's fury could still win him Pobedonostseff as well as all mighty forces in the Land of the Gleissen?'

'Protect the coldiron riches against the war which the reckless tsar has declared on the gleissen!'

'He will have to understand that in the frozen History, he has no way of defending such revolutionary change for long.' Pocięgło smacked his lips as he blew out smoke. Transferred to his left hand, his gloves cast an image on the boiserie of a sunlit chandelier entangled in a dozen thick limbs. 'Separating Siberia from the Russian Empire without Thaw –'

'Porfiry, sir, Count Schultz-Zimovy does not believe in the Mathematics of History.'

He bit his lips, or rather scabs on his lips.

'You must, must talk to your father!'

In the Kingdom of Ideas, the mathematician will be the most practical of men – for the time being, however, it is not History, not apoliteia that rules Siberia, Russia and the world. The best plans, most deeply thought-through criminal chess-games and mathematical conspiracies – come to nothing, because truth has not yet been completely separated from lies; it is not Ishmaels alone who live here, and despite everything, the germ of entropy always somehow impinges. Matter has *not yet frozen.*

'Eh, devil take it, to flee or not to flee, what's the point…'

He squeezed the arm.

'Benedykt, sir, don't do this! Get a grip. I know it looks like the sky has fallen in on your head, but it's not the end. Were you not in worse straits? As when they threw you off the Transsib into Asia? What? Did you give up then? Don't do this!'

He proffered another cigarette, already lit. Grasp it with trembling hand.

'For since there's no way to rely here even on reason, on logical necessities…,' drag on the cigarette, 'what remains? To prophecy from blackwickes, from frost patterns? To stand neath the Black Aurora like a dreamslave?'

'I'll take you with me,' he repeated. 'I too must leave the city. I attract people's attention; we'll sit it out. I've made my excuses in the firm. Put your skates on! I shouldn't have come; please appreciate that I do somehow feel guilty, though I never had any ill intent. But I'm not hanging around any longer. Well! I promise no creature comforts – but at least you'll be safe!'

Safe!

Thrust aside the hand of Porfiry Pocięgło.

'Leave me alone now.'

Offended, he waved his gloves in the smoke.

'What is it now? What's made you so prickly? A veritable thorny dragon, I swear to God!'

Flick the unsmoked cigarette into his shuba. He stepped back instinctively.

'Just because I'm caught in a trap, must I sell my gratitude for a song?' Rise to the feet. Stand no taller than Pocięgło, but liberated at least from a posture of helplessness and despondency. Pocięgło took another step back. 'Friend!' snarl at him with venomous contempt. 'Confidant! Helping hand!'

The Oblastnik stared goggle-eyed.

'What the devil's got into you!'

'Well go now, go, and celebrate your Glorious Free State of Svobodoslaviye!'

He blinked as dense umbriance flowed over his cheek. Breathing out, he performed a blurry movement with his bare hand before his face, as if removing the sticky murch from his own breath.

'I understand.' He took stock. 'You will never forgive me for your having let her go like that.'

Ten o'clock struck. Walk to the bedroom, draw the blinds and place a lighted naphtha lamp on the windowsill overlooking the Angara, betwixt fabric and frostglaze. Extinguish other lamps in the room. The snowstorm had as though lost ferocity; more pinpoints of light were visible on the river, as the night sky flashed with purer shades of black.

A dark shape darted across the room and stole between the feet – the tomcat. Lift it up and return to the drawing room. The beastie clung to the shirt, rubbing its head against the shirtfront. Whatever had come over it now? Lay it down by the hearth beside the gently snoring old Wielicka. But it crept at once under the table, tracing a figure of eight around the table-legs and climbing onto the knees as soon as the body settled on a chair under the clock.

Till Maciuś chased it away, only to take its place, yawning, heavy with sleep, stretching and wriggling – but no, he would not go back to bed. All the children were awake, due maybe to the raised adult voices, maybe to the general hum and hubbub of constant movement, or maybe to the tension already pervading the whole household; an atmosphere anticipating terrible yet inevitable news had infected them by some less obvious means. Marta Wielicka, hurriedly swathing herself in shawls and scarves, dashed to the neighbours, to an old tchinovnik family living two buildings away; she returned with reports of equally vague disturbances. The neighbours were rifling through old documents stowed in escritoires and hiding their gold. Tell no one of the tidings brought by Director Pocięgło, of that letter of recommendation to the scaffold. Meanwhile, Mr Jusche had arrived with more unpleasant rumours, namely that Jewish bankers were packing their families and riches overnight, clearly intending to escape Irkutsk as soon as possible. Wojsław Wielicki, having placed his silver pince-nez on his nose, sat at a table drafting letter upon letter and sending them out with even the youngest messenger-boys to all corners of the city. The servants scurried back and forth across the drawing room with coffee, tchay, fruit liqueur, cakes or evening butterschnitten for the guest. Andrey Jusche marched up and down on the creaking parquet waving his long arms. What's a-brewing! What's a-brewing! Maybe it would be wiser to flee for a time, hide one's Jewish head from the authorities? What think you, Wojsław, sir, are you staying? Wielicki was writing letters; Michasia, curled on his lap, blew from under his arm at the ink-blackened sheets and slipped him clean pieces of paper, totally absorbed in her function as junior clerk. Jusche collared in turn Modest Pavlovitch. And you, wise man, what say you? For what are you waiting? Where ought you to be sitting on a night like this, well, presumably not here? Lawyer Kuzmentsoff gobblegrowled into his beard and cast a furtive glance at Mr Jusche from under his brow. Precisely here, he said, I shall wait to see whether the governor general gives up the ghost or survives and remains in power.

Old Mrs Wielicka awoke; with an embroidery thread draped over her arthritic finger like a string of rosary beads, she began reciting a timid prayer into the fire: '*Omnem spem et consolationem meam, omnes angustias et miserias meas...*' The large clock ticked above the head; numbers tapped in the thoughts. Sit in silence, stroking Macius's tangled crop of hair, and relish with bitter satisfaction – in noble awareness of the experienced betrayal – that no fear is felt, in fact, no trembling at every slammed door or patter of servants' feet, no tense anticipation of the gendarmes' imminent arrival. If they come, then they come; if they don't, then they don't. Thinking once more – this being one of those moments – of Julia. Julia, father – neither of these figures from memory could be imagined quaking with fear before an uncertain future. Defeat – then defeat; too bad, it's happened, now we're on our road to katorga, or we'll jump from a window. That which exists not – the past, the future – holds no sway over them. No one puts them to shame. They are not fearless – yet what do they fear most of all? Most likely themselves. Both were building great designs – for an independent Poland, for a comfortable life – which, through no fault of their own, have never materialised. (But whose fault was that?) The clock struck eleven. At midnight, the lamp in the window has to be replaced by a blackwicke. Maybe the Yapontchiks will notice the sign, maybe have time to organise the escape. Or maybe not.

'Will there be levolution?' Macius asks, having wriggled into a ball on the other knee. (He dreams of left-o-lution as a kind of Piegnarian dragon devouring people, roubles and toys, and begetting only dreamslaves.) Will it come today? Not revolution, no. That's a different fairy story, one about a king. A story, story, tell us a story, uncle! he clamours at once. And so, a story is told – about an old king, who, captured by enemies, resorts to forbidden magical knowledge and flees from earthly persecution to underground lands, to the Upside-Down World, wherein a Black Sun with broken rays freezes pastures of iron, over which mammoths gallop, and where spirits grow fat on the shadows of life, until they reap enough strength from them to break through to the world above amidst the sons and daughters of Flesh. The king, having descended amongst mammoths, surrenders his body to the earth. Dozens of sorcerers and powerful men had tried it and not survived; a king, however, is a king. But under the Black Sun, he grew colder and colder with every day and began to freeze more and more in those meadows of rusty metal; he grew a beard like an icicle, his blood turned to cold stone, his hair frosted over, his skin became like mirror. When he tried to return from the unlicht into the light of day he rose up only as a great towering glacier, slow and unwieldy, moving glacier-like over the surface of the earth – people flickered around him like dancing glow-worms or fireflies, skip-scamp and they're gone; and if he succeeded in touching one, it would fade at once and die, frozen solid; and whenever he tried to talk to anyone, all that came out of him was the roar of a Siberian snowstorm; and whenever he thought of taking revenge on his former foes, he no longer even felt like revenge, he was that cold. So, what was he to do? Was he to freeze with the mammoths to the end of time? Ah, but the king had a valiant son – who had been too small to help when the king was seized by his enemies, but now he came at his father's bidding and… And how will the prince save him? Will he descend himself to the Underground World? He too will freeze. He'll approach his icy father – but there's no way to touch him; the gruesome frost will kill him on the spot, congealing his warm impressionable flesh. So how is the prince to extract his father from the land of the mammoths?

'By giving back the treasure,' Maciuś declared emphatically.

'Treasure?'

'Something in return for something. Then the thortherers will let him go.'

'But there's no sorcerer casting a spell on the king. The king went into the Ice of his own accord.'

'He has to buy the secret from the thortherer!' insisted the maltchik.

'No, no, the king was born that way.'

'But didn't he lose something? A gold ring, a magic sword, ah, a little cross on a chain? He must've lost something!'

'But, Sir Maciej! He went with nothing at all, stark naked.'

'Stark naked?' the fidget-pot giggled and squirmed on the knees, and again onto the left shoulder. 'A naked king?'

'That's right.'

'So maybe, maybe, maybe give him what's needed? What he hasn't got. What hasn't the king got the most?'

'Lies.'

Half an hour to midnight and the dead are flexing their bones; it's silent outside the window, whilst the whole heated house on Tsvetistaya Street creaks as Mademoiselle Filipov hurries upstairs, along corridors and through rooms like a whirlwind steaming with unlighted breath, scattering twinkling sparklets of snow all around. Halina Wielicka barely managed to stop her for a moment, just long enough for Mademoiselle Filipov to throw off shapka and kaleidoscopic spectacles and breathe a couple of words of explanation on the run. Piotruś Paweł, safely concealed behind his mother's skirts, followed the feverish Yankee devushka with great staring eyes.

Stand up, putting down Maciuś from the knees. Christine smiled palely at him but wasted no time on courtesies and greetings, blurting out at once in French:

'Four o'clock, before dawn, by the statue of Tsar Aleksandr, pack now!'

'Who?'

'The Tunguses on your sleds.'

'Has the governor's Mr Uriah been?'

'No.'

The Wielickis and Mr Jusche and even old Kuzmentsoff were listening intently. Invite Mademoiselle Filipov into the private chamber. Pull the door to, kicking the tomcat away with the foot. Switch on the single standard lamp; glintzen on the wall faded and slunk behind the furniture or into cracks in the floor.

'And you, Christine? Having turned against the tsar, the governor general will dispose first and foremost of Doctor Tesla; you're staying there under guard of his Cossacks. Was he protecting you from Pobedonostseff? He was protecting you for himself! One command from the Citadel and finito. Flee! The Transsib is closed, but the Tunguses should be loyal to me –'

She pulled off her gloves and threw her fur coat vigorously into an armchair. Her cheeks were rosy from frost; crystal snowflakes glittered on her heavy plait. She pursed her lips.

'What's this I'm hearing, Benedykt? you were involved in a plot against the governor's life?!'

'Whence such rumours, miss –'

'Porfiry Pocięgło called on us just now. Despite your warnings, Nikola has no intention obviously of fleeing, and when Director Pocięgło burst in… But what an insolent, impertinent man! By the way, what did you tell him about me? I thought he was going to kidnap us by storm, no longer the managing director – but a complete savage. Men!' she snorted, not entirely convincingly, wagging the dainty hand raised to her breast, only to force herself back to her previous her train of thought. 'But – but whatever entered your head!'

'But it wasn't like that…'

'What? maybe once again, as in the Trans-Siberian Express, you've been dressed in lies by an alien hand, so much so you didn't even notice when – and yet the lie hangs on you so well it leads everyone around you astray?'

'No.' This was not possible, not in the Land of the Gleissen. 'No, Christine. I have no idea what Porfiry told you, but, you see, in one respect he is definitely wrong: *here truth is created*.' The recent purchases from Rappaport's lay beside the chest of drawers. Pull out the leather sac de voyage and felt carryalls and begin to pack. Start by chucking the entire contents of the wardrobe onto the bed. In the semi-darkness of the winter night, beneath pale glintzen and in the pale glow of naphtha, behind blinds drawn against the blizzard – separate material goods from material goods, like life from life. 'Not everything that will be truth one day was always truth formerly, Christine; not every proposition that is true now was true yesterday, nor was one that was true yesterday also true the day before. There are propositions that become truths at a particular moment, propositions that are made into truths, whose truthfulness is created. I… I have been freezing. I have frozen. And only now – only now am I convinced into what, into whom.'

'Into whom?'

Smile melancholically, now without any tensity, without nerves and without fear.

'You can see for yourself.'

Proceed to the other side of the bed, where a servant had placed the boots ready-greased and stretched; the devushka recoiled hastily.

'And so,' she sniffed, 'it is nevertheless true.'

'It is true that Count Schultz took a stand against the tsar in order to carve out a State of Siberia for himself? We know not. But is the tsar mistaken to punish him for treason? No! Because Count Schultz is *that kind of man*. Whatever happened or not – what is material truth, the truth of matter, when compared to the truth of the idea, to spiritual truth? That my plans have collapsed and I won't find father, won't bargain with gleissen – of what significance is it? I have frozen as the Son of Frost. Eleven days since I last pumped off murch. I am playing History. Composing the Algorithmics of History. Calculating against the tsar. Such is the truth, Mademoiselle.'

She sat down in the armchair, flopping onto the crookedly spread shuba, a little girl in the embrace of a shaggy beast. A memory returned – from beyond the Ice, and so a memory of a past neither true nor false – of the first conversation with her, of the meeting on a Urals mountainside under European and Asian sky, of her disarming concern for Doctor Tesla. How had Christine Filipov frozen in the Land of the Gleissen? The rosy-cheeked angel of shame – will she ever freeze? If only she'd not been jilted at the governor general's ball…

'I owe you an apology.'

She raised her head.

'For what?'

'For my whole behaviour. At the ball and –'

'But really –'

'I don't want you to remember me as –'

'As what?'

'As an arrogant man.' Kneeling beside her, smack a kiss on the back of her cold little hand. '*Je suis désolé, pardonnez-moi, je vous en prie.*'

'You really have stopped pumping.'

Gaze met gaze, the symmetry of fatal intimacy was arising; yet avert not the eyes.

'Yes. What's more, Christine, I *do not want* to pump.'

She smiled; in this was falsehood – and she withdrew the smile.

'Tell me, but from the heart: why did you let Jelena go?'

'How could I not let her go to the sanatorium!'

She pouted.

'You know what I mean.'

'Yes.' Sigh. 'I can't give you an answer.'

'You don't want to!'

Grasp her hand.

'No, Christine, I want to, I want to. But… It is only here, only to gleisseniks, to people of Winter, only to them and to the Ishmaels that certainty is granted, this geometrical consistency of soul. After all, I was systematically pumping off murch at the time, I was a child of fire. And we, people of Summer, we, what are we… Smoke, butterflies, rainbows.' Blow from the bloated cheeks, waving aside the exhaled air with the other hand. 'We do something or don't do something, and then for the rest of our lives, we go over and over it again in our mind, asking why we behaved precisely in that way.

'I'm letting her go, I know not why; not letting her go, I know not why; I let her go or don't let her go, either way without a reason that I could express to you. I'm fleeing Irkutsk, I know not why; not fleeing, I know not why; fleeing or not fleeing, I can't say. I'm looking for my father, why – I'll not utter in words; not looking for my father, why – I'll not utter in words; looking or not looking, equally a mystery. I will do something evil, and find no argument within me for or against; do something good, and find no argument within me for or against; evil or good, neither with grounds that could be expressed in arguments this way or that.'

'The perfect justification for every wickedness!'

'I'm not justifying myself. I'm taking responsibility.'

'Responsibility? What responsibility? You believe, sir, that you exist not!'

'That's exactly it!' Wave the hand again.

Indignant, she wrenched away her hand. Return to the packing. Christine sat half-curled in the dark shuba, half-covered by shadow and glintz, constantly rubbing her unwarmed palms. The cat had squeezed into the room despite everything; it brushed against the devushka's legs and leaped at once onto the bed. Slap it with the rolled-up shirts. It bared its claws.

'I don't understand how you can…' she went on, talking into the air.

'He exists not, and yet he continues to work like others, to converse, to live amongst people...'

'You don't understand, miss... yet I have lived, life has been lived, in this way ever since birth. What has changed? Only that an additional point of view has arisen,' indicate above the back of the neck, 'a point at the back of the head whence everything can be seen as it truly is, that is in all its non-existence.'

'I don't believe you. It's a kind of madness.'

'On the contrary: it's precisely the route out of madness. All of us in Summer succumb to this delusion, to this fraud of the speech of men, customs and conventions: that we exist. Whereas the truth is clear to us from the very beginning, at the very beginning – from birth, in childhood: we do not say "I" until our mother, nanny, family, forces us to. Thereafter, the lie accumulates in layers on top of the lie, habits reinforce habits, until eventually, we completely forget that a different speech may be possible, a language that hinges not on the falsehoods of men, is not taken from distorted reflections in a mirror – the language of truth, the language of what precedes the "I" and words uttered by the "I". It doesn't even occur to us to ask ourselves the question...! There is a movement of the hand, and an object is picked up' – pick up a parcel of books tied with string – 'and we say: "I picked it up". And so, it goes on – we view the body in silver reflections, in the mirrors of other people's eyes, we tell it in their tongues, which likewise come from outside; we cram ourselves full of the sensory perceptions and thoughts of matter – and so it grows – "I am", "I am", "I am".'

'But now you're saying that no one exists!'

'Maybe there are such people... who think they exist and do exist for real. Those who have frozen completely in their own soletruth. Crystallised living truth. Maybe. But we – or rather, what language takes as implied by the word "we" – have so gorged our fill on matter that we take the concatenation of what the body thinks and what it feels as ultimate proof of existence.

'You have heard perhaps of surgical experiments where doctors cut a madman's brain in half. A crony of mine, training to be a physician, told me about such procedures. Thwack, and instead of one – you have two madmen. Such is the unshakable basis of every truth, that any knife can slice it in two! You're trying to understand my "madness"? Well, so perform the Gedankenexperiment in reverse: an anti-thwack. One madman – zero madmen.'

'You're taking those books with you?'

'The ones I've not yet read. For what else remains for me to do in my exile?'

'Exile?'

'Christine, allow me at least to try!' exclaim in an undertone. 'With Shtchekelnikoff, with people from the Observatory, with Stepan, with the help of the Tunguses – we'll take care of it somehow. At most he'll receive a knock to the head and be dragged out unconscious – but you will save his life!'

'Leave it be,' she said quietly. 'You know what kind of man he is.'

Laugh under the moustache.

'Yes.' Stare at her attentively. 'Think you, Christine, that I shall escape at all from the city?'

'A fatalist?'

'No, it's simply that all my designs till now… Well, let's say the Tunguses keep me alive in some out-of-the-way village – for a month? two months? In Irkutsk, meanwhile, everything could turn topsy-turvy and back again and inside out. Outside of the Land of the Gleissen, I would equip myself with the wireless telegraph, but here…' Tip onto the blanket the items brought from Warsaw, the mathematical scribblings, the original of the Pilsudtchiks' deciphered missive, the unfinished letter to Julia, Fryderyk Weltz's pack of cards…

Straighten the back.

'When you left, Christine – was the Hammer striking?'

She opened her mouth and swallowed the obvious; murch clouded her eyes.

'Yes,' she replied.

Quickly shuffle the cards and, still shuffling, begin to lay them out on the bed in rows.

'Good. I'll write you down a procedure for the doctor. I know not how far the Hammer reaches along the Ways of the Mammoths, but whilst it still can, let it strike.'

Sit down at the table and scrawl a few sentences in Latin. Mademoiselle Filipov tucked the note away carefully. She frowned, watching the cards as they were picked up from the bed.

'A joke? You're laughing.'

'*Oh, c'est rien.* A present from a non-existent friend.' Shrug the shoulders. 'Tricks of the mind, Christine, I told you how we're deceived by the memory of horoscopes fulfilled. You read a thousand horoscopes; you remember the one that comes true.' Shake the little box containing the Piatnik pack. 'A prophecy!' Snort sarcastically. 'Gift of fate!'

Dancing, bullets for the Grossmeister, cards from the hands of widow Weltz – they attract notice, for the contradictions between past and past can easily be shown, all in a single memory; but how many such details (or not even details as highly crucial events), originating from outside of frozen History, impersonate Truth totally unobserved? From outside of Winter, from outside the of Ice – Warsaw? Wilkówka?

father, mother? Bronek, Emilka, Julia? Was it? Or was it not? Either way, it's all lies.

Happy those begotten in the Land of the Gleissen! They don't have to remember, don't have to know truth – *they are the truth*. People say: 'it has frozen'. But who says it? Born gleisseniks won't know such a saying. At most: 'it has melted'.

Midnight struck. Remember the lamp and the blackwicke – is it worth it? Something flickered in the door slit – Maciuś was spying, his nose stuck to the frame. Shake the finger at him. Pad-pad-pad, he trotted away.

Light the blackwicke, set it on the windowsill in place of the lamp; after the curtains were drawn, it grew brighter in the bedchamber.

In a flash, Mademoiselle Christine grasped also this obvious thing.

'Who is it this time?'

'Piłsudski's Yapontchiks. I had an agreement with them to get you out safely. Did I not tell you, miss?'

'You really have frozen into it all along with your boots.'

'Bah! But if they should however –'

'I can't do it, Benedykt, you're the mathematician.' She slipped her arms into the shuba and rose to her feet. 'I must return to Nikola. You won't dream up some other stupidity, will you, as soon as I'm gone?'

Point to the luggage.

'It has frozen. Four o'clock by the statue of Emperor Aleksandr.'

'Good. For I was beginning to think you had no intention of saving yourself,' she sighed.

After that, there followed three short footfalls and a quick peck on the unshaven cheek.

'What was that for?' ask in amazement.

'My present! For your birthday! Benedykt!' she cried from the threshold and beyond the threshold, already swirling in a whirlwind of dark fur and bright plait, flying hurriedly back the way she'd come through rooms, down corridors and staircases, through the creaking house.

The valet carried the luggage to the hallway. (Six bundles in total and a suitcase – the acquisition of bourgeois goods here was plain to see.) Shtchekelnikoff was already asleep; the bonebreakers had woken him. He emerged sullen like a hangman hungover. Invite him aside and explain in simple words what and how.

'Meaning it were you, sir, as ordered the shanking of the governor.'

Confirm it not. Deny it not.

'Aha.' He nodded. 'All right. All right.'

He could equally well have whacked his bearlike chest with a mighty fist and roared: 'It has frozen!' And so, there was no need at all for the

Black Aurora in the sky, no need for dense murch between man and man; still less to dress things up in the awkward words of the language of the second kind, to search for metaphors, similes. You look and just know. Grasp in that moment, for the first time, the entire soletruth without any complex operations in the Mathematics of Character, through animal instinct alone – through a nose for truth – which people of the likes of Doctor Myśliwski or one-eyed Yerofey exploit ́ here with such ease. It comes as no surprise that the Martsynian responded to the desperate questions yelled above the empty grave with silence and symbolic gesture. For what can be explained here? That one man thinks truth is such, and another – something completely different? This is as much as can be comprehended by the child of Summer: a mere divergence of opinions. And yet – this is obvious – the truth is one, as hard as diamond, as certain as – as two and two make four.

It was only the Kotarbiński pump that had confused everything, overturned it, darkened it, split it into lies.

'The emperor.'

'The emperor. Well, a fine kettle of fish.' Shtchekelnikoff glanced with his saurian eye. 'I already said, time to go, Mr G.'

'Time.'

'So, what'll it be?'

'Four o'clock, the boulevard by the Angara.'

He extended his square paw; squeeze it firmly.

'No point in tempting the devil any longer.'

He went to harness the sleigh.

Just know: Tchingis Shtchekelnikoff.

Return upstairs to bid farewell to the Wielickis. Mr Jusche had taken his leave in the meantime and gone to panic in the company of another household; Marta too had slipped out again somewhere. Piotruś had fallen asleep in Wojsław's arms, half-suspended over his father's powerful shoulder, fingers interwoven in his beard. Wojsław rose to say goodbye without waking the little boy, with the child thus clinging to his chest; uttering no word, he held out his hand. Piotruś stirred in his sleep as Wielicki's right hand was shaken; stirred, moaned and put his thumb in his mouth. Maciuś and Michasia were watching instead from under the table, through large loops in the lace tablecloth.

Halina Wielicka brought warm freshly baked rolls from the kitchen wrapped in sweet-scented linen. Thank her softly, kiss her hands coated in flour. Impulsively, she drew the body to her in a heartfelt embrace; press the bent head into her bosom. Emotion welled in the throat, whetting the larynx and moistening the eyes. The unfrozen past flashed in the mind: Princess Blutskaya in the Trans-Siberian Express, all those former emotions.

'Still after your father?' whispered Halina. 'Why not go in search of mother instead?'

'I'm so sorry.' Clear the throat. 'I ought not to have endangered you and the children. I know… I'm not made for such a family, such a home. You've been too kind to me. Nothing better has ever – only –'

'Yes, yes, yes.'

Just know: Mrs Halina Wielicka.

She gave her blessing with a sign of the cross drawn on forehead and chest. Turn quickly towards the door with the warm package under-arm. Old Grzegorz handed the shuba, shapka, scarves. Pad-pad-pad behind the back. Peer through the frostoglazes. Maciuś and Michasia were standing in the doorway, round-eyed, the corners of their mouths turned down.

'Uncle will be back,' assure them, pulling on the gloves. 'He'll be back, he'll be back.'

But these were children of Winter, born gleisseniks. They turned away from the lie and fled in tears.

Shtchekelnikoff extinguished the lamps on the sleigh. The blizzard had completely subsided. Even the wind had blown away somewhere off the streets of Irkutsk, for huge snowdrifts and vast inclines of compact-ed brash-ice now loomed two storeys high neath the rainbow glow of frostoglaze lanterns like immovable monuments, like waves of a tumul-tuous ocean suddenly stilled in half-convulsion; and even the colours, greenish-blueish marine colours, assumed by that whole City of Ice nightscape neath its fresh coating of snow, were befitting. Immovable, yes, and silent too; the city was impossibly, inhumanly silent when traversed in the horse-drawn troika with Shtchekelnikoff at the helm wielding his whip, and the Grossmeister unsheathed in the coat pocket and clutched through a glove. Glance back at the celadon-hued vista of Tsvetistaya Street, lined with geometrical glintzen flashing off the buildings. Not a living soul nor living movement. 'Where to?' inquire into Tchingis's back, as the words resounded neath the star-studded sky like a groan echoing through a tserkoff. 'To the statue already?' 'Three hours, Mr G., we has to bide our time.' 'At this time of night? Where?' 'Where none'll be coming for ya, in the haunt of old murderers.'

The cutthroats' basement tavern was situated immediately on the far, Uysky side of the Angara, yet in truth there was no way of ascer-taining whether it really was the opposite bank or still the frozen river, where low-ceilinged cellars had been hewn directly out of the ice under the coal warehouses, and where vagabonds and homeless bandits of the blackest ilk whiled away cheerless nights over the vilest, cheapest vodka. Descend a crooked staircase chiselled out of the permafrost. The walls glowed with a dirty pearly sheen; here, in these walls, as well as in the ceiling, the Tchornoye Siyaniye had painted hypnotic forms resembling black-and-white seals, walruses, whales, wallowing in ice. More than one felon, drunk to the core, had glimpsed in that place a manifestation of the mammoths and thrown himself after them in his trance, smashing walls with bench or bottle, head or fist, stabbing them with knives or even firing from revolvers. Ice would freeze over them and unfreeze and refreeze. Here, Shtchekelnikoff pointed to a red trace from the gob of the Bilethirsty Swede, here – the bullet of Ivan Grigoryevitch Kut, also known as the Whorescraper, since he mobs and robs street girls in order to scrape together money for his ticket to Golden California; here – a strip of skin from the cheek of Jamjar Lipko; and here – my tooth. Tchingis rolled back his lip to reveal one of the picturesque hollows between his teeth. Grunt in appreciation. He called for vodka. The dive's owner rose from his pallet, opened the armoured strongbox and took out a bottle of half-frozen bootleg. Stuck in the belt of his Cossack shinel was a hatchet half an arshin in length. 'The door freezes,' explained Shtchekelnikoff and tore out the cork with jagged teeth.

Sip with caution. Having unhooked the fur coat, glance at the watch. Seventeen minutes past one. What to talk about for two and a half hours on a winter's night with a notorious criminal in a murderers' drinking-den?

Foul-smelling vapour hung in the air, the sort of mist exuded by damp walls and unwashed bodies. Breathe through the mask of the scarf. Remove only the oculars. Shadowy indistinct shapes floated in the mist and within the pearly walls.

'The Yapontchik you butchered the other day, outside Horczyński's –'

'Yeh?'

'I've gone round and round in my head wondering why you did it.' Laugh into the beard and tightly coiled scarf. 'And what Wielicki hired you for, and how much he paid.'

'You didn't see clearly.'

'No,' shake the head, 'I didn't see.'

He emptied his glass.

'A wonder them wolves ain't gobbled you up long ago, such a victim of his own naivety, you'll pardon the expression.'

'You felt sorry for me.'

'When an old un takes pity on a young un, the young don't forgive the old. Oh, that Jamjar Lipko once sheltered a famished half-savage from the frost, took him under his own roof, fed him without stint, led him around the city under his wing. Everyone saw, only not Lipko; they told him: leave that damn native alone, he can't even look ya straight in the eye. But Lipko were a stubborn sort. And so, one night, the savage stabbed Lipko to death and fled back into the taiga to his hunger.'

'Such a character.'

'Yep, such a character.'

Another shot of vodka.

'But you's a different specimen, Mr G.'

'Am I?'

Tchingis hunched over the tabletop, leering confidentially, like in some assassins' plot.

'A noble cad, that's what!'

'You don't say.'

'Listen, him as has survived is wiser because of it by divine decree than all them motherfuckers tucked up in their graves!' He puffed out unlicht. 'Truth is: seen one son of a bitch, seen 'em all.'

'I used to trudge them northern trails neath Sibirkhozheto's or not Sibirkhozheto's flag, under those commanders, these commanders, but one late spring I had this young un thrust on me, fresh from his European schools, a pale scraggy smooth-cheek, appointed as our chief surveyor. Well, so we sets off with our Mr Surveyor. At once, it's clear the maltchik's of thinner blood, superior blood, eh, noble. We all had fun at his expense, for he had no clue of the simplest Siberian things and no obedience amongst the men, and even went off to shit somewhere out of sight, he were that ashamed. He were also a man of few words, he'd start stuttering at once and then not speak for days; the most he could stammer was a few numbers between his teeth. Well, in this way we reached near Yakutsk, with two poor buggers severely frostbitten and half our stags devoured by wolves; we was meant to meet up there with the company's main expedition. Well, the camp, true, is standing, but utterly plundered, and our men left shot in the snow, buried already under fresh falls, as good as chewed to bits. Vagabonds had raided earlier. But it's still upward of two hundred versts to Yakutsk, and here scarcely a dribble of spiritus and hardly any grub; our animals keep lying down, and a new storm's on its way. Our chief guide saw what were afoot and merely spat; that were as much as we saw of him and our best three reindeer. Oho, methinks, it's curtains for Shtchekelnikoff. Meanwhile, our young surveyor pulls out his Nagant, aims at the younger guide, and says to us: he shall lead me to the city, we'll take one sled, you slaughter the last weak stag and weather the storm here with the rest of the equipment, and I shall find you again and bring help. And he took the sled and went. And a week later he returned with supplies and so rescued us all.'

'Well and?'

Shtchekelnikoff shot a glance.

'Nothing. Seen one son of a bitch, seen 'em all.'

'Pshaw! Tales of Siberian heroes to lift the spirits!'

He wagged his begloved finger. Bare the teeth behind the scarf.

'But what greater honour for a den of prestupniks and artisans,' he continued, 'cos any cardsharp, smuggler, receiver of stolen goods, bandit, revolutionary could've drunk here, but never the killer of a governor general and personal enemy of Batyushka Tsar!'

For one way or another, an unrealised action is truer than a realised. Unimportant is what you happen to have changed in the order of matter – arm, leg, arm, leg, arm, leg, until thou art laid in earth – important is the kind of man you've frozen as. In what do you reveal yourself the more: in the truth of matter or in its falsity, which reflects the truth of spirit?

Raise the glass.

'To our enemies!'

'To our enemies! May devils grease their arses!'

Hurl the glass at the wall. Shards gnawed into the permafrost. Ice will grow over them; they'll merge into the black-and-white backdrop as an eternal souvenir. Oh, behold: the vodka of the Son of Frost.

The Tunguses showed up by the statue of Aleksandr the Third well ahead of the appointed hour. Arrive there at a quarter to four. They were already waiting beside their long heavy-laden sled harnessed to four reindeer. The low sled, with its wide pliable runners and centre of gravity straining towards the ground, was destined not for the roads of Irkutsk but the wastes beyond Baikal. Gather from the hurried patter of Tigry Etmatoff and his two kinsmen that they had not driven from the Observatory without trouble, which had ended in some sort of fisticuffs. With whom had they come to blows? Tesla? Schultz's Cossacks? the tsar's troops sent by Prince Blutsky? Glintzen sparkled in sharp and wondrous elongated forms. In his military uniform, sword by his side, Tsar Aleksandr towered on his pedestal in soldierly pose above a massive sculpture of the double-headed eagle, poised to swoop on its prey below. Etmatoff was jumping up and down on the spot, highly excited. Raise the head, but the statue's countenance was no longer visible.

Fog in the meantime had clouded the city like leucoma an old man's eye. The famous forty-degree frost was dropping lower still, nearer even to minus seventy maybe at this hour of the night. The larynxes of the Tunguses, who were swaddled in skins and furs and rags with the narrowest of slits for eyes, swiftly froze as they passed from coughing to husky wheezing to watchful silence. Their steaming animals exuded angular clouds of shadow. Snow crunched underfoot like trampled glass, resoundingly clear in that empty, iridescent white infinity. Fog – the densest sour cream, milk-jelly fog – was sealing off squares, boulevards, prospects, as high as the rooftops of the tallest residential buildings. Even the spine of a gleiss freezing its way nearby along the Angara towards Konny Island was invisible. The Buryat glashatays had evidently also gone to ground, since the pulse of their shaman drums no longer ruffled the misty silence. Only kaleidoscopic floods of colour emanating from the frostoglaze streetlamps – and charcoal symphonies from the celestial organ-pipes of the Black Aurora – seeped through the fog.

Instruct the Tunguses in sign language to first drive safely out of town and then take charge of the redistribution and reloading of the luggage. '*Ila*?' Tigry croaked, and his voice went hoarse for good; wheezing, he waved his short arms in all directions, stirring up the shadows fluttering in the monumental glintz of Aleksandr the Third. Understand that he was asking where to drive outside of the city. Stand up in the sleigh behind Shtchekelnikoff and survey the nocturnal whiteness. For the truth was… truth was…

The fog held back their sounds till they'd ridden into the square itself and then released all at once: hooves on the snow, jingle-jangle of harnesses, click of gun mechanisms, animals' rasping breath and clipped military commands. Without pausing for thought, Shtchekelnikoff struck the middle horse of the troika, and the sleigh lurched forward. Thrown onto the luggage packs, scramble up from under the soft bundles and catch sight from above the sleigh-back of the silhouettes of half a dozen riders looming out of the rainbow fog like ghosts spat from a pit of nightmarish vapour. For the same colours flowed through fog and through snow, over horses and over soldiers, except they were seeping into and leaking out of their concrete outlines considerably faster. But this was no quick, pounding military charge; everything moved as if curiously compacted, as if in slow motion, like – like – like the shadows of the mammoths in the walls of the murderers' riverside den. Perhaps it wasn't such a good idea to have drunk vodka with Tchingis… Cling for dear life to the rocking sleigh. Shtchekelnikoff lashed the horses with his whip. Fog-coloured hussars were advancing through the nocturnal stillness at almost a walking pace; in front rode a tall officer, his drawn sabre shimmering. Recognise him despite his scarf-bound face, wound so tight that not even a moustache-tip poked out; recognise him from his shadow and glintz, obvious.

Two riders broke away, chasing the Tunguses' sled, which had swung in the meantime from Glavnaya Street onto Uritskovo. The soldiers were yelling at the natives to stop, their voices quickly swallowed by the fog. Captain Frett did not yell. The rainbow-coloured silhouettes of the hussars grew larger every second. One of them jerked his mount and stood up in the stirrups – a streetlamp illuminated a thickset, clumsy hollow-man with gun-barrel jutting from his forehead, more like one of Piegnar's goylems. Hold the breath, but no shot rang out. The soldier put aside his rifle and unsheathed his sabre. They all unsheathed their sabres – the Baikal hussars, ice hussars, entering the charge slashing and trampling, since the extreme cold jams the locks on their firearms. Shtchekelnikoff cracked his whip. To no avail, they'll be upon him in no time. Shooting – meaning out to kill on the spot. Captian Frett had taken the prince's orders as if they'd come from the holy tsar himself, and would carry them out to the letter; and it was no secret what truth Prince Blutsky-Osey had learned about Benedykt Gierosławski. A therefore B, therefore C, therefore D. Jump up to Tchingis, point to the left – he swerved off the boulevard onto an intersecting street running east. Bail out of the sleigh into a snowdrift immediately after the corner.

No time to get up and run away. Lie in deep snow where the body landed; the drift caved in at once and collapsed, burying everything, head included. Wrapped tightly in the shuba and scarf, feel nothing, not even the intensifying chill. Hear the gallop of four horses as if through a mantle of wax and featherdown; six breaths, and it sank into the fog. Count another twenty breaths and start to dig a way out of the rampart of snow.

Upright on the feet, retreat at once neath the wall of a residential house. Grasp only then that flight won't succeed – that there's no possibility of losing the pursuers on the streets of the City of Ice – since the past had been seen, that is, non-being had been seen. For in the kaleidoscopic, sour cream, heavily frozen fog, every movement, every transposed object left behind tunnels of non-fog, empty voids where fog had once been, sharp corridors carved out as though with a knife, composed of all the object's former existences. Retreating from the snowdrift to the wall, draw a streak of non-being the height and width of a man: the clearly existing contours of non-existence. Wave a hand. The waving hung, hangs and will continue to hang in the fog – until wind returns to Irkutsk from over Baikal, in other words until dawn.

How to flee when the past trails behind you like the negative of every bygone moment? After the hussars also were left huge covered corridors of non-fog, chiselled-out voids down the middle of the street, veering beyond the corner onto the embankment boulevard.

Enter thus into the horse-voids, the non-horses, and trot back inside them towards the statue of Aleksandr the Third.

Made to slow, however, after only a few steps to a hobbling walk – as every faster inhalation slashes throat and lungs to shreds. You won't conquer the frost: in the Land of the Gleissen, you measure temperature by the way people walk down the street (and whether they walk down the street at all). It rules out any vigorous movement that forces the body into sudden spurts; the clothing itself – thick, multi-layered and limb-constraining – makes any unencumbered step impossible. You sway from foot to foot like a rag doll stuffed to bursting, indeed like a straw-packed hollow-man. So now be a clever dick and try running like this!

Lean against the statue's pedestal. Here, entangled non-being was penetrating the present most powerfully. Non-sleighs, non-horses, non-people were being scattered to the four corners of the past: a moment that had frozen. Breathing slowly, steadily, extract the Grossmeister and unwind the last rag from the reptile-gun. Under the Black Aurora, it shone with the radiance of a holy icon. Listen out for the sound of sleighbells, hoof-beats on glass, human voices. Nothing. Hrrr-khrr, hrrr-khrr, hrr-khrr, only one sound of breathing. Squeeze tight the rimy eyelids. How did they get here, for crying out loud?! On departure from Tsvetistaya, the fog had not yet sealed the streets, so Frett could not have followed the non-being of Shtchekelnikoff's sleigh. When had Frett been unleashed on the city? – an hour ago, two? Did it mean Schultz had finally given up the ghost? Certainly, the captain had clear-cut orders from the prince: kill as soon as possible – it has frozen. Frett took his men and went… He never would have killed in front of the Wielickis; he'd have driven out of town. Did Kuzmentsoff or the Wielickis overhear Christine's words – when she gave the time and place of the rendezvous? No, no, they were no traitors – that too has frozen. So, what did Frett do? Three places where Benedykt Gierosławski might be found: Tsvetistaya Street seventeen, the Physical Observatory of the Imperial Academy of Sciences and Krupp's Cryophysics Laboratory in Zimny Nikolayevsk. So, what did he do? – well, he rode to the Observatory. Did the governor general's Cossacks admit him? Tesla would not have betrayed Gierosławski either. But – Engineer Jago! D therefore E, therefore F. And then it sufficed to pursue the Tunguses' non-existent sled. But the Tunguses had had a premonition – the Tchornoye Siyaniye was in the sky – they *saw* danger. *See* it too, in the glintz of Tsar Aleksandr the Third. And how did Frett know until what hour to wait, and when to charge out of the fog? Had an inadvertent sound given it away? A shout not in Buryat? No, Frett also *saw*. That certitude of soletruth, that necessity like logical compulsion, mesmerising under the Black Auroras, that obviousness of rational epiphanies experienced already on Old Zima Station… Bright outlines of mammoths flowing from a charcoal sun in the rainbow-hued soup of non-being. It has frozen.

Tshrrtook-twook, hooves on crusty shuga. Hide behind the pedestal.

Out of the fog came a saddled horse, riderless, with a shred of greatcoat caught in a stirrup, reins trailing on the ground. Limping, it turned onto Glavnaya Street and melted into the black rainbows. Tshrrtook-twook.

Think, think! (But cold has benumbed the brain.) Think, damn it! (Erk, now you're panicking!) Think! – what rescue here? Raise the head. No sickle Moon, no stars, nothing in the sky except kaleidoscopic fog and columns of unlicht. The Kingdom of Darkness is unfolding over the City of Ice. From the lofty heights of his hydraulic throne at the summit of the Sibirkhozheto Tower, Aleksandr Aleksandrovitch Pobedonostseff is reading cartographic omens from the foggy shapes beneath the Black Auroras –

Khhrr! Only he!

But which way to go? Wisest, true, would be to start moving inside the hussars' non-being, inside the hole hewn in present-time by past hussars, that is, by the ones who no longer exist – like that riderless horse – uphill along Glavnaya. Scramble out from behind the statue, stomp through the grainy firn; it burst underboot with the roar of a fairground firecracker. Walk with the head lowered, shoulders swinging from the momentum, legs scarcely bent at the knee. Twoopp-trwoop, twoop-trrookr. The Grossmeister shone in the gloved hand.

Irkutsk stood silent like a dream of Irkutsk. Shadowy phantoms of houses drifted from left and right. In fog, perspective breaks down rapidly: the buildings appeared to loom a good fifty to sixty arshins farther away, gigantic instead beyond the work of any human hand. In fog too, every impulse rapidly swells in the famished senses to the level of alarm. Wheel around in all directions and jump at every step, not from faint heart or schoolgirl nerves, but because even the slightest movement or minutest sound pierces the brain so powerfully. Any shadow, any flicker of a streetlamp, any crack of the expanding ice. Wander through the Irkutsk of nocturnal fogs as through the shaman's smoke; in the smoke float oily abassylar.

A shadow ahead – mammoth – dragon – Piegnar's freshest freak; leap clear of the corridor of non-fog. It was the riderless horse, the same horse with the shred of greatcoat in its stirrup, returning now along the path of its own non-being. Breathe in and out. The scarf had frozen to the beard and moustache thanks to moist breath mist; it couldn't be adjusted without ripping new growth out of the skin.

On, on, after the non-hussars. Frost was already cutting through the unty-boots and under the hare-skin wraps. No point in hastening the step; need to maintain a steady rhythm. Twoopp-trwoop. Think of that lonely race through night-time Yekaterinburg. Think of Shtchekelnikoff and the Tunguses – what had become of them? Think of Jelena Muklanowicz; it was painful to smile neath that cocoon of solid ice. Icicles stabbed the lungs like stilettos. The tunnel of non-fog veered to the right, towards the shadows of buildings. Light from a streetlamp blossomed gloriously in the milky suspension. The non-hussars are marching up and down by the wall. Advance one more step and catch sight, in the dazzling iridescent glow, of the armoured spidery massif of a gleiss sprawled across the middle of the street. Perpendicular waves of frost stood between it and the wall. For an hour already? Two? It was enough. There was no going round that way; another route, another street had to be found... Comprehend at last that the Sibirkhozheto Tower could not be reached on foot in fifty-degree frost. Breathe in and out for a second time. Hoarfrost was taking root between the teeth.

The gleiss was freezing over stalagmites and a web of black strings reaching as high as the second floor. Windows were dark. Drums of the shaman glashatays were not beating. Doors on both sides of the street were surely well secured (the criminal profession of hibernik-plunderer was rife in the cities of Winter). Glance at the icer for the last time. It was either coming up from under the ground or descending below – half its mass, its north-facing left half, rested directly on the glazed cobblestones. Whereas here, above the non-hussars, the glacius had splintered into a corona of a thousand fine and finer-still icespikes stretching high into the fog, far into the sky, as well as towards façades of buildings and streetlamps (those that were still functioning). Kaleidoscopes of cold colour danced on its vast shapeless body, spilling over its ovoid surfaces, as if some glacial pigment and not just an illusory reflection really were circulating within its crystal organism along with its helium blood.

Warning came from behind the back, from the glintz spreading its wings over the massif of the icer, from the light-play flashing on that pigment. Look back, half-rotating the body to that end. He was approaching with sabre already raised – the frostoglaze blade gleamed with all seven colours of the rainbow – leaning forward from behind his horse's head for slick clean slaughter, visage uncovered, black scarf streaming out behind his collar, frozen moustache tucked under goggle lenses bespattered with white, mouth wide open – out of which oozed an oily cloud of unlicht. On his jaw he had a gaping, bloody wound. The red of this blood was dripping onto his greatcoat – the grey-brown of which was seeping into horse hair – the blackness of which was flowing onto the ice – the whiteness of which was exploding into fog – the blue-green tints of which were sucked in by the blinding refulgence of the Grossmeister, as it was raised and aimed with straightened arm at the middle of Captain Frett's broad chest.

He tugged at the reins, tossed to the left in his saddle. His mount wheeled around obediently but seemed to trip or slide on the freshly encrusted paw or root or vein of the gleiss, as its front legs suddenly gave way beneath it, and it flew – a wild billowing coil of man and beast – catapulted into a snowdrift on the pavement, miraculously avoiding a streetlamp. The harrowing squeal of the horse pierced the fog. A cloud of jet-black snow rose from the spot where it fell. Stand and stare at the cloud, transfixed, spellbound, like a little child. Several long breaths passed before it began to drop to earth; hardening frost from the gleiss seeming to freeze the flakes already in mid-air.

On the following breath, the unhorsed Captain Frett stepped out of the cloud, now without shapka and goggles but still with that same rainbow sabre-scythe in his grip. Blackness washed over him where crystallised snow had previously clung. His moustache jutted out like a blood-stained wisp of icicle, steaming with blood.

A friend to whom you owe your life – thus it has frozen – and a foe come to rob you of it – thus it has frozen: what more can be said in such situations? And here too, here too, no room is left for a word in the language of the second kind; no place even for shame. There is only what's necessary, only what's obvious.

Captain Frett blinked, spat out unlichted snow, began to whirl the gleaming blade away from his chest, and darted beneath the glintz of the glacius. Fire at the hussar's belly. Ice tore him limb from limb.

Fall flat on the frozen ground, slide over crystalline cobbles. Too close! Curtains of inhuman frost closed overhead. The night crumpled and sagged as if suddenly viewed through warped glass. Something too had gone wrong with the hearing: a loud pop and then silence, though not silence as lack of sound, but silence as lack of any sense responsive to sound. Something had gone wrong with every thread of the senses connecting spirit and body: snapped or got so muddled that little or nothing penetrated to the spirit side. Lying supine on an Irkutsk street yet feeling nothing under back and shoulders, not even the clothes, not even that down there is a 'below' and up here, before the eyes, an 'above'. No feeling of external movement and no feeling of internal movement. No feeling of breathing. No feeling of time slipping by. The night came in waves, trapped within a sealed loop: a moment and another moment and another moment.

To get up. Whence this impulse? The body began to perform clumsy hollow-man gestures. Perceive a light blazing from the clenched right hand. The Grossmeister. No feeling in this hand, nor for that matter in the other.

All sense of direction was lost in the coloured fog. Stand up, turn around so as to venture a step across the ice, and only then see the massive, glistening black body of the gleiss – icicle, stalagmite, string, vein, medusa, belly – see it close at arm's length, half an arshin away. Curtains of frost fluttering like butterfly wings.

This white sweat trickling down the side of the glacius – is liquefied air.

This shadow neath the skin of the glacius – is helium moving spontaneously at a temperature where nothing moves.

This ice – is Truth materialised, matter cooled to below zero Kelvin.

Straighten the arm. It's enough to put a hand to an icicle.

Think of Mr Korzyński's finger.

Think of the finger, of the encoded letter from that other past, of all those dance routines impossible to know, of Nikola Tesla's resurrection, of different pasts not yet frozen. There are things that are made into truths, whose truthfulness is created.

Think that whatever way you look at it, death is inevitable: no organism of Summer can stand under a gleiss and survive.

The night was crumpling and sagging.

The Tchornoye Siyaniye was projecting huge glintzen from out of the glacius, beautiful and mesmerising.

Nestle close to the gleiss.

… Captain Frett, shot through and spattered in a star-shape of surgical icicles, was hanging suspended above the street, frozen into dozens of larger and hundreds of smaller pieces. The star-shape still held together his body, although anatomically incorrect, enabling a human form to be discerned nevertheless in the icebound shambles. Walk between thigh and guts, between head and a segment of spine, beneath the flying buttress of his bent arm still brandishing the frostoglaze sabre. The Grossmeister had ignited on its blade a million dazzling rainbows.

The hussars shielded their eyes from them as they approached. Both had lost their oculars somewhere. Why had they dismounted? Discern their animals at the edge of the fog, in the fog, retreating timidly into denser fog. The shorter hussar, the one with a bloodstained shoulder, took two steps forward and leapt back as if scalded, panting darkly. The taller hussar, the one with the rifle, blew into the lock of his weapon and took aim; but nothing came of it, the rifle failed to fire. He also ran back a few arshins, into the fog.

But the report from the Grossmeister was bound to summon the rest one way or another. It was essential to –

What? Shake the head. The plan was – what? To surrender to the protection of Pobedonostseff?

Emerge from the glintz of Captain Frett, and a first shock of pain shot up the arm to the back of the neck; it was hard to stay upright.

Forced to stagger. The shorter hussar, the one with the sabre, stared wide-eyed like a frightened bird, gathering himself to pounce and thrust. See in the shape of his glintz, cast by the Black Aurora, the whole necessity of the soldier's subsequent moves, the succession of logical inevitabilities. Step aside as if in sleep – like a dreamslave – grown sluggish amongst the sluggish. The hussar punched the air with his weapon.

He screamed and fled.

Now there remained only the fog and what lurked in the fog.

They were advancing to the very boundary of the streetlamp's paradisiacal light: mammoths, abassylar, Piegnar's goylems. Observe the colourful convulsions of the night. Let one of them finally step out and openly show its inhuman countenance. Let it leap out and snatch at the fog, at the smoke. How to beckon it more clearly? What sacrifice to make?

Wait patiently for the guide to the Underground World. Wait as long as strength allows, or the Frost – meaning, how long? A moment of drowsiness, a minute, two, a quarter of an hour, an hour, the rest of the night? Stand as if frozen to the middle of Glavnaya Street, tungetitum torch in hand, glintzen shimmering like coal-dust on clouds of white. A frigid mind won't testify to change, just as you won't engrave anything on diamond or impress information on perfectly ordered crystal. One moment merges into another; time adopts a circular shape, language ceases to convey complex thoughts. Hrrr-khrr, hrrr-khrr, hrrr-khrr, hrrr-khrr, hrrr-khrr.

Lying supine on the icy cobbles, a good twenty arshins from Frett and the gleiss, as the sleigh drew up; aquake with mortal shivering, doubled up, knees hammering into the chest, teeth chattering, arms thrashing helplessly in the snow. No breath wishing to enter the frozen windpipe. Unable to utter even a moan of suffering.

They lifted the shuddering body and laid it alongside the bloodsoaked Shtchekelnikoff, bound it swiftly in hare and reindeer skins, forced open the jaws and poured warm herbs down the throat. Swaddled the whole body in furs like a newborn babe. Star-studded sky and rainbow fog leapt up and down in the narrow eye-slit. Drift in and out of consciousness; again, and again. The sleigh gathered speed, faster and faster. Hear the swish of ice neath the runners and cries of the drivers – it was Polish, sounded like Polish. Once, an unshaven face appeared above the slit and displayed a toothless grin. Try to cry out in answer but only bite the lip and tongue. The shivering resembled more an epileptic fit; fiery acid coursed through the veins; the executioners had torn skin from flesh, ripped the body to pieces, crushed its bones and, in place of marrow, poured in liquid lead. Try to tell the grinning beardy that everything's understood – the lamp, the blackwicke at midnight, that Piłsudski also craves to steer History towards his own goals on the death of the governor general – but he hastily stuffed a chunk of animal fat into the open mouth, and no words were exchanged. In the sky overhead, the Tchornoye Siyaniye covered and uncovered the Baikal constellations. See no roofs, lanterns or rainbows emanating from frostoglaze streetlamps. Just one and then a second corpse mast. Relaxed now, the Yapontchiks laughed raucously at their ribald soldierly jokes. Tears of agony congealed in the eyes. Nothing, nothing had gone to plan. There'll be no finding father, no unfreezing father, no setting History to rights; for nothing, for nothing had Jelena been relinquished. Frozen to the core, chew on raw pork fat. Abandon the City of Ice.

CHAPTER THE NINTH

On a Lyednyak soul

He was laying out the patience cards.

'I had a bet with myself that if this patience comes out in my favour, then I shall be dictator of Poland.'

Sit down on a wall bench on the far side of the table, curling up in a reindeer hide. A large stove, sprawling over a quarter of the room like a sitting sultan, heated the cabin intensely; yet frost still sits in the bones. A colossal mauled wolfdog, barely able to open its eyes, was warming its old bones on the stove; whatever it took in of the world through its sense of smell, thus far was it still present in that world. As the room was traversed from door to kitchen, wherein Krzysztof and another Yapontchik were sitting over their cheese pirozhki, the dog raised its head and slowly rotated it in keeping with the commands of its nose; it was blind. Sit down, curl up in the hide, extract tobacco and paper, roll a leisurely cigarette. Morning sun falls from behind the shoulders, no need to screw up the eyes. He screwed up his eyes neath the bushy fused eyebrows – he, the one laying out the patience.

For there, beyond the window of the white interior – on the left flank, above the shoulder – there stretch fields of dazzling snow, of bright-blue coating as in a miniature watercolour, and farther away the boreal forest of conifers and cedar, high, dense, yet not completely swamped by the eiderdown of crystal powder, for first comes the blackness of shaded trunks, and only then – the high plateau of frozen crowns. Maybe it would be possible to walk on it, from which animals, squirrels and the occasional sable scamper away; they'd been spotted once or twice on the road from Irkutsk, against the backdrop of sky. And so, it soars – white, black, white – ever upward – to the sun almost, across entire steep mountainsides capped to the south by tapering pinnacles. A formation of triple peaks is visible from the small window – there sit the Yapontchik sentries, scanning the region through their binoculars and flashing warnings of alien wanderers. At night they light fires on the summits. A chain of beacons stretches for a good few-score versts all around. Tunka is a natural fortress. One back-breaking path to the east, one – to the west. Otherwise, you'll not reach it: mountains,

mountains, snow-bedecked frozen forests, and within them only the secret tracks of hunters. A dream hideout for anti-state fighters.

Yesterday, a walk was taken in the company of Krzysztof, also known as Adin, or Number One. He by no means occupied number-one position in the Japanese Legion; the nickname arose from his twisted neck. It seems he almost broke it and so he remained: contorted, dislocated, head facing down and to one side, twisted onto his shoulder, so that in profile, in outline, and no doubt also in his glintz neath the Black Auroras, Krzysztof (well-formed by nature and slender as a birch tree) was depicted as the first numeral: here the narrow torso straight and upright, but here – neck and head pointing earthwards at a sharp angle. Thus he trod aiming into the ground, crestfallen from his collarbone. Ask him what exactly happened – in what military brawl had he received the contusion? Adin merely sighed melancholically, thereby summarising in that sigh his whole life story. In this way, safe from the falsehoods of words, people can be known. Empty the lungs in equally heartfelt response, whilst penumbra blackened the breath-mist on the frosted lips.

Breathe the Siberian air, breathe the frost of unbounded Asia, breathe deeply, as on a vacation prescribed by doctors at an alpine spa. Life is different here – different the light, the sky, the colours; different the way time slides over the icy azure. Editor Wólkiewicz was right: there, in Irkutsk, people live by the minute clock, in a state of fervent tension – a moment missed is a moment lost – you can do more, you can do it faster, must do it faster! Do money? Do it, do it! This, that, whatever – anything, so long as you break out of inactivity, so long as success be added to success. Inactivity is the greatest sin. In the city, and all the more so in such a city – man is what he makes himself, what he has made himself. Noblemen escape to the country not because that's where they have estates and peasant souls under feudal domination, but because there they can be the more. Whatever he does or does not, a prince never ceases to be a prince. A city, on the other hand, an industrial, commercial, banking city – is the element of the Schultzes of this world.

'Any news of the governor? Which way is power tipping in Irkutsk?'

'Nothing new, Benedykt, sir,' said Adin. 'We were the last to come from the city, then nothing, silence.'

Silence above fields, silence above forests. Since there's no sound for measuring seconds and minutes, there's no regretting these seconds and minutes passing imperceptibly. In the city, vast impatience would have gripped a man already; he'd be girding himself for thought, for action, for some cruel necessity. But here – step outside, walk through fresh whiteness between huts, sinking to the knees in encumbering snow, leaving a regular four-print path, wading in crystalline frosty air... But for what? For this: in order to walk, in order to breathe. What time is it? Glance not at the watch. What day? Monday or Tuesday, twenty-fourth or twenty-fifth of November. Or twenty-sixth. Something like that. Thereabouts. More or less.

Abandoning the settlement, emerge from between the huts and skeletons of old yurts and climb the first hill below the forest so as to pause and view the open expanse stretching before the eyes, throbbing vibrantly in the sun. Leaning on the stick, raise the frostoglazes. One, two, three, six, a dozen, and still two more columns of smoke – signs of as many chimneys blackening the sky. Before the encroachment of the Ice, Tunka had numbered well over a hundred families, not including the transient Buryats; now there were probably more of Piłsudski's Yapontchiks than former settlers. There had been two tserkoffs, a wooden and a brick, goods warehouses for the Buryat and Mongolian steppe dwellers... Now there's only snow and ice and permafrost. What were people meant to live on? Once upon a time they'd lived off fishing and hunting; they bred cattle, yak, ponies and sheep. But you won't feed cattle on icicles. So, agriculture too is dying out in Winter. Krzysztof, having lit his pipe, likewise leaning on a trapper's stick, was telling how things looked no different throughout the Baikal Kray. Under the frosty sunlight, he pointed to where uluses of Buryat yurts had stood, and waxed lyrical on the life of Summer, on the customs of those days. You could always call at a Buryat tal, at villages of the oldest pagan tribe, where they'd entertain you with sour cream salamat porridge and tarasun brewed from cow's and mare's milk, very sour to the taste, but with a powerful kick... Yet who remains today? A few survivors, take a look, Benedykt – all the villages and small settlements across Siberia have suffered the same fate, whether they be ancient, indigenous, or those of eighteenth-century settlers, or recent ones of rural paupers re-settled from beyond the Urals by Stolypin. What was once the great and chief industry of Siberia – nature, Benedykt, nature, fruits of the taiga, produce of the earth, benefactions of the waters – hardly anyone lives off these today. Siberia relies on the heavy coldiron and tungetitum industries. In the Land of the Gleissen, folk are drawn from the provinces to cities, especially to Irkutsk. Food is brought in on long trains, which then transport in the opposite direction the treasures of Zimny Nikolayevsk. Everything's been turned around, stood on its head. (So spoke Number One, his moist gentle eyes staring out of the head hung low over his chest.) History has been turned around and needs to be set aright on old foundations.

'Don't believe what Comrade Wiktor told you. No one has such magic power over History.'

'Ah, so it's untrue you negotiated a good Thaw with Schultz-Zimovy?'

'Negotiated Thaw!' Sigh. Krzysztof shook his drooping head. There you have the whole story.

Silence above fields, silence above forests. No birds, for instance, are heard. Have all taken flight? Perished from unrelenting frost? Enter a cutting that leads from the Irkut gorge. The Irkut flows into the Angara close to Irkutsk, so for the first few versts of the ride from the city, the Yapontchiks had driven along the wide river course (before the Year of the Gleissen it also froze for at least seven months, transforming it into a convenient winter thoroughfare). There they had a rearguard base where they kept supplies, spare horses and reindeer, prepared in advance as behoves an army; there they were awaiting the remainder of their unit. After this, however, the journey continued for another two days through forests, along narrow alleyways between trees, so it could have been equally possible to go round in circles within a closed loop – maybe they did go round in circles – there was only the taiga, the taiga, the taiga: the white frozen silence.

Cedar, larch, fir, pine, birch, iced-through, snowed-over, icicle-bound – hence a forest, but a forest as if already half-transformed and redrawn to the landscape of the gleissen world. The lack not only of birds, but of all movement. Trees stir not, toss not their branches, tilt not their crowns. You wander through the taiga as if through a lace-work structure of geological formations. This is nature – but nature the farthest removed from man, scarred by life the most superficially. Stop and look back at the trail of foot and stick-prints, like pale letters etched on a cleaner-than-clean page after the nightly snowfalls. Tunka and its columns of smoke had disappeared already behind the vastness of the primordial forest. Silence, silence, motionlessness, whiteness, frost. Unwind the scarf from the beard, scoop air into the chest as water is scooped into a pail from a hole in the ice – and belch forth the foaming voice into the taiga. Chin resting on his sheepskin, Adin listened to the extended yell with an indulgent mien. A weak echo came back. Clear the throat, wipe the lips with the glove. No doubt they all yell.

Throughout all those months spent in Irkutsk, Siberia had not been truly felt; no real sense had there been of living in Siberia – the city is the city, Winter is Winter – only now is it felt, standing in lonely insignificance on the wide palette of the taiga, and despite being hemmed in on all sides by mountains, somehow boundless in its Asian enormity, under a wider-still sky, under a sky like a smooth Mongolian mug stuck in the ground, under a slanting sun… Siberia. Only now. How many words have been uttered in total to Adin since leaving the hut? Three-dozen maybe.

Stabbing at the heart was the first painful inkling of that 'Siberian soul sickness' which Filimon Romanovitch Zeytsoff had endeavoured to describe in the Trans-Siberian Express – how he met Sergey Andreyevitch Atchukhoff, how they recognised one another without words, understood one another beyond the language of the second kind… Here, neath the mountains of Asia, in pre-human nature. In the silence. For ordinarily, a man utters a word and half the attention has already departed from the man – from who he is – onto the true or false meaning of his word. More assiduous windbags manage to erase themselves almost totally from existence with floods of words, gushed out minute after minute, meaning after meaning. But just try to renounce your being in this silent ocean of white taiga, try to talk yourself down to zero under the sky of the mammoths…! Walk on with Krzysztof in companionable silence.

The old forester's hut, probably originally a hideout of contrabandists smuggling bloodstained gold beyond Baikal, was hidden behind ancient cedars, a hundred paces from the cutting. The Tunguses were under strict orders not to show their noses, so as not to be seen by the Tunka Buryats, which would at once provoke a needless brawl. On the far side of the Irkut – pointed out already by the Yapontchiks on the drive from Irkutsk – lie burial mounds containing the remains of heroes from some former Mongolian–Russian–Buryat war. Do the Ways of the Mammoths lead through Tunka? The legionaries shrugged their shoulders, shook their heads. Lay out at night the cards for sortilege patience, by the light of a tallow candle, to the rhythm of the well-wound-up watch, on a rough wooden surface – without result.

The sleds stood behind the hut; the reindeer were concealed neath a temporary lean-to. On a bench on the veranda, square head resting on the icicled balustrade, in the sunny frost, sat Shtchekelnikoff. Sit down next to him. Adin went to check on the indigenes. Shtchekelnikoff raised an eyelid, adjusted his bandage, adjusted his scarf, lowered the eyelid. On the trek from Tunka, the body had been sweating, now it was fagged out to the point of breathlessness, throat cut to ruination; only on pausing to catch deeper breath did it succumb for good to exhaustion. Post-chillage weakness had still not departed from the organism. Sit, breathing slowly, bent forward as far as the knees. Shtchekelnikoff raised his face to the sky, twisting on the bench and straining towards the sun like a vegetable in a cabbage patch. Clear the throat and return to the silent rhythm of breathing. White light from the frost pierced the pupils. Crystal rainbows glittered on icicles. One pale little cloud had got stuck below the horizon – show Shtchekelnikoff the cloudlet with the stretched-out hand. Shtchekelnikoff pointed to the icified crowns of the trees – scamper-scamper, a black-and-white ball of fur darted amongst the branches, an emaciated ermine, probably the last. Pull the frostoglazes back over the eyes; brightness poured over all the world, already softened and starting to melt. Breathe more and more slowly; frost caressed the cheeks like fir panicles. No desire was there to sleep – only a sense of falling into that same all-embracing peace in which words (as in sleep) are perfectly redundant, where words only get in the way. Tigry Etmatoff followed Adin outside; he'd been preparing a fresh portion of cedar-resin salve in a small clay pot. Tuck the salve under the shuba. Tigry smacked his lips in satisfaction, limped around the bench and flopped down on the other side, well pleased with himself, his round visage beaming smugly. Shtchekelnikoff gave him a furtive glance; the shaman bared his teeth gleefully. Lean against the quoin. Frost. Frost. Pure light. It will remain forever now, even if forgotten, unremembered, unsullied by words, bah, all the more powerful for it then: the brand of the gleiss. Memory of the Ice's touch. Although the gleiss could not have been touched; this past is distorted, refracted at the boundary of the milieu of Truth – like a sunray is refracted, split into colours, at the edge of a prism. (Mr Korzyński's finger.) The gleiss could not have been touched; yet nothing will ever take the experience away from the heart. True or false, realised or unrealised – it makes no differences. *In recollection there is no difference between the world and the world imagined.* Frost, frost remains in the bones. A patch of icy sun was swelling on the frostoglazes. White light from the frost pierced the pupils. Silence. The taiga. Siberia.

On the return journey, Krzysztof spoke but once. The hill with its view over Tunka was reclimbed; wintry shadows had begun to creep from behind buildings, trees and snowdrifts, the village swam in floods of oily black, whilst a small group of hunters waded through them with rifles slung over their backs, returning empty-handed from an expedition; Adin pointed them out in the communal square with his stick and in particular one tiny huntsman amongst them.

'When he talks to you,' said Adin, prising his head from his chest, shedding tears of murch, 'when he takes up a thought, you'll know.'

'I'll know?'

'Whether there'll be Thaw after this Winter. He scents it like a dog scents the gore of a wounded animal, through his nose, through his nerves.'

'The weakness of History, you mean.'

'Bah!' he chuckled. 'Our Old Man cut his eyeteeth on History.'

Since yesterday, however, no messenger had come from Irkutsk with fresh news. They were still waiting. Know from the conversations overheard, as well as from their blunt, openly exchanged remarks as Krzysztof and another Yapontchik now led from the hut by the church to this low shack: they were awaiting the return of the final unit, which was to report on the forces marching out of the Box. For the Old Man had informed them of a new operation. The destruction of another bridge? Blowing up of a train? If only History keels around favourably with the wind. If the patience comes out.

Light a cigarette. Lost in thought, he laid down a card and scratched at his copious beard. Swaddled in two thick sweaters, he seemed sturdier and broader in the shoulders, for he was not in fact of tall build. His ash-grey eyes were squinting from the sun. He ought perhaps to be wearing spectacles. He dragged a card down the length of his prominent nose, muttering something under his moustache. Back then, at the demonstration of the Battle Pump, he hadn't been recognised, despite his Eastern Borderlands accent and plainspoken words. Spit out the cigarette smoke. According to the arrest warrant – a wart on the edge of the right ear. Scrutinise him openly.

Then he glanced up in his typically focused but exasperated manner.

'I had a bet with myself that if this patience comes out, then I shall be dictator of Poland.'

Just know: Józef Piłsudski.

Flick ash into a bone ashtray. On the wall by the window, on a short bookshelf, stood a porcelain clock, a strangely elegant knick-knack in this coarse hut of rough-hewn logs in the last godforsaken hole of Siberia. The clock was broken; at least it had stopped at twenty minutes past seven. Above its round face was a photograph framed by ornamental foliage moulded into the porcelain as if in heraldic mantling: the portrait of a woman of exceptional charm. No doubt his wife, Maria, a famous beauty from Vilna, slain by Cossacks during the revolutionary disturbances in the Year of the Gleissen.

Piłsudski stroked his moustache and poured himself tchay into a stoneware mug.

'You may have noticed, sir,' he said, and shot a piercing look from under stormy eyebrows, 'that everything they call intuition, unconscious thought, is dwarfed by and disappears in the work of the intellect. People clutch at various tricks in order to liberate intuition – some pray, namely, or meditate, gaze at their navels, count rosary beads, others fall into a particular mechanistic rhythm of repeated actions, words and eventually thoughts. This enables them to fence off consciousness and push intuition front of stage. My mind, however, lives too rapidly, too fierily, to be tamed by such methods. Therefore, I occupy it with games of patience, force it to resolve its complexities. And not infrequently, I get up from a patience game with all my problems worked through unconsciously in the meantime. This is why I have often found courage to act where many would shrink, since I was sure or almost sure in advance that I would succeed.'

He had robbed trains, banks, gaols, tsarist government departments, on both sides of the Urals. He himself had escaped from prisons; raised prisoner rebellions – during his first exile, he'd incited a revolt in the Irkutsk prison; a bloody brawl ensued and his sentence was extended. He had shot tsarist dignitaries, military and aristocratic figures, in wars and in cities, by the hand of his people acting on his orders, or in person with his sawn-off Browning. He had travelled around the world agitating on Poland's behalf, collecting funds for the Polish cause, negotiating alliances in Poland's name – in Vienna, Zürich, Berlin, Paris, London, America, Japan, China. Created and lost secret partisan armies; created them anew almost in plain sight, especially here in Siberia after his second and third exile (from which, of course, he'd escaped). Blown up government buildings, military barracks, bridges, even exploded a dam. Disposed of enemies and competitors with equal ruthlessness without, it seems, entirely distinguishing between them. The Okhrana and Cossacks had had him a dozen times by the throat – yet he walked away unscathed. In Harbin, agents of Emperor Hirohito had him at gunpoint – yet he wriggled out on his word of honour.

'Dreamslaves also easily find within them this irrational certainty of the future.' Speak through the smoke.

'Perhaps you have heard of Engineer Ossowiecki. I have been convinced for a long time of the power of thought liberated from time and space. Stefan showed me –'

He laid down a card and suddenly snatched away his eyes. Glance over the shoulder and through the window directly into the blinding white. But it was not snow that struck the eyes with the colour of the sun.

'Adin!' shouted Piłsudski.

Krzysztof thrust his drooping head into the room. The Old Man pointed to the southern lights. Adin rushed outside at once summoning people.

Ask nothing. Piłsudski swallowed his tchay, wiped his moustache, beard.

'Your friend, Doctor Tesla –'

'He stayed behind.'

'Not far from Baikal there's this place about which tales circulate amongst the Buryats of how cold, slow, dark life flourishes even in the severest frosts, of how abassylar kidnap people and animals and carry them there to the Underground World, turning them into mammoths, and whoever –'

'I know that there is. I guessed. That is… I calculated.' Inhale radiant smoke. 'Father learned of it from you. At the start, he had only a few bottles of sazhayevka, nothing would have –'

'He himself wanted to!' Piłsudski threw down the card angrily. 'He went of his own accord!'

Laugh quietly.

'I know. By himself, no one else, he alone.'

'I shall give you a map –'

'Not so fast.' Raise the cigarette hand; the reindeer hide slipped from the shoulders. 'I'm in no hurry to enter the Ice. A suicidal venture.'

He frowned.

'It depends to whom. You sought me via Chruściński, you wished to speak to me, Mr Gierosławski. So, what now: you no longer desire it? To find your father?'

'To unfreeze father, rescue father… But what use is he to you, an unfrozen Gierosławski who talks not to gleissen?'

He winced.

'Something has made you badly distrust me. Have I ever harmed you?'

Extract from an inside breast pocket of the sheepskin a crumpled slip of paper, folded into eight. Straighten it out bit by bit on the table.

Piłsudski stared in confusion.

'What mathematics is this?'

'No mathematics, only an encoded letter from PPS-men in Warsaw to Filip Gierosławski, which I was to deliver to him here despite your tight guard.'

'And what do they supposedly write?'

'Spring of Nations – yes. Thaw from the Dnieper. Petersburg, Moscow, Kieff, Crimea – no. Japan – yes. The Party orders: time for amends – yes. Russia under the Ice. All means – yes. Be careful: Young Faction and Ottepyelniks against Winter. Defend the Gleissen. Don't believe the Old Man. A courier will come. Alive.'

'Aha.'

'I'm therefore thinking to myself,' continue slowly, 'that father could not have agreed wholeheartedly with your politics. Evidently, he wrote to his old comrades before he descended onto the Ways of the Mammoths. Arranged to correspond, in cypher. Maybe he was warning them precisely against Józef Piłsudski? For he'd been to the gleissen, and then a year went by, and a second, and a third, and a fourth – and what? You go on shooting at Cossacks in the Siberian wildernesses, but there is still no Poland, just as there wasn't before.'

'It's not so easy to bend History.'

'But the Ice, the Ice would have to retreat from it first! But here nothing – Winter is greater still. Unless you don't believe Berdyaeff – but then why strive at all for Thaw? Only for the sake of bringing down the coldiron industry? Huh?'

'I have a weak head for metaphysics; anyway, the logical abstractions of Marx also somehow do not suit my brain. I regard myself above all as a practical man, Mr Young Mathematician, and even if I don't take the whole of Berdyaeff's theory to be true, I can see nevertheless – precisely because I watch the practice – that there is something in it. History is unfolding differently from how everyone expected.' He turned around on his chair and pointed with a card (the Queen of Spades) to the book-shelf. 'Have a look at Seestern. Go on, take it down, take it down, have a peek.'

Stand up and remove a large tome. *1906: Der Zusammenbruch der alten Welt*, a reprint of the Leipzig 1907 edition, by a certain Ferdinand Grauthoff, hiding in the *editio princeps* under the nom de plume 'Seestern'. Flick through the introduction. The book seemingly predict-ed a war between the British Empire and Germany provoked by some absurd incident in colonial Samoa, in response to which the Royal Navy would attack Cuxhaven, thereby igniting a gigantic European conflict.

'You see, when I lived in Europe,' said the Old Man in the tone of a traditional storyteller, 'it struck me how in so many novels, from popular ones costing a few groschen to those printed in journals, how in so many novels published at that time – and in the preceding years – a future was portrayed upon which we'd all been most ardently counting: a great war between world powers, out of which the chance for a free Poland would emerge. I even tried to collect these novels – but it's hard to keep one's property together in such a life, a book here, a book there… There were scores of titles like this, if not hundreds. In German literature, English, French even. The novels of Curtis, Le Queux, Cole, Oppenheim, Eisenhart, Niemann, Heinrichka, Münch, Tracy, Bleibtreu. Chiefly about an invasion of Great Britain by Germany and various wars in the Hohenzollern Empire. There was also one in which the Japanese come to the rescue of the British. As for this here – take a look at the ending, at the denouement to the history of the war.'

Find a bookmark inserted between the well-read pages, and a frag-ment of the conclusion encircled in pencil.

The fate of the world no longer rests in the hands of the two naval powers of the Germanic race – Great Britain and Germany – but has passed on land into the hands of Russia, and at sea – of the United States of America. Saint Petersburg and Washington have taken the place of Berlin and London.

'A Great War hovers, was hovering over people's heads, and they felt it in Europe too before the Year of the Gleissen; the stench of gunpow-der hung in the air. Some even admitted it out loud; well, when they thought about it consciously, everyone was sure: a nervous combative spirit is on the rise, armies are preparing for severe tests in battle, warships are being built, heavy guns purchased; young men are eager for action, devushkas drag officers to the altar, and diplomats turn into spies. The dynamite had been planted, fuse cords laid, all that was lacking were the matches – well, and thus it has frozen.'

'But you don't belong, I assume, to the party which considers that History makes people, and not people History.'

'Have a look at... ah, no, I don't have it here. *On the Civilisations of Winter* by Feliks Konieczny. What is the subject of History? – civilisation, according to Konieczny, in other words a kind of tight-knit fusion of culture, laws, morality, religion exclusive to given peoples, their method of organising collective life.'

'It doesn't have to be the State.'

'Oh, it doesn't have to be. Take Jewish civilisation, for example, the oldest living civilisation in the world. Perhaps truly immortal! For herein lies the difference between civilisations and individual organisms, including human, in whose categories the Spenglers like to preach: for each individual organism of History is born, matures, blossoms and fades, grows decrepit and ultimately dies. But Konieczny claims: the laws of History are different from the laws of nature and all other systems known to man.'

'They require their own separate science. It that what you're saying? Their own precise algorithmics, based on entirely new rules.'

'Yes. Also, a civilisation can be immortal. Even when totally crushed, it may be reborn, rebuilt in visual, material instances. By what means? Well, by the very fact that a civilisation is not land and cities, not castles and factories, not even armies and million-strong populations – but first and foremost and above all: a healthy, cohesive fusion of morality, faith, law and custom.'

'A sporangium of ideas.'

'Yes! Everything stems from this! Including the nation as nation – for what is the nation without a true idea of the nation? Whilst he who builds on lies and falsehood will always be weaker than he who builds on truth. By the same token, a leader who relies in battle on false news, who is guided by false reports, is heading straight for defeat – by the same token too, a nation that derives its ideas from lies, is on course for inevitable ruin.'

'In Winter therefore –'

'In Winter a civilisation will not die.'

'But does it change in Winter? Will it recover? Will it extricate itself from the suffocating grip of other frozen civilisations?'

'This is precisely why, Benedykt, we need Thaw in the Kingdom and in Lithuania, in Galicia, but also in the whole of Austria-Hungary, as far as the Dnieper in the east – but no farther, not in Russia herself; the chance to recover, to modernise, cannot be given her.'

Put the book back in its place, sit down again on the bench, take out a fresh tobacco paper. White icy light shone from above the head; Piłsudski was sitting in it, the outline of his body clearly delineated, carved out from the backdrop by the contrasts in frosty dazzle. Like a monochrome figure depicted on a stained-glass window, motionless and deep in thought with the next card clasped between his fingers – frozen.

And see through him exactly as if he were a stained-glass window – that is, straight through.

How to liberate the Polish lands from all partition? Thaw is not enough; necessary too is precisely this great pan-European war – or universal Revolution advancing across the world according to the design of Bronstein-Trotsky. Piłsudski was trying to sell to the Japanese ideas for breaking up an unfrozen Romanoff Empire into national subdivisions, out of which would arise smaller independent countries, but also more distant powers that would not threaten Japan, like, for example, a Polish Federal Republic, not so very different from Jagiellonian Poland. Other conceptions involved the Congress Kingdom being annexed to the Habsburg Empire, but on equal terms, so that a new entity would be created: Austria–Hungary–Poland. Everything depended on how widely Poland could be torn from the jaws of History, in other words: on how far the Ice lets go.

… Because of these disagreements, the Polish Socialist Party had split: some PPS members had opted above all for Revolution, that is, for the unfreezing of the entire Russian Empire, others – for a national insurrection, that is, for the unfreezing of Poland and Lithuania. According to what Editor Wólkiewicz was saying and what the Yapontchiks say here, Piłsudski had persuaded the old Party and his Revolutionary Faction that only Russia under the Ice, shackled by archaic Byzantine practices of autocracy, Russia not rushing into the twentieth century, braced in eternal pre-revolutionary tension, only such a Russia would guarantee the unfrozen Poland a fair chance to develop her natural strengths as a state and take her natural place in Europe. All of which is a logical continuation of Piłsudski's dispute with the late Roman Dmowski of blessed memory, for on what carrion must the new Poland grow fat in order to become a great power? – not on Germany or Austria, but on the weakness of the frozen East. Besides, maybe Ziuk remains convinced that Russia released from under the Ice will by no means take the path of proletarian revolution, as the Young Ones believe, hence their dispute.

… But even the old PPS, which agrees with this reasoning, no longer has confidence in Piłsudski! *Don't believe the Old Man!* In what is Father Frost not meant to believe him?

Now, however, just know: Józef Piłsudski. Izydor Chruściński was right – he had perceived his soletruth.

'You really are a Lyednyak!'

He laid down the card.

'Mm-hmm?'

'Heart and soul – a Lyednyak! Why do you need the Ice in Russia? – so as to smear Poland again in ice, since Poland will arise only in the form that suits you!' Light a fresh cigarette. 'Let me guess: a State! A powerful state, oh, an efficient dictatorship, an independent country under your absolute control! It has already begun,' wave the hand about in the smoke, 'you are already building an army under your command, freezing people in hierarchical positions, I can see it after all; you won't enlie yourself, this is the truth about Józef Piłsudski.

'But Polish tradition –'

He exploded.

'Tradition-perdition!' he snorted, spraying spittle abundantly across the table and patience cards. 'You won't persuade me, sir, of the inanity that Poland cannot be Poland unless she tolerates her former squabbling and contentiousness, brawling and private feuds!'

He stood up and began marching from wall to wall and from wall to stove, noisily rattling his metal-shod military boots on the floor, so that the sobaka stirred and lifted its head, though still without opening its eyes; it sniffed after Piłsudski, uneasy.

'How are we to oppose the Russian State?' he asked, casting a brief glance out of the window. 'On what are we to rely? On spontaneous Romantic fits and starts, hot-headed chaos, revolutionary confusion? No! There's already been enough of this! Until a fighter submits to his commander's orders as to the word of the One God, we shall have no chance against the Russian Empire.'

'The military, then.'

'Military! It may seem to fusty civilians that so-called terrorists, fighters throwing bombs and smashing the oppressor State, are a force of chaos, extremists of Summer – yet nothing could be further from the truth! Harken to them well: with the exception of whole-hearted Bakuninists, they all stand behind the Ice, bah, behind an even colder State – except a different State, their State, constructed according to their dream. It's not my principle – it's the principle of every revolution. I blow up bridges? I blow up in order to build!'

'But what kind of choice is that: the State or the State?'

'Yes, I know, Poles are mistrustful of any bureaucracy and always favour anarchic, independent actions. We are the most civilian nation in the world! And we even brag about this abnegation of the state, this culture of statelessness!'

A quick stomping of feet resounded in the kitchen. The Old Man went to the door and exchanged a few words with someone; he withdrew, but, having withdrawn, immediately spun around and spat out an order over the threshold. The men stomped away.

Then they flashed past in the snow outside the window, running through Tunka: one, a second, a third, carrying rifles on their backs, belching out black breath-mist.

Snort mockingly.

'Indeed, it's as if your main aim were to organise men under your command in such a way that when sent into the fray, they'll carry out any order of higher authority without reflection, as if it really had come from God himself. Whenever I talk to anyone here, the answer is always the same: "it will be as the Old Man commands", "whichever way the Old Man says is best", "obey the Old Man". They're even reworking old national and religious songs to write in Józef Piłsudski! So here we have the ideal State! So here we have the dictator's dream: the obedience of Abraham.'

'Tell me, Mr Mathematician: shouldn't a soldier always obey orders from his commanding officer?'

'There are certainly orders which it is wrong to carry out irrespective of circumstances.'

'Killing the innocent.'

'Killing the innocent, yes,' answer him cautiously, blowing fresh smoke into the air.

'Who, however, can decide? Who possesses the right knowledge to judge the legal validity of war and methods of war?' Piłsudski paused by the stove and ruffled the dog's fur; the poor bow-wow licked his hand with an enthusiasm inspiring pity. 'You can see what times we live in: of agents single and double, Okhrana spies, conspirators, provocateurs and secret pacts stretching across continents, languages and civilisations. Look at what Polish independence hangs on. Who is able to embrace it with a single idea, a single narrative? Perhaps you can calculate Poland, Mr Gierosławski Junior?'

'Mm-hmm. Perhaps… No, I can't.'

'A soldier today who wants to decide independently on the battlefield – and the battlefield, as you well see, is the whole world – decide what belongs to a good war and what makes an evil war, such a soldier becomes a liability to the army and to its commander. Wars can no longer be waged according to the model of governments of Summer, that is, with the consent and understanding of the *levée en masse* of our noble brothers. Generals who explain the correctness and necessity of every move will lose to generals of the Ice, who are sure of their own mechanical effectiveness. Strategies that are openly declared and universally understood will lose to strategies that are secret and twofaced, in which only the leaders are complicit. Yet this still doesn't take into account the most obvious differences: that a leader is a leader because he sees farther, better, more sharply than any lower-ranked soldier. How differently would Bonaparte have fought had he performed only moves judged strategically and morally propitious by his rank-and-file! The laws of greatness are different from the laws of smallness.'

'So, this is how you lead your Riflemen along the path of terror: according to the Leader's word.'

'I would also prefer not to,' he sighed. 'I would prefer the necessary, ideal History.'

'Without leaders,' poke fun at him.

'And you imagine, sir, that I do it for myself, for some private interest? That power is an end in itself? Yet what did you write yourself in your *Apoliteia*? Had I desired only this thrill of power and absolute licence, I would have stuck with Summer.' He returned to the table, picked up a fresh card and cast his eyes over the patience. 'The right course for a leader is not mathematical calculation of his own and his opponent's forces, but risk. A leader must be able to reckon and dwell where reckoning has already lost certainty, where there are only probabilities. In Summer. For under the Ice – what remains? Mathematics, Mr Gierosławski.'

He laid down the card – and, tearing away his eyes, suddenly clouded over again, swelled with murch, grew hard as stone.

'But this is exactly what Poles need!' He clenched his fist. 'The Ice! The Ice!' He banged on the massive tabletop. 'The favourite argument of Poles is: emotion! The preferred position of Poles is: indecision! Only when frozen in their own powerful and necessary State, that is, cooled down and cured for good of all those Sarmatian brawls, of endless parliamentary blether, multiple cries of "liberum veto", anarchisation of the salons, the any-old-how and any-old-thinking of the Congress Kingdom, rat-like proliferation of factions and parties – only when in the clutch of the Ice, crushed by necessity – only then will be they be able to create a great Poland!'

'She will triumph, because she won't be able not to triumph!'

'Yes! Yes!'

Daemon of the Ice!

Leap up from the bench in order to break out of the tyrannical stereometry.

'And that's why they don't trust you! That's why they send warnings to Father Frost!'

Breathe, however, a sigh of relief. Pick up the bone ashtray, tap ash into it with measured, rhythmic strokes. Finding the internal rhythm – it always brings calm and detaches from fixations inflicted from without.

'Even if they all still thought you could do something real along those lines...' Mutter under the breath. 'But whatever you fancy in your own mind, you can't shift the Ice around the map of Europe single-handedly. But were you to send my pater to talk to the gleissen with such an instruction... Anyone in the PPS who believes Berdyaeff is now terrified with good reason to the bone.'

Tighten the fingers on the ashtray and cigarette, raise the eyes with conscious effort of will and body from the ash to Józef Piłsudski. He was staring straight ahead, stooping only slightly, burrowing deep into his soul in search of the slightest ember of shame.

'You have lived too long in the Russian land.' Tap the cigarette against the rim of the bowl. 'It's entered too deeply into you. Outside of the Ice you can't take people in this way; out of such poisoning with soletruth, are born sectarian castrates, pretenders, false tsars.'

'And from whom this harangue? What did you write yourself in your *Apoliteia*! The Ice State! The Un-State!' He wagged his finger like a grandfather telling off a mischievous grandson. 'I know you, sluggish intellectuals! On paper you vindicate every totalitarian system, and the more totalitarian, the greater the delight with which it's served up in pious, poetic words, Hegels, Marxes and Berdyaeffs; so that other progressive souls across the world will cry out in admiration in their cosy salons, and young ladies will wring their hands and fall into each other's arms, and immature young students will read it in the cafés with flushed cheeks... But as soon as anyone tries to realise that perfect and perfectly described project – then the blood drains at once from the gentleman intellectual and the genius covers his eyes: agh, the innocent victim, agh, agh, the corpse – how it stinks! how ugly! take it away from me!'

Slam the ashtray down on the windowsill.

'You have understood nothing! The whole point of apoliteia is to prevent one man from assuming power over another man, leaving all necessities directly to History – and not to create invincible dictators frozen in their dictatorship! Apoliteia is precisely freedom from such Daemons of Truth as you, sir!' level the finger at him, finger versus finger. 'From dictators, tsars, ministers, tchinovniks! There's no place in it any more for the free decisions of state rulers – there are only clear, obvious historical necessities!'

'Understood nothing?' Piłsudski smiled contemptuously from the depths of his beard. 'History rules – but who rules History, Mr

Gierosławski? *Who rules History*?' He walked around the table, moving four, three, two paces from the stove. 'You curse the governments of man, his dictatorships and empires – but a tsar, even the most powerful, with his million tchinovniks, million spies and agents, with his arsenal of extraordinary ukases, who is he in relation to the government of History? A helpless child! Almost an anarchist! But try opposing History, try bribing logical necessity, appeasing mathematics, threatening the idea…!'

'That's right! Here you see a man who will take control of the apparatus of government by History – such a man – a dictatorship, of which it's impossible to imagine a crueller – a tsardom, of which it's impossible to imagine a greater – the ultimate autarchy – autocracy equal to God's – such a man – such a man –'

Know not the moment when the retreat began from the Old Man, sweeping the reindeer hide off the bench, dropping the cigarette, eventually hitting the back against the wall – but he continued to approach, levelling his finger at the chest – the finger that had triumphed.

'Gierosławski!' yelled Piłsudski. 'Gierosławski! For this I sent you, for this I am sending you,' he screwed up his bony fist, 'for you to grab History by the muzzle!'

Cold, cold and colder still.

'And how many men did you send after father?!' Leap up to the table, wipe off the whole patience in one broad sweep; the cards fluttered like a flock of startled birds till the dog on the stove raised its head. 'Where would you find such an Ishmael as my pater? Whoever is a real toughgut won't obey you blindly! You won't bewitch an abassy! Those who would descend onto the Dorogi for you, for Pobedonostseff, for the tsar – will not descend!'

He smiled, now angelically calm.

'That is precisely why,' he said, 'I was so delighted to read your *Apoliteia*.' He extended an open hand. 'You quarrel, but with whom do you quarrel? – with your own self, not with me, for you already well know the truth about yourself. I do not have to convince you of anything. You yourself dream of the Ice. True? True. It has frozen. So go now and find Filip, show him yourself, talk to him honestly, like son to father, like Frost to Frost. Well.' He stepped forward energetically with that extended hand. 'After all I can see what kind of man you are.'

Cold, cold and colder still. Princess Blutskaya, she had been the first to know. Shake the head. What had happened that night on the street in Irkutsk? After all, the gleiss had not actually been touched – even if there was a memory of having touched the gleiss. Everything comes from a different, different past.

The Old Man was watching.

Lick the lips.

'They're to send a courier –'

'Never fear, he won't make it.'

Blink, smitten in the eye by the harsh crystalline white glare shining through the window behind the Old Man.

'Poland under the Ice.' Whisper the words.

'And the rest of the world you can keep for yourself.'

And so – above and beyond History – shake in the cold palm, the right hand of Józef Piłsudski.

Depart an hour later, racing the midday sun and the Cossacks. Adin and Ciecierkiewicz (Adin's bandy-legged comrade) led the way up steep forested slopes, first towards Shimki, a village set deeper still in the mountains where no living soul had been seen for years, so they claimed, since Winter had driven out all farmers long ago – and then from Shimki by means of a dramatic downhill slide to the provincial highroad, along which it is but a short hop to Baikal, to finally escape pursuit in the Primorsky mountains. For the Yapontchiks left behind in Tunka with the Old Man, it will be easier to slip away and melt into the taiga, unencumbered by baggage, equipment, supplies. Riding now with two equipages: the Tungus guides with their low sled, and then the team of four pulling the Yapontchiks' sled, adapted to the roadless wastes and icefields of Siberia. The luggage from Shtchekelnikoff's sleigh had been reloaded onto the latter, as had the chest with Tesla's small naphtha stove concealing the Kotarbiński pump and spools of coldiron cable. Adin and Ciecierkiewicz took the saddled reindeer and tore ahead half a verst, checking the passability after fresh snowfalls in the night. The higher into the mountains and deeper into the taiga, the harsher and more malevolent the frost. Snow crunches under the runners like split willow. No one says anything, everyone puffs shadowy breath, even the Tunguses. Shtchekelnikoff, turning around once from the reins, wheezed through his face-rags in a croaky halfwhisper: 'They'll recognise me. Caught no doubt the fart whose mug I beat the living daylights out of, he'd have blabbed. They'll hack me ter death, Mr G.' But apart from this, no one said a thing and shots could clearly be heard reverberating sporadically from the valley floor, borne on a protracted echo over the landscape of white nature. Count up to eighteen volleys. The path led up a ridge; between the high crests of sparser stone pine and cedar it was possible to see directly into the Tunka basin. The Cossacks had split up amongst the huts, examining the tracks leading into the forest. Another shot rang out – they retreated under cover. In such snow, only a blind man would be unable to read the trail left by two harnessed sleds, and Piłsudski had promised to repel this Cossack unit, or at least delay it sufficiently to allow the sleds to reach the provincial highroad in the meantime. Regret more than anything, however, that it hadn't been possible to wait for the report of those Yapontchiks tracked down by the Cossacks; and so, the situation in Irkutsk remains unknown, who is in power, onto whose side History has veered, and what orders have brought the soldiers here. Run the hands over the fur coat: feel for the Piatnik pack of cards belonging to Fryderyk Weltz. Tesla – is he alive? or dead? (Need to drive all the sooner down to where the Ways of the Mammoths run!) And beneath the cards in this same pocket – Piłsudski's hand-drawn map with directions to the Black Oasis, the open grave leading directly into the Underground World. The secret hydrography of Baikal will show you how to step down amongst the abassylar, Mr Gierosławski. And so, what now? – is a man to guzzle, gorge on tungetitum and pray for a happy freezing? No, no, no! There'll be no going there! The Cossacks fell out of the tserkoff, fired a concerted volley and rushed into the forest. Stand up in the sled and wave to Tigry to make haste. There'll be no going to the Black Oasis – so where to then? Shtchekelnikoff lashed his whip, the stags jerked as they sped uphill. Jump off into the snow, lightening the load. Icicled cedars leaned overhead. The Tungus sled had disappeared round a bend. From the valley below came the sound of a single shot and a deathly scream. Nowhere is there rescue, nowhere escape, nowhere a safe house. Snow, taiga, mountains, a man lost in Siberia. Trot alongside the sled, barely coughing even in the frost. Feel the frost too in the bones, in the smooth icy circulation around the internal curvatures of the body. The salve didn't always help. Run on in silence, in unlighted breath-mist, totting up in the head all the mistakes made; and thus, with every added blunder, the remembered past froze into a tangled, branchy, elaborately finessed figure, a baroque arabesque of hoar surrounding the already completely frozen Benedykt Gierosławski. For the irrefutable truth, the axis and root of every truth – is the present moment: this ice-benumbed zangisan, this snow-covered taiga and echo of distant firing, this pure clear sky, winter Sun, mountains under the Sun, and this reckless expedition in blind pursuit of Father Frost: steaming reindeer, overloaded sleds, Tigry Etmatoff and his worshippers of abassylar, Adin and the other bandy-legged Yapontchik, and also the good Shtchekelnikoff (and his knives).

On the jama-u-mu-kon bone

'*Emukol ela!*'
  '*Alatkal!*'
  '*Ili mat!*'

The Tunguses had espied something on Baikal. Step outside the tent into the frost, strapping the belt more tightly around the doubled-sided fur coat, binding the face in skins. Morning eight of the desperate Siberian odyssey – were the pursuers still hot on the trail? Adin and Ciecierkiewicz swore that any tracker would get lost five times over on the Baikal ice, in the blizzard, in the furious gales. Slide down the ice-encrusted slope to the rim of a fallen tree hollow, which opened up above icicled treetops onto the smooth infinity of the Sacred Sea. Tigry Etmatoff and his good cousin were squatting in the snow, staring into the whiteness that flowed from earth to sky and back again.

'*Ru, ru, ru,*' mumbled the shaman.

Remove the frostoglazes; the image of the ice lake suddenly froze. On the south-eastern horizon, where the indigenes were staring, stood a dark comma-shaped blot, a tiny smudge, like an old scratch on a fresco. It was one of those rare moments when the Baikal winds retreat into the mountains and snowy drapes no longer veil the countenance of the Sacred Sea. Had the vantage point been a little higher, the Cold Line itself would no doubt have been visible, perhaps also a goods train moving across the ice under coils of black smoke. Mm-hmm, or maybe no train would have been witnessed: are Irkutsk and Zimny Nikolayevsk still in contact with the rest of Siberia?

'Look, look!' Tigry's good cousin was waving his arms.

Strain the eyes. Is that mark on the horizon moving at all?

'*Syrga?*' ask the Tunguses. '*Lú-cza?*' This meant 'sled' and 'Russian' in Tungus.

The shaman passed his open hand horizontally across his chest, which was a gesture of negation.

'Who is it? Cossacks?'

The cousin started jabbering to Etmatoff, again they gazed at the horizon.

Shtchekelnikoff appeared on the slope with Ciecierkiewicz enveloped in steamy penumbras.

'Are we off, Mr G? Striking camp in a quarter-hour.'

'Wait, the lads have espied someone after us.'

Ciecierkiewicz rushed over to the Tunguses, performing on the ice the weirdest leaps and bounds, and stuck in his head between Tigry and his cousin; Ciecierkiewicz warbled away fluently in their tongue – most likely why Piłsudski had sent him with Adin.

Tchingis lit a cigarette.

'I were just saying: a-crawling in your tracks like they's a-crawling up your arse, no tearing away without blood.'

'Adin bet his life we'd already lost the Cossacks.'

Ciecierkiewicz stood up straight, waved his arms, came bounding up, unwound his scarf.

'They say it's not Cossacks.'

'Praise God!' sigh with relief.

'They say's it's a different pursuit.'

'Meaning, us, they're pursuing us?' The hackles went up.

'Tigry wants to fly to them along the Ways of the Mammoths.'

'First let's reach the Ways in the Middle World. Come evening, he can summon the spirits with his drum.'

Shtchekelnikoff puffed out the smokes of Lucifer.

'If another race be in the offing through this wintry Winter, then not on an empty stomach. You's as considered that one, Mr G?'

'How about that khutor in the mountains?'

'Half them gold prospectors and magpies bound for the Lena get their supplies from Lushtchy. Thirty versts of not the hardest road, we'll be there afore noon.'

'The news will get there ahead of us. Quieter go, farther be.'

'Hungry go, sooner drop. But we'll find something out for ourselves; perhaps they've got fresh news from the city. D'you really think all Siberia's watching us?'

'Well, someone was after us. And now – you can see for yourself.'

'After Polack terrorists! But with rations and reindeer fodder for two weeks – we won't even reach Kezhma.'

'But why would I go to Kezhma?'

Tchingis shoved the cigarette between his rags, spat out a stream of black smoke.

'But where is we going, Mr G? I know now to the Ways of the Mammoths, but – then where?'

Take a long look at white Baikal and at the distant blot described on that whiteness.

'We're upping sticks, Tchingis, upping sticks.'

The truth was: the relentless chase from Tunka had been losing pace due to the necessity of choosing a direction and announcing the rational aim of the expedition. But already yesterday, standing here in the camp, having stepped off gale-ridden Baikal, it was hard to avoid the questions of the Pilsudtchiks and Shtchekelnikoff; today an irrevocable decision has to be made. Therefore – the Black Oasis? the Black Oasis and death in the ice? Not on your life! But how else to draw near to father? On the first peaceful night, by the feeble light of the naphtha stove, the position of the Oasis had been plotted on Piłsudski's map in relation to the reported encounters with Batyushka Moroz. If Piłsudski was not mistaken, the tungetitum filtered out from subglacial Baikal emerges from the ground via hydrological ducts, carved by gleissen along the Ways of the Mammoths to the north-east of Baikal, directly behind the Baikal mountains, some one hundred versts from the spot where on the seventeenth and nineteenth of April this year, Engineer Di Pietro had come across father (if not some other abassylian) freezing his way along the paths of stone and clay. This was the most recent sighting recorded in the papers of Frantishek Markovitch Uriah. The thought occurred: was this abassylian observed by the Italian engineer – going to or coming from the Oasis? How quickly do people's metabolisms revolve on the Ways of the Mammoths? Frozen, pushed through geological formations by tides of helium – do people precipitate tungetitum from their organisms, so that they have to replenish it after a given time? But these are not organisms at all! This is not life! Or perhaps the Italian engineer saw someone entirely new, neither the pater, nor Crowley, nor the Dumb Ballooner, nor Kopytkin, but someone from a more recent, April freezing? Next day, another question came knocking at the brain cells: what exactly were Di Pietro and his companion doing there? What kind of surveys were they conducting in the Stanovoy highlands on the instructions of their firm or of Sibirkhozheto? In Uriah's papers, there is no word on such details. No doubt this is where the field of knowledge censored by Sibirkhozheto begins. Did the coldiron companies have no inkling of the riches amassed in Baikal? (Not to mention the riddle of this strange tungetitum which leaks out of the lake.) It could be wagered that this, amongst other things, was the reason for keeping the black hydrography of the Land of the Gleissen secret. And since the idea of the Black Oasis had been reached within a few weeks whilst demurching with the Kotarbiński pump and after only one visit to Olkhon Island, then the Sibirkhozheto engineers, even if thick-skulled gleisseniks, must have come across it somehow during the course of so many years. Why did Karol Bohdanowicz vanish? Where did that 'accident' happen to him, if not in the mountains above Baikal? And what did Czerski hear from the shamans, so that the tsar at once declared him a state criminal and put a reward on his head? Piłsudski should have been questioned as to whether it wasn't the Yapontchiks who helped Czerski to escape back in the day. If the dates were correctly remembered… Czerski was writing about the Buryats already ten years ago; he could have known Piłsudski from the time of the Old Man's escape from his third exile – after all, Piłsudski's Riflemen have been fighting in the Japanese Legion here throughout most of the second Russo-Japanese War; and therefore: Czerski told Piłsudski – Piłsudski told father – father descended to the Ways of the Mammoths. It could have been, could have been like that; it freezes very smoothly onto the present.

… Such were the dreams of the past dreamt at night in waking, buried under stinking animal skins, in the fug of a felt tent, listening to the grating snores of Adin, Ciecierkiewicz and Shtchekelnikoff. Despite the exhaustion, falling asleep often proved impossible for a long time. Try rearranging again Weltz's pack of cards, scratching zeros and zeros with the fingernail – for so far, all arrangements were coming out normally: even if Tesla were striking the Murch Hammer according to prescription, the wave of murch was radiating from the prototype too weakly for it easily to be read far from the Ways of the Mammoths. But there was no time to make a detour onto the Ways of the Mammoths – since the need now was to up sticks.

Krzysztof had brought binoculars; he pressed the instrument to his eyes, leaning backwards expressly to bring his nut on its broken neck into some kind of vertical position, and in this manner direct the binoculars towards Baikal.

'What d'you reckon?'

'They're on foot.'

'On foot?'

'And it seems without sleds. But in this direction, Benedykt, sir.'

Sigh blackly.

'Our bad luck. Shtchekelnikoff – to Lushtchy's!'

Tchingis whistled to the Tunguses. Within minutes the rest of the camp was struck and packed onto the sleds. Pull on topshoes made of bone and hide over the unty-boots, so as not to sink into drifts when having to jump off the sled and march alongside; this was terrain too uneven for skis. The Tunguses moved over the snow on so-called skates, that is, light wooden slats more than an arshin in length and three vershoks wide – but to wear such skates required exceptional skill and practice.

Take a good look around before leaving, making sure that nothing significant remained at the overnight site, that the natives and Pilsudtchiks had cleared away everything, even the piles of branches laid each evening under the tents. At once, however, snow would fall again and cover even the imprints left in the permafrost.

'*Ila?*' asked the shaman.

'To Lushtchy.' Point to Shtchekelnikoff. 'And then on to the Ways of the Mammoths. Understood?'

'Mamonty, mamonty,' Etmatoff mumbled into his skins, scraping his skates as if in confusion.

Yell to Tchingis; Tchingis cracked his whip and the sled moved off.

Maybe something really did happen there on the street on that last day in Irkutsk. After all, had the Yapontchiks or the Tunguses seen such truth about the Son of Frost as was remembered now, they wouldn't have let themselves be dragged for a single day across the wastes of Siberia. Remove for a moment both pairs of gloves, the two-fingered and five-fingered, take out the compass, watch, map and notebook, then record the time of day and direction of travel (jotting down half a word at a time between leaps of the sled), and also a comment on the alleged pursuers. Without guides who know the country, navigation here was practically impossible: the compass deceives through magnetic deflections of several tens of degrees, the Sun moves across the sky more than thirty degrees below its east–west path; but even so, everything can't be left to the mercy of the guides. Keep notes conscientiously every day. Read on the thermometer minus forty-seven degrees Celsius at dawn – the fingers should swiftly stiffen, feeling should depart the hand, the skin pale to milk-white. But this did not happen so quickly. The Tungus salves did not help, since evidently there was nothing for which they could help. It was a purely biological process, similar to that undergone by the young Mefody Pyelka.

Imagine, on the other hand, the effect of Mr Korzyński's finger. Truth had been touched and truth had frozen – but slightly different from the previous mendacious notions, adjusted to slightly different pasts and futures. Remember not change and remember not the former Benedykt Gierosławski, for how on earth would that be possible? – the truth is one, the soletruth – and this is the heart of Winter, not the Ukrainian steppes of Summer. Conclusions may be inferred at most from subtle discontinuities, from discrepancies with conclusions about the past based on what does not depend on memories. Which likewise belong to the newly frozen present, and like the body are more resistant to frost. For memories return of how the body used to shiver at the slightest whiff of chill, even during the journey in the Trans-Siberian Express – but were a fellow traveller from De Luxe standing here now, would he tell the same tale of Count Gyero-Saski, the Yekaterinburg frost, his falling off the train and the catastrophe on Old Zima Station? The past exists not.

In reality, therefore, no change has taken place. Change is possible only in History, but there is no History outside of the Ice – and there is no Benedykt Gierosławski from before the Frost.

Sometimes the thought occurs that despite everything, it is possible to train character through practice. Even if alethic capacity is a constant attribute with which a person is simply born – then despite poor physiological predispositions, much can be achieved in life through persistent training, through sheer tenacity, through rehearsing repeated experiences. If not from *how much* you freeze, then at least – *as whom* you freeze. Wasn't Atchukhoff saying as much in his final teaching on prayer?

How then to train the character? Seated sideways on the loaded sled, as it moved at this moment down a gentle slope in the mountain landscape, trying to reassemble with little conviction the Warsaw and pre-Warsaw memories; it was easier to summon those from the Transsib. How to train the character – well, there are scholastic methods: choose a topic and defend it in company to the bitter end. Any topic: this one, that one, a contrary one, and still another – the more, the better, the more varied, the better. Only in this way will you formulate and identify your own heartfelt convictions in matters of good and evil, religion and politics, people and the world: by clashing with other people's convictions. This is why Christians brought up amongst Christians are so insipid and woolly in their faith, so – melted down.

There are undoubtedly more brutal methods too, methods that rely on the direct breaking of shame. Here, however, the impulse has to come from outside – for who is the steward of their own shame? Only Jelena Muklanowicz perhaps. Suck in through the face-rags, frost that stings the mouth like diamond dust. Jelena! Here's the riddle: a devushka smeared in so many possibilities she looks at herself as at some childish fantasy, a tale served up half-seriously as flirtation – and yet she is real, oh, how real, real to the point of headache, real to the point of heartache. Truly, *un phénomène de la nature…*! A Lie come true! Was she really born thus – or did she make herself thus, tell her own life from beginning to end like Felitka Caoutchouc?

But what does this reflect about her to the man who falls for such a woman, who seeks such a woman?

'Tell me, Benedykt,' asks Krzysztof, flopping down on the other side of the sled, 'will we get there in time to return for the Nativity of Our Lord?'

'God willing, God willing.'

Which was the most honest truth, since indeed, salvation could only be envisaged now by the grace of heaven. Avert the frostoglazes from Adin so as to discourage his further questioning. The long haul from Tunka had obviously been a godsend: it had simply been an escape. But all of them – the Tunguses, the Yapontchiks, Shtchekelnikoff – had crawled across Siberia in wintertime with the sole aim of helping the Son of Frost to meet Father Frost, to hold talks with the gleissen, to negotiate History. And so, sooner or later, they would have to be confronted and frankly informed: we shan't find Father Frost, shan't save the world, we won't do anything at all on this ridiculous Siberian odyssey.

In the meantime, Tigry was being urged to lead onto the Ways of the Mammoths – this was the one and only chance: a sign from Tesla that affairs in Irkutsk had worked out fortuitously and it was safe to return.

Don't the companions of the odyssey, however, have their own secrets? Adin and Ciecierkiewicz have orders from the Old Man, which they'll not betray; no doubt he has instructed them to keep an eye on the proper course of negotiations with Father Frost, and censor any pacts towards Histories not in keeping with Piłsudski's thought.

But even the Tunguses – it was hard to believe that Uriah had discovered such originals at the drop of a hat. Amongst the books brought from Irkutsk read now in the tent neath storm and purga were two that treated of indigenous peoples (mainly, admittedly, Buryats). And so, in the eighteenth century, Tibetan Buddhism spread widely across Siberia. Grazers and herders and entire ulusus or irgens adopted this faith; monasteries and temples were built, in whose datsans the lamas provided spiritual care for the indigenous tribes, thereby gradually ousting the local shamans. As far as the Buryats were concerned, the dividing-line ran along Baikal: those from lands to the west of the Sacred Sea clung to the shamanic faith, but if they converted, then it was to Orthodox Christianity under the auspices of the Russian Tserkoff; it was from amongst these that Sibirkhozheto recruited its agents and soldiers of the Underground World. But the Tunguses must also have been caught up somehow in the clan administration project of Mikhail Speransky. So how many former-rite shamans still remained to them? and how many amongst these had so bizarrely turned to faith in abassylar?

Approach Tigry on this topic before the descent into the valley basin, beyond which stood Lushtchy's outpost. Snow on the shadowy slope was hard, ice-ridden, very slippery. The reindeer were reharnessed; first the Tunguses were to let down their lighter sleds. Help them with the roller-logs.

'How is it, Tigry, tell me, for there are no people in this world, after all, who admit to themselves that they're honestly working for evil.'

'*On?*' he replied in his own language.

'Well, you are not like Buryats. You believe gleissen are satanic abassylar, evil spirits of the Underground World, oopfkh, and yet, and yet – Mr Ciecierkiewicz, look where you're flailing your arms! – and yet you somehow worship them, protect them; now you are also helping me protect them against the emperor's wrath. So, how is it? And don't tell me you've got your corners mixed up, mountain and valley, hell and heaven, good and evil.

'Is it possible to honestly believe in blatant falsehood? Eh?'

The shaman began to limp alongside the sled, jabbering in his own language, nodding his tightly muffled head; then he approached Ciecierkiewicz and again spoke with him for a long time. Understand the words '*Un-Ilu*', or 'Ice', as well as '*hákin*', 'stomach', and '*bōm*', meaning 'narrow space'.

'He says it's a good thing that gleissen will freeze the Earth,' said

Ciecierkiewicz, thumping out a lively rhythm on his fur coat with his free hand. 'He says people are evil and have deserved the Ice. That the Dragon has to be awakened, he shall devour them all, and only in the belly of the Dragon, the Lord of the Ice, shall power be realised; he, Benedykt, shall digest and transform each one into a nice obedient mammoth.'

'In the belly of the Dragon,' mutter under the breath, whilst preventing the sled from sliding down the hillside, 'squeezed together like sardines in a can.'

'*Łot ajat ujdeni!*' enthused the shaman, ramming his wooden skates into the dark ice with every step. The Tunguses indeed often seemed like children, quick to slip into states of happiness or sorrow, quick to attach themselves to people or take offence. In this the shaman was no different from his cousins.

Tigry Etmatoff's two cousins (whom he sometimes called his brothers, brothers-in-law or other relatives and kin in the intricate Tungus family clans) were very alike in face and physique – identical barrel-bellied torsos on short legs, identical round countenances and narrow Mongolian eyes neath straight black hair – and when smothered in skins and furs, which they exchanged quite freely between themselves in the tent, they left next to nothing to distinguish one from another. Seek help in the fact that the lame-leg Etmatoff clearly harboured anger and great contempt towards one of the cousins, and because of this it was easy to point to the good or bad cousin.

Notice with surprise after several days, however, that a different one of his kinsmen was the object of animosity and the other was in favour.

It therefore remained the frozen truth that beside Tigry, there was a good and a bad cousin; however, this function of the shaman's sympathies and aversions operated on interchangeable variables.

'They're good, egh, good pagans,' panted Ciecierkiewicz. 'Filthy and smelly, but warm-hearted. Not like the darned Yakuts. Who are cunning thieves, crafty sweet-talkers. And such blackguards by nature: imagine, sir, a son buries his father alive in the earth, such is the loving send-off they give a parent in his old age. Khhrrr! For there's no such thing as death, only in the earth –'

'Hold on to this log.'

'All indigenes like to swill, but Yakuts are born drunks; meet a sober, and it's worth writing home about. And when –'

'Hold it!'

But Ciecierkiewicz suddenly felt a need to scratch beneath his shapka; the log restraining the sled on the ice slipped out of his one hand, and the whole weight swept down the mountainside. Shove under a pole to block the runners. '*Czuok, czuok!*' Tigry's cousins yelled at the reindeer from behind. An unattached bundle fell off the sled and tumbled into the valley, ten, twenty, thirty arshins, gathering speed...

'Chase it now!' snarl at Ciecierkiewicz.

The Pilsudtchik stood scratching his crown.

Ciecierkiewicz was a man of whom the parts had come unstuck, meaning everything in him walked on saliva and string, barely-barely as if on a blast of drunken air: whenever he took a step, it was manic, just like Saint Vitus's Dance; whenever he moved his head, then the head nearly dropped off; whenever he did anything more complex, then it was with so many excessive unnecessary gestures that the onlooker easily floundered in the unbridled chaos and lost track of what exactly Ciecierkiewicz did, or whether his work made the slightest sense. Even when resting, his fingers were constantly hopping about, his eyelids twitching, his knees trembling: a dumbshow bubbling on the surface of his physiognomy and erupting every second into vague grimaces. In this he was very like Ivan Petrukhoff, that is, like the memory of Ivan Petrukhoff from the governor general's ball. And umbriance framed him with a similar halo; soft and jellyfish-like.

A certain suspicion was had, a suspicion that could not be put to the test. Just as there exist people with a high teslectric structural constant, freaks with above-normal human capacity for Truth and Falsehood (like father and other abassylians), so, according to all statistical probability, there ought also to exist analogical *phénomènes de la nature* born at the other extreme of the alethic scale. Not living riddles like Miss Muklanowicz – but genuine children of Summer, people who never totally freeze in a given form of character, and of whom it's never possible to say in two-valued logic that they are like this or like that. Meaning, yes indeed, you can state with certainty: that they're wobbly, unspecific, that they've come unstuck.

What is their peculiar quality in the world? Do they really sink into entropy, into chance? Ciecierkiewicz seemed not to be distinguished by anything special. A few words had been exchanged with him at staging-posts and in the mornings (since in the tents of an evening, everyone was so tired they fell fast asleep, having barely swallowed something warm). Maybe, however, this is the whole point – for what is the contrary of exceptionality, of extraordinariness? Ciecierkiewicz, Ciecierkiewicz, a pang of conscience and scar of memory. Looking at him again now... isn't this how gleisseniks perceived Count Gyero-Saski in the Trans-Siberian Express? Here, it can be seen more plainly, because in contrast. And since, in the Land of the Gleissen, he has finally frozen – so what? Even before the incident with the gleiss, a strong conviction had been growing of not having being born at all as the alethic contrary to Petrukhoff; of being closer, on those graphs of

Tesla's, to Ciecierkiewicz than to the Ishmaels. Here it is, the structural constant of Benedykt Gierosławski. In the Black Oasis certain death awaits, there's no reason to go to the Oasis...

Sunlight sparkled on the ice-capped peaks, as smooth sharply cropped shadow crept over the mountainsides from the ridges, and flowed like black sugar-coating over the white sugar-coating of the snow. Whereas in the frostoglazes, the divide between gloom and glare grew blurry, as if someone were igniting the fire neath the iron stove-plate of the Baikal Country, it was enough to tilt the head further still, let the colours transfuse (though there remained in fact only two) and it became impossible in the wintry landscape to completely differentiate sky, crag, cloud, glacier, shadowy valley. Everything consisted of distorted patches of dazzling brightness, perfectly interchangeable. This journey through Siberia was like travelling through a charcoal sketch drawn on card, executed at phrenetic speed by a powerful hand: zigzags, jerky lines, arcs across half the horizon, broken geometric forms criss-crossing infinity. And between one and the backdrop of the next – miniscule human figures, likewise hastily and not very subtly depicted: with no faces, no fingers, no distinguishing marks, clumsy and cloddish, goylem-like, striding in coils of vapour.

The khutor of Nikolay Panteleymonovitch Lushtchy sat perched on a col above a deep valley, with a view opening eastward onto the vast white expanse of Baikal and a long section of the Cold Line. It was not Lushtchy's first railway posting. First, he had worked as a fireman on the Circum-Baikal Railway, several-score versts to the south of Port Baikal. When that line was still functioning, Lushtchy was responsible for maintaining the points and crossings in a state of usability, that is, unfrozen. The Transsib and Chinese Eastern Railway had been built on materials of Summer, only recently were the rails changed to coldiron; before this, men had to be hired to ensure the mechanisms functioned despite the severest frosts. Most often, therefore, they simply lit bonfires on the tracks. But even after the conversion to cold-iron, the problem did not completely disappear. Coldiron, admittedly, doesn't burst due to frost, won't freeze in the same way to stone, nor will mechanisms made of coldiron break down; yet an armour-plated excrescence of ice will immobilise any switch, and glaciuses have a special liking for railways. On Baikal there was a double problem – only a suicidal imbecile would light a bonfire near tracks laid on an ice-covered lake; hence the not-exactly-convenient, for other reasons, concentration of all branches of the Cold Line at Olkhon Station. After the closure of the Circum-Baikal, Nikolay Panteleymonovitch moved first to Olkhon, where – according to Siberian rumours – he tried to deal in opium powder on trains at the crossroads of Asia, cunningly hiding his merchandise of drugs from the ispravniks in the Baikal ice itself; such were the beginnings of Lushtchy's fortune. Later, first one and then another incident occurred on the Cold Line, and so on the orders of Governor General Schultz, railway strongholds began to be constructed on the summits of the Primorsky mountains. Because of the Baikal gales and snow-dust blizzards, which usually concealed the flat surface of the lake, communication depended on signals of light or unlicht: alongside sections of track 'eaten by ice', patrols rigged up unlicht searchbeams (for use during the day) and ordinary searchlights (for night) so as to alert the next position, which would then repeat the alarm along the line of mountain beacons, and in this way reach Port Baikal, Kultuk and Olkhon Station within a matter of minutes. This was not, however, a channel with any great throughput capacity. Doubt that Lushtchy ever received news from the opposite direction, that is, from Irkutsk.

The khutor had been built for the most part according to the Circum-Baikal method, that is, by the abundant use of explosives in the rock. Holes in the granite rockface were then patched up and in-walled, knocking out here and there windows and doors, whilst the main and only entrance on the ground level was fortified by a palisade, which also surrounded the farm buildings. Lushtchy, a merchant of the second Russian guild, guarded stringently his earnings from twenty years of black-market trading; here he kept warehouses full of goods of every kind, sold at shylock prices to travellers in need, distributed to geological and magpie camps across the western Baikal Country. But even from close-up, from fifty paces or so away, it wasn't easy to make out the rocky stronghold under its covering of snow and ice – except streams of smoke billowed from the uppermost openings in the rock, betraying the presence of warm life within.

Two thuggish guards with wolfdogs came out to meet halfway. Drive up to the palisade. There was a price to pay for everything, in-cluding allowing the animals into a heated shelter. Agree with Adin and Shtchekelnikoff that a brief stop would be possible. Step inside as a troika, without unwinding the face rags or removing the frostoglazes. All agreed not to reveal their countenances. The roubles were already counted, Adin was to pay. Speak only in Russian.

Inside, in the main hall, four men were standing by the fireplace, including a soldier in the uniform of a non-commissioned officer. Dogs were prowling everywhere, large, small, descended from wolves, de-scended from mongrels, collared or on the loose; it stank of rancid fat and urine. The good Shtchekelnikoff breathed deeply. 'Good to be back in native parts, always reeking of hay and farts!' Krzysztof went to select the supplies. Nikolay Panteleymonovitch Lushtchy, a mean-looking little man of shabby bearing and crooked glance, sat in a chamber adjoining the hall at a table covered in a white tablecloth, reading a newspaper. His bare feet lay stretched on a bench, whilst an old woman in black dress and tight-fitting cap tended to them with some sort of salves, the herbs of which filled the whole hall with a stench that stung the nose, penetrating even the sharp odour of ammonia. Cough into the scarf. Shtchekelnikoff nodded questioningly. Point to the newspaper. He went to inquire.

It was a mistake. Whatever prompted the idea of sending Tchingis Shtchekelnikoff on such a delicate mission that relied on words and not knives! Manage to avert the head at just the wrong moment, irritated by the piteous yelping of a puppy – an adolescent clad in embroidered rubashka and judging by his appearance: Lushtchy's son was frantically thrashing and kicking a little dog in the corner by a staircase leading up the rockface, hacking it to flesh and bone on the granite floor – avert the head at precisely the moment a separate howl and clatter suddenly came crashing from the opposite direction. Look back. Having knocked over a samovar and thrust aside the babushka, Shtchekelnikoff had Nikolay Panteleymonovitch splayed on his back on the table and was preparing to throttle him. Gospodin Lushtchy was lashing out with bare feet and tugging at the tablecloth like Lazarus caught in his shroud – which naturally did nothing to move the square-shaped thug bent over him. Yell loudly to Adin and pounce on Tchingis, cursing and pulling the cutthroat away. Eventually, he heaved a sigh and let go. Lushtchy came to on all fours and began squealing in whispers. Crammed into a passageway leading from the hall, his people gaped blankly. Lushtchy was no doubt urging them to take bloody revenge, but Shtchekelnikoff had flattened his larynx, and so it was impossible to make out the words of Nikolay Panteleymonovitch. Everyone would quickly grasp his meaning and intent, however. Extract the pocketbook with the rest of the roubles, brandish the banknotes. Krzysztof came running. 'Pay and we'll clear off!' hiss in his direction. Then, shielding him with the body and the diengi, shove Tchingis out of the rock interior and beyond the palisade in the direction of the sled. Shout to the Tunguses to run and fetch the supplies as quickly as possible. Ciecierkiewicz was talking to the wolfdog handlers; one of their dogs had already succeeded in biting him (his shuba had protected his hand). Urge him to turn around the sled for a swift escape. Drag Tchingis to the far side of the equipage, hiding him from view from the khutor behind the reindeer. 'What got into you! All you had to do was ask about news from the city!' Upon which, Shtchekelnikoff reached inside his shapeless sleeve and produced from under his armpit a ball of crumpled newspaper. Smooth out the paper on the knee. 'Still October's!' Miffed, hurl the *Herald* into the snow. 'But whyever did you strangle him, for God's sake!' Tchingis waved his hand. 'He said me a bad word.'

Escape in the end from Lushtchy's khutor alive, without admittedly taking all the supplies, although paying through the nose for those taken; as a parting gift, Lushtchy's hearties let rip a round of rifle-fire from windows hewn in the rock, scaring everyone to death.

… Learn a lot later that the brawl ended bloodlessly thanks only to the presence of that soldier, no doubt assigned to the railway outpost on the occasion of terrorist attacks.

Torment Tchingis at every stopping-place for the rest of the day with accusations and questions, why do such a stupid thing and what was it really about. Had he perhaps known Lushtchy before from some old criminal connections? Cease these feverish intellectual pursuits only at dusk, once the emotion had gone and it was possible to look again at things coldly, that is, in truth, and rely on a gleissenik's chilly instinct. Tchingis was busying himself about the pitched tent, angry and offended, no longer saying anything, awaiting any excuse to offload his fury on someone. He hadn't lied, hadn't hidden anything. He really did hurl himself at a stranger in order to throttle him – in the midst of severe trouble, surrounded by overwhelming power, to the undoing of himself and his companions – because that man had said a bad word to him. This was Tchingis Shtchekelnikoff through and through. Wasn't it known before? But what kind of man slits another man's throat in the middle of the street without hesitation? What kind of man volunteers for suicidal expeditions such as this? What kind of man is amused by nannying the Son of Frost and toying on a knife edge with all the powers of Siberia?

This too is the Mathematics of the Ice. You can't take the devil for a friend and then be surprised he's corrupted your kids, defiled a woman, tortured kittens for pure pleasure and shat on a shrine.

'Mr Shtchekelnikoff.'

'What?'

'Why was he battering that puppy?'

'Mm-hmm?'

'Lushtchy's maltchik was grinding that dog to a pulp.'

'Every man must have someun in this world as feels mortal terror at him and can be abused at will.'

It was a form of blindness, however: that inability to perceive the soletruth of character. Not to imply thereby the perspicacity of Doctor Myśliwski or Prosecutor Razbyesoff, but ordinary human familiarity with weaknesses, irrationality, madness. Already in the Trans-Siberian Express, this had been grappled with in various ways – Winter itself had to be entered for the simple model of Captain Privyezhensky to be calculated; a few dinners had to be consumed in the Wielicki household to be initiated at all into such reasoning.

On what precisely, however, does that special property of the Land of the Gleissen so depend – this feature of an environment so saturated with murch – that things once formulated in thought and language are manifested here in their soletruth, including people's individual characters? This was not after all a property of the mind, since no man acquired new cognitive abilities, nor did he become a great sage or expert in the mysteries of the soul. Nor was there any guarantee that at the crossroads of ignorance, we would turn onto the path of truth rather than falsehood. So whence this sharpness of vision amongst people steeped in murch?

Another nightly blizzard was brewing, a frequent occurrence now above Baikal, and the Yapontchiks advised overnighting in one tent, pitching it in the form of a large yurt, and erecting a shelter for the animals on the poles of the other. The Tunguses would have taken their dogs inside, but no dogs were brought from Tunka; the reindeer remained outside, burdened only by the wooden rattles around their necks so they wouldn't stray far. Light the stove, leaving the lid ajar to illuminate the interior. The chest with the other stove, the naphtha one adapted by Tesla, lay somewhere amongst the luggage spread in a ring around the inner walls of the tent. Remove not the furs; the yurt warms up so-so only when people are tightly huddled. The indigenous custom is to strip naked and dive in a heap under the skins; the Yapontchiks declined to practise it, regarding it as unhygienic in the extreme.

'Zmanda tyküllen,' declared the bad cousin as the last man to take cover in the tent and lace up the entrance. Krzysztof placed a kettle on the stove, chopped up frozen fish and sliced bread with a heavy saw. Having seated himself by the opposite wall, Tigry Etmatoff started his own fire: set before him a clay bowl, laid out plant kindling and other rubbish, sprinkling on various powders and herbs, spitting on them and pulling something out from his hair, which he also added to the mixture; he then set fire to the whole. An unpleasant stench spread throughout the yurt; the Christians swore as one man, sniffling from their runny noses.

Tigry chuckled and jabbered merrily and, reaching behind him, wrested from under the bundles a long bone drumstick and a drum covered in painted skin.

'He says we're above a mammoth path,' said Ciecierkiewicz, having thrown off his sheepskin and wrapped himself in a voluminous reindeer-hide kuklanka so that only his head protruded, his head and one hand as he tilted a small metal hip flask containing raw spirit into his beard, for it was his habit to warm himself every night into a state of total befuddlement; otherwise, he was unable to sleep on the march.

It was useless inquiring whether Ciecierkiewicz was such an un-stuck-uncoordinated fellow because he was familiar thanks to constant inebriation with the mild ailments associated with delirious states – or because he was simply unable to abide without his flask, as he was that kind of man: dishevelled, any-old-how. The sequence of events is meaningless, either way, there exists only truth frozen in the Now.

'But the coldiron trade hasn't come to a halt,' said Adin, as he brewed brick tchay.

'You spoke to someone at Lushtchy's?'

'Exchanged a couple of words before the brawl happened. Asked about prices and if they'd received fresh consignments from the city; well, because everything would be dearer, were there to be outright war; but I heard only that coldiron and tungetitum were holding their own.'

'This might rather mean that Blutsky-Osey had taken control of Irkutsk and Nikolayevsk by force for the tsar.'

'Pray rather that Lushtchy's not sent any of his gravediggers after us.'

'And where to tomorrow, Mr G?' croaked Tchingis.

'Wait a moment.' Raise the hand, demanding silence, and extract the Piatnik pack of cards from the sac de voyage. They saw what was about to follow; these coded patience games had been frequently tried.

Krzysztof, sighing melancholically, hung his head still lower; broken thus in two, he poured boiling water from the kettle held higher than his eyes. Steam misted the interior of the tent.

'How wide is this path?' inquire of Tigry.

'*Sotja birakan.*'

'He says narrow as a mountain torrent.'

'Mm-hmm.'

'Ain't you noted it on them secret maps of yours, Mr G? There, there or there, so many versts and that's it. Huh?'

Fortunately, Tigry began to bang on his drum. First, he sat for a while gazing into his fire, clutching a piece of meat above it, trembling bizarrely in body and face, hiccupping and coughing like a child; then a thicker sweat broke out on his cheeks, his eyelids dropped and a morbid shudder began to convulse him, a shudder, that is, his guiding spirits, 'the eight-legged guardians of the twelve uluses'. He then snatched up the drum.

Shtchekelnikoff was chewing the shavings as he scraped an ice-infested fish from tail to head with his long, narrow, bayonet-style knife. Take out the notebook and pencil, open the pocket watch on the reindeer skin alongside, shuffle the cards. Tchingis watched from under his brow with an expression of morose suspicion on his coarse visage – but this too was nothing out of the ordinary. A gleissenik ought never to be surprised that a man is as he is. It should have been foreseen how Shtchekelnikoff might react to Lushtchy and Lushtchy to Shtchekelnikoff, and this without any calculation, without the whole Mathematics of the Ice, but alone from 'looking', of which even the stupidest gleisseniks are capable.

The phenomenon was initially attributed to psychological or simply physiological causes ('an animal instinct for truth'!), the reasons for it being perceived in the long-lasting influence of murch on the electrics of the brain and similar mechanisms – namely, that all people living under the Ice manifest a tendency towards such harsh cut-and-dried categorisations, as well as sectarian fanaticism in the most trivial mundane matters. Now, however, months later, the phenomenon appeared to have much more in common with how the law of excluded middle varies in strength in Winter, within two-valued logic. In Summer, Aristotle's law that two contradictory propositions cannot at the same time be false, and that if one contradictory proposition is false, then the other must be true, has no power. In Summer, when you say, 'Every good devil has a tail', as well as 'Some good devils do not have tails', you will not find betwixt these two contradictory statements any truth. Under the Ice, however, all 'good devils' and similar self-refuting beings drop out of language, drop out of logic. All that remains is what the law of excluded middle has frozen in advance into sharp either-or. Therefore, just as you won't come across a good devil in the Land of the Ice, so too – you won't encounter a hare-hearted Timofey Schultz or a merciful, trusting Tchingis Shtchekelnikoff. A gleissenik looks and a gleissenik knows: Yea, yea, Nay, nay.

The logic of the Ice – the intensity of the teslectic field freezing the mind – precludes any thought of an object, person, idea, character that does not fit in its entirety into soletruth or its negation.

A man like Ciecierkiewicz – now making nervous clownish grimaces at his own reflection in the polished flask – would surely not be conspicuous in Summer by his posture and behaviour, and would not attract anyone's attention. But here, under the Ice, another man is unable to perceive him otherwise, think of him differently, apply different words to him and freeze him in different memory. Like every subject of a sentence governed by the principle of non-contradiction –

Pam-pwam! Pam-pwag! 'A mwooki dooki moowooki! owoooooki moowooki!' the scar-faced Tungus wails plaintively, swaying over the foul-smelling smoke and emitting every now and then, for the sake of variety, piercing animal noises. Lay out two-dozen cards, make a note of the distribution order – dot or dash, one or zero, according to its probability or improbability – then gather up the cards and reshuffle them with the rest of the pack, until the second hand of the silver watch has passed another twenty seconds; then again lay out a series of cards and put a mark. Pam-pwam! Pam-pwag! The good and the bad cousin, having lapped up the boiled tchay-water and thawed the fish on their tongues, had burrowed under the skins; now, in response to the shaman's rhythmic drumming and wailing, they resurfaced like mammoths conjured from below the earth, gradually, laboriously, ceasing to move for long intervals in their drowsiness. Etmatoff wasn't watching; his narrow eyes were closed, tightly shut, and even when he opened them, throwing back his head and flinging wide his slavering gob, they were rolled back to the whites and blind-sighted. The scars stitched into his cheeks in geometrical patterns glowed red as rowan-berries, as if roasted by the frost. Krzysztof was coughing, waving a hare-skin sock – the shaman's fire had so filled the yurt with smoke. Breathe through the mouth without lifting the eyes from the cards, closing the mind to the hypnotic melodies of the shaman's kamlaniye ritual. Zero, one, zero, one. According to prescription, the wave should be travelling along the Ways of the Mammoths at a frequency of three strokes per minute, meaning that even a very brief message required roughly a quarter of an hour to be sent; however, shorter periods of the wave would have unduly hindered the readings, curtailed the crests and troughs. The agreement was that messages should not exceed thirty signals. Reception therefore took about an hour: after fifteen or so shuffles of the cards, the rhythm of the wave could be felt and the end of a sequence recognised from the repetitions, whilst a second reading was still necessary for controlling distortions. So, only after having made a note in this way of a nearly a hundred zeros and ones derived from the distribution of the cards, insert underneath, expressed also in Morse code, the binary password assigned to Mademoiselle Filipoff and Doctor Tesla – 1011011011101111011111001001 – that is to say, AUFERSTEHUNG – in order to then decipher the original content in reverse operations of mathematical logic. Those which George Boole set forth in his *An Investigation of the Laws of Thought on Which are Founded the Mathematical Theories of Logic and Probabilities*, where, in order to express Aristotle's laws of logic in algebraic formulae, he chose two numerical representatives: 0 denoting Nothing and Never, hence 0 x y = 0 for every y, and 1 denoting the Universe and Eternity, hence 1 x y = y for every y. Using these symbols of Falsehood and Truth, simple calculations can therefore be performed, such as, for example, either-or operations, which always turn two zeros or two ones into a zero, and a one and a zero – into a one. As anybody can take readings of teslectric waves on the Ways of the Mammoths, it should have been anticipated that sooner or later, someone would hit on the idea of registering these fluctuations – hit on it precisely because the teslectric wave passes along the Ways of the Mammoths and every twenty seconds the weirdest combinations of ideas spark in any brain. Hence the cipher.

Tigry fell silent, having flown away (or maybe from exhaustion). Slip into the rhythm of shuffling and laying out the cards, not so very different from the rhythm of the drum and the shaman's moan: what it was all about, in the repeated sequences of movement, was detaching the spirit from the body – the body does its thing, and the spirit roams free. The roar of the gale and blizzard swelled, the tent walls shook. In a genuine yurt, an opening would be left at the apex for smoke to escape; winter in the Land of the Gleissen was far too harsh to voluntarily allow the slightest access to the frost. Smoke from the stove was led outside by a tight-fitting pipe, but the smoke from the shaman's fire, as well as the misty vapour of unlighted human breath – accumulated inside, benumbing, lulling to sleep, facilitating the hypnotic collapse. One, one, one.

Tigry awoke, having returned from his journey along the Ways of the Mammoths, and struck his drum once but hard, upon which the good and bad cousins began seething under the animal skins. Mr Ciecierkiewicz gave a start as if lashed by a whip, likewise wrested no doubt from some alcoholic hallucination. He cursed the Tungus. Tigry Etmatoff put away his drumstick, drank up the herbal tea from the little bowl and bared his teeth, brightening his sweaty cheeks in a broad grin. He began to explain something in earnest, slapping his thighs.

'He says devils are coming after –'

Raise the hand, demanding silence, without taking the eyes off the pocket watch. And quickly: card, card, card, half the pack in an astounding order of cold and hot colours – then the next number one jotted down in the notebook.

Eventually, loop the entire message twice. Three distortions had occurred, that is, incompatibilities in the reading of the wave or lack of wave – parallel versions of the decryption had to be accepted there. Lick the pencil. The very beginning… There is no beginning. Since assignation of a stop sign had been forgotten; besides, it would have attracted suspicion, since it was not covered by the cipher. So, there was nothing for it but to try another thirty reshuffles – until the meaning appeared.

Revolve in the head the binary sequences, like wax cylinders with musicians' recordings of truth and falsehood.

0101110100010101101100011001000
1011011011011110111111100100110
1110101111110101100111011101110
··· _·_· ···· ··_ _·.. _·_·· · _··· _

SCHULTZ LEBT.

Schultz lives. Don't return. Tsar all around. Tesla working here under arrest. We are waiting. The message went round in circles without beginning; so, the context and emphasis could be shifted within it at will. *We are waiting. Schultz lives. Don't return. Tsar all around. Tesla working here under arrest.* Or: *Tsar all around. Tesla working here under arrest. We are waiting. Schultz lives. Don't return.*

Schultz lives. That is, he is alive and in power, otherwise the emperor's rule wouldn't have stopped at the horizon, but Prince Blutsky would have reseized Irkutsk and Zimny Nikolayevsk and the entire Land of the Gleissen in the name of His Exaltedness Nikolay Aleksandrovitch. Meanwhile Schultz-Zimovy sits in the Box with his regiments, whilst the coldiron trade continues full steam ahead along the Trans-Siberian Railway as if nothing had happened, and diplomatic letters no doubt also travel from Baikal to the Neva Bay and back again. Schultz, especially until recovered from his near-fatal wound, will first and foremost woo Siberian industry, as well as watch over the punctual supply of imperial troops to the becalmed Japanese front: such is the former governor general's golden key, that of today's autocrat of Siberia, for he who controls the Transsib also holds a knife to the throat of Vladivostock and the whole of East Asia; therefore Saint Petersburg won't cut off Schultz from European Russia by blocking the Transsib anywhere before the Irkutsk guberniya. It's a tight clinch in which neither wrestler can flex his muscles more effectively, lest the other immediately counter with his own muscle power. (The politics of the Ice.) For the Japanese Empire itself also wishes to score, of course, from the new situation, and having spied an opportunity, will forget in a trice all peace treaties and solemn oaths. Schultz now has to guard the Transsib like the family jewels. And for this very reason, Józef Piłsudski and his Riflemen in the Japanese Legion will strive at all costs to blow up the railway. No doubt Schultz's first or second instruction on regaining consciousness was to send his Cossacks into Siberia to protect the Transsib and liquidate the Yapontchiks.

… *We are waiting.* They are waiting. For what are they waiting? Tesla is working, which goes without saying: otherwise, no message at all would be coming along the Ways of the Mammoths. (The message speaks of Tesla in the third person – so who was editing it, Mademoiselle Filipoff?) Sooner or later, however, Schultz will rid himself of the Serbian inventor. Gather up the cards, pack them away with the notebook. The tea had gone cold. Schultz is holding Nikola there as his next bargaining chip in his haggling with the tsar (how much will His Imperial Exaltedness give for keeping the Doctor of Summer alive with his gleissocidal knowledge in his head?) and with the local opposition (for whilst Tesla lives, the potentates of Sibirkhozheto cannot be safe from Thaw). But will Count Schultz realistically gain anything permanent from such haggling? An independent state…? Biding his time, blackmailing, playing on the freezing of the status quo. On the other hand, in order to react forcefully, Nikolay the Second would have to decide to send troops to a Baikal war… With Japan at his back? He won't do it. It's very difficult, however, to believe in any kind of meaningful political change under the Ice.

… And yet for a man to kidnap his own dominion by such methods is easiest in just such a feudal country, founded on the principle of autocracy, where there is no sanction over and above the sanction of power itself, no other sanction legitimising the rule of this or that autocrat. For he is chosen neither by the people nor by representatives of the people; here, the ruler depends not on the law (on the contrary: the law depends on him, his will is the law) and no measure of justice exists apart from this single one: he wields power, therefore such was God's will. A usurper that succeeds is God's anointed. Law, compromise and the contract between people have no force where everyone constantly seeks signs of Truth.

… And the tsar realises this perfectly – hence his eternal distrust and terror of his subjects, fear of talented ministers, generals, tchinovniks. Did Frantishek Markovitch Uriah not speak of it at the governor's ball? Gnaw into the raw fish, already so well thawed it sits on the tongue like a slimy half-dead snail. The principle of Truth organises Russian life in every sphere, from morality to high politics.

… Therefore, no one can say that Schultz, even after a definitive victory, would change anything here. Mr Pocięgło had outmanoeuvred himself. No morning star of freedom shall rise over the Land of the Gleissen. People had been living in the Governorate of Irkutsk, where Count Schultz-Zimovy held everyone by the scruff in the name of His Imperial Highness Nikolay the Second Aleksandrovitch – now they will live in the so-or-otherwise-called State of Irkutsk, where Count Schultz-Zimovy holds everyone by the scruff in the name of Count Schultz-Zimovy. Did the Oblastniks really believe they could unfreeze History with one smart carom made from outside of the Ice? Nothing will change. Symbol will replace symbol, but this won't affect the substance of the equation. There will always be a good cousin and a bad cousin.

… Chew on the abominable fish. Nothing will change and Schultz won't endeavour to change. Even were the negotiations on his behalf with the gleissen to –

'No way to kill them. They're already dead. They eat death.'

'What?'

Tigry Etmatoff was pounding with his fingers on the drum to indicate the gravity of his words.

'*Jokó-Awāhe, niu-un.*'

'He says, that, mm-hmm-er-er,' Ciecierkiewicz yawned widely, 'that Yakut Devils, six of them.'

Swallow, drink up the greasy wish-wash.

'Ask him if he knows who's sent them. The tsar? That is, the Okhrana, Prince Blutsky? Or Schultz?'

'He doesn't know.'

'Mm-hmm, anyway we'll lose them quickly in these blizzards.'

'He says they're not following tracks in the Middle World. A Yakut shaman, agh, is leading them.' Ciecierkiewicz took another swig and stretched out under his furs in a semi-recumbent pose, hitching his elbow in so doing onto the snoring Shtchekelnikoff, in response to which the latter drew back his great fist in his sleep and smashed it into the back of Ciecierkiewicz's neck. 'Ugh. He says that, mm-hmm, we should proceed under guard. He asks what you prophesied from the cards.'

Attempts had already been made to explain to them that this was no sortilege magic done in likeness of their shaman prophecies, from boiled and burned bones; but to no avail.

'It's science, understand? – sci-en-ce; no magic spells and superstitions.'

'He says, a-aaah, says it's higher spirits that choose the shaman, not the shaman who chooses.'

Then, mellowed by his successful out-of-body flight, Tigry Etmatoff floats into confidences of a yarn-spinning nature – in the confined, stuffy, smoked-filled tent, in sooty semi-darkness and oily damp, whilst the snowstorm rages outside and the frost hardens.

'From the beginning, from childhood, a shaman differs from other people, and suffers this difference every day: he sees the world differently, sees himself differently.'

'*Aja!*'

'A shaman has too many bones, one bone too many.'

'What?'

'*Jama u mu kon!*'

'A hundred and one. This bone is the hundredth-and-first, but, so I understand – this bone is always a kind of defect, a deformity. Either the shaman goes through a mortal illness in childhood, as a result of which he remains disfigured for the rest of his life, crippled. Or he is put to death and brought back to life by spirits in a time-honoured ancient ritual: reassembled out of not entirely the same material. Or – something breaks inside him. In any case, the hundred-and-first bone sets him apart from everyone else and handicaps him in daily life.'

'One leg shorter, for example.'

'*Aja!*'

'What's more, the shaman always sees how the invisible becomes detached from the visible. Mm-hmm, wait a moment –'

'Spirit from matter.' Grind on the gum the last snippet of fish, already completely devoid of taste.

Ciecierkiewicz and Etmatoff began jabbering again, assisted by their hands.

'Spirit from matter,' the Yapontchik belched at last. 'This world,' he waved his arm around the tent, 'crushes them, tortures them. It is forced, agh, forced upon them, they're doomed to it; it is the cause of their spiritual sickness.'

'*Aja!*'

'They feel it constantly. They try to break free, liberate themselves.'

'As a third soul,' mutter under the breath, 'to the Upper World.'

'A shaman,' continued Ciecierkiewicz, himself slipping into a yarn-spinning, sing-song lilt, 'lives under the power of invisible compulsions. He says: under the power of spirits. What a shaman does is not done by the shaman, but through the shaman. Yes?'

'*Aja!*' Tigry clapped his hands and pointed with a swift gesture, over the fire dying in the bowl, at the shuffling and laying out of the cards. He grinned broadly.

Did he still imagine some sort of shamanic ritual had been performed with the cards? That the Ways of the Mammoths had likewise been flown to – only with the aid of a pack of cards, pocket watch and notebook, instead of a drum?

'Tell him I'm a mathematician, not a shaman,' mutter to Ciecierkiewicz. Begin feeling with nervous movements for the tobacco and papers. The hand returned to the tea mug and clutched it tightly. 'I have as many bones as I should, I was not born with any deformity. Tell him to think rather of where to descend safely to some broader Ways of the Mammoths; I had distortions in my readings, a few times I had to guess the wave.'

'He says we shall approach from the Murin river along the Onot towards the Lena, to a trifurcation of the Ways. He says that's where you're sure to meet him.'

'What...?'

'*Agawūt-Ü-Nin!*'

This was too much.

'I have no idea where to look for Father Frost!' Fling the tea mug against the tent wall; it rebounded off a pole.' 'Understand, Tigry? All these maps, all these calculations, secret deliberations, investigations into father's black past, pacts with political devils – none of it is worth a fig! I have found out nothing! I am fleeing into Siberia because they're chasing me, but where to – where to – nowhere! But now I learn that for the time being I can't return to Irkutsk either. And also, that Schultz or the tsarist Okhrana are sending local trackers after me, some kind of corpse-eaters, so he says – well, what now?!' Tear at Ciecierkiewicz, who had not yet translated for Etmatoff and was merely gawping at the indecorous outburst with a foolish expression, offended expression. 'Well, what now?! I can't keep the truth from you any longer. There is no plan! Unless someone wants to volunteer for the icy grave, in which case be my guest, we can cross to the sources of Baikal tungetitum – who's willing?'

'Calm down,' Adin whispered from under his blanket.

'He says... he says, that –'

'Or perhaps he could shut up at last!' snarl at the shaman, curling up in the shuba and lying down on one side to sleep.

'He says that you like playing the wise man.'

'Pshaw!'

'Playing the wise man.' The Yapontchik breathed in smoke and coughed; the shaman was waiting. 'But why didn't you reckon that it would be the parent, first and foremost, who would want to find the *huta*, that is, his own son? He says, that –'

Here the drum of the crippled Tungus struck up again; Ciecierkiewicz began to translate the sung words:

'Wasn't it for this you left the City for open Winter? Wasn't it for this you demanded to be brought to the widest of the Ways? Half the heart in fire, half the heart in ice; you go to him so as not to reach him, seek him so as not to find. But how can a father who walks with abassylar remain blind to his son's black light? How can he not come out to meet him, when the *huta* comes to him with open arms? His dogs, wolves, bears – he speaks of spirits – shall lead him to you through the Underground World. All you have to do is meet him halfway, stretch out your hand, open the yurt. Call like a son to his father. At the parting of the mammoth ways. How can a father not come to his son? How can he not come? Even if he carries all *Un-Ilu* on his back. He shall come.'

On the measure of mirkdom

A murchometer is in the form of a rod ending in a dangling bow-shaped pendulum. Its method of usage is similar to that of rotary thermometers: you have to stand in an open space and spin the dangler. The rod is thick, with a coldiron 'bulb' under the bow – a small teslectric generator is located there with output set in advance and structure ensuring a standard structure constant, Q. The murchometer measures the pressure of the teslectric flow, U_w, released along the rod into the air. Since we know the specific absorbencies Q_1 and Q_2 (that is, of the constant of air), know the capacity of the generator as well as the pressure itself – then it's easy to calculate the final component of the equation: the intensity of the surrounding teslectric field. The lower the pressure on the murchometer, the less the difference in potentials. In the courtyard of the Physical Laboratory of the Imperial Academy of Sciences, on a day of calm skies, Tesla would read off the scale etched on the rod, one hundred and twenty point five mirks. Thus, he attributed to the gubernatorial city of Irkutsk an isoaletheia of nine ten-thousandths of a nocta. Walking north, towards the place of Impact, a systematic increase in the Frost was to be expected. Extract the murchometer from under Tesla's stove a day after descending from the mountains at a latitude of fifty-four degrees, and brandish the contraption at dawn above the head before striking camp, steaming with black breath mist neath a milk-white sun. (The Tunguses clutched at their iron amulets.) Then jot down the reading, freezing the calendar with a single stroke of the karandash.

7th December 1924, 116 mirks.

The Tunguses took the thing to be superstition, which came as no surprise, yet Shtchekelnikoff was also spotted stealthily making the sign of the cross. Whilst the Yapontchiks, supposedly educated Europeans and men experienced in the domain of the Ice, preferred always to be somewhere on the far side of the camp at times when the measurements were taken, behind the animals, behind the tents, with their backs turned. And whenever any attempt was made to question them, at first still in jocular tone, they slipped into evasive monosyllables.

How peculiarly the paths of science and superstitions intersect here! All jollity departed when it became clear they could in no way be separated: this pilgrimage was leading to Batyushka Moroz, who had descended onto the Ways of the Mammoths and, harnessed to a team of gleissen, was driving History. How to fully explain such a fairy tale in the language of science? Impossible and, in truth, it ought not even to be tried. However, this is precisely why the companions hastened obediently onward and did not rebel when it came out that they'd been led blindfold, senselessly – because they're prompted not by reason, not by rational calculation. Freeze as the Son of Frost, and these are the consequences.

And so, it's no longer only the cards in the evening, but also the murchometer at daybreak – the rituals of the mathematical shaman. Few words had been exchanged with the companions earlier, lest the lack of plan should be betrayed; now nothing was said at all – there being nothing to say: instead of fusing under the Frost with language of the first kind, the languages of the second kind had burst along the whole length of their seams. *These men were strangers all.* Watch them at the encampments and on the move in silent wonderment – as if through a reversed telescope that removes the object's image to an indeterminate distance. On the frostoglazes, their contours were washed out, since if the head weren't moved for a long while, they'd melt into shape-less puddles of white, and dissipate across the snowy plain and wide horizon: no trace remaining. Besides, what did survive in this abyss of white? Peoples and geographies were vanishing.

For these men were strangers all. The Tunguses – naturally, were indigenes. But the Pilsudtchiks too – melancholy Krzysztof and scat-ter-brained Ciecierkiewicz – met somewhere in the drawing rooms of Irkutsk, wouldn't be worth the briefest word, passed over by the gaze after an initial glance, after the shallowest touch of the *Gestalt* of their soletruth. And the good Shtchekelnikoff, who remained, until fatal ne-cessity ordained otherwise, as no more than a crudely sketched square silhouette: more words had been exchanged with him during that one evening spent in the ruffians' drinking-den under the ice than in all the previous months put together. They were strangers and would remain strangers, even were a whole long Siberian year to be spent with them under one tent. Strangers, not because they're unknown, but because of the totally alien geometry of their characters.

Understand better now Engineer Iertheim. The opposite of a friend is not an enemy, but a person you don't even notice, who at once drops completely from sight and memory. What of it that you spend a hundred long evenings with this Ciecierkiewicz, if all that connects you are banal words about the weather, reindeer, tchay and frostbitten fingers? And even were it possible to get to know him deeper – what gets known inspires no warmer emotion, floats past without trace.

Value now the remarkable unusualness of Jelena Muklanowicz. What transpired in the Trans-Siberian Express – or what was remembered of what transpired – was the connecting of symmetrical characters, the encounter of friend with friend. Before Miss Muklanowicz had been known at all, before she was first espied in her evening deshabille in the corridor of De Luxe, bah, before the train was even boarded – she was already a friend. Thereafter the words she spoke or spoke not, her lies and truths, gestures and omissions, despite being made still deep within Summer – were not and could not have been of the slightest significance. The cold Mathematics of Character had decided on every-thing in advance. Jelena had understood it better. *The meeting between one person and another is never boring: something authentic touches something authentic.*

And it would be a lie to maintain that here, in the Frost, the black-haired devushka was not thought about more and more obsessively. She would return in the early morn; intrude in the evenings; be projected off dazzling snow onto the frostoglazes during sled-ride or foot-march across the submontane taiga, so that the eyelids scarcely blinked. Riddle, phenomenon, true lie, woman. But first and foremost: phantom from the past. After all, she existed not. What existed was a warm mental wraith in the shape of a morbidly slender devushka flitting freely from memory to memory. Pleasant it was to forget after dusk, wrapped in the hareskin turban, nestling by the stove, in the dim ember afterglow parboiled at the margins of shadow – shadow here, shadow there, when suddenly, behold the beautiful wraith bent over the turban. Try to force open the eyes, raise a hand towards her... Asleep. She stroked the cheek with her cold palm. Sometimes, late at night, between Shtchekelnikoff's intermittent snores, hear her quiet consumptive cough. No Tchornoye Siyaniye stood in the sky, and no deeper dreams were dreamed. Miss Muklanowicz existed only insofar as she was thought about. In other words, more and more obsessively.

Still in the mountains, fear arose that this too could easily degenerate into the next addiction. For who was there to open the trap to – Adin, Shtchekelnikoff? (These men were strangers all.) Begin to talk to the delusions of memory. Could this be *loneliness* setting in? Loneliness had been unknown throughout all those Warsaw years spent on equations and theories, unknown in the desperate lostness in the Transsib, not sensed even in the solitary sojourn in Irkutsk; no such feeling was remembered. Now loneliness poisoned the soul: in the oppressive, suffocating proximity of strangers.

Prompted by panicked animal reactions – escape again into reading. In the books borrowed from the Polish Library, fellow countrymen (travellers and ethnologists) described the mysterious customs of diverse Siberian peoples; scraps of uncensored knowledge could be gleaned from the novels of Sieroszewski. After what Tigry had prattled, seek especially passages on the peculiarities of shamanism. In extensive quotations included in the Polish books, Russian works too had been salvaged, like *The Evolution of the Black Faith of the Yakut* by a certain Troshtchansky V.F., banned outright by Sibirkhozheto censors. Read – neath a cluster of larch icicles, neath an icy overhang during a stop in a ravine, by a fire dancing on resinous chippings – off cold paper that scrunched in the gloves like a great patch of hoarfrost.

In accounts of interviewed shamans, experiences would recur of discontinuity: there was always a particular moment in their lives when past was totally wrenched from future; but after they were stuck or stitched back together – they no longer quite fitted themselves. This dissonance, this blemish of internal rupture (like a hidden flaw in the disordered structure of a metal), this memory of not being quite frozen – this is what makes a person a shaman. Usually, it was death. The candidate to be a shaman would be dying – struck down by a grave feverish illness, consumed by spirits, cast into an airhole in the ice, drunk on a poisonous brew – after which he would return as someone already altered, that is, as a shaman. At the point of discontinuity, where their history broke off, new memories would blossom for the shamans: that they 'really were' born somewhere else, at some other time, with different parents, in a different ulus, under a different star; that they bore a different name; that their entire shamanic knowledge was not fresh or acquired but had been theirs from the very beginning, since they'd mastered it by living always as shamans (which none but they remember); that 'in reality', they'd spent more time with spirits in the Upper and Lower Worlds than amongst the living. Were customarily led through the moment of discontinuity by an animal spirit guide, a bear or enormous iron bird. There was talk of earth, iron and ice. There was talk of pain: of quartering, of scraping flesh off bones, of extracting internal organs, of replacing them with new ones made of stone and iron, of infusion with new blood; all of it painful. (Mutilation of memory accompanied memory of mutilation.)

On the evening of the seventh of December, at the camp not far from where a gleiss had half-frozen into a rockface, thrust under Tigry's nose a physical map of the region covering from the Primorsky mountains to Kuda, demanding he indicate the location of that crucial fork in the Ways of the Mammoths. Etmatoff pondered the map for a long while, rocking dejectedly on his heels, till it crossed the mind that he'd sunk again into some kind of trance; eventually, he stabbed at a point on the map with an iron bone. Lean forward, shining the nightlamp upon it.

'But's that's where we're standing right now!'

'To-mor-row,' he stammered, 'Near-ly there.'

'Words of the heathen fool the children; let in the heathen and Christians scarper,' muttered Shtchekelnikoff, hanging his ponging dirty-yellow socks on the tentpoles.

The good and bad cousin chuckled in agreement.

8th December 1924, 110 mirks.

On the Ways of the Mammoths stood the frozen carcass of a horse as well as the wreck of a European sleigh, half-reduced to ashes. The horse was still upright on three legs – one probably chewed off by wolves, before it utterly froze and was covered by a lump of solid ice.

Examine this statue for a long time, whilst the Yapontchiks and Tunguses pitched the tents and transferred the luggage.

'Here? Are you sure?'

'Da. Here,' Tigry confirmed and kicked his wooden skate into the crusty snow. 'Dorogi Ma-mon-toff,' he smacked his lips and opened wide his arms, as if showing off the length of a fish he'd just caught.

Apart from the corpse and wreck, nothing special distinguished the vicinity. Coniferous forest stretched from the north and north-east, mostly larch and pine, now heavily icebound; a plain of white opened towards the south. The eastern horizon, however, shot up above the taiga in the undulating line of the Primorsky mountains.

'How long... before he comes?'

The shaman waved his hands vigorously. (Recall how, in the clearing beside the Transsib, he had swept the spidery murch from the face – but who? it could hardly have been him.) He waved, rolled his eyes, scratched at his scars, waggled his shorter leg, and pointed in a ritual gesture to the north and to the earth. Understand he was about to descend onto the Ways in search of the pater.

Unbuckle the skis, walk around the sleigh entrapped in ice. Slightly tilted on its side, shoved by a runner neath the surface of the ground, its rear thrust up towards the Sun, scorched to charcoal, it was an image of pitiful ruin; many such roadside wrecks had been seen before at Warsaw's city limits, on the border between Summer and Winter. Wherefrom, however, had this one hailed – here, in the midst of the Onotsk Upland, precisely at a wide fork in the Ways of the Mammoths? The horse was standing with head thrown back as if about to whinny in panic, still in collar-harness and reins. Ice seemed to have surprised it mid-movement, as if it had no time to escape. Peer inside the sleigh, pressing the nose almost against the mass of milky crystal. Some sort of shapeless bundles lay there on the seats, long shadowy forms, obscured by dirt in the ice. Mortal remains of unlucky travellers? The puzzle was all the harder to solve, as there was no means of deducing the timescale from the material traces preserved in the ice: when had disaster struck this team? a month ago? a year? ten years? The shaft was broken off, the izvoztchik's seat had split. And why so much charred stuff? What had killed them – fire or frost? They'd caught fire as they travelled across Siberia, and suddenly – well, what could have happened?

With axe over shoulder, Shtchekelnikoff marched off to chop wood. (First a fire had to be lit in order to shift the petrified trunk.) If it came to waiting longer – maybe it would be wiser to organise some kind of cabin? Or at least pitch the yurts on wooden lattices, as custom dictated? Hiding inside the tent, take out the maps and reports of the Ministry of Winter. Whilst still at Tsvetistaya Street, the velocity had been calculated of Father Frost along the Ways of the Mammoths; 390 metres an hour, eight and three-quarter versts in twenty-four hours, assuming he doesn't sleep, doesn't get tired, doesn't stop (isn't living). But everything still depends on where Tigry Etmatoff's summons finds him (if it finds him). For this could be somewhere near Norilsk or beyond Yakutsk. Reckon quickly in the head. Taking as the starting-point the place of Impact, that is, the more-or-less geometrical centre of his wanderings as recorded by Uriah, results in a distance of 860 versts. When in that case will he arrive? At the earliest, in one hundred days (if he isn't alive).

... At this very moment he could be farther away, could be closer, but this calculation would appear the most likely. One hundred days, three and a half months. The supplies, according to Krzysztof's latest estimates, will last four weeks. Moss and dried lichen for the reindeer – longer, as long as they're not forced to make daily effort. So, what afterwards? The reindeer will surely unearth something for themselves from beneath the snow. Hunting is a possibility. Fat chance, however, that any living thing would come near a gun barrel on this plain of ice. It might be possible to purchase food and naphtha again for roubles at some out-of-the-way khutor or trading post. Without this time letting Tchingis loose on people and risking the Son of Frost being unmasked. But was it not a greater gamble to send the Yapontchiks alone with the diengi? And what if they're already waiting there at the trading post with the tsar's arrest warrants? For even were Count Schultz so minded, despite everything, to stick to the pact, this land is not his, the authority not his – but that of Nikolay Romanoff.

... Unless something has changed. If this be a wide fork in the Ways, then the wave flowing along them should be powerful – take out the deck of cards, open the pocket watch. Ciecierkiewicz was scraping fungus off the blisters on his feet stained by frostbite. Turn towards the wall, lay out the first row. Zero.

After an hour, it was clear that nothing had changed. *Don't return. Tsar all around. Tesla working here under arrest. We are waiting. Schultz lives.* Most likely they'd been sending this same message since the very beginning. Most likely Tesla had installed to this end some automatic gadget to regulate the Murch Hammer prototype. They themselves could have been arrested already and removed from the Observatory; Doctor Tesla and Mademoiselle Filipoff might even have been killed – whilst the Hammer continues to pound out the sequence in the teslectric field bequeathed to it mechanically. Until the Cossacks arrive and smash the contraption. Pam-pwam! Pam-pwag!

Raise the head suddenly. In the adjacent tent, Tigry is beating on his drum and ruckling through his teeth like a slaughtered beast. Put away the documents, tie up the notebook in rubber band and oilcloth, step out into the snow-white midday sun (a reflected ray shoots into the pupils bare of frostoglazes). On the northern horizon, in the direction of the Ice, from out of the Heart of Winter – a bank of inky-black clouds is swelling. A fresh snowstorm no doubt. Maybe it'll pass to one side; the wind has died down. Or maybe it's no natural meteorological phenomenon at all – maybe if you draw close enough, you'll glimpse with the naked eye a celestial reflection of the mysterious processes taking place within the Kingdom of Winter, beyond the Last Isotherm, where no human foot has yet trod and where only glowing shafts of murch burn amid mountains of tungetitum – in a Black Labyrinth, neath a sky of Black Auroras, on a field of black ice – in the fatherland of self-animating helium – where mathematical Truth may be touched – where gleissen flow like a river – and it's not possible, not possible to die –

Pwam-pwag! Shake the head. Here, above the wide Ways of the Mammoths, as the teslectric wave travels along them stretched between entropic extrema – any folly can suddenly leap to the head, the most banal thought warp in the most improbable associations. So as to return at once to the old order of noun, adjective and verb.

What herb-induced hallucinations and dreams does a Tungus false shaman invoke in such a place? Step inside his tent. A black stench hung in the air. Succumb to a fit of coughing. The reindeer hide fell back over the entrance and total darkness descended. There was a moment of panic – stumbling over something that suddenly moved, tripped up by a pair of legs – the good or bad cousin, stupefied by the kamlaniye ritual, was crawling silently around the yurt. Sink to the knees, cursing under the breath. *Dunda że-lē! Duuunda!* Etmatoff was howling as though burned alive. I massaged my bruised head (red blotches were spinning, the only radiance). 'Silence!' I yelled, irritated, as I ran my hand along the inner wall towards the exit. To let in at least a little light, a little air… Eventually, I pushed aside the reindeer hide and scrambled out on all fours. A black ray shot into the naked pupils. In the garden of iron, between apple trees of rust and pear trees of glowing embers stood a wooden guardhouse under the Romanoff emblem; a barrier separated one half of the grove from the other. I got to my feet, brushed down my white suit, approached, knocked. Into the unlicht of day loomed the Man in the Bowler Hat, completely holey and turned inside out. He said nothing, merely twisted his half-moustache; glanced at his cuff scrawled in milky scribbles and extended his hand. At first, I blinked in dismay – what does he want? – then I remembered. I took out my business-card holder, retrieved the card belonging to the Man in the Bowler Hat and placed it in his hand. He fixed a frosto-glaze monocle into his empty eye socket and lifted the card. Turned it over, examined the verso: the name *Benedykt Gierosławski* had been filled in. He nodded in satisfaction and kicked a stone lever, raising the barrier with its double-headed eagle. I stepped into the other half of the garden. From the branches, bird skeletons were rattling off chastushka tunes. The Black Sun with its angular rays burned more intensely here, frost whistled in the bones. I noticed I was bleeding white light: leaving puddles of shining grease on the ground. I stopped, which proved a tragic mistake, for this ground was too soft, too hungry, starved from fasting; it swallowed my feet, I couldn't take another step, swallowed me as far as the knees, as far as the loins, I tried resisting with my hands, it swallowed my hands too, all I could do was scream, so I screamed – it swallowed my mouth, swallowed my eyes, my whole head, the whole of me. Then it began to digest me, beginning not from my legs but from my innards, into which it reached through my forced-open mouth and unclenched anus. Earth, clay, gravel, stone – poured into me at a torturously slow, unbearable rate, one gramme per year, a kilogramme per century, until eventually – stuffed full, thoroughly digested – I so swelled verst upon verst, so expanded at my seams in the soil of the iron garden that I could touch the mountains to the east with one hand, and with the other – a volcano to the west; one foot was steeped in a lava lake, the other – in a mammoths' watering-hole. I lingered between them, cast in stone, until I sensed movement not my own in the geological masses; shivers, that is, gleissen ran down my spine. Magma-like thought struck the geological structures of the brain. I began to revolve neath the continental plate. And then, from out of hell, from behind my back – he laid his hand upon my shoulder.

9th December 1924, 109 mirks.

Shtchekelnikoff was suffering from the dismals. Shtchekelnikoff always gets the hump (such was the Shtchekelnikoff charm) but now it had so taken possession of him that he couldn't abide the presence of his fellow man; pumped up and fuelled by hatred, he rushed at the unfortunate's throat at the slightest word, slightest gesture, audible breath, with murder in his eyes. Two weeks in close proximity to his neighbours... What is the contrary of solitude for such a suspicious mistruster who sees evil everywhere and despises people? He took his axe, shag, hipflask of raw spirit, and escaped into the glassy white before the Sun was barely up.

Measure the intensity of the teslectric field (minimal fluctuation since yesterday). About to return to reading the books on Siberia, when the Yapontchiks crossed the path on their way from the reindeer.

'Benedykt, sir...,' Adin began with a moan, his bonce meekly drooping.

'What?'

'We have to agree on a date.'

'Aha, aha, a date!' Ciecierkiewicz leapt up alongside, blowing shadow out of his nostrils, ears and from under his shapka.

'Inside!'

'Here, here,' said Krzysztof.

'But why outside in the frost! The tent's empty.'

'Because in the frost you'll sooner say yea or yea.'

Oy, no doubt an order from Piłsudski.

'So, what's so troubling your souls, gentlemen, on such a fine morning?'

'You will wait here for your father, correct, Benedykt? But you know not when your father will come? You can't give a day?'

Lean on the rod of the murchometer mulling the thoughts.

'Well, Tigry claims that the pater has heard the summons and is on his way. Except that distances in the Underground World are quite unlike ours. The geography is different. And time is different, it flows differently. I did a little calculation of my own, and it seems safest to assume some time in March. But dates in May, June, can't be ruled out. Therefore, I was thinking of erecting a more lasting shelter here –'

'March! May!' Adin wrung his hands. 'This was not what was agreed, Benedykt! We go, we find, we do the business.'

'What, the Old Man told you to wind up quickly, before he launches some new brigandish offensive?'

'Why speak so badly of Ziuk?' Krzysztof said mournfully. 'Did he ever harm you? Did he not save you from prison and certain death?'

Brandish the murchometer.

'True, what does it matter now...' Recall the farewell handshake with Józef Piłsudski and that idiotic pact concluded with him, and for a moment relive the doubt: has it really frozen thus in Benedykt Gierosławski's own form, or did the accursed Piłsudski succeeded in beguiling the man with his brutal charm? 'You want to return? So, return!'

The Yapontchiks looked at one another; white bounced off white on their wide frostglaze goggles.

'Could you not write him a letter, Benedykt?'

'So that he won't be angry with you for not keeping an eye on me?'

'Well, we'll stay till Epiphany; we'll give you places and names so you can return on your own. But after that –'

'After that it's all the same? What's his latest plan that makes you so keen to go soldiering? Huh?'

'As if the Old Man ever confessed his plans to anyone...!' sighed Adin.

'Mm-hmm. But I told you Schultz is alive, holding Irkutsk.'

'You told us. Foreseen in the cards. Except that –'

'... but what the hell are you doing, for Christ's sake, did something bite you in the bott?'

Ciecierkiewicz was thrashing about in the snow, waving his arms and choking on hiccups of panic. Realise at last, however, that these convulsions had a concrete purpose: the Pilsudtchik was pointing to a spot behind the tents, towards the east – except that his hands were flying in arcs in all directions.

Glance over the top of the oculars. Shtchekelnikoff was charging back over the snow in huge leaps and bounds; the axe glinted fierily above his shoulder. Of its own accord, the hand jumped to the Grossmeister. He's deranged! Madness has caught up with him on the plain of white, he'll kill everyone! He fell amongst the tents, thrust his axe into the ice, reached his long arm through the opening in the hide, and drew out his double-barrelled gun in its fur case. He'll shoot us all down!

'They're a-coming for us, Mr G,' he panted. 'Brace yerselves, come on – don't stand here gawking like pricks on parade!'

Yell at the Tunguses. A moment of total chaos ensued as everyone grabbed their weapons, seized binoculars from one another, shouted questions and curses in three different languages, not knowing whether to strike camp and pack the sleds (there was no time) or fortify it as fast as possible against the enemy (there was no way). Although no one spoke of it, Etmatoff's words about pursuit coming from Baikal sat deep in their minds. Finally extract the Grossmeister; the basilisk revolver gently opalesced.

'Mr Ciecierkiewicz! Take the reindeer and flee into the forest!' If they shoot the animals, then they won't have to kill off the people. Ciecierkiewicz, fluttering unstuck between hysteria and heroism, was not what was wanted in the ranks under fire.

Snatch the binoculars from the bad cousin's hand as he ran past. Fact: four people on reindeer. But those on Baikal – Tigry said were on foot.

'Don't shoot till I say! Lower the barrel, devil take you!'

In the end, it transpired that all was the fault of the innate suspicions of Tchingis Shtchekelnikoff, who immediately saw thief or tsarist spy in any person encountered on the Siberian trail and reached for his knife or gun; such was his first reflex always and everywhere.

Whereas these were two magpies (one Russian, the other French) accompanied by their provodnik and an Orthodox priest, astray in the mountains, returning across Baikal to Irkutsk from the Stanovoy Highlands. They'd seen smoke on the white horizon and made a detour to exchange supplies.

'Maybe you've some spiritus to spare,' asked Vitaly Uskansky. 'Perhaps a bit of meat.'

Receive them in the heated tent; they removed their outer garments, warmed themselves by the stove. The priest's fingers were badly frostbitten, his countenance cruelly disfigured by wounds and scabs; the others' appearance was not much better. In accordance with the

trackers' camping custom, they examined one another for white blotches. It would have been good to ask where exactly they were headed, and
near which isotherm they'd been doing their magpie-prospecting, had
it not been a grave impertinence on the trail and valid cause for offence.

'But why not take the Cold Line from Olkhon Station?'

'Station's closed, surrounded by troops. They shoot at everyone, no
questions asked. Do you know what it's about?'

'The governor general is at war with the tsar. Whose soldiers are at
the station – Schultz's or those of His Imperial Exaltedness?'

'Bah!'

'Then you should have sought some lodging along the way.'

'We had no other intention,' Uskansky shook his head. 'Went especially to Lushtchy's khutor. Well, the Lord of Heaven had averted his
gaze. Lushtchy's khutor no longer exists.'

'What are you saying! We were there only…!'

'One big tomb,' said the priest, nervously sipping oily coffee.

'We thought the place had been abandoned, perhaps the army had
driven them out or something. But the gate stands wide open, frozen
dog carcasses strewn in the courtyard; we venture farther, and here's
one corpse, another corpse, murdered people.' The prospector crossed
himself. 'Women and children, everyone.'

'But totally unlike the work of robbers,' the Frenchman enjoined in
broken Russian. 'Like – like – like that of inhuman beasts.' He demonstrated, raising a dry biscuit to his mouth and biting into it violently.
'Torn apart, crushed, eaten away.'

'Eaten away?!'

He lacked the language to express it. But no matter, his meaning was
obvious. Had he said anything else – under such murch, the obviousness would have been grasped equally well.

'Corpse-easters,' muttered Shtchekelnikoff and took out his bayonet
to polish it.

Tigry Etmatoff scratched at his scars, extracted the iron medallions
from under his tunic, rattled his bone figurines. He threaded the animal
effigies between his fingers like rosary beads. '*Ru, ru, ru.*'

'We fled as fast as we could,' Uskansky concluded their account.

'Without giving the animals much rest.'

'No.'

'Mm-hmm.'

Before the red twilight – that is, in the Siberian afternoon hour – step
out of the yurt to smoke a cigarette. In order to avoid loneliness, people
had to be avoided first.

Feel at once the frost piercing the lungs like a surgical needle. Yet
inhale all the deeper the smoke and frozen air; there was a strange

indecent pleasure in it, as though the body were gradually becoming addicted to enduring low temperature: for a man feels more alive neath forty-below icespikes than in a fusty, stinking, overheated yurt. The sun was setting over snow-white Asia in total silence, unaccompanied even by wind. Scrunch, scrunch-ch-ch, glazed snow scrunched beneath the overshoes. Sit down on the lump of ice frozen around the upcast runner of the half-overturned sleigh. The shadows of the three tents were almost touching, stretching eastwards like long trains of a funeral pall. (The magpies are spending the night under their own canvas.) Outside without the frostglazes, with the naked eyes. The reindeer, combed for the night with horse-rakes, shone as if clad in diamond robes: ice crystals were swiftly forming on every hair of their coats. The first stars bore down from on high straight into the pupils. Blink, and hoarfrost on the lashes tickles the eyelids.

Corpse-eaters. Pagan fairy tales. Uskansky on reindeer, Yakuts on foot – he'd have had to have overtaken them unobserved somewhere between Lushtchy's rocky outpost and the Onot river… Fairy tales! Cough out smoke between the teeth. If, however, pursuit is indeed coming from Baikal – then any man who airily disregards all precautions and armed preparations is only asking for trouble. A hunting cabin at least, built of thick trunks, perhaps a semi-dugout, if the soil can be successfully warmed… After all, had tsarist trackers suddenly swooped today, instead of four needy travellers, there'd have been no holding out against them for long. Bah, there'd have been no holding out at all: Ciecierkiewicz unstuck from Ciecierkiewicz, Adin wringing his hands, the Tunguses panic-stricken, Shtchekelnikoff popping forthwith from his gun… one almighty fuckup. Whilst the place is as it is: there's nowhere to hide (except by fleeing into the forest) or raise a fortress. When a whole division descends like a ton of bricks together with the ispravnik, then it's clear we're done for. But four to six indigenous outlaws…? Have to stay right here for as long as possible. An abassy on the Ways of the Mammoth will always be slower. It remains therefore to wait and be hopeful.

… In other words, the same as from the beginning. Adjust the rag over the face and gaze around at the landscape as if at a black-and-white-and-red fresco, low and wide like the one on the wall of the Physical Observatory of the Imperial Academy of Sciences. It's hard not to feel lost. But no, this is not being lost, rather a burning sense of abandonment: fire, light, people, all delights and allurements of the warm world – have been chucked away, squandered, erased. Cold silent Siberia viewed from a lump of ice – this is what remains when life is robbed of all potential. Jelena Muklanowicz – snatched. The career at Krupp's – rejected. A secure, bourgeois family life – swapped for absurd ramblings across snowy wastes with a death sentence hanging over the head. Scientific ambitions – drained to a cesspit. Et cetera, the purgatorial litany goes on. And if it could only be said that such and such a calculation lay behind each decision, that such and such moral or rational argument had prevailed…! When there's nothing of the sort. Recall the past affixed in memory to this present – an image resembling snake-tracks in sand, zigzag after zigzag. Every plan is frustrated; every hope shattered and ground to atoms; every chance of normality broken across the knee. What strange kind of madness, what addiction! (Life is lived.)

… And all that remains in the end is: Siberia.

Fling the fag-end at the sleigh. The tiny glow slid over the crystal surface and was snuffled by darkness. Stand up, stabbed by an obscure suspicion. Horse, shaft, sleigh, ice – something jars here in the visual connections. Maybe it's the evening shadows, or maybe… Had the sleigh not shifted slightly? Had the horse not advanced half a step on its three legs?

Retreat to a distance of five, ten arshins; stare neath the last rays of the sun. Ice sculpture against Siberian backdrop. Nothing stirs as far as the eye can see. Silence, deadness, frost. Shudder neath the thick shuba. *Even if he carries all* Un-Ilu *on his back. He will come.*

Night flooded Asia.

10th December 1924, 101 mirks.

Don't return. Tsar all around. Tesla working here under arrest. We are waiting. Schultz lives. Don't return. Tsar all around.

First to raise the alarm were the Tunguses, *manoomoonanoomamoonoonan* and *akkoowookai*, rowdily hammering on the permafrost and thwacking the frozen walls of the tents. Wake up as if through clay, as if through honey, laboriously forcing a way towards consciousness. Very hard frost does not spark awareness – rather it lulls to sleep; such is the warning to all travellers on their Siberian odysseys: not to fall asleep from exhaustion out in the cold, not to lie down in the snow for a 'split second' to take breath. They won't rise again. Open the hoar-encrusted eyes – raise the stiffened hand – misty breath hovered in the crackling air. Every surface inside the yurt was coated in white rime. The fire in the stove barely glimmered. Yell croakily at Shtchekelnikoff. Sluggishly wrapping himself in two sheepskins, he crept outside. (Frost burst through the open flap like a cloud of smoke.) Prick up the ears. 'Time to get the arse out of here!' he cried. 'Glacier's upon us!'

… But there was still an hour to go before dawn. Step outside with lighted chipping; the French magpie was ablaze from a glintz prompted by the blackwicke in his gloved hand. Flickering images of ovoid shapes five, six arshins high loomed out of the night-time murk, towering over

men and tents. Etmatoff was dancing in the snow as patches of shamanic shadow leapt over the mirrorlike massifs. Ice, ice had sprung up from
under the earth. Stumble a little closer – it was no gleiss – it could be
approached and touched, right below a glacial overhang. The armour-
clad frost was pushing onward, but it was possible to stand still for a
moment with bated breath. Peer into the depths. The chipping in the
hand sputtered and went out. Dark sculptures, frozen coils of smoke
could nevertheless be seen within: the horse and sleigh locked in ice.
That overhang above – was a giant horse head. Walk around the outside
of the formation. Ninety-six paces. An icecradle just as it should be.

… In the rays of the rising sun, it was revealed in all its arctic beauty:
banks of permafrost, crests of icespikes, vistas of milky stalagmites,
spans of crystal, blocks of ice transparent yet coloured, embedded in one
another in drunken ranks. Sunlight was refracted on the icecradle into
a thousand rainbows. The shaman rampaged in them, foaming at the
mouth. Pass him by at a safe distance, unable to tear the eyes from the
massif of solid ice, from the mystery trapped within. Walk up to it time
and again glancing into the sunbright mirrors. The heart was pounding
as if chased at a gallop. In the mouth – a dry icicle of tongue. In the eyes
– rainbow sparks like mirror splinters, slashing to tears. In the lungs – a
snowstorm. In the head – a single, panic-stricken thought: is it him?
him? him? Not him. Walk up and peer inside. They were calling from
the camp – pay no heed. The magpies struck camp and went their own
way – barely notice. Snow began to fall in the sunshine – let it fall. Walk
up and peer inside. Him? him? him? Not him. He's not there. Inside
the icecradle were craters, shadowy rifts inflated by the flashing lights
of dawn, like the intraglacial corridors described by Mr Korzyński. But
how to enter when strength barely suffices to draw breath? How to step
into the heart of an icecradle and force steel air into the lungs… a knife
plunged below the ribs is less dangerous. And yet, on every approach,
a brief moment arose – just before the legs were restrained from taking
that extra step – when fear and reason were obscured by memory
of that final night in Irkutsk, memory like the reflection of someone
else's dream: the shining black belly of the glacius – the hand extended
towards the Ice – Truth garnered into the living body. What's a miserable icecradle beside that! A gleiss had been survived! And yet, on every
approach – stop at the boundary. The gaze ventured in a few arshins,
but soon floundered in ice debris, in the kefir suspension, in dazzling
kaleidoscopes. The horse and sleigh were discernible as hazy blots, but
the centre of the icecradle was located elsewhere. Peer inside in vain.
Him? Not him. For how could he have arrived so quickly? He couldn't
have. Fear and hope had muddied common sense. This is a fork in the
Ways of the Mammoths: is it any wonder that icecradles freeze up here

out of the ground? It should have been expected. Horse and sleigh – should have been expected. But Father Frost, when he comes, if he comes... The heart was pounding as if at a gallop.

The camp had to be moved beyond the severest cold. Decide to build a cabin near the forest by the simplest method, from unplaned trunks, with interlocking corners and no foundations, which could in no way be dug in ground frozen hard as granite. Besides, this is how houses were built for centuries on soil congealed by permafrost, by erecting on the icy surface boxlike structures that sag, when warmer times arrive, into an unstable mass; whole districts of wooden cots cave in, buckling and twisting. Which Shtchekelnikoff described at once in a tone of prophetic gloom, harking back to his frequent sojourns in Yakutsk affected by just such an architectural indisposition in years prior to Winter. This cabin, however, had to serve at most for a few months and was unlikely in the meantime to be threatened by thaw. Shtchekelnikoff grumbled and groused that Batyushka Moroz would come sooner than they could chop down the icebound trees and complete the task in such frost. He demonstrated how an axe bounces off a frozen-through trunk: like off coldiron.

Goad him on to work, however, and also the Pilsudtchiks and Tunguses – except for Tigry, who had not once throughout the day returned to full consciousness, but was celebrating his shaman rituals neath the icecradle, one soul abiding in this world, the other – in the yonder.

By dusk, six men, a dozen healthy arms, had succeeded in felling in all two larches and cutting into a thick fir. In the process, the bad cousin had set fire to his glove and Ciecierkiewicz almost chopped off his own feet. The need to warm the trunks before axing caused the greatest complications – for naturally, the ice and snow surrounding a tree melted first and the woodchopper suddenly found himself under an icicle-spiked monster about to land on his head, sunk to the waist in cold mud and enveloped by viscous, pungent smoke. A man ought not to wield an axe with frostoglazes over his eyes. But without the frostoglazes, a day spent from dawn to dusk under the open sky brought untold pain to the bedazzled sight, as well as a slight obsession with hypnotically twisted thoughts.

Shelter as the last man in the relocated tent and find Ciecierkiewicz curled up by the wall, in a huff, flickering with fierce umbriance and resembling for the first time, however, something akin to human stillness.

'Ciecierkiewicz, shattered soul, what ails you?'

'I'm listening to the hair growing in my ears.'

'He peeked into the icecradle,' said Adin. 'But wise priests have told: don't go near, don't look, don't believe.'

Sit down by the bedding, put aside the murchometer. Krzysztof watched the daily notes being recorded. Blow first on the fingers, however, for a long time and lay the palms on the stove.

'So, how is it?'

'Dropped eight mirks. Sudden jump in the intensity of murch. Mm-hmm,' glance at Ciecierkiewicz, 'maybe there's something in this. An icecradle crawls out, and the teslectricity leaps. Because it got him so suddenly –'

'I am asking about you,' Adin lowered his voice and head. 'This morning you seemed racked by some awful fever. Almost as if possessed.'

Lick the pencil-tip and calligraph the regular letters.

'Tigry spoke right,' the Yapontchik went on in a confidential undertone. 'You weren't expecting it. You said otherwise, but believed in truth that no such possibility existed.'

'Agh, *in truth…*,' mutter sneeringly.

'That you would find him. That he would find you.'

Slam the copybook closed.

'Then you've marked the secrets of my heart! I throw big diengi out of the window, bring political sentences down on my head, stake my life on a gamble, set out across icy wildernesses, the ultimate fool – but in truth, why no! I don't *in truth* want to save the pater at all!' spit in red-hot fury.

'Now, now, now,' Adin tried to mollify, 'don't fly into a rage. We're all a little shaken. After all, I can see you're a good man.'

'He sees!' taunt him. 'A good man!'

Adin smiled dolefully; murch sullied his blue lips.

'Had I such a father… I would also fear most the reflection in his eyes.'

Stare at him emptily.

These men were strangers all.

11th December 1924, 96 mirks.

Tsar all around. Prince in Aleksandrovsk. Attack. Schultz and Pobedonostseff. Tesla sick. Warrant out for Pocięgło. Don't return. Tsar all around. Prince in Aleksandrovsk. Attack.

Dream in the night that they rose in the night and killed. Why should they kill? In the dream, such a question didn't flash up at all. So, they rose, surrounded the camp bed and cudgelled to death. Observe it from above, from under the roof of the tent, with the salgyn-kut soul. Tchingis Shtchekelnikoff, Adin, Ciecierkiewicz. In the dream, it came as no surprise. Size them up in the morning with a frown, tight-lipped. Shtchekelnikoff was the first to go out to fell trees; join him at the forest rim, having laid out the cards and taken measurements. Pure icy sunlight shone like diamond on the surface of the icecradle a quarter-verst away.

'What measure d'you say, Mr G?' he rasped, thrusting his saw into a trunk.

'You think it's grown again?' Glance around at the refulgent rainbow icery. 'The measure leans towards Frost, towards power. Either the Tchornoye Siyanye is indeed above us, or the mammoths are beneath, or –'

'What?'

Adjust the gloves.

'It's starting to get to me –'

An old indigene, half-stooping, crept out from amongst the fir trees.

Shtchekelnikoff swung his great paw above his head and hurled the axe. It hacked into the old man up to the helve. The poor devil didn't even groan; he turned a somersault and fell flat on his back with the hatchet-shaft pointing skyward.

'Whatever have you…, for Christ's sake!'

'Didn't like the look of him,' muttered Tchingis.

Didn't like the look of him! Didn't like the look of him! Is it better to smash his skull with a chunk of wood, or at once grab the Grossmeister? Such a hardened slayer –

Five other half-naked savages emerged from the taiga, draped in rags and iron talismans. In their hands were spears and Berdan rifles. On the wide shoulders of the second from the left swayed the small head of black-eyed Mefody Pyelka. Murch was gushing from them in oily wreathes of night.

Shtchekelnikoff looked, coughed, spat, punched his chest with his fist and straightened his square shoulders.

'Got me knife.'

He had his knife.

On the corpse-eaters

Having shot and stabbed to death Shtchekelnikoff, they marched towards the camp.

Three remained. They took the guns of the Avahites disembowelled by Tchingis and loaded them as they marched, advancing slowly at the same stolid pace as on their thousand-mile wandering.

Manage in the meantime to unhook the shuba, extract and unpack the Grossmeister, shed the unwieldy glove, cock the gun, take aim –

And fire.

And succeed with wintry accuracy. The Avahite froze severed in two, that is, trapped inside a fir tree of ice: arm on one branch, head on another, leg above head. A second, swept up by a phalanx of frost, fell in deep snow and turned to ice just like that: heels towards the Sun.

Gritting the teeth, raise the still-living left hand and again cock the scorpion. The right hand, robbed of feeling, refused to bend to the will; kneeling down, enclose the snake's butt in both hands. The Pyelka Piegnarovian approached with raised spear. Shoot him in the chest. A red icicle pierced him like an angel's lance as a stalagspike the size of a cannon bore blew him up from within.

Get back on the feet. The Yapontchiks came running over. All around on the mosaic of corpses stood a coppice of ice shrapnel, trees of crystal needles, razors and star-shapes.

'Benedykt, sir, what's –'

'Who's that?!'

'Tchingis is dead,' clear the throat of black pitch. Thick murch spewed from the saurian barrel of the Grossmeister. Tuck it behind the belt neath the unhooked shuba.

Ciecierkiewicz tore his hunting rifle out of its case.

'Where? Who? Where? What? What? What?'

Try restraining his arm. He froze for a moment.

'It's the ones from Baikal, Etmatoff's devils. Someone has sent Piegnar's goylems after me. Probably the tsarist Okhrana. We should have put up corpse poles here. Where are our Tunguses?'

'Jumping around the icecradle,' Adin said, then slumped into white snow with his brain shot from his skull.

Ciecierkiewicz shrieked and fired blindly.

From behind the icebound grove loomed an Avahite with axe-hole in his chest. With clumsy fingers, he loaded a fresh cartridge into his Berdan rifle.

Something was likewise stirring in the snowdrift: the one frozen with heels in the air was scrambling out.

The Yakut's head impaled on a spike of the tree-explosion opened its eyes under the rime and began smacking its lips rhythmically.

Whilst the old Yakut, the limping one – couldn't cope with the cartridge, since he had eight fingers on his hand, each hailing from a different home.

'You won't kill them,' tell the Pilsudtchik. 'It's a matter for the shaman.'

But Ciecierkiewicz had come altogether unstuck, that is, lost his senses. Staring goggle-eyed at the lifeless pandemonium, he flung his rifle to the ground and rushed towards the camp, to the reindeer.

The old Yakut raised the Berdan to eye level and squeezed the trigger. It failed to fire. The Frost. (Or Murch Hammer.)

Mull over in the mind a stained-glass window of logical variants not unlike the pane coated in hoary arabesques. The reindeer. With reindeer, pursuers on foot could be speedily escaped – but for how far? There's no time to strike camp, muster supplies. They'll catch up. Whilst Etmatoff – should they kill him, then there'll be no chance.

Wheel around and run towards the icecradle.

Run through collapsing snow as if floundering in quicksand, from static pose to static pose. Glance not over the shoulder, for a bullet could hit the back any second; it was a wager with Death. One step, and another step, and another, and another, and still the body lives, still the white silence, and only the creak of permafrost and black ruckling breath.

A shot rang out. Stop still, leg raised ready to step. Over the white field floated the deathly scream of Ciecierkiewicz. Lower the leg.

One step, and another step, and another, and no glancing over the shoulder.

The Tunguses must have heard the shooting. Skin-clad silhouettes leapt out from behind the icecradle and disappeared again immediately. Shout once, twice. No reply.

A shot rang out. A bullet whistled past the shapka.

One step, and another step, and another.

Icecradle rainbows enfolded in butterfly wings; silken colours wiped away tears of exertion from the eyes.

Reach the first block of ice and tumble to the knees behind its screen, panting and coughing.

A Siberian fairy tale. Rub from the beard icicles of saliva. A Siberian fairy tale, goylems, Avahites, shamans, immortal corpse-eaters, fairy tale, fairy tale. (They called to one another out of the taiga in animal chants). Stand up. Reflected in the icecradle was a black silhouette with floral volcano bursting from its belly. Lay a bare hand automatically on the revolver butt. A fairy tale.

'Tigry!' Shout to him, walking round a corner of the ice-massif. 'Jokó-Awāhe! Ili mat! Bakturanegin!'

Tigry Etmatoff lowered the bone blade for a second time and slit the throat of the good cousin. Grinning gleefully through the foam frozen on his lips, he shook his head, rolled his eyes and limped away into the deep interior of the icecradle. Milky curtains of frost unfurled behind him like a funeral pall.

Walk slowly up to the crimson mandalas spattered on the trampled snow. Paintings in blood surrounded the small figures of the Tunguses tightly swathed in skins and furs; they lay in the same symmetrical configuration, one with head pointing towards the entrance of the icecradle, the other in the opposite direction. They were still steaming. Gore seeped still from the good cousin; his limbs still twitched. Butchered to death, he hadn't even squealed.

Etmatoff had brought them with him only to drain them of blood at a fitting moment before the gates of the Ice.

He had volunteered to Uriah for the Siberian odyssey with one purpose in mind: that the Son of Frost would open the doors to the abassylar.

For it had been said from the beginning: they bow before what they themselves see in plain truth as the greatest evil; they dream of eternal bondage in the belly of the Dragon.

It had been shown from the beginning: these inverted Tunguses – they are devils, whilst this friendly cutthroat – is a murderer, and this – this is death.

It had been known after all. No one was lying, no one was deceiving, there hadn't even been such possibility. The truth was pure, obvious. It had been seen very well.

And yet until now, it had been impossible to penetrate the barrier between knowledge and action, to translate the language of the first kind into the speech of men; there are things which may be known, but which cannot be told and judged. And hovering now above the carmine permafrost, belching forth graphite breath mist and pallid glintzen, stunned by desperation – is the milksop, dunderhead, child.

Krrshkip, trrshipp, Piegnar's goylems are on the march, their patch-work bodies staggering in the snow, brandishing their disproportionate limbs. The old Yakut raises again the hoar-encrusted Berdan rifle to his eye.

Trook.

Coldly make the sign of the cross and run inside the icecradle.

The narrow passage twisted every moment in crooked zigzags between walls of glaring sunlight, just as the icy labyrinth had taken shape in random cracks. Already after three turns, any sense was lost of the cardinal directions or position in relation to the entrance wall.

Within the frosted rainbows loomed ghostly forms, shadows in misty stone. Somewhere here a black steed was pulling a burned-out sleigh at geological speed. A Tungus shaman was running soaked in blood. Avahites were on the march. Somewhere here congealed Truth was flowing along the Ways of the Mammoths.

Stifle the breath with all might till the moment eventually passes un-noticed when the dam bursts and a first, then a second blast of Ice enters the lungs. Pause at a three-pronged fork in the glacier and notice only then how the Frost is already invading the chest every which way like an arctic waterfall. Press a cold hand to cold jacket. The movement left an afterimage of non-being in the air – there was no fog, yet somehow in this brilliant prismatic sunlight, in this sparkling million-faceted diamond, the past lingered a smidgen longer in full view, whilst the future slipped away in kaleidoscopes of bright colour. The Frost shot to the head like an intoxicating wine, and at once invoked thoughts of a ball in the Siberian sky, in Governor General Schultz-Zimovy's crystal palace; behind pillars of glass flashed the dazzling krasavitsa, Daughter of Winter. Greet her with a bow –

'Mr G...!'

Somewhere here Shtchekelnikoff's nut, frozen onto a Piegnarian patchwork, was baying for its ultimate victim, goaded by bloodthirsty yearning. Avahites are on the march.

Flee in panic through the labyrinth, blindly, instinctively.

Narrowly miss bumping into them from the momentum, as they approach in a long column led by the broad-shouldered specimen bearing Pyelka's head. He raised the spear seen reflected in the ice an instant before. Leap aside.

An instant, a fraction of a second, black breath on the tongue, crystal-clear thought in the skull. What to do?

Grossmeister in the hand. Fire at the goylems? It'll achieve nothing; frost is their element. Fire into the ice and bar their passage? They'll find a way, circle around it.

Only two bullets remained.

Tesla's Hammer strikes three times a minute – which means scarcely a few seconds at the peak of the wave.

But what other way out?

Retreat to a stalagspike and point the Grossmeister vertically at the ground. Fire between the feet.

The Frost –

– completely overgrew the small window looking out onto the courtyard well: ornamental flourishes and embroidered lace, geometrical patterns and splotches like flashes of sunlight photographed in rime. I turned up the lamp-wick, and it grew brighter in the room. A gale blew in the chimney. I put aside the unfinished letter to Julia and opened Alfred Teitelbaum's treatise *On Truth*. Someone knocked at the door. I instinctively grabbed the pocketbook – had Zygmunt paid Biernatowa this month's rent? I frowned in futile effort. What month is it anyway? Glance at the window: the window is frosted over, whilst outside the window it's obviously winter.

The knock was repeated.

'Come in!'

She entered and at once closed the door behind her. Cascades of fine snow spilled off her overcoat with its wide sable collar. I stood up; from her muff she took out a powerful, boyish little hand; I kissed the cold hand. On every finger shone a narrow band of gleaming coldiron inlaid with tungetitum.

'Have they been already?' she asked, surveying the space with a quick glance. The girlish countenance was ruddy from frost, as hair like golden wheat escaped from under her toque.

'Who?'

'The tchinovniks of Winter, the men in bowler hats.'

'No –'

'Let's go!'

She left no space for objection. She turned to the door; first, she peered out warily, but then, without tarrying a moment, strode into the corridor and rushed to the stairs, noisily clicking her heels. I hesitated above the first step. Then she turned again, nearly knocking me off my feet; we spun in a riot of sable, snow, frost and the young lady's pungent aroma. She hissed something between blue lips. I peered down over the warped banister. Huge cockroach shadows were drifting across the stairwell walls. Leaning deeper, I caught a glimpse of a broad silhouette in black shuba, in oval-shaped bowler. There were two of them, conducted by Biernatowa. Woop-dwoop, they set down their feet with the might of a drop-hammer; the lodging-house quaked neath the legs of the tchinovniks.

We ran to the coal stairs. Somehow the young woman knew these semi-dark interiors, the whole stinking anatomy of the boarding house deformed by architectural arthritis. She led with assurance, leaping two stairs at a time, brushing her coat against the hoar-infested bricks. Thus we descended one floor, a second, a third, a fourth, and only then did I realise that we were no longer in a Warsaw built by human hands. In the underground passage, above sewers frozen into black excrescences, shone monstrous stalactites and condensed dripstones of phosphorescent filth. Black-and-white steam gushed from pipes contorted into impossible knots. On bricks the size of royal coffers, the scratched-out signs of a prehistoric alphabet glistened with green mould. Beneath our feet, in the icy dung-heap and froth of impurities congealed into porcelain muck, I saw traces of feet and paws and organs alien to mammals of this earth. At a height of four metres, half-submerged in the masonry, a baby's head protruded from between the bricks.

The devushka leapt over a stony current and pointed to a low dark place between foundations that had crumbled like the pilasters of an antique tomb. I approached warily. It breathed putrefaction and the stench of rust. She gave me a vigorous shove. I entered half-bent. Darkness flowed over us in streams of cold oil. We walked down, then up, then down again, and then the directions got jumbled up. Splinters of ice rained down on us, a constant deluge of particles digested and excreted by the earth, including objects of human provenance: buttons, pins, tickets, apple cores, teeth, coins, clumps of hair, cigarette ends, crucifixes on chains, pebbles of frozen phlegm, broken-off chips of faience, stamps, household bells, brooches, toothpicks, fingerbones, glass eyes, rubbers, matches, combs, snuff boxes, sweets, toenails, pen nibs, rings, keys, rosaries, military dog tags, artificial jaws, iron tacks, torn photographs, shreds of love letters, anything left by people that might be found in gutters, on suburban rubbish tips, under street kerbs, in old wells or riverbeds. It had all worked its way laboriously through the earth's sieve and landed here, compacted at its confluence with a mightier stream. Every so often the downpour ceased or indeed gathered strength – following a violent tremor, when its hollow rumble rolled through the underground vaults. Then the devushka seized me by the hand, telling me to wait till the seismic disturbance subsided. Taking advantage of a calm moment, painfully craning my neck, I glanced upwards. Constellations of street footsteps were projected onto a sky of black clay; hazy outlines of cemetery tombs glowed feebly; geological fronts of basalt clouds staked out trajectories from conception to death. A broken child's rattle struck me on the nose and I lowered my head. 'We are on the Ways of the Mammoths.' 'Come.'

We came out inside a crypt amongst dead monarchs. On the catafalques were sculpted effigies of men stretched in posthumous poses, half-drowned in stone. I seemed to recognise the cold features of this one and that one or this one, recognise a distinct family likeness between them. They answered me with smooth unseeing gazes; one or other appeared almost to wink, move a granite tongue over cracked lips, prick up the ends of his moustache from under the mildew. They did not stir as we ran across to a door leading to the surface.

The young woman tugged helplessly at the handle; the door was locked. I reached under her toque; hair spilled over her sable collar and shoulders. Having unpicked the lock with a bent hairpin, I flung the metal on the floor. It rang once and fell silent. Everything returns to earth.

In the side nave, a hunchbacked sacristan was cleaning silver votive offerings before a statue of the Virgin. Kneeling and crossing myself, I sat in the first pew before the main altar adorned in the dark colour of Advent, neath a huge cross upon which Christ bled from heart and head, from hands and feet.

The devushka paused, looked about and turned around; she swiftly lost patience.

'You're not allowed to stop! You cannot stop!'

I touched my lips with my finger, enjoining her to be silent. The cross stood inclining over the altar; the Saviour's body hung arched in a half-bow. Droplets of blood the size of sparrows dripped into fabric glowing from the tongues of candles, plip, plop, it could be heard throughout the church; He must have shifted on His cross. A nun appeared, removed the full chalice and placed an empty one on the altar.

The smell of stale incense made me nauseous, the smell of incense and blood, like the reek of old iron. It made me double up; I held my head between my knees. Breathed through open mouth.

The young woman leant over me, put her arm around and covered me in the sable coat, shielding me with her scent from the church's poisons. With powerful hands, she pressed my temples.

'Remember and forget,' she whispered in my ear. 'I am releasing you from your oath! Have released you from your oath! You swore not! It has unfrozen – it has frozen.'

The touch of coldiron brought me to my senses. I drew myself up.

'I swore not…?'

'Come.'

We emerged into the night. Warsaw slept neath snow and gleissen. Haloes of woollen radiance swelled around the tall streetlamps; pale wraiths spun out of them on threads of winter gossamer. Shadows of Cossacks loomed in the white and black of snowclad, fogbound streets, always one crossroads farther ahead. The clatter of hooves on ice carried down avenues and alleys. Above the roofs of houses in their sleeping-caps of creamy snow smiled a one-eyed Moon.

The devushka chose the alleys – alleys, narrow lanes, dark court-yards, paths of thieves and spies. Thus we arrived at the backdoor of a two-storey mansion, which she opened without knocking and without key. Constantly urging me on, she cautiously climbed the stairs. I too set down my feet with extraordinary delicacy, fearing any sound that might betray us. People were sleeping in this house.

On the floor upstairs she shoved me into a side room and withdrew into the corridor.

At the last moment I grabbed her sleeve.

'Who –'

'Shhh! He'll be coming in a minute.'

Uproar had already broken out on the street; we could hear horses neighing, the angry shouts of police.

'Who are you?'

She stepped over the threshold and kissed me on the forehead. Ice exploded under my skull as I keeled onto a child's bed.

'Emilia.'

'But I would have recognised you!'

'We've never seen each other,' she said and fled, slamming the door.

Something was breathing, something was moving in the dark. I lay stock-still, straining my ears. Vulgar yells in Russian filled the house, screams and the thud of soldiers' boots and high-pitched women's voices and the crash of splitting wood. Someone was running along the upstairs corridor. I slunk against the wall. Then the door opened and into the room burst –

– a bright warm glow, tickling the eyelids and cheeks. Blink; the hoarfrost cracked. Cough; the icicles dropped off. Inhale air into the lungs; the ice armour let go. Scream and fall out onto the snow.

Everything was hurting. Roll onto the back. From the wall of the icecradle a mirrored face stared back, contorted into a grimace of suffering – except that it was a full arshin in length. Evening was come and the entire ice glowed pink, cherry-red, focusing lens-like the rays of the setting Sun. Sit down. Everything was hurting, but hurting as after a great effort, after a long run, not after torture maliciously destroying the body. And so, this is how to become a hibernik. Stand up and kick to bits the icicle wherein hung the Grossmeister. Then smash the matter frozen inside the revolver's internal mechanism by whacking it over the knee. Break open the reptile: one bullet left in the flower's calyx. Look around for the goylems built of frozen corpses.

Notice only then more facts incompatible with recent memory. The frozen horse and half-burned sleigh were on the left side, a few paces from the external wall of the icecradle. The icecradle had managed to shift a good thirty arshins. Shielding the eyes from the flood of sunlight, glance towards the camp. At the few stakes and single scrap of felt canvas blowing mournfully above fresh banks of snow, a miserable flapping flag. No trace of the reindeer.

In an unthinking reflex, wrench the watch chain from under the shuba, jacket and sweater. The watch had stopped of course, frozen. Shake the head, a boxer felled by God's right hook.

Single strands of puffy cloud hang in the evening sky.

No living thing stirs in the Onotsk wilderness.

Deathly silence wrests from the frost single rasps and sputters of shifting snow.

From horizon to horizon – no sign of the kingdom of men.

Far to the south-west – a single shell of tall gleiss.

Night pours out from behind the Primorsky mountains.

A day passed, or maybe a month, or maybe a year, or maybe a thousand years and in the meantime, the human race disappeared from the face of the planet. Whilst in Winter, under the Ice, nothing passes away and nothing new arrives. What is, is. Here, History freezes; but what sort of History is it, when no day differs from another day and everything persists in unruffled order? Truth is one and Truth changes not, since any change would mean change into Falsehood. Despite the memory, no bitten-off finger was discovered in the ice. Realise what this means: *to be that finger*. And everything outside the present moment – exists not.

Dragging the legs, shuffle towards the camp. Here and there bits of equipment, ice-encrusted shapes of baggage, broken tentpoles, runners of upturned sleds, rose out of the snow. Retrieve a coldiron rod from the Tunguses' cauldron-stand as well as a strong, heavy chip of wood. With their aid, chisel through the drift to the site of the Yapontchiks' tent. Dig out the small stove, an icy stack of reindeer hides, a crumpled tin can for medicaments and naphtha, a few frozen books and Adin's hunting bag. Walk around the outer rim of the camp. Poke with the rod wherever an unnatural irregularity was perceived. In this way were uncovered, amongst other things, the back leg of a reindeer and Ciecierkiewicz's clenched fist.

The sun was setting; return to the stove. Had it only been possible… to do what? Even if the stove wasn't totally damaged, even if enough firewood were found for it in time… Maybe one, perhaps two nights are survivable – but what then? Eventually, the legs gave way. Sink beneath the funereal banner of ossified thick felt. There are no reindeer; there is no way to return to people, to life. Maybe some odd leftovers might still be retrieved, supplies preserved in the ice. Then there are the reindeer carcasses. Then that horse. Then – Ciecierkiewicz. But when all corpses have been eaten…?

Feel with the hand neath the ever stiffer iced-through shuba. Cigarette case, matches – everything is wet and covered in hoar, whilst the hands shake and fingers disobey. Stare for a long time in dull amazement at the naked blue palm. Whatever happened to the gloves? Hiberniks too cannot survive any temperature. It will freeze. Cigarettes spill onto snow. Hah, now Emilia won't come, won't help…! An inauspicious shiver was swelling from deep inside the chest; muffle up inside the shuba, press the knees to the chin. Grind the teeth. The animal is trying to escape. Don't allow it out! Teardrops of pure crystal stab the eyes. Don't allow for this wild hysterical despair! In the presence of another human being, ever-dependable Shame would have to come to the rescue; without people, deliverance must be sought elsewhere. Begin to count the pulse throbbing in the temples. Turn the gaze upwards into the sky of Asia, towards the first stars – are these the familiar constellations? Can they be named? The eyes hang on the beautiful reflections blossoming off the icecradle. Attempt in the dim light to read the words and sentences of the books dug out of the snow. And so, still not recognising the icy figure of father broken off from the icecradle, lift in trembling hand the nearest book, frozen with pages open to heaven.

That very same day, before sunrise, Anhelli was seated on a lump of ice in a deserted spot when he espied two youths walking towards him.

From the light breeze that wafted off them, he sensed they were from God, and waited for what they would announce to him, expecting it to be death.

And when they greeted him like fellow earthlings, he said: I have recognised you, don't hide yourselves; you are Angels.

Are you come to comfort me? Or argue with the sorrow that has learned silence in solitude?

And the young men said unto him: Behold we are come to announce that today's sun shall still rise but tomorrow's shan't show itself above the earth.

We are come to announce the darkness of winter and horror greater than any men have ever known: solitude in darkness.

We are come to announce that your brothers have perished eating corpses, rabid from the blood of men: and you are the last.

PART IV

Un-Ilu

'And the sole object of all action is that which may be and may not be, which is neither necessary nor impossible, which lies in the realm of two-sided possibility; this is the realm of activity, of action; the realm of reality is not the realm of action, action ends where truth begins, truth ends where action begins. An omniscient being could not create anything, an omnipotent being not know anything.'

CHAPTER THE TENTH

On the coldest of fathers

The thirteenth day of December 1924 – let it be this day.

It has frozen.

Arms of Father – stalactite wings. Legs of Father – pillars of ice. Chest of Father – a glacial battleship. Genitals of Father – dark horn icicle. Head of Father – thousand-pood explosion of crystal thorns lacerating the sky. Index finger – glass rapier piercing the globe. Gazing open eye – pearl of angelic azure.

'Papa?'

He moves not.

Walk up to him. He won't turn his eyes.

Extend the hand. He belches forth frost.

Fear to touch him, this is the ice of death.

Sit down in the snow at father's feet.

Father stands in silence, a monumental figure of ice.

Spreading out from under the ground in a fan of sugar-crusted permafrost a good five arshins high, he obscures the last red glows of the icecradle, casting long deep shadow; sit in this shadow and raise the head as it rests on the knees, like a little child.

He gazes down from above, from on high, where he hangs suspended, frozen into blocks of ice sculpture magnifying his whole form in the style of the icecradle.

'Papa?'

He moves not. Air condenses on his massive bulk into white tears.

Sit humbly, motionless. A minute passes, two minutes, three – too slowly to perceive living movement; eventually the pater's gaze wheels around. He gazes down – sees.

Stand up. Remove the shapka. Scrape the rime off face and beard.

'It's me, Benedykt.'

He hears not, naturally, how could he hear? Yet he must have recognised his son at once – how could he not recognise him?

Stand in silence. It's impossible to approach, impossible to touch, impossible to hear or be heard.

Silence over Asia, nothing but darkness crackling on snow, running wild like gossamer.

Shudder.

Total night is about to fall, the icecradle will fade, father's glacial sculptures will fade.

He gazes down from above, silent as a gleiss.

Walk back to the buried camp, dig out a naphtha lighter from the hunting bag and remove the can of naphtha from the stove. Gather up a few wood chippings and the coldiron rod and head into the forest to the wood-felling site. Here everything lies buried in snow, icebound. Poke around with the rod for Shtchekelnikoff's axe. To no avail; there's no way of guessing where it was thrown by the Yakut. Gather up a few old broken branches, bits of bush covered in hoar. Carry it all to father. He, in the meantime, has shifted half an arshin in a wave of Frost, lowered his heavy head a little towards the earth: an immense Sun encircled by a crown of ice sabres and needles, each two arshins in length. He looks out from under dropped eyelids lined by razor-sharp lashes.

Light two bonfires, neath father's right and left hands. The flames reach nowhere near him; the smoke drifts as if deflected by cold air currents coming off him. Dusk has now descended completely, and the only light reflected on father's smooth glassy surfaces – not counting the faraway stars – is the glare of these two modest fires. They lend him the semblances of life: trembling flames, dancing shadows, flickering colours.

Beyond this – the lifeless backdrop of the Siberian night.

'Papa!'

He gazes down.

Shudder. Take out again the cigarette case. Light a deformed cigarette from a bonfire chipping. The tobacco tastes unusually bitter. Walk around father with blue-and-red hand shaking at the mouth. Stop at last beyond the fires and beyond father's gaze. The great star of his head rotates too slowly for his gaze's intent to be interpreted. This is the speech of stone – it can only crush with its granite mass, should you not escape in time.

The cigarette shrinks totally to ash. Chuck it in the direction of the fires, sit down again on the ice wrapped in the shuba, pulling the malakhay over the ears, winding the rags. The permafrost crackles in the dark. Father has bent his left thumb; now the crystal sword points into the sky. Try to twitch the toes inside the ice-logged overshoes, perceiving that nothing is felt in those toes at all. Realise there'll likely be no surviving this night. The uncontrolled shivering – is already hypothermia. Sasha Pavlitch had described it on many occasions. How a Siberian death comes upon you: first the biting chill and muscle disobedience, legs buckling under you, over-weak hands, then the disorientation and strange fear, then more shivering, getting stronger and stronger as teeth ring and the head tosses like an epileptic's, then a sense of being lost in time as well as horrendous pain; but then the pain recedes, the shivers recede, and you slowly begin to stiffen losing all feeling and consciousness, gradually resembling a corpse – until you resemble it thoroughly, utterly frozen to death. It's a matter of hours. There'll be no surviving this night.

Want to cry. Don't want to cry.

Father gazes down. (The star of thorns has swivelled around.)

Silence. Siberia. Ice.

Frost slices through the lungs and destroys the body.

The end.

For it can almost be seen how the whole remembered past has gradually been freezing onto this one necessary moment. Under father's gaze, truth comes to a standstill. This is the blessing of Batyushka Moroz. The greater the cold neath the skin and the slower the blood, the greater the certainty that no other meeting was possible in fact between the son and the coldest of fathers – only this: out in the godforsaken wastes, in a place cut off from other places, at a time cut off from other times, on the last tiny islet in an ocean of non-existence. And the more obvious it becomes that this entire, months-long journey in search of the parent had been nothing other than a mathematical reduction to the soletruth of Benedykt Gierosławski: first, in the Trans-Siberian Express, the amputation of all the false Benedykt Gierosławskis, of all the lies in which he'd lived in Summer like people driven by inertia live in their warm illusions, people who know not who they are, children born not of the blood of Ishmael; then, in Irkutsk, the amputation of all Benedykt Gierosławski's future hopes, of all other possible Benedykt Gierosławskis, who would easily have found happiness in denial, in rejecting the legacy of Ishmael – for this was how life was already being lived after all, having already almost become them, it had almost frozen; then finally, then now, on the surgical slab of Siberia, everything else has been chopped off: people, the world, History, Shame, past and future, even the certainty of life itself or further prospects for life. There remains cold naked soletruth served up on the blank slate of the Ice: a few digits, a few letters.

Only like this can Father Frost meet with the Son of Frost.

A few digits, a few letters… Leap to the feet, rush to one of the fires, wrest from the flames a long black chip. Step into the square of white snow directly beneath the million-pood gaze of father. The hands tremble, blood from the cracked lips freezes on the rags and beard, skin neath the ice-stiffened clothing tears off in slivers at every move.

Stop still, however, with the hand helplessly forlorn, stumped already in the place of the first word – for what word is it? what can be said here? Between father and son, under the Ice, that is, in absolute truth – what can be said here? In the language of the first kind – what remains to be said? Father is father, son is son – what else between them?

What can be said, now that everything can be said?

Look over the shoulder at father's face magnified in the fiery ice, at the furrowed brows under snow, clenched jaws, raised chin, steel nail of his pupil. The swords encircling his head split apart the constellations of Asia.

Draw with the charred wood on the snow in large letters:

FORGIVE

Father gazes down.

Geological thoughts solidify in the ice. Mountains of permafrost press against one another. Murch streams into light. Fiery blinks flash along the arshin-long needles. Father Frost has moved a finger.

The stalactite-rapier freezes over the ground, depositing in its wake a trail of crushed icicle on the surface of the permafrost.

G like a cracked eggshell with a hook, then U, then L composed of two crusty strokes, similarly T…

It lasts minutes and minutes.

GULTSFRGV

Reach for clean snow a step further on.

WHY

Father gazes down.

IAMIAMIAMIAMIAMIAMIAM

Interrupt to stop the frozen pattern stretching into eternity.

ALIVE

To this he responds not; he is silent, freezes in motionlessness.

Cramp wrenches at the shoulders. Grip the burned chip in both hands and trace firmly:

RETURN

Father gazes down.

The icicle letters slowly break off.

WNTRDONLIEM

LEOKADIA BOLEK IAM

NLIEM

Enlie him! Fling aside the burned chip, stride off into the murk. Reeling like a drunk. Impossible to cry, the eyelids freeze. Reach again for a cigarette – but it's too strenuous a business: first one, then a second, then a third cigarette slips between wooden fingers robbed of sensation. Stand with back to the fire and to father, for this is the whole world now – there's nothing beyond but the black infinity of Winter. Everything has been amputated, chopped off, subtracted from this one cold necessity. Try to evoke an image of Jelena Muklanowicz, but it's more like excavating a corpse from under the ice: a rigid form more like a stone effigy than a living being. It exists not.

Turn on the heel and retrieve the chip.

POLAND ICE PIŁSUDSKI GLEISSEN SPEAK

Wait in vain however for an answer in signs of earth. Instead – perceive it after a quarter of an hour – father lowers his open palm within a milky clump, flexes his dragged-down rocky shoulder. Murch drifts this night in thick waves. Comprehend the pater's half-gesture: it's an invitation, he has extended his hand in invitation.

For this he has come.

The world dances before the eyes. Take a step back and keel over. Stand up clumsily, the limbs wishing not to obey, bending at the least opportune moments, as the head jumps from side to side as on a rickety doll; hear a strange unhuman ruckle flowing between chattering teeth. Stagger to the campfire; fall again. Father gazes down from on high, one boulderlike hand held open; the other, formed of needles, prodding the earth with a spit seven arshins long. Judge and Pantocrator.

N L I E M

Enlie him. Enlie him! Strike the temple with the fist, in order to break free of the drowsy torpor. (Or maybe it's the peak of a wave on the Ways.) Rising on all fours, wedge the snout almost into the fire. A flame passes over the skin, a cat's warm tongue. *What hasn't the king got the most?*

Propping the body on the ice with the hands, hunched over like a monkey, shuffle towards the buried campsite. The felt banner indicates the spot. With broken tentpole and sliver of shovel-shaped ice, dig out from under the snowdrifts skins and furs frozen to stone, tearing off with mangled paws the shapeless clods of encrusted matter, lumps of frozen-though baggage. Attempt to shine a lighter; the lighter slips from the fingers. Try to guess: which boulder of solidified snow – is it this one? this one? that one? That one. Break open laboriously its sharp-edged shell, forfeiting nearly all strength and warmth – in order to eventually uncover at the bottom a packet of brick tchay turned to ice, along with a bag of salt.

A moment of breakdown ensues. Sink neath the flapping flag with empty heart and mind, drained of will. Silence, darkness, frost, it's all right to fall asleep, all right. Tiny flakes of snow fly into the face. Brush them away instinctively – there's no feeling in the fingers, nor in the nose, nor in cheek or forehead. Even the terrible shaking has ceased. All right, all right, all right, it's best this way.

No. Drag the body to the next lump of ice. Knock off the frozen crust with the reptilian grip of the Grossmeister. Barbed gurgling issuing from the larynx sets the tempo of strokes. The top of a travelling chest looms. Cut through the straps with a knife salvaged from the hunting bag, pry open the lid. It springs back with the crack of splitting glass. Inside is Doctor Tesla's stove.

Return to father, rolling the stove over snow and ice. The bonfires have died down; throw on the rest of the wood. Having placed the stove as close as possible to the flames, open the upper part of the construction and reach with clumsy hand under the empty naphtha reservoir. There should be a coldiron pin, which when pushed out will eject on hinges the Kotarbiński pump concealed below. In no way, however, can the pin be felt neath the fingers; these fingers are already those of a corpse. Endeavour to peer within through a chink in the casing. Endeavour to dislodge that goddamned pin from the inside with the coldiron rod. Endeavour to rip out the reservoir. All to no avail. In ultimate frustration, in despair beyond the bounds of hysteria, whack the stove blindly with the rod, hurling it back and forth through the fire and at father's feet and back again. Bawling at the same time incoherent curses, laughing and growling and moaning and babbling senselessly.

Father gazes down from on high with his cold eye, in stony silence.

Kicked for the umpteenth time, the stove falls apart. Stand for a long while in dull amazement, swaying like a drunk. Then seize hold of the pump, drag the abused mechanism towards one of the fires, examining it from all angles with obsessive tenderness; extract the spools of coldiron cable, press one prong into the aperture, snap, the cable slots in perfectly – clap almost for joy; check the container with the crystal murch battery, black as coal, and also the one with the second battery, this one white as snow; unwind the cable to its full length and turn the pump's power dial as a test, vrrr, it's working inside the flow dynamo – yes! yes! yes! Switch it off at once, grab the other end of the cable and, leaning on the rod, walk over to father. Without glancing up at all at the high overhang of his face, throw the cable at his legs. The cable slithers off the smooth ice. Throw it a second time. The same happens. The endpiece lacks insulation, a bare coldiron wire some three ver-shoks long; having straightened it on the rod, place it gently on the tongue of ice covering father's foot. Return to the pump, turn the dial. Vrrr, but nothing happens in any way obvious; the pump is too weak to suck out murch through the ice, besides the flow is now spreading over the entire formation and surely descending onto the very Ways of the Mammoths. Stand with arms dangling forlorn like pendulums, a monument to mental inertia, the apotheosis of a cretin. Snow is falling. Father gazes down. There's no way to scramble together a single original thought – frozen, everything has frozen, brain and reason and soul. With the deafening boom of interlocking glaciers, the whole fossilised past, that is, History, freezes onto the paralysed Now. For memory, only in memory does anything move, like maggots in a grave. So – so – so how did Tesla do it? Recall the scene on the Angara river below Konny Island, the demonstration of the Battle Pump: the machine's heavy arm with its coldiron claw plunged deep into the gleiss –

Wind the naked wire around the rod; the rod, ending in a long spike, serves to drive it to earth. Unravel the spare cable from the second spool and attach its naked end to the power dial of the pump. Strew smouldering ash onto the snow from the by-now-insensible hand and watch for the right pattern.

Run up to father, staggering, falling once and twice and thrice, hauling the two black snakes across the crystal white. Strength is needed, momentum is needed, there can be no stopping. (He gazes down.) Rush onto his feet, leap onto the crests of his knees, spring onto the slope of his thigh. Wielding the numb arm above the head ready to strike, only now raise the eyes.

Arms of Father – stalactite wings. Legs of Father – pillars of ice. Chest of Father – a glacial battleship. Genitals of Father – dark horn icicle. Head of Father – thousand-pood explosion of crystal thorns lacerating the sky. Index finger – glass rapier piercing the globe. Gazing open eye – pearl of angelic azure. Heart of Father – Truth set in stone.

Through ice and through murch, with all the strength still left from life – insert the prong. The other hand then jerks the cable, activating the pump: teslectic flow shoots along the wire with a silent bolt of shadow. And this pain alone is felt in the cadaverous right hand, as the body sinks into father's cold embrace.

On the Ice

At once it clutches the body in geological clench,
grinding flesh breaking bones locking
in mathematical trap father and son
not made for life not made for
movement breath words
thoughts, they also
freeze until
everything
comes
to a
halt

[space equivalent to 14 lines of type]
space equivalent to 14 lines of type
space equivalent to 14 lines of type
space equivalent to 14 lines of type
space equivalent to 14 lines of type
space equivalent to 14 lines of type
space equivalent to 14 lines of type
space equivalent to 14 lines of type
space equivalent to 14 lines of type
space equivalent to 14 lines of type
space equivalent to 14 lines of type
space equivalent to 14 lines of type
[space equivalent to 14 lines of type]
and
only
after a
while does
the hot blood
begin to jostle
the body, which I feel no
other than in suffering, that is, in the struggle for being,
for the coming into being of the body, for the coming into being of
me, for me myself, existing, if only in the foulest nethermost condition,
with mouth full of filth, drenched in mud, battered by stones, buried,
yet despite it, yet precisely because of it, yet all the more so – struggling
to force my way out to life, up to the surface, to the air and sun and sky
and people; thus, I tear my way out of darkness, blindly pull myself
out against the force of gravity, till the first gust of warm wind enters
my nostrils, and, reflected in a teardrop, an image of green morning
streams into my still gummy eye, under white cloud and blue sky, in the
rustle of trees and sough of grasses, heralded by a soaring hawk – for
it is spring.

On what cannot be known

I came out into the world amongst corpses. Balmy Siberia was flowing
with foetal waters from north, south, east and west. Steppe and taiga,
mountains and uplands, valleys and lowlands – everything stood in
mud. I crawled out of the mud; such is always the beginning: life out of
muck and clay.

I had stones in my mouth and sand in my ears, I had iron in my
palms. Rust had grown into my skin, it peeled off in flakes and spilled as

red dust when I took my first steps; rust, or maybe some other bloody secretion of the soil. All around me bones and entire body parts protruded from the ground: hands, legs. In a muddy puddle floated a human eye. A bird was pecking out fingers from amongst blades of young grass. I chased it away with iron. It rose off a mouldering skull and took flight. Grabbing a wisp of dark hair, I picked up the head. Father stared out from empty eye sockets, baring a toothless grin.

Such was my first resounding thought and first fully conscious action: to bury father. I found a dry spot and dug a pit. Then went to collect his body.

Having found a third hand (all of them right hands) and a fourth foot, I realised it wouldn't be possible to take out of Siberia only one death of my father. Everything dies and everything is born. The earth had digested the remains of the Yakuts and Tunguses; surely something also of the good Shchekelnikoff and the Yapontchiks lay scattered here in the mud, surely something too of former Siberians. A line of green taiga to the north-east corresponded to my memory of wintertime: I'd come out not far from the place where the icecradle had frozen up out of the ground. Here, father's remains were densest – his head, a hand, a bone – but the majority of our body parts are anonymous. Who shall recognise his own spine and pelvis, who own up to one of ten calves presented to him, even if clean and scarcely decayed, who point to the correct thumbs served in bundles of a dozen, bah, who give a police description of his own heart? All mysteries. We know not ourselves in the most literal, anatomical, material, butcherly sense. Indeed, we can rely only on Fyodorovians of future centuries and their automatic worms, for were it to come to it, left to ourselves, we'd make a thorough mess of our bodily resurrection just as we have of everything else.

I gathered up the body from the mud, similarly black from mud myself; there was nothing but filth and stench, muck and clay so that the body, unstuck into parts, seemed not in the least disgusting to my touch and warm embrace. In truth, none of the things subjected to my touch aroused disgust. Even the small flies furiously attacking me, shoving themselves up my nose, into my ears, into my mouth – the forever cursed Siberian gnus – even they seemed to me quite congenial by the very fact of their existence: they are, and that's good. Then I understood that for the first few hours since emerging into the world, I had persisted in a kind of desensitised euphoria, insofar as astonishment so powerful it was almost deafening can be called euphoria.

Only, therefore, after I'd fulfilled all obligations towards other people's bodies (the burial spot I marked with a mound of stones, intending to raise a cross there later) did I turn my attention to my own body. Having washed in a quagmire not far away, scraped off the clay accretions and fresh scabs beneath them, torn the soil and vegetable rot out of my hair and beard, I at last noticed things that should have moved me first and foremost. I was walking badly – indeed, I had a long wound down my right leg, stretching from thigh to knee and almost to my heel. The wound appeared to be healed, but the leg wasn't working properly, stepping distortedly, creaking at the joints, bending rather too violently; it looked considerably thinner and punier than the left. My feet meanwhile trod crookedly, since they were completely stripped of toes, probably frostbitten. Several fingers were missing besides from my hands (one on the left hand, two on the right; luckily, the thumbs were saved). I was also having trouble with my left eye; what I'd taken at first to be a mud clot proved in reality to be a dense adhesion of crushed skull bone, swollen bruise and suppurating eyelid; I saw nothing with my left eye and, in truth, wasn't sure whether an eyeball still rotated in there or a distended tuber of internal gangrene. I had also lost my left ear (though I could still hear through it). A looking glass would have come in handy, since in the viscid puddles, any reflection horrified with its monstrous caricaturisation. I saw how large patches of skin – on my hands, my thighs, my chest – had bizarrely changed colour, thanks most likely to near-fatal frostbite, for I resembled a living map of bogland, peat and heather. Some of these fragments remained insensitive to touch. Hard lumps were moving under my skin like small pebbles or armoured cockchafers. With my tongue I felt the inside of my mouth: the number of teeth on the left side differed from the right, the number of upper teeth from the lower. When I waved my arms, something jarred below the nape of my neck and hurt in my back – thus I realised that one shoulder-blade hung lower than the other and my arm didn't reach where an arm should reach. When I bent forwards, westerly shadows projected on the ground the outline of a slight hump.

But I was alive. Alive. Alive!

I scoured the land for the place where, in relation to the edge of the taiga, our camp should have stood. Of course, nothing significant jutted out above the grasses. Leaning on a piece of old iron (probably some fixture from that charred sleigh), I wandered across the flat. Swarms of insects flitted and hummed above the green vegetation, as well as magnificent tiger-coloured butterflies. On a fallen spruce trunk, a small chipmunk stood to attention, warming its stripy fur in the spring sunshine, blinking its coal-black eyes and opening wide its muzzle. I whistled. It merely turned its head. How long ago had Winter retreated? What year was it exactly?

I found relics of tentpoles. Rummaged in the earth, poked with the iron. Came across rotten wood and coldiron plates, the latter in fact very well preserved. From a hollow, I pulled out a few smouldered rags and two shapeless bits of hide. After an hour or two, I discovered a sandy dip between stones where most belongings from the Pilsudtchiks' tent had clearly drifted along with the melting snow, because there I plucked scraps of thick felt out of the sticky soil, along with two intact chests, the rusty barrel of a shotgun, a heap of putrid fur coats, the pitiful remains of a small stove and several pounds of other junk well mingled with gravel and clay.

One of the chests contained proviant; water had got inside, ruining the products. I uncovered a can of vitamin-rich fruit from the Mielke & Sohn factory. It made a decent impression, sounding solid and noiseless as it ought on shaking. I broke it open on a stone with the aid of the scrap iron. Mummified carcasses of fruit were revealed, now looking more like walnuts.

In the other chest were my own things, which I might have regarded as an exceptional stroke of good luck, were it not for the fact that here too water had seeped through. Fabric and paper disintegrated at the slightest touch, reduced to a uniform lump of muddy slush. All that had been saved was a package tightly wrapped in oilcloth and rubber band, in other words my notebook with its daily record of measurements. I undid the parcel, unexpectedly amused by this discovery.

The paper had yellowed, mouldered, and the handwriting had faded. Carefully I turned the pages. The final entry: *11th December 1924, 96 mirks. Tsar all around. Prince in Aleksandrovsk. Attack.* And so on. I laughed as I shook my head over the notebook. Underneath, held together by an elastic band, lay the Piatnik playing cards. I took them out and slowly shuffled them. Figures of kings and queens revealed their pale countenances, whilst their backgrounds over time had acquired the colour of antique ivory, become covered in a web of minute cracks like an old man's wrinkles. They still managed to gleam in the sunlight, however, emitting a reflected ray that made the eye blink. I looked up. The sun had not yet reached its zenith, it was not yet noon. Without watch, would I be able to keep up for half an hour the twenty-second rhythm?

Was Tesla's Murch Hammer prototype still beating at all in the Physical Laboratory of Irkutsk?

With a stick, I noted on the earth: zero, zero, zero, one, zero – and *Auferstehung.*

Schultz has sold Tesla. Flee. Pocięgło to the rescue. Pact with Pobedonostseff. Alliance of Lyednyaks. Winter holds.

But there were many distortions in this cyphered message, I had to guess a fair few of the signals. Besides, disturbances tended to increase in the rhythm of around thirteen waves, that is, for more than fourteen minutes, which came out very clearly in the control run. I grew lost in thought with the chin resting on the scrap iron, gazing at the chart scrawled in the mud.

Winter holds, right! The message is obviously not current. Is it possible that a wave travels still along the Ways years after the Hammer has been switched off? (What year is it?) The cryptograms were sent almost certainly by Mademoiselle Christine, no one was likely to have helped her, and if she'd asked Nikola, then he too is not the most shrewdly informed on mundane, political matters. One should therefore interpret this crypto-dispatch by compensating for their ignorance and naivety. Though even they wouldn't mistake Summer for Winter.

The possibility also exists that the message is mendacious.

Flee. Had they known about the Avahites… How were they to know? I did not believe, however, that any political calculations lay behind the mission of those deathless patchworks – were that the case, they'd have been sent first and foremost to hunt down Piłsudski, Pocięgło or other Oblastniks, anarchists, Siberian revolutionaries. For to whom did the fictitious power of the Son of Frost over History present the greatest threat? It was a matter of faith and not political reason. Such an order could have been given to the Okhrana by the tsar, tormented by a new nocturnal delirium neath the nightmares of the Winter Palace. Or by Rasputin.

One way or the other, none of it has the least significance now – for there is no longer a Son of Frost, no longer a Father Frost and no History. It has unfrozen.

I wiped the notation of ones and zeros from the earth.

Amongst the scraps of iron retrieved from the sandy dip was a lot of wire, from which it would have been possible to make snares; I knew in theory how they should work, and since the lesser wild-game of the forest had shown itself, it would have been worth using this method at least to hunt in the taiga; perhaps by evening I'd have caught some meat to roast on a spit. Searching through the wires and cables and steel slats, I came across the rather bent stick of the murchometer. I leant on it as a test – it withstood the strain. I wiped it with grass and a rag, picked out the sand and clay. And when I wound the dangler, the little teslectric dynamo inside began to whirr. Coldiron does not rust!

314 mirks.

There is no doubt: Summer.

I set off into the taiga. No regularity here typical of European forests: trunk, clearance, trunk and so on; nothing of that kind. The taiga is drunk; grown up on the eternal frost, it presents a natural disorder when unfrozen: trees actually stagger as if drunk, rooted so superficially in the former permafrost that the slightest breeze bends and topples them. That's why there are so many fallen trees, yet still growing despite being apparently felled: drunkard leaning on drunkard, but still alive, robust and branchy.

I found unripe berries on prickly bushes; I gorged on them unthinkingly, reckoning they were some sort of Siberian variety of buckthorn harmless to health that Doctor Konyeshin had told us about. For I suddenly felt hunger, as if an entirely new inner sense had been switched on inside me: as if the body spoke directly in its own organic dialect. Eat!

Of course, I immediately vomited. Spewed up the berries, acid from my stomach, sand and soil and tiny pebbles.

Then began again to gorge on the buckthorn.

After dusk, I returned there to check the wire traps – which again was hardly wise, since after dusk, I couldn't locate most of them. Besides, in only one of those recovered had anything been caught: a rat-like rodent little bigger than the chipmunk. To make matters worse, returning through the forest in the dark, I became entangled in willow and bird-cherry bushes and trod on a torn-off branch or sharp root, stabbing my foot. I was plainly limping.

Having spread what remained of the felt and hides on the broken tentpoles, I next spent half the night under this temporary wind-shelter trying to kindle a fire by the most primitive method, that is, without matches or lighter: grinding stone flint, rubbing stick against stick. Wondering, however, whether not to tuck into that raw forest rat.

When at last I'd struck sparks and built a slow-burning hearth out of a cloven stump so as to keep the fire going safely throughout the night, I roasted the rat, hastily skinning it with the aid of a coldiron plate, and devoured it within a few minutes whilst still hot, spitting out the tiny bones. Then with fingers caked in blood, soil and ash, I picked between my teeth for bits of stiff hair.

Then I lay down with belly facing the stars, my hunger appeased. The tough meat hit me in the bowels with a heavy blow; an armoured fist punched me from within. I belched once and twice. Something was gurgling and rumbling in the invisible organs; organic fluids and lubricants bubbled inside me; gases made their way through, winding up the clocks of putrefaction and springs of entropy. I laid a hand on my navel. On the axis of the world above revolved the bright life paths of Upper Land dwellers; the blood of angels burned through the black firmament. Under my fingers, I felt the soft earth around me. I came upon the murchometer and my notebook. I breathed freely.

I leafed through the yellowed pages in the glow of sluggish flames, marking the paper with sticky dirt. Before the first records from my Siberian odyssey, there were still notes to works on mathematical logic and commentaries on Kotarbiński and Teitelbaum – I'd completely forgotten them. Earlier still – some remininscences of Warsaw… I flicked through them indifferently, gliding my eyes over the faint calligraphy. I yawned; loose papers fell out. I lifted them to the light. The unfinished letter to Julia.

I wanted to laugh. I hiccupped loudly; an owl answered back. Which is the first page…? My God, how many I'd scribbled during all those months! Well over a dozen. The longest letter in the world. And it began – I read the very beginning – began from the moment when on returning to my lodgings from my last visit to Julia's home, where I'd yelled at her in her father's presence and declaimed out loud her whole snakelike perfidy, when on returning I started within a few minutes to sincerely regret it and wrestle with pangs of conscience, thrashing about in shackles of Shame. There was a bottle of caramel vodka lying to hand, inadvertently left by Zygmunt… I had begun the letter with a burning plea for forgiveness. *Do you still wish to set eyes on me?* But lacked the strength to write much more; my head flopped onto the tabletop, exhaustion and alcohol got the upper hand. In the morning, I added another sentence or two, and then went out into the city. And heard that Julia had thrown herself from a first-floor window, admittedly not a high one but disastrously breaking her vertebrae, and that she was now lying in the Infant Jesus hospital, most likely paralysed for life, neither dead nor alive. The second and third passages of the letter are about this. *You can't leave me like this before people and God!* I was already laughing out loud. A poor student's sufferings of the heart, a kopeck per page! How could I have written it in all seriousness? *I am praying for your recovery, everything will turn around, even you will forget it.* It rambled into ever more pitiful lies and illusions, for she never regained consciousness, whilst I was declaring to her on paper further solemn feelings, confessing my deepest secrets in the speech of men, spinning fantastical plans and daydreams that were already totally detached from the world and truth… Because I knew I would never send the letter. That no one would ever read it. I wrote to a Julia who existed not, existed not.

I flung the notebook and all pieces of paper into the fire. A flame shot out of the cloven stump into the starry firmament of Asia in a burst of merry sparks.

I stretched out on the hard earth, arranging my crooked bones for sleep; the blood of angels was shed far and wide over Siberia. Knowledge ends where action begins. Such order prevails under sun and moon that won't be expressed by language of the first kind. Activity, that is, change, is the nature of Falsehood; inaction, that is, unchangingness, is the nature of Truth. He, who would indeed know the full truth about himself, would step in so doing into the realm of ideas, of everlasting generalities, amongst syllogisms, logical conjunctions and bare numbers.

Father was finally close to this – finally, as he fled from life. Whilst he was still moving around in the world of matter, however, whilst he was active – was he concerned at all about the mathematics of his character? did he think about it even for a moment? No type of shame had access to him.

They knew him by his deeds. They knew him by his body.

Whoever craves knowledge of himself, craves death.

Whoever craves knowledge of the world – he craves life.

I fell asleep and slept the slumber of the healthy, until the trilling of birds and touch of spring sun roused me. I arose, gathered whatever might still prove useful, and set off into the world.

On the non-necessary

I went north, north-east, towards the Primorsky and Baikal mountains, towards the Lena river. The sun and vivid stars guided me through the warped geography, through the landscapes of the great Siberian thaw.

I saw whole river valleys and ravines buried neath landslides of mud, trees, stones, I saw mountains with torn-off sides, mountainsides pushed into folds by the hectare like waves of carpet, I saw the stripped-bare innards of those geological organisms with veins of watercourses, bones of rock, tissue of sand, muscles of clay – exposed to sunlight for the first time in millions of years.

I saw how sudden deluges flood a plain after spring rains, how modest rivulets, sparse mountain streams, rise a good three arshins in half a day, rushing in broad sweeps along new channels or no channel at all, flowing as a muddy front over grass, hills, clumps of trees.

I saw how after such inundation, Black Water descends from lands of old conflagrations, burned remnants accumulated under thawing ice from great Siberian fires that had changed swathes of taiga to charcoal desert, so large five European princedoms could be carved out of them. Black Water has the consistency of Tokai and colour of liquid murch; it absorbs all light and emits a colourless gloom.

I saw forests of trunks two arshins high, evenly chopped just above a man's head, as if some giant had stridden with his scythe through the taiga, reaping at a stroke a verst of primordial woodland to the height of a one-storey house.

I saw Tents of Earth: hillocks ten or more arshins wide and three arshins tall, into which you enter through clefts hacked in their green side like wounds; and within them: cold darkness and grey seams of unthawed ice above your head. I often slept in these Tents. There were many of them here, especially around Baikal: they'd been growing for years, gradually lifting up, pumped from below by ice, that is, by water transformed into ice under pressure, and also by compressed pockets of air. Then the ice and air receded leaving an empty Tent of Earth.

I saw craters in the midst of the taiga, as if someone had dropped bombs from an airship: great pits strewn roundabout with broken trees and scattered soil.

I saw whole fields of alases: depressions several arshins deep, some-times marking an irregularly configured plain with long versts between each, but sometimes grouped together by the dozen: hole, hole, hole, hole, like tracks left by the Mammoth of Mammoths, imprints of its feet.

I saw animal carcasses spat out from the ice, from the earth, and carried away by water, white and yellow bones, horse saddles, planks and whole fragments of wooden houses, the utensils of human trades, reindeer hides and rags, and also people's remains both naked and clothed – scattered following a sudden nocturnal flood in the midst of the plain, like toys fallen from the hole-ridden pockets of God. Thus, I acquired breeches with one and a half legs and a tattered hat: from a corpse, fresh yet ancient, barely decomposed. In a trouser pocket, it had a broken compass and a tchinovnik's stamp from the Harbin Customs House dated 1812.

I saw lightning bolts of spring storms slicing the dark navy sky from horizon to horizon with jagged claws, quarter-hour after quarter-hour, hour after hour; I walked under a mantle of lightning bolts.

On the eighth day, having consumed nothing for four days apart from herbs and mushrooms of dubious edibility, drinking muddy rain-water that made my stomach erupt in excruciating cramps – I began to lose consciousness. I began to faint on the march, collapsing inert, for which I paid eventually with a mighty bruise and torn skin on my forehead.

My head was spinning, I walked slowly, leaning heavily on the mur-chometer; I had to take longer rests. I fell over again and again and again; and sprained my wrist.

Boundless Siberia stretched before me in green plains, marshlands sparkling with a million sky-blue pools, vibrant spruce-and-larch taiga interspersed with white birch glades or darker islands of alder and cedar. The mountains were getting closer, embracing the horizon in muscular arms. Nowhere did I see a sign of man. And more and more often, this biblical fear came upon me: that I was indeed the last of the house of Seth. That the rest of the human race had perished – *eating corpses, rabid from the blood of men*, and that the same fate awaited me. Especially at night, vulnerable – alone in the dark. Hands shake and the heartbeat is shallow, rhythmless, just beneath the skin.

On the ninth day, I vomited blood. I trudged on, staggering and reeling. Covering no more than fifteen versts a day. Then the terrain grew damper still, and I floundered with every step.

On the tenth day, I lost consciousness during a shower of rain and fell into a dense quagmire, almost drowning. The wound on my right heel reopened – so I had to tread on toes I didn't have. Hallucinations, which I knew to be hallucinations, began to haunt me.

Later, the weakness in my legs and spinning head grew so intense it was faster and safer to move on hands and knees. Thus, I walked through another day and a half. Hallucinations, no longer distinguishable from waking, were haunting me.

I pushed on arshin after arshin, rise after rise – it was just as well the landscape was so hilly and the taiga veiled; thanks to this I could promise myself salvation beyond every near summit and then beyond the next and the next and the next. Water flowed in gullies between them; it was enough to lower my head and swallow the cold slush. I vomited mud and blood.

I crawled out onto a hillside above a trading post, and it was there that they found me.

Because I had on me an imperial tchinovnik's stamp and because Summer reigned there again, they took me in, dressed my wounds, fed me, let me sleep under a roof. When I finally woke up for good and thanked them for saving my life, they could hardly throw me out.

There had been four men at this merchants' trading post, set up to profit from the trade with prospectors, gold-diggers and magpies working in the Lena basin. One man had left the trading post to go to Kachug for news and instructions from his firm as well as fresh merchandise delivered there by river; three remained. One had gone to a prospectors' camp somewhere in the direction of old Vyerkholensk looking for gold and tungetitum and had not yet returned; two remained. They would barricade themselves in for the night in this cabin of thick cedar logs concealed under a hill, often keeping watch for hours by the window embrasures with rifles in their hands, lamps extinguished. Of a morning, the younger of the two, Alyosha, would take the dogs and go in search of their unreturned comrade, taking the opportunity to shoot a grouse or partridge, should the good Lord place the game right under the barrel. The older man, Gavrilo, would sit by his wireless receiver and attempt on the fragile Gropp tube to pick up Irkutsk, Harbin, Tomsk, Novosibirsk, Yakutsk or Vladivostock, whence short broadcasts were sometimes emitted into the ether. They had brought the radio there the previous summer, when the ice began to let go. Thaw had set in, and from the moment the Tchornoye Siyaniye disappeared from the skies once and for all, electromagnetic waves were travelling across the erstwhile Land of the Gleissen according to the same physics pertaining in the rest of the human world. That the apparatus was damaged and few comprehensible words could be heard was another matter. Turning the loudspeaker down to a whisper, Gavrilo would switch on the radio also at night – he liked to sit with his ear to the box; then he would sometimes catch Western music, that is, songs set to American melodies released into the ether by Royal Navy transmitters in Hong Kong and carried here at the midnight hour in magic tides of invisible waves. More often than not, buzzing noises reached the ears mingled with other buzzing noises, strange whiny serenades that changed tone, rhythm and tune whenever you moved nearer or farther away from the gadget, shook your hand or head, bent your body forward or back. It was a magical activity. We listened to the radio like this for hours. Somewhere out there in the darkness, on the heights, in the cosmic abysses, waves overlapped with waves – thus was born a new monster of whispered roars, wauling scratches. The traders had concealed the coldiron antenna in the branches of a birch tree growing on the roof of the hut. Alyosha slept at his sentry post by the window, hand on Mauser rifle, as the muffled tunes of ragtime or Dixieland jazz seeped into the Siberian night.

It was April 1930 and the Great War of Four Fleets was still raging in the Pacific, whilst the armies of Nikolay the Second Aleksandrovitch were crossing European Russia, scorching out Revolution with iron and fire. The old military treaties between the great powers, those diplomatic pacts of ruling houses binding Europe and her colonies in a web of artificial dependencies concluded as far back as Bismarck, had given way. In Asia, on the other hand, the Chinese emperor was slaughtering millions of his own mutinous peasants; the Emperor of Japan, having at last absorbed Korea, was fighting the Americans over Tchukotka. Siberia was governed by no one.

At night they were more talkative, that is, Gavrilo was, because Alyosha, as was the wont of faint-hearted peasants, mumbled and grumbled in the face of the unfamiliar, struggling to answer me in even a few words. Gavrilo, on the other hand, seemed glad of a fresh opportunity to chat. Not at once did he realise that I hailed from the Great Russian Heartland; first, he was deceived by that stamp, then he looked at the penumbra and took me for a gleissenik by blood and birth, and finally – for a magpie dealing for a long time in tungetitum. It was Summer, so I had to cut this short, swiftly and decisively: Benedykt Gierosławski, I said, pinning him with a frank Cyclopean

stare, Benedykt Gierosławski, a Pole with arrest warrants or even imperial convictions hanging over his head.

He believed me or believed me not. When I sat down for the first night
with him by the singing, softly whining radio set, he offered not-the-
worst tobacco and turned at once precisely to the tungetitum business.
Because these men have no idea what to do themselves, and await their
firm's instructions like words of the Saviour, for what if some belated
magpie should arrive with a sack of tungetitum, well what? – should
they buy? for how many roubles a pound? and blacktungets? Here, they
didn't know if they still fetched a high price at all. Last year, the Ice
industries had collapsed, and since then no new pricelists had been received. I ask if they've heard whether anyone in Siberia would now buy
tungetitum. Oy, it's a dark hour for all trade, Gospodin Yeroslavsky –
the old factor puffs on his pipe, adjusting the knobs on the radio. First
of all, devils take the gleissen and we no longer have coldiron; fortunes
are draining from Siberia. Then devils take the government and the
law, and you can no longer step onto the high road with goods to trade
or money earned from trade, because you'll be robbed at once by this
or that band of vagabonds, revolutionaries, Martsynians, Narodniks of
one hue or other, or simply thieves. In the end, people are less willing
to engage in any kind of business in such uncertain times. Who doesn't
have to, doesn't stick his nose out. It so happens that tungetitum is
harder for magpies to find now, especially blacktungets, for as the ice
thawed and snows melted, the waters rose, and everything is drowning
in mud, sinking into the soil.

... He says the Ice industry is dead – had he heard perhaps what had
become of Irkutsk and Zimny Nikolayevsk? A New Orleans orchestra
ripples in the radio and owls hoot in the blustering taiga, as Gavrilo tells
of the world's fate as overheard here in the Siberian wilderness. There's
no Zimny Nikolayevsk, Gospodin Yeroslavsky. Who rules in Irkutsk?
Who knows! And is the Trans-Siberian still running? Assuming some
army or other hasn't blown it up. And Governor Schultz-Zimovy? No
longer in power? Well, our lordling Schultz, tphoo, devil take him, vanished as long ago as the first riots, that is, in February of last year, on the
day of the Last Aurora when they began slaughtering each other there
in Irkutsk – so all news of him were lost, stabbed somewhere on the
quiet; been self-governing for over four years, quite long enough. And
Doctor Tesla? The factor knitted his bearlike brows. Who? And Prince
Blutsky-Osey? Gavrilo merely shook his head in a coil of tobacco
smoke. And Piłsudski? Again, who d'you mean? The famous Polish terrorist. A-ah, all them terrorists, sir, have crawled out onto the surface
and now openly lead their own armies; every settlement in the taiga
or major highway under a different banner: Red Army, Green Army,

Polish Regiments, German Regiments, Anarchist Fighters, Loyalist Fighters, gangs of paupers in a fresh wave of Martsynian fervour and even armed units of Chinamen and Hundreds of Buryat Cossacks led by False Atamans gone to the wild!

I listened unsurprised, with a sense of cold detachment from the world and from History. Once upon a time, I'd have got excited about it all and taken a feverish interest in every detail, but now – I inquire as if after the health of unloved maiden aunts. For at the end of the day, what else could I expect? Thaw is marching through History just as it marches through Siberian nature. *It has unfrozen.*

And from Europe, I ask lazily, having held my tongue throughout two jazz serenades, inhaling sharply from a lumpy cigarette – have you heard nothing from Europe? From Poland, for instance? He stares morosely. Here we have bandits, but in the Great Heartland there's war. Whilst I hear genuine sadness, genuine sadness in the voice of this old Siberian buried in the deepest wilderness – at the tidings of European Russia threatened by violent destruction. He had never been beyond the Urals, and so more Asian blood flows in Gavrilo, yet he grieved as if at news of disaster afflicting the parents of a friend. I was strangely affected by this – that it moved him more than me; that it was this that moved me. I gave him a friendly pat on the shoulder to console him. He cowered, responding from under his moustache with an ingratiating, doggy grin. For it was I who was the European.

Once on my feet again, having regained some strength, I began to go with Alyosha on nearby hunting walks. They lent me a gun, a light double-barrelled rifle, but accurate; for it was understood in and of itself that a gentleman from the Great Heartland was a proficient hunter. I told them at once this was untrue; that I had no great experience of handling a gun and had never gone after game. Did they believe me? It was Summer.

Alyosha knew every hollow and hillock, he'd grown up here; now, as they were laid bare from under the ice, he was getting to know them afresh. There were as yet few animals, they'd only begun returning after last year's thaws, birds first of all. Entranced like a child by a magic toy, he would show me flocks of birds stretched in formation across the sky, in high flight from distant lands; it was reflected in his eyes, only then full of joy and fearlessly open towards people. He knew, however, none of those species, could not name them, could not describe them, never having seen them before in life. Every day, he went out to discover a new exotic world like a traveller set down on the shore of a fantastical continent. The only difference being that not he but nature itself had been translocated – a new world was exploding beneath his feet every day. It so happened therefore that it was I who revealed the names and taught him the animal mythology (this is a wood grouse, which sometimes mates with the black grouse, which gives rise to infertile two-species crossbreeds; and this is the Manchurian izyubr, also known as maral, a type of Siberian deer that disappeared completely during the time of the Ice so that even Count Schultz had to give up hunting it), for I had come after all from their world. I was a European, it was Summer, and this was truth evenly mingled with falsehood.

Time passed; and I realised that I was not counting the passing time. I'd slipped into a routine. Gavrilo and Alyosha won't send me packing, I can linger here wandering o'er hill and through forest, learning how to shoot at squirrels, warming my bones in the sunshine and listening to night-time jazz on the crackling radio. No one shall find me. Besides, no one is looking for me. I lay down in lush juicy grass on a sunny mountainside above a brook, arms folded with my stick under my head, and watched the clouds inflated like balloons filing past above the taiga, first one, then a second, a third, then a procession of seven tied together in a long chain, then two roundish baby balloons, and a burst balloon, flaccid and fraying across half the sky... Alyosha's dog lay down beside me, thrusting its tongue out and panting heavily, happy from exhaustion after the chase with the young hunter. Blue midges swirled above the meadow. I waved my hand in front of my face. The movement was slow, disjointed, aimless – not to drive away the gnus, nor to shield the eyes from the Sun, nor to summon the dog... To fall asleep? Not fall asleep? Walk down and bathe in that cold, post-glacial stream? Or maybe climb a new mountain with Alyosha? Maybe go after elk? Maybe leave here for good, leave Siberia? Or maybe do nothing? The clouds covered me in soft shadows. Water babbled.

Thaw had come and nothing was any longer necessary, nothing had to be. No internal or external compulsion was giving me a definite future. I don't have to work in order to pay off debts, I am dead to the world anyway; I don't have to return at all to the old world. I have no family obligations; nor do I have obligations to the state – I have no family, I have no state. Nothing threatens me if I do or don't do this or that. Up till now I have always been frozen in the obvious: my Warsaw debts, the prikaz and threats of the Ministry of Winter, father. Life was lived. But now – everything is non-necessary, doesn't have to be, even life itself. The dog stretched itself on my chest; I blew in its nose. It licked me all over. The next cloud overshadowed us. The scent of warm grass and damp forest swelled in the nostrils. I thought: this is point zero, this is the beginning of the coordinate system.

For it begins from a supposedly simple and obvious thing, yet how few people have the courage for it. (Life is lived.) Namely, we ought really – in the depths of our soul, drawing not on models of reasoned argumentation but on simple peasant knowledge inscribed in muscles and bones – to become conscious of the *non-necessity* of our every action and inaction, of the non-necessity of each day lived in a particular way and not otherwise. (Life is lived.) That one gets up at eight o'clock and goes to the office – is not necessary, it doesn't have to be. That one lives in a city amongst people – doesn't have to be. That one works to earn money, spends money – doesn't have to be. That one gets married, brings up children – doesn't have to be. That one behaves in accordance with the law and morality, observes conventions and customs – doesn't have to be. That one walks on two legs – doesn't have to be. That one lives – (life is lived) – doesn't have to be!

To see this at once in all its obviousness, applied at once to each and every thing: it may be like this, it may be otherwise, whilst no means is truer than another.

To see it and accept it as the very first principle: *non-necessity*.

I tightened my hands on the back of the dog's neck; tightened my grip harder when it began to thrash about and scratch me with its claws. Its desperate squeal couldn't find a way out of its muzzle as it choked on its final breath.

Strangle a dog – why? Allow the creature to live – for what, supposedly? Do it or not do it – for what reason? There are no reasons. It'll snuff it or not snuff it – no difference. Behave in this way or that way – it amounts to the same. All roads are open, no one thing is more obvious than another thing. A dog's life, a man's life, one's own life – it's like rotating the letters of an unknown alphabet, like constellations in the sky, shapes of clouds above the forest: empty and absolutely non-necessary.

I can do everything; I don't have to do anything.

Then I thought of the Urals wolf and of Jelena Muklanowicz reaching out to the beast with her bare hand.

I tossed the dog away, rose to my feet, and just as I was, without taking anything else with me, without returning to the trading post, without looking back or answering Alyosha's calls – I set out for Kezhma.

To Kezhma was well over five hundred versts. I figured I would sail up the Lena at least as far as Ust-Kut and then avail myself of the Cold Line. This Second Roaming, however, unfolded differently. Descending off the Baikal mountains, the Lena is unnavigable even in the best of weathers. Before the Year of the Gleissen, great transports of tree trunks used to travel a long way north on it in the summer months – but now, first, no one was working at felling and no one was buying logs, and second, real deluges were still occurring as the Lena coughed up phlegm accumulated throughout the long winter: dirty-brown inundations of thick muddy suspension, cold post-glacial water, as well as millions of poods of soil and vegetation carried away by the icy landslide. From mountaintops along the river, I twice had occasion to observe the passage of such a wave, a spectacle out of the Book of Genesis; I stopped involuntarily and sat down, shielding my ears from the dragon's roar of nature liberated from the Ice. The Lena flows here through a very deep channel, in places between rock-stacks that shoot half a verst into the sky; then again it slackens its belt and sprawls indecorously in its wide bed. The low azure is reflected in its smooth mirror: here sky on sky, and here sky on earth. Then the rocks again slam shut; there the water roars most savagely. The rockfaces are arranged so regularly, however, in geological terraces like laboratory cross-sections of the earth's crust, that I often thought of this natural phenomenon, contrary to reason, as a creation of man: someone had designed it, someone had hewn a path for the current; someone had liked the colours of the wooded landscape above the curved river and the sharp evening shadows cast over it by the surgically incised rocks – had pictured it and made it come true. More than once, I fell asleep there by a dying bonfire above the Lena with my imagination full of geological shapes, drifting into gradual dreams of earth, rock and cold water-courses meandering in the dark neath Hephaestus's weighty blow.

In calmer tributaries of the Lena, I caught fish, having knocked a neat hook out of wire disentangled from a magpie's prospecting sieve with the aid of a stone and the murchometer. After the inundations of river phlegm, on the banks of oxbows, I found various pieces of equipment spat out of the earth along with its detritus. I ate fish from a gold panner's rusty bowl. I also had an aluminium can for water. One night, another Siberian traveller wandering along the Lena sat down to my fire and fish. He introduced himself by the name of Jan, said he was born in a Prague still subject to Emperor Franz Joseph; he'd come to Siberia to take up a position as manager of a mine, but now there's no longer a position and no longer a mine; now he's following a procession of crazed Martsynians who had abducted his wife and child – he draws out a huge revolver and aims at my chest demanding I swear I'm no Martsynian in any shape or form. At once the Trans-Siberian Express sprang to mind. I wound up the murchometer, 313 mirks, Summer. He must have seen my dark umbriance, that was why. I served him the rest of the fish and told him the story of the Son of Frost; one night sufficed. He did not shoot. In the morning, we made our way to Kachug.

Port and town were held by the people of a certain Fashuykin, who, so we heard, had once been a non-commissioned officer amongst the custodians of katorzhnik work gangs sent to fell the taiga on the banks of the Lena. After the Last Aurora, he had somehow mustered the guards along with the prisoners and vagabonds and, having joined forces, taken control of the entire navigation of the river. However, the same chaos and lawlessness that facilitated their self-government also caused trade across Russian Asia to wither for good, and so Fashuykin, instead of making an easy carefree fortune, had to labour to keep control of the town as well as protect and feed the people. We arrived there two days after the passage of the sectarian pilgrimage after which Jan was hurrying. Bloody skirmishes had taken place when the Martsynians tried to break into the town's depots and warehouses on the riverbank; Fashuykin's volunteer police force had resisted, firing across the river and shooting from windows of buildings, some of which had burned down. Fashuykin, a tall handsome thug in military shapka and wielding a whip, was patrolling the streets with his vagabond bodyguards, poking his nose in everywhere, yelling at the men in arms, goading those clearing away bodies, and bending over women and children who barred his way every moment with mournful requests; eventually, they would kiss his hands and, snivelling and blubbering, let themselves be led away by the sullen cutthroats, consoled despite everything. We witnessed such a scene on the embankment. Watch closely, I said to Jan, at how the United Free States of Siberia are born. He gave me an odd glance and pointed to the counter of a warehouse (which was not burned down). I squinted. A poster was hanging there, looking at a distance rather like the anti-Japanese wartime posters. I walked up to it. Someone had ripped off the bottom, a bullet had pierced the caption at the very top – there remained, however, what was most important. It was an appeal to the People of Siberia modelled on illustrated newspaper strips and delivered by a lumberjack of hardly Slavonic good looks. The lumberjack proclaimed from the poster that these lands and their riches were no longer in possession of the Emperor of All the Russias, but of the Siberian people – since on the seventeenth day of October 1929, in Tomsk, the United Free States of Siberia had been founded, handing democratic power to Siberians themselves. The Tomsk Declaration was signed by various political committees, including the New Narodniks and SR-Hangmen of Boris Savinkoff; first on the list, however, was the All-Siberian Regional Movement represented by Pocięgło P.D. Lower down, beneath the timber-cutter's left hand, it continued with a speech on the planned activities of the UFSS Provisional Government, part of which was missing. I asked Jan if he'd heard of this government. Who's chancellor? Not some Pole by any chance? However, Jan did not treat this state-building project with much seriousness. Parlour games for gentlemen politickers, he muttered, staring at the corpses being fished out of the river by indigenous bargemen. For why even try to spread such propaganda around the country – how many folk here can read, eh? Then he went off to the makeshift cemetery on the south side of town, to search there for his woman and child.

We wasted three days in Kachug waiting for an opportunity to take a boat downstream. Jan was the first to give up, preferring to hasten after the Martsynians on foot. There were hundreds of similar vagrants, all likewise without money, begging people for a warm meal and a roof over their heads. Money, besides, wouldn't have made a great deal of difference: as I swiftly observed, inflation had devoured the tsarist rouble shortly after the Thaw, and other European currencies didn't seem to fare much better, only the American dollar had retained its value, well, along with gold and diamonds. Fashuykin was paying for the town's clean-up and law enforcement in potatoes, turnips and onions as well as promissory notes from his Wood Syndicate. I worked for two days on the corpses; afterwards at least I ate my fill. The notes served to wipe my bum.

Jan lost patience and set out north along a timbering route. I caught up with him later roaming with a group of convicts who had fled from under Fashuykin's control and, making the most of their unexpected release by the Thaw, were attempting to return home to European Russia. There were many more of these would-be fugitives whose shackles had let go of their own accord when the Ice let go, and the fetters of the State also let go. Some had gone south, to Irkutsk, counting on travelling by Transsib or by sea via Vladivostock, or indeed planning to walk through Mongolia and Harbin and get fat on the Chinese Revolution. Others, like these companions of Jan, had set out immediately for Krasnoyarsk. Still others – the least numerous – having nowhere to return to and unable to find their bearings in the wider world, reckoned it wisest to wager on Fortune and remain under the wing of Fashuykin *et consortes*.

The company of former katorzhniks had one definite advantage: they won't die of starvation in the green taiga and no man travelling with them would die either. They ambushed a uniformed rider on the road, stealing his rifle and ammunition, and then managed to shoot a plump young stag. Which again became a reason to part with Jan, since he didn't wish to waste another day on preparing the animal and dressing the meat for a longer journey.

I caught up with the Czech several score versts farther on, already not far from Ust-Kut.

We were amazed to see on hills above the Lena, the encampment of some kind of military force. At first, we thought it was tsarist Cossacks, then – that it was a Cossack Hundred gone wild, then, as we counted from a distance more European faces – an organised band of ex-katorzhniks similar to Fashuykin's. They had erected a palisade, dug themselves in systematically, and had sentries with binoculars and at least two heavy Hiram Maxim machine guns, which were spotted by a young convict with recent experience of the Austrian Imperial-Royal Army. They had also erected a radio antenna mast. They were not wearing uniforms, which did not lessen the fears however of the ex-katorzhniks, who preferred to retreat into the taiga and bypass the camp from afar. I drew attention, however, to the fresh mud strewn everywhere on the shores of the Lena and the steel hull of a steamboat shining in the sunlight, its tail end protruding out of the mud. Opening wide my arms with a broad grin on my face, advancing slowly and steadily, I stepped out of the forest and walked towards the camp.

They shot me not down. More vagrants had converged on them; in such times, people seek above all safety, long to submit to authority. I had not taken ten paces inside when Jan sprang upon me, breaking from the sapper work which they clearly forced on all vagabonds here. A chief of guard appeared who did not understand Russian; I addressed him in French, which was what seemed to decide. Above the camp's main tent, a flag was flying that I didn't recognise even at close range – but this was because its colours were not those of a state or ruling dynasty, but of the mining company Société Minière de la Sibérie under the management control package of Empain-SPR. Édouard Louis Joseph Empain, in partnership with other large European and American firms who'd invested deeply in Siberia at the time of Stolypin's government and during the coldiron boom, had organised an expedition to evacuate these companies' employees and their families from defrosted Siberia. In Ust-Kut, there had been saltworks with an income of millions as well as the main tungetitum warehouses north of Kachug, whither all transports from magpieries close to the Last Isotherm used to come: on their way via the Cold Line across Baikal and Olkhon Island to Irkutsk. The rescue operation was being led by a sunburned Boer, Colonel van der Hek; he had recruited people even from Baron Empain's Egyptian expeditions and from Macao, experienced soldiers, many on French passports – I learnt that since Thaw, in contrast to the British, France had kept its alliance with the Russian Empire; the investments of French capitalists in the Russian lands had been too vast. Van der Hek's plan envisaged evacuation along the Lena, Yenisey and Ob to the northern ports, built during Winter for the needs of river and sea-ice transportation. They had steamers on each of these rivers as well as radio contact with them. The foreigners had left Ust-Kut according to instruction and assembled here with their families and belongings, to the south of the town; then two unforeseen events occurred: one, they collided with the wandering army of Martsynians, and two, the Lena coughed up a fresh helping of phlegm, sinking van der Hek's ship. As a result, Empain's expedition was stuck in this temporary fortress awaiting fresh transport and frightening away bands of vagrants.

Tossed by hysterical fatalistic mood swings, Jan had entered a phase of uncontrolled garrulity; within half a minute, he'd managed to blurt out to the chief of guard my entire life story. Whilst the latter, having heard that I'm Polish, a mathematician and a Krupp employee, escorted me to the colonel. The colonel chatted in a friendly manner over a glass of gin, asked me about this and that and then politely excused himself. No need to be an enmurched genius to realise that he'd gone to inquire via radio whether in the Berlin registers of Friedrich Krupp AG they had an employee named Gierosławski. It lasted till dusk and well into the night, when the connection improved; before questions and answers had passed to and fro on ether waves across half the world by telegraph cable, the stars of the Great Bear had lit up over Siberia and the yellow lantern of the moon travelled halfway to China. Colonel van der Hek found me before dawn, as I gazed from the landing stage of the palisade at the moon floating on the waves of the Lena. Bodies from Kachug had also collected in the sputum of the river; the moon turned over one corpse and then another in idle amusement; they bounced back dilated, distended, dangling their limbs. The Boer offered me a cigar from a steel etui. 'And so, German bureaucracy is functioning. Don't they now find themselves by chance on opposite sides of the front, Nikolay and Wilhelm?' 'In Germany there's a workers' revolution, they don't know themselves which side of the front they're on,' said van der Hek. '*Alors*, businessmen are always on the same side. Wars, politics, what do they signify when it comes to money? It'll flow just the same, find a way; the Société Minière de la Sibérie has big business interests also with Krupp. They checked, found two Gierosławskis. Made me assure them that it's not the elder. Baron Empain is sunning himself under the palm trees in Heliopolis; in this matter I come under Krupp's command.' 'My father is dead.' We smoked a cigar in silence listening to the slow breath of the taiga. The colonel was scrutinising me out of the corner of his eye, he smiled feebly when I caught him in close glance. 'You won't be returning to Europe,' he stated at last. 'No.' 'So where to?' 'Beyond Kezhma.' 'You won't get far on the Cold Line, the track is probably repaired, but immediately after Ust-Kut trains are being seized by the Church of Saint Martsyn. We can put you down in Kirensk. From there, you can go west, towards the Podkamennaya Tunguska river.' 'Thanks.' 'Never fear, sir, I shan't betray you to Krupp.' Only when he'd gone did I understand that van der Hek thought I intended, taking advantage of Thaw, to go now to the Last Isotherm, to the place of Impact. This idea immediately kindled a dozen other ideas from amongst my long-expired, melted plans and hopes. For maybe it was possible to freeze something back again...? I sat until dawn on the palisade, unhurriedly savouring one non-necessity after another, breaking them on the roof of my mouth with the tip of my tongue like communion wafer after communion wafer.

I reached Kezhma at the beginning of May, not without hardships – most of the permanent bridges had been torn down and no temporary bridges erected after Thaw; besides, everyone had grown so accustomed to winter roads along the frozen river-courses that the gushing spring waters suddenly became obstacles nigh impossible to overcome; versts and versts had to be added to a journey in order to cross any stream. Another problem arose from the fact that, like it or not, I was still following in the footsteps of that peasant army of Martsynians. I thought I'd parted company with them on the shores of the Lena, but no: just as Colonel van der Hek had said, they held the Cold Line beyond Ust-Kut. As I approached Kezhma, I encountered more and more Martsynians travelling in smaller groups – they were congregating from all over Siberia like animals drawn into a single horde by some unspoken instinct. In the end, however, I didn't even need to hide from them, for they saw the obvious, that I too – walking in this same direction – was their brother in faith. I did not deny it; this was enough. It was Summer.

Conversations by the nightly campfire came back to the same topic: they were congregating because a great assembly was to take place at the grave of the Holy Self-Glaciator with the participation of all the cold fathers, including Rasputin himself, now banished from Tsarskoe Selo and European Russia, an assembly including Rasputin's Church and all its renegade sects, heretic Martsynians; they were all congregating there in harmony, that is, without murdering each other on the road. (It was Summer.) Having innocently inquired about this and that, I then ventured the opinion that there was no real grave of Saint Martsyn, since no one knows what happened to Martsyn (they believe he went descended alive into the Ice); instead, they take Martsyn's old hermitage, ransacked by Cossacks on the orders of the tsar, as his symbolic grave. At that, my skin began to tingle, for I remembered namely where that hermitage stood.

I decided to procure a horse at any cost. In Kezhma, now half burned down, and even beforehand a rather unimpressive nondescript little town, the crowd of pilgrims was surging, seasoned with a large helping of human riff-raff borne here on the winds of History. According to van der Hek's maps and directions gleaned from Kezhma inhabitants, a march of at least a week still awaited me. The crowd was due to move off next day, whilst the first pilgrims had likely already reached their destination. That evening from the tserkoff bell tower, I had a look at the area. Bonfires flickered from horizon to horizon, those in the distance blazing more densely than stars in the sky. Tens of thousands of people were gathered here. How to feed such multitudes? How to maintain order? Sincere faith was not the remedy for everything. (Especially as it was Summer.) The Martsynian fathers were trying to establish order, rationing the food collected en route through violence, appointing guards... But only whilst on the move, only when heading towards a clearly defined goal, can such a mass of people be controlled.

I climbed into the belfry so as to observe the movements of those guards: they had horses. They also had firearms. I recalled how the ex-katorzhniks had knocked a rider out of his saddle in a forest ambush. One man could carry it out single-handed; I planned it very precisely. I lay in wait beyond the first bend in the forest road from Kezhma, the one most frequently chosen by mounted Martsynians. I selected a convenient hefty stick and located a tree leaning obligingly over the road. I scrambled onto a bough and waited, hidden in the nocturnal gloom, in the nocturnal rustle of the forest. My plan was simple and logical. One, two, three.

It didn't go to plan. (It was Summer.) Admittedly, I hit the rider with the stick, but he, instead of sliding smoothly out of the saddle, instinctively caught hold of that stick and dragged me along with him so that we collapsed together at high speed in a single heap; me, the Martsynian, the horse, the stick and the heavy bough. The Martsynian broke his neck, I knocked out a few of my teeth, and the horse shattered its legs. Before I'd managed to come to my senses over this ruffianly disaster, another rider coming from Kezhma loomed on the road. I dropped behind the terrified squealing steed and began screaming louder still for help in Martsyn's name. The rider drew near and stopped. I snatched the rifle from under the saddle and shot the man below the chin. Thus, I obtained a saddle horse, two guns and enough provisions for a week.

On the third day, in the late afternoon, I reached the Milky Pass. A sizeable throng had gathered already on the mountain meadows. The spot where Martsyn's hermitage had once been was surrounded by a stone circle; armed Cossack Martsynians were keeping guard. I cast my eyes upwards, above the thinning taiga, over the hills and sharp-edged crags. The black ruin of Professor Kryspin's sanatorium stood out against the sky above meadows and woods: a rotten tooth on the skyline of the jagged ridge. One glance and I knew: I was late by months, years.

I sat in the saddle, exhausted and sore from the forced gallopade, and gazed blankly for long minutes at that gloomy image projected against the darkening azure. Which grew gradually darker, like healthy skin flooded from beneath by violet bruising. A bloody sun drenched everything in cherry-red glow. The Siberian wind dug chill fingers into my beard and long hair. I stared motionless. Eventually, something thumped in my chest behind the breastbone – as if a stone tumour had dropped from my heart – and I tore away my eyes, tore away my thoughts; I dismounted, collapsed on the grass and fell into a dreamless sleep.

Thus, I was found by men from Rasputin's guard. This spontaneously formed praetorian watch of Grigory Yefimovitch consisted exclusively of hiberniks who had sworn allegiance to him; that all hiberniks from the ice-flock keepers were being encouraged to join was because of fear of the unforeseen dangers always aroused by a huge congregation driven by religious fervour, particularly when its object is a dispute over the most important things. A theological battle was about to take place. And because I looked as I looked and also arrived on a guardsman's horse with all his gear – I landed amongst the praetorians of the Holy Sinner. I had neither strength nor inclination to refuse. (Summer.) The Rasputinians had pitched their tents to the east of the hermitage, on the banks of a glacial stream. Hiberniks were washing in the bone-breakingly cold current; it was a form of ritual ablution, or so I understood from the unambiguous looks I received when I'd thrown my things on the bed under the tarpaulin. I also had to go and wash in the flowing frost. The water – thanks to the Sun slaughtered at that very moment in the firmament – was the shade of pig's blood. I pulled off my clothes. On the meadows below, hundreds of men, women and children were camped out. No one was watching. A Rasputinian bathing beside me had similarly frostbitten toes and skin hideously discoloured in patches, and many cruel wounds on his Mongolian physiognomy; and, just like me, was unable to straighten his body fully from its crippling distortions. We exchanged greetings in the name of the Cold God. He noticed my eye constantly fleeing towards the black ruin on the heights. 'There was a scientific clinic there for rich Europeans,' he said. 'They came to freeze themselves for the health of their bodies, treating as nothing the health of their souls. A single holy hermit impeded them!' So, I asked what the sanatorium had to do with Martsyn's hermitage. Well, Professor Kryspin complained to the imperial authorities that suspicious types were constantly gathering, making a bad impression on the patients, and so the authorities razed the hermitage to the ground. In return, in righteous anger, as soon as Thaw came and the State collapsed in Siberia, Rasputin the Most Cold ordered the health resort on the pass to be burned down. And so one night last year, the faithful broke into that house of western opulence, and laid the fuel. The servants of the sanatorium chased them out, but the fire was already spreading like a storm; the unbelievers and Papist reprobates were set alight. They held out for a few more weeks, sending in vain to the ispravniks for help; in the end they tried to sneak away by road to Kezhma, but the brotherhood captured them. They paid with their lives for their brazen godlessness. Cold be God!

The ice-cold water soothed my aching body; I'd have immersed myself fully had I been able, lain on the bottom neath the frosty current, with eye open to the purple clouds and greenness of low hills, I'd have frozen thus most willingly. Every subsequent non-necessity tormented me more. At the evening repast, first one and then another Martsynian would speak to me – I conducted conversations in silence. I moved slowly, petrified in poses of oblivion for long periods. Exhausted, dispirited, defeated, I'd have frozen then most willingly.

They accepted me like a brother.

After wanderings of many weeks and constant nervous tussles along the trail, I slept now long into the day, and went to bed soon after dusk. Energy had drained from me. Since nothing was necessary, everything was possible. I'd have frozen most willingly; but as I hadn't – I counted clouds, lying on the grass. Clearly, in this disposition of soul too, I wasn't so very different from Rasputin's hiberniks, since no one rebuked or upbraided me – or perhaps I merely turned a deaf ear without remembering – or perhaps I'd already chased away those who liked me not with my initial stare. I went down the mountain with the others whenever we needed to re-establish order amongst the pilgrims. The muzhiks treated the hiberniks with respect, usually a few angry words sufficed; once I had to deal a blow to some troublemakers with the murchometer. Several thousand Martsynians seemed to be arriving every day in those meadows. To me it was obvious that sooner or later such a multitude must explode in panic, hysteria or other ardent mass emotion – all the more so since they were already pumped up with religious gas, already ground down by inevitable starvation and penury. Some were ascetics, living solely on roots and water; some – Martsynian factions of Khlysts or Bogomils: they performed public acts of penitence; to the accompaniment of women's wails and children's sobs, they whipped themselves till they drew blood, cut themselves with 'belts of thorns', thrashed themselves with chains. Almost every group had its cold father, its 'holy old man' – usually easy to recognise as they were the most foul-smelling and pickled in filth. Their movements were nervous, their gazes feverish; they answered questions in biblical riddles or with follow-up questions devoid of any clear connection with the previous. Nearly each one managed, however, to express some peculiar wish: that no woman was to lie to the south of his bed, that psalms should be recited to him during sleep (otherwise he'd wake up as soon as Satan crawled into his dream), then again that the greatest sinner in the congregation should be presented to him forthwith (a seventy-year-old bookkeeper from Nizhneudinsk stepped forward).

The majority demanded ice. Obviously, no one had to hand even a tiny pellet of the frozen stuff.

It all sickened me horribly. So as not to have to commune with people, I applied to join the group responsible for building a refuge for Rasputin. We erected a single-chamber hut forty paces from the stone ring around the hermitage. Within the circle, beside the ruins of the hermit's sanctuary, the elders of the congregation were to confer.

We erected a hut; a hibernik carpenter stayed on to make furniture for it, a bed for the ice monk, a stool, tabletop, bench. Rasputin was to arrive within a day or two. In order to avoid people's eyes in the long afternoon, I took myself off into the forest. What began, however, as a flight from people soon turned into an amble through sunlit greenery, fragrant with healthy moisture, in soothing shadows that massaged the burning temples with their butterfly touch. Just as I used to amble through the woods near Wilkówka and my grandparents' estate, a child bereft of cares, bereft of reason, merely imbibing the dazzling world with all his senses, a sponge absorbing the world, a sponge absorbing the colours and sounds of unbridled matter... So much so you wish to remember such a childhood. Birds were singing. A warm spider's web stuck to my cheek. I drank water collected on mossy rock. Ants crawled into my boots. The forest roared in my head.

Inside the forest, I followed a twisting sandy path which led me up to the Milky Pass, to Professor Kryspin's sanatorium.

The Milky Pass – for when Winter lay over Siberia and gleissen trod the paths of men, this mountain chain, although not high, had formed a boundary and barrier for climatic currents: on the northern side, where slopes were gentler, an upland plain opened out and descended with no natural obstacles as far as the place of Impact, to the Lowest Isotherm; whilst differences in temperature, pressure, humidity, wind mechanisms and perhaps also the gradient of other black-physical forces, caused mists the thickness and consistency of milk to collect on the pass, and even flow over it onto the southern side, as Martsynians still filled with dread would relate – mists whose protracted touch was able to crush the hardest metals of Summer. I recalled how a sanatorium advertising brochure belonging to Jelena even contained a blurry photograph: of a mountain manor house above the milky vortices. Professor Kryspin informed of temperatures reaching below minus one hundred degrees Celsius. It was surely for this reason that Martsyn too had lived here for years in his burrow of stone, logs and ice: so as to be able to walk in and out of the Frost. Martsyn was here before Kryspin; it's possible that rumours in the newspapers about the hermit's peculiar habits actually gave the professor his idea. He'd tried treatments with cold before, developing the theories of Baron Larrey, the surgeon with

Napoleon's Moscow campaign, who observed in thousands of cases of soldiers' frozen organisms, the strangely beneficial effects of frost. With the coming of the Ice, however, cryotherapies acquired a totally new efficacy.

I entered the ruin through the main gate; it at least had survived undamaged. Through the wreckage of the mansion's great hall, I was able to cross directly to the back courtyard, where everything had burned to the ground and collapsed in a heap of rubble, two whole floors along with the roof; I picked my way through the rubbish, but from the depth of the pile I could deduce the architectural plan of the former building. The west wall was still standing as well as an observation tower on the east wing – hence the likeness to two black fangs protruding either side of an otherwise toothless jaw.

From the northern courtyard it was possible then to walk out through a wicket to the left or onto the hillside below. Above the slope, under the roof of a brick shed sculpted in waves and crests, an odd coldiron mechanism was concealed. I rapped it with the murchometer stick. It resounded like a cracked bell, rrrwoommm! scaring away two birds from the ruin. I examined the mechanism from all angles. It looked like a winch – but what sort of ropes had been wound on its inner drum? what driving-force made it rotate? With the sleeve of my rubashka, I wiped the dirt off the coldiron. On reading the inscription on the manufacturer's moulding, I burst out laughing. The winch had been produced in Zimny Nikolayevsk by Friedrich Krupp Frierteisen AG from the first brass coolbond of coldiron patented in the Holey Palace.

I walked to the top edge of the slope and sat on the low wall. The yellow-and-green panorama made the head spin, like the hypnotic effect of a first glimpse of open sea endlessly pounding the shore where you stand with massive fistfuls of water, a tiny human mite confronted by a monster. Here, the boundless ocean of Siberia spread before me. Tinged with beige and crimson, the sky thrust its swollen snout into a great bowl of grassy fields, dark swamps and succulent taiga. Between the upper and lower worlds, on one out-thrust of the Sun's tongue, birds were soaring in long constellations. I leaned on the stick and inhaled deeply the air of the new Asia. The scent and taste of damp earth entered again on my tongue, slid into my throat, clung to my sinuses. Everything is born of earth, no wonder it returns to me. That's how I thought then, it was Summer. The stick showed 310 mirks.

I sat there for maybe an hour, maybe two. From the meadows to the south, an echo reached me of the crazed roars of the Martsynian crowd; I had no desire to return to them. Lowering my eyes onto the slope immediately before me, I caught sight of a dark thread winding through the green. It was a coldiron line, released most likely from the winch mechanism; at its far end, a good quarter-verst farther on, loomed a boxlike shape. I guessed it was some kind of carriage – a sleigh? a luxury capsule? – in which Professor Kryspin used to lower patients into the Frost, striking them from his observation surgery with precise doses of curative cold. At first, I was caught off-guard, since I'd not noticed any rails on the slope or even a moderately straight pathway, only upturned trees, boulders and brushwood. Then I suddenly imagined the sanatorium functioning in Winter conditions: here lies a thick crust of ice, the capsule placed on runners slides downhill with no problem.

I left the courtyard by the side wicket. Two steps and I stood stock still – it was a cemetery. Well yes, not all illnesses were stopped by Professor Kryspin's miracle cure, and not all patients succumbing to illness were transported at great cost to necropolises in their own countries. The gravestones stood in even rows, manufactured according to a single model. (The thrifty professor no doubt ordered a large batch at wholesale discount.) Now, however, after the Thaw, some graves had sunk, caved in, as though sucked in from within; to others, the opposite had happened: they'd risen up, swelled. As a consequence, the headstones too had not stayed upright. Drunken taiga, drunken cemeteries, and people as if drunk… Everything is softening, coming unstuck, mel-mel-melting.

Farther on, beyond the rows of slanting stone slabs brought to their knees, on fallow land stretching onto the steep mountainside, was the other part of the graveyard. As I discovered when I trod on a piece of wood covered in weeds. I raked them back with the stick. A cross. Indeed, there were about a dozen such crude crosses, both Latin and Orthodox. They'd been knocked together at speed, as victims of the fire were hastily buried in the melting soil. Shoved in too shallowly, all the crosses had fallen flat following total Thaw, and were soon overgrown with fresh vegetation.

I remember smiling through black melancholy. Prompted by intuition of a future just as certain as the memory of things past – as if acting out my remembrance of the walk on Jerusalem Hill at the side of Leokadia Gwóźdź – I stomped through the weeds, inspecting the ground patiently and methodically with eye, foot and stick like a good gardener. Distorted family names were scratched on the crosses, with no date of death, often with no Christian names. I turned the inscribed boards to face the sun; sometimes I had to rub off clay, moss and fungus. I did it slowly, calmly, with the patience of an archaeologist. The certainty was so great.

Е. Муклянова

It was one of the farthest, on the very edge of the escarpment. A narrow mound strewn with crumbly stones, placed unevenly in relation to others, on the slope and at a crooked angle, half caved in. The shabby grave moved me by its unexpected association – her body had been so willowy, sickly, the fragile bones of her thin little hand barely hanging together neath the pale skin… She'd been stripped by maggots.

I stuck the cross back in the ground, recited *Eternal rest grant unto them* and strode down the hill to join the living.

Rasputin had arrived, hence the shouts and hullabaloo. At dusk, the cold fathers were to deliver their speeches – but fisticuffs and fierce arguments were already rife amongst the faithful; already they were spitting at one another, pummelling each other with curses and sticks. Pausing by the hiberniks' stream, I could read from on high, from the mob's spasms and swirls, the course of mystical currents and strength of particular heresies. A theological battle was about to take place. I hadn't realised to what great extent the Martsynian faith depended on former post-Raskol schisms, how much it drew on Old Believer traditions: in the Russian land, in the Russian people, there was such a terrible hunger for absolute truth which had to be satisfied one way or another.

I saw in the west, under the fir trees, Filippians and Martsynian Denisovans already wrangling with the Yervites, disciples of the State of Ice. Celibate Fedoseyans were thrashing followers of Lyubushkin and Akulina, advocates of free love. Communist Molokans were standing shoulder to shoulder against self-absorbed, sole-existent Palibots, known in Latin as Solipsists, at this moment clearly sharing the common dream. Jehovists were dislodging Church loyalists. Whereas the Rasputinians were sticking closely together, near to Martsyn's circle.

It was Summer – but what of it? For centuries here in Russia, they've been butchering one another, burning or burying alive, maiming and murdering in mirks below three hundred. Particularly the beardless youths and grey-haired elders of both sexes, for it is they who feel deepest the touch of Truth, the righteous anger that makes their blood boil at the very thought that people live alongside them who deny Truth, proclaim Untruth, bear witness against the Truth. In true belief there cannot be two Truths. Truth can only be faithfully repeated; and from this, falsehood shall be recognised, for falsehood varies, for there be more falsehoods than one. They pelted each other with mud and excrement, set children and dogs upon one another, hurled stones and spat out burning spittle – and still the speeches had not begun, still Rasputin had not yet made his appearance.

Grigory Yefimovitch was sitting in his hut, resting after his strenuous journey. At the evening meal (a modest repast of forest fruits and prosphora), I pricked up my ears. According to the least popular and most secretly circulating rumour, which I took nevertheless to be closest to the truth, Nikolay the Second had banished Rasputin and sentenced him after the sudden death of Tsarevitch Aleksey, caused by haemophilia, when Rasputin, in the course of one terrible night of incantations and wonderweaving ceremonies at Tsarskoe Selo, murdered in a drunken frenzy the empress's bosom friend Anna Vyrubova. The fact that Grigory Yefimovitch vociferously lamented the departure of the gleissen when the emperor was overjoyed at it did not speak in his favour; nor did the scandal of a large British bribe accepted by the ice monk for the Bosphorus Treaty – over which a war was now being waged in Europe, since Russia, Germany and Great Britain had finally come to blows over Turkey and the Black Sea. Rasputin was a Siberian by birth, from the village of Pokrovskoye in the Tobolsk Governorate; exploiting his friendship with another imposter at court, the doctor of Tibetan medicine Badamayev, a Buryat besides, he saved himself from his sorry plight by fleeing beyond the Urals. Here, he was to gather 'God's people' and return with this new force to the Great Russian Heartland, to Saint Petersburg, when armed conflict would destroy the Empire and His Imperial Exaltedness. At least this last rumour the hiberniks repeated openly.

Meanwhile, below the Milky Pass, it had reached the first murder: a Martsynian Ottepyelnik had strangled a Martsynian Bogomil in a polemical frenzy midway through the latter's testimony on the satanic nature of God the Creator. We were summoned at once to the crime scene in order to calm the crowd's emotions and prevent an outbreak of theological violence. There, whilst smashing raised heads and hands with a coldiron rod, calling for mercy in the name of Saint Martsyn, I was spotted from the crowd by Jan of Prague.

I saw that he'd recognised me. He signalled to me; I answered not. He pushed his way to the front row, to the very tree under which the corpse was lying (the murderer had already been dragged away to Martsyn's circle). 'Benedykt!' he yelled waving his arms, which only made him look like one of the rest. 'Benedykt! Gierosławski!' Eventually, he pushed up so close he almost screamed in my ear. 'What?' I growled. 'You have to help me! He'll listen to you!' 'What? Who?' It transpired that Jan had found his wife and child. The trouble was she'd acquired a taste for Truth in the meantime and wished to go nowhere with Jan. 'Bewitched by that doddering old swine!' the Czech lamented. 'Nadia gazes at him like at an icon, warms him in the night, kisses him on his legs, brings water to his lips in her own hands!' 'But what can I do? Leave me alone, man!'

I managed to shake him off, break free of his grasp. I yelled to the hiberniks not to wait for the word but get gone from there as soon as possible with the body. We withdrew across the stream, carrying the corpse on our shoulders.

It was high time. The Sun was sinking behind the mountainside, and the cold fathers were already gathering by the ruins of the hermitage. I tried to hide somewhere far from the crowd, but the senior guard claimed that 'people easily obey' me and that 'the shadow of the Ice is evident' upon me, and so stationed me at the entrance to the circle along with three hiberniks of more bearlike stature. I was handed an outmoded rifle and instructed to keep people at a distance of seven paces. I asked how long it would go on. The senior shrugged his shoulders. 'Today's the first day,' he said. I realised that at least one necessity was now clear: I had to escape whilst still alive.

The Sun went down, someone fired three shots into the air and an old man, naked as Death, stepped onto the boulders above me, the cold father of the Martsynian Postniks or Fasters. And so, the truthjoust commenced.

They spoke till they went hoarse or fell over, having lost balance in their homiletic overexcitement, or were dragged down or stoned. And since each and every Truth was an abominable heresy to the children of a dozen other Truths, I was sure stones would start flying from one side or another sooner or later. The only difference was whether a preacher was able to sense that moment, or was so enwrapped in his own words he'd lost all contact with the outside world. The latter sort had to be rescued by us – we guards would fire over the heads of the throng whilst people inside the circle pulled the prophet to the ground; the rescued men themselves loudly resisted rescue. Then we'd reload our guns in preparation for the next Revelation; the crowd would come a step nearer; and the next Martsynian gleissenik buzzing with murch would appear on the boulders. And so the night revolved.

After the first old man, soon pelted with stones, an Orthodox deacon stood above the human sea with a message, as it transpired, from an archimandrite – this one was dragged to the ground before he'd even managed to unfold the bumaga before his eyes. Then for a change, a doltish holy fool, an honest simpleton incapable of putting two sentences together logically, climbed onto the pulpit of rubble. To him, they all listened in great earnestness with mystical fever in their eyes, and to the end of his long gibberish no one raised an offended cry or leapt to murder the holy idiot.

Then a former monk from the Solovetsky Monastery came forward to spin the wordwheel. He did not contradict the yurodivy, since a proposition devoid of sense cannot be rationally denied – but straightaway declared only this: all misfortune stems from misinterpretation of the mathematics of the Apocalypse! As the holy fathers of Constantinople calculated, the world was created for a lifetime of seven thousand years, according to the Lord's reckoning of the Millennial day – 'for a thousand years in Thy sight are but as yesterday when it is past' – and as was also clearly written for the Russian people by Abraham of Smolensk, but, as we know from the Primary Chronicle, the Baptism of Rus took place in the 6496th year after Creation, and so the world ought to have ended without fail in the year 1491 of the Julian calendar – but it did not end! Did not end! How is that possible, I ask you, my brothers! Well, let us learn from Nikolay Berdyaeff how to see truth. Which is more trustworthy: holy mathematics or the witness of corrupt matter? Therefore, one of two things: either we are no longer alive and the world exists not, or History has never really reached the Year of our Lord 1491. This then is the task of the Ice and the role of gleissen: gleissen are angels sent from God to freeze us in historical progress until everything is fulfilled in preparation for the Second Coming. Why then were the great cities of Europe the most heavily iced-over, why did the severest Winter cover seats of human habitation? Because that's where History unfolds! They have been freezing us like this for centuries, without our being aware, and they go on freezing us, sometimes more feebly, sometimes more fiercely, so that generations replace generations, yet we are not much closer to the Kingdom of God – and this is the Truth.

Then came forward a Lyednyak Orthodox Martsynian Bogomil and declared that no, it is precisely the reverse, the Ice was a sign of the destruction of the Creation of Evil, according to Saint Martsyn's own words: since the world of flesh arose from the will and creative power of God-and-Satanael, for man is but the hideous ill-shapen pact between Satanael, who moulded this bestial dwelling for him out of flesh and bones and blood, and God the Father, who breathed life into it, and later sent into this evil world Christ the Logos. Yet what was the Ice if not the Logos congealed in matter, laying divine order and system on the disorder, sin and injustice of Satanael's Earth? The triumph of the Ice would mean the total destruction of the old world, open the first gates to the throne of Christ – for not in the year 1491, whichever way it's calculated, but here and now, before our very eyes, in the form of ice and gleissen we have seen the Beginning of the End, yes, in the cold Logos, the Lord came to us a second time – and this is the Truth.

Then came forward a Martsynian Lobushkovian who derived his faith from the Khlysts and said that no, this wasn't Christ at all – but only a trap for Christs, that is, for humans. For God is continually being incarnated in man, not just that once in Jesus, and flows constantly through us as the Holy Spirit, whilst the sign of a soul's perfection is total incarnation – as in the case of Danilo Filippovitch, who ascended into heaven alive, or Ivan Susloff, crucified three times and also whisked away into heaven, and all the Christs that came after them: Procopius Lupkin, Fyodor Savitsky or Avvakum Kopyloff, who was wont to hold one-to-one conversations with the Almighty. Man frozen in ice goes on existing, he dies not, but neither does he live, that is, he sins not; removed from time, from History, removed from evil, man is the perfect vessel for the Holy Spirit as well as the trap for ensnaring Christ. In the world of the Ice, movement of matter would have ultimately died out – only the Holy Spirit would have moved, blowing through people as through the pipes of an organ, playing beautiful melodies in praise of the Most High. That Thaw came, shattering this magnificent plan, is a sign that we led bad people to self-glaciation; evil, flawed vessels descended into the Ice – it was our mistake to push filthy souls towards the Dove; therefore, only through mortification, through purification and disembodiment, can we summon the icers back – and this is the Truth.

Then came forward a Martsynian Hilarionovite and cried that no, that quite the opposite is true: the vessels were too perfect! The virtuous outnumbered the sinners! Sodom was saved thanks to the just! The same as in precisely 1492, when God, persuaded by the heartfelt faith of Russian Christians, decided to revoke the prophesied decrees and call off the End of the World and Last Judgument. The Ice went on moving until a sufficient number of the Just, that is, Martsynians pure in spirit, had descended onto the Ways of the Mammoths – God saw the strength of the Russian people's faith and revoked the white annihilation – and this is the Truth.

Then came forward a holy old man from the Awayfacing Brothers and vehemently opposed his predecessor, raising his arthritic fists and flourishing his beard. Had they all forgotten the Prophecies of Saint Martsyn?! Had they grown so muddled in the head they can no longer distinguish the works of the True God from the words of the Evil-God Creator? Whose words shall tell us of the End of the World? There was to be fire, fire, which would burn everything, seas and lands, stones and air – and yet there was ice that froze everything. There was to be revelation of heavenly powers, of winged armies descending from on high in the glory of the Lord, to the sound of the trumpets of Archangels Michael and Gabriel – and yet there was revelation of underworld powers, of gleissen with dark mammoth blood freezing up out of hell, in deathly silence. There was to be resurrection of the just – and yet there was self-glaciation of the just. So, what sort of End of the World is it? End as Inversion! The Apocalypse stood on its head! Anti-Judgement and Anti-Redemption, further work of the Anti-God and return of the Antichrist – that's what the Ice was – this is the Truth!

This man fell of his own accord, having slipped as he sprang up ges-ticulating too wildly in his oratorial zeal. The hiberniks then ordered me from behind the stones to move the line of guards. I glanced in the direction of the stream, whence lights were moving. For people had seen Rasputin heading for Martsyn's circle and the crowd lunged forward.

We had no way of restraining them though we assumed a ferocious look, yelled threats and beat their legs, and again fired salvos over their heads. To no avail. There was just enough open field before us to swing a heavy rifle. And not even that – for leaping out of the throng, Jan fell upon me before I'd managed to position myself.

'Tear her from him whilst you're armed! He'll let her go! He has to!'

'You're crazy!'

'Or I'll hand you over! Tell them who you really are!'

'And they're sure to believe you!' I snorted and fled behind the stones so as to get out of his sight. Yes, I had to scutter from there as soon as possible.

Rasputin, surrounded by his cordon of sworn hiberniks, appeared between the boulders with head held high; his long beard and mane of grey hair shone silvery in the glow of torches and bonfires. He was wearing a black monk's habit with a wooden cross on his chest. He greeted the other cold fathers by kissing them three times on the cheeks, which every time prompted a loud roar of enthusiasm from the crowd; some kissed him additionally on the hand, to which he re-sponded by likewise kneeling and kissing their hands. At the sight of this, the assembled Martsynians almost burst into sobs.

He had huge, heavy hands with long muscular fingers; I saw from nearby how he stepped onto the boulders and blessed the congregation, his bare hand standing out as if severed against the backdrop of black.

He began quietly, and immediately everyone fell silent.

With moist eyes set deep in his head, he took the measure of the people as though they were the latest lost desperados at a private audi-ence, come to the Man of God in search of a miracle and conversion.

'My brothers! My sisters! Children sinners!

'It has forsaken us! It has departed! Wherefore? Wise men say why, wise men say otherwise – there is no, is no Ice! Reveal yourself, truth, to me! Come rightness of the word!

'Unto thee will I cry, O Lord; be not silent to me: Lest, if thou be silent to me, I become like them that go down into the pit. Draw me not away with the wicked, and with the workers of iniquity! Give them after the work of their hands; Render to them their desert, because they regard not the works of the Lord, nor the operation of his hands, He shall destroy them and not build them up.

'Blessed be the Lord! Because he hath heard the voice of my supplications! The Lord is my strength and my shield!

'Children sinners! Read in the Psalms what I harkened to in truth on the Holy Mount of Athos: so as not to be cast down together with the evildoers! so as not to be likened unto what is evil, through ignorance and confusion!

'Gather your blackest, most bilious thoughts and try to picture an image of the Antichrist, of what arouses the greatest horror. For what might it be? Who will he be?

'Will he be the one that does only evil? Aaah, yes, I see you putting your hands together – but only think! Glimpse the clear picture! Be this truth? Tremble in dread! The Antichrist does not bring truth, he brings no truth!

'For you see: he will be a beast capable in equal measure of the greatest good and the greatest evil! Not pure evil, which is an immutable truth and ORDER and tells us of God through open negation just as loudly as choirs of angels – but the CONFUSION of good and evil, truth and lies, the INDISTINGUISHABILITY of good from evil, truth from lies, heaven from hell – this is the mightiest horror! The horror of horrors!

'For the Antichrist is devil, angel and demon, light and dark, morning star and false star, lion and lamb, king and tormentor, false prophet and archpriest, benefactor and persecutor, purifier and defiler, safe haven and whirlpool, god to the godless, enemy to Christians, shepherd to those that love earth, persecutor of those that love God!

'And so, without the Ice, we dwell in Eternal Raskol, in Eternal Discord, in the confusion of everything with everything, in the motley that interweaves wickedness with piety – indistinguishable! – curse and blessing, torture and kindness, mercy and no mercy, gentleness and bestiality, disorder and decency – indistinguishable! – sobriety and harmfulness, the mortal and the eternal, the wolf and the lamb, the tripartite and the binary, the blessed tree and cursed tree, Orthodoxy and Catholicism – indistinguishable! – Papists and high priests, Western and Eastern, Lachs and Orthodox subdeacons, Poles and Tserkoff servants, holy relics and heretic corpses, holy icons and vile God paintings – indistinguishable! indistinguishable! indistinguishable!

'Whereas the Ice was restoring to us the order of the world of good and evil. Neither the Ice itself nor gleissen were the Antichrist or true God. But thanks only to the Ice could They exist at all, so that people might know Them! Otherwise, Christ is indistinguishable from the Antichrist, God from He Who is Not God – and as for truths, as you have heard, we have thousands of truths, as different from each other as each is true.

'The Ice, the kingdom of gleissen, Winter – only Winter is the world of truth and truth, of good and evil! But this, this, this everything which is outside of the Ice, is our terrible infinity of DISCORD and TURMOIL. Where we must live till the time comes, praying every day for the swift return of the Ice. So, I urge you too, children sinners, go with the Lord's blessing and love one another, for though reason shall lie, though the heart shall lie, the sin is lesser when lying for the sake of love, so sleep in the Lord, Amen.'

Afterwards, I stood for a long while lost in thought, stabbed involuntarily by Rasputin's words. People began to disperse; the holy voluptuary returned to his hut, led by the arm within his tight group of bodyguards – I sat down on the grass by Martsyn's circle, and squeezed tight my eye. Out of Confusion, out of Discord… against Order… For it had unfrozen, and they had drowned at once in Kotarbiński's purgatory, between truth and falsehood; it had unfrozen and there was no History. And the ruler of the Kingdom of Darkness foretold by Pobedonostseff – he it is who would wield Zeytsoff's switch: in whichever direction he yanks it, such shall be the good and evil that befall us, such the Truth and such the Necessity. He would stand against the Motley, bisect the world into Zero and One… The man who would seize control over the apparatus governing History – the tsardom of which it's impossible to imagine a greater – autocracy equal to God's – such a man… such a man… Perhaps I dozed off a bit then too. Because I didn't hear when they came for me – only when someone shook me did I raise an eyelid; and they were already standing over me, the morose hibernik guards armed with truncheons and rifles.

Immediately they snatched my shotgun. Stood me on my feet. Two words: Polack! Heretic! If they'd taken me forthwith into the wildwood, hanged me somewhere on the quiet, so long as it wasn't before the eyes of the Martsynian flock, I certainly wouldn't have had time to rally to the need for more vigorous resistance, escape, struggle. If only I'd noisily denied it…! It was Summer, there's no way their truth would have held up as the one and only. But I didn't even open my mouth. I allowed myself to be jerked and jostled, pulled and pushed; thanks to my stick, at least I didn't fall.

They led me not into the forest, however, but beyond the stream, to Rasputin's hut. The father of European hiberniks who'd come with Grigory Yefimovitch tried to throw me on my knees already on the threshold and tear the rubashka off my back, rip the belt out of my breeches, take away my stick and no doubt give me a thorough battering on entry just in case – but Rasputin restrained him with a single bearlike growl from inside the hut. I walked in unaided.

Three candles with wilting bent wicks burned on a table knocked together from uneven planks.

'Shut the door,' said the aged holy debauchee.

I pulled the door to and fastened the hasp. The slatted shutters were also closed so as to ensure the man of God some degree of privacy. Light from the three flames swilled out hundreds of shadows from his elongated horsey physiognomy, flowing now in the furrows of his deep wrinkles. He was sitting on a low bed, no doubt wishing to sleep; but was still in the black monkish garb, and only that face – which was too large – and those hands – which were too large – were conspicuous in the waxy semi-darkness. On a tabletop by the wall stood a solitary bottle – of water? moonshine? Still with its cork in.

'Have a seat, my son, have a seat.'

I sat down gingerly on a rickety stool.

Lifting my eyes again to Rasputin – he and I on the same level, he and I in the same cage – I saw how we were being caught in a solid geometry of confession, entreaty, profanity, forgiveness, crime.

Maybe this was the reason for the gloom, the blackness and candles, and in the gloom his two eyes gleaming like oily pearls – so as to capture his interlocutor and not let go. Suddenly I remembered all the tales of Rasputin's hypnotic powers, of instant healings neath his touch, of supernatural hot or cold suffusing people under his influence, of Petersburg ladies, courtiers, bishops, generals and even the tsarina and tsar themselves falling into friendship and love for him after their first meeting. Respectable aristocratic women would throw themselves at his feet, scurry towards him on all fours tucking up their skirts, offer themselves publicly to satisfy his desire – agents of the Okhrana sent to spy on him would submit to his orders –

'I had this revolver,' I said, 'this weapon that fired Ice, that is, it made Ice explode after the bullet had hit… I once shot a gleiss. What happened? The gleiss shattered, a leg was torn off. How was that possible? I mulled it over in my mind. Why doesn't the impact of ice upon ice produce more ice? Frost plus frost does not give fire. Not so?

'But today I heard your sermon on Confusion and understood this law of black physics: life is Disorderliness. All matter exists only insofar as it pollutes ideal Order. I. You. This table. These trees. Stones. Animals, people, the whole of nature, the cosmos above us. And also, gleissen.

'Cooling to absolute Orderliness, zero, one, zero, one, zero, one, to pure Yea and Nay – eradicates from being. I had a revolver that fired Truth.

'For in that universe of ice crystal, nothing exists and nothing changes, so there is no time even. In the beginning was the word, and that word, because it was different from cold Order, that word was a Lie, and thus matter arose and life and mankind: out of Falsehood, out of Confusion. In the words of Martsyn: the world was created by God the Liar, we exist thanks to the Lie – and this is the Truth!'

Rasputin slowly crossed himself, once, twice, thrice.

'You are the Pole Yeroslavsky, Father Frost.'

'Of his blood, yes.'

He thrust back his head, staring with grave attention – and his stare, now aimed into one pupil, had no need to leap to left and right – then grabbed hold of the cross on his chest; I thought he was mustering himself to perform exorcisms or bombard me with curses, when suddenly the spring inside him spun in the opposite direction and he unravelled into a broad ingratiating grin, shook his mane like a bewildered dog, bent over double in his sitting position, and placed a sticky kiss on the back of my crippled hand.

'I'm a sinner, I'm a sinner, I'm a sinner grovelling in the dust!'

Oh, how obvious these caroms are to someone who has himself practised the Mathematics of Character!

So instead of raising him up amid polite denials:

'Plead for forgiveness!' I barked.

He stole a furtive glance from under matted grey locks, himself now caught in invisible pincers.

'For me there is no forgiveness!' he whined, upping the stakes, and began to slobber over my hands still more. 'There is none, there is none! Not from people, maybe there shall be from the Highest – but here, in this quagmire of dung and sin... Only a man similarly steeped can embrace me and forgive.' Here he stole another furtive glance. 'You, you, sir!' He sank onto his knees, almost pulling me off the stool with the force of his huge well-fed body. 'You slew an innocent man.'

'Yes.'

'Surrendered to sinful delights of the flesh.'

'Yes.'

'Lied.'

'Yes.'

'Stole.'

'Yes.'

'Raised your hand, your word against your parent.'

'Yes.'

'Doubted in God's mercy.'

'Yes.'

'Renounced God, railed against God.'

'No.'

'Come here!' He drew me into his peasant arms, powerful despite his age. 'You know full well what news I bear from the beginning: re-demption through sin.' He raised his huge hand towards the ceiling. 'You see, there is no sin committed by you of which I too would not be guilty, you see. And therefore!' he roared, leaping to his feet. 'Precisely therefore! For in sin! For out of sin! For through sin!' He was gathering momentum, his advantage growing with every word; he gazed down from on high, screamed down from on high. 'Therefore! Therefore, God has given me –'

'Why did you order me killed?'

This tore the breath from his lungs.

He collapsed on the bed; the boards creaked.

'What...?'

'You were sending Martsynian brothers after me throughout the land. Did someone tell you I'm an Ottepyelnik?'

He gasped.

'And aren't you? You said yourself: the Ice is the enemy of all existence.'

'But I do not say that it's such a splendid thing – to exist.'

He was at a loss.

And quickly concealed it behind a grimace of mental effort.

'So, who are you? What exactly do you want?'

I hesitated. He had me here.

And like an old bloodhound, led on by many years' experience and instincts drilled to clockworklike surety, he leapt forward at once and embedded his fangs up to the roots.

'Eh, Yeroslavsky? What's he seeking here? Why's he wormed his way in amongst the Martsynian folk? Pretending to be one of the faithful? What does he want? Eh? What does he want!'

What does he want! I could have lied and maybe it would have even passed for truth, but I'd be stuck in the same trap, so I replied simply:

'Nothing.'

'Hah! Nothing! Does he imagine he's hit upon some numbskull! To what...'

He lapsed into silence. Stung me with his sharp eyes.

He added character to character and understood.

'Nothing. Well, Thaw's come, we have to rally together, close ranks, chill ourselves afresh; yes, a devout man can always rely on God, but the unbeliever, the doubter – how can he find firm ground in this swamp? Eh?' And he'd already clenched his jaws: 'Give me your hand! Lean on me! I'll be your steadfast rock!'

His shoulders seemed to broaden from the shadows and glintzen, the width of his pale countenance, the length of his arms – as he spread his hypnotic person over the whole darkness, so that no line separated his black robe from the gloom scuttling away from the candle flames. Rasputin, through Rasputin, and with Rasputin, and in Rasputin – the gaze bent towards him, the mind bowed to his.

'No,' I whispered.

'So, who?' he asked softly, gently, with a mildness that was suddenly womanish. 'So, what now? You will fall, my son, you've seen how they fall. Don't I know it? I have fallen myself. Stolen horses, chased after whores, drowned in vodka – for why not, eh? Why not? Gorge yourself, be sozzled, get laid – that's all.'

'The body cannot be the purpose of the body.'

'Well, what is then? Who is then? Where shall you go? Where lay down your head, before what altar find your dream? In whose pawnshop estimate your life? Who is going to give you truth by which to live?'

He bore down on me mercilessly – what remained to me other than to lie? Sooner or later, he'd pluck me out of my stubborn silence.

'I am,' I replied tearing my eye from his gaze.

'Uh?'

'I am!'

'You?'

'I am!' I snarled, and an icy shudder passed through me, for I suddenly sensed that this was no longer a lie, that I had in my grasp a force equal to the soletruth of Rasputin.

My eye returned to him. He was grinding his teeth.

I wiped the cold slobber off my hand. 'I am.'

He shook his head. Oy, it's not going to be so easy with Rasputin. Twice as many flickering glintzen crawl out onto his mug as buttery shadows from the yellow flames; murch hangs under his eyes in drunken sacks; a gleissenik's umbriance hovers about him on his cold breath. Of course, he doesn't call it by these names, expresses it not in logical theories – after all, this is the source of his extraordinary power over people, for Rasputin is well acquainted with the Algorithmics of Character, because he has lived so long himself neath the touch of the Ice.

'Madness,' he suddenly hissed, strangely cowering into himself and extending only one hand towards me, 'crrraziness, inescapable lunacy awaits you. It will come. It has come! I have cast out demons, fought with devils, spat in Lucifer's eyes; Christ the Lord Redeemer stood at my right hand, I bore his sweet breath upon my cheek, he embraced me tenderly and whispered in my ear: Go on, Grisha, go on! Don't listen to what they say, don't look at how they mock and point the finger. It is as nothing! Know no shame. What are people's glances? I stand by you! The mightiest of powers!

'When God whispers fondly in your ear, Mr Lach, that you should pay heed to nothing and do only as God commands – then you reckon no more according to the measure of churchly sins, nor watch from the level of the street!

'You have heard the very worst of me – yet it's true, all true! God stood by me! Do you understand?'

'What God commands is good, because God commanded it.'

'Yes! Yes! Yes!' Rasputin shifted on the bed with doggy movements, propping himself up on his hands and thrusting forward his muzzle, almost lolling out his tongue. 'To be blind drunk and puking – is a sin! But the Lord says: I stand by you! Do as I allow! And then I see that getting drunk too – is an entirely good thing.

'Robbing pure devotchkas of their virginity, seducing married women into adultery, surrendering to base lusts for whole nights and days – is a sin! But the Lord says: I am by your side! And then I see that this too – is a virtue.

'I have Truth!' he barked. 'I have Truth, so I am not afraid of the verdicts of men. To them too it's clear, that Truth, that God –'

'Until Thaw came!'

He began to howl, moan, tug at his beard, punch his crown with his fist.

'Wherefore did Batyushka Nikolay think to banish the gleissen! And now his young son has bled to death, his Empire is in flames, but the worst, the worst is that... Gospodin Yeroslavsky! What will protect you? You too obeyed His commandments when you led folk into the Ice, condemning to death whole villages and hamlets – and you knew: this way is good, this way is pleasing to the Lord. How shall you protect yourself when you're left all alone – "I am!", "I am!" – when it comes to doubting even the voice of God?

'Madness!' He smashed his grey nut against the wall. 'Madness!'

'There is no protection.' I shrugged my shoulders. 'We have all lived like this since we were expelled from Paradise. Whereas they that sink most often into lunacy are they that have tasted of the fruit of Truth, if only for a moment.'

'If the Ice returns not... Madness!'

'There exists this machine...'

He gave a suspicious look.

'Machine?'

'This invention, which relies on tungetitum and coldiron. For it's possible to pump oneself with Frost.'

He blinked slowly. Again, his strategy was turning against him: he'll ask about the pump and I'll have him trapped in a tight equation with only one possible solution.

He sat down, straightened his back, stroked his beard. The left-hand candle went out, he relit it from the neighbouring one.

For a long while he collected his thoughts, spluttering something to himself under his moustache.

'So you have no fear,' he grunted at last, having recalculated this way and that. 'I'll have you flogged. Stripped of your skin. Torn to shreds by horses!' He was gathering momentum again. 'I'll say you're a traitor to Martsyn and they'll eat you alive, hah! Well, what, have you no fear?'

'In that old manor on the pass,' I pointed with the stick to the north-facing wall, 'there was a Frost sanatorium, you had it burned down.'

'Uh?'

'You burned down half my soul.'

He crept forward, leaned over, excited.

'Some krasavitsa?'

'It's of no import.'

'Wifekin, eh?' He licked his lips. 'Kiddywinks perhaps?'

'It's of no import.'

He rubbed his muscular palms.

'Yes, yes, I am a murderer, I am a sinner, a sinner.' He grinned knowingly. 'I had it burned down, you're right, I burned it down.'

Oh, this was an exceptionally knotty tangle – this time Rasputin had succeeded in stirring in me extreme emotions, and I was forced to somehow betray them, if only in the tension of my muscles, comportment of my body, tautness of my lips, for the oaken boor was grinning still more broadly and almost clapping for joy.

'Poor Mr Yeroslavsky!'

I stood up and walked the length of a wall, back and forth, kicking the wood, dragging my knuckles over the needly splinters, waving my stick...

I glanced at it: 313 mirks.

I pressed the coldiron generator to my temple.

'I forgive you,' I said.

'What?'

'I forgive you.'

He bristled.

'Bull!'

I nodded.

'Devil fuck the forgiver!' He waved his arms about, exasperated. 'Now my wolves will tear you limb from limb!' He squirmed on the bedclothes, sat down on the stool, spun around on the stool... Stared at me from under his brow. 'Why, he's forgiven!' He pierced me with his hypnotic eyes, but I averted not my gaze, pressing the coldiron harder and harder into the nodular growth above my eye. 'Tphoo!' he spat resoundingly. 'Now my wolves will… Well, what? Oo-oo, Roman heretic!'

I had him, he won't break free; in the flickering semi-darkness, the lattice of glances both possible and necessary had slammed shut like a logic square of opposition: Yea, yea, Nay, nay.

He was still straining at the leash; to no avail. He bit into his wrist, eyeing me searchingly. Wiping away the black blood with a flap of his robe, he seized the cross and raised it in my direction as if offering it me to kiss or perhaps swear an oath. But in this too he barely lasted a few seconds. He let drop his arm, hung his head. I could hear him mumbling under his breath the fiercest imprecations. Coldiron burned into my forehead, as the miniscule teslectric dynamo continued rotating inside; I glanced at the scale: 311 mirks.

Rasputin began to laugh coarsely, beating his thighs with his fists – but here too he was defeated: five croaks and hysteria smashed his laughter into a panic-stricken giggle. He levelled his index finger at me. 'He lies! He lies!' I stared at him. He curled his fingers into a fist as they'd begun to tremble. Grabbed hold of the tabletop as if the table too were about to get the shudders. His back was bent and straining, readying for some great effort. 'Lies-lies-lies-lies…'. And then he sprang up, lifting and hurling the heavy furniture in a single move.

I dropped to the floor. The table thumped against the wall and crashed at my feet.

'Begone! My business!' roared Rasputin as the alarmed hiberniks banged at the door.

I scrambled up off the floorboards. Only one of the knocked-over candles was still burning; in the tiny hut, there remained of Rasputin mainly an enormous shadow splashed on the walls, ceiling, furniture.

'He lies!' he hissed. 'Lies!'

He seized the stool by the leg and hurled himself at me with that stool, lifting it like a lopsided cudgel.

'Well! And what now? Go on!' He walloped me from the left, walloped me from the right; I fell over and stood up. He'd surely broken a rib. 'Well? Well?' he growled, brandishing the massive stool. He'll reduce me to pulp. He swiped from below on my right; I hadn't shielded myself with the stick, and a thunderbolt shot along the nerves from my hip. I screamed in pain.

'Ah!' he triumphed. 'Now forgive! Now face up to yourself!'

And he went on thrashing me wherever the blows happened to fall, again and again and again – I retreated behind the upturned table, retreated behind the bed; he caught up with me even there – I shielded my head, shielded my knees; he crushed my fingers into the stick – I collapsed; he struck my back. He'll break my spine, kill me.

He kicked me into a corner.

'Well!' he roared. 'Come on! Forgive me! And this!' He whacked me on the arm; I let go the stick. 'And that!' He whacked me on my unprotected head; blood spilled into my eye. 'And this too, forgive! Hurry up! Forgive!'

Whack, whack, whack. I had a body built of fibres of pain, I existed solely as that pain.

'And who will offer you his hand now?!' Whack. 'Who bear the weight of the world on his shoulders?!' Whack. 'Who save you?!' Whack, whack.

I fumbled around in the dark for the stick and swung blindly with all my might. Again, it slipped from my hand as I struck. Rasputin groaned, something slumped heavily. I wiped my eye. He was clambering on all fours, choking; having sat down, he grabbed hold of his neck, of the jowl hidden neath his beard. I stood up, raised the stool, having to use both hands. Rasputin was red as a turkey, squealing something incomprehensible through his nose. I was in no doubt he'd soon come round; it would last only a moment. I swung the stool and struck him directly on the temple. He keeled onto the floor unconscious.

I sat down on the bed. My hands were shaking, the whole of me was shaking. Blood was oozing still from my forehead. It hurt me to inhale, hurt me to exhale, hurt with every movement. I picked up the bottle and tore out the cork with my teeth. Sniffed. Vodka stinking of iron. I took a gulp, two gulps. Gave way to a coughing fit.

He was coughing from the floor. Scraping the floorboards with his beard, he was crawling towards me, entangled in the black flaps of his habit, a bloodied shadow amid the shadows, his white hands like naked crabs. He wheezed louder and louder.

'Who-oo…! Who-oo is going to…! forgive….!'

I approached with the stool, stood astride the old man and walloped his back, breaking his neck.

'I am!' I snarled spitting blood and vodka. 'I am!'

I flung aside the stool, picked up the stick. Found the two remaining candles, lit them and stood them on the shutters. Running a hand over my head, I felt for open wounds. Clasped my broken fingers in my armpit, silently savouring the exquisite pain.

'Khhrrr. Krrr!'

I looked down. He had turned onto his back and was tugging at the cross on his chest, goggling with unseeing eyes at the ceiling.

I knelt over him and wedged the stick under his silvery chin; then I pressed on the murchometer and counted to two hundred, suffocating Rasputin and probably also utterly mangling his larynx. Then I checked again the old man's breathing – he was not breathing.

I got to my feet, dreadfully tired, aching all over. A further three gulps of the abominable spiritus vodka helped control the trembling and weakness threatening imminent faint: my tongue and palate were smarting, chill and heat flooding in turn into my arms and legs, my head was spinning. I bent over double, digging my palms into my thighs, breathing deeply. I ought to –

He'd got to his knees, rattling the cross against the wall. I ran over to him and clobbered him with the stick – his nut split open like a pumpkin; I clobbered him again, and again, and again – blood streamed over the white hair and black robe. He lay motionless with limbs splayed to the sides, head twisted, brain matter on the surface. I stopped only in order to vomit: the hiberniks' evening repast flew out of me, unripe berries, mushrooms and mouldy prosphora, flushed with gastric juices and vodka.

I pulled off the torn, puke-stained rubashka, wiping my face and broken lips with a clean scrap of the fabric. I gazed at Rasputin lying by the wall in shadow and my hands gradually ceased trembling. Dead, but perhaps alive. It was Summer, I knew after all what necessity is – that is, justice – that is, Truth. I cursed softly. He no longer lives, but maybe he lives.

I smashed the bottle and cut out Rasputin's heart from his breast.

Then I found the planks in the back wall for which we'd had insufficient nails when building; I prised one out with the stick, tore out two lower ones and squeezed through to the outside. I was amid the first trees of the taiga by the time someone peeked into the hut and proclaimed the death of Grigory Yefimovitch Rasputin. A long-drawn-out, almost animal groan passed through the mountain meadows in order to finally explode in a roar brimming with anger. Chaos reigned o'er the children of Truth.

That night, below the Milky Pass, above Martsyn's non-existent grave, more than four hundred disciples of the Ice gave up the ghost, trampled to death, clubbed to death, smothered to death, bitten to death. Not long afterwards, people began to speak of it as the Night of Martsyn's Judgement. For behold, Martsyn had arisen from out the Ways of the Mammoths and punished the usurper. The Pretender had not attained power: truth was not on his side.

It was Summer – but as such had it frozen.

On the founding of the first History Industry Company Ltd

The lift was out of action; they dragged me up a crooked spiral stairway. A second man was trying to break free, tossing from side to side, seemingly preferring to break his neck by hurling himself from the heights than be brought alive into the presence of the prime minister; he walked like a condemned man.

I looked back from the landing as armoured coldiron doors opened above us. Semenoff's Cossacks had already departed, the row of horsemen disappearing behind the ruins of the opposite towers. In the central crater (all that remained of the Holey Palace was a great Hole) a postglacial lake had formed; local children were launching model boats made of twigs and paper. The morning azure of the sky was reflected in the water, its bright glints enough to blind. I blinked as a single tear rolled down my cheek.

The corridors of the Crooked Tower were strewn with rubbish, broken fragments of office furniture, piles of waste paper. Like in a gutter in the street, they had collected by the walls on the rooms' lower sides. The angle of incline amounted to some twenty degrees, no more, which presented no problem when walking up or down in harmony with the tilt, but made traversing very uncomfortable. The condemned man stumbled once, twice and fell over; they began pulling him by the collar and hair, at which he whimpered vociferously, pitifully, beating his fists and heels against the walls. It transpired, however, that someone was living or working here – in rooms with spat-out windows, in chambers with collapsed ceilings – because every so often someone peeped into the corridor, startled by the piercing laments.

'Zeytsoff!'

They pushed me against a wall. I hollered again. Whatever was his first name? his patronymic? Zeytsoff, old madman!

The ex-katorzhnik, disciple of Atchukhoff, retreated, paused, frowned. Under his arm he carried a violin case; spectacles sat perched on his nose. Stooping now, he had aged significantly. His eyes squinted behind the lenses, striving unsuccessfully to match the voice to the physiognomy.

'Let go, you cur!' I snarled at the soldier. 'Zeytsoff, it's me, for Christ's sake, don't you remember throwing me headlong off the Transsib?'

The violin case fell from his arms as he keeled against the wall.

'Gospodin Yeroslavsky...?'

'But you're sober, eh?'

'Gospodin Yeroslavsky!'

'Tell him to get off my back!'

'God Almighty! You're alive!'

'Well come on, come on.'

The ruffians in green-and-white Free-Stater caps finally let go; I stood on my own two feet – but not for long, as Zeytsoff fell violently upon me and again I landed against the wall. Well, such a kindly nature, murders and rejoices with the same exhilaration. I allowed him to hug me for a moment.

Having stepped back, he wiped his eyeglasses and gazed beaming from ear to ear. Perhaps for the first time I was seeing him clean-shaven, which brought to light every abomination of his scarred phiz burned by the frost.

'Venyedikt Filipovitch! Dear God! What happened to you? We all buried you long ago!'

'Well, you weren't far off the truth.'

'But the way you look!' He wrung his hands. 'Did these hooligans make a mess of you?' And he glowered menacingly at the Free-Staters.

'No, no. I had various adventures along the way. Now I'm keen to see the prime minister; I caught up with this unit flying the States' colours by the Lena but somehow couldn't make myself understood... Well, at least I've made it. They told me he's based here.'

'Broken his leg. But please! Wash at least, pull yourself together! Have you anything to change into?' Again, he turned to the Free-Staters. 'Where's Gospodin Yeroslavsky's luggage?'

I snorted with laughter.

'Have them give back my stick!'

They gave it back.

'There, my luggage. Listen, Filimon Romanovitch, are you now a figure of some importance?'

'Eh, how could I be!' But at the same time, he waved angrily at the Free-Staters and they obediently withdrew at once, dragging with them their other prisoner, who remembered he was mortally terrified and began anew his aria of imploring sobs, the echo of which resounded throughout the empty tower. 'Odd jobs for the provisional authorities...' Zeytsoff picked up the violin case and led me up a frostoglaze staircase to the floor above. 'Well, you see, when you arranged that post for me as caretaker at Krupp's...'

'Yes?'

'They all fled with the Thaw, I mean the industrial people, the scientific people, officials and bourgeois; I saw from day to day, night to night, the towers going out all around me – but where had I to flee to? I stayed on as watchman, eventually the only man in the whole Five O'Clock Tower. But then it warmed up completely and the towers began to crumble one after another. My heart bled, Mr Yeroslavsky, I'm telling you, I couldn't look upon it. I searched for the governor's people, searched for people from Sibirkhozheto, from the city authorities – so as to organise something, do something... But everything had already melted; and you'd not have witnessed any firm grip on power here since the great icecradle collapsed. Well, so I got together with the hiberniks, coldmill workers who'd stayed on in Innokentyevskoye without work, even a few gendarmes and indigenes, and together we tried to save the towers. One of Thyssen's engineers turned up, experienced in permafrost timbering... You saw, sir, what we had to do to the mainstays: both deep inside and on the surface, and with concrete, but materials soon ran out, so we had to take them from mainstays lugged over from the towers that had already fallen... That was only at the end, mind, the first six crumbled at once, we also fought to save the Twelve O'Clock; in the end the Seven O'Clock and the One O'Clock also survived, on the opposite side.'

Meanwhile we'd finally reached the end of the corridor on the higher, northern side of the tower. Zeytsoff plucked a bunch of keys from under his heavily darned morning coat and opened a door. We entered a room. Once upon a time it had probably been a drawing room belonging to the director of a mighty ice concern. Amongst the furniture pushed against the southern wall I spied a chaise longue upholstered in leather and a beautiful dark-walnut bookstand. Books and porcelain lay scattered in the folds of an Afghan carpet.

I walked over to the broad window. All the panes were blown out; green chenille curtains fluttered between the casings. I raked them to the sides – and sunlight streamed into the ruined drawing room.

A bee attacked me; I chased it away with my stick, the dangler began to wind, 310 mirks. I sneezed. Shielding my eye with my hand, I stood in the shade to one side.

'But the One O'Clock also collapsed.' I pointed to the horizon beyond the Hole.

'It was still standing when they fought the Bolsheviks from the Tsentrosibir, the Central Committee of Siberian Soviets, as well as the tsarists. First, the Trotskyists climbed up there and fired at anything that came in sight. Oblastniks together with Savinkoff and his New Narodniks then drove out the Bolsheviks; there was a battle near Aleksandrovsk against the Imperial forces. Then they all withdrew to the Transsib line, and so for about a month the front ran through Irkutsk and the Angara. But the One O'Clock Tower was blown up by the Leninists after a Trotskyist sniper shot their commander.'

'So now Zimny Nikolayevsk is held by soldiers of the United Free States of Siberia.' I yawned. 'He's broken his leg, but I daresay receiving guests?'

'I'll go and inquire. In a moment I'll send a Chinaman with warm water and some clothes. Welcome to the kingdom of loot. And maybe you'd like a shave, eh? And proviant shall be found. Have a rest, you're exhausted. I'm off, I'm off.' And indeed, he hurried off, jangling his keys; the door slammed behind him of its own accord. I'd forgotten to ask about the violin.

Smiling involuntarily under my moustache, I flopped onto the chaise longue. And so, Thaw had arrived and upended the character enough in even such as Zeytsoff for the drunken Marxist Tolstoyan to strike within himself a spark of enterprising energy. I closed my eyes neath the warm caresses of the Sun. The bee buzzed above my head.

An elderly Chinaman brought a bowl and a bucket of boiled water, and also somebody's towels and bathroom accessories marked with the Latin initials: R.Z.W.; and for second course – four suitcases stuffed with men's clothing of not the worst quality. Amused, I rummaged through the contents trying to guess their provenance and owners' identities. In one suitcase I found a German prayerbook, in another – an *Astrological Handbook for the Businessman in Asia* in French. From this it emerged that it was unwise before the summer equinox in the Year of Our Lord 1930 to conclude larger transactions on the eastern side of the Urals with people born under the signs of Sagittarius, Aries and Capricorn. The superstitious industrialist had also equipped himself with *The Trader's Dreambook*, *Phrenology at Work and in Society*, as well as a *Stock-Exchange Tarot*. Underneath the books, however, I discovered three very flattering shirts the colour of silvery ash.

I shed my old clothes, devoured by filth, worn threadbare and stinking to high heaven. I scrubbed myself all over once and twice, and was on the point of grabbing the razor when the door in the lower wall opened and two Free-Staters crept in. Stark naked, I turned to face them with mug plastered in lather.

'What?!'

They recoiled, ashamed.

'The prime minister's secretary asked us to convey… They've booked you at noon for a quarter of an hour.'

'Good.'

Under the bookstand, I found fragments of a mirror, I chose the largest. When I'd shaved, I had my doubts. The growth had hidden to some extent the scars, the discolouring, the deformities; now everything had come to light, as with Zeytsoff.

Too bad. All hideous anyway. I chucked the improvised mirror out of the window.

I no longer bothered with my hair; instead of trimming it, I tied it back at the nape of my neck. I searched for underwear and a suit.

Everything was a tad too big or a tad too tight. The decision in the end was for trousers that had to be firmly secured with a belt and whose legs I had to turn up, and a single-breasted marengo jacket whose sleeves, when I held up my arms, slipped down almost as far as my elbows; only an astrological shirt fitted tolerably well. Instead of a cravat, I tied a white in a double Windsor knot.

I kept only my old footwear: high leather boots with cracked uppers which I'd pulled off a corpse by the Tunguska river.

I went out in search of a pocket watch. A young Russian, smoking a cigarette above the hole left by a stained-frostoglaze window (a breeze was gusting between it and other blown-out windows of the tower), offered me tobacco and rolling paper. We found ourselves discussing German literature and the beauty of Siberian nature. He promised to send me a well-versed man. Only then did I learn who he was, this handsome, smooth-skinned molodyets: minister of security in the government of the United Free States of Siberia. He asked about the umbriance on my shadowy side; he didn't know what it was, having arrived only post-Thaw from universities in the West and unacquainted with many gleisseniks apart from the prime minister. I told him that the very fact that his eyes were sensitive to unlicht bound him somehow to the Land of the Gleissen. This appealed to him. He lit another cigarette. They brought him some papers to sign; he ticked them with a chewed pencil-stub, resting them on a soldier's back and not reading them at all. Death sentences, I thought afterwards, and remembered my lamenting fellow prisoner. Who knows, were it not for Zeytsoff...

I returned to the room, I still had time for a nap. The obtrusive bee continued to disturb – sprawled on the chaise longue, I drifted in and out of warm consciousness. I got up, straightened my bones, peed out of the window. The children launching their little ships in the water-filled hollow left by the Holey Palace pointed me out to one another with their hands and waved, highly amused; I waved back in digni-fied fashion. Above the water swirled the Siberian gnus, a cloud of tiny midges, blindflies, gnats. Wild birds soared in the cloudless blue sky.

I rifled through the heap of books lying neath the overturned bookcase. Dictionaries, encyclopaedias, tomes published for special oc-casions. I returned to the suitcases containing looted clothes. Attached to the *Stock-Exchange Tarot* was a pocket deck of cards modelled on a Siberian version of Aleister Crowley's Egyptian Tarot. Crouched on my heels, counting rhythmically under my breath, I laid out two hundred sortilegious sequences on the bare coldiron floor. *Pocięgło saves. Pact with Pobedonostseff. Alliance of Lyednyaks. Winter holds. Schultz sold Tesla.* Interferences were more in evidence here, but because I already knew the essence of this murchogram, I could ignore the gaps and distortions. One thing was certain: it's not Tesla or Christine – an automatic Murch Hammer was already striking.

A Free-State apparatchik knocked at the door. We ascended to the roof.

The rooftop of the Seven O'Clock Tower had no balustrade surrounds, no protective barriers; having stopped on the sloping surface, I instinctively rammed in my stick to prevent myself from slipping. The wind inflated a flap of my jacket; I did up the button. A cleaned, polished sheet of coldiron cladding shone underfoot like the surface of a mercury lake; sunlight reflected off it in all directions with every step taken; it was like walking through the innards of a huge electric lightbulb. Mr Porfiry Pocięgło, prime minister of the Provisional Government of the United Free States of Siberia, sat at a circular table in the middle of the roof. Through black spectacles planted on his hawk nose, he was reading the documents served to him from his secretary's thick portfolio. Immobilised by splints, his leg lay stretched on a footstool upholstered in faded purple. Steely light swam all around Pocięgło; he was the wire filament of that lamp.

The secretary leaned over and whispered in his ear. Porfiry raised his head. I stood facing him.

'But who is it?' he snorted, amazed.

Full of consternation, the secretary and apparatchik exchanged glances. The Free-Stater grabbed me firmly by the arm.

I tapped the stick on the coldiron.

'I failed to buy you History from the gleissen,' I said, 'but I see you've managed well enough without me.'

He tore off the spectacles.

'Benedykt Gierosławski?! Is it you?! Really you?!'

I walked over to him, held out my hand.

'Allow me to squeeze the statesman's hand.'

He gazed at my three-fingered right hand, at the scars and deformities. Rising slightly from his armchair, he seized it in both palms, enfolding it a vigorous hearty clasp.

'I won't even ask. You've also been through a few things. Have a seat.'

He dismissed his people with a wave. I sat down on a wicker chair. Silver sails of light flapped all around, again my eye began to water – the world deliquesced into azure and green and this flickering silver, of this more than anything.

Pocięgło was also silent for a while.

'Let me offer you a drink,' he said gently, jingling a vodka carafe and glass. 'Siberian buckthorn liqueur mellowed for a year. It deadens any pain.'

Fumbling almost, I moistened my lips.

'I've eaten nothing for a second day.'

'My God, Benedykt Gierosławski...' He shook his head in disbelief. 'My wife will never believe me when I write to her.'

The glass slid from between my fingers. Trr-trr-trr-trroorrt! – it rolled across the roof and flew into the abyss.

'But she's dead!'

'What are you... Ah, yes, Jelena Muklanowicz! She was burned in that Ice Sanatorium, I know, I know.' He suddenly laughed, strangely relieved. 'My Chrissie, she would never... Ah, for you've not heard, have you? How many years is it? five? six?' In a state of excitement which didn't much suit Porfiry Pocięgło, he reached for his pocketbook. 'I'll show you, little Andrzej, Andrew, in this picture – at three months.'

'You married Christine Filipov.'

'I did, have a look. Taken last year in front of our house on Rua dos Pescadores.'

The photograph showed a beaming Christine Pocięgło dressed in a light-coloured loose-fitting frock, her face half-hidden in the shade of her straw hat, sitting with babe in arms on a bench in the garden of a villa. On her right is Porfiry himself, staring into the lens from the depths of his dark eye sockets with his habitual hawklike intensity. Whilst behind their backs, in the centre of the frame, looms the tall silhouette of Nikola Tesla. Now with silvery hair and what looks like a bony dried-up face, the inventor still holds himself erect and in that same distracted preoccupied pose, as if the portrait were taken at the last minute before he flees back to his secret experiments. Murch floods the folds and creases of his suit with dark ink; he stands engulfed in night. The house behind them is a magnificent building in the Hispanic colonial style, white-walled with long balconies on every floor. In the shade of an arcaded patio are numerous servants in livery or white aprons standing in two rows for the photograph. Fig and palm trees overhang the driveway on either side; hibiscus flowers with cupped open mouths gawp at the woman and baby.

'Congratulations.'

'He's shooting up fast, promising to be a strapping lad. Barely weaned and already a bunch of trouble! They write to me that –'

'Yes.' I gave back the photograph. Splashed some buckthorn liqueur into a fresh glass. My head, very light, was swaying on my neck like a balloon feebly secured against the wind. I swallowed sharply. Mm-hmm, perhaps it was due to the light impinging from everywhere. We sat like two blind lizards in a sun-drenched terrarium. 'You know, I'd happily throw you off this roof.'

Pocięgło put back his black spectacles.

'It didn't work out for you, huh?' he said softly. 'With your father –'

'Dead.'

'With Jelena –'

'Dead.'

'With History –'

'Likewise a corpse.'

I leaned against the back of my chair, opening wide my eyes and mouth to the blue sky above, waiting for a cold drop of that blue. Chirruping rainbows were massaging my temples; I could hear their brightly coloured sniggers and gurgles.

Porfiry well sensed my mood. He bided his time, leafing through the documents. He made a note of something in an exercise book with his fountain pen; the nib scratched pleasantly over the paper.

I said nothing, thrust back into the depression of non-necessity, of what doesn't have to be. A warm breeze rocked my head, liquid brightness trilled over my skin, pricking, stinging, biting. Mel-mel-melting… I smacked my lips noisily.

'You took them abroad.'

'Who? Ah! Yes. That night, when you fled from Irkutsk – at the time, to start with, I quarrelled with Christine dreadfully.' He laughed again. 'She'd have given her life for Nikola. In the end I wrenched them from Schultz, we escaped via Harbin, via China. When at the first signs of Thaw talks began with the British in Hong Kong, I naturally took advantage of the opportunity and entered Macau – and, well, by then there was no going back, ye-es. We got married there on the spot, in Saint Dominic's Church. Don't imagine, sir, it was a rushed job, done in improper haste – I was going to war, to an armed uprising, which might have ended badly in a thousand different ways.' He took out his cigarette case, rainbows flared on the Irkutsk coat of arms. He lit a cigarette. 'It still might end badly.'

'Look, Benedykt, at how stupid we were. With Jelena, I mean. If she hadn't snubbed me after our absurd deals at the Last Kopeck Club… Ah, forgive me, if you prefer not… Mm-hmmm.' He blew into the sun. 'You were calculating, I was calculating. It was Winter, well yes, there was the Ice, we probably couldn't have done otherwise. But… It's fire!' He shook a clenched fist below his black glasses. 'It's lust!' He thumped on the table till the crockery jangled and the papers leapt up, and a newspaper flew off. I pinned it down with my stick before the wind swept it from the rooftop. The *New Siberian Gazette*; I hadn't known they already had a post-Thaw press.

I gave it back to Pocięgło and returned to gazing into the blue.

'It's lust,' he repeated softly, 'that is, the simple symmetry of egotistical desires. You don't ask. Don't weigh up the chances. Don't switch on reason at all. Did I behave reasonably? Hardly! Reasonably would have meant waiting for the revolution and then proposing to Chrissie. But what did I do? Snapped my fingers, Benedykt. Snapped my fingers at all that!'

'Was it really our stupidity, then under the Ice?' My eyes strayed across the empty sky. 'Stupidity or reason had nothing to do with it, Porfiry, sir. What counted was what was true and what was false. That people fell in love – was not some hypnotic effect of the Black Auroras, but due to the law of two-valued logic. The same law that enabled us to judge with iron certainty according to the soletruth of people's characters, and you, sir, to set up carombolic conspiracies in History wrung from entropy.

'For the worst thing in feelings is that uncertainty, that torture of doubt and of being torn between YEA and NAY: she loves me, she loves me not, she loves me, she loves me not; and deeper still with regard to one's own self: am I in love, or does it merely seem to me that I'm in love? But all this is the curse of Summer, it's Kotarbiński love! In the Land of the Gleissen you had only two poles on the magnet of the soul, and most of those blunders and errors of judgement were unthinkable there, unfreezable. Only someone like me…' I shook my head. 'It wasn't stupidity, it was Doctor Tesla's murch pump.'

'But really!' he snorted. 'I haven't a clue what you're blathering about!'

'When did the stamp in your heart land upon Christine Filipov? As you were fleeing from Schultz, under the Ice, Porfiry, under the Ice.'

'Again, you want the reason the point to death. And yet you were right in what you said to us before: What is love? Something inexpressible in words. We have only people who behave like this or like that, so we say: it's because of love. But so long as they only pull excruciating faces, float under the Moon and write bad poetry – then what is it? Love? Hah! It's a drama about love! An image of love! A tale about love! Love in quotation marks!'

'So, who is she? Tesla's daughter, granddaughter – or his mistress?'

'Mistress!' He was genuinely offended. 'You can't mean it!'

I swung on my chair balancing back and forth with the stick.

'But Macau?' I clicked tongue against palate. 'He's up to something there.'

'Tesla? Well of course! Morgan Junior reached agreement with Nikolay Aleksandrovitch Romanoff; Nikola chose Macau on account of the Ways of the Mammoths in China, he set up his Great Hammer on the Ihla de Macau, on a hill in the centre. Morgan invested lavish capital in the *Tesla Tungetitum Company* whilst Nikola rented the Fortaleza da Guia from the Portuguese, a whole antiquated complex below the lighthouse, which now flashes in time to the rhythm of the Hammer strokes. The whole of Macau lives under the Hammer, all the gambling houses have closed, surgeons refuse to perform operations, whilst the Chinese go crazy with their dried-yarrow stalk divinations; the opium dens, on the other hand, are prospering magnificently.' Pocięgło waved his hand in a wide sweep taking in with his cigarette the ruins of Zimny Nikolayevsk, overgrown now with fresh greenery. 'Haven't you noticed? The Ice let go! History has moved on!'

Pshaw! A bubble burst, punctured inside my chest. I roared with laughter on a prolonged exhalation, at the sky, at the Sun.

'So, it wasn't me who killed Winter!'

Whereupon I collapsed in an attack of hiccups, half-hysterical, half-prompted by genuine amusement, which forced the unuttered words back into my voice box. For a while I could only gurgle like an idiot.

Porfiry measured me up and down with his black stare – at once I averted my eye back to the azure sky. Gradually my breathing calmed. The devil liberated from the bubble continued bouncing in my chest for another minute or two; I breathed him out in long puffs straight into silvery rainbow glares.

Porfiry clicked the lid of his watch.

'Later you must tell me everything –'

'Very well.' I sat up straight and wiped a tear from my eye; at that moment, Pocięgło and the roof of the Crooked Tower congealed. 'I have a deal to propose.'

'A deal?'

'A deal.' I clapped my hands. 'A plan for tidy profits. A means to make big money.'

He flicked ash to the wind.

'Benedykt, sir, I am now a servant of the State.'

'One doesn't preclude the other. Bah, the greatest fortunes are made on the State.'

'You jest!' His hackles were up. 'You never took the Oblastnik cause seriously from the beginning. But know that for me, it's the foremost idea: a free independent Siberia, a self-governing Siberian state, strong before the world's mighty powers!'

'I know, Mr Prime Minister, I know. But –'

'Look at it now and you see a wild country of adventurers, political exiles, illiterate peasants and superstitious autochthons, thousands of versts of cold wasteland stretching in every direction, the greatest wildernesses on earth where no human being has ever set foot; and what passed once for civilisation here, all this,' and again he waved his hand at the vast panorama stretching from the summit of the open Clock Tower, 'is sinking back into mud, as you see, the best people are running away. Yes? But I look at it a hundred years into the future – and glimpse a world power. The United Free States of Siberia!'

He inhaled tobacco smoke; glintzen shone for a second beneath his tarry eyeglasses and a dark umbriance spread over his long oval countenance, roasted under the Sun.

'But you hate the State!' he hissed. 'Apoliteia – you'd have: but people's governments, the governments of Summer – these you'd preferably forbid. Yet you say you're not a Lyednyak!'

'Because I'm not a Lyednyak, Porfiry, I'm not. Lyednyaks want to freeze and stop History in a form that's already familiar. But I –'

'A Lyednyak of the worst sort: living for the Ice, not for people! None of it bothers you in the least! Not Siberia, fine – but have you inquired at all about Poland?'

I bristled.

'What about Poland?'

He threw his cigarette butt into the rainbows.

'The same. In other words, nothing.'

He adjusted his splinted leg, pulled himself up in his chair.

'There is no Poland,' he said, clasping his hands under his chin. 'Only Poles tearing each other to pieces under foreign standards.'

'And Piłsudski? He had a pact –'

'Pact! Piłsudski has been made a general under Franz Ferdinand; now he can fight the tsar openly in battle – but do you imagine, sir, that Austria will hand him even a tiny piece of Poland as his own, in gratitude for his military services? The partitioning powers would first have to bleed to death themselves, in order for Piłsudski's legions or the various local sections of the Polish parties to suddenly become a force to reckon with in those lands for any significant length of time. Which, you have to admit, is an improbable turn of History.

'Whilst here – just look: land and State are for the taking. This is the second America, Gierosławski. A richer America! A more just America! Take for example the autochthons: the Americans slaughtered their indigenous peoples, but ours I shall give a role in government. The United Free States of Siberia!' He jabbed with his finger at the documents spread out in front of him. 'Buryats, Tunguses, all the indigenes, will have their own oblasts. No reservations, but seats in the Senate. Do you understand?' He crossed his hands on his chest. 'I am building a State here, making History with my own hands! And you come to me with promises of money...!

'Besides! I don't have time now, I am expecting Savinkoff; to hell with these SRs, they want to write again to Prince Georgy Yevgenyevitch, if indeed he still occupies his office as first minister of the Empire, for this too is has been changing very rapidly; we'll talk more tomorrow.' He calmed down. 'Well, I'm sorry it's so –'

'The PM's time is at a premium.'

He winced.

'Drop it.'

I smiled.

'Why so ashamed? You *are* the prime minister.'

We shook hands across the tabletop, in the deafening light.

'What became of the Wielickis?'

'I don't know, Benedykt. I had no information.'

I stood up reeling; again, I was saved by the stick.

'That liqueur of yours on an empty stomach…,' I muttered. I wiped away a tear with my cuff. 'How can you bear it here, truly, you could go blind…'

I was ushered away by the secretary who'd been waiting on the stairs with Boris Viktorovitch Savinkoff. Patting his high bald-spot with a sweaty handkerchief, the famous writer and terrorist eyed me up and down with a suspicious look. Revolutions, socialisms, anarchies, nationalisms – somehow, they'd all have to be brought together, fitted into one machine. It struck me that this might be a snag for Pocięgło: the return of History. Could the idea be sold in such packaging? I walked downstairs, pausing every few steps. It was Summer, these were the Ways of the Mammoths and the Great Murch Hammer was pounding in Macau uninterruptedly.

Hammer. Tesla must have laboriously sought this resonant frequency, after all – everything had begun from an impact.

My head was spinning. I should at least have found myself some sort of hat. This is how sunstroke manifests itself. I pressed the cold ferrule of the murchometer into my forehead.

Later on, during a meal prepared by Chinamen from the latest government plunder (the Free-Staters called it a 'state-building tax') and before I drew the green curtains and collapsed onto the chaise longue to sleep off my long exhaustion, Zeytsoff told me this and that about events of the last few years. Admittedly, I listened none too attentively, as my thoughts were revolving around the plan I intended to sell to Porfiry Pocięgło and Zeytsoff was recounting everything in characteristic Zeytsoff style, in his sing-song Russian lilt, in narrative spun out like an alcoholic hallucination… Past, what past? – Unfrozen, it exists not all the more. Maybe things were like this, maybe otherwise. What counts is what's beneath the fingers, what's in an embrace, what's under bodily control. I ate greedily, stuffing my gob with spicy meat baked in sour dough and salads mixed with cold fish and breads flavoured with nuts and fried rice-cakes and fresh potatoes baptised in butter; I choked, spat and went on eating. At the same time, at the corner of my mouth, I consumed History.

Chinese recipes, with Chinese spices and sauces, cooked by Chinese hands – well yes, there were now so many Chinamen here because war and historical turmoil were similarly raging behind the Great Wall. According to Zeytsoff, the National People's Party of China and United League had already amassed an army of over half a million, led by the 'peasant general' Lao Te, who had sworn to personally slit the throat of Emperor Puyi and eradicate everything of his blood. The Chinese Civil War front was moving north-west; first, Lao Te cut off the emperor from the ports. Anyway, that's how it appeared from the very beginning: the revolutionary forces were coming from the south, from Summer. Nanking and Canton were under control of the Kuomintang and Chen Duxiu's Chinese Trotskyists already before the Thaw. In 1926, the Portuguese negotiated a pact with the Kuomintang and Sun Yat-sen in Macau. Zeytsoff hinted unambiguously that some agreement was brokered between Doctor Sun's yellow Ottepyelniks, Morgan Junior and Doctor Tesla. The Great Murch Hammer began striking in 1928; at once the peasant rebellions commenced. In the summer of 1928, Winston Churchill, Minister of War of the British Crown, visited Tesla's laboratory in the Fortaleza da Guia. Meanwhile, parallel Russian–British talks on the Bosphorus and Balkan question took place in Oslo. The tsar found himself in an awkward position, unable to turn his back on either West or East. Schultz's secession and the Japanese threat had tied his hands in Asia. In 1929, the Ice let go in Irkutsk and Count Schultz vanished without trace; wasting no time, the Cherry Blossom Empire again attacked Korea as well as the eastern ports of the Russian Empire, entering China via Vladivostock on the way to Changchun and Harbin. In Mongolia, Buddhist holy men led the local inhabitants against the Chinese, Russians and all other foreigners. In Nanking, Doctor Sun's Tongmenhui announced the birth of the Chinese Republic; they debated a constitution for the Middle Kingdom, its first legitimate parliament, new taxes and new trading terms with the barbarians, as well as the size of the former emperor's pension. Nikolay the Second had to withdraw his armies from Europe and redeploy them beyond the Urals. Which in turn opened up an opportunity for the European powers too good to sit out peacefully; and so, following a brief ultimatum issued by London, war erupted over the Bosphorus and Dardanelles.

'So, who finally overthrew Count Zimovy?' I asked, stuffing myself with rice and fish. 'Mmm, the SRs? New Narodniks?'

'A-ah, Gospodin Yeroslavsky, after Thaw, few know what happened in Irkutsk. They don't even know what's happening now. There's a rumour going about that Schultz felt it coming in his bones and got his whole family out of Siberia before the day of the Last Aurora.'

'Meaning when?'

'In February, a year ago. I wasn't there, people told me. Unrest swelled in the wake of the accident on the Marmeladobahn: the melted ground sunk neath the tracks, a train full of proletariat crashed barely a few versts out of Irkutsk, and news spread that it was the work of Prince Blutsky's agents, that is, the tsar's, sent to bring the coldiron industry to its knees as swiftly as possible, and in so doing topple the count from his autocrat's throne. Such a rumour even suited Schultz's purposes, I mean, keeping it alive in ordinary folk's minds. But muzhik heads were already inflamed, the *Krasnoyarsk Worker* published fresh photographs of Trotsky in Ust-Kut, soviets were forming in towns, in villages… Well, Ottepyelniks at once began fighting Lyednyaks loyal to the emperor, whilst the count made the foolish mistake of sending heavy-handed Cossacks after the mob. What could be got away with under the Ice, could not be got away with in Summer: instead of disbanding and dispersing across the city, concealed in safehouses for fear of the authorities, the workers flocked together in seething anger and marched on the Box, led by a false Bronstein. Such was the end of Count Schultz, may the Lord absolve him of his countless sins.'

'Righteous wrath of the common people, mmm. The rabble chooses its Bastille goaded by the aesthetics of fear. Either the Box, or the Sibirkhozheto Tower, mmm.'

'Yes. Everyone in the Citadel at the time was hacked to pieces, soldiers or not soldiers, tchinovniks or not tchinovniks. But what exactly happened – who, where, how, by whose hands? God alone knows. The count even has no grave. Hence more poverty and bedlam in the city, for when summertime returned at last, everything crawled out of the unfrozen earth, corpses, carcasses, all manner of putrefaction; and severe pestilence descended on Irkutsk. And since it's killed off subsequent thousands and since they too had no one to give them a Christian burial or at least cremate them, because no government's had a strong grip on Siberia and its cities since Thaw – well, the contagion only intensified, and so more people died, rotting in their houses and streets, till the first natural frost arrived and shut down the furnace of disease and death for a few months. But now – it's all happening again. The prime minister calls it the City of Flies. Gnus torments us here as well but there… Typhus, cholera, jaundice, plague, whatever you choose to name. And so, for this reason, the Free-Staters are in no hurry to take Irkutsk. Whilst the fact that five armed parties of this or that hue still take turns to do battle there is a different matter altogether.'

I could imagine that picture of chaos and total anarchy; I'd surely seen many more such scenes of late than Zeytsoff. Often, it was hard to tell even which political project a particular armed gang was supporting, as they marched across Siberia pillaging and murdering, installing their own clownish governments in villages and little towns not yet razed to the ground. Ottepyelniks or Lyednyaks, for or against the tsarist autocracy – even this was impossible to determine. They'd enter the fray with the most peculiar slogans: 'For Tsar and Soviet power!' Utter confusion reigned, discord, unprecedented motley.

I asked Zeytsoff about the Trans-Siberian Railway; Colonel van der Hek had mentioned Red Cross convoys organised by various national Societies transporting women and children. Information had also reached me that the Japanese, honouring their agreement with Piłsudski, had rescued entire Polish orphanages and nurseries through Vladivostock. From my question, Zeytsoff probably took note that I was intending to convey myself out on the Transsib. With gloomy face, he explained how for fully two months military barricades were blocking the line between Irkutsk and the Ob river; thanks to the Japanese offensive, there was also no permanent connection with Vladivostock. Trains travel irregularly to Nertchinsk and Krasnoyarsk, but this too is uncertain, as Pobedonostseff has mined the tracks for fifty versts or so and threatens to blow up the railway. Two battles had already been fought between the New Narodniks and the Trotskyists over Port Baikal and the Baikal railway ferry.

'Besides, dozens of contradictory rumours reach us every day. We have functioning radios and telegraph cable open to the east. The day before yesterday they said that Hirohito had ordered a raid on Peking. Yesterday – that the Japanese had signed an alliance with Sun Yat-sen. Tomorrow, we'll no doubt learn that the Chinese emperor has abdicated. Or that America is fighting the Japanese fleet over Tchukotka. Prince Lvoff has been offering his resignation to the tsar more or less every other new moon. His Exaltedness Nikolay Aleksandrovitch sometimes accepts it, sometimes not, sometimes puts Georgy Yevgenyevitch under arrest and sometimes showers him with orders and implores him to return to office. In most cases, no one even knows who actually pulls the strings in Saint Petersburg. What difference does it make? One big shambles. Boris Viktorovitch was saying yesterday that the comrades had passed a new sentence on First Minister Lvoff; yet there are already seven or eight different factions within the Socialist Revolutionary Party, they excommunicate one another mercilessly, shoot envoys and apostates now on sight, since each one could be a suicide bomber in ideological disguise – only paper communication is still relatively safe. On Tuesday, we were in 'peace talks' with His Imperial Exaltedness, on Wednesday – we're implacable enemies of the Russian Empire. My head's splitting, Benedykt, sir.'

I had guzzled more than my fill of rice and History.

Around midnight, I was awoken by the sound of gunfire. Three or four shots; maybe I'd slept through quieter earlier. The shooting came from a distance, but its echo resounded across Zimny Nikolayevsk. I stood by the blown-out window facing the night and raked back the curtains. Scores of lights were burning; from above, against the dark backdrop, I could make out the ellipse outlining the former ring of Clock Towers and crescent of Innokentyevskoye Two. People were cooped up in the ruins or in what had been saved of the industrial edifices, as well as in shacks and shanties built from materials left by destroyed buildings that had sunk into the thawed earth. I pricked up my ears: someone down below was playing a flute. A child was crying. A typewriter was clacking away. A dog was barking. The night intensified everything fivefold, holding up its offerings to the ear – sounds and more sounds and more sounds – on a black cushion of silence. The wind licked the sweat from my skin; I hadn't realised I'd been sweating in my sleep. Again, I'd dreamed the underground nightmare. If people go crazy when buried alive neath the slab of their tomb, what can be said of the fellow cursed with bad luck immobilised forever neath the slab of a continent? I was thinking of a cigarette when the first lightning flashed. So, how was it then? Had I been woken by rifle shots – or the dry crack of thunderbolts? One hundred and thirty-one, one hundred and thirty-two, one hundred and thirty-three... a clap of thunder rolled over Zimny Nikolayevsk. The wind was pervaded by electric damp. I opened my mouth and breathed in air infused with the summer storm, a pungent ozone cocktail, *parfum de Tesla*. A second thunderclap – and the downpour burst. The rain didn't have to lash; tilted backwards, the tower lay supine beneath it. I stood there as the storm literally washed over me. Then I sat down in the middle of the empty coldiron floor and gawped at the streaks of rain swilling out shadows in the shadows; from the shape of their spray, I was able to guess the phases of the Hammers. The air grew chillier still. I stretched out on my back on the cold steel. It felt... pleasant.

Thunderclaps continued to rock the night.

'Give me the Ice,' I whispered. 'The Ice!'

In the morning, the secretary's pimply assistant came to see me and said the prime minister wouldn't find time before lunch, and most likely not until evening; I was to sit and wait. I went out into Nikolayevsk.

The Sun had returned in all its royal splendour, in robes of gold and white and azure blue, covering Siberia in a mantle of light. Puddles, sparkling profusely in the grass and swift-drying mud, stung me in the eye with their malign blinks. I stepped out of the shadow of the Crooked Tower and only then remembered about a hat. A dog ran up to me, sniffed me, stuck out its tongue, panted amicably. Someone whistled to it insistently from under the thicket of mainstays, cables, entangled coldiron scaffolding and whole engineering makeshift with which Zeytsoff and his lieutenants had rescued the Seven O'Clock Tower from subsiding into the softened ground. Now it was home to a hundred homeless people dwelling under canvas canopies or lopsided structures made from coldiron sheets. They were boiling water in kettles and battered samovars; there was an aroma of Chinese tea, and together with it – the sound of jangling glass, muffled prayers. Elderly Armenians were praising God neath the resurrected Sun.

Chinamen wound their way along the twisting paths between the shacks and ruins of Zimny Nikolayevsk, buying and selling all manner of goods in a barter of exchange, where their greatest turnover was in foul-smelling balms against the gnus or foodstuffs of the vilest quality; I saw a toothless babushka purchasing a none-too-fatty dog in exchange for a gold filling. Perhaps these paupers from under the tower were afraid that intentionally or unintentionally, I'd kidnap their lunch.

Several families who'd taken up residence under the half-broken wall of an industrial hall had started a small garden nearby, attempting to grow potatoes and cabbage. Someone always stood on guard armed with cudgel and knife. I exchanged courtesies with a handsome sentry in frockcoat and pince-nez. Before the Thaw, he'd been a court clerk in the Prosecutor's Office of the Criminal Chamber on an annual salary of four hundred and eighty roubles. He complained that Mongols had stolen his last wig.

Where the Ten O'Clock once stood, a family of Little Russians were keeping three wild birds of unknown species in cages. They were hurling stones and invectives across a heap of rumble at the devotchkas rescued from the Empress Maria Institute for Noble Maidens; allegedly, the young ladies had attempted to steal one of the birds in the night.

At the place of the Eleven O'Clock, beyond Zhiltsoff's former coldmill well (only a swampy depression remained), a clan of starved-to-death Tunguses were feeding their two reindeer alongside more than twenty horses belonging to the UFSS. The Provisional Government was paying for their services in salt and flour. Here I doubted the political acumen of Pocięgło and his cronies. For it was a peculiar method of establishing statehood: they're bringing half a vast continent under their control and plan to stand up to world powers – and yet they don't recognise their own citizens camped below their windows, trading with them as neighbours.

At the One O'Clock, on a pile of rubble left by the tower, neath a lopsided canopy and frostoglaze pane, a German doctor was receiving patients. A ruddy-faced nun in black habit was directing patients to him in the shade of the ruins, one at a time. The queue seemed to stretch as far as the next tower. Most of the people indeed looked like victims of infectious diseases, probably having left Irkutsk for that very reason. Pocięgło ought to introduce a quarantine law, otherwise Zimny Nikolayevsk would fall victim to the same epidemics as Irkutsk.

Walking along the rim of the Clock ring, I examined these poor wretches; none, overwhelmed by shame, averted their gaze from the vulture eye of curiosity. Those vociferously coughing and wheezing still clung to life – worse was with the silent and inert, basking with closed eyes in the sun, wrapped neath the burning sun in sheepskins and shubas. Children, of course, presented the saddest sight, pallid starvelings with brightly shining eyes, racked by cold fever, staring listlessly into space. I could have counted every month, every week of Ottepyel according to the sufferings and lives of innocent children. Certain types of injustice – certain types of evil – are impossible under the Ice. Herr Blutfeld was wrong: a rationally ordered world will strive towards a state of least suffering; it is against entropy that every living thing fights.

I was curious to know if the German took some kind of payment from them. They'd come empty-handed, had nothing. Maybe this is the origin of the State: it emerges from structures of spontaneous help. A few hobbledehoys had tied white cloths on their elbows and were distributing water, making sure everyone kept to their place in the queue, and establishing with the nun a hierarchy of diseases. The doctor, nun, volunteers – Pocięgło ought to bring them as soon as possible under the banner of the UFSS.

Two-thirds of the way down the queue, I espied a familiar countenance, the rugged ginger-haired fright impossible to forget: Mijnheer Iertheim was sitting on a leaky barrel. Chewing on the mouthpiece of his cracked pipe and warding off the gnus, he was reading an article from an obliquely torn sheet of newspaper. His bekesha, once white, now bore the colours of mud, grass, smoke and God knows what impurities.

I walked up to him. The newspaper was printed with ink of such dire quality that each and every letter was smeared to a smudgy ghost of itself, half-blown already off the page. The Dutchman sat hunched, frowning.

'What's new in politics? Are those Chinese still hanging in?'

He did not recognise me.

'Personally, I'm backing the Japs,' he mused. 'They at least aren't fighting amongst themselves.'

'Henrik, sir, the sun's blinding you.'

He stood up.

'Wait a moment... No.' He leant over me, looked me straight in the face. 'Yurotchkin?'

'What Yurotchkin! It's me, Gierosławski!'

He sprang back, tripped over the barrel and landed in the mud; wind snapped up the newspaper.

I gave him my hand.

'It's Benedykt, Engineer, Benedykt. Don't be afraid.'

We sat down on the barrel. Iertheim pulled out a dirty handkerchief, wiped his hands, blew his nose. I noticed his eyes watering with fresh moisture – he was moved by the very encounter with a familiar person; he too must have endured a tough fate in recent times. I also perceived blotches of murch under his eyes and a gleissenik's umbriance on his hair and matted beard, on his collar and sleeves. On his left sleeve he had dried blood.

'What happened? Are you wounded?'

'No, no.' He blew his nose again and tucked away the handkerchief. 'They killed my cook and the boy, I had to escape from Irkutsk.'

'Who?'

'Ah, the Leninists, Tsentrosibir.'

'What have you got to do with Leninists?'

'Nothing! Must one have anything to do with them?' He ground his teeth. 'You catch the eye of some bunch, then all's lost.'

'So why…?' I waved towards the One O'Clock Tower.

He removed the pipe from his mouth. His hands continued to tremble slightly.

'I'm afraid it'll now trigger an avalanche. As soon as the Ice lets go – whoomph! I shall disintegrate, crumble to bits,' he turned away, 'come unstuck.'

I grabbed him by the arm.

'What was your latest diagnosis?'

'I used to attend the Holy Trinity in Irkutsk. The doctor said it's not progressing. But, Benedykt, sir,' he drew me to him, and blew a quick whisper directly in my lacerated ear, 'but I've lost my dynamo, left behind in my flat in the city, I've not Frozen myself for nearly a week!'

'So, you built that manual teslectric generator.'

'Yes, I did! As you told me! And all went well for over a year, I had as much Winter as I needed. Until…' He let go of me. 'I can feel it beginning already.' He laid his hand on the bekesha squeezed tightly over his belly. 'It's begun.'

I pressed the cool ferrule of the stick to my temple. Give me the Ice, the Ice!

'Grab hold of this.'

'What?'

'Hold on to it. I'll wind it up. A bit clumsy, but…'

I rotated the murchometer till the little dynamo inside gathered momentum.

Engineer Iertheim knitted his shaggy brows.

'That's not –'

'No, it only measures the difference in potentials.' I read off the indication on the scale. 'Fifty-six mirks, mm-hmm.' I grabbed the end of the dangler myself and wound again. 'Thirty-one.'

'That's not our unit of measurement.'

'No, Nikola Tesla's.' I scratched the stumps left by my severed fingers. 'Khh-mm. Something tells me we won't establish the benchmark like this. Excuse me.'

I invited the two matrons standing next in line. They'd been watching us earlier, intrigued.

For them the murchometer showed identical readings: 301 mirks.

'Levels have almost evened out. A year and a half sufficed.'

'Deuced Thaw…,' Iertheim muttered from inside his beard.

I stood up.

'Thaw alters nothing, Henrik. Technology is technology. Man needs the Ice, man makes the Ice. Come on.'

'Where to namely?'

I pointed with the stick towards the Crooked Tower where green-and-white flags were streaming from the blown-out windows.

'Currently, I am staying with the Free-Staters. Guest of the prime minister. Whose headquarters was it, that of French companies? I can't believe we won't find material for a little tungetitum flow-generator for you. Well! Chin up!'

'And it's definitely safe?'

'You won't try and rub this lot up the wrong way, will you?'

The Free-Staters minding the stairs admitted us without blinking an eyelid; as to those upstairs, I had to yell and intimidate them with Pocięgło's name. I left Iertheim in my room, forbidding him to go out for the time being. I grabbed the first Chinaman that showed up and sent him for hot water and a fresh meal; of course, he pretended he hadn't understood, like all of them since Thaw – you had to speak in gestures.

I then went magpie-prospecting on my own around the tower, peering in turn into each of the mainly uninhabited rooms, and in this manner, three floors below, discovered the editorial offices of the *New Siberian Gazette*, where Mr Jeż Wólka-Wólkiewicz was in the process of preparing the latest issue for printing. Hunched over a typewriter click-clacking under his fingers, he was puffing black tobacco and humming a lively song. Above his desk, on the slanting wall, hung a framed photograph of Porfiry Pocięgło in military greatcoat, rifle under his arm, standing in the snow.

I recognised the editor from his badgerlike profile and silver-grey whiskers. I examined him for a few minutes from the threshold, until someone entered from a side door and asked what I wanted; Wólkiewicz glanced over his shoulder, snorted out smoke and resumed his typewriting. I left without a word.

In the afternoon, as Iertheim was tinkering in a corner over the suitcase of scrap-metal I'd collected for him, and I was sitting by the window chewing shag and shooing away an irksome blackfly, Zeytsoff knocked on the door.

'He says you know each other…,' he began, sticking in his head.

But he was immediately shoved aside as Editor Wólkiewicz himself swept into the room. His scrawny arms flung wide, he rushed up the sloping floor to greet me warmly and heartily, nearly tripping over the wire spread out by Iertheim.

'Well I never! Benedykt Gierosławski! I didn't recognise you! Only now! When I heard! Ooph! What a surprise! A joyous one! A joyous one!' And he lavished hugs on me.

I calmly pushed him away.

'And I told them so!' he went on, not in the least deflated. 'They didn't want to believe me when I said: Benedykt will emerge from this plight, they didn't catch the father, they won't catch the son. Mr Wielicki alone remained a similar optimist, for –'

'What became of the Wielickis?'

'A-ah, I don't know, I haven't been in Irkutsk since Thaw. I cleared out along with our leader.' He winked at me and pointed to the ceiling with his thumb. 'A great Pole, a great Siberian. Jeż, dear man, he says to me, our triumphs are as nothing if no one knows that a new state of Siberia exists. What do we need? We need a newspaper, a popular newspaper with a large circulation that reaches ordinary people. So, what happened? I rose to the occasion! Porfiry, sir,' here Jeż patted his decrepit chest with decrepit fist, 'you may count on Editor Wólka-Wólkiewicz!'

'So no longer Piłsudski.'

'We'll also have Piłsudski, never fear. But this issue –'

'It's a weekly? A daily?'

'Have you read it at all? Oh! Wait a moment!' and he sped downhill to the door.

I spat out of the window and cast an inquiring glance at Zeytsoff. The Russian shrugged his shoulders. I wiped the blackflies off my face, squashed the insects in my palm. Zeytsoff uncorked a bottle of moonshine. I shook my head in refusal.

Wólkiewicz returned. He handed me an as-yet-uncrumpled copy of the *Gazette*.

'The whole thing's in Russian,' I muttered.

'For Siberians! It has to be in Russian, the majority here speak Russian. That is, the majority don't speak it but, you understand, the literate ones...' He sat down on the neighbouring window frame, out of breath.

I flicked through the newspaper. The first four columns were filled with various high-flown Oblastnik declarations and political appeals; further on there was news from around the world, chiefly reports from the warfronts to east and west, not much more precise than the rumours relayed by Zeytsoff, except that they were conveyed in language skilfully imitating that of the tchinovniks; but after that it was a complete mishmash: farming prescriptions for 'new settlers of spring', recipes from a *Siberian Gastronomical Almanach* (black pottage made from stag blood, black sarana onion soup, weed salad, hawthorn-berry kasha), a Chinese horoscope, a caricature of Nikolay the Second lost at the crossroads of Europe with his trousers dropped to his ankles, an indistinct photograph (were the caption to be believed) showing the Vladivostock Massacre, two poems about Siberian nature and three pieces of prose, including an excerpt from the biography of Wacław Sieroszewski by Teodor Lewera.

'Whatever happened to him? Lewera and Sieroszewski are fierce competitors.'

'But that was before, Benedykt, before the Thaw.'

Thus I learned that Wacław Sieroszewski, a sworn Pilsudtchik, as soon as Piłsudski took his Yapontchiks to the Vistula to fight for the unfrozen Poland, forsook his pen for the rifle and joined the Legions. He was then killed in the first forest skirmish, fatally hit by a ricocheting bullet, leaving his Buryat wife and children without husband or father. Lewera was thereby rid of his Nemesis and the oppressive spirit of Siberian literature.

So what did he do next? He set about writing a hagiography of Wacław Sieroszewski.

'Clearly they weren't such great enemies,' Jeż concluded his story.

'Sieroszewski most likely didn't even notice Lewera,' I muttered, 'but Lewera suffered from a real obsession with Wacław Sieroszewski.' I read a few paragraphs of the biography. 'You don't see it, huh? Any image of soletruth when removed from the Ice begins to blur,' I folded the newspaper, 'like this smeary print.'

Wólkiewicz was perplexed. He quickly covered his confusion, however, with his next energetic movement and excited speech.

'But now, but this issue, you'll see,' he took a thick portfolio from under his arm, 'will be about our prime minister. Oh! I already have interviews with his old friends, his work colleagues, I've got his secondary-school report, a photograph of his confirmation, admittedly, not too, mm-hmm… And from the Siberian Metallurgical and Mining Company Kossowski and Boulanger. And from the beginning of the uprising. And earlier, from Hong Kong…'

He also had the same photograph that Porfiry had shown me the day before, as well as several similar taken at the same time in the same place. Christine Pocięgło was shielding herself from the tropical glare with her floppy hat; Doctor Tesla had laid his white-gloved hands on the shoulders of Christine and Porfiry and was bending towards baby Andrzej; a striped tomcat had climbed onto the bench and lain on Christine's lap, reaching out its paw to the child. Narrowing my eyes, I studied the photograph in the light of the low Sun.

'You visited them in Macau?'

'Hah, I accompanied Mr Pocięgło during the negotiations in Hong Kong, he took me with him –'

'So how was it at the wedding? It must have come out officially, who exactly Nikola Tesla is to Christine?'

'I was intrigued myself.' The old editor seized on the topic in a flash. 'I'd heard the gossip, but Morgan Junior's man, having drunk too much at the reception, told yet another tale. Perhaps you know it, Benedykt? For a given period, during the nineties of the past century, Doctor Tesla was the main attraction of the New York salons, enjoying the friendship of prominent personalities, Theodore Roosevelt, Mark Twain, Rudyard Kipling, our own Ignacy Paderewski, Augustus Saint-Gaudens or John Muir.

'Ah, I know, he told me.'

'Amongst others, Tesla became intimate with the Johnsons, a married couple with a firm footing in that high society, Robert and Katharine. By then, Katharine was already a mature woman and had two adolescent children. Hah, but Irish blood cools not till death.'

'They'd been carrying on for years, Benedykt. An odd romance, as odd as the lovers themselves. He was capable of not leaving his laboratory for weeks on end and living solely on lightning bolts and fantastical ideas; he used to write her long epistles. She would matchmake him with society women, often pushing forward other men's wives. She also didn't try very hard to hide it from her husband; whilst Doctor Tesla himself continued to enjoy warm relations with Mr Johnson.'

I squirted black saliva between my teeth.

'So, Christine is Tesla's daughter by this Mrs Johnson?'

'No, I should say not. Mrs Robert Johnson was too advanced in years. According to Morgan's man, another piece of gossip was also doing the rounds: that one of those affairs arranged by Katharine resulted in an illegitimate child, and Katharine, like a sui generis "black godmother", took it under her wing, giving it a home and education, whilst the Serbian genius travelled the globe, trotting from one moony enterprise to another.'

'So why "Filipov"?'

'Well, that's what Tesla called the Johnsons. Apparently, the name comes from some poem about a Serbian national hero. And so, for Tesla, Katharine was ever after "Madame Filipov". Besides, they didn't make any particular secret of it either, it's how he addressed her in society. You know yourself that our doctor is incapable of human intrigue, his mind is totally preoccupied by something else.'

'So, his daughter nevertheless... Does she acknowledge it herself?'

'Not likely! She hotly denies it! There are other rumours besides... *Alors, il n'y a que la verité qui blesse.*'

I gave Wólkiewicz a sharp look. He averted his gaze.

I lowered my eyes again to the photograph from Macau.

'Well, small wonder there's no extracting from her the soletruth of the past: she lives right next door to the constantly striking Great Murch Hammer. Mm-hmm. A nice-looking child.'

The half-true, half-false grandson of Nikola Tesla, conceived and born neath the Hammer, Andrzej Pocięgło: *l'Enfant de l'Été*. A strange shiver ran down my crooked backbone. I stared intently at the pale blotch of the baby's face, as if trying to decipher the visage of my mortal enemy, a general in a hostile army.

'But!' Jeż did not allow the silence to grow too long. 'I would have forgotten! Last time we met you asked me for something –'

'Last time we met, Mr Wólka?'

He gulped; his Adam's apple leapt birdlike – nevertheless the heartfelt smile did not vanish from his densely wrinkled countenance.

'You wished to know about Fishenstein – did you not? So, I made inquiries, for instance, about his family history. Did you know? He lost them all in the Great Fire of Irkutsk, but every one of them, his whole extended family: burned to death in their wooden house, which was one of the first to cave in. At the time, Abraham Fishenstein was attending some late-night business negotiations; he returns, and there's his house in flames, and his wife, kiddywinks, parents, brothers and sisters, cousins, all roasted alive – allegedly, they could be heard from the street, screaming. He ran into the fire.'

'His eye.'

'Just so. A beam came loose and fell on him, and then a firebrand or naked flame burned out the eye he now plugs with tungetitum. They dragged him out unconscious; clearly, he had saved no one. All of them, I tell you, went up in smoke.'

'In ash and dust.'

'Mm-hmm, yes.'

I slapped my cheek, squashing another blackfly into a bloody splodge on my skin.

'Well, many thanks, Mr Editor; it might indeed come in useful.'

His face lit up.

'At your service, at your service, pleased to be of assistance!'

'Though better not to overdo it, eh? No amount of gratitude can so shame me that I'd not be able to say always to your face: you're a traitor and louse in the pay of the Okhrana.'

Wólkiewicz leapt up violently, let go the portfolio and the rest of his papers, began waving his arms, flew up to me, glanced around the room, puffing out his chest like a cockerel, as if seeking witnesses to this insult, frowning and thrusting forward his chin in combative mode – but then changed strategy completely and sank in a twinkling into the pose of one unjustly wronged: mournful gaze from under dropped head, arms hanging limp, pain on the lips; he extends his hand in mute questioning. How could I say such a thing? What insensitivity and discourtesy, barefaced barbarism! Shame, shame, shame!

'What gave me pause for thought,' I said, refusing to be drawn into this dismal beggar's comedy, 'was the way you succeeded in so misleading everybody under the Ice, in deceiving and living so well in falsehood. Fellow Poles admitted you to sittings of the Last Kopeck Club, Doctor Myśliwski suspected nothing. But then I reversed cause and effect: the Okhrana came to you precisely because you had the trust of important people. Yet we clearly saw the flaw, the truth about this fatal flaw in your character: for why were you so angry, whence your constant irritation and touchiness towards people?' I wiped the blood from my cheek. 'The Mathematics of Character is unrelenting, Mr Wólka, you consent to betrayal and thereafter you're a traitor, betrayal is part of every equation. The only thing you can do is transfer it to the world's side. You have enormous resentment, you have grudges, pain and anger and ill-concealed rancour against the world, for you betrayed your friends. And it's no concern of mine what praiseworthy past you retain in your own memory. You betrayed your friends.' I stood up, spurning his outstretched hand. 'Such is the truth.'

He bridled.

'How dare you…!' He fell silent. His face writhed in a flurry of contradictory expressions like Petrukhoff's or Ciecierkiewicz's; it paused for a moment in pure despair, but from this too it melted. Wólkiewicz groaned indistinctly. Turning his eyes to the wall, he cleared his throat and whispered: 'You won't tell Pocięgło…'

'Traitor.'

'Benedykt, sir, for God's sake…'

'Traitor.'

He retreated a step.

'Have a heart…!'

I followed him.

'Traitor.'

'What's it to you now, there's no longer any Okhrana… I won't harm anyone, even if I…'

'Traitor.'

'Revenge, for the sake of filthy revenge, is that it?!'

'Traitor.'

Another step backwards and sudden anger:

'What d'you mean by this traitor, what traitor, where are your hard documents? I shan't permit such accusations, huh, perhaps you, sir, never spoke to the Ruskies, never came to an understanding with them, never took diengi from them?! Eh?! He's been found, the omniscient judge, the only one without sin!'

'Traitor.'

'We all had to somehow –'

'Traitor.'

'By what right, I ask, by what right! Only God in heaven –'

'Traitor.'

'Well, well, no need to be so Gierosławski-ish!'

'Traitor.'

A step backwards and now the tears:

'I'll leave, I'll leave, if that's what you want, what will you gain from an old man's suffering, I'm not much longer for this vale of –'

'Traitor.'

'It was such a piffling thing, how could I have known… they asked me… I didn't mean to hurt anyone –'

'Traitor.'

'You see, my whole life I've done what's best for the Fatherland, running risks for years in underground work, may people at least remember that, dear Benedykt –'

'Traitor.'

A step backwards –

– and he flew into the abyss, his legs undercut by the empty shutter; he tried in the final moment to cling still to the curtains and even grabbed one firmly in his fingers, but it tore like blotting-paper, and Mr Wólka-Wólkiewicz flew, flew into the abyss, in a flutter of soft fabric and shimmering sun-drenched green. He was – and was no more. He had fallen. I looked down. The Free-Staters were approaching the corpse with rifles raised.

Mijnheer Iertheim leant out of the window alongside. I caught him muttering something under his breath about Ishmael. He flinched when he saw that I'd heard; he was already opening his mouth to explain, but I walked past him without uttering a word.

I gathered up from the floor the documents scattered by the editor; they had slithered halfway across the room. Zeytsoff, setting aside the bottle and glass, handed me a few sheets of paper and a grey pamphlet.

'You needn't have,' he whispered.

'On this one I didn't lay a finger.'

'An old man. He begged for mercy...'

'It can't be helped. The truth is such: he was a traitor.'

Zeytsoff hung his head, mumbled something indistinct and walked out.

I returned to my seat in the window. Rolled myself a fat cigarette. The fingers remaining to me were very sure, calm. The Free-Staters had already dragged away Wólkiewicz's body from below the tower. I belched smoke at the confounded midges and mosquitoes. A red Sun was hiding behind the ruins of the Nine O'Clock Tower. The high-pitched cries of Chinese traders were exceptionally piercing at this time of day; the world grew rarefied in the evening stillness. I rested my occiput against the shutter-casing. A greasy, viscid melancholy was seeping into me from the oil paints of sky and Sun. But what's the sense in regretting that truth is as it is? What's the sense in weighing up variants of a past that exists not? (Whoever craves knowledge of himself, craves death.) This has to be shaken off! You can only feel so much remorse for things that could have gone differently.

I straightened my crooked backbone and pressed Wólkiewicz's portfolio of jumbled papers into the window frame with my knee. That dingy-looking pamphlet printed in a format half the size slipped out from between them. Stanisław Brzozowski, *Selected Works*. On page three was a handwritten dedication dated 1908: *For JWW – so that you may never forget the initial oaths.* I gave a smoky guffaw. That's a good one! Like minds amongst traitors! I'm curious to know what were their 'initial oaths'? What do traitors swear on? – on a Lie? on Teitelbaum's empty language?

I flicked through the pages. The future of Marxism, the might of revolutionary philosophy. Brzozowski at least seemed to understand History. *When we read philosophical writers from the pre-Kantian era, whether it be Descartes or Leibniz or the mystics Boehme and Spinoza, we are struck by the lack of historical atmosphere. Man is in direct touch with God, nature et cetera, as though thought had developed in some kind of extrahistorical void. The world is evil or the world is good. This is where the question stops.*

Whereas – *when a wild Yakut dies of hunger, not only the frost is to blame or the lack of fish in the river; also to blame is the primitive means of production that forms the bedrock of his life. To man, the world is always what he has made of it and what he has failed to make of it.* Man makes History; History does not make man. That is to say: History makes man insofar as man allows it to, insofar as he does not identify it as a force subordinate to his own force, and does not make use of this consciousness and power. Unlike in the time of the Greeks dreaming of the Circularity of History or Descartes drafting the absolute coordinates of the universe – all that remains for us is to surrender with heads humbly bowed to History flooding us with its wild currents, sweeping us away into the torrent.

But what can we change in the world so as to invalidate some forms of History and actuate others? Well, scientific progress, civilisational progress; this changes everything because there's no spell of History that would make people educated at universities, cross continents by train, receive information every day via radios and newspapers from dozens of different cultures, work in factories or electrified offices – that would stop falling into relations of slavery like in Pharaonic Egypt, or adopt tribal customs from prehistoric eras as their own. *Relations between man and the world depend on his own physiological organs and on the artificial organs, i.e., tools, which he has created. Since man has acquired in the course of humanity's historical development no new organs, all his progress would be confined within the limits described by his physiological organisation, were it not for the continual revolutionising influence of technological inventions and improvements.* But at the end of this process is – what? Nikolay Fyodoroff's automatic worms? It is not possible to acquire new organs and new senses, but it is possible to add tools that fulfil their functions.

For it is not naked man that moves forward in History, but man plus science.

A blackfly flew into my mouth; I spat it out. Bah, but I'd probably not feel those worms at all, were they even to crawl into my eyes in swarms... Machines visible only under a microscope, machines the size of bacilli. Abraham Fishenstein dreams of resurrecting his nearest and dearest from dust scattered by the wind in air, water and earth; madman he may be, but it is madmen such as he who contribute to the harnessing of History. Besides, the realisation of Fyodoroff's vision will also put an end to the Marxists' great design: people able to recreate themselves at will in whatever configuration of body and unbody they choose, in defiance of death, in defiance of time and space, will possess by this very ability total control over History. 'History' will simply become another name for man's actions that mould the world and man-within-it according to his own free will. Man will live in History as today he lives in Nature. *Man had to understand that even the nature in which he lives, nature conceived as the terrain of human activity, he himself fabricates in order to be able to pose another question: what is the aim of history, what is humanity to make of itself?*

Again this 'humanity'. I fired my cigarette butt at the Sun. Why can't Brzozowski comprehend that in Summer, agreement on even humanity's most general aims and purposes will never come about? It would be worth giving these philosophers a guided tour of one or other of the Martsynian truthjousts, or of those of other religious sectarians; they'd soon recognise the difference between the world of cold ideas and hot matter subjected to entropy. *It's not the world that has to solve what humanity is to be, but humanity itself that determines what to make of the world and of itself.* Bah! But try solving anything at all, now that the Ice has cracked and Truth has come apart at the seams.

Under the Ice – it could indeed be done. I lowered an eyelid, and the carmine glow of evening sealed it like sugar-coating over my living eye. Under the Ice – it could indeed be done, but how in actual fact was it to look in practice? I tried to compose a logical picture in my head and at once the memory returned of Pobedonostseff's prophetic dreams. For he who would control History in this way – a single man or some group of experts, it's of no consequence, so let's accept that it's one man – would determine for the whole Kingdom of Darkness not only the principles of power, principles of law and economy, but also everything that is obvious in the moral and religious and even aesthetic domains: the latter likewise make up the living tissue of History. The good-and-evil of the tribe of Moses wandering through the desert is one thing; quite another – the good-and-evil of the Empire of All the Russias. For has God changed in the meantime? No. It is men *who have shifted in History.*

The lord of the Kingdom of Darkness would wield in his hand that same lever of Good and Evil with which Zeytsoff ordered Jelena Muklanowicz to alter the course of the Trans-Siberian Express. I opened my eye, closed my eye, opened my eye – lever to the left, lever to the right.

But in practice, of course, it's not so easy. For how to assume control of an idea? *The human spirit imposes the world's laws through the hand. Thought, which has no relation to the hand, is an empty delusion.* It was only during the time of the gleissen that these or those people (and I too occasionally gave them credence) fancied that it was enough to bend Father Frost, the icers' shepherd, to their will, and the icers would freeze History for us according to a prescribed formula. But Thaw came and the fairy tale burst. *As long as we have no direct control over the influence of ideas on the world, the significance of ideas will depend wholly on their significance for mankind's productive powers.*

With scarred finger-stumps, I rubbed the stubble sprouting from under my skin; the wire brush scratched my brain, striking sparks. Because here, Brzozowski was not entirely right – for precisely Thaw, precisely this sudden dissolution of History in accordance with Berdyaeff's rule – had been prompted by nothing other than the direct influence of ideas on the world: why, Nikola Tesla had not struck ministerial offices and world parliaments with his Hammer, had not aimed a blow at matter –

'I have it!' cried Engineer Iertheim.

'It's freezing?'

'Wait, I've placed the tungetitum in the electromagnetic field, we'll see in a moment. But it's rotating smoothly and I have glintzen on the winding.'

I understand that for people whose entire physical work consists in writing, the thought that even the beauty of Shakespeare's plays or Plato's works has no significance in the face of blind and brutal matter and that because of this it would be desirable to uncover some mysterious connection between moral, aesthetic value and the forces of nature, is both painful and difficult to comprehend. As long as the only such connection, however, is the obedience that the human hand is able to impose on those forces of nature, all overcomings of Marxism are destined for the same repository wherein are held the works of alchemists and astrologers.

'Oh, Mijn God, Ijs, Ijs!' sang the Dutchman, rotating the lopsided coldiron drum. White hoar was spreading over the black physicist's palms as tarry umbriance danced about his stocky silhouette.

The only consistent attempt to overcome Marxism is magic.

As if a cold thunderbolt had shot through my own brain and backbone, I leapt to my feet flinging down Wólkiewicz's editorial papers, half of which flew out of the window. The Ice! I had said as much to Iertheim myself: Thaw alters nothing, technology is technology. Man needs the Ice, man makes the Ice! Man makes the Ice! Man makes History!

Well, here we know exactly the direct influence of ideas upon the world! Here we have a precise connection between the forces of nature and moral, aesthetic value and every other value: black physics!

'Perhaps, Benedykt, you'd like to?'

'No, I don't need to.' I breathed a sigh. 'Only don't overdo it. And better not leave the room. I have to go.'

'But what if they ask about the journalist?'

'What then? Tell them the truth.'

Porfiry Pocięgło, seated at his table in the middle of the sunny mirror of the rooftop, was eating supper in the company of a bearded priest; at the same time, a Mongolian barber-surgeon was examining the prime minister's broken leg under the table, rubbing in fresh balms, dressing it in fresh bandages. I waited on the stairs until both barber-surgeon and priest had descended. The Sun in the meantime had hidden its heavy head; only its golden purply-orange mane still hung in the sky, combed across half the horizon. The air was totally motionless and the gnus was raging, biting anything warm and living. Around Pocięgło's table, the Chinese servants had set up six incense burners, which belched forth smoke to ward off the mosquitoes. The rabid Siberian gnus is capable of quenching a fire, inundating it with insect ash.

'I feel as if I'm at an audience with Schultz-Zimovy.'

'Have a seat. Peckish?'

He had warm milk and black-cherry preserve and relatively soft bread, and also several bowls filled with various Chinese vegetable delicacies.

'Coffee?'

'Help yourself.' He pushed a tin in my direction.

'I can't remember when I last tasted coffee – mmm –'

'By the way, you haven't told me. Where have you been all these years?'

'On the Ways of the Mammoths.'

'Looking for your father?'

I inhaled the sharp cinnamon fragrance into my nostrils.

'Mmm, I found him, I found him. On the Ways of the Mammoth, Porfiry, in the Underworld.'

His facial expression did not change.

'And how is it with the pater?'

'Thaw.'

'Ah, yes. You said he was no longer alive. I'm very sorry.'

I raised my eyes.

'There's nothing to talk about as long as you take me for a madman.'

He burst out laughing. Something had snapped.

'All right, all right, Benedykt, just like old times! You're already bristling!'

'Or if you are not persuaded of my truth.' I drank up the rest of my coffee, set aside the faience cup and folded my empty hands symmetrically on the tabletop. I stared straight at Pocięgło, the trajectory of our gazes plotted as if by square and compasses. 'Am I telling the truth? Porfiry, sir! Your word. Am I truth?'

The reddish light was floundering in thick smoke, the moment moving forward at a snail's pace. I waited. My eye – his eyes.

'Give it me,' he croaked.

'We shall found a coldiron industrial company. Gierosławski,

Pocięgło and most likely a third person with respect to the finances; on that in a minute.'

'There is no coldiron industry.'

'So, when we found it, we shall have a monopoly.'

'There is no coldiron industry, there are no gleissen, there are no coldmills, there is no way to freeze through ores. It's finished.'

'I am starting it. I have the technology for coldiron production, all we need are tungetitum and electrical energy.' I slammed my open palm flat on the tabletop. 'Porfiry! Am I truth?'

He was fiddling with his black spectacles.

'Yes.'

'We shall found a company.'

'Why me? You could go to others with this.'

'You have people, you have military forces and tungetitum lands within reach. For first of all: you must order the Free-State army to occupy at once and secure the territory beyond the Last Isotherm. Thaw has come, yet the tungetitum has not melted, and by some miracle not disappeared from the Earth's surface; at most it's sunk a little into the mud. Do you remember the estimates made by Sibirkhozheto's geologists? Ninety per cent of the resources remained inaccessible to people. But now there's no longer a Last Isotherm, there's no Winter! But as soon as the secret of my technology leaks out, then everything will be decided by the size of resources. You shall send in the army, set up the cordon. And a bullet in the head for any smuggler.'

He put on the pitch-black glasses.

'You've been there.'

'I wandered there from Kezhma.'

'And what did you see?'

'Mountains of tungetitum, Porfiry, mountains of tungetitum.'

Mountains of tungetitum, landscapes ploughed through by black glaciers, smashed by the cudgel of the stars, nature utterly devastated by inhuman frost, congealed into ice-crystal and then crushed from crystal into grey powdery snow, into sand finer than sand, for at the very heart of the former Land of the Gleissen, on a perfectly flat plain purged of all life, there remain now – only these gigantic boulders, planted ever closer together, their bizarre fantastical shapes reaching into the sky… Take this sand in your hands, blow through your fingers – and tungetitum dust shall remain. You trample over tungetitum, sleep in the shadow of tungetitum, breathe tungetitum; the Sun rises and sets in a halo strung on tungetitum… During a storm, inky lightning bolts leap amongst the massifs of the Black Labyrinth and Frost comes hurtling in waves like a glass wall… Then, there – you can touch, taste, swallow Truth…

I breathed out.

'And I saw amongst them other wanderers,' I resumed, 'maybe they'd only strayed there out of curiosity – or maybe these were already scouts – from the Japanese Empire? sent by Harriman? or by that other general from the Caucasus who'd renounced his oath of allegiance to the Romanoffs? Whoever seizes control of those lands will possess the greatest fortune in the world. This political chaos won't last forever. We have to grasp the opportunity whilst there's still time.'

'Ye-es…' Pocięgło jerked his head to the left, to the right; purple magma flooded his spectacles. 'Clearly, you've totally failed to realise what you're inviting me into. I'd have hanged myself from a tree for such betrayal of the ideas for which hundreds of good men perished under my command. So that I might now enrich myself! Is this the sort of man you take me for?' He leant over the table as far as his stiffly splinted leg allowed. 'This sort of man?'

I smeared vegetable paste on a thick butterschnitte.

'No. You are a loyal upholder the State and for your sake, I include the State in this business.' I slurped more coffee. 'For you, for you I have History.'

'Same old story all over again! After the Ice –'

'What does it matter that History has unfrozen? What does it matter that the Ice has melted? Ssshh!' I raised the butterknife neath the smoke and bloody light, 'It's me who's speaking! What does it matter that we have Thaw? It was a kind of wild force of nature anyway, Porfiry, the Ice; it descended on us like a divine dispensation: we neither understood it nor managed to turn it to our advantage. What was the basis in practice for all those deliberations about man's control of History? A single Martsynian superstition about Father Frost! We even extracted coldiron in the fashion of hunters and nomads, like booty stolen on the off chance from a magical monster.'

'You have the technology.'

'I have the technology, indeed, but that's not the point. We will sell the coldiron or not sell it, we will make a fortune on it or not – that is, we will, we will make a fortune, but this is but a trifling detail, not the main idea, not why you will enter into this partnership.' I demolished the sandwich, cut another chunk of bread. 'Mm-hmm. Because I'm not talking merely about the next coldiron firm. I'm talking about the first company of the History industry. I am talking about the production of States and speculation on the stock market of Good and Evil. For you, I shall calculate and freeze the United Free States of Siberia before which all empires of the world shall bow.

'What does it matter that History has unfrozen? What does it matter that the Ice has melted? Since we have tungetitum and know the mechanisms of black physics. Just think for yourself.' I licked the sweet preserve off my fingers. 'First of all, as I said, we shall collect all the remaining tungetitum. But not in order to throw it onto the market, and convert it into fast cash. Of course, we'll allocate a little to the needs of the coldiron manufacturing technology. But above all... Just think: Nikola Tesla strikes with his Hammer in the destructive resonance of murch; and in this way he smashed the Ice, smashed the fetters of History. But we shall have a thousand, million, milliard times more tungetitum! We shall have everything we need: tungetitum, energy and knowledge, that is, maps of the Ways of the Mammoths, and me, who has walked them in the flesh, and also Baikal, which today is a veritable tungetitum storage cell – whilst I also know its outlet through the Ways. Porfiry, sir! Because of what did the Ice first stir? Because of what did History freeze?' I thumped my fist on the table, and again some utensil fell off and rolled into the abyss; neither of us averted his gaze. 'Because of the impact! Because of the conversion of kinetic and thermal energy within the tungetitum mass into teslectry, from which two-valued logic and its Biblical order, freezing away entropy to the level of Ice, spread in geological waves out of Siberia and across the globe. For all laws of murch-imbued matter have become closer to the laws of ideas, including the laws governing man, including History. But this was no divine miracle: take, sir, a tiny tungetitum hammer and strike – and you will also feel the Frost. So, what is needed? A mass of tungetitum sufficiently large, energy for conversion into pure murch, as well as the scientific knowhow for carrying it out. And then, once we have set up a whole system of Grosshammers at intervals along the Ways of the Mammoths, it's enough to calculate the appropriate sequences of strokes: more Ice here, less there, give History a free rein here, hold it back there... Petersburg – Moscow – Kieff – Crimea – Thaw to the Dnieper – Japan – Spring of Nations – Russia under the Ice. History trundles on in accordance with the coldest mechanics of ideas, from Truth to Truth.'

'But who will calculate this? you?'

'Did I not say that I am the Mathematician of History?' I wiped my mouth with a handkerchief. 'The United Free States of Siberia will be the most powerful, most majestic, most peaceful state on earth.'

'No need to over –'

'You don't understand. This is no empty political promise, no idle braggery. They will triumph, because they won't be able not to triumph. Such will be the *historical necessity*. Who will conquer a law of nature? Who will oppose gravity? They might as well rebel against the tyranny of Pythagoras's theorem or the autocracy of algebra.'

Pocięgło flashed his cigarette case; I thanked him, lit up.

'And you will keep an eye on the course of the Ice.' Porfiry tapped the cigarette case rhythmically on the tabletop. 'You will draft the History of the world.'

I blew out smoke, smoke to smoke. The sun set, blood flowed over Siberia; the light symphonies died out on the coldiron roof of the Crooked Tower, we sat amidst thickening shadows.

'*Je suis le Mathématicien de l'Histoire*,' I repeated.

He also lit a cigarette. Could he still see through his black spectacles? Why didn't he want to take them off?

'Apoliteia,' he muttered.

'Mm-hmm?'

'You were already planning it then?'

'How could I plan?'

'I don't know. With Tesla?' He was tapping the cigarette case faster and faster. 'Had he not first smashed the Ice, no one could have reached this tungetitum.'

'You're the one for great conspiracies, not me.'

'Yeh, and all you do is calculate the History of the world,' he sneered contemptuously. He inhaled deeply. 'The power of the State at the price of resignation from the State.'

'But you are not Piłsudski, you have in your sights the happiness of people of a thousand nations. What is the State? – a blunt instrument of History, sooner or later man would reject it anyway.'

'I am thinking.' Tap, tap, tap, tap. 'You wish to be director of this partnership, true?'

'Fifty per cent plus one more vote. Whereas you will be prime minister, president, whatever you –'

'Since you figure it that way.' Tap, tap, tap, tap. 'I shall provide the land and the people to harvest the tungetitum. You shall provide the knowledge; I recognise that it's the crucial thing. If –'

'How do you stand financially?'

'Me? Or my State?'

I waved my cigarette along the line of towers reduced to rubble.

'We have regressed here to commodity exchange, the rouble has plummeted, there's no economy, no commercial traffic going beyond the States' borders. We need some kind of backing in hard currency. Once the coldiron production is up and running, we'll be able to finance the building of the Grosshammer network from the profits, but in order to get off the ground in the first place, we need external capital. Time, Porfiry, is of the essence. Let's not deceive ourselves: if I don't set this up under the Ice of History, then loosed into the chaos of Summer, you'll have no way of protecting your States from the Russian Empire or Japan. What army will you put up against the armies of Hirohito?

Motley regiments of malnourished vagabonds? I must freeze us before the old-world powers have us by the throat. As soon as possible we should muster machines, materials, competent engineers. Capital is needed forthwith.'

'So, we'll start by releasing a little pure tungetitum onto the American market.'

'No, no, no! This we should not do! You have to look ten, twenty moves ahead. After all, as soon as I forge my Ice onto the world, in the capital cities of other powers they'll notice what's afoot and take remedial action.'

'Set up their own Hammers and Grosshammers.'

'No less.'

Pocięgło laughed hesitantly.

'You talk of historiosophical war, of some kind of global battles between philosophers of ideas, Mathematicians of History.'

'I don't give a damn about the Murch Hammers, any physicist with an oscillator is capable of introducing opposite-phase waves. But the Grosshammers of Russia, Japan, the United States of America, Great Britain, Germany, France or Austria-Hungary – these could interfere with my equations. Were the power ratio nine to one in my favour, then I should be able to manage with no problem; besides, they're unlikely to adopt a single concerted strategy. But the more tungetitum they have outside of our control, the more complex the Algorithmics of History. You may be sure that within a few years they'll have gathered all tungetitum from the free market or private hands into their own arsenals. Most probably, the tsar will simply nationalise it. We won't sell a gramme!'

'So, what's our solution then? Bring someone else into the partnership?' He pulled a wry face. 'But whom could we trust sufficiently to let him into the firm's deepest secrets and guarantee he won't betray them out of loyalty to his own state, nation, family? We're talking after all about an industrial company de facto ruling the country, bah, were it only the country...'

'There's nothing new under the Sun, for two centuries the East India Companies ruled half of Asia. As to the man, we have him: Abraham Fishenstein. Except that I have to find out if he's alive or dead.'

'He's alive.' Pocięgło flicked ash into an empty coffee cup. 'He's in Irkutsk.'

'Not fled? But not gone bust in the post-Thaw slump?'

'Fishenstein? Switzerland would have to go bust first. No, Fishenstein has an arrangement with Pobedonostseff and the Tsentrosibir; it seems he's even making money on the Thaw: he buys up land for groschen in the name of companies registered in Hong Kong, Macau or even

New York which exist only on paper.' Pocięgło sucked the smoke out of his cigarette end and smiled malevolently. 'I was planning to take it all from him by means of a single statute; the United Free States of Siberia have not signed any international agreements.'

'Tell him that anecdote on the anniversary of the foundation of our joint-stock company. Are you in touch with Irkutsk? We must send for Fishenstein.'

'But why him, Benedykt?'

'Because he too will enter into this for the sake of an idea.'

'The Siberian state? Control over History? I doubt it.'

'For the idea of victory over the Apocalypse, for the idea of universal resurrection.' I stretched my limbs in my chair; my crooked bones were reluctant to slot into place. 'Abraham Fishenstein is a staunch Fyodorovian, he'll do anything to further the progress of resurrection science.'

Pocięgło spread his hands questioningly.

'But what have we got to do with Fyodoroff?'

'First, we'll allocate a substantial cut of the profits to research into resurrection technologies. But second, and above all: I shall calculate History so that the visions of Nikolay Fyodoroff are realised as soon as possible. Fishenstein will receive a guarantee that – perhaps not during his lifetime, but – yes, that all his nearest and dearest will rise from the dead in the flesh. That is: for sure during his lifetime, since obviously he too will rise from the dead. He'll welcome them into his home, alive, immortal.'

Porfiry directed his black spectacles towards me and froze for a long time in the order of Sun and gnomon, stars and sextant. In the meantime, an evening breeze arose over Zimny Nikolayevsk, smoke from the steel incense-baskets drifted to the sides, floating between us above the table; but these were the only interruptions.

'And he'll take such a guarantee from you.'

I sat up straight.

'Porfiry, sir! Am I truth?'

He flung away the cigarette butt, removed the spectacles. His eyes had reddened, no doubt from the smoke.

'What makes me most afeard,' he whispered, 'is that you match these things to absolute truth.'

I stretched out my hand towards him.

'Deal.'

He adjusted his stiff leg, leaned over, squeezed my crippled hand.

'Deal.'

I struck my chest with my fist.

'It has frozen.'

He merely crossed himself.

'Good.' I poured myself the rest of the cold coffee and knocked it back. 'I already have one man in post, Engineer Henrik Iertheim, worked with me at Krupp; you won't find a better scientist initiated into black physics.'

Pocięgło waved indifferently.

'It's your business whom you employ. I know you know what you're doing.'

'When you send people to Irkutsk to fetch Fishenstein, have them search around for other survivors of the coldiron industry. I'll make a list in a moment. When are they leaving?'

He took out his watch.

'At a quarter to midnight at the earliest. The Podkamennaya Tunguska unit will go tomorrow, I have to assemble men, the majority are stationed by the rivers or along the Transsib.'

'You need Zeytsoff for anything? I'll take him as my handyman.'

Porfiry again gave permission with a wave.

'We must also think of a legal formula,' I continued. 'The commercial code of the Free States of Siberia is only now being written, but in the meantime, we have to freeze it on paper. That is, as soon as we've come to an agreement with Fishenstein. Do you have any friendly pettifoggers on side?'

'Are you quite sure, sir, you weren't planning it?'

'Mm-hmm? And what might you have unearthed in your memory?'

'Agh, Ünal Tayyib Fessar, for example. He was totally right about you. You denied it vehemently at the time. But what came out of it?'

'Those were lies, there in the Trans-Siberian Express in Summer – all lies.'

'Or on the steps with Mr Wielicki after leaving the Last Kopeck Club. You're a capitalist after all, Benedykt, body and soul an entrepreneur.'

'Lies, lies.'

'But you've made them truth.' He grinned a tad mockingly, a tad indulgently. 'No plans, nothing of the sort! Don't believe in the future. What was it you said? The future exists not.'

'The future exists not,' I repeated slowly. 'I can make of it whatever I will.' I clenched my half-fist. 'All my plans from before the Thaw melted into mud. Then I fashioned for myself new dreams. But if you're envisaging some Machiavellian plot… All I do is separate truth from lies.'

He coughed, spitting out smoke.

'I know. I read your *Apoliteia*. It's not a plan in the sense of my lame conspiracies… Rather as if coming from all directions at once, from front and back and sides –'

'From future and from past –'

'They arranged themselves to suit you –'

'Froze to me.'

'People, events, necessities.'

'Hoarfrost on the windowpane.'

'What?'

'Like hoarfrost on a windowpane.'

'Yes.' He swallowed hard. 'Certain things I remember, certain things I fill in for myself. You say: Abraham Fishenstein – so as to seize our founding capital from a man whom we shall purchase together with his soul in exchange for the Fyodorovian idea of universal resurrection. But I say: History manufactured *à la* Fyodoroff – so as you can resurrect your pater. Oh, and maybe Jelena Muklanowicz as well.' He rested his knuckles on the table, levelling at me his hawknose and dark, deep-set eyes. 'Now you tell me: Am I truth?'

I pointed with an unstraightened finger at the cylinder lying to Pocięgło's right, beyond a tumbler and sugar bowl.

'What have you there?'

He roused himself.

'Ah, Nikola gave it me as a present. So that I would know when to begin the uprising.'

'Take a look.'

He shrugged his shoulders.

'Summer.'

I rose to my feet.

'When the interferograph once again shows two points of light, ask me then about my plans for any distant future, and I shall tell you. Good night, partner.'

When I departed, the secretary and the Chinese servant approached Pocięgło. Porfiry sat motionless as they danced around him. The image was framed in smoke, stars covered it from above, whilst from below it had a mirrored reflection of the night. Pocięgło sat half-turned towards Zimny Nikolayevsk, elbow resting unsteadily amongst the crockery, other arm hanging loose, jacket uglily wrinkled across his back and neck, white shirt unbuttoned as far as the heart; clayey shadows had gummed up his eye sockets. A man overwhelmed, I thought to myself.

The thought was dispelled at once. I ran down the stairs leaping two at a time. Even without this my heart beat faster. I had won! It had succeeded! It had frozen, just as I wished!

I sent the first Free-Stater maltchik whom I encountered to find Zeytsoff. On a piece of clean paper, with pencil borrowed from Iertheim, I made a note of whom Pocięgło's men were to seek in Irkutsk. I had neither lamp nor candle; I sat in the window, wrote by the light of the stars. The gnus and the voices of refugees camping in the city's ruins floated up to me on waves of warm air. Once I raised my head and gazed at the panorama of Innokentyevskoye bonfires neath the bright constellations. Here will be our capital, I said to myself mentally, a new city, no longer with a tsarist name. Here will stand the headquarters of the History Industry Company. After all, the Ways of the Mammoths won't change their course through the earth's crust. Tall towers will once again shoot high into the sky; for black physics won't change, the same equations will indicate to us the safe heights. Except that it will be a city built from the beginning solely on architecture of the Kingdom of Darkness, on frozen-through materials. For instance, we won't be laying railway lines on the surface and exposing them like the Cold Line or Circum-Baikal to accidents – we shall construct overhead lines suspended on coldiron wires. Whilst from here, from my office –

Zeytsoff appeared. Mijnheer Iertheim, now fully bemurched, had fallen asleep in a lower corner, wrapped in his bekesha and a carpet; I pressed a finger to my lips, ordering the Russian to keep his voice down. He handed me several envelopes and whispered that it was post which had come for me still before Thaw, redirected to Krupp – Zeytsoff had kept it stashed away to the very end; he'd removed several boxes of books and company documents from the collapsed tower, now he remembered that there were also these letters. I thanked him heartily. I gave him the list; he cast an eye over it, narrowing his eyelids. He promised to bring me a naphtha lamp straightaway. He read through the list once more. I grabbed him by the arm and told him I was launching a new firm together with Prime Minister Pocięgło – would he like to work for me? And here he surprised me, for I'd been sure that he would rejoice effusively – but he hesitated, bit his lip and avoided my eyes before I trapped him in friendly confidences. What of it, Summer, I thought; he's no longer the same man. But Zeytsoff reflected for a moment, said he'd be pleased to, bowed and went out.

I tore open the first envelope. A prosecutor's summons from five years ago. Well yes, thanks to damned Wólka, I had taken part in an assassination attempt on the life of the governor general. Under the Romanoff Empire authorities, I am wanted as a state criminal with a stamped-and-sealed death sentence. No doubt to the end of my days, I shan't be free to leave the boundaries of the United Free States of Siberia. Maybe sent by Pocięgło on a diplomatic mission with immunity from arrest...

There were half a dozen more such tchinovnik letters; I threw them all out. Then I opened an envelope franked in a post office of the British Crown. The letter with no return address had wended its way to Baikal via Hong Kong and Vladivostock. I tilted it towards the bright stars of Asia.

29th October 1928
Fortaleza da Guia,
Cidade do Santo Nome de Deus de Macau

Benedykt, my friend,

Ingratitude is worse than theft, and time is a rushing torrent – I am writing to make a truce with an angry conscience. Yesterday I visited an old Chinaman, who read me divinations from the I Ching. When I last slept, I dreamed the very same. I see it in the sea and in the clouds and in the glintzen in my laboratory: that you are not amongst the living. But I am unable to reconcile myself to yet another wrong. You won't forgive me, nor give your consent. But write I must.

I am not a soulless man with his eye fixed solely on numbers and machines, as Christine often calls me resentfully, whilst you too, I imagine, could have retained a similar image in your heart. For we look differently at others from how we look at ourselves. Glimpsing in someone else's body, under someone else's name, the deeds, words, feelings of which we ourselves are no less guilty, we sometimes give an entirely contrary verdict; and not out of some rankling hypocrisy, but in sincere conviction of the truth. I am not saying that you would have behaved in the same way in my place (although – in all truth, you would have behaved in the same way). I mention it only so that you might see clearly now what motivates me. This letter is not an explanation; it is merely an instruction leading to explanation: look into yourself, and you will understand. Had we exchanged souls – would anyone have known the difference?

Only in later life do we learn what befell us in our youth. I had a brother, a hundred times more talented than I, who died still as a teenager, having fallen fatally from a horse. I often used to wonder whether I might have thrown myself with equal passion onto a different career path, directing all my energies into family life, for example, and happiness amongst people, into raising children and love for a woman. However, what distinguishes us – you and me and others like us – is a particular sensitivity to Truth, and to its highest kind, which does not come from examining inner spirituality or examining social life – we are not poets, judges, politicians, doctors – but from the deepest order of reality – we are mathematicians, physicists, chemists, discoverers of the mysteries of being and inventors of methods for exploiting the miraculous nature of the world. Is it possible to turn one's back on such Truth? Who amongst the seeing shall gouge out his eyes of his own free will, because he happens to live amid a million blind men? Thus, Plato wrote of us. These shadows – they are glintzen; this light – it is the unlicht.

It pleased God to carry out an experiment on the world entitled Nikola Tesla; the experiment is drawing to a close. There is a great thrill in the flesh when a storm gathers and the rumble swells in layers of the atmosphere; for a lightning strike is a finale infinitely short. Up until this moment, I was always convinced that the thunderclap had still to strike, that the real culmination was still ahead of me – but now I already see the shape of the lightning flash and hear a pre-echo of the thunderclap from which the earth shall tremble. Many of my previous enterprises I was not allowed to bring to completion, people or circumstances stood in my way; many I myself abandoned in the pursuit of more magnificent challenges; whilst those that succeeded were either scrupulously forgotten or ascribed to other men. But this one I shall not lose: it shall be I who smashes the Ice.

I will feel it in my heart with the first stroke of the machine: for in this manner, I will certainly also kill your Father. You would have done the same. Tell me: why? I am listening.

A full moon is gazing down on me through the palm trees and a grille in the ancient wall, shining from the west in the constellation of Aries. The Portuguese have put a guard on me. Below, in the port, a Royal Navy cutter awaits me. The tsar's people are negotiating with Lord Curzon's people. J.P. Morgan choked in the end on his own greed and gave up the ghost; now his son, having taken over the whole fortune, is repairing the sins of the father, paying attention above all to the interests of his steel concerns. So, I am writing this letter to you, since tomorrow at dawn I am to sail to them and say 'yes'. You won't read this, but I have to write and send it, before I break my word. From the very beginning, you wore that same badge of angry desperation as my nephew who insisted on becoming a boxer; I advised him against it, but he did not listen. He perished in the ring.

I pray that God may unite and reconcile you at least after death with your Father.

Nikol

Was it not worth replying? He'll find out anyway from Porfiry that I'm alive, but it would be only proper to send a heartfelt word. At once, however, I thought of my firm. The coldiron production technology was to benefit after all from Nikola Tesla's invention. Obviously, the United Free States of Siberia were under no obligation to respect foreign patents. All the same…

I tore open the next envelope. Bronek had written from Peru. He had received my letter but clearly replied only after some underground rag had landed in his hands, where I was mentioned as a political murderer wanted by the Empire. My brother's letter was a bizarre mixture of freshly ignited solicitude, bitter pangs of conscience and political invective. How could I have been so stupid! I won't help father by unleashing bloody plots against top-ranking tsarist tchinovniks! He must have anticipated, however, that his letter would pass through the hands of agents of the Third Department. Finally, he mentioned his family happiness (he had taken a wife from a Catholic family of German merchants who'd settled in Peru a century ago; now he's lecturing on the principles of modern architecture at the Universidad Nacional de San Agustín de Arequipa, in the White City at the feet of the White Volcano) and stretched out his hand in faint-hearted invitation. *Should the winds of Fortune ever blow you in this direction.*

Was it not worth replying? Eh, he'd sooner read it in the papers.

The last envelope was the largest; it had been bent, broken, rolled up many times, its dimensions were so awkward. This one I'd saved at the bottom of the bundle, for I'd noticed at once the name of Jelena Muklanowicz. In the meantime, the Chinaman brought a hooded naphtha lamp. I placed it on the floor and tied it with twine to the window. I sat down beside it, crossing my legs, and opened the envelope.

There was no letter inside, only a dozen or so sheets of art-paper with Jelena's pencil sketches. Mainly icy landscapes viewed from the height of the Milky Pass. I recognised the northern and southern slopes; the stream and ruins of Martsyn's hermitage obviously remained invisible under ice and snow. Below the windows, gleissen roamed across the frozen taiga. One drawing portrayed the sanatorium building neath downy caps and icicle-crowns, with shadows of human silhouettes in the windows. In another, an indistinct misshapen figure was ploughing through snowdrifts towards the line of frozen taiga; a gale lashed through the sketch in oblique strokes. (Everything was crumpled, wrinkled, faded.) Next sheet of paper: a black box in the sky. Next: ladies and gentlemen in evening dress with gloomy lifeless expressions seated at a long table. Next: a frozen man. Next: an empty black window. Next: a face in a frame.

I brought the lamp closer still. It was Jelena, she had drawn her self-portrait from her reflection in a tall oval mirror. Black hair loose to her shoulders, slender face, eyes morbidly large and disturbingly conspicuous neath brows distinctly charcoaled – these eyebrows were charcoaled. Around her neck, she had the same velvet choker with its ruby. On the left-hand side hovered some shapeless form – a fragment of someone else's silhouette? a piece of furniture? a shadow in the mirror? As if someone were looking over Jelena's shoulder, a second someone, or a third – Jelena painting alongside the Jelena reflected in the mirror; painters, after all, don't usually portray themselves as they actually see themselves, that is painting a picture in which they are painting a picture, in which they are painting a picture, in which… Hence it was a self-self-portrait; a self-portrait in quotation marks; a picture of truth in the Teitelbaum version. Miss Muklanowicz was staring directly into the pier glass, extending her right arm beyond the edge of the paper in an enigmatic gesture – pointing? summoning? repelling? She wasn't even looking there. What did it mean? I turned the sketch over this way and that, laid it on the floor, looked at it from above. And yet she could draw! Maybe it was a bit too expressive, executed too quickly and violently – she hadn't erased the bad lines but had corrected them with scores, hundreds of further hurried strokes – yet she had managed to capture the image and atmosphere of the picture. I scratched my blind eye. That arm raised to the side, out of sight, out of frame… Then I remembered. *Put out the light.* And the movement of her arm in the semi-dark compartment of the Trans-Siberian Express. Jelena Muklanowicz more real than Jelena Muklanowicz – it was her.

With whom had she duelled over truth and lies in the Ice Sanatorium? Whose blood had she tasted on her warm little tongue? To whom was she telling tales before she froze forever?

Smeared, bent, blurred. The past exists not – instead I have this drawing, a material object present in the now. I coughed. She wasn't smiling at all, lips compressed, nose slightly upturned. Blouse trimmed with lace on the high bodice… and something else at the edge. Not lace. Smeared, blurred. I worked it out letter by letter. A signature? No.

La Menzogna

'La Menzogna,' I said out loud, and Engineer Iertheim turned over in his sleep onto his other side. Below the tower a dog was barking, Russians were hurling verbal abuse at each other. In the flame of the lamp, the gnus sizzled. 'La Menzogna.'

Like water, like a wave, like froth.

In the afternoon of the day after next, the Free-Staters returned from Irkutsk. They did not bring Abraham Fishenstein. The Jew sat barricaded with armed men outside the city; it would have resulted in heavy shooting, had the prime minister issued orders to take the banker by force. In a sense it was understandable he wasn't keen to abandon a safe refuge for the sake of an obscure invitation from a political force hostile to the forces currently in control in Irkutsk. We arranged that I should write a letter to Fishenstein with a more detailed proposal, though without of course betraying any company secrets. The Free-Staters had brought with them Fishenstein's right-hand man, who was to hand him the letter.

Apart from him, they had found two skilled coldmill workers as well as a clerk who'd worked here in Zimny Nikolayevsk before the Thaw in the countinghouse of Belkoff-Zhiltsoff; all three accepted the work offer without hesitation. We lived in times when everyone was in fact unemployed. It was enough to promise protection, a roof over the head and hot meals; money was already a luxury.

Well, and the Free-Staters had also found Sasha Pavlitch.

As soon as I saw his name ticked off on the list, I had him brought to me.

He entered slightly stooping, squinting timidly behind his pince-nez (I was standing in front of the window, in the sunlight). He had lost weight since his days in Tesla's laboratory, shedding the last of his youthful softness. Beard-growth the colour of light ash covered his pockmarked phiz, which also worked to his advantage. Apart from that, however – the same Pavlitch.

Naturally, he did not recognise me.

'Sasha, rat doctor, it's me, Benedykt!'

He tottered over, removed the pince-nez, blinked, put back the pince-nez.

I crossed into shadow, opened wide my arms.

'Me!'

Only then did he burst into laughter.

'Alive!'

'Yes, alive!'

He fell into my embrace.

Immediately, however, he had to check again that he saw aright – he took a step back and stared goggle-eyed.

'Alive!'

'Alive!'

'Alive!'

'Alive!'

And so on; we tossed between us the word and our laughter, winding each other up in joy till we ran out of breath.

'Ooph, I don't believe it.'

'Yes, it's me, me, me.'

'But when those thugs with rifles came knocking at the door and started inquiring who worked in the Observatory, well, then I thought to myself: end of a beautiful life, bullet in the brain.'

'Sorry I jotted down their orders in such haste. But they didn't take by force, did they?'

'When a war mob comes for you, you don't wait till they directly threaten, you go quickly of your own accord. Or perhaps you don't know what it's like today? He who rules is the one with a Nagant in his hand.'

'There is no law.'

'There is no real authority.' He wiped his pince-nez again. 'Which means I'm now working – where? You have some business here with the Free-Staters?'

'Well yes, unless you wish otherwise. Wait, I'll tell you. I stashed away a little...'

Zeytsoff, local king of revolutionary plunder, had managed in the meantime to find me several pieces of Biedermeier furniture, at first glance entirely undamaged: an elegant small desk, chairs with rubber feet, an office cupboard, which we placed behind the bookcase fastening them to the slanting wall one behind the other, and also a light table. I strapped the table to the right-hand window; I could now eat with a view onto the sunlit ruins of melted industry. Zeytsoff had also brought me armfuls of papers left by the coldiron companies; I already had full shelves and six boxes to choose from. My desk and table were strewn with dried-out soaked documents.

I swept them onto the floor.

'A bottle, if please you.'

'To the miraculous resurrection!'

'Never was a truer word spoken!'

'Here's to!'

'Uh. And to, ahem, the success of my Company!'

'So now your guiding light is Mammon, eh?'

I raised my glass to the lopsided ceiling.

'The aim of money, dear Sasha, is not to have to earn money.'

We sat in a window facing the sky.

'In Irkutsk, they trade family jewels for a loaf of bread,' Pavlitch sighed.

'Fear not, by my side you too shall grow fat.'

'For what exactly would I be of use?'

'For what you're best qualified at: cases of life raised from ice. You shall be, take note, Director of the Department for War against the Apocalypse.' I refilled his glass. 'You shall realise Nikolay Fyodoroff's project to resurrect mankind. Or at least you'll begin its realisation. Mm-hmm?'

Sasha clung more firmly to the window casing.

'For the love of God, what sort of crazy enterprise are you launching?!' I told him.

Over the next bottle (Cossack sweetcorn vodka that reeked of burning), by which time he'd let both boots slip into the abyss and stowed away the pince-nez that kept slipping from his sweaty nose, Sasha became emotional and loud in his pity for me – whatever had happened to me, what terrible misfortunes had I experienced, what sufferings in body and soul, for I look as if I'd been broken on a wheel and dragged neath the scythes of Death, for such raven shadows of magisterial gloom hang over me – what's past won't return – youth, naivety, innocent eagerness – you poor wretch, Venyedikt, oy, poor wretch!'

It sufficed, however, to recount the meeting with father.

'And so, you descended in the flesh onto the Ways of the Mammoths!' He almost sprang towards me. 'What's it like down there? Huh? What did you see in the end?' He burped and clutched at his belly. 'Well, what does it feel like?'

'I often used to dream of descending to the Ways, yes.' I swung my leg back and hung it again outside. 'But it seems to me I only descended once for real.'

'And?'

'There is no "and". Man cannot live on the Ways of the Mammoths.' He winced sourly.

I waved my arms about incoherently.

'How do you describe ultimate truth, order compared to which no more perfect orderliness can exist? You say two words – and you've already destroyed it, since the second word is different from the first and so a change has taken place, and therefore – deviation from Truth!

'But in the gleissen world – not here on Earth where gleissen too are subject to partial Thaw and move about, transform, join and separate, but in the Ice below zero Kelvin – no transformation of Truth is possible there. All that is possible is the persistence of pure ideas.'

'In other words, what?'

I straightened my index finger. Sasha gawped at it, knitting his flaxen brows. The silence grew protracted. I stirred not.

He took a deep breath.

'This,' I said.

'What?'

Again, I said nothing. Finger. Motionlessness. Monotony of mirror-like symmetry.

He seemed to comprehend.

'The Ice,' he hiccupped, 'L-l-lyod.'

I raised the empty bottle to the Sun; dazzling sunshine scrambled over the thick glass. I held this telescope to my eye. It is possible, it is possible, to get drunk on light.

'The cold, Sasha, creeps into you like opium fever. As Pierre Schotcha used to say to me – it's true, you never forget, never cease to hanker. But I speak of real cold, of that gleissen-touch with which Professor Kryspin used to cure his patients and in which Martsynians experienced God. Why do hiberniks expressly expose themselves to cold? Eh? After all, it hurts, it always hurts everyone. But at the same time, it tugs with such mighty force – from the bones, from the guts, with animal instinct, with the longing written into the very nature of reality, like hunger or bodily craving – towards the Ice. It's man's first tropism, Sasha.'

'The Frost?'

'Order. Perfect orderliness. Truth!'

I flung the bottle at the Sun. It described a short arc and plunged below, missing the bottom edge of the Crooked Tower. We heard no clunk thereafter, only the curses of terrified soldiers.

'Like animals,' I groaned. 'We don't understand, don't even realise – and yet we cling to it; it tugs at us, lures us constantly. The Ice! The Ice! Everywhere, always, in every form and every guise, in every case and on every scale: in the fine arts, in architecture, in music, but also in politics, in religion, in legal, spiritual and doctrinal systems, as well as in the natural sciences, especially in physics and deductive reasoning – for a good mathematician will glimpse beauty and order in an equation before he glimpses Truth. Since they are the same things, Sasha, the very same things. And your work too: what did Nikolay Fyodoroff long for? Reversal of the laws of decomposition, retreat from this confusion, this oblivion in matter, which we call death.'

Pavlitch saluted briskly.

'Long live the Brotherhood of War on Entropy!'

I climbed down from the window to fetch the next bottle.

'But perhaps you'd like a bite to eat?'

Sasha glanced at his belly-button.

'Wouldn't say no, wouldn't say no.'

'I'll summon the Chinamen.'

Over sinewy duck with rice and raw herbs, I related the details of my meeting with the pater. Things I'd not told to anyone I divulged to Sasha Pavlitch. Although I didn't have to. But it began to flow – like blood gushing from a torn artery, sentence after sentence of thick, curdling sincerity.

The lines of our gazes trembled above the tilted tabletop. Sasha would flee and timidly return, whilst I thrust myself insolently into his eyes; let him say yea or yea, and I'd recognise at once the Truth.

'Mmmm,' for a long time he chewed the tough meat and his tough thoughts, 'mmm, but in the end – you succeeded, did you not? I mean, in unfreezing him.'

'I don't know.' I picked between my buckled teeth with a bone. 'It's hard to resist the idea that father knew everything. Just as he knew where to come out and meet me, so too he was aware of what was afoot in Irkutsk politics and in the emperor's plans and in Tesla's. He understood.' I spat into a napkin. 'Gleissen... I don't know if we can say that they understand anything, that they're capable of understanding. Look: if he hadn't been demurched first, perhaps my father wouldn't have allowed Thaw to happen at all, shifting the Ice and History accordingly. If indeed he really had such power of persuasion or control or scientific manipulation over the icers.

'But then again, I don't believe that the Kotarbiński pump, packed at the last minute for me by Nikola into a travelling stove, could have demurched father so effectively: it was a flow-generator made for people, not for mighty abassylar. Mm-hmm?'

'But – you stabbed him in the heart.'

I chuckled.

'He probably didn't even feel it.'

Sasha raised sad eyes. I shrugged my shoulders.

He pushed aside his plate, reached for the carafe of fruit liqueur, sniffed it. I offered him tobacco, we rolled cigarettes. I swung back and forth on the back legs of my chair.

'I often wonder... There, then, under the Ice, according to the Mathematics of Character... It could not have gone otherwise. He must have known.'

We smoked in silence.

Sasha pissed into a chamber pot and sat down again in the window. I sprawled on the chaise longue below, legs hooked over the armrests. Spun across the room, the threads of our gazes now hung thin and flabby between us like a summer cobweb.

A messenger glanced in, urgently reminding me about the letter to Fishenstein; I told him to return after dusk.

From on high, Sasha was observing the refugees as they bustled around the city like ants. Dangling his bare legs, he reminisced about Tchingis Shtchekelnikoff.

'Let's hope he won't surprise Saint Peter in some dark alley.' Pavlitch smirked in his boyish melancholic way. 'The few times I saw him, I was always terrified I'd somehow offended him and he'd rush at me with his fists.'

'He was a bad man.'

'But that they should hack him to pieces so…'

'What can even the greatest manslayer do against those unwilling to die?'

Sasha gave a snort, shook his head.

'Goylems? Corpses patched together?'

I assumed a serious expression.

'It's a type of black-biological engineering, a certain play on entropy, or so I believe.' I blew smoke up to the ceiling. 'Do you remember how, when we were drunk, we smashed the glass under the Small Murch Hammer? Or perhaps it has frozen differently for you? Mm-hmm? Well, and the story of Tesla's resurrection? Before they become the subject of science, such things form the gist of superstitions. The Ways of the Mammoths had their own pulse, tides and harmonies long before Doctor Tesla counted them, before he beat to their rhythm for the first time with his Hammer. Is it any wonder that simple-minded folk, confronted unexpectedly by such "miracles", descend into madness? An "Engineer of the Body", hah!

'Think: how did abassylians walk at all along the Ways of the Mammoths? What kind of life is possible for a human organism there in rock, in ice? I told you: none. The organism is not alive then. It flows with the blood of gleissen. Tesla was right from the very beginning: everything is a question of resonance, of the combination of frequencies. For change has to come from without: no one has ever extricated himself spontaneously from non-being. Waves, Sasha, flow and ebb tides, fre-quen-cies. Cr-cr-crackles… Affix your ear – no, some kind of special stethoscope – no, a radio receiver. Connect a radio receiver to the Ways of the Mammoths – and you will hear this unimaginably complex symphony of subtle whispers of teslectricity, just as in a Siberian radio at night you hear the slightest atmospheric crackle on the far side of the globe – cr-cr-crackles. Whilst every black whisper – is a gleiss freezing in tides of living helium; and every crackle – an abassylian that exists and exists not, bounced along the Ways from entropy to negentropy and back again.

'Understand now why the shamans beat their drums? Why they constantly beat, beat, beat their drums?

'Yes, Sasha, we are waves on the surface of the ocean, the frost pattern on the windowpane. Does someone exist, or does it only seem to him that he exists… In the Ice, he is an indestructible, eternally persisting being – like number, a mathematical theorem or syllogism. But is number alive? Does it change from second to second? Whilst every individual life is this: change, negation of one's own self from a moment ago, meaning a Lie. Believe me: a man on the Ways of the Mammoths lives not. He returns to life afterwards. Is put together again like broken glass.' I belched. 'And no doubt splinters sometimes get mixed up in the process.'

'You too are mixed up?'

This amused Sasha immensely. He scoffed for a long while; it passed off, but then he glanced down at me from above and again collapsed in gurgling cackles.

I clapped my hands.

'Well, that's enough, that's enough.'

He calmed down.

'A considerably simpler explanation,' he said, striving to assume the serious scientific tone and elevated mien of the scholarly biologist, 'is that instead of truth, you remember your hallucinations caused by hypothermia, by hunger, by despair. Frostridden people, pulled after a long time from the ice, retrieved from the threshold of cryonic death – tell all kinds of strange mystical tales. Also, there on the street in Irkutsk – you couldn't really have *touched* a gleiss; you would certainly have not lived. And as for remembering bizarre and extraordinary wonders… I have read many such accounts. And not just those of Martsynians, but significantly earlier ones. And you also claim that the Tunguses poisoned you on your journey with their soporific fumes. Therefore – how d'you put it? – as such has your past frozen.'

I twirled my hand and cigarette above my eye; the smoke wound itself into a beautiful coiling streamer.

'I was only sleeping.'

We fell silent. Gossamer threads of hesitant airy glances hung suspended between us in the evening light. At this time of day, the gnus, bred in the flooded crater, would rise and go crazy in search of warm nourishment. Sasha kept it vigorously at bay; but I was swatting insects on my skin every few minutes. A man also accustoms himself to the odour of his own blood, to this rotten perfume of life.

'Ah! You've not told me how it was with you. Weren't you supposed to return to Tomsk?'

'Eeee, everything broke off after Schultz-Zimovy's secession. Tomsk and the University of Tomsk were held already by the tsar, the border went along the Ob river. Moreover, Professor Yurkat stood by the count… After Doctor Tesla's flight, Schultz locked us in the Box for two months.'

'Because you allegedly helped Pocięgło?'

'That is, Schultz didn't throw us into prison. He shut us in rooms in the east wing. Maybe not he but his commissioner for emergency assignments, what's his name –'

'Uriah. But you were already under arrest in the Observatory, no?'

'It was like this.' Sasha turned to face me in the window casing, leaning down into the room. 'Immediately after you escaped the police investigation, Prince Blutsky left Irkutsk. We heard he was mustering the tsarist forces in Aleksandrovsk. Apparently, secret talks were going on via Pobedonostseff: between the prince, the count, the emperor and Sibirkhozheto. There was shooting in the unlicht outside the Observatory; the governor general's Cossacks protected us from a whole army of vagabonds. Blind fear overcame us all. Till one night Mr Pocięgło appears disguised as an ispravnik with a gubernatorial permit in his hand, and says the count has an order already prepared on his desk to banish Doctor Tesla. But, you understand, such banishment so that afterwards no one would even find his remains.'

'Well, it was only a question of time. Sibirkhozheto surely set the conditions: no Thaw and no blackmail by Thaw.'

'Prince Blutsky was to march with his Cossacks on Irkutsk, Mr Pocięgło said it was precisely to seize Tesla; rumours of imminent attack were circulating every day in the city. And then everything turned on its head: Nikola escaped, whilst Pobedonostseff came out in open support of a secessional alliance with the count; they signed a guarantee on the extraterritoriality of the Transsib, the coldindustrialists submitted a peace petition to His Most Serene Majesty with a contribution of ten million roubles, and Prince Blutsky withdrew to the Ob.' Sasha waved his hand, shooing away a blackfly; perhaps it was a gesture of total disorientation. 'Do you understand anything at all of this?'

'History, dear boy, History. Were the Ice still holding fast, I would calculate this and that – but now, after Thaw, seven versions of every fact are born every hour, none true, none false.'

'Who is it?'

'Mm-hmm?'

Turning around in the window frame, Sasha pointed with his cigarette to the west wall. In a tasteful mount, once occupied by an exploitation certificate issued by the Mining Directorate to a now defunct company, I had hung the black-and-white self-portrait of Jelena Muklanowicz.

'True, you didn't know her.'

'Ah, heartache!'

But here too, I was untouched by any shame.

'Yes.' I flicked ash into a coldiron tray. 'Poorly frozen memories.' Covering my face with my hand, I looked at the picture through the gap left by a missing finger. 'If only for this one thing, it's worth fighting for the Ice.'

'For what thing?'

'For this logical certainty of feelings. I had it in my sights from the beginning. After all, it's one of the fundamentals of the Mathematics of Character, perhaps the most important.'

Sasha shuffled up to the wall, brushing his long shadow over the boxes and furniture, put his nose to the picture and muttered something indistinct with the cigarette still between his lips.

'What?'

'But is it not a drawing sketched from imagination?' He drew his nail over crinkles in the paper.

'Why?'

'Such a living devushka exists not, *n'est-ce pas*?'

Meanwhile, I had slunk into a warm doze on the chaise longue.

'What's the difference, Sasha, we have Thaw anyway... And yet we two – think... We don't know each other very well, no... For even before you meet a person... Under the Ice... Friend, enemy, love, hatred – before you even saw a person, before they existed to your senses... Already Truth! Therefore, what's the difference...? Mathematics is everything...' I fell asleep.

The official inaugural meeting of the History Industry Company Gierosławski, Pocięgło and Fishenstein took place six days later, at noon sharp, on the sunlit mirror of the roof of the Crooked Tower.

Porfiry raised the first toast – not as the partnership's majority shareholder (I was the majority shareholder), but as Prime Minister of the United Free States of Siberia. He stood on his own legs for the occasion, supporting himself with his left hand on a cane. Spoke of the radiant future of the UFSS, of the mighty potential of Siberia's exceptional natural resources, of the right of Siberia's indigenous peoples to benefit from their God-given advantages in any form and any field of activity. We have the twentieth century, he said, Great Britain and Germany draw their strength not from exploiting the peasant, but from the work of their industrialists, from the wealth of their national syndicates. Therefore, the prime minister is setting an example by creating an economic infrastructure for the Free States of Siberia, by founding the History Industry Company GBF!

Applause. I also stood up. The Sun was shining fiercely beneath storm clouds. I raised my goblet full of light.

'For our Company's success will be inseparably linked to the political success of the Siberian state project – yes, exactly! The Company won't survive without the States and the States won't last without the Company! In celebrating one, we celebrate the other! We shall produce coldiron to sell to anyone, but History we shall sell to no one. Here is our national industry which we shall not surrender: in surrendering History, we would be surrendering our independence, for who amongst our neighbours, what other great power will allow us to survive here on the world map? Of all precious commodities, it is the most strictly regulated: History.

'And yet, dear friends, since there exist objective mechanisms of History as well as laws governing the sequence of historical events just as certain and calculable as the laws of chemistry, physics and biology, and these we already exploit for our own ends and convenience, for man controls Nature and not Nature man – since there exist such laws of History, it was only a matter of time before man would subordinate History to himself and devise technologies for steering historical events towards his own comfort and benefit.

'Who was first to found a business producing petroleum engines? Who first to mobilise a factory making electrical appliances? Who made fortunes on modern chemistry and machine weaving? Who milked the greatest riches from the coldiron technologies? These are as nothing beside the certain success of the first History Industry Company!'

Applause, thumping of feet, applause.

For greater pomp, I also quoted a few words of the Marquis de Condorcet from his eighteenth-century *Sketch for a Historical Picture of the Progress of the Human Spirit*: on how 'social mathematics' causes 'the truths of the moral and political sciences to become just as certain as those that comprise the system of the natural sciences,' et cetera, et cetera. Dazed and sweaty, a young journalist from the *New Siberian Gazette* was scrupulously taking notes. The prime minister had wished to come out entirely openly; well, he'd got his way.

Although throughout the entire two days of our tripartite negotiations I had sought to dissuade him, Pocięgło had resisted tooth and nail: either we come out openly before the world as a regular honest business, or he won't assist the Company with a single government soldier. I told him he's trading in pangs of conscience and exposing both the Company and his State to unnecessary risk. Porfiry, however, remained unbending.

Had he walled himself in like this in the actual negotiations, I would probably have had to make do with thirty or forty per cent. But eventually I understood that he did not want to take possession of the controlling stake in GPF.

This is how I solved the equation of Porfiry Pocięgło:

It is possible to acquire a State by force of arms, possible to build it from nothing, possible to gain it through centuries of torment, but he who buys the State from History without bloodshed, without pain, as a result of cold calculation and negotiations around a table – is not the owner of this State, but only its transitory lessee. What has been granted may be taken back. And even if there's no longer anyone to take back the State – the memory will remain in people's minds of the gracious sovereign who gave them a present; behind their backs for generations shall stand the ghost of the autocrat by whose grace they live in quasi-independence. They did not kill the tsar – the tsar allowed them to play at the State.

Having solved this equation, I signed without a word the document whereby I took possession of 50,001 of the 100,000 registered shares of the History Industry Company Gierosławski, Pocięgło and Fishenstein, on initial capital nominated in British pounds according to the honorary settlement of the shareholders. I knew: as soon as I freeze History, Pocięgło won't hesitate to kill me. Beneath the grimace on my scarred face, I concealed a twisted smile. For I knew also this: as soon as I freeze History, no one will kill me. Regicide is conceivable solely within defined cultures and defined historical formations. Besides, it's not about acting out some bloodthirsty theatre on the streets – hanging, shooting, burning, guillotining – but about guiding a people to such state of mind wherein they perform that drama naturally, of themselves, without the slightest whiff of theatricality. And then it's no longer a question of noose, guillotine, stake or firing squad – but of the idea controlling the epoch. Which is not created by any political murder; which is primal to murder and born of what is unseen, which can only take shape under the Grosshammers.

... I shall win, because I shan't be able to lose.

Throughout the negotiations, Fishenstein said the least. Whilst I banged on the table with my stick and yelled myself hoarse: 'Fifty-one! For me! On me! Mine! I! I!', the Jew merely stroked his grizzled beard and followed with his tungetitum eye the sugar-frosted clouds scudding across the firmament. He came to life when we discussed the matter of Doctor Tesla's involvement. For I had openly acknowledged that my discovery was made possible only because I'd enjoyed an exceptional position between the black physicists of Zimny Nikolayevsk and Tesla's Laboratory, and was conversant with the theories of both camps; I even admitted carrying out experiments on Tesla's patented equipment. Fishenstein demanded that Tesla should be given access to the profits. He was anxious moreover about the inventor's participation in the work against the Apocalypse. Allegedly, Nikola was carrying out resurrectionary experiments also in Macau, under the Great Hammer. Director Khavroff, who had fled immediately at the start of the Thaw and was travelling in countries of the Orient, had sent information that British newspapers in Hong Kong were writing about a peculiar 'corpselike plague' afflicting Macau. In turn, Porfiry, out of regard for Christine, wished to say no word against Tesla. The Hammer, however, prevailed: Tesla remained bound by his contract to destroy the Ice, yet GPF's first task must be to erect Hammers cancelling out the destructive resonances of the teslectric field induced by Tesla – it would be difficult to invite a man to join a project designed to foil the greatest triumph of his life. Besides, I myself had certain qualms. Healthy competition and the technological race, these Nikola would surely understand, but stealing ideas…? I was ready to restore before the world all honours due to the old man; as to financial compensation – we could, for example, buy up the patents for Tesla's fuel-less engines; here the electrical super-conductivity of coldiron might create new industrial opportunities. We would acquire the rights to them in exchange for Tesla's having a per-centage of the profits; even so we would still make money. Fishenstein nodded. As long as he was guaranteed realisation of Fyodoroff's resur-rection plan, he wasn't going to risk fierce bargaining over any other matter.

He wasn't keen either on delivering toasts. When the assembled guests stamped their feet and applauded him from the other side of the table, he rose heavily, muttered a few words of optimism in his strong accent and then flopped back into his chair. He did not rise from it again until the end of the rooftop celebration – except for the moment when a one-armed vagabond, reinvented by Editor Wólka-Wólkiewicz as the *Gazette*'s photographer, took it upon himself to arrange a commemorative picture. Zeytsoff held up a sail to screen us from the wind and sun. We stood as a troika for the occasion at the upper edge of the roof whilst the crippled photographer, bent over his camera, shouted directions: a little to the left, to the right, smile, gentlemen, smile!

It seemed to me at the time as if I were the only one of the Company owners genuinely delighted at its birth.

Porfiry spent the ensuing hours in lively discussions with the New Narodniks; Leninist and Trotskyist deputies had also attended the re-ception, as had someone with news from Harbin (rumours had reached us that Emperor Puyi wished to make use of the Transsib for a tac-tical transfer of his army beyond the rebel front). Towards evening, Engineer Iertheim appeared with a man whom he introduced as a former manager of the Holey Palace; the Dutchman had found him by the road to Usolye selling sachets of drinking water. The manager, once an eminent metallurgist, stood before me in stinking rags, clutching his cap in trembling hands, ravaged by poverty and ill fortune like an aged Gypsy; a hundred parched furrows twitched on his visage at the one fearful thought. Of course, I said, we'll take him; have someone bring him soap and garments. I was still sitting then with Fishenstein at the table – I grabbed the nearest lacquered tray of Chinese delicacies and handed it to the poor fellow. Tears welled in his eyes as he dribbled involuntarily; not the prettiest of sights. I gazed at him with a sunny smile. He bowed. And went away already more upright, lighter for not having Shame weigh so heavily on his back.

'The art of almsgiving,' I said to Fishenstein, 'depends on a capacity for absolute self-centredness. Why sit there so gloomy, as if the spirit had been wrung out of you?'

Fishenstein sighed heavily, his thick shoulders hunched neath the shiny ceremonial gabardine, narrowing the lids over his white-and-black eye.

'Yes, indeed, Mr Gierosławski is powerful, I am pleased, pleased, except that I'm always thinking stupidly to myself as well: you are pleased, Fishenstein, but were you not Fishenstein, but some other Jew, equally pious and conversant with the Word of God, would you then be so pleased, eh? And I'm already less pleased, because what pleases only Fishenstein pleases only Fishenstein, but that which would gladden every Jew on earth, bah, what am I saying! – which would gladden every person – only this thing would surely gladden the Lord. If you do something against your neighbour – you bring him no joy, so you bring no joy to the Lord either. But to do something that would be kind to every person born of man and woman... Have you ever done such a thing? Eh?'

'Our History Industry Company,' I said, mechanically twirling my stick, 'I sincerely believe will bring good to the whole of humanity. That is, History calculated by me will be civilised History, tamed, comfortable and benign. For up till now, we've been living in the wild, Fishenstein, living in the wild.'

The Jew shook his massive head, as the jewel of the night flashed neath his grizzled mane worthy of Isaiah or Moses.

'Ay, for you see, Mr Gierosławski, all wisdom comes from God. But knowledge – not all is from Him. The tree of the knowledge of good and evil, of which our first Parents partook, God did not say was dangerous because it bears falsehood in its fruit, but because it bears truth. Man strives after wisdom, which always proves healthy to his soul, but the man who strives after knowledge – knows not whether he's headed for heaven or hell. Any activity which changes the image of the world and man in the world, propelling him towards new cognizance – is a great gamble for his soul. Is it wise, therefore, for a pious Jew to sacrifice his life in order to pluck the next fruit off the tree of knowledge? It is not wise. Not wise.

'And yet the world changes also without us, and despite us; one way or another man changes; we ourselves, living in the world and amongst people, change. Thirty years ago – who thought about ice metals, who designed coldiron engines, who dreamed of gleissen and tungetitum and unlicht? On an earth ruled by the Ice our grandchildren will live differently. We live differently from our forefathers. Can we stand against History as a work of Evil and renounce everything that comes from dangerous knowledge? Undoubtedly, those farthest from error are the shepherds who spend their lives amongst sheep in pure pastures green, where nothing changes from generation to generation, not even the cut of their raiment.

'History, however, passes them by; History happens outside of them. Who of the Martsynians were right: those who maintained that History flows according to God's idea only under the truth of the Ice, or those who said that the Ice stopped History in its natural tracks? Because now, I'm thinking to myself in my stupidity, there is no longer any History at all. That this is the end, that History has broken off, been smashed to pieces, come crashing down. The Messiah won't come to his chosen people, nor will the dead arise in the shape of your Revelation. The last days have already been – now we have what comes after the end of time, that is, not the reign of the History of God, but the reign of the History of Man. *Now we are manufacturing History.* The History Industry Company Gierosławski, Pocięgło and Fishenstein! And if we pluck also this fruit of knowledge, then all the dead shall rise amongst the living – not in order to fulfil the Fyodorovian vision of the Christists, but just because man has dreamt it up. Will it be wise? Will it be good? It will be possible – and therefore necessary, Mr Gierosławski.' He slurped his cold tea. 'And you, sir, shall calculate it for me.'

'I shall calculate it for you.'

Rain began to spit and we all moved downstairs, inside the tower. In my room, Sasha Pavlitch had wound up the screechy gramophone (Zeytsoff's latest prize loot). We had records of German arias and military marches, and also one of Russian folk songs; the latter played non-stop. As I descended, some people were already dancing by the light of the naphtha lamp and candles spaced at intervals on the sloping furniture. I recognised one of our coldmill foremen; the women were volunteers attached to the UFSS government or wives of Free-Staters. At first, I wanted to drive them out but was in too good a mood and so turned a blind eye. In the adjacent room, a game of cards was underway. I peeked in there with a glass in my hand; and immediately withdrew. The rain was falling more heavily and as I retreated to the far end of the corridor, the steely jangle of drops battering the tower almost stifled the lively folk melody. In the shadows, a molodyets in dishevelled uniform was locked in embrace with a well-endowed devushka of Mongolian features, both panting loudly. The drumming of the rain drowned my footsteps; they did not hear me approach. I stood and watched, sipping the harsh alcohol. The ghost of the night of the governor's ball perched on my shoulder and fuddled my eye: body plus body plus body plus body... *usque ad nauseam.* A plump little hand was rummaging in the man's unbuttoned breeches. I rattled the murchometer against the wall and bawled at them that they were making an obscene spectacle. They skedaddled, blushing with shame.

I returned to my room. The foreman had vanished somewhere, new revellers had appeared; I knew no one. I set aside the empty glass on a box of geological maps, and flung my stick neath the chaise longue. Work, after all, awaited me, piles of papers to look through, decisions to make; the Black Oasis had to be occupied, a cordon demarcated around the Last Isotherm, transport extended to the main tungetitum deposits. Pocięgło's advisers were already quarrelling amongst themselves: whether to lay a railway line or rely on the water courses; and there'd be a problem too with conveyance of the transmutation machines, industrial Unlicht Bombs and largescale teslectrical inductors for the Grosshammers. Via Vladivostock and the Transsib to Baikal? There was a second proposal: since Porfiry had such a good arrangement with Harriman, best would be to purchase the heavy equipment through the mediation of Harriman's agents in America, with money from Fishenstein's local banks, and supply it at once via Tchukotka and the Alaskan Tunnel. This would be quickest and safest, on condition however that the turmoil of war dies down and Harriman finally opens the tunnel for use and the Northern Line is built from Nikolayevsk-on-Amur. Meanwhile, I had to play my cards in such a way that Harriman's men would be unable to deduce to the very end with total certainty, from specifications in the orders, the essence of the 'warm' coldmill process.

... Everything was still fluid, not yet completely frozen, written out as hypothetical tasks and rainbow possibilities. Each variant required a scrupulous plan; documents proliferated of their own accord; no wonder tchinovniks and bureaucrats flourish in Summer. Boxes of maps, boxes of documents calligraphed in pale ink... Meanwhile my head was roaring, as the Free-Staters caroused around me to the screeching music.

My hands were empty. I closed my eyes. The song began anew. Someone jostled me. A scent of invigorating fresh moisture pervaded the air. I walked up to the window neath the evening twilight. As they dance on the sloping floor, they're all naturally dragged downwards; here, free space is left. Rain quickly drenched my jacket and shirt. I drew my hand across my face. Any excitement and all my good humour were utterly washed away.

Pavlitch returned.

'Did you have to install that howling machine in my room?' I muttered grouchily.

'Mademoiselle Filipov said you like dancing.'

'I shall finally have to submit an official *démenti* in regard to this matter.'

Pavlitch was holding an elegant small chest encrusted with coloured stones. He winked at me and lifted the lid. I peeped inside. The case was full of blacktungets.

'From where…?'

'Word got out the day before yesterday. The Chinamen down below are now buying up tungetitum from people. This collection went for two chickens and ten pounds of rice.'

'And you bought it…?'

'The Chinaman's wife had contracted malaria, he was looking for quinine, knows that we have a doctor here for the prime minister. He was offering his last imperials; they're no longer going for fifteen roubles apiece but for their weight in gold. And as for the box itself, look: cornelian, nephrite, topaz. Song Dynasty! How many years ago, a thousand? Allegedly from Lord Elgin's booty from the Second Opium War, from Peking's Garden of Perfect Clarity! Oh! Now's the time for such opportunities, if anyone has goods to dispose of or at least a semblance of power, then you can acquire real treasures for almost nothing. Thaw! Everything's on the move!'

'But – malaria! We have to do something about this swamp in the Holey Palace.'

Sasha stopped beside me.

'It was here you threw him off, mm-hmm?' He pretended to look into the abyss. 'Brrr.'

'Who told you such nonsense…?'

'The lad from the *Gazette*. They went afterwards to Pocięgło to complain. Do you know what he said to them?'

'What?'

'That you'll be tried, once the courts have been set up and the law written.'

'Ah, that he entertains such a hope, I can well believe.' I thrust out my head neath the driving rain; the drops cut into my densely scarred skin. 'Not in such trivial cases as this, but you've no doubt heard what they say of a public figure: "History shall judge him". What does this mean? That it won't be people doing the judging. That there is a measure of events applicable on such a large scale that it can't be used within a timeframe of less than a century; and that events measured against this scale give an evaluation so obvious that the prejudices of the evaluators or their contraries no longer carry any weight – the measure leads to soletruth with iron logic. But – we have to wait in order to see. For operations on a scale of years, weeks, days – we lack the precise mental apparatus. No one has yet written a textbook of the Mathematics of History. They even argue over the axioms. History shall judge – but not today, not tomorrow, not this year; in Summer, it freezes so slow-ow-ly. We have been living in the muddy torrent, Sasha, living between a non-existent past and a non-existent future, on the shifting sands of Kotarbiński's half-truths. Come, feel this rain. How stuffy it is in here!'

Engineer Iertheim came staggering towards us, fighting his way between the dancers. Under his arm, he carried a portfolio. He stopped beyond the reach of the drizzle and waved the portfolio at us.

'What've you got there?'

'An historic picture!' He glanced around the room in the flickering light, around the walls painted in leaping shadows. 'Where to put...' He walked up to Jelena's self-portrait, fingered the frame. 'In the Holy Trinity, there's a woman like this who gives injections...' He took out a large photograph from the portfolio and held it against the wall. 'Yes. Yes. Mm-hmm.'

'Show us.'

We peered over his shoulder. The commemorative photograph depicted the troika of Company founders: Porfiry in elegant light-coloured suit with Free-State cockade in his lapel, leaning forward into the lens, rigidly supported on his cane, his visage rendered fiercely determined as if by this very effort; Abraham Fishenstein neath his mane of grizzled hair, beard spread across his chest like a white dicky, skull pierced clean through by a cold void in place of his tungetitum eye; myself standing in the middle, the shortest of the three: a blot of unlicht shaped like a man, arms and legs still a kind of smudgy grey, but the face – coal-black. Behind us hung an overcast sky, and beneath it the Asiatic horizon and blurry ruins of the industrial city.

In the bottom right-hand corner of the photograph was the Company's emblem: the swirling initials GPF. Pocięgło's secretaries were no doubt already designing the official rubber stamps, business cards and stationery.

'Only the date is missing,' I said.

'Twenty-eighth of June nineteen thirty, Zimny Nikolayevsk. The founding of the first History Industry Company. Benedykt Gierosławski, Porfiry Pocięgło, Abraham Fishenstein. Did I leave my tools here with you...? Wait, I'll pin it with a piece of wire. Mm-hmmm.'

'Zeytsoff will find us some old framed picture, we'll swap them over.' Sasha shook his head.

'Zeytsoff's already had more than enough for one day. I saw him with his violin case on the floor below.'

'Is he really learning the violin?'

'Eeee, not in the slightest. In one half he keeps refills of various vodkas, in the other – works of lyric poetry, sentimental verse. I came upon him like that yesterday. He sits sunning himself, opens the case, takes out the little book and a bottle, and whoosh – he takes flight!' Sasha puffed up his cheeks. 'An artist!'

I winced.

'They'll ruin that record.'

'Wait a moment, wait, we'll fix it.'

Sasha went to tinker with the turntable. I sat down in the window. Had it not been raining, I'd have lit a cigarette; I preferred to get soaked, far more pleasant. The gramophone stopped, and the dancers raised a resounding wail; Pavlitch put on an overture with drums and trumpets at which they whistled and stomped in protest; he stopped this music too. Beseeching shouts and moans began. Someone pointed a Nagant at Sasha, others seized the armed hothead around the waist and carried him out into the corridor; at once the crowd thinned, it grew brighter. I noticed a fat Buryat in Free-Stater cap and mud-covered jackboots asleep on my chaise longue. I merely sighed. Mijnheer Iertheim, rocking on widely parted legs like an old skipper at a port, mouth and beard full of wire and pins, was fixing the commemorative photograph alongside Miss Muklanowicz's drawing. A semi-naked Cossack, with hammer and plough tattooed on his chest on a triple-barred red cross, took out a mouth organ and began playing a Cossack dance. Shadows flitted over the walls and skewed ceiling. In the doorway below, shrunken and warped by some absurd trick of perspective, loomed Zeytsoff. I waved to him. Filimon Romanovitch, leaning into an upward charge as if resisting a tremendous hurricane, came ever closer in successive bursts of light projected from under shadows and between dancers; fifteen, ten, five paces from me – a figure in a lopsided box of rickety dazzle-and-dark mosaic. The higher he rose in the sick geometry, the slower and more laborious his step; but, bent double, he did not raise his head. Finally, he must have summoned all his strength, almost taking off from a semi-squatting position, monkey arms outstretched before him –

The little nephrite chest struck him in the ribs. Zeytsoff fell by the window, I leapt up just as the knife landed at my feet.

Sasha came running over, trod on Zeytsoff's hands. Choking on the pins, the Dutchman grabbed hold of his legs.

Zeytsoff lashed out and spat. His shattered spectacles slid from his nose. He was drunk, but in Zeytsoff's case, this was a circumstance much more aggravating. Having curled up snake-like, he freed his left arm and pointed a trembling finger at me.

'Him! Him!'

Pavlitch glanced inquiringly.

I shrugged my shoulders.

'That's Zeytsoff for you.' I picked up the knife, ran my thumb along the blade. Razor sharp. 'From time to time, blood rushes to his head and Filimon hurls himself at me with murderous intent; then he falls at my feet, tears his heart to shreds and begs for forgiveness.' I summoned the Free-Staters who had stopped still in their dance, stunned by the next theatrical display of frenzied violence. 'Lock him up somewhere, let him recover.'

They dragged him kicking towards the bottom of the mosaic box of drunken contours.

'Him!' Zeytsoff rattled hoarsely. 'Him!'

Until he disappeared together with them into the distorted lower corner.

I handed Sasha the little chest.

'Spasibo.'

'Mpfkh khmykh?' asked Mijnheer Iertheim.

'Who can tell? Perhaps it had to do with the traitorous editor.' I tapped the knife against my chin. 'Where did you eventually...' I glanced at Jelena's drawing. *La Menzogna*. Why was Zeytsoff able to take me by surprise in the first place, so that I failed to see the murderer in him until the last minute? *La Menzogna*.

'Spit it out!' I levelled the knife at the Dutchman.

He spat it out.

'Where did you see her?' I snarled. 'At the Holy Trinity Hospital? But look closer! Well!'

Quickly returning to his senses, the black physicist cast his eyes over Jelena's self-portrait.

'Well... maybe like her.' He blinked, examining it from close up. 'No. Not her after all. Except for that hair. And maybe the eyes... Not her, Benedykt, sir.'

I plunged the knife into the bookstand.

'Tomorrow morning I'm going to Irkutsk.'

Pavlitch bridled.

'Don't be crazy! Are you looking for trouble? He said it's not her!'

'So what?'

Sasha smashed his head in despair into the Chinese antique.

'You said yourself she's no longer alive!'

'Dead, but perhaps alive.'

'You were at her graveside!'

'Don't you see?' In one sweeping gesture, I encompassed the evening cityscape of Zimny Nikolayevsk under the rain. 'We have Thaw!'

'What of it –'

'We have Thaw!' I returned my eye to the faded sketch. Jelena was pointing with outstretched hand at something out of sight, which did not exist. There was no smile on her lips, no irony. *La Menzogna*. Lies truer than Truth. 'We have Thaw. Dead – but perhaps alive. Perhaps alive.'

Mijnheer Iertheim disentangled the last piece of wire from his beard. 'It's not her.'

'No matter.'

'He's gone mad,' groaned Pavlitch.

I leaned outside into the rain, which was growing colder and colder. Was Pocięgło right? Had I somehow *frozen* all this to myself? I hadn't planned it. And what I had planned, had not succeeded and turned my well-reasoned plans into a laughing stock. The past exists not, the future exists not. But the hoarfrost on the windowpane also plans nothing; in ice crystal there is no thought organising the surrounding structure. And yet the structure arranges itself around the crystal according to predetermined necessity – like the anti-entropic order of molecules in a cooled metal. Father, the Martsynians. Tesla, black physics, Krupp, the new coldiron technology. Piłsudski, the Ways of the Mammoths. The Fyodorovians, Fishenstein. Chronic poverty, insolent tchinovniks, the Trans-Siberian Express, the Ministry of Winter, the Kingdom of Darkness, apoliteia, Rasputin, the History Industry Company. Melted father, resurrected father. Jelena Muklanowicz. And even such trivial things as Weltz's playing cards or the ability to ballroom dance. True or false? True or false?

I let the rain wash it off me.

Before dawn, dressed already for my journey, I went down to see Zeytsoff. They had locked him up downstairs, on the first level of the building, in a corner cell without window (so he couldn't jump out). Outside the door, a Free-Stater was dozing with a Berdan rifle at his elbow. I ordered him to open and bring a lamp.

The ex-katorzhnik gradually awoke, crushed by the stony weight of his hangover. Eventually, he sat upright on the bare floor, in the lower corner, having drawn his knees up under his chin and wrapped his arms around his legs. I crouched opposite him, by the upper wall. It was enough to say nothing for a while; he himself sank into penitential mood.

He whacked his occiput against some wooden furniture, once, twice.

'Be gone!' he moaned. 'Don't look! Don't look!'

'Well, what?'

'Tphoo, Satan!'

I crossed myself slowly.

'Filimon Romanovitch, what's got into you?'

'You don't have God in your heart!'

I pressed the murchometer to my temple.

'I have God in my reason.'

'Satan!'

'Have I ever done you harm? When? What?'

He shaded his eyes, blinded perhaps after the dark night.

'That I failed to kill you then in the train...!' he wailed. 'That I allowed you to live...!'

Aha! His penitential remorse was not because of the murder attempt, but – because it had been unsuccessful.

I sighed heavily.

'It's surely due to Thaw. We already went through this in Summer.'

'But then I didn't see that you really would *manufacture* History!' He cast a furtive glance from under his sleeve. 'That you'd build machines for this purpose, that you'd put together a whole science, that you'd place yourself at the helm of the course of history and *calculate* it according to your own designs: this is necessary, this is impossible – and as such will it be! this is good, this is bad – and as such will it be! this is beautiful, this is ugly – and as such will it be! this is redemption, this is damnation – thus will they be divided! this is heaven, this is hell – thus the blind masses will go! for Russia and the world – apoliteia; for people – the dreamslaves' fate! And no escape! No thought of escape! There won't even be anyone to throw bombs at – when you calculate your HISTORICAL NECESSITIES!' Again, he covered his eyes. 'Horror, horror! Mankind's ideal tyrant! Mechanic of satanocracy!'

I reiterated what he'd asked me about then, before he threw me off the Express into Asia.

'Have you forgotten your Marxist dogmas? You believed in them after all. Berdyaeff also believed. Man will take control of History sooner or later.'

'Maybe he will take control – but what you are doing, Venyedikt Filipovitch, is condemning the whole of humanity to eternal damnation! History is the only method of communication between God and man, yet henceforth, it won't be God speaking to us through the centuries and human history, but – a mathematician from Warsaw!' Again, he began to bang his head against the wall. 'Mathematician from Warsaw!' Whack! 'A sick idealist!' Whack! 'Venyedikt Yeroslavsky!'

'You're an incurable idealist yourself!' I muttered.

'Me? I believe in ideas for people, out of love for people – out of this long-suffering, crazy Russian love for people! But you, you believe in ideas for the sake of ideas, out of love for ideas, you live already amongst ideas! And such will be your History, such will be your apoliteia: the Ice! the Ice! Paradise of bookkeepers and soulless slaves!'

I forced myself to put bad emotions aside and weigh up Zeytsoff's words according to reason alone. (And at once I thought: but indeed, you should have got angry! Too late.)

For in what could the Atchukhovian possibly be right... After all, a certain obvious truth rang in his words. All those students living every day amongst books because they can't live amongst people, living amongst words, numbers and ideas because there is no life for them amongst warm bodies, as in warm bodies they find only objects of disgust and bestiality – in contrast to an idealised notion of bodies... Thinkers, inventors, seekers of every epoch after Truth, all those Nikola Teslas who never married and sooner perceive the beauty of a mathematically describable machine than the immature, unfinished beauty of a Miss Filipov – all those who push the world forward with their heartfelt passions – who shape the image of the future world... Of what do they dream, of what do they muse? What do they desire in the powerhouses of their wound-up hearts? The Ice! The Ice! The world and man under the Ice, History under the Ice! Then indeed they will be the most practical, the most pragmatic of men – when language of the first kind shall coincide with language of the second kind – when there'll no longer be the slightest difference between the reality of ideas and the reality of matter.

Under the Ice, no inventiveness, no originality, will be possible – but under the Ice these won't be needed, since truth of thought will correspond directly to truth of experience, and an operation on ideas telling of the world will be reduced to a simple operation on an abacus. In fact, abacuses of ideas, ideometers – these will surely arise first. In the Kingdom of Darkness, a philosopher will be a mathematician, and a mathematician – a thunder-wielding general. The stereometry of gazes will become the universally understood language, and Teitelbaum's language, by then the only possible one – the tool of absolute Truth.

'Truth, Zeytsoff,' I said out loud. 'It will be a world of realised Truth. Would such Truth be unpleasing to God?'

'Were God concerned about truth, he'd have created slide-rules instead of people!'

And he spat at me filthy phlegm.

I stood up, retrieved the lamp. He went on cracking his head against the wall. Whack, whack, whack.

'Why did you not come to me, why did you not say?' I asked softly. Silence now hung between us, silence befitting confessor and sinner. He cowered at my feet. 'Why did you not confess what sits in your soul? Do you really see in me such a tyrant that only a stiletto can get through to me, that I would feel nothing in my heart but a cold blade? We know each other after all.'

'I knew you, yes. Then, under the Ice. But now. When you've

returned after so many years. What do I know? Gospodin Yeroslavsky, Company Director!' He ground his rotten teeth. 'How can it be that you arrive with empty pockets and they give you millions, the first chairman of an industry as vast as the state, and that they buy from you secret technologies taken at your word and build their whole politics on one word about future History calculated by you, on this one word from you. How can it be! You wrote that *Apoliteia*, yes. You are the son of Father Frost, yes. You stand in the black glow, yes, already in the Express you were like a gleissenik. But does this explain anything? How can it be, Venyedikt Filipovitch!' He stared at me with wild eyes. 'Hah, you haven't even asked yourself the question, to you it's so obvious! Nor do you look in mirrors. You hoodwinked them instantly. Like all your predecessors: our Russian usurpers, prophets of the land, holy men, like Martsyn, like your Piłsudski, like Rasputin – like Rasputin – Rasputin!' Here again he began to spit. 'You have blinded them with your black Truth! I know it, already from the Marxian brotherhood, Trotsky himself – who is he? A damned Mathematician of History!'

I left. Yawning, the Free-Stater locked the dark cell.

The noise carried after me as I walked away up the corridor: the rhythmical thudding and infernal wail of a downtrodden soul.

'Mathematician! Bozhe moy, that I failed to kill the viper…! Mathematician! I knew!' Zeytsoff howled out of the depths of the crooked steel well. 'Mathematician! Mathematician! Matheeemaaatiiician…!'

On the collective soul and dictatorship of mercy

Rain had blurred the image of the city; colours and shapes flowed over my pupils like frostglaze. We rode into left-bank Irkutsk from the side of the poor suburbs, over the Kaya and Irkut rivers and past Kayskaya mountain, and into the northern neighbourhoods of the Uysky quarter. It had been raining non-stop almost all day, our horses were slithering in mud. The City of Tiger and Sable was swimming in rain, softened, insubstantial. First to tumble had been the corpse masts; I glimpsed not a single one on the Moscow Highway, nor at the city toll-gates, nor in the Uysky district. At least in the ferocious frost, the views had been sharp and vivid, clear as far as the horizon in transparent crystalline air; with the advent of Thaw, God had wiped the windowpane with a filthy rag.

The Free-Staters chose the left bank since in recent weeks it had been of little interest to the main political forces holding Irkutsk in the grip of revolutionary terror. In the slums of northern Uysky – all I saw were rows of low booths and shacks sunk into wet earth, draped already in earthen colours – there had arisen the Peasants' Self-Help Party; the party was not, however, aspiring to state power or engaging in bloody skirmishes with the Leninists, Trotskyists, Monarchists and National Democrats; it was concerned only with feeding Irkutsk's poor, almost three-quarters of whom were paupers recently torn from the land. Pocięgło's Free-Staters had an arrangement with the peasants: twice we were stopped in the rain and immediately released after a brief exchange. Words seeped into the rain and I failed to hear these hurried conversations with muzhiks armed with cudgels and chains. We rode through the city like half-disembodied spirits, through a submarine landscape; cottages, mud huts and rented townhouses drifted by to left and right, rain-coloured, soil-coloured, uneven, sprawling, blurry. In a world without straight lines, Truth flees from sight; a man watches and knows little of what he sees, even when he sees it.

We pulled up at a coal warehouse in a side street off Kieshtinsky Prospect. Two Free-Staters went to check the bridge. Only the Shelekhoff was still standing; all older, weaker constructions were destroyed by an icefloe at the beginning of the thaws; the Pontoon Bridge had floated away to the Arctic Ocean. Sometimes it was possible to cross freely via the Shelekhoff, but at other times the revolutionaries would fire from the eastern bank without warning; but then again, in some periods, a payment in kind had been enough to obtain a pass. The Free-Staters sloped off somewhere, intending to return in an hour. We unsaddled and rubbed down the horses. I swallowed some warm raw spirit, lit a cigarette... but then had nothing to do, and so I went out for a stroll. A man returns to a city after many years; the city has moved on in time, the man has moved on in time, and the map of wrinkles and scars has to be walked afresh. Somewhere around here off Kieshtinsky Prospect stood The Devil's Hand...

The streetlamps were not burning, only now did I notice. I almost bumped into one such coldiron post. I raised my head. A streetlamp, of course! I glanced around involuntarily at Old Irkutsk, at the overcast sky: is that a cloud of unlicht there obscuring the Sibirkhozheto Tower? But the rain was obscuring it far more tightly, I couldn't make out at all the cupolas of Christ the Saviour Sobor, absolutely nothing of right-bank Irkutsk. The city had dissolved into a complex of dark-blue leaden blotches like posthumous haemorrhages on a dead man's skin – as on earth, so too in heaven.

At a given moment I must have taken a wrong turn – I'd crept into some alleyway, piled as high as the first floor with decomposing rubbish. I retraced my steps. In my final glance back, I spied in the heap of refuse the outline of a man: human refuse had also been thrown there. How many had died in Irkutsk of infectious diseases, how many – of hunger? I recoiled, shielding my mouth with the sleeve of my coat. As in a winter fog, so too now, behind the curtains of rain, pedestrians flitted along the streets of Irkutsk almost without seeing one another. I tried to examine the faces no longer covered by frostoglaze spectacles and shawls. They'd grown emaciated with unwholesome skin and dark bruises neath the eyes, not from murch but from long months of undernourishment… Whilst Irkutsk was still exporting coldiron riches to the world, it could afford to import into Winter every kind of foodstuff; but now, when order and stability had broken down, there was nothing with which to buy wheat and rice, and no one to do the buying – the very idea of trade had been suspended in this time of revolution. Siberian agriculture had not yet properly awoken; first the peasants had to be driven out of cities and back to the land, to farms assigned to them as their own property by the state, to steppe and taiga parcelled out for free. Porfiry had it all drawn up in legal schemes, ready to put into action. The parties controlling Irkutsk had managed to issue several instructions for Agricultural Reform – each threatening cruel punishments should anyone obey a dissident instruction; the peasants' lack of enthusiasm was hardly surprising. Obviously, as soon as the Ice once again shackles Siberia, agriculture will have to be entrusted rather to the Kingdom of Darkness, to those cloud-capped farms working on tungetitum soil, under heavy unlicht…

In The Devil's Hand, it was more crowded than I remembered. Or maybe these were simply times when everyone spent whole days here in the downstairs saloon, having nothing to do in a city steeped in chaos and numbing destitution. I was curious to see how the landlord settled accounts with his customers – in what currency? for what prices? and was he able to find food for them at all? Having hung up my drenched coat by the door and put aside my stick, I sat down at a free table by the window. Tobacco smoke filled the whole room with warm haze, smoke as well as steam from the gently puffing samovars. The tchay was for everyone. Beneath the photograph of Aleister Crowley, some gentlemen of European appearance were dividing out a portion of bone-dry yellow cheese on a monogrammed handkerchief; toothpicks served as measures. A Siberian (that is, a half-Asiatic), dressed in a thick, inelegantly cut suit of Shetland wool, sitting at the table where once had lain the unfinished chess game between Crowley and Father Platon, was cleaning and oiling a dismantled Mosin rifle. Bedside him, by the cold stove, a dozy old man was soaking his feet in a tin basin. I'd barely sat down when an Armenian with childlike eyes approached and inquired if I'd arrived with the Transsib. I was amazed. Is the Transsib still running? The Armenian was a petty trader in 'bargain goods', now out of work. Everyone here was waiting for the Transsib to reopen as if it were a sign from God. Any train from Vladivostock was cause for celebration. Behind the Siberian with the Mosin-Nagant stood a radio receiver; during hours when broadcasts were transmitted from Harbin and the Ob, the guests and their local acquaintances would congregate in order to listen to world news; at night they picked up signals from Hong Kong or farther afield. I asked about the tidings from Europe. The Armenian was able to say only that Franz Ferdinand had signed some 'Cracow Armistice' with Nikolay the Second Aleksandrovitch in order to create a special anti-revolutionary alliance. Apparently, Lwów was in flames. The summer in Europe had been exceptionally dry and hot.

A gigantic Chinaman was distributing tea in filigree cups. I didn't even have my pocketbook on me, let alone honest diengi. I threw up my hands and said I wouldn't be paying. He nodded his bald head and placed a hot cup in front of me. I thanked him. Naturally, there was no sugar, honey, salt, milk or sour cream. Half-mouldered lemon and orange peels were dipped in the tchay. Teeth, said the Armenian and bared a gap-toothed grin. Teeth are falling out. Then a gendarme in a mud-bespattered, mismatched uniform burst in from the steaming rainswept street. Gentlemen, he cried, and the coffee house hubbub fell silent. Gentlemen, a new revolution is coming! Following which he produced a crumpled sheet from under his arm and spread it across his chest. I looked: *The New Siberian Gazette*. It showed a reproduction of the celebratory photograph, luckily of such poor quality that it could equally well have portrayed three fir trees instead of three men. The gendarme read out a propaganda article by the press organ of the UFSS. Even before he'd finished, a fierce discussion had flared in the saloon of The Devil's Hand. 'History Industry Company'! What's that supposed to mean, dammit! But at this mention, the Armenian's eyes began to sparkle. They want to produce coldiron! Ayayay, then there'll be a new market for tungetitum! However, one man and then another correctly observed that for this, Pocięgło needs above all to control the Trans-Siberian Line. Therefore, he must hasten with all speed to Irkutsk and come to an arrangement with Pobedonostseff and the Tsentrosibir. Again, they'll be fighting over the city! The men crossed themselves, invoked God's mercy, spat. At which the grandad with his feet in the water awoke. Pocięgło, he hissed, Pocięgło, Fishenstein, Gierosławski. Well, look at them, two are Polacks and the third – as good as a Polack because a Jew! Such conspiracy against the emperor, against Russia...! Send the scourge packing from the Empire! The Siberian stroked the old man's head with his massive paw – calm down, batyushka, the Empire's no more.

The clock struck the hour. I made my apologies, stood up; it was time to go. The Armenian scrutinised me as I put on my coat – could he have recognised me? He couldn't. Raising my collar, I stepped out into the rain, my boots voluptuously sucking in the mud. Where was Kieshtinsky Prospect, where the Angara, which way to the Free-Staters…? I glanced about. A lack of straight lines – but this was more than an optical illusion caused by foul weather; these buildings really were crooked and deformed, really had subsided and collapsed. The tavern across the street, oh look: the left wall had already sunk to midway up the window; give it a little longer, and the bay window and balcony will drop into the street. I looked back at The Devil's Hand to see if any of the hotel wings had likewise slipped into the ground. The Armenian was standing in the doorway with an umbrella over his head, staring at me intently. I saluted him by pressing the murchometer to my temple. He seemed confused. Excuse me, sir, what… I shrugged my shoulders. Have we met before? The businessman approached cautiously. I don't believe you arrived with the Transsib at all, he confessed, whispering through the dense rain. It's as if I've seen you somewhere before… You're a man of the Black Aurora, I recognised it. I muttered something non-committal. He drew closer still, hiding me under the umbrella. Tried to read my face like a codebook. Don't you know the rumour? he asked through the rain. There are so many rumours now, so many new rumours since the Thaw! And some are true, and some clearly false, and some both one and the other. That when the omens are good, he comes down into the city and wanders alone amongst the people, unrecognised, unknown, alien, as he sits for a moment now here, now there, eavesdropping, straining his ears, conversing frankly, gathering into his mouth the smack and spirit of the city. No one addresses him by name – since no one had ever seen with their own eyes the named man. Is it he or not he? He? He? Not he. Pobedonostseff!

I walked away without a word. Pausing at bends in the road, once, twice, to check that the Armenian wasn't following me; but no. The Free-Staters were waiting with a man in a rubber cape. The Shelekhoff is under the barrels of Reptey's gang, this man will convey you across the Angara, go. We'll wait here till midnight of the second day, as agreed; after that, go to the fifth mile of the Marmeladobahn, or leave a message at Pelevin's warehouse. I thanked them, bid them farewell. The caped man introduced himself first as Lev, but then as Pavel, as if he'd forgotten he'd already given me a name. Most likely both were false. Along the way, he described the political map of the city; a new branch of the Socialist Revolutionaries had entered an alliance with the National Democrats and yesterday they'd taken the Muravyoff Station and the station warehouses. The Central Executive Committee of Siberian Soviets had occupied the seventeenth-century monastery in Znamenskoye, handing over the nuns to the amusement of a crowd of vagabonds recruited under the red flag. The Trotskyists had gained control of the city's cesspools. There'd been gunfire over the water supply; the Monarchists were attacking the water carts.

Were this merely some European city, a city in a country between cities tightly bunched on the map! For how long could they go on pummelling each other? a few weeks? The arrangement of external forces would drive things in this or that direction; the situation in the country or situation of neighbouring states would force the victory of one or other side. But Irkutsk, but such a Siberian metropolis half-suspended all alone in Asiatic infinity upon the tenuous thread of the Transsib – I understood it well – here we have a world totally cut off from the world; months, years go by before necessity from east or west tips the scales of history. In the meantime, everything revolves in insubstantialities, half-victories, and half-defeats; such is the incomplete Revolution, History according to Kotarbiński.

We descended to the Angara shore at the height of the old railway bridge, before the bend eastward in the river. With difficulty, through curtains of rain flapping in the wind, I could make out the contours of right-bank Irkutsk. The city – the outline of its shadow – the remembrance of a city. The current was surprisingly peaceful, waves swelled to no more than half an arshin. Water in the Angara was the colour of old mud. Lev Pavel's two helpers had dragged out their boat onto a gravelly sandbank; we pushed it into the river as a foursome. Should anything happen, Lev Pavel breathed in my ear as we began to row, should anything happen, say you were there to fetch medicines. What d'you mean – should anything happen? Is it a crime in the eyes of the revolutionary parties: to cross to the other side of the city? Worse, he wheezed. Treason!

The softened profile of Old Irkutsk gradually emerged against a bespattered sky. We landed below the scenic boulevard. Three flashes of light at an even-numbered hour, said Lev Pavel and rowed away on his return journey; I'd barely had time to leap out onto solid ground. Maltchiks smeared in grime were observing me from over the balustrade above. I made a wolfish face. Their solemn lips twitched not; nor did their wide-open eyes blink.

I climbed to street level, steeped in mud up to my knees. In the distance, at the southern extremity of the boulevard, the statue of Tsar Aleksandr the Third lay toppled and half-smashed on the pavement; bits of the emperor's feet jutted from the empty quadrangular pedestal. Midway along the boulevard towered a huge pile of furniture, household utensils, broken sleighs, books and loose papers; on top, like cherries adorning a gateau, the massacred bodies of naked men shone red. Whilst on a magisterial armchair pitched in the centre of the empty space, a young man of perhaps sixteen years sat reading a book under an umbrella; across his knees he had two rifles laid barrel to stock. I turned down the first side street as fast as I could.

The streetlamps were not burning – something else had been burning on them until the rain snuffed out the flames. Irkutsk was upholding the tradition of corpse masts; the revolutionaries were hanging the bourgeoisie on lampposts, dousing them in naphtha and hurling torches at them; smoking charcoal effigies remained, unrecognisable beyond their general human shape. None of the few pedestrians raised their heads to look at them – this was different from the corpse masts of the Buryat shamans at which everyone had gawped in disgust, yet gawped nevertheless as at a tourist attraction. But the citizens of Irkutsk walked now with eyes pinned to the ground beneath their feet, terrified by the very possibility of establishing any kind of contact with another human being. They'd erased themselves from existence as far as they could. I look not, see not, shan't be seen, there is no me. Glued to walls, flashing past as far as possible from the roadway, with arms dangling and heads hung over their chests. Washed away by the rain, emitting no sound; even their footsteps could not be heard. No one engaged in conversation.

At the intersection with Glavnaya Street, I perceived several clear silhouettes on the lampposts: they'd been hanged already in the rain. I recognised a man in a green batiste waistcoat swinging below the windows of the erstwhile seat of the District Court: Mayor Szostakiewicz. And so, they'd found him nevertheless! Pocięgło maintained that Bolesław Szostakiewicz had escaped to Harbin at the beginning of the Thaw – evidently, he'd preferred to remain despite everything in his own city, for good or ill. That is, for ill, for ill.

However, not all the hanged men can be former politicians or industrialists suddenly pulled from their hiding places. Even as I looked along the rain-shrouded street, I could see about a dozen corpses strung up on lampposts. Throughout a whole year of anarchy, the Irkutsk rebels would have managed to hang every single person on their blacklists. So, whom are they hanging and burning now, if not the class enemies, religious blasphemers and servants of the former regime?

Well, clearly, they have to hang someone. How else shall a de-iced man recognise in matter the shifting fronts of ideas? For which party controls this week the northern districts of Old Irkutsk beyond Glavnaya? Such is the new war on the Ways of the Mammoths: not indigenous tribes, but political movements. Not in order to banish hostile spirits, but to bring about the ruin of other men's historical projects

– do they erect corpse masts over Irkutsk. Sometimes the world of the body prevails, other times – the world of the spirit. But the battle is one and the same.

To the foot of a boy hanged at the next crossroads, a board had been tied stating that he'd been sentenced by the Workers' Soviet for possessing 'private bread'; from this I realised I was in Leninist territory. For I already knew from the Free-Staters that because of the famine prevailing in the Baikal country, the Tsentrosibir had ordained that only food rationed and officially allocated by it was legal; food originating from any other source must be handed over to the Committee, whilst the punishment for private consumption is death. Eating food has become a public activity, known as 'common nutrition', permitted exclusively under the strict control of the people's authorities. All overly violent movements of the jaw or furtive swallows are suspect. People relieving themselves during night-time hours are subject to immediate physiological inspection. A plan exists to weigh every inhabitant of Irkutsk and continually balance out all organic mass under Tsentrosibir control. The Marxist reckoners were already out with their abacuses to measure Matter.

Most of the edifices near the Holy Trinity Hospital had caved in, as if trampled on from the sky; one presented a picture of total ruin, a façade charred black, windows blown out. Flames had also licked at the hospital itself, leaving tigerlike stripes on its vast brick body between tear-stained panes of frostoglaze and milky glass.

I had barely entered the entrance hall and caught my balance on the sloping, undulating floor – when a long-drawn-out rumble swept through the vicinity and the ground shook. The young braves in Tsentrosibir armbands, who'd been guarding the front door, ran out into the street, only to return a moment later with news that half of Christ the Saviour Sobor had collapsed. One or two crossed themselves involuntarily. A fat commissar came running, soaked to the skin, and took the young soldiers of the revolution with him, as well as every Leninist he recognised by face: guards had to be quickly mobilised before people rushed to steal tungetitum from the shattered cupola. Which means that tungetitum is again in demand in Irkutsk. A good sign, I thought, History is settling into its bearings.

At this my optimism evaporated. I was stopped by a jackanapes with as many as three Leninist armbands on his bandaged arm, bored by spitting from a distance into a rusty spittoon; and when I refused him a cigarette, he began to puff and blow menacingly and mutter caustic political jibes. Why such a reaction? Jelena Muklanowicz would have said that I'd again behaved arrogantly, unaware even of my arrogance. I calculated in my head. Then I asked the Leninist how long he'd been there, in the Holy Trinity. He boasted of being shot in three places. He showed me: arm, shoulder, side above the hip. I undid my coat and took from under my sweater the tortoiseshell portfolio packed in canvas. Take a look, have you seen this girl here in the hospital? She assists with the wounded instead of the sisters. The Leninist fixed his eyes on Jelena's self-portrait, suddenly touched and commiserating in the Russian way. Ah, you're looking for your beloved! I nodded, avoiding words in the language of the second kind. He stared at the sketch for a very long time, claiming in the end that he'd not seen such a young woman.

But! Don't despair needlessly, Comrade, I may have seen her, may not have seen her, may have forgotten – though a krasavitsa like that wouldn't have slipped my memory. Well, you have to ask a reliable person. Come on, come on, we'll check with the matron, she must know all the volunteers coming into the hospital.

Thus we set off in search of the matron; the wounded communist had suddenly received a new combat mission and threw himself into the work with revolutionary zeal. We climbed first to the third floor, where the chief matron normally resided; from there they sent us to surgery. Greater chaos than usual prevailed in the surgical ward (as I was swiftly assured by the Leninist, who was himself a tad shocked). Not only did no one know very much; they were all so run off their feet moreover to notice what they knew not. The Committee's militia had begun to bring in victims from the Sobor; everywhere was full of mud, blood and mud-coloured bodily fluids. For the Sobor had not collapsed in the smooth orderly fashion of a felled house of cards. The foundations had sunk into the thawed, waterlogged ground on one side, and onto this side had 'slid' part of the monumental basilica, burying half the district under rubble. In carts and on horseback, in wheelbarrows and in the arms of rescued neighbours – the wounded finally reached the Holy Trinity, dying or already dead, and whom only a doctor could pronounce dead in order for their family to believe it. And even then, they'd not believe it at once: dead, but perhaps alive. I walked up and down in this storm of screaming, wailing and human tragedy with Miss Muklanowicz's sketch in my hand like the next relative of a chance victim, stunned by sudden calamity, clutching in blind hope at a holy icon. I tried to ask the doctors, the sisters. Even if they answered, then it was absentmindedly and in obvious hurry. (None of them recognised Jelena.)

Things calmed down a little towards evening. The communist comrade reappeared to offer shag and inform me of a brilliant new plan. For who, namely, apart from the chief matron, absolutely has to see every person working in the hospital? Why, the special commissar assigned by the Committee to the hospital who undersigns the permits in the Committee's name! 'And I've known Vasyl Petrovitch since the days we worked together as waiters,' the Leninist assured me, 'we'll soon solve it.'

And so, we went to see the special commissar of the Tsentrosibir. Vasyl Petrovitch indeed recognised his wounded comrade, though he showed no inclination to recall their former bond of friendship. Asked if he'd ever written out a hospital pass for this particular devushka, name of Jelena Muklanowicz or any other, he began at once to inquire, narrowing his bloodshot eyes: but who is she? and who's he that asks? and why such concern? and in whose political interest? a krasavitsa – but why's she wearing such bourgeois clothes? Polish, you say? Polish? And then I did a very foolish thing, because I confessed to Vasyl Petrovitch my real name and the real circumstances surrounding the affair. But it was Summer, and he too had been born none too bright – he failed to make the connection, hadn't realised, no glintz outlined the obvious. In the end, Vasyl examined Jelena's self-portrait honestly and declared that no such a citizen had ever received a bumaga from him, nor any woman like her.

I thanked him, stepped out into the corridor. Dead. I flung the rest of the shag into the spittoon. The little Leninist was still trying to comfort me. I sat down on a stool by a white-blinded window and straightened my scoliotic back. In the hospital it stank of chemicals and stale blood. A mouldy humidity hung in the air. Outside the window, rain drummed louder and louder. Leaning on the sill, I could feel the chill wafting through chinks in the brickwork, I was drawn to this chill. Over the walls ran zigzag cracks, out of which grinned the brown gums of bricks and teeth of crumbling mortar. The whole of Irkutsk was caving in.

What now, asks the tenderhearted communist, perhaps you could go and check with her relatives? I shrug my shoulders. She has no relatives. We will wait for the matron. Perhaps Vasyl didn't tell us the truth? Well, he told it, told it not, for does any kind of truth exist at all now…? I spit almost dryly. The Leninist maltchik sees that the matter is plainly one of the soul, so he invents fantastical consolations. But maybe your friend got it wrong and mistook her for a patient! Maybe she wasn't a volunteer listed in the registers, only helped once or twice when visiting out of the kindness of her heart; and he saw her then and so thought she was a volunteer. Is she ill with something? Well, you see! Maybe she came to visit someone. Maybe it happened, besides, after the front shifted, when the Trotskyists or SR-bombers were holding the Holy Trinity and some of the personnel quit, afraid of being accused of treason; and so they're all mostly volunteers now – for who's going to pay them a salary? will they earn a living from curing the sick? No! Behold the morning star of communism: selfless assistance to a stranger in need. Whilst anyone who tries to exploit the suffering and dying is right to flee before the people's justice! So fled the former head physician Kesselman, who first put me together again; so fled the famous surgeon Busansky, doctors Voromy, Konyeshin, Alholz-Streier, Director Putaszkiewicz himself, having allegedly emptied the hospital's coffers beforehand; oh, for such as these at once the rope and lamppost –

Konyeshin! So, Doctor Konyeshin was working here? And what happened to him afterwards? The Leninist leapt to his feet and immediately ran to find out: Konyeshin left with the Nationalists, stayed at the former City Infirmary. But, so what? Why d'you care about this doctor? You're no longer looking for the devushka?

I ran out into the street, hurriedly concealing the drawing. It was raining cats and dogs. I set off eastward intending to take the first turning south. Shots reached me at the junction; people ran past, hiding behind bends and street corners. After the Sobor catastrophe, they're preparing for a restless night; the Trotskyists will want to take advantage of this opportunity. I took a roundabout route via Bolshaya and Ivanovskaya Streets. In the demolished Vtoroff covered passage, an armed band on horseback was lurking with loaded rifles under cloaks, waiting only for the signal to attack. I had no idea whether these were still Leninists or already the vanguard of some other history-makers. It was too dark, and even without the rain lashing my face, all that could be descried were anonymous silhouettes, shadows upon shadows.

And so it was street after street. Someone chasing someone, someone shooting someone, someone calling someone through the storm… Wooboom, wooboom, wooboom! Lightning flashed in the sky above Irkutsk, and I saw that I was standing before the building of the Physical Observatory of the Imperial Academy of Sciences. Behind me, in the city, the revolutionaries were still firing zealously; people who'd been hit were screaming, a child was crying, a saddle horse neighing in panic. Wooboom, a tremor passed through the earth from the strokes of the Murch Hammer. I entered the building.

The main hall of the Observatory had split in two, the whole western flank lay in ruins. I picked my way through the rubble, supporting myself with the stick. It was hard to make out anything in the twilight… I lit a match. A young stag gazing into a green lake glanced up at me from a chipped-off fragment of the fresco. Wooboom! Why had no one switched off Doctor Tesla's prototype? It's been striking for years since his flight. Were they afraid of this infernal machine? Out of ordinary superstition? Sasha had not mentioned what happened here afterwards; he'd not returned to the place since the fall of the Citadel. And yet in the apparatus alone lie poods of tungetitum!

I did not enter the murky corridors or step through doors twisted in mute hysteria in the cloven walls. Darkness and silence; the abandoned temple of science. Ghosts of teslectricity and after-images of gleissen mourned in corners. All that could be heard were thick streams of leaking rain. Something scampered away in the gloom, shuffled past, squealed. I did not light another match. Cat? Mouse? Rat? Or perhaps vagabonds of some kind live here, maybe other people hiding from the street battles.

I clambered onto a high obstacle reaching halfway up my chest and jumped down on the far side. The exit into the courtyard was blocked by a gigantic mound of small bits of garbage glued firmly together with mud and gravel. I would have had to squeeze under the architrave on all fours, crawl my way through. I returned to the previous bend, entered a side chamber; if my memory had frozen correctly, this was the space behind Tesla's storeroom where he used to test his black coil – in the longer wall, there should be two windows overlooking the courtyard. I tapped on the wall with my stick, counting the paces from the corner. At last, a window frame – but no panes: the sinking building had forced the frostglaze out of the casings. I pushed – the shutter fell off its hinges. Wooboom. I looked out into the courtyard. Shshshshshshshshshshsh.

A single lightning bolt struck. I saw nothing. Wooboom! A second lightning bolt struck. A hundred tiny eyes flickered, fixed directly on me. Thrown backwards, I almost tripped over. The rats stood motionless under the driving rain, frozen as on a photograph burned out by flash: all on their hind legs, upright, all with snouts facing in one direction. Wooboom! Moving instead was the ram of the Murch Hammer, and with each stroke, a wave of shivers passed through the animals, as if someone had crumpled and wrenched that photograph. My heart leapt into my mouth. What in fact had happened later to the rodents used by Sasha Pavlitch in his teslectric experiments? Here in the Observatory, everything was just as on the day of Nikola's flight. The Hammer prototype was still functioning, fastened by coldiron cables to the flow-generators that were pumping teslectrical energy out of the Ways of the Mammoths. It seems no one let the animals out of their cages, they remained locked in. But – the Hammer was functioning. One extremum of the teslectric wave had been sufficient... Wooboom!

Garlands of rubbish, bizarrely twisted braids of wire now hung from these cables with talismans of human civilisation entwined within them: pencils, pens, coins, keys, screw-tops, corks, combs, toothpicks, cigarette tubes, monocles, springs, a hundred other odds and ends.

I withdrew slowly from the window, fearing to rupture that uncanny bond holding the rats in herdlike stupor. Eventually it was cut off by the wall. Then I turned on my heels and ran to the exit, stumbling over rubble and banging my shins.

Judging by the echoes of shots smothered by the rain, the street battles had shifted east, in the direction of the Northern Station. I ran across to the south side of Glavnaya Street. After some two hundred paces I passed the remains of a barricade blocking the roadway and pavements. A dead horse and a dead dog lay side by side on the pavement in a composition worthy of Goya. I was transfixed. A bullet whizzed past nearby, ricocheting off a cobble. I rushed towards a gate. It transpired that two SRs were hiding in the well-yard, one bleeding under his shirt, the other with three revolvers tucked into his belt, but each revolver now had an empty cylinder. They showed me the passage to a back gate that opened onto an alleyway leading west and told me to keep to the Angara side. Who's that shooting, I asked. They didn't know. And why are there never any lights burning in the windows? People are afraid and hide behind blackwickes. Look out for patches of unlicht, that's where the battle is.

I ran out westward. I realised I was going to have to trace a wide arc through half of Irkutsk on my walk to the City Infirmary. On a neogothic building at a corner, I noticed the Novy Rolmeyer sign (the windows of the shop itself were boarded up) and so I realised that I was standing on a level with Konny Island and had Zamorskaya and Tsvetistaya Streets directly to my right.

Long stretches of Tsvetistaya seemed completely deserted. An uncomfortable foreboding already stung me several houses earlier when I saw, within the dismal framework of night-time drizzle, only burned-out shells of buildings; the whole riverside from number eleven onwards presented just such a picture. The buildings overlooking the Angara bank had served as military defences during the initial, fiercest battles for control of Irkutsk, immediately after the Thaw.

The Wielickis' house yawned in inky darkness out of empty window sockets. At least the mansard roof was intact. One half of the gate was swinging on a single hinge, moaning pitifully in the wind. I climbed the cracked staircase to the first floor. Painful it was to superimpose on this image of devastation, memories of bright warm days spent with the Wielicki family. On the right the kitchen, the servants' rooms – I stepped inside. The floor was torn up, the parquet charred, the stove smashed. In a doorway to the left, a white stain loomed before my eyes – fungus of some kind had already managed in the damp to spread long tendrils over the ruin. With my stick, I rummaged through plasterwork and upturned floorboards. Birds had built their nests here. Filth lay strewn by the walls, there was a stench of excrement. Water was trickling through cracks and fissures in the walls and ceilings.

The second floor. Everything had been plundered, and what they'd not taken – they'd chopped up and burned. Sideboards in the drawing room, the tall grandfather clock, walnut cupboards – nothing but chips and charcoal remained. Where once Wojsław Wielicki had played on a Sunday afternoon with his children on the chaise longue, there was now a puddle of mud wherein floated the half-eaten carcass of a crow. Empty cartridge cases lay scattered beneath a crooked window. I turned with one eye open towards the rain-drenched night, with the other – towards the non-existent past. Here – the drawing room; there – the dining room; there again – Mr Wielicki's study. The children would come running, the mixing bowl would be rattling, there'd be a scent of rice kutia and bitter tchay, the clock would chime, old Mrs Wielicka would be muttering her rosary, a fire would be roaring in the stove. Yes, no, yes, no. A cold rain blew as the mouldering relics of bourgeois prosperity crunched beneath my boots. Where once Halina Wielicka had sat in an armchair with her embroidery frame or knitting, there gaped a hole with jagged edges: an entire chimney stack had slipped into the rubble below when the bearing wall caved in. I went from door to door. In the Wielickis' bedroom – the burned frame of a nuptial bed. In my bedroom – the residue of an enormous bonfire. I raked in the ashy mud with the murchometer. What had they not burned here; even porcelain, pictures and mirrors, had been thrown onto a heap. I nudged the broken figurine of an Indian elephant; it rolled across the threshold and slid into a black hole. I understood what I was looking for, impelled by nervous melancholy, fearing to find it: their remains, some trace of the Wielickis' calamitous end, material proof. For had they had time to leave calmly, they'd surely have taken more things with them. In the library, some of the books had escaped the fire; later they'd decayed, mouldered, disintegrated, exposed to foul weather and burning sun. A few title pages were still legible. *In Desert and Wilderness. 101 Parlour Games. Hoarfrost. Samarkand Diary.* In a corner lay the next carcass. I poked it with my stick. No, it was the sodden plush and rags of a child's teddy bear. Someone had ripped open the belly of Mr Fuffluck and then discarded the wrecked toy. Were they searching for Wielicki's wealth in Michasia's soft plaything? Had he not handed it over amicably? Unless they'd hanged him first, together with Irkutsk's most prominent bourgeoisie, immediately after Thaw. I had not paid attention to whether any corpses were hanging from lampposts on Tsvetistaya. I walked over to an east-facing window.

Just in time to snoop on the next act of relentless revolution. Three armed youths were threatening a fourth at gunpoint, belonging no doubt to a different political truth. It was happening on the other side of the street; I saw only their backs. They were binding the poor fellow's hands. Had thrown a rope over the lamppost – their whole hanging technique worked out to a tee: having attached a stone to one end of the rope, they threw the stone over the crossbar of the post. The condemned youth was prepared; first he yelled something at them, but they stuffed his gob with a fistful of mud.

Now the noose is around his neck; two of the hangmen catch hold of the opposite end of the rope, ready to pull at the signal –

A horse detachment suddenly fell upon them from out of the rain, only four riders, but this was more than enough: they mowed down the man pointing his barrel at the condemned man, shot one of the hangmen, and chased the other against a wall. How swiftly Truth revolves in the unfrozen current of History! The might-have-been victim, released from his tethers, now seized hold of that third hangman and dragged him kicking under the lamppost. The noose had already been made fast – he attached the free end of the rope to the saddle of one of the riders – all he had to do was spur on the horse – so that I leaned out of the window, for such is the execution fever gripping even the casual spectator in a thrill of passion; spitting out the mud, the rescued man tightened the halter around the neck of his executioner –

A floorboard gave way beneath me, bricks showered down, I crashed to the first floor.

When I recovered from the shock and rose to my knees, aching all over, feeling with my fingers for broken bones, they were already standing over me with rifles levelled. I raised my hands. If I could only get to my feet, make eye-to-eye contact; after all, I had no weapon or incriminating documents –

Just to be on the safe side, they beat me up first until I dropped unconscious.

My second eye, the only eye still able to see, swelled as a consequence, which I couldn't feel, immersed as I was in pain distributed evenly throughout my body; my first thought on regaining the rest of my senses was that sight would never be regained, because they'd blinded me, therefore I can't see. And only then did I feel genuine terror! Terror and fury and animal desire for revenge – hogtied, I began to toss and turn on the uneven surface, battering furniture and walls, yelling threats and curses. Until someone approached (I heard footsteps) and again whacked me on the crown of my head, and again I drowned in unconsciousness.

Later I was more sensible. Restored to consciousness, I lay still and merely twisted my head from side to side, hitting the floorboards; in this way I located the specific pain in my smashed eyelid and blood blister swelling on the eye. I pierced it on a sharp splinter. Felt warmth flow over my face. I began to struggle with the eyelid: if only a millimetre, if only a tiny slit onto the brightness of day – wham, red light shot into my pupil. I turned on my side in order to gaze from this wormlike position, drenched in blood, and through blood, at my prison.

I found myself in a long space whose opposite wall was fitted with a row of tall frostoglaze windows, over which only reflections of internal images scrambled. The night outside was dark, stormy; I could hear the regular clatter of rain and rumbles of distant thunder. Inside, mean-while, electric lamps were burning, weakly, as though only one in five; however, it was the first electricity I'd seen in Irkutsk since Thaw, even in the Holy Trinity Hospital they made do without.

At both ends of the room, coldiron spiral staircases led above and below, and someone was constantly running up and down, mainly armed men wearing red-and-black armbands. I tried to remember the revolutionary colour code as explained by the Free-Staters. Green and white was the UFSS, red – the Leninists, black and white – the National-Democrats, and black and red – Trotsky's communists, was that right?

I was not their only prisoner. By the wall to my right lay three wretch-es in an even worse condition than my own, for their hands were tied behind their backs and they had sacks over their heads. However, after about a quarter of an hour, several strapping lads appeared with Berdan rifles and dragged these three to their feet, no doubt for summary ex-ecution. I trembled.

To my left, on the other hand, I had an animal cage wherein lay a naked corpse savagely mutilated, covered in wounds, scabs and bruises, with amputated left foot and sawn-off fingers. That is, I thought ini-tially it was a corpse – but at a certain moment, he stirred and crawled around in his cage to face me, peering with blood-encrusted eye... So that I shuddered in amazement and involuntary disgust, which was hard to explain, since it was clearly only the life in this butchery that struck me as abhorrent; death I would have stomached. But he per-ceived that I saw him and smiled moreover a toothless smile, baring his mangled gums. On his bulging high forehead were four gashes made as if by the claws of a bird of prey. A lock of silvery hair had caked above his split nose. Breathing, he whistled through bizarre holes in his face. A colourless sticky substance oozed from his ear.

'Welcome to Purgatory,' he wheezed through the bars of his cage; he coughed again, whistled, after which he chuckled goofily, and then, in a brief flash of unlicht, I recognised the tortured cripple: Frantishek Markovitch Uriah.

We know each other from the Box, I say to him, I used to see Your Esteemed Nobleness regarding official matters, what happened? Whilst he: khrry-khrry-khrry – this is the chuckle of Mr Uriah, he's laughing;

and then I understood another thing: Frantishek Markovitch had gone out of his mind.

How long had they held him like this in cruel incarceration? Inquiring warily, one word at a time, I extracted his tale of woe: they seized him immediately after Thaw, not Trotskyists at all, but a unit of Lyednyak royalists, who at that time were still a force to be reckoned with in Irkutsk; they wanted above all to punish Count Schultz for unpardonable treason against His Imperial Exaltedness, and Mr Uriah had cropped up as the governor general's primary confidant, from whom they could wrest the secret of the traitor's hiding place by whatever means possible. For the Lyednyaks, not having seen the count's corpse with their own eyes, did not believe the tidings of his death and were determined to torment poor Frantishek until he revealed the secret. Except that Frantishek knew no secret. Count Schultz-Zimovy was no longer alive. Thaw came, rumour equalled rumour equalled truth. He spoke, but there was no way of convincing them. Had he known anything, he'd have confessed on day one. And so – they tortured him for weeks. It was then that he began to lose his mind. He told me all this not in plain words, obviously, but the story was clear: they'd tortured him not to the point of Truth, but to the point of total unfreezing. He went mad. Then they sold him to the Leninists.

At first, the Leninists intended to use him in a show trial of people's justice, but soon realised that they'd only make a mockery of the trial by putting up such a defendant to public view as an example. But to kill him just like that without any use and with no political decision – they couldn't afford this either. So, they kept him in a dark cellar, feeding him maggots and offal, until the fronts of the street revolution shifted and that whole quarter of the city was occupied by Trotskyists. At their hands, Mr Uriah experienced fresh sufferings, for there was no agreement amongst the Trotskyists themselves as to their political path in Siberia; various conspiratorial and intra-conspiratorial groups were arguing with one another, each citing the teachings of Leff Davidovitch Bronstein. Thus, as one lot were already hoisting Uriah onto a lamppost, another swept in and said no, we'll trade the life of the governor's confidant for the benefit of the Revolution! And so, he ended up in this animal cage, crammed into it like an animal – like a wolfdog or greyhound, kept for weeks in four-legged pose. Whilst the Trotskyists bargained with Pobedonostseff for one more train, for safe passage to Tomsk, for concessions on energy. But Pobedonostseff, it seems, made light of Frantishek Markovitch. Uriah bared his gums with doggish pride. He never did appreciate me, khrry-khrry. They're keeping me for goulash, for goulash, when hunger reaches the throat of the Revolution, then they'll eat me, khrry-khrry-khrry.

And whilst I was thus exchanging whispers and mad chuckles with the brutalised gubernatorial tchinovnik, one of the Trotskyists paid us a visit by the wall, dressed in tight-fitting leather jacket with three bullet holes in the chest, and carrying a gasoline lamp above his head. I fell silent when I perceived the movement of shadows on the wooden surfaces. He stood still, swayed on the heels of his shiny high-topped Cossack boots, leaned over and held the hot lampshade to my temple. I jerked backwards. He grabbed hold of a jacket-tail, pulled me into the sitting position and began searching my pockets. They'd already taken my pocketbook earlier on. This fighter, however, was more scrupulous. Every so often he glanced in my eye; and I had the odd impression that I knew this black-haired youth from somewhere, with his coarse visage frozen neath angry furrows, with bushy moustache concealing the mouth, with his work-worn palms, hardened by corns. Was it him? Him? Not him. Under the canvas, he found the tortoiseshell portfolio with Jelena's drawing, took it, opened it, shone the lamp over the sheet of paper, smiling to himself above his Gypsy growth. I uttered a cry of empty protest – and he dealt me a left-handed swipe without even clenching his fist. Yet the skin below my blind eye broke as from a cut. As he walked away, I caught sight in the lamp-glow of a bright star on his ring finger: a band with a huge diamond, now sticky with blood. Which I easily recognised from cold memory – was it? it was! – as the diamond of the Great Moguls once belonging to Wojsław Wielicki.

The floor shook and a shudder passed through the whole building, the panes rattled in the window casings: a train had ridden past. They were holding us somewhere not far from a railway line – were not Innokentyevskoye and all those workers' settlements to the south of Muravyoff Station under Trotskyist control? I lay despondent and oppressed by increasingly gloomy thoughts. They had murdered everyone; they will murder me. A specialist at frittering away plans calculated algorithmically! He had History laid out before him on his desk, but no, he himself had to crawl into the deepest entropy! A warm trickle was snailing its way down my cheek, sorely irritating the nerves on my skin; I wiped my face on the floorboards. Pain, pain, pain. Uriah watched me with his wild eye. Stupid, he hissed, stupid, they're all stupid! See how they dance, how they blind one another with golden spoils, how they yawn neath crystal chandeliers, puff up themselves up with their krasavitsas, with their orders and decorations! Where now the princes, generals, admirals? Where are they now? Purgatory!

Indeed, where are they now? I asked the gone-to-the-dogs commissioner about Prince Blutsky-Osey. After all, he'd stood at the beginning with the tsarist forces in Aleksandrovsk, but then, after that strange pact between Pobedonostseff and Count Schultz-Zimovy, he retreated to the Ob. Had the emperor not given him any instructions after Thaw? At this, Frantishek Markovitch shook his cage, hammering on the bars in sudden hysteria. Khrry! Khrry! Khrry! Prince Blutsky! His own wife tried to poison him! Such was the Lyednyak pact with Pobedonostseff, and such the power of Count Zimovy on the throne of Siberia: the Ice! the Ice! But it cracked. And now they will gobble me up. Khrry!

I closed my eye. He was already completely unfrozen, memory oozing from his ears. It could have been as he said, it could have been otherwise. I fumbled in my tethers with clumsy fingers – no, I won't unravel them. I tensed my muscles. I won't break free. Every other moment, someone was walking past, if not across the long room itself, then on the staircase to left or right; I won't escape like this. If I only knew what those tall windows looked down upon… Frostoglaze won't shatter easily, but perhaps it may be possible to force out a window together with its frame and jump outside – but what if this be the second or third high storey and there's nothing on the ground, only a chasm? I'll break my neck. But maybe not. Maybe I'll land on a slagheap or roof or goods wagon in a siding. I opened my eye. Leap up, run for it, ten paces, whack, a black window. Then what to do? Will it succeed? not succeed? Will I survive? not survive? To jump? or not to jump? Before they come and lead me to a lamppost or, worse still, lock me in a cage and drive me insane. I bit my tongue. True or false? True or false?

They came before I'd utterly frozen in this. The one with the Dutch diamond and two more bruisers – they stood me on my feet, untied my bonds. Dragged me away without a word. I offered no resistance, merely squinted from under my swollen eyelid at the nearby windows.

We did not reach the stairs. They shoved me into a cluttered office, a square cubicle neath a naked bulb casting yellow light, containing not a single stool, but instead three tabletops laden with newspapers, proclamations, underground pamphlets, books worn out by endless re-reading. There was no window in the main wall, which I ascertained at once with passive despair. Instead, a huge daub of a poster hung on it portraying a muscular Worker with rolled-up sleeves, trampling a rat representing Monarchy on a street pavement, and all this against a background of black twin cupolas and a skeletal tower. Even the lettering was identical to that on the propaganda posters from the time of the Japanese war. *Nationwide Revolution!* And a lot of grey symbolising red.

The diamond molodyets thrust a heavy telephone receiver into my hand, then went out, slamming the narrow door behind him. I stared at it, dumbfounded. They had a telephone here! Which, apparently, really worked. They'd managed to extend the wires after Thaw – but where to? Surely not beyond the city limits.

I pressed the chill metal to my pain-wracked hearing.

Eeeeyoooooo, vee-eeeeeey, ooeeeeeeyoo… Weeee-ee-eeeesk! Krkkk.

An electric wind was blowing down the cable. I laid aside the receiver, stole up to the door – they were standing immediately on the other side, talking. What to do? A situation without open solutions, all variables locked in a box. Combination after combination had to be checked one by one.

I sat down on the paper-strewn tabletop, it creaked loudly. Something coughed in the telephone. I counted to ten and again lifted the receiver.

Klee-eeeeyoooooo! Ooooooyzzzzzz! Krkhhr, trtrtr, krkkk. Tshtk!

I gulped.

'Aleksandr Aleksandrovitch?'

Krkhhrrr.

'Venyedikt Filipovitch.'

Ooeeooeeooeeeeeeeeeeeeeeeee….

Give me the Ice! I clenched my dislocated fingers, hunched my crooked back. C, therefore D, therefore E. I had introduced myself at the Holy Trinity using my real name. Pobedonostseff holds a knife to the Transsib, also no doubt to the city power station; who knows what else he's managed to line with dynamite. Everyone has to negotiate with him. He has spies here, there and everywhere; always did have. Certainly, news about the History Industry Company Gierosławski, Pocięgło & Fishenstein reached him before anyone else. Now he hears of Gierosławski care of the Leninists. Hears of the Trotskyist prisoner seized on Tsvetistaya. He tells them to check – they find Jelena's portrait.

He will try to strike a deal. What does he want? The Kingdom of Darkness?

I spat red phlegm into a corner.

'How are your dreams, Aleksandr Aleksandrovitch? What does Irkutsk prophesy for you now?'

He was silent for a long time.

'Forget everything,' he said at last. 'Your Pocięgło… Is anyone else listening?'

'No. I don't know. There's no one with me.'

'I gave orders it should be in private… I will give them twenty-four hours from Blagoveshchensk to the Ob, they'll let you go free. And as soon as the Free-Staters take Irkutsk, you'll give me free passage under the flag of the Free States of Siberia.'

'Where to?'

'Wherever.'

'There's a condition. We shall have maps of all your mines.'

'I shan't blow up myself.'

'But afterwards, afterwards.'

'So then on the border.'

'On the border. *D'accord*. It has frozen.'

'It has frozen, God willing, it will freeze.'

I breathed a sigh.

'So, what now, is that all?'

Krkhhrrr.

'Aleksandr Aleksandrovitch?'

Eeeeyoooooo, vee-eeeeeey, ooeeeeeeyoo…

'Aleksandr Aleksandrovitch, but what about your Kingdom of Darkness? Do you no longer want to witness the triumphal return of the Ice? What about your dreams, your great visions which you told me about friend to friend? I was to sit at your side. Things have swung around. Eh?'

Ooeeooeeooeeeeeeeeeeeeeeeee….

'Aleksandr Aleksandrovitch!' Something isn't quite right here. Obviously, we have Summer, I can no longer calculate someone's character with total certainty, especially a man like Pobedonostseff. Nevertheless… Is it possible to so break the algorithmics of the soul? It doesn't add up! The calculations are all wrong! 'What happened there? Tell me. Still before Thaw. I hear you arranged with Princess Blutskaya-Osey to assassinate the prince with poison. What sort of truth is that?'

Krkhrrr.

'Gospodin Yeroslavsky…'

'But tell me, tell me!'

'You know that His Princely Highness was dead against you from the start. I heard there were matters still from your journey in the Express. And as soon as word got out –'

'He sent his hussars after me!'

'And this was his first great annoyance, because you killed one of his men, a good man. But the princess, the princess and… and I… we wanted above all to protect the Ice, to defend the gleissen. And you, Gospodin Yeroslavsky. But the prince, that is, the emperor –'

'So it was you who sent that army of vagabonds after Tesla!'

'But you see! Was I not right? You ought to be grateful to me! That you should so side with the doctor of lightning – is contrary to all reason, contrary to logic, for you stand at opposite poles in ideas, he is thrashing the Ice, whilst you want to construct out of the Ice your apoliteia – you're fighting on different sides of the front – where's the logic in that?'

'How many times have I told you, Gospodin Pobedonostseff? He's my friend!'

'*Les amis de mes amis sont mes ennemis – mais c'est absurde!* My God, that I should not have had him removed earlier, when I still could! Now he boasts in newspapers all over the world: "The Man Who Smashed the Ice"! *Quel bouffon!*'

'And yet you were mediating between Count Schultz and Prince Blutsky.'

'Agh, that's not how it was. The prince was already preparing for a general assault; we decided that the princess would give him poisoned tea, I sent Mr Ziel with a fast-acting chemical, but he was seized by the okhranniks, I don't know if he talked, well, the princess certainly talked. Imagine the turmoil in the old prince's mind! He swiftly despatched his wife to some secure clinic for nervous conditions, and unleashed Geist's special sleuths to track down the Son of Frost; the princess had told him so many things about the victory of the Ice and the Poles named Gierosławski...! But His Princely Highness had already lost heart for Siberia and political, military questions. Then Tesla gave Count Schultz the slip and it was all over.'

'And you went into open alliance with the Count, and Siberia declared independence.'

'What could I do? Without the Ice –'

'You are dying.'

I rubbed the wound on my temple with the receiver. The plump Worker from the poster on the opposite wall gazed at me with bright eyes, his stubby fingers like frankfurters wrapped around a rifle, his dumpling face spilling over the collar of his white shirt. The thing is, all of them here must have been anticipating Revolution. At most, the Thaw merely liberated History frozen till then. Schultz, after all, had moved his family abroad beforehand. Pobedonostseff had secretly mined hundreds of miles of railway track. And what, and now –

Yet why exactly should the chairman of Sibirkhozheto's board of directors wish to mine the Transsib? This would have been a perfect argument in Count Schultz-Zimovy's negotiations with the tsar, since the cutting-off of Saint Petersburg from the Empire's Pacific ports posed for Tsar Nikolay the greatest threat – but what was Pobedonostseff playing at here...?

And since it was only the Ice that had kept him alive in his otherwise mortal illness – how come he'd survived for over a year after Thaw? How come?

What is he really up to, perched at the summit of his tower, in the midst of a city occupied by fighters of parties equally hostile to him, and warding them off day by day through blackmail?

I squeezed tight my bruised eye. I am standing on the platform in Old Zima, whiteout all around; anyone can be he, whom he's turned from a lie into truth, riding out of Summer into the Land of the Gleissen,

whereas I have to draw conclusions above all from what does not exist
– from what exists not – exists not – never existed –

Eeeeyoooooo, vee-eeeeeey, ooeeeeeeyoo… Weeee-ee-eeeesk!

'Why don't you ransom your loyal servant Frantishek Markovitch,
Count?'

Krkhrrr! Krkhrrr! Krkhrrr!

'What use the governor general's servant to Pobedonostseff?'

'He's suffering infernal torment here.'

Ooeeooeeooeeeeeeeeeeeeeeeee….

'I know.'

But he won't run the risk, it would arouse suspicion. What use the
governor general's servant to Pobedonostseff?

And he won't confess to me out loud. How can he know who's
listening?

For with whom am I conversing? With the electric wind, with a wave
of sound rasping down a cable, with a metallic whistle modulated on
hidden speaking trumpets. What I do not see, what I do not experience
directly – is not. The past, the future – is a blank. Did I really stand face
to face with Aleksandr Aleksandrovitch Pobedonostseff? Did I ever
speak with such a sole-existent man?

I pressed my forehead against the cool bakelite. Give me the Ice!
Give me the Ice!

Maybe he really did die shortly after Thaw, maybe that's what indeed
transpired. Fleeing from the murderous mob, where else was Schultz to
turn other than to the hideout in the sky of his anti-Ottepyelnik ally?
Therefore, by some miracle, he reaches the Sibirkhozheto Tower on the
revolutionary night, but there – who does he find? Pobedonostseff's
corpse frozen to the hydraulic throne? It could have been like that,
could have been.

No one had seen his countenance, no one had heard his naked voice.
After the death of his Angel – how many people, apart from his faithful
Buryat servants, had free access to him? What could be simpler than to
take the place of the fresh mortal remains?

Could it have been like that? No, probably not. Someone, after all,
had to speak through the coldiron trumpets; a living hand had to
depress the grating levers in order to issue an initial instruction and
admit the count to the unlighted summit and before the throne of darkness. Schultz arrived, paused, demanded asylum and… Pobedonostseff
refused? wanted to throw him to the crowds for them to devour? they
quarrelled, the count forced his way between the machines, reached
the body – it could have been like that – reached the body, and what?
killed him? He killed him. In order then to hide behind the mask of the
Invisible One, behind the mask of His name.

And so, from then on, it's not Pobedonostseff who speaks with the voice of Pobedonostseff, not Pobedonostseff who rules through Pobedonostseff's coldiron. For who will tell the difference? No one had seen the face of Aleksandr Aleksandrovitch Pobedonostseff. No one had calculated his character.

But – no one had seen the face of Aleksandr Aleksandrovitch Pobedonostseff since his very arrival in Irkutsk!

Where to stop the suspicion, at what point draw the line? (Give me the Ice! Give me the Ice!). When we lose our measure of truth – what decides? Anything.

And yet –

'Did Pobedonostseff ever exist?'

'What?'

'Did he exist?' I cleared my throat. 'Such a singular man: the natchalnik of Sibirkhozheto. You must at least have seen the dead body.'

'But…!'

'Unrecognisable, yes.'

I walked around the table and towards the wall, as far as the cord would allow. My aching body, smashed on all sides, burned with every movement. But this is good, these are attributes of entropy: if you can't calculate – you have to guess. More movement, more pain, more disorder in the brain matter.

Schultz/Pobedonostseff coughed thickly.

'You think that –'

'You replaced him smoothly after all, and no one put two and two together, isn't that it? Tell me, did you ever see him with your own eyes during his lifetime?'

Eeeeyooooooo, vee-eeeeeey, ooeeeeeeeyoo…

'Did they ever meet openly: Pobedonostseff and Count Schultz. That's what I'm asking.'

'In Saint Petersburg, years ago, at a dinner at Prime Minister Struve's.'

'But here, in Irkutsk!'

'According to what Rasputin and his ilk spread at court… there was this faith, this hope… many people travelled to the Land of the Gleissen suffering from incurable illnesses. There are also more embarrassing complaints, when a man avoids his nearest and dearest from the start, retreats into shadow, erases himself. You understand after all.'

'I faced the same thing on my train journey from Summer…' I banged the edge of my hand on the edge of the tabletop; the papers slid off, the metallic innards of the telephone jangled. A fresh stream of pain swept through my body. 'I should have suspected! This modus operandi is more than obvious. Especially under the Ice: what betrays a greater truth about you than the lie coming from yourself? This is how you proclaim yourself to the world. And he openly admitted to me that he used this method to send an agent after Tesla disguised as a Flemish journalist. Such was the truth! Such was Pobedonostseff's genuine method! Such the truest lie!

'He arrived mortally sick and died soon afterwards, or was helped to die somehow. As he'd already hidden himself from the world, the world didn't find out. Did they hire a man to sit at the summit of the tower behind the trumpets and pneumatic apparatuses and relay their orders in his enciphered voice? Or maybe they themselves took it in turns to play this role, a day at a time, a week at a time?'

'Who?'

'The Siberian Coldiron Industrial Company! The directors on the board!' I pressed the receiver to my ear, my forehead to the wooden furniture, my swelling eye to a cold nail. A blind man with head jammed into a wall, a battering-ram of intellectual stupidity against the obtuseness of matter. So, this is why my deductions leading from the agent-cum-murderer to Pobedonostseff broke down: there was no sole truth of character standing behind his orders. They decided amongst themselves, voted, did their calculations, inferred from the necessity of saving their coldiron fortunes, percentage by percentage, rouble by rouble, share packet by share packet.

'The City of Ice was ruled from the beginning by money! Directly ruled by the Ice and by coldiron, by fluctuations in the Harbin exchange rates and geological wars on the Ways of the Mammoths! No individual man, but Necessity – not the tsar's word, which they obeyed only insofar as they had to – and not Aleksandr Aleksandrovitch Pobedonostseff. Who existed not, existed not, existed not!'

Ooee-eewww-eeee-eeeesk…

Krkhrrr.

'But… ooeeooeeee… you speak… weeeezg!… of this… Kingdom of Darkness… eeeeeeeeeeee… and your friendship in the project of the future world of the Ice… who… wee-eeeeeey… if not… eezg!… Well, who? The board of directors? Did they vote on those dreams? Sell themselves shares in the planned friendship?'

Indeed, who mused, who dreamed? If he existed not – whose truth did he tell in those lies? What secret of the collective soul did he reveal in his zealous sermon on the Kingdom of Darkness, preached from behind glintzen and unlicht, from behind the clattering steel – he, the frost pattern proliferating amongst the Sibirkhozheto directors, he, the Man Who Never Was?

Of what does Sibirkhozheto dream? Of what do listed companies and multibillion corporations muse? What icy nightmares drive the bureaucratic souls of joint-stock companies, *Sociétés Anonymes* and *Aktiengesellschaften*?

On that day, at the top of the coldiron tower – I had conversed with a bodyless, brainless entity, not even with a mechanical creature, not with machine intelligence, not with some Leibnizian reckoner operating on gears and dials; allegiance and friendship were offered me by someone totally different, by something totally different… Just as we are children of matter, blossoming upwards from where we are into worlds of ideas, so it was born amongst ideas, and reaches only hesitatingly from where it is, into matter. The Child of History, setting off up the gradient of historical necessity with the same naturalness as we walk between the rooms of a brick-built house.

As its herald and sole confidant, it finds – whom? The castrate Angel, a man already almost severed from his body, detached from matter. And as its friend, it seeks – whom? The Mathematician, the Algorithmist of Ideas, the non-existent Benedykt Gierosławski.

That it happened to grow up on the nourishment of money… Others like it will grow up on pure politics, on war, still others – on study of the natural sciences. Organisms built from ideas instead of proteins. For the time being, there are no names for them, there is no language.

'Well, we won't get to the truth now anyway. It has unfrozen.'

Krkhhr, trtrtr, krkkkk, kkhh-kaar! This was the laughter of Schultz/Pobedonostseff.

'Agh, agh, but I know how it is: Count Schultz is dead, no longer alive!' and goes on laughing.

I shan't get to the truth. Maybe Schultz is enlying Pobedonostseff, or maybe Pobedonostseff is enlying Schultz. It may be so and it may be so. It *is* both so and so.

Summer.

I beat my head against the wall. Eeeeeeyooooooooo! Outside, rain rattles on sheet-iron roofs, drums on timber. I open my eye. The yeasty Revolutionary flexes his muscles.

Exhalation.

But does any of this matter anyway…? As long as we live to see the return of the Ice. Let there be truth and falsehood, being and non-being, One and Zero.

'I give you my word. And now tell them to let me go.'

'… ooeeooeeee… always… vyooeeeezzz… Yeroslavsky's… eezzzz… word!'

I laid down the receiver beside the apparatus, knocked on the door. The diamond brute eyed me up and down with his butcher's gaze, passing me without a word in the doorway. He listened for a moment to the voice wheezing down the wire. Then went to fetch his superiors, leaving me with two other sentries. I waited patiently.

An older Trotskyist appeared, probably roused from slumber, he had such a befuddled look to start with. Evidently, he was not well informed about the affair: first of all, he consulted with the diamond bully, then talked for a long while to Schultz/Pobedonostseff. Eventually, he hung up, and dismissed the fighters from the room with a wave. He buttoned his crumpled jacket, lit a cigarette… I blinked, putting together his blurred image on my pupil. He was observing me closely, coughing into the palm cupped before his mouth. Only then did something begin to freeze in my mind's eye – playing cards, a parrot, AGG, no, that one had been as bald as your knee.

I cleared my throat.

'You used to be editor of *The Irkutsk News*.'

He handed me a cigarette, proffered a light. I inhaled. He squinted, blinded by the yellow lightbulb.

'Maybe I should keep you in order to bargain with Pocięgło, Gospodin Yeroslavsky…'

'A nice trade in live wares now passes through Lev Davidovitch's hands. Why not hang me straightaway on a lamppost.'

'Egh, Polacks.' He flicked ash into the hollow of his other palm. 'Don't name-drop before my eyes, Trotsky has stayed overnight with me many a time, I'm on the List of the Four Hundred.'

'An elite conspiracy!' I smiled with lips taut with blood. 'How do you make a proletarian revolution in a country with no proletariat? Well, with the Jewish intelligentsia, which knows what's best for the proletariat without being that proletariat. How does it know? From historical calculations. But whosoever takes on the Mathematics of History not as a cold impartial scholar focused solely on numbers and on the internal beauty of algorithms, but as a missionary, a sectarian, blinded aforehand by his own sacred soletruth and formulating everything according to it, fighting his own truthjoust against the world – will never get a good result. The suffering of the simple man has eaten into the hearts of thin-skinned students, so they set about converting Russia to the new Marxist religion. The arithmetic of humanists!' I snorted. 'Well, so now you have the people's justice and a new world order: hunger, terror, corpses on the streets and humans locked in animal cages, kept like animals.'

The Trotskyist editor stretched his limbs, endeavouring to shake off his exhaustion, the fatigue from body and mind.

'I don't have the nerves for any of you people…' He sat down on the table, but this recast him in a shorter posture; he noticed and stood up. 'You're an intelligent educated man after all, I read your article, you must know that the idea itself is just. The task, however, is to reconcile the world to the idea. Had Pobedonostseff not mined the Transsib, had the Bolsheviks not broken the revolutionary covenant, were it not for the Japanese blockades and the Chinese war, were it not for the autocrat's anti-Japanese Pacific Pact with the Americans, were there no epidemics constantly in the city… Just look at the mud, the pulp, the chaos, the mulch. The world won't allow us to realise the idea!'

'Because you began it all from the wrong end: first you have to surrender the world into the total power of ideas, and only then set about engineering history.'

'We shall notify your Company of our first order,' the crumpled editor spat with acid sarcasm, and on that note our conversation ended, for the diamond fighter had returned with my belongings. They gave back my coat, stick, pocketbook, the tortoiseshell portfolio with Jelena's portrait, even the box of sodden cigarette tubes.

The former editor caught my sidelong scowls at the ring glittering on the swaggerer's hand and then suddenly, straight out of his drowsiness, out of his senile exhaustion, he exploded in sputtering anger, bellowing such a torrent of curses, vituperations, death threats and spirts of foul language that the youngster sprang to attention and froze before him in the centre of the office, arms by his sides, eyes to the ceiling, humbly awaiting the boyar's verdict, blasted to stone. I recalled the tchinovnik outbursts of Commissioner Schembuch. The boorishness of these semiservile, feudal relationships will still haunt Russians for a long while to come, whichever way History turns. It is precisely this pulp and mulch which is at variance with ideological projects when built on entropy. Come the Kingdom of God as envisaged by Filimon Romanovitch Zeytsoff, and Russian angels will be filling in each other's mugs likewise and spitting out insults according to the heavenly pecking order from the highest-ranked downwards, pickled on warm vodka and sweating red neath their snow-white feathers.

Eventually, the editor tore the ring from the fighter's finger and kicked him out of the office.

'From whom did he steal it?' I asked, fastening my coat, wiping the blood off my face with a sleeve and carefully massaging my bruised eye.

He shrugged his shoulders.

'Tailors, cobblers, ragpickers,' he puffed, 'there you have it, such is their concept of the people's justice: take from the rich man. Why be surprised at the ignorance of the poor? Well, go, go, we have to dispatch you lest Pobedonostseff seek an excuse. Where were you heading?'

'To the City Infirmary.'

They delivered me to the boundary of the quarter held by the National Democrats, stretching from the old landing-stage beyond Baikalskaya

Street, immediately to the west of Innokentyevskoye. In the meantime, rain had been pouring harder still; thick clouds had sealed the night sky over Irkutsk and the city was blotted out by shadows deeper than shadow: a single dark stain, a smeary daub, blackness sprawling into an oily neither-this-nor-that. This was as much as I saw with my eye tightly sealed by swelling, bathed in rain and pink discharge: how it swims, how it spills from contour into contour, worse still, how it bursts every line of the contour. I wore no frostoglaze spectacles – the city was dissolving of its own accord.

I limped through the boundary streets, hiding under walls. Lights were burning in the turrets and mansards of the City Infirmary; thanks to these alone, I recognised the building. As after the fire in 1879 and Great Fire of 1910, many young architects inspired by new world fashions were brought to Irkutsk so that they might change the aspect of the Baikal metropolis. At the beginning of the Ice era, additional factors came into play: coldiron technology and safety measures against gleissen; the restorations proceeded too quickly, however, to be significantly reflected in the image of the city centre. But the rebuilding of the City Infirmary was delayed for two years on account of embezzlement scandals; in the end, the Red Cross Society in East Siberia contributed funds of its own and placed the hospital under management of the Congregation of the Sisters of Mercy. Meanwhile, it received an entirely modern design and an edifice befitting more the cityscape of Zimny Nikolayevsk: built on a first storey a dozen arshins above the ground, on coldiron pillars chilled into open-work patterns, within walls encased by huge frostoglaze panels, with dozens of neogothic bay windows and secessionist plant designs sprouting between them, embellished in pilasters and reliefs.

Lights were burning in the east wing; only when approaching the building itself, did I see that a darker wing had sunk into the thawed ground – not very far, perhaps an arshin, but enough to totally unravel the multi-storey structure and force the great sheets of frostoglaze out of their casings. Just as a gangrenous, moribund limb is amputated from an organism, so too the withered part of the hospital had been amputated from its healthy part. Life and light were milling to the right of the stairs and lift shaft.

Where, however, even greater chaos reigned than at the Holy Trinity. First of all, immediately on entering from the hallway, I chanced upon a heartrending scene, as two sobbing women tussled over a filthy bundle, themselves pulled from the queue by the sisters; some men joined the scuffle as did even an impulsive young man with a gun. I gave it a wide berth. A kind soul of a sister, who saw me in the registration office and then proceeded to tie clean bandages around my injured head, pouring on hydrogen peroxide or some other bug-killer, told me the tragedy was the result of rat-bite fever: the child had died and had to be cremated, as otherwise infection would spread. There was a crematorium in the dark wing.

I took out the sketch from the canvas (it slipped and slipped again between my swollen fingers). Such a young woman, and such a doctor, name of Konyeshin – do you know them, sister?

'Doctor Konyeshin operates in number seven.'

Naturally, she was mistaken. In suite number seven (whose theatres were numbered however 7A, 7Б and 7B), no operations could have taken place: these rooms were already located beyond the line of scission, wind was driving rain through gouged-out windows and onto equipment piled by the lower walls. I walked around the entire operating floor. The fact that I could wander freely at will, a man off the street, in a coat still dripping with water, testified more than anything to the general state of chaos and anarchy – here a sawn-off leg, there ten beds full of poor wretches groaning in agony, here a mountain of red bandages heaped on disembowelled guts, there a complicated child delivery, here chest and ribs gaping wide open, there a queue of bedraggled survivors from the night-time shelling – and no one even raised an eyebrow at my presence. The sisters tottered back and forth with hands full, passing people in the corridors without paying them attention. The gentlemen doctors – I counted four working at that hour, all it was possible to muster on that bloody night of war – were calling in raised voices for these or those medicaments, for water, for light, for clean rags and a helping hand. Arched stained-glass panels above the doors portrayed Gospel scenes, mainly of healing the sick or exorcising demons; Jesus was always there with his back turned, distinguished only by the brightness of His silhouette.

In theatre number 3Б (the Gadarene swine), Doctor Konyeshin, as he cut open the lung of a pot-bellied fatty, whose head had been bandaged into a ball, was shouting for drainage tubes and thread; I found them three rooms farther on. The sister assisting Konyeshin thanked me without letting go a throbbing tangle of veins from her fingers inserted into the patient's chest. It stank of naphtha, blood and putrefaction, above all of naphtha: the operating table was surrounded by lamps emitting smoke as high as the ceiling. 'Don't block the light, don't block the light!' growled the red-haired doctor, moving with his tongue a short fag-end on his lip as soon as I approached the table. I walked around the room below the frostoglaze windows, wading through mounds of congealed dressings and rags, shredded clothing and body scraps. 'Doctor, sir,' I asked, supporting myself against a coldiron olive tree inbuilt between the tall panes, for my head had begun to spin from my great fatigue, from the constant pain and tension. 'Doctor, sir, where will I find Miss Muklanowicz?' 'Not now,' he barked, 'not now! Wait, she only helps in the daytime, I don't know the address. Her shift starts at seven. Mm-mm, he'll die on me yet, the son of a bitch!'

I sat on a stool in the corner. My fever abated; I cooled down. Blood flowed into my legs, into my drooping hands. The stick tapped on the parquet floor. I had to press my head into the wall, otherwise it would have rolled off my neck to right or left. The dressing on my eye slipped lower and lower, so now I could see the scene in the honey-coloured lamplight – with the doctor glimmering in his silver-rimmed glasses, apron bespattered with organic fluids, the white sister and enormous body ripped open on the operating table – I saw half of it, a quarter, an eighth. The doctor worked inside the breathing body with the motions of a master chef, chopping carrot and slicing beetroot for the hundred-thousandth time: one, two, three, four, cut, transfer, extract, stitch. He consulted with the sister wordlessly, as they performed the centuries-old ritual on the body, nothing new between man and matter. How he had advanced in years – grown thin, emaciated, haggard; his once luxuriant sideburns too had shrivelled, the left now intersected by a broad milky-white scar; thus, Doctor Konyeshin had lost, had forfeited his former symmetry... I closed the dressing over my eye.

I woke neath the cold light of a rainy dawn.

I tore off the bandage.

'What time is it?!'

'Quarter past six.' Doctor Konyeshin was rummaging with his scalpel in the fatty's chest, gradually loosening the clamps, removing the drains, forceps and tweezers, clasps and clips, but doing it all lacka-daisically, perfunctorily with one hand, whilst the other held high a fresh cigarette. 'According to the rules, I ought to chuck you out, but – the rotter's kicked the bucket anyway.' He inhaled, inclined his head almost horizontally and blew smoke towards the ceiling. 'Agh, like in my youth! Almost like my days at the front.'

The echo of a single gunshot, muffled by rain, reached us from the street.

Koneyshin chuckled, then he flicked ash onto the corpse's heart and raised towards me a pure, sober gaze – sober as only a man can be at a milky translucent dawn after a sleepless night: nerves on the surface, skin like parchment, brain throbbing in an open skull.

'Aren't you perhaps one of them? What do you want from Mademoiselle Jelena?'

'Everything.' I stood up and stretched out my hand across the oper-ating table. 'Benedykt Gierosławski.'

'You?' He levelled his lancet at me, narrowing his left eye and aiming along a straight line above his spectacle lenses. 'Yeroslavsky. Yeroslavsky? Yeroslavsky. Come, show me your face! Mm-hmmm. Well, they must have given you a good drubbing.'

He transferred the lancet to his other palm, wiped his right on his apron and shook my proffered hand.

'You were going to treat the White Plague in the Pacific ports,' I said.

'It seems that Doctor Tesla has cured them. Boom, boom, boom. But I got stuck in Irkutsk halfway into my journey as I tried to return to Europe on the Trans-Siberian Express; it wasn't a sensible idea. Mm-hmmm.' He inhaled again. 'Yes, I remember you well. *Franchement*, I often wondered afterwards what became of that business with your pater and with History. And now, here he is, the great Nikola Tesla... Mm-hmmm.' He scrutinised me through the smoke. 'Is it not true? Why, you did distort the course of history, did redirect the Ice. Not by persuading the gleissen through your father, as everyone expected, but earlier, during your journey on the Trans-Siberian Express. Fate was bent on Doctor Tesla's death and the long reign of the Ice, now it can be seen clearly, yet you, sir – let me count – you obstinately saved Tesla: once, from the attempt on his life by the traitorous okhran-nik, secondly, by raising him from the dead, thirdly, by discovering the bomber in time – time and again you rescued Tesla from the fate destined for him.'

'Jelena told you this.'

'I've heard it also from others. When the Serb declared himself in Macau... Mm-hmmm.'

I lowered my eyes.

'Yes, I have the same impression. That the most important things already happened on the journey in the Express.'

He was silent, blowing out acrid smoke.

I took off my coat, threw it over my shoulder. On the blurred horizon above the city, beyond the frostglaze panel where everything still swam in the rain, brighter, more dazzling patches were flicker-ing. There in the west, to the south of the Uysky district – probably in Glazkovo, something was on fire. The wet weather had brought to the City of Thaw at least this blessing: it stifled the conflagrations after a night of truthjousts.

My eye returned involuntarily to the entrails of the dissected corpse. The first flies were buzzing about. In Zygmunt's anatomical atlases, it had all looked so different, *duodenum, jejunum, ileum*, almost like dia-grams of industrial machines: that part is for this, this part for that, this serves such-and-such purpose, whilst that is attached to this. Yet here: it's as if someone had stirred inside the man with a big primitive ladle, one great bigos, one brownish-reddish-yellowish-violet mush with tougher chunks of meat caught inside. Man arose out of mud and bears mud within him.

'Show me.' Doctor Konyeshin strode towards me from the feet of the corpse, reached for my beard, my cheek.

I pushed him away.

'It's nothing!'

'Maybe it could be straightened out… Those are bad adhesions. Who did the trepanations?'

'No one.'

He continued eyeing me up and down with a sceptical look.

'What of it,' I snorted, 'still dabbling in phrenology?'

He slowly removed his apron.

'Before in the train, you seemed so…'

'What?'

He threw the apron into the autoclave and performed a vapid, empty gesture with his arm and cigarette

'Without qualities.'

I laughed.

'I know.'

He glanced suspiciously. The scales tipped in my favour, lines converged in my eye; the eye held Doctor Konyeshin trapped in that moment like an insect in amber.

He shuddered.

'You've supposedly acquired vast worldly wisdom, eh?'

'Worldly wisdoms I leave to rabbis and old harlots. Let us say I have uncovered several laws governing the Mathematics of Character.'

'For example?'

'A man's character arises through subtraction.'

His suspicion mounted with every second. Now he was circumventing me in a safe arc, at a distance of five paces, like a matador stalking a bull. His hand with the smoking cigarette served as his muleta. The livid pot-bellied corpse as a screen.

'Mademoiselle Jelena showed me what they've been writing about you recently. Here every newspaper is brazen propaganda, lies upon lies. But I remember also Director Pocięgło. Today you're doing Oblastnik politics together. Mm-hmmm.'

'I don't consider myself a politician, if that's what you're asking. Politics is an obsolete craft.'

The asymmetrical doctor paused and rested his foot on the crossbar of the operating table. The last drops of life dripped from the dissected fatty. Konyeshin leaned across him towards me, trying to strike a pose of intimacy, of familiarity, of unserious confidences.

'So, what will it be?' he asked softly.

'What?'

'This new Siberian state of Director Pocięgło. A republic? Some kind of institutionalised anarchy? A union of Narodnik zemstvos? Or maybe communism? Or perhaps Pocięgło will appoint himself autocrat? Tell me.'

'To tell the truth...'

'What, don't they know yet?'

I swept my arm and coat in a wide gesture, embracing the whole dissolved city.

'But how it is supposed to freeze of its own accord?'

I raised the murchometer, wound it briskly, glanced at the scale, 366 mirks. An aquamarine river was flowing beyond the frostoglaze panes.

'For sure it'll begin with some kind of democracy,' I muttered. 'If only to draw our darling revolutionaries away from Saint-Simon *et consortes*. With time, the reformed SRs and Struvists will gain the upper hand. Voting, parties, elections – these will freeze first; then the political asceticism of Proudhon, Bakunin and Kropotkin will lose its attraction.' I clicked my tongue. 'Democracy, yes, democracy.'

The asymmetrical doctor winced in disgust.

'You speak of democracy, sir, as if it were a kind of ideology and carried within it some content, aim, ideal; I hear it all the time from local hotheads here dreaming of the guillotine for the Tsar Batyushka. Yet nothing could be more mistaken! Democracy is an empty mould, within which a thousand miscellaneous substances may freeze, both good and evil. It's the same with a knife,' he grabbed hold of the dirty scalpel and brandished it over the corpse, 'the knife in itself is neither good nor evil: you can slice an apple with it, operate on a patient, but you can also thrust it under a man's ribs in a tavern brawl and deprive him of his life. The democracy of cannibals will introduce to parliament ideas of the equal division of corpses. The democracy of the merciful will vote down pardons for cannibals. Whilst the democracy of children – will choose whatever the adults induce it to.'

'The instrument, however, doesn't remain ultimately impartial when it comes to the aim. What you carry out with a knife, you don't carry out with a hammer, and vice versa. There are certain ideas that blossom better in democracy, and there are those that wilt and wither. The same applies to other systems of government, like monarchy or autocracy.

'You see, Doctor, the first thing in the practice of the Algorithmics of History is to learn how to read ideas from low-level matter. We already talked about this with Zeytsoff in the Express – were you present then? – about fashions, melodies, customs, tastes. What is this?' I raised before me the mud-caked, blood-soaked coat, 'A coat. But take a look at the cut: longer? shorter? has it a collar? what type of fastening? how do the lapels lie? what kind of pockets? square or raglan sleeves? to cut open or not cut open the flaps? indent the waist – by how much? Count the buttons. And what are they made of: bone? horn? wood? metal? And how many rows are there? Where's the belt, where the waist, what kind of buckle? What colour? What kind of material? All these are not random eruptions of a tailor's fantasy, unconstrained by utilitarian necessity, but signs of the zeitgeist, that is, of the ideas controlling people in every sphere of life. For there is no separate idea for politics, and a different one – for music, a different one – for gastronomical art, a different one – for architectural fashion or fancy goods. The idea encompasses everything. Therefore, *par example*, the advent of a great European war can be read about years in advance in cheap popular novels, the type published in print runs of hundreds of thousands. Whilst officers' greatcoats, vatermörder collars and tight corsets – they similarly reflect a single truth. That which is unseen precedes that which is seen, Monsieur le Docteur. First idea ousts idea, and only then does the tailor think to himself: "No, better trim the coat to fit the strict fashion, add tabs, shoulder-straps and a wider belt made of leather, so it'll sell faster". My task is to express this in numbers and concrete symbols, to place the idea behind tailor or tsar within the system of the Algorithmics of History.

'Yes, my dear Doctor, this is exactly how I regard democracy.' I pointed the murchometer stick at the coat; the gesture was purely theatrical, taken straight from the show of a parlour magician. 'Coat. Democracy. *Voilà!*

'I can put it on, take it off. I am not a politician. Politics and politicians are variables in my equations.'

A sister peeped into the room bringing papers in a linen portfolio. Doctor Konyeshin took the hospital documents from her. Having done up the buttons on his shirt-cuffs and wiped the lenses of his glasses, he quickly ticked off item after item, muttering to himself under his breath.

'But what about order, but what about the State!' he suddenly cried, startling the sister. 'These you will not provide by democracy alone, Mr Yeroslavsky! Soon you and Director Pocięgło will understand this: people are unable to govern themselves. There is as much order and justice as there is concrete power over man.' He returned the documents to the sister. Having stubbed out his cigarette butt on the coldiron moulding of a creeper vine, he wiped the steamy frostoglaze with his sleeve. 'Especially now, especially here. Will you start from democracy? You will end on the scrapheap!'

He sighed, grew sad. Removed his spectacles; now he was staring at the city through waves of hazy colour with the squint eyes of a myopic, from under puckered red brows; the stern ruddy visage of the iron bourgeois branded by an expression of agonised concern. Agh, I had forgotten that for the doctor, History was a personal matter, that he took these things to heart; the doctor had unfinished business with History, it had gnawed deep into his soul.

'No,' he whispered. 'You won't succeed. How many of them here still swim in it after the Thaw? Democracy is a cauldron only a fraction more solid. You'll brew nothing in it.

'Just look! How it melts, degenerates. Hegel was wrong. History progresses downwards from what is necessary, hard, logical – to what is unclear, soft, random. From theocracies, through absolute divine-right monarchies, constitutional monarchies and eventually to democracies; but after that – after that there is only communism and nihilism and anarchy. Which can be seen most clearly here, in Russia, where the first order held – frozen – for so long and where now, suddenly, everything is melting at once into this human mud, into this – this – this fetid muck. Look out of the window. Look!

'This Thaw is a natural disaster of History!'

I stood beside him, a step away from the tall windowpane, before a heap of rags that stank of the corpse, leaning on my stick. The fire in Glazkovo had died down and no living colour now penetrated the perpendicular puddles of drizzle splashing against the frostoglaze. Irkutsk was slowly trickling into the gutters.

'Never fear, Doctor. It will freeze.'

'You don't say?'

'Did you not urge me to do this when we were still in the train? Your dreams shall come true: man will straighten out History into an ideal, mathematical order.'

'You don't say...'

'Apoliteia shall come about.'

'Apoliteia?'

Doctor Konyeshin did not know my article. There had been no Konyeshin in Irkutsk at the time, he arrived after Thaw. What had Jelena told him? Clearly not everything.

So, I repainted for him in dry, dispassionate words – or so I thought – the concept of the rule of History, of the Un-State and highest order, in which no man has power to oppress and torment another man; and also my practical way of realising it: through the technologies of the Ice, in a future offering the pancosmic immortality of Fyodoroff, the whole Kingdom of Darkness, wherein people will at last wrest themselves from the slavery of the body, dwelling already amidst pure ideas – matter shall equal spirit; language of the second kind shall equal language of the first kind. *It is the spirit that giveth life, the flesh profiteth nothing.*

Therefore, no State. No earthly power, no tsars, no tchinovniks. No physical suffering. No poverty. No lies. No injustice. Truth calculable at first glance. No death. No Dostoyevskyisms in the soul. Love as sure as mathematics, mathematics as sure as love. Enough Ice to still preserve life; enough life to enjoy the heavenly order of the Ice.

I was expecting that Konyeshin of all people would grasp the thing in a trice, that he would fathom to the core the whole diamond beauty of the vision – was it not he who had sermonised to me with passion: find a way of curing History! take the responsibility upon yourself! judge according to your own reason! pay no attention to temptations flowing from the world of the senses, from the life which is thus but could be otherwise! take History upon yourself! – was it not he? He, he, he! He it was who shouted loudest: History can exist only under the Ice! He, he had called for History designed by man!

Yet now – he is silent, tightens his lips, folds his arms across his chest... Knows not what to say. Rubs his hunched shoulders through his flimsy shirt. A shudder passes through him.

'When you put it in those terms...'

'What?' I smirked quietly, covering my burning disappointment in laughter. 'Have you got cold feet, Doctor?'

'I spoke to you of repairing, of *curing* History.' Wrenching his gaze from the swimming city, he glanced at me from close by. 'For this, however, you need to have a doctor's soul... Not... a mathematician's.' He chewed over some harsh thought for a while. 'What will it look like? Have you thought it through? How will people live from day to day? Who perchance will govern them? In the Express, you did not betray such convictions.'

I bristled.

'Do you not remember your quarrel with Herr Blutfeld? You must possess this memory, I can't be the only one left with it, *n'est-ce pas*?'

He nodded.

I took a breath.

'*Alors*, precisely apoliteia is the only possible solution to your dispute: freedom from the tyranny of man over man, and at the same time, I'm telling you, Order and Truth saving humanity from all this poverty, injustice, all these non-necessary deaths and sufferings.

'For you are mistaken, Doctor, History over the centuries has lost none of its strength and coherence. Here in Russia, you have a twisted view of things, Frost has entered your bones; intensified teslectrical pressure has accustomed you to Truth. But it's going in the opposite direction.

'Look. Take an Egyptian building the pyramids in Pharaonic times: he didn't feel History at all; he was born and died in the same world, under the same political system and religion, under the immovable stars.

'But Roman citizens at the time of the Republic, or Christians of Charlemagne's and Barbarossa's Europe – they already felt the first pressures of History, for History was already manifesting itself beyond the will of rulers: they were conscious, for instance, that they lived in the twilight or dawn of a certain culture; that one civilisation ousts another civilisation, that blood swills out blood, new peoples replace former peoples, cult slays cult and a young God casts down from heaven the decrepit gods. But why should these historical systems fall away into oblivion? wherein lies the advantage of their successors? It was still not discernible; changes took place over generations; the movement of History was palpable but still unable to be described, unable to be measured.

'But then came the Age of Reason and revolutions made with revolutionary consciousness, on the basis of revolutionary theories – History plucked out specific individuals with its fingers. Already within a single lifetime, you could see the world pupating – not according to this or that decision taken by a ruler, not according to someone's private plan or a chance event of Nature, but out of *historical necessity*.

'And now it has speeded up even more, now you read about the movements of History in the newspapers. Who told Stolypin to introduce agricultural reform, to lease to peasants their own land beyond the Urals, to harness the landed aristocracy into new economic systems, to invent new methods of taxation? Neither Tsarskoye Selo nor the Tauride Palace was well-disposed. But it had to be done: otherwise, Russia would have lost out to countries that had modernised without delay. You see it more clearly still in the changes in military art: did someone suddenly tell them all to order dreadnoughts from the shipyards, instead of old ironclads? No. But it's obvious: whoever does not go along with History, will lose out, whilst History will consume them one way or another, bitten through, chewed over, crushed to a uniform pulp. Yet this was demonstrated perfectly following the advent of the Ice technologies, when within a few short years the weathercocks of science, of economics, of progress swung around on every continent. Could they not have swung around? Physics is physics. History is History.

'So, multiply this by ten, a hundred, a thousand, and see it magnified in details of everyday bourgeois life. For what will the State still be needed? For what – tchinovniks? For what – politicians? History will don their suits and their functions. Taxes – there'll be only such taxes as have to be: neither higher, for we'll lose out in commercial competition to states with lower taxes, nor slashed to zero, for without taxes we won't maintain social order. The law – will be strictly dictated by the era's obvious realities: the Code of Hammurabi won't be realised in twentieth-century Switzerland, nor the Bill of Rights amongst naked savages of the South who create fire by rubbing stones. Maybe parliaments will survive as entertainment for the populace; colourful tub-thumpers will be elected for their singularity, whilst their pseudo-political shows will amuse the mob with bedchamber scandals, with the hatred of one character for another, or with exalted arguments over national colours or tunes for the national anthem, totally lacking in significance when it comes to money or science, or the happiness of ordinary citizens. Since the time of apoliteia is imminent.

'History shall rule.'

He fled from me in his eyes. Rrrrrwoom, this time the tremor passed through the very building causing everything to shake, walls and equipment and medical instruments, whilst the corpse on the operating table belched forth the last of its gases. An earthquake? They often occur near Baikal, especially since Thaw, or so I heard. But no, it was probably only the permafrost letting go, the frozen matter near the surface that lets go the quickest.

'So how do you intend in turn to govern History?' asked the irregular doctor, standing wider on his legs. 'If this whole inevitable apoliteia is also a foregone conclusion –'

'Ah, but ask yourself the question, Doctor: what is it that makes History reveal precisely such necessities?' I leant more heavily on the murchometer. 'You know the habits of Nature. That the butterfly is born of the caterpillar, and not the caterpillar of the butterfly; biology decides it, according to its own specific laws and dependences. But what historical biology determines that the chivalric, noble estate must transform into the bourgeoisie, and not the other way around? that dynastic fiefdoms are turned into nation-states – and not the other way around? that industry destroys the landed aristocracy – why, why not the other way around?'

'God has ordained it so…'

'You said yourself that you don't need God for anything!' I cried triumphantly.

He drew in air, but did not reply. No truth remained under his feet upon which he could oppose my Mathematics of History.

Why was he resisting me? Why denying his own words as they flowed from my mouth? Most likely, he couldn't have said himself, not in the language of the second kind.

'Yet the Ice showed us, my dear Doctor,' I continued, already calmer, 'how it's possible to influence the biology of History as well. And how sooner or later, we will be living in History designed by man. If not I, then someone else would have thought of it first. The Kingdom of Darkness awaits its lord. In the end, one way or another, matter will become as one with ideas, that is, with number, whilst History will become our natural environment, our air and bread, the sole centre of human life.

'*Monsieur le docteur, vous comprenez, vous!* You remember in Zeytsoff's parable that lever for switching the points for the train of History.' I raised my stick to the height of my eye, swung it to the left, swung it to the right. 'Did God forbid killing because killing is evil – or is killing evil, because God forbade killing?'

On hearing this *dictum*, Konyeshin grew flustered. Looking down at his feet, he walked over to the washbasin, poured himself water, but did not wash his hands; he turned around, leaning his back against the porcelain. His eyes shot about the chaotic theatre, carefully avoiding me. Eventually, they stopped on the naked human remains displayed in the middle.

'So how shall it be then, Mr Yeroslavsky? will killing be evil?'

I extricated myself from the rags by the window and walked up to the table, cutting into the doctor's gaze. The taste and odour of death, that sweet putrefaction not so very different to the human senses from the gamey smack of tenderised venison, pleasant after all, entered my mouth, settled in my saliva, stuck to my palate. I gulped once and twice. The sickly graveyard perfume both attracted and repelled. Who is able to restrain himself from scratching a sore fresh wound? The patient's huge belly, dissected by Konyeshin's hand, bared its moist interior, reminiscent in the white early-morning light of an open grave – even a worm was moving inside, that is, a fly. His head was tightly packed instead in linen bandages. I laid my crippled hand upon this blind tuber and patted tenderly the soulless meat through the clean shroud.

'Again, you wish to urge me to something? Ask for something?'

Konyeshin approached hesitatingly from the other side of the table, took in his palm the dangling hand of the corpse, then laid it symmetrically alongside – without, however, finally releasing his clasp with the dead man.

'For the dictatorship of mercy,' he whispered.

But he was unable to look me straight in the eye.

As I departed, I paused again in the doorway and wheeled around under the swine possessed by the demon.

'And yet you have rubbed shoulders with History,' I said in a deliberately lighter tone. 'And yet you have touched its flesh in motion, felt the fabric of History beneath your fingers. Did you not dream of this,

Doctor? To exert an influence even to the slightest degree. Well, you have exerted an influence upon me.'

Doctor Konyeshin continued to stand over the patient whom he'd been unable to save, eyeing up and down the ghastliness of matter with sad eyes. A blurred sun delineated him from behind through rain and frostglaze, setting alight his red sideburns.

He buttoned his shirt to the neck.

'I'm cold.'

Having extracted again Miss Muklanowicz's now severely creased and sodden drawing, I began once more to walk around the infirmary, questioning the sisters and indeed anyone who didn't have the look of a patient. Some said they'd never set eyes on such a devushka, others on the contrary, that there was a girl like that who'd died, and others still who recognised their own relative in her; I no longer cared. Even the sight of wards full of unfortunates dying from their wounds or from plague or from smallpox could not spoil my mood. In hospital, the hours after dawn are a time of vocal suffering: those who've survived the night wake up and greet the new day with groans, coughing, dry sobs, but most often with endless litanies of dull, mechanical, spat-out curses; women recite litanies of prayers. The filthy melody of their hoarse distorted voices blends with the scent of medicinal chemicals and stench of human bodies lying in sweat, urine, faeces and blood. You want to pit your strength against the emperor of the flesh – so drop in first to a hospital.

In a ward below a stained-glass panel portraying a woman with clay vases under seven black shadows, I heard a familiar voice, a male voice uttering German words, which resonated at once in my memory with a long echo. Bittan von Asenhoff! I stopped still, turned on my heels. Bed on the left, bed on the right, bed by the wall – it is he who speaks. I draw near. I did not recognise him from his body; his voice was intact, but of von Asenhoff's body there was but a shred. He had kicked off a blanket and sheet soaked in blood and pus, and lay now with shirt rolled up to his chest, naked apart from this, except for a wide bandage over his belly, which he was nevertheless trying to rip off, but lacked the strength for ripping off dressings; his emaciated skeleton was veiled in skin like a fish bladder. Of the Prussian aristocrat's countenance, not even the sharp nose remained – his nose was broken, his cheeks sunken, dotted with uneven tufts of old grey stubble. A toothless hundred-year-old gaffer clinging to life's dregs with trembling claw-like fingers.

'*Es wurde mir schwarz vor den Augen, Katya... wurde mir dunkel...*'

I stood beside him but he saw me not. With wide-open eyes, he stared at the cracked wall. He stank to high heaven. A large stain of unwiped faeces was visible underneath him on the mattress. His ulcerated genitals resembled rather a nest of subterranean worms. A thick brown substance was oozing from beneath the bandage.

I touched his shoulder. 'Herr Bittan?' But did he hear me at all? He was calling for his Katya. Probably for weeks on end, he'd been dwelling in hallucinations entirely detached from life.

Raising my eyes, however, I espied Katya coming from the doorway with basin and towel. She sat down on a stool beside the bed, wrung out hot water from the towel and, having rolled up the sleeve of his grey caftan, began to wash the old man. She didn't spare me a glance. Her bright-golden hair – now no longer golden, but grey – was tied neath a linen cap from which disorderly strands were now escaping. On her furrowed face etched by a thousand cares, no trace survived of her girlish joy, nor shadow of her innocent smile. Had I passed her in the corridor, I'd have taken her for a cleaner.

'What's the matter with him?' I asked quietly.

'Peasant pitchfork.'

Von Asenhoff was waving his arms and legs about uncoordinatedly beyond the bedframe, I withdrew slightly.

'I knew him,' I said, 'years ago, before the Thaw, when he still – when at Pussy Court –'

'You did not know him,' she cut in.

He managed to find her hand and clung to it with all his might.

'*Es dunkelt, meine Katze, es ist so finster…*'

She freed herself carefully.

'Maybe his relatives,' I began, 'surely he has money abroad, he can't be –'

'He gave it all away.'

'What happened?'

'Thaw.'

I scrutinised them for a long while. It was a most egregiously obscene thing, yet none of us showed any shame.

'You stayed with him,' I murmured.

'He paid me,' she replied indifferently, 'so that I wouldn't leave him alone in the darkness.'

'Paid you? Yet – he gave it all away.'

'Go, he'll die anyway, you won't get anything, go, go.'

I showed her Jelena's drawing. Katya glanced at it, then pointed with her wet hand to a fat sister in the ward opposite.

'I've often seen her with her. Will you hang her?'

'What? No!'

'Aha.'

Then, very gently, she began to wash the face of Bittan von Asenhoff.

The plump sister confessed that Jelena Muklanowicz did not work there at all; she came herself for some sort of tests and was well acquainted with Doctor Konyeshin. But she often helps on daytime shifts when extra hands are needed for the patients. But will she come today? Probably not. So where does she live? Here the sister began to stretch her feeble memory. In a boarding house, if I'm not mistaken. On Italyanskaya Street? Ispanskaya?

The rest I was able to freeze for myself. I thanked the nurse and ran down the long staircase into the rain.

From there to Gretchesky Pereulok was not far; it was impossible to count, however, how many alternate waves of electric euphoria and black hopelessness swept over me. With every footstep taken in the morning light, split into rainbows by the damp air – I was elated by certainty of the impending meeting with Jelena. Whilst every footstep taken under heavy cloud, in the shadow of a building hunched over a street – I was crushed to the ground, driven into mud, trampled by a mammoth. As if in me too, the City of Thaw, the City of Mud and Decay had at last managed to unfreeze. So that I wanted to grab the butt of the murchometer and measure the temperature of my own character; so that I wanted to find some mirror and look at myself in it with the eye of a stranger. Porfiry Pocięgło's mute fear touched me not at all, Zeytsoff's drunken passion slid off me like the rain, but the timorous doubting of Doctor Konyeshin – this I felt, this I had taken to heart. And then here was Herr Bittan von Asenhoff, steadfast knight of the flesh, dying in the flesh no differently after all from Sergey Atchukhoff... *Es ist so finster...* It grew dark – grew light – grew dark. Whoever craves knowledge of himself craves death – yet I was on my way to Kirytchkina's boarding house, wondering whether Filimon Romanovitch did manage to utter some obscure truth about me. Whether Doctor Konyeshin's terror stems, despite everything, from the rights of reason, from those rights which cannot be expressed in the speech of men. And whether what really awaits me at the helm of History is: *the darkness of winter and horror greater than any men have ever known: solitude in darkness?*

On us

I discovered Kirytchkina's boarding house in a state of half-burned ruin. Bare bricks peered from under patches of scorched façade. I climbed the stairwell, which had collapsed onto the street like a split-open tree mouldering from within, to the first floor. Blown off its hinges, the door to the rooms once rented by Jelena and her aunt swung mournfully in the rain-soaked wind. I merely glanced inside – at ransacked shells of furniture, at rotten carcasses of birds, at ash and fungus – and went back down. With the coldiron stick, I banged on the landlord's door. After long minutes of relentless drumming, someone – a man – yelled at me through the thick wood to get lost, for he had two loaded hagbuts in there and an army pistol at the ready. I inquired about Miss Muklanowicz from upstairs. He said he knew nothing. I inquired about Kirytchkina. He said she perished in the flames on the night the Citadel was taken.

The rain fell and fell. I hid on the landing beneath an overhang of surviving roof; I sat in a corner, wrapped in my coat. Thrum, thrum, thrum, thrum. At least it won't freeze.

I was awakened by the patter of cork heels on brick. I opened my eye. She was climbing the stairs, heavy bag in one hand; in the other – a half-folded umbrella. She had already passed me, climbing higher. The hood of her dark cape concealed the profile of her countenance.

I leapt to my feet, hobbled after her, supporting myself on the rubble with the stick.

She heard me. On the landing above, she spun around, stepping away from the wall. She let go the umbrella, which rolled down the stairs. I grabbed hold of it, and then a shot rang out and a bullet whistled right above my shoulder.

I raised my hands.

'It's me!'

Held in a man's chamois glove, the revolver did not tremble. She hadn't recognised me. She'll shoot me dead.

'Jelena… *qualsivoglia!*'

She recognised me. Recognised me not. Recognised me. Recognised me not. Recognised me.

She lowered the gun.

I walked up to her, handed back the umbrella. Having put away the short-barrelled revolver, she reached with her other hand for the umbrella, and then a black lightning-bolt of unlicht shot from me to her along the coldiron of the stick. Stung by icy teslectricity, the devushka uttered a muffled shriek – thus I recognised the voice of Jelena Muklanowicz.

I slipped the hood from her head. My God, how haggard she'd become, how emaciated. I touched her cheek with my three-fingered hand, kissed her on the forehead still wet from the rain. She no longer smelt of jasmine.

'Jelenka.'

She nestled close. I picked up the bag. She pointed to the ruins upstairs. We climbed the narrow steps to the loft above the burned-out apartments. The loft seemed no better; it was possible, however, to walk across the twisted floorboards to the other side, where a door reinforced with coldiron loomed in the brick wall, with both lock and padlock. Jelena took out her keys.

She had two garret rooms adjoining the wall of the taller, neighbouring house. The smaller, where she rustled up modest meals on a naphtha stove, had no window; the window of the larger chamber, wherein stood a bed, sideboard and a few more solid items of furniture rescued from Kirytchkina's apartments, looked out onto Gretchesky Pereulok and the same northerly panorama of Old Irkutsk that I recalled from my visits to the boarding house from years ago.

I took off my coat. She sat me on a chair, and herself sat down on the bed opposite. She restrained me when I raised my hand, did nothing but observe me, for a minute, two minutes, too long to count, as it stretched into a moment removed from time; she sat and stared, following me with her birdlike gaze – dark eyes, raven-black brows, pale skin, pale lips, her little tongue with its smooth tip poking out between teeth – until in the end she herself reached out and, having removed her gloves, began to trace her bony fingers, frozen to the marrow, over my hair, over my wounds and scars, over my blind eye and uneven cheeks… But without shame, but under eyes totally shameless and devoid of pity, like a cripple a cripple – for on the left side of her neck she had an ugly scald mark, whilst her left eyelid twitched slightly in a constant nervous tick, which I remembered not from the former Jelena Muklanowicz, entropy had also entered into her – therefore, like cripple a cripple. I wanted to tell her that they're only bodies – what truth can come between us from them, Jelena, what truth can be found in matter? – and I opened my mouth, but she was already waiting, lurking on my chin; she stole onto my tongue and nestled under gum and cheek – I bit – ah, now she smiled broadly – I licked the blood off her dirty fingers. Jelena sighed in deep relief; I saw the weights drop from her, the tension retreat, the eyelid close.

Melted, at peace, she snuggled down on the unmade bed like a child in a cradle, just as she was in her muddy boots and wet clothes, and fell asleep.

I continued to sit and watch over her. Covered her with a plaid blanket. She was breathing evenly. I wound the hair that kept falling on her face behind her ear. In her sleep, she licked her lips. I rose for a moment to light the cast-iron stove; then returned at once to my post. Raindrops tapped on the windowpanes and sill; a draft blew through the loft, rattling the floorboards outside the door – but all of it was muffled, softened, more and more distant. The room grew gradually warmer. I fell asleep. Woke up. Fell asleep. Woke up. Shadows changed on the walls and chest-of-drawers; hours must have passed. Jelena Muklanowicz was sleeping beside me, an arm's length away. I reached out with my hand and touched her lightly through the plaid – shoulder, hip, knee, neck, clenched fist. I kept falling asleep and waking up. Nothing pinned my thoughts to this timeless moment – for I had before me a vast crystal of frozen memory to survey in the sunlight spreading from the window, a vast crystal of events, people, places, words and deeds, all perfectly arranged, frozen into a totally chilled structure, organised around my remembered-existing past like a high-quality Nikolayevsk coolbond: zero, one, zero, one, zero, one, the tchinovniks from the Warsaw Ministry of Winter, the Transsib, Jelena, Tesla, Zeytsoff, Doctor Konyeshin, Pocięgło, Captain Privyezhensky, the Underground World, Irkutsk, Schultz, Fishenstein, Wielicki, Shtchekelnikoff, the Tunguses, Piłsudski, my father, Rasputin, and again Irkutsk, again Konyeshin, again Jelena, again – zero, one, zero, one, zero – I kept falling asleep and waking up.

In the other room I found full buckets and demijohns; I put a kettle on the stove, found also some coarse lye soap and had a wash, making very sparing use of the water. Noiselessly, I ferreted through shelves, bottles and tins. There was a little flour mixed with sawdust, some petrified salt, compressed brick tea, a handful of dried fruit from an unknown plant, rancid fat in an earthenware jar, a few bulbs of wild garlic… Whilst that day, Jelena had brought a dozen sprouted potatoes, two onions and a jugful of black chokeberries. I peeled the potatoes, clumsily working the knife, and set a pan of water on the flame… But Jelena continued to sleep. I brewed tea. Add salt? The crumbling crystals slipped through the holes in my fist and sped over the tabletop. Heavy with sleep, I watched them arrange themselves on the yellow oilcloth into symmetrical patterns. I gathered them up and scattered them afresh. And again. And again. Those hammers are striking, striking uninterruptedly, whilst here in Irkutsk, even in its short waves the small prototype drowns out Tesla's Great Hammer. Moments of extreme entropy will occur, those flashes of impossible thoughts, impossible associations, impossible feelings, lasting but a second. The antidote to the Ice. Were it only possible… It eluded me. I stood and waited without moving, in the same pose, staring at the same spot on the oilcloth, turning over in my mind the same images. Wooboom. Were it only possible… on the throne of the Kingdom of Darkness – to think the unthought, to feel the unfelt – to step beyond oneself – to be at the same time oneself and someone else – to lie – to lie – to lie in truth. Wooboom. I collected up every grain of salt.

She had beautiful teacups, painted in the Chinese style, made of finest porcelain. I sat down again by the bed, blowing onto the steaming tea. Jelena was breathing with open mouth, her cheeks coloured by feverish blushes. I adjusted the plaid. The rain had eased a little; silence descended on the old building, silence and bright sunshine beating in rainbow shafts through the frostoglaze. The hand lifting the teacup moved so slowly… See, Alfred: this is all that really exists: here, now.

I fell asleep and woke up.

She was standing over me with a knife in her hand, silver sunlight brimming along its blade.

I caught her in my one living eye. She was staring entirely consciously, lost for a long while in thought. How long had she been standing thus? She'd already removed her outer clothing, was clad in a simple white blouse and woollen skirt. The knife faltered in her hand. The steel stereometry of gazes, however, held firm. I moved not, smiled not.

She returned to the cooker, to the saucepan on the flame.

Her tea had gone completely cold. I went to brew a fresh cup. Miss Muklanowicz busied herself with the potato soup.

We ate in silence. There was no second chair; later, Jelena sat on my knees when I moved to the window. Eventually, the rain stopped; rainbows were splashed across the city. It was a warm, summer afternoon. She played with my hair tied back at the nape of my neck. I pressed her hand to my dry lips. Shots rang out from the direction of Tikhvinsky Square and the banking quarter; a riderless horse galloped past along the pavement. The Sibirkhozheto Tower, disproportionately crowned in a huge mace of darkness, shook, then began, unbearably slowly, to describe its own black bow against the rainbowed sky, preserving however – to the very end, to the very earth – the geometrical integrity of its structure. We did not hear the crash. It capsized towards the east, towards the Moscow Triumphal Arch and Jerusalem Hill. A moment later, the chimneys of the new cadet school collapsed. The whole of Irkutsk had been built on permafrost; yet this was not the natural geology of Transbaikal. Judging by the roofs visible from the garret window, we could observe: that house is crooked, this one leaning, that one sunken, this one washed away. Straight lines and regular corners were harder and harder to find. We sat in the warmth with our pungent, salty tea and watched as the Frost's old powers came tumbling down.

Then more shots rang out as inky darkness spread towards Gretchesky Pereulok from the heart of the city, so deeply wounded by the downfall of Schultz/Pobedonostseff. Had he really carried out his threat and ordered, in case of his death, the detonation of mines laid neath the Trans-Siberian Railway tracks? One way or another, a new truthjoust is hotting up. It was still light and Irkutsk's residents were sheltering as best they could, and, whatever else they lacked, they still had plenty of blackwickes. A lake of darkness was inundating district after district. Jelena also took a stub-end in ceramic surround from the sideboard, placed it in the window and lit it. Whoosh, unlicht dropped upon us like a velvet cape; we cowered neath a flap of the wizard's cloak, where now no one could see us. We could see each other only by halves, in halves illuminated by a glintz leaping over the wall to our right. And so, although she sat on my knee and nestled against my chest, I could see only one half of Jelena Muklanowicz, a profile taken out of nothingness; her other half existed not.

And she, half-existing, saw but half of me.

'Of that former young man, you have only an eye.'

'No great price to pay, Jelena, no great price. When I think... Did you go to Tsvetistaya? The Wielickis, their children – did they survive? are they alive?'

'Yes, no, don't know.'

'Thaw, yes. Agh, I had the same with you.'

'Oh?'

'I saw your grave at Kryspin's sanatorium. Only later... Thaw, Summer, everything has unfrozen; and now again, you're both the consumptive immersed in romances and the criminal on the train – and what better way to close all investigations and stop all pursuits than to bury yourself there under your stolen name? But here in Irkutsk you ran into Doctor Konyeshin, who knows you from the Express, a sick young woman, well, and so the name came back to life.'

She moved her fingers over the furrows, burrows and sores on my forehead.

'But which Jelena was Benedykt seeking?'

I clasped her tighter. 'Understand this,' I whispered. 'I need such a woman by my side – a woman indeed – the kind of a woman who is as capable of laying down her life for me as of thrusting a knife into my heart.'

'How oddly you speak. "I need such a woman"?'

I drew her into the dark, onto the side of non-being.

'By my side, by the throne of the Kingdom of Darkness,' I whispered. 'Such a woman, the Queen of Summer: loyal companion and traitor, friend and enemy – indistinguishable! – mother and infanticide, shield of truth and sword of lies, lady of mercy and mistress of extermination – indistinguishable! – naïve lover and calculating old hag, frivolous girl and picture of cunning wisdom, bleeding heart and rock of Golgotha – woman and woman.'

She broke away onto the side of light.

'Benedykt Gierosławski can't even propose!'

'You know what I speak of, you showed Doctor Konyeshin the newspapers articles, you know my plans, you see the truth about the History Industry Company. This won't simply be our private Sibirkhozheto. It's not about material wealth.'

'I know.' She smiled faintly. 'You didn't inherit it; it didn't fall to the Son of Frost from the lies bequeathed by his father. It all springs from your own deeds, from your own character.'

'Don't try to wriggle out. It was counted unto you. From the beginning – yes, it was – for your own deeds, Jelena, for your own character.'

'How so?'

I spun her around again on the boundary between unlicht and light. 'The Urals wolf.'

'Wolf!' Her glance was swift. 'But you called that – what? courage? foolish bravado? Shamelessness. Would I otherwise have knocked on the door of your compartment, that of a strange man?'

'And earlier too: it was you after all who broke in, rummaged through my luggage – unless my memory deceives me? But you also remember!'

'Yes.' She turned her gaze towards the past, that is, into non-being. 'I read that long letter of yours to false love. I knew you before we met.'

'Before we met… As I said, it was counted unto you: friend, enemy, love, hatred.' I gently tut-tutted. 'But reading other people's letters… Too bad, maybe in Summer it really can't be otherwise. Except – why break especially into my compartment? At the very beginning – you didn't know me at all then. So why?'

'Why especially into yours?' She laughed. 'Into others as well.'

'But – why?'

'*Because I could.*' She grew serious. 'Do you understand, Benedykt? Well, don't you know what medicine I sought in the Ice? "By the throne of the Kingdom of Darkness", how nice – but think you, sir, that at the last moment I shall withdraw the knife? Just so that you know what you're asking, so you're not taken later by surprise! I shan't withdraw it. At any moment – at whatever moment I choose – with no reason, Benedykt, with no reason – *because I can*. What are you asking of me? I shan't withdraw it! Shan't withdraw it! It's no longer a game between two strangers on a journey, no longer a night of innocent lies and truths. Once I stand by your side – make no mistake, sir: this Jelena will be standing there, and that one too.'

I instinctively sought her other eye; the black-and-white half-images only misled, I knew not which Jelena to address: the existing or the non-existing.

It had unfrozen, I hesitated.

'Yet you are not a cold criminal; you cannot so enlie yourself. Cannot so enlie these blushing cheeks, this trembling voice, all these questioning glances and bodily uncertainties.'

'Of what are you talking?' She was miffed. 'Are unshaven brutes and venomous shrews the only ones capable of evil? vulgar, brazen people devoid of delicate feelings, with insensitive souls and infallible bodies?

You've let yourself be seduced by Romantic poetry, by tear-jerking theatre!'

'But – have you ever done a truly evil thing?'

'What I've done is of no importance!' Jelena, the existing one, was irritated. 'Why pretend, Benedykt? If I have not stolen, not cheated and not killed, it's not because these are evil – but because I so *chose*, because that's precisely what I wanted: not to steal, not to cheat, not to kill. But nothing prevented me, nothing outside of myself, nothing within me. *I could have done it.* Not a single further thought, not a scrap more effort, nothing.

'What did you used to say yourself? Truth or falsehood – what's the difference? The unrealised is truer than the realised. Dostoyevsky's Raskolnikoff is a plaything for well-behaved children. Wherefore the axes, wherefore the dead bodies, wherefore the necessity to prove yourself in material deeds? You said so yourself! That which is unseen precedes that which is seen. First of all, murder is written into character, then – maybe – maybe! – murder is realised. Because what does it alter: shall I do it? shall I do it not? I am *such a person.*

'Do you understand?' She dug her bony fingers into my shoulder. 'Capable of the highest sanctity as of the lowest ignominy. From infinity to infinity. Nothing will restrain me. Not because I don't know what is good and what is evil. I know. But – because I can. I can. I CAN.

'Isn't it just such a Queen of Summer that you seek?'

My whole life is like that moment by the thawed stream with hands tightening around the dog's neck – my whole life with knife dripping blood in one hand and loving heart proffered in the other; here is truth and here is truth, there is no difference.

I swept Jelena into a powerful embrace, clasped her with all my strength. She trembled a while longer; then the trembling ceased. She was breathing rapidly; the breathing calmed. Her fingers strayed now here, now there; the fingers came to a halt. Her eyelid leapt; her eyelid stopped. I moved us deeper into the unlicht. Slowly, slowly, slowly, she froze.

'Benedykt…,' she whispered; it was as much as she could manage before a fit of coughing interrupted her.

I pressed my head to her bosom, my half-ear against the soft textured fabric of her blouse, and felt relief only when I'd heard the rasp of fatal consumption mounting in her chest.

The model: Miss Jelena Muklanowicz. A young girl from a good home, beloved daughter of a respectable bourgeois family, apple of Papa's eye, Mama's pet, a quick-witted toddler bursting with vital energy. But – sickness arrives. Sickness arrives, a first, second, tenth protracted malady, unspecific, overflowing from influenza into angina, from angina into anaemia, from anaemia into influenza... The sickness is in the devotchka herself; fevers and fainting fits are the symptoms of her body. You cure one symptom, others attack. The family spares no money, leaves no stone unturned, summons famous doctors, sends the girl to clinics and fashionable spas, funds every miraculous cure, hires qualified nurses so that the little darling can have the best hospital treatment in the comfort of her own bed. May she not even get up! May she not go out! Not move unneedfully! What's left for Jelenka for years to come? A view from the window, books telling fictions about the world, and the words of her visitors.

... Thus begins her first obsession with freedom: what she doesn't live through, she imagines as lived – equally true. A boundary exists to mental effort and spiritual engagement beyond which there is no difference for a person's character between the deed and the deed imagined. For this reason, the Lord God equally forbade adultery and dreaming of adultery. You did it, you did it not – for the soul, it's one sin; this way or that, you are already someone different. And there's no need either to plunge a knife into a living heart; the genuine possibility, in this way genuinely lived, is sufficient. And what Jelena did not experience, lying there for weeks and months and years, trapped neath her sealed bell-jar! Great loves as in salacious romances. Affairs and scandals. Marriages, motherhood, old age, sorrow and euphoria. Journeys. Trains, escapes, crimes, police investigations, trials. She loved and hated, fought and suffered, conquered and fell helpless victim, lied, committed adultery, killed, betrayed. For she could. (Because she couldn't.)

... And thus begins her second obsession with freedom: as there is no difference between the deed and the deed imagined, no boundary remains to be overstepped – since Jelena Muklanowicz has already done everything (although she's not done it), knows the thrill, feeling and thoughts accompanying it, knows the paths of the soul. She has trodden them far and wide. First, she makes herself a skeleton key from a hairpin or brooch and opens the door to the room wherein they imprison her for her own good. Freedom! That's how it begins. She *can*, and so she escapes for night-time strolls around the silent house, ferrets in sideboards and servants' cubbyholes, savours on the sly forbidden sweetmeats, tries alcoholic drinks and tobacco. She *can*, and so she breaks into rooms and other people's secrets, into their studies, writing desks, bureaus; reads other people's letters, diaries, sucking the life out of them to the very core. She *can*, and so she spies on them hidden also during the day – on their trickery, dirty deeds, puny fears, love affairs, acts of petty nobility. She *can*, and so she lies: about this, about that, about important things and unimportant, whenever it's possible, how far it's possible, to the very limits of lying. Every open possibility is a temptation of freedom that can't be resisted. There's no need for causes, reasons, motives, they'd only bring fresh limitations and constraints; they're obsolete. *Jelena Muklanowicz can.* She did it not, but she did it. Falsehood truer than truth.

I pushed Jelena into the glintz spreading on my right in an electric puddle; she spun around on my knees, rolling her skirt up high. She was breathing hoarsely, whilst her breath, sticking to my face like a damp handkerchief, already smelled distinctly of wet leaves.

'I shall take you at once to Nikolayevsk,' I said, 'away from this swamp of History. I still have unfinished business here with a certain cobbler... But then, so long as it's at an even-numbered hour –'

'You have it all figured out in advance!'

'About History? Yes.'

'Oh. And is there perhaps also a place for Poland in these equations of yours?'

'The colour of flags, the name of the currency, anthems and languages – are not what's most important in life, Jelena. But, what can I do, I have this agreement with Piłsudski... Let our Old Man fight there and win his State. It's not important now. Now – I am taking you away from here and –'

'But aren't you going to ask me, Benedykt? Have I agreed to these crazy great plans of yours? Nothing is –'

One crippled hand on her neck, by the scald mark, the other crippled hand making its way along her leg and up the holey stocking to her thigh – till the astonished devushka opened her eyes wide, arrested in hesitation between possibility and possibility.

'I'm not going to ask,' I snarled. 'My plans for the world are something else: good that you understand them. But what I plan for you – is my business!' I drew the head bent over me closer still, so that not only by our breath but also by our bare skin, we mingled in matter. Jelena resisted not, but I squeezed so hard that she'd have had no freedom at all, even had she wished to resist with all her might. 'Have you ever experienced, Jelena, such passion devouring the soul – desire, which consumes you unconditionally – not because you desire, but because you are desired?'

Rapid gunshots and terrified yells reached us from outside, from beyond the light and unlicht, from History. An anguished horse was neighing.

Jelena caught her breath.

'In those days you weren't so... decided.'

'Decided? In those days I existed not!'

She tried to laugh; began to cough.

'So, you're not ashamed after all to express the truth out loud! You have words to tell of untellable things!

I shook my head.

'Living in Summer, Jelenka, we never learn the language of ideas and never see clearly the truth about reality. Whereas we know the truth of our words about reality.' I leant into non-being, in order to better see the half-existing woman, eye to eye. 'When I say that I love you – do I love you? – but I am telling the truth when I say that I love you.'

Meanwhile History was drawing nearer and nearer; in the darkness, the boots of Revolution clattered on the cobbles, timber split under rifle butts, glass shattered.

Jelena sank back neath the undulating surface of the unlicht.

'All right, I will stand by you in Winter as the honest lie, protect you from your mathematics so that you don't end up like your hapless father, yes. But, Benek, but before you set your machines in motion, before you freeze History… What salvation for me?' She coughed painfully. She floundered deeper and deeper in dark non-being, clinging to my collar, my sleeves, my wounds and scabs, sinking in her burning fever into the cool murch. 'The Ice!' she whispered breathlessly. 'The Ice! What now the Ice to me?'

'I am.'

May 2005–April 2007

EX LIBRIS

Mottos to all parts of the novel as well as several quotations in the text are taken from Tadeusz Kotarbiński's article 'Zagadnienie istnienia przyszłości [The Problem of the Existence of the Future]', which appeared in the journal *Przegląd Filozoficzny*, vol. 16, 1913.

Passages relating to Józef Piłsudski are based on his 'Pomnik Kata' (*Robotnik*, 1898–1899); letter to the editor of *Przedświt*, 1893, no. 5; speech delivered in Poznań on 12 October 1919; *Odezwa do robotników w sprawie pomnika Mickiewicza w Warszawie*, 16 December 1898; speeches delivered to Legionaries at congresses in Kraków on 5 August 1922 and Lwów (Lviv) on 5 August 1923; *Memoriał o organizacji werbunku do Polskiej Siły Zbrojnej*, 26 December 1916; interview given to *Tygodnik Ilustrowany*, 6 January 1917; speech on the occasion of the interment of Juliusz Słowacki's remains in the Wawel Cathedral crypt, 28 June 1927; interview with Artur Śliwiński published posthumously (*Niepodległość*, vol. 18, 1938); and on the books *Komendant-Wychowawca* by Karol Lilienfeld-Krzewski (Warsaw, 1919) and *Józef Piłsudski w życiu codziennym* by Maria Jehanne Wielopolska (Kraków, ca 1937).

Also quoted are fragments from Nikolay Fyodoroff [Mikołaj Fiodorow], *Filozofia wspólnego czynu* [*The Philosophy of the Common Task*], translated from Russian to Polish by Cezary Wodziński (Kęty, 2012), and from Deacon Fyodor (*O poznanii antikhristovoi prelesti*), translated by Elżbieta Przybył in her book *W cieniu Antychrysta. Idee staroobrzędowców w XVII w.* (Kraków, 1999).

Dukaj's paraphrase of the poem by Sergey Yesyenin 'Snezhnaya ravina, belaya luna', his slightly adapted version of Adam Mickiewicz's poem 'Śniło się zima', as well as fragments from Fyodor Tyutchev's poem 'Silentium' and Juliusz Słowacki's *Anhelli* are rendered in English here by Ursula Phillips.

Quotations from Stanisław Brzozowski are taken from his essay *Drogi i zadania nowoczesnej filozofii* [*The Ways and Tasks of Modern Philosophy*], completed in April 1906, published during 1906–1907 in *Przegląd Społeczny*.

Excerpts from the late-seventeenth-century travellers to China Adam Brandt and Evert Ysbrants Ides are quoted (slightly adapted) from facsimile reprints of English translations in: *Beschreibung seiner grosser chinesischen Reise* = *A Journal of the Embassy from Moscow to China Overland* [by] Adam Brand; Evert Ysbrants Ides, *Three Years'*

Travels from Moscow Overland to Peking (Richmond: Curzon, 2000). The quotations from Marco Polo are based on *The Travels of Marco Polo/Book 4/Chapter 21* [sic], translated by Henry Yule.

Phrases from the Tungus language are based on early-twentieth-century aural transcriptions made by Kazimierz Grochowski and listed in the Polish–Tungus glossary compiled by Kajdański in *Dzienniki syberyjskie podróży Kazimierza Grochowskiego (1910–1914)*, compiled and edited by Edward Kajdański (Lublin, 1986).

GLOSSARY

abaasy (pl. abassylar), shaman term for evil spirit(s)
arshin, obsolete Russian unit of measurement equivalent to 71.12 cm
babotchka, butterfly
babushka, grandma or old woman
banya, bathhouse
batyushka, as in Batyushka Tsar/Batyushka Moroz, Father, literally
    Little Father
blacktunget, shaman amulet made of tungetitum
blackwicke, 'candle' that emits unlicht
blizzarder, poker-like game aiming for the coldest, lowest-valued
    hand
bumaga, paper or document
bumazhnik, pocketbook
chastushka, traditional Russian four-line verse, often satirical, using
    a standard rhyme scheme: ABAB, ABCB or AABB.
coldindustrialist, entrepreneur of the ice industries
coldiron, iron modified and super-strengthened by the Ice
coldmill, supercooling plant where elements are iced through
coolbond, alloy formed not by heating but by cooling
dastan, Buddhist university monastery
desyatina, Russian land measurement roughly equivalent to 2.7 acres
devotchka, little girl
devushka, girl or young woman
diengi, money
Duma, the Russian parliament
freezeworks, black "fireworks"
frostoglaze, unbreakable cold-resistant glasslike material
frostoglazes, spectacles or goggles made of frostoglaze
Fyodorovian, disciple of Nikolay Fyodorovitch Fydoroff
glashatay, herald or town crier
glacius, another term for gleiss
gleiss (pl. gleissen), exceptionally cold frosty matter appearing to
    move or pass through solid phenomena
glintz (pl. glintzen), unlicht shadow
gnus, Siberian midge and mosquito cloud
guberniya, large administrative unit in tsarist Russia, a province or
    governorate

hiberniks, people able to withstand extreme cold
hoartin, tin made super-strong by the passage of ice
icecradle, ice structure into which and out of which gleissen pass
interferograph, instrument for observing changes in light phenomena
irgen, similar to ulus, but smaller
ispravnik, regional police chief
izvoztchik, driver of horse-drawn cab or sleigh
Kadet, member of the Constitutional Democratic Party
kamlaniye, shaman chanting ritual for invoking spirits
kartyozhnik, habitual cardplayer
katorga, hard-labour penal servitude
katorzhnik, person sentenced to katorga, a convict
katzenjammer, hangover
khanshin, distilled liquor similar to Chinese baijiu
kholodnik, coldmill worker
kholodny (adj.), 'cold' in Russian
khutir, Ukrainian farmstead or rural settlement
khutor, Russian farmstead or rural settlement
kibitka, hooded sledge or wagon in which convicts were transported
    to Siberia
korobotchka, traditional folk dance
krasavitsa, beautiful woman
lyod, in Russian: ice
Lyednyak (from Lyod = the Ice), advocate of retaining the Ice and the
    conservative status quo
magpiery, prospecting site
magpies, coldiron and tungetitum prospectors
malakhay, traditional conical-crowned fur hat with earflaps and
    animal tail
maltchik, boy
Martsynians, followers of Saint Martsyn, a sectarian hermit
mirk(s), unit of measurement in black physics
molodyets, fine fellow or woman
moroz, frost
murch, form of black energy
murchometer, instrument for measuring levels of murch
muzhik, peasant
Narodniks, intelligentsia campaigning for the rights of the common
    people (narod), supporters of the People's Will Party (Narodnaya
    Volya)
natchalnik, head of an organisation or government department
nachalstvo, collective word for the management or authorities
oblast, large provincial administrative division within a guberniya,

usually in the imperial peripheries
Oblastnik, advocate of an independent Siberia
Okhrana, tsarist security police
okhrannik, functionary of the Okhrana
oryeshki, walnut-shaped cookies
Ottepyel, Thaw
Ottepyelnik, advocate of Thaw and political liberalisation
paravoz, steam locomotive
Pilsudtchik, comrade of Józef Piłsudski
pirozhki, dough pockets or dumplings with various filings
PPS-men, members of Piłsudski's Polish Socialist Party (Polska
    Partia Socjalistyczna)
pood, obsolete Russian unit of weight equivalent to 16.38 kilogrammes
prestupnik, criminal
prikaz, official administrative order
provodnik, conductor
putevoditel, guidebook or brochure
rayon, local administrative unit
rubashka, Russian-style traditional shirt
samovar, traditional Russian urn for boiling water and preparing tea
sarafan, traditional sleeveless full-length pinafore dress
sazhayevka, type of vodka (derived here from 'sazha', meaning soot)
shapka, cap usually of fur
shuba, fur coat
shuga, snow sludge
Sibirkhozheto, the Siberian Coldiron Industrial Company (Sibirskoye
    Kholod-Zhelezopromyshlennoye Tovarishtchestvo)
Skopets (pl. Skoptsy), religious castrate(s)
sobor, cathedral
SR-men (or SRs), supporters of the Socialist Revolutionary Party
Sybirak, Polish katorzhnik and political exile
tchay, tea
tcheburyeki, lamb pasties
tchinovnik, functionary in the tsarist bureaucracy
Tchornoye Siyaniye, the Black Aurora or Atra Aurora
teslectricity, physical force discovered by Nikola Tesla
Tolstoyan, follower of the religious teachings of writer Leff
    Nikolayevitch Tolstoy
troika (lit. and fig.), carriage or sleigh drawn by three horses, a
    threesome
Trotskyites, followers of Trotsky (Leff Davidovitch Bronstein)
Trudoviks, breakaway 'Labour' faction of the Socialist Revolutionary
    Party

tserkoff, church
tsviker, pince-nez
tungetitum, element appearing after the Impact of June 1908
ukase, tsarist government decree
ulus, indigenous community or village in parts of Siberia
unlicht, negation of light
uyezd, tsarist administrative unit within a guberniya, usually rural
vershok, obsolete Russian measurement of length equivalent to 4.45
    cm
verst, obsolete Russian measurement of length equivalent to 1.067 km
Yapontchik, comrade of Piłsudski fighting on the Japanese side
zemstvo, regional elective assembly in tsarist Russia
zima, winter (in Polish and Russian)
zimny (adj.), in Polish: cold, in Russian: winter
zolotnik, obsolete Russian unit of weight equivalent to 4.26 grammes

ABOUT THE AUTHOR AND TRANSLATOR

JACEK DUKAJ read his first Stanislaw Lem novel at the age of six, published his first short story at the age of fourteen and has gone on to publish six novels, five novellas and three short story collections. He is a six-time winner of the Janusz A. Zajdel Award, a four-time winner of the Jerzy Zulawski Award and a winner of a European Literary Award and a Koscielski Award. A short animated movie by Tomasz Baginski based on this short story Katedra (The Cathedral) was nominated for an Academy Award in 2003. Dukaj lives in Cracow.

URSULA PHILLIPS is an award-winning British translator of Polish literary and academic works and a writer on Polish literary history with background in both Russian and Polish studies and a doctorate in Polish nineteenth-century literature. She has co-edited five volumes of critical essays on aspects of Polish literature and has been instrumental in introducing the work of Polish female authors to an Anglophone readership both academic and general. Translations include works by nineteenth- and early-twentieth-century writers Maria Wirtemberska, Narcyza Żmichowska, Zofia Nałkowska, Pola Gojawiczyńska and Maria Kuncewiczowa, as well as contemporaries Wiesław Myśliwski, Agnieszka Taborska and Piotr Paziński.

TRANSLATOR'S POSTSCRIPT

Translating the 'Untranslatable'

At the beginning of this project, the author of Ice deemed his novel 'untranslatable', since he regarded certain challenges in the transfer from Polish to English as impossible to resolve in cultural as well as linguistic terms. In addition, the translator is confronted by a secondary exchange between Polish and Russian, influenced by aspects of shared history but also cultural separateness, thereby involving tensions and hierarchies between themselves which are also difficult to convey to Anglophone readers. After five years of dedicated work and frequent discussions with the author himself, it is hard to disagree: particular elements appear impossible, i.e. untranslatable, at least initially. This does not mean, however, that on some wider level, the novel as a whole cannot be rendered into English. After all, no translation is ever a carbon copy, compromises have to be made; every literary translation is at best an approximation, an impression of the original, one of an indefinite number of possible versions. It is a question of degree, and this novel just happens to be more complex than many others.

There is much talk in translation criticism about what is 'lost' in translation, as if translation were always an inferior activity to original writing. Yet translation is itself writing, in which something may also be gained or at least creatively reconstructed. As such, it is one of the arts of the possible. Translating Ice, a work brimming with translation challenges on every page, has certainly taken me to the limits of the possible. And despite the so-called 'untranslatables', I believe it has been feasible to create a version in English that conveys if not all, then at least most aspects of the original: the story plot, characters historical and fictional, historical contexts, contrasting political standpoints and religious visions, underlying philosophical inspirations and speculations, mathematical and logical assumptions, science real and invented, imagined industries and technologies, the Siberian landscapes and indigenous peoples, as well as the fantastical architecture of the Ice itself. Although the stylistic aspects in particular present massive problems, my translation despite everything is a very close translation.

The greatest problems lie in the transfer of the Polish language itself (its syntax, grammar, particular idiosyncrasies) into English, that is in the fundamental structural differences between the two languages and the frequent lack of exact equivalents. I had an immediate problem, for example, in that there is no satisfactory English adjective derived from 'ice' that fits all the contexts in which Dukaj employs the Polish 'lodowy'; 'icy' is usable only in specific circumstances and does not necessarily imply 'made of ice' as well as 'covered in ice' or 'icebound' (sometimes 'ice' itself sufficed as an adjective). Polish is a very compact language reliant on dense combinations of verbs, nouns, verbal nouns, pronouns, adverbs, adjectives and prepositions; like other Slavonic languages, it is highly inflected, allowing much more flexibility than in English in the arrangement of elements in a sentence, which therefore has implications for style, especially in poetry or poetic prose. Also, Polish, again like other Slavonic languages, lacks the articles 'the' and 'a'. Just taking into consideration the necessary introduction of these into an English narrative, along with the fact that English verb forms often comprise two, three or even four elements (whereas Polish usually has only one), gives some idea of how it can expand in translation as well as lose its compactness.

In fact, length is a crucial factor in the current context. The narrative covers over 1000 pages. Any translation decision has to render it equally energetic on page 1000 as on page one. To achieve the latter, individual sentences should not be too long in English. This is a fundamental problem since it is acceptable in Polish, following a comma, i.e. within one and the same sentence, to introduce a fresh main clause with new subject and predicate, whereas English prefers to start a new sentence. Dukaj's text contains many passages with very long sentences sometimes stretching to whole paragraphs or even pages; the idea of breaking them down into many shorter sentences, however, seemed to me too drastic an intervention, hence my introduction throughout of semicolons. Also, with regard to length and 'energetic' style, I decided to reduce the ubiquitous 'padding' words that appear in the original (such as: przecie, przecież, już, jednak); these may sound fine in the original narrative, but when repeated constantly in English feel stylistically clumsy and redundant (how many 'howevers' or 'after alls' or 'alreadys' can be tolerated on one page?) At the same time, I have tried to preserve something of the Polish sentence structure and cadences. Whilst my text has to flow as comfortably and naturally as possible, it does not have to read as if it were originally written in English; it is a foreign text and so to some extent should remain foreign in order to convey the atmosphere and cultural specifics of the original.

These problems confront the translator of any work from Polish into English, but in the case of *Ice* they are compounded by the verbal acrobatics of the author who exploits these grammatical characteristics, as well as interactions between Polish and Russian, in order to create a distinctive individual style that characterises the entire narrative. These fall into four main categories: use of the Polish reflexive particle 'się' to create an 'impersonal' first-person narrative; the incorporation of Russian words and phrases into the Polish narrative (note this is integration, not a switching between the two languages); the use of archaisms that contribute to conveying the atmosphere of the historical setting; the introduction of a large number of neologisms relating mostly to alternative natural phenomena and to the development in response of scientific research and the ice technologies based upon it.

The particle 'się' is an integral element of Polish reflexive verbs. It fulfils a similar function to the Russian suffix -ся but differs in that it is not attached to the verb and can move around the sentence within certain limits. Many Polish verbs are reflexive, for example: śmiać się (to laugh), mylić się (to make a mistake), kąpić się (to have a bath). This is regular usage that feels entirely familiar to a Polish native speaker. However, when used with third person *neuter* endings (Polish has three grammatical genders: masculine, feminine and neuter; endings decline in the past tense) and linked to a non-reflexive verb, 'się' creates an impersonal, or even generalised sense that renders the actual subjectivity or agency obscure. It removes obvious personal agency from the construction; and as such, it can also be a way of conveying passive voice. In this respect, constructions with 'się' function in roughly the same way as the German 'man', usually translated into English by the impersonal 'one'. Although this usage, i.e. third person neuter constructions with 'się' attached to any verb, is grammatically possible in Polish and not infrequently encountered, its usage as the main narrative technique throughout a long novel is unfamiliar and does not feel immediately natural. It feels strange until the reader adjusts, e.g. czytało się (one read, it was read, people were reading, yet used here not to convey those meanings, but rather to mean: *I read*; but the real subject is concealed). This is the form adopted by Dukaj. And when an actual reflexive verb appears in his narrative, such as those mentioned above, 'się' occurs twice: 'się śmiało się,' which indeed seems odd to a Polish reader. There is no reason, therefore, why the chosen translation should not also feel odd, at least initially, in English.

The crucial point to note, however, is that the narrative voice in *Ice*, that of the protagonist, twenty-four-year-old Polish student of mathematics and logic Benedykt Gierosławski, is *always* a first-person one. The whole narrative is written by him, from his perspective, filtered through his mind, reactions and speculations. It is not a third-person narrative. Yet it uses a third-person grammatical form, which thereby avoids the use of first-person indicators, including the pronouns 'I' and 'me' as well as masculine past-tense endings. Readers will come to understand that this underpins his philosophical speculations about 'non-existence' that run through the book. What we have is an impersonal first-person narrative. Its usage begins towards the end of Chapter the First, when the narrator transfers from regular first-person endings (here in the non-gendered present tense) to third-person endings: 'Nie istnieję. Nie istnieje się' (I do not exist. Exist not). Regular first-person forms return not long into Chapter the Tenth, approximately one hundred pages from the end of the novel, after a most significant event (not to be divulged to readers here). There are also various points in the narrative where first-person endings reappear, in the present tense or in the past (gendered masculine), namely in passages where Benedykt Gierosławski relates his own dreams.

So how to translate this narrative form into English, a language which does not possess a reflexive particle? The brief example above provides a clue (Exist not). There are several options, all of which I experimented with. Constructions using 'one' (czytało się > one read, meaning here 'I read' without investing the statement with subjectivity) were rejected for two reasons: first, 'one' itself is a subject, albeit impersonal, whereas obvious subjectivity needs to be suppressed; second, the usage occurs so frequently (multiple times on a single page) that constant repetition of the construction with 'one' would be stylistically unsustainable. I then considered the use of gerunds: czytało się > reading, which appears to remove agency, thus concealing the subject; although Gierosławski refers to himself, the gerund conveys neither tense nor gender. However, this is also unsatisfactory since it would cause confusion with other, standard uses of gerunds, and would again become unsustainable thanks to frequent repetition (how many '-ings' in constant close succession are digestible?).

I eventually decided on a form that I have not seen used elsewhere, though it could have been without my knowledge. The solution consists ideally of one word, conveys the semantic element of the verb, and makes obvious that Gierosławski is referring to himself (I repeat: he uses a third-person grammatical form to write a first-person narrative). I take the purely semantic element of an infinitive and omit indicators of person, gender and tense; hence: read, go, eat, think, decide, freeze, exist. Often this sounds like an imperative, which is not out of kilter with Gierosławski's assertions about his own non-existing, making him appear indecisive and lacking in agency. I then place this truncated form of the verb at the very beginning of every sentence in which it occurs, this being my signal to the reader that the narrative voice is now referring to himself; other characters are identified by regular grammatical rules. In order to distinguish statements relating exclusively to Gierosławski, I have also avoided the past tense, e.g. I have not used: went, ate, froze, thought, decided, existed etc, because without a pronoun, these words could refer to other characters, causing confusion. My usage may feel odd when first encountered (as it does in the Polish) but the persevering reader will adjust (as Polish readers have done). This solution works, I would estimate, in about eighty per cent of instances; in cases where it cannot be satisfactorily applied, such as in certain negative statements, I have preferred constructions such as: there was no reading, there was no eating, or passive constructions: no decision was made; and/or where the narrator Gierosławski is himself the object of a verb, when different formulations proved necessary in context to avoid any use of 'me'. Some especially tricky instances required a separate impersonal construction; for example: pomyślało się, literally: it was thought, which I have rendered with such phrases as: 'the thought occurred' or 'it sprang to mind'. In his reported conversations interspersed within the narrative, the narrator of course uses the pronouns 'I' and 'me', but he suppresses them in the actual narrative.

The interaction between Polish and Russian is equally complex. As I indicated above, this is not a case of frequent switching between languages or of one person speaking Polish and another Russian. The language is basically Polish with a significant number of Russian words and phrases woven into it, incorporated into a natural flow and transcribed not in Cyrillic but in the Latin alphabet adapted to the Polish ear and orthography. As related Slavonic languages, they can be smoothly manipulated in this way. Readers of the Polish original, even if they do not know Russian, can understand this 'mixed' language because of the recognisability of shared Slavonic roots. I have tried to understand how it functions through reference to the historical context. Dukaj's book is set in late Tsarist Russia (or rather in its alternative imagined extension into the 1920s), to which parts of the former Polish-Lithuanian Commonwealth (partitioned in the second half of the eighteenth century) remained subject until 1917 (in fact), except that in his alternative reality neither the First World War nor the Russian revolutions of February and October 1917 have taken place — the empire continues. All across the empire, including in the western guberniyas, the language of public discourse, intensified after the crushing of the 1863-1864 Uprising, was exclusively Russian: it was the language of administration, courts, army, police, education, commerce; it was visible everywhere from in official documents to shop signs. Therefore, one can imagine how Russian words became integrated into the everyday speech of the empire's Polish subjects. I found it helpful to understand the phenomenon in this mundane way. I appreciate, however, that Dukaj had more grandiose stylistic ambitions; but he is creating a distinctive poetics which cannot be fully reproduced in English. This is clearly one of the 'untranslatables,' an aspect of his novel 'lost' in translation. There is no language close enough to English with similarly common roots with which it could be integrated in a comparable way. My task anyway was to translate from Polish, not Russian, so how was I to deal with the many Russianisms in the text? Leaving them untranslated or translating as if the narrative consisted of a single language (thus giving the impression to Anglophone readers that the original was written in pure literary Polish) did not seem to me to be satisfactory options.

My solution, inevitably inadequate, has been to translate most of the Russian but retain certain words so as to preserve something of a Russian flavour (bumaga, diengi, ispravnik, izvoztchik, natchalnik, okhrannik, parovoz, provodnik, putevoditel, samovar, shuba, tchay, tchinovnik, troika, and so on). I have tried to ensure that their meaning is clear from the context in which they appear, or swiftly becomes clear, to readers unfamiliar with Russian. For such readers, these words may function like neologisms, of which there are likewise very many in this novel (see below). I have deliberately chosen not to qualify them in situ with an explanatory gloss, which would be cumbersome stylistically and feel contrived; and not to use italics (because to Dukaj's characters, they were not 'foreign' but part of their natural discourse); it is important that the narrative flows naturally, absorbing these words into a sentence as if they were automatically part of it, and not artificially inserted. After consultation with the author, it was agreed that there would be no explanations in footnotes; a separate glossary has been provided that also includes neologisms.

Some of these chosen words are culturally loaded, imbued with centuries of historical experience, thus making them doubly difficult to render in English. So, this is another area where we encounter the 'untranslatable'. A good example is the word 'katorga'. Such phrases as 'hard labour' or 'exile to a penal settlement' do not convey the political and emotional connotations the word has for Poles who were dispatched to Siberia, often forever, thousands of miles from home. Benedykt Gierosławski's father Filip is a case in point. I chose therefore to retain the word (similar in this case in Russian and Polish) in the hope that it conveys something of the human trauma associated with it. 'Katorga' was suffered, however, also by Russian dissidents, represented in the novel by the ex-katorznhik Filimon Romanovitch Zeytsoff, a former Marxist turned religious fanatic. A 'katorzhnik' (a convict) refers to anyone condemned to hard-labour exile. In *Ice*, however, we also frequently encounter the word 'Sybirak', which refers specifically to a Polish political 'katorzhnik' and derives from 'Sybir', the Polish term for Siberia used in this context. I have likewise preserved these in the translation so as to distinguish their loaded connotations from the more neutral 'Siberia' and 'Siberian'.

The language of *Ice* also conveys hierarchies and tensions in the power relationships between Poles and Russians under the tsarist system, wherein 'Poland' did not exist as a separate entity but constituted a partitioned and occupied nation whose culture and language were subjected to varying degrees of repression. Controls were also experienced by other subject peoples within the Russian Empire, including the Tunguses and other indigenous Siberians represented in the novel. The great variety of Polish individuals featured in the novel, however, both historical and fictional, are not portrayed as victims; on the contrary, Poles got everywhere in the Russian Empire and some grew rich on it, like Dukaj's Polish entrepreneurs in Irkutsk. On the other hand, already from the opening scenes, when Benedykt Gierosławski is taken from his student digs by the functionaries of the tsarist Ministry of Winter (Warsaw branch) and brought before the minister himself, he is forced to confront the overwhelming nature of Russian administrative power, codified since the days of Peter I into a strict hierarchy of ranks and functions, as were other state institutions such as the church and the army. Likewise, when Benedykt attends the Ministry in Irkutsk. In addition, there are many instances throughout the book where he is patronised as a Pole by Russians, such as by the condescending Privyezhensky, an army captain whom he encounters in the Trans-Siberian Express. How is this effect achieved? In ways which it is difficult to reproduce in English, because the historical experience of hierarchical bureaucracy is different and the language itself lacks powerful equivalents, for example in compulsory forms of address to superiors (see below). It is necessary for the translator to compensate by emphasising instead harshness and abruptness of tone or threatening mannerisms and gestures.

A general problem, pertinent in this context, is the lack of alternatives in English for the various Russian and Polish words expressing 'you'; again, the two languages differ between themselves. In Polish especially, class and social divisions, various gradations of power, disrespect and condescension, can be enhanced by the way 'you' is expressed. Put briefly, Russian has 'ty', the singular second-person form used primarily between close relatives, friends and peers, but also towards a lower-class person (relative to the speaker) such as a peasant, thereby indicating social or indeed administrative superiority; and plural 'vy'. 'Vy' functions not only as the plural of 'ty' but as the standard 'polite' form of you, used when addressing individuals. Polish usage is more complex. It also has 'ty' used in much the same way as in Russian. But standard (polite) forms of address use the third person (pan, pani, and plural forms panowie, panie or państwa, with third-person verbs). 'Wy' (second-person) is used mainly as the plural of 'ty'; it can be offensive when addressing an individual. So, when Russian officials in *Ice* address Gierosławski as 'wy', this implies disrespect towards a Polish subject they feel free to treat as they please. Polish also has forms that express superiority and disrespect. A form frequently used by Poles in *Ice* is 'pan' (third person when addressing a man) followed by a second-person singular verb (otherwise used with 'ty'); the force of this combination is somewhere between the standard third-person form and direct 'ty' form. It often appears in Polish nineteenth-century literary texts, so this is one element also contributing to the 'archaism' of the narrative, of which more in a moment. These subtleties cannot be rendered by unqualified English 'you'; other means have to be emphasised or introduced, as suggested above, to convey the speaker's position and attitude vis-à-vis the addressee.

Attempts have been made over the years to formalise English-language equivalents for the official terms of address prescribed in the tsarist table of ranks for the army, church and civil service and imposed on the Russian nobility by Peter I (1722), from nineteenth-century Isabel Hapgood (1890) to Robert Chandler (2005) to Angelo Segrillo (2016) to Wikipedia (https://en.wikipedia.org/wiki/Table_of_Ranks). While I have been guided by these as by the helpful suggestions of colleagues who translate from Russian today, I have not applied any one set of suggestions exclusively or systematically. I have reservations about transferring into the context of *Ice*, forms of address well-established in English in non-Russian contexts. The use, for example, of 'Your High Excellency' and 'Your Excellency' for the highest-ranked officials in the civil service is too closely associated, in my opinion, with ambassadors. Nevertheless, when Dukaj has Count Schultz-Zimovy specifically addressed as 'Ekscelencjo', I have kept 'Excellency'.

Similarly with the widespread use of 'Your Honour' or 'Your Worship' as forms of address for lower-ranking tsarist officials. I associate 'Your Honour' with addressing a judge, and 'Your Worship' with a mayor; these formulations may work of course in other translations but are inappropriate to the scenes portrayed in *Ice*, where precisely the power invested in the rank itself is being emphasised; the narrative is not objective, everything is filtered through the first-person narrative of Benedykt Gierosławski, a powerless subject at the receiving end of official whims. Instead, I have preferred 'Your Esteemed Nobleness' and 'Your Highly Esteemed Nobleness' for 'Vashe blagorodiye' and 'Vashe vysokoblagorodiye' respectively, judging these to be more accessible to English readers than Hapgood's more literal (though contemporary)

'Your Well Born' and 'Your High Well Born'. These decisions were reinforced by the author's concern that Anglicisms such as 'Your Honour' not only introduce alien cultural associations, but also water down the exaggerated impact of the Russian expressions. Interestingly, there are also occasions, for example on the long train journey, when Gierosławski himself, travelling first class, is addressed by lowly functionaries (conductors, waiters, hairdressers) as 'Your Esteemed Nobleness', thereby reflecting their (mis-)perception of him as rich and upper-class.

Outside of the table of ranks, and used for princes and counts, the form 'Vashe siyatelstvo' (sometimes rendered as 'Your Radiance') also appears. Here I have preferred: Your Illustriousness. I felt this alternative rachets up the way in which a petitioner or lower functionary not only has to show due respect to superiors but also ingratiate himself. For the same reason, I have sometimes translated 'Vashe Imperatorskoe Velitchestvo' addressed to the tsar himself as 'Your Imperial Exaltedness' rather than 'Your Imperial Majesty'. In addition to these Russian forms of address, the novel also contains native Polish forms, some of which are also translations of Russian ones (Wasza Wysokość, Your Highness, which I have kept for princes such as Prince Blutsky and Princess Blutskaya), but also others historically established in Polish such as Wasza Wielmość and Wasza Wielmożność, hence another 'archaising' element. Here, I have preferred simply: Your Lordship. When used with 'pan' or 'pani', more in descriptions than forms of address, I have preferred 'honourable' (wielmożny pan Fessar, wielmożny Aleksandr Aleksandrovitch > the honourable Mr Fessar, the honourable Aleksandr Aleksandrovitch).

How to transcribe, or transliterate Russian has likewise been challenging, as standard English-language schemes, albeit also into the Latin alphabet, differ from Polish ones, which are obviously done with Polish orthography and pronunciation in mind. I therefore found myself mentally converting Dukaj's Polonised Russianisms back into Cyrillic and then transcribing them into English. Today, the preferred transliteration scheme for academic journals and online library catalogues is that of the Library of Congress or an adaptation of it. But I have not used this because it would be unsuited to the early twentieth-century setting of the novel. After researching contemporaneous entries in the British Library (formerly British Museum) catalogue and noting the variants, I decided to adopt a combination of different practices that seemed to me both appropriate to the historical period and assimilable for present-day Anglophone readers unfamiliar with Russian. I basically follow British Standard with some modifications so as to preserve something of the 'archaic' style of the narrative. For example, I have used -ff (not -v) for Russian -в whenever it occurs in final position, where it is devoiced, as was often done in the nineteenth and early-twentieth centuries (preserved today for instance in Rachmaninoff); it commonly appears at the end of male surnames, hence: Berdyaeff, Fyodoroff, Zeytsoff, Shtchekelnikoff; and -tch for Russian -ч (preserved in Tchaikovsky as well as in present-day transliteration into French), hence: Tchingis, devotchka, tchinovnik, Filip Filipovitch, Sasha Pavlitch. For Russian surnames that in Russian script would end in -ый or -ский, I have consistently used -y or -sky. This is my marker to readers that the character is Russian; I have deliberately introduced this distinction for clarity, since all such male names appear in Dukaj's text as -ski. I have not changed the Polish names; they appear in my translation as in the original, accents and all; hence in the translation, an ending in -ski (as opposed to -sky) indicates that the name is Polish. Likewise with the female characters, Halina Wielicka is Polish, the Princess Blutskaya is Russian (even though in the original she appears as Blutska). On the whole, this is transliteration rather than phonetic transcription though they often coincide. The Russian letter ё, which appears in the all-important word 'Лёд' (Ice), I have rendered as -yo, hence 'Lyod'; when it appears in Polish (Lód), I have translated into English. There was one place where I preferred a phonetic transcription over transliteration since the latter could have introduced an unwanted association: one of Piłsudski's companions is nicknamed Adin (Number One); I have kept the Russian pronunciation of the unstressed *o* rather than transliterated as Odin (there are no Norse gods in this novel). In some cases of Russians' personal names whose roots would appear to be Germanic, such as Schembuch, Schotcha, Jusche, Schultz (all these forms exist on the internet), I have transcribed as such and not used Dukaj's Polonised forms (Szembuch, Szocza, Jusze, Szulc).

The ways in which Russian appears in the text are connected with Dukaj's general attempt to promote archaism as a major feature of his style. Once again, I am confronted with the more-or-less untranslatable and the need to find compromises in order to convey something approximating the original.

It is hard to define what exactly is meant by 'archaism' (use of old-fashioned or obsolete language) in relation to this book. At the same time, is important to realise that what Dukaj creates in *Ice* is a construction, an artificial product of imagination made in 2007, not a reflection of an historically attested living language, although it does combine many elements of obsolete orthography, outmoded forms of address and arcane vocabulary. Its purpose is to contribute to recreating the ambience of late nineteenth-century/early-twentieth imperial Russia, the so-called Belle Epoque, alongside other recreated contemporaneous elements such as architecture, street scenes, interiors, furnishings, fashions, clothes. This is the point I clung to in trying to reproduce what could not be conveyed in reconstructed 'archaic' English.

On starting to read the novel, the reader of the Polish original is struck immediately by the appearance of the text. The visual aspect is a significant factor, since Dukaj employs standard Polish orthography from before the reforms of 1936, that is in the nineteenth and early twentieth centuries (he does not employ Old Polish forms from earlier centuries). The changes affected certain letters and also certain grammatical endings; the most significant: consonants were to be followed by i where j had formerly been in use (except after c, s and z); the distinction between adjective endings in *-ym*, *-ymi* and *-em*, *-emi* was abolished, leaving only *-ym* and *-ymi*. As these were and are very frequent usages, the reforms dramatically altered the way a text appears on the page. To those who regularly read nineteenth- or early twentieth-century Polish-language publications, the old orthography and grammar are familiar, but to the majority of readers they are not. They feel antiquated and give a sense of the distant past. Given also the impact on language of the intervening communist era, it is understandable that today's Polish speakers might feel far-removed from the orthography of Dukaj's book.

In order to create a similar distancing effect in English, we have to go back much further than the turn of the nineteenth and twentieth centuries, as far as the conventions of the mid- or even early eighteenth century. When we speak of such 'archaism' in English, it cannot be applied to the historical setting of Dukaj's novel without creating an enormous anachronism, because the contrast between our contemporary English and early twentieth-century English is nowhere near as great as it is in Polish. So, exactly what period of English are we looking to? That of Blake, Defoe, Swift, Milton, Shakespeare? But it will not do to impose the language of these writers on a narrative stemming from late imperial Russia. The author indicated to me that an inspiration for him had been the novel by Thomas Pynchon *Mason & Dixon* (1997). Here, Pynchon uses such orthographic conventions as capitalising the first letter of nouns and ending many past-tense verbs with apostrophe d instead of the later *-ed* (dress'd, smil'd, exclaim'd). This language, like Dukaj's archaism, is a construction, yet in Pynchon's case arguably appropriate to the period and cultural setting of his novel: the action takes place between England and America in 1760s-1780s.

So, what to do? I decided to use Victorian and early twentieth-century literary English as my inspiration, this being closer to the time when the fictional Gierosławski wrote his narrative. I was careful not to use any word or expression that would not have been used before 1930; my text should therefore not feel unduly modern or present-day.

I do appreciate the possibility, however, that in the alternative reality, Gierosławski's manuscript could theoretically have lain undiscovered for some time, found by a reader only in the far distant future, by which time his language might indeed have felt as 'archaic' as Swift or Defoe (or Pynchon). But I stand by my contention that Gierosławski's narrative should be rendered in a style of English appropriate to the time in which it arose (probably sometime in the early 1930s of *Ice*'s alternative reality).

The fourth stylistic issue, and the last to be discussed in this postscript, are the many neologisms in Dukaj's original. This was also challenging, but unlike the problems discussed above, it gave scope for greater freedom, flexibility and invention. Sometimes I would ponder for weeks or months, in the middle of the night or on a train, seeking satisfactory equivalents; other times, terms occurred suddenly without too much effort. It is difficult therefore to be systematic in describing the neologisms, since the way I arrived at solutions was often arbitrary, unconscious, intuitive.

My starting point was to examine how the various neologisms, or at least a significant number of them, are constructed in the original. Semantic word-building is a feature of Slavonic languages that can be used to great effect. Many neologisms in Ice depend on indicators such as prefixes that relate to light, darkness, and the negation of light. For example, they may contain the prefix: *ćmi-* (indicating darkness, murk, gloom): *ćmiatło* (unlicht), *ćmieczka* (blackwicke), *ćmiecz* (murch); while others have: *świ-* (indicating light), as in: *światło* (the regular Polish word for 'light') or *świecień* (glintz). The neologism *ćmiatło* is created by replacing the prefix in *światło* with the 'opposite' prefix *ćmi-*; *ćmiatło* is the negation of light (distinct from *ciemność*, the regular Polish word for 'darkness' which also appears frequently in this novel), in other words *unlight*, *non-light* or (my choice) *unlicht*.

I attempted initially to tabulate potential English equivalents based on prefixes; however, this purely linguistic approach soon became academic and felt contrived. I was rescued by the author who suggested I take a less scientific approach and imagine what these phenomena might look like when seen for the first time by a non-specialist, and then try to describe them to someone who had not seen them. Hence *świecień*, another of the above neologisms, became not the literal light-shadow (the combination of prefix *świ-* plus *cień* the Polish word for 'shadow') but: *glintz* (plural *glintzen*), indicating what appears to be an intense flash (glint) of light, i.e. the bright 'shadow' of *unlicht*, of non-light. Also noted above, *ćmieczka* is similarly created by substituting *świ-* for *ćmi-*: *świeczka* (the regular Polish word for 'candle') becomes *ćmieczka* ('blackwicke', where again I prefer visual appearance over a purely linguistic alternative). The case of *ćmiecz* (for which I, have invented: *murch*) is slightly different (there is no Polish word *świecz*). Again, the visual aspect is key: never precisely defined, 'murch' is a form of dark energy fundamental to black physics. It is not a liquid as such, but the word connotes to the Polish word for a liquid or fluid *ciecz*. In English, the *ćmi-* element is rendered by the suggestion of 'murk'. In the case of this word, many other words, especially verbs, are derived from it, which also points to the flexibility and diversity of verbal prefixes; these I have translated by adding roughly equivalent English prefixes: hence, to enmurch, bemurch, immurch, demurch.

One of the key neologisms and one of the first encountered by the reader is: *luty*, plural: *lute*, which are initially unexplained, slow-moving, gigantic and extremely cold masses of frosty matter that threaten the cities of Europe, and emanate from the epicentre of the Ice in Siberia. The word on first sight is puzzling since *luty* is the regular Polish word for February. The association, however, is not without etymological foundation, since it derives from an older meaning of 'severe' or 'bleak' and has common roots with the Russian лютый (lyuty) meaning 'ferocious', 'fierce', 'cruel' or (of frost) 'sharp'. The Polish *luty* also contains phonetically within it, the Polish word for ice, *lód*, which is pronounced 'loot' as in *lute* (*ó* is pronounced similarly to *u* while *d* in final position is devoiced to sound like *t*), even though there is no actual etymological connection. I wanted to find therefore a term for the *lute* that also contains a word for ice. My choice of *gleiss* (plural *gleissen*), note with double 's', is Germanic-sounding, but not a real German word, similarly to *unlicht* and *glintz*. The neologism connotes to words in English associated with ice, such as *glacier*, *glaciation*. And it contains 'eis' within it. As with *glintz*, plural in -*en* feels natural.

In searching beyond strictly English terminology for something still north European but more exotic and mysterious, I wanted to avoid any association with Tolkien (Dukaj's book is not a fantasy of this ilk); German provided a good option because, as Benedykt Gierosławski occasionally mentions in his narrative, the common language of social interaction, spoken for example at mealtimes, of the travellers in the De Luxe carriages of the Trans-Siberian Express, is not Russian or French, but German. My use of German-like words is limited to these: *gleiss*, *glintz*, *unlicht*. In other cases (some based on Polish, some on Russian, and some on common roots), mostly connected with the ice science and new technologies and industries based upon it, I have invented terms in English, although some are close translations; one of the two crucially important 'new' elements *zimnazo* (derived from *zimny*, Polish for 'cold' and *żelazo* meaning 'iron') I have simply rendered as *coldiron* (as one word), whilst the second crucial element *tungetitum*, I have left as just this (Tesla himself uses it in an English description of one his inventions, see Chapter the Third). Meanings of others should be clear in context, although a glossary has been provided.

Unsurprisingly, a few neologisms have proved untranslatable, and so have required a corresponding neologism that describes their function without conveying the associations the original might have for Polish readers. A good example is the 'icecradle', the term I have adopted to denote the massive moving ice structure into which gleissen enter and exit, as distinct from their 'nest' or 'cluster'. The word used in Polish is *soplicowo*, albeit uncapitalised. It connotes to the Polish word for 'icicle', *sopel*, but it is also the name of the manor at the centre of Adam Mickiewicz's epic poem *Pan Tadeusz* (1834) familiar to most Polish readers. Left as such, it would not be comprehensible to most Anglophones.

This postscript has described the most difficult, namely the stylistic challenges of translating *Ice*. Although more straightforward to deal with, the content also required considerable research into the various scientific and philosophical inspirations, for which the correct terminology had to be established. The fields of Russian and Polish history are more familiar to me, but still required consultation with colleagues more expert than myself on specific topics. Dukaj also ventures occasionally into Turkish, Chinese, Buryat and Tungus references, where advice was likewise needed. I wish therefore to express my gratitude to the author for our many discussions in person and by email since the very beginning of the translation project; his input has undoubtedly improved the final product. I likewise thank the following colleagues for their advice and support at various points during the past five years: Helen Beer, Kasia Beresford, Tim Button, Robert Chandler, Felix Corley, Pamela Davidson, Jim Dingley, Simon Dixon, Maureen Freely, Nicky Harman, Gerard T. Kapolka, Sebastian Leśniewski, Catherine MacRobert, Antoni Mikocki, Anne Thompson-Ahmadova, Anna Zaranko.

Ursula Phillips, February 2024